P9-CRZ-258

ZANE GREY

FIVE COMPLETE NOVELS

ZANE GREY

FIVE COMPLETE NOVELS

Riders of the Purple Sage

To the Last Man

The Thundering Herd

The Hash Knife Outfit

West of the Pecos

AVENEL BOOKS · NEW YORK

This edition is published by Avenel Books,
distributed by Crown Publishers, Inc.,
by arrangement with Harper & Row, Publishers, Inc.

a b c d e f g h

AVENEL 1980 EDITION

Manufactured in the United States of America

Library of Congress Cataloging in Publication Data

Grey, Zane, 1872–1939.
Five complete novels.

CONTENTS: Riders of the purple sage.—To the last
man.—The thundering herd. [etc.]
1. Western stories. I. Title.
PZ3.G87Fk [PS3513.R6545] 813'.52 80-17742
ISBN: 0-517-322218
ISBN: 0-517-32220X (lib. bdg.)

CONTENTS

Riders of the Purple Sage

CHAPTER ONE
Lassiter

A SHARP CLIP-CLOP of iron-shod hoofs deadened and died away, and clouds of yellow dust drifted from under the cottonwoods out over the sage.

Jane Withersteen gazed down the wide purple slope with dreamy and troubled eyes. A rider had just left her and it was his message that held her thoughtful and almost sad, awaiting the churchmen who were coming to resent and attack her right to befriend a Gentile.

She wondered if the unrest and strife that had lately come to the little village of Cottonwoods was to involve her. And then she sighed, remembering that her father had founded this remotest border settlement of southern Utah and that he had left it to her. She owned all the ground and many of the cottages. Withersteen House was hers, and the great ranch, with its thousands of cattle, and the swiftest horses of the sage. To her belonged Amber Spring, the water which gave verdure and beauty to the village and made living possible on that wild purple upland waste. She could not escape being involved by whatever befell Cottonwoods.

That year, 1871, had marked a change which had been gradually coming in the lives of the peace loving Mormons of the border. Glaze—Stone Bridge—Sterling, villages to the north, had risen against the invasion of Gentile settlers and the forays of rustlers. There had been opposition to the one and fighting with the other. And now Cottonwoods had begun to wake and bestir itself and grown hard.

Jane prayed that the tranquillity and sweetness of her life would not be permanently disrupted. She meant to do so much more for her people than she had done. She wanted the sleepy quiet pastoral days to last always. Trouble between the Mormons and the Gentiles of the community would make her unhappy. She was Mormon-born, and she was a friend to poor and unfortunate Gentiles. She wished only to go on doing good and being happy. And she thought of what that great ranch meant to her. She loved it all—the grove of cottonwoods, the old stone house, the amber-tinted water, and the droves of shaggy, dusty horses and mustangs, the sleek, clean-limbed, blooded racers, and the browsing herds of cattle and the lean, sun-browned riders of the sage.

While she waited there she forgot the prospect of untoward change. The bray of a lazy burro broke the afternoon quiet, and it was comfortingly suggestive of the drowsy farmyard, and the open corrals, and the green alfalfa fields. Her clear sight intensified the purple sage-slope as it rolled before her. Low swells of prairie-like ground sloped up to the west. Dark, lonely cedar-trees, few and far between, stood out strikingly, and at long distances ruins of red rocks. Farther on, up the gradual slope, rose a broken wall, a huge monument, looming dark purple and stretching its solitary, mystic way, a wavering line that faded in the north. Here to the westward was the light and color and beauty. Northward the slope descended to a dim line of cañons from which rose an up-flinging of the earth, not mountainous, but a vast heave of purple uplands, with ribbed and fan-shaped walls, castle-crowned cliffs, and gray escarpments. Over it all crept the lengthening, waning afternoon shadows.

The rapid beat of hoofs recalled Jane Withersteen to the question at hand. A group of riders cantered up the lane, dismounted, and threw their bridles. They were seven in number, and Tull, the leader, a tall, dark man, was an elder of Jane's church.

"Did you get my message?" he asked, curtly.

"Yes," replied Jane.

"I sent word I'd give that rider Venters half an hour to come down to the village. He didn't come."

"He knows nothing of it," said Jane. "I didn't tell him. I've been waiting here for you."

"Where is Venters?"

"I left him in the courtyard."

"Here, Jerry," called Tull, turning to his men, "take the gang and fetch Venters out here if you have to rope him."

The dusty-booted and long-spurred riders clanked noisily into the grove of cottonwoods and disappeared in the shade.

"Elder Tull, what do you mean by this?" demanded Jane. "If you must arrest Venters you might have the courtesy to wait till he leaves my home. And if you do arrest him it will be adding insult to injury. It's absurd to accuse Venters of being mixed up in that shooting fray in the village last night. He was with me at the time. Besides, he let me take charge of his guns. You're only using this as a pretext. What do you mean to do to Venters?"

"I'll tell you presently," replied Tull. "But first tell me why you defend this worthless rider?"

"Worthless!" exclaimed Jane, indignantly. "He's nothing of the kind. He was the best rider I ever had. There's not a reason why I shouldn't champion him and every reason why I should. It's no little shame to me, Elder Tull, that through my friendship he has roused the enmity of my people and become an outcast. Besides, I owe him eternal gratitude for saving the life of little Fay."

"I've heard of your love for Fay Larkin and that you intend to adopt her. But—Jane Withersteen, the child is a Gentile!"

"Yes. But, Elder, I don't love the Mormon children any less because I love a Gentile child. I shall adopt Fay if her mother will give her to me."

"I'm not so much against that. You can give the child Mormon teaching," said Tull. "But I'm sick of seeing this fellow Venters hang around you. I'm going to put a stop to it. You've so much love to throw away on these beggars of Gentiles that I've an idea you might love Venters."

Tull spoke with the arrogance of a Mormon whose power could not be brooked and with the passion of a man in whom jealousy had kindled a consuming fire.

"Maybe I do love him," said Jane. She felt both fear and anger stir her heart. "I'd never thought of that. Poor fellow! he certainly needs some one to love him."

"This'll be a bad day for Venters unless you deny that," returned Tull, grimly.

Tull's men appeared under the cottonwoods and led a young man out into the lane. His ragged clothes were those of an outcast. But he stood tall and straight, his wide shoulders flung back, with the muscles of his bound arms rippling and a blue flame of defiance in the gaze he bent on Tull.

For the first time Jane Withersteen felt Venters's real spirit. She wondered if she would love this splendid youth. Then her emotion cooled to the sobering sense of the issue at stake.

"Venters, will you leave Cottonwoods at once and forever?" asked Tull, tensely.

"Why?" rejoined the rider.

"Because I order it."

Venters laughed in cool disdain.

The red leaped to Tull's dark cheek.

"If you don't go it means your ruin," he said, sharply.

"Ruin!" exclaimed Venters, passionately. "Haven't you already ruined me? What do you call ruin? A year ago I was a rider. I had horses and cattle of my own. I had a good name in Cottonwoods. And now when I come into the village to see this woman you set your men on me. You hound me. You trail me as if I were a rustler. I've no more to lose—except my life."

"Will you leave Utah?"

"Oh! I know," went on Venters, tauntingly, "it galls you, the idea of beautiful Jane Withersteen being friendly to a poor Gentile. You want her all yourself. You're a wiving Mormon. You have use for her—and Withersteen House and Amber Spring and seven thousand head of cattle!"

Tull's hard jaw protruded, and rioting blood corded the veins of his neck.

"Once more. Will you go?"

"No!"

"Then I'll have you whipped within an inch of your life," replied Tull, harshly. "I'll turn you out in the sage. And if you ever come back you'll get worse."

Venters's agitated face grew coldly set and the bronze changed to gray.

Jane impulsively stepped forward. "Oh! Elder Tull!" she cried. "You won't do that!"

Tull lifted a shaking finger toward her.

"That'll do from you. Understand, you'll not be allowed to hold this boy to a friendship that's offensive to your Bishop. Jane Withersteen, your father left you wealth and power. It has turned your head. You haven't yet come to see the place of Mormon women. We've reasoned with you, borne with you. We've patiently waited. We've let you have your fling, which is more than I ever saw granted to a Mormon woman. But you haven't come to your senses. Now, once for all, you can't have any further friendship with Venters. He's going to be whipped, and he's got to leave Utah!"

"Oh! Don't whip him! It would be dastardly!" implored Jane, with slow certainty of her failing courage.

Tull always blunted her spirit, and she grew conscious that she had feigned a boldness which she did not possess. He loomed up now in different guise, not as a jealous suitor, but embodying the mysterious despotism she had known from childhood—the power of her creed.

"Venters, will you take your whipping here or would you rather go out in the sage?" asked Tull. He smiled a flinty smile that was more than inhuman, yet seemed to give out of its dark aloofness a gleam of righteousness.

"I'll take it here—if I must," said Venters. "But by God!—Tull, you'd better kill me outright. That'll be a dear whipping for you and your praying Mormons. You'll make me another Lassiter!"

The strange glow, the austere light which radiated from Tull's face, might have been a holy joy at the spiritual conception of exalted duty. But there was something more in him, barely hidden, a something personal and sinister, a deep of himself, an engulfing abyss. As his religious mood was fanatical and inexorable, so would his physical hate be merciless.

"Elder, I—I repent my words," Jane faltered. The religion in her, the long habit of obedience, of humility, as well as agony of fear, spoke in her voice. "Spare the boy!" she whispered.

"You can't save him now," replied Tull, stridently.

Her head was bowing to the inevitable. She was grasping the truth, when suddenly there came, in inward constriction, a hardening of gentle forces within her breast. Like a steel bar it was, stiffening all that had been soft and weak in her. She felt a birth in her of something new and unintelligible. Once more her strained gaze sought the sage-slopes. Jane Withersteen loved that wild and purple wilderness. In times of sorrow it had been her strength, in happiness its beauty was her continual delight. In her extremity she found herself murmuring, "Whence cometh my help!" It was a prayer, as if forth from those lonely purple reaches and walls of red and clefts of blue might ride a fearless man, neither creed-bound nor creed-mad, who would hold up a restraining hand in the faces of her ruthless people.

The restless movements of Tull's men suddenly quieted down. Then followed a low whisper, a rustle, a sharp exclamation.

"Look!" said one, pointing to the west.

"A rider!"

Jane Withersteen wheeled and saw a horseman, silhouetted against the western sky, coming riding out of the sage. He had ridden down from the left, in the golden glare of the sun, and had been unobserved till close at hand. An answer to her prayer!

"Do you know him? Does any one know him?" questioned Tull, hurriedly.

His men looked and looked, and one by one shook their heads.

"He's come from far," said one.

"Thet's a fine hoss," said another.

"A strange rider."

"Huh! he wears black leather," added a fourth.

With a wave of his hand, enjoining silence, Tull stepped forward in such a way that he concealed Venters.

The rider reined in his mount, and with a lithe forward-slipping action appeared to reach the ground in one long step. It was a peculiar movement in its quickness and inasmuch that while performing it the rider did not swerve in the slightest from a square front to the group before him.

"Look!" hoarsely whispered one of Tull's companions. "He packs two black-butted guns—low down—they're hard to see—black agin them black chaps."

"A gun-man!" whispered another. "Fellers, careful now about movin' your hands."

The stranger's slow approach might have been a mere leisurely manner of gait or the cramped short steps of a rider unused to walking; yet, as well, it could have been the guarded advance of one who took no chances with men.

"Hello, stranger!" called Tull. No welcome was in this greeting, only a gruff curiosity.

The rider responded with a curt nod. The wide brim of a black sombrero cast a dark shade over his face. For a moment he closely regarded Tull and his comrades, and then, halting in his slow walk, he seemed to relax.

"Evenin', ma'am," he said to Jane, and removed his sombrero with quaint grace.

Jane, greeting him, looked up into a face that she trusted instinctively and which riveted her attention. It had all the characteristics of the range rider's—the leanness, the red burn of the sun, and the set changelessness that came from years of silence and solitude. But it was not these which held her; rather the intensity of his gaze, a strained weariness, a piercing wistfulness of keen, gray sight, as if the man was forever looking for that which he never found. Jane's subtle woman's intuition, even in that brief instant, felt a sadness, a hungering, a secret.

"Jane Withersteen, ma'am?" he inquired.

"Yes," she replied.

"The water here is yours?"

"Yes."

"May I water my horse?"

"Certainly. There's the trough."

"But mebbe if you knew who I was—" He hesitated, with his glance on the listening men. "Mebbe you wouldn't let me water him—though I ain't askin' none for myself."

"Stranger, it doesn't matter who you are. Water your horse. And if you are thirsty and hungry come into my house."

"Thanks, ma'am. I can't accept for myself—but for my tired horse—"

Trampling of hoofs interrupted the rider. More restless movements on the part of Tull's men broke up the little circle, exposing the prisoner Venters.

"Mebbe I've kind of hindered somethin'—for a few moments, perhaps?" inquired the rider.

"Yes," replied Jane Withersteen, with a throb in her voice.

She felt the drawing power of his eyes; and then she saw him look at the bound Venters, and at the men who held him, and their leader.

"In this here country all the rustlers an' thieves an' cut throats an' gun-throwers an' all-round no-good men jest happen to be Gentiles. Ma'am, which of the no-good class does that young feller belong to?"

"He belongs to none of them. He's an honest boy."

"You *know* that, ma'am?"

"Yes—yes."

"Then what has he done to get tied up that way?"

His clear and distinct question, meant for Tull as well as for Jane Withersteen, stilled the restlessness and brought a momentary silence.

"Ask him," replied Jane, her voice rising high.

The rider stepped away from her, moving out with the same slow, measured stride in which he had approached, and the fact that his action placed her wholly to one side, and him no nearer to Tull and his men, had a penetrating significance.

"Young feller, speak up," he said to Venters.

"Here, stranger, this's none of your mix," began Tull. "Don't try any interference. You've been asked to drink and eat. That's more than you'd have got in any other village of the Utah border. Water your horse and be on your way."

"Easy—easy—I ain't interferin' yet," replied the rider. The tone of his voice had undergone a change. A different man had spoken. Where, in addressing Jane, he had been mild and gentle, now, with his first speech to Tull, he was dry, cool, biting. "I've jest stumbled onto a queer deal. Seven Mormons all packin' guns, an' a Gentile tied with a rope, an' a woman who swears by his honesty! Queer, ain't that?"

"Queer or not, it's none of your business," retorted Tull.

"Where I was raised a woman's word was law. I ain't quite outgrowed that yet."

Tull fumed between amaze and anger.

"Meddler, we have a law here something different from woman's whim—Mormon law! . . . Take care you don't transgress it."

"To hell with your Mormon law!"

The deliberate speech marked the rider's further change, this time from kindly interest to an awakening menace. It produced a transformation in Tull and his companions. The leader gasped and staggered backward at a blasphemous affront to an institution he held most sacred. The man Jerry, holding the horses, dropped the bridles and froze in his tracks. Like posts the other men stood, watchful-eyed, arms hanging rigid, all waiting.

"Speak up now, young man. What have you done to be roped that way?"

"It's a damned outrage!" burst out Venters. "I've done no wrong. I've offended this Mormon Elder by being a friend to that woman."

"Ma'am, is it true—what he says?" asked the rider of Jane; but his quiveringly alert eyes never left the little knot of quiet men.

"True? Yes, perfectly true," she answered.

"Well, young man, it seems to me that bein' a friend to such a woman would be what you wouldn't want to help an' couldn't help. . . . What's to be done to you for it?"

"They intend to whip me. You know what that means—in Utah!"

"I reckon," replied the rider, slowly.

With his gray glance cold on the Mormons, with the restive bit-champing of the horses, with Jane failing to repress her mounting agitations, with Venters standing pale and still, the tension of the moment tightened. Tull broke the spell with a laugh, a laugh without mirth, a laugh that was only a sound betraying fear.

"Come on, men!" he called.

Jane Withersteen turned again to the rider.

"Stranger, can you do nothing to save Venters?"

"Ma'am, you ask me to save him—from your own people?"

"Ask you? I beg of you!"

"But you don't dream who you're askin'."

"Oh, sir, I pray you—save him!"

"These are Mormons, an' I . . ."

"At—at any cost—save him. For I—I care for him!"

Tull snarled. "You love-sick fool! Tell your secrets. There'll be a way to teach you what you've never learned. . . . Come men, out of here!"

"Mormon, the young man stays," said the rider.

Like a shot his voice halted Tull.

"What!"

"He stays."

"Who'll keep him? He's my prisoner!" cried Tull, hotly. "Stranger, again I tell you—don't mix here. You've meddled enough. Go your way now or—"

"Listen! . . . He stays."

Absolute certainty, beyond any shadow of doubt, breathed in the rider's low voice.

"Who are you? We are seven here."

The rider dropped his sombrero and made a rapid movement, singular in that it left him somewhat crouched, arms bent and stiff, with the big black gun-sheaths swung round to the fore.

"Lassiter!"

It was Venters's wondering, thrilling cry that bridged the fateful connection between the rider's singular position and the dreaded name.

Tull put out a groping hand. The life of his eyes dulled to the gloom with which men of his fear saw the approach of death. But death, while it hovered over him, did not descend, for the rider waited for the twitching fingers, the downward flash of hand that did not come. Tull, gathering himself together, turned to the horses, attended by his pale comrades.

CHAPTER TWO
Cottonwoods

Venters appeared too deeply moved to speak the gratitude his face expressed. And Jane turned upon the rescuer and gripped his hands. Her smiles and tears seemingly dazed him. Presently, as something like calmness returned, she went to Lassiter's weary horse.

"I will water him myself," she said, and she led the horse to a trough under a huge old cottonwood. With nimble fingers she loosened the bridle and removed the bit. The horse snorted and bent his head. The trough was of solid stone, hollowed out, mosscovered and green and wet and cool, and the clear brown water that fed it spouted and splashed from a wooden pipe.

"He has brought you far to-day?"

"Yes, ma'am, a matter of over sixty miles, mebbe seventy."

"A long ride—a ride that— Ah, he is blind!"

"Yes, ma'am," replied Lassiter.

"What blinded him?"

"Some men once roped him an' tied him, an' then held white-iron close to his eyes."

"Oh! Men? You mean devils. . . . Were they your enemies—Mormons?"

"Yes, ma'am."

"To take revenge on a horse! Lassiter, the men of my creed are unnaturally cruel. To my everlasting sorrow I confess it. They have been driven, hated, scourged till their hearts have hardened. But we women hope and pray for the time when our men will soften."

"Beggin' your pardon, ma'am—that time will never come."

"Oh, it will! . . . Lassiter, do you think Mormon women wicked? Has your hand been against them, too?"

"No. I believe Mormon women are the best and noblest, the most long-sufferin', and the blindest, unhappiest women on earth."

"Ah!" She gave him a grave, thoughtful look. "Then you will break bread with me?"

Lassiter had no ready response, and he uneasily shifted his weight from one leg to another, and turned his sombrero round and round in his hands. "Ma'am," he began, presently, "I reckon your kindness of heart makes you overlook things. Perhaps I ain't well known hereabouts, but back up North there's Mormons who'd rest oneasy in their graves at the idea of me sittin' to table with you."

"I dare say. But—will you do it, anyway?" she asked.

"Mebbe you have a brother or relative who might drop in an' be offended, an' I wouldn't want to—"

"I've not a relative in Utah that I know of. There's no one with a right to question my actions." She turned smilingly to Venters. "You will come in, Bern, and Lassiter will come in. We'll eat and be merry while we may."

"I'm only wonderin' if Tull an' his men'll raise a storm down in the village," said Lassiter, in his last weakening stand.

"Yes, he'll raise the storm—after he has prayed," replied Jane. "Come."

She led the way, with the bridle of Lassiter's horse over her arm. They entered a grove and walked down a wide path shaded by great low-branching cottonwoods. The last rays of the setting sun sent golden bars through the leaves. The grass was deep and rich; welcome contrast to sage-tired eyes. Twittering quail darted across the path, and from a tree-top somewhere a robin sang its evening song, and on the sill air floated the freshness and murmur of flowing water.

The home of Jane Withersteen stood in a circle of cottonwoods, and was a flat, long, red-stone structure with a covered court in the center through which flowed a lively stream of amber-colored water. In the massive blocks of stone and heavy timbers and solid doors and shutters showed the hand of a man who had builded against pillage and time; and in the flowers and mosses lining the stone-bedded stream, in the bright colors of rugs and blankets on the court floor, and the cozy corner with hammock and books, and the clean-linened table, showed the grace of a daughter who lived for happiness and the day at hand.

Jane turned Lassiter's horse loose in the thick grass. "You will want him to be near you," she said, "or I'd have him taken to the alfalfa fields." At her call appeared women who began at once to bustle about, hurrying to and fro, setting the table. Then Jane, excusing herself, went within.

She passed through a huge low-ceiled chamber, like the inside of a fort, and into a smaller one where a bright wood-fire blazed in an old open fireplace, and from this into her own room. It had the same comfort as was manifested in the home-like outer court; moreover, it was warm and rich in soft hues.

Seldom did Jane Withersteen enter her room without looking into her mirror. She knew she loved the reflection of that beauty which since early childhood she had never been allowed to forget. Her relatives and friends, and later a horde of Mormon and Gentile suitors, had fanned the flame of natural vanity in her. So that at twenty-eight she scarcely thought at all of her wonderful influence for good in the little community where her father had left her practically its beneficent landlord; but cared most for the dream and the assurance and the allurement of her beauty. This time, however, she gazed into her glass with more than the usual happy motive, without the usual slight conscious smile. For she was thinking of more than the desire to be fair in her own eyes, in those of her friend; she wondered if she were to seem fair in the eyes of this Lassiter, this man whose name had crossed the long, wild brakes of stone and plains of sage, this gentle-voiced, sad-faced man who was a hater and a killer of Mormons. It was not now her usual half-conscious vain obsession that actuated her as she hurriedly changed her riding-dress to one of white, and then looked long at the stately form with its gracious contours, at the fair face with its strong chin and full firm lips, at the dark-blue, proud, and passionate eyes.

"If by some means I can keep him here a few days, a week—he will never kill another Mormon," she mused. "Lassiter! . . . I shudder when I think of that name, of him. But when I look at the man I forget who he is—I almost like him. I remember only that he saved Bern. He has suffered. I wonder what it was—did he love a Mormon woman once? How splendidly he championed us poor misunderstood souls! Somehow he knows—much."

Jane Withersteen joined her guests and bade them to her board. Dismissing her woman, she waited upon them with her own hands. It was a bountiful supper and a strange company. On her right sat the ragged and half-starved Venters; and though blind eyes could have seen what he counted for in the sum of her happiness, yet he looked the gloomy outcast his allegiance had made him, and about him there was the shadow of the ruin presaged by Tull. On her left sat black-leather-garbed Lassiter looking like a man in a dream. Hunger was not with him, nor composure, nor speech, and when he twisted in frequent unquiet movements the heavy guns that he had not removed knocked against the table-legs. If it had been otherwise possible to forget the presence of Lassiter those telling little jars would have rendered it unlikely. And Jane Withersteen talked and smiled and laughed with all the dazzling play of lips and eyes that a beautiful, daring woman could summon to her purpose.

When the meal ended, and the men pushed back their chairs, she leaned closer to Lassiter and looked square into his eyes.

"Why did you come to Cottonwoods?"

Her question seemed to break a spell. The rider arose as if he had just remembered himself and had tarried longer than his wont.

"Ma'am, I have hunted all over the southern Utah and Nevada for—somethin'. An' through your name I learned where to find it—here in Cottonwoods."

"My name! Oh, I remember. You did know my name when you spoke first. Well, tell me where you heard it and from whom?"

"At the little village—Glaze, I think it's called—some fifty miles or more west of here. An' I heard it from a Gentile, a rider who said you'd know where to tell me to find—"

"What?" she demanded, imperiously, as Lassiter broke off.

"Milly Erne's grave," he answered low, and the words came with a wrench.

Venters wheeled in his chair to regard Lassiter in amazement, and Jane slowly raised herself in white, still wonder.

"Milly Erne's grave?" she echoed, in a whisper. "What do you know of Milly Erne, my best-beloved friend—who died in my arms? What were you to her?"

"Did I claim to be anythin'?" he inquired. "I know people—relatives—who have long wanted to know where she's buried. That's all."

"Relatives? She never spoke of relatives, except a brother who was shot in Texas. Lassiter, Milly Erne's grave is in a secret burying ground on my property."

"Will you take me there? . . . You'll be offendin' Mormons worse than by breakin' bread with me."

"Indeed yes, but I'll do it. Only we must go unseen. To-morrow, perhaps."

"Thank you, Jane Withersteen," replied the rider, and he bowed to her and stepped backward out of the court.

"Will you not stay—sleep under my roof?" she asked.

"No, ma'am, an' thanks again. I never sleep indoors. An' even if I did there's that gatherin' storm in the village below. No, no. I'll go to the sage. I hope you won't suffer none for your kindness to me."

"Lassiter," said Venters, with a half-bitter laugh, "my bed, too, is the sage. Perhaps we may meet out there."

"Mebbe so. But the sage is wide an' I won't be near. Good night."

At Lassiter's low whistle the black horse whinnied, and carefully picked his blind way out of the grove. The rider did not bridle him, but walked beside him, leading him by touch of hand, and together they passed slowly into the shade of the cottonwoods.

"Jane, I must be off soon," said Venters. "Give me my guns. If I'd had my guns—"

"Either my friend or the Elder of my church would be lying dead," she interposed.

"Tull would be—surely."

"Oh, you fierce-blooded, savage youth! Can't I teach you forbearance, mercy? Bern, it's divine to forgive your enemies. 'Let not the sun go down upon thy wrath.'"

"Hush! Talk to me no more of mercy or religion—after to-day. To-day this strange coming of Lassiter left me still a man, and now I'll die a man! . . . Give me my guns."

Silently she went into the house, to return with a heavy cartridge-belt and gun-filled sheath and a long rifle; these she handed to him, and as he buckled on the belt she stood before him in silent eloquence.

"Jane," he said, in gentler voice, "don't look so. I'm not going out to murder your churchman. I'll try to avoid him and all his men. But can't you see I've reached the end of my rope? Jane, you're a wonderful woman. Never was there a woman so unselfish and good. Only you're blind in one way. . . . Listen!"

From behind the grove came the clicking sound of horses in a rapid trot.

"Some of your riders," he continued. "It's getting time for the night shift. Let us go out to the bench in the grove and talk there."

It was still daylight in the open, but under the spreading cottonwoods shadows were obscuring the lanes. Venters drew Jane off from one of these into a shrub-lined trail, just wide enough for the two to walk abreast, and in a roundabout way led her far from the house to a knoll on the edge of the grove. Here in a secluded nook was a bench from which, through an opening in the tree-tops, could be seen the sage-slope and the wall of rock and the dim lines of cañons. Jane had not spoken since Venters had shocked her with his first harsh speech; but all the way she had clung to his arm, and now, as he stopped and laid his rifle against the bench, she still clung to him.

"Jane, I'm afraid I must leave you."

"Bern!" she cried.

"Yes, it looks that way. My position is not a happy one—I can't feel right—I've lost all—"

"I'll give you anything you—"

"Listen, please. When I say loss I don't mean what you think. I mean loss of good-will, good name—that which would have enabled me to stand up in this village without bitterness. Well, it's too late. . . . Now, as to the future, I think you'd do best to give me up. Tull is implacable. You ought to see from his intention to-day that— But you can't see. Your blindness—your damned religion!

. . . Jane, forgive me—I'm sore within and something rankles. Well, I fear that invisible hand will turn its hidden work to your ruin."

"Invisible hand? Bern!"

"I mean your Bishop." Venters said it deliberately and would not release her as she started back. "He's the law. The edict went forth to ruin me. Well, look at me! It'll now go forth to compel you to the will of the Church."

"You wrong Bishop Dyer. Tull is hard, I know. But then he has been in love with me for years."

"Oh, your faith and your excuses! You can't see what I know—and if you did see it you'd not admit it to save your life. That's the Mormon of you. These elders and bishops will do absolutely any deed to go on building up the power and wealth of their church, their empire. Think of what they've done to the Gentiles here, to me—think of Milly Erne's fate!"

"What do you know of her story?"

"I know enough—all, perhaps, except the name of the Mormon who brought her here. But I must stop this kind of talk."

She pressed his hand in response. He helped her to a seat beside him on the bench. And he respected a silence that he divined was full of woman's deep emotion, beyond his understanding.

It was the moment when the last ruddy rays of the sunset brightened momentarily before yielding to twilight. And for Venters the outlook before him was in some sense similar to a feeling of his future, and with searching eyes he studied the beautiful purple, barren waste of sage. Here was the unknown and the perilous. The whole scene impressed Venters as a wild, austere, and mighty manifestation of nature. And as it somehow reminded him of his prospect in life, so it suddenly resembled the woman near him, only in her there were greater beauty and peril, a mystery more unsolvable, and something nameless that numbed his heart and dimmed his eye.

"Look! A rider!" exclaimed Jane, breaking the silence. "Can that be Lassiter?"

Venters moved his glance once more to the west. A horseman showed dark on the sky-line, then merged into the color of the sage.

"It might be. But I think not—that fellow was coming in. One of your riders, more likely. Yes, I see him clearly now. And there's another."

"I see them, too."

"Jane, your riders seem as many as the bunches of sage. I ran into five yesterday 'way down near the trail to Deception Pass. They were with the white herd."

"You still go to that cañon? Bern, I wish you wouldn't. Oldring and his rustlers live somewhere down there."

"Well, what of that?"

"Tull has already hinted to your frequent trips into Deception Pass."

"I know." Venters uttered a short laugh. "He'll make a rustler of me next. But, Jane, there's no water for fifty miles after I leave here, and the nearest is in the cañon. I must drink and water my horse. There! I see more riders. They are going out."

"The red herd is on the slope, toward the Pass."

Twilight was fast falling. A group of horsemen crossed the dark line of low ground to become more distinct as they climbed the slope. The silence broke to a clear call from an incoming rider, and, almost like the peal of a hunting-horn, floated back the answer. The outgoing riders moved swiftly, came sharply into sight as they topped a ridge to show wild and black above the horizon, and then passed down, dimming into the purple of the sage.

"I hope they don't meet Lassiter," said Jane.

"So do I," replied Venters. "By this time the riders of the night shift know what happened to-day. But Lassiter will likely keep out of their way."

"Bern, who is Lassiter? He's only a name to me—a terrible name."

"Who is he? I don't know, Jane. Nobody I ever met knows him. He talks a little like a Texan, like Milly Erne. Did you note that?"

"Yes. How strange of him to know of her! And she lived here ten years and has been dead two. Bern, what do you know of Lassiter? Tell me what he has done—why you spoke of him to Tull—threatening to become another Lassiter yourself?"

"Jane, I only heard things, rumors, stories, most of which I disbelieved. At Glaze his name was known, but none of the riders or ranchers I knew there ever met him. At Stone Bridge I never heard him mentioned. But at Sterling and villages north of there he was spoken of often. I've never been in a village which he had been known to visit. There were many conflicting stories about him and his doings. Some said he had shot up this and that Mormon village, and others denied it. I'm inclined to believe he has, and you know how Mormons hide the truth. But there was one feature about Lassiter upon which all agree—that he was what riders in this country call a gun-man. He's a man with a marvelous quickness and accuracy in the use of a Colt. And now that I've seen him I know more. Lassiter was born without fear. I watched him with eyes which saw him my friend. I'll never forget the moment I recognized him from what had been told me of his crouch before the draw. It was then I yelled his name. I believe that yell saved Tull's life. At any rate, I know this, between Tull and death then there was not the breadth of the littlest hair. If he or any of his men had moved a finger downward . . ."

Venters left his meaning unspoken, but at the suggestion Jane shuddered.

The pale afterglow in the west darkened with the merging of twilight into night. The sage now spread out black and gloomy. One dim star glimmered in the southwest sky. The sound of trotting horses had ceased, and there was silence broken only by a faint, dry pattering of cottonwood leaves in the soft night wind.

Into this peace and calm suddenly broke the high-keyed yelp of a coyote, and from far off in the darkness came the faint answering note of a trailing mate.

"Hello! the sage-dogs are barking," said Venters.

"I don't like to hear them," replied Jane. "At night, sometimes, when I lie awake, listening to the long mourn or breaking bark or wild howl, I think of you asleep somewhere in the sage, and my heart aches."

"Jane, you couldn't listen to sweeter music, nor could I have a better bed."

"Just think! Men like Lassiter and you have no home, no comfort, no rest, no place to lay your weary heads. Well! . . . Let us be patient. Tull's anger may cool, and time may help us. You might do some service to the village—who can tell? Suppose you discovered the long-unknown hiding-place of Oldring and his band, and told it to my riders? That would disarm Tull's ugly hints and put you in favor. For years my riders have trailed the tracks of stolen cattle. You know as well as I how dearly we've paid for our ranges in this wild country. Oldring drives our cattle down into the network of deceiving cañons, and somewhere far to the north or east he drives them up and out to Utah markets. If you will spend time in Deception Pass try to find the trails."

"Jane, I've thought of that. I'll try."

"I must go now. And it hurts, for now I'll never be sure of seeing you again. But to-morrow, Bern?"

"To-morrow surely. I'll watch for Lassiter and ride in with him."

"Good night."

Then she left him and moved away, a white, gliding shape that soon vanished in the shadows.

Venters waited until the faint slam of a door assured him she had reached the house; and then, taking up his rifle, he noiselessly slipped through the bushes, down the knoll, and on under the dark trees to the edge of the grove. The sky was now turning from gray to blue; stars had begun to lighten the earlier blackness; and from the wide flat sweep before him blew a cool wind, fragrant with the breath of sage. Keeping close to the edge of the cottonwoods, he went swiftly and silently westward. The grove was long, and he had not reached the end when he heard something that brought him to a halt. Low padded thuds told him horses were coming this way. He sank down in the gloom, waiting, listening. Much before he had expected, judging from sound, to his amazement he descried horsemen near at hand. They were riding along the border of the sage, and instantly he knew the hoofs of the horses were muffled. Then the pale starlight afforded him indistinct sight of the riders. But his eyes were keen and used to the dark, and by peering closely he recognized the huge bulk and black-bearded visage of Oldring and the lithe, supple form of the rustler's lieutenant, a masked rider. They passed on; the darkness swallowed them. Then, farther out on the sage, a dark, compact body of horsemen went by, almost without sound, almost like specters, and they, too, melted into the night.

CHAPTER THREE
Amber Spring

No unusual circumstances was it for Oldring and some of his men to visit Cottonwoods in the broad light of day, but for him to prowl about in the dark with the hoofs of his horses muffled meant that mischief was brewing. Moreover, to Venters the presence of the masked rider with Oldring seemed especially ominous. For about this man there was mystery; he seldom rode through the village, and when he did ride through it was swiftly; riders seldom met by day on the sage; but wherever he rode there always followed deeds as dark and mysterious as the mask he wore. Oldring's band did not confine themselves to the rustling of cattle.

Venters lay low in the shade of the cottonwoods, pondering this chance meeting, and not for many moments did he consider it safe to move on. Then, with sudden impulse, he turned the other way and went back along the grove. When he reached the path leading to Jane's home he decided to go down to the village. So he hurried onward, with quick soft steps. Once beyond the grove he entered the one and only street. It was wide, lined with tall poplars, and under each row of trees, inside the foot-path, were ditches where ran the water from Jane Withersteen's spring.

Between the trees twinkled lights of cottage candles, and far down flared bright windows of the village stores. When Venters got closer to these he saw knots of men standing together in earnest conversation. The usual lounging on the corners and benches and steps was not in evidence. Keeping in the shadow, Venters went closer and closer until he could hear voices. But he could not distinguish what was said. He recognized many Mormons, and looked hard for Tull and his men, but looked in vain. Venters concluded that the rustlers had not passed along the village street. No doubt these earnest men were discussing Lassiter's coming. But Venters felt positive that Tull's intention toward himself that day had not been and would not be revealed.

So Venters, seeing there was little for him to learn, began retracing his steps. The church was dark, Bishop Dyer's home next to it was also dark, and likewise Tull's cottage. Upon almost any night at this hour there would be lights here, and Venters marked the unusual omission.

As he was about to pass out of the street to skirt the grove, he once more slunk down at the sound of trotting horses. Presently he descried two mounted men riding toward him. He hugged the shadow of a tree. Again the starlight, brighter now, aided him, and he made out Tull's stalwart figure, and beside him the short, froglike shape of the rider Jerry. They were silent, and they rode on to disappear.

Venters went his way with busy, gloomy mind, revolving events of the day, trying to reckon those brooding in the night. His thoughts overwhelmed him. Up in that dark grove dwelt a woman who had been his friend. And he skulked about her home, gripping a gun stealthily as an Indian, a man without place or people or purpose. Above her hovered the shadow of grim, hidden, secret power. No queen could have given more royally out of a bounteous store than Jane Withersteen gave her people, and likewise to those unfortunates whom her people hated. She asked only the divine right of all women—freedom; to love and to live as her heart willed. And yet prayer and her hope were vain.

"For years I've seen a storm clouding over her and the village of Cottonwoods," muttered Venters, as he strode on. "Soon it'll burst. I don't like the prospects." That night the villagers whispered in the street—and night-riding rustlers muffled horses—and Tull was at work in secret—and out there in the sage hid a man who meant something terrible—Lassiter!

Venters passed the black cottonwoods, and, entering the sage, climbed the gradual slope. He kept his direction in line with a western star. From time to time he stopped to listen and heard only the usual familiar bark of coyote and sweep of wind and rustle of sage. Presently a low jumble of rocks loomed up darkly somewhat to his right, and, turning that way, he whistled softly. Out of the rocks glided a dog that leaped and whined about him. He climbed over rough, broken rock, picking his way carefully, and then went down. Here it was darker, and sheltered from the wind. A white object guided him. It was another dog, and this one was asleep, curled up between a saddle and a pack. The animal awoke and thumped his tail in greeting. Venters placed the saddle for a pillow, rolled in his blankets, with his face upward to the stars. The white dog snuggled close to him. The other whined and pattered a few yards to the rise of ground and there crouched on guard. And in that wild covert Venters shut his eyes under the great white stars and intense vaulted blue, bitterly comparing their loneliness to his own, and fell asleep.

When he awoke, day had dawned and all about him was bright steel-gray. The air had a cold tang. Arising, he greeted the fawning dogs and stretched his cramped body, and then, gathering together bunches of dead sage sticks, he lighted a fire. Strips of dried beef held to the blaze for a moment served him and the dogs. He drank from a canteen. There was nothing else in his outfit; he had grown used to a scant fire. Then he sat over the fire, palms outspread, and waited. Waiting had been his chief occupation for months, and he scarcely knew what he waited for, unless it was the passing of the hours. But now he sensed action in the immediate present; the day promised another meeting with Lassiter and Jane, perhaps news of the rustlers; on the morrow he meant to take the trail to Deception Pass.

And while he waited he talked to his dogs. He called them Ring and Whitie; they were sheep-dogs, half collie, half deerhound, superb in build, perfectly trained. It seemed that in his fallen fortunes these dogs understood the nature of their value to him, and governed their affection and faithfulness accordingly. Whitie watched him with somber eyes of love, and Ring, crouched on the little rise of ground above, kept tireless guard. When the sun rose, the white dog took the place of the other, and Ring went to sleep at his master's feet.

By and by Venters rolled up his blankets and tied them and his meager pack together, then climbed out to look for his horse. He saw him, presently, a little way off in the sage, and went to fetch him. In that country, where every rider boasted of a fine mount and was eager for a race, where thoroughbreds dotted the wonderful grazing ranges, Venters rode a horse that was sad proof of his misfortunes.

Then, with his back against a stone, Venters faced the east, and, stick in hand and idle blade, he waited. The glorious sunlight filled the valley with purple fire. Before him, to left, to right, waving, rolling, sinking, rising, like low swells of a purple sea, stretched the sage. Out of the grove of cottonwoods, a green patch on the purple, gleamed the dull red of Jane Withersteen's old stone house. And from there extended the wide green of the village gardens and orchards marked by the graceful poplars; and farther down shone the deep, dark richness of the alfalfa fields. Numberless red and black and white dots speckled the sage, and these were cattle and horses.

So, watching and waiting, Venters let the time wear away. At length he saw a horse rise above a ridge, and he knew it to be Lassiter's black. Climbing to the highest rock, so that he would show against the sky-line, he stood and waved his hat. The almost instant turning of Lassiter's horse attested to the quickness of that rider's eye. Then Venters climbed down, saddled his horse, tied on his pack, and, with a word to his dogs, was about to ride out to meet Lassiter, when he concluded to wait for him there, on higher ground, where the outlook was commanding.

It had been long since Venters had experienced friendly greeting from a man. Lassiter's warmed in him something that had grown cold from neglect. And when he had returned it, with a strong grip of the iron hand that held his, and met the gray eyes, he knew that Lassiter and he were to be friends.

"Venters, let's talk awhile before we go down there," said Lassiter, slipping his bridle. "I ain't in no hurry. Them's sure fine dogs you've got." With a rider's eye he took in the points of Venters's horse, but did not speak his thought. "Well, did anythin' come off after I left you last night?"

Venters told him about the rustlers.

"I was snug hid in the sage," replied Lassiter, "an' didn't see or hear no one. Oldrin's got a high hand here, I reckon. It's no news up in Utah how he holes in canons an' leaves no track." Lassiter was silent a moment. "Me and Oldrin' wasn't exactly strangers some years back when he drove cattle into Bostil's Ford, at the head of the Rio Virgin. But he got harassed there an' now he drives some place else."

"Lassiter, you knew him? Tell me, is he Mormon or Gentile?"

"I can't say. I've knowed Mormons who pretended to be Gentiles."

"No Mormon ever pretended that unless he was a rustler," declared Venters.

"Mebbe so."

"It's a hard country for any one, but hardest for Gentiles. Did you ever know or hear of a Gentile prospering in a Mormon community?"

"I never did."

"Well, I want to get out of Utah. I've a mother living in Illinois. I want to go home. It's eight years now."

The older man's sympathy moved Venters to tell his story. He had left Quincy, run off to seek his fortune in the gold fields, had never gotten any farther than Salt Lake City, wandered here and there as helper, teamster, shepherd, and drifted southward over the divide and across the barrens and up the rugged plateau through the passes to the last border settlements. Here he became a rider of the sage, had stock of his own, and for a time prospered, until chance threw him in the employ of Jane Withersteen.

"Lassiter, I needn't tell you the rest."

"Well, it'd be no news to me. I know Mormons. I've seen their women's strange love an' patience an' sacrifice an' silence an' what I call madness for their idea of God. An' over against that I've seen the tricks of men. They work hand in hand, all together, an' in the dark. No man can hold out against them, unless he takes to packin' guns. For Mormons are slow to kill. That's the only good I ever seen in their religion. Venters, take this from me, these Mormons ain't just right in their minds. Else could a Mormon marry one woman when he already has a wife, an' call it duty?"

"Lassiter, you think as I think," returned Venters.

"How'd it come then that you never throwed a gun on Tull or some of them?" inquired the rider, curiously.

"Jane pleaded with me, begged me to be patient, to overlook. She even took my guns from me. I lost all before I knew it," replied Venters, with the red color in his face. "But, Lassiter, listen. Out of the wreck I saved a Winchester, two Colts, and plenty of shells. I packed these down into Deception Pass. There, almost every day for six months, I have practiced with my rifle till the barrel burnt my hands. Practiced the draw—the firing of a Colt, hour after hour!"

"Now that's interestin' to me," said Lassiter, with a quick uplift of his head and a concentration of his gray gaze on Venters. "Could you throw a gun before you began that practicin'?"

"Yes. And now . . ." Venters made a lightning-swift movement.

Lassiter smiled, and then his bronzed eyelids narrowed till his eyes seemed mere gray slits. "You'll kill Tull!" He did not question; he affirmed.

"I promised Jane Withersteen I'd try to avoid Tull. I'll keep my word. But sooner or later Tull and I will meet. As I feel now, if he even looks at me I'll draw!"

"I reckon so. There'll be hell down there, presently." He paused a moment and flicked a sage-brush with his quirt. "Venters, seein' as you're considerable worked up, tell me Milly Erne's story."

Venters's agitation stilled to the trace of suppressed eagerness in Lassiter's query.

"Milly Erne's story? Well, Lassiter, I'll tell you what I know. Milly Erne had been in Cottonwoods years when I first arrived there, and most of what I tell you happened before my arrival. I got to know her pretty well. She was a slip of a woman, and crazy on religion. I conceived an idea that I never mentioned—I thought she was at heart more Gentile than Mormon. But she passed as a Mormon, and certainly she had the Mormon woman's locked lips. You know, in every Mormon village there are women who seem mysterious to us, but about Milly there was more than the ordinary mystery. When she came to Cottonwoods she had a beautiful little girl whom she loved passionately. Milly was not known openly in Cottonwoods as a Mormon wife. That she really was a Mormon wife I have no doubt. Perhaps the Mormon's other wife or wives would not acknowledge Milly. Such things happen in these villages. Mormon wives wear yokes, but they get jealous. Well, whatever had brought Milly to this country—love or madness of religion—she repented of it. She gave up teaching the village school. She quit the church. And she began to fight Mormon upbringing for her baby girl. Then the Mormons put on the screws—slowly, as is their way. At last the child disappeared. Lost, was the report. The child was stolen, I know that. So do you. That wrecked Milly Erne. But she lived on in hope. She became a slave. She worked her heart and soul and life out to get back her child. She never heard of it again. Then she sank. . . . I can see her now, a frail thing, so transparent you could almost look through her—white like ashes—and her eyes! . . . Her eyes have always haunted me. She had one real friend—Jane Withersteen. But Jane couldn't mend a broken heart, and Milly died."

For moments Lassiter did not speak, or turn his head.

"The man!" he exclaimed, presently, in husky accents.

"I haven't the slightest idea who the Mormon was," replied Venters; "nor has any Gentile in Cottonwoods."

"Does Jane Withersteen know?"

"Yes. But a red-hot running-iron couldn't burn that name out of her!"

Without further speech Lassiter started off, walking his horse, and Venters followed with his dogs. Half a mile down the slope they entered a luxuriant growth of willows, and soon came into an open space carpeted with grass like deep green velvet. The rushing of water and singing of birds filled their ears. Venters led his comrade to a shady bower and showed him Amber Spring. It was a magnificent outburst of clear, amber water pouring from a dark, stone-lined hole. Lassiter knelt and drank, lingered there to drink again. He made no comment, but Venters did not need words. Next to his horse a rider of the sage loved a spring. And this spring was the most beautiful and remarkable known to the upland riders of southern Utah. It was the spring that made old Withersteen a feudal lord and now enabled his daughter to return the toll which her father had exacted from the toilers of the sage.

The spring gushed forth in a swirling torrent, and leaped down joyously to make its swift way along a willow-skirted channel. Moss and ferns and lilies overhung its green banks. Except for the rough-hewn stones that held and directed the water, this willow thicket and glade had been left as nature had made it.

Below were artificial lakes, three in number, one above the other in banks of raised earth; and round about them rose the lofty green-foliaged shafts of poplar trees. Ducks dotted the glassy surface of the lakes; a blue heron stood motionless on a water-gate; kingfishers darted with shrieking flight along the shady banks; a white hawk sailed above; and from the trees and shrubs came the song of robins and cat-birds. It was all in strange contrast to the endless slopes of lonely sage and the wild rock environs beyond. Venters thought of the woman who loved the birds and the green of the leaves and the murmur of the water.

Next on the slope, just below the third and largest lake, were corrals and a wide stone barn and open sheds and coops and pens. Here were clouds of dust, and cracking sounds of hoofs, and romping colts and heehawing burros. Neighing horses trampled to the corral fences. And from the little windows of the barn projected bobbing heads of bays and blacks and sorrels. When the two men entered the immense barnyard, from all around the din increased. This welcome, however, was not seconded by the several men and boys who vanished on sight.

Venters and Lassiter were turning toward the house when Jane appeared in the lane leading a horse. In riding-skirt and blouse she seemed to have lost some of her statuesque proportions, and looked more like a girl rider than the mistress of Withersteen. She was brightly smiling, and her greeting was warmly cordial.

"Good news," she announced. "I've been to the village. All is quiet. I expected—I don't know what. But there's no excitement. And Tull has ridden out on his way to Glaze."

"Tull gone?" inquired Venters, with surprise. He was wondering what could have taken Tull away. Was it to avoid another meeting with Lassiter that he went? Could it have any connection with the probably nearness of Oldring and his gang?

"Gone, yes, thank goodness," replied Jane. "Now I'll have peace for a while. Lassiter, I want you to see my horses. You are a rider, and you must be a judge of horseflesh. Some of mine have Arabian blood. My father got his best strain in Nevada from Indians who claimed their horses were bred down from the original stock left by the Spaniards."

"Well, ma'am, the one you've been ridin' takes my eye," said Lassiter, as he walked round the racy, clean-limbed, and fine-pointed roan.

"Where are the boys?" she asked, looking about. "Jerd, Paul, where are you? Here, bring out the horses."

The sound of dropping bars inside the barn was the signal for the horses to jerk their heads in the windows, to snort and stamp. Then they came pounding out of the door, a file of thoroughbreds, to plunge about the barnyard, heads and tails up, manes flying. They halted afar off, squared away to look, came slowly forward with whinnies for their mistress, and doubtful snorts for the strangers and their horses.

"Come—come—come," called Jane, holding out her hands. "Why Bells—Wrangle, where are your manners? Come, Black Star—come, Night. Ah, you beauties! My racers of the sage!"

Only two came up to her; those she called Night and Black Star. Venters never looked at them without delight. The first was soft dead black, the other glittering black, and they were perfectly matched in size, both being high and long-bodied, wide through the shoulders, with lithe, powerful legs. That they were a woman's pets showed in the gloss of skin, the fineness of mane. It showed, too, in the light of big eyes and the gentle reach of eagerness.

"I never seen their like," was Lassiter's encomium, "an' in my day I've seen a sight of horses. Now, ma'am, if you was wantin' to make a long an' fast ride across the sage—say to elope—"

Lassiter ended there with dry humor, yet behind that was meaning. Jane blushed and made arch eyes at him.

"Take care, Lassiter, I might think that a proposal," she replied, gaily. "It's dangerous to propose elopement to a Mormon woman. Well, I was expecting you. Now will be a good hour to show you Milly Erne's grave. The day-riders have gone, and the night-riders haven't come in. Bern, what do you make of that? Need I worry? You know I have to be made worry."

"Well, it's not usual for the night shift to ride in so late," replied Venters, slowly, and his glance sought Lassiter's. "Cattle are usually quiet after dark. Still, I've known even a coyote to stampede your white herd."

"I refuse to borrow trouble. Come," said Jane.

They mounted, and, with Jane in the lead, rode down the lane, and, turning off into a cattle trail, proceeded westward. Venters's dogs trotted behind them. On this side of the ranch the outlook was different from that on the other; the immediate foreground was rough and the sage more rugged and less colorful; there were no dark-blue lines of cañons to hold the eye, nor any uprearing rock walls. It was a long roll and slope into gray obscurity. Soon Jane left the trail and rode into the sage, and presently she dismounted and threw her bridle. The men did likewise. Then, on foot, they followed her, coming out at length on the rim of a low escarpment. She passed by several little ridges of earth to halt before a faintly defined mound. It lay in the shade of a sweeping sage-brush close to the edge of the promontory; and a rider could have jumped his horse over it without recognizing a grave.

"Here!"

She looked sad as she spoke, but she offered no explanation for the neglect of an unmarked, uncared-for grave. There was a little bunch of pale, sweet lavender daisies, doubtless planted there by Jane.

"I only come here to remember and to pray," she said. "But I leave no trail!"

A grave in the sage! How lonely this resting-place of Milly Erne! The cottonwoods or the alfalfa fields were not in sight, nor was there any rock or ridge or cedar to lend contrast to the monotony. Gray slopes, tinging the purple, barren and wild, with the wind waving the sage, swept away to the dim horizon.

Lassiter looked at the grave and then out into space. At that moment he seemed a figure of bronze.

Jane touched Venters's arm and led him back to the horses.

"Bern!" cried Jane, when they were out of hearing. "Suppose Lassiter were Milly's husband—the father of that little girl lost so long ago!"

"It might be, Jane. Let us ride on. If he wants to see us again he'll come."

So they mounted and rode out to the cattle trail and began to climb. From the height of the ridge, where they had started down, Venters looked back. He did not see Lassiter, but his glance, drawn irresistibly farther out on the gradual slope, caught sight of a moving cloud of dust.

"Hello, a rider!"

"Yes, I see," said Jane.

"That fellow's riding hard. Jane, there's something wrong."

"Oh yes, there must be. . . . How he rides!"

The horse disappeared in the sage, and then puffs of dust marked his course.

"He's short-cut on us—he's making straight for the corrals."

Venters and Jane galloped their steeds and reined in at the turning of the lane. This lane led down to the right of the grove. Suddenly into its lower entrance flashed a bay horse. Then Venters caught the fast rhythmic beat of pounding hoofs. Soon his keen eye recognized the swing of the rider in his saddle.

"It's Judkins, your Gentile rider!" he cried. "Jane, when Judkins rides like that it means hell!"

CHAPTER FOUR
Deception Pass

The rider thundered up and almost threw his foam-flecked horse in the sudden stop. He was a giant form, and with fearless eyes.

"Judkins, you're all bloody!" cried Jane, in affright. "Oh, you've been shot!"

"Nothin' much, Miss Withersteen. I got a nick in the shoulder. I'm some wet an' the hoss's been throwin' lather, so all this ain't blood."

"What's up?" queried Venters, sharply.

"Rustlers sloped off with the red herd."

"Where are my riders?" demanded Jane.

"Miss Withersteen, I was alone all night with the herd. At daylight this mornin' the rustlers rode down. They began to shoot at me on sight. They chased me hard an' far, burnin' powder all the time, but I got away."

"Jud, they meant to kill you," declared Venters.

"Now I wonder," returned Judkins. "They wanted me bad. An' it ain't regular for rustlers to waste time chasin' one rider."

"Thank heaven you got away," said Jane. "But my riders—where are they?"

"I don't know. The night-riders weren't there last night when I rode down, an' this mornin' I met no day-riders."

"Judkins! Bern they've been set upon—killed by Oldring's men!"

"I don't think so," replied Venters, decidedly. "Jane, your riders haven't gone out in the sage."

"Bern, what do you mean?" Jane Withersteen turned deathly pale.

"You remember what I said about the unseen hand?"

"Oh! . . . Impossible!"

"I hope so. But I fear—" Venters finished, with a shake of his head.

"Bern, you're bitter; but that's only natural. We'll wait to see what's happened to my riders. Judkins, come to the house with me. Your wound must be attended to."

"Jane, I'll find out where Oldring drives the herd," vowed Venters.

"No, no! Bern, don't risk it now—when the rustlers are in such shooting mood."

"I'm going. Jud, how many cattle in that red herd?"

"Twenty-five hundred head."

"Whew! What on earth can Oldring do with so many cattle? Why, a hundred head is a big steal. I've got to find out."

"Don't go," implored Jane.

"Bern, you want a hoss thet can run. Miss Withersteen, if it's not too bold of me to advise, make him take a fast hoss or don't let him go."

"Yes, yes, Judkins. He must ride a horse that can't be caught. Which one—Black Star—Night?"

"Jane, I won't take either," said Venters, emphatically. "I wouldn't risk losing one of your favorites."

"Wrangle, then?"

"Thet's the hoss," replied Judkins. "Wrangle can outrun Black Star an' Night. You'd never believe it, Miss Withersteen, but I know. Wrangle's the biggest an' fastest hoss on the sage."

"Oh no, Wrangle can't beat Black Star. But, Bern, take Wrangle, if you will go. Ask Jerd for anything you need. Oh, be watchful, careful. . . . God speed you!"

She clasped his hand, turned quickly away, and went down the lane with the rider.

Venters rode to the barn, and, leaping off, shouted for Jerd. The boy came running. Venters sent him for meat, bread, and dried fruits, to be packed in saddlebags. His own horse he turned loose into the nearest corral. Then he went for Wrangle. The giant sorrel had earned his name for a trait the opposite of amiability. He came readily out of the barn, but once in the yard he broke from

Venters, and plunged about with ears laid back. Venters had to rope him, and then he kicked down a section of fence, stood on his hind legs, crashed down and fought the rope. Jerd returned to lend a hand.

"Wrangle don't git enough work," said Jerd, as the big saddle went on. "He's unruly when he's corralled, an' wants to run. Wait till he smells the sage!"

"Jerd, this horse is an iron-jawed devil. I never straddled him but once. Run? Say, he's swift as wind!"

When Venters's boot touched the stirrup the sorrel bolted, giving him the rider's flying mount. The swing of this fiery horse recalled to Venters days that were not really long past, when he rode into the sage as the leader of Jane Withersteen's riders. Wrangle pulled hard on a tight rein. He galloped out of the lane, down the shady border of the grove, and hauled up at the watering-trough, where he pranced and champed his bit. Venters got off and filled his canteen while the horse drank. The dogs, Ring and Whitie, came trotting up for their drink. Then Venters remounted and turned Wrangle toward the sage.

A wide, white trail wound away down the slope. One keen, sweeping glance told Venters that there was neither man nor horse nor steer within the limit of his vision, unless they were lying down in the sage. Ring loped in the lead and Whitie loped in the rear. Wrangle settled gradually into an easy swinging canter, and Venters's thoughts, now that the rush and flurry of the start were past, and the long miles stretched before him, reverted to a calm reckoning of late singular coincidences.

There was the night ride of Tull's, which, viewed in the light of subsequent events, had a look of his covert machinations; Oldring and his Masked Rider and his rustlers riding muffled horses; the report that Tull had ridden out that morning with his man Jerry on the trail to Glaze, the strange disappearance of Jane Withersteen's riders, the unusually determined attempt to kill the one Gentile still in her employ, an intention frustrated, no doubt, only by Judkin's magnificent riding of her racer, and lastly the driving of the red herd. These events, to Venters's color of mind, had a dark relationship. Remembering Jane's accusation of bitterness, he tried hard to put aside his rancor in judging Tull. But it was bitter knowledge that made him see the truth. He had felt the shadow of an unseen hand; he had watched till he saw its dim outline, and then he had traced it to a man's hate, to the rivalry of a Mormon Elder, to the power of a Bishop, to the long, far-reaching arm of a terrible creed. That unseen hand had made its first move against Jane Withersteen. Her riders had been called in, leaving her without help to drive seven thousand head of cattle. But to Venters it seemed extraordinary that the power which had called in these riders had left so many cattle to be driven by rustlers and harried by wolves. For hand in glove with that power was an insatiate greed; they were one and the same.

"What can Oldring do with twenty-five hundred head of cattle?" muttered Venters. "Is he a Mormon? Did he meet Tull last night? It looks like a black plot to me. But Tull and his churchmen wouldn't ruin Jane Withersteen unless the Church was to profit by that ruin. Where does Oldring come in? I'm going to find out about these things."

Wrangle did the twenty-five miles in three hours and walked little of the way. When he had gotten warmed up he had been allowed to choose his own gait. The afternoon had well advanced when Venters struck the trail of the red herd and found where it had grazed the night before. Then Venters rested the horse and used his eyes. Near at hand were a cow and a calf and several yearlings, and farther out in the sage some straggling steers. He caught a glimpse of coyotes skulking near the cattle. The slow, sweeping gaze of the rider failed to find other living things within the field of sight. The sage about him was breast-high to his horse, oversweet with its warm, fragrant breath, gray where it waved to the light, darker where the wind left it still, and beyond the wonderful haze-purple lent by distance. Far across that wide waste began the slow lift of uplands through which Deception Pass cut its tortuous many-cañoned way.

Venters raised the bridle of his horse and followed the broad cattle trail. The crushed sage resembled the path of a monster snake. In a few miles of travel he passed several cows and calves that had escaped the drive. Then he stood on the last high bench of the slope with the floor of the valley beneath. The opening of the cañon showed in a break of the sage, and the cattle trail paralleled it as far as he could see. That trail led to an undiscovered point where Oldring drove cattle into the pass, and many a rider who had followed it had never returned. Venters satisfied himself that the rustlers had not deviated from their usual course, and then he turned at right angles off the cattle trail and made for the head of the pass.

The sun lost its heat and wore down to the western horizon, where it changed from white to gold and rested like a huge ball about to roll on its golden shadows down the slope. Venters watched the lengthening of the rays and bars, and marveled at his own league-long shadow. The sun sank. There was instant shading of brightness about him, and he saw a kind of cold purple bloom creep ahead of him to cross the cañon, to mount the opposite slope and chase and darken and bury the last golden flare of sunlight.

Venters rode into a trail that he always took to get down into the cañon. He dismounted and found no tracks but his own made days previous. Nevertheless he sent the dog Ring ahead and waited. In a little while Ring returned. Whereupon Venters led his horse on to the break in the ground.

The opening into Deception Pass was one of the remarkable natural phenomena in a country remarkable for vast slopes of sage, uplands insulated by gigantic red walls, and deep cañons of mysterious source and outlet. Here the valley floor was level, and here opened a narrow chasm, a ragged vent in yellow walls of stone. The trail down the five hundred feet of sheer depth always tested Venters's nerve. It was bad going for even a burro. But Wrangle, as Venters led him, snorted defiance or disgust rather than fear, and, like a hobbled horse on the jump, lifted his ponderous iron-shod fore hoofs and crashed down over the first rough step. Venters warmed to greater admiration of the sorrel; and, giving him a loose bridle, he stepped down foot by foot. Oftentimes the stones and shale started by Wrangle buried Venters to his knees; again he was hard put to it to dodge a rolling boulder; there were times when he could not see Wrangle for dust, and once he and the horse rode a sliding shelf of yellow, weathered cliff. It was a trail on which there could be no stops, and, therefore, if perilous, it was at least one that did not take long in the descent.

Venters breathed lighter when that was over, and felt a sudden assurance in the success of his enterprise. For at first it had been a reckless determination to achieve something at any cost, and now it resolved itself into an adventure worthy of all his reason and cunning, and keenness of eye and ear.

Piñon pines clustered in little clumps along the level floor of the pass. Twilight had gathered under the walls. Venters rode into the trail and up the cañon. Gradually the trees and caves and objects low down turned black, and this blackness moved up the walls till night enfolded the pass, while day still lingered above. The sky darkened; and stars began to show, at first pale and then bright. Sharp notches of the rim-wall, biting like teeth into the blue, were landmarks by which Venters knew where his camping site lay. He had to feel his way through a thicket of slender oaks to a spring where he watered Wrangle and drank himself. Here he unsaddled and turned Wrangle loose, having no fear that the horse would leave the thick, cool grass adjacent to the spring. Next he satisfied his own hunger, fed Ring and Whitie, and, with them curled beside him, composed himself to await sleep.

There had been a time when night in the high altitude of these Utah uplands had been satisfying to Venters. But that was before the oppression of enemies had made the change in his mind. As a rider guarding the herd he had never thought of the night's wildness and loneliness; as an outcast, now when the full silence set in, and the deep darkness, and trains of radiant stars shone cold and calm, he lay with an ache in his heart. For a year he had lived as a black fox, driven from his kind. He longed for the sound of a voice, the touch of a hand. In the daytime there was riding from place to place, and the gun practice to which something drove him, and other tasks that at least necessitated action; at night, before he won sleep, there was strife in his soul. He yearned to leave the endless sage slopes, the wilderness of cañons; and it was in the lonely night that this yearning grew unbearable. It was then that he reached forth to feel Ring or Whitie, immeasurably grateful for the love and companionship of two dogs.

On this night the same old loneliness beset Venters, the old habit of sad thought and burning unquiet had its way. But from it evolved a conviction that his useless life had undergone a subtle change. He had sensed it first when Wrangle swung him up to the high saddle, he knew it now when he lay in the gateway of Deception Pass. He had no thrill of adventure, rather a gloomy perception of great hazard, perhaps death. He meant to find Oldring's retreat. The rustlers had fast horses, but none that could match Wrangle. Venters knew no rustler could creep upon him at night when Ring and Whitie guarded his hiding-place. For the rest, he had eyes and ears, and a long rifle and an unerring aim, which he meant to use. Strangely his foreshadowing of change did not hold a thought of the killing of Tull. It related only to what was to happen to him in Deception Pass; and he could no more lift the veil of that mystery than tell where the trails led to in that unexplored cañon. Moreover, he did not care. And at length, tired out by stress of thought, he fell asleep.

When his eyes unclosed, day had come again, and he saw the rim of the opposite wall tipped with the gold of sunrise. A few moments sufficed for the morning's simple camp duties. Near at hand he found Wrangle, and to his surprise the horse came to him. Wrangle was one of the horses that left his viciousness in the home corral. What he wanted was to be free of mules and burros and steers, to roll in dust-patches, and then to run down the wide, open, windy sage-plains, and at night browse and sleep in the cool wet grass of a springhole. Jerd knew the sorrel when he said of him, "Wait till he smells the sage!"

Venters saddled and led him out of the oak thicket, and, leaping astride, rode up the cañon, with Ring and Whitie trotting behind. An old grass-grown trail followed the course of a shallow wash where flowed a thin stream of water. The cañon was a hundred rods wide; its yellow walls were perpendicular; it had abundant sage and a scant growth of oak and piñon. For five miles it held to a comparatively straight bearing, and then began a heightening of rugged walls and a deepening of the floor. Beyond this point of sudden change in the character of the cañon Venters had never explored, and here was the real door to the intricacies of Deception Pass.

He reined Wrangle to a walk, halted now and then to listen, and then proceeded cautiously with shifting and alert gaze. The cañon assumed proportions that dwarfed those of its first ten miles. Venters rode on and on, not losing in the interest of his wide surroundings any of his caution or keen search for tracks or sight of living thing. If there ever had been a trail here, he could not find it. He rode through sage and clumps of piñon trees and grassy plots where long-petaled purple lilies bloomed. He rode through a dark constriction of the pass no wider than the lane in the grove at Cottonwoods. And he came out into a great amphitheater into which jutted huge towering corners of a confluence of intersecting cañons.

Venters sat his horse, and, with a rider's eye, studied this wild cross-cut of huge stone gullies. Then he went on, guided by the course of running water. If it had not been for the main stream of water flowing north he would never have been able to tell which of those many openings was a continuation of the pass. In crossing this amphitheater he went by the mouths of five cañons, fording little streams that flowed into the larger one. Gaining the outlet which he took to be the pass, he rode on again under overhanging walls. One side was dark in shade, the other light in sun. This narrow passageway turned and twisted and opened into a valley that amazed Venters.

Here again was a sweep of purple sage, richer than upon the higher levels. The valley was miles long, several wide, and inclosed by unscalable walls. But it was the background of this valley that so forcibly struck him. Across the sage-flat rose a strange up-flinging of yellow rocks. He could not tell which were close and which were distant. Scrawled mounds of stone, like mountain waves, seemed to roll up to steep bare slopes and towers.

In this plain of sage Venters flushed birds and rabbits, and when he had proceeded about a mile he caught sight of the bobbing white tails of a herd of running antelope. He rode along the edge of the stream which wound toward the western end of the slowly looming mounds of stone. The high slope retreated out of sight behind the nearer projection. To Venters the valley appeared to have been filled in by a mountain of melted stone that had hardened in strange shapes of rounded outline. He followed the stream till he lost it in a deep cut. Therefore Venters quit the dark slit which baffled further search in that direction, and rode out along the curved edge of stone where it met the sage. It was not long before he came to a low place, and here Wrangle readily climbed up.

All about him was ridgy roll of wind-smoothed, rain-washed rock. Not a tuft of grass or a bunch of sage colored the dull rust-yellow. He saw where, to the right, this uneven flow of stone ended in a blunt wall. Leftward, from the hollow that lay at his feet, mounted a gradual slow-swelling slope to a great height topped by leaning, cracked, and ruined crags. Not for some time did he grasp the wonder of that acclivity. It was no less than a mountain-side, glistening in the sun like polished granite, with cedar-trees springing as if by magic out of the denuded surface. Winds had swept it clear of weathered shale, and rains had washed it free of dust. Far up the curved slope its beautiful lines broke to meet the vertical rim-wall, to lose its grace in a different order and color of rock, a stained yellow cliff of cracks and caves and seamed crags. And straight before Venters was a scene less striking but more significant to his keen survey. For beyond a mile of the bare, hummocky rock began the valley of sage, and the mouths of cañons, one of which surely was another gateway into the pass.

* * *

He got off his horse, and, giving the bridle to Ring to hold, he commenced a search for the cleft where the stream ran. He was not successful and concluded the water dropped into an underground passage. Then he returned to where he had left Wrangle, and led him down off the stone to the sage. It was a short ride to the opening cañons. There was no reason for a choice of which one to enter. The one he rode into was a clear, sharp shaft in yellow stone a thousand feet deep, with wonderful wind-worn caves low down and high above buttressed and turreted ramparts. Farther on Venters came into a region where deep indentations marked the line of cañon walls. These were huge, cove-like blind pockets extending back to a sharp corner with a dense growth of underbrush and trees.

Venters penetrated into one of these offshoots, and, as he had hoped, he found abundant grass. He had to bend the oak saplings to get his horse through. Deciding to make this a hiding-place if he could find water, he worked back to the limit of the shelving walls. In a little cluster of silver spruces he found a spring. This inclosed nook seemed an ideal place to leave his horse and to camp at night, and from which to make stealthy trips on foot. The thick grass hid his trail; the dense growth of oaks in the opening would serve as a barrier to keep Wrangle in, if, indeed, the luxuriant browse would not suffice for that. So Venters, leaving Whitie with the horse, called Ring to his side, and, rifle in hand, worked his way out to the open. A careful photographing in mind of the formation of the bold outlines of rimrock assured him he would be able to return to his retreat even in the dark.

Bunches of scattered sage covered the center of the cañon, and among these Venters threaded his way with the step of an Indian. At intervals he put his hand on the dog and stopped to listen. There was a drowsy hum of insects, but no other sound disturbed the warm midday stillness. Venters saw ahead a turn, more abrupt than any yet. Warily he rounded this corner, once again to halt bewildered.

The cañon opened fan-shaped into a great oval of green and gray growths. It was the hub of an oblong wheel, and from it, at regular distances, like spokes, ran the outgoing cañons. Here a dull red color predominated over the fading yellow. The corners of wall bluntly rose, scarred and scrawled, to taper into towers and serrated peaks and pinnacled domes.

Venters pushed on more heedfully than ever. Toward the center of this circle the sage-brush grew smaller and farther apart. He was about to sheer off to the right, where thickets and jumbles of fallen rock would afford him cover, when he ran right upon a broad cattle trail. Like a road it was, more than a trail; and the cattle tracks were fresh. What surprised him more, they were wet! He pondered over this feature. It had not rained. The only solution to this puzzle was that the cattle had been driven through water, and water deep enough to wet their legs.

Suddenly Ring growled low. Venters rose cautiously and looked over the sage. A band of straggling horsemen were riding across the oval. He sank down, startled and trembling. "Rustlers!" he muttered. Hurriedly he glanced about for a place to hide. Near at hand there was nothing but sage-brush. He dared not risk crossing the open patches to reach the rocks. Again he peeped over the sage. The rustlers—four—five—seven—eight in all, were approaching, but not directly in line with him. That was relief for a cold deadness which seemed to be creeping inward along his veins. He crouched down with bated breath and held the bristling dog.

He heard the click of iron-shod hoofs on stone, the coarse laughter of men, and then voices gradually dying away. Long moments passed. Then he rose. The rustlers were riding into a cañon. Their horses were tired, and they had several pack animals; evidently they had traveled far. Venters doubted that they were the rustlers who had driven the red herd. Oldring's band had split. Venters watched these horsemen disappear under a bold cañon wall.

The rustlers had come from the northwest side of the oval. Venters kept a steady gaze in that direction, hoping, if there were more, to see from what cañon they rode. A quarter of an hour went by. Reward for his vigilance came when he descried three more mounted men, far over to the north. But out of what cañon they had ridden it was too late to tell. He watched the three ride across the oval and round the jutting red corner where the others had gone.

"Up that cañon!" exclaimed Venters. "Oldring's den! I've found it!"

A knotty point for Venters was the fact that the cattle tracks all pointed west. The broad trail came from the direction of the cañon into which the rustlers had ridden, and undoubtedly the cattle had been driven out of it across the oval. There were no tracks pointing the other way. It had been in his mind that Oldring had driven the red herd toward the rendezvous, and not from it. Where did that broad trail come down into the pass, and where did it lead? Venters knew he wasted time in pondering the question, but it held a fascination not easily dispelled. For many years Oldring's mysterious entrance and exit to Deception Pass had been all-absorbing topics to sage-riders.

All at once the dog put an end to Venters's pondering. Ring sniffed the air, turned slowly in his tracks with a whine, and then growled. Venters wheeled. Two horsemen were within a hundred yards, coming straight at him. One, lagging behind the other, was Oldring's Masked Rider.

Venters cunningly sank, slowly trying to merge into sage-brush. But, guarded as his action was, the first horse detected it. He stopped short, snorted, and shot up his ears. The rustler bent forward, as if keenly peering ahead. Then, with a swift sweep, he jerked a gun from its sheath and fired.

The bullet zipped through the sage-brush. Flying bits of wood struck Venters, and the hot, stinging pain seemed to lift him in one leap. Like a flash the blue barrel of his rifle gleamed level and he shoot once—twice.

The foremost rustler dropped his weapon and toppled from his saddle, to fall with his foot catching in a stirrup. The horse snorted wildly and plunged away, dragging the rustler through the sage.

The Masked Rider huddled over his pommel, slowly swaying to one side, and then, with a faint, strange cry, slipped out of the saddle.

CHAPTER FIVE
The Masked Rider

Venters looked quickly from the fallen rustlers to the cañon where the others had disappeared. He calculated on the time needed for running horses to return to the open, if their riders heard shots. He waited breathlessly. But the estimated time dragged by and no riders appeared. Venters began presently to believe that the rifle reports had not penetrated into the recesses of the cañon, and felt safe for the immediate present.

He hurried to the spot where the first rustler had been dragged by his horse. The man lay in deep grass, dead, jaw fallen, eyes protruding—a sight that sickened Venters. The first man at whom he had ever aimed a weapon he had shot through the heart. With the clammy sweat oozing from every pore Venters dragged the rustler in among some boulders and covered him with slabs of rock. Then he smoothed out the crushed trail in grass and sage. The rustler's horse had stopped a quarter of a mile off and was grazing.

When Venters rapidly strode toward the Masked Rider not even the cold nausea that gripped him could wholly banish curiosity. For he had shot Oldring's infamous lieutenant, whose face had never been seen. Venters experienced a grim pride in the feat. What would Tull say to this achievement of the outcast who rode too often to Deception Pass?

Venters's curious eagerness and expectation had not prepared him for the shock he received when he stood over a slight, dark figure. The rustler wore the black mask that had given him his name, but he had no weapons. Venters glanced at the drooping horse; there were no gun-sheaths on the saddle.

"A rustler who didn't pack guns!" muttered Venters. "He wears no belt. He couldn't pack guns in that rig. . . . Strange!"

A low, gasping intake of breath and a sudden twitching of body told Venters the rider still lived.

"He's alive! . . . I've got to stand here and watch him die. And I shot an unarmed man."

Shrinkingly Venters removed the rider's wide sombrero and the black cloth mask. This action disclosed bright chestnut hair, inclined to curl, and a white, youthful face. Along the lower line of cheek and jaw was a clear demarcation, where the brown of tanned skin met the white that had been hidden from the sun.

"Oh, he's only a boy! . . . What! Can he be Oldring's Masked Rider?"

The boy showed signs of returning consciousness. He stirred; his lips moved; a small brown hand clenched in his blouse.

Venters knelt with a gathering horror of his deed. His bullet had entered the rider's right breast, high up to the shoulder. With hands that shook, Venters untied a black scarf and ripped open the blood-wet blouse.

First he saw a gaping hole, dark red against a whiteness of skin, from which welled a slender red stream. Then the graceful, beautiful swell of a woman's breast!

"A woman!" he cried. "A girl! . . . I've killed a girl!"

She suddenly opened eyes that transfixed Venters. They were fathomless blue. Consciousness of death was there, a blended terror and pain, but no consciousness of sight. She did not see Venters. She stared into the unknown.

Then came a spasm of vitality. She writhed in a torture of reviving strength, and in her convulsions she almost tore from Venters's grasp. Slowly she relaxed and sank partly back. The ungloved hand sought the wound, and pressed so hard that her wrist half buried itself in her bosom. Blood trickled between her spread fingers. And she looked at Venters with eyes that saw him.

He cursed himself and the unerring aim of which he had been so proud. He had seen that look in the eyes of a crippled antelope which he was about to finish with his knife. But in her it had infinitely more—a revelation of mortal spirit. The instinctive clinging to life was there, and the divining helplessness and the terrible accusation of the stricken.

"Forgive me! I didn't know!" burst out Venters.

"You shot me—you've killed me!" she whispered, in panting gasps. Upon her lips appeared a fluttering, bloody froth. By that Venters knew the air in her lungs was mixing with blood. "Oh, I knew—it would—come—some day! . . . Oh, the burn! . . . Hold me—I'm sinking—it's all dark. . . . Ah, God! . . . Mercy—"

Her rigidity loosened in one long quiver and she lay back limp, still, white as snow, with closed eyes.

Venters thought then that she died. But the faint pulsation of her breast assured him that life yet lingered. Death seemed only a matter of moments, for the bullet had gone clear through her. Nevertheless, he tore sageleaves from a bush, and, pressing them tightly over her wounds, he bound the black scarf round her shoulder, tying it securely under her arm. Then he closed the blouse, hiding from his sight that blood-stained, accusing breast.

"What—now?" he questioned, with flying mind. "I must get out of here. She's dying—but I can't leave her."

He rapidly surveyed the sage to the north and made out no animate object. Then he picked up the girl's sombrero and the mask. This time the mask gave him as great a shock as when he first removed it from her face. For in the woman he had forgotten the rustler, and this black strip of felt-cloth established the identity of Oldring's Masked Rider. Venters had solved the mystery. He slipped his rifle under her, and, lifting her carefully upon it, he began to retrace his steps. The dog trailed in his shadow. And the horse, that had stood dropping by, followed without a call. Venters chose the deepest tufts of grass and clumps of sage on his return. From time to time he glanced over his shoulder. He did not rest. His concern was to avoid jarring the girl and to hide his trail. Gaining the narrow cañon, he turned and held close to the wall till he reached his hiding-place. When he entered the dense thicket of oaks he was hard put to it to force a way through. But he held his burden almost upright, and by slipping sidewise and bending the saplings he got in. Through sage and grass he hurried to the grove of silver spruces.

He laid the girl down, almost fearing to look at her. Though marble pale and cold, she was living. Venters then appreciated the tax that long carry had been to his strength. He sat down to rest. Whitie sniffed at the pale girl and whined and crept to Venters's feet. Ring lapped the water in the runway of the spring.

Presently Venters went out to the opening, caught the horse, and, leading him through the thicket, unsaddled him and tied him with a long halter. Wrangle left his browsing long enough to whinny and toss his head. Venters felt that he could not rest easily till he had secured the other rustler's horse; so, taking his rifle and calling for Ring, he set out. Swiftly yet watchfully he made his way through the cañon to the oval and out to the cattle trail. What few tracks might have betrayed him he obliterated, so only an expert tracker could have trailed him. Then, with many a wary backward glance across the sage, he started to round up the rustler's horse. This was unexpectedly easy. He led the horse to lower ground, out of sight from the opposite side of the oval, along the shadowy western wall, and so on into his cañon and secluded camp.

The girl's eyes were open; a feverish spot burned in her cheeks; she moaned something unintelligible to Venters, but he took the movement of her lips to mean that she wanted water. Lifting her head, he tipped the canteen to her lips. After that she again lapsed into unconsciousness or a weakness which was its counterpart. Venters noted, however, that the burning flush had faded into the former pallor.

The sun set behind the high cañon rim, and a cool shade darkened the walls. Venters fed the dogs and put a halter on the dead rustler's horse. He allowed Wrangle to browse free. This done, he cut spruce boughs and made a lean-to for the girl. Then, gently lifting her upon a blanket, he folded the sides over her. The other blanket he wrapped about his shoulders and found a comfortable seat against a spruce-tree that upheld the little shack. Ring and Whitie lay near at hand, one asleep, the other watchful.

Venters dreaded the night's vigil. At night his mind was active, and this time he had to watch and think and feel beside a dying girl whom he had all but murdered. A thousand excuses he invented for himself, yet not one made any difference in his act or his self-reproach.

It seemed to him that when night fell black he could see her white face so much more plainly.

"She'll go, presently," he said, "and be out of agony—thank God!"

Every little while certainty of her death came to him with a shock; and then he would bend over and lay his ear on her breast. Her heart still beat.

The early night blackness cleared to the cold starlight. The horses were not moving, and no sound disturbed the deathly silence of the cañon.

"I'll bury her here," thought Venters, "and let her grave be as much a mystery as her life was."

For the girl's few words, the look of her eyes, the prayer, had strangely touched Venters.

"She was only a girl," he soliloquized. "What was she to Oldring? Rustlers don't have wives nor sisters nor daughters. She was bad—that's all. But somehow . . . well, she may not have willingly become the companion of rustlers. That prayer of hers to God for mercy! . . . Life is strange and cruel. I wonder if other members of Oldring's gang are women? Likely enough. But what was his game? Oldring's Mask Rider! A name to make villagers hide and lock their doors. A name credited with a dozen murders, a hundred forays, and a thousand stealings of cattle. What part did the girl have in this? It may have served Oldring to create mystery."

Hours passed. The white stars moved across the narrow strip of dark blue sky above. The silence awoke to the low hum of insects. Venters watched the immovable white face, and as he watched, hour by hour waiting for death, the infamy of her passed from his mind. He thought only of the sadness, the truth of the moment. Whoever she was—whatever she had done—she was young and she was dying.

The after-part of the night wore on interminably. The starlight failed and the gloom blackened to the darkest hour. "She'll die at the gray of dawn," muttered Venters, remembering some old woman's fancy. The blackness paled to gray, and the gray lightened and day peeped over the eastern rim. Venters listened at the breast of the girl. She still lived. Did he only imagine that her heart beat stronger, ever so slightly, but stronger? He pressed his ear closer to her breast. And he rose with his own pulse quickening.

"If she doesn't die soon—she's got a chance—the barest chance—to live," he said.

He wondered if the internal bleeding had ceased. There was no more film of blood upon her lips. But no corpse could have been whiter. Opening her blouse, he untied the scarf, and carefully picked away the sageleaves from the wound in her shoulder. It had closed. Lifting her lightly, he ascertained that the same was true of the hole where the bullet had come out. He reflected on the fact that clean wounds closed quickly in the healing upland air. He recalled instances of riders who had been cut and shot, apparently to fatal issues; yet the blood had clotted, the wounds closed, and they had recovered. He had no way to tell if internal hemorrhage still went on, but he believed that it had stopped. Otherwise she would surely not have lived so long. He marked the entrance of the bullet, and concluded that it had just touched the upper lobe of her lung. Perhaps the wound in the lung had also closed. As he began to wash the blood stains from her breast and carefully rebandage the wound, he was vaguely conscious of a strange, grave happiness in the thought that she might live.

Broad daylight and a hint of sunshine high on the cliff-rim to the west brought him to consideration of what he had better do. And while busy with his few camp tasks he revolved the thing in his mind. It would not be wise for him to remain long in his present hiding-place. And if he intended to follow the cattle trail and try to find the rustlers he had better make a move at once. For he knew that rustlers, being riders, would not make much of a day's or night's absence from camp for one or two of their number; but when the missing ones failed to show up in reasonable time there would be a search. And Venters was afraid of that.

"A good tracker could trail me," he muttered. "And I'd be cornered here. Let's see. Rustlers are a lazy set when they're not on the ride. I'll risk it. Then I'll change my hiding-place."

He carefully cleaned and reloaded his guns. When he rose to go he bent a long glance down upon the unconscious girl. Then, ordering Whitie and Ring to keep guard, he left the camp.

The safest cover lay close under the wall of the cañon, and here through the dense thickets Venters made his slow, listening advance toward the oval. Upon gaining the wide opening he decided to cross it and follow the left wall till he came to the cattle trail. He scanned the oval as keenly as if hunting for antelope. Then, stooping, he stole from one cover to another, taking advantage of rocks and bunches of sage, until he had reached the thickets under the opposite wall. Once there, he exercised extreme caution in his surveys of the ground ahead, but increased his speed when moving. Dodging from bush to bush, he passed the mouths of two cañons, and in the entrance of a third cañon he crossed a wash of swift, clear water, to come abruptly upon the cattle trail.

It followed the low bank of the wash, and, keeping it in sight, Venters hugged the line of sage and thicket. Like the curves of a serpent the cañon wound for a mile or more and then opened into a valley. Patches of red showed clear against the purple of sage, and farther out on the level dotted strings of red led away to the wall of rock.

"Ha, the red herd!" exclaimed Venters.

Then dots of white and black told him there were cattle of other colors in this inclosed valley. Oldring, the rustler, was also a rancher. Venters's calculating eye took count of stock that outnumbered the red herd.

"What a range!" went on Venters. "Water and grass enough for fifty thousand head, and no riders needed!"

After his first burst of surprise and rapid calculation Venters lost no time there, but slunk again into the sage on his back trail. With the discovery of Oldring's hidden cattle-range had come enlightenment on several problems. Here the rustler kept his stock; here was Jane Withersteen's red herd; here were the few cattle that had disappeared from the Cottonwoods slopes during the last two years. Until Oldring had driven the red herd his thefts of cattle for that time had not been more than enough to supply meat for his men. Of late no drives had been reported from Sterling or the villages north. And Venters knew that the riders had wondered at Oldring's inactivity in that particular field. He and his band had been active enough in their visits to Glaze and Cottonwoods; they always had gold; but of late the amount gambled away and drunk and thrown away in the villages had given rise to much conjecture. Oldring's more frequent visits had resulted in new saloons, and where there had formerly been one raid or shooting fray in the little hamlets there were now many. Perhaps Oldring had another range farther on up the pass, and from there drove the cattle to distant Utah towns where he was little known. But Venters came finally to doubt this. And, from what he had learned in the last few days, a belief began to form in Venters's mind that Oldring's intimidations of the villages and the mystery of the Masked Rider, with his alleged evil deeds, and the fierce resistance offered any trailing riders, and the rustling of cattle—these things were only the craft of the rustler-chief to conceal his real life and purpose and work in Deception Pass.

And like a scouting Indian Venters crawled through the sage of the oval valley, crossed trail after trail on the north side, and at last entered the cañon out of which headed the cattle trail, and into which he had watched the rustlers disappear.

If he had used caution before, now he strained every nerve to force himself to creeping stealth and to sensitiveness of ear. He crawled along so hidden that he could not use his eyes except to aid himself in the toilsome progress through the brakes and ruins of cliff-wall. Yet from time to time, as he rested, he saw the massive red walls growing higher and wilder, more looming and broken. He made note of the fact that he was turning and climbing. The sage and thickets of oak and brakes of alder gave place to piñon pine growing out of rocky soil. Suddenly a low, dull murmur assailed his ears. At first he thought it was thunder, then the slipping of a weathered slope of rock. But it was incessant, and as he progressed it filled out deeper and from a murmur changed into a soft roar.

"Falling water," he said. "There's volume to that. I wonder if it's the stream I lost."

The roar bothered him, for he could hear nothing else. Likewise, however, no rustlers could hear him. Emboldened by this, and sure that nothing but a bird could see him, he arose from his hands and knees to hurry on. An opening in the piñons warned him that he was nearing the height of slope.

He gained it, and dropped low with a burst of astonishment. Before him stretched a short cañon with rounded stone floor bare of grass or sage or tree, and with curved, shelving walls. A broad rippling stream flowed toward him, and at the back of the cañon a waterfall burst from a wide rent in the cliff, and, bounding down in two green steps, spread into a long white sheet.

If Venters had not been indubitably certain that he had entered the right cañon his astonishment would not have been so great. There had been no breaks in the walls, no side cañons entering this one where the rustlers' tracks and the cattle trail had guided him, and, therefore, he could not be wrong. But here the cañon ended, and presumably the trails also.

"That cattle trail headed out of here," Venters kept saying to himself. "It headed out. Now what I want to know is how on earth did cattle ever get in here?"

If he could be sure of anything it was of the careful scrutiny he had given that cattle track, every hoofmark of which headed straight west. He was now looking east at an immense round boxed corner of cañon down which tumbled a thin, white veil of water, scarcely twenty yards wide. Somehow, somewhere, his calculations had gone wrong. For the first time in years he found himself doubting his rider's skill in finding tracks, and his memory of what he had actually seen. In his anxiety to keep under cover he must have lost himself in this offshoot of Deception Pass, and thereby, in some unaccountable manner, missed the cañon with the trails. There was nothing else for him to think. Rustlers could not fly, nor cattle jump down thousand-foot precipices. He was only proving what the sage-riders had long said of this labyrinthine system of deceitful cañons and valleys—trails led down into Deception Pass, but no rider had ever followed them.

On a sudden he heard above the soft roar of the waterfall an unusual sound that he could not define. He dropped flat behind a stone and listened. From the direction he had come swelled something that resembled a strange muffled pounding and splashing and ringing. Despite his nerve the chill sweat began to dampen his forehead. What might not be possible in this stone-walled maze of mystery? The unnatural sound passed beyond him as he lay gripping his rifle and fighting for coolness. Then from the open came the sound, now distinct and different. Venters recognized a hobblebell of a horse, and the cracking of iron on submerged stones, and the hollow splash of hoofs in water.

Relief surged over him. His mind caught again at realities, and curiosity prompted him to peep from behind the rock.

In the middle of the stream waded a long string of packed burrows driven by three superbly mounted men. Had Venters met these dark-clothed, dark-visaged, heavily armed men anywhere in Utah, let alone in this robbers' retreat, he would have recognized them as rustlers. The discerning eye of a rider saw the signs of a long, arduous trip. These men were packing in supplies from one of the northern villages. They were tired, and their horses were almost played out, and the burros plodded on, after the manner of their kind when exhausted, faithful and patient, but as if every weary, splashing, slipping step would be their last.

All this Venters noted in one glance. After that he watched with a thrilling eagerness. Straight at the waterfall the rustlers drove the burros, and straight through the middle, where the water spread into a fleecy, thin film like dissolving smoke. Following closely, the rustlers rode into this white mist, showing in bold black rélief for an instant, and then they vanished.

Venters drew a full breath that rushed out in brief and sudden utterance.

"Good Heaven! Of all the holes for a rustler! . . . There's a cavern under that waterfall, and a passageway leading out to a cañon beyond. Oldring hides in there. He needs only to guard a trail leading down from the sage-flat above. Little danger of this outlet to the pass being discovered. I stumbled on it by luck, after I had given up. And now I know the truth of what puzzled me most—why that cattle trail was wet!"

He wheeled and ran down the slope, and out to the level of the sage-brush. Returning, he had no time to spare, only now and then, between dashes, a moment when he stopped to cast sharp eyes ahead. The abundant grass left no trace of his trail. Short work he made of the distance to the circle of cañons. He doubted that he would ever see it again; he knew he never wanted to; yet he looked at the red corners and towers with the eyes of a rider picturing landmarks never to be forgotten.

Here he spent a panting moment in a slow-circling gaze of the sage-oval and the gaps between the bluffs. Nothing stirred except the gentle wave of the tips of the brush. Then he pressed on past the mouths of several cañons and over ground new to him, now close under the eastern wall. This latter part proved to be easy traveling, well screened from possible observation from the north and west, and he soon covered it and felt safer in the deepening shade of his own cañon. Then the huge, notched bulge of red rim loomed over him, a mark by which he knew again the deep cove where his camp lay hidden. As he penetrated the thicket, safe again for the present, his thoughts reverted to the girl he had left there. The afternoon had far advanced. How would he find her? He ran into camp, frightening the dogs.

The girl lay with wide-open, dark eyes, and they dilated when he knelt beside her. The flush of fever shone in her cheeks. He lifted her and held water to her dry lips, and felt an inexplicable sense of lightness as he saw her swallow in a slow, choking gulp. Gently he laid her back.

"Who—are—you?" she whispered, haltingly.

"I'm the man who shot you," he replied.

"You'll—not—kill me—now?"

"No, no."

"What—will—you—do—with me?"

"When you get better—strong enough—I'll take you back to the cañon where the rustlers ride through the waterfall."

As with a faint shadow from a flitting wing overhead, the marble whiteness of her face seemed to change.

"Don't—take—me—back—there!"

CHAPTER SIX
The Mill-Wheel of Steers

Meantime, at the ranch, when Judkins's news had sent Venters on the trail of the rustlers, Jane Withersteen led the injured man to her house and with skilled fingers dressed the gunshot wound in his arm.

"Judkins, what do you think happened to my riders?"

"I—I'd rather not say," he replied.

"Tell me. Whatever you'll tell me I'll keep to myself. I'm beginning to worry about more than the loss of a herd of cattle. Venters hinted of—but tell me, Judkins."

"Well, Miss Withersteen, I think as Venters thinks—your riders have been called in."

"Judkins! . . . By whom?"

"You know who handles the reins of your Mormon riders."

"Do you dare insinuate that my churchmen have ordered in my riders?"

"I ain't insinuatin' nothin', Miss Withersteen," answered Judkins, with spirit. "I know what I'm talking about. I didn't want to tell you."

"Oh, I can't believe that! I'll not believe it! Would Tull leave my herds at the mercy of rustlers and wolves just because—because—? No, no! It's unbelievable."

"Yes, thet particular thing's onheard of around Cottonwoods. But, beggin' pardon, Miss Withersteen, there never was any other rich Mormon woman here on the border, let alone one thet's taken the bit between her teeth."

That was a bold thing for the reserved Judkins to say, but it did not anger her. This rider's crude hint of her spirit gave her a glimpse of what others might think. Humility and obedience had been hers always. But had she taken the bit between her teeth? Still she wavered. And then, with a quick spurt of warm blood along her veins, she thought of Black Star when he got the bit fast between his iron jaws and ran wild in the sage. If she ever started to run! Jane smothered the glow and burn within her, ashamed of a passion for freedom that opposed her duty.

"Judkins, go to the village," she said, "and when you have learned anything definite about my riders please come to me at once."

When he had gone Jane resolutely applied her mind to a number of tasks that of late had been neglected. Her father had trained her in the management of a hundred employees and the working of gardens and fields; and to keep record of the movements of cattle and riders. And beside the many duties she had added to this work was one of extreme delicacy, such as required all her tact and ingenuity. It was an unobtrusive, almost secret aid which she rendered to the Gentile families of the village. Though Jane Withersteen never admitted so to herself, it amounted to no less than a system of charity. But for her invention of numberless kinds of employment, for which there was no actual need, these families of Gentiles, who had failed in a Mormon community, would have starved.

In aiding these poor people Jane thought she deceived her keen churchmen, but it was a kind of deceit for which she did not pray to be forgiven. Equally as difficult was the task of deceiving the Gentiles, for they were as proud as they were poor. It had been a great grief to her to discover how these people hated her people; and it had been a source of great joy that through her they had come to soften in hatred. At any time this work called for a clearness of mind that precluded anxiety and worry; but under the present circumstances it required all her vigor and obstinate tenacity to pin her attention upon her task.

Sunset came, bringing with the end of her labor a patient calmness and power to wait that had not been hers earlier in the day. She expected Judkins, but he did not appear. Her house was always quiet; to-night, however, it seemed unusually so. At supper her women served her with a silent assiduity; it spoke what their sealed lips could not utter—the sympathy of Mormon women. Jerd came to her with the key of the great door of the stone stable, and to make his daily report about the horses. One of his daily duties was to give Black Star and Night and the other racers a ten-mile run. This day it had been omitted, and the boy grew confused in explanations that she had not asked for. She did inquire if he would return on the morrow, and Jerd, in mingled surprise and relief, assured her he would always work for her. Jane missed the rattle and trot, canter and gallop of the incoming riders on the hard trails. Dusk shaded the grove where she walked; the birds ceased singing; the wind sighed through the leaves of the cottonwoods, and the running water murmured down its stone-bedded channel. The glimmering of the first star was like the peace and beauty of the night. Her faith welled up in her heart and said that all would soon be right in her little world. She pictured Venters about his lonely camp-fire sitting between his faithful dogs. She prayed for his safety, for the success of his undertaking.

Early the next morning one of Jane's women brought in word that Judkins wished to speak to her. She hurried out, and in her surprise to see him armed with rifle and revolver, she forgot her intention to inquire about his wound.

"Judkins! Those guns? You never carried guns."

"It's high time, Miss Withersteen," he replied. "Will you come into the grove? It ain't jest exactly safe for me to be seen here."

She walked with him into the shade of the cottonwoods.

"What do you mean?"

"Miss Withersteen, I went to my mother's house last night. While there, some one knocked, an' a man asked for me. I went to the door. He wore a mask. He said I'd better not ride any more for Jane Withersteen. His voice was hoarse an' strange, disguised, I reckon, like his face. He said no more, an' ran off in the dark."

"Did you know who he was?" asked Jane, in a low voice.

"Yes."

Jane did not ask to know; she did not want to know; she feared to know. All her calmness fled at a single thought.

"Thet's why I'm packin' guns," went on Judkins. "For I'll never quit ridin' for you, Miss Withersteen, till you let me go."

"Judkins, do you want to leave me?"

"Do I look thet way? Give me a hoss—a fast hoss, an' send me out on the sage."

"Oh, thank you, Judkins! You're more faithful than my own people. I ought not accept your loyalty—you might suffer more through it. But what in the world can I do? My head whirls. The wrong to Venters—the stolen herd—these masks, threats, this coil in the dark! I can't understand! But I feel something dark and terrible closing in around me."

"Miss Withersteen, it's all simple enough," said Judkins, earnestly. "Now please listen—an' beggin' your pardon—jest turn thet deaf Mormon ear aside, an' let me talk clear an' plain in the other. I went around to the saloons an' the stores an' the loafin' places yesterday. All your riders are in. There's talk of a vigilance band organized to hunt down rustlers. They call themselves 'The Riders.' Thet's the report—thet's the reason given for your riders leavin' you. Strange thet only a few riders of other ranchers joined the band! An' Tull's man, Jerry Card he's the leader. I seen him an' his hoss. He 'ain't been to Glaze. I'm not easy to fool on the looks of a hoss thet's traveled the sage. Tull an' Jerry didn't ride to Glaze! . . . Well, I met Blake an' Dorn, both good friends of mine, usually, as far as their Mormon lights will let 'em go. But these fellers couldn't fool me, an' they didn't try very hard. I asked them, straight out like a man, why they left you like thet. I didn't forget to mention how you nursed Blake's poor old mother when she was sick, an' how good you was to Dorn's kids. They looked ashamed, Miss Withersteen. An' they jest froze up—thet dark set look thet makes them strange an' different to me. But I could tell the difference between thet first natural twinge of conscience an' the later look of some secret thing. An' the difference I caught was thet they couldn't help themselves. They hadn't no say in the matter. They looked as if their bein' unfaithful to you was bein' faithful to a higher duty. An' there's the secret. Why, it's as plain as—as sight of my gun here."

"Plain! . . . My herds to wander in the sage—to be stolen! Jane Withersteen a poor woman! Her head to be brought low and her spirit broken! . . . Why, Judkins, it's plain enough."

"Miss Withersteen, let me get what boys I can gather, an' hold the white herd. It's on the slope now, not ten miles out—three thousand head, an' all steers. They're wild, an' likely to stampede at the pop of a jack-rabbit's ears. We'll camp right with them, an' try to hold them."

"Judkins, I'll reward you some day for your service, unless all is taken from me. Get the boys and tell Jerd to give you pick of my horses, except Black Star and Night. But—do not shed blood for my cattle nor heedlessly risk your lives."

Jane Withersteen rushed to the silence and seclusion of her room, and there could not longer hold back the bursting of her wrath. She went stone-blind in the fury of a passion that had never before showed its power. Lying upon her bed, sightless, voiceless, she was a writhing, living flame. And she tossed there while her fury burned and burned, and finally burned itself out.

Then, weak and spent, she lay thinking, not of the oppression that would break her, but of this new revelation of self. Until the last few days there had been little in her life to rouse passions. Her forefathers had been Vikings, savage chieftains who bore no cross and brooked no hindrance to their will. Her father had inherited that temper; and at times, like antelope fleeing before fire on the slope, his people fled from his red rages. Jane Withersteen realized that the spirit of wrath and war had lain dormant in her. She shrank from black depths hitherto unsuspected. The one thing in man or woman that she scorned above all scorn, and which she could not forgive, was hate. Hate headed a flaming pathway straight to hell. All in a flash, beyond her control there had been in her a birth of fiery hate. And the man who had dragged her peaceful and loving spirit to this degradation was a minister of God's word, an Elder of her church, the counselor of her beloved Bishop.

The loss of herds and ranges, even of Amber Spring and the Old Stone House, no longer concerned Jane Withersteen; she faced the foremost thought of her life, what she now considered the mightiest problem—the salvation of her soul.

She knelt by her bedside and prayed; she prayed as she had never prayed in all her life—prayed to be forgiven for her sin; to be immune from that dark, hot hate; to love Tull as her minister, though she could not love him as a man; to do her duty by her church and people and those dependent upon her bounty; to hold reverence of God and womanhood inviolate.

When Jane Withersteen rose from that storm of wrath and prayer for help she was serene, calm, sure—a changed woman. She would do her duty as she saw it, live her life as her own truth guided her. She might never be able to marry a man of her choice, but she certainly never would become the wife of Tull. Her churchmen might take her cattle and horses, ranges and fields, her corrals and stables, the house of Withersteen and the water that nourished the village of Cottonwoods; but they could not force her to marry Tull, they could not change her decision or break her spirit. Once resigned to further loss, and sure of herself, Jane Withersteen attained a peace of mind that had not been hers for a year. She forgave Tull, and felt a melancholy regret over what she knew he considered duty, irrespective of his personal feeling for her. First of all, Tull, as he was a man, wanted her for himself; and secondly, he hoped to save her and her riches for his church. She did not believe that Tull had been actuated solely by his minister's zeal to save her soul. She doubted her interpretation of one of his dark sayings—that if she were lost to him she might as well be lost to heaven. Jane Withersteen's common sense took arms against the binding limits of her religion; and she doubted that her Bishop, whom she had been taught had direct communication with God—would damn her soul for refusing to marry a Mormon. As for Tull and his churchmen, when they had harassed her, perhaps made her poor, they would find her unchangeable, and then she would get back most of what she had lost. So she reasoned, true at last to her faith in all men, and in their ultimate goodness.

The clank of iron hoofs upon the stone courtyard drew her hurriedly from her retirement. There, beside his horse, stood Lassiter, his dark apparel and the great black gun-sheaths contrasting singularly with his gentle smile. Jane's active mind took up her interest in him and her half-determined desire to use what charm she had to foil his evident design in visiting Cottonwoods. If she could mitigate his hatred of Mormons, or at least keep him from killing more of them, not only would she would get back most of what she had lost. So she reasoned, true at last to her faith in all men, and in their ultimate goodness.

"Mornin', ma'am," he said, black sombrero in hand.

"Lassiter, I'm not an old woman, or even a madam," she replied, with her bright smile. "If you can't say Miss Withersteen—call me Jane."

"I reckon Jane would be easier. First names are always handy for me."

"Well, use mine, then. Lassiter, I'm glad to see you. I'm in trouble."

Then she told him of Judkin's return, of the driving of the red herd, of Venters's departure on Wrangle, and the calling-in of her riders.

"'Pears to me you're some smilin' an' pretty for a woman with so much trouble," he remarked.

"Lassiter! Are you paying me compliments? But, seriously, I've made up my mind not to be miserable. I've lost much, and I'll lose more. Nevertheless, I won't be sour, and I hope I'll never be unhappy—again."

Lassiter twisted his hat round and round, as was his way, and took his time in replying.

"Women are strange to me. I got to back-trailin' myself from them long ago. But I'd like a game woman. Might I ask, seein' as how you take this trouble, if you're goin' to fight?"

"Fight! How? Even if I would, I haven't a friend except that boy who doesn't dare stay in the village."

"I make bold to say, ma'am—Jane—that there's another, if you want him."

"Lassiter! . . . Thank you. But how can I accept you as a friend? Think! Why, you'd ride down into the village with those terrible guns and kill my enemies—who are also my churchmen."

"I reckon I might be riled up to jest about that," he replied, dryly.

She held out both hands to him.

"Lassiter! I'll accept your friendship—be proud of it—return it—if I may keep you from killing another Mormon."

"I'll tell you one thing," he said, bluntly, as the gray lightning formed in his eyes. "You're too good a woman to be sacrificed as you're goin' to be. . . . No, I reckon you an' me can't be friends on such terms."

In her earnestness she stepped closer to him, repelled yet fascinated by the sudden transition of his moods. That he would fight for her was at once horrible and wonderful.

"You came here to kill a man—the man whom Milly Erne—"

"The man who dragged Milly Erne to hell—put it that way! . . . Jane Withersteen, yes, that's why I came here. I'd tell so much to no other livin' soul. . . . There're things such a woman as you'd never dream of—so don't mention her again. Not till you tell me the name of the man!"

"Tell you! I? Never!"

"I reckon you will. An' I'll never ask you. I'm a man of strange beliefs an' ways of thinkin', an' I seem to see into the future an' feel things hard to explain. The trail I've been followin' for so many years was twisted an' tangled, but it's straightenin' out now. An', Jane Withersteen, you crossed it long ago to ease poor Milly's agony. That, whether you want or not, makes Lassiter your friend. But you cross it now strangely to mean somethin' to me—God knows what!—unless by your noble blindness to incite me to greater hatred of Mormon men."

Jane felt swayed by a strength that far exceeded her own. In a clash of wills with this man she would go to the wall. If she were to influence him it must be wholly through womanly allurement. There was that about Lassiter which commanded her respect; she had abhorred his name; face to face with him, she found she feared only his deeds. His mystic suggestion, his foreshadowing of something that she was to mean to him, pierced deep into her mind. She believed fate had thrown in her way the lover or husband of Milly Erne. She believed that through her an evil man might be reclaimed. His allusion to what he called her blindness terrified her. Such a mistaken idea of his might unleash the bitter, fatal mood she sensed in him. At any cost she must placate this man; she knew the die was cast, and that if Lassiter did not soften to a woman's grace and beauty and wiles, then it would be because she could not make him.

"I reckon you'll hear no more such talk from me," Lassiter went on, presently. "Now, Miss Jane, I rode in to tell you that your herd of white steers is down on the slope behind them big ridges. An' I seen somethin' goin' on that'd be mighty interestin' to you, if you could see it. Have you a field-glass?"

"Yes, I have two glasses. I'll get them and ride out with you. Wait, Lassiter, please," she said, and hurried within. Sending word to Jerd to saddle Black Star and fetch him to the court, she then went to her room and changed to the riding-clothes she always donned when going into the sage. In this male attire her mirror showed her a jaunty, handsome rider. If she expected some little need of admiration from Lassiter, she had no cause for disappointment. The gentle smile that she liked, which made of him another person, slowly overspread his face.

"If I didn't take you for a boy!" he exclaimed. "It's powerful queer what difference clothes make. Now I've been some scared of your dignity, like when the other night you was all in white, but in this rig—"

Black Star came pounding into the court, dragging Jerd half off his feet, and he whistled at Lassiter's black. But at sight of Jane all his defiant lines seemed to soften, and with tosses of his beautiful head he whipped his bridle.

"Down, Black Star, down," said Jane.

He dropped his head, and, slowly lengthening, he bent one foreleg, then the other, and sank to his knees. Jane slipped her left foot in the stirrup, swung lightly into the saddle, and Black Sar rose with a ringing stamp. It was not easy for Jane to hold him to a canter through the grove, and like the wind he broke when he saw the sage. Jane let him have a couple of miles of free running on the open trail, and then she coaxed him in and waited for her companion. Lassiter was not long in catching up, and presently they were riding side by side. It reminded her how she used to ride with Venters. Where was he now? She gazed far down the slope to the curved purple lines of Deception Pass, and involuntarily shut her eyes with a trembling stir of nameless fear.

"We'll turn off here," Lassiter said, "an' take to the sage a mile or so. The white herd is behind them big ridges."

"What are you going to show me?" asked Jane. "I'm prepared—don't be afraid."

He smiled as if he meant that bad news came swiftly enough without being presaged by speech.

When they reached the lee of a rolling ridge Lassiter dismounted, motioning to her to do likewise. They left the horses standing, bridles down. Then Lassiter, carrying the field-glasses, began to lead the way up the slow rise of ground. Upon nearing the summit he halted her with a gesture.

"I reckon we'd see more if we didn't show ourselves against the sky," he said. "I was here less than an hour ago. Then the herd was seven or eight miles south, an' if they 'ain't bolted yet—"

"Lassiter! . . . Bolted?"

"That's what I said. Now let's see."

Jane climbed a few more paces behind him and then peeped over the ridge. Just beyond began a shallow swale that deepened and widened into a valley and then swung to the left. Following the undulating sweep of sage, Jane saw the straggling lines and then the great body of the white herd. She knew enough about steers, even at a distance of four or five miles, to realize that something was in the wind. Bringing her field-glass into use, she moved it slowly from left to right, which action swept the whole herd into range. The stragglers were restless; the more compactly massed steers were browsing. Jane brought the glass back to the big sentinels of the herd, and she saw them trot with quick steps, stop short and toss wide horns, look everywhere, and then trot in another direction.

"Judkins hasn't been able to get his boys together yet," said Jane. "But he'll be there soon. I hope not too late. Lassiter, what's frightening those big leaders?"

"Nothin' jest on the minute," replied Lassiter. "Them steers are quietin' down. They've been scared, but not bad yet. I reckon the whole herd has moved a few miles this way since I was here."

"They didn't browse that distance—not in less than an hour. Cattle aren't sheep."

"No, they jest run it, an' that looks bad."

"Lassiter, what frightened them?" repeated Jane, impatiently.

"Put down your glass. You'll see at first better with a naked eye. Now look along them ridges on the other side of the herd, the ridges where the sun shines bright on the sage. . . . That's right. Now look an' look hard an' wait."

Long-drawn moments of straining sight rewarded Jane with nothing save the low, purple rim of ridge and the shimmering sage.

"It's begun again!" whispered Lassiter, and he gripped her arm. "Watch. . . . There, did you see that?"

"No, no. Tell me what to look for?"

"A white flash—a kind of pin-point of quick light—a gleam as from sun shinin' on somethin' white."

Suddenly Jane's concentrated gaze caught a fleeting glint. Quickly she brought her glass to bear on the spot. Again the purple sage, magnified in color and size and wave, for long moments irritated her with its monotony. Then from out of the sage on the ridge flew up a broad, white object, flashed in the sunlight, and vanished. Like magic it was, and bewildered Jane.

"What on earth is that?"

"I reckon there's some one behind that ridge throwin' up a sheet or a white blanket to reflect the sunshine."

"Why?" queried Jane, more bewildered than ever.

"To stampede the herd," replied Lassiter, and his teeth clicked.

"Ah!" She made a fierce, passionate movement, clutched the glass tightly, shook as with the passing of a spasm, and then dropped her head. Presently she raised it to greet Lassiter with something like a smile. "My righteous brethren are at work again," she said, in scorn. She had stifled the leap of her wrath, but for perhaps the first time in her life a bitter derision curled her lips. Lassiter's cool gray eyes seemed to pierce her. "I said I was prepared for anything; but that was hardly true. But why would they—anybody stampede my cattle?"

"That's a Mormon's godly way of bringin' a woman to her knees."

"Lassiter, I'll die before I ever bend my knees. I might be led; I won't be driven. Do you expect the herd to bolt?"

"I don't like the looks of them big steers. But you can never tell. Cattle sometimes stampede as easily as buffalo. Any little flash or move will start them. A rider gettin' down an' walkin' toward them sometimes will make them jump an' fly. Then again nothin' seems to scare them. But I reckon that white flare will do the biz. It's a new one on me, an' I've seen some ridin' an' rustlin'. It jest takes one of them God-fearin' Mormons to think of devilish tricks."

"Lassiter, might not this trick be done by Oldring's men?" asked Jane, ever grasping at straws.

"It might be, but it ain't," replied Lassiter. "Oldring's an honest thief. He don't skulk behind ridges to scatter your cattle to the four winds. He rides down on you, an' if you don't like it you can throw a gun."

Jane bit her tongue to refrain from championing men who at the very moment were proving to her that they were little and mean compared even with rustlers.

"Look! . . . Jane, them leadin' steers have bolted. They're drawin' the stragglers, an' that'll pull the whole herd."

Jane was not quick enough to catch the details called out by Lassiter, but she saw the line of cattle lengthening. Then, like a stream of white bees pouring from a huge swarm, the steers stretched out from the main body. In a few moments, with astonishing rapidity, the whole herd got into motion. A faint roar of trampling hoofs came to Jane's ears, and gradually swelled; low, rolling clouds of dust began to rise above the sage.

"It's a stampede, an' a hummer," said Lassiter.

"Oh, Lassiter! The herd's running with the valley! It leads into the cañon! There's a straight jump-off!"

"I reckon they'll run into it, too. But that's a good many miles yet. An' Jane, this valley swings round almost north before it goes east. That stampede will pass within a mile of us."

The long, white, bobbing line of steers streaked swiftly through the sage, and a funnel-shaped dust-cloud arose at a low angle. A dull rumbling filled Jane's ears.

"I'm thinkin' of millin' that herd," said Lassiter. His gray glance swept up the slope to the west. "There's some specks an' dust way off toward the village. Mebbe that's Judkins an' his boys. It ain't likely he'll get here in time to help. You'd better hold Black Star here on this high ridge."

He ran to his horse and, throwing off saddle-bags and tightening the cinches, he leaped astride and galloped straight down across the valley.

Jane went for Black Star and, leading him to the summit of the ridge, she mounted and faced the valley with excitement and expectancy. She had heard of milling stampeded cattle, and knew it was a feat accomplished by only the most daring riders.

The white herd was now strung out in a line two miles long. The dull rumble of thousands of hoofs deepened into continuous low thunder, and as the steers swept swiftly closer the thunder became a heavy roll. Lassiter crossed in a few moments the level of the valley to the eastern rise of ground and there waited the coming of the herd. Presently, as the head of the white line reached a point opposite to where Jane stood, Lassiter spurred his black into a run.

Jane saw him take a position on the off side of the leaders of the stampede, and there he rode. It was like a race. They swept on down the valley, and when the end of the white line neared Lassiter's first stand the head had begun to swing round to the west. It swung slowly and stubbornly, yet surely, and gradually assumed a long, beautiful curve of moving white. To Jane's amaze she saw the leaders swinging, turning till they headed back toward her and up the valley. Out to the right of these wild, plunging steers ran Lassiter's black, and Jane's keen eye appreciated the fleet stride and sure-footedness of the blind horse. Then it seemed that the herd moved in a great curve, a huge half-moon, with the points of head and tail almost opposite, and a mile apart. But Lassiter relentlessly crowded the leaders, sheering them to the left, turning them little by little. And the dust-blinded wild followers plunged on madly in the tracks of their leaders. This ever-moving, ever-changing curve of steers rolled toward Jane, and when below her, scarce half a mile, it began to narrow and close into a circle. Lassiter had ridden parallel with her position, turned toward her, then aside, and now he was riding directly away from her, all the time pushing the head of that bobbing line inward.

It was then that Jane, suddenly understanding Lassiter's feat, stared and gasped at the riding of this intrepid man. His horse was fleet and tireless, but blind. He had pushed the leaders around and around till they were about to turn in on the inner side of the end of that line of steers. The leaders were already running in a circle; the end of the herd was still running almost straight. But soon they would be wheeling. Then, when Lassiter had the circle formed, how would he escape? With Jane Withersteen prayer was as ready as praise; and she prayed for this man's safety. A circle of dust began to collect. Dimly, as through a yellow veil, Jane saw Lassiter press the leaders inward to close the gap in the sage. She lost sight of him in the dust; again she thought she saw the black, riderless now, rear and drag himself and fall. Lassiter had been thrown—lost! Then he reappeared running out of the dust into the sage. He had escaped, and she breathed again.

Spellbound, Jane Withersteen watched this stupendous mill-wheel of steers. Here was the milling of the herd. The white running circle closed in upon the open space of sage. And the dust circles closed above into a pall. The ground quaked and the incessant thunder of pounding hoofs rolled on. Jane felt deafened, yet she thrilled to a new sound. As the circle of sage lessened the steers began to bawl, and when it closed entirely there came a great upheaval in the center, and a terrible thumping of heads and clicking of horns. Bawling, climbing, goring, the great mass of steers on the inside wrestled in a crashing din, heaved and groaned under the pressure. Then came a deadlock. The inner strife ceased, and the hideous roar and crash. Movement went on in the outer circle, and that, too, gradually stilled. The white herd had come to a stop, and the pall of yellow dust began to drift away on the wind.

Jane Withersteen waited on the ridge with full and grateful heart. Lassiter appeared, making his weary way toward her through the sage. And up on the slope Judkins rode into sight with his troop of boys. For the present, at least, the white herd would be looked after.

When Lassiter reached her and laid his hand on Black Star's mane, Jane could not find speech.

"Killed—my—hoss," he panted.

"Oh! I'm sorry," cried Jane. "Lassiter! I know you can't replace him, but I'll give you any one of my racers—Bells, or Night, even Black Star."

"I'll take a fast hoss, Jane, but not one of your favorites," he replied. "Only—will you let me have Black Star now an' ride him over there an' head off them fellers who stampeded the herd?"

He pointed to several moving specks of black and puffs of dust in the purple sage.

"I can head them off with this hoss, an' then—"

"Then, Lassiter?"

"They'll never stampede no more cattle."

"Oh! No! No! . . . Lassiter, I won't let you go!"

But a flush of fire flamed in her cheeks, and her trembling hands shook Black Star's bridle, and her eyes fell before Lassiter's.

CHAPTER SEVEN
The Daughter of Withersteen

"Lassiter, will you be my rider?" Jane had asked him.

"I reckon so," he had replied.

Few as the words were, Jane knew how infinitely much they implied. She wanted him to take charge of her cattle and horses and ranges, and save them if that were possible. Yet, though she could not have spoken aloud all she meant, she was perfectly honest with herself. Whatever the price to be paid, she must keep Lassiter close to her; she must shield from him the man who had lured Milly Erne to Cottonwoods. In her fear she so controlled her mind that she did not whisper this Mormon's name to her own soul, she did not even think it. Besides, beyond this thing she regarded as a sacred obligation thrust upon her, was the need of a helper, of a friend, of a champion in this critical time. If she could rule this gun-man, as Venters had called him, if she could even keep him from shedding blood, what strategy to play his name and his presence against the game of oppression her churchmen were waging against her? Never would she forget the effect upon Tull and his men when Venters shouted Lassiter's name. If she could not wholly control Lassiter, then what she could do might put off the fatal day.

One of her safe racers was a dark bay, and she called him Bells because of the way he struck his iron shoes on the stones. When Jerd led out this slender, beautifully built horse Lassiter suddenly became all eyes. A rider's love of a thoroughbred shone in them. Round and round Bells he walked, plainly weakening all the time in his determination not to take one of Jane's favorite racers.

"Lassiter, you're half horse, and Bells sees it already," said Jane, laughing. "Look at his eyes. He likes you. He'll love you, too. How can you resist him? Oh, Lassiter, but Bells can run! It's nip and tuck between him and Wrangle, and only Black Star can beat him. He's too spirited a horse for a woman. Take him. He's yours."

"I jest am weak where a hoss's concerned," said Lassiter. "I'll take him, an' I'll take your orders, ma'am."

"Well, I'm glad, but never mind the ma'am. Let it still be Jane."

From that hour, it seemed, Lassiter was always in the saddle, riding early and late; and coincident with his part in Jane's affairs the days assumed their old tranquillity. Her intelligence told her this was only the lull before the storm, but her faith would not have it so.

She resumed her visits to the village, and upon one of these she encountered Tull. He greeted her as he had before any trouble came between them, and she, responsive to peace if not quick to forget, met him halfway with manner almost cheerful. He regretted the loss of her cattle; he assured her that the vigilantes which had been organized would soon rout the rustlers; when that had been accomplished her riders would likely return to her.

"You've done a headstrong thing to hire this man Lassiter," Tull went on, severely. "He came to Cottonwoods with evil intent."

"I had to have somebody. And perhaps making him my rider may turn out best in the end for the Mormons of Cottonwoods."

"You mean to stay his hand?"

"I do—if I can."

"A woman like you can do anything with a man. That would be well, and would atone in some measure for the errors you have made."

He bowed and passed on. Jane resumed her walk with conflicting thoughts. She resented Elder Tull's cold, impassive manner that looked down upon her as one who had incurred his just displeasure. Otherwise he would have been the same calm, dark-browed, impenetrable man she had known for ten years. In fact, except when he had revealed his passion in the matter of the seizing of Venters, she had never dreamed he could be other than the grave, reproving preacher. He stood out now a strange, secretive man. She would have thought better of him if he had picked up the threads of their quarrel where they had parted. Was Tull what he appeared to be? The question flung itself involuntarily over Jane Withersteen's inhibitive habit of faith without question. And she refused to answer it. Tull could not fight in the open. Venters had said, Lassiter had said, that her Elder shirked fight and worked in the dark. Just now in this meeting Tull had ignored the fact that he had sued, exhorted, demanded that she marry him. He made no mention of Venters. His manner was that of the minister who had been outraged, but who overlooked the frailties of a woman. Beyond question he seemed unutterably aloof from all knowledge of pressure being brought to bear upon her, absolutely guiltless of any connection with secret power over riders, with night journeys, with rustlers and stampedes of cattle. And that convinced her again of unjust suspicions. But it was convincement through an obstinate faith. She shuddered as she accepted it, and that shudder was the nucleus of a terrible revolt.

Jane turned into one of the wide lanes leading from the main street and entered a huge, shady yard. Here were sweet-smelling clover, alfalfa, flowers, and vegetables, all growing in happy confusion. And like these fresh green things were the dozens of babies, tots, toddlers, noisy urchins, laughing girls, a whole multitude of children of one family. For Collier Brandt, the father of all this numerous progeny, was a Mormon with four wives.

The big house where they lived was old, solid, picturesque, the lower part built of logs, the upper of rough clapboards, with vines growing up the outside stone chimneys. There were many wooden-shuttered windows, and one pretentious window of glass, proudly curtained in white. As this house had four mistresses, it likewise had four separate sections, not one of which communicated with another, and all had to be entered from the outside.

In the shade of a wide, low, vine-roofed porch Jane found Brandt's wives entertaining Bishop Dyer. They were motherly women, of comparatively similar ages, and plain-featured, and just at this moment anything but grave. The Bishop was rather tall, of stout build, with iron-gray hair and beard, and eyes of light blue. They were merry now; but Jane had seen them when they were not, and then she feared him as she had feared her father.

The woman flocked around her in welcome.

"Daughter of Withersteen," said the Bishop, gaily, as he took her hand, "you have not been prodigal of your gracious self of late. A Sabbath without you at service! I shall reprove Elder Tull."

"Bishop, the guilt is mine. I'll come to you and confess," Jane replied, lightly; but she felt the undercurrent of her words.

"Mormon love-making!" exclaimed the Bishop, rubbing his hands. "Tull keeps you all to himself."

"No. He is not courting me."

"What? The laggard! If he does not make haste I'll go a-courting myself up to Withersteen House."

There was laughter and further bantering by the Bishop, and then mild talk of village affairs, after which he took his leave, and Jane was left with her friend, Mary Brandt.

"Jane, you're not yourself. Are you sad about the rustling of the cattle? But you have so many, you are so rich."

Then Jane confided in her, telling much, yet holding back her doubts of fear.

"Oh, why don't you marry Tull and be one of us?"

"But, Mary, I don't love Tull," said Jane, stubbornly.

"I don't blame you for that. But, Jane Withersteen, you've got to choose between the love of man and love of God. Often we Mormon women have to do that. It's not easy. The kind of happiness you want I wanted once. I never got it, nor will you, unless you throw away your soul. We've all watched your affair with Venters in fear and trembling. Some dreadful thing will come of it. You don't want him hanged or shot—or treated worse, as that Gentile boy was treated in Glaze for fooling round a Mormon woman. Marry Tull. It's your duty as a Mormon. You'll feel no rapture as his wife—but think of Heaven! Mormon women don't marry for what they expect on earth. Take up the cross, Jane. Remember your father found Amber Spring, built these old houses, brought Mormons here, and fathered them. You are the daughter of Withersteen!"

Jane left Mary Brandt and went to call upon other friends. They received her with the same glad welcome as had Mary, lavished upon her the pent-up affection of Mormon women, and let her go with her ears ringing of Tull, Venters, Lassiter, of duty to God and glory in Heaven.

"Verily," murmured Jane, "I don't know myself when, through all this, I remain unchanged—nay, more fixed of purpose."

She returned to the main street and bent her thoughtful steps toward the center of the village. A string of wagons drawn by oxen was lumbering along. These "sage-freighters," as they were called, hauled grain and flour and merchandise from Sterling; and Jane laughed suddenly in the midst of her humility at the thought that they were her property, as was one of the three stores for which they freighted goods. The water that flowed along the path at her feet, and turned into each cottage-yard to nourish garden and orchard, also was hers, no less her private property because she chose to give it free. Yet in this village of Cottonwoods, which her father had founded and which she maintained, she was not her own mistress; she was not able to abide by her own choice of a husband. She was the daughter of Withersteen. Suppose she proved it, imperiously! But she quelled that proud temptation at its birth.

Nothing could have replaced the affection which the village people had for her; no power could have made her happy as the pleasure her presence gave. As she went on down the street, past the stores with their rude platform entrances, and the saloons, where tired horses stood with bridles dragging, she was again assured of what was the bread and wine of life to her—that she was loved. Dirty boys playing in the ditch, clerks, teamsters, riders, loungers on the corners, ranchers on dusty horses, little girls running errands, and women hurrying to the stores all looked up at her coming with glad eyes.

Jane's various calls and wandering steps at length led her to the Gentile quarter of the village. This was at the extreme southern end, and here some thirty Gentile families lived in huts and shacks and log-cabins and several dilapidated cottages. The fortunes of these inhabitants of Cottonwoods could be read in their abodes. Water they had in abundance, and therefore grass and fruit-trees and patches of alfalfa and vegetable gardens. Some of the men and boys had a few stray cattle, others obtained such intermittent employment as the Mormons reluctantly tendered them. But none of the families was prosperous, many were very poor, and some lived only by Jane Withersteen's beneficence.

As it made Jane happy to go among her own people, so it saddened her to come in contact with these Gentiles. Yet that was not because she was unwelcome; here she was gratefully received by the women, passionately by the children. But poverty and idleness, with their attendant wretchedness and sorrow, always hurt her. That she could alleviate this distress more now than ever before proved the adage that it was an ill wind that blew nobody good. While her Mormon riders were in her employ she had found few Gentiles who would stay with her, and now she was able to find employment for all the men and boys. No little shock was it to have man after man tell her that he dare not accept her kind offer.

"It won't do," said one Carson, an intelligent man who had seen better days. "We've had our warning. Plain and to the point! Now there's Judkins, he packs guns, and he can use them, and so can the daredevil boys he's hired. But they've little responsibility. Can we risk having our homes burned in our absence?"

Jane felt the stretching and chilling of the skin of her face as the blood left it.

"Carson, you and the others rent these houses?" she asked.

"You ought to know, Miss Withersteen. Some of them are yours."

"I know? . . . Carson, I never in my life took a day's labor for rent or a yearling calf or a bunch of grass, let alone gold."

"Bivens, your store-keeper, sees to that."

"Look here, Carson," went on Jane, hurriedly, and now her cheeks were burning. "You and Black and Willet pack your goods and move your families up to my cabins in the grove. They're far more comfortable than these. Then go to work for me. And if aught happens to you there I'll give you money—gold enough to leave Utah!"

The man choked and stammered, and then, as tears welled into his eyes, he found the use of his tongue and cursed. No gentle speech could ever have equaled that curse in eloquent expression of what he felt for Jane Withersteen. How strangely his look and tone reminded her of Lassiter!

"No, it won't do," he said, when he had somewhat recovered himself. "Miss Withersteen, there are things that you don't know, and there's not a soul among us who can tell you."

"I seem to be learning many things, Carson. Well, then, will you let me aid you—say till better times?"

"Yes, I will," he replied, with his face lighting up. "I see what it means to you, and you know what it means to me. Thank you! And if better times ever came I'll be only too happy to work for you."

"Better times will come. I trust God and have faith in man. Good day, Carson."

The lane opened out upon the sage-inclosed alfalfa fields, and the last habitation, at the end of that lane of hovels, was the meanest. Formerly it had been a shed; now it was a home. The broad leaves of a wide-spreading cottonwood sheltered the sunken roof of weathered boards. Like an Indian hut, it had one floor. Round about it were a few scanty rows of vegetables, such as the hand of a weak woman had time and strength to cultivate. This little dwelling-place was just outside the village limits, and the widow who lived there had to carry her water from the nearest irrigation ditch. As Jane Withersteen entered the unfenced yard a child saw her, shrieked with joy, and came tearing toward her with curls flying. This child was a little girl of four called Fay. Her name suited her, for she was an elf, a sprite, a creature so fairy-like and beautiful that she seemed unearthly.

"Muvver sended for oo," cried Fay, as Jane kissed her, "an' oo never tome."

"I didn't know, Fay; but I've come now."

Fay was a child of outdoors, of the garden and ditch and field, and she was dirty and ragged. But rags and dirt did not hide her beauty. The one thin little bedraggled garment she wore half covered her fine, slim body. Red as cherries were her cheeks and lips; her eyes were violet blue, and the crown of her childish loveliness was the curling golden hair. All the children of Cottonwoods were Jane Withersteen's friends; she loved them all. But Fay was dearest to her. Fay had few playmates, for among the Gentile children there were none near her age, and the Mormon children were forbidden to play with her. So she was a shy, wild, lonely child.

"Muvver's sick," said Fay, leading Jane toward the door of the hut.

Jane went in. There was only one room, rather dark and bare, but it was clean and neat. A woman lay upon a bed.

"Mrs. Larkin, how are you?" asked Jane, anxiously.

"I've been pretty bad for a week, but I'm better now."

"You haven't been here all alone—with no one to wait on you?"

"Oh no! My women neighbors are kind. They take turns coming in."

"Did you send for me?"

"Yes, several times."

"But I had no word—no messages ever got to me."

"I sent the boys, and they left word with your women that I was ill and would you please come."

A sudden deadly sickness seized Jane. She fought the weakness, as she fought to be above suspicious thoughts, and it passed, leaving her conscious of her utter impotence. That, too, passed as her spirit rebounded. But she had again caught a glimpse of dark underhand domination, running its secret lines this time into her own household. Like a spider in the blackness of night an unseen hand had begun to run these dark lines, to turn and twist them about her life, to plait and weave a web. Jane Withersteen knew it now, and in the realization further coolness and sureness came to her, and the fighting courage of her ancestors.

"Mrs. Larkin, you're better, and I'm so glad," said Jane. "But may I not do something for you—a turn at nursing, or send you things, or take care of Fay?"

"You're so good. Since my husband's been gone what would have become of Fay and me but for you? It was about Fay that I wanted to speak to you. This time I thought surely I'd die, and I was worried about Fay. Well, I'll be around all right shortly, but my strength's gone and I won't live long. So I may as well speak now. You remember you've been asking me to let you take Fay and bring her up as your daughter?"

"Indeed yes, I remember. I'll be happy to have her. But I hope the day—"

"Never mind that. The day'll come—sooner or later. I refused your offer, and now I'll tell you why."

"I know why," interposed Jane. "It's because you don't want her brought up as a Mormon."

"No, it wasn't altogether that." Mrs. Larkin raised her thin hand and laid it appealingly on Jane's. "I don't like to tell you. But—it's this: I told all my friends what you wanted. They know you, care for you, and they said for me to trust Fay to you. Women will talk, you know. It got to the ears of Mormons—gossip of your love for Fay and your wanting her. And it came straight back to me, in jealousy, perhaps, that you wouldn't take Fay as much for love of her as because of your religious duty to bring up another girl for some Mormon to marry."

"That's a damnable lie!" cried Jane Withersteen.

"It was what made me hesitate," went on Mrs. Larkin, "but I never believed it at heart. And now I guess I'll let you—"

"Wait! Mrs. Larkin, I may have told little white lies in my life, but never a lie that mattered, that hurt any one. Now believe me. I love little Fay. If I had her near me I'd grow to worship her. When I asked for her I thought only of that love. . . . Let me prove this. You and Fay come to live with me. I've such a big house, and I'm so lonely. I'll help nurse you, take care of you. When you're better you can work for me. I'll keep little Fay and bring her up—without Mormon teaching. When she's grown, if she should want to leave me, I'll send her, and not empty-handed, back to Illinois where you came from. I promise you."

"I knew it was a lie," replied the mother, and she sank back upon her pillow with something of peace in her white, worn face. "Jane Withersteen, may Heaven bless you! I've been deeply grateful to you. But because you're a Mormon I never felt close to you till now. I don't know much about religion as religion, but your God and my God are the same."

CHAPTER EIGHT
Surprise Valley

Back in that strange cañon, which Venters had found indeed a valley of surprises, the wounded girl's whispered appeal, almost a prayer, not to take her back to the rustlers crowned the events of the last few days with a confounding climax. That she should not want to return to them staggered Venters. Presently, as logical thought returned, her appeal confirmed his first impression—that she was more unfortunate than bad—and he experienced a sensation of gladness. If he had known before that Oldring's Masked Rider was a woman his opinion would have been formed and he would have considered her abandoned. But his first knowledge had come when he lifted a white face quivering in a convulsion of agony; he had heard God's name whispered by blood-stained lips; through her solemn and awful eyes he had caught a glimpse of her soul. And just now had come the entreaty to him, "Don't—take—me—back—there!"

Once for all Venters's quick mind formed a permanent conception of this poor girl. He based it, not upon what the chances of life had made her, but upon the revelation of dark eyes that pierced the infinite, upon a few pitiful, halting words that betrayed failure and wrong and misery, yet breathed the truth of a tragic fate rather than a natural leaning to evil.

"What's your name?" he inquired.

"Bess," she answered.

"Bess what?"

"That's enough—just Bess."

The red that deepened in her cheeks was not all the flush of fever. Venters marveled anew, and this time at the tint of shame in her face, at the momentary drooping of long lashes. She might be a rustler's girl, but she was still capable of shame; she might be dying, but she still clung to some little remnant of honor.

"Very well, Bess. It doesn't matter," he said. "But this matters—what shall I do with you?"

"Are—you—a rider?" she whispered.

"Not now. I was once. I drove the Withersteen herds. But I lost my place—lost all I owned—and now I'm—I'm sort of outcast. My name's Bern Venters."

"You won't—take me—to Cottonwoods—or Glaze? I'd be—hanged."

"No, indeed. But I must do something with you. For it's not safe for me here. I shot that rustler who was with you. Sooner or later he'll be found, and then my tracks. I must find a safer hiding-place where I can't be trailed."

"Leave me—here."

"Alone—to die!"

"Yes."

"I will not." Venters spoke shortly with a kind of ring in his voice.

"What—do you want—to do—with me?" Her whispering grew difficult, so low and faint that Venters had to stoop to hear her.

"Why, let's see," he replied slowly. "I'd like to take you some place where I could watch by you, nurse you, till you're all right again."

"And—then?"

"Well, it'll be time to think of that when you're cured of your wound. It's a bad one. And—Bess, if you don't want to live—if you don't fight for your life—you'll never—"

"Oh! I want—to live! I'm afraid—to die. But I'd rather—die—than go back—to—to—"

"To Oldring?" asked Venters, interrupting her in turn.

Her lips moved in an affirmative.

"I promise not to take you back to him or to Cottonwoods or to Glaze."

The mournful earnestness of her gaze suddenly shone with unutterable gratitude and wonder. And as suddenly Venters found her eyes beautiful as he had never seen or felt beauty. They were as dark blue as the sky at night. Then the flashing changed to a long, thoughtful look, in which there was a wistful, unconscious searching of his face, a look that trembled on the verge of hope and trust.

"I'll try—to live," she said. The broken whisper just reached his ears. "Do what—you want—with me."

"Rest then—don't worry—sleep," he replied.

Abruptly he arose, as if words had been decision for him, and with a sharp command to the dogs he strode from the camp. Venters was conscious of an indefinite conflict of change within him. It seemed to be a vague passing of old moods, a dim coalescing of new forces, a moment of inexplicable transition. He was both cast down and uplifted. He wanted to think and think of the meaning, but he resolutely dispelled emotion. His imperative need at present was to find a safe retreat, and this called for action.

So he set out. It still wanted several hours before dark. This trip he turned to the left and wended his skulking way southward a mile or more to the opening of the valley, where lay the strange scrawled rocks. He did not, however, venture boldly out into the open sage, but clung to the right-hand wall and went along that till its perpendicular line broke into the long incline of bare stone.

Before proceeding farther he halted, studying the strange character of this slope and realizing that a moving black object could be seen far against such background. Before him ascended a gradual swell of smooth stone. It was hard, polished, and full of pockets worn by centuries of eddying rain-water. A hundred yards up began a line of grotesque cedar-trees, and they extended along the slope clear to its most southerly end. Beyond that end Venters wanted to get, and he concluded the cedars, few as they were, would afford some cover.

Therefore he climbed swiftly. The trees were farther up than he had estimated, though he had from long habit made allowance for the deceiving nature of distances in that country. When he gained the cover of cedars he paused to rest and look, and it was then he saw how the trees sprang from holes in the bare rock. Ages of rain had run down the slope, circling, eddying in depressions, wearing deep round holes. There had been dry seasons, accumulations of dust, wind-blown seeds, and cedars rose wonderfully out of solid rock. But these were not beautiful cedars. They were gnarled, twisted into weird contortions, as if growth were torture, dead at the tops, shrunken, gray, and old. Theirs had been a bitter fight, and Venters felt a strange sympathy for them. This country was hard on trees—and men.

He slipped from cedar to cedar, keeping them between him and the open valley. As he progressed, the belt of trees widened, and he kept to its upper margin. He passed shady pockets half full of water, and, as he marked the location for possible future need, he reflected that there had been no rain since the winter snows. From one of these shady holes a rabbit hopped out and squatted down, laying its ears flat.

Venters wanted fresh meat now more than when he had only himself to think of. But it would not do to fire his rifle there. So he broke off a cedar branch and threw it. He crippled the rabbit, which started to flounder up the slope. Venters did not wish to lose the meat, and he never allowed crippled game to escape, to die lingeringly in some covert. So after a careful glance below, and back toward the cañon, he began to chase the rabbit.

The fact that rabbits generally ran uphill was not new to him. But it presently seemed singular why this rabbit, that might have escaped downward, chose to ascend the slope. Venters knew then that it had a burrow higher up. More than once he jerked over to seize it, only in vain. for the rabbit by renewed effort eluded his grasp. Thus the chase continued on up the bare slope. The farther Venters climbed the more determined he grew to catch his quarry. At last, panting and sweating, he captured the rabbit at the foot of a steeper grade. Laying his rifle on the bulge of rising stone, he killed the animal and slung it from his belt.

Before starting down he waited to catch his breath. He had climbed far up that wonderful smooth slope, and had almost reached the base of yellow cliff that rose skyward, a huge scarred and cracked bulk. It frowned down upon him as if to forbid further ascent. Venters bent over for his rifle, and, as he picked it up from where it leaned against the steeper grade, he saw several little nicks cut in the solid stone.

They were only a few inches deep and about a foot apart. Venters began to count them—one—two—three—four—on up to sixteen. That number carried his glance to the top of his first bulging bench of cliff-base. Above, after a more level offset, was still steeper slope, and the line of nicks kept on, to wind round a projecting corner of wall.

A casual glance would have passed by these little dents; if Venters had not known what they signified he would never have bestowed upon them the second glance. But he knew they had been cut there by hand, and, though age-worn, he recognized them as steps cut in the rock by the cliff-dwellers. With a pulse beginning to beat and hammer away his calmness, he eyed that indistinct line of steps, up to where the buttress of wall hid further sight of them. He knew that behind the corner of stone would be a cave or a crack which could never be suspected from below. Chance, that had sported with him of late, now directed him to a probable hiding-place. Again he laid aside his rifle, and, removing boots and belt, he began to walk up the steps. Like a mountain goat, he was agile, sure-footed, and he mounted the first bench without bending to use his hands. The next ascent took grip of fingers as well as toes, but he climbed steadily, swiftly, to reach the projecting corner, and slipped around it. Here he faced a notch in the cliff. At the apex he turned abruptly into a ragged vent that split the ponderous wall clear to the top, showing a narrow streak of blue sky.

At the base this vent was dark, cool, and smelled of dry, musty dust. It zigzagged so that he could not see ahead more than a few yards at a time. He noticed tracks of wildcats and rabbits in the dusty floor. At every turn he expected to come upon a huge cavern full of little square stone houses, each with a small aperture like a staring dark eye. The passage lightened and widened, and opened at the foot of a narrow, steep, ascending chute.

Venters had a moment's notice of the rock, which was of the same smoothness and hardness as the slope below, before his gaze went irresistibly upward to the precipitous walls of this wide ladder of granite. These were ruined walls of yellow sandstone, and so split and splintered, so overhanging with great sections of balancing rim, so impending with tremendous crumbling crags, that Venters caught his breath sharply, and, appalled, he instinctively recoiled as if a step upward might jar the ponderous cliffs from their foundation. Indeed, it seemed that these ruined cliffs were but awaiting a breath of wind to collapse and come tumbling down. Venters hesitated. It would be a foolhardy man who risked his life under the leaning, waiting avalanches of rock in that gigantic split. Yet how many years had they leaned there without falling! At the bottom of the incline was an immense heap of weathered sandstone all crumbling to dust, but there were no huge rocks as large as houses, such as rested so lightly and frightfully above, waiting patiently and inevitably to crash down. Slowly split from the parent rock by the weathering process, and carved and sculptured by ages of wind and rain, they waited their moment. Venters felt how foolish it was for him to fear these broken walls; to fear that, after they had endured for thousands of years, the moment of his passing should be the one for them to slip. Yet he feared it.

"What a place to hide!" muttered Venters. "I'll climb—I'll see where this thing goes. If only I can find water!"

With teeth tight shut he essayed the incline. And as he climbed he bent his eyes downward. This, however, after a little grew impossible; he had to look to obey his eager, curious mind. He raised his glance and saw light between row on row of shafts and pinnacles and crags that stood out from the main wall. Some leaned against the cliff, others against each other; many stood sheer and alone; all were crumbling, cracked, rotten. It was a place of yellow, ragged ruin. The passage narrowed as he went up; it became a slant, hard for him to stick on; it was smooth as marble. Finally he surmounted it, surprised to find the walls still several hundred feet high, and a narrow gorge leading down on the other side. This was a divide between two inclines, about twenty yards wide. At one side stood an enormous rock. Venters gave it a second glance, because it rested on a pedestal. It attracted closer attention. It was like a colossal pear of stone standing on its stem. Around the bottom were thousands of little nicks just distinguishable to the eye. They were marks of stone hatchets. The cliff-dwellers had chipped and chipped away at this boulder till it rested its tremendous bulk upon a mere pin-point of its surface. Venters pondered. Why had the little stone-men hacked away at that big boulder? It bore no semblance to a statue or an idol or a godhead or a sphinx. Instinctively he put his hands on it and pushed; then his shoulder and heaved. The stone seemed to groan, to stir, to grate, and then to move. It tipped a little downward and hung balancing for a long instant, slowly returned, rocked slightly, groaned, and settled back to its former position.

Venters divined its significance. It had been meant for defense. The cliff-dwellers, driven by dreaded enemies to this last stand, had cunningly cut the rock until it balanced perfectly, ready to be dislodged by strong hands. Just below it leaned a tottering crag that would have toppled, starting an avalanche on an acclivity where no sliding mass could stop. Crags and pinnacles, splintered cliffs, and leaning shafts and monuments, would have thundered down to block forever the outlet to Deception Pass.

"That was a narrow shave for me," said Venters, soberly. "A balancing rock! The cliff-dwellers never had to roll it. They died, vanished, and here the rock stands, probably little changed. . . . But it might serve another lonely dweller of the cliffs. I'll hide up here somewhere, if I can only find water."

He descended the gorge on the other side. The slope was gradual, the space narrow, the course straight for many rods. A gloom hung between the up-sweeping walls. In a turn the passage narrowed to scarce a dozen feet, and here was darkness of night. But light shone ahead; another abrupt turn brought day again, and then wide open space.

Above Venters loomed a wonderful arch of stone bridging the cañon rims, and through the enormous round portal gleamed and glistened a beautiful valley shining under sunset gold reflected by surrounding cliffs. He gave a start of surprise. The valley was a cove a mile long, half that wide, and its enclosing walls were smooth and stained, and curved inward, forming great caves. He decided that its floor was far higher than the level of Deception Pass and the intersecting cañons. No purple sage colored this valley floor. Instead there were the white of aspens, streaks of branch and slender trunk glistening from the green of leaves, and the darker green of oaks, and through the middle of this forest, from wall to wall, ran a winding line of brilliant green which marked the course of cottonwoods and willows.

"There's water here—and this is the place for me," said Venters. "Only birds can peep over those walls. I've gone Oldring one better."

Venters waited no longer, and turned swiftly to retrace his steps. He named the cañon Surprise Valley and the huge boulder that guarded the outlet Balancing Rock. Going down he did not find himself attended by such fears as had beset him in the climb; still, he was not easy in mind and could not occupy himself with plans of moving the girl and his outfit until he had descended to the notch. There he rested a moment and looked about him. The pass was darkening with the approach of night. At the corner of the wall, where the stone steps turned, he saw a spur of rock that would serve to hold the noose of a lasso. He needed no more aid to scale that place. As he intended to make the move under cover of darkness, he wanted most to be able to tell where to climb up. So, taking several small stones with him, he stepped and slid down to the edge of the slope where he had left his rifle and boots. He placed the stones some yards apart. He left the rabbit lying upon the bench where the steps began. Then he addressed a keen-sighted, remembering gaze to the rim-wall above. It was serrated, and between two spears of rock, directly in line with his position, showed a zigzag crack that at night would let through the gleam of sky. This settled, he put on his belt and boots and prepared to descend. Some consideration was necessary to decide whether or not to leave his rifle there. On the return, carrying the girl and a pack, it would be added encumbrance; and after debating the matter he left the rifle leaning against the bench. As he went straight down the slope he halted every few rods to look up at his mark on the rim. It changed, but he fixed each change in his memory. When he reached the first cedar-tree, he tied his scarf upon a dead branch, and then hurried toward camp, having no more concern about finding his trail upon the return trip.

Darkness soon emboldened and lent him greater speed. It occurred to him, as he glided into the grassy glade near camp and heard the whinny of a horse, that he had forgotten Wrangle. The big sorrel could not be gotten into Surprise Valley. He would have to be left here.

Venters determined at once to lead the other horses out through the thicket and turn them loose. The farther they wandered from this cañon the better it would suit him. He easily descried Wrangle through the gloom, but the others were not in sight. Venters whistled low for the dogs, and when they came trotting to him he sent them out to search for the horses, and followed. It soon developed that they were not in the glade nor the thicket. Venters grew cold and rigid at the thought of rustlers having entered his retreat. But the thought passed, for the demeanor of Ring and Whitie reassured him. The horses had wandered away.

Under the clump of silver spruces a denser mantle of darkness, yet not so thick that Venters's night-practiced eyes could not catch the white oval of a still face. He bent over it with a slight suspension of breath that was both caution lest he frighten her and chill uncertainty of feeling lest he find her dead. But she slept, and he arose to renewed activity.

He packed his saddle-bags. The dogs were hungry, they whined about him and nosed his busy hands; but he took no time to feed them nor to satisfy his own hunger. He slung the saddle-bags over his shoulders and made them secure with his lasso. Then he wrapped the blankets closer about the girl and lifted her in his arms. Wrangle whinnied and thumped the ground as Venters passed him with the dogs. The sorrel knew he was being left behind, and was not sure whether he liked it or not. Venters went on and entered the thicket. Here he had to feel his way in pitch blackness and to wedge his progress between the close saplings. Time meant little to him now that he had started, and he edged along with slow side movement till he got clear of the thicket. Ring and Whitie stood waiting for him. Taking to the open aisles and patches of the sage, he walked guardedly, careful not to stumble or step in dust or strike against spreading sage-branches.

If he were burdened he did not feel it. From time to time, when he passed out of the black lines of shade into the wan starlight, he glanced at the white face of the girl lying in his arms. She had not awakened from her sleep or stupor. He did not rest until he cleared the black gate of the cañon. Then he leaned against a stone breast-high to him and gently released the girl from his hold. His brow and hair and the palms of his hands were wet, and there was a kind of nervous contraction of his muscles. They seemed to ripple and string tense. He had a desire to hurry and no sense of fatigue. A wind blew the scent of sage in his face. The first early blackness of night passed with the brightening of the stars. Somewhere back on his trail a coyote yelped, splitting the dead silence. Venters's faculties seemed singularly acute.

He lifted the girl again and pressed on. The valley afforded better traveling than the cañon. It was lighter, freer of sage, and there were no rocks. Soon, out of the pale gloom shone a still paler thing, and that was the low swell of slope. Venters mounted it, and his dogs walked beside him. Once upon the stone he slowed to snail pace, straining his sight to avoid the pockets and holes. Foot by foot he went up. The weird cedars, like great demons and witches chained to the rock and writhing in silent anguish, loomed up with wide and twisting naked arms. Venters crossed this belt of cedars, skirted the upper border, and recognized the tree he had marked, even before he saw his waving scarf.

Here he knelt and deposited the girl gently, feet first, and slowly laid her out full length. What he feared was to reopen one of her wounds. If he gave her a violent jar, or slipped and fell! But the supreme confidence so strangely felt that night admitted no such blunders.

The slope before him seemed to swell into obscurity, to lose its definite outline in a misty, opaque cloud that shaded into the over-shadowing wall. He scanned the rim where the serrated points speared the sky, and he found the zigzag crack. It was dim, only a shade lighter than the dark ramparts; but he distinguished it, and that served.

Lifting the girl, he stepped upward, closely attending to the nature of the path under his feet. After a few steps he stopped to mark his line with the crack in the rim. The dogs clung closer to him. While chasing the rabbit this slope had appeared interminable to him; now, burdened as he was, he did not think of length or height or toil. He remembered only to avoid a misstep and to keep his direction. He climbed on, with frequent stops to watch the rim, and before he dreamed of gaining the bench he bumped his knees into it, and saw, in the dim gray light, his rifle and the rabbit. He had come straight up without mishap or swerving off his course, and his shut teeth unlocked.

As he laid the girl down in the shallow hollow of the little ridge, with her white face upturned, she opened her eyes. Wide, staring, black, at once like both the night and the stars, they made her face seem still whiter.

"Is—it—you?" she asked, faintly.

"Yes," replied Venters.

"Oh! Where—are we?"

"I'm taking you to a safe place where no one will ever find you. I must climb a little here and call the dogs. Don't be afraid. I'll soon come for you."

She said no more. Her eyes watched him steadily for a moment and then closed. Venters pulled off his boots and then felt for the little steps in the rock. The shade of the cliff above obscured the point he wanted to gain, but he could see dimly a few feet before him. What he had attempted with care he now went at with surpassing lightness. Buoyant, rapid, sure, he attained the corner of wall and slipped around it. Here he could not see a hand before his face, so he groped along, found a little flat space, and there removed the saddle-bags. The lasso he took back with him to the corner and looped the noose over the spur of rock.

"Ring—Whitie—come," he called, softly.

Low whines came up from below.

"Here! Come, Whitie—Ring," he repeated, this time sharply.

Then followed scraping of claws and pattering of feet; and out of the gray gloom below him swiftly climbed the dogs to reach his side and pass beyond.

Venters descended, holding to the lasso. He tested its strength by throwing all his weight upon it. Then he gathered the girl up, and, holding her securely in his left arm, he began to climb, at every few steps jerking his right hand upward along the lasso. It sagged at each forward movement he made, but he balanced himself lightly during the interval when he lacked the support of a taut rope. He climbed as if he had wings, the strength of a giant, and knew not the sense of fear. The sharp corner of cliff seemed to cut out of the darkness. He reached it and the protruding shelf, and then, entering the black shade of the notch, he moved blindly but surely to the place where he had left the saddle-bags. He heard the dogs, though he could not see them. Once more he carefully placed the girl at his feet. Then, on hands and knees, he went over the little flat space, feeling for stones. He removed a number, and, scraping the deep dust into a heap, he unfolded the outer blanket from around the girl and laid her upon this bed. Then he went down the slope again for his boots, rifle, and the rabbit, and, bringing also his lasso with him, he made short work of that trip.

"Are—you—there?" The girl's voice came low from the blackness.

"Yes," he replied, and was conscious that his laboring breast made speech difficult.

"Are we—in a cave?"

"Yes."

"Oh, listen! . . . The waterfall! . . . I hear it! You've brought me back!"

Venters heard a murmuring moan that one moment swelled to a pitch almost softly shrill and the next lulled to a low, almost inaudible sigh.

"That's—wind blowing—in the—cliffs," he panted. "You're far—from Oldring's—cañon."

The effort it cost him to speak made him conscious of extreme lassitude following upon great exertion. It seemed that when he lay down and drew his blanket over him the action was the last before utter prostration. He stretched inert, wet, hot, his body one great strife of throbbing, stinging nerves and bursting veins. And there he lay for a long while before he felt that he had begun to rest.

Rest came to him that night, but no sleep. Sleep he did not want. The hours of strained effort were now as if they had never been, and he wanted to think. Earlier in the day he had dismissed an inexplicable feeling of change; but now, when there was no longer demand on his cunning and strength and he had time to think, he could not catch the illusive thing that had sadly perplexed as well as elevated his spirit.

Above him, through a V-shaped cleft in the dark rim of the cliff, shone the lustrous stars that had been his lonely accusers for a long, long year. To-night they were different. He studied them. Larger, whiter, more radiant they seemed; but that was not the difference he meant. Gradually it came to him that the distinction was not one he saw, but one he felt. In this he divined as much of the baffling change as he thought would be revealed to him then. And as he lay there, with the singing of the cliff-winds in his ears, the white stars above the dark, bold vent, the difference which he felt was that he was no longer alone.

CHAPTER NINE
Silver Spruce and Aspens

The rest of that night seemed to Venters only a few moments of starlight, a dark overcasting of sky, an hour or so of gray gloom, and then the lighting of dawn.

When he had bestirred himself, feeding the hungry dogs and breaking his long fast, and had repacked his saddle-bags, it was clear daylight, though the sun had not tipped the yellow wall in the east. He concluded to make the climb and descent into Surprise Valley in one trip. To that end he tied his blanket upon Ring and gave Whitie the extra lasso and the rabbit to carry. Then, with the rifle and saddle-bags slung upon his back, he took up the girl. She did not awaken from heavy slumber.

That climb up under the rugged, menacing brows of the broken cliffs, in the face of a grim, leaning boulder that seemed to be weary of its age-long wavering, was a tax on strength and nerve that Venters felt equally with something sweet and strangely exulting in its accomplishment. He did not pause until he gained the narrow divide and there he rested. Balancing Rock loomed huge, cold in the gray light of dawn, a thing without life, yet it spoke silently to Venters: "I am waiting to plunge down, to shatter and crash, roar and boom, to bury your trail, and close forever the outlet to Deception Pass!"

On the descent of the other side Venters had easy going, but was somewhat concerned because Whitie appeared to have succumbed to temptation, and while carrying the rabbit was also chewing on it. And Ring evidently regarded this as an injury to himself, especially as he had carried the heavier load. Presently he snapped at one end of the rabbit and refused to let go. But his action prevented Whitie from further misdoing, and then the two dogs pattered down, carrying the rabbit between them.

Venters turned out of the gorge, and suddenly paused stock-still, astounded at the scene before him. The curve of the great stone bridge had caught the sunrise, and through the magnificent arch burst a glorious stream of gold that shone with a long slant down into the center of Surprise Valley. Only through the arch did any sunlight pass, so that all the rest of the valley lay still asleep, dark green, mysterious, shadowy, merging its level into walls as misty and soft as morning clouds.

Venters then descended, passing through the arch, looking up at its tremendous height and sweep. It spanned the opening to Surprise Valley, stretching in almost perfect curve from rim to rim. Even in his hurry and concern Venters could not but feel its majesty, and the thought came to him that the cliff-dwellers must have regarded it as an object of worship.

Down, down, down Venters strode, more and more feeling the weight of his burden as he descended, and still the valley lay below him. As all other cañons and coves and valleys had deceived him, so had this deep, nestling oval. At length he passed beyond the slope of weathered stone that spread fan-shape from the arch, and encountered a grassy terrace running to the right and about on a level with the tips of the oaks and cottonwoods below. Scattered here and there upon this shelf were clumps of aspens, and he walked through them into a glade that surpassed, in beauty and adaptability for a wild home, any place he had ever seen. Silver spruces bordered the base of a precipitous wall that rose loftily. Caves indented its surface, and there were no detached ledges or weathered sections that might dislodge a stone. The level ground, beyond the spruces, dropped down into a little ravine. This was one dense line of slender aspens from which came the low splashing of water. And the terrace, lying open to the west, afforded unobstructed view of the valley of green treetops.

For his camp Venters chose a shady, grassy plot between the silver spruces and the cliff. Here, in the stone wall, had been wonderfully carved by wind or washed by water several deep caves above the level of the terrace. They were clean, dry, roomy. He cut spruce boughs and made a bed in the largest cave and laid the girl there. The first intimation that he had of her being aroused from sleep or lethargy was a low call for water.

He hurried down into the ravine with his canteen. It was a shallow, grass-green place with aspens growing up everywhere. To his delight he found a tiny brook of swift-running water. Its faint tinge of amber reminded him of the spring at Cottonwoods, and the thought gave him a little shock. The water was so cold it made his fingers tingle as he dipped the canteen. Having returned to the cave, he was glad to see the girl drink thirstily. This time he noted that she could raise her head slightly without his help.

"You were thirsty," he said. "It's good water. I've found a fine place. Tell me—how do you feel?"

"There's pain—here," she replied, and moved her hand to her left side.

"Why, that's strange! Your wounds are on your right side. I believe you're hungry. Is the pain a kind of dull ache—a gnawing?"

"It's like—that."

"Then it's hunger." Venters laughed, and suddenly caught himself with a quick breath and felt again a little shock. When had he laughed? "It's hunger," he went on. "I've had that gnaw many a time. I've got it now. But you mustn't eat. You can have all the water you want, but no food just yet."

"Won't I—starve?"

"No, people don't starve easily. I've discovered that. You must lie perfectly still and rest and sleep—for days."

"My hands—are dirty; my face feels—so hot and sticky; my boots hurt." It was her longest speech as yet, and it trailed off in a whisper.

"Well, I'm a fine nurse!"

It annoyed him that he had never thought of these things. But then awaiting her death and thinking of her comfort were vastly different matters. He unwrapped the blanket which covered her. What a slender girl she was! No wonder he had been able to carry her miles and pack her up that slippery ladder of stone. Her boots were of soft, fine leather, reaching clear to her knees. He recognized the make as one of a bootmaker in Sterling. Her spurs, that he had stupidly neglected to remove, consisted of silver frames and gold chains, and the rowels, large as silver dollars, were fancifully engraved. The boots slipped off rather hard. She wore heavy woollen rider's stockings, half length, and these were pulled up over the ends of her short trousers. Venters took off the stockings to note her little feet were red and swollen. He bathed them. Then he removed his scarf and bathed her face and hands.

"I must see your wounds now," he said, gently.

She made no reply, but watched him steadily as he opened her blouse and untied the bandage. His strong fingers trembled a little as he removed it. If the wounds had reopened! A chill struck him as he saw the angry red bullet-mark, and a tiny stream of blood winding from it down her white breast. Very carefully he lifted her to see that the wound in her back had closed perfectly. Then he washed the blood from her breast, bathed the wound, and left it unbandaged, open to the air.

Her eyes thanked him.

"Listen," he said, earnestly. "I've had some wounds, and I've seen many. I know a little about them. The hole in your back has closed. If you lie still three days the one in your breast will close and you'll be safe. The danger from hemorrhage will be over."

He had spoken with earnest sincerity, almost eagerness.

"Why—do you—want me—to get well?" she asked, wonderingly.

The simple question seemed unanswerable except on grounds of humanity. But the circumstances under which he had shot this strange girl, the shock and realization, the waiting for death, the hope, had resulted in a condition of mind wherein Venters wanted her to live more than he had ever wanted anything. Yet he could not tell why. He believed the killing of the rustler and the subsequent excitement had disturbed him. For how else could he explain the throbbing of his brain, the heat of his blood, the undefined sense of full hours, charged, vibrant with pulsating mystery where once they had dragged in loneliness?

"I shot you," he said, slowly, "and I want you to get well so I shall not have killed a woman. But—for your own sake, too—"

A terrible bitterness darkened her eyes, and her lips quivered.

"Hush," said Venters. "You've talked too much already."

In her unutterable bitterness he saw a darkness of mood that could not have been caused by her present weak and feverish state. She hated the life she had led, that she probably had been compelled to lead. She had suffered some unforgivable wrong at the hands of Oldring. With that conviction Venters felt a flame throughout his body, and it marked the rekindling of fierce anger and ruthlessness. In the past long year he had nursed resentment. He had hated the wilderness—the loneliness of the uplands. He had waited for something to come to pass. It had come. Like an Indian stealing horses he had skulked into the recesses of the cañons. He had found Oldring's retreat; he had killed a rustler; he had shot an unfortunate girl, then had saved her from this unwitting act, and he meant to save her from the consequent wasting of blood, from fever and weakness. Starvation he had to fight for her and for himself. Where he had been sick at the letting of blood, now he remembered it in grim, cold calm. And as he lost that softness of nature, so he lost his fear of men. He would watch for Oldring, biding his time, and he would kill this great black-bearded rustler who had held a girl in bondage, who had used her to his infamous ends.

Venters surmised this much of the change in him—idleness had passed; keen, fierce vigor flooded his mind and body; all that had happened to him at Cottonwoods seemed remote and hard to recall; the difficulties and perils of the present absorbed him, held him in a kind of spell.

First, then, he fitted up the little cave adjoining the girl's room for his own comfort and use. His next work was to build a fireplace of stones and to gather a store of wood. That done, he spilled the contents of his saddle-bags upon the grass and took stock. His outfit consisted of a small-handled axe, a hunting-knife, a large number of cartridges for rifle or revolver, a tin plate, a cup, and a fork and spoon, a quantity of dried beef and dried fruits, and small canvas bags containing tea, sugar, salt, and pepper. For him alone this supply would have been bountiful to begin a sojourn in the wilderness, but he was no longer alone. Starvation in the uplands was not an unheard-of thing; he did not, however, worry at all on that score, and feared only his possible inability to supply the needs of a woman in a weakened and extremely delicate condition.

If there was no game in the valley—a contingency he doubted—it would not be a great task for him to go by night to Oldring's herd and pack out a calf. The exigency of the moment was to ascertain if there were game in Surprise Valley. Whitie still guarded the dilapidated rabbit, and Ring slept near by under a spruce. Venters called Ring and went to the edge of the terrace, and there halted to survey the valley.

He was prepared to find it larger than his unstudied glances had made it appear; for more than a casual idea of dimensions and a hasty conception of oval shape and singular beauty he had not had time. Again the felicity of the name he had given the valley struck him forcibly. Around the red perpendicular walls, except under the great arc of stone, ran a terrace fringed at the cliff-base by silver spruces; below that first terrace sloped another wider one densely overgrown with aspens, and the center of the valley was a level circle of oaks and alders, with the glittering green line of willows and cottonwood dividing it in half. Venters saw a number and variety of birds flitting among the trees. To his left, facing the stone bridge, an enormous cavern opened in the wall; and low down, just above the tree-tops, he made out a long shelf of cliff-dwellings, with little black, staring windows or doors. Like eyes they were, and seemed to watch him. The few cliff-dwellings he had seen—all ruins—had left him with haunting memory of age and solitude and of something past. He had come, in a way, to be a cliff-dweller himself, and those silent eyes would look down upon him, as if in surprise that after thousands of years a man had invaded the valley. Venters felt sure that he was the only white man who had ever walked under the shadow of the wonderful stone bridge, down into that wonderful valley with its circle of caves and its terraced rings of silver spruce and aspens.

The dog growled below and rushed into the forest. Venters ran down the declivity to enter a zone of light shade streaked with sunshine. The oak-trees were slender, none more than half a foot thick, and they grew close together, intermingling their branches. Ring came running back with a rabbit in his mouth. Venters took the rabbit and, holding the dog near him, stole softly on. There were fluttering of wings among the branches and quick bird-notes, and rustling of dead leaves and rapid patterings. Venters crossed well-worn trails marked with fresh tracks; and when he had stolen on a little farther he saw many birds and running quail, and more rabbits than he could count. He had not penetrated the forest of oaks for a hundred yards, had not approached anywhere near the line of willows and cottonwoods which he knew grew along a stream. But he had seen enough to know that Surprise Valley was the home of many wild creatures.

Venters returned to camp. He skinned the rabbits, and gave the dogs the one they had quarreled over, and the skin of this he dressed and hung up to dry, feeling that he would like to keep it. It was a particularly rich, furry pelt with a beautiful white tail. Venters remembered that but for the bobbing of that white tail catching his eye he would not have espied the rabbit, and he would never have discovered Surprise Valley. Little incidents of chance like this had turned him here and there in Deception Pass; and now they had assumed to him the significance and direction of destiny.

His good fortune in the matter of game at hand brought to his mind the necessity of keeping it in the valley. Therefore he took the axe and cut bundles of aspens and willows, and packed them up under the bridge to the narrow outlet of the gorge. Here he began fashioning a fence, by driving aspens into the ground and lacing them fast with willows. Trip after trip he made down for more building material, and the afternoon had passed when he finished the work to his satisfaction. Wildcats might scale the fence, but no coyote could come in to search for prey, and no rabbits or other small game could escape from the valley.

Upon returning to camp he set about getting his supper at ease, around a fine fire, without hurry or fear of discovery. After hard work that had definite purpose, this freedom and comfort gave him peculiar satisfaction. He caught himself often, as he kept busy round the camp-fire, stopping to glance at the quiet form in the cave, and at the dogs stretched cozily near him, and then out across the beatiful valley. The present was not yet real to him.

While he ate, the sun set beyond a dip in the rim of the curved wall. As the morning sun burst wondrously through a grand arch into this valley, in a golden, slanting shaft, so the evening sun, at the moment of setting, shone through a gap of cliffs, sending down a broad red burst to brighten the oval with a blaze of fire. To Venters both sunrise and sunset were unreal.

A cool wind blew across the oval, waving the tips of oaks, and, while the light lasted, fluttering the aspen leaves into millions of facets of red, and sweeping the graceful spruces. Then with the wind soon came a shade and a darkening, and suddenly the valley was gray. Night came there quickly after the sinking of the sun. Venters went softly to look at the girl. She slept, and her breathing was quiet and slow. He lifted Ring into the cave, with stern whisper for him to stay there on guard. Then he drew the blanket carefully over her and returned to the camp-fire.

Though exceedingly tired, he was yet loath to yield to lassitude, but this night it was not from listening, watchful vigilance; it was from a desire to realize his position. The details of his wild environment seemed the only substance of a strange dream. He saw the darkening rims, the gray oval turning black, the undulating surface of forest, like a rippling lake, and the spear-pointed spruces. He heard the flutter of aspen leaves and the soft, continuous splash of falling water. The melancholy note of a cañon bird broke clear and lonely from the high cliffs. Venters had no name for this night singer, and he had never seen one; but the few notes, always pealing out just at darkness, were as familiar to him as the cañon silence. Then they ceased, and the rustle of leaves and the murmur of water hushed in a growing sound that Venters fancied was not of earth. Neither had he a name for this, only it was inexpressibly wild and sweet. The thought came that it might be a moan of the girl in her last outcry of life, and he felt a tremor shake him. But no! This sound was not human, though it was like despair. He began to doubt his sensitive perceptions, to believe that he half-dreamed what he thought he heard. Then the sound swelled with the strengthening of the breeze, and he realized it was the singing of the wind in the cliffs.

By and by a drowsiness overcame him, and Venters began to nod, half asleep, with his back against a spruce. Rousing himself and calling Whitie, he went to the cave. The girl lay barely visible in the dimness. Ring crouched beside her, and the patting of his tail on the stone assured Venters that the dog was awake and faithful to his duty. Venters sought his own bed of fragrant boughs; and as he lay back, somehow grateful for the comfort and safety, the night seemed to steal away from him and he sank softly into intangible space and rest and slumber.

Venters awakened to the sound of melody that he imagined was only the haunting echo of dream music. He opened his eyes to another surprise of this valley of beautiful surprises. Out of his cave he saw the exquisitely fine foliage of the silver spruces crossing a round space of blue morning sky; and in this lacy leafage fluttered a number of gray birds with black and white stripes and long tails. They were mocking-birds, and they were singing as if they wanted to burst their throats. Venters listened. One long, silver-tipped branch dropped almost to his cave, and upon it, within a few yards of him, sat one of the graceful birds. Venters saw the swelling and quivering of its throat in song. He arose, and when he slid down out of his cave the birds fluttered and flew farther away.

Venters stepped before the opening of the other cave and looked in. The girl was awake, with wide eyes and listening look, and she had a hand on Ring's neck.

"Mocking-birds!" she said.

"Yes," replied Venters, "and I believe they like our company."

"Where are we?"

"Never mind now. After a little I'll tell you."

"The birds woke me. When I heard them—and saw the shiny trees—and the blue sky—and then a blaze of gold dropping down—I wondered—"

She did not complete her fancy, but Venters imagined he understood her meaning. She appeared to be wandering in mind. Venters felt her face and hands and found them burning with fever. He went for water, and was glad to find it almost as cold as if flowing from ice. That water was the only medicine he had, and he put faith in it. She did not want to drink, but he made her swallow, and then he bathed her face and head and cooled her wrists.

The day began with the heightening of the fever. Venters spent the time reducing her temperature, cooling her hot cheeks and temples. He kept close watch over her, and at the least indication of restlessness, that he knew led to tossing and rolling of the body, he held her tightly, so no violent move could reopen her wounds. Hour after hour she babbled and laughed and cried and moaned in delirium; but whatever her secret was she did not reveal it. Attended by something somber for Venters, the day passed. At night in the cool winds the fever abated and she slept.

The second day was a repetition of the first. On the third he seemed to see her wither and waste away before his eyes. That day he scarcely went from her side for a moment, except to run for fresh, cool water; and he did not eat. The fever broke on the fourth day and left her spent and shrunken, a slip of a girl with life only in her eyes. They hung upon Venters with a mute observance, and he found hope in that.

To rekindle the spark that had nearly flickered out, to nourish the little life and vitality that remained in her, was Venters's problem. But he had little resource other than the meat of the rabbits and quail; and from these he made broths and soups as best he could, and fed her with a spoon. It came to him that the human body, like the human soul, was a strange thing and capable of recovering from terrible shocks. For almost immediately she showed faint signs of gathering strength. There was one more waiting day, in which he doubted, and spent long hours by her side as she slept, and watched the gentle swell of her breast rise and fall in breathing, and the wind stir the tangled chestnut curls. On the next day he knew that she would live.

Upon realizing it he abruptly left the cave and sought his accustomed seat against the trunk of a big spruce, where once more he let his glance stray along the sloping terraces. She would live, and the somber gloom lifted out of the valley, and he felt relief that was pain. Then he roused to the call of action, to the many things he needed to do in the way of making camp fixtures and utensils, to the necessity of hunting food, and the desire to explore the valley.

But he decided to wait a few more days before going far from camp, because he fancied that the girl rested easier when she could see him near at hand. And on the first day her languor appeared to leave her in a renewed grip of life. She awoke stronger from each short slumber; she ate greedily, and she moved about in her bed of boughs; and always, it seemed to Venters, her eyes followed him. He knew now that her recovery would be rapid. She talked about the dogs, about the caves, the valley, about how hungry she was, till Venters silenced her, asking her to put off further talk till another time. She obeyed, but she sat up in her bed, and her eyes roved to and fro, and always back to him.

Upon the second morning she sat up when he awakened her, and would not permit him to bathe her face and feed her, which actions she performed for herself. She spoke little, however, and Venters was quick to catch in her the first intimations of thoughtfulness and curiosity and appreciation of her situation. He left camp and took Whitie out to hunt for rabbits. Upon his return he was amazed and somewhat anxiously concerned to see his invalid sitting with her back to a corner of the cave and her bare feet swinging out. Hurriedly he approached, intending to advise her to lie down again, to tell her that perhaps she might overtax her strength. The sun shone upon her, glinting on the little head with its tangle of bright hair and the small, oval face with its pallor, and dark-blue eyes underlined by dark-blue circles. She looked at him and he looked at her. In that exchange of glances he imagined each saw the other in some different guise. It seemed impossible to Venters that this frail girl could be Oldring's Masked Rider. It flashed over him that he had made a mistake which presently she would explain.

"Help me down," she said.

"But—are you well enough?" he protested. "Wait—a little longer."

"I'm weak—dizzy But I want to get down."

He lifted her—what a light burden now!—and stood her upright beside him, and supported her as she essayed to walk with halting steps. She was like a stripling of a boy; the bright, small head scarcely reached his shoulder. But now, as she clung to his arm, the rider's costume she wore did not contradict, as it had done at first, his feeling of her femininity. She might be the famous Masked Rider of the uplands, she might resemble a boy; but her outline, her little hands and feet, her hair, her big eyes and tremulous lips, and especially a something that Venters felt as a subtle essence rather than what he saw, proclaimed her sex.

She soon tired. He arranged a comfortable seat for her under the spruce that overspread the camp-fire.

"Now tell me—everything," she said.

He recounted all that had happened from the time of his discovery of the rustlers in the cañon up to the present moment.

"You shot me—and now you've saved my life?"

"Yes. After almost killing you I've pulled you through."

"Are you glad?"

"I should say so!"

Her eyes were unusually expressive, and they regarded him steadily; she was unconscious of that mirroring of her emotions, and they shone with gratefulness and interest and wonder and sadness.

"Tell me about yourself?" she asked.

He made this a briefer story, telling of his coming to Utah, his various occupations till he became a rider, and then how the Mormons had practically driven him out of Cottonwoods, an outcast.

Then, no longer able to withstand his own burning curiosity, he questioned her in turn.

"Are you Oldring's Masked Rider?"

"Yes," she replied, and dropped her eyes.

"I knew it—I recognized your figure—and mask, for I saw you once. Yet I can't believe it! . . . But you never *were* really that rustler, as we riders knew him? A thief—a marauder—a kidnapper of women—a murderer of sleeping riders!"

"No! I never stole—or harmed any one—in all my life. I only rode and rode—"

"But why—why?" he burst out. "Why the name? I understand Oldring made you ride. But the black mask—the mystery—the things laid to your hands—the threats in your infamous name—the night-riding credited to you—the evil deeds deliberately blamed on you and acknowledged by rustlers—even Oldring himself! Why? Tell me why?"

"I never knew that," she answered low. Her drooping head straightened, and the large eyes, larger now and darker, met Venters's with a clear, steadfast gaze in which he read truth. It verified his own conviction.

"Never knew? That's strange! Are you a Mormon?"

"No."

"Is Oldring a Mormon?"

"No."

"Do you—care for him?"

"Yes. I hate his men—his life—sometimes I almost hate him!"

Venters paused in his rapid-fire questioning, as if to brace himself to ask for a truth that would be abhorrent for him to confirm, but which he seemed driven to hear.

"What are—what *were* you to Oldring?"

Like some delicate thing suddenly exposed to blasting heat, the girl wilted; her head dropped, and into her white, wasted cheeks crept the red of shame.

Venters would have given anything to recall that question. It seemed so different—his thought when spoken. Yet her shame established in his mind something akin to the respect he had strangely been hungering to feel for her.

"D—n that question!—forget it!" he cried, in a passion of pain for her and anger at himself. "But once and for all—tell me—I know it, yet I want to hear you say so—you couldn't help yourself?"

"Oh no."

"Well, that makes it all right with me," he went on, honestly. "I—I want you to feel that . . . you see—we've been thrown together—and—and I want to help you—not hurt you. I thought life had been cruel to me, but when I think of yours I feel mean and little for my complaining. Anyway, I was a lonely outcast. And now! . . . I don't see very clearly what it all means. Only we are here—together. We've got to stay here, for long, surely till you are well. But you'll never go back to Oldring. And I'm sure helping you will help me, for I was sick in mind. There's something now for me to do. And if I can win back your strength—then get you away, out of this wild country—help you somehow to a happier life—just think how good that'll be for me!"

CHAPTER TEN
Love

During all these waiting days Venters, with the exception of the afternoon when he had built the gate in the gorge, had scarcely gone out of sight of camp and never out of hearing. His desire to explore Surprise Valley was keen, and on the morning after his long talk with the girl he took his rifle and, calling Ring, made a move to start. The girl lay back in a rude chair of boughs he had put together for her. She had been watching him, and when he picked up the gun and called the dog Venters thought she gave a nervous start.

"I'm only going to look over the valley," he said.

"Will you be gone long?"

"No," he replied, and started off. The incident set him thinking of his former impression that, after her recovery from fever, she did not seem at ease unless he was close at hand. It was fear of being alone, due, he concluded, most likely to her weakened condition. He must not leave her much alone.

As he strode down the sloping terrace, rabbits scampered before him, and the beautiful valley quail, as purple in color as the sage on the uplands, ran fleetly along the ground into the forest. It was pleasant under the trees, in the gold-flecked shade, with the whistle of quail and twittering of birds everywhere. Soon he had passed the limit of his former excursions and entered new territory. Here the woods began to show open glades and brooks running down from the slope, and presently he emerged from shade into the sunshine of a meadow. The shaking of the high grass told him of the running of animals, what species he could not tell, but from Ring's manifest desire to have a chase they were evidently some kind wilder than rabbits. Venters approached the willow and cottonwood belt that he had observed from the height of slope. He penetrated it to find a considerable stream of water and great half-submerged mounds of brush and sticks, and all about him were old and new gnawed circles at the base of the cottonwoods.

"Beaver!" he exclaimed. "By all that's lucky! The meadow's full of beaver! How did they ever get here?"

Beaver had not found a way into the valley by the trail of the cliff-dwellers, of that he was certain; and he began to have more than curiosity as to the outlet or inlet of the stream. When he passed some dead water, which he noted was held by a beaver-dam, there was a current in the stream, and it flowed west. Following its course, he soon entered the oak forest again, and passed through to find himself before massed and jumbled ruins of cliff-wall. There were tangled thickets of wild plum-trees and other thorny growths that made passage extremely laborsome. He found innumerable tracks of wildcats and foxes. Rustlings in the thick undergrowth told him of stealthy movements of these animals. At length his further advance appeared futile, for the reason that the stream disappeared in a split at the base of immense rocks over which he could not climb. To his relief he concluded that though beaver might work their way up the narrow chasm where the water rushed in, it would be impossible for men to enter the valley there.

This western curve was the only part of the valley where the walls had been split asunder, and it was a wildly rough and inaccessible corner. Going back a little way, he leaped the stream and headed toward the southern wall. Once out of the oaks he found again the low terrace of aspens, and above that the wide, open terrace fringed by silver spruces. This side of the valley contained the wind or water worn caves. As he pressed on, keeping to the upper terrace, cave after cave opened out of the cliff; now a large one, now a small one. Then yawned, quite suddenly and wonderfully above him, the great cavern of the cliff-dwellers.

It was still a goodly distance, and he tried to imagine, if it appeared so huge from where he stood, what it would be when he got there. He climbed the terrace and then faced a long, gradual ascent of weathered rock and dust, which made climbing too difficult for attention to anything else. At length he entered a zone of shade, and looked up. He stood just within the hollow of a cavern so immense that he had no conception of its real dimensions. The curved roof, stained by ages of leakage, with buff and black and rust-colored streaks, swept up and loomed higher and seemed to soar to the rim of the cliff. Here again was a magnificent arch, such as formed the grand gateway to the valley, only in this instance it formed the dome of a cave instead of the span of a bridge.

Venters passed onward and upward. The stones he dislodged rolled down with strange, hollow crack and roar. He had climbed a hundred rods inward, and yet he had not reached the base of the shelf where the cliff-dwellings rested, a long half-circle of connected stone house, with little dark holes that he had fancied were eyes. At length he gained the base of the shelf, and here found steps cut in the rock. These facilitated climbing, and as he went up he thought how easily this vanished race of men might once have held that stronghold against an army. There was only one possible place to ascend, and this was narrow and steep.

Venters had visited cliff-dwellings before, and they had been in ruins, and of no great character or size but this place was of proportions that stunned him, and it had not been desecrated by the hand of man, nor had it been crumbled by the hand of time. It was a stupendous tomb. It had been a city. It was just as it had been left by its builders. The little houses were there, the smoke-blackened stains of fires, the pieces of pottery scattered about cold hearths, the stone hatchets; and stone pestles and mealing-stones lay beside round holes polished by years of grinding maize—lay there as if they had been carelessly dropped yesterday. But the cliff-dwellers were gone!

Dust! They were dust on the floor or at the foot of the shelf, and their habitations and utensils endured. Venters felt the sublimity of that marvelous vaulted arch, and it seemed to gleam with a glory of something that was gone. How many years had passed since the cliff-dwellers gazed out across the beautiful valley as he was gazing now? How long had it been since women ground grain in those polished holes? What time had rolled by since men of an unknown race lived, loved, fought, and died there? Had an enemy destroyed them? Had disease destroyed them, or only that greatest destroyer—time? Venters saw a long line of blood-red hands painted low down upon the yellow roof of stone. Here was strange portent, if not an answer to his queries. The place oppressed him. It was light, but full of a transparent gloom. It smelled of dust and musty stone, of age and disuse. It was sad. It was solemn. It had the look of a place where silence had become master and was now irrevocable and terrible and could not be broken. Yet, at the moment, from high up in the carved crevices of the arch, floated down the low, strange wail of wind—a knell indeed for all that had gone.

Venters, sighing, gathered up an armful of pottery, such pieces as he thought strong enough and suitable for his own use, and bent his steps toward camp. He mounted the terrace at an opposite point to which he had left. He saw the girl looking in the direction he had gone. His footsteps made no sound in the deep grass, and he approached close without her being aware of his presence. Whitie lay on the ground near where she sat, and he manifested the usual actions of welcome, but the girl did not notice them. She seemed to be oblivious to everything near at hand. She made a pathetic figure drooping there, with her sunny hair contrasting so markedly with her white, wasted cheeks and her hands listlessly clasped and her little bare feet propped in the framework of the rude seat. Venters could have sworn and laughed in one breath at the idea of the connection between this girl and Oldring's Masked Rider. She was the victim of more than accident of fate—a victim to some deep plot the mystery of which burned him. As he stepped forward with a half-formed thought that she was absorbed in watching for his return, she turned her head and saw him. A swift start, a change rather than rush of blood under her white cheeks, a flashing of big eyes that fixed their glance upon him, transformed her face in that single instant of turning; and he knew she had been watching for him, that his return was the one thing in her mind. She did not smile; she did not flush; she did not look glad. All these would have meant little compared to her indefinite expression. Venters grasped the peculiar, vivid, vital something that leaped from her face. It was as if she had been in a dead, hopeless clamp of inaction and feeling, and had been suddenly shot through and through with quivering animation. Almost it was as if she had returned to life.

And Venters thought with lightning swiftness, "I've saved her—I've unlinked her from that old life—she was watching as if I were all she had left on earth—she belongs to me!" The thought was startlingly new. Like a blow it was in an unprepared moment. The cheery salutation he had ready for her died unborn, and he tumbled the pieces of pottery awkwardly on the grass, while some unfamiliar, deep-seated emotion, mixed with pity and glad assurance of his power to succor her, held him dumb.

"What a load you had!" she said. "Why, they're pots and crocks! Where did you get them!"

Venters laid down his rifle, and, filling one of the pots from his canteen, he placed it on the smoldering campfire.

"Hope it'll hold water," he said, presently. "Why, there's an enormous cliff-dwelling just across here. I got the pottery there. Don't you think we needed something? That tin cup of mine has served to make tea, broth, soup—everything."

"I noticed we hadn't a great deal to cook in."

She laughed. It was the first time. He liked that laugh, and though he was tempted to look at her, he did not want to show his surprise or his pleasure.

"Will you take me over there, and all around in the valley—pretty soon when I'm well?" she added.

"Indeed I shall. It's a wonderful place. Rabbits so thick you can't step without kicking one out. And quail, beaver, foxes, wildcats. We're in a regular den. But—haven't you ever seen a cliff-dwelling?"

"No. I've heard about them, though. The—the men say the Pass is full of old houses and ruins."

"Why, I should think you'd have run across one in all your riding around," said Venters. He spoke slowly, choosing his words carefully, and he essayed a perfectly casual manner, and pretended to be busy assorting pieces of pottery. She must have no cause again to suffer shame for curiosity of his. Yet never in all his days had he been so eager to hear the details of anyone's life.

"When I rode—I rode like the wind," she replied, "and never had time to stop for anything."

"I remember that day I—I met you in the Pass—how dusty you were, how tired your horse looked. Were you always riding?"

"Oh, no. Sometimes not for months, when I was shut up in the cabin."

Venters tried to subdue a hot tingling.

"You were shut up, then?" he asked, carelessly.

"When Oldring went away on his long trips—he was gone for months sometimes—he shut me up in the cabin."

"What for?"

"Perhaps to keep me from running away. I always threatened that. Mostly, though, because the men got drunk at the villages. But they were always good to me. I wasn't afraid."

"A prisoner! That must have been hard on you?"

"I liked that. As long as I can remember I've been locked up there at times, and those times were the only happy ones I ever had. It's a big cabin, high up on a cliff, and I could look out. Then I had dogs and pets I had tamed, and books. There was a spring inside, and food stored, and the men brought me fresh meat. Once I was there one whole winter."

It now required deliberation on Venters's part to persist in his unconcern and to keep at work. He wanted to look at her, to volley questions at her.

"As long as you can remember—you've lived in Deception Pass?" he went on.

"I've a dim memory of some other place, and women and children; but I can't make anything of it. Sometimes I think till I'm weary."

"Then you can read—you have books?"

"Oh yes, I can read, and write, too, pretty well. Oldring is educated. He taught me, and years ago an old rustler lived with us, and he had been something different once. He was always teaching me."

"So Oldring takes long trips," mused Venters. "Do you know where he goes?"

"No. Every year he drives cattle north of Sterling—then does not return for months. I heard him accused once of living two lives—and he killed the man. That was at Stone Bridge."

Venters dropped his apparent task and looked up with an eagerness he no longer strove to hide.

"Bess," he said, using her name for the first time, "I suspected Oldring was something besides a rustler. Tell me, what's his purpose here in the Pass? I believe much that he has done was to hide his real work here."

"You're right. He's more than a rustler. In fact, as the men say, his rustling cattle is now only a bluff. There's gold in the cañons!"

"Ah!"

"Yes, there's gold, not in great quantities, but gold enough for him and his men. They wash for gold week in and week out. Then they drive a few cattle and go into the villages to drink and shoot and kill—to bluff the riders."

"Drive a few cattle! But, Bess, the Withersteen herd, the red herd—twenty-five hundred head! That's not a few. And I tracked them into a valley near here."

"Oldring never stole the red herd. He made a deal with Mormons. The riders were to be called in, and Oldring was to drive the herd and keep it till a certain time—I won't know when—then drive it back to the range. What his share was I didn't hear."

"Did you hear *why* that deal was made?" queried Venters.

"No. But it was a trick of Mormons. They're full of tricks. I've heard Oldring's men tell about Mormons. Maybe the Withersteen woman wasn't minding her halter! I saw the man who made the deal. He was a little, queer-shaped man, all humped up. He sat his horse well. I heard one of our men say afterward there was no better rider on the sage than this fellow. What was the name? I forget."

"Jerry Card?" suggested Venters.

"That's it. I remember—it's a name easy to remember—and Jerry Card appeared to be on fair terms with Oldring's men."

"I shouldn't wonder," replied Venters, thoughtfully. Verification of his suspicions in regard to Tull's underhand work—for the deal with Oldring made by Jerry Card assuredly had its inception in the Mormon Elder's brain, and had been accomplished through his orders—revived in Venters a memory of hatred that had been smothered by press of other emotions. Only a few days had elapsed since the hour of his encounter with Tull, yet they had been forgotten and now seemed far off, and the interval one that now appeared large and profound with incalculable change in his feelings. Hatred of Tull still existed in his heart; but it had lost its white heat. His affection for Jane Withersteen had not changed in the least; nevertheless, he seemed to view it from another angle and see it as another thing—what, he could not exactly define. The recalling of these two feelings was to Venters like getting glimpses into a self that was gone; and the wonder of them—perhaps the change which was too elusive for him—was the fact that a strange irritation accompanied the memory and desire to dismiss it from mind. And straightway he did dismiss it, to return to thoughts of his significant present.

"Bess, tell me one more thing," he said. "Haven't you known any women—any young people?"

"Sometimes there were women with the men; but Oldring never let me know them. And all the young people I ever saw in my life was when I rode fast through the villages."

Perhaps that was the most puzzling and thought-provoking thing she had yet said to Venters. He pondered, more curious the more he learned, but he curbed his inquisitive desires, for he saw her shrinking on the verge of that shame, the causing of which had occasioned him such self-reproach. He would ask no more. Still he had to think, and he found it difficult to think clearly. This sad-eyed girl was so utterly different from what it would have been reason to believe such a remarkable life would have made her. On this day he had found her simple and frank, as natural as any girl he had ever known. About her there was something sweet. Her voice was low and well modulated. He could not look into her face, meet her steady, unabashed, yet wistful eyes, and think of her as the woman she had confessed herself. Oldring's Masked Rider sat before him, a girl dressed as a man. She had been made to ride at the head of infamous forays and drives. She had been imprisoned for many months of her life in an obscure cabin. At times the most vicious of men had been her companions; and the vilest of women, if they had not been permitted to approach her, had, at least, cast their shadows over her. But—but in spite of all this—there thundered at Venters some truth that lifted its voice higher than the clamoring facts of dishonor, some truth that was the very life of her beautiful eyes; and it was innocence.

In the days that followed, Venters balanced perpetually in mind this haunting conception of innocence over against the cold and sickening fact of an unintentional yet actual gift. How could it be possible for the two things to be true? He believed the latter to be true, and he would not relinquish his conviction of the former; and these conflicting thoughts augmented the mystery that appeared to be a part of Bess. In those ensuing days, however, it became clear as clearest light that Bess was rapidly regaining strength; that, unless reminded of her long association with Oldring, she seemed to have forgotten it; that, like an Indian who lives solely from moment to moment, she was utterly absorbed in the present.

Day by day Venters watched the white of her face slowly change to brown, and the wasted cheeks fill out by imperceptible degrees. There came a time when he could just trace the line of demarcation between the part of her face once hidden by a mask and that left exposed to wind and sun. When that line disappeared in clear bronze tan it was as if she had been washed clean of the stigma of Oldring's Masked Rider. The suggestion of the mask always made Venters remember; now that it was gone he seldom thought of her past. Occasionally he tried to piece together the several stages of strange experience and to make a whole. He had shot a masked outlaw the very sight of whom had been ill omen to riders; he had carried off a wounded woman whose bloody lips quivered in prayer; he had nursed what seemed a frail, shrunken boy; and now he watched a girl whose face had become strangely sweet, whose dark-blue eyes were ever upon him without boldness, without shyness, but with a steady, grave, and growing light. Many times Venters found the clear gaze embarrassing to him, yet, like wine, it had an exhilarating effect. What did she think when she looked at him so? Almost he believed she had no thought at all. All about her and the present there in Surprise Valley, and the dim yet subtly impending future, fascinated Venters and made him thoughtful as all his lonely vigils in the sage had not.

Chiefly it was the present that he wished to dwell upon; but it was the call of the future which stirred him to action. No idea had he of what that future had in store for Bess and him. He began to think of improving Surprise Valley as a place to live in, for there was no telling how long they would be compelled to stay there. Venters stubbornly resisted the entering into his mind of an insistent thought that, clearly realized, might have made it plain to him that he did not want to leave Surprise Valley at all. But it was imperative that he consider practical matters; and whether or not he was destined to stay long there, he felt the immediate need of a change of diet. It would be necessary for him to go farther afield for a variety of meat, and also that he soon visit Cottonwoods for a supply of food.

It occurred again to Venters that he could go to the cañon where Oldring kept his cattle, and at little risk he could pack out some beef. He wished to do this, however, without letting Bess know of it till after he had made the trip. Presently he hit upon the plan of going while she was asleep.

That very night he stole out of camp, climbed up under the stone bridge, and entered the outlet to the Pass. The gorge was full of luminous gloom. Balancing Rock loomed dark and leaned over the pale descent. Transformed in the shadowy light, it took shape and dimensions of a spectral god waiting—waiting for the moment to hurl himself down upon the tottering walls and close forever the outlet to Deception Pass. At night more than by day Venters felt something fearful and fateful in that rock, and that it had leaned and waited through a thousand years to have somehow to deal with his destiny.

"Old man, if you must roll, wait till I get back to the girl, and then roll!" he said, aloud, as if the stones were indeed a god.

And those spoken words, in their grim note to his ear, as well as contents to his mind, told Venters that he was all but drifting on a current which he had not power nor wish to stem.

Venters exercised his usual care in the matter of hiding tracks from the outlet, yet it took him scarcely an hour to reach Oldring's cattle. Here sight of many calves changed his original intention, and instead of packing out meat he decided to take a calf out alive. He roped one, securely tied its feet, and swung it over his shoulder. Here was an exceedingly heavy burden, but Venters was powerful—he could take up a sack of grain and with ease pitch it over a pack-saddle—and he made long distance without resting. The hardest work came in the climb up to the outlet and on through to the valley. When he had accomplished it, he became fired with another idea that again changed his intention. He would not kill the calf, but keep it alive. He would go back to Oldring's herd and pack out more calves. Thereupon he secured the calf in the best available spot for the moment and turned to make a second trip.

When Venters got back to the valley with another calf, it was close upon daybreak. He crawled into his cave and slept late. Bess had no inkling that he had been absent from camp nearly all night, and only remarked solicitously that he appeared to be more tired than usual, and more in the need of sleep. In the afternoon Venters built a gate across a small ravine near camp, and here corralled the calves; and he succeeded in completing his task without Bess being any the wiser.

That night he made two more trips to Oldring's range, and again on the following night, and yet another on the next. With eight calves in his corral, he concluded that he had enough; but it dawned upon him then that he did not want to kill one. "I've rustled Oldring's cattle," he said, and laughed. He noted then that all the calves were red. "Red!" he exclaimed. "From the red herd. I've stolen Jane Withersteen's cattle! . . . That's about the strangest thing yet."

One more trip he undertook to Oldring's valley, and this time he roped a yearling steer and killed it and cut out a small quarter of beef. The howling of coyotes told him he need have no apprehension that the work of his knife would be discovered. He packed the beef back to camp and hung it upon a spruce-tree. Then he sought his bed.

On the morrow he was up bright and early, glad that he had a surprise for Bess. He could hardly wait for her to come out. Presently she appeared and walked under the spruce. Then she approached the camp-fire. There was a tinge of healthy red in the bronze of her cheeks, and her slender form had begun to round out in graceful lines.

"Bess, didn't you say you were tired of rabbit?" inquired Venters. "And quail and beaver?"

"Indeed I did."

"What would you like?"

"I'm tired of meat, but if we have to live on it I'd like some beef."

"Well, how does that strike you?" Venters pointed to the quarter hanging from the spruce-tree. "We'll have fresh beef for a few days, then we'll cut the rest into strips and dry it."

"Where did you get that?" asked Bess, slowly.

"I stole that from Oldring."

"You went back to the cañon—you risked—" While she hesitated the tinge of bloom faded out of her cheeks.

"It wasn't any risk, but it was hard work."

"I'm sorry I said I was tired of rabbit. Why! How—When did you get that beef?"

"Last night."

"While I was asleep?"

"Yes."

"I woke last night sometime—but I didn't know."

Her eyes were widening, darkening with thought, and whenever they did so the steady, watchful, seeing gaze gave place to the wistful light. In the former she saw as the primitive woman without thought; in the latter she looked inward, and her gaze was the reflection of a troubled mind. For long Venters had not seen that dark change, that deepening of blue, which he thought was beautiful and sad. But now he wanted to make her think.

"I've done more than pack in that beef," he said. "For five nights I've been working while you slept. I've got eight calves corralled near a ravine. Eight calves, all alive and doing fine!"

"You went five nights!"

All that Venters could make of the dilation of her eyes, her slow pallor, and her exclamation, was fear—fear for herself or for him.

"Yes. I didn't tell you, because I knew you were afraid to be left alone."

"Alone?" She echoed his word, but the meaning of it was nothing to her. She had not even thought of being left alone. It was not, then, fear for herself, but for him. This girl, always slow of speech and action, now seemed almost stupid. She put forth a hand that might have indicated the groping of her mind. Suddenly she stepped swiftly to him, with a look and touch that drove from him any doubt of her quick intelligence or feeling.

"Oldring has men watch the herds—they would kill you. You must never go again!"

When she had spoken, the strength and the blaze of her died, and she swayed toward Venters.

"Bess, I'll not go again," he said, catching her.

She leaned against him, and her body was limp and vibrated to a long, wavering tremble. Her face was upturned to his. Woman's face, woman's eyes, woman's lips—all acutely and blindly and sweetly and terribly truthful in their betrayal! But as her fear was instinctive, so was her clinging to this one and only friend.

Venters gently put her from him and steadied her upon her feet; and all the while his blood raced wild, and a thrilling tingle unsteadied his nerve, and something—that he had seen and felt in her—that he could not understand—seemed very close to him, warm and rich as a fragrant breath, sweet as nothing had ever before been sweet to him.

With all his will Venters strove for calmness and thought and judgment unbiased by pity, and reality unswayed by sentiment. Bess's eyes were still fixed upon him with all her soul bright in that wistful light. Swiftly, resolutely he put out of mind all of her life except what had been spent with him. He scorned himself for the intelligence that made him still doubt. He meant to judge her as she had judged him. He was face to face with the inevitableness of life itself. He saw destiny in the dark, straight path of her wonderful eyes. Here was the simplicity, the sweetness of a girl contending with new and strange and enthralling emotions; here the living truth of innocence; here the blind terror of a woman confronted with the thought of death to her savior and protector. All this Venters saw, but, besides, there was in Bess's eyes a slow-dawning consciousness that seemed about to break out in glorious radiance.

"Bess, are you thinking?" he asked.

"Yes—oh yes!"

"Do you realize we are here alone—man and woman?"

"Yes."

"Have you thought that we may make our way out to civilization, or we may have to stay here—alone—hidden from the world all our lives?"

"I never thought—till now."

"Well, what's your choice—to go—or to stay here—alone with me?"

"Stay!" New-born thought of self, ringing vibrantly in her voice, gave her answer singular power.

Venters trembled, and then swiftly turned his gaze from her face—from her eyes. He knew what she had only half divined—that she loved him.

CHAPTER ELEVEN
Faith and Unfaith

At Jane Withersteen's home the promise made to Mrs. Larkin to care for little Fay had begun to be fulfilled. Like a gleam of sunlight through the cottonwoods was the coming of the child to the gloomy house of Withersteen. The big, silent halls echoed with childish laughter. In the shady court, where Jane spent many of the hot July days, Fay's tiny feet pattered over the stone flags and splashed in the amber stream. She prattled incessantly. What difference, Jane thought, a child made in her home! It had never been a real home, she discovered. Even the tidiness and neatness she had so observed, and upon which she had insisted to her women, became, in the light of Fay's smile, habits that now lost their importance. Fay littered the court with Jane's books and papers, and other toys her fancy improvised, and many a strange craft went floating down the little brook.

And it was owing to Fay's presence that Jane Withersteen came to see more of Lassiter. The rider had for the most part kept to the sage. He rode for her, but he did not seek her except on business; and Jane had to acknowledge in pique that her overtures had been made in vain. Fay, however, captured Lassiter the moment he first laid eyes on her.

Jane was present at the meeting, and there was something about it which dimmed her sight and softened her toward this foe of her people. The rider had clanked into the court, a tired yet wary man, always looking for the attack upon him that was inevitable and might come from any quarter; and he had walked right upon little Fay. The child had been beautiful even in her rags and amid the surroundings of the hovel in the sage, but now, in a pretty white dress, with her shining curls brushed and her face clean and rosy, she was lovely. She left her play and looked up at Lassiter.

If there was not an instinct for all three of them in that meeting, an unreasoning tendency toward a closer intimacy, then Jane Withersteen believed she had been subject to a queer fancy. She imagined any child would have feared Lassiter. And

Fay Larkin had been a lonely, a solitary elf of the sage, not at all an ordinary child, and exquisitely shy with strangers. She watched Lassiter with great, round, grave eyes, but showed no fear. The rider gave Jane a favorable report of cattle and horses; and as he took the seat to which she invited him, little Fay edged as much as half an inch nearer. Jane replied to his look of inquiry and told Fay's story. The rider's gray, earnest gaze troubled her. Then he turned to Fay and smiled in a way that made Jane doubt her sense of the true relation of things. How could Lassiter smile so at a child when he had made so many children fatherless? But he did smile, and to the gentleness she had seen a few times he added something that was infinitely sad and sweet. Jane's intuition told her that Lassiter had never been a father; but if life ever so blessed him he would be a good one. Fay, also, must have found that smile singularly winning. For she edged closer and closer, and then, by way of feminine capitulation, went to Jane, from whose side she bent a beautiful glance upon the rider.

Lassiter only smiled at her.

Jane watched them, and realized that now was the moment she should seize, if she was ever to win this man from his hatred. But the step was not easy to take. The more she saw of Lassiter the more she respected him, and the greater her respect the harder it became to lend herself to mere coquetry. Yet as she thought of her great motive, of Tull, and of that other whose name she had schooled herself never to think of in connection with Milly Erne's avenger, she suddenly found she had no choice. And her creed gave her boldness far beyond the limit to which vanity would have led her.

"Lassiter, I see so little of you now," she said, and was conscious of heat in her cheeks.

"I've been ridin' hard," he replied.

"But you can't live in the saddle. You come in sometimes. Won't you come here to see me—oftener?"

"Is that an order?"

"Nonsense! I simply ask you to come to see me when you find time."

"Why?"

The query once heard was not so embarrassing to Jane as she might have imagined. Moreover, it established in her mind a fact that there existed actually other than selfish reasons for her wanting to see him. And as she had been bold, so she determined to be both honest and brave.

"I've reasons—only one of which I need mention," she answered. "If it's possible I want to change you toward my people. And on the moment I can conceive of little I wouldn't do to gain that end."

How much better and freer Jane felt after that confession! She meant to show him that there was one Mormon who could play a game or wage a fight in the open.

"I reckon," said Lassiter, and he laughed.

It was the best in her, if the most irritating, that Lassiter always aroused.

"Will you come?" She looked into his eyes, and for the life of her could not quite subdue any imperiousness that rose with her spirit. "I never asked so much of any man—except Bern Venters."

"'Pears to me that you'd run no risk, or Venters, either. But mebbe that doesn't hold good for me."

"You mean it wouldn't be safe for you to be often here? You look for ambush in the cottonwoods?"

"Not that so much."

At this juncture little Fay sidled over to Lassiter.

"Has oo a little dirl?" she inquired.

"No, lassie," replied the rider.

Whatever Fay seemed to be searching for in Lassiter's sun-reddened face and quiet eyes she evidently found. "Oo tan tum to see me," she added, and with that, shyness gave place to friendly curiosity. First his sombrero with its leather band and silver ornaments commanded her attention; next his quirt, and then the clinking, silver spurs. These held her for some time, but presently, true to childish fickleness, she left off playing with them to look for something else. She laughed in glee as she ran her little hands down the slippery, shiny surface of Lassiter's leather chaps. Soon she discovered one of the hanging gun-sheaths, and she dragged it up and began tugging at the huge black handle of the gun. Jane Withersteen repressed an exclamation. What significance there was to her in the little girl's efforts to dislodge that heavy weapon! Jane Withersteen saw Fay's play and her beauty and her love as most powerful allies to her own woman's part in a game that suddenly had acquired a strange zest and a hint of danger. And as for the rider, he appeared to have forgotten Jane in the wonder of this lovely child playing about him. At first he was much the shyer of the two. Gradually her confidence overcame his backwardness, and he had the temerity to stroke her golden curls with a great hand. Fay rewarded his boldness with a smile, and when he had gone to the extreme of closing that great hand over her little brown one, she said, simply, "I like oo!"

Sight of his face then made Jane oblivious for the time to his character as a hater of Mormons. Out of the mother longing that swelled her breast she divined the child hunger in Lassiter.

He returned the next day, and the next; and upon the following he came both at morning and at night. Upon the evening of this fourth day Jane seemed to feel the breaking of a brooding struggle in Lassiter. During all these visits he had scarcely a word to say, though he watched her and played absent-mindedly with Fay. Jane had contented herself with silence. Soon little Fay substituted for the expression of regard, "I like oo," a warmer and more generous one, "I love oo."

Thereafter Lassiter came oftener to see Jane and her little protégée. Daily he grew more gentle and kind, and gradually developed a quaintly merry mood. In the morning he lifted Fay upon his horse and let her ride as he walked beside her to the edge of the sage. In the evening he played with the child at an infinite variety of games she invented, and then, oftener than not, he accepted Jane's invitation to supper. No other visitor came to Withersteen House during those days. So that in spite of watchfulness he never forgot, Lassiter began to show he felt at home there. After the meal they walked into the grove of cottonwoods or up by the lakes, and little Fay held Lassiter's hand as much as she held Jane's. Thus a strange relationship was established, and Jane liked it. At twilight they always returned to the house, where Fay kissed them and went in to her mother. Lassiter and Jane were left alone.

Then, if there were anything that a good woman could do to win a man and still preserve her self-respect, it was something which escaped the natural subtlety of a woman determined to allure. Jane's vanity, that after all was not great, was soon satisfied with Lassiter's silent admiration. And her honest desire to lead him from his dark, blood-stained path would never have blinded her to what she owed herself. But the driving passion of her religion, and its call to save Mormons' lives, one life in particular, bore Jane Withersteen close to an infringement of her womanhood. In the beginning she had reasoned that her appeal to Lassiter must be through the senses. With whatever means she possessed in the way of adornment she enhanced her beauty. And she stooped to artifices that she knew were unworthy of her, but which she deliberately chose to employ. She made herself a girl in every variable mood wherein a girl might be desirable. In those moods she was not above the methods of an inexperienced though natural flirt. She kept close to him whenever opportunity afforded; and she was forever playfully, yet passionately underneath the surface, fighting him for possession of the great black guns. These he would never yield to her. And so in that manner their hands were often and long in contact. The more of simplicity that she sensed in him the greater the advantage she took.

She had a trick of changing—and it was not altogether voluntary—from this gay, thoughtless, girlish coquettishness to the silence and the brooding, burning mystery of a woman's mood. The strength and passion and fire of her were in her eyes, and she so used them that Lassiter had to see this depth in her, this haunting promise more fitted to her years than to the flaunting guise of a wilful girl.

The July days flew by. Jane reasoned that if it were possible for her to be happy during such a time, then she was happy. Little Fay completely filled a long aching void in her heart. In fettering the hands of this Lassiter she was accomplishing the greatest good of her life, and to do good even in a small way rendered happiness to Jane Withersteen. She had attended the regular Sunday services of her church; otherwise she had not gone to the village for weeks. It was unusual that none of her churchmen or friends had called upon her of late; but it was neglect for which she was glad. Judkins and his boy riders had experienced no difficulty in driving the white herd. So these warm July days were free of worry, and soon Jane hoped she had passed the crisis; and for her to hope was presently to trust, and then to believe. She thought often of Venters, but in a dreamy, abstract way. She spent hours teaching and playing with little Fay. And the activity of her mind centered around Lassiter. The direction she had given her will seemed to blunt any branching off of thought from that straight line. The mood came to obsess her.

In the end, when her awakening came, she learned that she had builded better than she knew. Lassiter, though kinder and gentler than ever, had parted with his quaint humor and his coldness and his tranquillity to become a restless and unhappy man. Whatever the power of his deadly intent toward Mormons, that passion now had a rival, the one equally burning and consuming. Jane Withersteen had one moment of exultation before the dawn of a strange uneasiness. What if she had made of herself a lure, at tremendous cost to him and to her, and all in vain!

That night in the moonlit grove she summoned all her courage and, turning suddenly in the path, she faced Lassiter and leaned close to him, so that she touched him and her eyes looked up to his.

"Lassiter! . . . Will you do anything for me?"

In the moonlight she saw his dark, worn face change, and by that change she seemed to feel him immovable as a wall of stone.

Jane slipped her hands down to the swinging gunsheaths, and when she had locked her fingers around the huge, cold handles of the guns, she trembled as with a chilling ripple over all her body.

"May I take your guns?"

"Why?" he asked, and for the first time to her his voice carried a harsh note. Jane felt his hard, strong hands close round her wrists. It was not wholly with intent that she leaned toward him, for the look of his eyes and the feel of his hands made her weak.

"It's no trifle—no woman's whim—it's deep—as my heart. Let me take them?"

"Why?"

"I want to keep you from killing more men—Mormons. You must let me save you from more wickedness—more wanton bloodshed—" Then the truth forced itself falteringly from her lips. "You must—let—me—help me to keep my vow to Milly Erne. I swore to her—as she lay dying—that if ever any one came here to avenge her—I swore I would stay his hand. Perhaps I—I alone can save the—the man who—who—Oh, Lassiter! . . . I feel that I can't change you—then soon you'll be out to kill—and you'll kill by instinct—and among the Mormons you kill will be the one—who . . . Lassiter, if you care a little for me—let me—for my sake—let me take your guns!"

As if her hands had been those of a child, he unclasped their clinging grip from the handles of his guns, and, pushing her away, he turned his gray face to her in one look of terrible realization and then strode off into the shadows of the cottonwoods.

When the first shock of her futile appeal to Lassiter had passed, Jane took his cold, silent condemnation and abrupt departure not so much as a refusal to her entreaty as a hurt and stunned bitterness for her attempt at his betrayal. Upon further thought and slow consideration of Lassiter's past actions, she believed he would return and forgive her. The man could not be hard to a woman, and she doubted that he could stay away from her. But at the point where she had hoped to find him vulnerable she now began to fear he was proof against all persuasion. The iron and stone quality that she had early suspected in him had actually cropped out as an impregnable barrier. Nevertheless, if Lassiter remained in Cottonwoods she would never give up her hope and desire to change him. She would change him if she had to sacrifice everything dear to her except hope of heaven. Passionately devoted as she was to her religion, she had yet refused to marry a Mormon. But a situation had developed wherein self paled in the great white light of religious duty of the highest order. That was the leading motive, the divinely spiritual one; but there were other motives, which, like tentacles, aided in drawing her will to the acceptance of a possible abnegation. And through the watches of that sleepless night Jane Withersteen, in fear and sorrow and doubt, came finally to believe that if she must throw herself into Lassiter's arms to make him abide by "Thou shalt not kill!" she would yet do well.

In the morning she expected Lassiter at the usual hour, but she was not able to go at once to the court, so she sent little Fay. Mrs. Larkin was ill and required attention. It appeared that the mother, from the time of her arrival at Withersteen House, had relaxed and was slowly losing her hold on life. Jane had believed that absence of worry and responsibility coupled with good nursing and comfort would mend Mrs. Larkin's broken health. Such, however, was not the case.

When Jane did get out to the court, Fay was there alone, and at the moment embarking on a dubious voyage down the stone-lined amber stream upon a craft of two brooms and a pillow. Fay was as delightfully wet as she could possibly wish to get.

Clatter of hoofs distracted Fay and interrupted the scolding she was gleefully receiving from Jane. The sound was not the light-spirited trot that Bells made when Lassiter rode him into the outer court. This was slower and heavier, and Jane did not recognize in it any of her other horses. The appearance of Bishop Dyer startled Jane. He dismounted with his rapid, jerky motion, flung the bridle, and, as he turned toward the inner court and stalked up on the stone flags, his boots rang. In his authoritative front, and in the red anger unmistakably flaming in his face, he reminded Jane of her father.

"Is that the Larkin pauper?" he asked, bruskly, without any greeting to Jane.

"It's Mrs. Larkin's little girl," replied Jane, slowly.

"I hear you intend to raise the child?"

"Yes."

"Of course you mean to give her Mormon bringing-up?"

"No!"

His questions had been swift. She was amazed at a feeling that some one else was replying for her.

"I've come to say a few things to you." He stopped to measure her with stern, speculative eye.

Jane Withersteen loved this man. From earliest childhood she had been taught to revere and love bishops of her church. And for ten years Bishop Dyer had been the closest friend and counselor of her father, and for the greater part of that period her own friend and Scriptural teacher. Her interpretation of her creed and her religious activity in fidelity to it, her acceptance of mysterious and holy Mormon truths, were all invested in this Bishop. Bishop Dyer as an entity was next to God. He was God's mouthpiece to the little Mormon community at Cottonwoods. God revealed himself in secret to this mortal.

And Jane Withersteen suddenly suffered a paralyzing affront to her consciousness of reverence by some strange, irresistible twist of thought wherein she saw this Bishop as a man. And the train of thought hurdled the rising, crying protests of that other self whose poise she had lost. It was not her Bishop who eyed her in curious measurement. It was a man who tramped into her presence without removing his hat, who had no greeting for her, who had no semblance of courtesy. In looks, as in action, he made her think of a bull stamping cross-grained into a corral. She had heard of Bishop Dyer forgetting the minister in the fury of a common man, and now she was to feel it. The glance by which she measured him in turn momentarily veiled the divine in the ordinary. He looked a rancher; he was booted, spurred, and covered with dust; he carried a gun at his hip, and she remembered that he had been known to use it. But during the long moment while he watched her there was nothing commonplace in the slow-gathering might of his wrath.

"Brother Tull has talked to me," he began. "It was your father's wish that you marry Tull, and my order. You refused him?"

"Yes."

"You would not give up your friendship with that tramp Venters?"

"No."

"But you'll do as *I* order!" he thundered. "Why, Jane Withersteen, you are in danger of becoming a heretic! You can thank your Gentile friend for that. You face the damning of your soul to perdition."

In the flux and reflux of the whirling torture of Jane's mind, that new, daring spirit of hers vanished in the old habitual order of her life. She was a Mormon, and the Bishop regained ascendance.

"It's well I got you in time, Jane Withersteen. What would your father have said to these goings-on of yours? He would have put you in a stone cage on bread and water. He would have taught you something about Mormonism. Remember, you're a *born* Mormon. There have been Mormons who turned heretic—damn their souls!—but no born Mormon ever left us yet. Ah, I see your shame. Your faith is not shaken. You are only a wild girl." The Bishop's tone softened. "Well, it's enough that I got to you in time. . . . Now tell me about this Lassiter. I hear strange things."

"What do you wish to know?" queried Jane.

"About this man. You hired him?"

"Yes, he's riding for me. When my riders left me I had to have any one I could get."

"Is it true what I hear—that he's a gun-man, a Mormon-hater, steeped in blood?"

"True—terribly true, I fear."

"But what's he doing here in Cottonwoods? This place isn't notorious enough for such a man. Sterling and the villages north, where there's universal gun-packing and fights every day—where there are more men like him, it seems to me they would attract him most. We're only a wild, lonely border settlement. It's only recently that the rustlers have made killings here. Nor have there been saloons till lately, nor the drifting in of outcasts. Has not this gun-man some special mission here?"

Jane maintained silence.

"Tell me," ordered Bishop Dyer, sharply.

"Yes," she replied.

"Do you know what it is?"

"Yes."

"Tell me that."

"Bishop Dyer, I don't want to tell."

He waved his hand in an imperative gesture of command. The red once more leaped to his face, and in his steel-blue eyes glinted a pin point of curiosity.

"That first day," whispered Jane, "Lassiter said he came here to find—Milly Erne's grave!"

With downcast eyes Jane watched the swift flow of the amber water. She saw it and tried to think of it, of the stones, of the ferns; but, like her body, her mind was in a leaden vise. Only the Bishop's voice could release her. Seemingly there was silence of longer duration than all her former life.

"For what—else?" When Bishop Dyer's voice did cleave the silence it was high, curiously shrill, and on the point of breaking. It released Jane's tongue, but she could not lift her eyes.

"To kill the man who persuaded Milly Erne to abandon her home and her husband—and her God!"

With wonderful distinctness Jane Withersteen heard her own clear voice. She heard the water murmur at her feet and flow on to the sea; she heard the rushing of all the waters in the world. They filled her ears with low, unreal murmurings—these sounds that deadened her brain and yet could not break the long and terrible silence. Then, from somewhere—from an immeasurable distance—came a slow, guarded, clinking, clanking step. Into her it shot electrifying life. It released the weight upon her numbed eyelids. Lifting her eyes she saw—ashen, shaken, stricken—not the Bishop but the man! And beyond him, from round the corner came that soft, silvery step. A long black boot with a gleaming spur swept into sight—and then Lassiter! Bishop Dyer did not see, did not hear: he stared at Jane in the throes of sudden revelation.

"Ah, I understand!" he cried, in hoarse accents. "That's why you made love to this Lassiter—to bind his hands!"

It was Jane's gaze riveted upon the rider that made Bishop Dyer turn. Then clear sight failed her. Dizzily, in a blur, she saw the Bishop's hand jerk to his hip. She saw gleam of blue and spout of red. In her ears burst a thundering report. The court floated in darkening circles around her, and she fell into utter blackness.

The darkness lightened, turned to slow-drifing haze, and lifted. Through a thin film of blue smoke she saw the rough-hewn timbers of the court roof. A cool, damp touch moved across her brow. She smelled powder, and it was that which galvanized her suspended thought. She moved, to see that she lay prone upon the stone flags with her head on Lassiter's knee, and he was bathing her brow with water from the stream. The same swift glance, shifting low, brought into range of her sight a smoking gun and splashes of blood.

"Ah-h!" she moaned, and was drifting, sinking again into darkness, when Lassiter's voice arrested her.

"It's all right, Jane. It's all right."

"Did—you—kill—him?" she whispered.

"Who? That fat party who was here? No. I didn't kill him."

"Oh! . . . Lassiter!"

"Say! It was queer for you to faint. I thought you were such a strong woman, not faintish like that. You're all right now—only some pale. I thought you'd never come to. But I'm awkward round women folks. I couldn't think of anythin'."

"Lassiter! . . . the gun there! . . . the blood!"

"So that's troublin' you. I reckon it needn't. You see it was this way. I come round the house an' seen that fat party an' heard him talkin' loud. Then he seen me, an' very impolite goes straight for his gun. He oughtn't have tried to throw a gun on me—whatever his reason was. For that's meetin' me on my own grounds. I've seen runnin' molasses that was quicker n' him. Now I didn't know who he was, visitor or friend or relation of yours, though I seen he was a Mormon all over, an' I couldn't get serious about shootin'. So I winged him—put a bullet through his arm as he was pullin' at his gun. An' he dropped the gun there, an' a little blood. I told him he'd introduced himself sufficient, an' to please move out of my vicinity. An' he went."

Lassiter spoke with slow, cool, soothing voice, in which there was a hint of levity, and his touch, as he continued to bathe her brow, was gentle and steady. His impassive face, and the kind, gray eyes, further stilled her agitation.

"He drew on you first, and you deliberately shot to cripple him—you wouldn't kill him—you—*Lassiter?"*

"That's about the size of it."

Jane kissed his hand.

All that was calm and cool about Lassiter instantly vanished.

"Don't do that! I won't stand it! An' I don't care a damn who that fat party was."

He helped Jane to her feet and to a chair. Then with the wet scarf he had used to bathe her face he wiped the blood from the stone flags and, picking up the gun, he threw it upon a couch. With that he began to pace the court, and his silver spurs jangled musically, and the great gun-sheaths softly brushed against his leather chaps.

"So—it's true—what I heard him say?" Lassiter asked, presently halting before her. "You made love to me—to bind my hands?"

"Yes," confessed Jane. It took all her woman's courage to meet the gray storm of his glance.

"All these days that you've been so friendly an' like a pardner—all these evenin's that have been so bewilderin' to me—your beauty—an'—an' the way you looked an' came close to me—they were woman's tricks to bind my hands?"

"Yes."

"An' your sweetness that seemed so natural, an' your throwin' little Fay an' me so much together—to make me love the child—all that was for the same reason?"

"Yes."

Lassiter flung his arms—a strange gesture for him.

"Mebbe it wasn't much in your Mormon thinkin', for you to play that game. But to ring the child in—that was hellish!"

Jane's passionate, unheeding zeal began to loom darkly.

"Lassiter, whatever my intention in the beginning, Fay loves you dearly—and I—I've grown to—to like you."

"That's powerful kind of you, now," he said. Sarcasm and scorn made his voice that of a stranger. "An' you sit there an' look me straight in the eyes! You're a wonderful strange woman, Jane Withersteen."

"I'm not ashamed, Lassiter. I told you I'd try to change you."

"Would you mind tellin' me just what you tried?"

"I tried to make you see beauty in me and be softened by it. I wanted you to care for me so that I could influence you. It wasn't easy. At first you were stone-blind. Then I hoped you'd love little Fay, and through that come to feel the horror of making children fatherless."

"Jane Withersteen, either you're a fool or noble beyond my understandin'. Mebbe you're both. I know you're blind. What you meant is one thing—what you *did* was to make me love you."

"Lassiter!"

"I reckon I'm a human bein', though I never loved any one but my sister, Milly Erne. That was long—"

"Oh, are you Milly's brother?"

"Yes, I was, an' I loved her. There never was any one but her in my life till now. Didn't I tell you that long ago I back-trailed myself from women? I was a Texas ranger till—till Milly left home, an' then I became somethin' else—Lassiter! For years I've been a lonely man set on one thing. I came here an' met you. An' now I'm not the man I was. The change was gradual, an' I took no notice of it. I understand now that never-satisfied longin' to see you, listen to you, watch you, feel you near me. It's plain now why you were never out of my thoughts. I've had no thoughts but of you. I've lived an' breathed for you. An' now when I know what it means—what you've done—I'm burnin' up with hell's fire!"

"Oh, Lassiter—no—no—you don't love me that way!" Jane cried.

"If that's what love is, then I do."

"Forgive me! I didn't mean to make you love me like that. Oh, what a tangle of our lives! You—Milly Erne's brother! And I—heedless, mad to melt your heart toward Mormons. Lassiter, I may be wicked but not wicked enough to hate. If I couldn't hate Tull, could I hate you?"

"After all, Jane, mebbe you're only blind—Mormon blind. That only can explain what's close to selfishness—"

"I'm not selfish. I despise the very word. If I were free—"

"But you're not free. Not free of Mormonism. An' in playin' this game with me you've been unfaithful."

"Un-faithful!" faltered Jane.

"Yes, I said unfaithful. You're faithful to your Bishop an' unfaithful to yourself. You're false to your womanhood an' true to your religion. But for a savin' innocence you'd have made yourself low an' vile—betrayin' yourself, betrayin' me—all to bind my hands an' keep me from snuffin' out Mormon life. It's your damned Mormon blindness."

"Is it vile—is it blind—is it only Mormonism to save human life? No, Lassiter, that's God's law, divine, universal for all Christians."

"The blindness I mean is blindness that keeps you from seein' the truth. I've known many good Mormons. But some are blacker than hell. You won't see that even when you know it. Else, why all this blind passion to save the life of that—that. . . ."

Jane shut out the light, and the hands she held over her eyes trembled and quivered against her face.

"Blind—yes, an' let me make it clear an' simple to you," Lassiter went on, his voice losing its tone of anger. "Take, for instance, that idea of yours last night when you wanted my guns. It was good an' beautiful, an' showed your heart—but—why, Jane, it was crazy. Mind I'm assumin' that life to me is as sweet as to any other man. An' to preserve that life is each man's first an' closest thought. Where would any man be on this border without guns? Where, especially, would Lassiter be? Well, I'd be under the sage with thousands of other men now livin' an' sure better men than me. Gun-packin' in the West since the Civil War has growed into a kind of moral law. An' out here on this border it's the difference between a man an' somethin' not a man. Look what you takin' Venters's guns from him all but made him! Why, your churchmen carry guns. Tull has killed a man an' drawed on others. Your Bishop has shot a half dozen men, an' it wasn't through prayers of his that they recovered. An' to-day he'd have shot me if he'd been quick enough on the draw. Could I walk or ride down into Cottonwoods without my guns? This is a wild time, Jane Withersteen, this year of our Lord eighteen seventy-one."

"No time—for a woman!" exclaimed Jane, brokenly. "Oh, Lassiter, I feel helpless—lost—and don't know where to turn. If I *am* blind—then—I need some one—a friend—you, Lassiter—more than ever!"

"Well, I didn't say nothin' about goin' back on you, did I?"

CHAPTER TWELVE
The Invisible Hand

Jane received a letter from Bishop Dyer, not in his own handwriting, which stated that the abrupt termination of their interview had left him in some doubts as to her future conduct. A slight injury had incapacitated him from seeking another meeting at present, the letter went on to say, and ended with a request which was virtually a command, that she call upon him at once.

The reading of the letter acquainted Jane Withersteen with the fact that something within her had all but changed. She sent no reply to Bishop Dyer nor did she go to see him. On Sunday she remained absent from the service—for the second time in years—and though she did not actually suffer there was a dead-lock of feelings deep within her, and the waiting for a balance to fall on either side was almost as bad as suffering. She had a gloomy expectancy of untoward circumstances, and with it a keen-edged curiosity to watch developments. She had a half-formed conviction that her future conduct—as related to her churchmen—was beyond her control and would be governed by their attitude toward her. Something was changing in her, forming, waiting for decision to make it a real and fixed thing. She had told Lassiter that she felt helpless and lost in the fateful tangle of their lives; and now she feared that she was approaching the same chaotic condition of mind in regard to her religion. It appalled her to find that she questioned phases of that religion. Absolute faith had been her serenity. Though leaving her faith unshaken, her serenity had been disturbed, and now it was broken by open war between her and her ministers. That something within her—a whisper—which she had tried in vain to hush had become a ringing voice, and it called to her to wait. She had transgressed no laws of God. Her churchmen, however invested with the power and the glory of a wonderful creed, however they sat in inexorable judgment of her, must now practice toward her the simple, common, Christian virtue they professed to preach, "Do unto others as you would have others do unto you!"

Jane Withersteen, waiting in darkness of mind, remained faithful still. But it was darkness that must soon be pierced by light. If her faith were justified, if her churchmen were trying only to intimidate her, the fact would soon be manifest, as would their failure, and then she would redouble her zeal toward them and toward what had been the best work of her life—work for the welfare and happiness of those among whom she lived, Mormon and Gentile alike. If that secret, intangible power closed its toils round her again, if that great invisible hand moved here and there and everywhere, slowly paralyzing her with its mystery and its inconceivable sway over her affairs, then she would know beyond doubt that it was not chance, nor jealousy, nor intimidation, nor ministerial wrath at her revolt, but a cold and calculating policy thought out long before she was born, a dark, immutable will of whose empire she and all that was hers was but an atom.

The might come her ruin. Then might come her fall into black storm. Yet she would rise again, and to the light. God would be merciful to a driven woman who had lost her way.

A week passed. Little Fay played and prattled and pulled at Lassiter's big black guns. The rider came to Withersteen House oftener than ever. Jane saw a change in him, though it did not relate to his kindness and gentleness. He was quieter and more thoughtful. While playing with Fay or conversing with Jane he seemed to be possessed of another self that watched with cool, roving eyes, that listened, listened always as if the murmuring amber stream brought messages, and the moving leaves whispered something. Lassiter never rode Bells into the court any more, nor did he come by the lane or the paths. When he appeared it was suddenly and noiselessly out of the dark shadow of the grove.

"I left Bells out in the sage," he said, one day at the end of that week. "I must carry water to him."

"Why not let him drink at the trough or here?" asked Jane, quickly.

"I reckon it'll be safer for me to slip through the grove. I've been watched when I rode in from the sage."

"Watched? By whom?"

"By a man who thought he was well hid. But my eyes are pretty sharp. An', Jane," he went on, almost in a whisper, "I reckon it'd be a good idea for us to talk low. You're spied on here by your women."

"Lassiter!" she whispered in turn. "That's hard to believe. My women love me."

"What of that?" he asked. "Of course they love you. But they're Mormon women."

Jane's old, rebellious loyalty clashed with her doubt.

"I won't believe it," she replied, stubbornly.

"Well then, just act natural an' talk natural, an' pretty soon—give them time to hear us—pretend to go over there to the table, an' then quick-like make a move for the door an' open it."

"I will," said Jane, with heightened color. Lassiter was right; he never made mistakes; he would not have told her unless he positively knew. Yet Jane was so tenacious of faith that she had to see with her own eyes, and so constituted that to employ even such small deceit toward her women made her ashamed, and angry for her shame as well as theirs. Then a singular thought confronted her that made her hold up this simple ruse—which hurt her, though it was well justified—against the deceit she had wittingly and eagerly used toward Lassiter. The difference was staggering in its suggestion of that blindness of which he had accused her. Fairness and justice and mercy, that she had imagined were anchor-cables to hold fast her soul to righteousness, had not been hers in the strange, biased duty that had so exalted and confounded her.

Presently Jane began to act her little part, to laugh and play with Fay, to talk of horses and cattle to Lassiter. Then she made deliberate mention of a book in which she kept records of all pertaining to her stock, and she walked slowly toward the table, and when near the door she suddenly whirled and thrust it open. Her sharp action nearly knocked down a woman who had undoubtedly been listening.

"Hester," said Jane, sternly, "you may go home, and you need not come back."

Jane shut the door and returned to Lassiter. Standing unsteadily, she put her hand on his arm. She let him see that doubt had gone, and how this stab of disloyalty pained her.

"Spies! My own women! . . . Oh, miserable!" she cried, with flashing, tearful eyes.

"I hate to tell you," he replied. By that she knew he had long spared her. "It's begun again—that work in the dark."

"Nay, Lassiter—it never stopped!"

So bitter certainty claimed her at last, and trust fled Withersteen House and fled forever. The women who owed much to Jane Withersteen changed not in love for her, nor in devotion to their household work, but they poisoned both by a thousand acts of stealth and cunning and duplicity. Jane broke out once and caught them in strange, stone-faced, unhesitating falsehood. Thereafter she broke out no more. She forgave them because they were driven. Poor, fettered, and sealed Hagars, how she pitied them! What terrible thing bound them and locked their lips, when they showed neither consciousness of guilt toward their benefactress nor distress at the slow wearing apart of long-established and dear ties?

"The blindness again!" cried Jane Withersteen. "In my sisters as in me! . . . O God!"

There came a time when no words passed between Jane and her women. Silently they went about their household duties, and secretly they went about the underhand work to which they had been bidden. The gloom of the house and the gloom of its mistress, which darkened even the bright spirit of little Fay, did not pervade these women. Happiness was not among them, but they were aloof from gloom. They spied and listened; they received and sent secret messengers; and they stole Jane's books and records, and finally the papers that were deeds of her possessions. Through it all they were silent, rapt in a kind of trance. Then one by one, without leave or explanation or farewell, they left Withersteen House, and never returned.

Coincident with this disappearance Jane's gardeners and workers in the alfalfa fields and stable men quit her, not even asking for their wages. Of all her Mormon employees about the great ranch only Jerd remained. He went on with his duty, but talked no more of the change than if it had never occurred.

"Jerd," said Jane, "what stock you can't take care of turn out in the sage. Let your first thought be for Black Star and Night. Keep them in perfect condition. Run them every day and watch them always."

Though Jane Withersteen gave them such liberality, she loved her possessions. She loved the rich, green stretches of alfalfa, and the farms, and the grove, and the old stone house, and the beautiful, ever-faithful amber spring, and every one of a myriad of horses and colts and burros and fowls down to the smallest rabbit that nipped her vegetables; but she loved best her noble Arabian steeds. In common with all riders of the upland sage Jane cherished two material things—the cold, sweet, brown water that made life possible in the wilderness and the horses which were a part of that life. When Lassiter asked her what Lassiter would be without his guns he was assuming that his horse was part of himself. So Jane loved Black Star and Night because it was her nature to love all beautiful creatures—perhaps all living things; and then she loved them because she herself was of the sage and in her had been born and bred the rider's instinct to rely on his four-footed brother. And when Jane gave Jerd the order to keep her favorites trained down to the day it was a half-conscious admission that presaged a time when she would need her fleet horses.

Jane had now, however, no leisure to brood over the coils that were closing round her. Mrs. Larkin grew weaker as the August days began; she required constant care, there was little Fay to look after; and such household work as was imperative. Lassiter put Bells in the stable with the other racers, and directed his efforts to a closer attendance upon Jane. She welcomed the change. He was always at hand to help, and it was her fortune to learn that his boast of being awkward around women had its root in humility and was not true.

His great, brown hands were skilled in a multiplicity of ways which a woman might have envied. He shared Jane's work, and was of especial help to her in nursing Mrs. Larkin. The woman suffered most at night, and this often broke Jane's rest. So it came about that Lassiter would stay by Mrs. Lassiter during the day, when she needed care, and Jane would make up the sleep she lost in night-watches. Mrs. Larkin at once took kindly to the gentle Lassiter, and, without ever asking who or what he was, praised him to Jane. "He's a good man and loves children," she said. How sad to hear this truth spoken of a man whom Jane thought lost beyond all redemption! Yet ever and ever Lassiter towered above her, and behind or through his black, sinister figure shone something luminous that strangely affected Jane. Good and evil began to seem incomprehensibly blended in her judgment. It was her belief that evil could not come forth from good; yet here was a murderer who dwarfed in gentleness, patience, and love any man she had ever known.

She had almost lost track of her more outside concerns when early one morning Judkins presented himself before her in the courtyard.

Thin, hard, burnt, bearded, with the dust and sage thick on him, with his leather wrist-bands shining from use, and his boots worn through on the stirrup side, he looked the rider of riders. He wore two guns and carried a Winchester.

Jane greeted him with surprise and warmth, set meat and bread and drink before him; and called Lassiter out to see him. The men exchanged glances, and the meaning of Lassiter's keen inquiry and Judkins's bold reply, both unspoken, was not lost upon Jane.

"Where's your hoss?" asked Lassiter, aloud.

"Left him down the slope," answered Judkins. "I footed it in a ways, an' slept last night in the sage. I went to the place you told me you 'most always slept, but didn't strike you."

"I moved up some, near the spring, an' now I go there nights."

"Judkins—the white herd?" queried Jane, hurriedly.

"Miss Withersteen, I make proud to say I've not lost a steer. Fer a good while after thet stampede Lassiter milled we hed no trouble. Why, even the sage dogs left us. But it's begun agin—thet flashin' of lights over ridge tips, an' queer puffin' of smoke, an' then at night strange whistles an' noises. But the herd's acted magnificent. An' my boys, say, Miss Withersteen, they're only kids, but I ask no better riders. I got the laugh in the village fer takin' them out. They're a wild lot, an' you know boys hev more nerve than grown men, because they don't know what danger is. I'm not denyin' there's danger. But they glory in it, an' mebbe I like it myself—anyway, we'll stick. We're goin' to drive the herd on the far side of the first break of Deception Pass. There's a great round valley over there, an' no ridges or piles of rocks to aid these stampeders. The rains are due. We'll hev plenty of water fer a while. An' we can hold thet herd from anybody except Oldrin'. I come in fer supplies. I'll pack a couple of burros an' drive out after dark to-night."

"Judkins, take what you want from the store-room. Lassiter will help you. I—I can't thank you enough . . . but—wait."

Jane went to the room that had once been her father's, and from a secret chamber in the thick stone wall she took a bag of gold, and, carrying it back to the court, she gave it to the rider.

"There, Judkins, and understand that I regard it as little for your loyalty. Give what is fair to your boys, and keep the rest. Hide it. Perhaps that would be wisest."

"Oh . . . Miss Withersteen!" ejaculated the rider. "I couldn't earn so much in—in ten years. It's not right—I oughtn't take it."

"Judkins, you know I'm a rich woman. I tell you I've few faithful friends. I've fallen upon evil days. God only knows what will become of me and mine! So take the gold."

She smiled in understanding of his speechless gratitude, and left him with Lassiter. Presently she heard him speaking low at first, then in louder accents emphasized by the thumping of his rifle on the stones. "As infernal a job as even you, Lassiter, ever heerd of."

"Why, son," was Lassiter's reply, "this breakin' of Miss Withersteen may seem bad to you, but it ain't bad—yet. Some of these wall-eyed fellers who look jest as if they was walkin' in the shadow of Christ himself, right down the sunny road, now they can think of things an' do things that are really hell-bent."

Jane covered her ears and ran to her own room, and there like a caged lioness she paced to and fro till the coming of little Fay reversed her dark thoughts.

The following day, a warm and muggy one threatening rain, while Jane was resting in the court, a horseman clattered through the grove and up to the hitching-rack. He leaped off and approached Jane with the manner of a man determined to execute a difficult mission, yet fearful of its reception. In the gaunt, wiry figure and the lean, brown face Jane recognized one of her Mormon riders, Blake. It was he of whom Judkins had long since spoken. Of all the riders ever in her employ Blake owed her the most, and as he stepped before her, removing his hat and making manly efforts to subdue his emotion, he showed that he remembered.

"Miss Withersteen, mother's dead," he said.

"Oh—Blake!" exclaimed Jane, and she could say no more.

"She died free from pain in the end, and she's buried—resting at last, thank God! . . . I've come to ride for you again, if you'll have me. Don't think I mentioned mother to get your sympathy. When she was living and your riders quit, I had to also. I was afraid of what might be done—said to her. . . . Miss Withersteen, we can't talk of—of what's going on now—"

"Blake, do you know?"

"I know a great deal. You understand, my lips are shut. But without explanation or excuse I offer my services. I'm a Mormon—I hope a good one. But—there are some things! . . . It's no use, Miss Withersteen, I can't say any more—what I'd like to. But will you take me back?"

"Blake! . . . You know what it means?"

"I don't care. I'm sick of—of—I'll show you a Mormon who'll be true to you!"

"But, Blake—how terribly you might suffer for that!"

"Maybe. Aren't you suffering now?"

"God knows indeed I am!"

"Miss Withersteen, it's a liberty on my part to speak so, but I know you pretty well—know you'll never give in. I wouldn't if I were you. And I—I must—Something makes me tell you the worst is yet to come. That's all. I absolutely can't say more. Will you take me back—let me ride for you—show everybody what I mean?"

"Blake, it makes me happy to hear you. How my riders hurt me when they quit!" Jane felt the hot tears well to her eyes and splash down upon her hands. "I thought so much of them—tried so hard to be good to them. And not one was true. You've made it easy to forgive. Perhaps many of them really feel as you do, but dare not return to me. Still, Blake, I hesitate to take you back. Yet I want you so much."

"Do it, then. If you're going to make your life a lesson to Mormon women, let me make mine a lesson to the men. Right is right. I believe in you, and here's my life to prove it."

"You hint it may mean your life!" said Jane, breathless and low.

"We won't speak of that. I want to come back. I want to do what every rider aches in his secret heart to do for you. . . . Miss Withersteen, I hoped it'd not be necessary to tell you that my mother on her deathbed told me to have courage. She knew how the thing galled me—she told me to come back. . . . Will you take me?"

"God bless you, Blake! Yes, I'll take you back. And will you—will you accept gold from me?"

"Miss Withersteen!"

"I just gave Judkins a bag of gold. I'll give you one. If you will not take it you must not come back. You might ride for me a few months—weeks—days till the storm breaks. Then you'd have nothing, and be in disgrace with your people. We'll forearm you against poverty, and me against endless regret. I'll give you gold which you can hide—till some future time."

"Well, if it pleases you," replied Blake. "But you know I never thought of pay. Now, Miss Withersteen, one thing more. I want to see this man Lassiter. Is he here?"

"Yes, but, Blake—what— Need you see him? Why?" asked Jane, instantly worried. "I can speak to him—tell him about you."

"That won't do. I want to—I've got to tell him myself. Where is he?"

"Lassiter is with Mrs. Larkin. She is ill. I'll call him," answered Jane, and going to the door she softly called for the rider. A faint, musical jingle preceded his step—then his tall form crossed the threshold.

"Lassiter, here's Blake, an old rider of mine. He has come back to me and he wishes to speak to you."

Blake's brown face turned exceedingly pale.

"Yes, I had to speak to you," he said, swiftly. "My name's Blake. I'm a Mormon and a rider. Lately I quit Miss Withersteen. I've come to beg her to take me back. Now I don't know you, but I know—what you are. So I've this to say to your face. It would never occur to this woman to imagine—let alone suspect me to be a spy. She couldn't think it might just be a low plot to come here and shoot you in the back. Jane Withersteen hasn't that kind of a mind. . . . Well, I've not come for that. I want to help her—to pull a bridle along with Judkins and—and you. The thing is—do you believe me?"

"I reckon I do," replied Lassiter. How this slow, cool speech contrasted with Blake's hot, impulsive words! "You might have saved some of your breath. See here, Blake, cinch this in your mind. Lassiter has met some square Mormons! An' mebbe—"

"Blake," interrupted Jane, nervously anxious to terminate a colloquy that she perceived was an ordeal for him. "Go at once and fetch me a report of my horses."

"Miss Withersteen! . . . You mean the big drove—down in the sage-cleared fields?"

"Of course," replied Jane. "My horses are all there, except the blooded stock I keep here."

"Haven't you heard—then?"

"Heard? No! What's happened to them?"

"They're gone, Miss Withersteen, gone these ten days past. Dorn told me, and I rode down to see for myself."

"Lassiter—did you know?" asked Jane, whirling to him.

"I reckon so. . . . But what was the use to tell you?"

It was Lassiter turning away his face and Blake studying the stone flags at his feet that brought Jane to the understanding of what she betrayed. She strove desperately, but she could not rise immediately from such a blow.

"My horses! My horses! What's become of them?"

"Dorn said the riders report another drive by Oldring. . . . And I trailed the horses miles down the slope toward Deception Pass."

"My red herd's gone! My horses gone! The white herd will go next. I can stand that. But if I lost Black Star and Night, it would be like parting with my own flesh and blood. Lassiter—Blake—am I in danger of losing my racers?"

"A rustler—or—or anybody stealin' hosses of yours would most of all want the blacks," said Lassiter. His evasive reply was affirmative enough. The other rider nodded gloomy acquiescence.

"Oh! Oh!" Jane Withersteen choked, with violent utterance.

"Let me take charge of the blacks?" asked Blake. "One more rider won't be any great help to Judkins. But I might hold Black Star and Night, if you put such store on their value."

"Value! Blake, I love my racers. Besides, there's another reason why I mustn't lose them. You go to the stables. Go with Jerd every day when he runs the horses, and don't let them out of your sight. If you would please me—win my gratitude, guard my black racers."

When Blake had mounted and ridden out of the court Lassiter regarded Jane with the smile that was becoming rarer as the days sped by.

"'Pears to me, as Blake says, you do put some store on them hosses. Now I ain't gainsayin' that the Arabians are the handsomest hosses I ever seen. But Bells can beat Night, an' run neck an' neck with Black Star."

"Lassiter, don't tease me now. I'm miserable—sick. Bells is fast, but he can't stay with the blacks, and you know it. Only Wrangle can do that."

"I'll bet that big raw-boned brute can more'n show his heels to your black racers. Jane, out there in the sage, on a long chase, Wrangle could kill your favorites."

"No, no," replied Jane, impatiently. "Lassiter, why do you say that so often? I know you've teased me at times, and I believe it's only kindness. You're always trying to keep my mind off worry. But you mean more by this repeated mention of my racers?"

"I reckon so." Lassiter paused, and for the thousandth time in her presence moved his black sombrero round and round, as if counting the silver pieces on the band. "Well, Jane, I've sort of read a little that's passin' in your mind."

"You think I might fly from my home—from Cottonwoods—from the Utah border?"

"I reckon. An' if you ever do an' get away with the blacks I wouldn't like to see Wrangle left here on the sage. Wrangle could catch you. I know Venters had him. But you can never tell. Mebbe he hasn't got him now. . . . Besides—things are happenin', an' somethin' of the same queer nature might have happened to Venters."

"God knows you're right! . . . Poor Bern, how long he's gone! In my trouble I've been forgetting him. But, Lassiter, I've little fear for him. I've heard my riders say he's as keen as a wolf. . . . As to your reading my thoughts—well, your suggestion makes an actual thought of what was only one of my dreams. I believe I dreamed of flying from this wild borderland, Lassiter. I've strange dreams. I'm not always practical and thinking of my many duties, as you said once. For instance—if I dared—if I dared I'd ask you to saddle the blacks and ride away with me—and hide me."

"Jane!"

The rider's sunburnt face turned white. A few times Jane had seen Lassiter's cool calm broken—when he had met little Fay, when he had learned how and why he had come to love both child and mistress, when he had stood beside Milly Erne's grave. But one and all they could not be considered in the light of his present agitation. Not only did Lassiter turn white—not only did he grow tense, not only did he lose his coolness, but also he suddenly, violently, hungrily took her into his arms and crushed her to his breast.

"Lassiter!" cried Jane, trembling. It was an action for which she took sole blame. Instantly, as if dazed, weakened, he released her. "Forgive me!" went on Jane. "I'm always forgetting your—your feelings. I thought of you as my faithful friend. I'm always making you out more than human . . . only, let me say—I meant that—about riding away. I'm wretched, sick of this—this— Oh, something bitter and black grows on my heart!"

"Jane, the hell—of it," he replied, with deep intake of breath, "is you *can't* ride away. Mebbe realizin' it accounts for my grabbin' you—that way, as much as the crazy boy's rapture your words gave me. I don't understand myself. . . . But the hell of this game is—you *can't* ride away."

"Lassiter! . . . What on earth do you mean? I'm an absolutely free woman."

"You ain't absolutely anythin' of the kind. . . . I reckon I've got to tell you!"

"Tell me all. It's uncertainty that makes me a coward. It's faith and hope—blind love, if you will, that makes me miserable. Every day I awake believing—still believing. The day grows, and with it doubts, fears, and that black bat hate that bites hotter and hotter into my heart. Then comes night—I pray—I pray for all, and for myself—I sleep—and I awake free once more, trustful, faithful, to believe—to hope! Then, O my God! I grow and live a thousand years till night again! . . . But if you want to see me a woman, tell me why I can't ride away—tell me what more I'm to lose—tell me the worst."

"Jane, you're watched. There's no single move of yours, except when you're hid in your house, that ain't seen by sharp eyes. The cottonwood grove's full of creepin', crawlin' men. Like Indians in the grass. When you rode, which wasn't often lately, the sage was full of sneakin' men. At night they crawl under your windows, into the court, an' I reckon into the house. Jane Withersteen, you know, never locked a door! This here grove's a hummin' bee-hive of mysterious happenin's. Jane, it ain't so much that these spies keep out of my way as me keepin' out of theirs. They're goin' to try to kill me. That's plain. But mebbe I'm as hard to shoot in the back as in the face. So far I've seen fit to watch only. This all means, Jane, that you're a marked woman. You can't get away—not now. Mebbe later, when you're broken, you might. But that's sure doubtful. Jane, you're to lose the cattle that's left—your home an' ranch—an' Amber Spring. You can't even hide a sack of gold! For it couldn't be slipped out of the house, day or night, an' hid or buried, let alone be rid off with. You may lose all. I'm tellin' you, Jane, hopin' to prepare you, if the worst does come. I told you once before about that strange power I've got to feel things."

"Lassiter, what can I do?"

"Nothin', I reckon, except know what's comin' an' wait an' be game. If you'd let me make a call on Tull, an' a long-deferred call on—"

"Hush! . . . Hush!" she whispered.

"Well, even that wouldn't help you any in the end."

"What does it mean? Oh, what does it mean? I am my father's daughter—a Mormon, yet I can't see! I've not failed in religion—in duty. For years I've given with a free and full heart. When my father died I was rich. If I'm still rich it's because I couldn't find enough ways to become poor. What am I, what are my possessions to set in motion such intensity of secret oppression?"

"Jane, the mind behind it all is an empire builder."

"But, Lassiter, I would give freely—all I own to avert this—this wretched thing. If I gave—that would leave me with faith still. Surely my—my churchmen think of my soul? If I lose my trust in them—"

"Child, be still!" said Lassiter, with a dark dignity that had in it something of pity. "You are a woman, fine an' big an' strong, an' your heart matches your size. But in mind you're a child. I'll say a little more—then I'm done. I'll never mention this again. Among many thousands of women you're one who has bucked against your churchmen. They tried you out, an' failed of persuasion, an' finally of threats. You meet now the cold steel of a will as far from Christlike as the universe is wide.

You're to be broken. Your body's to be held, given to some man, made, if possible, to bring children into the world. But your soul? . . . What do they care for your soul?"

CHAPTER THIRTEEN
Solitude and Storm

In his hidden valley, Venters awakened from sleep, and his ears rang with innumerable melodies from full-throated mocking-birds, and his eyes opened wide upon the glorious golden shaft of sunlight shining through the great stone bridge. The circle of cliffs surrounding Surprise Valley lay shrouded in morning mist, a dim blue low down along the terraces, a creamy, moving cloud along the ramparts. The oak forest in the center was a plumed and tufted oval of gold.

He saw Bess under the spruces. Upon her complete recovery of strength she always rose with the dawn. At the moment she was feeding the quail she had tamed. And she had begun to tame the mocking-birds. They fluttered among the branches overhead, and some left off their songs to flit down and shyly hop near the twittering quail. Little gray and white rabbits crouched in the grass, now nibbling, now laying long ears flat and watching the dogs.

Venters's swift glance took in the brightening valley, and Bess and her pets, and Ring and Whitie. It swept over all to return again and rest upon the girl. She had changed. To the dark trousers and blouse she had added moccasins of her own make, but she no longer resembled a boy. No eye could have failed to mark the rounded contours of a woman. The change had been to grace and beauty. A glint of warm gold gleamed from her hair, and a tint of red shone in the clear dark brown of cheeks. The haunting sweetness of her lips and eyes, that earlier had been illusive, a promise, had become a living fact. She fitted harmoniously into that wonderful setting; she was like Surprise Valley—wild and beautiful.

Venters leaped out of his cave to begin the day.

He had postponed his journey to Cottonwoods until after the passing of the summer rains. The rains were due soon. But until their arrival and the necessity for his trip to the village he sequestered in a far corner of mind all thought of peril, of his past life, and almost that of the present. It was enough to live. He did not want to know what lay hidden in the dim and distant future. Surprise Valley had enchanted him. In this home of the cliff-dwellers there were peace and quiet and solitude, and another thing, wondrous as the golden morning shaft of sunlight, that he dared not ponder over long enough to understand.

The solitude he had hated when alone he had now come to love. He was assimilating something from this valley of gleams and shadows. From this strange girl he was assimilating more.

The day at hand resembled many days gone before. As Venters had no tools with which to build, or to till the terraces, he remained idle. Beyond the cooking of the simple fare there were no tasks. And as there were no tasks, there was no system. He and Bess began one thing, to leave it; to begin another, to leave that; and then do nothing but lie under the spruces and watch the great cloud-sails majestically move along the ramparts, and dream and dream. The valley was a golden, sunlit world. It was silent. The sighing wind and the twittering quail and the singing birds, even the rare and seldom-occurring hollow crack of a sliding weathered stone, only thickened and deepened that insulated silence.

Venters and Bess had vagrant minds.

"Bess, did I tell you about my horse Wrangle?" inquired Venters.

"A hundred times," she replied.

"Oh, have I? I'd forgotten. I want you to see him. He'll carry us both."

"I'd like to ride him. Can he run?"

"Run? He's a demon. Swiftest horse on the sage! I hope he'll stay in that cañon."

"He'll stay."

They left camp to wander along the terraces, into the aspen ravines, under the gleaming walls. Ring and Whitie wandered in the fore, often turning, often trotting back, open-mouthed and solemn-eyed and happy. Venters lifted his gaze to the grand archway over the entrance to the valley, and Bess lifted hers to follow his, and both were silent. Sometimes the bridge held their attention for a long time. To-day a soaring eagle attracted them.

"How he sails!" exclaimed Bess. "I wonder where his mate is?"

"She's at the nest. It's on the bridge in a crack near the top. I see her often. She's almost white."

They wandered on down the terrace, into the shady, sun-flecked forest. A brown bird fluttered crying from a bush. Bess peeped into the leaves.

"Look! A nest and four little birds. They're not afraid of us. See how they open their mouths. They're hungry."

Rabbits rustled the dead brush and pattered away. The forest was full of a drowsy hum of insects. Little darts of purple, that were running quail, crossed the glades. And a plaintive, sweet peeping came from the coverts. Bess's soft step disturbed a sleeping lizard that scampered away over the leaves. She gave chase and caught it, a slim creature of nameless color but of exquisite beauty.

"Jewel eyes," she said. "It's like a rabbit—afraid. We won't eat you. There—go."

Murmuring water drew their steps down into a shallow shaded ravine where a brown brook brawled softly over mossy stones. Multitudes of strange, gray frogs with white spots and black eyes lined the rocky bank and leaped only at close approach. Then Venters's eye descried a very thin, very long green snake coiled round a sapling. They drew closer and closer till they could have touched it. The snake had no fear and watched them with scintillating eyes.

"It's pretty," said Bess. "How tame! I thought snakes always ran."

"No. Even the rabbits didn't run here till the dogs chased them."

On and on they wandered to the wild jumble of massed and broken fragments of cliff at the west end of the valley. The roar of the disappearing stream dinned in their ears. Into this maze of rocks they threaded a tortuous way, climbing, descending, halting to gather wild plums and great lavender lilies, and going on at the will of fancy. Idle and keen perceptions guided them equally.

"Oh, let us climb there!" cried Bess, pointing upward to a small space of terrace left green and shady between huge abutments of broken cliff. And they climbed to the nook and rested and looked out across the valley to the curling column of blue smoke from their campfire. But the cool shade and the rich grass and the fine view were not what they had climbed for. They could not have told, although whatever had drawn them was well-satisfying. Light, sure-footed as a mountain goat, Bess pattered down at Venters's heels; and they went on, calling the dogs, eyes dreamy and wide, listening to the wind and the bees and the crickets and the birds.

Part of the time Ring and Whitie led the way, then Venters, then Bess; and the direction was not an object. They left the sun-streaked shade of the oaks, brushed the long grass of the meadows, entered the green and fragrant swaying willows, to stop, at length, under the huge old cottonwoods where the beavers were busy.

Here they rested and watched. A dam of brush and logs and mud and stones backed the stream into a little lake. The round, rough beaver houses projected from the water. Like the rabbits, the beavers had become shy. Gradually, however, as Venters and Bess knelt low, holding the dogs, the beavers emerged to swim with logs and gnaw at cottonwoods and pat mud walls with their paddle-like tails, and, glossy and shiny in the sun, to go on with their strange, persistent industry. They were the builders. The lake was a mud-hole, and the immediate environment a scarred and dead region, but it was a wonderful home of wonderful animals.

"Look at that one—he puddles in the mud," said Bess. "And there! See him dive! Hear them gnawing! I'd think they'd break their teeth. How's it they can stay out of the water and under the water?"

And she laughed.

Then Venters and Bess wandered farther, and, perhaps not all unconsciously this time, wended their slow steps to the cave of the cliff-dwellers, where she liked best to go.

The tangled thicket and the long slant of dust and little chips of weathered rock and the steep bench of stone and the worn steps all were arduous work for Bess in the climbing. But she gained the shelf, gasping, hot of cheek, glad of eye, with her hand in Venters's. Here they rested. The beautiful valley glittered below with its millions of wind-turned leaves bright-faced in the sun, and the mighty bridge towered heavenward, crowned with blue sky. Bess, however, never rested for long. Soon she was exploring, and Venters followed; she dragged forth from corners and shelves a multitude of crudely fashioned and painted pieces of pottery, and he carried them. They peeped down into the dark holes of the kivas, and Bess gleefully dropped a stone and waited for the long-coming hollow sound to rise. They peeped into the little globular houses, like mud-wasp nests, and wondered if these had been store-places for grain, or baby cribs, or what; and they crawled into the larger houses and laughed when they bumped their heads on the low roofs, and they dug in the dust of the floors. And they brought from dust and darkness armloads of treasure which they carried to the light. Flints and stones and strange curved sticks and pottery they found; and twisted grass rope that crumbled in their hands, and bits of whitish stone which crushed to powder at a touch and seemed to vanish in the air.

"That white stuff was bone," said Venters, slowly. "Bones of a cliff-dweller."

"No!" exclaimed Bess.

"Here's another piece. Look! . . . Whew! dry, powdery smoke! That's bone."

Then it was that Venters's primitive, childlike mood, like a savage's, seeing, yet unthinking, gave way to the encroachment of civilized thought. The world had not been made for a single day's play or fancy or idle watching. The world was old. Nowhere could be gotten a better idea of its age than in this gigantic silent tomb. The gray ashes in Venters's hand had once been bone of a human being like himself. The pale gloom of the cave had shadowed people long ago. He saw that Bess had received the same shock—could not in moments such as this escape her feeling, living, thinking destiny.

"Bern, people have *lived* here," she said, with wide, thoughtful eyes.

"Yes," he replied.

"How long ago?"

"A thousand years and more."

"What were they?"

"Cliff-dwellers. Men who had enemies and made their homes high out of reach."

"They had to fight?"

"Yes."

"They fought for—what?"

"For life. For their homes, food, children, parents—for their women!"

"Has the world changed any in a thousand years?"

"I don't know—perhaps a little."

"Have men?"

"I hope so—I think so."

"Things crowd into my mind," she went on, and the wistful light in her eyes told Venters the truth of her thoughts. "I've ridden the border of Utah. I've seen people—know how they live—but they must be few of all who are living. I had my books and I studied them. But all that doesn't help me any more. I want to go out into the big world and see it. Yet I want to stay here more. What's to become of us? Are we cliff-dwellers? We're alone here. I'm happy when I don't think. These—these bones that fly into dust—they make me sick and a little afraid. Did the people who lived here once have the same feelings as we have? What was the good of their living at all? They're gone! What's the meaning of it all—of us?"

"Bess, you ask more than I can tell. It's beyond me. Only there was laughter here once—and now there's silence. There was life—and now there's death. Men cut these little steps, made these arrow-heads and mealing-stones, plaited the ropes we found, and left their bones to crumble in our fingers. As far as time is concerned it might all have been yesterday. We're here to-day. Maybe we're higher in the scale of human beings—in intelligence. But who knows? We can't be any higher in the things for which life is lived at all."

"What are they?"

"Why—I suppose relationship, friendship—love."

"Love!"

"Yes. Love of man for woman—love of woman for man. That's the nature, the meaning, the best of life itself."

She said no more. Wistfulness of glance deepened into sadness.

"Come, let us go," said Venters.

Action brightened her. Beside him, holding his hand, she slipped down the shelf, ran down the long, steep slant of sliding stones, out of the cloud of dust, and likewise out of the pale gloom.

"We beat the slide," she cried.

The miniature avalanche cracked and roared, and rattled itself into an inert mass at the base of the incline. Yellow dust like the gloom of the cave, but not so changeless, drifted away on the wind; the roar clapped in echo from the cliff, returned, went back, and came again to die in the hollowness. Down on the sunny terrace there was a different atmosphere. Ring and Whitie leaped around Bess. Once more she was smiling, gay, and thoughtless, with the dream-mood in the shadow of her eyes.

"Bess, I haven't seen that since last summer. Look!" said Venters, pointing to the scalloped edge of rolling purple clouds that peeped over the western wall. "We're in for a storm."

"Oh, I hope not. I'm afraid of storms."

"Are you? Why?"

"Have you ever been down in one of these walled-up pockets in a bad storm?"

"No, now I think of it, I haven't."

"Well, it's terrible. Every summer I get scared to death and hide somewhere in the dark. Storms up on the sage are bad, but nothing to what they are down here in the cañons. And in this little valley—why, echoes can rap back and forth so quick they'll split our ears."

"We're perfectly safe here, Bess."

"I know. But that hasn't anything to do with it. The truth is I'm afraid of lightning and thunder, and thunder-claps hurt my head. If we have a bad storm, will you stay close to me?"

"Yes."

When they got back to camp the afternoon was closing, and it was exceedingly sultry. Not a breath of air stirred the aspen leaves, and when these did not quiver the air was indeed still. The dark-purple clouds moved almost imperceptibly out of the west.

"What have we for supper?" asked Bess.

"Rabbit."

"Bern, can't you think of another new way to cook rabbit?" went on Bess, with earnestness.

"What do you think I am—a magician?" retorted Venters.

"I wouldn't dare tell you. But, Bern, do you want me to turn into a rabbit?"

There was a dark-blue, merry flashing of eyes and a parting of lips; then she laughed. In that moment she was naïve and wholesome.

"Rabbit seems to agree with you," replied Venters. "You are well and strong—and growing very pretty."

Anything in the nature of compliment he had never before said to her, and just now he responded to a sudden curiosity to see its effect. Bess stared as if she had not heard aright, slowly blushed, and completely lost her poise in happy confusion.

"I'd better go right away," he continued, "and fetch supplies from Cottonwoods."

A startlingly swift change in the nature of her agitation made him reproach himself for his abruptness.

"No, no, don't go!" she said. "I didn't mean—that about the rabbit. I—I was only trying to be—funny. Don't leave me all alone!"

"Bess, I must go sometime."

"Wait then. Wait till after the storms."

The purple cloud-bank darkened the lower edge of the setting sun, crept up and up, obscuring its fiery red heart, and finally passed over the last ruddy crescent of its upper rim.

The intense dead silence awakened to a long, low, rumbling roll of thunder.

"Oh!" cried Bess, nervously.

"We've had big black clouds before this without rain," said Venters. "But there's no doubt about that thunder. The storms are coming. I'm glad. Every rider on the sage will hear that thunder with glad ears."

Venters and Bess finished their simple meal and the few tasks around the camp, then faced the open terrace, the valley, and the west, to watch and await the approaching storm.

It required keen vision to see any movement whatever in the purple clouds. By infinitesimal degrees the dark cloud-line merged upward into the golden-red haze of the afterglow of sunset. A shadow lengthened from under the western wall across the valley. As straight and rigid as steel rose the delicate spear-pointed silver spruces; the aspen leaves, by nature pendant and quivering, hung limp and heavy; no slender blade of grass moved. A gentle splashing of water came from the ravine. Then again from out of the west sounded the low, dull, and rumbling roll of thunder.

A wave, a ripple of light, a trembling and turning of the aspen leaves, like the approach of a breeze on the water, crossed the valley from the west; and the lull and the deadly stillness and the sultry air passed away on a cool wind.

The night bird of the cañon, with clear and melancholy notes, announced the twilight. And from all along the cliffs rose the faint murmur and moan and mourn of the wind singing in the caves. The bank of clouds now swept hugely out of the western sky. Its front was purple and black, with gray between, a bulging, mushrooming, vast thing instinct with storm. It had a dark, angry, threatening aspect. As if all the power of the winds were pushing and piling behind, it rolled ponderously across the sky. A red flare burned out instantaneously, flashed from the west to east, and died. Then from the deepest black of the purple cloud burst a boom. It was like the bowling of a huge boulder along the crags and ramparts, and seemed to roll on and fall into the valley to bound and bang and boom from cliff to cliff.

"Oh!" cried Bess, with her hands over her ears. "What did I tell you?"

"Why, Bess, be reasonable!" said Venters.

"I'm a coward."

"Not quite that, I hope. It's strange you're afraid. I love a storm."

"I tell you a storm down in these cañons is an awful thing. I know Oldring hated storms. His men were afraid of them. There was one who went deaf in a bad storm, and never could hear again."

"Maybe I've lots to learn, Bess. I'll lose my guess if this storm isn't bad enough. We're going to have heavy wind first, then lightning and thunder, then the rain. Let's stay out as long as we can."

The tips of the cottonwoods and the oaks waved to the east, and the rings of aspens along the terraces twinkled their myriad of bright faces in fleet and glancing gleam. A low roar rose from the leaves of the forest, and the spruces swished in the rising wind. It came in gusts, with light breezes between. As it increased in strength the lulls shortened in length till there was a strong and steady blow all the time, and violent puffs at intervals, and sudden whirling currents. The clouds spread over the valley, rolling swiftly and low, and twilight faded into a sweeping darkness. Then the singing of the wind in the caves drowned the swift roar of rustling leaves; then the song swelled to a mourning, moaning wail; then with the gathering power of the wind the wail changed to a shriek. Steadily the wind strengthened and constantly the strange sound changed.

The last bit of blue sky yielded to the onsweep of clouds. Like angry surf the pale gleams of gray, amid the purple of that scuddling front, swept beyond the eastern rampart of the valley. The purple deepened to black. Broad sheets of lightning flared over the western wall. There were not yet any ropes or zigzag streaks darting down through the gathering darkness. The storm center was still beyond Surprise Valley.

"Listen! . . . Listen!" cried Bess, with her lips close to Venters's ear. "You'll hear Oldring's knell!"

"What's that?"

"Oldring's knell. When the wind blows a gale in the caves it makes what the rustlers call Oldring's knell. They believe it bodes his death. I think he believes so, too. It's not like any sound on earth. . . . It's beginning. Listen!"

The gale swooped down with a hollow unearthly howl. It yelled and pealed and shrilled and shrieked. It was made up of a thousand piercing cries. It was a rising and a moving sound. Beginning at the western break of the valley, it rushed along each gigantic cliff, whistling into the caves and cracks, to mount in power, to bellow a blast through the great stone bridge. Gone, as into an engulfing roar of surging waters, it seemed to shoot back and begin all over again.

It was only wind, thought Venters. Here sped and shrieked the sculptor that carved out the wonderful caves in the cliffs. It was only a gale, but as Venters listened, as his ears became accustomed to the fury and strife, out of it all or through it or above it pealed low and perfectly clear and persistently uniform a strange sound that had no counterpart in all the sounds of the elements. It was not of earth or of life. It was the grief and agony of the gale. A knell of all upon which it blew!

Black night enfolded the valley. Venters could not see his companion, and knew of her presence only through the tightening hold of her hand on his arm. He felt the dogs huddle closer to him. Suddenly the dense, black vault overhead split asunder to a blue-white, dazzling streak of lightning. The whole valley lay vividly clear and luminously bright in his sight. Upreared, vast and magnificent, the stone bridge glimmered like some grand god of storm in the lightning's fire. Then all flashed black again—blacker than pitch—a thick, impenetrable coal-blackness. And there came a ripping, crashing report. Instantly an echo resounded with clapping crash. The initial report was nothing to the echo. It was a terrible, living, reverberating, detonating crash. The wall threw the sound across, and could have made no greater roar if it had slipped in avalanche. From cliff to cliff the echo went on crashing retort and banged in lessening power, and boomed in thinner volume, and clapped weaker and weaker till a final clap could not reach across the waiting cliff.

In the pitchy darkness Venters led Bess, and, groping his way, by feel of hand found the entrance to her cave and lifted her up. On the instant a blinding flash of lightning illumined the cave and all about him. He saw Bess's face white now, with dark, frightened eyes. He saw the dogs leap up, and he followed suit. The golden glare vanished; all was black; then came the splitting crack and the infernal din of echoes.

Bess shrank closer to him and closer, found his hands, and pressed them tightly over her ears, and dropped her face upon his shoulder, and hid her eyes.

Then the storm burst with a succession of ropes and streaks and shafts of lightning, playing continuously, filling the valley with a broken radiance; and the cracking shots followed each other swiftly till the echoes blended in one fearful, deafening crash.

Venters looked out upon the beautiful valley—beautiful now as never before—mystic in its transparent, luminous gloom, weird in the quivering, golden haze of lightning. The dark spruces were tipped with glimmering lights; the aspens bent low in the winds, as waves in a tempest at sea; the forest of oaks tossed wildly and shone with gleams of fire. Across the valley the huge cavern of the cliff-dwellers yawned in the glare, every little black window as clear as at noonday; but the night and the storm added to their tragedy. Flung arching to the black clouds, the great stone bridge seemed to bear the brunt of the storm. It caught the full fury of the rushing wind. It lifted its noble crown to meet the lightning. Venters thought of the eagles and their lofty nest in a niche under the arch. A driving pall of rain, black as the clouds, came sweeping on to obscure the bridge and the gleaming walls and the shining valley. The lightning played incessantly, streaking down through opaque darkness of rain. The roar of the wind, with its strange knell and the recrashing echoes, mingled with the roar of the flooding rain, and all seemingly were deadened and drowned in a world of sound.

In the dimming pale light Venters looked down upon the girl. She had sunk into his arms, upon his breast, burying her face. She clung to him. He felt the softness of her, and the warmth, and the quick heave of her breast. He saw the dark, slender, graceful outline of her form. A woman lay in his arms! And he held her closer. He who had been alone in the sad, silent watches of the night was not now and never must be again alone. He who had yearned for the touch of a hand felt the long tremble and the heart-beat of a woman. By what strange chance had she come to love him! By what change—by what marvel had she grown into a treasure!

No more did he listen to the rush and roar of the thunder-storm. For with the touch of clinging hands and the throbbing bosom he grew conscious of an inward storm—the tingling of new chords of thought, strange music of unheard, joyous bells, sad dreams dawning to wakeful delight, dissolving doubt, resurging hope, force, fire, and freedom, unutterable sweetness of desire. A storm in his breast—a storm of real love.

CHAPTER FOURTEEN
West Wind

When the storm abated Venters sought his own cave, and late in the night, as his blood cooled and the stir and throb and thrill subsided, he fell asleep.

With the breaking of dawn his eyes unclosed. The valley lay drenched and bathed, a burnished oval of glittering green. The rain-washed walls glistened in the morning light. Waterfalls of many forms poured over the rims. One, a broad, lacy sheet, thin as smoke, slid over the western notch and struck a ledge in its downward fall, to bound into broader leap, to burst far below into white and gold and rosy mist.

Venters prepared for the day, knowing himself a different man.

"It's a glorious morning," said Bess, in greeting.

"Yes. After the storm the west wind," he replied.

"Last night was I—very much of a baby?" she asked, watching him.

"Pretty much."

"Oh, I couldn't help it!"

"I'm glad you were afraid."

"Why?" she asked, in slow surprise.

"I'll tell you some day," he answered, soberly. Then around the camp-fire and through the morning meal he was silent; afterward he strolled thoughtfully off alone along the terrace. He climbed a great yellow rock raising its crest among the spruces, and there he sat down to face the valley and the west.

"I love her!"

Aloud he spoke—unburdened his heart—confessed his secret. For an instant the golden valley swam before his eyes, and the walls waved, and all about him whirled with tumult within.

"I love her! . . . I understand now."

Reviving memory of Jane Withersteen and thought of the complications of the present amazed him with proof of how far he had drifted from his old life. He discovered that he hated to take up the broken threads, to delve into dark problems and difficulties. In this beautiful valley he had been living a beautiful dream. Tranquillity had come to him, and the joy of solitude, and interest in all the wild creatures and crannies of this incomparable valley—and love. Under the shadow of the great stone bridge God had revealed Himself to Venters.

"The world seems very far away," he muttered, "but it's there—and I'm not yet done with it. Perhaps I never shall be. . . . Only—how glorious it would be to live here always and never think again!"

Whereupon the resurging reality of the present, as if in irony of his wish, steeped him instantly in contending thought. Out of it all he presently evolved these things: he must go to Cottonwoods; he must bring supplies back to Surprise Valley; he must cultivate the soil and raise corn and stock, and, most imperative of all, he must decide the future of the girl who loved him and whom he loved. The first of these things required tremendous effort, the last one, concerning Bess, seemed simply and naturally easy of accomplishment. He would marry her. Suddenly, as from roots of poisonous fire, flamed up the forgotten truth concerning her. It seemed to wither and shrivel up all his joy on its hot, tearing way to his heart. She had been Oldring's Masked Rider. To Venters's question, "What were you to Oldring?" she had answered with scarlet shame and drooping head.

"What do I care who she is or what she was!" he cried, passionately. And he knew it was not his old self speaking. It was this softer, gentler man who had awakened to new thoughts in the quiet valley. Tenderness, masterful in him now, matched the absence of joy and blunted the knife-edge of entering jealousy. Strong and passionate effort of will, surprising him, held back the poison from piercing his soul.

"Wait! . . . Wait!" he cried, as if calling. His hand pressed his breast, and he might have called to the pang there. "Wait! It's all so strange—so wonderful. Anything can happen. Who am I to judge her? I'll glory in my love for her. But I can't tell it—can't give up to it."

Certainly he could not then decide her future. Marrying her was impossible in Surprise Valley and in any village south of Sterling. Even without the mask she had once worn she would easily have been recognized as Oldring's Rider. No man who had ever seen her would forget her, regardless of his ignorance as to her sex. Then more poignant than all other argument was the fact that he did not want to take her away from Surprise Valley. He resisted all thought of that. He had brought her to the most beautiful and wildest place of the uplands; he had saved her, nursed her back to strength, watched her bloom as one of the valley lilies; he knew her life there to be pure and sweet—she belonged to him, and he loved her. Still these were not all the reasons why he did not want to take her away. Where could they go? He feared the rustlers—he feared the riders—he feared the Mormons. And if he should ever succeed in getting Bess safely away from these immediate perils, he feared the sharp eyes of women and their tongues, the big outside world with its problems of existence. He must wait to decide her future, which, after all, was deciding his own. But between her future and his something hung impending. Like Balancing Rock, which waited darkly over the steep gorge, ready to close forever the outlet to Deception Pass, that nameless thing, as certain yet intangible as fate, must fall and close forever all doubts and fears of the future.

"I've dreamed," muttered Venters, as he rose. "Well, why not? . . . To dream is happiness! But let me just once see this clearly, wholly; then I can go on dreaming till the thing falls. I've got to tell Jane Withersteen. I've dangerous trips to take. I've work here to make comfort for this girl. She's mine. I'll fight to keep her safe from that old life. I've already seen her forget it. I love her. And if a beast ever rises in me I'll burn my hand off before I lay it on her with shameful intent. And, by God! sooner or later I'll kill the man who hid her and kept her in Deception Pass!"

As he spoke the west wind softly blew in his face. It seemed to soothe his passion. That west wind was fresh, cool, fragrant, and it carried a sweet, strange burden of far-off things—tidings of life in other climes, of sunshine asleep on other walls—of other places where reigned peace. It carried, too, sad truth of human hearts and mystery—of promise and hope unquenchable. Surprise Valley was only a little niche in the wide world whence blew that burdened wind. Bess was only one of millions at the mercy of unknown motive in nature and life. Content had come to Venters in the valley; happiness had breathed in the slow, warm air; love as bright as light had hovered over the walls and descended to him; and now on the west wind came a whisper of the eternal triumph of faith over doubt.

"How much better I am for what has come to me!" he exclaimed. "I'll let the future take care of itself. Whatever falls, I'll be ready."

Venters retraced his steps along the terrace back to camp, and found Bess in the old familiar seat, waiting and watching for his return.

"I went off by myself to think a little," he explained.

"You never looked that way before. What—what is it? Won't you tell me?"

"Well, Bess, the fact is I've been dreaming a lot. This valley makes a fellow dream. So I forced myself to think. We can't live this way much longer. Soon I'll simply have to go to Cottonwoods. We need a whole pack train of supplies. I can get—"

"Can you go safely?" she interrupted.

"Why, I'm sure of it. I'll ride through the Pass at night. I haven't any fear that Wrangle isn't where I left him. And once on him—Bess, just wait till you see that horse!"

"Oh, I want to see him—to ride him. But—but, Bern, this is what troubles me," she said. "Will—will you come back?"

"Give me four days. If I'm not back in four days you'll know I'm dead. For that only shall keep me."

"Oh!"

"Bess, I'll come back. There's danger—I wouldn't lie to you—but I can take care of myself."

"Bern, I'm sure—oh, I'm sure of it! All my life I've watched hunted men. I can tell what's in them. And I believe you can ride and shoot and see with any rider of the sage. It's not—not that I—fear."

"Well, what is it, then?"

"Why—why—why should you come back at all?"

"I couldn't leave you here alone."

"You might change your mind when you get to the village—among old friends—"

"I won't change my mind. As for old friends—" He uttered a short, expressive laugh.

"Then—there—there must be a—a woman!" Dark red mantled the clear tan of temple and cheek and neck. Her eyes were eyes of shame, upheld a long moment by intense, straining search for the verification of her fear. Suddenly they drooped, her head fell to her knees, her hands flew to her hot cheeks.

"Bess—look here," said Venters, with a sharpness due to the violence with which he checked his quick, surging emotion.

As if compelled against her will—answering to an irresistible voice—Bess raised her head, looked at him with sad, dark eyes, and tried to whisper with tremulous lips.

"There's no woman," went on Venters, deliberately holding her glance with his. "Nothing on earth, barring the chances of life, can keep me away."

Her face flashed and flushed with the glow of a leaping joy; but like the vanishing of a gleam it disappeared to leave her as he had never beheld her.

"I am nothing—I am lost—I am nameless!"

"Do you *want* me to come back?" he asked, with sudden stern coldness. "Maybe *you* want to go back to Oldring!"

That brought her erect, trembling and ashy pale, with dark, proud eyes and mute lips refuting his insinuation.

"Bess, I beg your pardon. I shouldn't have said that. But you angered me. I intend to work—to make a home for you here—to be a—a brother to you as long as ever you need me. And you must forget what you are—were—I mean, and be happy. When you remember that old life you are bitter, and it hurts me."

"I was happy—I shall be very happy. Oh, you're so good that—that it kills me! If I think, I can't believe it. I grow sick with wondering *why.* I'm only a *let me say it*—only a lost, nameless—girl of the rustlers. *Oldring's Girl,* they called me. That you should save me—be so good and kind—want to make me happy—why, it's beyond belief. No wonder I'm wretched at the thought of your leaving me. But I'll be wretched and bitter no more. I promise you. If only I could repay you even a little—"

"You've repaid me a hundredfold. Will you believe me?"

"Believe you! I couldn't do else."

"Then listen! . . . Saving you, I saved myself. Living here in this valley with you, I've found myself. I've learned to think while I was dreaming. I never troubled myself about God. But God, or some wonderful spirit, has whispered to me here. I absolutely deny the truth of what you say about yourself. I can't explain it. There are things too deep to tell. Whatever the terrible wrongs you've suffered, God holds you blameless. I see that—feel that in you every moment you are near me. I've a mother and a sister 'way back in Illinois. If I could I'd take you to them—to-morrow."

"*If it were true!* Oh, I might—I might lift my head!" she cried.

"Lift it then—you child. For I swear it's true."

She did lift her head with the singular wild grace always a part of her actions, with that old unconscious intimation of innocence which always tortured Venters, but now with something more—a spirit rising from the depths that linked itself to his brave words.

"I've been thinking—too," she cried, with quivering smile and swelling breast. "I've discovered myself—too. I'm young—I'm alive—I'm so full—oh! I'm a woman!"

"Bess, I believe I can claim credit of that last discovery—before you," Venters said, and laughed.

"Oh, there's more—there's something I must tell you."

"Tell it, then."

"When will you go to Cottonwoods?"

"As soon as the storms are past, or the worst of them."

"I'll tell you before you go. I can't now. I don't know how I shall then. But it must be told. I've never let you leave me without knowing. For in spite of what you say there's a chance you mightn't come back."

Day after day the west wind blew across the valley. Day after day the clouds clustered gray and purple and black. The cliffs sang and the caves rang with Oldring's knell, and the lightning flashed, the thunder rolled, the echoes crashed and crashed, and the rains flooded the valley. Wild flowers sprang up everywhere, swaying with the lengthening grass on the terraces, smiling wanly from shady nooks, peeping wondrously from year-dry crevices of the walls. The valley bloomed into a paradise. Every single moment, from the breaking of the gold bar through the bridge at dawn on to the reddening of rays over the western wall, was one of colorful change. The valley swam in thick, transparent haze, golden at dawn, warm and white at noon, purple in the twilight. At the end of every storm a rainbow curved down into the leaf-bright forest to shine and fade and leave lingeringly some faint essence of its rosy iris in the air.

Venters walked with Bess, once more in a dream, and watched the lights change on the walls, and faced the wind from out of the west.

Always it brought softly to him strange, sweet tidings of far-off things. It blew from a place that was old and whispered of youth. It blew down the grooves of time. It brought a story of the passing hours. It breathed low of fighting men and praying women. It sang clearly the song of love. That ever was the burden of its tidings—youth in the shady woods, waders through the wet meadows, boy and girl at the hedgerow stile, bathers in the booming surf, sweet, idle hours on grassy, windy hills, long strolls down moonlit lanes—everywhere in far-off lands, fingers locked and bursting hearts and longing lips—from all the world tidings of unquenchable love.

Often, in these hours of dreams he watched the girl, and asked himself of what was she dreaming? For the changing light of the valley reflected its gleam and its color and its meaning in the changing light of her eyes. He saw in them infinitely more than he saw in his dreams. He saw thought and soul and nature—strong vision of life. All tidings the west wind blew from distance and age he found deep in those dark-blue depths, and found them mysteries solved. Under their wistful shadow he softened, and in the softening felt himself grow a sadder, a wiser, and a better man.

While the west wind blew its tidings, filling his heart full, teaching him a man's part, the days passed, the purple clouds changed to white, and the storms were over for that summer.

"I must go now," he said.

"When?" she asked.

"At once—to-night."

"I'm glad the time has come. It dragged at me. Go—for you'll come back the sooner."

Late in the afternoon, as the ruddy sun split its last flame in the ragged notch of the western wall, Bess walked with Venters along the eastern terrace, up the long, weathered slope, under the great stone bridge. They entered the narrow gorge to climb around the fence long before built there by Venters. Farther than this she had never been. Twilight had already fallen in the gorge. It brightened to waning shadow in the wider ascent. He showed her Balancing Rock, of which he had often told her, and explained its sinister leaning over the outlet. Shuddering, she looked down the long, pale incline with its closed-in, toppling walls.

"What an awful trail! Did you carry me up here?"

"I did, surely," replied he.

"It frightens me, somehow. Yet I never was afraid of trails. I'd ride anywhere a horse could go, and climb where he couldn't. But there's something fearful here. I feel as—as if the place was watching me."

"Look at this rock. It's balanced here—balanced perfectly. You know I told you the cliff-dwellers cut the rock, and why. But they're gone and the rock waits. Can't you see—feel how it waits here? I moved it once, and I'll never dare again. A strong heave would start it. Then it would fall and bang, and smash that crag, and jar the walls, and close forever the outlet to Deception Pass!"

"Ah! When you come back I'll steal up here and push and push with all my might to roll the rock and close forever the outlet to the Pass!" She said it lightly, but in the undercurrent of her voice was a heavier note, a ring deeper than any ever given mere play of words.

"Bess! . . . You can't dare me! Wait till I come back with supplies—then roll the stone."

"I—was—in—fun." Her voice now throbbed low. "Always you must be free to go when you will. Go now . . . this place presses on me—stifles me."

"I'm going—but you had something to tell me?"

"Yes. . . . Will you—come back?"

"I'll come if I live."

"But—but you mightn't come?"

"That's possible, of course. It'll take a good deal to kill me. A man couldn't have a faster horse or keener dog. And, Bess, I've guns, and I'll use them if I'm pushed. But don't worry."

"I've faith in you. I'll not worry until after four days. Only—because you mightn't come—I *must* tell you—"

She lost her voice. Her pale face, her great, glowing, earnest eyes, seemed to stand alone out of the gloom of the gorge. The dog whined, breaking the silence.

"I *must* tell you—because you mightn't come back," she whispered. "You *must* know what—what I think of your goodness—of you. Always I've been tongue-tied. I seemed not to be grateful. It was deep in my heart. Even now—if I were other than I am—I couldn't tell you. But I'm nothing—only a rustler's girl—nameless—infamous. You've saved me—and I'm—I'm yours to do with as you like. . . . With all my heart and soul—I love you!"

CHAPTER FIFTEEN
Shadows on the Sage-Slope

In the cloudy, threatening, waning summer days shadows lengthened down the sage-slope, and Jane Withersteen likened them to the shadows gathering and closing in around her life.

Mrs. Larkin died, and little Fay was left an orphan with no known relative. Jane's love redoubled. It was the saving brightness of a darkening hour. Fay turned now to Jane in childish worship. And Jane at last found full expression for the mother-longing in her heart. Upon Lassiter, too, Mrs. Larkin's death had some subtle reaction. Before, he had often, without explanation, advised Jane to send Fay back to any Gentile family that would take her in. Passionately and reproachfully and wonderingly Jane had refused even to entertain such an idea. And now Lassiter never advised it again, grew sadder and quieter in his contemplation of the child, and infinitely more gentle and loving. Sometimes Jane had a cold, inexplicable sensation of dread when she saw Lassiter watching Fay. What did the rider see in the future? Why did he, day by day, grow more silent, calmer, cooler, yet sadder in prophetic assurance of something to be?

No doubt, Jane thought, the rider, in his almost superhuman power of foresight, saw behind the horizon the dark, lengthening shadows that were soon to crowd and gloom over him and her and little Fay. Jane Withersteen awaited the long-deferred breaking of the storm with a courage and embittered calm that had come to her in her extremity. Hope had not died. Doubt and fear, subservient to her will, no longer gave her sleepless nights and tortured days. Love remained. All that she had loved she now loved the more. She seemed to feel that she was defiantly flinging the wealth of her love in the face of misfortune and of hate. No day passed but she prayed for all—and most fervently for her enemies. It troubled her that she had lost, or had never gained, the whole control of her mind. In some measure reason and wisdom and decision were locked in a chamber of her brain, awaiting a key. Power to think of some things was taken from her. Meanwhile, abiding a day of judgment, she fought ceaselessly to deny the bitter drops in her cup, to tear back the slow, the intangibly slow growth of a hot, corrosive lichen eating into her heart.

On the morning of August 10th, Jane, while waiting in the court for Lassiter, heard a clear, ringing report of a rifle. It came from the grove, somewhere toward the corrals. Jane glanced out in alarm. The day was dull, windless, soundless. The leaves of the cottonwoods drooped, as if they had foretold the doom of Withersteen House and were now ready to die and drop and decay. Never had Jane seen such shade. She pondered on the meaning of the report. Revolver shots had of late cracked from different parts of the grove—spies taking snap-shots at Lassiter from a cowardly distance! But a rifle report meant more. Riders seldom used rifles. Judkins and Venters were the exceptions she called to mind. Had the men who hounded her hidden in her grove, taken to the rifle to rid her of Lassiter, her last friend? It was probable—it was likely. And she did not share his cool assumption that his death would never come at the hands of a Mormon. Long had she expected it. His constancy to her, his singular reluctance to use the fatal skill for which he was famed—both now plain to all Mormons—laid him open to inevitable assassination. Yet what charm against ambush and aim and enemy he seemed to bear about him! No, Jane reflected, it was not charm; only a wonderful training of eye and ear, and sense of impending peril. Nevertheless that could not forever avail against secret attack.

That moment a rustling of leaves attracted her attention; then the familiar clinking accompaniment of a slow, soft, measured step, and Lassiter walked into the court.

"Jane, there's a fellow out there with a long gun," he said, and, removing his sombrero, showed his head bound in a bloody scarf.

"I heard the shot; I knew it was meant for you. Let me see—you can't be badly injured?"

"I reckon not. But mebbe it wasn't a close call! . . . I'll sit here in this corner where nobody can see me from the grove." He untied the scarf and removed it to show a long, bleeding furrow above his left temple.

"It's only a cut," said Jane. "But how it bleeds! Hold your scarf over it just a moment till I come back."

She ran into the house and returned with bandages; and while she bathed and dressed the wound Lassiter talked.

"That fellow had a good chance to get me. But he must have flinched when he pulled the trigger. As I dodged down I saw him run through the trees. He had a rifle. I've been expectin' that kind of gun play. I reckon now I'll have to keep a little closer hid myself. These fellers all seem to get chilly or shaky when they draw a bead on me, but one of them might jest happen to hit me."

"Won't you go away—leave Cottonwoods as I've begged you to—before some one does happen to hit you?" she appealed to him.

"I reckon I'll stay."

"But, oh, Lassiter—your blood will be on my hands!"

"See here, lady, look at your hands now, right now. Aren't they fine, firm, white hands? Aren't they bloody now? Lassiter's blood! That's a queer thing to stain your beautiful hands. But if you could only see deeper you'd find a redder color of blood. Heart color, Jane!"

"Oh! . . . My friend!"

"No, Jane, I'm not one to quit when the game grows hot, no more than you. This game, though, is new to me, an' I don't know the moves yet, else I wouldn't have stepped in front of that bullet."

"Have you no desire to hunt the man who fired at you—to find him—and—and kill him?"

"Well, I reckon I haven't any great hankerin' for that."

"Oh, the wonder of it! . . . I knew—I prayed—I trusted. Lassiter, I almost gave—all myself to soften you to Mormons. Thank God, and thank you, my friend. . . . But, selfish woman that I am, this is no great test. What's the life of one of those sneaking cowards to such a man as you? I think of your great hate toward him who— I think of your life's implacable purpose. Can it be—"

"Wait! . . . Listen!" he whispered. "I hear a hoss."

He rose noiselessly, with his ear to the breeze. Suddenly he pulled his sombrero down over his bandaged head and, swinging his gun-sheaths round in front, he stepped into the alcove.

"It's a hoss—comin' fast," he added.

Jane's listening ear soon caught a faint, rapid, rhythmic beat of hoofs. It came from the sage. It gave her a thrill that she was at a loss to understand. The sound rose stronger, louder. Then came a clear, sharp difference when the horse passed from the sage trail to the hard-packed ground of the grove. It became a ringing run—swift in its bell-like clatterings, yet singular in longer pause than usual between the hoofbeats of a horse.

"It's Wrangle! . . . It's Wrangle!" cried Jane Withersteen. "I'd know him from a million horses!"

Excitement and thrilling expectancy flooded out all Jane Withersteen's calm. A tight band closed round her breast as she saw the giant sorrel flit in reddish-brown flashes across the openings in the green. Then he was pounding down the lane—

thundering into the court—crashing his great iron-shod hoofs on the stone flags. Wrangle it was surely but shaggy and wild-eyed, and sage-streaked, with dust-caked lather staining his flanks. He reared and crashed down and plunged. The rider leaped off, threw the bridle, and held hard on a lasso looped round Wrangle's head and neck. Jane's heart sank as she tried to recognize Venters in the rider. Something familiar struck her in the lofty stature, in the sweep of powerful shoulders. But this bearded, long-haired, unkempt man, who wore ragged clothes patched with pieces of skin, and boots that showed bare legs and feet—this dusty, dark, and wild rider could not possibly be Venters.

"Whoa, Wrangle, old boy! Come down. Easy now. So—so—so. You're home, old boy, and presently you can have a drink of water you'll remember."

In the voice Jane knew the rider to be Venters. He tied Wrangle to the hitching-rack and turned to the court.

"Oh, Bern! . . . You wild man!" she exclaimed.

"Jane—Jane, it's good to see you! Hello, Lassiter! Yes, it's Venters."

Like rough iron his hard hand crushed Jane's. In it she felt the difference she saw in him. Wild, rugged, unshorn—yet how splendid! He had gone away a boy—he had returned a man. He appeared taller, wider of shoulder, deeper-chested, more powerfully built. But was that only her fancy—he had always been a young giant—was the change one of spirit? He might have been absent for years, proven by fire and steel, grown like Lassiter, strong and cool and sure. His eyes—were they keener, more flashing than before?—met hers with clear, frank, warm regard, in which perplexity was not, nor discontent, nor pain.

"Look at me long as you like," he said, with a laugh. "I'm not much to look at. And, Jane, neither you nor Lassiter, can brag. You're paler than I ever saw you. Lassiter, here, he wears a bloody bandage under his hat. That reminds me. Some one took a flying shot at me down in the sage. It made Wrangle run some. . . . Well, perhaps you've more to tell me than I've got to tell you."

Briefly, in few words, Jane outlined the circumstances of her undoing in the weeks of his absence.

Under his beard and bronze she saw his face whiten in terrible wrath.

"Lassiter—what held you back?"

No time in the long period of fiery moments and sudden shocks had Jane Withersteen ever beheld Lassiter as calm and serene and cool as then.

"Jane had gloom enough without my addin' to it by shootin' up the village," he said.

As strange as Lassiter's coolness was Venters's curious, intent scrutiny of them both, and under it Jane felt a flaming tide wave from bosom to temples.

"Well—you're right," he said, with slow pause. "It surprises me a little, that's all."

Jane sensed then a slight alteration in Venters, and what it was, in her own confusion, she could not tell. It had always been her intention to acquaint him with the deceit she had fallen to in her zeal to move Lassiter. She did not mean to spare herself. Yet now, at the moment, before these riders, it was an impossibility to explain.

Venters was speaking somewhat haltingly, without his former frankness. "I found Oldring's hiding-place and your red herd. I learned—I know—I'm sure there was a deal between Tull and Oldring." He paused and shifted his position and his gaze. He looked as if he wanted to say something that he found beyond him. Sorrow and pity and shame seemed to contend for mastery over him. Then he raised himself and spoke with effort. "Jane, I've cost you too much. You've almost ruined yourself for me. It was wrong, for I'm not worth it. I never deserved such friendship. Well, maybe it's not too late. You must give me up. Mind, I haven't changed. I am just the same as ever. I'll see Tull while I'm here, and tell him to his face."

"Bern, it's too late," said Jane.

"I'll *make* him believe!" cried Venters, violently.

"You ask me to break our friendship?"

"Yes. If you don't, I shall."

"Forever?"

"Forever!"

Jane sighed. Another shadow had lengthened down the sage-slope to cast further darkness upon her. A melancholy sweetness pervaded her resignation. The boy who had left her had returned a man, nobler, stronger, one in whom she divined something unbending as steel. There might come a moment later when she would wonder why she had not fought against his will, but just now she yielded to it. She liked him as well—nay, more, she thought, only her emotions were deadened by the long, menacing wait for the bursting storm.

Once before she had held out her hand to him—when she gave it; now she stretched it tremblingly forth in acceptance of the decree circumstance had laid upon them. Venters bowed over it, kissed it, pressed it hard, and half stifled a sound very like a sob. Certain it was that when he raised his head tears glistened in his eyes.

"Some—women—have a hard lot," he said, huskily. Then he shook his powerful form, and his rags lashed about him. "I'll say a few things to Tull—when I meet him."

"Bern—you'll not draw on Tull? Oh, that must not be! Promise me—"

"I promise you this," he interrupted, in stern passion that thrilled while it terrorized her. "If you say one more word for that plotter I'll kill him as I would a mad coyote!"

Jane clasped her hands. Was this fire-eyed man the one whom she had once made as wax to her touch? Had Venters become Lassiter and Lassiter Venters?

"I'll—say no more," she faltered.

"Jane, Lassiter once called you blind," said Venters. "It must be true. But I won't upbraid you. Only don't rouse the devil in me by praying for Tull! I'll try to keep cool when I meet him. That's all. Now there's one more thing I want to ask of you—the last. I've found a valley down in the Pass. It's a wonderful place. I intend to stay there. It's so hidden I believe no one can find it. There's good water, and browse, and game. I want to raise corn and stock. I need to take in supplies. Will you give them to me?"

"Assuredly. The more you take the better you'll please me—and perhaps the less my—my enemies will get."

"Venters, I reckon you'll have trouble packin' anythin' away," put in Lassiter.

"I'll go at night."

"Mebbe that wouldn't be best. You'd sure be stopped. You'd better go early in the mornin'—say, just after dawn. That's the safest time to move round here."

"Lassiter, I'll be hard to stop," returned Venters, darkly.

"I reckon so."

"Bern," said Jane, "go first to the riders' quarters and get yourself a complete outfit. You're a—a sight. Then help yourself to whatever else you need—burros, packs, grain, dried fruits, and meat. You must take coffee and sugar and flour—all kinds of supplies. Don't forget corn and seeds. I remember how you used to starve. Please—please take all you can pack away from here. I'll make a bundle for you, which you mustn't open till you're in your valley. How I'd like to see it! To judge by you and Wrangle, how wild it must be!"

Jane walked down into the outer court and approached the sorrel. Upstarting, he laid back his ears and eyed her.

"Wrangle—dear old Wrangle," she said, and put a caressing hand on his matted mane. "Oh, he's wild, but he knows me! Bern, can he run as fast as ever?"

"Run? Jane, he's done sixty miles since last night at dark, and I could make him kill Black Star right now in a ten-mile race."

"He never could," protested Jane. "He couldn't even if he was fresh."

"I reckon mebbe the best hoss'll prove himself yet," said Lassiter, "an', Jane, if it ever comes to that race I'd like you to be on Wrangle."

"I'd like that, too," rejoined Venters. "But, Jane, maybe Lassiter's hint is extreme. Bad as your prospects are, you'll surely never come to the running point."

"Who knows!" she replied, with mournful smile.

"No, no, Jane, it can't be so bad as all that. Soon as I see Tull there'll be a change in your fortunes. I'll hurry down to the village. . . . Now don't worry."

Jane retired to the seclusion of her room. Lassiter's subtle forecasting of disaster, Venters's forced optimism, neither remained in mind. Material loss weighed nothing in the balance with other losses she was sustaining. She wondered dully at her sitting there, hands folded listlessly, with a kind of numb deadness to the passing of time and the passing of her riches. She thought of Venters's friendship. She had not lost that, but she had lost him. Lassiter's friendship—that was more than love—it would endure, but soon he, too, would be gone. Little Fay slept dreamlessly upon the bed, her golden curls streaming over the pillow. Jane had the child's worship. Would she lose that, too? And if she did, what then would be left? Conscience thundered at her that there was left her religion. Conscience thundered that she should be grateful on her knees for this baptism of fire; that through misfortune, sacrifice, and suffering her soul might be fused pure gold. But the old, spontaneous, rapturous spirit no more exalted her. She wanted to be a woman—not a martyr. Like the saint of old who mortified his flesh, Jane Withersteen had in her the temper for heroic martyrdom, if by sacrificing herself she could save the souls of others. But here the damnable verdict blistered her that the more she sacrificed herself the blacker grew the souls of her churchmen. There was something terribly wrong with her soul, something terribly wrong with her churchmen and her religion. In the whirling gulf of her thought there was yet one shining light to guide her, to sustain her in her hope; and it was that, despite her errors and her frailties and her blindness, she had one absolute and unfaltering hold on ultimate and supreme justice. That was love. "Love your enemies as yourself!" was a divine word, entirely free from any church or creed.

Jane's meditations were disturbed by Lassiter's soft, tinkling step in the court. Always he wore the clinking spurs. Always he was in readiness to ride. She passed out and called him into the huge, dim hall.

"I think you'll be safer here. The court is too open," she said.

"I reckon," replied Lassiter. "An' it's cooler here. The day's sure muggy. Well, I went down to the village with Venters."

"Already! Where is he?" queried Jane, in quick amaze.

"He's at the corrals. Blake's helpin' him get the burros an' packs ready. That Blake is a good fellow."

"Did—did Bern meet Tull?"

"I guess he did," answered Lassiter, and he laughed dryly.

"Tell me! Oh, you exasperate me! You're so cool, so calm! For Heaven's sake, tell me what happened!"

"First time I've been in the village for weeks," went on Lassiter, mildly. "I reckon there 'ain't been more of a show for a long time. Me an' Venters walkin' down the road! It was funny. I ain't sayin' anybody was particular glad to see us. I'm not much thought of hereabouts, an' Venters he sure looks like what you called him, a wild man. Well, there was some runnin' of folks before we got to the stores. Then everybody vamoosed except some surprised rustlers in front of a saloon. Venters went right in the stores an' saloons, an' of course I went along. I don't know which tickled me the most—the actions of many fellers we met, or Venters's nerve. Jane, I was downright glad to be along. You see *that* sort of thing is my element, an' I've been away from it for a spell. But we didn't find Tull in one of them places. Some Gentile feller at last told Venters he'd find Tull in that long buildin' next to Parson's store. It's a kind of meetin'-room; and sure enough, when we peeped in, it was half full of men.

"Venters yelled: 'Don't anybody pull guns! We ain't come for that!' Then he tramped in, an' I was some put to keep alongside him. There was a hard, scrapin' sound of feet, a loud cry, an' then some whisperin', an' after that stillness you could cut with a knife. Tull was there, an' that fat party who once tried to throw a gun on me, an' other important-lookin' men, an' that little frog-legged feller who was with Tull the day I rode in here. I wish you could have seen their faces, 'specially Tull's an' the fat party's. But there ain't no use of me tryin' to tell you how they looked.

"Well, Venters an' I stood there in the middle of the room, with that batch of men all in front of us, an' not a blamed one of them winked an eyelash or moved a finger. It was natural, of course, for me to notice many of them packed guns. That's a way of mine, first noticin' them things. Venters spoke up, an' his voice sort of chilled an' cut, an' he told Tull he had a few things to say."

Here Lassiter paused while he turned his sombrero round and round, in his familiar habit, and his eyes had the look of a man seeing over again some thrilling spectacle, and under his red bronze there was strange animation.

"Like a shot, then, Venters told Tull that the friendship between you an' him was all over, an' he was leaving your place. He said you'd both of you broken off in the hope of propitiatin' your people, but you hadn't changed your mind otherwise, an' never would.

"Next he spoke up for you. I ain't goin' to tell you what he said. Only—no other woman who ever lived ever had such tribute! You had a champion, Jane, an' never fear that those thick-skulled men don't know you now. It couldn't be otherwise. He spoke the ringin', lightnin' truth. . . . Then he accused Tull of the underhand, miserable robbery of a helpless woman. He told Tull where the red herd was, of a deal made with Oldrin', that Jerry Card had made the deal. I thought Tull was goin' to drop, an' that little frog-legged cuss, he looked some limp an' white. But Venters's voice would have kept anybody's legs from bucklin'. I was stiff myself. He went on an' called Tull—called him every bad name ever known to a rider, an' then some. He cursed Tull. I never hear a man get such a cursin'. He laughed in scorn at the idea of Tull bein' a minister. He said Tull an' a few more dogs of hell builded their empire out of the hearts of such innocent an' God-fearin' women as Jane Withersteen. He called Tull a binder of women, a callous beast who hid behind a mock mantle of righteousness—an' the last an' lowest coward on the face of the earth. To prey on weak women through their religion—that was the last unspeakable crime!

"Then he finished, an' by this time he'd almost lost his voice. But his whisper was enough. 'Tull,' he said, '*she* begged me not to draw on you to-day. *She* would pray for you if you burned her at the stake. . . . But listen! . . . I swear if you and I ever come face to face again, I'll kill you!'

"We backed out of the door then, an' up the road. But nobody follered us."

Jane found herself weeping passionately. She had not been conscious of it till Lassiter ended his story, and she experienced exquisite pain and relief in shedding tears. Long had her eyes been dry, her grief deep; long had her emotions been dumb. Lassiter's story put her on the rack; the appalling nature of Venters's act and speech had no parallel as an outrage; it was worse than bloodshed. Men like Tull had been shot, but had one ever been so terribly denounced in public? Overmounting her horror, an uncontrollable, quivering passion shook her very soul. It was sheer human glory in the deed of a fearless man. It was hot, primitive instinct to live—to fight. It was a kind of mad joy in Venters's chivalry. It was close to the wrath that had first shaken her in the beginning of this war waged upon her.

"Well, well, Jane, don't take it that way," said Lassiter, in evident distress. "I had to tell you. There's some things a feller jest can't keep. It's strange you give up on hearin' that, when all this long time you've been the gamest woman I ever seen. But I don't know women. Mebbe there's reason for you to cry. I know this—nothin' ever rang in my soul an' so filled it as what Venters did. I'd like to have done it, but—I'm only good for throwin' a gun, an' it seems you hate that. . . . Well, I'll be goin' now."

"Where?"

"Venters took Wrangle to the stable. The sorrel's shy a shoe, an' I've got to help hold the big devil an' put on another."

"Tell Bern to come for the pack I want to give him—and—and to say good-by," called Jane, as Lassiter went out.

Jane passed the rest of that day in a vain endeavor to decide what and what not to put in the pack for Venters. This task was the last she would ever perform for him, and the gifts were the last she would ever make him. So she picked and chose and rejected, and chose again, and often paused in sad revery, and began again, till at length she filled the pack.

It was about sunset, and she and Fay had finished supper and were sitting in the court, when Venters's quick steps rang on the stones. She scarcely knew him, for he had changed the tattered garments, and she missed the dark beard and long hair. Still he was not the Venters of old. As he came up the steps she felt herself pointing to the pack, and heard herself speaking words that were meaningless to her. He said good-by; he kissed her, released her, and turned away. His tall figure blurred in her sight, grew dim through dark, streaked vision, and then he vanished.

Twilight fell around Withersteen House, and dusk and night. Little Fay slept; but Jane lay with strained, aching eyes. She heard the wind moaning in the cottonwoods and mice squeaking in the walls. The night was interminably long, yet she prayed to hold back the dawn. What would another day bring forth? The blackness of her room seemed blacker for the sad, entering gray of morning light. She heard the chirp of awakening birds, and fancied she caught a faint clatter of hoofs. Then low, dull, distant, throbbed a heavy gunshot. She had expected it, was waiting for it; nevertheless, an electric shock checked her heart, froze the very living fiber of her bones. That vise-like hold on her faculties apparently did not relax for a long time, and it was a voice under her window that released her.

"Jane! . . . Jane!" softly called Lassiter.

She answered somehow.

"It's all right. Venters got away. I thought mebbe you'd heard that shot, an' I was worried some."

"What was it—who fired?"

"Well—some fool feller tried to stop Venters out there in the sage—an' he only stopped lead! . . . I think it'll be all right. I haven't seen or heard of any other fellers round. Venters'll go through safe. An', Jane, I've got Bells saddled, an' I'm going to trail Venters. Mind, I won't show myself unless he falls foul of somebody an' needs me. I want to see if this place where he's goin' is safe for him. He says nobody can track him there. I never seen the place yet I couldn't track a man to. Now, Jane, you stay indoors while I'm gone, an' keep close watch on Fay. Will you?"

"Yes! Oh yes!"

"An' another thing, Jane," he continued, then paused for long—"another thing—if you ain't here when I come back—if you're *gone*—don't fear, I'll trail you—I'll find you."

"My dear Lassiter, where could I be gone—as you put it?" asked Jane, in curious surprise.

"I reckon you might be somewhere. Mebbe tied in an old barn—or corralled in some gulch—or chained in a cave! *Milly Erne was*—till she give in! Mebbe that's news to you. . . . Well, if you're gone I'll hunt for you."

"No, Lassiter," she replied, sadly and low. "If I'm gone just forget the unhappy woman whose blinded selfish deceit you repaid with kindness and love."

She heard a deep, muttering curse, under his breath, and then the silvery tinkling of his spurs as he moved away.

Jane entered upon the duties of that day with a settled, gloomy calm. Disaster hung in the dark clouds, in the shade, in the humid west wind. Blake, when he reported, appeared without his usual cheer; and Jerd wore a harassed look of a worn and worried man. And when Judkins put in appearance, riding a lame horse, and dismounted with the cramp of a rider, his dust-covered figure and his darkly grim, almost dazed expression told Jane of dire calamity. She had no need of words.

"Miss Withersteen, I have to report—loss of the—white herd," said Judkins, hoarsely.

"Come, sit down; you look played out," replied Jane, solicitously. She brought him brandy and food, and while he partook of refreshments, of which he appeared badly in need, she asked no questions.

"No one rider—could hev done more—Miss Withersteen," he went on, presently.

"Judkins, don't be distressed. You've done more than any other rider. I've long expected to lose the white herd. It's no surprise. It's in line with other things that are happening. I'm grateful for your service."

"Miss Withersteen, I knew how you'd take it. But if anythin', that makes it harder to tell. You see, a feller wants to do so much fer you, an' I'd got fond of my job. We hed the herd a ways off to the north of the break in the valley. There was a big level an' pools of water an' tip-top browse. But the cattle was in a high nervous condition. Wild—as wild as antelope! You see, they'd been so scared they never slept. I ain't a-goin' to tell you of the many tricks that were pulled off out there in the sage. But there wasn't a day for weeks thet the herd didn't get started to run. We allus managed to ride 'em close an' drive 'em back an' keep 'em bunched.

Honest, Miss Withersteen, them steers was *thin.* They was *thin* when water and grass was everywhere. *Thin* at this season—thet'll tell you how your steers was pestered. Fer instance, one night a strange runnin' streak of fire run right through the herd. That streak was a coyote—*with an oiled an' blazin' tail!* Fer I shot it an' found out. We had hell with the herd that night, an' if the sage an' grass hadn't been wet—we, hosses, steers, an' all would hev burned up. But I said I wasn't goin' to tell you any of the tricks. . . . Strange now, Miss Withersteen, when the stampede did come it was from natural cause—jest a whirlin' devil of dust. You've seen the like often. An' this wasn't no big whirl, fer the dust was mostly settled. It had dried out in a little swale, an' ordinarily no steer would ever hev run fer it. But the herd was nervous an' wild. An' jest as Lassiter said, when that bunch of white steers got to movin' they was as bad as buffalo. I've seen some buffalo stampedes back in Nebraska, an' this bolt of the steers was the same kind.

"I tried to mill the herd jest as Lassiter did. But I wasn't equal to it, Miss Withersteen. I don't believe the rider lives who could hev turned thet herd. We kept along of the herd fer miles, an' more 'n one of my boys tried to get the steers a-millin'. It wasn't no use. We got off level ground, goin' down, an' then the steers ran somethin' fierce. We left the little gullies an' washes level-full of dead steers. Finally I saw the herd was makin' to pass a kind of low pocket between ridges. There was a hog-back—as we used to call 'em—a pile of rocks stickin' up, and I saw the herd was goin' to split round it, or swing out to the left. An' I wanted 'em to go to the right so mebbe we'd be able to drive 'em into the pocket. So, with all my boys except three, I rode hard to turn the herd a little to the right. We couldn't budge 'em. They went on an' split round the rocks, an' the most of 'em was turned sharp to the left by a deep wash we hedn't seen—hed no chance to see.

"The other three boys—Jimmy Vail, Joe Willis, an' thet little Cairns boy—a nervy kid! they, with Cairns leadin', tried to buck thet herd round to the pocket. It was a wild, fool idee. I couldn't do nothin'. The boys got hemmed in between the steers an' the wash—thet they hedn't no chance to see, either. Vail an' Willis was run down right before our eyes. An' Cairns, who rode a fine hoss, he did some ridin' I never seen equaled, an' would hev beat the steers if there'd been any room to run in. I was high up an' could see how the steers kept spillin' by twos an' threes over into the wash. Cairns put his hoss to a place thet was too wide fer any hoss, an' broke his neck an' the hoss's too. We found that out after, an' as fer Vail an' Willis—two thousand steers ran over the poor boys. There wasn't much left to pack home fer burying! . . . An', Miss Withersteen, thet all happened yesterday, an' I believe, if the white herd didn't run over the wall of the Pass, it's runnin' yet."

On the morning of the second day after Judkins's recital, during which time Jane remained indoors a prey to regret and sorrow for the boy riders, and a new and now strangely insistent fear for her own person, she again heard what she had missed more than she dared honestly confess—the soft, jingling step of Lassiter. Almost overwhelming relief surged through her, a feeling as akin to joy as any she could have been capable of in those gloomy hours of shadow, and one that suddenly stunned her with the significance of what Lassiter had come to mean to her. She had begged him, for his own sake, to leave Cottonwoods. She might yet beg that, if her weakening courage permitted her to dare absolute loneliness and helplessness, but she realized now that if she were left alone her life would become one long, hideous nightmare.

When his soft steps clinked into the hall, in answer to her greeting, and his tall, black-garbed form filled the door, she felt an inexpressible sense of immediate safety. In his presence she lost her fear of the dim passageways of Withersteen House and of every sound. Always it had been that, when he entered the court or the hall, she had experienced a distinctly sickening but gradually lessening shock at sight of the huge black guns swinging at his sides. This time the sickening shock again visited her, it was, however, because a revealing flash of thought told her that it was not alone Lassiter who was thrillingly welcome, but also his fatal weapons. They meant so much. How she had fallen—how broken and spiritless must she be—to have still the same old horror of Lassiter's guns and his name, yet feel somehow a cold, shrinking protection in their law and might and use.

"Did you trail Venters—find his wonderful valley?" she asked, eagerly.

"Yes, an' I reckon it's sure a wonderful place."

"Is he safe there?"

"That's been botherin' me some. I trackled him an' part of the trail was the hardest I ever tackled. Mebbe there's a rustler or somebody in this country who's as good at trackin' as I am. If that's so Venters ain't safe."

"Well tell me all about Bern and his valley."

To Jane's surprise Lassiter showed disinclination for further talk about his trip. He appeared to be extremely fatigued. Jane reflected that one hundred and twenty miles, with probably a great deal of climbing on foot, all in three days, was enough to tire any rider. Moreover, it presently developed that Lassiter had returned in a mood of singular sadness and preoccupation. She put it down to a moodiness over the loss of her white herd and the now precarious condition of her fortune.

Several days passed, and as nothing happened, Jane's spirits began to brighten. Once in her musings she thought that this tendency of hers to rebound was as sad as it was futile. Meanwhile, she had resumed her walks through the grove with little Fay.

One morning she went as far as the sage. She had not seen the slope since the beginning of the rains, and now it bloomed a rich deep purple. There was a high wind blowing, and the sage tossed and waved and colored beautifully from light to dark. Clouds scudded across the sky and their shadows sailed darkly down the sunny slope.

Upon her return toward the house she went by the lane to the stables, and she had scarcely entered the great open space with its corrals and sheds when she saw Lassiter hurriedly approaching. Fay broke from her and, running to a corral fence, began to pat and pull the long, hanging ears of a drowsy burro.

One look at Lassiter armed her for a blow.

Without a word he led her across the wide yard to the rise of the ground upon which the stable stood.

"Jane—look!" he said, and pointed to the ground.

Jane glanced down, and again, and upon steadier vision made out splotches of blood on the stones, and broad, smooth marks in the dust, leading out toward the sage.

"What made these?" she asked.

"I reckon somebody has dragged dead or wounded men out to where there was hosses in the sage."

"Dead—or—wounded—men!"

"I reckon—Jane, are you strong? Can you bear up?"

His hands were gently holding hers, and his eyes—suddenly she could no longer look into them. "Strong?" she echoed, trembling. "I—I will be."

Up on the stone-flag drive, nicked with the marks made by the iron-shod hoofs of her racers, Lassiter led her, his grasp ever growing firmer.

"Where's Blake—and—and Jerb?" she asked, haltingly.

"I don't know where Jerb is. Bolted, most likely," replied Lassiter, as he took her through the stone door. "But Blake—poor Blake! He's gone forever! . . .Be prepared, Jane."

With a cold prickling of her skin, with a queer thrumming in her ears, with fixed and staring eyes, Jane saw a gun lying at her feet with chamber swung and empty, and discharged shells scattered near.

Outstretched upon the stable floor lay Blake, ghastly white—dead—one hand clutching a gun and the other twisted in his bloody blouse.

"Whoever the thieves were, whether your people or rustlers—Blake killed some of them!" said Lassiter.

"Thieves?" whispered Jane.

"I reckon. Hoss-thieves! . . . Look!" Lassiter waved his hand toward the stalls.

The first stall—Bell's stall—was empty. All the stalls were empty. No racer whinnied and stamped greeting to her. Night was gone! Black Star was gone!

CHAPTER SIXTEEN
Gold

As Lassiter had reported to Jane, Venters "went through" safely, and after a toilsome journey reached the peaceful shelter of Surprise Valley. When finally he lay wearily down under the silver spruces, resting from the strain of dragging packs and burros up the slope and through the entrance to Surprise Valley, he had leisure to think, and a great deal of the time went in regretting that he had not been frank with his loyal friend, Jane Withersteen.

But, he kept continually recalling, when he had stood once more face to face with her and had been shocked at the change in her and had heard the details of her adversity, he had not had the heart to tell her of the closer interest which had entered his life. He had not lied; yet he had kept silence.

Bess was in transports over the stores of supplies and the outfit he had packed from Cottonwoods. He had certainly brought a hundred times more than he had gone for; enough, surely, for years, perhaps to make permanent home in the valley. He saw no reason why he need ever leave there again.

After a day of rest he recovered his strength and shared Bess's pleasure in rummaging over the endless packs, and began to plan for the future. And in this planning, his trip to Cottonwoods, with its revived hate of Tull and consequent unleashing of fierce passions, soon faded out of mind. By slower degrees his friendship for Jane Withersteen and his contrition drifted from the active preoccupation of his present thought to a place in memory, with more and more infrequent recalls.

And as far as the state of his mind was concerned, upon the second day after his return, the valley, with its golden hues and purple shades, the speaking west wind and the cool, silent night, and Bess's watching eyes with their wonderful light, so wrought upon Venters that he might never have left them at all.

That very afternoon he set to work. Only one thing hindered him upon beginning, though it in no wise checked his delight, and that in the multiplicity of tasks planned to make a paradise out of the valley he could not choose the one with which to begin. He had to grow into the habit of passing from one dreamy pleasure to another, like a bee going from flower to flower in the valley, and he found this wandering habit likely to extend to his labors. Nevertheless, he made a start.

At the outset he discovered Bess to be both a considerable help in some ways and a very great hindrance in others. Her excitement and joy were spurs, inspirations; but she was utterly impracticable in her ideas, and she flitted from one plan to another with bewildering vacillation. Moreover, he fancied that she grew more eager, youthful, and sweet; and he marked that it was far easier to watch her and listen to her than it was to work. Therefore he gave her tasks that necessitated her going often to the cave where he had stored his packs.

Upon the last of these trips, when he was some distance down the terrace and out of sight of camp, he heard a scream, and then the sharp barking of the dogs.

For an instant he straightened up, amazed. Danger for her had been absolutely out of his mind. She had seen a rattlesnake—or a wildcat. Still she would not have been likely to scream at sight of either; and the barking of the dogs was ominous. Dropping his work, he dashed back along the terrace. Upon breaking through a clump of aspens he saw the dark form of a man in the camp. Cold, then hot, Venters burst into frenzied speed to reach his guns. He was cursing himself for a thoughtless fool when the man's tall form became familiar and he recognized Lassiter. Then the reversal of emotions changed his run to a walk; he tried to call out, but his voice refused to carry; when he reached camp there was Lassiter staring at the white-faced girl. By that time Ring and Whitie had recognized him.

"Hello, Venters! I'm makin' you a visit," said Lassiter, slowly. "An' I'm surprised to see you've a—a young feller for company."

One glance had sufficed for the keen rider to read Bess's real sex, and for once his cool calm had deserted him. He stared till the white of Bess's cheeks flared into crimson. That, if it were needed, was the concluding evidence of her femininity; for it went fittingly with her sun-tinted hair and darkened, dilated eyes, the sweetness of her mouth, and the striking symmetry of her slender shape.

"Heavens! Lassiter!" panted Venters, when he caught his breath. "What relief—it's only you! How—in the name of all—that's wonderful—did you ever get here?"

"I trailed you. We—I wanted to know where you was, if you had a safe place. So I trailed you."

"Trailed me," cried Venters, bluntly.

"I reckon. It was some of a job after I got to them smooth rocks. I was all day trackin' you up to them little cut steps in the rock. The rest was easy."

"Where's your hoss? I hope you hid him."

"I tied him in them queer cedars down on the slope. He can't be seen from the valley."

"That's good. Well, well! I'm completely dumfounded. It was my idea that no man could track me in here."

"I reckon. But if there's a tracker in these uplands as good as me he can find you."

"That's bad. That'll worry me. But, Lassiter, now you're here I'm glad to see you. And—and my companion here is not a young fellow! . . . Bess, this is a friend of mine. He saved my life once."

The embarrassment of the moment did not extend to Lassiter. Almost at once his manner, as he shook hands with Bess, relieved Venters and put the girl at ease.

After Venters's words and one quick look at Lassiter, her agitation stilled, and, though she was shy, if she were conscious of anything out of the ordinary in the situation, certainly she did not show it.

"I reckon I'll only stay a little while," Lassiter was saying. "An' if you don't mind troublin', I'm hungry. I fetched some biscuits along, but they're gone. Venters, this place is sure the wonderfullest ever seen. Them cut steps on the slope! That outlet into the gorge! An' it's like climbin' up through hell into heaven to climb through that gorge into this valley! There's a queer-lookin' rock at the top of the passage. I didn't have time to stop. I'm wonderin' how you ever found this place. It's sure interestin'."

During the preparation and eating of dinner Lassiter listened mostly, as was his wont, and occasionally he spoke in his quaint and dry way. Venters noted, however, that the rider showed an increasing interest in Bess. He asked her no questions, and only directed his attention to her while she was occupied and had no opportunity to observe his scrutiny. It seemed to Venters that Lassiter grew more and more absorbed in his study of Bess, and that he lost his coolness in some strange, softening sympathy. Then, quite abruptly, he arose and announced the necessity for his early departure. He said good-by to Bess in a voice gentle and somewhat broken, and turned hurriedly away. Venters accompanied him, and they had traversed the terrace, climbed the weathered slope, and passed under the stone bridge before either spoke again.

Then Lassiter put a great hand on Venters's shoulder and wheeled him to meet a smoldering fire of gray eyes.

"Lassiter, I couldn't tell Jane! I couldn't," burst out Venters, reading his friend's mind. "I tried. But I couldn't. She wouldn't understand, and she has troubles enough. And I love the girl!"

"Venters, I reckon this beats me. I've seen some queer things in my time, too. This girl—who is she?"

"I don't know."

"Don't know! What is she, then?"

"I don't know that, either. Oh, it's the strangest story you ever heard. I must tell you. But you'll never believe."

"Venters, women were always puzzles to me. But for all that, if this girl ain't a child, an' as innocent, I'm no fit person to think of virtue an' goodness in anybody. Are you goin' to be square with her?"

"I am—so help me God!"

"I reckoned so. Mebbe my temper oughtn't led me to make sure. But, man, she's a woman in all but years. She's sweeter 'n the sage."

"Lassiter, I know, I know. And the *hell* of it is that in spite of her innocence and charm she's—she's not what she seems!"

"I wouldn't want to—of course, I couldn't call you a liar, Venters," said the older man.

"What's more, she was Oldring's Masked Rider!"

Venters expected to floor his friend with that statement, but he was not in any way prepared for the shock his words gave. For an instant he was astounded to see Lassiter stunned; then his own passionate eagerness to unbosom himself, to tell the wonderful story, precluded any other thought.

"Son, tell me all about this," presently said Lassiter as he seated himself on a stone and wiped his moist brow.

Thereupon Venters began his narrative at the point where he had shot the rustler and Oldring's Masked Rider, and he rushed through it, telling all, not holding back even Bess's unreserved avowal of her love or his deepest emotions.

"That's the story," he said, concluding. "I love her, though I've never told her. If I did tell her I'd be ready to marry her, and that seems impossible in this country. I'd be afraid to risk taking her anywhere. So I intend to do the best I can for her here."

"The longer I live the stranger life is," mused Lassiter, with downcast eyes. "I'm reminded of somethin' you once said to Jane about hands in her game of life. There's that unseen hand of power, an' Tull's black hand, an' my red one, an' your indifferent one, an' the girl's little brown, helpless one. An', Venters, there's another one that's all-wise an' all-wonderful. *That's* the hand guidin' Jane Withersteen's game of life! . . .Your story's one to daze a far clearer head than mine. I can't offer no advice, even if you asked for it. Mebbe I can help you. Anyway, I'll hold Oldrin' up when he comes to the village, an' find out about this girl. I knew the rustler years ago. He'll remember me."

"Lassiter, if I ever meet Oldring I'll kill him!" cried Venters, with sudden intensity.

"I reckon that'd be perfectly natural," replied the rider.

"Make him think Bess is dead—as she is to him and that old life."

"Sure, sure, son. Cool down now. If you're goin' to begin pullin' guns on Tull an' Oldin' you want to be cool. I reckon, though, you'd better keep hid here. Well, I must be leavin'."

"One thing, Lassiter. You'll not tell Jane about Bess? Please don't!"

"I reckon not. But I wouldn't be afraid to bet that after she'd got over anger at your secrecy—Venters, she'd be furious once in her life!—she'd think more of you. I don't mind sayin' for myself that I think you're a good deal of a man."

In the further ascent Venters halted several times with the intention of saying good-by, yet he changed his mind and kept on climbing till they reached Balancing Rock. Lassiter examined the huge rock, listened to Venters's idea of its position and suggestion, and curiously placed a strong hand upon it.

"Hold on!" cried Venters. "I heaved at it once and have never gotten over my scare."

"Well, you do seem uncommon nervous," replied Lassiter, much amused. "Now, as for me, why I always had the funniest notion to roll stones! When I was a kid I did it, an' the bigger I got the bigger stones I'd roll. Ain't that funny? Honest—even now I often get off my hoss just to tumble a big stone over a precipice, an' watch it drop, an' listen to it bang an' boom. I've started some slides in my time, an' don't you forget it. I never seen a rock I wanted to roll as bad as this one! Wouldn't there jest be roarin', crashin' hell down that trail?"

"You'd close the outlet forever!" exclaimed Venters. "Well, good-by, Lassiter. Keep my secret and don't forget me. And be mighty careful how you get out of the valley below. The rustlers' cañon isn't more than three miles up the Pass. Now you've tracked me here, I'll never feel safe again."

In his descent to the valley, Venters's emotion, roused to stirring pitch by the recital of his love story, quieted gradually, and in its place came a sober, thoughtful mood. All at once he saw that he was serious, because he would never more regain his sense of security while in the valley. What Lassiter could do another skilful tracker might duplicate. Among the many riders with whom Venters had ridden he recalled no one who could have taken his trail at Cottonwoods and have followed it to the edge of the bare slope in the pass, let alone up that glistening smooth stone.

Lassiter, however, was not an ordinary rider. Instead of hunting cattle tracks he had likely spent a goodly portion of his life tracking men. It was not improbable that among Oldring's rustlers there was one who shared Lassiter's gift for trailing. And the more Venters dwelt on this possibility the more perturbed he grew.

Lassiter's visit, moreover, had a disquieting effect upon Bess, and Venters fancied that she entertained the same thought as to future seclusion. The breaking of their solitude, though by a well-meaning friend, had not only dispelled all its dream and much of its charm, but had instilled a canker of fear. Both had seen the footprint in the sand.

Venters did no more work that day. Sunset and twilight gave way to night, and the cañon bird whistled its melancholy notes, and the wind sang softly in the cliffs, and the camp-fire blazed and burned down to red embers. To Venters a subtle difference was apparent in all of these, or else the shadowy change had been in him. He hoped that on the morrow this slight depression would have passed away.

In that measure, however, he was doomed to disappointment. Furthermore, Bess reverted to a wistful sadness that he had not observed in her since her recovery. His attempt to cheer her out of it resulted in dismal failure, and consequently in a darkening of his own mood. Hard work relieved him; still, when the day had passed, his unrest returned. Then he set to deliberate thinking, and there came to him the startling conviction that he must leave Surprise Valley and take Bess with him. As a rider he had taken many chances, and as an adventurer in Deception Pass he had unhesitatingly risked his life; but now he would run no preventable hazard of Bess's safety and happiness, and he was too keen not to see that hazard. It gave him a pang to think of leaving the beautiful valley just when he had the means to establish a permanent and delightful home there. One flashing thought tore in hot temptation through his mind—why not climb up into the gorge, roll Balancing Rock down the trail, and close forever the outlet to Deception Pass? "That was the beast in me—showing his teeth!" muttered Venters, scornfully. "I'll just kill him good and quick! I'll be fair to this girl, if it's the last thing I do on earth!"

Another day went by, in which he worked less and pondered more and all the time covertly watched Bess. Her wistfulness had deepened into downright unhappiness, and that made his task to tell her all the harder. He kept the secret another day, hoping by some chance she might grow less moody, and to his exceeding anxiety she fell into far deeper gloom. Out of his own secret and the torment of it he divined that she, too, had a secret and the keeping of it was torturing her. As yet he had no plan thought out in regard to how or when to leave the valley, but he decided to tell her the necessity of it and to persuade her to go. Furthermore, he hoped his speaking out would induce her to unburden her own mind.

"Bess, what's wrong with you?" he asked.

"Nothing," she answered, with averted face.

Venters took hold of her gently, though masterfully, forced her to meet his eyes.

"You can't look at me and lie," he said. "Now—what's wrong with you? You're keeping something from me. Well, I've got a secret, too, and I intend to tell it presently."

"Oh—I *have* a secret. I was crazy to tell you when you came back. That's why I was so silly about everything. I kept holding my secret back—gloating over it. But when Lassiter came I got an idea—that changed my mind. Then I hated to tell you."

"Are you going to now?"

"Yes—yes. I was coming to it. I tried yesterday, but you were so cold. I was afraid. I couldn't keep it much longer."

"Very well, most mysterious lady, tell your wonderful secret."

"You needn't laugh," she retorted, with a first glimpse of reviving spirit. "I can take the laugh out of you in one second."

"It's a go."

She ran through the spruces to the cave, and returned carrying something which was manifestly heavy. Upon nearer view he saw that whatever she held with such evident importance had been bound up in a black scarf he well remembered. That alone was sufficient to make him tingle with curiosity.

"Have you any idea what I did in your absence?" she asked.

"I imagine you lounged about, waiting and watching for me," he replied, smiling. "I've my share of conceit, you know."

"You're wrong. I worked. Look at my hands." She dropped on her knees close to where he sat, and, carefully depositing the black bundle, she held out her hands. The palms and inside of her fingers were white, puckered, and worn.

"Why, Bess, you've been fooling in the water," he said.

"Fooling? Look here!" With deft fingers she spread open the black scarf, and the bright sun shone upon a dull, glittering heap of gold.

"Gold!" he ejaculated.

"Yes, gold! See, pounds of gold! I found it—washed it out of the stream—picked it out grain by grain, nugget by nugget!"

"Gold!" he cried.

"Yes. Now—now laugh at my secret!"

For a long minute Venters gazed. Then he stretched forth a hand to feel if the gold was real.

"Gold!" he almost shouted. "Bess, there are hundreds—thousands of dollars' worth here!"

He leaned over to her, and put his hand, strong and clenching now, on hers.

"Is there more where this came from?" he whispered.

"Plenty of it, all the way up the stream to the cliff. You know I've often washed for gold. Then I've heard the men talk. I think there's no great quantity of gold here, but enough for—for a fortune for *you.*"

"That—was—your—secret!"

"Yes. I hate gold. For it makes men mad. I've seen them drunk with joy and dance and fling themselves around. I've seen them curse and rave. I've seen them fight like dogs and roll in the dust. I've seen them kill each other for gold."

"Is that why you hated to tell me?"

"Not—not altogether." Bess lowered her head. "It was because I knew you'd never stay here long after you found gold."

"You were afraid I'd leave you?"

"Yes."

"Listen! . . . You great, simple child! Listen . . . You sweet, wonderful, wild, blue-eyed girl! I was tortured by my secret. It was that I knew we—*we* must leave the valley. We can't stay here much longer. I couldn't think how we'd get away—out of the country—or how we'd live, if we ever got out. I'm a beggar. That's why I kept my secret. I'm poor. It takes money to make way beyond Sterling. We couldn't ride horses or burros or walk forever. So while I knew we must go, I was distracted over how to go and what to do. *Now!* We've gold! Once beyond Sterling, we'll be safe from rustlers. We've no others to fear.

"Oh! Listen! Bess!" Venters now heard his voice ringing high and sweet, and he felt Bess's cold hands in his crushing grasp as she leaned toward him pale, breathless. "This is how much I'd leave you! You made me live again! I'll take you away—far away from this wild country. You'll begin a new life. You'll be happy. You shall see cities, ships, people. You shall have anything your heart craves. All the shame and sorrow of your life shall be forgotten—as if they had never been. This is how much I'd leave you here alone—you sad-eyed girl. I love you! Didn't you know it? How could you fail to know it? I love you! I'm free! I'm a man—a man you've made—no more a beggar! . . . Kiss me! This is how much I'd leave you here alone—you beautiful, strange, unhappy girl. But I'll make you happy. What—what do I care for—your past! I love you! I'll take you home to Illinois—to my mother. Then I'll take you to far places. I'll make up all you've lost. Oh, I know you love me—knew it before you told me. And it changed my life. And you'll go with me, not as my companion as you are here, nor my sister, but, Bess, darling! . . . *As my wife!*"

CHAPTER SEVENTEEN
Wrangle's Race Run

The plan eventually decided upon by the lovers was for Venters to go to the village, secure a horse and some kind of a disguise for Bess, or at least less striking apparel than her present garb, and to return post-haste to the valley. Meanwhile, she would add to their store of gold. Then they would strike the long and perilous trail to ride out of Utah. In the event of his inability to fetch back a horse for her, they intended to make the giant sorrel carry double. The gold, a little food, saddle blankets, and Venters's guns were to compose the light outfit with which they would make the start.

"I love this beautiful place," said Bess. "It's hard to think of leaving it."

"Hard! Well, I should think so," replied Venters. "Maybe—in years—" But he did not complete in words his thought that might be possible to return after many years of absence and change.

Once again Bess bade Venters farewell under the shadow of Balancing Rock, and this time it was with whispered hope and tenderness and passionate trust. Long after he had left her, all down through the outlet to the Pass, the clinging clasp of her arms, the sweetness of her lips, and the sense of a new and exquisite birth of character in her remained hauntingly and thrillingly in his mind. The girl who had sadly called herself nameless and nothing had been marvelously transformed in the moment of his avowal of love. It was something to think over, something to warm his heart, but for the present it had absolutely to be forgotten so that all his mind could be addressed to the trip so fraught with danger.

He carried only his rifle, revolver, and a small quantity of bread and meat; and thus lightly burdened, he made swift progress down the slope and out into the valley. Darkness was coming on, and he welcomed it. Stars were blinking when he reached his old hiding-place in the split of cañon wall, and by their aid he slipped through the dense thickets to the grassy enclosure. Wrangle stood in the center of it with his head up, and he appeared black and of gigantic proportions in the dim light. Venters whistled softly, began a slow approach, and then called. The horse snorted and, plunging away with dull, heavy sound of hoofs, he disappeared in the gloom. "Wilder than ever!" muttered Venters. He followed the sorrel into the narrowing split between the walls, and presently had to desist because he could not see a foot in advance. As he went back toward the open Wrangle jumped out of an ebony shadow of cliff and like a thunderbolt shot huge and black past him down into the starlit glade. Deciding that all attempts to catch Wrangle at night would be useless, Venters repaired to the shelving rock where he had hidden saddle and blanket, and there went to sleep.

The first peep of day found him stirring, and as soon as it was light enough to distinguish objects, he took his lasso off his saddle and went out to rope the sorrel. He espied Wrangle at the lower end of the cove and approached him in a perfectly natural manner. When he got near enough, Wrangle evidently recognized him, but was too wild to stand. He ran up the glade and on into the narrow lane between the walls. This favored Venters's speedy capture of the horse, so, coiling his noose ready to throw, he hurried on. Wrangle let Venters get to within a hundred feet and then he broke. But as he plunged by, rapidly getting into his stride, Venters made a perfect throw with the rope. He had time to brace himself for the shock; nevertheless, Wrangle threw him and dragged him several yards before halting.

"You wild devil," said Venters, as he slowly pulled Wrangle up. "Don't you know me? Come now—old fellow—so—so—"

Wrangle yielded to the lasso and then to Venters's strong hand. He was as straggly and wild-looking as a horse left to roam free in the sage. He dropped his long ears and stood readily to be saddled and bridled. But he was exceedingly sensitive, and quivered at every touch and sound. Venters led him to the thicket, and, bending the close saplings to let him squeeze through, at length reached the open. Sharp survey in each direction assured him of the usual lonely nature of the cañon; then he was in the saddle, riding south.

Wrangle's long, swinging canter was a wonderful ground-gainer. His stride was almost twice that of an ordinary horse, and his endurance was equally remarkable. Venters pulled him in occasionally, and walked him up the stretches of rising ground and along the soft washes. Wrangle had never yet shown any indication of distress while Venters rode him. Nevertheless, there was now reason to save the horse; therefore Venters did not resort to the hurry that had characterized his former trip. He camped at the last water in the Pass. What distance that was to Cottonwoods he did not know; he calculated, however, that it was in the neighborhood of fifty miles.

Early in the morning he proceeded on his way, and about the middle of the forenoon reached the constricted gap that marked the southerly end of the Pass, and through which led the trail up to the sage-level. He spied out Lassiter's tracks in the dust, but no others, and dismounting, he straightened out Wrangle's bridle and began to lead him up the trail. The short climb, more severe on beast than on man, necessitated a rest on the level above, and during this he scanned the wide purple reaches of slope.

Wrangle whistled his pleasure at the smell of the sage. Remounting, Venters headed up the white trail with the fragrant wind in his face. He had proceeded for perhaps a couple of miles when Wrangle stopped with a suddenness that threw Venters heavily against the pommel.

"What's wrong, old boy?" called Venters, looking down for a loose shoe or a snake or a foot lamed by a picked-up stone. Unrewarded, he raised himself from his scrutiny. Wrangle stood stiff, head high, with his long ears erect. Thus guided, Venters swiftly gazed ahead to make out a dust-clouded, dark group of horsemen riding down the slope. If they had seen him, it apparently made no difference in their speed or direction.

"Wonder who they are!" exclaimed Venters. He was not disposed to run. His cool mood tightened under grip of excitement as he reflected that, whoever the approaching riders, were, they could not be friends. He slipped out of the saddle and led Wrangle behind the tallest sage-brush. It might serve to conceal them until the riders were close enough for him to see who they were; after that he would be indifferent to how soon they discovered him.

After looking to his rifle and ascertaining that it was in working order, he watched, and as he watched, slowly the force of a bitter fierceness, long dormant, gathered ready to flame into life. If those riders were not rustlers he had forgotten how rustlers looked and rode. On they came, a small group, so compact and dark that he could not tell their number. How unusual that their horses did not see Wrangle! But such failure, Venters decided, was owing to the speed with which they were traveling. They moved at a swift canter affected more by rustlers than by riders. Venters grew concerned over the possibility that these horsemen would actually ride down on him before he had a chance to tell what to expect. When they were within three hundred yards he deliberately led Wrangle out into the trail.

Then he heard shots, and the hard scrape of sliding hoofs, and saw horses rear and plunge back with up-flung heads and flying manes. Several little white puffs of smoke appeared sharply against the black background of riders and horses, and shots rang out. Bullets struck far in front of Venters, and whipped up the dust and then hummed low into the sage. The range was great for revolvers, but whether the shots were meant to kill or merely to check advance, they were enough to fire that waiting ferocity in Venters. Slipping his arm through the bridle, so that Wrangle could not get away, Venters lifted his rifle and pulled the trigger twice.

He saw the first horseman lean sideways and fall. He saw another lurch in his saddle and heard a cry of pain. Then Wrangle, plunging in fright, lifted Venters and nearly threw him. He jerked the horse down with a powerful hand and leaped into the saddle. Wrangle plunged again, dragging his bridle, that Venters had not had time to throw in place. Bending over with a swift movement, he secured it and dropped the loop over the pommel. Then, with grinding teeth, he looked to see what the issue would be.

The band had scattered so as not to afford such a broad mark for bullets. The riders faced Venters, some with red-belching guns. He heard a sharper report, and just as Wrangle plunged again he caught the whizz of a leaden missile that would have hit him but for Wrangle's sudden jump. A swift, hot wave, turning cold, passed over Venters. Deliberately he picked out the one rider with a carbine, and killed him. Wrangle snorted shrilly and bolted into the sage. Venters let him run a few rods, then with iron arm checked him.

Five riders, surely rustlers, were left. One leaped out of the saddle to secure his fallen comrade's carbine. A shot from Venters, which missed the man but sent the dust flying over him, made him run back to his horse. Then they separated. The crippled rider went one way; the one frustrated in his attempt to get the carbine rode another; Venters thought he made out a third rider, carrying a strange-appearing bundle and disappearing in the sage. But in the rapidity of action and vision he could not discern what it was. Two riders with three horses swung out to the right. Afraid of the long rifle—a burdensome weapon seldom carried by rustlers or riders—they had been put to rout.

Suddenly Venters discovered that one of the two men last noted was riding Jane Withersteen's horse Bells—the beautiful bay racer she had given to Lassiter. Venters uttered a savage outcry. Then the small, wiry, frog-like shape of the second rider, and the ease and grace of his seat in the saddle—things so strikingly incongruous—grew more and more familiar in Venters's sight.

"Jerry Card!" cried Venters.

It was indeed Tull's right-hand man. Such a white hot wrath inflamed Venters that he fought himself to see with clearer gaze.

"It's Jerry Card!" he exclaimed, instantly. *"And he's riding Black Star and leading Night!"*

The long-kindling, stormy fire in Venters's heart burst into flame. He spurred Wrangle, and as the horse lengthened his stride Venters slipped cartridges into the magazine of his rifle till it was once again full. Card and his companion were now half a mile or more in advance, riding easily down the slope. Venters marked the smooth gait, and understood it when Wrangle galloped out of the sage into the broad cattle trail, down which Venters had once tracked Jane Withersteen's red herd. This hard-packed trail, from years of use, was as clean and smooth as a road. Venters saw Jerry Card look back over his shoulder; the other rider did likewise. Then the three racers lengthened their stride to the point where the swinging canter was ready to break into a gallop.

"Wrangle, the race's on," said Venters, grimly. "We'll canter with them and gallop with them and run with them. We'll let them set the pace."

Venters knew he bestrode the strongest, swiftest, most tireless horse ever ridden by any rider across the Utah uplands. Recalling Jane Withersteen's devoted assurance that Night could run neck and neck with Wrangle, and Black Star could show his heels to him, Venters wished that Jane were there to see the race to recover her blacks and in the unqualified superiority of the giant sorrel. Then Venters found himself thankful that she was absent, for he meant that race to end in Jerry Card's death. The first flush, the raging of Venters's wrath, passed, to leave him in sullen, almost cold possession of his will. It was a deadly mood, utterly foreign to his nature, engendered, fostered, and released by the wild passions of wild men in a wild country. The strength in him then—the thing rife in him that was not hate, but something as remorseless—might have been the fiery fruition of a whole lifetime of vengeful quest. Nothing could have stopped him.

Venters thought out the race shrewdly. The rider on Bells would probably drop behind and take to the sage. What he did was of little moment to Venters. To stop Jerry Card, his evil hidden career as well as his present flight, and then to catch the blacks—that was all that concerned Venters. The cattle trail wound for miles and miles down the slope. Venters saw with a rider's keen vision ten, fifteen, twenty miles of clear purple sage. There were no on-coming riders or rustlers to aid Card. His only chance to escape lay in abandoning the stolen horses and creeping away in the sage to hide. In ten miles Wrangle could run Black Star and Night off their feet, and in fifteen he could kill them outright. So Venters held the sorrel in, letting Card make the running. It was a long race that would save the blacks.

In a few miles of that swinging canter Wrangle had crept appreciably closer to the three horses. Jerry Card turned again, and when he saw how the sorrel had gained, he put Black Star to a gallop. Night and Bells, on either side of him, swept into his stride.

Venters loosened the rein on Wrangle and let him break into a gallop. The sorrel saw the horses ahead and wanted to run. But Venters restrained him. And in the gallop he gained more than in the canter. Bells was fast in that gait, but Black Star and Night had been trained to run. Slowly Wrangle closed the gap down to a quarter of a mile, and crept closer and closer.

Jerry Card wheeled once more. Venters distinctly saw the red flash of his red face. This time he looked long. Venters laughed. He knew what passed in Card's mind. The rider was trying to make out what horse it happened to be that thus gained on Jane Withersteen's peerless racers. Wrangle had so long been away from the village that not improbably Jerry had forgotten. Besides, whatever Jerry's qualifications for his fame as the greatest rider of the sage, certain it was that his best point was not far-sightedness. He had not recognized Wrangle. After what must have been a searching gaze he got his comrade to face about. This action gave Venters amusement. It spoke so surely of the fact that neither Card nor the rustler actually knew their danger. Yet if they kept to the trail—and the last thing such men would do would be to leave it—they were both doomed.

This comrade of Card's whirled far around in his saddle, and he even shaded his eyes from the sun. He, too, looked long. Then, all at once, he faced ahead again and, bending lower in the saddle, began to fling his right arm up and down. That flinging Venters knew to be the lashing of Bells. Jerry also became active. And the three racers lengthened out into a run.

"Now, Wrangle!" cried Venters. "Run, you big devil! Run!"

Venters laid the reins on Wrangle's neck and dropped the loop over the pommel. The sorrel needed no guiding on that smooth trail. He was surer-footed in a run than at any other fast gait, and his running gave the impression of something devilish. He might now have been actuated by Venters's spirit; undoubtedly his savage running fitted the mood of his rider. Venters bent forward, swinging with the horse, and gripped his rifle. His eye measured the distance between him and Jerry Card.

In less than two miles of running Bells began to drop behind the blacks, and Wrangle began to overhaul him. Venters anticipated that the rustler would soon take to the sage. Yet he did not. Not improbably he reasoned that the powerful sorrel could more easily overtake Bells in the heavier going outside of the trail. Soon only a few hundred yards lay between Bells and Wrangle. Turning in his saddle, the rustler began to shoot, and the bullets beat up little whiffs of dust. Venters raised his rifle, ready to take snap shots, and waited for favorable opportunity when Bells was out of line with the forward horses. Venters had it in him to kill these men as if they were skunk-bitten coyotes, but also he had restraint enough to keep from shooting one of Jane's beloved Arabians.

No great distance was covered, however, before Bells swerved to the left, out of line with Black Star and Night. Then Venters, aiming high and waiting for the pause between Wrangle's great strides, began to take snap shots at the rustler. The fleeing rider presented a broad target for a rifle, but he was moving swiftly forward and bobbing up and down. Moreover, shooting from Wrangle's back was shooting from a thunderbolt. And added to that was the danger of a low-placed bullet taking effect on Bells. Yet, despite these considerations, making the shot exceedingly difficult, Venters's confidence, like his implacability, saw a speedy and fatal termination of that rustler's race. On the sixth shot the rustler threw up his arms and took a flying tumble off his horse. He rolled over and over, hunched himself to a half-erect position, fell, and then dragged himself into the sage. As Venters went thundering by he peered keenly into the sage, but caught no sign of the man. Bells ran a few hundred yards, slowed up, and had stopped when Wrangle passed him.

Again Venters began slipping fresh cartridges into the magazine of his rifle, and his hand was so sure and steady that he did not drop a single cartridge. With the eye of a rider and the judgment of a marksman he once more measured the distance between him and Jerry Card. Wrangle had gained, bringing him into rifle range. Venters was hard put to it now not to shoot, but thought it better to withhold his fire. Jerry, who, in anticipation of a running fusillade, had huddled himself into a little twisted ball on Black Star's neck, now surmising that this pursuer would make sure of not wounding one of the blacks, rose to his natural seat in the saddle.

In his mind perhaps, as certainly as in Venters's, this moment was the beginning of the real race.

Venters leaned forward to put his hand on Wrangle's neck; then backward to put it on his flank. Under the shaggy, dusty hair trembled and vibrated and rippled a wonderful muscular activity. But Wrangle's flesh was still cold. What a cold-blooded brute, thought Venters, and felt in him a love for the horse he had never given to any other. It would not have been humanly possible for any rider, even though clutched by hate or revenge or a passion to save a loved one or fear of his own life, to be astride the sorrel, to swing with his swing, to see his magnificent stride and hear the rapid thunder of his hoofs, to ride him in that race and not glory in the ride.

So, with his passion to kill still keen and unabated, Venters lived out that ride, and drank a rider's sage-sweet cup of wildness to the dregs.

When Wrangle's long mane, lashing in the wind, stung Venters in the cheek, the sting added a beat to his flying pulse. He bent a downward glance to try to see Wrangle's actual stride, and saw only twinkling, darting streaks and the white rush of the trail. He watched the sorrel's savage head, pointed level, his mouth still closed and dry, but his nostrils distended as if he were snorting unseen fire. Wrangle was the horse for a race with death. Upon each side Venters saw the sage merged into a sailing, colorless wall. In front sloped the lay of ground with its purple breadth split by the white trail. The wind, blowing with heavy, steady blast into his face, sickened him with enduring, sweet odor, and filled his ears with a hollow, rushing roar.

Then for the hundredth time he measured the width of space separating him from Jerry Card. Wrangle had ceased to gain. The blacks were proving their fleetness. Venters watched Jerry Card, admiring the little rider's horsemanship. He had the incomparable seat of the upland rider, born in the saddle. It struck Venters that Card had changed his position, or the position of the horses. Presently Venters remembered positively that Jerry had been leading Night on the right-hand side of the trail. The racer was now on the side to the left. No—it was Black Star. But, Venters argued in amaze, Jerry had been mounted on Black Star. Another clearer, keener gaze assured Venters that Black Star was really riderless. Night now carried Jerry Card.

"He's changed from one to the other!" ejaculated Venters, realizing the astounding feat with unstinted admiration. "Changed at full speed! Jerry Card, that's what you've done unless I'm drunk on the smell of sage. But I've got to see the trick before I believe it."

Thenceforth, while Wrangle sped on, Venters glued his eyes to the little rider. Jerry Card rode as only he could ride. Of all the daring horsemen of the uplands, Jerry was the one rider fitted to bring out the greatness of the blacks in that long race. He had them on a dead run, but not yet at the last strained and killing pace. From time to time he glanced backward, as a wise general in retreat calculating his chances and the power and speed of pursuers, and the moment for the last desperate burst. No doubt, Card, with his life at stake, gloried in that race, perhaps more wildly than Venters. For he had been born to the sage and the saddle and the wild. He was more than half horse. Not until the last call—the sudden up-flashing instinct of self-preservation—would he lose his skill and judgment and nerve and the spirit of that race. Venters seemed to read Jerry's mind. That little crime-stained rider was actually thinking of his horses, husbanding their speed, handling them with knowledge of years, glorying in their beautiful, swift, racing stride, and wanting them to win the race when his own life hung suspended in quivering balance. Again Jerry whirled in his saddle and the sun flashed red on his face. Turning, he drew Black Star closer and closer toward Night, till they ran side by side, as one horse. Then Card raised himself in the saddle, slipped out of the stirrups, and, somehow twisting himself, leaped upon Black Star. He did not even lose the swing of the horse. Like a leech he was there in the other saddle, and as the horses separated, his right foot, that had been apparently doubled under him, shot down to catch the stirrup. The grace and dexterity and daring of that rider's act won something more than admiration from Venters.

For the distance of a mile Jerry rode Black Star and then changed back to Night. But all Jerry's skill and the running of the blacks could avail little more against the sorrel.

Venters peered far ahead, studying the lay of the land. Straight-away for five miles the trail stretched, and then it disappeared in hummocky ground. To the right, some few rods, Venters saw a break in the sage, and this was the rim of Deception Pass. Across the dark cleft gleamed the red of the opposite wall. Venters imagined that the trail went down into the Pass somewhere north of those ridges. And he realized that he must and would overtake Jerry Card in this straight course of five miles.

Cruelly he struck his spurs into Wrangle's flanks. A light touch of spur was sufficient to make Wrangle plunge. And now, with a ringing, wild snort, he seemed to double up in muscular convulsions and to shoot forward with an impetus that almost unseated Venters. The sage blurred by, the trail flashed by, and the wind robbed him of breath and hearing. Jerry Card turned once more. And the way he shifted to Black Star showed he had to make his last desperate running. Venters aimed to the side of the trail and sent a bullet puffing the dust beyond Jerry. Venters hoped to frighten the rider and get him to take to the sage. But Jerry returned the shot, and his ball struck dangerously close in the dust at Wrangle's flying feet. Venters held his fire then, while the rider emptied his revolver. For a mile, with Black Star leaving Night behind and doing his utmost, Wrangle did not gain; for another mile he gained little, if at all. In the third he caught up with the now galloping Night and began to gain rapidly on the other black.

Only a hundred yards now stretched between Black Star and Wrangle. The giant sorrel thundered on—and on—and on. In every yard he gained a foot. He was whistling through his nostrils, wringing wet, flying lather, and as hot as fire. Savage as ever, strong as ever, fast as ever, but each tremendous stride jarred Venters out of the saddle! Wrangle's power and spirit and momentum had begun to run him off his legs. Wrangle's great race was nearly won—and run. Venters seemed to see the expanse before him as a vast, sheeted, purple plain sliding under him. Black Star moved in it as a blur. The rider, Jerry Card, appeared a mere dot bobbing dimly. Wrangle thundered on—on—on! Venters felt the increase in quivering, straining shock after every leap. Flecks of foam flew into Venters's eyes, burning him, making him see all the sage as red. But in that red haze he saw, or seemed to see, Black Star suddenly riderless and with broken gait. Wrangle thundered on to change his pace with a violent break. Then Venters pulled him hard. From run to gallop, gallop to canter, canter to trot, trot to walk, and walk to stop, the great sorrel ended his race.

Venters looked back. Black Star stood riderless in the trail. Jerry Card had taken to the sage. Far up the white trail Night came trotting faithfully down. Venters leaped off, still half blind, reeling dizzily. In a moment he had recovered sufficiently to have a care for Wrangle. Rapidly he took off the saddle and bridle. The sorrel was reeking, heaving, whistling, shaking. But he had still the strength to stand, and for him Venters had no fears.

As Venters ran back to Black Star he saw the horse stagger on shaking legs into the sage and go down in a heap. Upon reaching him Venters removed the saddle and bridle. Black Star had been killed on his legs, Venters thought. He had no hope for the stricken horse. Black Star lay flat, covered with bloody froth, mouth wide, tongue hanging, eyes glaring, and all his beautiful body in convulsions.

Unable to stay there to see Jane's favorite racer die, Venters hurried up the trail to meet the other black. On the way he kept a sharp lookout for Jerry Card. Venters imagined the rider would keep well out of range of the rifle, but, as he would be lost on the sage without a horse, not improbably he would linger in the vicinity on the chance of getting back one of the blacks. Night soon came trotting up, hot and wet and run out. Venters led him down near the others, and unsaddling him, let him loose to rest. Night wearily lay down in the dust and rolled, proving himself not yet spent.

Then Venters sat down to rest and think. Whatever the risk, he was compelled to stay where he was, or comparatively near, for the night. The horses must rest and drink. He must find water. He was now seventy miles from Cottonwoods, and, he believed, close to the cañon where the cattle trail must surely turn off and go down into the Pass. After a while he rose to survey the valley.

He was very near to the ragged edge of a deep cañon into which the trail turned. The ground lay in uneven ridges divided by washes, and these sloped into the cañon. Following the cañon line, he saw where its rim was broken by other intersecting cañons, and farther down red walls and yellow cliffs leading toward a deep blue cleft that he made sure was Deception Pass. Walking out a few rods to a promontory, he found where the trail went down. The descent was gradual, along a stone-walled trail, and Venters felt sure that this was the place where Oldring drove cattle into the Pass. There was, however, no indication at all that he ever had driven cattle out at this point. Oldring had many holes to his burrow.

In searching round in the little hollows Venters, much to his relief, found water. He composed himself to rest and eat some bread and meat, while he waited for a sufficient time to elapse so that he could safely give the horses a drink. He judged the hour to be somewhere around noon. Wrangle lay down to rest and Night followed suit. So long as they were down Venters intended to make no move. The longer they rested the better, and the safer it would be to give them water. By and by he forced himself to go over to where Black Star lay, expecting to find him dead. Instead he found the racer partially if not wholly recovered. There was recognition, even fire, in his big black eyes. Venters was overjoyed. He sat by the black for a long time. Black Star presently labored to his feet with a heave and a groan, shook himself, and snorted for water. Venters repaired to the little pool he had found, filled his sombrero, and gave the racer a drink. Black Star gulped it at one draught, as if it were but a drop, and pushed his nose into the hat and snorted for more. Venters now led Night down to drink, and after a further time Black Star also. Then the blacks began to graze.

The sorrel had wandered off down the sage between the trail and the cañon. Once or twice he disappeared in little swales. Finally Venters concluded Wrangle had grazed far enough, and, taking his lasso, he went to fetch him back. In crossing from one ridge to another he saw where the horse had made muddy a pool of water. It occurred to Venters then that Wrangle had drunk his fill, and did not seem the worse for it, and might be anything but easy to catch. And, true enough, he could not come within roping reach of the sorrel. He tried for an hour, and gave up in disgust. Wrangle did not seem so wild as simply perverse. In a quandary Venters returned to the other horses, hoping much, yet doubting more, that when Wrangle had grazed to suit himself he might be caught.

As the afternoon wore away Venters's concern diminished, yet he kept close watch on the blacks and the trail and the sage. There was no telling of what Jerry Card might be capable. Venters sullenly acquiesced to the idea that the rider had been too quick and too shrewd for him. Strangely and doggedly, however, Venters clung to his foreboding of Card's downfall.

The wind died away; the red sun topped the far distant western rise of slope; and the long, creeping purple shadows lengthened. The rims of the cañons gleamed crimson and the deep clefts appeared to belch forth blue smoke. Silence enfolded the scene.

It was broken by a horrid, long-drawn scream of a horse and the thudding of heavy hoofs. Venters sprang erect and wheeled south. Along the cañon rim, near the edge, came Wrangle, once more in thundering flight.

Venters gasped in amazement. Had the wild sorrel gone mad? His head was high and twisted, in a most singular position for a running horse. Suddenly Venters descried a frog-like shape clinging to Wrangle's neck. Jerry Card! Somehow he had straddled Wrangle and now stuck like a huge burr. But it was his strange position and the sorrel's wild scream that shook Venters's nerves. Wrangle was pounding toward the turn where the trail went down. He plunged onward like a blind horse. More than one of his leaps took him to the very edge of the precipice.

Jerry Card was bent forward with his teeth fast in the front of Wrangle's nose! Venters saw it, and there flashed over him a memory of this trick of a few desperate riders. He even thought of one rider who had worn off his teeth in this terrible hold to break or control desperate horses. Wrangle had indeed gone mad. The marvel was what guided him. Was it the half-brute, the more than half-horse instinct of Jerry Card? Whatever the mystery, it was true. And in a few more rods Jerry would have the sorrel turning into the trail leading down into the cañon.

"No—Jerry!" whispered Venters, stepping forward and throwing up the rifle. He tried to catch the little humped, frog-like shape over the sights. It was moving too fast; it was too small. Yet Venters shot once . . . twice . . . the third time . . . four times . . . five! All wasted shots and precious seconds!

With a deep-muttered curse Venters caught Wrangle through the sights and pulled the trigger. Plainly he heard the bullet thud. Wrangle uttered a horrible strangling sound. In swift death action he whirled, and with one last splendid leap he cleared the cañon rim. And he whirled downward with the little frog-like shape clinging to his neck!

There was a pause which seemed never ending, a shock, and an instant's silence.

Then up rolled a heavy crash, a long roar of sliding rocks dying away in distant echo, then silence unbroken.

Wrangle's race was run.

CHAPTER EIGHTEEN
Oldring's Knell

Some forty hours or more later Venters created a commotion in Cottonwoods by riding down the main street on Black Star and leading Bells and Night. He had come upon Bells grazing near the body of a dead rustler, the only incident of his quick ride into the village.

Nothing was farther from Venters's mind than bravado. No thought came to him of the defiance and boldness of riding Jane Withersteen's racers straight into the archplotter's stronghold. He wanted men to see the famous Arabians; he wanted men to see them dirty and dusty, bearing all the signs of having been driven to their limit; he wanted men to see and to know that the thieves who had ridden them out into the sage had not ridden them back. Venters had come for that and for more—he wanted to meet Tull face to face; if not Tull, then Dyer; if not Dyer, then anyone in the secret of these master conspirators. Such was Venters's passion. The meeting with the rustlers, the unprovoked attack upon him, the spilling of blood, the recognition of Jerry Card and the horses, the race, and that last plunge of mad Wrangle—all these things, fuel on fuel to the smoldering fire, had kindled and swelled and leaped into living flame. He could have shot Dyer in the midst of his religious services at the alter; he could have killed Tull in front of wives and babes.

He walked the three racers down the broad, green-bordered village road. He heard the murmur of running water from Amber Spring. Bitter waters for Jane Withersteen! Men and women stopped to gaze at him and the horses. All knew him; all knew the blacks and the bay. As well as if it had been spoken, Venters read in the faces of men the intelligence that Jane Withersteen's Arabians had been known to have been stolen. Venters reined in and halted before Dyer's residence. It was a low, long, stone structure resembling Withersteen House. The spacious front yard was green and luxuriant with grass and flowers; gravel walks led to the huge porch; a well-trimmed hedge of purple sage separated the yard from the church grounds; birds sang in the trees, water flowed musically along the walks; and there were glad, careless shouts of children. For Venters the beauty of this home, and the serenity and its apparent happiness, all turned red and black. For Venters a shade overspread the lawn, the flowers, the old vine-clad stone house. In the music of the singing birds, in the murmur of the running water, he heard an ominous sound. Quiet beauty—sweet music—innocent laughter! By what monstrous abortion of fate did these abide in the shadow of Dyer?

Venters rode on and stopped before Tull's cottage. Women stared at him with white faces and then flew from the porch. Tull himself appeared at the door, bent low, craning his neck. His dark face flashed out of sight; the door banged; a heavy bar dropped with a hollow sound.

Then Venters shook Black Star's bridle, and, sharply trotting, led the other horses to the center of the village. Here at the intersecting streets and in front of the stores he halted once more. The usual lounging atmosphere of that prominent corner was not now in evidence. Riders and ranchers and villagers broke up what must have been absorbing conversation. There was a rush of many feet, and then the walk was lined with faces.

Venters's glance swept down the line of silent stone-faced men. He recognized many riders and villagers, but none of those he had hoped to meet. There was no expression in the faces turned toward him. All of them knew him, most were inimical, but there were few who were not burning with curiosity and wonder in regard to the return of Jane Withersteen's racers. Yet all were silent. Here were the familiar characteristics—masked feeling—strange secretiveness—expressionless expression of mystery and hidden power.

"Has anybody here seen Jerry Card?" queried Venters, in a loud voice.

In reply there came not a word, not a nod or shake of head, not so much as dropping eye or twitching lip—nothing but a quiet, stony stare.

"Been under the knife? You've a fine knife-wielder here—one Tull, I believe! . . . Maybe you've all had your tongues cut out?"

This passionate sarcasm of Venters brought no response, and the stony calm was as oil on the fire within him.

"I see some of you pack guns, too!" he added, in biting scorn. In the long, tense pause, strung keenly as a tight wire, he sat motionless on Black Star. "All right," he went on. "Then let some of you take this message to Tull. Tell him I've seen Jerry Card! . . . Tell him Jerry Card *will never return!*"

Thereupon, in the same dead calm, Venters backed Black Star away from the curb, into the street, and out of range. He was ready now to ride up to Withersteen House and turn the racers over to Jane.

"Hello, Venters!" a familiar voice cried, hoarsely, and he saw a man running toward him. It was the rider Judkins who came up and gripped Venters's hand. "Venters, I could hev dropped when I seen them hosses. But thet sight ain't a marker to the looks of you. What's wrong? Hev you gone crazy? You must be crazy to ride in here this way—with them hosses—talkin' thet way about Tull an' Jerry Card."

"Jud, I'm not crazy—only mad clean through," replied Venters.

"Wal, now, Bern, I'm glad to hear some of your old self in your voice. Fer when you come up you looked like the corpse of a dead rider with fire fer eyes. You hed thet crowd too stiff fer throwin' guns. Come, we've got to hev a talk. Let's go up the lane. We ain't much safe here."

Judkins mounted Bells and rode with Venters up to the cottonwood grove. Here they dismounted and went among the trees.

"Let's hear from you first," said Judkins. "You fetched back them hosses. Thet *is* the trick. An', of course, you got Jerry the same as you got Horne."

"Horne!"

"Sure. He was found dead yesterday all chewed by coyotes, an' he'd been shot plumb center."

"Where was he found?"

"At the split down the trail—you know where Oldrin's cattle trail runs off north from the trail to the pass."

"That's where I met Jerry and the rustlers. What was Horne doing with them? I thought Horne was an honest cattle-man."

"Lord—Bern, don't ask me thet! I'm all muddled now tryin' to figure things."

Venters told of the fight and the race with Jerry Card and its tragic conclusion.

"I knowed it! I knowed all along that Wrangle was the best hoss!" exclaimed Judkins, with his lean face working and his eyes lighting. "Thet was a race! Lord, I'd like to hev seen Wrangle jump the cliff with Jerry. An' thet was good-by to the grandest hoss an' rider ever on the sage! . . . But, Bern, after you got the hosses why'd you want to bolt right in Tull's face?"

"I want him to know. An' if I can get to him I'll—"

"You can't get near Tull," interrupted Judkins. "Thet vigilante bunch hev taken to bein' bodyguard for Tull an' Dyer, too."

"Hasn't Lassiter made a break yet?" inquired Venters, curiously.

"Naw!" replied Judkins, scornfully. "Jane turned his head. He's mad in love over her—follers her like a dog. He ain't no more Lassiter! He's lost his nerve; he doesn't look like the same feller. It's village talk. Everybody knows it. He hasn't thrown a gun, an' he won't!"

"Jud, I'll bet he does," replied Venters, earnestly. "Remember what I say. This Lassiter is something more than a gun-man. Jud, he's big—he's great! . . . I feel that in him. God help Tull and Dyer when Lassiter does go after them. For horses and riders and stone walls won't save them."

"Wal, hev it your way, Bern. I hope you're right. Nat'rully I've been some sore on Lassiter fer gittin' soft. But I ain't denyin' his nerve, or whatever's great in him thet sort of paralyzes people. No later 'n this mornin' I seen him saunterin' down the lane, quiet an' slow. An' like his guns he comes black—*black,* thet's Lassiter. Wal, the crowd on the corner never batted an eye, an' I'll gamble my hoss thet there wasn't one who hed a heartbeat till Lassiter got by. He went in Snell's saloon, an' as there wasn't no gun play I had to go in, too. An' there, darn my pictures, if Lassiter wasn't standin' to the bar, drinkin' an' talkin' with Oldrin'."

"Oldring!" whispered Venters. His voice, as all fire and pulse within him, seemed to freeze.

"Let go my arm!" exclaimed Judkins. "Thet's my bad arm. Sure it was Oldrin'. What the hell's wrong with you, anyway? Venters, I tell you somethin's wrong. You're whiter 'n a sheet. You can't be *scared* of the rustler. I don't believe you've got a scare in you. Wal, now, jest let me talk. You know I like to talk, an' if I'm slow I allus git there sometime. As I said, Lassiter was talkin' chummy with Oldrin'. There wasn't no hard feelin's. An' the gang wasn't payin' no pertic'lar attention. But like a cat watchin' a mouse I hed my eyes on them two fellers. It was strange to me, thet confab. I'm gittin' to think a lot, fer a feller who doesn't know much. There's been some queer deals lately an' this seemed to me the queerest. These men stood to the bar alone, an' so close their big gun-hilts butted together. I seen Oldrin' was some surprised at first, an' Lassiter was cool as ice. They talked, an' presently at somethin' Lassiter said the rustler bawled out a curse, an' then he jest fell up against the bar, an' sagged there. The gang in the saloon looked around an' laughed, an' thet's about all. Finally Oldrin' turned, and it was easy to see somethin' hed shook him. Yes, sir, thet big rustler—you know he's as broad as he is long, an' the powerfulest build of a man—yes, sir, the nerve had been taken out of him. Then, after a little, he began to talk an' said a lot to Lassiter, an' by an' by it didn't take much of an eye to see thet Lassiter was gittin' hit hard. I never seen him anyway but cooler 'n ice—till then. He seemed to be hit harder 'n Oldrin', only he didn't roar out thet way. He jest kind of sunk in, an' looked an' looked, an' he didn't see a livin' soul in thet saloon. Then he sort of come to, an' shakin' hands—mind you, *shakin' hands* with Oldrin'—he went out. I couldn't help thinkin' how easy even a boy could hev dropped the great gun-man then! . . . Wal, the rustler stood at the bar fer a long time, an' he was seein' things far off, too; then he come to an' roared fer whisky, an' gulped a drink thet was big enough to drown me."

"Is Oldring here now?" whispered Venters. He could not speak above a whisper. Judkins's story had been meaningless to him.

"He's at Snell's yet. Bern, I hevn't told you yet thet the rustlers hev been raisin' hell. They shot up Stone Bridge an' Glaze, an' fer three days they've been here drinkin' an gamblin' an' throwin' of gold. These rustlers hev a pile of gold. If it was gold dust or nugget gold I'd hev reason to think, but it's new coin gold, as if it had jest come from the United States treasury. An' the coin's genuine. Thet's all been proved. The truth is Oldrin's on a rampage. A while back he lost his Masked Rider, an' they say he's wild about thet. I'm wonderin' if Lassiter could hev told the rustler anythin' about thet little masked, hard-ridin' devil. Ride! He was most as good as Jerry Card. An', Bern, I've been wonderin' if you know—"

"Judkins, you're a good fellow," interrupted Venters. "Some day I'll tell you a story. I've no time now. Take the horses to Jane."

Judkins stared, and then, muttering to himself, he mounted Bells, and stared again at Venters, and then, leading the other horses, he rode into the drove and disappeared.

Once, long before, on the night Venters had carried Bess through the cañon and up into Surprise Valley, he had experienced the strangeness of faculties singularly, tinglingly acute. And now the same sensation recurred. But it was different in that he felt cold, frozen, mechanical, incapable of free thought, and all about him seemed unreal, aloof, remote. He hid his rifle in the sage, marking its exact location with extreme care. Then he faced down the lane and strode toward the center of the village. Perceptions flashed upon him, the faint, cold touch of the breeze, a cold, silvery tinkle of flowing water, a cold sun shining out of a cold sky, song of birds and laugh of children, coldly distant. Cold and intangible were all things in earth and heaven. Colder and tighter stretched the skin over his face; colder and harder grew the polished butts of his guns; colder and steadier became his hands as he wiped the clammy sweat from his face or reached low to his gun-sheaths. Men meeting him in the walk gave him wide berth. In front of Bevin's store a crowd melted apart for his passage, and their faces and whispers were faces and whispers of a dream. He turned a corner to meet Tull face to face, eye to eye. As once before he had seen this man pale to a ghastly, livid white, so again he saw the change. Tull stopped in his tracks, with right hand raised and shaking. Suddenly it dropped, and he seemed to glide aside, to pass out of Venters's sight. Next he saw many horses with bridles down—all clean-limbed, dark bays or blacks—rustlers' horses! Loud voices and boisterous laughter, rattle of dice and scrape of chair and clink of gold, burst in mingled din from an open doorway. He stepped inside.

With the sight of smoke-hazed room and drinking, cursing, gambling, dark-visaged men, reality once more dawned upon Venters.

His entrance had been unnoticed, and he bent his gaze upon the drinkers at the bar. Dark-clothed, dark-faced men they all were, burned by the sun, bow-legged as were most riders of the sage, but neither lean nor gaunt. Then Venters's gaze passed to the tables, and swiftly it swept over the hard-featured gamesters, to alight upon the huge, shaggy, black head of the rustler chief.

"Oldring!" he cried, and to him his voice seemed to split a bell in his ears.

It stilled the din.

That silence suddenly broke to the scrape and crash of Oldring's chair as he rose; and then, while he passed, a great gloomy figure, again the thronged room stilled in silence yet deeper.

"Oldring, a word with you!" continued Venters.

"Ho! What's this?" boomed Oldring, in frowning scrutiny.

"Come outside, alone. A word with you—*from your Masked Rider!"*

Oldring kicked a chair out of his way and lunged forward with a stamp of heavy boot that jarred the floor. He waved down his muttering, rising men.

Venters backed out of the door and waited, hearing, as no sound had ever before struck into his soul, the rapid, heavy steps of the rustler.

Oldring appeared, and Venters had one glimpse of his great breadth and bulk, his gold-buckled belt with hanging guns, his high-top boots with gold spurs. In that moment Venters had a strange, unintelligible curiosity to see Oldring alive. The rustler's broad brow, his large black eyes, his sweeping beard, as dark as the wing of a raven, his enormous width of shoulder and depth of chest, his whole splendid presence so wonderfully charged with vitality and force and strength, seemed to afford Venters an unutterable fiendish joy because for that magnificent manhood and life he meant cold and sudden death.

"Oldring, Bess is alive! But she's dead to you—dead to the life you made her lead—dead as you will be in one second!"

Swift as lightning Venters's glance dropped from Oldring's rolling eyes to his hands. One of them, the right swept out, then toward his gun—and Venters shot him through the heart.

Slowly Oldring sank to his knees, and the hand, dragging at the gun, fell away. Venters's strangely acute faculties grasped the meaning of that limp arm, of the swaying hulk, of the gasp and heave, of the quivering beard. But was that awful spirit in the black eyes only one of vitality?

"Man—why—didn't—you—wait? Bess—was—" Oldring's whisper died under his beard, and with a heavy lurch he fell foward.

Bounding swiftly away, Venters fled around the corner, across the street, and, leaping a hedge, he ran through yard, orchard, and garden to the sage. Here, under cover of the tall brush, he turned west and ran on to the place where he had hidden his rifle. Securing that, he again set out into a run, and, circling through the sage, came up behind Jane Withersteen's stable and corrals. With laboring, dripping chest, and pain as of a knife thrust in his side, he stopped to regain his breath, and while resting his eyes roved around in search of a horse. Doors and windows of the stable were open wide and had a deserted look. One dejected, lonely burro stood in the near corral. Strange indeed was the silence brooding over the once happy, noisy home of Jane Withersteen's pets.

He went into the corral, exercising care to leave no tracks, and led the burro to the watering-trough. Venters, though not thirsty, drank till he could drink no more. Then, leading the burro over hard ground, he struck into the sage and down the slope.

He strode swiftly, turning from time to time to scan the slope for riders. His head just topped the level of sage-brush, and the burro could not have been seen at all. Slowly the green of Cottonwoods sank behind the slope, and at last a wavering line of purple sage met the blue of sky.

To avoid being seen, to get away, to hide his trail—these were the sole ideas in his mind as he headed for Deception Pass; and he directed all his acuteness of eye and ear, and the keenness of a rider's judgment for distance and ground, to stern accomplishment of the task. He kept to the sage far to the left of the trail leading into the Pass. He walked ten miles and looked back a thousand times. Always the graceful, purple wave of sage remained wide and lonely, a clear, undotted waste. Coming to a stretch of rocky ground, he took advantage of it to cross the trail and then continued down on the right. At length he persuaded himself that he would be able to see riders mounted on horses before they could see him on the little burro, and he rode bareback.

Hour by hour the tireless burro kept to his faithful, steady trot. The sun sank and the long shadows lengthened down the slope. Moving veils of purple twilight crept out of the hollows and, mustering and forming on the levels, soon merged and shaded into night. Venters guided the burro nearer to the trail, so that he could see its white line from the ridges, and rode on through the hours.

Once down in the Pass without leaving a trail, he would hold himself safe for the time being. When late in the night he reached the break in the sage, he sent the burro down ahead of him, and started an avalanche that all but buried the animal at the bottom of the trail. Bruised and battered as he was, he had a moment's elation, for he had hidden his tracks. Once more he mounted the burro and rode on. The hour was the blackest of the night when he made the thicket which inclosed his old camp. Here he turned the burro loose in the grass near the spring, and then lay down on his old bed of leaves.

He felt only vaguely, as outside things, the ache and burn and throb of the muscles of his body. But a dammed-up torrent of emotion at last burst its bounds, and the hour that saw his release from immediate action was one that confounded him in the reaction of his spirit. He suffered without understanding why. He caught glimpses into himself, into unlit darkness of soul. The fire that had blistered him and the cold which had frozen him now united in one torturing possession of his mind and heart, and like a fiery steed with ice-shod feet, ranged his being, ran rioting through his blood, trampling the resurging good, dragging ever at the evil.

Out of the subsiding chaos came a clear question. What had happened? He had left the valley to go to Cottonwoods. Why? It seemed that he had gone to kill a man—Oldring! The name riveted his consciousness upon the one man of all men upon earth whom he had wanted to meet. He had met the rustler. Venters recalled the smoky haze of the saloon, the dark-visaged men, the huge Oldring. He saw him step out of the door, a splendid specimen of manhood, a handsome giant with purple-black and sweeping beard. He remembered inquisitive gaze of falcon eyes. He heard himself repeating: *"Oldring, Bess is alive! But she's dead to you,"* and he felt himself jerk, and his ears throbbed to the thunder of a gun, and he saw the giant sink slowly to his knees. Was that only the vitality of him—that awful light in the eyes—only the hard-dying life of a tremendously powerful brute? A broken whisper, strange as death: *"Man—why—didn't—you wait! Bess—was—"* And Oldring plunged face forward, dead.

"I killed him," cried Venters, in remembering shock. "But it wasn't *that.* Ah, the look in his eyes and his whisper!"

Herein lay the secret that had clamored to him through all the tumult and stress of his emotions. What a look in the eyes of a man shot through the heart! It had been neither hate nor ferocity nor fear of men nor fear of death. It had been no passionate, glinting spirit of a fearless foe, willing shot for shot, life for life, but lacking physical power. Distinctly recalled now, never to be forgotten, Venters saw in Oldring's magnificent eyes the rolling of great, glad surprise—softness—love! Then came a shadow and the terrible superhuman striving of his spirit to speak. Oldring, shot through the heart, had fought and forced back death, not for a moment in which to shoot or curse, but to whisper strange words.

What words for a dying man to whisper? Why had not Venters waited? For what? That was no plea for life. It was regret that there was not a moment of life left in which to speak. Bess was— Herein lay renewed torture for Venters. What had Bess been to Oldring? The old question, like a specter, stalked from its grave to haunt him. He had overlooked, he had forgiven, he had loved, and he had forgotten; and now, out of the mystery of a dying man's whisper rose again that perverse, unsatisfied, jealous uncertainty. Bess had loved that splendid, black-crowned giant—by her own confession she had loved him; and in Venters's soul again flamed up the jealous hell. Then into the clamoring hell burst the shot that had killed Oldring, and it rang in a wild, fiendish gladness, a hateful, vengeful joy. That passed to the memory of the love and light in Oldring's eyes and the mystery in his whisper. So the changing, swaying emotions fluctuated in Venters's heart.

This was the climax of his year of suffering and the crucial struggle of his life. And when the gray dawn came he rose, a gloomy, almost heartbroken man, but victor over evil passions. He could not change the past; and, even if he had not loved Bess with all his soul, he had grown into a man who would not change the future he had planned for her. Only, and once for all, he must know the truth, know the worst, stifle all these insistent doubts and subtle hopes and jealous fancies, and kill the past by knowing truly what Bess had been to Oldring. For that matter he knew—he had always known, but he must hear it spoken. Then, when they had safely gotten out of that wild country to take up a new and an absorbing life, she would forget, she would be happy, and through that, in the years to come, he could not but find life worth living.

All day he rode slowly and cautiously up the Pass, taking time to peer around corners, to pick out hard ground and grassy patches, and to make sure there was no one in pursuit. In the night sometime he came to the smooth, scrawled rocks dividing the valley, and here set the burro at liberty. He walked beyond, climbed the slope and the dim, starlit gorge. Then, weary to the point of exhaustion, he crept into a shallow cave and fell asleep.

In the morning, when he descended the trail, he found the sun was pouring a golden stream of light through the arch of the great stone bridge. Surprise Valley, like a valley of dreams, lay mystically soft and beautiful, awakening to the golden flood which was rolling away its slumberous bands of mist, brightening its walled faces.

While yet far off he discerned Bess moving under the silver spruces, and soon the barking of the dogs told him that they had seen him. He heard the mocking-birds singing in the trees, and then the twittering of the quail. Ring and Whitie came bounding toward him, and behind them ran Bess, her hands outstretched.

"Bern! You're back! You're back!" she cried, in joy that rang of her loneliness.

"Yes, I'm back," he said, as she rushed to meet him.

She had reached out for him when suddenly, as she saw him closely, something checked her, and as quickly all her joy fled, and with it her color, leaving her pale and trembling.

"Oh! What's happened?"

"A good deal has happened, Bess. I don't need to tell you what. And I'm played out. Worn out in mind more than body."

"Dear—you look strange to me!" faltered Bess.

"Never mind that. I'm all right. There's nothing for you to be scared about. Things are going to turn out just as we have planned. As soon as I'm rested we'll make a break to get out of the country. Only now, right now, I must know the truth about you."

"Truth about me?" echoed Bess, shrinkingly. She seemed to be casting back into her mind for a forgotten key. Venters himself, as he saw her, received a pang.

"Yes—the truth. Bess, don't misunderstand. I haven't changed that way. I love you still. I'll love you more afterward. Life will be just as sweet—sweeter to us. We'll be—be married as soon as ever we can. We'll be happy—but there's a devil in me. A perverse, jealous devil! Then I've queer fancies. I forgot for a long time. Now all those fiendish little whispers of doubt and faith and fear and hope come torturing me again. I've got to kill them with the truth."

"I'll tell you anything you want to know," she replied, frankly.

"Then, by Heaven! we'll have it over and done with! . . . Bess—did Oldring love you?"

"Certainly he did."

"Did—did you love him?"

"Of course. I told you so."

"How can you tell it so lightly?" cried Venters, passionately. "Haven't you any sense of—of—" He choked back speech. He felt the rush of pain and passion. He seized her in rude, strong hands and drew her close. He looked straight into her dark-blue eyes. They were shadowing with the old wistful light, but they were as clear as the limpid water of the spring. They were earnest, solemn in unutterable love and faith and abnegation. Venters shivered. He knew he was looking into her soul. He knew she could not lie in that moment; but that she might tell the truth, looking at him with those eyes, almost killed his belief in purity.

"What are—what were you to—to Oldring?" he panted, fiercely.

"I am his daughter," she replied, instantly.

Venters slowly let go of her. There was a violent break in the force of his feeling—then creeping blankness.

"What—was it—you said?" he asked, in a kind of dull wonder.

"I am his daughter."

"Oldring's daughter?" queried Venters, with life gathering in his voice.

"Yes."

With a passionately awakening start he grasped her hands and drew her close.

"All the time—you've been Oldring's daughter?"

"Yes, of course all the time—always."

"But Bess, you told me—you let me think—I made out you were—a—so—so ashamed."

"It is my shame," she said, with voice deep and full, and now the scarlet fired her cheek. "I told you—I'm nothing—nameless—just Bess, Oldring's girl!"

"I know—I remember. But I never thought—" he went on, hurriedly, huskily. "That time—when you lay dying—you prayed—you—somehow I got the idea you were bad."

"Bad?" she asked, with a little laugh.

She looked up with a faint smile of bewilderment and the absolute unconsciousness of a child. Venters gasped in the gathering might of the truth. She did not understand his meaning.

"Bess! Bess!" He clasped her in his arms, hiding her eyes against his breast. She must not see his face in that moment. And he held her while he looked out across the valley. In his dim and blinded sight, in the blur of golden light and moving mist, he saw Oldring. She was the rustler's nameless daughter. Oldring had loved her. He had so guarded her, so kept her from women and men and knowledge of life that her mind was as a child's. That was part of the secret—part of the mystery. That was the wonderful truth. Not only was she not bad, but good, pure, innocent above all innocence in the world—the innocence of lonely girlhood.

He saw Oldring's magnificent eyes, inquisitive, searching—softening. He saw them flare in amaze, in gladness, with love, then suddenly strain in terrible effort of will. He heard Oldring whisper and saw him sway like a log and fall. Then a million bellowing, thundering voices—gunshots of conscience, thunderbolts of remorse—dinned horribly in his ears. He had killed Bess's father. Then a rushing wind filled his ears like a moan of wind in the cliffs, a knell indeed—Oldring's knell.

He dropped to his knees and hid his face against Bess, and grasped her with the hands of a drowning man.

"My God! . . . My God! . . . Oh, Bess! . . . Forgive me! Never mind what I've done—what I've thought. But forgive me. I'll give you my life. I'll live for you. I'll love you. Oh, I do love you as no man ever loved a woman. I want you to know—to remember that I fought a fight for you—however blind I was. I thought—I thought—never mind what I thought—but I loved you—I asked you to marry me. Let that—let me have that to hug to my heart. Oh, Bess, I was driven! And I might have known! I could not rest nor sleep till I had this mystery solved. God! how things work out!"

"Bern, you're weak—trembling—you talk wildly," cried Bess. "You've overdone your strength. There's nothing to forgive. There's no mystery except your love for me. You have come back to me!"

And she clasped his head tenderly in her arms and pressed it closely to her throbbing breast.

CHAPTER NINETEEN
Fay

At the home of Jane Withersteen Little Fay was climbing Lassiter's knee.

"Does oo love me?" she asked.

Lassiter, who was as serious with Fay as he was gentle and loving, assured her in earnest and elaborate speech that he was her devoted subject. Fay looked thoughtful and appeared to be debating the duplicity of men or searching for a supreme test to prove this cavalier.

"Does oo love my new muvver?" she asked, with bewildering suddenness.

Jane Withersteen laughed, and for the first time in many a day she felt a stir of her pulse and warmth in her cheek.

It was a still drowsy summer of afternoon, and the three were sitting in the shade of the wooded knoll that faced the sage-slope. Little Fay's brief spell of unhappy longing for her mother—the childish, mystic gloom—had passed, and now where Fay was there were prattle and laughter and glee. She had emerged from sorrow to be the incarnation of joy and loveliness. She had grown supernaturally sweet and beautiful. For Jane Withersteen the child was an answer to prayer, a blessing, a possession infinitely more precious than all she had lost. For Lassiter, Jane divined that little Fay had become a religion.

"Does oo love my new muvver?" repeated Fay.

Lassiter's answer to this was a modest and sincere affirmative.

"Why don't oo marry my new muvver an' be my favver?"

Of the thousands of questions put by little Fay to Lassiter that was the first he had been unable to answer.

"Fay—Fay, don't ask questions like that," said Jane.

"Why?"

"Because," replied Jane. And she found it strangely embarrassing to meet the child's gaze. It seemed to her that Fay's violet eyes looked through her with piercing wisdom.

"Oo love him, don't oo?"

"Dear child—run and play," said Jane, "but don't go too far. Don't go from this little hill."

Fay pranced off wildly, joyous over freedom that had not been granted her for weeks.

"Jane, why are children more sincere than grown-up persons?" asked Lassiter.

"Are they?"

"I reckon so. Little Fay there—she sees things as they appear on the face. An Indian does that. So does a dog. An' an Indian an' a dog are most of the time right in what they see. Mebbe a child is always right."

"Well, what does Fay see?" asked Jane.

"I reckon you know. I wonder what goes on in Fay's mind when she sees part of the truth with the wise eyes of a child, an' wantin' to know more, meets with strange falseness from you? Wait! You are false in a way, though you're the best woman I ever knew. What I want to say is this. Fay has taken you're pretendin' to—to care for me for the thing it looks on the face. An' her little formin' mind asks questions. An' the answers she gets are different from the looks of things. So she'll grow up, gradually takin' on that falseness, an' be like the rest of the women, an' men, too. An' the truth of this falseness to life is proved by your appearin' to love me when you don't. Things aren't what they seem."

"Lassiter, you're right. A child should be told the absolute truth. But—is that possible? I haven't been able to do it, and all my life I've loved the truth, and I've prided myself upon being truthful. Maybe that was only egotism. I'm learning much, my friend. Some of those blinding scales have fallen from my eyes. And—and as to caring for you, I think I care a great deal. How much, how little, I couldn't say. My heart is almost broken, Lassiter. So now is not a good time to judge of affection. I can still play and be merry with Fay. I can still dream. But when I attempt serious thought I'm dazed. I don't think. I don't care any more. I don't pray! . . . Think of that, my friend! But in spite of my numb feeling I believe I'll rise out of all this dark agony a better woman, with greater love of man and God. I'm on the rack now; I'm senseless to all but pain, and growing dead to that. Sooner or later I shall rise out of this stupor. I'm waiting the hour."

"It'll soon come, Jane," replied Lassiter, soberly. "Then I'm afraid for you. Years are terrible things, an' for years you've been bound. Habit of years is strong as life itself. Somehow, though, I believe as you—that you'll come out of it all a finer woman. I'm waitin', too. An' I'm wonderin'—I reckon, Jane, that marriage between us is out of all human reason?"

"Lassiter! . . . My dear friend! . . . It's impossible for us to marry."

"Why—as Fay says?" inquired Lassiter, with gentle persistence.

"Why! I never thought why. But it's not possible. I am Jane, daughter of Withersteen. My father would rise out of his grave. I'm of Mormon birth. I'm being broken. But I'm still a Mormon woman. And you—you are Lassiter!"

"Mebbe I'm not so much Lassiter as I used to be."

"What was it you said? Habit of years is strong as life itself! You can't change the one habit—the purpose of your life. For you still pack those black guns! You still nurse your passion for blood."

A smile, like a shadow, flickered across his face.

"No."

"Lassiter, I lied to you. But I beg of you—don't you lie to me. I've great respect for you. I believe you're softened toward most, perhaps all, my people except— But when I speak of your purpose, your hate, your guns, I have only him in mind. I don't believe you've changed."

For answer he unbuckled the heavy cartridge-belt, and laid it with the heavy, swing gun-sheaths in her lap.

"Lassiter!" Jane whispered, as she gazed from him to the black, cold guns. Without them he appeared shorn of strength, defenseless, a smaller man. Was she Delilah? Swiftly, conscious of only one motive—refusal to see this man called craven by his enemies—she rose, and with blundering fingers buckled the belt round his waist where it belonged.

"Lassiter, *I* am a coward."

"Come with me out of Utah—where I can put away my guns an' be a man," he said. "I reckon I'll prove it to you then! Come! You've got Black Star back, an' Night an' Bells. Let's take the racers an' little Fay, an' ride out of Utah. The hosses an' the child are all you have left. Come!"

"No, no, Lassiter. I'll never leave Utah. What would I do in the world with my broken fortunes and my broken heart? I'll never leave these purple slopes I love so well."

"I reckon I ought to 've knowed that. Presently you'll be livin' down here in a hovel, an' presently Jane Withersteen will be a memory. I only wanted to have a chance to show you how a man—*any* man—can be better 'n he was. If we left Utah I could prove—I reckon I could prove this thing you call love. It's strange, an' hell an' heaven at once, Jane Withersteen. 'Pears to me that you've thrown away your big heart on love—love of religion an' duty an' churchmen, an' riders an' poor families an' poor children! Yet you can't see what love is—how it changes a person! . . . Listen, an' in tellin' you Milly Erne's story I'll show you how love changed her.

"Milly an' me was children when our family moved from Missouri to Texas, an' we growed up in Texas ways same as if we'd been born there. We had been poor, an' there we prospered. In time the little village where we went became a town, an' strangers an' new families kept movin' in. Milly was the belle them days. I can see her now, a little girl no bigger 'n a bird, an' as pretty. She had the finest eyes, dark blue-black when she was excited, an' beautiful all the time. You remember Milly's eyes! An' she had light-brown hair with streaks of gold, an' a mouth that every feller wanted to kiss.

"An' about the time Milly was the prettiest an' the sweetest, along came a young minister who began to ride some of a race with the other fellers for Milly. An' he won. Milly had always been strong on religion, an' when she met Frank Erne she went in heart an' soul for the salvation of souls. Fact was, Milly, through study of the Bible an' attendin' church an' revivals, went a little out of her head. It didn't worry the old folks none, an' the only worry to me was Milly's everlastin' prayin' an' workin' to save my soul. She never converted me, but we was the best of comrades, an' I reckon no brother an' sister ever loved each other better. Well, Frank Erne an' me hit up a great friendship. He was a strappin' feller, good to look at, an' had the most pleasin' ways. His religion never bothered me, for he could hunt an' fish an' ride an' be a good feller. After buffalo once, he come pretty near to savin' my life. We got to be thick as brothers, an' he was the only man I ever seen who I thought was good enough for Milly. An' the day they were married I got drunk for the only time in my life.

"Soon after that I left home—it seems Milly was the only one who could keep me home—an' I went to the bad, as to prosperin'. I saw some pretty hard life in the Pan Handle, an' then I went North. In them days Kansas an' Nebraska was as bad, come to think of it, as these days right here on the border of Utah. I got to be pretty handy with guns. An' there wasn't many riders as could beat me ridin'. An' I can say all modest-like that I never seen the white man who could track a hoss or a steer or a man with me. Afore I knowed it two years slipped by, an' all at once I got homesick, an' pulled a bridle south.

"Things at home had changed. I never got over that home-comin'. Mother was dead an' in her grave. Father was a silent, broken man, killed already on his feet. Frank Erne was a ghost of his old self, through with workin', through with preachin', almost through with livin', an' Milly was gone! . . . It was a long time before I got the story. Father had no mind left, an' Frank Erne was *afraid* to talk. So I had to pick up what'd happened from different people.

"It 'pears that soon after I left home another preacher come to the little town. An' he an' Frank become rivals. This feller was different from Frank. He preached some other kind of religion, and he was quick an' passionate, where Frank was slow an' mild. He went after people, women specially. In looks he couldn't compare to Frank Erne, but he had power over women. He had a voice, an' he talked an' talked an' preached an' preached. Milly fell under his influence. She became mightily interested in his religion. Frank had patience with her, as was his way, an' let her be as interested as she liked. All religions were devoted to one God, he said, an' it wouldn't hurt Milly none to study a different point of view. So the new preacher often called on Milly, an' sometimes in Frank's absence. Frank was a cattle-man between Sundays.

"Along about this time an incident come off that I couldn't get much light on. A stranger come to town, an' was seen with the preacher. This stranger was a big man with an eye like blue ice, an' a beard of gold. He had money, an' he 'peared a man of mystery, an' the town went to buzzin' when he disappeared about the same time as a young woman known to be mightily interested in the new preacher's religion. Then, presently, along comes a man from somewheres in Illinois, an' he up an' spots this preacher as a famous Mormon proselyter. That ri'led Frank Erne as nothin' ever before, an' from rivals they come to be bitter enemies. An' it ended in Frank goin' to the meetin'-house where Milly was listenin', an' before her an' everybody else he called that preacher—called him, well, almost as hard as Venters called Tull here sometime back. An' Frank followed up that call with a hoss-whippin', an' he drove the proselyter out of town.

"People noticed, so 'twas said, that Milly's sweet disposition changed. Some said it was because she would soon become a mother, an' others said she was pinin' after the new religion. An' there was women who said right out that she was pinin' after the Mormon. Anyway, one mornin' Frank rode in from one of his trips, to find Milly gone. He had no real near neighbors—livin' a little out of town—but those who was nearest said a wagon had gone by in the night, an' there was the wagon tracks an' hoss tracks an' man tracks. The news spread like wildfire that Milly had run off from her husband. Everybody but Frank believed it an' wasn't slow in tellin' why she run off. Mother had always hated that strange streak of Milly's, takin' up with the new religion as she had, an' she believed Milly ran off with the Mormon. That hastened mother's death, an' she died unforgivin'. Father wasn't the kind to bow down under disgrace or misfortune, but he had surpassin' love for Milly, an' the loss of her broke him.

"From the minute I heard of Milly's disappearance I never believed she went off of her own free will. I knew Milly, an' I knew she *couldn't* have done that. I stayed at home awhile, tryin' to make Frank Erne talk. But if he knowed anythin' then he wouldn't tell it. So I set out to find Milly. An' I tried to get on the trail of that proselyter. I knew if I ever struck a town he'd visited that I'd get a trail. I knew, too, that nothin' short of hell would stop his proselytin'. An' I rode from town to town. I had a blind faith that somethin' was guidin' me. An' as the weeks an' months went by I growed into a strange sort of a man, I guess. Anyway, people were afraid of me. Two yars after that, way over in a corner of Texas, I struck a town where my man had been. He'd jest left. People said he came to that town *without* a woman. I back-trailed my man through Arkansas an' Mississippi, an' the old trail got hot again in Texas. I found the town where he first went after leavin' home. An' here I got track of Milly. I found a cabin where she had given birth to her baby. There was no way to tell whether she'd been kept a prisoner or not. The feller who owned the place was a mean, silent sort of a skunk, an' as I was leavin' I jest took a chance an' left my mark on him. Then I went home again.

"It was to find I hadn't any home, no more. Father had been dead a year. Frank Erne still lived in the house where Milly had left him. I stayed with him awhile, an' I grew old watchin' him. His farm had gone to weed, his cattle had strayed or been rustled, his house weathered till it wouldn't keep out rain nor wind. An' Frank set on the porch and whittled sticks, an' day by day wasted away. There was times when he ranted about like a crazy man, but mostly he was always sittin' an' starin' with eyes that made a man curse. I figured Frank had a secret fear that I needed to know. An' when I told him I'd trailed Milly for near three years an' had got trace of her, an' saw where she'd had her baby, I thought he would drop dead at my feet. An' when he'd come round more natural-like he begged me to *give up* the trail. But he wouldn't explain. So I let him alone, an' watched him day an' night.

"An' I found there was one thing still precious to him, an' it was a little drawer where he kept his papers. This was in the room where he slept. An' it 'peared he seldom slept. But after bein' patient I got the contents of that drawer an' found two letters from Milly. One was a long letter written a few months after her disappearance. She had been bound an' gagged an' dragged away from her home by three men, an' she named them—Hurd, Metzger, Slack. They was strangers to her. She was taken to the little town where I found trace of her two years after. But she didn't send the letter from that town. There she was penned in. 'Peared that the proselyter, who had, of course, come on the scene, was not runnin' any risks of losin' her. She went on to say that for a time she was out of her head, an' when she got right again all that kept her alive was the baby. It was a beautiful baby, she said, an' all she thought an' dreamed of was somehow to get baby back to its father, an' then she'd thankfully lay down and die. An' the letter ended abrupt, in the middle of a sentence, an' it wasn't signed.

"The second letter was written more than two years after the first. It was from Salt Lake City. It simply said that Milly had heard her brother was on her trail. She asked Frank to tell her brother to give up the search because if he didn't she would suffer in a way too horrible to tell. She didn't beg. She just stated a fact an' made the simple request. An' she ended that letter by sayin' she would soon leave Salt Lake City with the man she had come to love, an' would never be heard of again.

"I recognized Milly's handwritin', an' I recognized her way of puttin' things. But that second letter told me of some great change in her. Ponderin' over it, I felt at last she'd either come to love that feller an' his religion, or some terrible fear made her lie an' say so. I couldn't be sure which. But, of course, I meant to find out. I'll say here, if I'd known Mormons then as I do now I'd left Milly to her fate. For mebbe she was right about what she'd suffer if I kept on her trail. But I was young an' wild them days. First I went to the town where she'd first been taken, an' I went to the place where she'd been kept. I got that skunk who owned the place, an' took him out in the woods, an' made him tell all he knowed. That wasn't much as to length, but it was pure hell's-fire in substance. This time I left him some incapacitated for any more skunk work short of hell. Then I hit the trail for Utah.

"That was fourteen years ago. I saw the incomin' of most of the Mormons. It was a wild country an' a wild time. I rode from town to town, village to village, ranch to ranch, camp to camp. I never stayed long in one place. I never had but one idea. I never rested. Four years went by, an' I knowed every trail in northern Utah. I kept on an' as time went by, an' I'd begun to grow old in my search, I had firmer, blinder faith in whatever was guidin' me. Once I read about a feller who sailed the seven seas an' traveled the world, an' he had a story to tell, an' whenever he seen the man to whom he must tell that story he knowed him on sight. I was like that, only I had a question to ask. An' always I knew the man of whom I must ask. So I never really lost the trail, though for many years it was the dimmest trail ever followed by any man.

"Then come a change in my luck. Along in Central Utah I rounded up Hurd, an' I whispered somethin' in his ear, an' watched his face, an' then throwed a gun against his bowels. An' he died with his teeth so tight shut I couldn't have pried them open with a knife. Slack an' Metzger that same year both heard me whisper the same question, an' neither would they speak a word when they lay dyin'. Long before I'd learned no man of this breed or class—or God knows what—would give up any secrets! I had to see in a man's fear of death the connections with Milly Erne's fate. An' as the years passed at long intervals I would find such a man.

"So as I drifted on the long trail down into southern Utah my name preceded me, an' I had to meet a people prepared for me, an' ready with guns. They made me a gun-man. An' that suited me. In all this time signs of the proselyter an' the giant with the blue-ice eyes an' the gold beard seemed to fade dimmer out of the trail. Only twice in ten years did I find a trace of that mysterious man who had visited the proselyter at my home village. What he had to do with Milly's fate was beyond all hope for me to learn, unless my guidin' spirit led me to him! As for the other man, I knew, as sure as I breathed an' the stars shone an' the wind blew, that I'd meet him some day.

"Eighteen years I've been on the trail. An' it led me to the last lonely village of the Utah border. Eighteen years! . . . I feel pretty old now. I was only twenty when I hit that trail. Well, as I told you, back here a ways a Gentile said Jane

Withersteen could tell me about Milly Erne an' show me her grave!"

The low voice ceased, and Lassiter slowly turned his sombrero round and round, and appeared to be counting the silver ornaments on the band. Jane, leaning toward him, sat as if petrified, listening intently, waiting to hear more. She could have shrieked, but power of tongue and lips were denied her. She saw only this sad, gray, passion-worn man, and she heard only the faint rustling of the leaves.

"Well, I came to Cottonwoods," went on Lassiter, "an' you showed me Milly's grave. An' though your teeth have been shut tighter 'n them of all the dead men lyin' back along that trail, jest the same you told me the secret I've lived these eighteen years to hear! Jane, I said you'd tell me without ever me askin'. I didn't need to ask my question here. The day, you remember, when that fat party throwed a gun on me in your court, an'—"

"Oh! Hush!" whispered Jane, blindly holding up her hands.

"I seen in your face that Dyer, now a bishop, was the proselyter who ruined Milly Erne!"

For an instant Jane Withersteen's brain was a whirling chaos, and she recovered to find herself grasping at Lassiter like one drowning. And as if by a lightning stroke she sprang from her dull apathy into exquisite torture.

"It's a lie! Lassiter! No, no!" she moaned. "I swear—you're wrong!"

"Stop! You'd perjure yourself! But I'll spare you that. You poor woman! Still blind! Still faithful! . . . Listen. *I know.* Let that settle it. An' I give up my purpose!"

"What is it—you say?"

"I give up my purpose. I've come to see an' feel differently. I can't help poor Milly. An' I've outgrowed revenge. I've come to see I can be no judge for men. I can't kill a man jest for hate. Hate ain't the same with me since I loved you and little Fay."

"Lassiter! You mean you won't kill him?" Jane whispered.

"No."

"For my sake?"

"I reckon. I can't understand, but I'll respect your feelin's."

"Because you—oh, because you love me? . . . Eighteen years! You were that terrible Lassiter! And *now*—because you love me?"

"That's it, Jane."

"Oh, you'll make me love you! How can I help but love you? My heart must be stone. But—oh, Lassiter, wait, wait! Give me time. I'm not what I was. Once it was so easy to love. Now it's easy to hate. Wait! My faith in God—*some* God—still lives. By it I see happier times for you, poor passion-swayed wanderer! For me—a miserable, broken woman. I loved your sister Milly. I *will* love you. I can't have fallen so low—I can't be so abandoned by God—that I've no love left to give you. Wait! Let us forget Milly's sad life. Ah, I knew it as no one else on earth! There's one thing I shall tell you—if you are at my death-bed, but I can't speak now."

"I reckon I don't want to hear no more," said Lassiter.

Jane leaned against him; as if some pent-up force had rent its way out, she fell into a paroxysm of weeping. Lassiter held her in silent sympathy. By degrees she regained composure, and she was rising, sensible of being relieved of a weighty burden, when a sudden start on Lassiter's part alarmed her.

"I heard hosses—hosses with muffled hoofs!" he said; and he got up guardedly.

"Where's Fay?" asked Jane, hurriedly glancing round the shady knoll. The bright-haired child, who had appeared to be close all the time, was not in sight.

"Fay!" called Jane.

No answering shout of glee. No patter of flying feet. Jane saw Lassiter stiffen.

"Fay—oh—Fay!" Jane almost screamed.

The leaves quivered and rustled; a lonesome cricket chirped in the grass; a bee hummed by. The silence of the waning afternoon breathed hateful portent. It terrified Jane. When had silence been so infernal?

"She's—only—strayed—out—of earshot," faltered Jane, looking at Lassiter.

Pale, rigid as a statue, the rider stood, not in listening, searching posture, but in one of doomed certainty. Suddenly he grasped Jane with an iron hand, and, turning his face from her gaze, he strode with her from the knoll.

"See—Fay played here last—a house of stones an' sticks. . . . An' here's a corral of pebbles with leaves for hosses," said Lassiter, stridently, and pointed to the ground. "Back an' forth she trailed here. . . . See, she's buried somethin'—a dead grasshopper—there's a tombstone . . . she pulled bark off this cottonwood . . . look in the dust of the path—the letters you taught her—she's drawn pictures of birds an' hosses an' people. . . . Look, a cross! Oh, Jane, *your* cross!"

Lassiter dragged Jane on, and as if from a book read the meaning of little Fay's trail. All the way down the knoll, through the shrubbery, round and round a cottonwood, Fay's vagrant fancy left records of her sweet musings and innocent play. Long had she lingered round a bird-nest to leave therein the gaudy wing of a butterfly. Long had she played beside the running stream, sending adrift vessels freighted with pebbly cargo. Then she had wandered through the deep grass, her tiny feet scarcely turning a fragile blade, and she had dreamed beside some old faded flowers. Thus her steps led her into the broad lane. The little dimpled imprints of her bare feet showed clean-cut in the dust; they went a little way down the lane; and then, at a point where they stopped, the great tracks of a man led out from the shrubbery and returned.

CHAPTER TWENTY
Lassiter's Way

Footprints told the story of little Fay's abduction. In anguish Jane Withersteen turned speechlessly to Lassiter, and, confirming her fears, she saw him gray-faced, aged all in a moment, stricken as if by a mortal blow.

Then all her life seemed to fall about her in wreck and ruin.

"It's all over," she heard her voice whisper. "It's ended. I'm going—I'm going—"

"Where?" demanded Lassiter, suddenly looming darkly over her.

"To—to those cruel men—"

"Speak names!" thundered Lassiter.

"To Bishop Dyer—to Tull," went on Jane, shocked into obedience.

"Well—what for?"

"I want little Fay. I can't live without her. They've stolen her as they stole Milly Erne's child. I must have little Fay. I want only her. I give up. I'll go and tell Bishop Dyer—I'm broken. I'll tell him I'm ready for the yoke—only give me back Fay—and—and I'll marry Tull!"

"Never!" hissed Lassiter.

His long arm leaped at her. Almost running, he dragged her under the cottonwoods, across the court, into the huge hall of Withersteen House, and he shut the door with a force that jarred the heavy walls. Black Star and Night and Bells, since their return, had been locked in this hall, and now they stamped on the stone floor.

Lassiter released Jane and like a dizzy man swayed from her with a hoarse cry and leaned shaking against a table where he kept his rider's accoutrements. He began to fumble in his saddle-bags. His action brought a clinking, metallic sound—the rattling of gun-cartridges. His fingers trembled as he slipped cartridges into an extra belt. But as he buckled it over the one he habitually wore his hands became steady. This second belt contained two guns, smaller than the black ones swinging low, and he slipped them round so that his coat hid them. Then he fell to swift action. Jane Withersteen watched him, fascinated but uncomprehending; and she saw him rapidly saddle Black Star and Night. Then he drew her into the light of the huge windows, standing over her, gripping her arm with fingers like cold steel.

"Yes, Jane, it's ended—but you're not goin' to Dyer! . . . *I'm goin' instead!"*

Looking at him—he was so terrible of aspect—she could not comprehend his words. Who was this man with the face gray as death, with eyes that would have made her shriek had she the strength, with the strange, ruthlessly bitter lips? Where was the gentle Lassiter? What was this presence in the hall, about him, about her—this cold, invisible presence?

"Yes, it's ended, Jane," he was saying, so awfully quiet and cool and implacable, "an' I'm goin' to make a little call. I'll lock you in here, an' when I get back have the saddle-bags full of meat an' bread. An' be ready to ride!"

"Lassiter!" cried Jane.

Desperately she tried to meet his gray eyes, in vain; desperately she tried again, fought herself as feeling and thought resurged in torment, and she succeeded; and then she knew.

"No—no—no!" she wailed. "You said you'd foregone your vengeance. You promised not to kill Bishop Dyer."

"If you want to talk to me about him—leave off the Bishop. I don't understand that name, or its use."

"Oh, hadn't you foregone your vengeance on—on Dyer?"

"Yes."

"But—your actions—your words—your guns—your terrible looks! . . . They don't seem foregoing vengeance?"

"Jane, now it's justice."

"You'll—kill him?"

"If God lets me live another hour! If not God—then the devil who drives me!"

"You'll kill him—for yourself—for your vengeful hate?"

"No!"

"For Milly Erne's sake?"

"No."

"For little Fay's?"

"No!"

"Oh—for whose?"

"For yours!"

"His blood on my soul!" whispered Jane, and she fell to her knees. This was the long-pending hour of fruition. And the habit of years—the religious passion of her life—leaped from lethargy, and the long months of gradual drifting to doubt were as if they had never been. "If you spill his blood it'll be on my soul—and on my father's. Listen." And she clasped his knees, and clung there as he tried to raise her. "Listen. Am I nothing to you?"

"Woman—don't trifle at words! I love you! An' I'll soon prove it!"

"I'll give myself to you—I'll ride away with you—marry you, if only you'll spare him?"

His answer was a cold, ringing, terrible laugh.

"Lassiter—I'll love you. Spare him!"

"No!"

She sprang up in despairing, breaking spirit, and encircled his neck with her arms, and held him in an embrace that he strove vainly to loosen. "Lassiter, would you kill me? I'm fighting my last fight for the principles of my youth—love of religion, love of father. You don't know—you can't guess the truth, and I can't speak it! I'm losing all. I'm changing. All I've gone through is nothing to this hour. Pity me—help me in my weakness. You're strong again—oh, so cruelly, coldly strong! You're killing me. I see you—feel you as some other Lassiter! My master, be merciful—spare him!"

His answer was a ruthless smile.

She clung the closer to him, and leaned her panting breast on him, and lifted her fact to his. "Lassiter, *I do love you!* It's leaped out of my agony. It comes suddenly with a terrible blow of truth. You are a man! I never knew it till now. Some wonderful change came to me when you buckled on these guns and showed that gray, awful face. I loved you then. All my life I've loved, but never as now. No woman can love like a broken woman. If it were not for one thing—just one thing—and yet! I *can't* speak it—I'd glory in your manhood—the lion in you that means to slay for me. Believe me—and spare Dyer. Be merciful—great as it's in you to be great. . . . Oh, listen and believe—I have nothing, but I'm a woman—a beautiful woman, Lassiter—a passionate, loving woman—and I love you! Take me—hide me in some wild place—and love me and mend my broken heart. Spare him and take me away."

She lifted her face closer and closer to his, until their lips nearly touched, and she hung upon his neck, and with strength almost spent pressed and still pressed her palpitating body to his.

"Kiss me!" she whispered, blindly.

"No—not at your price!" he answered. His voice had changed or she had lost clearness of hearing.

"Kiss me! . . . Are you a man? Kiss me and save me!"

"Jane, you never played fair with me. But now you're blisterin' your lips—blackenin' your soul with lies!"

"By the memory of my mother—by my Bible—no! No, I *have* no Bible! But by my hope of heaven I swear I love you!"

Lassiter's gray lips formed soundless words that meant even her love could not avail to bend his will. As if the hold of her arms was that of a child's he loosened it and stepped away.

"Wait! Don't go! Oh, hear a last word! . . . May a more just and merciful God than the God I was taught to worship judge me—forgive me—save me! For I can no longer keep silent! . . . Lassiter, in pleading for Dyer I've been pleading more for my father. My father was a Mormon master, close to the leaders of the church. It was my father who sent Dyer out to proselyte. It was my father who had the blue-ice eye and the beard of gold. It was my father you got trace of in the past years.

Truly, Dyer ruined Milly Erne—dragged her from her home—to Utah—to Cottonwoods. *But it was for my father!* If Milly Erne was ever wife of a Mormon that Mormon was my father! I never knew—never will know whether or not she was a wife. Blind I may be, Lassiter—fanatically faithful to a false religion I may have been, but I know justice, and my father is beyond human justice. Surely he is meeting just punishment—somewhere. Always it has appalled me—the thought of your killing Dyer for my father's sins. So I have prayed!"

"Jane, the past is dead. In my love for you I forgot the past. This thing I'm about to do ain't for myself or Milly or Fay. It's not because of anythin' that ever happened in the past, but for what is happenin' right *now. It's for you! . . .* An' listen. Since I was a boy I've never thanked God for anythin'. If there is a God—an' I've come to believe it—I thank Him now for the years that made me Lassiter! . . . I can reach down an' feel these big guns, an' know what I can do with them. An', Jane, only one of the miracles Dyer professes to believe in can save him!"

Again for Jane Withersteen came the spinning of her brain in darkness, and as she whirled in endless chaos she seemed to be falling at the feet of a luminous figure—a man—Lassiter—who had saved her from herself, who could not be changed, who would slay rightfully. Then she slipped into utter blackness.

When she recovered from her faint she became aware that she was lying on a couch near the window in her sitting-room. Her brow felt damp and cold and wet; some one was chafing her hands; she recognized Judkins, and then saw that his lean, hard face wore the hue and look of excessive agitation.

"Judkins!" Her voice broke weakly.

"Aw, Miss Withersteen, you're comin' round fine. Now jest lay still a little. You're all right; everythin's all right."

"Where is—he?"

"Who?"

"Lassiter!"

"You needn't worry none about him."

"Where is he? Tell me—instantly."

"Wal, he's in the other room patchin' up a few triflin' bulletholes."

"Ah! . . . Bishop Dyer?"

"When I seem him last—a matter of half an hour ago, he was on his knees. He was some busy, *but* he wasn't prayin'!"

"How strangely you talk! I'll sit up. I'm—well, strong again. Tell me. Dyer on his knees! What was he doing?"

"Wal, beggin' your pardon fer blunt talk, Miss Withersteen, Dyer was on his knees an' *not* prayin'. You remember his big, broad hands? You've seen 'em raised in blessin' over old gray men an' little curly-haired children like—like Fay Larkin! Come to think of thet, I disremember ever hearin' of his liftin' his big hands in blessin' over a *woman.* Wal, when I seen him last—jest a little while ago—he was on his knees, *not* prayin', as I remarked—an' he was pressin' his big hands over some bigger wounds."

"Man, you drive me mad! Did Lassiter kill Dyer?"

"Yes."

"Did he kill Tull?"

"No. Tull's out of the village with most of his riders. He's expected back before evenin'. Lassiter will hev to git away before Tull an' his riders come in. It's sure death fer him here. An' wuss fer you, too, Miss Withersteen. There'll be some of an uprisin' when Tull gits back."

"I shall ride away with Lassiter. Judkins, tell me all you saw—all you know about this killing." She realized, without wonder or amaze, how Judkins's one word, affirming the death of Dyer—that the catastrophe had fallen—had completed the change whereby she had been molded or beaten or broken into another woman. She felt calm, slightly cold, strong as she had not been strong since the first shadow fell upon her.

"I jest saw about all of it, Miss Withersteen, an' I'll be glad to tell if you'll only hev patience with me," said Judkins, earnestly. "You see, I've been pecooliarly interested, an' nat'rully I'm some excited. An' I talk a lot thet mebbe ain't necessary, but I can't help thet.

"I was at the meetin'-house where Dyer was holdin' court. You know he allus acts as magistrate an' judge when Tull's away. An' the trial was fer tryin' what's left of my boy riders—thet helped me hold your cattle—fer a lot of hatched-up things the boys never did. We're used to thet, an' the boys wouldn't hev minded bein' locked up fer a while, or hevin' to dig ditches, or whatever the judge laid down. You see, I divided the gold you give me among all my boys, an' they all hid it, an' they all feel rich. Howsomever, court was adjourned before the judge passed sentence. Yes, ma'am, court was adjourned some strange an' quick, much as if lightnin' hed struck the meetin'-house.

"I hed trouble attendin' the trial, but I got in. There was a good many people there, all my boys, an' Judge Dyer with his several clerks. Also he hed with him the five riders who've been guardin' him pretty close of late. They was Carter, Wright, Jengessen, an' two new riders from Stone Bridge. I didn't hear their names, but I heard they was handy men with guns an' they looked more like rustlers than riders. Anyway, there they was, the five all in a row.

"Judge Dyer was tellin' Willie Kern, one of my best an' steadiest boys—Dyer was tellin' him how there was a ditch opened near Willie's home lettin' water through his lot, where it hadn't ought to go. An' Willie was tryin' to git a word in to prove he wasn't at home all the day it happened—which was true, as I know—but Willie couldn't git a word in, an' then Judge Dyer went on layin' down the law. An' all at onct he happened to look down the long room. An' if ever any man turned to stone he was thet man.

"Nat'rully I looked back to see what hed acted so powerful strange on the judge. An' there, half-way up the room, in the middle of the wide aisle, stood Lassiter! All white an' black he looked, an' I can't think of anythin' he resembled, onless it's death. Venters made thet same room some still an' chilly when he called Tull; but this was different. I give my word, Miss Withersteen, thet I went cold to my very marrow. I don't know why. But Lassiter had a way about him thet's awful. He spoke a word—a name—I couldn't understand it, though he spoke clear as a bell. I was too excited, mebbe. Judge Dyer must hev understood it, an' a lot more thet was mystery to me, for he pitched forrard out of his chair right onto the platform.

"Then them five riders, Dyer's bodyguards, they jumped up an' two of them thet I found out afterward were the strangers from Stone Bridge, they piled right out of a winder, so quick you couldn't catch your breath. It was plain they wasn't Mormons.

"Jengessen, Carter, an' Wright eyed Lassiter, for what must hev been a second an' seemed like an hour, an' they went white an' strung. But they didn't weaken nor lose their nerve.

"I hed a good look at Lassiter. He stood sort of stiff, bendin' a little, an' both his arms were crooked, an' his hands looked like a hawk's claws. But there ain't no tellin' how his eyes looked. I know this, though, an' thet is his eyes could read the mind of any man about to throw a gun. An' in watchin' him, of course, I couldn't see the three men go fer their guns. An' though I was lookin' right at Lassiter—lookin' hard—I couldn't see how he drawed. He was quicker 'n eyesight—thet's all. But I seen the red spurtin' of his guns, an' heard his shots jest the very littlest instant before I heard the shots of the riders. An' when I turned, Wright an' Carter was down, an' Jengessen, who's tough like a steer, was pullin' the trigger of a wabblin' gun. But it was plain he was shot through, plumb center. An' sudden he fell with a crash, an' his gun clattered on the floor.

"Then there was a hell of a silence. Nobody breathed. Sartin I didn't, anyway. I saw Lassiter slip a smokin' gun back in a belt. But he hadn't throwed either of the big black guns, an' I thought thet strange. An' all this was happenin' quick—you can't imagine how quick.

"There come a scrapin' on the floor an' Dyer got up, his face like lead. I wanted to watch Lassiter, but Dyer's face, onct I seen it like thet, glued my eyes. I seen him go fer his gun—why, I could hev done better—quicker—an' then there was a thunderin' shot from Lassiter, an' it hit Dyer's right arm, an' his gun went off as it dropped. He looked at Lassiter like a cornered sage-wolf, an' sort of howled, an' reached down fer his gun. He'd jest picked it off the floor an' was raisin' it when another thunderin' shot almost tore thet arm off—so it seemed to me. The gun dropped again an' he went down on his knees, kind of flounderin' after it. It was some strange an' terrible to see his awful earnestness. Why would such a man cling so to life? Anyway, he got the gun with left hand an' was raisin' it, pullin' trigger in his madness, when the third thunderin' shot hit his left arm, an' he dropped the gun again. But thet left arm wasn't useless yet, fer he grabbed up the gun, an' with a shakin' aim thet would hev been pitiful to me—in any other man—he began to shoot. One wild bullet struck a man twenty feet from Lassiter. An' it killed thet man, as I seen afterward. Then come a bunch of thunderin' shots—nine I calkilated after, fer they come so quick I couldn't count them—an' I knew Lassiter hed turned the black guns loose on Dyer.

"I'm tellin' you straight, Miss Withersteen, fer I want you to know. Afterward you'll git over it. I've seen some soul-rackin' scenes on this Utah border, but this was the awfulest. I remember I closed my eyes, an' fer a minute I thought of the strangest things, out of place there, such as you'd never dream would come to mind. I saw the sage, an' runnin' hosses—an' thet's the beautifulest sight to me—an' I saw dim things in the dark, an' there was a kind of hummin' in my ears. An' I remember distinctly—fer it was what made all these things whirl out of my mind an' opened my eyes—I remember distinctly it was the smell of gunpowder.

"The court had about adjourned fer thet judge. He was on his knees, an' he wasn't prayin'. He was gaspin' and tryin' to press his big, floppin', crippled hands over his body. Lassiter had sent all those last thunderin' shots through his body. Thet was Lassiter's way.

"An' Lassiter spoke, an' if I ever forgit his words I'll never forgit the sound of his voice.

"'*Proselyter,* I reckon you'd better call quick on thet God who reveals Hisself to you on earth, because He won't be visitin' the place you're goin' to!'

"An' then I seen Dyer look at his big, hangin' hands thet wasn't big enough fer the last work he set them to. An' he looked up at Lassiter. An' then he stared horrible at somethin' thet wasn't Lassiter, nor anyone there, nor the room, nor the branches of purple sage peepin' into the winder. Whatever he seen, it was with the look of a man who *discovers* somethin' too late. Thet's a terrible look! . . . An' with a horrible *understandin'* cry he slid forrard on his face."

Judkins paused in his narrative, breathing heavily while he wiped his perspiring brow.

"Thet's about all," he concluded. "Lassiter left the meetin'-house an' I hurried to catch up with him. He was bleedin' from three gunshots, none of them much to bother him. An' we come right up here. I found you layin' in the hall, an' I hed to work some over you."

Jane Withersteen offered up no prayer for Dyer's soul.

Lassiter's step sounded in the hall—the familiar soft, silver-clinking step—and she heard it with thrilling new emotions in which was a vague joy in her very fear of him. The door opened, and she saw him, the old Lassiter, slow, easy, gentle, cool, yet not exactly the same Lassiter. She rose, and for a moment her eyes blurred and swam in tears.

"Are you—all—all right?" she asked, tremulously.

"I reckon."

"Lassiter, I'll ride away with you. Hide me till danger is past—till we are forgotten—then take me where you will. Your people shall be my people, and your God my God!"

He kissed her hand with the quaint grace and courtesy that came to him in rare moments.

"Black Star an' Night are ready," he said simply.

His quiet mention of the black racers spurred Jane to action. Hurrying to her room, she changed to her rider's suit, packed her jewelry, and the gold that was left, and all the woman's apparel for which there was space in the saddle-bags, and then returned to the hall. Black Star stamped his iron-shod hoofs and tossed his beautiful head, and eyed her with knowing eyes.

"Judkins, I give Bells to you," said Jane. "I hope you will always keep him and be good to him."

Judkins mumbled thanks that he could not speak fluently, and his eyes flashed.

Lassiter strapped Jane's saddle-bags upon Black Star, and led the racers out into the court.

"Judkins, you ride with Jane out into the sage. If you see any riders comin' shout quick twice. An', Jane, *don't look back!* I'll catch up soon. We'll get to the break onto the Pass before midnight, an' then wait until mornin' to go down."

Black Star bent his graceful neck and bowed his noble head, and his broad shoulders yielded as he knelt for Jane to mount.

She rode out of the court beside Judkins, through the grove, across the wide lane into the sage, and she realized that she was leaving Withersteen House forever, and she did not look back. A strange, dreamy, calm peace pervaded her soul. Her doom had fallen upon her, but, instead of finding life no longer worth living she found it doubly significant, full of sweetness as the western breeze, beautiful and unknown as the sage-slope stretching its purple sunset shadows before her. She became aware of Judkins's hand touching hers; she heard him speak a husky good-by; then into the place of Bells shot the dead-black, keen, racy nose of Night, and she knew Lassiter rode beside her.

"Don't—look—back!" he said, and his voice, too, was not clear.

Facing straight ahead, seeing only the waving, shadowy sage, Jane held out her gauntleted hand, to feel it enclosed in strong clasp. So she rode on without a backward glance at the beautiful grove of Cottonwoods. She did not seem to think of the past, of what she left forever, but of the color and mystery and wildness of the sage-slope leading down to Deception Pass, and of the future. She watched the shadows lengthen down the slope; she felt the cool west wind sweeping by from the rear; and she wondered at low, yellow clouds sailing swiftly over her and beyond.

"Don't—look—back!" said Lassiter.

Thick-driving belts of smoke traveled by on the wind, and with it came a strong, pungent odor of burning wood.

Lassiter had fired Withersteen House! But Jane did not look back.

A misty veil obscured the clear, searching gaze she had kept steadfastly upon the purple slope and the dim lines of cañons. It passed, as passed the rolling clouds of smoke, and she saw the valley deepening into the shades of twilight. Night came on, swift as the fleet racers, and stars peeped out to brighten and grow, and the huge, windy, eastern heave of sage-level paled under a rising moon and turned to silver. Blanched in moonlight, the sage yet seemed to hold its hue of purple and was infinitely more wild and lonely. So the night hours wore on, and Jane Withersteen never once looked back.

CHAPTER TWENTY-ONE
Black Star and Night

The time had come for Venters and Bess to leave their retreat. They were at great pains to choose the few things they would be able to carry with them on the journey out of Utah.

"Bern, whatever kind of a pack's this, anyhow?" questioned Bess, rising from her work with reddened face.

Venters, absorbed in his own task, did not look up at all, and in reply said he had brought so much from Cottonwoods that he did not recollect the half of it.

"A woman packed this!" Bess exclaimed.

He scarcely caught her meaning, but the peculiar tone of her voice caused him instantly to rise, and he saw Bess on her knees before an open pack which he recognized as the one given him by Jane.

"By George!" he ejaculated, guiltily, and then at sight of Bess's face he laughed outright.

"A woman packed this," she repeated, fixing woeful, tragic eyes on him.

"Well, is that a crime?"

"There—there *is* a woman, after all!"

"Now, Bess—"

"You've lied to me!"

Then and there Venters found it imperative to postpone work for the present. All her life Bess had been isolated, but she had inherited certain elements of the eternal feminine.

"But there *was* a woman and you *did* lie to me," she kept repeating, after he had explained.

"What of that? Bess, I'll get angry at you in a moment. Remember you've been pent up all your life. I venture to say that if you'd been out in the world you'd have had a dozen sweethearts and have told many a lie before this."

"I wouldn't anything of the kind," declared Bess, indignantly.

"Well—perhaps not lie. But you'd have had the sweethearts. You couldn't have helped that—being so pretty."

This remark appeared to be a very clever and fortunate one; and the work of selecting and then of stowing all the packs in the cave went on without further interruption.

Venters closed up the opening of the cave with a thatch of willows and aspens, so that not even a bird or a rat could get in to the sacks of grain. And this work was in order with the precaution habitually observed by him. He might not be able to get out of Utah, and have to return to the valley. But he owed it to Bess to make the attempt, and in case they were compelled to turn back he wanted to find that fine store of food and grain intact. The outfit of implements and utensils he packed away in another cave.

"Bess, we have enough to live here all our lives," he said once, dreamily.

"Shall I go roll Balancing Rock?" she asked, in light speech, but with deep-blue fire in her eyes.

"No—no."

"Ah, you don't forget the gold and the world," she sighed.

"Child, you forget the beautiful dresses and the travel—and everything."

"Oh, I want to go. But I want to stay!"

"I feel the same way."

They let the eight calves out of the corral, and kept only two of the burros Venters had brought from Cottonwoods. These they intended to ride. Bess freed all her pets—the quail and rabbits and foxes.

The last sunset and twilight and night were both the sweetest and saddest they had ever spent in Surprise Valley. Morning brought keen exhilaration and excitement. When Venters had saddled the two burros, strapped on the light packs and the two canteens, the sunlight was dispersing the lazy shadows from the valley. Taking a last look at the caves and the silver spruces, Venters and Bess made a reluctant start, leading the burros. Ring and Whitie looked keen and knowing. Something seemed to drag at Venters's feet and he noticed Bess lagged behind. Never had the climb from terrace to bridge appeared so long.

Not till they reached the opening of the gorge did they stop to rest and take one last look at the valley. The tremendous arch of stone curved clear and sharp in outline against the morning sky. And through it streaked the golden shaft. The valley seemed an enchanted circle of glorious veils of gold and wraiths of white and silver haze and dim, blue, moving shade—beautiful and wild and unreal as a dream.

"We—we can—th—think of it—always—re—remember," sobbed Bess.

"Hush! Don't cry. Our valley has only fitted us for a better life somewhere. Come!"

They entered the gorge and he closed the willow gate. From rosy, golden morning light they passed into cool, dense gloom. The burros pattered up the trail with little hollow-cracking steps. And the gorge widened to narrow outlet and the gloom lightened to gray. At the divide they halted for another rest. Venters's keen, remembering gaze searched Balancing Rock, and the long incline, and the cracked toppling walls, but failed to note the slightest change.

The dogs led the descent; then came Bess leading her burro; then Venters leading his. Bess kept her eyes bent downward. Venters, however, had an irresistible desire to look upward at Balancing Rock. It had always haunted him, and now he wondered if he were really to get through the outlet before the huge stone thundered down. He fancied that would be a miracle. Every few steps he answered to the strange, nervous fear and turned to make sure the rock still stood like a giant statue. And, as he descended, it grew dimmer in his sight. It changed form; it swayed; it nodded darkly; and at last, in his heightened fancy, he saw it heave and roll. As in a dream when he felt himself falling yet knew he would never fall, so he saw this long-standing thunder-bolt of the little stone-men plunge down to close forever the outlet to Deception Pass.

And while he was giving way to unaccountable dread imaginations the descent was accomplished without mishap.

"I'm glad that's over," he said, breathing more freely. "I hope I'm by that hanging rock for good and all. Since almost the moment I first saw it I've had an idea that it was waiting for me. Now, when it does fall, if I'm thousands of miles away, I'll hear it."

With the first glimpses of the smooth slope leading down to the grotesque cedars and out to the Pass, Venters's cool nerve returned. One long survey to the left, then one to the right, satisfied his caution. Leading the burros down to the spur of rock, he halted at the steep incline.

"Bess, here's the bad place, the place I told you about, with the cut steps. You start down, leading your burro. Take your time and hold on to him if you slip. I've got a rope on him and a half-hitch on this point of rock, so I can let him down safely. Coming up here was a killing job. But it'll be easy going down."

Both burros passed down the difficult stairs cut by the cliff-dwellers, and did it without a misstep. After that the descent down the slope and over the mile of scrawled, ripped, and ridged rock required only careful guidance, and Venters got the burros to level ground in a condition that caused him to congratulate himself.

"Oh, if we only had Wrangle!" exclaimed Venters. "But we're lucky. That's the worst of our trail passed. We've only men to fear now. If we get up in the sage we can hide and slip along like coyotes."

They mounted and rode west through the valley and entered the cañon. From time to time Venters walked, leading his burro. When they got by all the cañons and gullies opening into the Pass they went faster and with fewer halts. Venters did not confide in Bess the alarming fact that he had seen horses and smoke less than a mile up one of the intersecting cañons. He did not talk at all. And long after he had passed this cañon and felt secure once more in the certainty that they had been unobserved he never relaxed his watchfulness. But he did not walk any more, and he kept the burros at a steady trot. Night fell before they reached the last water in the Pass and they made camp by starlight. Venters did not want the burros to stray, so he tied them with long halters in the grass near the spring. Bess, tired out and silent, laid her head in a saddle and went to sleep between the two dogs. Venters did not close his eyes. The cañon silence appeared full of the low, continuous hum of insects. He listened until the hum grew into a roar, and then, breaking the spell, once more he heard it low and clear. He watched the stars and the moving shadows, and always his glance returned to the girl's dimly pale face. And he remembered how white and still it had once looked in the starlight. And again stern thought fought his strange fancies. Would all his labor and his love be for naught? Would he lose her, after all? What did the dark shadow around her portend? Did calamity lurk on that long upland trail through the sage? Why should his heart swell and throb with nameless fear? He listened to the silence, and told himself that in the broad light of day he could dispel this leaden-weighted dread.

At the first hint of gray over the eastern rim he awoke Bess, saddled the burros, and began the day's travel. He wanted to get out of the Pass before there was any chance of riders coming down. They gained the break as the first red rays of the rising sun colored the rim.

For once, so eager was he to get up to level ground, he did not send Ring or Whitie in advance. Encouraging Bess to hurry, pulling at his patient, plodding burro, he climbed the soft, steep trail.

Brighter and brighter grew the light. He mounted the last broken edge of rim to have the sun-fired, purple sage-slope burst upon him as a glory. Bess panted up to his side, tugging on the halter of her burro.

"We're up!" he cried, joyously. "There's not a dot on the sage. We're safe. We'll not be seen! Oh, Bess—"

Ring growled and sniffed the keen air and bristled. Venters clutched at his rifle. Whitie sometimes made a mistake, but Ring never. The dull thud of hoofs almost deprived Venters of power to turn and see from where disaster threatened. He felt his eyes dilate as he stared at Lassiter leading Black Star and Night out of the sage, with Jane Withersteen, in rider's costume, close beside them.

For an instant Venters felt himself whirl dizzily in the center of vast circles of sage. He recovered partially, enough to see Lassiter standing with a glad smile and Jane riveted in astonishment.

"Why, Bern!" she exclaimed. "How good it is to see you! We're riding away, you see. The storm burst—and I'm a ruined woman! . . . I thought you were alone."

Venters, unable to speak for consternation, and bewildered out of all sense of what he ought or ought not to do, simply stared at Jane.

"Son, where are you bound for?" asked Lassiter.

"Not safe—where I was. I'm—we're going out of Utah—back East," he found tongue to say.

"I reckon this meetin's the luckiest thing that ever happened to you an' to me—an' to Jane—an' to Bess," said Lassiter, coolly.

"Bess!" cried Jane, with a sudden leap of blood to her pale cheek.

It was entirely beyond Venters to see any luck in that meeting.

Jane Withersteen took one flashing, woman's glance at Bess's scarlet face, at her slender, shapely form.

"Venters! is this a girl—a woman?" she questioned, in a voice that stung.

"Yes."

"Did you have her in that wonderful valley?"

"Yes, but Jane—"

"All the time you were gone?"

"Yes, but I couldn't tell—"

"Was it for *her* you asked me to give you supplies? Was it for *her* that you wanted to make your valley a paradise?"

"Oh—Jane—"

"Answer me."

"Yes."

"Oh, you liar!" And with these passionate words Jane Withersteen succumbed to fury. For the second time in her life she fell into the ungovernable rage that had been her father's weakness. And it was worse than his, for she was a jealous woman—jealous even of her friends.

As best he could, he bore the brunt of her anger. It was not only his deceit to her that she visited upon him, but her betrayal by religion, by life itself.

Her passion, like fire at white heat, consumed itself in little time. Her physical strength failed, and still her spirit attempted to go on in magnificent denunciation of those who had wronged her. Like a tree cut deep into its roots, she began to quiver and shake, and her anger weakened into despair. And her ringing voice sank into a broken, husky whisper. Then, spent and pitiable, upheld by Lassiter's arm, she turned and hid her face in Black Star's mane.

Numb as Venters was when at length Jane Withersteen lifted her head and looked at him, he yet suffered a pang.

"Jane, the girl is innocent!" he cried.

"Can you expect me to believe that?" she asked, with weary, bitter eyes.

"I'm not that kind of a liar. And you know it. If I lied—if I kept silent when honor should have made me speak, it was to spare you. I came to Cottonwoods to tell you. But I couldn't add to your pain. I intended to tell you I had come to love this girl. But, Jane, I hadn't forgotten how good you were to me. I haven't changed at all toward you. I prize your friendship as I always have. But, however it may look to you—don't be unjust. The girl is innocent. Ask Lassiter."

"Jane, she's jest as sweet an' innocent as little Fay," said Lassiter. There was a faint smile upon his face and beautiful light.

Venters saw, and knew that Lassiter saw, how Jane Withersteen's tortured soul wrestled with hate and threw it—with scorn, doubt, suspicion, and overcame all.

"Bern, if in my misery I accused you unjustly, I crave forgiveness," she said. "I'm not what I once was. Tell me—who is this girl?"

"Jane, she is Oldring's daughter, and his Masked Rider. Lassiter will tell you how I shot her for a rustler, saved her life—all the story. It's a strange story, Jane, as wild as the sage. But it's true—true as her innocence. That you must believe!"

"Oldring's Masked Rider! Oldring's daughter!" exclaimed Jane. "And she's innocent! You ask me to believe much. If this girl is—is what you say, how could she be going away with the man who killed her father?"

"Why did you tell that?" cried Venters, passionately.

Jane's question had roused Bess out of stupefaction. Her eyes suddenly darkened and dilated. She stepped toward Venters and held up both hands as if to ward off a blow.

"Did—did you kill Oldring?"

"I did, Bess, and I hate myself for it. But you know I never dreamed he was your father. I thought he'd wronged you. I killed him when I was madly jealous."

For a moment Bess was shocked into silence.

"But he was my father!" she broke out, at last. "And now I must go back—I can't go with you. It's all over—that beautiful dream. Oh, I *knew* it couldn't come true. You can't take me now."

"If you forgive me, Bess, it'll all come right in the end!" implored Venters.

"It can't be right. I'll go back. After all, I loved him. He was good to me. I can't forget that."

"If you go back to Oldring's men I'll follow you, and then they'll kill me," said Venters, hoarsely.

"Oh no, Bern, you'll not come. Let me go. It's best for you to forget me. I've brought you only pain and dishonor."

She did not weep. But the sweet bloom and life died out of her face. She looked haggard and sad, all at once stunted; and her hands dropped listlessly; and her head drooped in slow, final acceptance of a hopeless fate.

"Jane, look there!" cried Venters, in despairing grief. "Need you have told her? Where was all your kindness of heart? This girl has had a wretched, lonely life. And I'd found a way to make her happy. You've killed it. You've killed something sweet and pure and hopeful, just as sure as you breathe."

"Oh, Bern! It was a slip. I never thought—I never thought!" replied Jane. "How could I tell she didn't know?"

Lassiter suddenly moved forward, and with the beautiful light on his face now strangely luminous, he looked at Jane and Venters and then let his soft, bright gaze rest on Bess.

"Well, I reckon you've all had your say, an' now it's Lassiter's turn. Why, I was jest prayin' for this meetin'. Bess, jest look here."

Gently he touched her arm and turned her to face the others, and then outspread his great hand to disclose a shiny, battered gold locket.

"Open it," he said, with a singularly rich voice.

Bess complied, but listlessly.

"Jane—Venters—come closer," went on Lassiter. "Take a look at the picture. Don't you know the woman?"

Jane, after one glance, drew back.

"Milly Erne!" she cried, wonderingly.

Venters, with tingling pulse, with something growing on him, recognized in the faded miniature portrait the eyes of Milly Erne.

"Yes, that's Milly," said Lassiter, softly. "Bess, did you ever see her face—look hard—with all your heart an' soul?"

"The eyes seem to haunt me," whispered Bess. "Oh, I can't remember—they're eyes of my dreams—but—but—"

Lassiter's strong arm went round her and he bent his head.

"Child, I thought you'd remember her eyes. They're the same beautiful eyes you'd see if you looked in a mirror or a clear spring. They're your mother's eyes. You are Milly Erne's child. Your name is Elizabeth Erne. You're not Oldring's daughter. You're the daughter of Frank Erne, a man once my best friend. Look! Here's his picture beside Milly's. He was handsome, an' as fine an' gallant a Southern gentleman as I ever seen. Frank came of an old family. You come of the best of blood, lass, and blood tells."

Bess slipped through his arm to her knees and hugged the locket to her bosom, and lifted wonderful, yearning eyes.

"It—can't—be—true!"

"Thank God, lass, it *is* true," replied Lassiter. "Jane an' Bern here—they both recognize Milly. They see Milly in you. They're so knocked out they can't tell you, that's all."

"Who are you?" whispered Bess.

"I reckon I'm Milly's brother an' your uncle! . . . Uncle Jim! Ain't that fine?"

"Oh, I can't believe— Don't raise me! Bern, let me kneel. I see truth in your face—in Miss Withersteen's. But let me hear it all—all on my knees. Tell me *how* it's true!"

"Well, Elizabeth, listen," said Lassiter. "Before you was born your father made a mortal enemy of a Mormon named Dyer. They was both ministers an' come to be rivals. Dyer stole your mother away from her home. She gave birth to you in Texas eighteen years ago. Then she was taken to Utah, from place to place, an' finally to the last border settlement—Cottonwoods. You was about three years old when you was taken away from Milly. She never knew what had become of you. But she lived a good while hopin' and prayin' to have you again. Then she gave up an' died. An' I may as well put in here your father died ten years ago. Well, I spent my time tracin' Milly, an' some months back I landed in Cottonwoods. An' jest lately I learned all about you. I had a talk with Oldrin' an' told him you was dead, an' he told me what I had so long been wantin' to know. It was Dyer, of course, who stole you from Milly. Part reason he was sore because Milly refused to give you Mormon teachin', but mostly he still hated Frank Erne so infernally that he made a deal with Oldrin' to take you an' bring you up as an infamous rustler an' rustler's girl. The idea was to break Frank Erne's heart if he ever came to Utah—to show him his daughter with a band of low rustlers. Well—Oldrin' took you, brought you up from childhood, an' then made you his Masked Rider. He made you infamous. He kept that part of the contract, but he learned to love you as a daughter an' never let any but his own men know you was a girl. I heard him say that with my own ears, an' I saw his big eyes grow dim. He told me how he had guarded you always, kept you locked up in his absence, was always at your side or near you on those rides that made you famous on the sage. He said he an' an old rustler whom he trusted had taught you how to read an' write. They selected the books for you. Dyer had wanted you brought up the vilest of the vile! An' Oldrin' brought you up the innocentest of the innocent. He said you didn't know what vileness was. I can hear his big voice tremble now as he said it. He told me how the men—rustlers an' outlaws—who from time to time tried to approach you familiarly—he told me how he shot them dead. I'm tellin' you this 'specially because you've showed such shame—sayin' you was nameless an' all that. Nothin' on earth can be wronger than that idea of yours. An' the truth of it is here. Oldrin' swore to me that if Dyer died, releasin' the contract, he intended to hunt up your father an' give you back to him. It seems Oldrin' wasn't all bad, an' he sure loved you."

Venters leaned forward in passionate remorse.

"Oh, Bess! I know Lassiter speaks the truth. For when I shot Oldring he dropped to his knees and fought with unearthly power to speak. And he said: 'Man—why—didn't—you—wait? Bess was—' Then he fell dead. And I've been haunted by his look and words. Oh, Bess, what a strange, splendid thing for Oldring to do! It all seems impossible. But, dear, you really are not what you thought."

"Elizabeth Erne!" cried Jane Withersteen. "I loved your mother and I see her in you!"

What had been incredible from the lips of men became, in the tone, look, and gesture of a woman, a wonderful truth for Bess. With little tremblings of all her slender body she rocked to and fro on her knees. The yearning wistfulness of her eyes changed to solemn splendor of joy. She believed. She was realizing happiness. And as the process of thought was slow, so were the variations of her expression. Her eyes reflected the transformation of her soul. Dark, brooding, hopeless belief—clouds of gloom—drifted, paled, vanished in glorious light. An exquisite rose flush—a glow—shone from her face as she slowly began to rise from her knees. A spirit uplifted her. All that she had held as base dropped from her.

Venters watched her in joy too deep for words. By it he divined something of what Lassiter's revelation meant to Bess, but he knew he could only faintly understand. That moment when she seemed to be lifted by some spiritual transfiguration was the most beautiful moment of his life. She stood with parted, quivering lips, with hands tightly clasping the locket to her heaving breast. A new conscious pride of worth dignified the old wild, free grace and poise.

"Uncle Jim!" she said, tremulously, with a different smile from any Venters had ever seen on her face.

Lassiter took her into his arms.

"I reckon. It's powerful fine to hear that," replied Lassiter, unsteadily.

Venters, feeling his eyes grow hot and wet, turned away, and found himself looking at Jane Withersteen. He had almost forgotten her presence. Tenderness and sympathy were fast hiding traces of her agitation. Venters read her mind—felt the reaction of her noble heart—saw the joy she was beginning to feel at the happiness of others. And suddenly blinded, choked by his emotions, he turned from her also. He knew what she would do presently; she would make some magnificent amend for her anger; she would give some manifestation of her love; probably all in a moment, as she had loved Milly Erne, so would she love Elizabeth Erne.

"'Pears to me, folks, that we'd better talk a little serious now," remarked Lassiter, at length. "Time flies."

"You're right," replied Venters, instantly. "I'd forgotten time—place—danger. Lassiter, you're riding away. Jane's leaving Withersteen House?"

"Forever," replied Jane.

"I fired Withersteen House," said Lassiter.

"Dyer?" questioned Venters, sharply.

"I reckon where Dyer's gone there won't be any kidnappin' of girls."

"Ah! I knew it. I told Judkins— And Tull?" went on Venters, passionately.

"Tull wasn't around when I broke loose. By now he's likely on our trail with his riders."

"Lassiter, you're going into the Pass to hide till all this storm blows over?"

"I reckon that's Jane's idea. I'm thinkin' the storm'll be a powerful long time blowin' over. I was comin' to join you in Surprise Valley. You'll go back now with me?"

"No. I want to take Bess out of Utah. Lassiter, Bess found gold in the valley. We've a saddle-bag full of gold. If we can reach Sterling—"

"Man! How're you ever goin' to do that? Sterlin' is a hundred miles."

"My plan is to ride on, keeping sharp lookout. Somewhere up the trail we'll take to the sage and go round Cottonwoods and then hit the trail again."

"It's a bad plan. You'll kill the burros in two days."

"Then we'll walk."

"That's more bad an' worse. Better go back down the Pass with me."

"Lassiter, this girl has been hidden all her life in that lonely place," went on Venters. "Oldring's men are hunting me. We'd not be safe there any longer. Even if we would be I'd take this chance to get her out. I want to marry her. She shall have some of the pleasures of life—see cities and people. We've gold—we'll be rich. Why, life opens sweet for both of us. And, by Heaven! I'll get her out or lose my life in the attempt!"

"I reckon if you go on with them burros you'll lose your life all right. Tull will have riders all over this sage. You can't get out on them burros. It's a fool idea. That's not doin' best by the girl. Come with me an' take chances on the rustlers."

Lassiter's cool argument made Venters waver, not in determination to go, but in hope of success.

"Bess, I want you to know. Lassiter says the trip's almost useless now. I'm afraid he's right. We've got about one chance in a hundred to go through. Shall we take it? Shall we go on?"

"We'll go on," replied Bess.

"That settles it, Lassiter."

Lassiter spread wide his hands, as if to signify he could do no more, and his face clouded.

Venters felt a touch on his elbow. Jane stood beside him with a hand on his arm. She was smiling. Something radiated from her, and like an electric current accelerated the motion of his blood.

"Bern, you'd be right to die rather than not take Elizabeth out of Utah—out of this wild country. You must do it. You'll show her the great world, with all its wonders. Think how little she has seen! Think what delight is in store for her! You have gold; you will be free; you will make her happy. What a glorious prospect! I share it with you. I'll think of you—dream of you—pray for you."

"Thank you, Jane," replied Venters, trying to steady his voice. "It does look bright. Oh, if we were only across that wide, open waste of sage!"

"Bern, the trip's as good as made. It'll be safe—easy. It'll be a glorious ride," she said, softly.

Venters stared. Had Jane's troubles made her insane? Lassiter, too, acted queerly, all at once beginning to turn his sombrero round in hands that actually shook.

"You are a rider. She is a rider. This will be the ride of your lives," added Jane, in that same soft undertone, almost as if she were musing to herself.

"Jane!" he cried.

"I give you Black Star and Night!"

"Black Star and Night!" he echoed.

"It's done. Lassiter, put our saddle-bags on the burros."

Only when Lassiter moved swiftly to execute her bidding did Venters's clogged brain grasp at literal meanings. He leaped to catch Lassiter's busy hands.

"No, no! What are you doing?" he demanded, in a kind of fury. "I won't take her racers. What do you think I am? It'd be monstrous. Lassiter! stop it, I say! . . . You've got her to save. You've miles and miles to go. Tull is trailing you. There are rustlers in the Pass. Give me back that saddle-bag!"

"Son—cool down," returned Lassiter, in a voice he might have used to a child. But the grip with which he tore away Venters's grasping hands was that of a giant. "Listen—you fool boy! Jane's sized up the situation. The burros'll do for us. We'll sneak along an' hide. I'll take your dogs an' your rifle. Why, it's the trick. The blacks are yours, an' sure as I can throw a gun you're goin' to ride safe out of the sage."

"Jane—stop him—please stop him," gasped Venters. "I've lost my strength. I can't do—anything. This is hell for me! Can't you see that? I've ruined you—it was through me you lost all. You've only Black Star and Night left. You love these horses. Oh! I know how you must love them now! And—you're trying to give them to me. To help me out of Utah! To save the girl I love!"

"That will be my glory."

Then in the white, rapt face, in the unfathomable eyes, Venters saw Jane Withersteen in a supreme moment. This moment was one wherein she reached up to the height for which her noble soul had ever yearned. He, after disrupting the calm tenor of her peace, after bringing down on her head the implacable hostility of her churchmen, after teaching her a bitter lesson of life—he was to be her salvation. And he turned away again, this time shaken to the core of his soul. Jane Withersteen was the incarnation of selflessness. He experienced wonder and terror, exquisite pain and rapture. What were all the shocks life had dealt him compared to the thought of such loyal and generous friendship?

And instantly, as if by some divine insight, he knew himself in the remaking—tried, found wanting; but stronger, better, surer—and he wheeled to Jane Withersteen, eager, joyous, passionate, wild, exalted. He bent to her; he left tears and kisses on her hands.

"Jane, I—I can't find words—now," he said. "I'm beyond words. Only—I understand. And I'll take the blacks."

"Don't be losin' no more time," cut in Lassiter. "I ain't certain, but I think I seen a speck up the sage-slope. Mebbe I was mistaken. But, anyway, we must all be movin'. I've shortened the stirrups on Black Star. Put Bess on him."

Jane Withersteen held out her arms.

"Elizabeth Erne!" she cried, and Bess flew to her.

How inconceivably strange and beautiful it was for Venters to see Bess clasped to Jane Withersteen's breast!

Then he leaped astride Night.

"Venters, ride straight on up the slope," Lassiter was saying, "an' if you don't meet any riders keep on till you're a few miles from the village, then cut off in the sage an' go round to the trail. But you'll most likely meet riders with Tull. Jest keep right on till you're jest out of gunshot an' then make your cut-off into the sage. They'll ride after you, but it won't be no use. You can ride, an' Bess can ride. When you're out of reach turn on round to the west, an' hit the trail somewhere. Save the hosses all you can, but don't be afraid. Black Star and Night are good for a hundred miles before sundown, if you have to push them. You can get to Sterlin' by night if you want. But better make it along about to-morrow mornin'. When you get through the notch on the Glaze trail, swing to the right. You'll be able to see both Glaze an' Stone Bridge. Keep away from them villages. You won't run no risk of meetin' any of Oldrin's rustlers from Sterlin' on. You'll find water in them deep hollows north of the Notch. There's an old trail there, not much used, an' it leads to Sterlin'. That's your trail. An' one thing more. If Tull pushes you—or keeps on persistent-like, for a few miles—jest let the blacks out an' lose him an' his riders."

"Lassiter, may we meet again!" said Venters, in a deep voice.

"Son, it ain't likely—it ain't likely. Well, Bess Oldrin'—Masked Rider—Elizabeth Erne—now you climb on Black Star. I've heard you could ride. Well, every rider loves a good horse. An', lass, there never was but one that could beat Black Star."

"Ah, Lassiter, there never was any horse that could beat Black Star," said Jane, with the old pride.

"I often wondered—mebbe Venters rode out that race when he brought back the blacks. Son, was Wrangle the best hoss?"

"No, Lassiter," replied Venters. For this lie he had his reward in Jane's quick smile.

"Well, well, my hoss-sense ain't always right. An' here I'm talkin' a lot, wastin' time. It ain't so easy to find an' lose a pretty niece all in one hour! Elizabeth—good-by!"

"Oh, Uncle Jim! . . . Good-by!"

"Elizabeth Erne, be happy! Good-by," said Jane.

"Good-by—oh—good-by!"

In lithe, supple action Bess swung up to Black Star's saddle.

"Jane Withersteen! . . . Good-by!" called Venters hoarsely.

"Bern—Bess—riders of the purple sage—good-by!"

CHAPTER TWENTY-TWO
Riders of the Purple Sage

Black Star and Night, answering to spur, swept swiftly westward along the white, slow-rising, sage-bordered trail. Venters heard a mournful howl from Ring, but Whitie was silent. The blacks settled into their fleet, long-striding gallop. The wind sweetly fanned Venters's hot face. From the summit of the first low-swelling ridge he looked back. Lassiter waved his hand; Jane waved her scarf. Venters replied by standing in his stirrups and holding high his sombrero. Then the dip of the ridge hid them. From the height of the next he turned once more. Lassiter, Jane, and the burros had disappeared. They had gone down into the Pass. Venters felt a sensation of irreparable loss.

"Bern—look!" called Bess, pointing up the long slope.

A small, dark, moving dot split the line where purple sage met blue sky. That dot was a band of riders.

"Pull the black, Bess."

They slowed from gallop to canter, then to trot. The fresh and eager horses did not like the check.

"Bern, Black Star has great eyesight."

"I wonder if they're Tull's riders. They might be rustlers. But it's all the same to us."

The black dot grew to a dark patch moving under low dust-clouds. It grew all the time, though very slowly. There were long periods when it was in plain sight, and intervals when it dropped behind the sage. The blacks trotted for half an hour, for another half-hour, and still the moving patch appeared to stay on the horizon line. Gradually, however, as time passed, it began to enlarge, to creep down the slope, to encroach upon the intervening distance.

"Bess, what do you make them out?" asked Venters. "I don't think they're rustlers."

"They're sage-riders," replied Bess. "I see a white horse and several grays. Rustlers seldom ride any horses but bays and blacks."

"That white horse is Tull's. Pull the black, Bess. I'll get down and cinch up. We're in for some riding. Are you afraid?"

"Not now," answered the girl, smiling.

"You needn't be. Bess, you don't weigh enough to make Black Star know you're on him. I won't be able to stay with you. You'll leave Tull and his riders as if they were standing still."

"How about you?"

"Never fear. If I can't stay with you I can still laugh at Tull."

"Look, Bern! They've stopped on that ridge. They see us."

"Yes. But we're too far yet for them to make out who we are. They'll recognize the blacks first. We've passed most of the ridges and the thickest sage. Now, when I give the word, let Black Star go and ride!"

Venters calculated that a mile or more still intervened between them and the riders. They were approaching at a swift canter. Soon Venters recognized Tull's white horse, and concluded that the riders had likewise recognized Black Star and Night. But it would be impossible for Tull yet to see that the blacks were not ridden by Lassiter and Jane. Venters noted that Tull and the line of horsemen, perhaps ten or twelve in number, stopped several times and evidently looked hard down the slope. It must have been a puzzling circumstance for Tull. Venters laughed grimly at the thought of what Tull's rage would be when he finally discovered the trick. Venters meant to sheer out into the sage before Tull could possibly be sure who rode the blacks.

The gap closed to a distance to half a mile. Tull halted. His riders came up and formed a dark group around him. Venters thought he saw him wave his arms, and was certain of it when the riders dashed into the sage, to right and left of the trail. Tull had anticipated just the move held in mind by Venters.

"Now Bess!" shouted Venters. "Strike north. Go round those riders and turn west."

Black Star sailed over the low sage, and in a few leaps got into his stride and was running. Venters spurred Night after him. It was hard going in the sage. The horses could run as well there, but keen eyesight and judgment must constantly be used by the riders in choosing ground. And continuous swerving from aisle to aisle between the brush, and leaping little washes and mounds of the pack-rats, and breaking through sage, made rough riding. When Venters had turned into a long aisle he had time to look up at Tull's riders. They were now strung out into an extended line riding northeast. And, as Venters and Bess were holding due north, this meant, if the horses of Tull and his riders had the speed and the staying power, they would head the blacks and turn them back down the slope. Tull's men were not saving their mounts; they were driving them desperately. Venters feared only an accident to Black Star or Night, and skilful riding would mitigate possibility of that. One glance ahead served to show him that Bess could pick a course through the sage as well as he. She looked neither back nor at the running riders, and bent forward over Black Star's neck and studied the ground ahead.

It struck Venters, presently, after he had glanced up from time to time, that Bess was drawing away from him as he had expected. He had, however, only thought of the light weight Black Star was carrying and of his superior speed; he saw now that the black was being ridden as never before, except when Jerry Card lost the race to Wrangle. How easily, gracefully, naturally, Bess sat her saddle! She could ride! Suddenly Venters remembered she had said she could ride. But he had not dreamed she was capable of such superb horsemanship. Then all at once, flashing over him, thrilling him, came the recollection that Bess was Oldring's Masked Rider.

He forgot Tull—the running riders—the race. He let Night have a free rein and felt him lengthen out to suit himself, knowing he would keep to Black Star's course, knowing that he had been chosen by the best rider now on the upland sage. For Jerry Card was dead. And fame had rivaled him with only one rider, and that was the slender girl who now swung so easily with Black Star's stride. Venters had abhorred her notoriety, but now he took passionate pride in her skill, her daring, her power over a horse. And he delved into his memory, recalling famous rides which he had heard related in the villages and round the camp-fires. Oldring's Masked Rider! Many times this strange rider, at once well known and unknown, had escaped pursuers by matchless riding. He had to run the gantlet of vigilantes down the main street of Stone Bridge, leaving dead horses and dead rustlers behind. He had jumped his horse over the Gerber Wash, a deep, wide ravine separating the fields of Glaze from the wild sage. He had been surrounded north of Sterling; and he had broken through the line. How often had been told the story of day stampedes, of night raids, of pursuit, and then how the Masked Rider, swift as the wind, was gone in the sage! A fleet, dark horse—a slender, dark form—a black mask—a driving run down the slope—a dot on the purple sage—a shadowy, muffled steed disappearing in the night!

And this Masked Rider of the uplands had been Elizabeth Erne!

The sweet sage wind rushed in Venters's face and sang a song in his ears. He heard the dull, rapid beat of Night's hoofs; he saw Black Star drawing away, farther and farther. He realized both horses were swinging to the west. Then gunshots in the rear reminded him of Tull. Venters looked back. Far to the side, dropping behind, trooped the riders. They were shooting. Venters saw no puffs or dust, heard no whistling bullets. He was out of range. When he looked back again Tull's riders had given up pursuit. The best they could do, no doubt, had been to get near enough to recognize who really rode the blacks. Venters saw Tull drooping in his saddle.

Then Venters pulled Night out of his running stride. Those few miles had scarcely warmed the black, but Venters wished to save him. Bess turned, and, though she was far away, Venters caught the white glint of her waving hand. He held Night to a trot and rode on, seeing Bess and Black Star, and the sloping upward stretch of sage, and from time to time the receding black riders behind. Soon they disappeared behind a ridge, and he turned no more. They would go back to Lassiter's trail and follow it, and follow in vain. So Venters rode on, with the wind growing sweeter to taste and smell, and the purple sage richer and the sky bluer in his sight; and the song in his ears ringing. By and by Bess halted to wait for him, and he knew she had come to the trail. When he reached her it was to smile at sight of her standing with arms round Black Star's neck.

"Oh, Bern! I love him!" she cried. "He's beautiful; he knows; and how he can run! I've had fast horses. But Black Star! . . . Wrangle never beat him!"

"I'm wondering if I didn't dream that. Bess, the blacks are grand. What it must have cost Jane—ah!—well, when we get out of this wild country with Star and Night, back to my old home in Illinois, we'll buy a beautiful farm with meadows and springs and cool shade. There we'll turn the horses free—free to roam and browse and drink—never to feel a spur again—never to be ridden!"

"I would like that," said Bess.

They rested. Then, mounting, they rode side by side up the white trail. The sun rose higher behind them. Far to the left a low line of green marked the site of Cottonwoods. Venters looked once and looked no more. Bess gazed only straight ahead. They put the blacks to the long, swinging rider's canter, and at times pulled them to a trot, and occasionally to a walk. The hours passed, the miles slipped behind, and the wall of rock loomed in the fore. The Notch opened wide. It was a rugged, stony pass, but with level and open trail, and Venters and Bess ran the blacks through it. An old trail led off to the right, taking the line of the wall, and this Venters knew to be the trail mentioned by Lassiter.

The little hamlet, Glaze, a white and green patch in the vast waste of purple, lay miles down the slope much like the Cottonwoods slope, only this descended to the west. And miles farther west a faint green spot marked the location of Stone Bridge. All the rest of that world was seemingly smooth, undulating sage, with no ragged lines of cañons to accentuate its wildness.

"Bess, we're safe—we're free!" said Venters. "We're alone on the sage. We're half way to Sterling."

"Ah! I wonder how it is with Lassiter and Miss Withersteen."

"Never fear, Bess. He'll outwit Tull. He'll get away and hide her safely. He might climb into Surprise Valley, but I don't think he'll go so far."

"Bern, will we ever find any place like our beautiful valley?"

"No. But, dear, listen. We'll go back some day, after years—ten years. Then we'll be forgotten. And our valley will be just as we left it."

"What if Balancing Rock falls and closes the outlet to the Pass?"

"I've thought of that. I'll pack in ropes and ropes. And if the outlet's closed we'll climb up the cliffs and over them to the valley and go down on rope ladders. It could be done. I know just where to make the climb, and I'll never forget."

"Oh yes, let us go back!"

"It's something sweet to look forward to. Bess, it's like all the future looks to me."

"Call me—Elizabeth," she said, shyly.

"Elizabeth Erne! It's a beautiful name. But I'll never forget Bess. Do you know—have you thought that very soon—by this time to-morrow—you will be Elizabeth Venters?"

So they rode on down the old trail. And the sun sloped to the west, and a golden sheen lay on the sage. The hours sped now; the afternoon waned. Often they rested the horses. The glisten of a pool of water in a hollow caught Venters's eye, and here he unsaddled the blacks and let them roll and drink and browse. When he and Bess rode up out of the hollow the sun was low, a crimson ball, and the valley seemed veiled in purple fire and smoke. It was that short time when the sun appeared to rest before setting, and silence, like a cloak of invisible life, lay heavy on all that shimmering world of sage.

They watched the sun begin to bury its red curve under the dark horizon.

"We'll ride on till late," he said. "Then you can sleep a little, while I watch and graze the horses. And we'll ride into Sterling early to-morrow. We'll be married! . . . We'll be in time to catch the stage. We'll tie Black Star and Night behind—and then—for a country not wild and terrible like this!"

"Oh, Bern! . . . But look! The sun is setting on the sage—the last time for us till we dare come again to the Utah border. Ten years! Oh, Bern, look, so you will never forget!"

Slumbering, fading purple fire burned over the undulating sage ridges. Long streaks and bars and shafts and spears fringed the far western slope. Drifting, golden veils mingled with low, purple shadows. Colors and shades changed in slow, wondrous transformation.

Suddenly Venters was startled by a low, rumbling roar—so low that it was like the roar in a sea-shell.

"Bess, did you hear anything?" he whispered.

"No."

"Listen! . . . Maybe I only imagined— *Ah!"*

Out of the east or north, from remote distance, breathed an infinitely low, continuously long sound—deep, weird, detonating, thundering, deadening—dying.

CHAPTER TWENTY-THREE
The Fall of Balancing Rock

Through tear-blurred sight Jane Withersteen watched Venters and Elizabeth Erne and the black racers disappear over the ridge of sage.

"They're gone!" said Lassiter. "An' they're safe now. An' there'll never be a day of their comin' happy lives but what they'll remember Jane Withersteen an'—an' Uncle Jim! . . . I reckon, Jane, we'd better be on our way."

The burros obediently wheeled and started down the break with little, cautious steps, but Lassiter had to leash the whining dogs and lead them. Jane felt herself bound in a feeling that was neither listlessness nor indifference, yet which rendered her incapable of interest. She was still strong in body, but emotionally tired. That hour at the entrance to Deception Pass had been the climax of her suffering—the flood of her wrath—the last of her sacrifice—the supremity of her love—and the attainment of peace. She thought that if she had little Fay she would not ask any more of life.

Like an automaton she followed Lassiter down the steep trail of dust and bits of weathered stone; and when the little slides moved with her or piled around her knees she experienced no alarm. Vague relief came to her in the sense of being enclosed between dark stone walls, deep hidden from the glare of the sun, from the glistening sage. Lassiter lengthened the stirrup straps on one of the burros and bade her mount and ride close to him. She was to keep the burro from cracking his little hard hoofs on stones. Then she was riding on between dark, gleaming walls. There were quiet and rest and coolness in this cañon. She noted indifferently that they passed close under shady, bulging shelves of cliff, through patches of grass and sage and thicket and groves of slender trees, and over white, pebbly washes, and around masses of broken rock. The burros trotted tirelessly; the dogs, once more free, pattered tirelessly; and Lassiter led on with never a stop, and at every open place he looked back. The shade under the walls gave place to sunlight. And presently they came to a dense thicket of slender trees, through which they passed to rich, green grass and water. Here Lassiter rested the burros for a little while, but he was restless, uneasy, silent, always listening, peering under the trees. She dully reflected that enemies were behind them—before them; still the thought awakened no dread or concern or interest.

At his bidding she mounted and rode on close to the heels of his burro. The cañon narrowed; the walls lifted their rugged rims higher; and the sun shone down hot from the center of the blue stream of sky above. Lassiter traveled slower, with more exceeding care as to the ground he chose, and he kept speaking low to the dogs. They were now hunting-dogs—keen, alert, suspicious, sniffing the warm breeze. The monotony of the yellow walls broke in change of color and smooth surface, and the rugged outline of rims grew craggy. Splits appeared in deep breaks, and gorges running at right angles, and then the pass opened wide at a junction of intersecting cañons.

Lassiter dismounted, led his burro, called the dogs close, and proceeded at snail pace through dark masses of rock and dense thickets under the left wall. Long he watched and listened before venturing to cross the mouths of side cañons. At length he halted, tied his burro, lifted a warning hand to Jane, and then slipped away among the boulders, and, followed by the stealthy dogs, disappeared from sight. The time he remained absent was neither short nor long to Jane Withersteen.

When he reached her side again he was pale, and his lips were set in a hard line, and his gray eyes glittered coldly. Bidding her dismount, he led the burros into a covert of stones and cedars, and tied them.

"Jane, I've run into the fellers I've been lookin' for, an' I'm goin' after them," he said.

"Why?" she asked.

"I reckon I won't take time to tell you."

"Couldn't we slip by without being seen?"

"Likely enough. But that ain't my game. An' I'd like to know, in case I don't come back, what you'll do."

"What can I do?"

"I reckon you can go back to Tull. Or stay in the Pass an' be taken off by rustlers. Which'll you do?"

"I don't know. I can't think very well. But I believe I'd rather be taken off by rustlers."

Lassiter sat down, put his head in his hands, and remained for a few moments in what appeared to be deep and painful thought. When he lifted his face it was haggard, lined, cold as sculptured marble.

"I'll go. I only mentioned that chance of my not comin' back. I'm pretty sure to come."

"Need you risk so much? Must you fight more? Haven't you shed enough blood?"

"I'd like to tell you why I'm goin'," he continued, in coldness he had seldom used to her. She remarked it, but it was the same to her as if he had spoken with his old gentle warmth. "But I reckon I won't. Only, I'll say that mercy an' goodness, such as is in you, though they're the grand things in human nature, can't be lived up to on this Utah border. Life's hell out here. You think—or you used to think—that your religion made this life heaven. Mebbe them scales on your eyes has dropped now. Jane, I wouldn't have you no different, an' that's why I'm going to try to hide you somewhere in this Pass. I'd like to hide many more women, for I've come to see there are more like you among your people. An' I'd like you to see jest how hard an' cruel this border life is. It's bloody. You'd think churches an' churchmen would make it better. They make it worse. You give names to things—bishops, elders, ministers, Mormonism, duty, faith, glory. You dream—or you're driven mad. I'm a man, an' I know. I name fanatics, followers, blind women, oppressors, thieves, ranchers, rustlers, riders. An' we have—what you've lived through these last months. It can't be helped. But it can't last always. An' remember this—some day the border'll be better, cleaner, for the ways of men like Lassiter!"

She saw him shake his tall form erect, look at her strangely and steadfastly, and then, noiselessly, stealthily slip away amid the rocks and trees. Ring and Whitie, not being bidden to follow, remained with Jane. She felt extreme weariness, yet somehow it did not seem to be of her body. And she sat down in the shade and tried to think. She saw a creeping lizard, cactus flowers, the drooping burros, the resting dogs, an eagle high over a yellow crag. Once the meanest flower, a color, the flight of the bee, or any living thing had given her deepest joy. Lassiter had gone off, yielding to his incurable blood lust, probably to his own death; and she was sorry, but there was no feeling in her sorrow.

Suddenly from the mouth of the cañon just beyond her rang out a clear, sharp report of a rifle. Echoes clapped. Then followed a piercingly high yell of anguish, quickly breaking. Again echoes clapped, in grim imitation. Dull revolver shots—hoarse yells—pound of hoofs—shrill neighs of horses—commingling of echoes—and again silence! Lassiter must be busily engaged, thought Jane, and no chill trembled over her, no blanching tightened her skin. Yes, the border was a bloody place. But life had always been bloody. Men were blood-spillers. Phases of the history of the world flashed through her mind—Greek and Roman wars, dark, mediæval times, the crimes in the name of religion. On sea, on land, everywhere—shooting, stabbing, cursing, clashing, fighting men! Greed, power, oppression, fanaticism, love, hate, revenge, justice, freedom—for these, men killed one another.

She lay there under the cedars, gazing up through the delicate lacelike foliage at the blue sky, and she thought and wondered and did not care.

More rattling shots disturbed the noonday quiet. She heard a sliding of weathered rock, a hoarse shout of warning, a yell of alarm, again the clear, sharp crack of the rifle, and another cry that was a cry of death. Then rifle reports pierced a dull volley of revolver shots. Bullets whizzed over Jane's hiding-place; one struck a stone and whined away in the air. After that, for a long time, succeeded desultory shots; and then they ceased under long, thundering fire from heavier guns.

Sooner or later, then, Jane heard the cracking of horses' hoofs on the stones, and the sound came nearer and nearer. Silence intervened until Lassiter's soft, jingling step assured her of his approach. When he appeared he was covered with blood.

"All right, Jane," he said. "I come back. An' don't worry."

With water from a canteen he washed the blood from his face and hands.

"Jane, hurry now. Tear my scarf in two, an' tie up these places. That hole through my hand is some inconvenient, worse 'n this cut over my ear. There—you're doin' fine! Not a bit nervous—no tremblin'. I reckon I ain't done your courage justice. I'm glad you're brave jest now—you'll need to be. Well, I was hid pretty good, enough to keep them from shootin' me deep, but they was slingin' lead close all the time. I used up all the rifle shells, an' then I went after them. Mebbe you heard. It was then I got hit. I had to use up every shell in my own gun, an' they did, too, as I seen. Rustlers an' Mormons, Jane! An' now I'm packin' five bullet holes in my carcass, an' guns without shells. Hurry, now."

He unstrapped the saddle-bags from the burros, slipped the saddles and let them lie, turned the burros loose, and, calling the dogs, led the way through stones and cedars to an open where two horses stood.

"Jane, are you strong?" he asked.

"I think so. I'm not tired," Jane replied.

"I don't mean that way. Can you bear up?"

"I think I can bear anything."

"I reckon you look a little cold an' thick. So I'm preparin' you."

"For what?"

"I didn't tell you why I jest had to go after them fellers. I couldn't tell you. I believe you'd have died. But I can tell you now—if you'll bear up under a shock?"

"Go on, my friend."

"I've got little Fay! Alive—bad hurt—but she'll live!"

Jane Withersteen's dead-locked feeling, rent by Lassiter's deep, quivering voice, leaped into an agony of sensitive life.

"Here," he added, and showed her where little Fay lay on the grass.

Unable to speak, unable to stand, Jane dropped on her knees. By that long, beautiful golden hair Jane recognized the beloved Fay. But Fay's loveliness was gone. Her face was drawn and looked old with grief. But she was not dead—her heart beat—and Jane Withersteen gathered strength and lived again.

"You see I jest had to go after Fay," Lassiter was saying, as he knelt to bathe her little pale face. "But I reckon I don't want no more choices like the one I had to make. There was a crippled feller in that bunch, Jane. Mebbe Venters crippled him. Anyway, that's why they were holdin' up here. I seen little Fay first thing, an' was hard put to it to figure out a way to get her. An' I wanted hosses, too. I had to take chances. So I crawled close to their camp. One feller jumped a hoss with little Fay, an' when I shot him, of course she dropped. She's stunned an' bruised—she fell right on her head. Jane, she's comin' to! She ain't bad hurt!"

Fay's long lashes fluttered; her eyes opened. At first they seemed glazed over. They looked dazed by pain. Then they quickened, darkened, to shine with intelligence—bewilderment—memory—and sudden wonderful joy.

"Muvver—Jane!" she whispered.

"Oh, little Fay, little Fay!" cried Jane, lifting, clasping the child to her.

"Now, we've got to rustle!" said Lassiter, in grim coolness. "Jane, look down the Pass!"

Across the mounds of rock and sage Jane caught sight of a band of riders filing out of the narrow neck of the Pass; and in the lead was a white horse, which, even at a distance of a mile or more, she knew.

"Tull!" she almost screamed.

"I reckon. But, Jane, we've still got the game in our hands. They're ridin' tired hosses. Venters likely give them a chase. He wouldn't forget that. An' we've fresh hosses."

Hurriedly he strapped on the saddle-bags, gave quick glance to girths and cinches and stirrups, then leaped astride.

"Lift little Fay up," he said.

With shaking arms Jane complied.

"Get back your nerve, woman! This's life or death now. Mind that. Climb up! Keep your wits. Stick close to me. Watch where your hoss 's goin an' ride!"

Somehow Jane mounted; somehow found strength to hold the reins, to spur, to cling on, to ride. A horrible quaking, craven fear possessed her soul. Lassiter led the swift flight across the wide space, over washes, through sage, into a narrow cañon where the rapid clatter of hoofs rapped sharply from the walls. The wind roared in her ears; the gleaming cliffs swept by; trail and sage and grass moved under her. Lassiter's bandaged, blood-stained face turned to her; he shouted encouragement; he looked back down the Pass; he spurred his horse. Jane clung on, spurring likewise. And the horses settled from hard, furious gallop into a long-striding, driving run. She had never ridden at anything like that pace; desperately she tried to get the swing of the horse, to be of some help to him in that race, to see the best of the ground and guide him into it. But she failed of everything except to keep her seat in the saddle, and to spur and spur. At times she closed her eyes, unable to bear sight of Fay's golden curls streaming in the wind. She could not pray; she could not rail; she no longer cared for herself. All of life, of good, of use in the world, of hope in heaven centered in Lassiter's ride with little Fay to safety. She would have tried to turn the iron-jawed brute she rode; she would have given herself to that relentless, dark-browed Tull. But she knew Lassiter would turn with her, so she rode on and on.

Whether that run was of moments or hours Jane Withersteen could not tell. Lassiter's horse covered her with froth that blew back in white streams. Both horses ran their limit, were allowed to slow down in time to save them, and went on dripping, heaving, staggering.

"Oh, Lassiter, we must run—we must run!"

He looked back, saying nothing. The bandage had blown from his head, and blood trickled down his face. He was bowing under the strain of injuries, of the ride, of his burden. Yet how cool and gray he looked—how intrepid!

The horses walked, trotted, galloped, ran, to fall again to walk. Hours sped or dragged. Time was an instant—an eternity. Jane Withersteen felt hell pursuing her, and dared not look back for fear she would fall from her horse.

"Oh, Lassiter! Is he coming?"

The grim rider looked over his shoulder, but said no word. Little Fay's golden hair floated on the breeze. The sun shone; the walls gleamed; the sage glistened. And then it seemed the sun vanished, the walls shaded, the sage paled. The horses walked—trotted—galloped—ran—to fall again to walk. Shadows gathered under shelving cliffs. The cañon turned, brightened, opened into long, wide, wall enclosed valley. Again the sun, lowering in the west, reddened the sage. Far ahead round, scrawled stone appeared to block the Pass.

"Bear up, Jane, bear up!" called Lassiter. "It's our game, if you don't weaken."

"Lassiter! Go on—*alone!* Save little Fay!"

"Only with you!"

"Oh!— I'm a coward—a miserable coward! I can't fight or think or hope or pray! I'm lost! Oh, Lassiter, look back! Is he coming? I'll not—hold out—"

"Keep your breath, woman, an' ride not for yourself or for me, but for Fay!"

A last breaking run across the sage brought Lassiter's horse to a walk.

"He's done," said the rider.

"Oh, no—no!" moaned Jane.

"Look back, Jane, look back. Three—four miles we've come across this valley, an' no Tull yet in sight. Only a few more miles!"

Jane looked back over the long stretch of sage, and found the narrow gap in the wall, out of which came a file of dark horses with a white horse in the lead. Sight of the riders acted upon Jane as a stimulant. The weight of cold, horrible terror lessened. And, gazing forward at the dogs, at Lassiter's limping horse, at the blood on his face, at the rocks growing nearer, last at Fay's golden hair, the ice left her veins, and slowly, strangely, she gained hold of strength that she believed would see her to the safety Lassiter promised. And, as she gazed, Lassiter's horse stumbled and fell.

He swung his leg and slipped from the saddle.

"Jane, take the child," he said, and lifted Fay up. Jane clasped her arms suddenly strong. "They're gainin'," went on Lassiter, as he watched the pursuing riders. "But we'll beat 'em yet."

Turning with Jane's bridle in his hand, he was about to start when he saw the saddle-bag on the fallen horse.

"I've jest about got time," he muttered, and with swift fingers that did not blunder or fumble he loosened the bag and threw it over his shoulder. Then he started to run, leading Jane's horse, and he ran, and trotted, and walked, and ran again. Close ahead now Jane saw a rise of bare rock. Lassiter reached it, searched along the base, and, finding a low place, dragged the weary horse up and over round, smooth stone. Looking backward, Jane saw Tull's white horse not a mile distant, with riders strung out in a long line behind him. Looking forward, she saw more valley to the right, and to the left a towering cliff. Lassiter pulled the horse and kept on.

Little Fay lay in her arms with wide-open eyes—eyes which were still shadowed by pain, but no longer fixed, glazed in terror. The golden curls blew across Jane's lips; the little hands feebly clasped her arm; a ghost of a troubled, trustful smile hovered round the sweet lips. And Jane Withersteen awoke to the spirit of a lioness.

Lassiter was leading the horse up a smooth slope toward cedar-trees of twisted and bleached appearance. Among these he halted.

"Jane, give me the girl an' get down," he said. As if it wrenched him he unbuckled the empty black guns with a strange air of finality. He then received Fay in his arms and stood a moment looking backward. Tull's white horse mounted the ridge of round stone, and several bays or blacks followed. "I wonder what he'll think when he sees them empty guns. Jane, bring your saddle-bag and climb after me."

A glistening, wonderful bare slope, with little holes, swelled up and up to lose itself in a frowning yellow cliff. Jane closely watched her steps and climbed behind Lassiter. He moved slowly. Perhaps he was only husbanding his strength. But she saw drops of blood on the stone, and then she knew. They climbed and climbed without looking back. Her breast labored; she began to feel as if little points of fiery steel were penetrating her side into her lungs. She heard the panting of Lassiter and the quicker panting of the dogs.

"Wait—here," he said.

Before her rose a bulge of stone, nicked with little cut steps, and above that a corner of yellow wall, and overhanging that a vast, ponderous cliff.

The dogs pattered up, disappeared round the corner. Lassiter mounted the steps with Fay, and he swayed like a drunken man, and he too disappeared. But instantly he returned alone, and half ran, half slipped down to her.

Then from below pealed up hoarse shouts of angry men. Tull and several of his riders had reached the spot where Lassiter had parted with his guns.

"You'll need that breath—mebbe!" said Lassiter, facing downward, with glittering eyes.

"Now, Jane, the last pull," he went on. "Walk up them little steps. I'll follow an' steady you. Don't think. Jest go. Little Fay's above. Her eyes are open. She jest said to me, *'Where's muvver Jane?'* "

Without a fear or a tremor or a slip or a touch of Lassiter's hand Jane Withersteen walked up that ladder of cut steps.

He pushed her round the corner of the wall. Fay lay, with wide staring eyes, in the shade of a gloomy wall. The dogs waited. Lassiter picked up the child and turned into a dark cleft. It zig-zagged. It widened. It opened. Jane was amazed at a wonderfully smooth and steep incline leading up between ruined, splintered, toppling walls. A red haze from the setting sun filled this passage. Lassiter climbed with slow, measured steps, and blood dripped from him to make splotches on the white stone. Jane tried not to step in his blood, but was compelled, for she found no other footing. The saddle-bag began to drag her down; she gasped for breath; she thought her heart was bursting. Slower, slower yet the rider climbed, whistling as he breathed. The incline widened. Huge pinnacles and monuments of stone stood alone, leaning fearfully. Red sunset haze shone through cracks where the wall had split. Jane did not look high, but she felt the overshadowing of broken rims above. She felt that it was a fearful, menacing place. And she climbed on in heartrending effort. And she fell beside Lassiter and Fay at the top of the incline in a narrow, smooth divide.

He staggered to his feet—staggered to a huge, leaning rock that rested on a small pedestal. He put his hand on it—the hand that had been shot through—and Jane saw the blood drip from the ragged hole. Then he fell.

"Jane—I—can't—do—it!" he whispered.

"What?"

"Roll the—stone! . . . All my—life I've loved—to roll stones—an' now I—can't!"

"What of it? You talk strangely. Why roll that stone?"

"I planned to—fetch you here—to roll this stone. See! It'll smash the crags—loosen the walls—close the outlet!"

As Jane Withersteen gazed down that long incline, walled in by crumbling cliffs, awaiting only the slightest jar to make them fall asunder, she saw Tull appear at the bottom and begin to climb. A rider followed him—another—and another.

"See! Tull! The riders!"

"Yes—they'll get us—now."

"Why? Haven't you the strength left to roll the stone?"

"Jane—it ain't that—I've lost my nerve!"

"*You!* . . . Lassiter!"

"I wanted to roll it—meant to—but I—can't. Venters's valley is down behind here. We could—live there. But if I roll the stone—we're shut in for always. I don't dare. I'm thinkin' of you!"

"Lassiter! Roll the stone!" she cried.

He arose, tottering, but with set face, and again he placed the bloody hand on the Balancing Rock. Jane Withersteen gazed from him down the passageway. Tull was climbing. Almost, she thought, she saw his dark, relentless face. Behind him more riders climbed. What did they mean for Fay—for Lassiter—for herself?

"*Roll the stone! . . . Lassiter, I love you!*"

Under all his deathly pallor, and the blood, and the iron of seared cheek and lined brow, worked a great change. He placed both hands on the rock and then leaned his shoulder there and braced his powerful body.

"ROLL THE STONE!"

It stirred, it groaned, it grated, it moved; and with a slow grinding, as of wrathful relief, began to lean. It had waited ages to fall, and now was slow in starting. Then, as if suddenly instinct with life, it leaped hurtingly down to alight on the steep incline, to bound more swiftly into the air, to gather momentum, to plunge into the lofty leaning crag below. The crag thundered into atoms. A wave of air—a splitting shock! Dust shrouded the sunset red of shaking rims; dust shrouded Tull as he fell on his knees with uplifted arms. Shafts and monuments and sections of wall fell majestically.

From the depths there rose a long-drawn rumbling roar. The outlet to Deception Pass closed forever.

[illegible]

[illegible] from a distance.

[illegible]

[illegible]

[illegible]

[illegible]

[illegible]

[illegible]

[illegible]

[illegible]

[illegible]

[illegible]

[illegible]

[illegible]

[illegible]

To the Last Man

FOREWORD

It was inevitable that in my efforts to write romantic history of the great West I should at length come to the story of a feud. For long I have steered clear of this rock. But at last I have reached it and must go over it, driven by my desire to chronicle the stirring events of pioneer days.

Even to-day it is not possible to travel into the remote corners of the West without seeing the lives of people still affected by a fighting past. How can the truth be told about the pioneering of the West if the struggle, the fight, the blood be left out? It cannot be done. How can a novel be stirring and thrilling, as were those times, unless it be full of sensation? My long labors have been devoted to making stories resemble the times they depict. I have loved the West for its vastness, its contrast, its beauty and color and life, for its wildness and violence, and for the fact that I have seen how it developed great men and women who died unknown and unsung.

In this materialistic age, this hard, practical, swift, greedy age of realism, it seems there is no place for writers of romance, no place for romance itself. For many years all the events leading up to the great war were realistic, and the war itself was horribly realistic, and the aftermath is likewise. Romance is only another name for idealism; and I contend that life without ideals is not worth living. Never in the history of the world were ideals needed so terribly as now. Walter Scott wrote romance; so did Victor Hugo; and likewise Kipling, Hawthorne, Stevenson. It was Stevenson, particularly, who wielded a bludgeon against the realists. People live for the dream in their hearts. And I have yet to know anyone who has not some secret dream, some hope, however dim, some storied wall to look at in the dusk, some painted window leading to the soul. How strange indeed to find that the realists have ideals and dreams! To read them one would think their lives held nothing significant. But they love, they hope, they dream, they sacrifice, they struggle on with that dream in their hearts just the same as others. We all are dreamers, if not in the heavy-lidded wasting of time, then in the meaning of life that makes us work on.

It was Wordsworth who wrote, "The world is too much with us"; and if I could give the secret of my ambition as a novelist in a few words it would be contained in that quotation. My inspiration to write has always come from nature. Character and action are subordinated to setting. In all that I have done I have tried to make people see how the world is too much with them. Getting and spending they lay waste to their powers, with never a breath of the free and wonderful life of the open!

So I come back to the main point of this foreword, in which I am trying to tell why and how I came to write the story of a feud notorious in Arizona as the Pleasant Valley War.

Some years ago Mr. Harry Adams, a cattleman of Vermajo Park, New Mexico, told me he had been in the Tonto Basin of Arizona and thought I might find interesting material there concerning this Pleasant Valley War. His version of the war between cattlemen and sheepmen certainly determined me to look over the ground. My old guide, Al Doyle of Flagstaff, had led me over half of Arizona, but never down into that wonderful wild and rugged basin between the Mogollon Mesa and the Mazatzal Mountains. Doyle had long lived on the frontier and his version of the Pleasant Valley War differed markedly from that of Mr. Adams. I asked other old timers about it, and their remarks further excited my curiosity.

Once down there, Doyle and I found the wildest, most rugged, roughest, and most remarkable country either of us had visited; and the few inhabitants were like the country. I went in ostensibly to hunt bear and lion and turkey, but what I really was hunting for was the story of that Pleasant Valley War. I engaged the services of a bear hunter who had three strapping sons as reserved and strange and aloof as he was. No wheel tracks of any kind had ever come within miles of their cabin. I spent two wonderful months hunting game and reveling in the beauty and grandeur of that Rim Rock country, but I came out knowing no more about the Pleasant Valley War. These Texans and their few neighbors, likewise from Texas, did not talk. But all I saw and felt only inspired me the more. This trip was in the fall of 1918.

The next year I went again with the best horses, outfit and men the Doyles could provide. And this time I did not ask any questions. But I rode horses—some of them too wild for me—and packed a rifle many a hundred miles, riding sometimes thirty and forty miles a day, and I climbed in and out of the deep cañons, desperately staying at the heels of one of those long-legged Texans. I learned the life of those backwoodsmen, but I did not get the story of the Pleasant Valley War. I had, however, won the friendship of that hardy people.

In 1920 I went back with a still larger outfit, equipped to stay as long as I liked. And this time, without my asking it, different natives of the Tonto came to tell me about the Pleasant Valley War. No two of them agreed on anything concerning it, except that only one of the active participants survived the fighting. Whence comes my title, *To the Last Man.* Thus I was swamped in a mass of material out of which I could only flounder to my own conclusion. Some of the stories told me are singularly tempting to a novelist. But, though I believe them myself, I cannot risk their improbability to those who have no idea of the wildness of wild men at a wild time. There really was a terrible and bloody feud, perhaps the most deadly and least known in all the annals of the West. I saw the ground, the cabins, the graves, all so darkly suggestive of what must have happened.

I never learned the truth of the cause of the Pleasant Valley War, or if I did hear it I had no means of recognizing it. All the given causes were plausible and convincing. Strange to state, there is still secrecy and reticence all over the Tonto Basin as to the facts of this feud. Many descendents of those killed are living there now. But no one likes to talk about it. Assuredly many of the incidents told me really occurred, as, for example, the terrible one of the two women, in the face of relentless enemies, saving the bodies of their dead husbands from being devoured by wild hogs. Suffice it to say that this romance is true to my conception of the war, and I base it upon the setting I learned to know and love so well, upon the strange passions of primitive people, and upon my instinctive reaction to the facts and rumors that I gathered.

ZANE GREY.

Avalon, California,
April, 1921.

CHAPTER ONE

AT THE END of a dry, uphill ride over barren country Jean Isbel unpacked to camp at the edge of the cedars where a little rock cañon, green with willow and cottonwood, promised water and grass.

His animals were tired, especially the pack mule that had carried a heavy load; and with slow heave of relief they knelt and rolled in the dust. Jean experienced something of relief himself as he threw off his chaps. He had not been used to hot, dusty, glaring days on the barren lands. Stretching his long length beside a tiny rill of clear water that tinkled over the red stones, he drank thirstily. The water was cool, but it had an acrid taste—an alkali bite that he did not like. Not since he had left Oregon had he tasted clear, sweet, cold water; and he missed it just as he longed for the stately shady forests he had loved. This wild, endless Arizona land bade fair to earn his hatred.

By the time he had leisurely completed his tasks twilight had fallen and coyotes had begun their barking. Jean listened to the yelps and to the moan of the cool wind in the cedars with a sense of satisfaction that these lonely sounds were familiar. This cedar wood burned into a pretty fire and the smell of its smoke was newly pleasant.

"Reckon maybe I'll learn to like Arizona," he mused, half aloud. "But I've a hankerin' for waterfalls an' dark-green forests. Must be the Indian in me. . . . Anyway, dad needs me bad, an' I reckon I'm here for keeps."

Jean threw some cedar branches on the fire, in the light of which he opened his father's letter, hoping by repeated reading to grasp more of its strange portent. It had been two months in reaching him, coming by traveler, by stage and train, and then by boat, and finally by stage again. Written in lead pencil on a leaf torn from an old ledger, it would have been hard to read even if the writing had been more legible.

"Dad's writin' was always bad, but I never saw it so shaky," said Jean, thinking aloud.

GRASS VALLY, ARIZONA.

SON JEAN,—Come home. Here is your home and here your needed. When we left Oregon we all reckoned you would not be long behind. But its years now. I am growing old, son, and you was always my steadiest boy. Not that you ever was so dam steady. Only your wildness seemed more for the woods. You take after mother, and your brothers Bill and Guy take after me. That is the red and white of it. Your part Indian, Jean, and that Indian I reckon I am going to need bad. I am rich in cattle and horses. And my range here is the best I ever seen. Lately we have been losing stock. But that is not all nor so bad. Sheepmen have moved into the Tonto and are grazing down on Grass Vally. Cattlemen and sheepmen can never bide in this country. We have bad times ahead. Reckon I have more reasons to worry and need you, but you must wait to hear that by word of mouth. Whatever your doing, chuck it and rustle for Grass Vally so to make here by spring. I am asking you to take pains to pack some guns and a lot of shells. And hide them in your outfit. If you meet anyone when your coming down into the Tonto, listen more than you talk. And last, son, dont let anything keep you in Oregon. Reckon you have a sweetheart, and if so fetch her along. With love from your dad,

GASTON ISBEL.

Jean pondered over this letter. Judged by memory of his father, who had always been self-sufficient, it had been a surprise and somewhat of a shock. Weeks of travel and reflection had not helped him to grasp the meaning between the lines.

"Yes, dad's growin' old," mused Jean, feeling a warmth and a sadness stir in him. "He must be 'way over sixty. But he never looked old. . . . So he's rich now an' losin' stock, an' goin' to be sheeped off his range. Dad could stand a lot of rustlin', but not much from sheepmen."

The softness that stirred in Jean merged into a cold, thoughtful earnestness which had followed every perusal of his father's letter. A dark, full current seemed flowing in his veins, and at times he felt it swell and heat. It troubled him, making him conscious of a deeper, stronger self, opposed to his careless, free, and dreamy nature. No ties had bound him in Oregon, except love for the great, still forests and the thundering rivers; and this love came from his softer side. It had cost him a wrench to leave. And all the way by ship down the coast to San Diego and across the Sierra Madres by stage, and so on to this last overland travel by horseback, he had felt a retreating of the self that was tranquil and happy and a dominating of this unknown somber self, with its menacing possibilities. Yet despite a nameless regret and a loyalty to Oregon, when he lay in his blankets he had to confess a keen interest in his adventurous future, a keen enjoyment of this stark, wild Arizona. It appeared to be a different sky stretching in dark, star-spangled dome over him—closer, vaster, bluer. The strong fragrance of sage and cedar floated over him with the camp-fire smoke, and all seemed drowsily to subdue his thoughts.

At dawn he rolled out of his blankets and, pulling on his boots, began the day with a zest for the work that must bring closer his calling future. White, crackling frost and cold, nipping air were the same keen spurs to action that he had known in the uplands of Oregon, yet they were not wholly the same. He sensed an exhilaration similar to the effect of a strong, sweet wine. His horse and mule had fared well during the night, having been much refreshed by the grass and water of the little cañon. Jean mounted and rode into the cedars with gladness that at last he had put the endless leagues of barren land behind him.

The trail he followed appeared to be seldom traveled. It led, according to the meager information obtainable at the last settlement, directly to what was called the Rim, and from there Grass Valley could be seen down in the Basin. The ascent of the ground was so gradual that only in long, open stretches could it be seen. But the nature of the vegetation showed Jean how he was climbing. Scant, low, scraggy cedars gave place to more numerous, darker, greener, bushier ones, and these to high, full-foliaged, green-berried trees. Sage and grass in the open flats grew more luxuriously. Then came the piñons, and presently among them the checker-barked junipers. Jean hailed the first pine tree with a hearty slap on the brown, rugged bark. It was a small dwarf pine struggling to live. The next one was larger, and after that came several, and beyond them pines stood up everywhere above the lower trees. Odor of pine needles mingled with the other dry smells that made the wind pleasant to Jean. In an hour from the first line of pines he had ridden beyond the cedars and piñons into a slowly thickening and deepening forest. Underbrush appeared scarce except in ravines, and the ground in open patches held a bleached grass. Jean's eye roved for sight of squirrels, birds, deer, or any moving creature. It appeared to be a dry, uninhabited forest. About midday Jean halted at a pond of surface water, evidently melted snow, and gave his animals a drink. He saw a few old deer tracks in the mud and several huge bird tracks new to him which he concluded must have been made by wild turkeys.

The trail divided at this pond. Jean had no idea which branch he ought to take. "Reckon it doesn't matter," he muttered, as he was about to remount. His horse was standing with ears up, looking back along the trail. Then Jean heard the clip-clop of trotting hoofs, and presently espied a horseman.

Jean made a pretense of tightening his saddle girths while he peered over his horse at the approaching rider. All men in this country were going to be of exceeding interest to Jean Isbel. This man at a distance rode and looked like all the Arizonians Jean had seen, he had a superb seat in the saddle, and he was long and lean. He wore a huge black sombrero and a soiled red scarf. His vest was open and he was without a coat.

The rider came trotting up and halted several paces from Jean.

"Hullo, stranger!" he said, gruffly.

"Howdy yourself!" replied Jean. He felt an instinctive importance in the meeting with the man. Never had sharper eyes flashed over Jean and his outfit. He had a dust-colored, sun-burned face, long, lean, and hard, a huge sandy mustache that hid his mouth, and eyes of piercing light intensity. Not very much hard Western experience had passed by this man, yet he was not old, measured by years. When he dismounted Jean saw he was tall, even for an Arizonian.

"Seen your tracks back a ways," he said, as he slipped the bit to let his horse drink. "Where bound?"

"Reckon I'm lost, all right," replied Jean. "New country for me."

"Shore. I seen thet from your tracks an' your last camp. Wal, where was you headin' for before you got lost?"

The query was deliberately cool, with a dry, crisp ring. Jean felt the lack of friendliness or kindliness in it.

"Grass Valley. My name's Isbel," he replied, shortly.

The rider attended to his drinking horse and presently rebridled him; then with a long swing of leg he appeared to step into the saddle.

"Shore I knowed you was Jean Isbel," he said. "Everybody in the Tonto has heerd old Gass Isbel sent fer his boy."

"Well then, why did you ask?" inquired Jean, bluntly.

"Reckon I wanted to see what you'd say."

"So? All right. But I'm not carin' very much for what *you* say."

Their glances locked steadily then and each measured the other by the intangible conflict of spirit.

"Shore thet's natural," replied the rider. His speech was slow, and the motions of his long, brown hands, as he took a cigarette from his vest, kept time with his words. "But seein' you're one of the Isbels, I'll hev my say whether you want it or not. My name's Colter an' I'm one of the sheepmen Gass Isbel's riled with."

"Colter. Glad to meet you," replied Jean. "An' I reckon who riled my father is goin' to rile me."

"Shore. If thet wasn't so you'd not be an Isbel," returned Colter, with a grim little laugh. "It's easy to see you ain't run into any Tonto Basin fellers yet. Wal, I'm goin' to tell you thet your old man gabbed like a woman down at Greaves's store. Bragged aboot you an' how you could fight an' how you could shoot an' how you could track a hoss or a man! Bragged how you'd chase every sheep herder back up on the Rim. . . . I'm tellin' you because we want you to git our stand right. We're goin' to run sheep down in Grass Valley."

"Ahuh! Well, who's we?" queried Jean, curtly.

"Wha-at? . . . We—I mean the sheepmen rangin' this Rim from Black Butte to the Apache country."

"Colter, I'm a stranger in Arizona," said Jean, slowly. "I know little about ranchers or sheepmen. It's true my father sent for me. It's true, I dare say, that he bragged, for he was given to bluster an' blow. An' he's old now. I can't help it if he bragged about me. But if he has, an' if he's justified in his stand against you sheepmen, I'm goin' to do my best to live up to his brag."

"I get your hunch. Shore we understand each other, an' thet's a powerful help. You take my hunch to your old man," replied Colter, as he turned his horse away toward the left. "Thet trail leadin' south is yours. When you come to the Rim you'll see a bare spot down in the Basin. Thet'll be Grass Valley."

He rode away out of sight into the woods. Jean leaned against his horse and pondered. It seemed difficult to be just to this Colter, not because of his claims, but because of a subtle hostility that emanated from him. Colter had the hard face, the masked intent, the turn of speech that Jean had come to associate with dishonest men. Even if Jean had not been prejudiced, if he had known nothing of his father's trouble with these sheepmen, and if Colter had met him only to exchange glances and greetings, still Jean would never have had a favorable impression. Colter grated upon him, roused an antagonism seldom felt.

"Heigho!" sighed the young man. "Good-by to huntin' and fishin'! Dad's given me a man's job."

With that he mounted his horse and started the pack mule into the right-hand trail. Walking and trotting, he traveled all afternoon, toward sunset getting into heavy forest of pine. More than one snow bank showed white through the green, sheltered on the north slopes of shady ravines. And it was upon entering this zone of richer, deeper forestland that Jean sloughed off his gloomy forebodings. These stately pines were not the giant firs of Oregon, but any lover of the woods could be happy under them. Higher still he climbed until the forest spread before and around him like a level park, with thicketed ravines here and there on each side. And presently that deceitful level led to a higher bench upon which the pines towered, and were matched by beautiful trees he took for spruce. Heavily barked, with regular spreading branches, these conifers rose in symmetrical shape to spear the sky with silver plumes. A graceful gray-green moss, waved like veils from the branches. The air was not so dry and it was colder, with a scent and touch of snow. Jean made camp at the first likely site, taking the precaution to unroll his bed some little distance from his fire. Under the softly moaning pines he felt comfortable, having lost the sense of an immeasurable open space falling away from all around him.

The gobbling of wild turkeys awakened Jean, "Chug-a-lug, chug-a-lug, chug-a-lug-chug." There was not a great difference between the gobble of a wild turkey and that of a tame one. Jean got up, and taking his rifle went out into the gray obscurity of dawn to try to locate the turkeys. But it was too dark, and finally when daylight came they appeared to be gone. The mule had strayed, and, what with finding it and cooking breakfast and packing, Jean did not make a very early start. On this last lap of his long journey he had slowed down. He was weary of hurrying; the change from weeks in the glaring sun and dust-laden wind to this sweet cool darkly green and brown forest was very welcome; he wanted to linger along the shaded trail. This day he made sure would see him reach the Rim. By and by he lost the trail. It had just worn out from lack of use. Every now and then Jean would cross an old trail, and as he penetrated deeper into the forest every damp or dusty spot showed tracks of turkey, deer, and bear. The amount of bear sign surprised him. Presently his keen nostrils were assailed by a smell of sheep, and soon he rode into a broad sheep trail. From the tracks Jean calculated that the sheep has passed there the day before.

An unreasonable antipathy seemed born in him. To be sure he had been prepared to dislike sheep, and that was why he was unreasonable. But on the other hand this band of sheep had left a broad bare swath, weedless, grassless, flowerless, in their wake. Where sheep grazed they destroyed. That was what Jean had against them.

An hour later he rode to the crest of a long parklike slope, where new green grass was sprouting and flowers peeped everywhere. The pines appeared far apart; gnarled oak trees showed rugged and gray against the green wall of woods. A white strip of snow gleamed like a moving stream away down in the woods.

Jean heard the musical tinkle of bells and the baa-baa of sheep and the faint, sweet bleating of lambs. As he rode toward these sounds a dog ran out from an oak thicket and barked at him. Next Jean smelled a camp fire and soon he caught sight of a curling blue column of smoke, and then a small peaked tent. Beyond the clump of oaks Jean encountered a Mexican lad carrying a carbine. The boy had a swarthy, pleasant face, and to Jean's greeting he replied, *"Buenas dias."* Jean understood little Spanish, and about all he gathered by his simple queries was that the lad was not alone—and that it was "lambing time."

This latter circumstance grew noisily manifest. The forest seemed shrilly full of incessant baas and plaintive bleats. All about the camp, on the slope, in the glades, and everywhere, were sheep. A few were grazing; many were lying down; most of them were ewes suckling white fleecy little lambs that staggered on their feet. Everywhere Jean saw tiny lambs just born. Their pin-pointed bleats pierced the heavier baa-baa of their mothers.

Jean dismounted and led his horse down toward the camp, where he rather expected to see another and older Mexican, from whom he might get information. The lad walked with him. Down this way the plaintive uproar made by the sheep was not so loud.

"Hello there!" called Jean, cheerfully, as he approached the tent. No answer was forthcoming. Dropping his bridle, he went on, rather slowly, looking for some one to appear. Then a voice from one side startled him.

"Mawnin', stranger."

A girl stepped out from beside a pine. She carried a rifle. Her face flashed richly brown, but she was not Mexican. This fact, and the sudden conviction that she had been watching him, somewhat disconcerted Jean.

"Beg pardon—miss," he floundered. "Didn't expect to see a—girl. . . . I'm sort of lost—lookin' for the Rim—an' thought I'd find a sheep herder who'd show me. I can't savvy this boy's lingo."

While he spoke it seemed to him an intentness of expression, a strain relaxed from her face. A faint suggestion of hostility likewise disappeared. Jean was not even sure that he had caught it, but there had been something that now was gone.

"Shore I'll be glad to show y'u," she said.

"Thanks, miss. Reckon I can breathe easy now," he replied. "It's a long ride from San Diego. Hot an' dusty! I'm pretty tired. An' maybe this woods isn't good medicine to achin' eyes!"

"San Diego! Y'u're from the coast?"

"Yes."

Jean had doffed his sombrero at sight of her and he still held it, rather deferentially, perhaps. It seemed to attract her attention.

"Put on y'ur hat, stranger. . . . Shore I can't recollect when any man bared his haid to me." She uttered a little laugh in which surprise and frankness mingled with a tint of bitterness.

Jean sat down with his back to a pine, and, laying the sombrero by his side, he looked at her, conscious of a singular eagerness, as if he wanted to verify by close scrutiny a first hasty impression. If there had been an instinct in his meeting with Colter, there was more in this. The girl half sat, half leaned against a log, with the shiny carbine across her knees. She had a level, curious gaze upon him, and Jean had never met one just like it. Her eyes were rather a wide oval in shape, clear and steady, with shadows of thought in their amber-brown depths. They seemed to look through Jean, and his gaze dropped first. Then it was he saw her ragged homespun skirt and a few inches of brown, bare ankles, strong and round, and crude worn-out moccasins that failed to hide the shapeliness of her feet. Suddenly she drew back her stockingless ankles and ill-shod little feet. When Jean lifted his gaze again he found her face half averted and a stain of red in the gold tan of her cheek. That touch of embarrassment somehow removed her from this strong, raw, wild woodland setting. It changed her poise. It detracted from the curious, unabashed, almost bold, look that he had encountered in her eyes.

"Reckon you're from Texas," said Jean, presently.

"Shore am," she drawled. She had a lazy Southern voice, pleasant to hear. "How'd y'u-all guess that?"

"Anybody can tell a Texan. Where I came from there were a good many pioneers an' ranchers from the old Lone Star state. I've worked for several. An', come to think of it, I'd rather hear a Texas girl talk than anybody."

"Did y'u know many Texas girls?" she inquired, turning again to face him.

"Reckon I did—quite a good many."

"Did y'u go with them?"

"Go with them? Reckon you mean keep company. Why, yes, I guess I did—a little," laughed Jean. "Sometimes on a Sunday or a dance once in a blue moon, an' occasionally a ride."

"Shore that accounts," said the girl, wistfully.

"For what?" asked Jean.

"Y'ur bein' a gentleman," she replied, with force. "Oh, I've not forgotten. I had friends when we lived in Texas. . . . Three years ago. Shore it seems longer. Three miserable years in this damned country!"

Then she bit her lip, evidently to keep back further unwitting utterance to a total stranger. And it was that biting of her lip that drew Jean's attention to her mouth. It held beauty of curve and fullness and color that could not hide a certain sadness and bitterness. Then the whole flashing brown face changed for Jean. He saw that it was young, full of passion and restraint, possessing a power which grew on him. This, with her shame and pathos and the fact that she craved respect, gave a leap to Jean's interest.

"Well, I reckon you flatter me," he said, hoping to put her at ease again. "I'm only a rough hunter an' fisherman—woodchopper an' horse tracker. Never had all the school I needed—nor near enough company of nice girls like you."

"Am I nice?" she asked, quickly.

"You sure are," he replied, smiling.

"In these rags," she demanded, with a sudden flash of passion that thrilled him. "Look at the holes." She showed rips and worn-out places in the sleeves of her buckskin blouse, through which gleamed a round, brown arm. "I sew when I have anythin' to sew with. . . . Look at my skirt—a dirty rag. An' I have only one other to my name. . . . Look!" Again a color tinged her cheeks, most becoming, and giving the lie to her action. But shame could not check her violence now. A dammed-up resentment seemed to have broken out in flood. She lifted the ragged skirt almost to her knees. "No stockings! No shoes! . . . How can a girl be nice when she has no clean, decent woman's clothes to wear?"

"How—how can a girl . . ." began Jean. "See here, miss, I'm beggin' your pardon for—sort of stirrin' you to forget yourself a little. Reckon I understand. You don't meet many strangers an' I sort of hit you wrong—makin' you feel too much—an' talk too much. Who an' what you are is none of my business. But we met. . . . An' I reckon somethin' has happened—perhaps more to me than to you. . . . Now let me put you straight about clothes an' women. Reckon I know most women love nice things to wear an' think because clothes make them look pretty that they're nicer or better. But they're wrong. You're wrong. Maybe it'd be too much for a girl like you to be happy without clothes. But you can be—you are just as nice, an'—an' fine—an', for all you know, a good deal more appealin' to some men."

"Stranger, y'u shore must excuse my temper an' the show I made of myself," replied the girl, with composure. "That, to say the least, was not nice. An' I don't want anyone thinkin' better of me than I deserve. My mother died in Texas, an' I've lived out heah in this wild country—a girl alone among rough men. Meetin' y'u today makes me see what a hard lot they are—an' what it's done to me."

Jean smothered his curiosity and tried to put out of his mind a growing sense that he pitied her, liked her.

"Are you a sheep herder?" he asked.

"Shore I am now an' then. My father lives back heah in a cañon. He's a sheepman. Lately there's been herders shot at. Just now we're short an' I have to fill in. But I like shepherdin' an' I love the woods, and the Rim Rock an' all the Tonto. If they were all, I'd shore be happy."

"Herders shot at!" exclaimed Jean, thoughtfully. "By whom? An' what for?"

"Trouble brewin' between the cattlemen down in the Basin an' the sheepmen up on the Rim. Dad says there'll shore be hell to pay. I tell him I hope the cattlemen chase him back to Texas."

"Then— Are you on the ranchers' side?" queried Jean, trying to pretend casual interest.

"No. I'll always be on my father's side," she replied, with spirit. "But I'm bound to admit I think the cattlemen have the fair side of the argument."

"How so?"

"Because there's grass everywhere. I see no sense in a sheepman goin' out of his way to surround a cattleman an' sheep off his range. That started the row. Lord knows how it'll end. For most all of them heah are from Texas."

"So I was told," replied Jean. "An' I heard 'most all these Texans got run out of Texas. Any truth in that?"

"Shore I reckon there is," she replied, seriously. "But, stranger, it might not be healthy for y'u to say that anywhere. My dad, for one, was not run out of Texas. Shore I never can see why he came heah. He's accumulated stock, but he's not rich nor so well off as he was back home."

"Are you goin' to stay here always?" queried Jean, suddenly.

"If I do so it'll be in my grave," she answered, darkly. "But what's the use of thinkin'? People stay places until they drift away. Y'u can never tell. . . . Well, stranger, this talk is keepin' y'u."

She seemed moody now, and a note of detachment crept into her voice. Jean rose at once and went for his horse. If this girl did not desire to talk further he certainly had no wish to annoy her. His mule had strayed off among the bleating sheep. Jean drove it back and then led his horse up to where the girl stood. She appeared taller and, though not of robust build, she was vigorous and lithe, with something about her that fitted the place. Jean was loath to bid her good-by.

"Which way is the Rim?" he asked, turning to his saddle girths.

"South," she replied, pointing. "It's only a mile or so. I'll walk down with y'u. . . . Suppose y'u're on the way to Grass Valley?"

"Yes; I've relatives there," he returned. He dreaded her next question, which he suspected would concern his name. But she did not ask. Taking up her rifle she turned away. Jean strode ahead to her side. "Reckon if you walk I won't ride."

So he found himself beside a girl with the free step of a mountaineer. Her bare, brown head came up nearly to his shoulder. It was a small, pretty head, graceful, well held, and the thick hair on it was a shiny, soft brown. She wore it in a braid, rather untidily and tangled, he thought, and it was tied with a string of buckskin. Altogether her apparel proclaimed poverty.

Jean let the conversation languish for a little. He wanted to think what to say presently, and then he felt a rather vague pleasure in stalking beside her. Her profile was straight cut and exquisite in line. From this side view the soft curve of lips could not be seen.

She made several attempts to start conversation, all of which Jean ignored, manifestly to her growing constraint. Presently Jean, having decided what he wanted to say, suddenly began: "I like this adventure. Do you?"

"Adventure! Meetin' me in the woods?" And she laughed the laugh of youth. "Shore you must be hard up for adventure, stranger."

"Do you like it?" he persisted, and his eyes searched the half-averted face.

"I might like it," she answered, frankly, "if—if my temper had not made a fool of me. I never meet anyone I care to talk to. Why should it not be pleasant to run across some one new—some one strange in this heah wild country?"

"We are as we are," said Jean, simply. "I didn't think you made a fool of yourself. If I thought so, would I want to see you again?"

"Do y'u?" The brown face flashed on him with surprise, with a light he took for gladness. And because he wanted to appear calm and friendly, not too eager, he had to deny himself the thrill of meeting those changing eyes.

"Sure I do. Reckon I'm overbold on such short acquaintance. But I might not have another chance to tell you, so please don't hold it against me."

This declaration over, Jean felt relief and something of exultation. He had been afraid he might not have the courage to make it. She walked on as before, only with her head bowed a little and her eyes downcast. No color but the gold-brown tan and the blue tracery of veins showed in her cheeks. He noticed then a slight swelling quiver of her throat; and he became alive to its graceful contour, and to how full and pulsating it was, how nobly it set into the curve of her shoulder. Here in her quivering throat was the weakness of her, the evidence of her sex, the womanliness that belied the mountaineer stride and the grasp of strong brown hands on a rifle. It had an effect on Jean totally inexplicable to him, both in the strange warmth that stole over him and in the utterance he could not hold back.

"Girl, we're strangers, but what of that? We've met, an' I tell you it means somethin' to me. I've known girls for months an' never felt this way. I don't know who you are an' I don't care. You betrayed a good deal to me. You're not happy. You're lonely. An' if I didn't want to see you again for my own sake I would for yours. Some things you said I'll not forget soon. I've got a sister, an' I know you have no brother. An I reckon . . ."

At this juncture Jean in his earnestness and quite without thought grasped her hand. The contact checked the flow of his speech and suddenly made him aghast at his temerity. But the girl did not make any effort to withdraw it. So Jean, inhaling a deep breath and trying to see through his bewilderment, held on bravely. He imagined he felt a faint, warm, returning pressure. She was young, she was friendless, she was human. By this hand in his Jean felt more than ever the loneliness of her. Then, just as he was about to speak again, she pulled her hand free.

"Heah's the Rim," she said, in her quaint Southern drawl. "An' there's y'ur Tonto Basin."

Jean had been intent only upon the girl. He had kept step beside her without taking note of what was ahead of him. At her words he looked up expectantly, to be struck mute.

He felt a sheer force, a downward drawing of an immense abyss beneath him. As he looked afar he saw a black basin of timbered country, the darkest and wildest he had ever gazed upon, a hundred miles of blue distance across to an unflung mountain range, hazy purple against the sky. It seemed to be a stupendous gulf surrounded on three sides by bold, undulating lines of peaks, and on his side by a wall so high that he felt lifted aloft on the rim of the sky.

"Southeast y'u see the Sierra Anchas," said the girl, pointing. "That notch in the range is the pass where sheep are driven to Phoenix an' Maricopa. Those big rough mountains to the south are the Mazatzals. Round to the west is the Four Peaks Range. An' y'u're standin' on the Rim."

Jean could not see at first just what the Rim was, but by shifting his gaze westward he grasped this remarkable phenomenon of nature. For leagues and leagues a colossal red and yellow wall, a rampart, a mountain-faced cliff, seemed to zigzag westward. Grand and bold were the promontories reaching out over the void. They ran toward the westering sun. Sweeping and impressive were the long lines slanting away from them, sloping darkly spotted down to merge into the black timber. Jean had never seen such a wild and rugged manifestation of nature's depths and upheavals. He was held mute.

"Stranger, look down," said the girl.

Jean's sight was educated to judge heights and depths and distances. This wall upon which he stood sheered precipitously down, so far that it made him dizzy to look, and then the craggy broken cliffs merged into red-slided, cedar-greened slopes running down and down into gorges choked with forests, and from which soared up a roar of rushing waters. Slope after slope, ridge beyond ridge, cañon merging into cañon—so the tremendous bowl sunk away to its black, deceiving depths, a wilderness across which travel seemed impossible.

"Wonderful!" exclaimed Jean.

"Indeed it is!" murmured the girl. "Shore that is Arizona. I reckon I love *this*. The heights an' depths—the awfulness of its wilderness!"

"An' you want to leave it?"

"Yes an' no. I don't deny the peace that comes to me heah. But not often do I see the Basin, an' for that matter, one doesn't live on grand scenery."

"Child, even once in a while—this sight would cure any misery, if you only see. I'm glad I came. I'm glad you showed it to me first."

She too seemed under the spell of a vastness and loneliness and beauty and grandeur that could not but strike the heart.

Jean took her hand again. "Girl, say you will meet me here," he said, his voice ringing deep in his ears.

"Shore I will," she replied, softly, and turned to him. It seemed then that Jean saw her face for the first time. She was beautiful as he had never known beauty. Limned against that scene, she gave it life—wild, sweet, young life—the poignant meaning of which haunted yet eluded him. But she belonged there. Her eyes were again searching him, as if for some lost part of herself, unrealized, never known before. Wondering, wistful, hopeful, glad—they were eyes that seemed surprised, to reveal part of her soul.

Then her red lips parted. Their tremulous movement was a magnet to Jean. An invisible and mighty force pulled him down to kiss them. Whatever the spell had been, that rude, unconscious action broke it.

He jerked away, as if he expected to be struck. "Girl—I—I"—he gasped in amaze and sudden-dawning contrition—"I kissed you—but I swear it wasn't intentional—I never thought. . . ."

The anger that Jean anticipated failed to materialize. He stood, breathing hard, with a hand held out in unconscious appeal. By the same magic, perhaps, that had transfigured her a moment past, she was now invested again by the older character.

"Shore I reckon my callin' y'u a gentleman was a little previous," she said, with a rather dry bitterness. "But, stranger, yu're sudden."

"You're not insulted?" asked Jean, hurriedly.

"Oh, I've been kissed before. Shore men are all alike."

"They're not," he replied, hotly, with a subtle rush of disillusion, a dulling of enchantment. "Don't you class me with other men who've kissed you. I wasn't myself when I did it an' I'd have gone on my knees to ask your forgiveness. . . . But now I wouldn't—an' I wouldn't kiss you again, either—even if you—you wanted it."

Jean read in her strange gaze what seemed to him a vague doubt, as if she was questioning him.

"Miss, I take that back," added Jean, shortly. "I'm sorry. I didn't mean to be rude. It was a mean trick for me to kiss you. A girl alone in the woods who's gone out of her way to be kind to me! I don't know why I forgot my manners. An' I ask your pardon."

She looked away then, and presently pointed far out and down into the Basin.

"There's Grass Valley. That long gray spot in the black. It's about fifteen miles. Ride along the Rim that way till y'u cross a trail. Shore y'u can't miss it. Then go down."

"I'm much obliged to you," replied Jean, reluctantly accepting what he regarded as his dismissal. Turning his horse, he put his foot in the stirrup, then, hesitating, he looked across the saddle at the girl. Her abstraction, as she gazed away over the purple depths suggested loneliness and wistfulness. She was not thinking of that scene spread so wondrously before her. It struck Jean she might be pondering a subtle change in his feeling and attitude, something he was conscious of, yet could not define.

"Reckon this is good-by," he said, with hesitation.

"Adios, señor," she replied, facing him again. She lifted the little carbine to the hollow of her elbow and, half turning, appeared ready to depart.

"Adios means good-by?" he queried.

"Yes, good-by till to-morrow or good-by forever. Take it as y'u like."

"Then you'll meet me here day after to-morrow?" How eagerly he spoke, on impulse, without a consideration of the intangible thing that had changed him!

"Did I say I wouldn't?"

"No. But I reckoned you'd not care to after—" he replied, breaking off in some confusion.

"Shore I'll be glad to meet y'u. Day after to-morrow about mid-afternoon. Right heah. Fetch all the news from Grass Valley."

"All right. Thanks. That'll be—fine," replied Jean, and as he spoke he experienced a buoyant thrill, a pleasant lightness of enthusiasm, such as always stirred boyishly in him at a prospect of adventure. Before it passed he wondered at it and felt unsure of himself. He needed to think.

"Stranger, shore I'm not recollectin' that y'u told me who y'u are," she said.

"No, reckon I didn't tell," he returned. "What difference does that make? I said I didn't care who or what you are. Can't you feel the same about me?"

"Shore—I felt that way," she replied, somewhat nonplussed, with the level brown gaze steadily on his face. "But now y'u make me think."

"Let's meet without knowin' any more about each other than we do now."

"Shore. I'd like that. In this big wild Arizona a girl—an' I reckon a man—feels so insignificant. What's a name, anyhow? Still, people an' things have to be distinguished. I'll call y'u 'Stranger' an' be satisfied—if y'u say it's fair for y'u not to tell who y'u are."

"Fair! No, it's not," declared Jean, forced to confession. "My name's Jean—Jean Isbel."

"Isbel!" she exclaimed, with a violent start. "Shore y'u can't be son of old Gass Isbel. . . . I've seen both his sons."

"He has three," replied Jean, with relief, now the secret was out. "I'm the youngest. I'm twenty-four. Never been out of Oregon till now. On my way—"

The brown color slowly faded out of her face, leaving her quite pale, with eyes that began to blaze. The suppleness of her seemed to stiffen.

"My name's Ellen Jorth," she burst out, passionately. "Does it mean anythin' to y'u?"

"Never heard it in my life," protested Jean. "Sure I reckoned you belonged to the sheep raisers who're on the outs with my father. That's why I had to tell you I'm Jean Isbel. . . . Ellen Jorth. It's strange an' pretty. . . . Reckon I can be just as good a—a friend to you—"

"No Isbel can ever be a friend to me," she said, with bitter coldness. Stripped of her ease and her soft wistfulness, she stood before him one instant, entirely another girl, a hostile enemy. Then she wheeled and strode off into the woods.

Jean, in amaze, in consternation, watched her swiftly draw away with her lithe, free step, wanting to follow her, wanting to call to her; but the resentment roused by her suddenly avowed hostility held him mute in his tracks. He watched her disappear, and when the brown-and-green wall of forest swallowed the slender gray form he fought against the insistent desire to follow her, and fought in vain.

CHAPTER TWO

But Ellen Jorth's moccasined feet did not leave a distinguishable trail on the springy pine needle covering of the ground, and Jean could not find any trace of her.

A little futile searching to and fro cooled his impulse and called pride to his rescue. Returning to his horse, he mounted, rode out behind the pack mule to start it along, and soon felt the relief of decision and action. Clumps of small pines grew thickly in spots on the Rim, making it necessary for him to skirt them; at which times he lost sight of the purple basin. Every time he came back to an opening through which he could see the wild ruggedness and colors and distances, his appreciation of their nature grew on him. Arizona from Yuma to the Little Colorado had been to him an endless waste of wind-scoured, sun-blasted barrenness. This black-forested rock-rimmed land of untrodden ways was a world that in itself would satisfy him. Some instinct in Jean called for a lonely, wild land, into the fastnesses of which he could roam at will and be the other strange self that he had always yearned to be but had never been.

Every few moments there intruded into his flowing consciousness the flashing face of Ellen Jorth, the way she had looked at him, the things she had said. "Reckon I was a fool," he soliloquized, with an acute sense of humiliation. "She never saw how much in earnest I was." And Jean began to remember the circumstances with a vividness that disturbed and perplexed him.

The accident of running across such a girl in that lonely place might be out of the ordinary—but it had happened. Surprise had made him dull. The charm of her appearance, the appeal of her manner, must have drawn him at the very first, but he had not recognized that. Only at her words, "Oh, I've been kissed before," had his feelings been checked in their heedless progress. And the utterance of them had made a difference he now sought to analyze. Some personality in him, some voice, some idea had begun to defend her even before he was conscious that he had arraigned her before the bar of his judgment. Such defense seemed clamoring in him now and he forced himself to listen. He wanted, in his hurt pride to justify his amazing surrender to a sweet and sentimental impulse.

He realized now that at first glance he should have recognized in her look, her poise, her voice the quality he called thoroughbred. Ragged and stained apparel did not prove her of a common sort. Jean had known a number of fine and wholesome girls of good family; and he remembered his sister. This Ellen Jorth was that kind of a girl irrespective of her present environment. Jean championed her loyally, even after he had gratified his selfish pride.

It was then—contending with an intangible and stealing glamour, unreal and fanciful, like the dream of a forbidden enchantment—that Jean arrived at the part in the little woodland drama where he had kissed Ellen Jorth and had been unrebuked. Why had she not resented this action? Dispelled was the illusion he had been dreamily and nobly constructing. "Oh, I've been kissed before!" The shock to him now exceeded his first dismay. Half bitterly she had spoken, and wholly scornful of herself, or of him, or of all men. For she had said all men were alike. Jean chafed under the smart of that, a taunt every decent man hated. Naturally every happy and healthy young man would want to kiss such red, sweet lips. But if those lips had been for others—never for him! Jean reflected that not since childish games had he kissed a girl—until this brown-faced Ellen Jorth came his way. He wondered at it. Moreover, he wondered at the significance he placed upon it. After all, was it not merely an accident? Why should he remember? Why should he ponder? What was the faint, deep, growing thrill that accompanied some of his thoughts?

Riding along with busy mind, Jean almost crossed a well-beaten trail, leading through a pine thicket and down over the Rim. Jean's pack mule led the way without being driven. And when Jean reached the edge of the bluff one look down was enough to fetch him off his horse. That trail was steep, narrow, clogged with stones, and as full of sharp corners as a crosscut saw. Once on the descent with a packed mule and a spirited horse, Jean had no time for mind wanderings and very little for occasional glimpses out over the cedar tops to the vast blue hollow asleep under a westering sun.

The stones rattled, the dust rose, the cedar twigs snapped, the little avalanches of red earth slid down, the iron-shod hoofs rang on the rocks. This slope had been narrow at the apex in the Rim where the trail led down a crack, and it widened in fan shape as Jean descended. He zigzagged down a thousand feet before the slope benched into dividing ridges. Here the cedars and junipers failed and pines once more hid the sun. Deep ravines were black with brush. From somewhere rose a roar of running water, most pleasant to Jean's ears. Fresh deer and bear tracks covered old ones made in the trail.

Those timbered ridges were but billows of that tremendous slope that now sheered above Jean, ending in a magnificent yellow wall of rock, greened in niches, stained by weather rust, carved and cracked and caverned. As Jean descended farther the hum of bees made melody, the roar of rapid water and the murmur of a rising breeze filled him with the content of the wild. Sheepmen like Colter and girls like Ellen Jorth and all that seemed promising or menacing in his father's letter could never change the Indian in Jean. So he thought. Hard upon that conclusion rushed another—one which troubled with its stinging revelation. Surely these influences he had defied were just the ones to bring out in him the Indian he had sensed but had never known. The eventful day had brought new and bitter food for Jean to reflect upon.

The trail landed him in the boulder-strewn bed of a wide cañon, where the huge trees stretched a canopy of foliage which denied the sunlight, and where a beautiful brook rushed and foamed. Here at last Jean tasted water that rivaled his Oregon springs. "Ah," he cried, "that sure is good!" Dark and shaded and ferny and mossy was this streamway; and everywhere were tracks of game, from the giant spread of a grizzly bear to the tiny, birdlike imprints of a squirrel. Jean heard familiar sounds of deer crackling the dead twigs; and the chatter of squirrels was incessant. This fragrant, cool retreat under the Rim brought back to him the dim recesses of Oregon forests. After all, Jean felt that he would not miss anything that he had loved in the Cascades. But what was the vague sense of all not being well with him—the essence of a faint regret—the insistence of a hovering shadow? And then flashed again, etched more vividly by the repetition in memory, a picture of eyes, of lips—of something he had to forget.

Wild and broken as this rolling Basin floor had appeared from the Rim, the reality of traveling over it made that first impression a deceit of distance. Down here all was on a big, rough, broken scale. Jean did not find even a few rods of level ground. Boulders as huge as houses obstructed the stream bed; spruce trees eight feet thick tried to lord it over the brawny pines; the ravine was a veritable cañon from which occasional glimpses through the foliage showed the Rim as a lofty red-tipped mountain peak.

Jean's pack mule became frightened at scent of a bear or lion and ran off down the rough trail, imperiling Jean's outfit. It was not an easy task to head him off nor, when that was accomplished, to keep him to a trot. But his fright and succeeding skittishness at least made for fast traveling. Jean calculated that he covered ten miles under the Rim before the character of ground and forest began to change.

The trail had turned southeast. Instead of gorge after gorge, red-walled and choked with forest, there began to be rolling ridges, some high; others were knolls; and a thick cedar growth made up for a falling off of pine. The spruce had long disappeared. Juniper thickets gave way more and more to the beautiful manzanita; and soon on the south slopes appeared cactus and a scrubby live oak. But for the well-broken trail, Jean would have fared ill through this tough brush.

Jean espied several deer, and again a coyote, and what he took to be a small herd of wild horses. No more turkey tracks showed in the dusty patches. He crossed a number of tiny brooklets, and at length came to a place where the trail ended or merged in a rough road that showed evidence of considerable travel. Horses, sheep, and cattle had passed along there that day. This road turned southward, and Jean began to have pleasurable expectations.

The road, like the trail, led down grade, but no longer at such steep angles, and was bordered by cedar and piñon, jack-pine and juniper, mescal and manzanita. Quite sharply, going around a ridge, the road led Jean's eye down to a small open flat of marshy, or at least grassy, ground. This green oasis in the wilderness of red and timbered ridges marked another change in the character of the Basin. Beyond that the country began to spread out and roll gracefully, its dark-green forest interspersed with grassy parks, until Jean headed into a long, wide gray-green valley surrounded by black-fringed hills. His pulses quickened here. He saw cattle dotting the expanse, and here and there along the edge log cabins and corrals.

As a village, Grass Valley could not boast of much, apparently, in the way of population. Cabins and houses were widely scattered, as if the inhabitants did not care to encroach upon one another. But the one store, built of stone, and stamped also with the characteristic isolation, seemed to Jean to be a rather remarkable edifice. Not exactly like a fort did it strike him, but if it had not been designed for defense it certainly gave that impression, especially from the long, low side with its dark eye-like windows about the height of a man's shoulder. Some rather fine horses were tied to a hitching rail. Otherwise dust and dirt and age and long use stamped this Grass Valley store and its immediate environment.

Jean threw his bridle, and, getting down, mounted the low porch and stepped into the wide open door. A face, gray against the background of gloom inside, passed out of sight just as Jean entered. He knew he had been seen. In front of the long, rather low-ceilinged store were four men, all absorbed, apparently, in a game of checkers. Two were playing and two were looking on. One of these, a gaunt-faced man past middle age, casually looked up as Jean entered. But the moment of that casual glance afforded Jean time enough to meet eyes he instinctively distrusted. They masked their penetration. They seemed neither curious nor friendly. They saw him as if he had been merely thin air.

"Good evenin'," said Jean.

After what appeared to Jean a lapse of time sufficient to impress him with a possible deafness of these men, the gaunt-faced one said, "Howdy, Isbel!"

The tone was impersonal, dry, easy, cool, laconic, and yet it could not have been more pregnant with meaning. Jean's sharp sensibilities absorbed much. None of the slouch-sombreroed, long-mustached Texans—for so Jean at once classed them—had ever seen Jean, but they knew him and knew that he was expected in Grass Valley. All but the one who had spoken happened to have their faces in shadow under the wide-brimmed black hats. Motley-garbed, gun-belted, dusty-booted, they gave Jean the same impression of latent force that he had encountered in Colter.

"Will somebody please tell me where to find my father, Gaston Isbel?" inquired Jean, with as civil a tongue as he could command.

Nobody paid the slightest attention. It was the same as if Jean had not spoken. Waiting, half amused, half irritated, Jean shot a rapid glance around the store. The place had felt bare; and Jean, peering back through gloomy space, saw that it did not contain much. Dry goods and sacks littered a long rude counter; long rough shelves divided their length into stacks of canned foods and empty sections; a low shelf back of the counter held a generous burden of cartridge boxes, and next to it stood a rack of rifles. On the counter lay open cases of plug tobacco, the odor of which was second in strength only to that of rum.

Jean's swift-roving eye reverted to the men, three of whom were absorbed in the greasy checkerboard. The fourth man was the one who had spoken and he now deigned to look at Jean. Not much flesh was there stretched over his bony, powerful physiognomy. He stroked a lean chin with a big mobile hand that suggested more of bridle holding than familiarity with a bucksaw and plow handle. It was a lazy hand. The man looked lazy. If he spoke at all it would be with lazy speech. Yet Jean had not encountered many men to whom he would have accorded more potency to stir in him the instinct of self-preservation.

"Shore," drawled this gaunt-faced Texan, "old Gass lives aboot a mile down heah." With slow sweep of the big hand he indicated a general direction to the south; then, appearing to forget his questioner, he turned his attention to the game.

Jean muttered his thanks and, striding out, he mounted again, and drove the pack mule down the road. "Reckon I've run into the wrong folks to-day," he said. "If I remember dad right he was a man to make an' keep friends. Somehow I'll bet there's goin' to be hell." Beyond the store were some rather pretty and comfortable homes, little ranch houses back in the coves of the hills. The road turned west and Jean saw his first sunset in the Tonto Basin. It was a pageant of purple clouds with silver edges, and background of deep rich gold. Presently Jean met a lad driving a cow. "Hello, Johnny!" he said, genially, and with a double purpose. "My name's Jean Isbel. By Golly! I'm lost in Grass Valley. Will you tell me where my dad lives?"

"Yep. Keep right on, an' y'u cain't miss him," replied the lad, with a bright smile. "He's lookin' fer y'u."

"How do you know, boy?" queried Jean, warmed by that smile.

"Aw, I know. It's all over the valley thet y'u'd ride in ter-day. Shore I wus the one thet tole yer dad an' he give me a dollar."

"Was he glad to hear it?" asked Jean, with a queer sensation in his throat.

"Wall, he plumb was."

"An' who told you I was goin' to ride in to-day?"

"I heerd it at the store," replied the lad, with an air of confidence. "Some sheepmen was talkin' to Greaves. He's the storekeeper. I was settin' outside, but I heerd. A Mexican come down off the Rim ter-day an' he fetched the news." Here the lad looked furtively around, then whispered. "An' thet greaser was sent by somebody. I never heerd no more, but them sheepmen looked pretty plumb sour. An' one of them, comin' out, give me a kick, darn him. It shore is the luckedest day fer us cowmen."

"How's that, Johnny?"

"Wal, that's shore a big fight comin' to Grass Valley. My dad says so an' he rides fer yer dad. An' if it comes now y'u'll be heah."

"Ahuh!" laughed Jean. "An' what then, boy?"

The lad turned bright eyes upward. "Aw, now, yu'all cain't come thet on me. Ain't y'u an Injun, Jean Isbel? Ain't y'u a hoss tracker thet rustlers cain't fool? Ain't y'u a plumb dead shot? Ain't y'u wuss'ern a grizzly bear in a rough-an'-tumble? . . . Now ain't y'u, shore?"

Jean bade the flattering lad a rather sober good day and rode on his way. Manifestly a reputation somewhat difficult to live up to had preceded his entry into Grass Valley.

Jean's first sight of his future home thrilled him through. It was a big, low, rambling log structure standing well out from a wooded knoll at the edge of the valley. Corrals and barns and sheds lay off at the back. To the fore stretched broad pastures where numberless cattle and horses grazed. At sunset the scene was one of rich color. Prosperity and abundance and peace seemed attendant upon that ranch; lusty voices of burros braying and cows bawling seemed welcoming Jean. A hound bayed. The first cool touch of wind fanned Jean's cheek and brought a fragrance of wood smoke and frying ham.

Horse in the pasture romped to the fence and whistled at these newcomers. Jean espied a white-faced black horse that gladdened his sight. "Hello, Whiteface! I'll sure straddle you," called Jean. Then up the gentle slope he saw the tall figure of his father—the same as he had seen him thousands of times, bareheaded, shirt sleeved, striding with long step. Jean waved and called to him.

"Hi, you prodigal!" came the answer. Yes, the voice of his father—and Jean's boyhood memories flashed. He hurried his horse those last few rods. No—dad was not the same. His hair shone gray.

"Here I am, dad," called Jean, and then he was dismounting. A deep, quiet emotion settled over him, stilling the hurry, the eagerness, the pang in his breast.

"Son, I shore am glad to see you," said his father, and wrung his hand. "Wal, wal, the size of you! Shore you've grown, an' how you favor your mother."

Jean felt in the iron clasp of hand, in the uplifting of the handsome head, in the strong, fine light of piercing eyes that there was no difference in the spirit of his father. But the old smile could not hide lines and shades strange to Jean.

"Dad, I'm as glad as you," replied Jean, heartily. "It seems long we've been parted, now I see you. Are you well, dad, an' all right?"

"Not complainin', son. I can ride all day same as ever," he said. "Come. Never mind your hosses. They'll be looked after. Come meet the folks. . . . Wal, wal, you got heah at last."

On the porch of the house a group awaited Jean's coming, rather silently, he thought. Wide-eyed children were there, very shy and watchful. The dark face of his sister corresponded with the image of her in his memory. She appeared taller, more womanly, as she embraced him. "Oh, Jean, Jean, I'm glad you've come!" she cried, and pressed him close. Jean felt in her a woman's anxiety for the present as well as affection for the past. He remembered his aunt Mary, though he had not seen her for years. His half brothers, Bill and Guy, had changed but little except perhaps to grow lean and rangy. Bill resembled his father, though his aspect was jocular rather than serious. Guy was smaller, wiry, and hard as rock, with snapping eyes in a brown, still face, and he had the bow-legs of a cattleman. Both had married in Arizona. Bill's wife, Kate, was a stout, comely little woman, mother of three of the children. The other wife was young, a strapping girl, red headed and freckled, with wonderful lines of pain and strength in her face. Jean remembered, as he looked at her, that some one had written him about the tragedy in her life. When she was only a child the Apaches had murdered all her family. Then next to greet Jean were the little children, all shy, yet all manifestly impressed by the occasion. A warmth and intimacy of forgotten home emotions flooded over Jean. Sweet it was to get home to these relatives who loved him and welcomed him with quiet gladness. But there seemed more. Jean was quick to see the shadow in the eyes of the women in that household and to sense a strange reliance which his presence brought.

"Son, this heah Tonto is a land of milk an' honey," said his father, as Jean gazed spellbound at the bounteous supper.

Jean certainly performed gastronomic feats on this occasion, to the delight of Aunt Mary and the wonder of the children. "Oh, he's starv-ved to death," whispered one of the little boys to his sister. They had begun to warm to this stranger uncle. Jean had no chance to talk, even had he been able to, for the meal-time showed a relaxation of restraint and they all tried to tell him things at once. In the bright lamplight his father looked easier and happier as he beamed upon Jean.

After supper the men went into an adjoining room that appeared most comfortable and attractive. It was long, and the width of the house, with a huge stone fireplace, low ceiling of hewn timbers and walls of the same, small windows with inside shutters of wood, and home-made table and chairs and rugs.

"Wal, Jean, do you recollect them shootin'-irons?" inquired the rancher, pointing above the fireplace. Two guns hung on the spreading deer antlers there. One was a musket Jean's father had used in the war of the rebellion and the other was a long, heavy, muzzle-loading flintlock Kentucky rifle with which Jean had learned to shoot.

"Reckon I do, dad," replied Jean, and with reverent hands and a rush of memory he took the old gun down.

"Jean, you shore handle thet old arm some clumsy," said Guy Isbel, dryly. And Bill added a remark to the effect that perhaps Jean had been leading a luxurious and tame life back there in Oregon, and then added, "But I reckon he's packin' that six-shooter like a Texan."

"Say, I fetched a gun or two along with me," replied Jean, jocularly. "Reckon I near broke my poor mule's back with the load of shells an' guns. Dad, what was the idea askin' me to pack out an arsenal?"

"Son, shore all shootin' arms an' such are at a premium in the Tonto," replied his father. "An' I was givin' you a hunch to come loaded."

His cool, drawling voice seemed to put a damper upon the pleasantries. Right there Jean sensed the charged atmosphere. His brothers were bursting with utterance about to break forth, and his father suddenly wore a look that recalled to Jean critical times of days long past. But the entrance of the children and the women folk put an end to confidences. Evidently the youngsters were laboring under subdued excitement. They preceded their mother, the smallest boy in the lead. For him this must have been both a dreadful and a wonderful experience, for he seemed to be pushed forward by his sister and brother and mother, and driven by yearnings of his own. "There now, Lee. Say, 'Uncle Jean, what did you fetch us?'"

The lad hesitated for a shy, frightened look at Jean, and then, gaining something from his scrutiny of his uncle, he toddled forward and bravely delivered the question of tremendous importance.

"What did I fetch you, hey?" cried Jean, in delight, as he took the lad up on his knee. "Wouldn't you like to know? I didn't forget, Lee. I remembered you all. Oh! the job I had packin' your bundle of presents. . . . Now, Lee, make a guess."

"I dess you fetched a dun," replied Lee.

"A dun!—I'll bet you mean a gun," laughed Jean. "Well, you four-year-old Texas gunman! Make another guess."

That appeared too momentous and entrancing for the other two youngsters, and, adding their shrill and joyous voices to Lee's, they besieged Jean.

"Dad, where's my pack?" cried Jean. "These young Apaches are after my scalp."

"Reckon the boys fetched it onto the porch," replied the rancher.

Guy Isbel opened the door and went out. "By golly! heah's three packs," he called. "Which one do you want, Jean?"

"It's a long, heavy bundle all tied up," replied Jean.

Guy came staggering in under a burden that brought a whoop from the youngsters and bright gleams to the eyes of the women. Jean lost nothing of this. How glad he was that he had tarried in San Francisco because of a mental picture of this very reception in far-off wild Arizona.

When Guy deposited the bundle on the floor it jarred the room. It gave forth metallic and rattling and crackling sounds.

"Everybody stand back an' give me elbow room," ordered Jean, majestically. "My good folks, I want you all to know this is somethin' that doesn't happen often. The bundle you see here weighed about a hundred pounds when I packed it on my shoulder down Market Street in Frisco. It was stolen from me on shipboard. I got it back in San Diego an' licked the thief. It rode on a burro from San Diego to Yuma an' once I thought the burro was lost for keeps. It came up the Colorado River from Yuma to Ehrenberg an' there went on top of a stage. We got chased by bandits an' once when the horses were gallopin' hard it near rolled off. Then it went on the back of a pack horse an' helped wear him out. An' I reckon it would be somewhere else now if I hadn't fallen in with a freighter goin' north from Phoenix to the Santa Fe Trail. The last lap when it sagged the back of a mule was the riskiest an' full of the narrowest escapes. Twice my mule bucked off his pack an' left my outfit scattered. Worst of all, my precious bundle made the mule top heavy comin' down that place back here where the trail seems to drop off the earth. There I was hard put to keep sight of my pack. Sometimes it was on top an' other times the mule. But it got here at last. . . . An' now I'll open it."

After this long and impressive harangue, which at least augmented the suspense of the women and worked the children into a frenzy, Jean leisurely untied the many knots round the bundle and unrolled it. He had packed that bundle for just such travel as it had sustained. Three cloth-bound rifles he laid aside, and with them a long, very heavy package tied between two thin wide boards. From this came a metallic clink. "Oo, I know what dem is!" cried Lee, breaking the silence of suspense. Then Jean, tearing open a long flat parcel, spread before the mute, rapt-eyed youngsters such magnificent things as they had never dreamed of—picture books, mouth-harps, dolls, a toy gun and a toy pistol, a wonderful whistle and a fox horn, and last of all a box of candy. Before these treasures on the floor, too magical to be touched at first, the two little boys and their sister simply knelt. That was a sweet, full moment for Jean; yet even that was clouded by the something which shadowed these innocent children fatefully born in a wild place at a wild time. Next Jean gave to his sister the presents he had brought her—beautiful cloth for a dress, ribbons and a bit of lace, handkerchiefs and buttons and yards of linen, a sewing case and a whole box of spools of thread, a comb and brush and mirror, and lastly a Spanish brooch inlaid with garnets. "There, Ann," said Jean, "I confess I asked a girl friend in Oregon to tell me some things my sister might like." Manifestly there was not much difference in girls. Ann seemed stunned by this munificence, and then awakening, she hugged Jean in a way that took his breath. She was not a child any more, that was certain. Aunt Mary turned knowing eyes upon Jean. "Reckon you couldn't have pleased Ann more. She's engaged, Jean, an' where girls are in that state these things mean a heap. . . . Ann, you'll be married in that!" And she pointed to the beautiful folds of material that Ann had spread out.

"What's this?" demanded Jean. His sister's blushes were enough to convict her, and they were mightily becoming, too.

"Here, Aunt Mary," went on Jean, "here's yours, an' here's somethin' for each of my new sisters." This distribution left the women as happy and occupied, almost, as the children. It also left another package, the last one in the bundle. Jean laid hold of it and, lifting it, he was about to speak when he sustained a little shock of memory. Quite distinctly he saw two little feet, with bare toes peeping out of worn-out moccasins, and then round, bare symmetrical ankles that had been scratched by brush. Next he saw Ellen Jorth's passionate face as she looked when she had made the violent action so disconcerting to him. In this happy moment the memory seemed farther off than a few hours. It had crystallized. It annoyed while it drew him. As a result he slowly laid this package aside and did not speak as he had intended to.

"Dad, I reckon I didn't fetch a lot for you an' the boys," continued Jean. "Some knives, some pipes an' tobacco. An' sure the guns."

"Shore, you're a regular Santa Claus, Jean," replied his father. "Wal, wal, look at the kids. An' look at Mary. An' for the land's sake look at Ann! Wal, wal, I'm gettin' old. I'd forgotten the pretty stuff an' gimcracks that mean so much to women. We're out of the world heah. It's just as well you've lived apart from us, Jean, for comin' back this way, with all that stuff, does us a lot of good. I cain't say, son, how obliged I am. My mind has been set on the hard side of life. An' it's shore good to forget—to see the smiles of the women an' the joy of the kids."

At this juncture a tall young man entered the open door. He looked a rider. All about him, even his face, except his eyes, seemed old, but his eyes were young, fine, soft, and dark.

"How do, y'u-all!" he said, evenly.

Ann rose from her knees. Then Jean did not need to be told who this newcomer was.

"Jean, this is my friend, Andrew Colmor."

Jean knew when he met Colmor's grip and the keen flash of his eyes that he was glad Ann had set her heart upon one of their kind. And his second impression was something akin to the one given him in the road by the admiring lad. Colmor's estimate of him must have been a monument built of Ann's eulogies. Jean's heart suffered misgivings. Could he live up to the character that somehow had forestalled his advent in Grass Valley? Surely life was measured differently here in the Tonto Basin.

The children, bundling their treasures to their bosoms, were dragged off to bed in some remote part of the house, from which their laughter and voices came back with happy significance. Jean forthwith had an interested audience. How eagerly these lonely pioneer people listened to news of the outside world! Jean talked until he was hoarse. In their turn his hearers told him much that had never found place in the few and short letters he had received since he had been left in Oregon. Not a word about sheepmen or any hint of rustlers! Jean marked the omission and thought all the more seriously of probabilities because nothing was said. Altogether the evening was a happy reunion of a family of which all living members were there present. Jean grasped that this fact was one of significant satisfaction to his father.

"Shore we're all goin' to live together heah," he declared. "I started this range. I call most of this valley mine. We'll run up a cabin for Ann soon as she says the word. An' you, Jean, where's your girl? I shore told you to fetch her."

"Dad, I didn't have one," replied Jean.

"Wal, I wish you had," returned the rancher. "You'll go courtin' one of these Tonto hussies that I might object to."

"Why, father, there's not a girl in the valley Jean would look twice at," interposed Ann Isbel, with spirit.

Jean laughed the matter aside, but he had an uneasy memory. Aunt Mary averred, after the manner of relatives, that Jean would play havoc among the women of the settlement. And Jean retorted that at least one member of the Isbels should hold out against folly and fight and love and marriage, the agents which had reduced the family to these few present. "I'll be the last Isbel to go under," he concluded.

"Son, you're talkin' wisdom," said his father. "An' shore that reminds me of the uncle you're named after. Jean Isbel! . . . Wal, he was my youngest brother an' shore a fire-eater. Our mother was a French creole from Louisiana, an' Jean must have inherited some of his fightin' nature from her. When the war of the rebellion started Jean an' I enlisted. I was crippled before we ever got to the front. But Jean went through three years before he was killed. His company had orders to fight to the last man. An' Jean fought an' lived long enough just to be that last man."

At length Jean was left alone with his father.

"Reckon you're used to bunkin' outdoors?" queried the rancher, rather abruptly.

"Most of the time," replied Jean.

"Wal, there's room in the house, but I want you to sleep out. Come get your beddin' an' gun. I'll show you."

They went outside on the porch, where Jean shouldered his roll of tarpaulin and blankets. His rifle, in its saddle sheath, leaned against the door. His father took it up and, half pulling it out, looked at it by the starlight. "Forty-four, eh? Wal, wal, there's shore no better, if a man can hold straight." At the moment a big gray dog trotted up to sniff at Jean. "An' heah's your bunkmate, Shepp. He's part lofer, Jean. His mother was a favorite shepherd dog of mine. His father was a big timber wolf that took us two years to kill. Some bad wolf packs runnin' this Basin."

The night was cold and still, darkly bright under the moon and stars; the smell of hay seemed to mingle with that of cedar. Jean followed his father round the house and up a gentle slope of grass to the edge of the cedar line. Here several trees with low-sweeping thick branches formed a dense, impenetrable shade.

"Son, your uncle Jean was scout for Liggett, one of the greatest rebels the South had," said the rancher. "An' you're goin' to be scout for the Isbels of Tonto. Reckon you'll find it 'most as hot as your uncle did. . . . Spread your bed inside. You can see out, but no one can see you. Reckon there's been some queer happenin's 'round heah lately. If Shepp could talk he'd shore have lots to tell us. Bill an' Guy have been sleepin' out, trailin' strange hoss tracks, an' all that. But shore whoever's been prowlin' around heah was too sharp for them. Some bad, crafty, light-steppin' woodsmen 'round heah, Jean. . . . Three mawnin's ago, just after daylight, I stepped out the back door an' some one of these sneaks I'm talkin' aboot took a shot at me. Missed my head a quarter of an inch! To-morrow I'll show you the bullet hole in the doorpost. An' some of my gray hairs that're stickin' in it!"

"Dad!" ejaculated Jean, with a hand outstretched. "That's awful! You frighten me."

"No time to be scared," replied his father, calmly. "They're shore goin' to kill me. That's why I wanted you home. . . . In there with you, now! Go to sleep. You shore can trust Shepp to wake you if he gets scent or sound. . . . An' good night, my son. I'm sayin' that I'll rest easy to-night."

Jean mumbled a good night and stood watching his father's shining white head move away under the starlight. Then the tall, dark form vanished, a door closed, and all was still. The dog Shepp licked Jean's hand. Jean felt grateful for that warm touch. For a moment he sat on his roll of bedding, his thought still locked on the shuddering revelation of his father's words, "They're shore goin' to kill me." The shock of inaction passed. Jean pushed his pack in the dark opening and, crawling inside, he unrolled it and made his bed.

When at length he was comfortably settled for the night he breathed a long sigh of relief. What bliss to relax! A throbbing and burning of his muscles seemed to begin with his rest. The cool starlit night, the smell of cedar, the moan of wind, the silence—all were real to his senses. After long weeks of long, arduous travel he was home. The warmth of the welcome still lingered, but it seemed to have been pierced by an icy thrust. What lay before him? The shadow in the eyes of his aunt, in the younger, fresher eyes of his sister—Jean connected that with the meaning of his father's tragic words. Far past was the morning that had been so keen, the breaking of camp in the sunlit forest, the riding down the brown aisles under the pines, the music of bleating lambs that had called him not to pass by. Thought of Ellen Jorth recurred. Had he met her only that morning? She was up there in the forest, asleep under the starlit pines. Who was she? What was her story? That savage fling of her skirt, her bitter speech and passionate flaming face—they haunted Jean. They were crystallizing into simpler memories, growing away from his bewilderment, and therefore at once sweeter and more doubtful. "Maybe she meant differently from what I thought," Jean soliloquized. "Anyway, she was honest." Both shame and thrill possessed him at the recall of an insidious idea—dare he go back and find her and give her the last package of gifts he had brought from the city? What might they mean to poor, ragged, untidy, beautiful Ellen Jorth? The idea grew on Jean. It could not be dispelled. He resisted stubbornly. It was bound to go to its fruition. Deep into his mind had sunk an impression of her need—a material need that brought spirit and pride to abasement. From one picture to another his memory wandered, from one speech and act of hers to another, choosing, selecting, casting aside, until clear and sharp as the stars shone the words, "Oh, I've been kissed before!" That stung him now. By whom? Not by one man, but by several, by many, she had meant. Pshaw! he had only been sympathetic and drawn by a strange girl in the woods. To-morrow he would forget. Work there was for him in Grass Valley. And he reverted uneasily to the remarks of his father until at last sleep claimed him.

A cold nose against his cheek, a low whine, awakened Jean. The big dog Shepp was beside him, keen, wary, intense. The night appeared far advanced toward dawn. Far away a cock crowed; the near-at-hand one answered in clarion voice. "What is it, Shepp?" whispered Jean, and he sat up. The dog smelled or heard something suspicious to his nature, but whether man or animal Jean could not tell.

CHAPTER THREE

The morning star, large, intensely blue-white, magnificent in its dominance of the clear night sky, hung over the dim, dark valley ramparts. The moon had gone down and all the other stars were wan, pale ghosts.

Presently the strained vacuum of Jean's ears vibrated to a low roar of many hoofs. It came from the open valley, along the slope to the south. Shepp acted as if he wanted the word to run. Jean laid a hand on the dog. "Hold on, Shepp," he whispered. Then hauling on his boots and slipping into his coat Jean took his rifle and stole out into the open. Shepp appeared to be well trained, for it was evident that he had a strong natural tendency to run off and hunt for whatever had roused him. Jean thought it more than likely that the dog scented an animal of some kind. If there were men prowling around the ranch Shepp might have been just as vigilant, but it seemed to Jean that the dog would have shown less eagerness to leave him, or none at all.

In the stillness of the morning it took Jean a moment to locate the direction of the wind, which was very light and coming from the south. In fact that little breeze had borne the low roar of trampling hoofs. Jean circled the ranch house to the right and kept along the slope at the edge of the cedars. It struck him suddenly how well fitted he was for work of this sort. All the work he had ever done, except for his few years in school, had been in the open. All the leisure he had ever been able to obtain had been given to his ruling passion for hunting and fishing. Love of the wild had been born in Jean. At this moment he experienced a grim assurance of what his instinct and his training might accomplish if directed to a stern and daring end. Perhaps his father understood this; perhaps the old Texan had some little reason for his confidence.

Every few paces Jean halted to listen. All objects, of course, were indistinguishable in the dark-gray obscurity, except when he came close upon them. Shepp showed an increasing eagerness to bolt out into the void. When Jean had traveled half a mile from the house he heard a scattered trampling of cattle on the run, and farther out a low strangled bawl of a calf. "Ahuh!" muttered Jean. "Cougar or some varmint pulled down that calf." Then he discharged his rifle in the air and yelled with all his might. It was necessary then to yell again to hold Shepp back.

Thereupon Jean set forth down the valley, and tramped out and across and around, as much to scare away whatever had been after the stock as to look for the wounded calf. More than once he heard cattle moving away ahead of him, but he could not see them. Jean let Shepp go, hoping the dog would strike a trail. But Shepp neither gave tongue nor came back. Dawn began to break, and in the growing light Jean searched around until at last he stumbled over a dead calf, lying in a little bare wash where water ran in wet seasons. Big wolf tracks showed in the soft earth. "Lofers," said Jean, as he knelt and just covered one track with his spread hand. "We had wolves in Oregon, but not as big as these. . . . Wonder where that half-wolf dog, Shepp, went. Wonder if he can be trusted where wolves are concerned. I'll bet not, if there's a she-wolf runnin' around."

Jean found tracks of two wolves, and he trailed them out of the wash, then lost them in the grass. But, guided by their direction, he went on and climbed a slope to the cedar line, where in the dusty patches he found the tracks again. "Not scared much," he muttered, as he noted the slow trotting tracks. "Well, you old gray lofers, we're goin' to clash." Jean knew from many a futile hunt that wolves were the wariest and most intelligent of wild animals in the quest. From the top of a low foothill he watched the sun rise; and then no longer wondered why his father waxed eloquent over the beauty and location and luxuriance of this grassy valley. But it was large enough to make rich a good many ranchers. Jean tried to restrain any curiosity as to his father's dealings in Grass Valley until the situation had been made clear.

Moreover, Jean wanted to love this wonderful country. He wanted to be free to ride and hunt and roam to his heart's content; and therefore he dreaded hearing his father's claims. But Jean threw off forebodings. Nothing ever turned out so badly as it presaged. He would think the best until certain of the worst. The morning was gloriously bright, and already the frost was glistening wet on the stones. Grass Valley shone like burnished silver dotted with innumerable black spots. Burros were braying their discordant messages to one another; the colts were romping in the fields; stallions were whistling; cows were bawling. A cloud of blue smoke hung low over the ranch house, slowly wafting away on the wind. Far out in the valley a dark group of horsemen were riding toward the village. Jean glanced thoughtfully at them and reflected that he seemed destined to harbor suspicion of all men new and strange to him. Above the distant village stood the darkly green foothills leading up to the craggy slopes, and these ending in the Rim, a red, black-fringed mountain front, beautiful in the morning sunlight, lonely, serene, and mysterious against the level skyline. Mountains, ranges, distances unknown to Jean, always called to him—to come, to seek, to explore, to find, but no wild horizon ever before beckoned to him as this one. And the subtle vague emotion that had gone to sleep with him last night awoke now hauntingly. It took effort to dispel the desire to think, to wonder.

Upon his return to the house, he went around on the valley side, so as to see the place by light of day. His father had built for permanence; and evidently there had been three constructive periods in the history of that long, substantial, picturesque log house. But few nails and little sawed lumber and no glass had been used. Strong and skillful hands, axes and a crosscut saw, had been the prime factors in erecting this habitation of the Isbels.

"Good mawnin', son," called a cheery voice from the porch. "Shore we-all heard you shoot; an' the crack of that forty-four was as welcome as May flowers."

Bill Isbel looked up from a task over a saddle girth and inquired pleasantly if Jean ever slept of nights. Guy Isbel laughed and there was warm regard in the gaze he bent on Jean.

"You old Indian!" he drawled, slowly. "Did you get a bead on anythin'?"

"No. I shot to scare away what I found to be some of your lofers," replied Jean. "I heard them pullin' down a calf. An' I found tracks of two whoppin' big wolves. I found the dead calf, too. Reckon the meat can be saved. Dad, you must lose a lot of stock here."

"Wal, son, you shore hit the nail on the haid," replied the rancher. "What with lions an' bears an' lofers—an' two-footed lofers of another breed—I've lost five thousand dollars in stock this last year."

"Dad! You don't mean it!" exclaimed Jean, in astonishment. To him that sum represented a small fortune.

"I shore do," answered his father.

Jean shook his head as if he could not understand such an enormous loss where there were keen able-bodied men about. "But that's awful, dad. How could it happen? Where were your herders an' cowboys? An' Bill and Guy?"

Bill Isbel shook a vehement fist at Jean and retorted in earnest, having manifestly been hit in a sore spot. "Where was me an' Guy, huh? Wal, my Oregon brother, we was heah, all year, sleepin' more or less aboot three hours out of every twenty-four—ridin' our boots off—an' we couldn't keep down that loss."

"Jean, you-all have a mighty tumble comin' to you out heah," said Guy, complacently.

"Listen, son," spoke up the rancher. "You want to have some hunches before you figure on our troubles. There's two or three packs of lofers, an' in winter time they are hell to deal with. Lions thick as bees, an' shore bad when the snow's on. Bears will kill a cow now an' then. An' whenever an' old silvertip comes mozyin' across from the Mazatzals he kills stock. I'm in with half a dozen cattlemen. We all work together, an' the whole outfit cain't keep these vermints down. Then two years ago the Hash Knife Gang come into the Tonto."

"Hash Knife Gang? What a pretty name!" replied Jean. "Who're they?"

"Rustlers, son. An' shore the real old Texas brand. The old Lone Star State got too hot for them, an' they followed the trail of a lot of other Texans who needed a healthier climate. Some two hundred Texans around heah, Jean, an' maybe a matter of three hundred inhabitants in the Tonto all told, good an' bad. Reckon it's aboot half an' half."

A cheery call from the kitchen interrupted the conversation of the men.

"You come to breakfast."

During the meal the old rancher talked to Bill and Guy about the day's order of work; and from this Jean gathered an idea of what a big cattle business his father conducted. After breakfast Jean's brothers manifested keen interest in the new rifles. These were unwrapped and cleaned and taken out for testing. The three rifles were forty-four calibre Winchesters, the kind of gun Jean had found most effective. He tried them out first, and the shots he made were satisfactory to him and amazing to the others. Bill had used an old Henry rifle. Guy did not favor any particular rifle. The rancher pinned his faith to the famous old single-shot buffalo gun, mostly called *needle* gun. "Wal, reckon I'd better stick to mine. Shore you cain't teach an old dog new tricks. But you boys may do well with the forty-fours. Pack 'em on your saddles an' practice when you see a coyote."

Jean found it difficult to convince himself that this interest in guns and marksmanship had any sinister propulsion back of it. His father and brothers had always been this way. Rifles were as important to pioneers as plows, and their skillful use was an achievement every frontiersman tried to attain. Friendly rivalry had always existed among the members of the Isbel family: even Ann Isbel was a good shot. But such proficiency in the use of firearms—and life in the open that was correlative with it—had not dominated them as it had Jean. Bill and Guy Isbel were born cattlemen—chips of the old block. Jean began to hope that his father's letter was an exaggeration, and particularly that the fatalistic speech of last night, "they are goin' to kill me," was just a moody inclination to see the worst side. Still, even as Jean tried to persuade himself of this more hopeful view, he recalled many references to the peculiar reputation of Texans for gun-throwing, for feuds, for never-ending hatreds. In Oregon the Isbels had lived among industrious and peaceful pioneers from all over the States; to be sure, the life had been rough and primitive, and there had been fights on occasions, though no Isbel had ever killed a man. But now they had become fixed in a wilder and sparsely settled country among men of their own breed. Jean was afraid his hopes had only sentiment to foster them. Nevertheless, he forced back a strange, brooding, mental state and resolutely held up the brighter side. Whatever the evil conditions existing in Grass Valley, they could be met with intelligence and courage, with an absolute certainty that it was inevitable they must pass away. Jean refused to consider the old, fatal law that at certain wild times and wild places in the West certain men had to pass away to change evil conditions.

"Wal, Jean, ride around the range with the boys," said the rancher. "Meet some of my neighbors, Jim Blaisdell, in particular. Take a look at the cattle. An' pick out some hosses for yourself."

"I've seen one already," declared Jean quickly. "A black with white face. I'll take him."

"Shore you know a hoss. To my eye he's my pick. But the boys don't agree. Bill 'specially has degenerated into a fancier of pitchin' hosses. Ann can ride that black. You try him this mawnin'. . . . An', son, enjoy yourself."

True to his first impression, Jean named the black horse Whiteface and fell in love with him before ever he swung a leg over him. Whiteface appeared spirited, yet gentle. He had been trained instead of being broken. Of hard hits and quirts and spurs he had no experience. He liked to do what his rider wanted him to do.

A hundred or more horses grazed in the grassy meadow, and as Jean rode on among them it was a pleasure to see stallions throw heads and ears up and whistle or snort. Whole troops of colts and two-year-olds raced with flying tails and manes.

Beyond these pastures stretched the range, and Jean saw the gray-green expanse speckled by thousands of cattle. The scene was inspiring. Jean's brothers led him all around, meeting some of the herders and riders employed on the ranch, one of whom was a burly, grizzled man with eyes reddened and narrowed by much riding in wind and sun and dust. His name was Evarts and he was father of the lad whom Jean had met near the village. Evarts was busily skinning the calf that had been killed by the wolves. "See heah, y'u Jean Isbel," said Evarts, "it shore was aboot time y'u come home. We-all heahs y'u hev an eye fer tracks. Wal, mebbe y'u can kill Old Gray, the lofer thet did this job. He's pulled down nine calves an' yearlin's this last two months thet I know of. An' we've not hed the spring round-up."

Grass Valley widened to the southeast. Jean would have been backward about estimating the square miles in it. Yet it was not vast acreage so much as rich pasture that made it such a wonderful range. Several ranches lay along the western slope of this section. Jean was informed that open parks and swales, and little valleys nestling among the foothills, wherever there was water and grass, had been settled by ranchers. Every summer a few new families ventured in.

Blaisdell struck Jean as being a lionlike type of Texan, both in his broad, bold face, his huge head with its upstanding tawny hair like a mane, and in the speech and force that betokened the nature of his heart. He was not as old as Jean's father. He had a rolling voice, with the same drawling intonation characteristic of all Texans, and blue eyes that still held the fire of youth. Quite a marked contrast he presented to the lean, rangy, hard-jawed, intent-eyed men Jean had begun to accept as Texans.

Blaisdell took time for a curious scrutiny and study of Jean, that, frank and kindly as it was, and evidently the adjustment of impressions gotten from hearsay, yet bespoke the attention of one used to judging men for himself, and in this particular case having reasons of his own for so doing.

"Wal, you're like your sister Ann," said Blaisdell. "Which you may take as a compliment, young man. Both of you favor your mother. But you're an Isbel. Back in Texas there are men who never wear a glove on their right hands, an' shore I reckon if one of them met up with you sudden he'd think some graves had opened an' he'd go for his gun."

Blaisdell's laugh pealed out with deep, pleasant roll. Thus he planted in Jean's sensitive mind a significant thought-provoking idea about the past-and-gone Isbels.

His further remarks, likewise, were exceedingly interesting to Jean. The settling of the Tonto Basin by Texans was a subject often in dispute. His own father had been in the first party of adventurous pioneers who had traveled up from the south to cross over the Reno Pass of the Mazatzals into the Basin. "Newcomers from outside get impressions of the Tonto accordin' to the first settlers they meet," declared Blaisdell. "An' shore it's my belief these first impressions never change. Just so strong they are! Wal, I've heard my father say there were men in his wagon train that got run out of Texas, but he swore he wasn't one of them. So I reckon that sort of talk held good for twenty years, an' for all the Texans who emigrated, except, of course, such notorious rustlers as Daggs an' men of his ilk. Shore we've got some bad men heah. There's no law. Possession used to mean more than it does now. Daggs an' his Hash Knife Gang have begun to hold forth with a high hand. No small rancher can keep enough stock to pay for his labor."

At the time of which Blaisdell spoke there were not many sheepmen and cattlemen in the Tonto, considering its vast area. But these, on account of the extreme wildness of the broken country, were limited to the comparatively open Grass Valley and its adjacent environs. Naturally, as the inhabitants increased and stock raising grew in proportion the grazing and water rights became matters of extreme importance. Sheepmen ran their flocks up on the Rim in summer time and down into the Basin in winter time. A sheepman could throw a few thousand sheep round a cattleman's ranch and ruin him. The range was free. It was as fair for sheepmen to graze their herds anywhere as it was for cattlemen. This of course did not apply to the few acres of cultivated ground that a rancher could call his own; but very few cattle could have been raised on such limited area. Blaisdell said that the sheepmen were unfair because they could have done just as well, though perhaps at more labor, by keeping to the ridges and leaving the open valley and little flats to the ranchers. Formerly there had been room enough for all; now the grazing ranges were being encroached upon by sheepmen newly come to the Tonto. To Blaisdell's way of thinking the rustler menace was more serious than the sheeping-off of the range, for the simple reason that no cattleman knew exactly who the rustlers were and for the more complex and significant reason that the rustlers did not steal sheep.

"Texas was overstocked with bad men an' fine steers," concluded Blaisdell. "Most of the first an' some of the last have struck the Tonto. The sheepmen have now got distributin' points for wool an' sheep at Maricopa an' Phoenix. They're shore waxin' strong an' bold."

"Ahuh! . . . An' what's likely to come of this mess?" queried Jean.

"Ask your dad," replied Blaisdell.

"I will. But I reckon I'd be obliged for your opinion."

"Wal, short an' sweet it's this: Texas cattlemen will never allow the range they stocked to be overrun with sheepmen."

"Who's this man Greaves?" went on Jean. "Never run into anyone like him."

"Greaves is hard to figure. He's a snaky customer in deals. But he seems to be good to the poor people 'round heah. Says he's from Missouri. Ha-ha! He's as much Texan as I am. He rode into the Tonto without even a pack to his name. An' presently he builds his stone house an' freights supplies in from Phoenix. Appears to buy an' sell a good deal of stock. For a while it looked like he was steerin' a middle course between cattlemen an' sheepmen. Both sides made a rendezvous of his store, where he heard the grievances of each. Laterly he's leanin' to the sheepmen. Nobody has accused him of that yet. But it's time some cattleman called his bluff."

"Of course there are honest an' square sheepmen in the Basin?" queried Jean.

"Yes, an' some of them are not unreasonable. But the new fellows that dropped in on us the last few years—they're the ones we're goin' to clash with."

"This—sheepman, Jorth?" went on Jean, in slow hesitation, as if compelled to ask what he would rather not learn.

"Jorth must be the leader of this sheep faction that's harryin' us ranchers. He doesn't make threats or roar around like some of them. But he goes on raisin' an' buyin' more an' more sheep. An' his herders have been grazin' down all around us this winter. Jorth's got to be reckoned with."

"Who is he?"

"Wal, I don't know enough to talk aboot. Your dad never said so, but I think he an' Jorth knew each other in Texas years ago. I never saw Jorth but once. That was in Greaves's barroom. Your dad an' Jorth met that day for the first time in this country. Wal, I've not known men for nothin'. They just stood stiff an' looked at each other. Your dad was aboot to draw. But Jorth made no sign to throw a gun."

Jean saw the growing and weaving and thickening threads of a tangle that had already involved him. And the sudden pang of regret he sustained was not wholly because of sympathies with his own people.

"The other day back up in the woods on the Rim I ran into a sheepman who said his name was Colter. Who is he?"

"Colter? Shore he's a new one. What'd he look like?"

Jean described Colter with a readiness that spoke volumes for the vividness of his impressions.

"I don't know him," replied Blaisdell. "But that only goes to prove my contention—any fellow runnin' wild in the woods can say he's a sheepman."

"Colter surprised me by callin' me by my name," continued Jean. "Our little talk wasn't exactly friendly. He said a lot about my bein' sent for to run sheep herders out of the country."

"Shore, that's all over," replied Blaisdell, seriously. "You're a marked man already."

"What started such rumor?"

"Shore you cain't prove it by me. But it's not taken as rumor. It's got to the sheepmen as hard as bullets."

"Ahuh! That accunts for Colter's seemin' a little sore under the collar. Well, he said they were goin' to run sheep over Grass Valley, an' for me to take that hunch to my dad."

Blaisdell had his chair tilted back and his heavy boots against a post of the porch. Down he thumped. His neck corded with a sudden rush of blood and his eyes changed to blue fire.

"The hell he did!" he ejaculated, in furious amaze.

Jean gauged the brooding, rankling hurt of this old cattleman by his sudden break from the cool, easy Texan manner. Blaisdell cursed under his breath, swung his arms violently, as if to throw a last doubt or hope aside, and then relapsed to his former state. He laid a brown hand on Jean's knee.

"Two years ago I called the cards," he said, quietly. "It means a Grass Valley war."

Not until late that afternoon did Jean's father broach the subject uppermost in his mind. Then at an opportune moment he drew Jean away into the cedars out of sight.

"Son, I shore hate to make your home-comin' unhappy," he said, with evidence of agitation, "but so help me God I have to do it!"

"Dad, you called me Prodigal, an' I reckon you were right. I've shirked my duty to you. I'm ready now to make up for it," replied Jean, feelingly.

"Wal, wal, shore that's fine-spoken, my boy. . . . Let's set down heah an' have a long talk. First off, what did Jim Blaisdell tell you?"

Briefly Jean outlined the neighbor rancher's conversation. Then Jean recounted his experience with Colter and concluded with Blaisdell's reception of the sheepman's threat. If Jean expected to see his father rise up like a lion in his wrath he made a huge mistake. This news of Colter and his talk never struck even a spark from Gaston Isbel.

"Wal," he began, thoughtfully, "reckon there are only two points in Jim's talk I need touch on. There's shore goin' to be a Grass Valley war. An' Jim's idea of the cause of it seems to be pretty much the same as that of all the other cattlemen. It'll go down a black blot on the history page of the Tonto Basin as a war between rival sheepmen an' cattlemen. Same old fight over water an' grass! . . . Jean, my son, that is wrong. It'll not be a war between sheepmen an' cattlemen. But a war of honest ranchers against rustlers maskin' as sheep raisers! . . . Mind you, I don't belittle the trouble between sheepmen an' cattlemen in Arizona. It's real an' it's vital an' it's serious. It'll take law an' order to straighten out the grazin' question. Some day the government will keep sheep off of cattle ranges. . . . So get things right in your mind, my son. You can trust your dad to tell the absolute truth. In this fight that'll wipe out some of the Isbels—maybe all of them—you're on the side of justice and right. Knowin' that, a man can fight a hundred times harder than he who knows he is a liar an' a thief."

The old rancher wiped his perspiring face and breathed slowly and deeply. Jean sensed in him the rise of a tremendous emotional strain. Wonderingly he watched the keen lined face. More than material worries were at the root of brooding, mounting thoughts in his father's eyes.

"Now next take what Jim said aboot your comin' to chase these sheep-herders out of the valley. . . . Jean, I started that talk. I had my tricky reasons. I know these greaser sheep herders an' I know the respect Texans have for a gunman. Some say I bragged. Some say I'm an old fool in his dotage, ravin' aboot a favorite son. But they are people who hate me an' are afraid. True, son, I talked with a purpose, but shore I was mighty cold an' steady when I did it. My feelin' was that you'd do what I'd do if I were thirty years younger. No, I reckoned you'd do more. For I figured on your blood. Jean, you're Indian, an' Texas an' French, an' you've trained yourself in the Oregon woods. When you were only a boy, few marksmen I ever knew could beat you, an' I never saw your equal for eye an' ear, for trackin' a hoss, for all the gifts that make a woodsman. . . . Wal, rememberin' this an' seein' the trouble ahaid for the Isbels, I just broke out whenever I had a chance. I bragged before men I'd reason to believe would take my words deep. For instance, not long ago I missed some stock, an', happenin' into Greaves's place on Saturday night, I shore talked loud. His barroom was full of men an' some of them were in my black book. Greaves took my talk a little testy. He said. 'Wal, Gass, mebbe you're right aboot some of these cattle thieves livin' among us, but ain't they jest as liable to be some of your friends or relatives as Ted Meeker's or mine or any one around heah?' That was where Greaves an' me fell out. I yelled at him: 'No, by God, they're not! My record heah an' that of my people is open. The least I can say for you, Greaves, an' your crowd, is that your records fade away on dim trails.' Then he said, nasty-like, 'Wal, if you could work out all the dim trails in the Tonto you'd shore be surprised.' An' then I roared. Shore that was the chance I was lookin' for. I swore the trails he hinted of would be tracked to the holes of the rustlers who made them. I told him I had sent for you an' when you got heah these slippery, mysterious thieves, whoever they were, would shore have hell to pay. Greaves said he hoped so, but he was afraid I was partial to my Indian son. Then we had hot words. Blaisdell got between us. When I was leavin' I took a partin' fling at him. 'Greaves, you ought to know the Isbels, considerin' you're from Texas. Maybe you've got reasons for throwin' taunts at my claims for my son Jean. Yes, he's got Indian in him an' that'll be the worse for the men who will have to meet him. I'm tellin' you, Greaves, Jean Isbel is the black sheep of the family. If you ride down his record you'll find he's shore in line to be another Poggin, or Reddy Kingfisher, or Hardin', or any of the Texas gunmen you ought to remember. . . . Greaves, there are men rubbin' elbows with you right heah that my Indian son is goin' to track down!' "

Jean bent his head in stunned cognizance of the notoriety with which his father had chosen to affront any and all Tonto Basin men who were under the ban of his suspicion. What a terrible reputation and trust to have saddled upon him! Thrills and strange, heated sensations seemed to rush together inside Jean, forming a hot ball of fire that threatened to explode. A retreating self made feeble protests. He saw his own pale face going away from this older, grimmer man.

"Son, if I could have looked forward to anythin' but blood spillin' I'd never have given you such a name to uphold," continued the rancher. "What I'm goin' to tell you now is my secret. My other sons an' Ann have never heard it. Jim Blaisdell suspects there's somethin' strange, but he doesn't know. I'll shore never tell anyone else but you. An' you must promise to keep my secret now an' after I am gone."

"I promise," said Jean.

"Wal, an' now to get it out," began his father, breathing hard. His face twitched and his hands clenched. "The sheepman heah I have to reckon with is Lee Jorth, a lifelong enemy of mine. We were born in the same town, played together as children, an' fought with each other as boys. We never got along together. An' we both fell in love with the same girl. It was nip an' tuck for a while. Ellen Sutton belonged to one of the old families of the South. She was a beauty, an' much courted, an' I reckon it was hard for her to choose. But I won her an' we became engaged. Then the war broke out. I enlisted with my brother Jean. He advised me to marry Ellen before I left. But I would not. That was the blunder of my life. Soon after our partin' her letters ceased to come. But I didn't distrust her. That was a terrible time an' all was confusion. Then I got crippled an' put in a hospital. An' in aboot a year I was sent back home."

At this juncture Jean refrained from further gaze at his father's face.

"Lee Jorth had gotten out of goin' to war," went on the rancher, in lower, thicker voice. "He'd married my sweetheart, Ellen. . . . I knew the story long before I got well. He had run after her like a hound after a hare. . . . An' Ellen married him. Wal, when I was able to get aboot I went to see Jorth an' Ellen. I confronted them. I had to know why she had gone back on me. Lee Jorth hadn't changed any with all his good fortune. He'd made Ellen believe in my dishonor. . . . But, I reckon, lies or no lies, Ellen Sutton was faithless. In my absence he had won her away from me. An' I saw that she loved him as she never had me. I reckon that killed all my generosity. If she'd been imposed upon an' weaned away by his lies an' had regretted me a little I'd have forgiven, perhaps. But she worshiped him. She was his slave. An' I, wal, I learned what hate was.

"The war ruined the Suttons, same as so many Southerners. Lee Jorth went in for raisin' cattle. He'd gotten the Sutton range an' after a few years he began to accumulate stock. In those days every cattleman was a little bit of a thief. Every cattleman drove in an' branded calves he couldn't swear was his. Wal, the Isbels were the strongest cattle raisers in that country. An' I laid a trap for Lee Jorth, caught him in the act of brandin' calves of mine I'd marked, an' I proved him a thief. I made him a rustler. I ruined him. We met once. But Jorth was one Texan not strong on the draw, at least against an Isbel. He left the country. He had friends an' relatives an' they started him at stock raisin' again. But he began to gamble an' he got in with a shady crowd. He went from bad to worse an' then he came back home. When I saw the change in proud, beautiful Ellen Sutton, an' how she still worshiped Jorth, it shore drove me near mad between pity an' hate. . . . Wal, I reckon in a Texan hate outlives any other feelin'. There came a strange turn of the wheel an' my fortunes changed. Like most young bloods of the day, I drank an' gambled. An' one night I run across Jorth an' a card-sharp friend. He fleeced me. We quarreled. Guns were thrown. I killed my man. . . . Aboot that period the Texas Rangers had come into existence. . . . An', son, when I said I never was run out of Texas I wasn't holdin' to strict truth. I rode out on a hoss.

"I went to Oregon. There I married soon, an' there Bill and Guy were born. Their mother did not live long. An' next I married your mother, Jean. She had some Indian blood, which, for all I could see, made her only the finer. She was a wonderful woman an' gave me the only happiness I ever knew. You remember her, of course, an' those home days in Oregon. I reckon I made another great blunder when I moved to Arizona. But the cattle country had always called me. I had heard of this wild Tonto Basin an' how Texans were settlin' there. An' Jim Blaisdell sent me word to come—that this shore was a garden spot of the West. Wal, it is. An' your mother was gone—

"Three years ago Lee Jorth drifted into the Tonto. An', strange to me, along aboot a year or so after his comin' the Hash Knife Gang rode up from Texas. Jorth went in for raisin' sheep. Along with some other sheepmen he lives up in the Rim cañons. Somewhere back in the wild brakes is the hidin' place of the Hash Knife Gang. Nobody but me, I reckon, associates Colonel Jorth, as he's called, with Daggs an' his gang. Maybe Blaisdell an' a few others have a hunch. But that's no matter. As a sheepman Jorth has a legitimate grievance with the cattlemen. But what could be settled by a square consideration for the good of all an' the future Jorth will never settle. He'll never settle because he is now no longer an honest man. He's in with Daggs. I cain't prove this, son, but I know it. I saw it in Jorth's face when I met him that day with Greaves. I saw more. I shore saw what he is up to. He'd never meet me at an even break. He's dead set on usin' this sheep an' cattle feud to ruin my family an' me, even as I ruined him. But he means more, Jean. This will be a war between Texans, an' a bloody war. There are bad men in this Tonto—some of the worst that didn't get shot in Texas. Jorth will have some of these fellows. . . . Now, are we goin' to wait to be sheeped off our range an' to be murdered from ambush?"

"No, we are not," replied Jean, quietly.

"Wal, come down to the house," said the rancher, and led the way without speaking until he halted by the door. There he placed his finger on a small hole in the wood at about the height of a man's head. Jean saw it was a bullet hole and that a few gray hairs stuck to its edges. The rancher stepped closer to the door-post, so that his head was within an inch of the wood. Then he looked at Jean with eyes in which there glinted dancing specks of fire, like wild sparks.

"Son, this sneakin' shot at me was made three mawnin's ago. I recollect movin' my haid just when I heard the crack of a rifle. Shore was surprised. But I got inside quick."

Jean scarcely heard the latter part of his speech. He seemed doubled up inwardly, in hot and cold convulsions of changing emotion. A terrible hold upon his consciousness was about to break and let go. The first shot had been fired and he was an Isbel. Indeed, his father had made him ten times an Isbel. Blood was thick. His father did not speak to dull ears. The strife of rising tumult in him seemed the effect of years of calm, of peace in the woods, of dreamy waiting for he knew not what. It was the passionate primitive life in him that had awakened to the call of blood ties.

"That's aboot all, son," concluded the rancher. "You understand now why I feel they're goin' to kill me. I feel it heah." With solemn gesture he placed his broad hand over his heart. "An, Jean, strange whispers come to me at night. It seems like your mother was callin' or tryin' to warn me. I cain't explain these queer whispers. But I know what I know."

"Jorth has his followers. You must have yours," replied Jean, tensely.

"Shore, son, an' I can take my choice of the best men heah," replied the rancher, with pride. "But I'll not do that. I'll lay the deal before them an' let them choose. I reckon it'll not be a long-winded fight. It'll be short an' bloody, after the way of Texans. I'm lookin' to you, Jean, to see that an Isbel is the last man!"

"My God—dad! is there no other way? Think of my sister Ann—of my brothers' wives—of—of other women! Dad, these damned Texas feuds are cruel, horrible!" burst out Jean, in passionate protest.

"Jean, would it be any easier for our women if we let these men shoot us down in cold blood?"

"Oh no—no, I see, there's no hope of—of. . . . But, dad, I wasn't thinkin' about myself. I don't care. Once started I'll—I'll be what you bragged I was. Only it's so hard to—to give in."

Jean leaned an arm against the side of the cabin and, bowing his face over it, he surrendered to the irresistible contention within his breast. And as if with a wrench that strange inward hold broke. He let down. He went back. Something that was boyish and hopeful—and in its place slowly rose the dark tide of his inheritance, the savage instinct of self-preservation bequeathed by his Indian mother, and the fierce, feudal blood lust of his Texan father.

Then as he raised himself, gripped by a sickening coldness in his breast, he remembered Ellen Jorth's face as she had gazed dreamily down off the Rim—so soft, so different, with tremulous lips, sad, musing, with far-seeing stare of dark eyes, peering into the unknown, the instinct of life still unlived. With confused vision and nameless pain Jean thought of her.

"Dad, it's hard on—the—the young folks," he said, bitterly. "The sins of the father, you know. An' the other side. How about Jorth? Has he any children?"

What a curious gleam of surprise and conjecture Jean encountered in his father's gaze!

"He has a daughter. Ellen Jorth. Named after her mother. The first time I saw Ellen Jorth I thought she was a ghost of the girl I had loved an' lost. Sight of her was like a blade in my side. But the looks of her an' what she is—they don't gibe. Old as I am, my heart—Bah! Ellen Jorth is a damned hussy!"

Jean Isbel went off alone into the cedars. Surrender and resignation to his father's creed should have ended his perplexity and worry. His instant and burning resolve to be as his father had represented him should have opened his mind to slow cunning, to the craft of the Indian, to the development of hate. But there seemed to be an obstacle. A cloud in the way of vision. A face limned on his memory.

Those damning words of his father's had been a shock—how little or great he could not tell. Was it only a day since he had met Ellen Jorth? What had made all the difference? Suddenly like a breath the fragrance of her hair came back to him. Then the sweet coolness of her lips! Jean trembled. He looked around him as if he were pursued or surrounded by eyes, by instincts, by fears, by incomprehensible things.

"Ahuh! That must be what ails me," he muttered. "The look of her—an' that kiss—they've gone hard with me. I should never have stopped to talk. An' I'm goin' to kill her father an' leave her to God knows what."

Something was wrong somewhere. Jean absolutely forgot that within the hour he had pledged his manhood, his life to a feud which could be blotted out only in blood. If he had understood himself he would have realized that the pledge was no more thrilling and unintelligible in its possibilities than this instinct which drew him irresistibly.

"Ellen Jorth! So—my dad calls her a damned hussy! So—that explains the—the way she acted—why she never hit me when I kissed her. An' her words, so easy an' cool-like. Hussy? That means she's bad—bad! Scornful of me—maybe disappointed because my kiss was innocent! It was, I swear. An' all she said: 'Oh, I've been kissed before.'"

Jean grew furious with himself for the spreading of a new sensation in his breast that seemed now to ache. Had he become infatuated, all in a day, with this Ellen Jorth? Was he jealous of the men who had the privilege of her kisses? No! But his reply was hot with shame, with uncertainty. The thing that seemed wrong was outside of himself. A blunder was no crime. To be attracted by a pretty girl in the woods—to yield to an impulse was no disgrace, nor wrong. He had been foolish over a girl before, though not to such a rash extent. Ellen Jorth had stuck in his consciousness, and with her a sense of regret.

Then swiftly rang his father's bitter words, the revealing: "But the looks of her an' what she is—they don't gibe!" In the import of these words hid the meaning of the wrong that troubled him. Broodingly he pondered over them.

"The looks of her. Yes, she was pretty. But it didn't dawn on me at first. I—I was sort of excited. I liked to look at her, but didn't think." And now consciously her face was called up, infinitely sweet and more impelling for the deliberate memory. Flash of brown skin, smooth and clear; level gaze of dark, wide eyes, steady, bold, unseeing; red curved lips, sad and sweet; her strong, clean, fine face rose before Jean, eager and wistful one moment, softened by dreamy musing thought and the next stormily passionate, full of hate, full of longing, but the more mysterious and beautiful.

"She looks like that, but she's bad," concluded Jean, with bitter finality. "I might have fallen in love with Ellen Jorth if—if she'd been different."

But the conviction forced upon Jean did not dispel the haunting memory of her face nor did it wholly silence the deep and stubborn voice of his consciousness. Later that afternoon he sought a moment with his sister.

"Ann, did you ever meet Ellen Jorth?" he asked.

"Yes, but not lately," replied Ann.

"Well, I met her as I was ridin' along yesterday. She was herdin' sheep," went on Jean, rapidly. "I asked her to show me the way to the Rim. An' she walked with me a mile or so. I can't say the meetin' was not interestin', at least to me. . . . Will you tell me what you know about her?"

"Sure, Jean," replied his sister, with her dark eyes fixed wonderingly and kindly on his troubled face. "I've heard a great deal, but in this Tonto Basin I don't believe all I hear. What I know I'll tell you. I first met Ellen Jorth two years ago. We didn't know each other's names then. She was the prettiest girl I ever saw. I liked her. She liked me. She seemed unhappy. The next time we met was at a round-up. There were other girls with me and they snubbed her. But I left them and went around with her. That snub cut her to the heart. She was lonely. She had no friends. She talked about herself—how she hated the people, but loved Arizona. She had nothin' fit to wear. I didn't need to be told that she'd been used to better things. Just when it looked as if we were goin' to be friends she told me who she was and asked me my name. I told her. Jean, I couldn't have hurt her more if I'd slapped her face. She turned white. She gasped. And then she ran off. The last time I saw her was about a year ago. I was ridin' a short-cut trail to the ranch where a friend lived. And I met Ellen Jorth ridin' with a man I'd never seen. The trail was overgrown and shady. They were ridin' close and didn't see me right off. The man had his arm round her. She pushed him away. I saw her laugh. Then he got hold of her again and was kissin' her when his horse shied at sight of mine. They rode by me then. Ellen Jorth held her head high and never looked at me."

"Ann, do you think she's a bad girl?" demanded Jean, bluntly.

"Bad? Oh, Jean!" exclaimed Ann, in surprise and embarrassment.

"Dad said she was a damned hussy."

"Jean, dad hates the Jorths."

"Sister, I'm askin' you what you think of Ellen Jorth. Would you be friends with her if you could?"

"Yes."

"Then you don't believe she's bad."

"No. Ellen Jorth is lonely, unhappy. She has no mother. She lives alone among rough men. Such a girl can't keep men from handlin' her and kissin' her. Maybe she's too free. Maybe she's wild. But she's honest, Jean. You can trust a woman to tell. When she rode past me that day her face was white and proud. She was a Jorth and I was an Isbel. She hated herself—she hated me. But no bad girl could look like that. She knows what's said of her all around the valley. But she doesn't care. She'd encourage gossip."

"Thank you, Ann," replied Jean, huskily. "Please keep this—this meetin' of mine with her all to yourself, won't you?"

"Why, Jean, of course I will."

Jean wandered away again, peculiarly grateful to Ann for reviving and upholding something in him that seemed a wavering part of the best of him—a chivalry that had demanded to be killed by judgment of a righteous woman. He was conscious of an uplift, a gladdening of his spirit. Yet the ache remained. More than that, he found himself plunged deeper into conjecture, doubt. Had not the Ellen Jorth incident ended? He denied his father's indictment of her and accepted the faith of his sister. "Reckon that's aboot all, as dad says," he soliloquized. Yet was that all? He paced under the cedars. He watched the sun set. He listened to the coyotes. He lingered there after the call for supper; until out of the tumult of his conflicting emotions and ponderings there evolved the staggering consciousness that he must see Ellen Jorth again.

CHAPTER FOUR

Ellen Jorth hurried back into the forest, hotly resentful of the accident that had thrown her in contact with an Isbel.

Disgust filled her—disgust that she had been amiable to a member of the hated family that had ruined her father. The surprise of this meeting did not come to her while she was under the spell of stronger feeling. She walked under the trees, swiftly, with head erect, looking straight before her, and every step seemed a relief.

Upon reaching camp, her attention was distracted from herself. Pepe, the Mexican boy, with the two shepherd dogs, was trying to drive sheep into a closer bunch to save the lambs from coyotes. Ellen loved the fleecy, tottering little lambs, and at this season she hated all the prowling beast of the forest. From this time on for weeks the flock would be besieged by wolves, lions, bears, the last of which were often bold and dangerous. The old grizzlies that killed the ewes to eat only the milk-bags were particularly dreaded by Ellen. She was a good shot with a rifle, but had orders from her father to let the bears alone. Fortunately, such sheep-killing bears were but few, and were left to be hunted by men from the ranch. Mexican sheep herders could not be depended upon to protect their flocks from bears. Ellen helped Pepe drive in the stragglers, and she took several shots at coyotes skulking along the edge of the brush. The open glade in the forest was favorable for herding the sheep at night and the dogs could be depended upon to guard the flock, and in most cases to drive predatory beasts away.

After this task, which brought the time to sunset, Ellen had supper to cook and eat. Darkness came, and a cool night wind set in. Here and there a lamb bleated plaintively. With her work done for the day, Ellen sat before a ruddy camp fire, and found her thoughts again centering around the singular adventure that had befallen her. Disdainfully she strove to think of something else. But there was nothing that could dispel the interest of her meeting with Jean Isbel. Thereupon she impatiently surrendered to it, and recalled every word and action which she could remember. And in the process of this meditation she came to an action of hers, recollection of which brought the blood tingling to her neck and cheeks, so unusually and burningly that she covered them with her hands. "What did he think of me?" she mused, doubtfully. It did not matter what he thought, but she could not help wondering. And when she came to the memory of his kiss she suffered more than the sensation of throbbing scarlet cheeks. Scornfully and bitterly she burst out, "Shore he couldn't have thought much good of me."

The half hour following this reminiscence was far from being pleasant. Proud, passionate, strong-willed Ellen Jorth found herself a victim of conflicting emotions. The event of the day was too close. She could not understand it. Disgust and disdain and scorn could not make this meeting with Jean Isbel as if it had never been. Pride could not efface it from her mind. The more she reflected, the harder she tried to forget, the stronger grew a significance of interest. And when a hint of this dawned upon her consciousness she resented it so forcibly that she lost her temper, scattered the camp fire, and went into the little teepee tent to roll in her blankets.

Thus settled snug and warm for the night, with a shepherd dog curled at the opening of her tent, she shut her eyes and confidently bade sleep end her perplexities. But sleep did not come at her invitation. She found herself wide awake, keenly sensitive to the sputtering of the camp fire, the tinkling of bells on the rams, the bleating of lambs, the sough of wind in the pines, and the hungry sharp bark of coyotes off in the distance. Darkness was no respecter of her pride. The lonesome night with its emphasis of solitude seemed to induce clamoring and strange thoughts, a confusing ensemble of all those that had annoyed her during the daytime. Not for long hours did sheer weariness bring her to slumber.

Ellen awakened late and failed of her usual alacrity. Both Pepe and the shepherd dog appeared to regard her with surprise and solicitude. Ellen's spirit was low this morning; her blood ran sluggishly; she had to fight a mournful tendency to feel sorry for herself. And at first she was not very successful. There seemed to be some kind of pleasure in reveling in melancholy which her common sense told her had no reason for existence. But states of mind persisted in spite of common sense.

"Pepe, when is Antonio comin' back?" she asked.

The boy could not give her a satisfactory answer. Ellen had willingly taken the sheep herder's place for a few days, but now she was impatient to go home. She looked down the green-and-brown aisles of the forest until she was tired. Antonio did not return. Ellen spent the day with the sheep; and in the manifold task of caring for a thousand new-born lambs she forgot herself. This day saw the end of lambing-time for that season. The forest resounded to a babel of baas and bleats. When night came she was glad to go to bed, for what with loss of sleep, and weariness she could scarcely keep her eyes open.

The following morning she awakened early, bright, eager, expectant, full of bounding life, strangely aware of the beauty and sweetness of the scented forest, strangely conscious of some nameless stimulus to her feelings.

Not long was Ellen in associating this new and delightful variety of sensations with the fact that Jean Isbel had set to-day for his ride up to the Rim to see her. Ellen's joyousness fled; her smiles faded. The spring morning lost its magic radiance.

"Shore there's no sense in my lyin' to myself," she soliloquized, thoughtfully. "It's queer of me—feelin' glad about him—without knowin'. Lord! I must be lonesome! To be glad of seein' an Isbel, even if he is different!"

Soberly she accepted the astounding reality. Her confidence died with her gayety; her vanity began to suffer. And she caught at her admission that Jean Isbel was different; she resented it in amaze; she ridiculed it; she laughed at her naïve confession. She could arrive at no conclusion other than that she was a weak-minded, fluctuating, inexplicable little fool.

But for all that she found her mind had been made up for her, without consent or desire, before her will had been consulted; and that inevitably and unalterably she meant to see Jean Isbel again. Long she battled with this strange decree. One moment she won a victory over this new curious self, only to lose it the next. And at last out of her conflict there emerged a few convictions that left her with some shreds of pride. She hated all Isbels, she hated any Isbel, and particularly she hated Jean Isbel. She was only curious—intensely curious to see if he would come back, and if he did come what he would do. She wanted only to watch him from some covert. She would not go near him, not let him see her or guess of her presence. Thus she assuaged her hurt vanity—thus she stifled her miserable doubts.

Long before the sun had begun to slant westward toward the mid-afternoon Jean Isbel had set as a meeting time Ellen directed her steps through the forest to the Rim. She felt ashamed of her eagerness. She had a guilty conscience that no strange thrills could silence. It would be fun to see him, to watch him, to let him wait for her, to fool him.

Like an Indian, she chose the soft pine-needle mats to tread upon, and her light-moccasined feet left no trace. Like an Indian also she made a wide detour, and reached the Rim a quarter of a mile west of the spot where she had talked with Jean Isbel; and here, turning east, she took care to step on the bare stones. This was an adventure, seemingly the first she had ever had in her life. Assuredly she had never before come directly to the Rim without halting to look, to wonder, to worship. This time she scarcely glanced into the blue abyss. All absorbed was she in hiding her tracks. Not one chance in a thousand would she risk. The Jorth pride burned even while the feminine side of her dominated her actions. She had some difficult rocky points to cross, then windfalls to round, and at length reached the covert she desired. A rugged yellow point of the Rim stood somewhat higher than the spot Ellen wanted to watch. A dense thicket of jack pines grew to the very edge. It afforded an ambush that even the Indian eyes Jean Isbel was credited with could never penetrate. Moreover, if by accident she made a noise and excited suspicion, she could retreat unobserved and hide in the huge rocks below the Rim, where a ferret could not locate her.

With her plan decided upon, Ellen had nothing to do but wait, so she repaired to the other side of the pine thicket and to the edge of the Rim where she could watch and listen. She knew that long before she saw Isbel she would hear his horse. It was altogether unlikely that he would come on foot.

"Shore, Ellen Jorth, y'u're a queer girl," she mused. "I reckon I wasn't well acquainted with y'u."

Beneath her yawned a wonderful deep cañon, rugged and rocky with but few pines on the north slope, thick with dark green timber on the south slope. Yellow and gray crags, like turreted castles, stood up out of the sloping forest on the side opposite her. The trees were all sharp, spear pointed. Patches of light green aspens showed strikingly against the dense black. The great slope beneath Ellen was serrated with narrow, deep gorges, almost cañons in themselves. Shadows alternated with clear bright spaces. The mile-wide mouth of the cañon opened upon the Basin, down into a world of wild timbered ranges and ravines, valleys and hills, that rolled and tumbled in dark-green waves to the Sierra Anchas.

But for once Ellen seemed singularly unresponsive to this panorama of wildness and grandeur. Her ears were like those of a listening deer, and her eyes continually reverted to the open places along the Rim. At first, in her excitement, time flew by. Gradually, however, as the sun moved westward, she began to be restless. The soft thud of dropping pine cones, the rustling of squirrels up and down the shaggy-barked spruces, the cracking of weathered bits of rock, these caught her keen ears many times and brought her up erect and thrilling. Finally she heard a sound which resembled that of an unshod hoof on stone. Stealthily then she took her rifle and slipped back through the pine thicket to the spot she had chosen. The little pines were so close together that she had to crawl between their trunks. The ground was covered with a soft bed of pine needles, brown and fragrant. In her hurry she pricked her ungloved hand on a sharp pine cone and drew the blood. She sucked the tiny wound. "Shore I'm wonderin' if that's a bad omen," she muttered, darkly thoughtful. Then she resumed her sinuous approach to the edge of the thicket, and presently reached it.

Ellen lay flat a moment to recover her breath, then raised herself on her elbows. Through an opening in the fringe of buck brush she could plainly see the promontory where she had stood with Jean Isbel, and also the approaches by which he might come. Rather nervously she realized that her covert was hardly more than a hundred feet from the promontory. It was imperative that she be absolutely silent. Her eyes searched the openings along the Rim. The gray form of a deer crossed one of these, and she concluded it had made the sound she had heard. Then she lay down more comfortably and waited. Resolutely she held, as much as possible, to her sensorial perceptions. The meaning of Ellen Jorth lying in ambush just to see an Isbel was a conundrum she refused to ponder in the present. She was doing it, and the physical act had its fascination. Her ears, attuned to all the sounds of the lonely forest, caught them and arranged them according to her knowledge of woodcraft.

A long hour passed by. The sun had slanted to a point halfway between the zenith and the horizon. Suddenly a thought confronted Ellen Jorth: "He's not comin'," she whispered. The instant that idea presented itself she felt a blank sense of loss, a vague regret—something that must have been disappointment. Unprepared for this, she was held by surprise for a moment, and then she was stunned. Her spirit, swift and rebellious, had no time to rise in her defense. She was a lonely, guilty, miserable girl, too weak for pride to uphold, too fluctuating to know her real self. She stretched there, burying her face in the pine needles, digging her fingers into them, wanting nothing so much as that they might hide her. The moment was incomprehensible to Ellen, and utterly intolerable. The sharp pine needles, piercing her wrists and cheeks, and her hot heaving breast, seemed to give her exquisite relief.

The shrill snort of a horse sounded near at hand. With a shock Ellen's body stiffened. Then she quivered a little and her feelings underwent swift change. Cautiously and noiselessly she raised herself upon her elbows and peeped through the opening in the brush. She saw a man tying a horse to a bush somewhat back from the Rim. Drawing a rifle from its saddle sheath he threw it in the hollow of his arm and walked to the edge of the precipice. He gazed away across the Basin and appeared lost in contemplation or thought. Then he turned to look back into the forest, as if he expected some one.

Ellen recognized the lithe figure, the dark face so like an Indian's. It was Isbel. He had come. Somehow his coming seemed wonderful and terrible. Ellen shook as she leaned on her elbows. Jean Isbel, true to his word, in spite of her scorn, had come back to see her. The fact seemed monstrous. He was an enemy of her father.

Long had range rumor been bandied from lip to lip—old Gass Isbel had sent for his Indian son to fight the Jorths. Jean Isbel—son of a Texan—unerring shot—peerless tracker—a bad and dangerous man! Then there flashed over Ellen a burning thought—if it were true, if he was an enemy of her father's, if a fight between Jorth and Isbel was inevitable, she ought to kill this Jean Isbel right there in his tracks as he boldly and confidently waited for her. Fool he was to think she would come. Ellen sank down and dropped her head until the strange tremor of her arms ceased. That dark and grim flash of thought retreated. She had not come to murder a man from ambush, but only to watch him, to try to see what he meant, what he thought, to allay a strange curiosity.

After a while she looked again. Isbel was sitting on an upheaved section of the Rim, in a comfortable position from which he could watch the openings in the forest and gaze as well across the west curve of the Basin to the Mazatzals. He had composed himself to wait. He was clad in a buckskin suit, rather new, and it certainly showed off to advantage, compared with the ragged and soiled apparel Ellen remembered. He did not look so large. Ellen was used to the long, lean, rangy Arizonians and Texans. This man was built differently. He had the widest shoulders of any man she had ever seen, and they made him appear rather short. But his lithe, powerful limbs proved he was not short. Whenever he moved the muscles rippled. His hands were clasped round a knee—brown, sinewy hands, very broad, and fitting the thick muscular wrists. His collar was open, and he did not wear a scarf, as did the men Ellen knew. Then her intense curiosity at last brought her steady gaze to Jean Isbel's head and face. He wore a cap, evidently of some thin fur. His hair was straight and short, and in color a dead raven black. His complexion was dark, clear tan, with no trace of red. He did not have the prominent cheek bones nor the high-bridged nose usual with white men who were part Indian. Still he had the Indian look. Ellen caught that in the dark, intent, piercing eyes, in the wide, level, thoughtful brows, in the stern impassiveness of his smooth face. He had a straight, sharp-cut profile.

Ellen whispered to herself: "I saw him right the other day. Only, I'd not admit it. . . . The finest-lookin' man I ever saw in my life is a damned Isbel! . . . Was that what I come out heah for?"

She lowered herself once more and, folding her arms under her breast, she reclined comfortably on them, and searched out a smaller peephole from which she could spy upon Isbel. And as she watched him the new and perplexing side of her mind waxed busier. Why had he come back? What did he want of her? Acquaintance, friendship, was impossible for them. He had been respectful, deferential toward her, in a way that had strangely pleased, until the surprising moment when he had kissed her. That had only disrupted her rather dreamy pleasure in a situation she had not experienced before. All the men she had met in this wild country were rough and bold; most of them had wanted to marry her, and, failing that, they had persisted in amorous attentions not particularly flattering or honorable. They were a bad lot. And contact with them had dulled some of her sensibilities. But this Jean Isbel had seemed a gentleman. She struggled to be fair, trying to forget her antipathy, as much as to understand herself as to give him due credit. True, he had kissed her, crudely and forcibly. But that kiss had not been an insult. Ellen's finer feeling forced her to believe this. She remembered the honest amaze and shame and contrition with which he had faced her, trying awkwardly to explain his bold act. Likewise she recalled the subtle swift change in him at her words, "Oh, I've been kissed before!" She was glad she had said that. Still—was she glad, after all?

She watched him. Every little while he shifted his gaze from the blue gulf beneath him to the forest. When he turned thus the sun shone on his face and she caught the piercing gleam of his dark eyes. She saw, too, that he was listening. Watching and listening for her! Ellen had to still a tumult within her. It made her feel very young, very shy, very strange. All the while she hated him because he manifestly expected her to come. Several times he rose and walked a little way into the woods. The last time he looked at the westering sun and shook his head. His confidence had gone. Then he sat and gazed down into the void. But Ellen knew he did not see anything there. He seemed an image carved in the stone of the Rim, and he gave Ellen a singular impression of loneliness and sadness. Was he thinking of the miserable battle his father had summoned him to lead—of what it would cost—of its useless pain and hatred? Ellen seemed to divine his thoughts. In that moment she softened toward him, and in her soul quivered and stirred an intangible something that was like pain, that was too deep for her understanding. But she felt sorry for an Isbel until the old pride resurged. What if he admired her? She remembered his interest, the wonder and admiration, the growing light in his eyes. And it had not been repugnant to her until he disclosed his name. "What's in a name?" she mused, recalling poetry learned in her girlhood. "'A rose by any other name would smell as sweet'. . . . He's an Isbel—yet he might be splendid—noble. . . . Bah! He's not—and I'd hate him anyhow."

All at once Ellen felt cold shivers steal over her. Isbel's piercing gaze was directed straight at her hiding place. Her heart stopped beating. If he discovered her there she felt that she would die of shame. Then she became aware that a blue jay was screeching in a pine above her, and a red squirrel somewhere near was chattering his shrill annoyance. These two denizens of the woods could be depended upon to espy the wariest hunter and make known his presence to their kind. Ellen had a moment of more than dread. This keen-eyed, keen-eared Indian might see right through her brushy covert, might hear the throbbing of her heart. It relieved her immeasurably to see him turn away and take to pacing the promontory, with his head bowed and his hands behind his back. He had stopped looking off into the forest. Presently he wheeled to the west, and by the light upon his face Ellen saw that the time was near sunset. Turkeys were beginning to gobble back on the ridge.

Isbel walked to his horse and appeared to be untying something from the back of his saddle. When he came back Ellen saw that he carried a small package apparently wrapped in paper. With this under his arm he strode off in the direction of Ellen's camp and soon disappeared in the forest.

For a little while Ellen lay there in bewilderment. If she had made conjectures before, they were now multiplied. Where was Jean Isbel going? Ellen sat up suddenly. "Well, shore this heah beats me," she said. "What did he have in that package? What was he goin' to do with it?"

It took no little will power to hold her there when she wanted to steal after him through the woods and find out what he meant. But his reputation influenced even her and she refused to pit her cunning in the forest against his. It would be better to wait until he returned to his horse. Thus decided, she lay back again in her covert and gave her mind over to pondering curiosity. Sooner than she expected she espied Isbel approaching through the forest, empty handed. He had not taken his rifle. Ellen averted her glance a moment and thrilled to see the rifle leaning against a rock. Verily Jean Isbel had been far removed from hostile intent that day. She watched him stride swiftly up to his horse, untie the halter, and mount. Ellen had an impression of his arrowlike straight figure, and sinuous grace and ease. Then he looked back at the promontory, as if to fix a picture of it in his mind, and rode away along the Rim. She watched him out of sight. What ailed her? Something was wrong with her, but she recognized only relief.

When Isbel had been gone long enough to assure Ellen that she might safely venture forth she crawled through the pine thicket to the Rim on the other side of the point. The sun was setting behind the Black Range, shedding a golden glory over the Basin. Westward the zigzag Rim reached like a streamer of fire into the sun. The vast promontories jutted out with blazing beacon lights upon their stone-walled faces. Deep down, the Basin was turning shadowy dark blue, going to sleep for the night.

Ellen vent swift steps toward her camp. Long shafts of gold preceded her through the forest. Then they paled and vanished. The tips of pines and spruces turned gold. A hoarse-voiced old turkey gobbler was booming his chug-a-lug from the highest ground, and the softer chick of hen turkeys answered him. Ellen was almost breathless when she arrived. Two packs and a couple of lop-eared burros attested to the fact of Antonio's return. This was good news for Ellen. She heard the bleat of lambs and tinkle of bells coming nearer and nearer. And she was glad to feel that if Isbel had visited her camp, most probably it was during the absence of the herders.

The instant she glanced into her tent she saw the package Isbel had carried. It lay on her bed. Ellen stared blankly. "The—the impudence of him!" she ejaculated. Then she kicked the package out of the tent. Words and action seemed to liberate a dammed-up hot fury. She kicked the package again, and thought she would kick it into the smoldering camp-fire. But somehow she stopped short of that. She left the thing there on the ground.

Pepe and Antonio hove in sight, driving in the tumbling woolly flock. Ellen did not want them to see the package, so with contempt for herself, and somewhat lessening anger, she kicked it back into the tent. What was in it? She peeped inside the tent, devoured by curiosity. Neat, well wrapped and tied packages like that were not often seen in the Tonto Basin. Ellen decided she would wait until after supper, and at a favorable moment lay it unopened on the fire. What did she care what it contained? Manifestly it was a gift. She argued that she was highly incensed with this insolent Isbel who had the effrontery to approach her with some sort of present.

It developed that the usually cheerful Antonio had returned taciturn and gloomy. All Ellen could get out of him was that the job of sheep herder had taken on hazards inimical to peace-loving Mexicans. He had heard something he would not tell. Ellen helped prepare the supper and she ate in silence. She had her own brooding troubles. Antonio presently told her that her father had said she was not to start back home after dark. After supper the herders repaired to their own tents, leaving Ellen the freedom of her camp-fire. Wherewith she secured the package and brought it forth to burn. Feminine curiosity rankled strong in her breast. Yielding so far as to shake the parcel and press it, and finally tear a corner off the paper, she saw some words written in lead pencil. Bending nearer the blaze, she read, "For my sister Ann." Ellen gazed at the big, bold hand-writing, quite legible and fairly well done. Suddenly she tore the outside wrapper completely off. From printed words on the inside she gathered that the package had come from a store in San Francisco. "Reckon he fetched home a lot of presents for his folks—the kids—and his sister," muttered Ellen. "That was nice of him. Whatever this is he shore meant it for sister Ann. . . . Ann Isbel. Why, she must be that black-eyed girl I met and liked so well before I knew she was an Isbel. . . . His sister!"

Whereupon for the second time Ellen deposited the fascinating package in her tent. She could not burn it up just then. She had other emotions besides scorn and hate. And memory of that soft-voiced, kind-hearted, beautiful Isbel girl checked her resentment. "I wonder if he is like his sister," she said, thoughtfully. It appeared to be an unfortunate thought. Jean Isbel certainly resembled his sister. "Too bad they belong to the family that ruined dad."

Ellen went to bed without opening the package or without burning it. And to her annoyance, whatever way she lay she appeared to touch this strange package. There was not much room in the little tent. First she put it at her head beside her rifle, but when she turned over her cheek came in contact with it. Then she felt as if she had been stung. She moved it again, only to touch it presently with her hand. Next she flung it to the bottom of her bed, where it fell upon her feet, and whatever way she moved them she could not escape the pressure of this undesirable and mysterious gift.

By and by she fell asleep, only to dream that the package was a caressing hand stealing about her, feeling for hers, and holding it with soft, strong clasp. When she awoke she had the strangest sensation in her right palm. It was moist, throbbing, hot, and the feel of it on her cheek was strangely thrilling and comforting. She lay awake then. The night was dark and still. Only a low moan of wind in the pines and the faint tinkle of a sheep bell broke the serenity. She felt very small and lonely lying there in the deep forest, and, try how she would, it was impossible to think the same then as she did in the clear light of day. Resentment, pride, anger—these seemed abated now. If the events of the day had not changed her, they had at least brought up softer and kinder memories and emotions than she had known for long. Nothing hurt and saddened her so much as to remember the gay, happy days of her childhood, her sweet mother, her old home. Then her thought returned to Isbel and his gift. It had been years since anyone had made her a gift. What could this one be? It did not matter. The wonder was that Jean Isbel should bring it to her and that she could be perturbed by its presence. "He meant it for his sister and so he thought well of me," she said, in finality.

Morning brought Ellen further vacillation. At length she rolled the obnoxious package inside her blankets, saying that she would wait until she got home and then consign it cheerfully to the flames. Antonio tied her pack on a burro. She did not have a horse, and therefore had to walk the several miles to her father's ranch.

She set off at a brisk pace, leading the burro and carrying her rifle. And soon she was deep in the fragrant forest. The morning was clear and cool, with just enough frost to make the sunlit grass sparkle as if with diamonds. Ellen felt fresh, buoyant, singularly full of life. Her youth would not be denied. It was pulsing, yearning. She hummed an old Southern tune and every step seemed one of pleasure in action, of advance toward some intangible future happiness. All the unknown of life before her called. Her heart beat high in her breast and she walked as one in a dream. Her thoughts were swift-changing, intimate, deep, and vague, not of yesterday or today, nor of reality.

The big, gray, white-tailed squirrels crossed ahead of her on the trail, scampered over the piny ground to hop on tree trunks, and there they paused to watch her pass. The vociferous little red squirrels barked and chattered at her. From every thicket sounded the gobble of turkeys. The blue jays squalled in the tree tops. A deer lifted its head from browsing and stood motionless, with long ears erect, watching her go by.

Thus happily and dreamily absorbed, Ellen covered the forest miles and soon reached the trail that led down into the wild brakes of Chevelon Cañon. It was rough going and less conducive to sweet wanderings of mind. Ellen slowly lost them. And then a familiar feeling assailed her, one she never failed to have upon returning to her father's ranch—a reluctance, a bitter dissatisfaction with her home, a loyal struggle against the vague sense that all was not as it should be.

At the head of this cañon in a little, level, grassy meadow stood a rude one-room log shack, with a leaning red-stone chimney on the outside. This was the abode of a strange old man who had long lived there. His name was John Sprague and his occupation was raising burros. No sheep or cattle or horses did he own, not even a dog. Rumor had said Sprague was a prospector, one of the many who had searched that country for the Lost Dutchman gold mine. Sprague knew more about the Basin and Rim than any of the sheepmen or ranchers. From Black Butte to the Cibique and from Chevelon Butte to Reno Pass he knew every trail, cañon, ridge, and spring, and could find his way to them on the darkest night. His fame, however, depended mostly upon the fact that he did nothing but raise burros, and would raise none but black burros with white faces. These burros were the finest bred in all the Basin and were in great demand. Sprague sold a few every year. He had made a present of one to Ellen, although he hated to part with them. This old man was Ellen's one and only friend.

Upon her trip out to the Rim with the sheep, Uncle John, as Ellen called him, had been away on one of his infrequent visits to Grass Valley. It pleased her now to see a blue column of smoke lazily lifting from the old chimney and to hear the discordant bray of burros. As she entered the clearing Sprague saw her from the door of his shack.

"Hello, Uncle John!" she called.

"Wal, if it ain't Ellen!" he replied, heartily. "When I seen thet white-faced jinny I knowed who was leadin' her. Where you been, girl?"

Sprague was a little, stoop-shouldered old man, with grizzled head and face, and shrewd gray eyes that beamed kindly on her over his ruddy cheeks. Ellen did not like the tobacco stain on his grizzled beard nor the dirty, motley, ragged, ill-smelling garb he wore, but she had ceased her useless attempts to make him more cleanly.

"I've been herdin' sheep," replied Ellen. "And where have y'u been, uncle? I missed y'u on the way over."

"Been packin' in some grub. An' I reckon I stayed longer in Grass Valley than I recollect. But thet was only natural, considerin'—"

"What?" asked Ellen, bluntly, as the old man paused.

Sprague took a black pipe out of his vest pocket and began rimming the bowl with his fingers. The glance he bent on Ellen was thoughtful and earnest, and so kind that she feared it was pity. Ellen suddenly burned for news from the village.

"Wal, come in an' set down, won't you?" he asked.

"No, thanks," replied Ellen, and she took a seat on the chopping block. "Tell me, uncle, what's goin' on down in the Valley?"

"Nothin' much yet—except talk. An' there's a heap of thet."

"Humph! There always was talk," declared Ellen, contemptuously. "A nasty, gossipy, catty hole, that Grass Valley!"

"Ellen, thar's goin' to be war—a bloody war in the ole Tonto Basin," went on Sprague seriously.

"War! . . . Between whom?"

"The Isbels an' their enemies. I reckon most people down thar, an' sure all the cattlemen, air on old Gass's side. Blaisdell, Gordon, Fredericks, Blue—they'll all be in it."

"Who are they goin' to fight?" queried Ellen, sharply.

"Wal, the open talk is thet the sheepmen are forcin' this war. But thar's talk not so open, an' I reckon not very healthy for any man to whisper hyarbouts."

"Uncle John, y'u needn't be afraid to tell me anythin'," said Ellen. "I'd never give y'u away. Y'u've been a good friend to me."

"Reckon I want to be, Ellen," he returned, nodding his shaggy head. "It ain't easy to be fond of you as I am an' keep my mouth shet. . . . I'd like to know somethin'. Hev you any relatives away from hyar thet you could go to till this fight's over?"

"No. All I have, so far as I know, are right heah."

"How aboot friends?"

"Uncle John, I have none," she said, sadly, with bowed head.

"Wal, wal, I'm sorry. I was hopin' you might git away."

She lifted her face. "Shore y'u don't think I'd run off if my dad got in a fight?" she flashed.

"I hope you will."

"I'm a Jorth," she said, darkly, and dropped her head again.

Sprague nodded gloomily. Evidently he was perplexed and worried, and strongly swayed by affection for her.

"Would you go away with me?" he asked. "We could pack over to the Mazatzals an' live thar till this blows over."

"Thank y'u, Uncle John. Y'u're kind and good. But I'll stay with my father. His troubles are mine."

"Ahuh! . . . Wal, I might hev reckoned so. . . . Ellen, how do you stand on this hyar sheep an' cattle question?"

"I think what's fair for one is fair for another. I don't like sheep as much as I like cattle. But that's not the point. The range is free. Suppose y'u had cattle and I had sheep. I'd feel as free to run my sheep anywhere as y'u were to run your cattle."

"Right. But what if you throwed your sheep round my range an' sheeped off the grass so my cattle would hev to move or starve?"

"Shore I wouldn't throw my sheep round y'ur range," she declared, stoutly.

"Wal, you've answered half of the question. An' now supposin' a lot of my cattle was stolen by rustlers, but not a single one of your sheep. What'd you think then?"

"I'd shore think rustlers chose to steal cattle because there was no profit in stealin' sheep."

"Egzactly. But wouldn't you hev a queer idee aboot it?"

"I don't know. Why queer? What're y'u drivin' at, Uncle John?"

"Wal, wouldn't you git kind of a hunch thet the rustlers was—say a leetle friendly toward the sheepmen?"

Ellen felt a sudden vibrating shock. The blood rushed to her temples. Trembling all over, she rose.

"Uncle John!" she cried.

"Now, girl, you needn't fire up thet way. Set down an don't—"

"Dare y'u insinuate my father has—"

"Ellen, I ain't insinuatin' nothin'," interrupted the old man. "I'm jest askin' you to think. Thet's all. You're 'most grown into a young woman now. An' you've got sense. Thar's bad times ahead, Ellen. An' I hate to see you mix in them."

"Oh, y'u do make me think," replied Ellen, with smarting tears in her eyes. "Y'u make me unhappy. Oh, I know my dad is not liked in this cattle country. But it's unjust. He happened to go in for sheep raising. I wish he hadn't. It was a mistake. Dad always was a cattleman till we came heah. He made enemies—who—

who ruined him. And everywhere misfortune crossed his trail. . . . But, oh, Uncle John, my dad is an honest man."

"Wal, child, I—I didn't mean to—to make you cry," said the old man, feelingly, and he averted his troubled gaze. "Never mind what I said. I'm an old meddler. I reckon nothin' I could do or say would ever change what's goin' to happen. If only you wasn't a girl! . . . Thar I go ag'in. Ellen, face your future an' fight your way. All youngsters hev to do thet. An' it's the right kind of fight thet makes the right kind of man or woman. Only you must be sure to find yourself. An' by thet I mean to find the real, true, honest-to-God best in you an' stick to it an' die fightin' for it. You're a young woman, almost, an' a blamed handsome one. Which means you'll hev more trouble an' a harder fight. This country ain't easy on a woman when once slander has marked her."

"What do I care for the talk down in that Basin?" returned Ellen. "I know they think I'm a hussy. I've let them think it. I've helped them to."

"You're wrong, child," said Sprague, earnestly. "Pride an' temper! You must never let anyone think bad of you, much less help them to."

"I hate everybody down there," cried Ellen, passionately. "I hate them so I'd glory in their thinkin' me bad. . . . My mother belonged to the best blood in Texas. I am her daughter. I know *who and what I am.* That uplifts me whenever I meet the sneaky, sly suspicions of these Basin people. It shows me the difference between them and me. That's what I glory in."

"Ellen, you're a wild, headstrong child," rejoined the old man, in severe tones. "Word has been passed ag'in' your good name—your honor. . . . An' hevn't you given cause fer thet?"

Ellen felt her face blanch and all her blood rush back to her heart in sickening force. The shock of his words was like a stab from a cold blade. If their meaning and the stern, just light of the old man's glance did not kill her pride and vanity they surely killed her girlishness. She stood mute, staring at him, with her brown, trembling hands stealing up toward her bosom, as if to ward off another and a mortal blow.

"Ellen!" burst out Sprague, hoarsely. "You mistook me. Aw, I didn't mean—what you think, I swear. . . . Ellen, I'm old an' blunt. I ain't used to wimmen. But I've love for you, child, an' respect, jest the same as if you was my own. . . . An' I *know* you're good. . . . Forgive me. . . . I meant only hevn't you been, say, sort of—careless?"

"Care-less?" queried Ellen, bitterly and low.

"An' powerful thoughtless an'—an' blind—lettin' men kiss you an' fondle you—when you're really a growed-up woman now?"

"Yes—I have," whispered Ellen.

"Wal, then, why did you let them?"

"I—I don't know. . . . I didn't think. The men never let me alone—never—never! I got tired everlastingly pushin' them away. And sometimes—when they were kind—and I was lonely for something I—I didn't mind if one or another fooled round me. I never thought. It never looked as y'u have made it look. . . . Then—those few times ridin' the trail to Grass Valley—when people saw me—then I guess I encouraged such attentions. . . . Oh, I must be—I am a shameless little hussy!"

"Hush thet kind of talk," said the old man, as he took her hand. "Ellen, you're only young an' lonely an' bitter. No mother—no friends—no one but a lot of rough men! It's a wonder you hev kept yourself good. But now your eyes are open, Ellen.

They're brave an' beautiful eyes, girl, an' if you stand by the light in them you will come through any trouble. An' you'll be happy. Don't ever forgit that. Life is hard enough, God knows, but it's unfailin' true in the end to the man or woman who finds the best in them an' stands by it."

"Uncle John, y'u talk so—so kindly. Y'u make me have hope. There seemed really so little for me to live for—hope for. . . . But I'll never be a coward again—nor a thoughtless fool. I'll find some good in me—or make some—and never fail it, come what will. I'll remember your words. I'll believe the future holds wonderful things for me. . . . I'm only eighteen. Shore all my life won't be lived heah. Perhaps this threatened fight over sheep and cattle will blow over. . . . Somewhere there must be some nice girl to be a friend—a sister to me. . . . And maybe some man who'd believe, in spite of all they say—that I'm not a hussy."

"Wal, Ellen, you remind me of what I was wantin' to tell you when you just got here. . . . Yestiddy I heerd you called thet name in a barroom. An' thar was a fellar thar who raised hell. He near killed one man an' made another plumb eat his words. An' he scared thet crowd stiff."

Old John Sprague shook his grizzled head and laughed, beaming upon Ellen as if the memory of what he had seen had warmed his heart.

"Was it—y'u?" asked Ellen, tremulously.

"Me? Aw, I wasn't nowhere. Ellen, this fellar was quick as a cat in his actions an' his words was like lightnin'."

"Who?" she whispered.

"Wal, no one else but a stranger jest come to these parts—an Isbel, too. Jean Isbel."

"Oh!" exclaimed Ellen, faintly.

"In a barroom full of men—almost all of them in sympathy with the sheep crowd—most of them on the Jorth side—this Jean Isbel resented an insult to Ellen Jorth."

"No!" cried Ellen. Something terrible was happening to her mind or her heart.

"Wal, he sure did," replied the old man, "an' it's goin' to be good fer you to hear all about it."

CHAPTER FIVE

Old John Sprague launched into his narrative with evident zest.

"I hung round Greaves' store most of two days. An' I heerd a heap. Some of it was jest plain ole men's gab, but I reckon I got the drift of things concernin' Grass Valley. Yestiddy mornin' I was packin' my burros in Greaves' back yard, takin' my time carryin' out supplies from the store. An' as last when I went in I seen a strange fellar was thar. Strappin' young man—not so young, either—an' he had on buckskin. Hair black as my burros, dark face, sharp eyes—you'd took him fer an Injun. He carried a rifle—one of them new forty-fours—an' also somethin' wrapped in paper thet he seemed partickler careful about. He wore a belt round his middle an' thar was a bowie-knife in it, carried like I've seen scouts an' Injun fighters hev on the frontier in the 'seventies. That looked queer to me, an' I reckon to the rest of the crowd thar. No one overlooked the big six-shooter he packed Texas fashion. Wal, I didn't hev no idee this fellar was an Isbel until I heard Greaves call him thet.

"'Isbel,' said Greaves, 'reckon your money's counterfeit hyar. I cain't sell you anythin'.'

"'Counterfeit? Not much,' spoke up the young fellar, an' he flipped some gold twenties on the bar, where they rung like bells. 'Why not? Ain't this a store? I want a cinch strap.'

"Greaves looked particular sour thet mornin'. I'd been watchin' him fer two days. He hedn't hed much sleep fer I hed my bed back of the store, an' I heerd men come in the night an' hev long confabs with him. Whatever was in the wind hedn't pleased him none. An' I calkilated thet young Isbel wasn't a sight good fer Greaves' sore eyes, anyway. But he paid no more attention to Isbel. Acted jest as if he hedn't heerd Isbel say he wanted a cinch strap.

"I stayed inside the store then. Thar was a lot of fellars I'd seen, an' some I knowed. Couple of card games goin', an' drinkin', of course. I soon gathered thet the general atmosphere wasn't friendly to Jean Isbel. He seen thet quick enough, but he didn't leave. Between you an' me I sort of took a likin' to him. An' I sure watched him as close as I could, not seemin' to, you know. Reckon they all did the same, only you couldn't see it. It got jest about the same as if Isbel hedn't been in thar, only you knowed it wasn't really the same. Thet was how I got the hunch the crowd was all sheepmen or their friends. The day before I'd heerd a lot of talk about this young Isbel, an' what he'd come to Grass Valley fer, an' what a bad hombre he was. An' when I seen him I was bound to admit he looked his reputation.

"Wal, pretty soon in come two more fellars, an' I knowed both of them. You know them, too, I'm sorry to say. Fer I'm comin' to the facts now thet will shake you. The first fellar was your father's Mexican foreman, Lorenzo, and the other was Simm Bruce. I reckon Bruce wasn't drunk, but he'd sure been lookin' on red licker. When he seen Isbel darn me if he didn't swell an' bustle all up like a mad ole turkey gobbler.

"'Greaves,' he said, 'if thet fellar's Jean Isbel I ain't hankerin' fer the company y'u keep.' An' he made no bones of pointin' right at Isbel. Greaves looked up dry an' sour an' he bit out spiteful-like: 'Wal, Simm, we ain't hed a hell of a lot of choice in this heah matter. Thet's Jean Isbel shore enough. Mebbe you can persuade him thet his company an' his custom ain't wanted round heah!'

"Jean Isbel set on the counter an' took it all in, but he didn't say nothin'. The way he looked at Bruce was sure enough fer me to see thet thar might be a surprise any minnit. I've looked at a lot of men in my day, an' can sure feel events comin'. Bruce got himself a stiff drink an' then he straddles over the floor in front of Isbel.

"'Air you Jean Isbel, son of ole Gass Isbel?' asked Bruce, sort of lolling back an' givin' a hitch to his belt.

"'Yes sir, you've identified me,' said Isbel, nice an' polite.

"'My name's Bruce. I'm rangin' sheep heahabouts, an' I hev interest in Kurnel Lee Jorth's bizness.'

"'Hod do, Mister Bruce,' replied Isbel, very civil an' cool as you please. Bruce hed an eye fer the crowd thet was now listenin' an' watchin'. He swaggered closer to Isbel.

"'We heerd y'u come into the Tonto Basin to run us sheepmen off the range. How aboot thet?'

"'Wal, you heerd wrong,' said Isbel, quietly. 'I came to work fer my father. Thet work depends on what happens.'

"Bruce began to get redder of face, an' he shook a husky hand in front of Isbel. 'I'll tell y'u this heah, my Nez Perce Isbel—' an' when he sort of choked fer more wind Greaves spoke up, 'Simm, I shore reckon thet Nez Perce handle will stick.' An' the crowd haw-hawed. Then Bruce got goin' ag'in. 'I'll tell y'u this heah, Nez Perce. Thar's been enough happen already to run y'u out of Arizona.'

"'Wal, you don't say! What, fer instance?" asked Isbel, quick an' sarcastic.

"Thet made Bruce bust out puffin' an' spittin': 'Wha-tt, fer instance? Huh! Why, y'u dam half-breed, y'u'll git run out fer makin' up to Ellen Jorth. Thet won't go in this heah country. Not fer any Isbel.'

"'You're a liar,' called Isbel, an' like a big cat he dropped off the counter. I heerd his moccasins pat soft on the floor. An' I bet to myself that he was as dangerous as he was quick. But his voice an' his looks didn't change even a leetle.

"'I'm not a liar,' yelled Bruce. 'I'll make y'u eat thet. I can prove what I say. . . . Y'u was seen with Ellen Jorth—up on the Rim—day before yestiddy. Y'u was watched. Y'u was with her. Y'u made up to her. Y'u grabbed her an' kissed her! . . . An' I'm heah to say, Nez Perce, that y'u're a marked man on this range.'

"'Who saw me?' asked Isbel, quiet an' cold. I seen then thet he'd turned white in the face.

"'Yu cain't lie out of it,' hollered Bruce, wavin' his hands. 'We got y'u daid to rights. Lorenzo saw y'u—follered y'u—watched y'u.' Bruce pointed at the grinnin' greaser. 'Lorenzo is Kurnel Jorth's foreman. He seen y'u maulin' of Ellen Jorth. An' when he tells the Kurnel an' Tad Jorth an' Jackson Jorth! . . . Haw! Haw! Haw! Why, hell'd be a cooler place fer yu then this heah Tonto.'

"Greaves an' his gang hed come round, sure tickled clean to thar gizzards at this mess. I noticed, howsomever, thet they was Texans enough to keep back to one side in case this Isbel started any action. . . . Wal, Isbel took a look at Lorenzo. Then with one swift grab he jerked the little greaser off his feet an' pulled him close. Lorenzo stopped grinnin'. He began to look a leetle sick. But it was plain he hed right on his side.

"'You say you saw me?' demanded Isbel.

"'*Si,* señor,' replied Lorenzo.

"'What did you see?'

"'I see señor an' señorita. I hide by manzanita. I see señorita like grande señor ver mooch. She like señor keese. She—'

"Then Isbel hit the little greaser a back-handed crack in the mouth. Sure it was a crack! Lorenzo went over the counter backward an' landed like a pack load of wood. An' he didn't git up.

"'Mister Bruce,' said Isbel, 'an' you fellars who heered thet lyin' greaser, I did meet Ellen Jorth. An' I lost my head. I—I kissed her. . . . But it was an accident. I meant no insult. I apologized—I tried to explain my crazy action. . . . Thet was all. The greaser lied. Ellen Jorth was kind enough to show me the trail. We talked a little. Then—I suppose—because she was young an' pretty an' sweet—I lost my head. She was absolutely innocent. Thet damned greaser told a bare-faced lie when he said she liked me. The fact was she despised me. She said so. An' when she learned I was Jean Isbel she turned her back on me an' walked away.'"

At this point of his narrative the old man halted as if to impress Ellen not only with what just had been told, but particularly with what was to follow. The reciting of this tale had evidently given Sprague an unconscious pleasure. He glowed. He seemed to carry the burden of a secret that he yearned to divulge. As for Ellen, she was deadlocked in breathless suspense. All her emotions waited for the end. She begged Sprague to hurry.

"Wal, I wish I could skip the next chapter an' hev only the last to tell," rejoined the old man, and he put a heavy, but solicitous, hand upon hers. . . . "Simm Bruce haw-hawed loud an' loud. . . . 'Say, Nez Perce,' he calls out, most insolent-like, 'we air too good sheepmen heah to hev the wool pulled over our eyes. We shore know what y'u meant by Ellen Jorth. But y'u wasn't smart when y'u told her y'u was Jean Isbel! . . . Haw-haw!'

"Isbel flashed a strange, surprised look from the red-faced Bruce to Greaves and to the other men. I take it he was wonderin' if he'd heerd right or if they'd got the same hunch thet 'd come to him. An' I reckon he determined to make sure.

"'Why wasn't I smart?' he asked.

"'Shore y'u wasn't smart if y'u was aimin' to be one of Ellen Jorth's lovers,' said Bruce, with a leer. 'Fer if y'u hedn't give y'urself away y'u could hev been easy enough.'

"Thar was no mistakin' Bruce's meanin' an' when he got it out some of the men thar laughed. Isbel kept lookin' from one to another of them. Then facin' Greaves, he said, deliberately: 'Greaves, this drunken Bruce is excuse enough fer a show-down. I take it that you are sheepmen, an' you're goin' on Jorth's side of the fence in the matter of this sheep rangin'.'

"'Wal, Nez Perce, I reckon you hit plumb center,' said Greaves, dryly. He spred wide his big hands to the other men, as if to say they'd might as well own the jig was up.

"'All right. You're Jorth's backers. Have any of you a word to say in Ellen Jorth's defense? I tell you the Mexican lied. Believin' me or not doesn't matter. But this vile-mouthed Bruce hinted against thet girl's honor.'

"Ag'in some of the men laughed, but not so noisy, an' there was a nervous shufflin' of feet. Isbel looked sort of queer. His neck had a bulge round his collar. An' his eyes was like black coals of fire. Greaves spread his big hands again, as if to wash them of this part of the dirty argument.

"'When it comes to any wimmen I pass—much less play a hand fer a wildcat like Jorth's gurl,' said Greaves, sort of cold an' thick. 'Bruce shore ought to know her. Accordin' to talk heahaboots an' what *he* says, Ellen Jorth has been his gurl fer two years.'

"Then Isbel turned his attention to Bruce an' I fer one begun to shake in my boots.

"'Say thet to me!' he called.

"'Shore she's my gurl, an' thet's why I'm a-goin' to hev y'u run off this range.'

"Isbel jumped at Bruce. 'You damned drunken cur! You vile-mouthed liar! . . . I may be an Isbel, but by God you cain't slander thet girl to my face!'. . . . Then he moved so quick I couldn't see what he did. But I heerd his fist hit Bruce. It sounded like an ax ag'in' a beef. Bruce fell clear across the room. An' by Jinny when he landed Isbel was thar. As Bruce staggered up, all bloody-faced, bellowin' an' spittin' out teeth Isbel eyed Greaves's crowd an' said: 'If any of y'u make a move it'll mean gun-play.' Nobody moved, thet's sure. In fact, none of Greaves's outfit was packin' guns, at least in sight. When Bruce got all the way up—he's a tall fellar—why Isbel took a full swing at him an' knocked him back across the room ag'in' the counter. Y'u know when a fellar's hurt by the way he yells. Bruce got thet second smash right on his big red nose. . . . I never seen any one so quick as Isbel. He vaulted over thet counter jest the second Bruce fell back on it, an' then, with Greaves's gang in front so he could catch any moves of theirs, he jest slugged Bruce right an' left, an' banged his head on the counter. Then as Bruce sunk limp an' slipped down, lookin' like a bloody sack, Isbel let him fall to the floor. Then he vaulted back over the counter. Wipin' the blood off his hands, he throwed his kerchief down in Bruce's face. Bruce wasn't dead or bad hurt. He'd jest been beaten bad. He was moanin' an' slobberin'. Isbel kicked him, not hard, but jest sort of disgustful. Then he faced thet crowd. 'Greaves, thet's what I think of your Simm Bruce. Tell him next time he sees me to run or pull a gun.' An' then Isbel grabbed his rifle an' package off the counter an' went out. He didn't even look back. I seen him mount his horse an' ride away. . . . Now, girl, what hev you to say?"

Ellen could only say good-by and the word was so low as to be almost inaudible. She ran to her burro. She could not see very clearly through tear-blurred eyes, and her shaking fingers were all thumbs. It seemed she had to rush away—somewhere, anywhere—not to get away from old John Sprague, but from herself—this palpitating, bursting self whose feet stumbled down the trail. All—all seemed ended for her. That interminable story! It had taken so long. And every minute of it she had been helplessly torn asunder by feelings she had never known she possessed. This Ellen Jorth was an unknown creature. She sobbed now as she dragged the burro down the cañon trail. She sat down only to rise. She hurried only to stop. Driven, pursued, barred, she had no way to escape the flaying thoughts, no time or will to repudiate them. The death of her girlhood, the rending aside of a veil of maiden mystery only vaguely instinctively guessed, the barren, sordid truth of her life as seen by her enlightened eyes, the bitter realization of the vileness of men of her clan in contrast to the manliness and chivalry of an enemy, the hard facts of unalterable repute as created by slander and fostered by low minds, all these were forces in a cataclysm that had suddenly caught her heart and whirled her through changes immense and agonizing, to bring her face to face with reality, to force upon her suspicion and doubt of all she had trusted, to warn her of the dark, impending horror of a tragic bloody feud, and lastly to teach her the supreme truth at once so glorious and so terrible—that she could not escape the doom of womanhood.

About noon that day Ellen Jorth arrived at the Knoll, which was the location of her father's ranch. Three cañons met there to form a larger one. The Knoll was a symmetrical hill situated at the mouth of the three cañons. It was covered with brush and cedars, with here and there lichened rocks showing above the bleached grass. Below the Knoll was a wide, grassy flat or meadow through which a willow-bordered stream cut its rugged boulder-strewn bed. Water flowed abundantly at this season, and the deep washes leading down from the slopes attested to the fact of cloudbursts and heavy storms. This meadow valley was dotted with horses and cattle, and meandered away between the timbered slopes to lose itself in a green curve. A singular feature of this cañon was that a heavy growth of spruce trees covered the slope facing northwest; and the opposite slope, exposed to the sun and therefore less snowbound in winter, held a sparse growth of yellow pines. The ranch house of Colonel Jorth stood round the rough corner of the largest of the three cañons, and rather well hidden, it did not obtrude its rude and broken-down log cabins, its squalid surroundings, its black mud-holes of corrals upon the beautiful and serene meadow valley.

Ellen Jorth approached her home slowly, with dragging, reluctant steps; and never before in the three unhappy years of her existence there had the ranch seemed so bare, so uncared for, so repugnant to her. As she had seen herself with clarified eyes, so now she saw her home. The cabin that Ellen lived in with her father was a single-room structure with one door and no windows. It was about twenty feet square. The huge, ragged, stone chimney had been built on the outside, with the wide open fireplace set inside the logs. Smoke was rising from the chimney. As Ellen halted at the door and began unpacking her burro she heard the loud, lazy laughter of men. An adjoining log cabin had been built in two sections, with a wide roofed hall or space between them. The door in each cabin faced the other, and there was a tall man standing in one. Ellen recognized Daggs, a neighbor sheepman, who evidently spent more time with her father than at his own home, wherever that was. Ellen had never seen it. She heard this man drawl, "Jorth, heah's your kid come home."

Ellen carried her bed inside the cabin, and unrolled it upon a couch built of boughs in the far corner. She had forgotten Jean Isbel's package, and now it fell out under her sight. Quickly she covered it. A Mexican woman, relative of Antonio, and the only servant about the place, was squatting Indian fashion before the fireplace, stirring a pot of beans. She and Ellen did not get along well together, and few words ever passed between them. Ellen had a canvas curtain stretched upon a wire across a small triangular corner, and this afforded her a little privacy. Her possessions were limited in number. The crude square table she had constructed herself. Upon it was a little old-fashioned walnut-framed mirror, a brush and comb, and a dilapidated ebony cabinet which contained odds and ends the sight of which always brought a smile of derisive self-pity to her lips. Under the table stood an old leather trunk. It had come with her from Texas, and contained clothing and belongings of her mother's. Above the couch on pegs hunt her scant wardrobe. A tiny shelf held several worn-out books.

When her father slept indoors, which was seldom except in winter, he occupied a couch in the opposite corner. A rude cupboard had been built against the logs next to the fireplace. It contained supplies and utensils. Toward the center, somewhat closer to the door, stood a crude table and two benches. The cabin was dark and smelled of smoke, of the stale odors of past cooked meals, of the mustiness of dry, rotting timber. Streaks of light showed through the roof where the rough-hewn shingles had split or weathered. A strip of bacon hung upon one side of the cupboard, and upon the other a haunch of venison. Ellen detested the Mexican woman because she was dirty. The inside of the cabin presented the same unkempt appearance usual to it after Ellen had been away for a few days. Whatever Ellen had lost during the retrogression of the Jorths, she had kept her habits of cleanliness, and straightway upon her return she set to work.

The Mexican woman sullenly slouched away to her own quarters outside and Ellen was left to the satisfaction of labor. Her mind was as busy as her hands. As she cleaned and swept and dusted she heard from time to time the voices of the men, the clip-clop of shod horses, the bellow of cattle. And a considerable time elapsed before she was disturbed.

A tall shadow darkened the doorway.

"Howdy, little one!" said a lazy, drawling voice. "So y'u-all got home?"

Ellen looked up. A superbly built man leaned against the doorpost. Like most Texans, he was light haired and light eyed. His face was lined and hard. His long, sandy mustache hid his mouth and drooped with a curl. Spurred, booted, belted, packing a heavy gun low down on his hip, he gave Ellen an entirely new impression. Indeed, she was seeing everything strangely.

"Hello, Daggs!" replied Ellen. "Where's my dad?"

"He's playin' cairds with Jackson an' Colter. Shore's playin' bad, too, an' it's gone to his haid."

"Gamblin'?" queried Ellen.

"Mah child, when'd Kurnel Jorth ever play for fun?" said Daggs, with a lazy laugh. "There's a stack of gold on the table. Reckon yo' uncle Jackson will win it. Colter's shore out of luck."

Daggs stepped inside. He was graceful and slow. His long spurs clinked. He laid a rather compelling hand on Ellen's shoulder.

"Heah, mah gal, give us a kiss," he said.

"Daggs, I'm not your girl," replied Ellen as she slipped out from under his hand.

Then Daggs put his arm round her, not with violence or rudeness, but with an indolent, affectionate assurance, at once bold and self-contained. Ellen, however, had to exert herself to get free of him, and when she had placed the table between them she looked him square in the eyes.

"Daggs, y'u keep your paws off me," she said.

"Aw, now, Ellen, I ain't no bear," he remonstrated. "What's the matter, kid?"

"I'm not a kid. And there's nothin' the matter. Y'u're to keep your hands to yourself, that's all."

He tried to reach her across the table, and his movements were lazy and slow, like his smile. His tone was coaxing.

"Mah dear, shore you set on my knee just the other day, now, didn't you?"

Ellen felt the blood sting her cheeks.

"I was a child," she returned.

"Wal, listen to this heah grown-up young woman. All in a few days! . . . Doon't be in a temper, Ellen. . . . Come, give us a kiss."

She deliberately gazed into his eyes. Like the eyes of an eagle, they were clear and hard, just now warmed by the dalliance of the moment, but there was no light, no intelligence in them to prove he understood her. The instant separated Ellen immeasurably from him and from all of his ilk.

"Daggs, I was a child," she said. "I was lonely—hungry for affection—I was innocent. Then I was careless, too, and thoughtless when I should have known better. But I hardly understood y'u men. I put such thoughts out of my mind. I know now—know what y'u mean—what y'u have made people believe I am."

"Ahuh! Shore I get your hunch," he returned, with a change of tone. "But I asked you to marry me?"

"Yes y'u did. The first day y'u got heah to my dad's house. And y'u asked me to marry y'u after y'u found y'u couldn't have your way with me. To y'u the one didn't mean any more than the other."

"Shore I did more than Simm Bruce an' Colter," he retorted. "They never asked you to marry."

"No, they didn't. And if I could respect them at all I'd do it because they didn't ask me."

"Wal, I'll be dog-goned!" ejaculated Daggs, thoughtfully, as he stroked his long mustache.

"I'll say to them what I've said to y'u," went on Ellen. "I'll tell dad to make y'u let me alone. I wouldn't marry one of y'u—y'u loafers to save my life. I've my suspicions about y'u. Y'u're a bad lot."

Daggs changed subtly. The whole indolent nonchalance of the man vanished in an instant.

"Wal, Miss Jorth, I reckon you mean we're a bad lot of sheepmen?" he queried, in the cool, easy speech of a Texan.

"No," flashed Ellen. "Shore I don't say sheepmen. I say y'u're a *bad lot.*"

"Oh, the hell you say!" Daggs spoke as he might have spoken to a man; then turning swiftly on his heel he left her. Outside he encountered Ellen's father. She heard Daggs speak: "Lee, your little wildcat is shore heah. An' take mah hunch. Somebody has been talkin' to her."

"Who has?" asked her father, in his husky voice. Ellen knew at once that he had been drinking.

"Lord only knows," replied Daggs. "But shore it wasn't any friends of ours."

"We cain't stop people's tongues," said Jorth, resignedly.

"Wal, I ain't so shore," continued Daggs, with his slow, cool laugh. "Reckon I never yet heard any daid men's tongues wag."

Then the musical tinkle of his spurs sounded fainter. A moment later Ellen's father entered the cabin. His dark, moody face brightened at the sight of her. Ellen knew she was the only person in the world left for him to love. And she was sure of his love. Her very presence always made him different. And through the years, the darker their misfortunes, the farther he slipped away from better days, the more she loved him.

"Hello, my Ellen!" he said, and he embraced her. When he had been drinking he never kissed her. "Shore I'm glad you're home. This heah hole is bad enough any time, but when you're gone it's black. . . . I'm hungry."

Ellen laid food and drink on the table; and for a little while she did not look directly at him. She was concerned about this new searching power of her eyes. In relation to him she vaguely dreaded it.

Lee Jorth had once been a singularly handsome man. He was tall, but did not have the figure of a horseman. His dark hair was streaked with gray, and was white over his ears. His face was sallow and thin, with deep lines. Under his round, prominent, brown eyes, like deadened furnaces, were blue swollen welts. He had a bitter mouth and weak chin, not wholly concealed by gray mustache and pointed beard. He wore a long frock coat and a wide-brimmed sombrero, both black in color, and so old and stained and frayed that along with the fashion of them they betrayed that they had come from Texas with him. Jorth always persisted in wearing a white linen shirt, likewise a relic of his Southern prosperity, and to-day it was ragged and soiled as usual.

Ellen watched her father eat and waited for him to speak. It occurred to her strangely that he never asked about the sheep or the new-born lambs. She divined with a subtle new woman's intuition that he cared nothing for his sheep.

"Ellen, what riled Daggs?" inquired her father, presently. "He shore had fire in his eye."

Long ago Ellen had betrayed an indignity she had suffered at the hands of a man. Her father had nearly killed him. Since then she had taken care to keep her troubles to herself. If her father had not been blind and absorbed in his own brooding he would have seen a thousand things sufficient to inflame his Southern pride and temper.

"Daggs asked me to marry him again and I said he belonged to a bad lot," she replied.

Jorth laughed in scorn. "Fool! . . . My God! Ellen, I must have dragged you low—that every damned ru—er—sheepman—who comes along thinks he can marry you."

At the break in his words, the incompleted meaning, Ellen dropped her eyes. Little things once never noted by her were now come to have a fascinating significance.

"Never mind, dad," she replied. "They cain't marry me."

"Daggs said somebody had been talkin' to you. How aboot that?"

"Old John Sprague has just gotten back from Grass Valley," said Ellen. "I stopped in to see him. Shore he told me all the village gossip."

"Anythin' to interest me?" he queried, darkly.

"Yes, dad, I'm afraid a good deal," she said, hesitatingly. Then in accordance with a decision Ellen had made she told him of the rumored war between sheepmen and cattlemen; that old Isbel had Blaisdell, Gordon, Fredericks, Blue and other well-known ranchers on his side; that his son Jean Isbel had come from Oregon with a wonderful reputation as fighter and scout and tracker; that it was no secret how Colonel Lee Jorth was at the head of the sheepmen; that a bloody war was sure to come."

"Hah!" exclaimed Jorth, with a stain of red in his sallow cheek. "Reckon none of that is news to me. I knew all that."

Ellen wondered if he had heard of her meeting with Jean Isbel. If not he would hear as soon as Simm Bruce and Lorenzo came back. She decided to forestall them.

"Dad, I met Jean Isbel. He came into my camp. Asked the way to the Rim. I showed him. We—we talked a little. And shore were gettin' acquainted when—when he told me who he was. Then I left him—hurried back to camp."

"Colter met Isbel down in the woods," replied Jorth, ponderingly. "Said he looked like an Indian—a hard an' slippery customer to reckon with."

"Shore I guess I can indorse what Colter said," returned Ellen, dryly. She could have laughed aloud at her deceit. Still she had not lied.

"How'd this heah young Isbel strike you?" queried her father, suddenly glancing up at her.

Ellen felt the slow, sickening, guilty rise of blood in her face. She was helpless to stop it. But her father evidently never saw it. He was looking at her without seeing her.

"He—he struck me as different from men heah," she stammered.

"Did Sprague tell you aboot this half-Indian Isbel—aboot his reputation?"

"Yes."

"Did he look to you like a real woodsman?"

"Indeed he did. He wore buckskin. He stepped quick and soft. He acted at home in the woods. He had eyes black as night and sharp as lightnin'. They shore saw about all there was to see."

Jorth chewed at his mustache and lost himself in brooding thought.

"Dad, tell me, is there goin' to be a war?" asked Ellen, presently.

What a red, strange, rolling flash blazed in his eyes! His body jerked.

"Shore. You might as well know."

"Between sheepmen and cattlemen?"

"Yes."

"With y'u, dad, at the haid of one faction and Gaston Isbel the other?"

"Daughter, you have it correct, so far as you go."

"Oh! . . . Dad, can't this fight be avoided?"

"You forget you're from Texas," he replied.

"Cain't it be helped?" she repeated, stubbornly.

"No!" he declared, with deep, hoarse passion.

"Why not?"

"Wal, we sheepmen are goin' to run sheep anywhere we like on the range. An' cattlemen won't stand for that."

"But, dad, it's so foolish," declared Ellen, earnestly. "Y'u sheepmen do not have to run sheep over the cattle range."

"I reckon we do."

"Dad, that argument doesn't go with me. I know the country. For years to come there will be room for both sheep and cattle without overrunnin'. If some of the range is better in water and grass, then whoever got there first should have it. That shore is only fair. It's common sense, too."

"Ellen, I reckon some cattle people have been prejudicin' you," said Jorth, bitterly.

"Dad!" she cried, hotly.

This had grown to be an ordeal for Jorth. He seemed a victim of contending tides of feeling. Some will or struggle broke within him and the change was manifest. Haggard, shifty-eyed, with wabbling chin, he burst into speech.

"See heah, girl. You listen. There's a clique of ranchers down in the Basin, all those you named, with Isbel at their haid. They have resented sheepmen comin' down into the valley. They want it all to themselves. That's the reason. Shore there's another. All the Isbels are crooked. They're cattle an' horse thieves—have been for years. Gaston Isbel always was a maverick rustler. He's gettin' old now an' rich, so he wants to cover his tracks. He aims to blame this cattle rustlin' an' horse stealin' on to us sheepmen, an' run us out of the country."

Gravely Ellen Jorth studied her father's face, and the newly found truth-seeing power of her eyes did not fail her. In part, perhaps in all, he was telling lies. She shuddered a little, loyally battling against the insidious convictions being brought to fruition. Perhaps in his brooding over his failures and troubles he leaned toward false judgments. Ellen could not attach dishonor to her father's motives or speeches. For long, however, something about him had troubled her, perplexed her. Fearfully she believed she was coming to some revelation, and, despite her keen determination to know, she found herself shrinking.

"Dad, mother told me before she died that the Isbels had ruined you," said Ellen, very low. It hurt her so to see her father cover his face that she could hardly go on. "If they ruined you they ruined all of us. I know what we had once—what we lost again and again—and I see what we are come to now. Mother hated the Isbels. She taught me to hate the very name. But I never knew how they ruined you—or why—or when. And I want to know now."

Then it was not the face of a liar that Jorth disclosed. The present was forgotten. He lived in the past. He even seemed younger in the revivifying flash of hate that made his face radiant. The lines burned out. Hate gave him back the spirit of his youth.

"Gaston Isbel an' I were boys together in Weston, Texas," began Jorth, in swift passionate voice. "We went to school together. We loved the same girl your mother. When the war broke out she was engaged to Isbel. His family was rich. They influenced her people. But she loved me. When Isbel went to war she married me. He came back an' faced us. God! I'll never forget that. Your mother confessed her unfaithfulness—by Heaven! She taunted him with it. Isbel accused me of winnin' her by lies. But she took the sting out of that. . . . Isbel never forgave her an' he hounded me to ruin. He made me out a card sharp, cheatin' my best friends. I was disgraced. Later he tangled me in the courts—he beat me out of property—an' last by convictin' me of rustlin' cattle he run me out of Texas."

Black and distorted now, Jorth's face was a spectacle to make Ellen sick with a terrible passion of despair and hate. The truth of her father's ruin and her own were enough. What mattered all else? Jorth beat the table with fluttering, nerveless hands that seemed all the more significant for their lack of physical force.

"An' so help me God, it's got to be wiped out in blood!" he hissed.

That was his answer to the wavering and nobility of Ellen. And she in her turn had no answer to make. She crept away into the corner behind the curtain, and there on her couch in the semidarkness she lay with strained heart, and a resurging, unconquerable tumult in her mind. And she lay there from the middle of that afternoon until the next morning.

When she awakened she expected to be unable to rise—she hoped she could not—but life seemed multiplied in her, and inaction was impossible. Something young and sweet and hopeful that had been in her did not greet the sun this morning. In their place was a woman's passion to learn for herself, to watch events, to meet what must come, to survive.

After breakfast, at which she sat alone, she decided to put Isbel's package out of the way, so that it would not be subjecting her to continual annoyance. The moment she picked it up the old curiosity assailed her.

"Shore I'll see what it is, anyway," she muttered, and with swift hands she opened the package. The action disclosed two pairs of fine, soft shoes, of a style she had never seen, and four pairs of stockings, two of strong, serviceable wool, and the others of a finer texture. Ellen looked at them in amaze. Of all things in the world, these would have been the last she expected to see. And, strangely, they were what she wanted and needed most. Naturally, then, Ellen made the mistake of taking them in her hands to feel their softness and warmth.

"Shore! He saw my bare legs! And he brought me these presents he'd intended for his sister. . . . He was ashamed for me—sorry for me. . . . And I thought he looked at me bold-like, as I'm used to be looked at heah! Isbel or not, he's shore . . ."

But Ellen Jorth could not utter aloud the conviction her intelligence tried to force upon her.

"It'd be a pity to burn them," she mused. "I cain't do it. Sometime I might send them to Ann Isbel."

Whereupon she wrapped them up again and hid them in the bottom of the old trunk, and slowly, as she lowered the lid, looking darkly, blankly at the wall, she whispered: "Jean Isbel! . . . I hate him!"

Later when Ellen went outdoors she carried her rifle, which was unusual for her, unless she intended to go into the woods.

The morning was sunny and warm. A group of shirt-sleeved men lounged in the hall and before the porch of the double cabin. Her father was pacing up and down, talking forcibly. Ellen heard his hoarse voice. As she approached he ceased talking and his listeners relaxed their attention. Ellen's glance ran over them swiftly—Daggs, with his superb head, like that of a hawk, uncovered to the sun; Colter with his lowered, secretive looks, his sand-gray lean face; Jackson Jorth, her uncle, huge, gaunt, hulking, with white in his black beard and hair, and the fire of a ghoul in his hollow eyes; Tad Jorth, another brother of her father's, younger, red of eye and nose, a weak-chinned drinker of rum. Three other limber-legged Texans lounged there, partners of Daggs, and they were sun-browned, light-haired, blue-eyed men singularly alike in appearance, from their dusty high-heeled boots to their broad black sombreros. They claimed to be sheepmen. All Ellen could be sure of was that Rock Wells spent most of his time there, doing nothing but look for a chance to waylay her; Springer was a gambler; and the third, who answered to the strange name of Queen, was a silent, lazy, watchful-eyed man who never wore a glove on his right hand and who never was seen without a gun within easy reach of that hand.

"Howdy, Ellen. Shore you ain't goin' to say good mawnin' to this heah bad lot?" drawled Daggs, with good-natured sarcasm.

"Why, shore! Good morning, y'u hard-working industrious *mañana* sheep raisers," replied Ellen, coolly.

Daggs stared. The others appeared taken back by a greeting so foreign from any to which they were accustomed from her. Jackson Jorth let out a gruff haw-haw. Some of them doffed their sombreros, and Rock Wells managed a lazy, polite good morning. Ellen's father seemed most significantly struck by her greeting, and the least amused.

"Ellen, I'm not likin' your talk," he said, with a frown.

"Dad, when y'u play cards don't y'u call a spade a spade?"

"Why, shore I do."

"Well, I'm calling spades spades."

"Ahuh!" grunted Jorth, furtively dropping his eyes. "Where you goin' with your gun? I'd rather you hung round heah now."

"Reckon I might as well get used to packing my gun all the time," replied Ellen. "Reckon I'll be treated more like a man."

Then the event Ellen had been expecting all morning took place. Simm Bruce and Lorenzo rode around the slope of the Knoll and trotted toward the cabin. Interest in Ellen was relegated to the background.

"Shore they're bustin' with news," declared Daggs.

"They been ridin' some, you bet," remarked another.

"Huh!" exclaimed Jorth. "Bruce shore looks queer to me."

"Red liquor," said Tad Jorth, sententiously. "You-all know the brand Greaves hands out."

"Naw, Simm ain't drunk," said Jackson Jorth. "Look at his bloody shirt."

The cool, indolent interest of the crowd vanished at the red color pointed out by Jackson Jorth. Daggs rose in a single springy motion to his lofty height. The face Bruce turned to Jorth was swollen and bruised, with unhealed cuts. Where his right eye should have been showed a puffed dark purple bulge. His other eye, however, gleamed with hard and sullen light. He stretched a big shaking hand toward Jorth.

"Thet Nez Perce Isbel beat me half to death," he bellowed.

Jorth stared hard at the tragic, almost grotesque figure, at the battered face. But speech failed him. It was Daggs who answered Bruce.

"Wall, Simm, I'll be damned if you don't look it."

"Beat you! What with?" burst out Jorth explosively.

"I thought he was swingin' an ax, but Greaves swore it was his fists," bawled Bruce, in misery and fury.

"Where was your gun?" queried Jorth, sharply.

"Gun? Hell!" exclaimed Bruce, flinging wide his arms. "Ask Lorenzo. He had a gun. An' he got a biff in the jaw before my turn come. Ask him?"

Attention thus directed to the Mexican showed a heavy discolored swelling upon the side of his olive-skinned face. Lorenzo looked only serious.

"Hah! Speak up," shouted Jorth, impatiently.

"Señor Isbel heet me ver quick," replied Lorenzo, with expressive gesture. "I see thousand stars—then moocho black—all like night."

At that some of Daggs's men lolled back with dry crisp laughter. Daggs's hard face rippled with a smile. But there was no humor in anything for Colonel Jorth.

"Tell us what come off. Quick!" he ordered. "Where did it happen? Why? Who saw it? What did you do?"

Bruce lapsed into a sullen impressiveness. "Wal, I happened in Greaves's store an' run into Jean Isbel. Shore was lookin' fer him. I had my mind made up what to do, but I got to shootin' off my gab instead of my gun. I called him Nez Perce—an' I throwed all thet talk in his face about old Gass Isbel sendin' fer him—an' I told him he'd get run out of the Tonto. Reckon I was jest warmin' up. . . . But then it all happened. He slugged Lorenzo jest one. An' Lorenzo slid peaceful-like to bed behind the counter. I hadn't time to think of throwin' a gun before he whaled into me. He knocked out two of my teeth. An' I swallered one of them."

Ellen stood in the background behind three of the men and in the shadow. She did not join in the laugh that followed Bruce's remarks. She had known that he would lie. Uncertain yet of her reaction to this, but more bitter and furious as he revealed his utter baseness, she waited for more to be said.

"Wal, I'll be doggoned," drawled Daggs.

"What do you make of this kind of fightin'?" queried Jorth.

"Darn if I know," replied Daggs in perplexity. "Shore an' sartin it's not the way of a Texan. Mebbe this young Isbel really is what old Gass swears he is. Shore Bruce ain't nothin' to give an edge to a real gun fighter. Looks to me like Isbel bluffed Greaves an' his gang an' licked your men without throwin' a gun."

"Maybe Isbel doesn't want the name of drawin' first blood," suggested Jorth.

"That'd be like Gass," spoke up Rock Wells, quietly. "I onct rode fer Gass in Texas."

"Say, Bruce," said Daggs, "was this heah palaverin' of yours an' Jean Isbel's aboot the old stock dispute? Aboot his father's range an' water. An' partickler aboot sheep?"

"Wal—I—I yelled a heap," declared Bruce, haltingly, "but I don't recollect all I said—I was riled. . . . Shore, though it was the same old argyment thet's been fetchin' us closer an' closer to trouble."

Daggs removed his keen hawklike gaze from Bruce. "Wal, Jorth, all I'll say is this. If Bruce is tellin' the truth we ain't got a hell of a lot to fear from this young Isbel. I've known a heap of gun fighters in my day. An' Jean Isbel don't run true to class. Shore there never was a gunman who'd risk cripplin' his right hand by sluggin' anybody."

"Wal," broke in Bruce, sullenly. "You-all can take it daid straight or not. I don't give a damn. But you've shore got my hunch that Nez Perce Isbel is liable to handle any of you fellars jest as he did me, an' jest as easy. What's more, he's got Greaves figgered. An' you-all know thet Greaves is as deep in—"

"Shut up that kind of gab," demanded Jorth, stridently. "An' answer me. Was the row in Greaves's barroom aboot sheep?"

"Aw, hell! I said so, didn't I?" shouted Bruce, with a fierce uplift of his distorted face.

Ellen strode out from the shadow of the tall men who had obscured her.

"Bruce, y'u're a liar," she said, bitingly.

The surprise of her sudden appearance seemed to root Bruce to the spot. All but the discolored places on his face turned white. He held his breath a moment, then expelled it hard. His effort to recover from the shock was painfully obvious. He stammered incoherently.

"Shore y'u're more than a liar, too," cried Ellen, facing him with blazing eyes. And the rifle, gripped in both hands, seemed to declare her intent of menace. "That row was not about sheep. . . . Jean Isbel didn't beat y'u for anythin' about sheep. . . . Old John Sprague was in Greaves's store. He heard y'u. He saw Jean Isbel beat y'u as y'u deserved. . . . An' he told *me!"*

Ellen saw Bruce shrink in fear of his life; and despite her fury she was filled with disgust that he could imagine she would have his blood on her hands. Then she divined that Bruce saw more in the gathering storm in her father's eyes than he had to fear from her.

"Girl, what the hell are y'u sayin'?" hoarsely called Jorth, in dark amaze.

"Dad, y'u leave this to me," she retorted.

Daggs stepped beside Jorth, significantly on his right side. "Let her alone Lee," he advised, coolly. "She's shore got a hunch on Bruce."

"Simm Bruce, y'u cast a dirty slur on my name," cried Ellen, passionately.

It was then that Daggs grasped Jorth's right arm and held it tight. "Jest what I thought," he said. "Stand still, Lee. Let's see the kid make him showdown."

"That's what Jean Isbel beat y'u for," went on Ellen. "For slandering a girl who wasn't there. . . . Me! Y'u rotten liar!"

"But, Ellen, it wasn't all lies," said Bruce, huskily. "I was half drunk—an' horrible jealous. . . . You know Lorenzo seen Isbel kissin' you. I can prove thet."

Ellen threw up her head and a scarlet wave of shame and wrath flooded her face. "Yes," she cried, ringingly. "He saw Jean Isbel kiss me. Once! . . . An' it was the only decent kiss I've had in years. He meant no insult. I didn't know who he was. An' through his kiss I learned a difference between men. . . . Y'u made Lorenzo lie. An' if I had a shred of good name left in Grass Valley you dishonored it. . . . Y'u made *him* think I was your girl! Damn y'u! I ought to kill y'u. . . . Eat your words now—take them back—or I'll cripple y'u for life!"

Ellen lowered the cocked rifle toward his feet.

"Shore, Ellen, I take back—all I said," gulped Bruce. He gazed at the quivering rifle barrel and then into the face of Ellen's father. Instinct told him where his real peril lay.

Here the cool and tactful Daggs showed himself master of the situation.

"Heah, listen!" he called. "Ellen, I reckon Bruce was drunk an' out of his haid. He's shore ate his words. Now, we don't want any cripples in this camp. Let him alone. Your dad got me heah to lead the Jorths, an' that's my say to you. . . . Simm, you're shore a low-down, lyin' rascal. Keep away from Ellen after this or I'll bore you myself. . . . Jorth, it won't be a bad idee for you to forget you're a Texan till you cool off. Let Bruce stop some Isbel lead. Shore the Jorth-Isbel war is aboot on, an' I reckon we'd be smart to believe old Gass's talk aboot his Nez Perce son."

CHAPTER SIX

From this hour Ellen Jorth bent all of her lately awakened intelligence and will to the only end that seemed to hold possible salvation for her. In the crisis sure to come she did not want to be blind or weak. Dreaming and indolence, habits born in her which were often a comfort to one as lonely as she, would ill fit her for the hard test she divined and dreaded. In the matter of her father's fight she must stand by him whatever the issue or the outcome; in what pertained to her own principles, her womanhood, and her soul she stood absolutely alone.

Therefore, Ellen put dreams aside, and indolence of mind and body behind her. Many tasks she found, and when these were done for a day she kept active in other ways, thus earning the poise and peace of labor.

Jorth rode off every day, sometimes with one or two of the men, often with a larger number. If he spoke of such trips to Ellen it was to give an impression of visiting the ranches of his neighbors or the various sheep camps. Often he did not return the day he left. When he did get back he smelled of rum and appeared heavy from need of sleep. His horses were always dust and sweat covered. During his absences Ellen fell victim to anxious dread until he returned. Daily he grew darker and more haggard of face, more obsessed by some impending fate. Often he stayed up late, haranguing with the men in the dim-lit cabin, where they drank and smoked, but seldom gambled any more. When the men did not gamble something immediate and perturbing was on their minds. Ellen had not yet lowered herself to the deceit and suspicion of eavesdropping, but she realized that there was a climax approaching in which she would deliberately do so.

In those closing May days Ellen learned the significance of many things that previously she had taken as a matter of course. Her father did not run a ranch. There was absolutely no ranching done, and little work. Often Ellen had to chop wood herself. Jorth did not possess a plow. Ellen was bound to confess that the evidence of this lack dumfounded her. Even old John Sprague raised some hay, beets, turnips. Jorth's cattle and horses fared ill during the winter. Ellen remembered how they used to clean up four-inch oak saplings and aspens. Many of them died in the snow. The flocks of sheep, however, were driven down into the Basin in the fall, and across the Reno Pass to Phoenix and Maricopa.

Ellen could not discover a fence post on the ranch, nor a piece of salt for the horses and cattle, nor a wagon, nor any sign of a sheep-shearing outfit. She had never seen any sheep sheared. Ellen could never keep track of the many and different horses running loose and hobbled round the ranch. There were droves of horses in the woods, and some of them wild as deer. According to her long-established understanding, her father and her uncles were keen on horse trading and buying.

Then the many trails leading away from the Jorth ranch—these grew to have a fascination for Ellen; and the time came when she rode out on them to see for herself where they led. The sheep ranch of Daggs, supposed to be only a few miles across the ridges, down in Bear Cañon, never materialized at all for Ellen. This circumstance so interested her that she went up to see her friend Sprague and got him to direct her to Bear Cañon, so that she would be sure not to miss it. And she rode from the narrow, maple-thicketed head of it near the Rim down all its length. She found no ranch, no cabin, not even a corral in Bear Cañon. Sprague said there was only one cañon by that name. Daggs had assured her of the exact location on his place, and so had her father. Had they lied? Were they mistaken in the cañon? There were many cañons, all heading up near the Rim, all running and widening down for miles through the wooded mountain, and vastly different from the deep, short, yellow-walled gorges that cut into the Rim from the Basin side. Ellen investigated the cañons within six or eight miles of her home, both to east and to west. All she discovered was a couple of old log cabins, long deserted. Still, she did not follow out all the trails to their ends. Several of them led far into the deepest, roughest, wildest brakes of gorge and thicket that she had seen. No cattle or sheep had ever been driven over these trails.

This riding around of Ellen's at length got to her father's ears. Ellen expected that a bitter quarrel would ensue, for she certainly would refuse to be confined to the camp; but her father only asked her to limit her riding to the meadow valley, and straightway forgot all about it. In fact, his abstraction one moment, his intense nervousness the next, his harder drinking and fiercer harangues with the men, grew to be distressing for Ellen. They presaged his further deterioration and the ever-present evil of the growing feud.

One day Jorth rode home in the early morning, after an absence of two nights. Ellen heard the clip-clop of horses long before she saw them.

"Hey, Ellen. Come out heah," called her father.

Ellen left her work and went outside. A stranger had ridden in with her father, a young giant whose sharp-featured face appeared marked by ferret-like eyes and a fine, light, fuzzy beard. He was long, loose jointed, not heavy of build, and he had the largest hands and feet Ellen had ever seen. Next Ellen espied a black horse they had evidently brought with them. Her father was holding a rope halter. At once the black horse struck Ellen as being a beauty and a thoroughbred.

"Ellen, heah's a horse for you," said Jorth with something of pride. "I made a trade. Reckon I wanted him myself, but he's too gentle for me an' maybe a little small for my weight."

Delight visited Ellen for the first time in many days. Seldom had she owned a good horse, and never one like this.

"Oh, dad!" she exclaimed, in her gratitude.

"Shore, he's yours on one condition," said her father.

"What's that?" asked Ellen, as she laid caressing hands on the restless horse.

"You're not to ride him out of the cañon."

"Agreed. . . . All daid black, isn't he, except that white face? What's his name, dad?"

"I forgot to ask," replied Jorth, as he began unsaddling his own horse. "Slater, what's this heah black's name?"

The lanky giant grinned. "I reckon it was Spades."

"Spades?" ejaculated Ellen, blankly. "What a name! . . . Well, I guess it's as good as any. He's shore black."

"Ellen, keep him hobbled when you're not ridin' him," was her father's parting advice as he walked off with the stranger.

Spades was wet and dusty and his satiny skin quivered. He had fine, dark, intelligent eyes that watched Ellen's every move. She knew how her father and his friends dragged and jammed horses through the woods and over the rough trails. It did not take her long to discover that this horse had been a pet. Ellen cleaned his coat and brushed him and fed him. Then she fitted her bridle to suit his head and saddled him. His evident response to her kindness assured her that he was gentle, so she mounted and rode him, to discover he had the easiest gait she had ever experienced. He walked and trotted to suit her will, but when left to choose his own gait he fell into a graceful little pace that was very easy for her. He appeared quite ready to break into a run at her slightest bidding, but Ellen satisfied herself on this first ride with his slower gaits.

"Spades, y'u've shore cut out my burro Jinny," said Ellen, regretfully. "Well, I reckon women are fickle."

Next day she rode up the cañon to show Spades to her friend John Sprague. The old burro breeder was not at home. As his door was open, however, and a fire smoldering, Ellen concluded he would soon return. So she waited. Dismounting, she left Spades free to graze on the new green grass that carpeted the ground. The cabin and little level clearing accentuated the loneliness and wildness of the forest. Ellen always liked it here and had once been in the habit of visiting the old man often. But of late she had stayed away, for the reason that Sprague's talk and his news and his poorly hidden pity depressed her.

Presently she heard hoof beats on the hard, packed trail leading down the cañon in the direction from which she had come. Scarcely likely was it that Sprague should return from this direction. Ellen thought her father had sent one of the herders for her. But when she caught a glimpse of the approaching horseman, down in the aspens, she failed to recognize him. After he had passed one of the openings she heard his horse stop. Probably the man had seen her; at least she could not otherwise account for his stopping. The glimpse she had of him had given her the impression that he was bending over, peering ahead in the trail, looking for tracks. Then she heard the rider come on again, more slowly this time. At length the horse trotted out into the opening, to be hauled up short. Ellen recognized the buckskin-clad figure, the broad shoulders, the dark face of Jean Isbel.

Ellen felt prey to the strangest quaking sensation she had ever suffered. It took violence of her new-born spirit to subdue that feeling.

Isbel rode slowly across the clearing toward her. For Ellen his approach seemed singularly swift—so swift that her surprise, dismay, conjecture, and anger obstructed her will. The outwardly calm and cold Ellen Jorth was a travesty that mocked her—that she felt he would discern.

The moment Isbel drew close enough for Ellen to see his face she experienced a strong, shuddering repetition of her first shock of recognition. He was not the same. The light, the youth was gone. This, however, did not cause her emotion. Was it not a sudden transition of her nature to the dominance of hate? Ellen seemed to feel the shadow of her unknown self standing with her.

Isbel halted his horse. Ellen had been standing near the trunk of a fallen pine and she instinctively backed against it. How her legs trembled! Isbel took off his cap and crushed it nervously in his bare, brown hand.

"Good mornin', Miss Ellen!" he said.

Ellen did not return his greeting, but queried, almost breathelessly, "Did y'u come by our ranch?"

"No. I circled," he replied.

"Jean Isbel! What do y'u want heah?" she demanded.

"Don't you know?" he returned. His eyes were intensely black and piercing. They seemed to search Ellen's very soul. To meet their gaze was an ordeal that only her rousing fury sustained.

Ellen felt on her lips a scornful allusion to his half-breed Indian traits and the reputation that had preceded him. But she could not utter it.

"No" she replied.

"It's hard to call a woman a liar," he returned, bitterly. "But you must be—seein' you're a Jorth."

"Liar! Not to y'u, Jean Isbel," she retorted. "I'd not lie to y'u to save my life."

He studied her with keen, sober, moody intent. The dark fire of his eyes thrilled her.

"If that's true, I'm glad," he said.

"Shore it's true. I've no idea why y'u came heah."

Ellen did have a dawning idea that she could not force into oblivion. But if she ever admitted it to her consciousness, she must fail in the contempt and scorn and fearlessness she chose to throw in this man's face.

"Does old Sprague live here?" asked Isbel.

"Yes. I expect him back soon. . . . Did y'u come to see him?"

"No. . . . Did Sprague tell you anythin' about the row he saw me in?"

"He—did not," replied Ellen, lying with stiff lips. She who had sworn she could not lie! She felt the hot blood leaving her heart, mounting in a wave. All her conscious will seemed impelled to deceive. What had she to hide from Jean Isbel? And a still, small voice replied that she had to hide the Ellen Jorth who had waited for him that day, who had spied upon him, who had treasured a gift she could not destroy, who had hugged to her miserable heart the fact that he had fought for her name.

"I'm glad of that," Isbel was saying, thoughtfully.

"Did you come heah to see me?" interrupted Ellen. She felt that she could not endure this reiterated suggestion of fineness, of consideration in him. She would betray herself—betray what she did not even realize herself. She must force other footing—and that should be the one of strife between the Jorths and Isbels.

"No—honest, I didn't, Miss Ellen," he rejoined, humbly. "I'll tell you, presently, why I came. But it wasn't to see you. . . . I don't deny I wanted . . . but that's no matter. You didn't meet me that day on the Rim."

"Meet y'u!" she echoed, coldly. "Shore y'u never expected me?"

"Somehow I did," he replied, with those penetrating eyes on her. "I put somethin' in your tent that day. Did you find it?"

"Yes," she replied, with the same casual coldness.

"What did you do with it?"

"I kicked it out, of course," she replied.

She saw him flinch.

"And you never opened it?"

"Certainly not," she retorted, as if forced. "Doon't y'u know anythin' about—about people? . . . Shore even if y'u are an Isbel y'u never were born in Texas."

"Thank God I wasn't!" he replied. "I was born in a beautiful country of green meadows and deep forests and white rivers, not in a barren desert where men live dry and hard as the cactus. Where I come from men don't live on hate. They can forgive."

"Forgive! . . . Could y'u forgive a Jorth?"

"Yes, I could."

"Shore that's easy to say—with the wrongs all on your side," she declared, bitterly.

"Ellen Jorth, the first wrong was on your side," retorted Jean, his voice full. "Your father stole my father's sweetheart—by lies, by slander, by dishonor, by makin' terrible love to her in his absence."

"It's a lie," cried Ellen, passionately.

"It is not," he declared, solemnly.

"Jean Isbel, I say y'u lie!"

"No! *I* say you've been lied to," he thundered.

The tremendous force of his spirit seemed to fling truth at Ellen. It weakened her.

"But—mother loved dad—best."

"Yes, afterward. No wonder, poor woman! . . . But it was the action of your father and your mother that ruined all these lives. You've got to know the truth, Ellen Jorth. . . . All the years of hate have borne their fruit. God Almighty can never save us now. Blood must be spilled. The Jorths and the Isbels can't live on the same earth. . . . And you've got to know the truth because the worst of this hell falls on you and me."

The hate that he spoke of alone upheld her.

"Never, Jean Isbel!" she cried. "I'll never know truth from y'u. . . . I'll never share anythin' with y'u—not even hell."

Isbel dismounted and stood before her, still holding his bridle reins. The bay horse champed his bit and tossed his head.

"Why do you hate me so?" he asked. "I just happen to be my father's son. I never harmed you or any of your people. I met you . . . fell in love with you in a flash—though I never knew it till after. . . . Why do you hate me so terribly?"

Ellen felt a heavy, stifling pressure within her breast. "Y'u're an Isbel. . . . Doon't speak of love to me."

"I didn't intend to. But your—your hate seems unnatural. And we'll probably never meet again. . . . I can't help it. I love you. Love at first sight! Jean Isbel and Ellen Jorth! Strange, isn't it? . . . It was all so strange. My meetin' you so lonely and unhappy, my seein' you so sweet and beautiful, my thinkin' you so good in spite of—"

"Shore it was strange," interrupted Ellen, with scornful laugh. She had found her defense. In hurting him she could hide her own hurt. "Thinking me so good in spite of— Ha-ha! And I said I'd been kissed before!"

"Yes, in spite of everything," he said.

Ellen could not look at him as he loomed over her. She felt a wild tumult in her heart. All that crowded to her lips for utterance was false.

"Yes—kissed before I met you—and since," she said, mockingly. "And I laugh at what y'u call love, Jean Isbel."

"Laugh if you want—but believe it was sweet, honorable—the best in me," he replied, in deep earnestness.

"Bah!" cried Ellen, with all the force of her pain and shame and hate.

"By Heaven, you must be different from what I thought!" exclaimed Isbel, huskily.

"Shore if I wasn't, I'd make myself. . . . Now, Mister Jean Isbel, get on your horse an' go!"

Something of composure came to Ellen with these words of dismissal, and she glanced up at him with half-veiled eyes. His changed aspect prepared her for some blow.

"That's a pretty black horse."

"Yes," replied Ellen, blankly.

"Do you like him?"

"I—I love him."

"All right, I'll give him to you then. He'll have less work and kinder treatment than if I used him. I've got some pretty hard rides ahead of me."

"Y'u—y'u give—" whispered Ellen, slowly stiffening.

"Yes. He's mine," replied Isbel. With that he turned to whistle. Spades threw up his head, snorted, and started forward at a trot. He came faster the closer he got, and if ever Ellen saw the joy of a horse at sight of a beloved master she saw it then. Isbel laid a hand on the animal's neck and caressed him, then, turning back to Ellen, he went on speaking: "I picked him from a lot of fine horses of my father's. We got along well. My sister Ann rode him a good deal. . . . He was stolen from our pasture day before yesterday. I took his trail and tracked him up here. Never lost his trail till I got to your ranch, where I had to circle till I picked it up again."

"Stolen—pasture—tracked him up heah?" echoed Ellen, without any evidence of emotion whatever. Indeed, she seemed to have been turned to stone.

"Trackin' him was easy. I wish for your sake it'd been impossible," he said, bluntly.

"For my sake?" she echoed, in precisely the same tone.

Manifestly that tone irritated Isbel beyond control. He misunderstood it. With a hand far from gentle he pushed her bent head back so he could look into her face.

"Yes, for your sake!" he declared, harshly. "Haven't you sense enough to see that? . . . What kind of a game do you think you can play with me?"

"Game? . . . Game of what?" she asked.

"Why, a—a game of ignorance—innocence—any old game to fool a man who's tryin' to be decent."

This time Ellen mutely looked her dull, blank questioning. And it inflamed Isbel.

"You know your father's a horse thief!" he thundered.

Outwardly Ellen remained the same. She had been prepared for an unknown and a terrible blow. It had fallen. And her face, her body, her hands, locked with the supreme fortitude of pride and sustained by hate, gave no betrayal of the crashing, thundering ruin within her mind and soul. Motionless she leaned there, meeting the piercing fire of Isbel's eyes, seeing in them a righteous and terrible scorn. In one flash the naked truth seemed blazed at her. The faith she had fostered died a sudden death. A thousand perplexing problems were solved in a second of whirling, revealing thought.

"Ellen Jorth, you know your father's in with this Hash Knife Gang of rustlers," thundered Isbel.

"Shore," she replied, with the cool, easy, careless defiance of a Texan.

"You know he's got this Daggs to lead his faction against the Isbels?"

"Shore."

"You know this talk of sheepmen buckin' the cattlemen is all a blind?"

"Shore," reiterated Ellen.

Isbel gazed darkly down upon her. With his anger spent for the moment, he appeared ready to end the interview. But he seemed fascinated by the strange look of her, by the incomprehensible something she emanated. Havoc gleamed in his pale, set face. He shook his dark head and his broad hand went to his breast.

"To think I fell in love with such as you!" he exclaimed, and his other hand swept out in a tragic gesture of helpless pathos and impotence.

The hell Isbel had hinted at now possessed Ellen—body, mind, and soul. Disgraced, scorned by an Isbel! Yet loved by him! In that divination there flamed up a wild, fierce passion to hurt, to rend, to flay, to fling back upon him a stinging agony. Her thought flew upon her like whips. Pride of the Jorths! Pride of the old Texan blue blood! It lay dead at her feet, killed by the scornful words of the last of that family to whom she owed her degradation. Daughter of a horse thief and rustler! Dark and evil and grim set the forces within her, accepting her fate, damning her enemies, true to the blood of the Jorths. The sins of the father must be visited upon the daughter.

"Shore y'u might have had me—that day on the Rim—if y'u hadn't told your name," she said, mockingly, and she gazed into his eyes with all the mystery of a woman's nature.

Isbel's powerful frame shook as with an ague. "Girl, what do you mean?"

"Shore, I'd have been plumb fond of havin' y'u make up to me," she drawled. It possessed her now with irresistible power, this fact of the love he could not help. Some fiendish woman's satisfaction dwelt in her consciousness of her power to kill the noble, the faithful, the good in him.

"Ellen Jorth, you lie!" he burst out, hoarsely.

"Jean, shore I'd been a toy and a rag for these rustlers long enough. I was tired of them. . . . I wanted a new lover. . . . And if y'u hadn't give yourself away—"

Isbel moved so swiftly that she did not realize his intention until his hard hand smote her mouth. Instantly she tasted the hot, salty blood from a cut lip.

"Shut up, you hussy!" he ordered, roughly. "Have you no shame? . . . My sister Ann spoke well of you. She made excuses—she pitied you."

That for Ellen seemed the culminating blow under which she almost sank. But one moment longer could she maintain this unnatural and terrible poise.

"Jean Isbel—go along with y'u," she said, impatiently. "I'm waiting heah for Simm Bruce!"

At last it was as if she struck his heart. Because of doubt of himself and a stubborn faith in her, his passion and jealousy were not proof against this last stab. Instinctive subtlety inherent in Ellen had prompted the speech that tortured Isbel. How the shock to him rebounded on her! She gasped as he lunged for her, too swift for her to move a hand. One arm crushed round her like a steel band; the other, hard across her breast and neck, forced her head back. Then she tried to wrestle away. But she was utterly powerless. His dark face bent down closer and closer. Suddenly Ellen ceased trying to struggle. She was like a stricken creature paralyzed by the piercing, hypnotic eyes of a snake. Yet in spite of her terror, if he meant death by her, she welcomed it.

"Ellen Jorth, I'm thinkin' yet—you lie!" he said, low and tense between his teeth.

"No! No!" she screamed, wildly. Her nerve broke there. She could no longer meet those terrible black eyes. Her passionate denial was not only the last of her shameful deceit; it was the woman of her, repudiating herself and him, and all this sickening, miserable situation.

Isbel took her literally. She had convinced him. And the instant held blank horror for Ellen.

"By God—then I'll have somethin'—of you anyway!" muttered Isbel, thickly.

Ellen saw the blood bulge in his powerful neck. She saw his dark, hard face, strange now, fearful to behold, come lower and lower, till it blurred and obstructed her gaze. She felt the swell and ripple and stretch—then the bind of his muscles, like huge coils of elastic rope. Then with savage rude force his mouth closed on hers. All Ellen's senses reeled, as if she were swooning. She was suffocating. The spasm passed, and a bursting spurt of blood revived her to acute and terrible consciousness. For the endless period of one moment he held her so that her breast seemed crushed. His kisses burned and bruised her lips. And then, shifting violently to her neck, they pressed so hard that she choked under them. It was as if a huge bat had fastened upon her throat.

Suddenly the remorseless binding embraces—the hot and savage kisses—fell away from her. Isbel had let go. She saw him throw up his hands, and stagger back a little, all the while with his piercing gaze on her. His face had been dark purple: now it was white.

"No—Ellen Jorth," he panted, "I don't—want any of you—that way." And suddenly he sank on the log and covered his face with his hands. "What I loved in you—was what I thought—you were."

Like a wildcat Ellen sprang upon him, beating him with her fists, tearing at his hair, scratching his face, in a blind fury. Isbel made no move to stop her, and her violence spent itself with her strength. She swayed back from him, shaking so that she could scarcely stand.

"Y'u—damned—Isbel!" she gasped, with hoarse passion. "Y'u insulted me!"

"Insulted you? . . ." laughed Isbel, in bitter scorn. "It couldn't be done."

"Oh! . . . I'll *kill* y'u!" she hissed.

Isbel stood up and wiped the red scratches on his face. "Go ahead. There's my gun," he said, pointing to his saddle sheath. "Somebody's got to begin this Jorth-Isbel feud. It'll be a dirty business. I'm sick of it already. . . . Kill me! . . . First blood for Ellen Jorth!"

Suddenly the dark grim tide that had seemed to engulf Ellen's very soul cooled and receded, leaving her without its false strength. She began to sag. She stared at Isbel's gun. "Kill him," whispered the retreating voices of her hate. But she was as powerless as if she were still held in Jean Isbel's giant embrace.

"I—I want to—kill y'u," she whispered, "but I cain't. . . . Leave me."

"You're no Jorth—the same as I'm no Isbel. We oughtn't be mixed in this deal," he said, somberly. "I'm sorrier for you than I am for myself. . . . You're a girl. . . . You once had a good mother—a decent home. And this life you've led here—mean as it's been—is nothin' to what you'll face now. Damn the men that brought you to this! I'm goin' to kill some of them."

With that he mounted and turned away. Ellen called out for him to take his horse. He did not stop nor look back. She called again, but her voice was fainter, and Isbel was now leaving at a trot. Slowly she sagged against a tree, lower and lower. He headed into the trail leading up the cañon. How strange a relief Ellen felt! She watched him ride into the aspens and start up the slope, at last to disappear in the pines. It seemed at the moment that he took with him something which had been hers. A pain in her head dulled the thoughts that wavered to and fro. After he had gone she could not see so well. Her eyes were tired. What had happened to her? There was blood on her hands. Isbel's blood! She shuddered. Was it an omen? Low she sank against the tree and closed her eyes.

Old John Sprague did not return. Hours dragged by—dark hours for Ellen Jorth lying prostrate beside the tree, hiding the blue sky and golden sunlight from her eyes. At length the lethargy of despair, the black dull misery wore away; and she gradually returned to a condition of coherent thought.

What had she learned? Sight of the black horse grazing near seemed to prompt the trenchant replies. Spades belonged to Jean Isbel. He had been stolen by her father or by one of her father's accomplices. Isbel's vaunted cunning as a tracker had been no idle boast. Her father was a horse thief, a rustler, a sheepman only as a blind, a consort of Daggs, leader of the Hash Knife Gang. Ellen well remembered the ill repute of that gang, way back in Texas, years ago. Her father had gotten in with this famous band of rustlers to serve his own ends—the extermination of the Isbels. It was all very plain now to Ellen.

"Daughter of a horse thief an' rustler!" she muttered.

And her thoughts sped back to the days of her girlhood. Only the very early stage of that time had been happy. In the light of Isbel's revelation and many changes of residence, the sudden moves to unsettled parts of Texas, the periods of poverty and sudden prosperity, all leading to the final journey to this God-forsaken Arizona—these were now seen in their true significance. As far back as she could remember her father had been a crooked man. And her mother had known it. He had dragged her to her ruin. That degradation had killed her. Ellen realized that with poignant sorrow, with a sudden revolt against her father. Had Gaston Isbel truly and dishonestly started her father on his downhill road? Ellen wondered. She hated the Isbels with unutterable and growing hate, and yet she had it in her to think, to ponder, to weigh judgments in their behalf. She owed it to something in herself to be fair. But what did it matter who was to blame for the Jorth-Isbel feud? Somehow Ellen was forced to confess that deep in her soul it mattered terribly. To be true to herself—the self that she alone knew—she must have right on her side. If the Jorths were guilty, and she clung to them and their creed, then she would be one of them.

"But I'm not," she mused, aloud. "My name's Jorth, an' I reckon I have bad blood. . . . But it never came out in me till to-day. I've been honest. I've been good—yes, *good,* as my mother taught me to be—in spite of all. . . . Shore my pride made me a fool. . . . An' now have I any choice to make? I'm a Jorth. I must stick to my father."

All this summing up, however, did not wholly account for the pang in her breast.

What had she done that day? And the answer beat in her ears like a great throbbing hammer-stroke. In an agony of shame, in the throes of hate, she had perjured herself. She had sworn away her honor. She had basely made herself vile. She had struck ruthlessly at the great heart of a man who loved her. Ah! That thrust had rebounded to leave this dreadful pang in her breast. Loved her? Yes, the strange truth, the insupportable truth! She had to contend now, not with her father and her disgrace, not with the baffling presence of Jean Isbel, but with the mysteries of her own soul. Wonder of all wonders was it that such love had been born for her. Shame worse than all other shame was it that she would kill it by a poisoned lie. By what monstrous motive had she done that? To sting Isbel as he had stung her! But that had been base. Never could she have stooped so low except in a moment of tremendous tumult. If she had done sore injury to Isbel what had she done to herself? How strange, how tenacious had been his faith in her honor! Could she ever forget? She must forget it. But she could never forget the way he had scorned those vile men in Greaves's store—the way he had beaten Bruce for defiling her name—the way he had stubbornly denied her own insinuations. She was a woman now. She had learned something of the complexity of a woman's heart. She could not change nature. And all her passionate being thrilled to the manhood of her defender. But even while she thrilled she acknowledged her hate. It was the contention between the two that caused the pang in her breast. "An' now what's left for me?" murmured Ellen. She did not analyze the significance of what had prompted that query. The most incalculable of the day's disclosures was the wrong she had done herself. "Shore I'm done for, one way or another. . . . I must stick to Dad . . . or kill myself?"

Ellen rode Spades back to the ranch. She rode like the wind. When she swung out of the trail into the open meadow in plain sight of the ranch her appearance created a commotion among the loungers before the cabin. She rode Spades at a full run.

"Who's after you?" yelled her father, as she pulled the black to a halt. Jorth held a rifle. Daggs, Colter, the other Jorths were there, likewise armed, and all watchful, strung with expectancy.

"Shore nobody's after me," replied Ellen. "Cain't I run a horse around heah without being chased?"

Jorth appeared both incensed and relieved.

"Hah! . . . What you mean, girl, runnin' like a streak right down on us? You're actin' queer these days, an' you look queer. I'm not likin' it."

"Reckon these are queer times—for the Jorths," replied Ellen, sarcastically.

"Daggs found strange horse tracks crossin' the meadow," said her father. "An' that worried us. Some one's been snoopin' around the ranch. An' when we seen you runnin' so wild we shore thought you was bein' chased."

"No. I was only trying out Spades to see how fast he could run," returned Ellen. "Reckon when we do get chased it'll take some running to catch me."

"Haw! Haw!" roared Daggs. "It shore will, Ellen."

"Girl, it's not only your runnin' an' your looks that's queer," declared Jorth, in dark perplexity. "You talk queer."

"Shore, dad, y'u're not used to hearing spades called spades," said Ellen, as she dismounted.

"Humph!" ejaculated her father, as if convinced of the uselessness of trying to understand a woman. "Say, did you see any strange horse tracks?"

"I reckon I did. And I know who made them."

Jorth stiffened. All the men behind him showed a sudden intensity of suspense.

"Who?" demanded Jorth.

"Shore it was Jean Isbel," replied Ellen, coolly. "He came up heah tracking his black horse."

"Jean—Isbel—trackin'—his—black horse," repeated her father.

"Yes. He's not overrated as a tracker, that's shore."

Blank silence ensued. Ellen cast a slow glance over her father and the others, then she began to loosen the cinches of her saddle. Presently Jorth burst the silence with a curse, and Daggs followed with one of his sardonic laughs.

"Wal, boss, what did I tell you?" he drawled.

Jorth strode to Ellen, and, whirling her around with a strong hand, he held her facing him.

"Did y'u see Isbel?"

"Yes," replied Ellen, just as sharply as her father had asked.

"Did y'u talk to him?"

"Yes."

"What did he want up heah?"

"I told y'u. He was tracking the black horse y'u stole."

Jorth's hand and arm dropped limply. His sallow face turned a livid hue. Amaze merged into discomfiture and that gave place to rage. He raised a hand as if to strike Ellen. And suddenly Daggs's long arm shot out to clutch Jorth's wrist. Wrestling to free himself, Jorth cursed under his breath. "Let go, Daggs," he shouted, stridently. "Am I drunk that you grab me?"

"Wal, y'u ain't drunk, I reckon," replied the rustler, with sarcasm. "But y'u're shore some things I'll reserve for your private ear."

Jorth gained a semblance of composure. But it was evident that he labored under a shock.

"Ellen, did Jean Isbel see this black horse?"

"Yes. He asked me how I got Spades an' I told him."

"Did he say Spades belonged to him?"

"Shore I reckon he proved it. Y'u can always tell a horse that loves its master."

"Did y'u offer to give Spades back?"

"Yes. But Isbel wouldn't take him."

"Hah! . . . An' why not?"

"He said he'd rather I kept him. He was about to engage in a dirty, blood-spilling deal, an' he reckoned he'd not be able to care for a fine horse. . . . I didn't want Spades. I tried to make Isbel take him. But he rode off. . . . And that's all there is to that."

"Maybe it's not," replied Jorth, chewing his mustache and eying Ellen with dark, intent gaze. "Y'u've met this Isbel twice."

"It wasn't any fault of mine," retorted Ellen.

"I heah he's sweet on y'u. How aboot that?"

Ellen smarted under the blaze of blood that swept to neck and cheek and temple. But it was only memory which fired this shame. What her father and his crowd might think were matters of supreme indifference. Yet she met his suspicious gaze with truthful blazing eyes.

"I heah talk from Bruce an' Lorenzo," went on her father. "An' Daggs heah—"

"Daggs nothin'!" interrupted that worthy. "Don't fetch me in. I said nothin' an' I think nothin'."

"Yes, Jean Isbel *was* sweet on me, dad . . . but he will never be again," returned Ellen, in low tones. With that she pulled her saddle off Spades and, throwing it over her shoulder, she walked off to her cabin.

Hardly had she gotten indoors when her father entered.

"Ellen, I didn't know that horse belonged to Isbel," he began, in the swift, hoarse, persuasive voice so familiar to Ellen. "I swear I didn't. I bought him—traded with Slater for him. . . . Honest to God, I never had any idea he was stolen! . . . Why, when y'u said 'that horse y'u stole,' I felt as if y'u'd knifed me. . . ."

Ellen sat at the table and listened while her father paced to and fro and, by his restless action and passionate speech, worked himself into a frenzy. He talked incessantly, as if her silence was condemnatory and as if eloquence alone could convince her of his honesty. It seemed that Ellen saw and heard with keener faculties than ever before. He had a terrible thirst for her respect. Not so much for her love, she divined, but that she would not see how he had fallen!

She pitied him with all her heart. She was all he had, and he was all the world to her. And so, as she gave ear to his long, illogical rigmarole of argument and defense, she slowly found that her pity and her love were making vital decisions for her. As of old, in poignant moments, her father lapsed at last into a denunciation of the Isbels and what they had brought him to. His sufferings were real, at least, in Ellen's presence. She was the only link that bound him to long-past happier times. She was her mother over again—the woman who had betrayed another man for him and gone with him to her ruin and death.

"Dad, don't go on so," said Ellen, breaking in upon her father's rant. "I will be true to y'u—as my mother was. . . . I am a Jorth. Your place is my place—your fight is my fight. . . . Never speak of the past to me again. If God spares us through this feud we will go away and begin all over again, far off where no one ever heard of a Jorth. . . . If we're not spared we'll at least have had our whack at these damned Isbels."

CHAPTER SEVEN

During June Jean Isbel did not ride far away from Grass Valley.

Another attempt had been made upon Gaston Isbel's life. Another cowardly shot had been fired from ambush, this time from a pine thicket bordering the trail that led to Blaisdell's ranch. Blaisdell heard this shot, so near his home was it fired. No trace of the hidden foe could be found. The ground all around that vicinity bore a carpet of pine needles which showed no trace of footprints. The supposition was that this cowardly attempt had been perpetrated, or certainly instigated, by the Jorths. But there was no proof. And Gaston Isbel had other enemies in the Tonto Basin besides the sheep clan. The old man raged like a lion about this sneaking attack on him. And his friend Blaisdell urged an immediate gathering of their kin and friends. "Let's quit ranchin' till this trouble's settled," he declared. "Let's arm an' ride the trails an' meet these men half-way. . . . It won't help our side any to wait till you're shot in the back." More than one of Isbel's supporters offered the same advice.

"No; we'll wait till we know for shore," was the stubborn cattleman's reply to all these promptings.

"Know! Wal, hell! Didn't Jean find the black hoss up at Jorth's ranch?" demanded Blaisdell. "What more do we want?"

"Jean couldn't swear Jorth stole the black."

"Wal, by thunder, I can swear to it!" growled Blaisdell. "An' we're losin' cattle all the time. Who's stealin' 'em?"

"We've always lost cattle ever since we started ranchin' heah."

"Gas, I reckon y'u want Jorth to start this fight in the open."

"It'll start soon enough," was Isbel's gloomy reply.

Jean had not failed altogether in his tracking of lost or stolen cattle. Circumstances had been against him, and there was something baffling about this rustling. The summer storms set in early, and it had been his luck to have heavy rains wash out fresh tracks that he might have followed. The range was large and cattle were everywhere. Sometimes a loss was not discovered for weeks. Gaston Isbel's sons were now the only men left to ride the range. Two of his riders had quit because of the threatened war, and Isbel had let another go. So that Jean did not often learn that cattle had been stolen until their tracks were old. Added to that was the fact that this Grass Valley country was covered with horse tracks and cattle tracks. The rustlers, whoever they were, had long been at the game, and now that there was reason for them to show their cunning they did it.

Early in July the hot weather came. Down on the red ridges of the Tonto it was hot desert. The nights were cool, the early mornings were pleasant, but the day was something to endure. When the white cumulus clouds rolled up out of the southwest, growing larger and thicker and darker, here and there coalescing into a black thundercloud, Jean welcomed them. He liked to see the gray streamers of rain hanging down from a canopy of black, and the roar of rain on the trees as it approached like a trampling army was always welcome. The grassy flats, the red ridges, the rocky slopes, the thickets of manzanita and scrub oak and cactus were dusty, glaring, throat-parching places under the hot summer sun. Jean longed for the cool heights of the Rim, the shady pines, the dark sweet verdure under the silver spruces, the tinkle and murmur of the clear rills. He often had another longing, too, which he bitterly stifled.

Jean's ally, the keen-nosed shepherd dog, had disappeared one day, and had never returned. Among men at the ranch there was a difference of opinion as to what had happened to Shepp. The old rancher thought he had been poisoned or shot; Bill and Guy Isbel believed he had been stolen by sheep herders, who were always stealing dogs; and Jean inclined to the conviction that Shepp had gone off with the timber wolves. The fact was that Shepp did not return, and Jean missed him.

One morning at dawn Jean heard the cattle bellowing and trampling out in the valley; and upon hurrying to a vantage point he was amazed to see upward of five hundred steers chasing a lone wolf. Jean's father had seen such a spectacle as this, but it was a new one for Jean. The wolf was a big gray and black fellow, rangy and powerful, and until he got the steers all behind him he was rather hard put to it to keep out of their way. Probably he had dogged the herd, trying to sneak in and pull down a yearling, and finally the steers had charged him. Jean kept along the edge of the valley in the hope they would chase him within range of a rifle. But the wary wolf saw Jean and sheered off, gradually drawing away from his pursuers.

Jean returned to the house for his breakfast, and then set off across the valley. His father owned one small flock of sheep that had not yet been driven up on the Rim, where all the sheep in the country were run during the hot, dry summer down on the Tonto. Young Evarts and a Mexican boy named Bernardino had charge of this flock. The regular Mexican herder, a man of experience, had given up his job; and these boys were not equal to the task of risking the sheep up in the enemies' stronghold.

This flock was known to be grazing in a side draw, well up from Grass Valley, where the brush afforded some protection from the sun, and there was good water and a little feed. Before Jean reached his destination he heard a shot. It was not a rifle shot, which fact caused Jean a little concern. Evarts and Bernardino had rifles, but, to his knowledge, no small arms. Jean rode up on one of the black-brushed conical hills that rose on the south side of Grass Valley, and from there he took a sharp survey of the country. At first he made out only cattle, and bare meadowland, and the low encircling ridges and hills. But presently up toward the head of the valley he descried a bunch of horsemen riding toward the village. He could not tell their number. That dark moving mass seemed to Jean to be instinct with life, mystery, menace. Who were they? It was too far for him to recognize horses, let alone riders. They were moving fast, too.

Jean watched them out of sight, then turned his horse downhill again, and rode on his quest. A number of horsemen like that was a very unusual sight around Grass Valley at any time. What then did it portend now? Jean experienced a little shock of uneasy dread that was a new sensation for him. Brooding over this he proceeded on his way, at length to turn into the draw where the camp of the sheep herders was located. Upon coming in sight of it he heard a hoarse shout. Young Evarts appeared running frantically out of the brush. Jean urged his horse into a run and soon covered the distance between them. Evarts appeared beside himself with terror.

"Boy! what's the matter?" queried Jean, as he dismounted, rifle in hand, peering quickly from Evarts's white face to the camp, and all around.

"Ber-nardino! Ber-nardino!" gasped the boy, wringing his hands and pointing.

Jean ran the few remaining rods to the sheep camp. He saw the little teepee, a burned-out fire, a half-finished meal—and then the Mexican lad lying prone on the ground, dead, with a bullet hole in his ghastly face. Near him lay an old six-shooter.

"Whose gun is that?" demanded Jean, as he picked it up.

"Ber-nardino's," replied Evarts, huskily. "He—he jest got it—the other day."

"Did he shoot himself accidentally?"

"Oh no! No! He didn't do it—atall."

"Who did, then?"

"The men—they rode up—a gang—they did it," panted Evarts.

"Did you know who they were?"

"No. I couldn't tell. I saw them comin' an' I was skeered. Bernardino had gone fer water. I run an' hid in the brush. I wanted to yell, but they come too close. . . . Then I heerd them talkin'. Bernardino come back. They 'peared friendly-like. Thet made me raise up to look. An' I couldn't see good. I heerd one of them ask Bernardino to let him see his gun. An' Bernardino handed it over. He looked at the gun an' haw-hawed, an' flipped it up in the air, an' when it fell back in his hand it—it went off bang! . . . An' Bernardino dropped. . . . I hid down close. I was skeered stiff. I heerd them talk more, but not what they said. Then they rode away. . . . An' I hid there till I seen y'u comin'."

"Have you got a horse?" queried Jean, sharply.

"No. But I can ride one of Bernardino's burros."

"Get one. Hurry over to Blaisdell. Tell him to send word to Blue and Gordon and Fredericks to ride like the devil to my father's ranch. Hurry now!"

Young Evarts ran off without reply. Jean stood looking down at the limp and pathetic figure of the Mexican boy. "By Heaven!" he exclaimed, grimly, "the Jorth-Isbel war is on! . . . Deliberate, cold-blooded murder! I'll gamble Daggs did this job. He's been given the leadership. He started it. . . . Bernardino, greaser or not, you were a faithful lad, and you won't go long unavenged."

Jean had no time to spare. Tearing a tarpaulin out of the teepee he covered the lad with it and then ran for his horse. Mounting, he galloped down the draw, over the little red ridges, out into the valley, where he put his horse to a run.

Action changed the sickening horror that sight of Bernardino had engendered. Jean even felt a strange grim relief. The long, dragging days of waiting were over. Jorth's gang had taken the initiative. Blood had begun to flow. And it would continue to flow now till the last man of one faction stood over the dead body of the last man of the other. Would it be a Jorth or an Isbel? "My instinct was right," he muttered, aloud. "That bunch of horses gave me a queer feelin'." Jean gazed all around the grassy, cattle-dotted valley he was crossing so swiftly, and toward the village, but he did not see any sign of the dark group of riders. They had gone on to Greaves's store, there, no doubt, to drink and to add more enemies of the Isbels to their gang. Suddenly across Jean's mind flashed a thought of Ellen Jorth. "What'll become of her? . . . What'll become of all the women? My sister? . . . The little ones?"

No one was in sight around the ranch. Never had it appeared more peaceful and pastoral to Jean. The grazing cattle and horses in the foreground, the haystack half eaten away, the cows in the fenced pasture, the column of blue smoke lazily ascending, the cackle of hens, the solid, well-built cabins—all these seemed to repudiate Jean's haste and his darkness of mind. This place was his father's farm.

There was not a cloud in the blue, summer sky.

As Jean galloped up the lane some one saw him from the door, and then Bill and Guy and their gray-headed father came out upon the porch. Jean saw how he waved the womenfolk back, and then strode out into the lane. Bill and Guy reached his side as Jean pulled up his heaving horse to a halt. They all looked at Jean, swiftly and intently, with a little, hard, fiery gleam strangely identical in the eyes of each. Probably before a word was spoken they knew what to expect.

"Wal, you shore was in a hurry," remarked the father.

"What the hell's up?" queried Bill, grimly.

Guy Isbel remained silent and it was he who turned slightly pale. Jean leaped off his horse.

"Bernardino has just been killed—murdered with his own gun."

Gaston Isbel seemed to exhale a long-dammed, bursting breath that let his chest sag. A terrible deadly glint, pale and cold as sunlight on ice, grew slowly to dominate his clear eyes.

"A-huh!" ejaculated Bill Isbel, hoarsely.

Not one of the three men asked who had done the killing. They were silent a moment, motionless, locked in the secret seclusion of their own minds. Then they listened with absorption to Jean's brief story.

"Wal, that lets us in," said his father. "I wish we had more time. Reckon I'd done better to listen to you boys an' have my men close at hand. Jacobs happened to ride over. That makes five of us besides the women."

"Aw, dad, you don't reckon they'll round us up heah?" asked Guy Isbel.

"Boys, I always feared they might," replied the old man. "But I never really believed they'd have the nerve. Shore I ought to have figured Daggs better. This heah secret bizness an' shootin' at us from ambush looked aboot Jorth's size to me. But I reckon now we'll have to fight without our friends."

"Let them come," said Jean. "I sent for Blaisdell, Blue, Gordon, and Fredericks. Maybe they'll get here in time. But if they don't it needn't worry us much. We can hold out here longer than Jorth's gang can hang around. We'll want plenty of water, wood, and meat in the house."

"Wal, I'll see to that," rejoined his father. "Jean, you go out close by, where you can see all around, an' keep watch."

"Who's goin' to tell the women?" asked Guy Isbel.

The silence that momentarily ensued was an eloquent testimony to the hardest and saddest aspect of this strife between men. The inevitableness of it in no wise detracted from its sheer uselessness. Men from time immemorial had hated, and killed one another, always to the misery and degradation of their women. Old Gaston Isbel showed this tragic realization in his lined face.

"Wal, boys, I'll tell the women," he said. "Shore you needn't worry none aboot them. They'll be game."

Jean rode away to an open knoll a short distance from the house, and here he stationed himself to watch all points. The cedared ridge back of the ranch was the one approach by which Jorth's gang might come close without being detected, but even so, Jean could see them and ride to the house in time to prevent a surprise. The moments dragged by, and at the end of an hour Jean was in hopes that Blaisdell would soon come. These hopes were well founded. Presently he heard a clatter of hoofs on hard ground to the south, and upon wheeling to look he saw the friendly neighbor coming fast along the road, riding a big white horse. Blaisdell carried a rifle in his hand, and the sight of him gave Jean a glow of warmth. He was one of the Texans who would stand by the Isbels to the last man. Jean watched him ride to the house—watched the meeting between him and his lifelong friend. There floated out to Jean old Blaisdell's roar of rage.

Then out on the green of Grass Valley, where a long, swelling plain swept away toward the village, there appeared a moving dark patch. A bunch of horses! Jean's body gave a slight start—the shock of sudden propulsion of blood through all his veins. Those horses bore riders. They were coming straight down the open valley, on the wagon road to Isbel's ranch. No subterfuge nor secrecy nor sneaking in that advance! A hot thrill ran over Jean.

"By Heaven! They mean business!" he muttered. Up to the last moment he had unconsciously hoped Jorth's gang would not come boldly like that. The verifications of all a Texan's inherited instincts left no doubts, no hopes, no illusions—only a grim certainty that this was not conjecture nor probability, but fact. For a moment longer Jean watched the slowly moving dark patch of horsemen against the green background, then he hurried back to the ranch. His father saw him coming—strode out as before.

"Dad—Jorth is comin'," said Jean, huskily. How he hated to be forced to tell his father that! The boyish love of old had flashed up.

"Whar?" demanded the old man, his eagle gaze sweeping the horizon.

"Down the road from Grass Valley. You can't see from here."

"Wal, come in an' let's get ready."

Isbel's house had not been constructed with the idea of repelling an attack from a band of Apaches. The long living room of the main cabin was the one selected for defense and protection. This room had two windows and a door facing the lane, and a door at each end, one of which opened into the kitchen and the other into an adjoining and later-built cabin. The logs of this main cabin were of large size, and the doors and window coverings were heavy, affording safer protection from bullets than the other cabins.

When Jean went in he seemed to see a host of white faces lifted to him. His sister Ann, his two sisters-in-law, the children, all mutely watched him with eyes that would haunt him.

"Wal, Blaisdell, Jean says Jorth an' his precious gang of rustlers are on the way heah," announced the rancher.

"Damn me if it's not a bad day fer Lee Jorth!" declared Blaisdell.

"Clear off that table," ordered Isbel, "an' fetch out all the guns an' shells we got."

Once laid upon the table these presented a formidable arsenal, which consisted of the three new .44 Winchesters that Jean had brought with him from the coast; the enormous buffalo, or so-called "needle" gun, that Gaston Isbel had used for years; a Henry rifle which Blaisdell had brought, and half a dozen six-shooters. Piles and packages of ammunition littered the table.

"Sort out these heah shells," said Isbel. "Everybody wants to get hold of his own."

Jacobs, the neighbor who was present, was a thick-set, bearded man, rather jovial among those lean-jawed Texans. He carried a .44 rifle of an old pattern. "Wal, boys, if I'd knowed we was in fer some fun I'd hev fetched more shells. Only got one magazine full. Mebbe them new .44's will fit my gun."

It was discovered that the ammunition Jean had brought in quantity fitted Jacob's rifle, a fact which afforded peculiar satisfaction to all the men present.

"Wal, shore we're lucky," declared Gaston Isbel.

The women sat apart, in the corner toward the kitchen, and there seemed to be a strange fascination for them in the talk and action of the men. The wife of Jacobs was a little woman, with homely face and very bright eyes. Jean thought she would be a help in that household during the next doubtful hours.

Every moment Jean would go to the window and peer out down the road. His companions evidently relied upon him, for no one else looked out. Now that the suspense of days and weeks was over, these Texans faced the issue with talk and act not noticeably different from those of ordinary moments.

At last Jean espied the dark mass of horsemen out in the valley road. They were close together, walking their mounts, and evidently in earnest conversation. After several ineffectual attempts Jean counted eleven horses, every one of which he was sure bore a rider.

"Dad, look out!" called Jean.

Gaston Isbel strode to the door and stood looking, without a word.

The other men crowded to the windows. Blaisdell cursed under his breath. Jacobs said: "By Golly! Come to pay us a call!" The women sat motionless, with dark, strained eyes. The children ceased their play and looked fearfully to their mother.

When just out of rifle shot of the cabins the band of horsemen halted and lined up in a half circle, all facing the ranch. They were close enough for Jean to see their gestures, but he could not recognize any of their faces. It struck him singularly that not one of them wore a mask.

"Jean, do you know any of them?" asked his father.

"No, not yet. They're too far off."

"Dad, I'll get your old telescope," said Guy Isbel, and he ran out toward the adjoining cabin.

Blaisdell shook his big, hoary head and rumbled out of his bull-like neck, "Wal, now you're heah, you sheep fellars, what are you goin' to do aboot it?"

Guy Isbel returned with a yard-long telescope, which he passed to his father. The old man took it with shaking hands and leveled it. Suddenly it was as if he had been transfixed; then he lowered the glass, shaking violently, and his face grew gray with an exceeding bitter wrath.

"Jorth!" he swore, harshly.

Jean had only to look at his father to know that recognition had been like a mortal shock. It passed. Again the rancher leveled the glass.

"Wal, Blaisdell, there's our old Texas friend, Daggs," he drawled, dryly. "An' Greaves, our honest storekeeper of Grass Valley. An' there's Stonewall Jackson Jorth. An' Tad Jorth, with the same old red nose! . . . An', say, damn if one of that gang isn't Queen, as bad a gun fighter as Texas ever bred. Shore I thought he'd been killed in the Big Bend country. So I heard. . . . An' there's Craig another respectable sheepman of Grass Valley. Haw-haw. . . . An', wal, I don't recognize any more of them."

Jean forthwith took the glass and moved it slowly across the faces of that group of horsemen. "Simm Bruce," he said, instantly. "I see Colter. And, yes, Greaves is there. I've seen the man next to him—face like a ham. . . ."

"Shore that is Craig," interrupted his father.

Jean knew the dark face of Lee Jorth by the resemblance it bore to Ellen's, and the recognition brought a twinge. He thought, too, that he could tell the other Jorths. He asked his father to describe Daggs and then Queen. It was not likely that Jean would fail to know these several men in the future. Then Blaisdell asked for the telescope and, when he got through looking and cursing, he passed it on to others, who, one by one, took a long look, until finally it came back to the old rancher.

"Wal, Daggs is wavin' his hand heah an' there, like a general aboot to send out scouts. Haw-haw! . . . An' 'pears to me he's not overlookin' our hosses. Wal, that's natural for a rustler. He'd have to steal a hoss or a steer before goin' into a fight or to dinner or to a funeral."

"It'll be his funeral if he goes to foolin' 'round them hosses," declared Guy Isbel, peering anxiously out of the door.

"Wal, son, shore it'll be somebody's funeral," replied his father.

Jean paid but little heed to the conversation. With sharp eyes fixed upon the horsemen, he tried to grasp at their intention. Daggs pointed to the horses in the pasture lot that lay between him and the house. These animals were the best on the range and belonged mostly to Guy Isbel, who was the horse fancier and trader of the family. His horses were his passion.

"Looks like they'd do some horse stealin'," said Jean.

"Lend me that glass," demanded Guy, forcefully. He surveyed the band of men for a long moment, then he handed the glass back to Jean.

"I'm goin' out there after my hosses," he declared.

"No!" exclaimed his father.

"That gang come to steal an' not to fight. Can't you see that? If they meant to fight they'd do it. They're out there arguin' about my hosses."

Guy picked up his rifle. He looked sullenly determined and the gleam in his eye was one of fearlessness.

"Son, I know Daggs," said his father. "An' I know Jorth. They've come to kill us. It'll be shore death for y'u to go out there."

"I'm goin', anyhow. They can't steal my hosses out from under my eyes. An' they ain't in range."

"Wal, Guy, you ain't goin' alone," spoke up Jacobs, cheerily, as he came forward.

The red-haired young wife of Guy Isbel showed no change in her grave face. She had been reared in a stern school. She knew men in times like these. But Jacobs's wife appealed to him, "Bill, don't risk your life for a horse or two."

Jacobs laughed and answered, "Not much risk," and went out with Guy. To Jean their action seemed foolhardy. He kept a keen eye on them and saw instantly when the band became aware of Guy's and Jacobs's entrance into the pasture. It took only another second then to realize that Daggs and Jorth had deadly intent. Jean saw Daggs slip out of his saddle, rifle in hand. Others of the gang did likewise, until half of them were dismounted.

"Dad, they're goin' to shoot," called out Jean, sharply. "Yell for Guy and Jacobs. Make them come back."

The old man shouted; Bill Isbel yelled; Blaisdell lifted his stentorian voice.

Jean screamed piercingly: "Guy! Run! Run!"

But Guy Isbel and his companion strode on into the pasture, as if they had not heard, as if no menacing horse thieves were within miles. They had covered about a quarter of the distance across the pasture, and were nearing the horses, when Jean saw red flashes and white puffs of smoke burst out from the front of that dark band of rustlers. Then followed the sharp, rattling crack of rifles.

Guy Isbel stopped short, and, dropping his gun, he threw up his arms and fell headlong. Jacobs acted as if he had suddenly encountered an invisible blow. He had been hit. Turning, he began to run and ran fast for a few paces. There were more quick, sharp shots. He let go of his rifle. His running broke. Walking, reeling, staggering, he kept on. A hoarse cry came from him. Then a single rifle shot pealed out. Jean heard the bullet strike. Jacobs fell to his knees, then forward on his face.

Jean Isbel felt himself turned to marble. The suddenness of this tragedy paralyzed him. His gaze remained riveted on those prostrate forms.

A hand clutched his arm—a shaking woman's hand, slim and hard and tense.

"Bill's—killed!" whispered a broken voice. "I was watchin'. . . . They're both dead!"

The wives of Jacobs and Guy Isbel had slipped up behind Jean and from behind him they had seen the tragedy.

"I asked Bill—not to—go," faltered the Jacobs woman, and, covering her face with her hands, she groped back to the corner of the cabin, where the other women, shaking and white, received her in their arms. Guy Isbel's wife stood at the window, peering over Jean's shoulder. She had the nerve of a man. She had looked out upon death before.

"Yes, they're dead," she said, bitterly. "An' how are we goin' to get their bodies?"

At this Gaston Isbel seemed to rouse from the cold spell that had transfixed him.

"God, this is hell for our women," he cried out, hoarsely. "My son—my son! . . . Murdered by the Jorths!" Then he swore a terrible oath.

Jean saw the remainder of the mounted rustlers get off, and then all of them leading their horses, they began to move around to the left.

"Dad, they're movin' round," said Jean.

"Up to some trick," declared Bill Isbel.

"Bill, you make a hole through the back wall, say aboot the fifth log up," ordered the father. "Shore we've got to look out."

The elder son grasped a tool, and scattering the children, who had been playing near the back corner, he began to work at the point designated. The little children backed away with fixed, wondering, grave eyes. The women moved their chairs, and huddled together as if waiting and listening.

Jean watched the rustlers until they passed out of his sight. They had moved toward the sloping, brushy ground to the north and west of the cabins.

"Let me know when you get a hole in the back wall," said Jean, and he went through the kitchen and cautiously out another door to slip into a low-roofed, shed-like end of the rambling cabin. This small space was used to store winter firewood. The chinks between the walls had not been filled with adobe clay, and he could see out on three sides. The rustlers were going into the juniper brush. They moved out of sight, and presently reappeared without their horses. It looked to Jean as if they intended to attack the cabins. Then they halted at the edge of the brush and held a long consultation. Jean could see them distinctly, though they were too far distant for him to recognize any particular man. One of them, however, stood and moved apart from the closely massed group. Evidently, from his strides and gestures, he was exhorting his listeners. Jean concluded this was either Daggs or Jorth. Whoever it was had a loud, coarse voice, and this and his actions impressed Jean with a suspicion that the man was under the influence of the bottle.

Presently Bill Isbel called Jean in a low voice. "Jean, I got the hole made, but we can't see anyone."

"I see them," Jean replied. "They're havin' a powwow. Looks to me like either Jorth or Daggs is drunk. He's arguin' to charge us, an' the rest of the gang are holdin' back. . . . Tell dad, an' all of you keep watchin'. I'll let you know when they make a move."

Jorth's gang appeared to be in no hurry to expose their plan of battle. Gradually the group disintegrated a little; some of them sat down; others walked to and fro. Presently two of them went into the brush, probably back to the horses. In a few moments they reappeared, carrying a pack. And when this was deposited on the ground all the rustlers sat down around it. They had brought food and drink. Jean had to utter a grim laugh at their coolness; and he was reminded of many dare-devil deeds known to have been perpetrated by the Hash Knife Gang. Jean was glad of a reprieve. The longer the rustlers put off an attack the more time the allies of the Isbels would have to get here. Rather hazardous, however, would it be now for anyone to attempt to get to the Isbel cabins in the daytime. Night would be more favorable.

Twice Bill Isbel came through the kitchen to whisper to Jean. The strain in the large room, from which the rustlers could not be seen, must have been great. Jean told him all he had seen and what he thought about it. "Eatin' an' drinkin'!" ejaculated Bill. "Well, I'll be—! That'll jar the old man. He wants to get the fight over."

"Tell him I said it'll be over too quick—for us—unless we are mighty careful," replied Jean, sharply.

Bill went back muttering to himself. Then followed a long wait, fraught with suspense, during which Jean watched the rustlers regale themselves. The day was hot and still. And the unnatural silence of the cabin was broken now and then by the gay laughter of the children. The sound shocked and haunted Jean. Playing children! Then another sound, so faint he had to strain to hear it, disturbed and saddened him—his father's slow tread up and down the cabin floor, to and fro, to and fro. What must be in his father's heart this day!

At length the rustlers rose and, with rifles in hand, they moved as one man down the slope. They came several hundred yards closer, until Jean, grimly cocking his rifle, muttered to himself that a few more rods closer would mean the end of several of that gang. They knew the range of a rifle well enough, and once more sheered off at right angles with the cabin. When they got even with the line of corrals they stooped down and were lost to Jean's sight. This fact caused him alarm. They were, of course, crawling up on the cabins. At the end of that line of corrals ran a ditch, the bank of which was high enough to afford cover. Moreover, it ran along in front of the cabins, scarcely a hundred yards, and it was covered with grass and little clumps of brush, from behind which the rustlers could fire into the windows and through the clay chinks without any considerable risk to themselves. As they did not come into sight again, Jean concluded he had discovered their plan. Still, he waited awhile longer, until he saw faint, little clouds of dust rising from behind the far end of the embankment. That discovery made him rush out, and through the kitchen to the large cabin, where his sudden appearance startled the men.

"Get back out of sight!" he ordered, sharply, and with swift steps he reached the door and closed it. "They're behind the bank out there by the corrals. An' they're goin' to crawl down the ditch closer to us. . . . It looks bad. They'll have grass an' brush to shoot from. We've got to be mighty careful how we peep out."

"Ahuh! All right," replied his father. "You women keep the kids with you in that corner. An' you all better lay down flat."

Blaisdell, Bill Isbel, and the old man crouched at the large window, peeping through cracks in the rough edges of the logs. Jean took his post beside the small window, with his keen eyes vibrating like a compass needle. The movement of a blade of grass, the flight of a grasshopper could not escape his trained sight.

"Look sharp now!" he called to the other men. "I see dust. . . . They're workin' along almost to that bare spot on the bank. . . . I saw the tip of a rifle . . . a black hat . . . more dust. They're spreadin' along behind the bank."

Loud voices, and then thick clouds of yellow dust, coming from behind the highest and brushiest line of the embankment, attested to the truth of Jean's observation, and also to a reckless disregard of danger.

Suddenly Jean caught a glint of moving color through the fringe of brush. Instantly he was strung like a whipcord.

Then a tall, hatless and coatless man stepped up in plain sight. The sun shone on his fair, ruffled hair. Daggs!

"Hey, you —— —— Isbels!" he bawled, in magnificent derisive boldness. "Come out an' fight!"

Quick as lightning Jean threw up his rifle and fired. He saw tufts of fair hair fly from Daggs's head. He saw the squirt of red blood. Then quick shots from his comrades rang out. They all hit the swaying body of the rustler. But Jean knew with a terrible thrill that his bullet had killed Daggs before the other three struck. Daggs fell forward, his arms and half his body resting over the embankment. Then the rustlers dragged him back out of sight. Hoarse shouts rose. A cloud of yellow dust drifted away from the spot.

"Daggs!" burst out Gaston Isbel. "Jean, you knocked off the top of his haid. I seen that when I was pullin' trigger. Shore we over heah wasted our shots."

"God! he must have been crazy or drunk—to pop up there—an' brace us that way," said Blaisdell, breathing hard.

"Arizona is bad for Texans," replied Isbel, sardonically. "Shore it's been too peaceful heah. Rustlers have no practice at fightin.' An' I reckon Daggs forgot."

"Daggs made as crazy a move as that of Guy an' Jacobs," spoke up Jean. "They were overbold, an' he was drunk. Let them be a lesson to us."

Jean had smelled whisky upon his entrance to this cabin. Bill was a hard drinker, and his father was not immune. Blaisdell, too, drank heavily upon occasions. Jean made a mental note that he would not permit their chances to become impaired by liquor.

Rifles began to crack, and puffs of smoke rose all along the embankment for the space of a hundred feet. Bullets whistled through the rude window casing and spattered on the heavy door, and one split the clay between the logs before Jean, narrowly missing him. Another volley followed, then another. The rustlers had repeating rifles and they were emptying their magazines. Jean changed his position. The other men profited by his wise move. The volleys had merged into one continuous rattling roar of rifle shots. Then came a sudden cessation of reports, with silence of relief. The cabin was full of dust, mingled with the smoke from the shots of Jean and his companions. Jean heard the stifled breaths of the children. Evidently they were terror-stricken, but they did not cry out. The women uttered no sound.

A loud voice pealed from behind the embankment.

"Come out an' fight! Do you Isbels want to be killed like sheep?"

This sally gained no reply. Jean returned to his post by the window and his comrades followed his example. And they exercised extreme caution when they peeped out.

"Boys, don't shoot till you see one," said Gaston Isbel. "Maybe after a while they'll get careless. But Jorth will never show himself."

The rustlers did not again resort to volleys. One by one, from different angles, they began to shoot, and they were not firing at random. A few bullets came straight in at the windows to pat into the walls; a few others ticked and splintered the edges of the windows; and most of them broke through the clay chinks between the logs. It dawned upon Jean that these dangerous shots were not accident. They were well aimed, and most of them hit low down. The cunning rustlers had some unerring riflemen and they were picking out the vulnerable places all along the front of the cabin. If Jean had not been lying flat he would have been hit twice. Presently he conceived the idea of driving pegs between the logs, high up, and, kneeling on these, he managed to peep out from the upper edge of the window. But this position was awkward and difficult to hold for long.

He heard a bullet hit one of his comrades. Whoever had been struck never uttered a sound. Jean turned to look. Bill Isbel was holding his shoulder, where red splotches appeared on his shirt. He shook his head at Jean, evidently to make light of the wound. The women and children were lying face down and could not see what was happening. Plain it was that Bill did not want them to know. Blaisdell bound up the bloody shoulder with a scarf.

Steady firing from the rustlers went on, at the rate of one shot every few minutes. The Isbels did not return these. Jean did not fire again that afternoon. Toward sunset, when the besiegers appeared to grow restless or careless, Blaisdell fired at something moving behind the brush; and Gaston Isbel's huge buffalo gun boomed out.

"Wal, what're they goin' to do after dark, an' what're *we* goin' to do?" grumbled Blaisdell.

"Reckon they'll never charge us," said Gaston.

"They might set fire to the cabins," added Bill Isbel. He appeared to be the gloomiest of the Isbel faction. There was something on his mind.

"Wal, the Jorths are bad, but I reckon they'd not burn us alive," replied Blaisdell.

"Hah!" ejaculated Gaston Isbel. "Much you know aboot Lee Jorth. He would skin me alive an' throw red-hot coals on my raw flesh."

So they talked during the hour from sunset to dark. Jean Isbel had little to say. He was revolving possibilities in his mind. Darkness brought a change in the attack of the rustlers. They stationed men at four points around the cabins; and every few minutes one of these outposts would fire. These bullets embedded themselves in the logs, causing but little anxiety to the Isbels.

"Jean, what you make of it?" asked the old rancher.

"Looks to me this way," replied Jean. "They're set for a long fight. They're shootin' just to let us know they're on the watch."

"Ahuh! Wal, what're you goin' to do aboot it?"

"I'm goin' out there presently."

Gaston Isbel grunted his satisfaction at this intention of Jean's.

All was pitch dark inside the cabin. The women had water and food at hand. Jean kept a sharp lookout from his window while he ate his supper of meat, bread, and milk. At last the children, worn out by the long day, fell asleep. The women whispered a little in their corner.

About nine o'clock Jean signified his intention of going out to reconnoitre.

"Dad, they've got the best of us in the daytime," he said, "but not after dark."

Jean buckled on a belt that carried shells, a bowie knife, a revolver, and with rifle in hand he went out through the kitchen to the yard. The night was darker than usual, as some of the stars were hidden by clouds. He leaned against the log cabin, waiting for his eyes to become perfectly adjusted to the darkness. Like an Indian, Jean could see well at night. He knew every point around cabins and sheds and corrals, every post, log, tree, rock, adjacent to the ranch. After perhaps a quarter of an hour watching, during which time several shots were fired from behind the embankment and one each from the rustlers at other locations, Jean slipped out on his quest.

He kept in the shadow of the cabin walls, then the line of orchard trees, then a row of currant bushes. Here, crouching low, he halted to look and listen. He was now at the edge of the open ground, with the gently rising slope before him. He could see the dark patches of cedar and juniper trees. On the north side of the cabin a streak of fire flashed in the blackness, and a shot rang out. Jean heard the bullet hit the cabin. Then silence enfolded the lonely ranch and the darkness lay like a black blanket. A low hum of insects pervaded the air. Dull sheets of lightning illumined the dark horizon to the south. Once Jean heard voices, but could not tell from which direction they came. To the west of him then flared out another rifle shot. The bullet whistled down over Jean to thud into the cabin.

Jean made a careful study of the obscure, gray-black open before him and then the background to his rear. So long as he kept the dense shadows behind him he could not be seen. He slipped from behind his covert and, gliding with absolutely noiseless footsteps, he gained the first clump of junipers. Here he waited patiently and motionlessly for another round of shots from the rustlers. After the second shot from the west side Jean sheered off to the right. Patches of brush, clumps of juniper, and isolated cedars covered this slope, affording Jean a perfect means for his purpose, which was to make a detour and come up behind the rustler who was firing from that side. Jean climbed to the top of the ridge, descended the opposite slope, made his turn to the left, and slowly worked up behind the point near where he expected to locate the rustler. Long habit in the open, by day and night, rendered his sense of direction almost as perfect as sight itself. The first flash of fire he saw from this side proved that he had come straight up toward his man. Jean's intention was to crawl up on this one of the Jorth gang and silently kill him with a knife. If the plan worked successfully, Jean meant to work round to the next rustler. Laying aside his rifle, he crawled forward on hands and knees, making no more sound than a cat. His approach was slow. He had to pick his way, be careful not to break twigs nor rattle stones. His buckskin garments made no sound against the brush. Jean located the rustler sitting on the top of the ridge in the center of an open space. He was alone. Jean saw the dull-red end of the cigarette he was smoking. The ground on the ridge top was rocky and not well adapted for Jean's purpose. He had to abandon the idea of crawling up on the rustler. Whereupon, Jean turned back, patiently and slowly, to get his rifle.

Upon securing it he began to retrace his course, this time more slowly than before, as he was hampered by the rifle. But he did not make the slightest sound, and at length he reached the edge of the open ridge top, once more to espy the dark form of the rustler silhouetted against the sky. The distance was not more than fifty yards.

As Jean rose to his knee and carefully lifted his rifle round to avoid the twigs of a juniper he suddenly experienced another emotion besides the one of grim, hard wrath at the Jorths. It was an emotion that sickened him, made him weak internally, a cold, shaking, ungovernable sensation. Suppose this man was Ellen

Jorth's father! Jean lowered the rifle. He felt it shake over his knee. He was trembling all over. The astounding discovery that he did not want to kill Ellen's father—that he could not do it—awakened Jean to the despairing nature of his love for her. In this grim moment of indecision, when he knew his Indian subtlety and ability gave him a great advantage over the Jorths, he fully realized his strange, hopeless, and irresistible love for the girl. He made no attempt to deny it any longer. Like the night and the lonely wilderness around him, like the inevitableness of this Jorth-Isbel feud, this love of his was a thing, a fact, a reality. He breathed to his own inward ear, to his soul he could not kill Ellen Jorth's father. Feud or no feud, Isbel or not, he could not deliberately do it. And why not? There was no answer. Was he not faithless to his father? He had no hope of ever winning Ellen Jorth. He did not want the love of a girl of her character. But he loved her. And his struggle must be against the insidious and mysterious growth of that passion. It swayed him already. It made him a coward. Through his mind and heart swept the memory of Ellen Jorth, her beauty and charm, her boldness and pathos, her shame and her degradation. And the sweetness of her outweighed the boldness. And the mystery of her arrayed itself in unquenchable protest against her acknowledged shame. Jean lifted his face to the heavens, to the pitiless white stars, to the infinite depths of the dark-blue sky. He could sense the fact of his being an atom in the universe of nature. What was he, what was his revengeful father, what were hate and passion and strife in comparison to the nameless something, immense and everlasting, that he sensed in this dark moment?

But the rustlers—Daggs—the Jorths—they had killed his brother Guy—murdered him brutally and ruthlessly. Guy had been a playmate of Jean's—a favorite brother. Bill had been secretive and selfish. Jean had never loved him as he did Guy. Guy lay dead down there on the meadow. This feud had begun to run its bloody course. Jean steeled his nerve. The hot blood crept back along his veins. The dark and masterful tide of revenge waved over him. The keen edge of his mind then cut out sharp and trenchant thoughts. He must kill when and where he could. This man could hardly be Ellen Jorth's father. Jorth would be with the main crowd, directing hostilities. Jean could shoot this rustler guard and his shot would be taken by the gang as the regular one from their comrade. Then swiftly Jean leveled his rifle, covered the dark form, grew cold and set, and pressed the trigger. After the report he rose and wheeled away. He did not look nor listen for the result of his shot. A clammy sweat wet his face, the hollow of his hands, his breast. A horrible, leaden, thick sensation oppressed his heart. Nature had endowed him with Indian gifts, but the exercise of them to this end had caused a revolt in his soul.

Nevertheless, it was the Isbel blood that dominated him. The wind blew cool on his face. The burden upon his shoulders seemed to lift. The clamoring whispers grew fainter in his ears. And by the time he had retraced his cautious steps back to the orchard all his physical being was strung to the task at hand. Something had come between his reflective self and this man of action.

Crossing the lane, he took to the west line of sheds, and passed beyond them into the meadow. In the grass he crawled silently away to the right, using the same precaution that had actuated him on the slope, only here he did not pause so often, nor move so slowly. Jean aimed to go far enough to the right to pass the end of the embankment behind which the rustlers had found such efficient cover. This ditch had been made to keep water, during spring thaws and summer storms, from pouring off the slope to flood the corrals.

Jean miscalculated and found he had come upon the embankment somewhat to the left of the end, which fact, however, caused him no uneasiness. He lay there awhile to listen. Again he heard voices. After a time a shot pealed out. He did not see the flash, but he calculated that it had come from the north side of the cabins.

The next quarter of an hour discovered to Jean that the nearest guard was firing from the top of the embankment, perhaps a hundred yards distant, and a second one was performing the same office from a point apparently only a few yards farther on. Two rustlers close together! Jean had not calculated upon that. For a little while he pondered on what was best to do, and at length decided to crawl round behind them, and as close as the situation made advisable.

He found the ditch behind the embankment a favorable path by which to stalk these enemies. It was dry and sandy, with borders of high weeds. The only drawback was that it was almost impossible for him to keep from brushing against the dry, invisible branches of the weeds. To offset this he wormed his way like a snail, inch by inch, taking a long time before he caught sight of the sitting figure of a man, black against the dark-blue sky. This rustler had fired his rifle three times during Jean's slow approach. Jean watched and listened a few moments, then wormed himself closer and closer, until the man was within twenty steps of him.

Jean smelled tobacco smoke, but could see no light of pipe or cigarette, because the fellow's back was turned.

"Say, Ben," said this man to his companion sitting hunched up a few yards distant, "shore it strikes me queer thet Somers ain't shootin' any over thar."

Jean recognized the dry, drawling voice of Greaves, and the shock of it seemed to contract the muscles of his whole thrilling body, like that of a panther about to spring.

CHAPTER EIGHT

"I was shore thinkin' thet same," said the other man.

"An', say, didn't thet last shot sound too sharp fer Somers's forty-five?"

"Come to think of it, I reckon it did," replied Greaves.

"Wal, I'll go around over thar an' see."

The dark form of the rustler slipped out of sight over the embankment.

"Better go slow an' careful," warned Greaves. "An' only go close enough to call Somers. . . . Mebbe thet damn half-breed Isbel is comin' some Injun on us."

Jean heard the soft swish of footsteps through wet grass. Then all was still. He lay flat, with his cheek on the sand, and he had to look ahead and upward to make out the dark figure of Greaves on the bank. One way or another he meant to kill Greaves, and he had the will power to resist the strongest gust of passion that had ever stormed his breast. If he arose and shot the rustler, that act would defeat his plan of slipping on around upon the other outposts who were firing at the cabins. Jean wanted to call softly to Greaves, "You're right about the half-breed!" but then, as he wheeled aghast, to kill him as he moved. But it suited Jean to risk leaping upon the man. Jean did not waste time in trying to understand the strange, deadly instinct that gripped him at the moment. But he realized then he had chosen the most perilous plan to get rid of Greaves.

Jean drew a long, deep breath and held it. He let go of his rifle. He rose, silently as a lifting shadow. He drew the bowie knife. Then with light, swift bounds he glided up the bank. Greaves must have heard a rustling—a soft, quick pad of moccasin, for he turned with a start. And that instant Jean's left arm darted like a striking snake round Greaves's neck and closed tight and hard. With his right hand free, holding the knife, Jean might have ended the deadly business in just one move. But when his bared arm felt the hot, bulging neck something terrible burst out of the depths of him. To kill this enemy of his father's was not enough! Physical contact had unleashed the savage soul of the Indian. Yet there was more, and as Jean gave the straining body a tremendous jerk backward, he felt the same strange thrill, the dark joy that he had known when his fist had smashed the face of Simm Bruce. Greaves had leered—he had corroborated Bruce's vile insinuation about Ellen Jorth. So it was more than hate that actuated Jean Isbel.

Greaves was heavy and powerful. He whirled himself, feet first, over backward, in a lunge like that of a lassoed steer. But Jean's hold held. They rolled down the bank into the sandy ditch, and Jean landed uppermost, with his body at right angles with that of his adversary.

"Greaves, your hunch was right," hissed Jean. "It's the half-breed. . . . An' I'm goin' to cut you—first for Ellen Jorth—an' then for Gaston Isbel!"

Jean gazed down into the gleaming eyes. Then his right arm whipped the big blade. It flashed. It fell. Low down, as far as Jean could reach, it entered Greaves's body.

All the heavy, muscular frame of Greaves seemed to contract and burst. His spring was that of an animal in terror and agony. It was so tremendous that it broke Jean's hold. Greaves let out a strangled yell that cleared, swelling wildly, with a hideous mortal note. He wrestled free. The big knife came out. Supple and swift, he got to his knees. He had his gun out when Jean reached him again. Like a bear Jean enveloped him. Greaves shot, but he could not raise the gun, nor twist it far enough. Then Jean, letting go with his right arm, swung the bowie. Greaves's strength went out in an awful, hoarse cry. His gun boomed again, then dropped from his hand. He swayed. Jean let go. And that enemy of the Isbels sank limply in the ditch. Jean's eyes roved for his rifle and caught the starlit gleam of it. Snatching it up, he leaped over the embankment and ran straight for the cabins. From all around yells of the Jorth faction attested to their excitement and fury.

A fence loomed up gray in the obscurity. Jean vaulted it, darted across the lane into the shadow of the corral, and soon gained the first cabin. Here he leaned to regain his breath. His heart pounded high and seemed too large for his breast. The hot blood beat and surged all over his body. Sweat poured off him. His teeth were clenched tight as a vise, and it took effort on his part to open his mouth so he could breathe more freely and deeply. But these physical sensations were as nothing compared to the tumult of his mind. Then the instinct, the spell, let go its grip and he could think. He had avenged Guy, he had depleted the ranks of the Jorths, he had made good the brag of his father, all of which afforded him satisfaction. But these thoughts were not accountable for all that he felt, especially for the bitter-sweet sting of the fact that death to the defiler of Ellen Jorth could not efface the doubt, the regret which seemed to grow with the hours.

Groping his way into the woodshed, he entered the kitchen and, calling low, he went on into the main cabin.

"Jean! Jean!" came his father's shaking voice.

"Yes, I'm back," replied Jean.

"Are—you—all right?"

"Yes. I think I've got a bullet crease on my leg. I didn't know I had it till now. . . . It's bleedin' a little. But it's nothin'."

Jean heard soft steps and some one reached shaking hands for him. They belonged to his sister Ann. She embraced him. Jean felt the heave and throb of her breast.

"Why, Ann, I'm not hurt," he said, and held her close. "Now you lie down an' try to sleep."

In the black darkness of the cabin Jean led her back to the corner and his heart was full. Speech was difficult, because the very touch of Ann's hands had made him divine that the success of his venture in no wise changed the plight of the women.

"Wal, what happened out there?" demanded Blaisdell.

"I got two of them," replied Jean. "That fellow who was shootin' from the ridge west. An' the other was Greaves."

"Hah!" exclaimed his father.

"Shore then it was Greaves yellin'," declared Blaisdell. "By God, I never heard such yells! Whad 'd you do, Jean?"

"I knifed him. You see, I'd planned to slip up on one after another. An' I didn't want to make noise. But I didn't get any farther than Greaves."

"Wal, I reckon that'll end their shootin' in the dark," muttered Gaston Isbel. "We've got to be on the lookout for somethin' else—fire, most likely."

The old rancher's surmise proved to be partially correct. Jorth's faction ceased the shooting. Nothing further was seen or heard from then. But this silence and apparent break in the siege were harder to bear than deliberate hostility. The long, dark hours dragged by. The men took turns watching and resting, but none of them slept. At last the blackness paled and gray dawn stole out of the east. The sky turned rose over the distant range and daylight came.

The children awoke hungry and noisy, having slept away their fears. The women took advantage of the quiet morning hour to get a hot breakfast.

"Maybe they've gone away," suggested Guy Isbel's wife, peering out of the window. She had done that several times since daybreak. Jean saw her somber gaze search the pasture until it rested upon the dark, prone shape of her dead husband, lying face down in the grass. Her look worried Jean.

"No, Esther, they've not gone yet," replied Jean. "I've seen some of them out there at the edge of the brush."

Blaisdell was optimistic. He said Jean's night work would have its effect and that the Jorth contingent would not renew the siege very determinedly. It turned out, however, that Blaisdell was wrong. Directly after sunrise they began to pour volleys from four sides and from closer range. During the night Jorth's gang had thrown earth banks and constructed log breastworks, from behind which they were now firing. Jean and his comrades could see the flashes of fire and streaks of smoke to such good advantage that they began to return the volleys.

In half an hour the cabin was so full of smoke that Jean could not see the womenfolk in their corner. The fierce attack then abated somewhat, and the firing became more intermittent, and therefore more carefully aimed. A glancing bullet cut a furrow in Blaisdell's hoary head, making a painful, though not serious wound. It was Esther Isbel who stopped the flow of blood and bound Blaisdell's head, a task which she performed skillfully and without a tremor. The old Texan could not sit still during this operation. Sight of the blood on his hands, which he tried to rub off, appeared to inflame him to a great degree.

"Isbel, we got to go out thar," he kept repeating, "an' kill them all."

"No, we're goin' to stay heah," replied Gaston Isbel. "Shore I'm lookin' for Blue an' Fredericks an' Gordon to open up out there. They ought to be heah, an' if they are y'u shore can bet they've got the fight sized up."

Isbel's hopes did not materialize. The shooting continued without any lull until about midday. Then the Jorth faction stopped.

"Wal, now what's up?" queried Isbel. "Boys, hold your fire an' let's wait."

Gradually the smoke wafted out of the windows and doors, until the room was once more clear. And at this juncture Esther Isbel came over to take another gaze out upon the meadows. Jean saw her suddenly start violently, then stiffen, with a trembling hand outstretched.

"Look!" she cried.

"Esther, get back," ordered the old rancher. "Keep away from that window."

"What the hell!" muttered Blaisdell. "She sees somethin', or she's gone dotty."

Esther seemed turned to stone. "Look! The hogs have broken into the pasture! . . . They'll eat Guy's body!"

Everyone was frozen with horror at Esther's statement. Jean took a swift survey of the pasture. A bunch of big black hogs had indeed appeared on the scene and were rooting around in the grass not far from where lay the bodies of Guy Isbel and Jacobs. This herd of hogs belonged to the rancher and was allowed to run wild.

"Jane, those hogs—" stammered Esther Isbel, to the wife of Jacobs. "Come! Look! . . . Do y'u know anythin' about hogs?"

The woman ran to the window and looked out. She stiffened as had Esther.

"Dad, will those hogs—eat human flesh?" queried Jean, breathlessly.

The old man stared out of the window. Surprise seemed to hold him. A completely unexpected situation had staggered him.

"Jean—can you—can you shoot that far?" he asked, huskily.

"To those hogs? No, it's out of range."

"Then, by God, we've got to stay trapped in heah an' watch an awful sight," ejaculated the old man, completely unnerved. "See that break in the fence! . . . Jorth's done that. . . . To let in the hogs!"

"Aw, Isbel, it's not so bad as all that," remonstrated Blaisdell, wagging his bloody head. "Jorth wouldn't do such a hell-bent trick."

"It's shore done."

"Wal, mebbe the hogs won't find Guy an' Jacobs," returned Blaisdell, weakly. Plain it was that he only hoped for such a contingency and certainly doubted it.

"Look!" cried Esther Isbel, piercingly. "They're workin' straight up the pasture!"

Indeed, to Jean it appeared to be the fatal truth. He looked blankly, feeling a little sick. Ann Isbel came to peer out of the window and she uttered a cry. Jacobs's wife stood mute, as if dazed.

Blaisdell swore a mighty oath. "—— —— ——! Isbel, we cain't stand heah an' watch them hogs eat our people!"

"Wal, we'll have to. What else on earth can we do?"

Esther turned to the men. She was white and cold, except her eyes, which resembled gray flames.

"Somebody can run out there an' bury our dead men," she said.

"Why, child, it'd be shore death. Y'u saw what happened to Guy an' Jacobs. . . . We've jest got to bear it. Shore nobody needn't look out—an' see."

Jean wondered if it would be possible to keep from watching. The thing had a horrible fascination. The big hogs were rooting and tearing in the grass, some of them lazy, others nimble, and all were gradually working closer and closer to the bodies. The leader, a huge, gaunt boar, that had fared ill all his life in this barren country, was scarcely fifty feet away from where Guy Isbel lay.

"Ann, get me some of your clothes, an' a sunbonnet—quick," said Jean, forced out of his lethargy. "I'll run out there disguised. Maybe I can go through with it."

"No!" ordered his father, positively, and with dark face flaming. "Guy an' Jacobs are dead. We cain't help them now."

"But, dad—" pleaded Jean. He had been wrought to a pitch by Esther's blaze of passion, by the agony in the face of the other woman.

"I tell y'u no!" thundered Gaston Isbel, flinging his arms wide.

"I will go!" cried Esther, her voice ringing.

"You won't go alone!" instantly answered the wife of Jacobs, repeating unconsciously the words her husband had spoken.

"You stay right heah," shouted Gaston Isbel, hoarsely.

"I'm goin'," replied Esther. "You've no hold over me. My husband is dead. No one can stop me. I'm goin' out there to drive those hogs away an' bury him."

"Esther, for Heaven's sake, listen," replied Isbel. "If y'u show yourself outside, Jorth an' his gang will kill y'u."

"They may be mean, but no white men could be so low as that."

Then they pleaded with her to give up her purpose. But in vain! She pushed them back and ran out through the kitchen with Jacobs's wife following her. Jean turned to the window in time to see both women run out into the lane. Jean looked fearfully, and listened for shots. But only a loud, "Haw! Haw!" came from the watchers outside. That coarse laugh relieved the tension in Jean's breast. Possibly the Jorths were not as black as his father painted them. The two women entered an open shed and came forth with a shovel and spade.

"Shore they've got to hurry," burst out Gaston Isbel.

Shifting his gaze, Jean understood the import of his father's speech. The leader of the hogs had no doubt scented the bodies. Suddenly he espied them and broke into a trot.

"Run, Esther, run!" yelled Jean, with all his might.

That urged the women to flight. Jean began to shoot. The hog reached the body of Guy. Jean's shots did not reach nor frighten the beast. All the hogs now had caught a scent and went ambling toward their leader. Esther and her companion passed swiftly out of sight behind a corral. Loud and piercingly, with some awful note, rang out their screams. The hogs appeared frightened. The leader lifted his long snout, looked, and turned away. The others had halted. Then they, too, wheeled and ran off.

All was silent then in the cabin and also outside wherever the Jorth faction lay concealed. All eyes manifestly were fixed upon the brave wives. They spaded up the sod and dug a grave for Guy Isbel. For a shroud Esther wrapped him in her shawl. Then they buried him. Next they hurried to the side of Jacobs, who lay some yards away. They dug a grave for him. Mrs. Jacobs took off her outer skirt to wrap round him. Then the two women labored hard to lift him and lower him. Jacobs was a heavy man. When he had been covered his widow knelt beside his grave. Esther went back to the other. But she remained standing and did not look as if she prayed. Her aspect was tragic—that of a woman who had lost father, mother, sisters, brother, and now her husband, in this bloody Arizona land.

The deed and the demeanor of these wives of the murdered men surely must have shamed Jorth and his followers. They did not fire a shot during the ordeal nor give any sign of their presence.

Inside the cabin all were silent, too. Jean's eyes blurred so that he continually had to wipe them. Old Isbel made no effort to hide his tears. Blaisdell nodded his shaggy head and swallowed hard. The women sat staring into space. The children, in round-eyed dismay, gazed from one to the other of their elders.

"Wal, they're comin' back," declared Isbel, in immense relief. "An' so help me—Jorth let them bury their daid!"

The fact seemed to have been monstrously strange to Gaston Isbel. When the women entered the old man said, brokenly: "I'm shore glad. . . . An' I reckon I was wrong to oppose you . . . an' wrong to say what I did aboot Jorth."

No one had any chance to reply to Isbel, for the Jorth gang, as if to make up for lost time and surcharged feelings of shame, renewed the attack with such a persistent and furious volleying that the defenders did not risk a return shot. They all had to lie flat next to the lowest log in order to keep from being hit. Bullets rained in through the window. And all the clay between the logs low down was shot away. This fusillade lasted for more than an hour, then gradually the fire diminished on one side and then on the other until it became desultory and finally ceased.

"Ahuh! Shore they've shot their bolt," declared Gaston Isbel.

"Wal, I doon't know aboot that," returned Blaisdell, "but they've shot a hell of a lot of shells."

"Listen," suddenly called Jean. "Somebody's yellin'."

"Hey, Isbel!" came in loud, hoarse voice. "Let your women fight for you."

Gaston Isbel sat up with a start and his face turned livid. Jean needed no more to prove that the derisive voice from outside had belonged to Jorth. The old rancher lunged up to his full height and with reckless disregard of life he rushed to the window. "Jorth," he roared, "I dare you to meet me—man to man!"

This elicited no answer. Jean dragged his father away from the window. After that a waiting silence ensued, gradually less fraught with suspense. Blaisdell started conversation by saying he believed the fight was over for that particular time. No one disputed him. Evidently Gaston Isbel was loath to believe it. Jean, however, watching at the back of the kitchen, eventually discovered that the Jorth gang had lifted the siege. Jean saw them congregate at the edge of the brush, somewhat lower down than they had been the day before. A team of mules, drawing a wagon, appeared on the road, and turned toward the slope. Saddled horses were led down out of the junipers. Jean saw bodies, evidently of dead men, lifted into the wagon, to be hauled away toward the village. Seven mounted men, leading four riderless horses, rode out into the valley and followed the wagon.

"Dad, they've gone," declared Jean. "We had the best of this fight. . . . If only Guy an' Jacobs had listened!"

The old man nodded moodily. He had aged considerably during these two trying days. His hair was grayer. Now that the blaze and glow of the fight had passed he showed a subtle change, a fixed and morbid sadness, a resignation to a fate he had accepted.

The ordinary routine of ranch life did not return for the Isbels. Blaisdell returned home to settle matters there, so that he could devote all his time to this feud. Gaston Isbel sat down to wait for the members of his clan.

The male members of the family kept guard in turn over the ranch that night. Another day dawned. It brought word from Blaisdell that Blue, Fredericks, Gordon, and Colmor were all at his house, on the way to join the Isbels. The news appeared greatly to rejuvenate Gaston Isbel. But his enthusiasm did not last long.

Impatient and moody by turns, he paced or moped around the cabin, always looking out, sometimes toward Blaisdell's ranch, but mostly toward Grass Valley.

It struck Jean as singular that neither Esther Isbel nor Mrs. Jacobs suggested a reburial of their husbands. The two bereaved women did not ask for assistance, but repaired to the pasture, and there spent several hours working over the graves. They raised mounds, which they sodded, and then placed stones at the heads and feet. Lastly, they fenced in the graves.

"I reckon I'll hitch up an' drive back home," said Mrs. Jacobs, when she returned to the cabin. "I've much to do an' plan. Probably I'll go to my mother's home. She's old an' will be glad to have me."

"If I had any place to go to I'd sure go," declared Esther Isbel, bitterly.

Gaston Isbel heard this remark. He raised his face from his hands, evidently both nettled and hurt.

"Esther, shore that's not kind," he said.

The red-haired woman—for she did not appear to be a girl any more—halted before his chair and gazed down at him, with a terrible flare of scorn in her gray eyes.

"Gaston Isbel, all I've got to say to you is this," she retorted, with the voice of a man. "Seein' that you an' Lee Jorth hate each other, why couldn't you act like men? . . . You damned Texans, with your bloody feuds, draggin' in every relation, every friend to murder each other! That's not the way of Arizona men. . . . We've all got to suffer—an' we women will be ruined for life—because *you* had differences with Jorth. If you were half a man you'd go out an' kill him yourself, an' not leave a lot of widows an' orphaned children!"

Jean himself writhed under the lash of her scorn. Gaston Isbel turned a dead white. He could not answer her. He seemed stricken with merciless truth. Slowly dropping his head, he remained motionless, a pathetic and tragic figure; and he did not stir until the rapid beat of hoofs denoted the approach of horsemen. Blaisdell appeared on his white charger, leading a pack animal. And behind rode a group of men, all heavily armed, and likewise with packs.

"Get down an' come in," was Isbel's greeting. "Bill—you look after their packs. Better leave the hosses saddled."

The booted and spurred riders trooped in, and their demeanor fitted their errand. Jean was acquainted with all of them. Fredericks was a lanky Texan, the color of dust, and he had yellow, clear eyes, like those of a hawk. His mother had been an Isbel. Gordon, too, was related to Jean's family, though distantly. He resembled an industrious miner more than a prosperous cattleman. Blue was the most striking of the visitors, as he was the most noted. A little, shrunken gray-eyed man, with years of cowboy written all over him, he looked the quiet, easy, cool, and deadly Texan he was reputed to be. Blue's Texas record was shady, and was seldom alluded to, as unfavorable comment had turned out to be hazardous. He was the only one of the group who did not carry a rifle. But he packed two guns, a habit not often noted in Texans, and almost never in Arizonians.

Colmor, Ann Isbel's fiancé, was the youngest member of the clan, and the one closest to Jean. His meeting with Ann affected Jean powerfully, and brought to a climax an idea that had been developing in Jean's mind. His sister devotedly loved this lean-faced, keen-eyed Arizonian; and it took no great insight to discover that Colmor reciprocated her affection. They were young. They had a long life before them. It seemed to Jean a pity that Colmor should be drawn into this war. Jean watched them, as they conversed apart; and he saw Ann's hands creep up to Colmor's breast, and he saw her dark eyes, eloquent, hungry, fearful, lifted with queries her lips did not speak. Jean stepped beside them, and laid an arm over both their shoulders.

"Colmor, for Ann's sake you'd better back out of this Jorth-Isbel fight," he whispered.

Colmor looked insulted. "But, Jean, it's Ann's father," he said. "I'm almost one of the family."

"You're Ann's sweetheart, an', by Heaven, I say you oughtn't to go with us!" whispered Jean.

"Go—with—you," faltered Ann.

"Yes. Dad is goin' straight after Jorth. Can't you tell that? An' there'll be one hell of a fight."

Ann looked up into Colmor's face with all her soul in her eyes, but she did not speak. Her look was noble. She yearned to guide him right, yet her lips were sealed. And Colmor betrayed the trouble of his soul. The code of men held him bound, and he could not break from it, though he divined in that moment how truly it was wrong.

"Jean, your dad started me in the cattle business," said Colmor, earnestly. "An' I'm doin' well now. An' when I asked him for Ann he said he'd be glad to have me in the family. . . . Well, when this talk of fight come up, I asked your dad to let me go in on his side. He wouldn't hear of it. But after a while, as the time passed an' he made more enemies, he finally consented. I reckon he needs me now. An' I can't back out, not even for Ann."

"I would if I were you," replied Jean, and knew that he lied.

"Jean, I'm gamblin' to come out of the fight," said Colmor, with a smile. He had no morbid fears nor presentiments, such as troubled Jean.

"Why, sure—you stand as good a chance as anyone," rejoined Jean. "It wasn't that I was worryin' about so much."

"What was it, then?" asked Ann, steadily.

"If Andrew *does* come through alive he'll have blood on his hands," returned Jean, with passion. "He can't come through without it. . . . I've begun to feel what it means to have killed my fellow men. . . . An' I'd rather your husband an' the father of your children never felt that."

Colmor did not take Jean as subtly as Ann did. She shrunk a little. Her dark eyes dilated. But Colmor showed nothing of her spiritual reaction. He was young. He had wild blood. He was loyal to the Isbels.

"Jean, never worry about my conscience," he said, with a keen look. "Nothin' would tickle me any more than to get a shot at every damn one of the Jorths."

That established Colmor's status in regard to the Jorth-Isbel feud. Jean had no more to say. He respected Ann's friend and felt poignant sorrow for Ann.

Gaston Isbel called for meat and drink to be set on the table for his guests. When his wishes had been complied with the women took the children into the adjoining cabin and shut the door.

"Hah! Wal, we can eat an' talk now."

First the newcomers wanted to hear particulars of what had happened. Blaisdell had told all he knew and had seen, but that was not sufficient. They plied Gaston Isbel with questions. Laboriously and ponderously he rehearsed the experiences of the fight at the ranch, according to his impressions. Bill Isbel was exhorted to talk, but he had of late manifested a sullen and taciturn disposition. In spite of Jean's vigilance Bill had continued to imbibe red liquor. Then Jean was called upon to relate all he had seen and done. It had been Jean's intention to keep his mouth shut, first for his own sake and, secondly, because he did not like to talk of his deeds. But when thus appealed to by these somber-faced, intent-eyed men he divined that the more carefully he described the cruelty and baseness of their enemies, and the more vividly he presented his participation in the first fight of the feud the more strongly he would bind these friends to the Isbel cause. So he talked for an hour, beginning with his meeting with Colter up on the Rim and ending with an account of his killing Greaves. His listeners sat through this long narrative with unabated interest and at the close they were leaning forward, breathless and tense.

"Ah! So Greaves got his desserts at last," exclaimed Gordon.

All the men around the table made comments, and the last, from Blue, was the one that struck Jean forcibly.

"Shore thet was a strange an' a hell of a way to kill Greaves. Why'd you do thet, Jean?"

"I told you. I wanted to avoid noise an' I hoped to get more of them."

Blue nodded his lean, eagle-like head and sat thoughtfully, as if not convinced of anything save Jean's prowess. After a moment Blue spoke again.

"Then, goin' back to Jean's tellin' aboot trackin' rustled cattle, I've got this to say. I've long suspected thet somebody livin' right heah in the valley has been drivin' off cattle an' dealin' with rustlers. An' now I'm shore of it."

This speech did not elicit the amaze from Gaston Isbel that Jean expected it would.

"You mean Greaves or some of his friends?"

"No. They wasn't none of them in the cattle business, like we are. Shore we all knowed Greaves was crooked. But what I'm figgerin' is thet some so-called honest man in our settlement has been makin' crooked deals."

Blue was a man of deeds rather than words, and so much strong speech from him, whom everybody knew to be remarkably reliable and keen, made a profound impression upon most of the Isbel faction. But, to Jean's surprise, his father did not rave. It was Blaisdell who supplied the rage and invective. Bill Isbel, also, was strangely indifferent to this new element in the condition of cattle dealing. Suddenly Jean caught a vague flash of thought, as if he had intercepted the thought of another's mind, and he wondered—could his brother Bill know anything about this crooked work alluded to by Blue? Dismissing the conjecture, Jean listened earnestly.

"An' if it's true it shore makes this difference—we cain't blame all the rustlin' on to Jorth," concluded Blue.

"Wal, it's not true," declared Gaston Isbel, roughly. "Jorth an' his Hash Knife Gang are at the bottom of all the rustlin' in the valley for years back. An' they've got to be wiped out!"

"Isbel, I reckon we'd all feel better if we talk straight," replied Blue, coolly. "I'm heah to stand by the Isbels. An' y'u know what thet means. But I'm not heah to fight Jorth because he may be a rustler. The others may have their own reasons, but mine is this—you once stood by me in Texas when I was needin' friends. Wal, I'm standin' by y'u now. Jorth is your enemy, an' so he is mine."

Gaston Isbel bowed to this ultimatum, scarcely less agitated than when Esther Isbel had denounced him. His rabid and morbid hate of Jorth had eaten into his heart to take possession there, like the parasite that battened upon the life of its victim. Blue's steely voice, his cold, gray eyes, showed the unbiased truth of the man, as well as his fidelity to his creed. Here again, but in a different manner, Gaston Isbel had the fact flung at him that other men must suffer, perhaps die, for his hate. And the very soul of the old rancher apparently rose in passionate revolt against the blind, headlong, elemental strength of his nature. So it seemed to Jean, who, in love and pity that hourly grew, saw through his father. Was it too late? Alas! Gaston Isbel could never be turned back! Yet something was altering his brooding, fixed mind.

"Wal," said Blaisdell, gruffly, "let's get down to business. . . . I'm for havin' Blue be foreman of this heah outfit, an' all of us to do as he says."

Gaston Isbel opposed this selection and indeed resented it. He intended to lead the Isbel faction.

"All right, then. Give us a hunch what we're goin' to do," replied Blaisdell.

"We're goin' to ride off on Jorth's trail—an' one way or another—kill him—*kill him!* . . . I reckon that'll end the fight."

What did old Isbel have in his mind? His listeners shook their heads.

"No," asserted Blaisdell. "Killin' Jorth might be the end of your desires, Isbel, but it'd never end *our* fight. We'll have gone too far. . . . If we take Jorth's trail from heah it means we've got to wipe out that rustler gang, or stay to the last man."

"Yes, by God!" exclaimed Fredericks.

"Let's drink to thet!" said Blue. Strangely they all turned to this Texas gunman, instinctively recognizing in him the brain and heart, and the past deeds, that fitted him for the leadership of such a clan. Blue had all in life to lose, and nothing to gain. Yet his spirit was such that he could not lean to all the possible gain of the future, and leave a debt unpaid. Then his voice, his look, his influence were those of a fighter. They all drank with him, even Jean, who hated liquor. And this act of drinking seemed the climax of the council. Preparations were at once begun for their departure on Jorth's trail.

Jean took but little time for his own needs. A horse, a blanket, a knapsack of meat and bread, a canteen, and his weapons, with all the ammunition he could pack, made up his outfit. He wore his buckskin suit, leggings, and moccasins. Very soon the cavalcade was ready to depart. Jean tried not to watch Bill Isbel say good-by to his children, but it was impossible not to. Whatever Bill was, as a man, he was father of those children, and he loved them. How strange that the little ones seemed to realize the meaning of this good-by! They were grave, somber-eyed, pale up to the last moment, then they broke down and wept. Did they sense that their father would never come back? Jean caught that dark, fatalistic presentiment. Bill Isbel's convulsed face showed that he also caught it. Jean did not see Bill say good-by to his wife. But he heard her. Old Gaston Isbel forgot to speak to the children, or else could not. He never looked at them. And his good-by to Ann was as if he were only riding to the village for a day. Jean saw woman's love, woman's intuition, woman's grief in her eyes. He could not escape her. "Oh, Jean! oh, brother!" she whispered as she enfolded him. "It's awful! It's wrong! Wrong! Wrong! . . . Good-by! . . . If killing *must* be—see that y'u kill the Jorths! . . . Good-by!"

Even in Ann, gentle and mild, the Isbel blood spoke at last. Jean gave Ann over to the pale-faced Colmor, who took her in his arms. Then Jean fled out to his horse. This cold-blooded devastation of a home was almost more than he could bear. There was love here. What would be left?

Colmor was the last one to come out to the horses. He did not walk erect, nor as one whose sight was clear. Then, as the silent, tense, grim men mounted their horses, Bill Isbel's eldest child, the boy, appeared in the door. His little form seemed instinct with a force vastly different from grief. His face was the face of an Isbel.

"Daddy—kill 'em all!" he shouted, with a passion all the fiercer for its incongruity to the treble voice.

So the poison had spread from father to son.

CHAPTER NINE

Half a mile from the Isbel ranch the cavalcade passed the log cabin of Evarts, father of the boy who had tended sheep with Bernardino.

It suited Gaston Isbel to halt here. No need to call! Evarts and his son appeared so quickly as to convince observers that they had been watching.

"Howdy, Jake!" said Isbel. "I'm wantin' a word with y'u alone."

"Shore, boss, git down an' come in," replied Evarts.

Isbel led him aside, and said something forcible that Jean divined from the very gesture which accompanied it. His father was telling Evarts that he was not to join the Isbel-Jorth war. Evarts had worked for the Isbels a long time, and his faithfulness, along with something stronger and darker, showed in his rugged face as he stubbornly opposed Isbel. The old man raised his voice: "No, I tell you. An' that settles it."

They returned to the horses, and, before mounting, Isbel, as if he remembered something, directed his somber gaze on young Evarts.

"Son, did you bury Bernardino?"

"Dad an' me went over yestiddy," replied the lad. "I shore was glad the coyotes hadn't been round."

"How aboot the sheep?"

"I left them there. I was goin' to stay, but bein' all alone—I got skeered. . . . The sheep was doin' fine. Good water an' some grass. An' this ain't time for varmints to hang round."

"Jake, keep your eye on that flock," returned Isbel. "An' if I shouldn't happen to come back y'u can call them sheep yours. . . . I'd like your boy to ride up to the village. Not with us, so anybody would see him. But afterward. We'll be at Abel Meeker's."

Again Jean was confronted with an uneasy premonition as to some idea or plan his father had not shared with his followers. When the cavalcade started on again Jean rode to his father's side and asked him why he had wanted the Evarts boy to come to Grass Valley. And the old man replied that, as the boy could run to and fro in the village without danger, he might be useful in reporting what was going on at Greaves's store, where undoubtedly the Jorth gang would hold forth. This appeared reasonable enough, therefore Jean smothered the objection he had meant to make.

The valley road was deserted. When, a mile farther on, the riders passed a group of cabins, just on the outskirts of the village, Jean's quick eye caught sight of curious and evidently frightened people trying to see while they avoided being seen. No doubt the whole settlement was in a state of suspense and terror. Not unlikely this dark, closely grouped band of horsemen appeared to them as Jorth's gang had looked to Jean. It was an orderly, trotting march that manifested neither hurry nor excitement. But any Western eye could have caught the singular aspect of such a group, as if the intent of the riders was a visible thing.

Soon they reached the outskirts of the village. Here their approach had been watched for or had been already reported. Jean saw men, women, children peeping from behind cabins and from half-opened doors. Farther on Jean espied the dark figures of men, slipping out the back way through orchards and gardens and running north, toward the center of the village. Could these be friends of the Jorth crowd, on the way with warnings of the approach of the Isbels? Jean felt convinced of it. He was learning that his father had not been absolutely correct in his estimation of the way Jorth and his followers were regarded by their neighbors. Not improbably there were really many villagers who, being more interested in sheep raising than in cattle, had an honest leaning toward the Jorths. Some, too, no doubt, had leanings that were dishonest in deed if not in sincerity.

Gaston Isbel led his clan straight down the middle of the wide road of Grass Valley until he reached a point opposite Abel Meeker's cabin. Jean espied the same curiosity from behind Meeker's door and windows as had been shown all along the road. But presently, at Isbel's call, the door opened and a short, swarthy man appeared. He carried a rifle.

"Howdy, Gass!" he said. "What's the good word?"

"Wal, Abel, it's not good, but bad. An' it's shore started," replied Isbel. "I'm askin' y'u to let me have your cabin."

"You're welcome. I'll send the folks 'round to Jim's," returned Meeker. "An' if y'u want me, I'm with y'u, Isbel."

"Thanks, Abel, but I'm not leadin' any more kin an' friends into this heah deal."

"Wal, jest as you say. But I'd like damn bad to jine with y'u. . . . My brother Ted was shot last night."

"Ted! Is he daid?" ejaculated Isbel, blankly.

"We can't find out," replied Meeker. "Jim says thet Jeff Campbell said thet Ted went into Greaves's place last night. Greaves allus was friendly to Ted, but Greaves wasn't thar—"

"No, he shore wasn't," interrupted Isbel, with a dark smile, "an' he never will be there again."

Meeker nodded with slow comprehension and a shade crossed his face.

"Wal, Campbell claimed he'd heerd from some one who was thar. Anyway, the Jorths were drinkin' hard, an' they raised a row with Ted—same old sheep talk—an' somebody shot him. Campbell said Ted was thrown out back, an' he was shore he wasn't killed."

"Ahuh! Wal, I'm sorry, Abel, your family had to lose in this. Maybe Ted's not bad hurt. I shore hope so. . . . An' y'u an' Jim keep out of the fight, anyway."

"All right, Isbel. But I reckon I'll give y'u a hunch. If this heah fight lasts long the whole damn Basin will be in it, on one side or t'other."

"Abe, you're talkin' sense," broke in Blaisdell. "An' that's why we're up heah for quick action."

"I heerd y'u got Daggs," whispered Meeker, as he peered all around.

"Wal, y'u heerd correct," drawled Blaisdell.

Meeker muttered strong words into his beard. "Say, was Daggs in thet Jorth outfit?"

"He *was*. But he walked right into Jean's forty-four. . . . An' I reckon his carcass would show some more."

"An' whar's Guy Isbel?" demanded Meeker.

"Daid an' buried, Abel," replied Gaston Isbel. "An' now I'd be obliged if y'u'll hurry your folks away, an' let us have your cabin an' corral. Have y'u got any hay for the hosses?"

"Shore. The barn's half full," replied Meeker, as he turned away. "Come on in."

"No. We'll wait till you've gone."

When Meeker had gone, Isbel and his men sat their horses and looked about them and spoke low. Their advent had been expected, and the little town awoke to the imminence of the impending battle. Inside Meeker's house there was the sound of indistinct voices of women and the bustle incident to a hurried vacating.

Across the wide road people were peering out on all sides, some hiding, others walking to and fro, from fence to fence, whispering in little groups. Down the wide road, at the point where it turned, stood Greaves's fort-like stone house. Low, flat, isolated, with its dark, eye-like windows, it presented a forbidding and sinister aspect. Jean distinctly saw the forms of men, some dark, others in shirt sleeves, come to the wide door and look down the road.

"Wal, I reckon only aboot five hundred good hoss steps are separatin' us from that outfit," drawled Blaisdell.

No one replied to his jocularity. Gaston Isbel's eyes narrowed to a slit in his furrowed face and he kept them fastened upon Greaves's store. Blue, likewise, had a somber cast of countenance, not, perhaps, any darker nor grimmer than those of his comrades, but more representative of intense preoccupation of mind. The look of him thrilled Jean, who could sense its deadliness, yet could not grasp any more. Altogether, the manner of the villagers and the watchful pacing to and fro of the Jorth followers and the silent, boding front of Isbel and his men summed up for Jean the menace of the moment that must very soon change to a terrible reality.

At a call from Meeker, who stood at the back of the cabin, Gaston Isbel rode into the yard, followed by the others of his party. "Somebody look after the hosses," ordered Isbel, as he dismounted and took his rifle and pack. "Better leave the saddles on, leastways till we see what's comin' off."

Jean and Bill Isbel led the horses back to the corral. While watering and feeding them, Jean somehow received the impression that Bill was trying to speak, to confide in him, to unburden himself of some load. This peculiarity of Bill's had become marked when he was perfectly sober. Yet he had never spoken or even begun anything unusual. Upon the present occasion, however, Jean believed that his brother might have gotten rid of his emotion, or whatever it was, had they not been interrupted by Colmor.

"Boys, the old man's orders are for us to sneak round on three sides of Greaves's store, keepin' out of gunshot till we find good cover, an' then crawl closer an' to pick off any of Jorth's gang who shows himself."

Bill Isbel strode off without a reply to Colmor.

"Well, I don't think so much of that," said Jean, ponderingly. "Jorth has lots of friends here. Somebody might pick us off."

"I kicked, but the old man shut me up. He's not to be bucked ag'in' now. Struck me as powerful queer. But no wonder."

"Maybe he knows best. Did he say anythin' about what he an' the rest of them are goin' to do?"

"Nope. Blue taxed him with that an' got the same as me. I reckon we'd better try it out, for a while, anyway."

"Looks like he wants us to keep out of the fight," replied Jean, thoughtfully. "Maybe, though . . . Dad's no fool. Colmor, you wait here till I get out of sight.

I'll go round an' come up as close as advisable behind Greaves's store. You take the right side. An' keep hid."

With that Jean strode off, going around the barn, straight out the orchard lane to the open flat, and then climbing a fence to the north of the village. Presently he reached a line of sheds and corrals, to which he held until he arrived at the road. This point was about a quarter of a mile from Greaves's store, and around the bend. Jean sighted no one. The road, the fields, the yards, the backs of the cabins all looked deserted. A blight had settled down upon the peaceful activities of Grass Valley. Crossing the road, Jean began to circle until he came close to several cabins, around which he made a wide detour. This took him to the edge of the slope, where brush and thickets afforded him a safe passage to a line directly back of Greaves's store. Then he turned toward it. Soon he was again approaching a cabin of that side, and some of its inmates descried him. Their actions attested to their alarm. Jean half expected a shot from this quarter, such were his growing doubts, but he was mistaken. A man, unknown to Jean, closely watched his guarded movements and then waved a hand, as if to signify to Jean that he had nothing to fear. After this act he disappeared. Jean believed that he had been recognized by some one not antagonistic to the Isbels. Therefore he passed the cabin and, coming to a thick scrub oak tree that offered shelter, he hid there to watch. From this spot he could see the back of Greaves's store, at a distance probably too far for a rifle bullet to reach. Before him, as far as the store, and on each side, extended the village common. In front of the store ran the road. Jean's position was such that he could not command sight of this road down toward Meeker's house, a fact that disturbed him. Not satisfied with this stand, he studied his surroundings in the hope of espying a better. And he discovered what he thought would be a more favorable position, although he could not see much farther down the road. Jean went back around the cabin and, coming out into the open to the right, he got the corner of Greaves's barn between him and the window of the store. Then he boldly hurried into the open, and soon reached an old wagon, from behind which he proposed to watch. He could not see either window or door of the store, but if any of the Jorth contingent came out the back way they would be within reach of his rifle. Jean took the risk of being shot at from either side.

So sharp and roving was his sight that he soon espied Colmor slipping along behind the trees some hundred yards to the left. All his efforts to catch a glimpse of Bill, however, were fruitless. And this appeared strange to Jean, for there were several good places on the right from which Bill could have commanded the front of Greaves's store and the whole west side.

Colmor disappeared among some shrubbery, and Jean seemed left alone to watch a deserted, silent village. Watching and listening, he felt that the time dragged. Yet the shadows cast by the sun showed him that, no matter how tense he felt and how the moments seemed hours, they were really flying.

Suddenly Jean's ears rang with the vibrant shock of a rifle report. He jerked up, strung and thrilling. It came from in front of the store. It was followed by revolver shots, heavy, booming. Three he counted, and the rest were too close together to enumerate. A single hoarse yell pealed out, somehow trenchant and triumphant. Other yells, not so wild and strange, muffled the first one. Then silence clapped down on the store and the open square.

Jean was deadly certain that some of the Jorth clan would show themselves. He strained to still the trembling those sudden shots and that significant yell had caused him. No man appeared. No more sounds caught Jean's ears. The suspense, then, grew unbearable. It was not that he could not wait for an enemy to appear but that he could not wait to learn what had happened. Every moment that he stayed there, with hands like steel on his rifle, with eyes of a falcon, but added to a dreadful, dark certainty of disaster. A rifle shot swiftly followed by revolver shots! What could they mean? Revolver shots of different caliber, surely fired by different men! What could they mean? It was not these shots that accounted for Jean's dread, but the yell which had followed. All his intelligence and all his nerve were not sufficient to fight down the feeling of calamity. And at last, yielding to it, he left his post, and ran like a deer across the open, through the cabin yard, and around the edge of the slope to the road. Here his caution brought him to a halt. Not a living thing crossed his vision. Breaking into a run, he soon reached the back of Meeker's place and entered, to hurry forward to the cabin.

Colmor was there in the yard, breathing hard, his face working, and in front of him crouched several of the men with rifles ready. The road, to Jean's flashing glance, was apparently deserted. Blue sat on the doorstep, lighting a cigarette. Then on the moment Blaisdell strode to the door of the cabin. Jean had never seen him look like that.

"Jean—look—down the road," he said, brokenly, and with big hand shaking he pointed down toward Greaves's store.

Like lightning Jean's glance shot down—down—down—until it stopped to fix upon the prostrate form of a man, lying in the middle of the road. A man of lengthy build, shirt-sleeved arms flung wide, white head in the dust—dead. Jean's recognition was as swift as his sight. His father! They had killed him! The Jorths! It was done. His father's premonition of death had not been false. And then, after these flashing thoughts, came a sense of blankness, momentarily almost oblivion, that gave place to rending of the heart. That pain Jean had known only at the death of his mother. It passed, this agonizing pang, and its icy pressure yielded to a rushing gust of blood, fiery as hell.

"Who—did it?" whispered Jean.

"Jorth!" replied Blaisdell, huskily. "Son, we couldn't hold your dad back. . . . We couldn't. He was like a lion. . . . An' he throwed his life away! Oh, if it hadn't been for that it'd not be so awful. Shore, we come heah to shoot an' be shot. But not like that. . . . By God, it was murder—murder!"

Jean's mute lips framed a query easily read.

"Tell him, Blue. I cain't," continued Blaisdell, and he tramped back into the cabin.

"Set down, Jean, an' take things easy," said Blue, calmly. "You know we all reckoned we'd git plugged one way or another in this deal. An' shore it doesn't matter how much a fellar gits it. All thet ought to bother us is to make shore the other outfit bites the dust—same as your dad had to."

Under this man's tranquil presence, all the more quieting because it seemed to be so deadly sure and cool, Jean felt the uplift of his dark spirit, the acceptance of fatality, the mounting control of faculties that must wait. The little gunman seemed to have about his inert presence something that suggested a rattlesnake's inherent knowledge of its destructiveness. Jean sat down and wiped his clammy face.

"Jean, your dad reckoned to square accounts with Jorth, an' save us all," began Blue, puffing out a cloud of smoke. "But he reckoned too late. Mebbe years ago—or even not long ago—if he'd called Jorth out man to man there'd never been any Jorth-Isbel war. Gaston Isbel's conscience woke too late. That's how I figger it."

"Hurry! Tell me—how it—happened," panted Jean.

"Wal, a little while after y'u left I seen your dad writin' on a leaf he tore out of a book—Meeker's Bible, as y'u can see. I thought thet was funny. An' Blaisdell gave me a hunch. Pretty soon along comes young Evarts. The old man calls him out of our hearin' an' talks to him. Then I seen him give the boy somethin', which I afterward figgered was what he wrote on the leaf out of the Bible. Me an' Blaisdell both tried to git out of him what thet meant. But not a word. I kept watchin' an' after a while I seen young Evarts slip out the back way. Mebbe half an hour I seen a bare-legged kid cross the road an' go into Greaves's store. . . . Then shore I tumbled to your dad. He'd sent a note to Jorth to come out an' meet him face to face, man to man! . . . Shore it was like readin' what your dad had wrote. But I didn't say nothin' to Blaisdell. I jest watched."

Blue drawled these last words, as if he enjoyed remembrance of his keen reasoning. A smile wreathed his thin lips. He drew twice on the cigarette and emitted another cloud of smoke. Quite suddenly then he changed. He made a rapid gesture—the whip of a hand, significant and passionate. And swift words followed:

"Colonel Lee Jorth stalked out of the store—out into the road—mebbe a hundred steps. Then he halted. He wore his long black coat an' his wide black hat, an' he stood like a stone.

"'What the hell!' burst out Blaisdell, comin' out of his trance.

"The rest of us jest looked. I'd forgot your dad, for the minnit. So had all of us. But we remembered soon enough when we seen him stalk out. Everybody had a hunch then. I called him. Blaisdell begged him to come back. All the fellars had a say. No use! Then I shore cussed him an' told him it was plain as day thet Jorth didn't hit me like an honest man. I can sense such things. I knew Jorth had a trick up his sleeve. I've not been a gun fighter fer nothin'.

"Your dad had no rifle. He packed his gun at his hip. He jest stalked down thet road like a giant, goin' faster an' faster, holdin' his head high. It shore was fine to see him. But I was sick. I heerd Blaisdell groan, an' Fredericks thar cussed somethin' fierce. . . . When your dad halted—I reckon aboot fifty steps from Jorth—then we all went numb. I heerd your dad's voice—then Jorth's. They cut like knives. Y'u could shore heah the hate they hed fer each other."

Blue had become a little husky. His speech had grown gradually to denote his feeling. Underneath his serenity there was a different order of man.

"I reckon both your dad an' Jorth went fer their guns at the same time—an even break. But jest as they drew, some one shot a rifle from the store. Must hev been a forty-five seventy. A big gun! The bullet must have hit your dad low down, aboot the middle. He acted thet way, sinkin' to his knees. An' he was wild in shootin'—so wild thet he must hev missed. Then he wabbled—an' Jorth run in a dozen steps, shootin' fast, till your dad fell over. . . . Jorth run closer, bent over him, an' then straightened up with an Apache yell, if I ever heerd one. . . . An' then Jorth backed slow—lookin' all the time—backed to the store, an' went in."

Blue's voice ceased. Jean seemed suddenly released from an impelling magnet that now dropped him to some numb, dizzy depth. Blue's lean face grew hazy. Then Jean bowed his head in his hands, and sat there, while a slight tremor shook all his muscles at once. He grew deathly cold and deathly sick. This paroxysm slowly wore away, and Jean grew conscious of a dull amaze at the apparent deadness of his spirit. Blaisdell placed a huge, kindly hand on his shoulder.

"Brace up, son!" he said, with voice now clear and resonant. "Shore it's what your dad expected—an' what we all must look for. . . . If y'u was goin' to kill

Jorth before—think how —— —— shore y'u're goin' to kill him now."

"Blaisdell's talkin'," put in Blue, and his voice had a cold ring. "Lee Jorth will never see the sun rise ag'in!"

These calls to the primitive in Jean, to the Indian, were not in vain. But even so, when the dark tide rose in him, there was still a haunting consciousness of the cruelty of this singular doom imposed upon him. Strangely Ellen Jorth's face floated back in the depths of his vision, pale, fading, like the face of a spirit floating by.

"Blue," said Blaisdell, "let's get Isbel's body soon as we dare, an' bury it. Reckon we can, right after dark."

"Shore," replied Blue. "But y'u fellars figger thet out. I'm thinkin' hard. I've got somethin' on my mind."

Jean grew fascinated by the looks and speech and action of the little gunman. Blue, indeed, had something on his mind. And it boded ill to the men in that dark square stone house down the road. He paced to and fro in the yard, back and forth on the path to the gate, and then he entered the cabin to stalk up and down, faster and faster, until all at once he halted as if struck, to upfling his right arm in a singular fierce gesture.

"Jean, call the men in," he said, tersely.

They all filed in, sinister and silent, with eager faces turned to the little Texan. His dominance showed markedly.

"Gordon, y'u stand in the door an' keep your eye peeled," went on Blue. . . . "Now, boys, listen! I've thought it all out. This game of man huntin' is the same to me as cattle raisin' is to y'u. An' my life in Texas all comes back to me, I reckon, in good stead fer us now. I'm goin' to kill Lee Jorth! Him first, an' mebbe his brothers. I had to think of a good many ways before I hit on one I reckon will be shore. It's got to be *shore.* Jorth has got to die! Wal, heah's my plan. . . . Thet Jorth outfit is drinkin' some, we can gamble on it. They're not goin' to leave thet store. An' of course they'll be expectin' us to start a fight. I reckon they'll look fer some such siege as they held round Isbel's ranch. But we shore ain't goin' to do thet. I'm goin' to surprise thet outfit. There's only one man among them who is dangerous, an' thet's Queen. I know Queen. But he doesn't know me. An' I'm goin' to finish my job before he gets acquainted with me. After thet, all right!"

Blue paused a moment, his eyes narrowing down, his whole face setting in hard cast of intense preoccupation, as if he visualized a scene of extraordinary nature.

"Wal, what's your trick?" demanded Blaisdell.

"Y'u all know Greaves's store," continued Blue. "How them winders have wooden shutters thet keep a light from showin' outside? Wal, I'm gamblin' thet as soon as it's dark Jorth's gang will be celebratin'. They'll be drinkin' an' they'll have a light, an' the winders will be shut. They're not goin' to worry none aboot us. Thet store is like a fort. It won't burn. An' shore they'd never think of us chargin' them in there. Wal, as soon as it's dark, we'll go round behind the lots an' come up jest acrost the road from Greaves's. I reckon we'd better leave Isbel where he lays till this fight's over. Mebbe y'u'll have more 'n him to bury. We'll crawl behind them bushes in front of Coleman's yard. An' heah's where Jean comes in. He'll take an ax, an' his guns, of course, an' do some of his Injun sneakin' round to the back of Greaves's store. . . . An', Jean, y'u must do a slick job of this. But I reckon it'll be easy fer you. Back there it'll be dark as pitch, fer anyone lookin' out of the store. An' I'm figgerin y'u can take your time an' crawl right up. Now if y'u don't remember how Greaves's back yard looks I'll tell y'u."

Here Blue dropped on one knee to the floor and with a finger he traced a map of

Greaves's barn and fence, the back door and window, and especially a break in the stone foundation which led into a kind of cellar where Greaves stored wood and other things that could be left outdoors.

"Jean, I take particular pains to show y'u where this hole is," said Blue, "because if the gang runs out y'u could duck in there an' hide. An' if they run out into the yard—wal, y'u'd make it a sorry run fer them. . . . Wal, when y'u've crawled up close to Greaves's back door, an' waited long enough to see an' listen—then you're to run fast an' swing your ax smash ag'in' the winder. Take a quick peep in if y'u want to. It might help. Then jump quick an' take a swing at the door. Y'u'll be standin' to one side, so if the gang shoots through the door they won't hit y'u. Bang thet door good an' hard. . . . Wal, now's where I come in. When y'u swing thet ax I'll shore run fer the front of the store. Jorth an' his outfit will be some attentive to thet poundin' of yours on the back door. So I reckon. An' they'll be *lookin'* thet way. I'll run in—yell—an' throw my guns on Jorth."

"Humph! Is that all?" ejaculated Blaisdell.

"I reckon thet's all an' I'm figgerin' it's a hell of a lot," responded Blue, dryly. "Thet's what Jorth will think."

"Where do we come in?"

"Wal, y'u all can back me up," replied Blue, dubiously. "Y'u see, my plan goes as far as killin' Jorth—an' mebbe his brothers. Mebbe I'll get a crack at Queen. But I'll be shore of Jorth. After thet all depends. Mebbe it'll be easy fer me to get out. An' if I do y'u fellars will know it an' can fill thet storeroom full of bullets."

"Wal, Blue, with all due respect to y'u, I shore don't like your plan," declared Blaisdell. "Success depends upon too many little things any one of which might go wrong."

"Blaisdell, I reckon I know this heah game better than y'u," replied Blue. "A gun fighter goes by instinct. This trick will work."

"But suppose that front door to Greaves's store is barred," protested Blaisdell.

"It hasn't got any bar," said Blue.

"Y'u're shore?"

"Yes, I reckon," replied Blue.

"Hell, man! Aren't y'u takin' a terrible chance?" queried Blaisdell.

Blue's answer to that was a look that brought the blood to Blaisdell's face. Only then did the rancher really comprehend how the little gunman had taken such desperate chances before, and meant to take them now, not with any hope or assurance of escaping with his life, but to live up to his peculiar code of honor.

"Blaisdell, did y'u ever heah of me in Texas?" he queried, dryly.

"Wal, no, Blue, I cain't swear I did," replied the rancher, apologetically. "An' Isbel was always sort of mysterious aboot his acquaintance with you."

"My name's not Blue."

"Ahuh! Wal, what is it, then—if I'm safe to ask?" returned Blaisdell, gruffly.

"It's King Fisher," replied Blue.

The shock that stiffened Blaisdell must have been communicated to the others. Jean certainly felt amaze, and some other emotion not fully realized, when he found himself face to face with one of the most notorious characters ever known in Texas—an outlaw long supposed to be dead.

"Men, I reckon I'd kept my secret if I'd any idee of comin' out of this Isbel-Jorth war alive," said Blue. "But I'm goin' to cash. I feel it heah. . . . Isbel was my friend. He saved me from bein' lynched in Texas. An' so I'm goin' to kill Jorth. Now I'll take it kind of y'u—if any of y'u come out of this alive—to tell who I was an' why I was on the Isbel side. Because this sheep an' cattle war—this talk of Jorth an' the Hash Knife Gang—it makes me sick. I *know* there's been crooked work on Isbel's side, too. An' I never want it on record thet I killed Jorth because he was a rustler."

"By God, Blue! it's late in the day for such talk," burst out Blaisdell, in rage and amaze. "But I reckon y'u know what y'u're talkin' aboot. . . . Wal, I shore don't want to heah it."

At this juncture Bill Isbel quietly entered the cabin, too late to hear any of Blue's statement. Jean was positive of that, for as Blue was speaking those last revealing words Bill's heavy boots had resounded on the gravel path outside. Yet something in Bill's look or in the way Blue averted his lean face or in the entrance of Bill at that particular moment, or all these together, seemed to Jean to add further mystery to the long secret causes leading up to the Jorth-Isbel war. Did Bill know what Blue knew? Jean had an inkling that he did. And on the moment, so perplexing and bitter, Jean gazed out the door, down the deserted road to where his dead father lay, white-haired and ghastly in the sunlight.

"Blue, you could have kept that to yourself, as well as your real name," interposed Jean, with bitterness. "It's too late now for either to do any good. . . . But I appreciate your friendship for dad, an' I'm ready to help carry out your plan."

That decision of Jean's appeared to put an end to protest or argument from Blaisdell or any of the others. Blue's fleeting dark smile was one of satisfaction. Then upon most of this group of men seemed to settle a grim restraint. They went out and walked and watched; they came in again, restless and somber. Jean thought that he must have bent his gaze a thousand times down the road to the tragic figure of his father. That sight roused all emotions in his breast, and the one that stirred there most was pity. The pity of it! Gaston Isbel lying face down in the dust of the village street! Patches of blood showed on the back of his vest and one white-sleeved shoulder. He had been shot through. Every time Jean saw this blood he had to stifle a gathering of wild, savage impulses.

Meanwhile the afternoon hours dragged by and the village remained as if its inhabitants had abandoned it. Not even a dog showed on the side road. Jorth and some of his men came out in front of the store and sat on the steps, in close convening groups. Every move they made seemed significant of their confidence and importance. About sunset they went back into the store, closing door and window shutters. Then Blaisdell called the Isbel faction to have food and drink. Jean felt no hunger. And Blue, who had kept apart from the others, showed no desire to eat. Neither did he smoke, though early in the day he had never been without a cigarette between his lips.

Twilight fell and darkness came. Not a light showed anywhere in the blackness.

"Wal, I reckon it's aboot time," said Blue, and he led the way out of the cabin to the back of the lot. Jean strode behind him, carrying his rifle and an ax. Silently the other men followed. Blue turned to the left and led through the field until he came within sight of a dark line of trees.

"Thet's where the road turns off," he said to Jean. "An' heah's the back of Coleman's place. . . . Wal, Jean, good luck!"

Jean felt the grip of a steel-like hand, and in the darkness he caught the gleam of Blue's eyes. Jean had no response in words for the laconic Blue, but he wrung the hard, thin hand and hurried away in the darkness.

Once alone, his part of the business at hand rushed him into eager thrilling action. This was the sort of work he was fitted to do. In this instance it was important, but it seemed to him that Blue had coolly taken the perilous part. And this cowboy with gray in his thin hair was in reality the great King Fisher! Jean marveled at the fact. And he shivered all over for Jorth. In ten minutes—fifteen, more or less, Jorth would lie gasping bloody froth and sinking down. Something in the dark, lonely, silent, oppressive summer night told Jean this. He strode on swiftly. Crossing the road at a run, he kept on over the ground he had traversed during the afternoon, and in a few moments he stood breathing hard at the edge of the common behind Greaves's store.

A pin point of light penetrated the blackness. It made Jean's heart leap. The Jorth contingent were burning the big lamp that hung in the center of Greaves's store. Jean listened. Loud voices and coarse laughter sounded discord on the melancholy silence of the night. What Blue had called his instinct had surely guided him aright. Death of Gaston Isbel was being celebrated by revel.

In a few moments Jean had regained his breath. Then all his faculties set intensely to the action at hand. He seemed to magnify his hearing and his sight. His movements made no sound. He gained the wagon, where he crouched a moment.

The ground seemed a pale, obscure medium, hardly more real than the gloom above it. Through this gloom of night, which looked thick like a cloud, but was really clear, shone the thin, bright point of light, accentuating the black square that was Greaves's store. Above this stood a gray line of tree foliage, and then the intensely dark-blue sky studded with white, cold stars.

A hound bayed lonesomely somewhere in the distance. Voices of men sounded more distinctly, some deep and low, others loud, unguarded, with the vacant note of thoughtlessness.

Jean gathered all his forces, until sense of sight and hearing were in exquisite accord with the suppleness and lightness of his movements. He glided on about ten short, swift steps before he halted. That was as far as his piercing eyes could penetrate. If there had been a guard stationed outside the store Jean would have seen him before being seen. He saw the fence, reached it, entered the yard, glided in the dense shadow of the barn until the black square began to loom gray—the color of stone at night. Jean peered through the obscurity. No dark figure of a man showed against that gray wall—only a black patch, which must be the hole in the foundation mentioned. A ray of light now streaked out from the little black window. To the right showed the wide, black door.

Farther on Jean glided silently. Then he halted. There was no guard outside. Jean heard the clink of a cup, the lazy drawl of a Texan, and then a strong, harsh voice—Jorth's. It strung Jean's whole being tight and vibrating. Inside he was on fire while cold thrills rippled over his skin. It took tremendous effort of will to hold himself back another instant to listen, to look, to feel, to make sure. And that instant charged him with a mighty current of hot blood, straining, throbbing, damming.

When Jean leaped this current burst. In a few swift bounds he gained his point halfway between door and window. He leaned his rifle against the stone wall. Then he swung the ax. Crash! The window shutter split and rattled to the floor inside. The silence then broke with a hoarse, "What's thet?"

With all his might Jean swung the heavy ax on the door. Smash! The lower half caved in and banged to the floor. Bright light flared out the hole.

"Look out!" yelled a man, in loud alarm. "They're batterin' the back door!"

Jean swung again, high on the splintered door. Crash! Pieces flew inside.

"They've got axes," hoarsely shouted another voice. "Shove the counter ag'in' the door."

"No!" thundered a voice of authority that denoted terror as well. "Let them come in. Pull your guns an' take to cover!"

"They ain't comin' in," was the hoarse reply. "They'll shoot in on us from the dark."

"Put out the lamp!" yelled another.

Jean's third heavy swing caved in part of the upper half of the door. Shouts and curses intermingled with the sliding of benches across the floor and the hard shuffle of boots. This confusion seemed to be split and silenced by a piercing yell, of different caliber, of terrible meaning. It stayed Jean's swing—caused him to drop the ax and snatch up his rifle.

"Don't anybody move!"

Like a steel whip this voice cut the silence. It belonged to Blue. Jean swiftly bent to put his eye to a crack in the door. Most of those visible seemed to have been frozen into unnatural positions. Jorth stood rather in front of his men, hatless and coatless, one arm outstretched, and his dark profile set toward a little man just inside the door. This man was Blue. Jean needed only one flashing look at Blue's face, at his leveled, quivering guns, to understand why he had chosen this trick.

"Who're—you?" demanded Jorth, in husky pants.

"Reckon I'm Isbel's right-hand man," came the biting reply. "Once tolerable well known in Texas. . . . *King Fisher!*"

The name must have been a guarantee of death. Jorth recognized this outlaw and realized his own fate. In the lamplight his face turned a pale greenish white. His outstretched hand began to quiver down.

Blue's left gun seemed to leap up and flash red and explode. Several heavy reports merged almost as one. Jorth's arm jerked limply, flinging his gun. And his body sagged in the middle. His hands fluttered like crippled wings and found their way to his abdomen. His death-pale face never changed its set look nor position toward Blue. But his gasping utterance was one of horrible mortal fury and terror. Then he began to sway, still with that strange, rigid set of his face toward his slayer, until he fell.

His fall broke the spell. Even Blue, like the gunman he was, had paused to watch Jorth in his last mortal action. Jorth's followers began to draw and shoot. Jean saw Blue's return fire bring down a huge man, who fell across Jorth's body. Then Jean, quick as the thought that actuated him, raised his rifle and shot at the big lamp. It burst in a flare. It crashed to the floor. Darkness followed—a blank, thick, enveloping mantle. Then red flashes of guns emphasized the blackness. Inside the store there broke loose a pandemonium of shots, yells, curses, and thudding boots. Jean shoved his rifle barrel inside the door and, holding it low down, he moved it to and fro while he worked lever and trigger until the magazine was empty. Then, drawing his six-shooter, he emptied that. A roar of rifles from the front of the store told Jean that his comrades had entered the fray. Bullets zipped through the door he had broken. Jean ran swiftly round the corner, taking care to sheer off a little to the left, and when he got clear of the building he saw a line of flashes in the middle of the road. Blaisdell and the others were firing into the door of the store. With nimble fingers Jean reloaded his rifle. Then swiftly he ran across the road and down to get behind his comrades. Their shooting had slackened. Jean saw dark forms coming his way.

"Hello, Blaisdell!" he called, warningly.

"That y'u, Jean?" returned the rancher, looming up. "Wal, we wasn't worried aboot y'u."

"Blue?" queried Jean, sharply.

A little, dark figure shuffled past Jean. "Howdy, Jean!" said Blue, dryly. "Y'u shore did your part. Reckon I'll need to be tied up, but I ain't hurt much."

"Colmor's hit," called the voice of Gordon, a few yards distant. "Help me, somebody!"

Jean ran to help Gordon uphold the swaying Colmor. "Are you hurt—bad?" asked Jean, anxiously. The young man's head rolled and hung. He was breathing hard and did not reply. They had almost to carry him.

"Come on, men!" called Blaisdell, turning back toward the others who were still firing. "We'll let well enough alone. . . . Fredericks, y'u an' Bill help me find the body of the old man. It's heah somewhere."

Farther on down the road the searchers stumbled over Gaston Isbel. They picked him up and followed Jean and Gordon, who were supporting the wounded Colmor. Jean looked back to see Blue dragging himself along in the rear. It was too dark to see distinctly; nevertheless, Jean got the impression that Blue was more severely wounded than he claimed to be. The distance to Meeker's cabin was not far, but it took what Jean felt to be a long and anxious time to get there. Colmor apparently rallied somewhat. When this procession entered Meeker's yard, Blue was lagging behind.

"Blue, how air y'u?" called Blaisdell, with concern.

"Wal, I got—my boots—on—anyhow," replied Blue, huskily.

He lurched into the yard and slid down on the grass and stretched out.

"Man! Y'u're hurt bad!" exclaimed Blaisdell. The others halted in their slow march and, as if by tacit, unspoken word, lowered the body of Isbel to the ground. Then Blaisdell knelt beside Blue. Jean left Colmor to Gordon and hurried to peer down into Blue's dim face.

"No, I ain't—hurt," said Blue, in a much weaker voice. "I'm—jest killed! . . . It was Queen! . . . Y'u all heerd me—Queen was—only bad man in that lot. I knowed it. . . . I could—hev killed him. . . . But I was—after Lee Jorth—an' his brothers. . . ."

Blue's voice failed there.

"Wal!" ejaculated Blaisdell.

"Shore was funny—Jorth's face—when I said—King Fisher," whispered Blue. "Funnier—when I bored—him through. . . . But it—was—Queen—"

His whisper died away

"Blue!" called Blaisdell, sharply. Receiving no answer, he bent lower in the starlight and placed a hand upon the man's breast.

"Wal, he's gone. . . . I wonder if he really was the old Texas King Fisher. No one would ever believe it. . . . But if he killed the Jorths, I'll shore believe him."

CHAPTER TEN

Two weeks of lonely solitude in the forest had worked incalculable change in Ellen Jorth.

Late in June her father and her two uncles had packed and ridden off with Daggs, Colter, and six other men, all heavily armed, some somber with drink, others hard and grim with a foretaste of fight. Ellen had not been given any orders. Her father had forgotten to bid her good-by or had avoided it. Their dark mission was stamped on their faces.

They had gone and, keen as had been Ellen's pang, nevertheless, their departure was a relief. She had heard them bluster and brag so often that she had her doubts of any great Jorth-Isbel war. Barking dogs did not bite. Somebody, perhaps on each side, would be badly wounded, possibly killed, and then the feud would go on as before, mostly talk. Many of her former impressions had faded. Development had been so rapid and continuous in her that she could look back to a day-by-day transformation. At night she had hated the sight of herself and when the dawn came she would rise, singing.

Jorth had left Ellen at home with the Mexican woman and Antonio. Ellen saw them only at meal times, and often not then, for she frequently visited old John Sprague or came home late to do her own cooking.

It was but a short distance up to Sprague's cabin, and since she had stopped riding the black horse, Spades, she walked. Spades was accustomed to having grain, and in the mornings he would come down to the ranch and whistle. Ellen had vowed she would never feed the horse and bade Antonio to do it. But one morning Antonio was absent. She fed Spades herself. When she laid a hand on him and when he rubbed his nose against her shoulder she was not quite so sure she hated him. "Why should I?" she queried. "A horse cain't help it if he belongs to—to—" Ellen was not sure of anything except that more and more it grew good to be alone.

A whole day in the lonely forest passed swiftly, yet it left a feeling of long time. She lived by her thoughts. Always the morning was bright, sunny, sweet and fragrant and colorful, and her mood was pensive, wistful, dreamy. And always, just as surely as the hours passed, thought intruded upon her happiness, and thought brought memory, and memory brought shame, and shame brought fight. Sunset after sunset she had dragged herself back to the ranch, sullen and sick and beaten. Yet she never ceased to struggle.

The July storms came, and the forest floor that had been so sear and brown and dry and dusty changed as if by magic. The green grass shot up, the flowers bloomed, and along the cañon beds of lacy ferns swayed in the wind and bent their graceful tips over the amber-colored water. Ellen haunted these cool dells, these pine-shaded, mossy-rocked ravines where the brooks tinkled and the deer came down to drink. She wandered alone. But there grew to be company in the aspens and the music of the little waterfalls. If she could have lived in that solitude always, never returning to the ranch home that reminded her of her name, she could have forgotten and have been happy.

She loved the storms. It was a dry country and she had learned through years to welcome the creamy clouds that rolled from the southwest. They came sailing and clustering and darkening at last to form a great, purple, angry mass that appeared to lodge against the mountain rim and burst into dazzling streaks of lightning and gray palls of rain. Lightning seldom struck near the ranch, but up on the Rim there was never a storm that did not splinter and crash some of the noble pines. During the storm season sheep herders and woodsmen generally did not camp under the pines. Fear of lightning was inborn in the natives, but for Ellen the dazzling white streaks or the tremendous splitting, crackling shock, or the thunderous boom and rumble along the battlements of the Rim had no terrors. A storm eased her breast. Deep in her heart was a hidden gathering storm. And somehow, to be out when the elements were warring, when the earth trembled and the heavens seemed to burst asunder, afforded her strange relief.

The summer days became weeks, and farther and farther they carried Ellen on the wings of solitude and loneliness until she seemed to look back years at the self she had hated. And always, when the dark memory impinged upon peace, she fought and fought until she seemed to be fighting hatred itself. Scorn of scorn and hate of hate! Yet even her battles grew to be dreams. For when the inevitable retrospect brought back Jean Isbel and his love and her cowardly falsehood she would shudder a little and put an unconscious hand to her breast and utterly fail in her fight and drift off down to vague and wistful dreams. The clean and healing forest, with its whispering wind and imperious solitude, had come between Ellen and the meaning of the squalid sheep ranch, with its travesty of home, its tragic owner. And it was coming between her two selves, the one that she had been forced to be and the other that she did not know—the thinker, the dreamer, the romancer, the one who lived in fancy the life she loved.

The summer morning dawned that brought Ellen strange tidings. They must have been created in her sleep, and now were realized in the glorious burst of golden sun, in the sweep of creamy clouds across the blue, in the solemn music of the wind in the pines, in the wild screech of the blue jays and the noble bugle of a stag. These heralded the day as no ordinary day. Something was going to happen to her. She divined it. She felt it. And she trembled. Nothing beautiful, hopeful, wonderful could ever happen to Ellen Jorth. She had been born to disaster, to suffer, to be forgotten, and die alone. Yet all nature about her seemed a magnificent rebuke to her morbidness. The same spirit that came out there with the thick, amber light was in her. She lived, and something in her was stronger than mind.

Ellen went to the door of her cabin, where she flung out her arms, driven to embrace this nameless purport of the morning. And a well-known voice broke in upon her rapture.

"Wal, lass, I like to see you happy an' I hate myself fer comin'. Because I've been to Grass Valley fer two days an' I've got news."

Old John Sprague stood there, with a smile that did not hide a troubled look.

"Oh! Uncle John! You startled me," exclaimed Ellen, shocked back to reality. And slowly she added: "Grass Valley! News?"

She put out an appealing hand, which Sprague quickly took in his own, as if to reassure her.

"Yes, an' not bad so far as you Jorths are concerned," he replied. "The first Jorth-Isbel fight has come off. . . . Reckon you remember makin' me promise to tell you if I heerd anythin'. Wal, I didn't wait fer you to come up."

"So," Ellen heard her voice calmly saying. What was this lying calm when there seemed to be a stone hammer at her heart? The first fight—not so bad for the Jorths! Then it had been bad for the Isbels. A sudden, cold stillness fell upon her senses.

"Let's sit down—outdoors," Sprague was saying. "Nice an' sunny this—mornin'. An' besides, I left Grass Valley in the night—an' I'm tired. But excoose me from hangin' round thet village last night! There was shore—"

"Who—who was killed?" interrupted Ellen, her voice breaking low and deep.

"Guy Isbel an' Bill Jacobs on the Isbel side, an' Daggs, Craig, an' Greaves on your father's side," stated Sprague, with something of awed haste.

"Ah!" breathed Ellen, and she relaxed to sink back against the cabin wall.

Sprague seated himself on the log beside her, turning to face her, and he seemed burdened with grave and important matters.

"I heerd a good many conflictin' stories," he said, earnestly. "The village folks is all skeered an' there's no believin' their gossip. But I got what happened straight from Jake Evarts. The fight come off day before yestiddy. Your father's gang rode down to Isbel's ranch. Daggs was seen to be wantin' some of the Isbel hosses, so Evarts says. An' Guy Isbel an' Jacobs run out in the pasture. Daggs an' some others shot them down . . ."

"Killed them—that way?" put in Ellen, sharply.

"So Evarts says. He was on the ridge an' swears he seen it all. They killed Guy an' Jacobs in cold blood. No chance fer their lives—not even to fight! . . . Wal, then they surrounded the Isbel cabin. The fight lasted all thet day an' all night an' the next day. Evarts says Guy an' Jacobs laid out thar all this time. An' a herd of hogs broke in the pasture an' was eatin' the dead bodies . . ."

"My God!" burst out Ellen. "Uncle John, y'u shore cain't mean my father wouldn't stop fightin' long enough to drive the hogs off an' bury those daid men?"

"Evarts says they stopped fightin', all right, but it was to watch the hogs," declared Sprague. "An' then, what d' ye think? The wimminfolks come out—the red-headed one, Guy's wife, an' Jacobs's wife—they drove the hogs away an' buried their husbands right there in the pasture. Evarts says he seen the graves."

"It is the women who can teach these bloody Texans a lesson," declared Ellen, forcibly.

"Wal, Daggs was drunk, an' he got up from behind where the gang was hidin', an' dared the Isbels to come out. They shot him to pieces. An' thet night some one of the Isbels shot Craig, who was alone on guard. . . . An' last—this here's what I come to tell you—Jean Isbel slipped up in the dark on Greaves an' knifed him."

"Why did y'u want to tell me that particularly?" asked Ellen, slowly.

"Because I reckon the facts in the case are queer—an' because, Ellen, your name was mentioned," announced Sprague, positively.

"My name—mentioned?" echoed Ellen. Her horror and disgust gave way to a quickening process of thought, a mounting astonishment. "By whom?"

"Jean Isbel," replied Sprague, as if the name and the fact were momentous.

Ellen sat still as a stone, her hands between her knees. Slowly she felt the blood recede from her face, prickling her skin down below her neck. That name locked her thought.

"Ellen, it's a mighty queer story—too queer to be a lie," went on Sprague. "Now you listen! Evarts got this from Ted Meeker. An' Ted Meeker heerd it from Greaves, who didn't die till the next day after Jean Isbel knifed him. An' your dad shot Ted fer tellin' what he heerd. . . . No, Greaves wasn't killed outright. He was cut somethin' turrible—in two places. They wrapped him all up an' next day packed him in a wagon back to Grass Valley. Evarts says Ted Meeker was friendly with Greaves an' went to see him as he was layin' in his room next to the store. Wal, accordin' to Meeker's story, Greaves came to an' talked. He said he was sittin' there in the dark, shootin' occasionally at Isbel's cabin, when he heerd a rustle behind him in the grass. He knowed some one was crawlin' on him. But before he could get his gun around he was jumped by what he thought was a grizzly bear. But it was a man. He shut off Greaves's wind an' dragged him back in the ditch. An' he said: 'Greaves, it's the half-breed. An' he's goin' to cut you—*first for Ellen Jorth!* an' then for Gaston Isbel!' . . . Greaves said Jean ripped him with a bowie knife. . . . An' thet was all Greaves remembered. He died soon after tellin' this story. He must hev fought awful hard. Thet second cut Isbel gave him went clear through him. . . . Some of the gang was thar when Greaves talked, an' naturally they wondered why Jean Isbel said 'first for Ellen Jorth.' . . . Somebody remembered thet Greaves had cast a slur on your good name, Ellen. An' then they had Jean Isbel's reason fer sayin' thet to Greaves. It caused a lot of talk. An' when Simm Bruce busted in some of the gang haw-hawed him an' said as how he'd get the third cut from Jean Isbel's bowie. Bruce was half drunk an' he began to cuss an' rave about Jean Isbel bein' in love with his girl. . . . As bad luck would have it, a couple of more fellars come in an' asked Meeker questions. He jest got to thet part, 'Greaves, it's the half-breed, an' he's goin' to cut you—*first for Ellen Jorth,'* when in walked your father! . . . Then it all had to come out—what Jean Isbel had said an' done—an' why. How Greaves had backed Simm Bruce in slurrin' you!"

Sprague paused to look hard at Ellen.

"Oh! Then—what did dad do?" whispered Ellen.

"He said, 'By God! half-breed or not, there's one Isbel who's a man! An' he killed Bruce on the spot an' gave Meeker a nasty wound. Somebody grabbed him before he could shoot Meeker again. They threw Meeker out an' he crawled to a neighbor's house, where he was when Evarts seen him."

Ellen felt Sprague's rough but kindly hand shaking her. "An' now what do you think of Jean Isbel?" he queried.

A great, unsurmountable wall seemed to obstruct Ellen's thought. It seemed gray in color. It moved toward her. It was inside her brain.

"I tell you, Ellen Jorth," declared the old man, "thet Jean Isbel loves you—loves you turribly—an' he believes you're good."

"Oh no—he doesn't!" faltered Ellen.

"Wal, he jest does."

"Oh, Uncle John, he cain't believe that!" she cried.

"Of course he can. He does. You are good—good as gold, Ellen, an' he knows it. . . . What a queer deal it all is! Poor devil! To love you thet turribly an' hev to fight your people! Ellen, your dad had it correct. Isbel or not, he's a man. . . . An' I say what a shame you two are divided by hate. Hate thet you hed nothin' to do with." Sprague patted her head and rose to go. "Mebbe thet fight will end the trouble. I reckon it will. Don't cross bridges till you come to them, Ellen. . . . I must hurry back now. I didn't take time to unpack my burros. Come up soon. . . . An', say, Ellen, don't think hard any more of thet Jean Isbel."

Sprague strode away, and Ellen neither heard nor saw him go. She sat perfectly motionless, yet had a strange sensation of being lifted by invisible and mighty power. It was like movement felt in a dream. She was being impelled upward when her body seemed immovable as stone. When her blood beat down this deadlock of all her physical being and rushed on and on through her veins it gave her an irresistible impulse to fly, to sail through space, to run and run and run.

And on the moment the black horse, Spades, coming from the meadow, whinnied at sight of her. Ellen leaped up and ran swiftly, but her feet seemed to be stumbling. She hugged the horse and buried her hot face in his mane and clung to him. Then just as violently she rushed for her saddle and bridle and carried the heavy weight as easily as if it had been an empty sack. Throwing them upon him, she buckled and strapped with strong, eager hands. It never occurred to her that she was not dressed to ride. Up she flung herself. And the horse, sensing her spirit, plunged into strong, free gait down the cañon trail.

The ride, the action, the thrill, the sensations of violence were not all she needed. Solitude, the empty aisles of the forest, the far miles of lonely wilderness—were these the added all? Spades took a swinging, rhythmic lope up the winding trail. The wind fanned her hot face. The sting of whipping aspen branches was pleasant. A deep rumble of thunder shook the sultry air. Up beyond the green slope of the cañon massed the creamy clouds, shading darker and darker. Spades loped on the levels, leaped the washes, trotted over the rocky ground, and took to a walk up the long slope. Ellen dropped the reins over the pommel. Her hands could not stay set on anything. They pressed her breast and flew out to caress the white aspens and to tear at the maple leaves, and gather the lavender juniper berries, and came back again to her heart. Her heart that was going to burst or break! As it had swelled, so now it labored. It could not keep pace with her needs. All that was physical, all that was living in her had to be unleashed.

Spades gained the level forest. How the great, brown-green pines seemed to bend their lofty branches over her, protectively, understandingly. Patches of azure-blue sky flashed between the trees. The great white clouds sailed along with her, and shafts of golden sunlight, flecked with gleams of falling pine needles, shone down through the canopy overhead. Away in front of her, up the slow heave of forest land, boomed the heavy thunderbolts along the battlements of the Rim.

Was she riding to escape from herself? For no gait suited her until Spades was running hard and fast through the glades. Then the pressure of dry wind, the thick odor of pine, the flashes of brown and green and gold and blue, the soft, rhythmic thuds of hoofs, the feel of the powerful horse under her, the whip of spruce branches on her muscles contracting and expanding in hard action—all these sensations seemed to quell for the time the mounting cataclysm in her heart.

The oak swales, the maple thickets, the aspen groves, the pine-shaded aisles, and the miles of silver spruce all sped by her, as if she had ridden the wind; and through the forest ahead shone the vast open of the Basin, gloomed by purple and silver cloud, shadowed by gray storm, and in the west brightened by golden sky.

Straight to the Rim she had ridden, and to the point where she had watched Jean Isbel that unforgetable day. She rode to the promontory behind the pine thicket and beheld a scene which stayed her restless hands upon her heaving breast.

The world of sky and cloud and earthly abyss seemed one of storm-sundered grandeur. The air was sultry and still, and smelled of the peculiar burnt-wood odor caused by lightning striking trees. A few heavy drops of rain were pattering down from the thin, gray edge of clouds overhead. To the east hung the storm—a black cloud lodged against the Rim, from which long, misty veils of rain streamed down into the gulf. The roar of rain sounded like the steady roar of the rapids of a river. Then a blue-white, piercingly bright, ragged streak of lightning shot down out of the black cloud. It struck with a splitting report that shocked the very wall of rock under Ellen. Then the heavens seemed to burst open with thundering crash and close with mighty thundering boom. Long roar and longer rumble rolled away to the eastward. The rain poured down in roaring cataracts.

The south held a panorama of purple-shrouded range and cañon, cañon and range, on across the rolling leagues to the dim, lofty peaks, all canopied over with angry, dusky, low-drifting clouds, horizon-wide, smoky, and sulphurous. And as Ellen watched, hands pressed to her breast, feeling incalculable relief in sight of this tempest and gulf that resembled her soul, the sun burst out from behind the long bank of purple cloud in the west and flooded the world there with golden lightning.

"It is for me!" cried Ellen. "My mind—my heart—my very soul. . . . Oh, I know! I know now! . . . I love him—love him—love him!"

She cried it out to the elements. "Oh, I love Jean Isbel—an' my heart will burst or break!"

The might of her passion was like the blaze of the sun. Before it all else retreated, diminished. The suddenness of the truth dimmed her sight. But she saw clearly enough to crawl into the pine thicket, through the clutching, dry twigs, over the mats of fragrant needles to the covert where she had once spied upon Jean Isbel. And here she lay face down for a while, hands clutching the needles, breast pressed hard upon the ground, stricken and spent. But vitality was exceeding strong in her. It passed, that weakness of realization, and she awakened to the consciousness of love.

But in the beginning it was not consciousness of the man. It was new, sensorial life, elemental, primitive, a liberation of a million inherited instincts, quivering and physical, over which Ellen had no more control than she had over the glory of the sun. If she thought at all it was of her need to be hidden, like an animal, low down near the earth, covered by green thicket, lost in the wildness of nature. She went to nature, unconsciously seeking a mother. And love was a birth from the depths of her, like a rushing spring of pure water, long underground, and at last propelled to the surface by convulsion.

Ellen gradually lost her tense rigidity and relaxed. Her body softened. She rolled over until her face caught the lacy, golden shadows cast by sun and bough. Scattered drops of rain pattered around her. The air was hot, and its odor was that of dry pine and spruce fragrance penetrated by brimstone from the lightning. The nest where she lay was warm and sweet. No eye save that of nature saw her in her abandonment. An ineffable and exquisite smile wreathed her lips, dreamy, sad, sensuous, the supremity of unconscious happiness. Over her dark and eloquent eyes, as Ellen gazed upward, spread a luminous film, a veil. She was looking intensely, yet she did not see. The wilderness enveloped her with its secretive, elemental sheaths of rock, of tree, of cloud, of sunlight. Through her thrilling skin poured the multiple and nameless sensations of the living organism stirred to supreme sensitiveness. She could not lie still, but all her movements were gentle, involuntary. The slow reaching out of her hand, to grasp at nothing visible, was similar to the lazy stretching of her limbs, to the heave of her breast, to the ripple of muscle.

Ellen knew not what she felt. To live that sublime hour was beyond thought. Such happiness was like the first dawn of the world to the sight of man. It had to do with bygone ages. Her heart, her blood, her flesh, her very bones were filled with instincts and emotions common to the race before intellect developed, when the savage lived only with his sensorial perceptions. Of all happiness, joy, bliss, rapture to which man was heir, that of intense and exquisite preoccupation of the senses, unhindered and unburdened by thought, was the greatest. Ellen felt that which life meant with its inscrutable design. Love was only the realization of her mission on the earth.

The dark storm cloud with its white, ragged ropes of lightning and down-streaming gray veils of rain, the purple gulf rolling like a colored sea to the dim mountains, the glorious golden light of the sun—these had enchanted her eyes with her beauty of the universe. They had burst the windows of her blindness. When she crawled into the green-brown covert it was to escape too great perception. She needed to be encompassed by close tangible things. And there her body paid the tribute to the realization of life. Shock, convulsion, pain, relaxation, and then unutterable and insupportable sensing of her environment and the heart! In one way she was a wild animal alone in the woods, forced into the mating that meant reproduction of its kind. In another she was an infinitely higher being shot through and through with the most resistless and mysterious transport that life could give to flesh.

And when that spell slackened its hold there wedged into her mind a consciousness of the man she loved—Jean Isbel. Then emotion and thought strove for mastery over her. It was not herself or love that she loved, but a living man. Suddenly he existed so clearly for her that she could see him, hear him, almost feel him. Her whole soul, her very life cried out to him for protection, for salvation, for love, for fulfillment. No denial, no doubt marred the white blaze of her realization. From the instant that she had looked up into Jean Isbel's dark face she had loved him. Only she had not known. She bowed now, and bent, and humbly quivered under the mastery of something beyond her ken. Thought clung to the beginnings of her romance—to the three times she had seen him. Every look, every word, every act of his returned to her now in the light of the truth. Love at first sight! He had sworn it, bitterly, eloquently, scornful of her doubts. And now a blind, sweet, shuddering ecstasy swayed her. How weak and frail seemed her body—too small, too slight for this monstrous and terrible engine of fire and lightning and fury and glory—her heart! It must burst or break. Relentlessly memory pursued Ellen, and her thoughts whirled and emotion conquered her. At last she quivered up to her knees as if lashed to action. It seemed that first kiss of Isbel's, cool and gentle and timid, was on her lips. And her eyes closed and hot tears welled from under her lids. Her groping hands found only the dead twigs and the pine boughs of the trees. Had she reached out to clasp him? Then hard and violent on her mouth and cheek and neck burned those other kisses of Isbel's, and with the flashing, stinging memory came the truth that now she would have bartered her soul for them. Utterly she surrendered to the resistlessness of this love. Her loss of mother and friends, her wandering from one wild place to another, her lonely life among bold and rough men, had developed her for violent love. It overthrew all pride, it engendered humility, it killed hate. Ellen wiped the tears from her eyes, and as she knelt there she swept to her breast a fragrant spreading bough of pine needles. "I'll go to him," she whispered. "I'll tell him of—of my—my love. I'll tell him to take me away—away to the end of the world—away from heah—before it's too late!"

It was a solemn, beautiful moment. But the last spoken words lingered hauntingly. "Too late?" she whispered.

And suddenly it seemed that death itself shuddered in her soul. Too late! It was too late. She had killed his love. That Jorth blood in her—that poisonous hate—had chosen the only way to strike this noble Isbel to the heart. Basely, with an abandonment of womanhood, she had mockingly perjured her soul with a vile lie. She writhed, she shook under the whip of this inconceivable fact. Lost! Lost! She wailed her misery. She might as well be what she had made Jean Isbel think she was. If she had been shamed before, she was now abased, degraded, lost in her own sight. And if she would have given her soul for his kisses, she now would have killed herself to earn back his respect. Jean Isbel had given her at sight the deference that she had unconsciously craved, and the love that would have been her salvation. What a horrible mistake she had made of her life! Not her mother's blood, but her father's—the Jorth blood—had been her ruin.

Again Ellen fell upon the soft pine-needle mat, face down, and she groveled and burrowed there, in an agony that could not bear the sense of light. All she had suffered was as nothing to this. To have awakened to a splendid and uplifting love for a man whom she had imagined she hated, who had fought for her name and had killed in revenge for the dishonor she had avowed—to have lost his love and what was infinitely more precious to her now in her ignominy—his faith in her purity—this broke her heart.

CHAPTER ELEVEN

When Ellen, utterly spent in body and mind, reached home that day a melancholy, sultry twilight was falling. Fitful flares of sheet lightning swept across the dark horizon to the east. The cabins were deserted. Antonio and the Mexican woman were gone. The circumstances made Ellen wonder, but she was too tired and too sunken in spirit to think long about it or to care. She fed and watered her horse and left him in the corral. Then, supperless and without removing her clothes, she threw herself upon the bed, and at once sank into heavy slumber.

Sometime during the night she awoke. Coyotes were yelping, and from that sound she concluded it was near dawn. Her body ached; her mind seemed dull. Drowsily she was sinking into slumber again when she heard the rapid clip-clop of trotting horses. Startled, she raised her head to listen. The men were coming back. Relief and dread seemed to clear her stupor.

The trotting horses stopped across the lane from her cabin, evidently at the corral where she had left Spades. She heard him whistle. From the sound of hoofs she judged the number of horses to be six or eight. Low voices of men mingled with thuds and cracking of straps and flopping of saddles on the ground. After that the heavy tread of boots sounded on the porch of the cabin opposite. A door creaked on its hinges. Next a slow footstep, accompanied by a clinking of spurs, approached Ellen's door, and a heavy hand banged upon it. She knew this person could not be her father.

"Hullo, Ellen!"

She recognized the voice as belonging to Colter. Somehow its tone, or something about it, sent a little shiver down her spine. It acted like a revivifying current. Ellen lost her dragging lethargy.

"Hey, Ellen, are y'u there?" added Colter, in louder voice.

"Yes. Of course I'm heah," she replied. "What do y'u want?"

"Wal—I'm shore glad y'u're home," he replied. "Antonio's gone with his squaw. An' I was some worried aboot y'u."

"Who's with y'u, Colter?" queried Ellen, sitting up.

"Rock Wells an' Springer. Tad Jorth was with us, but we had to leave him over heah in a cabin."

"What's the matter with him?"

"Wal, he's hurt tolerable bad," was the slow reply.

Ellen heard Colter's spurs jangle, as if he had uneasily shifted his feet.

"Where's dad an' Uncle Jackson?" asked Ellen.

A silence pregnant enough to augment Ellen's dread finally broke to Colter's voice, somehow different. "Shore they're back on the trail. An' we're to meet them where we left Tad."

"Are y'u goin' away again?"

"I reckon. . . . An', Ellen, y'u're goin' with us."

"I am not," she retorted.

"Wal, y'u are, if I have to pack y'u," he replied, forcibly. "It's not safe heah any more. That damned half-breed Isbel with his gang are on our trail."

That name seemed like a red-hot blade at Ellen's leaden heart. She wanted to fling a hundred queries on Colter, but she could not utter one.

"Ellen, we've got to hit the trail an' hide," continued Colter, anxiously. "Y'u mustn't stay heah alone. Suppose them Isbels would trap y'u! . . . They'd tear your clothes off an' rope y'u to a tree. Ellen, shore y'u're goin'. . . . Y'u heah me!"

"Yes—I'll go," she replied, as if forced.

"Wal—that's good," he said, quickly. "An' rustle tolerable lively. We've got to pack."

The slow jangle of Colter's spurs and his slow steps moved away out of Ellen's hearing. Throwing off the blankets, she put her feet to the floor and sat there a moment staring at the blank nothingness of the cabin interior in the obscure gray of dawn. Cold, gray, dreary, obscure—like her life, her future! And she was compelled to do what was hateful to her. As a Jorth she must take to the unfrequented trails and hide like a rabbit in the thickets. But the interest of the moment, a premonition of events to be, quickened her into action.

Ellen unbarred the door to let in the light. Day was breaking with an intense, clear, steely light in the east through which the morning star still shone white. A ruddy flare betokened the advent of the sun. Ellen unbraided her tangled hair and brushed and combed it. A queer, still pang came to her at sight of pine needles tangled in her brown locks. Then she washed her hands and face. Breakfast was a matter of considerable work and she was hungry.

The sun rose and changed the gray world of forest. For the first time in her life Ellen hated the golden brightness, the wonderful blue of sky, the scream of the eagle and the screech of the jay; and the squirrels she had always loved to feed were neglected that morning.

Colter came in. Either Ellen had never before looked attentively at him or else he had changed. Her scrutiny of his lean, hard features accorded him more Texan attributes than formerly. His gray eyes were as light, as clear, as fierce as those of an eagle. And the sand gray of his face, the long, drooping, fair mustache hid the secrets of his mind, but not its strength. The instant Ellen met his gaze she sensed a power in him that she instinctively opposed. Colter had not been so bold nor so rude as Daggs, but he was the same kind of man, perhaps the more dangerous for his secretiveness, his cool, waiting inscrutableness.

"'Mawnin', Ellen!" he drawled. "Y'u shore look good for sore eyes."

"Don't pay me compliments, Colter," replied Ellen. "An' your eyes are not sore."

"Wal, I'm shore sore from fightin' an' ridin' an' layin' out," he said, bluntly.

"Tell me—what's happened," returned Ellen.

"Girl, it's a tolerable long story," replied Colter. "An' we've no time now. Wait till we get to camp."

"Am I to pack my belongin's or leave them heah?" asked Ellen.

"Reckon y'u'd better leave—them heah."

"But if we did not come back—"

"Wal, I reckon it's not likely we'll come—soon," he said, rather evasively.

"Colter, I'll not go off into the woods with just the clothes I have on my back."

"Ellen, we shore got to pack all the grub we can. This shore ain't goin' to be a visit to neighbors. We're shy pack hosses. But y'u make up a bundle of belonging's y'u care for, an' the things y'u'll need bad. We'll throw it on somewhere."

Colter stalked away across the lane, and Ellen found herself dubiously staring at his tall figure. Was it the situation that struck her with a foreboding perplexity or was her intuition steeling her against this man? Ellen could not decide. But she had to go with him. Her prejudice was unreasonable at this portentous moment. And she could not yet feel that she was solely responsible to herself.

When it came to making a small bundle of her belongings she was in a quandary. She discarded this and put in that, and then reversed the order. Next in preciousness to her mother's things were the long-hidden gifts of Jean Isbel. She could part with neither.

While she was selecting and packing this bundle Colter again entered and, without speaking, began to rummage in the corner where her father kept his possessions. This irritated Ellen.

"What do y'u want there?" she demanded.

"Wal, I reckon your dad wants his papers—an' the gold he left heah—an' a change of clothes. Now doesn't he?" returned Colter, coolly.

"Of course. But I supposed y'u would have me pack them."

Colter vouchsafed no reply to this, but deliberately went on rummaging, with little regard for how he scattered things. Ellen turned her back on him. At length, when he left, she went to her father's corner and found that, as far as she was able to see, Colter had taken neither paper nor clothes, but only the gold. Perhaps, however, she had been mistaken, for she had not observed Colter's departure closely enough to know whether or not he carried a package. She missed only the gold. Her father's papers, old and musty, were scattered about, and these she gathered up to slip in her own bundle.

Colter, or one of the men, had saddled Spades, and he was now tied to the corral fence, champing his bit and pounding the sand. Ellen wrapped bread and meat inside her coat, and after tying this behind her saddle she was ready to go. But evidently she would have to wait, and, preferring to remain outdoors, she stayed by her horse. Presently, while watching the men pack, she noticed that Springer wore a bandage round his head under the brim of his sombrero. His motions were slow and lacked energy. Shuddering at the sight, Ellen refused to conjecture. All too soon she would learn what had happened, and all too soon, perhaps, she herself would be in the midst of another fight. She watched the men. They were making a hurried slipshod job of packing food supplies from both cabins. More than once she caught Colter's gray gleam of gaze on her, and she did not like it.

"I'll ride up an' say good-by to Sprague," she called to Colter.

"Shore y'u won't do nothin' of the kind," he called back.

There was authority in his tone that angered Ellen, and something else which inhibited her anger. What was there about Colter with which she must reckon? The other two Texans laughed aloud, to be suddenly silenced by Colter's harsh and lowered curses. Ellen walked out of hearing and sat upon a log, where she remained until Colter hailed her.

"Get up an' ride," he called.

Ellen complied with this order and, riding up behind the three mounted men, she soon found herself leaving what for years had been her home. Not once did she look back. She hoped she would never see the squalid, bare pretension of a ranch again.

Colter and the other riders drove the pack horses across the meadow, off of the trails, and up the slope into the forest. Not very long did it take Ellen to see that Colter's object was to hide their tracks. He zigzagged through the forest, avoiding the bare spots of dust, the dry, sun-baked flats of clay where water lay in spring, and he chose the grassy, open glades, the long, pine-needle matted aisles. Ellen rode at their heels and it pleased her to watch for their tracks. Colter manifestly had been long practiced in this game of hiding his trail, and he showed the skill of a rustler. But Ellen was not convinced that he could ever elude a real woodsman. Not improbably, however, Colter was only aiming to leave a trail difficult to follow and which would allow him and his confederates ample time to forge ahead of pursuers. Ellen could not accept a certainty of pursuit. Yet Colter must have expected it, and Springer and Wells also, for they had a dark, sinister, furtive demeanor that strangely contrasted with the cool, easy manner habitual to them.

They were not seeking the level routes of the forest land, that was sure. They rode straight across the thick-timbered ridge down into another cañon, up out of that, and across rough, rocky bluffs, and down again. These riders headed a little to the northwest and every mile brought them into wilder, more rugged country, until Ellen, losing count of cañons and ridges, had no idea where she was. No stop was made at noon to rest the laboring, sweating pack animals.

Under circumstances where pleasure might have been possible Ellen would have reveled in this hard ride into a wonderful forest ever thickening and darkening. But the wild beauty of glade and the spruce slopes and the deep, bronze-walled cañons left her cold. She saw and felt, but had no thrill, except now and then a thrill of alarm when Spades slid to his haunches down some steep, damp, piny declivity.

All the woodland, up and down, appeared to be richer, greener as they traveled farther west. Grass grew thick and heavy. Water ran in all ravines. The rocks were bronze and copper and russet, and some had green patches of lichen.

Ellen felt the sun now on her left cheek and knew that the day was waning and that Colter was swinging farther to the northwest. She had never before ridden through such heavy forest and down and up such wild cañons. Toward sunset the deepest and ruggedest cañon halted their advance. Colter rode to the right, searching for a place to get down through a spruce thicket that stood on end. Presently he dismounted and the others followed suit. Ellen found she could not lead Spades because he slid down upon her heels, so she looped the end of her reins over the pommel and left him free. She herself managed to descend by holding to branches and sliding all the way down that slope. She heard the horses cracking the brush, snorting and heaving. One pack slipped and had to be removed from the horse, and rolled down. At the bottom of this deep, green-walled notch roared a stream of water. Shadowed, cool, mossy, damp, this narrow gulch seemed the wildest place Ellen had ever seen. She could just see the sunset-flushed, gold-tipped spruces far above her. The men repacked the horse that had slipped his burden, and once more resumed their progress ahead, now turning up this cañon. There was no horse trail, but deer and bear trails were numerous. The sun sank and the sky darkened, but still the men rode on; and the farther they traveled the wilder grew the aspect of the cañon.

At length Colter broke a way through a heavy thicket of willows and entered a side cañon, the mouth of which Ellen had not even descried. It turned and widened, and at length opened out into a round pocket, apparently inclosed, and as lonely and isolated a place as even pursued rustlers could desire. Hidden by jutting wall and thicket of spruce were two old log cabins joined together by roof and attic floor, the same as the double cabin at the Jorth ranch.

Ellen smelled wood smoke, and presently, on going round the cabins, saw a bright fire. One man stood beside it gazing at Colter's party, which evidently he had heard approaching.

"Hullo, Queen!" said Colter. "How's Tad?"

"He's holdin' on fine," replied Queen, bending over the fire, where he turned pieces of meat.

"Where's father?" suddenly asked Ellen, addressing Colter.

As if he had not heard her, he went on wearily loosening a pack.

Queen looked at her. The light of the fire only partially shone on his face. Ellen could not see its expression. But from the fact that Queen did not answer her question she got further intimation of an impending catastrophe. The long, wild ride had helped prepare her for the secrecy and taciturnity of men who had resorted to flight. Perhaps her father had been delayed or was still off on the deadly mission that had obsessed him; or there might, and probably was, darker reason for his absence. Ellen shut her teeth and turned to the needs of her horse. And presently, returning to the fire, she thought of her uncle.

"Queen, is my uncle Tad heah?" she asked.

"Shore. He's in there," replied Queen, pointing at the nearer cabin.

Ellen hurried toward the dark doorway. She could see how the logs of the cabin had moved awry and what a big, dilapidated hovel it was. As she looked in, Colter loomed over her—placed a familiar and somehow masterful hand upon her. Ellen let it rest on her shoulder a moment. Must she forever be repulsing these rude men among whom her lot was cast? Did Colter mean what Daggs had always meant? Ellen felt herself weary, weak in body, and her spent spirit had not rallied. Yet, whatever Colter meant by his familiarity, she could not bear it. So she slipped out from under his hand.

"Uncle Tad, are y'u heah?" she called into the blackness. She heard the mice scamper and rustle and she smelled the musty, old, woody odor of a long-unused cabin.

"Hello, Ellen!" came a voice she recognized as her uncle's, yet it was strange. "Yes. I'm heah—bad luck to me! . . . How're y'u buckin' up, girl?"

"I'm all right, Uncle Tad—only tired an' worried. I—"

"Tad, how's your hurt?" interrupted Colter.

"Reckon I'm easier," replied Jorth, wearily, "but shore I'm in bad shape. I'm still spittin' blood. I keep tellin' Queen that bullet lodged in my lungs—but he says it went through."

"Wal, hang on, Tad!" replied Colter, with a cheerfulness Ellen sensed was really indifferent.

"Oh, what the hell's the use!" exclaimed Jorth. "It's all—up with us—Colter!"

"Wal, shut up, then," tersely returned Colter. "It ain't doin' y'u or us any good to holler."

Tad Jorth did not reply to this. Ellen heard his breathing and it did not seem natural. It rasped a little—came hurriedly—then caught in his throat. Then he spat. Ellen shrunk back against the door. He was breathing through blood.

"Uncle, are y'u in pain?" she asked.

"Yes, Ellen—it burns like hell," he said.

"Oh! I'm sorry. . . . Isn't there something I can do?"

"I reckon not. Queen did all anybody could do for me—now—unless it's pray."

Colter laughed at this—the slow, easy, drawling laugh of a Texan. But Ellen felt pity for this wounded uncle. She had always hated him. He had been a drunkard, a gambler, a waster of her father's property; and now he was a rustler and a fugitive, lying in pain, perhaps mortally hurt.

"Yes, Uncle—I will pray for y'u," she said, softly.

The change in his voice held a note of sadness that she had been quick to catch.

"Ellen, y'u're the only good Jorth—in the whole damned lot," he said. "God! I see it all now. . . . We've dragged y'u to hell!"

"Yes, Uncle Tad, I've shore been dragged some—but not yet—to hell," she responded, with a break in her voice.

"Y'u will be—Ellen—unless—"

"Aw, shut up that kind of gab, will y'u?" broke in Colter, harshly.

It amazed Ellen that Colter should dominate her uncle, even though he was wounded. Tad Jorth had been the last man to take orders from anyone, much less a rustler of the Hash Knife Gang. This Colter began to loom up in Ellen's estimate as he loomed physically over her, a lofty figure, dark motionless, somehow menacing.

"Ellen, has Colter told y'u yet—aboot—aboot Lee an' Jackson?" inquired the wounded man.

The pitch-black darkness of the cabin seemed to help fortify Ellen to bear further trouble.

"Colter told me dad an' Uncle Jackson would meet us heah," she rejoined, hurriedly.

Jorth could be heard breathing in difficulty, and he coughed and spat again, and seemed to hiss.

"Ellen, he lied to y'u. They'll never meet us—heah!"

"Why not?" whispered Ellen.

"Because—Ellen—" he replied, in husky pants, "your dad an'—uncle Jackson—are daid—an' buried!"

If Ellen suffered a terrible shock it was a blankness, a deadness, and a slow, creeping failure of sense in her knees. They gave way under her and she sank on the grass against the cabin wall. She did not faint nor grow dizzy nor lose her sight, but for a while there was no process of thought in her mind. Suddenly then it was there—the quick, spiritual rending of her heart—followed by a profound emotion of intimate and irretrievable loss—and after that grief and bitter realization.

An hour later Ellen found strength to go to the fire and partake of the food and drink her body sorely needed.

Colter and the men waited on her solicitously, and in silence, now and then stealing furtive glances at her from under the shadow of their black sombreros. The dark night settled down like a blanket. There were no stars. The wind moaned fitfully among the pines, and all about that lonely, hidden recess was in harmony with Ellen's thoughts.

"Girl, y'u're shore game," said Colter, admiringly. "An' I reckon y'u never got it from the Jorths."

"Tad in there—he's game," said Queen, in mild protest.

"Not to my notion," replied Colter. "Any man can be game when he's croakin', with somebody around. . . . But Lee Jorth an' Jackson—they always was yellow clear to their gizzards. They was born in Louisiana—not Texas. . . . Shore they're no more Texans than I am. Ellen heah, she must have got another strain in her blood."

To Ellen their words had no meaning. She rose and asked, "Where can I sleep?"

"I'll fetch a light presently an' y'u can make your bed in there by Tad," replied Colter.

"Yes, I'd like that."

"Wal, if y'u reckon y'u can coax him to talk you're shore wrong," declared Colter, with that cold timbre of voice that struck like steel on Ellen's nerves. "I cussed him good an' told him he'd keep his mouth shut. Talkin' makes him cough an' that fetches up the blood. . . . Besides, I reckon I'm the one to tell y'u how your dad an' uncle got killed. Tad didn't see it done, an' he was bad hurt when it happened. Shore all the fellars left have their idee aboot it. But I've got it straight."

"Colter—tell me now," cried Ellen.

"Wal, all right. Come over heah," he replied, and drew her away from the camp fire, out in the shadow of gloom. "Poor kid! I shore feel bad aboot it." He put a long arm around her waist and drew her against him. Ellen felt it, yet did not offer any resistance. All her faculties seemed absorbed in a morbid and sad anticipation.

"Ellen, y'u shore know I always loved y'u—now don't y'u?" he asked, with suppressed breath.

"No, Colter. It's news to me—an' not what I want to heah."

"Wal, y'u may as well heah it right now," he said. "It's true. An' what's more—your dad gave y'u to me before he died."

"What! Colter, y'u must be a liar."

"Ellen, I swear I'm not lyin'," he returned, in eager passion. "I was with your dad last an' heard him last. He shore knew I'd loved y'u for years. An' he said he'd rather y'u be left in my care than anybody's."

"My father gave me to y'u in marriage!" ejaculated Ellen, in bewilderment.

Colter's ready assurance did not carry him over this point. It was evident that her words somewhat surprised and disconcerted him for the moment.

"To let me marry a rustler—one of the Hash Knife Gang!" exclaimed Ellen, with weary incredulity.

"Wal, your dad belonged to Daggs's gang, same as I do," replied Colter, recovering his cool ardor.

"No!" cried Ellen.

"Yes, he shore did, for years," declared Colter, positively. "Back in Texas. An' it was your dad that got Daggs to come to Arizona."

Ellen tried to fling herself away. But her strength and her spirit were ebbing, and Colter increased the pressure of his arm. All at once she sank limp. Could she escape her fate? Nothing seemed left to fight with or for.

"All right—don't hold me—so tight," she panted. "Now tell me how dad was killed . . . an' who—who—"

Colter bent over so he could peer into her face. In the darkness Ellen just caught the gleam of his eyes. She felt the virile force of the man in the strain of his body as he pressed her close. It all seemed unreal—a hideous dream—the gloom, the moan of the wind, the weird solitude, and this rustler with hand and will like cold steel.

"We'd come back to Greaves's store," Colter began. "An' as Greaves was daid we all got free with his liquor. Shore some of us got drunk. Bruce was drunk, an' Tad in there—he was drunk. Your dad put away more 'n I ever seen him. But shore he wasn't exactly drunk. He got one of them weak an' shaky spells. He cried an' he wanted some of us to get the Isbels to call off the fightin'. . . . He shore was ready to call it quits. I reckon the killin' of Daggs—an' then the awful way Greaves was cut up by Jean Isbel—took all the fight out of your dad. He said to me, 'Colter, we'll take Ellen an' leave this heah country—an' begin life all over again—where no one knows us.'"

"Oh, did he really say that? . . . Did he—really mean it?" murmured Ellen, with a sob.

"I'll swear it by the memory of my daid mother," protested Colter. "Wal, when night come the Isbels rode down on us in the dark an' began to shoot. They smashed in the door—tried to burn us out—an' hollered around for a while. Then they left an' we reckoned there'd be no more trouble that night. All the same we kept watch. I was the soberest one an' I bossed the gang. We had some quarrels aboot the drinkin'. Your dad said if we kept it up it'd be the end of the Jorths. An' he planned to send word to the Isbels next mawnin' that he was ready for a truce. An' I was to go fix it up with Gaston Isbel. Wal, your dad went to bed in Greaves's room, an' a little while later your uncle Jackson went in there, too. Some of the men laid down in the store an' went to sleep. I kept guard till aboot three in the mawnin'. An' I got so sleepy I couldn't hold my eyes open. So I waked up Wells an' Slater an' set them on guard, one at each end of the store. Then I laid down on the counter to take a nap."

Colter's low voice, the strain and breathlessness of him, the agitation with which he appeared to be laboring, and especially the simple, matter-of-fact detail of his story, carried absolute conviction to Ellen Jorth. Her vague doubt of him had been created by his attitude toward her. Emotion dominated her intelligence. The images, the scenes called up by Colter's words, were as true as the gloom of the wild gulch and the loneliness of the night solitude—as true as the strange fact that she lay passive in the arm of a rustler.

"Wal, after a while I woke up," went on Colter, clearing his throat. "It was gray dawn. All was as still as death. . . . An' somethin' shore was wrong. Wells an' Slater had got to drinkin' again an' now laid daid drunk or asleep. Anyways, when I kicked them they never moved. Then I heard a moan. It came from the room where your dad an' uncle was. I went in. It was just light enough to see. Your uncle Jackson was layin' on the floor—cut half in two—daid as a door nail. . . . Your dad lay on the bed. He was alive, breathin' his last. . . . He says, 'That half-breed Isbel—knifed us—while we slept!' . . . The winder shutter was open. I seen where Jean Isbel had come in an' gone out. I seen his moccasin tracks in the dirt outside an' I seen where he'd stepped in Jackson's blood an' tracked it to the winder. Y'u shore can see them bloody tracks yourself, if y'u go back to Greaves's store. . . . Your dad was goin' fast. . . . He said, 'Colter—take care of Ellen,' an I reckon he meant a lot by that. He kept sayin', 'My God! if I'd only seen Gaston Isbel before it was too late!' an' then he raved a little, whisperin' out of his haid. . . . An' after that he died. . . . I woke up the men, an' aboot sunup we carried your dad an' uncle out of town an' buried them. . . . An' them Isbels shot at us while we were buryin' our daid! That's where Tad got his hurt. . . . Then we hit the trail for Jorth's ranch. . . . An' now, Ellen, that's all my story. Your dad was ready to bury the hatchet with his old enemy. An' that Nez Perce Jean Isbel, like the sneakin' savage he is, murdered your uncle an' your dad. . . . Cut him horrible—made him suffer tortures of hell—all for Isbel revenge!"

When Colter's husky voice ceased Ellen whispered through lips as cold and still as ice, "Let me go . . . leave me—heah—alone!"

"Why, shore! I reckon I understand," replied Colter. "I hated to tell y'u. But y'u had to heah the truth aboot that half-breed. . . . I'll carry your pack in the cabin an' unroll your blankets."

Releasing her, Colter strode off in the gloom. Like a dead weight, Ellen began to slide until she slipped down full length beside the log. And then she lay in the cool, damp shadow, inert and lifeless so far as outward physical movement was concerned. She saw nothing and felt nothing of the night, the wind, the cold, the falling dew. For the moment or hour she was crushed by despair, and seemed to see herself sinking down and down into a black, bottomless pit, into an abyss where murky tides of blood and furious gusts of passion contended between her body and her soul. Into the stormy blast of hell! In her despair she longed, she ached for death. Born of infidelity, cursed by a taint of evil blood, further cursed by higher instinct for good and happy life, dragged from one lonely and wild and sordid spot to another, never knowing love or peace or joy or home, left to the companionship of violent and vile men, driven by a strange fate to love with unquenchable and insupportable love a half-breed, a savage, an Isbel, the hereditary enemy of her people, and at last the ruthless murderer of her father—what in the name of God had she left to live for? Revenge! An eye for an eye! A life for a life! But she could not kill Jean Isbel. Woman's love could turn to hate, but not the love of Ellen Jorth. He could drag her by the hair in the dust, beat her, and make her a thing to loathe, and cut her mortally in his savage and implacable thirst for revenge—but with her last gasp she would whisper she loved him and that she had lied to him to kill his faith. It was that—his strange faith in her purity—which had won her love. Of all men, that he should be the one to recognize the truth of her, the womanhood yet unsullied—how strange, how terrible, how overpowering! False, indeed, was she to the Jorths! False as her mother had been to an Isbel! This agony and destruction of her soul was the bitter Dead Sea fruit—the sins of her parents visited upon her.

"I'll end it all," she whispered to the night shadows that hovered over her. No coward was she—no fear of pain or mangled flesh or death or the mysterious hereafter could ever stay her. It would be easy, it would be a last thrill, a transport of self-abasement and supreme self-proof of her love for Jean Isbel to kiss the Rim rock where his feet had trod and then fling herself down into the depths. She was the last Jorth. So the wronged Isbels would be avenged.

"But he would never know—never know—I lied to him!" she wailed to the night wind.

She was lost—lost on earth and to hope of heaven. She had right neither to live nor to die. She was nothing but a little weed along the trail of life, trampled upon, buried in the mud. She was nothing but a single rotten thread in a tangled web of love and hate and revenge. And she had broken.

Lower and lower she seemed to sink. Was there no end to this gulf of despair? If Colter had returned he would have found her a rag and a toy—a creature degraded, fit for his vile embrace. To be thrust deeper into the mire—to be punished fittingly for her betrayal of a man's noble love and her own womanhood—to be made an end of, body, mind, and soul.

But Colter did not return.

The wind mourned, the owls hooted, the leaves rustled, the insects whispered their melancholy night song, the camp-fire flickered and faded. Then the wild forestland seemed to close imponderably over Ellen. All that she wailed in her despair, all that she confessed in her abasement, was true, and hard as life could be—but she belonged to nature. If nature had not failed her, had God failed her? It was there—the lonely land of tree and fern and flower and brook, full of wild birds and beasts, where the mossy rocks could speak and the solitude had ears, where she had always felt herself unutterably a part of creation. Thus a wavering spark of hope quivered through the blackness of her soul and gathered light.

The gloom of the sky, the shifting clouds of dull shade, split asunder to show a glimpse of a radiant star, piercingly white, cold, pure, a steadfast eye of the universe, beyond all understanding and illimitable with its meaning of the past and the present and the future. Ellen watched it until the drifting clouds once more hid it from her strained sight.

What had that star to do with hell? She might be crushed and destroyed by life, but was there not something beyond? Just to be born, just to suffer, just to die—could that be all? Despair did not loose its hold on Ellen, the strife and pang of her breast did not subside. But with the long hours and the strange closing in of the forest around her and the fleeting glimpse of that wonderful star, with a subtle divination of the meaning of her beating heart and throbbing mind, and, lastly, with a voice thundering at her conscience that a man's faith in a woman must not be greater, nobler, than her faith in God and eternity—with these she checked the dark flight of her soul toward destruction.

CHAPTER TWELVE

A chill, gray, somber dawn was breaking when Ellen dragged herself into the cabin and crept under her blankets, there to sleep the sleep of exhaustion.

When she awoke the hour appeared to be late afternoon. Sun and sky shone through the sunken and decayed roof of the old cabin. Her uncle, Tad Jorth, lay upon a blanket bed upheld by a crude couch of boughs. The light fell upon his face, pale, lined, cast in a still mold of suffering. He was not dead, for she heard his respiration.

The floor underneath Ellen's blankets was bare clay. She and Jorth were alone in this cabin. It contained nothing besides their beds and a rank growth of weeds along the decayed lower logs. Half of the cabin had a rude ceiling of rough-hewn boards which formed a kind of loft. This attic extended through to the adjoining cabin, forming the ceiling of the porch-like space between the two structures. There was no partition. A ladder of two aspen saplings, pegged to the logs, and with braces between for steps, led up to the attic.

Ellen smelled wood smoke and the odor of frying meat, and she heard the voices of men. She looked out to see that Slater and Somers had joined their party—an addition that might have strengthened it for defense, but did not lend her own situation anything favorable. Somers had always appeared the one best to avoid.

Colter espied her and called her to "Come an' feed your pale face." His comrades laughed, not loudly, but guardedly, as if noise was something to avoid. Nevertheless, they awoke Tad Jorth, who began to toss and moan on the bed.

Ellen hurried to his side and at once ascertained that he had a high fever and was in critical condition. Every time he tossed he opened a wound in his right breast, rather high up. For all she could see, nothing had been done for him except the binding of a scarf round his neck and under his arm. This scant bandage had worked loose. Going to the door, she called out:

"Fetch me some water." When Colter brought it, Ellen was rummaging in her pack for some clothing or towel that she could use for bandages.

"Weren't any of y'u decent enough to look after my uncle?" she queried.

"Huh! Wal, what the hell!" rejoined Colter. "We shore did all we could. I reckon y'u think it wasn't a tough job to pack him up the Rim. He was done for then an' I said so."

"I'll do all I can for him," said Ellen.

"Shore. Go ahaid. When I get plugged or knifed by that half-breed I shore hope y'u'll be round to nurse me."

"Y'u seem to be pretty shore of your fate, Colter."

"Shore as hell!" he bit out, darkly. "Somers saw Isbel an' his gang trailin' us to the Jorth ranch."

"Are y'u goin' to stay heah—an' wait for them?"

"Shore I've been quarrelin' with the fellars out there over that very question. I'm for leavin' the country. But Queen, the damn gun fighter, is daid set to kill that cowman, Blue, who swore he was King Fisher, the old Texas outlaw. None but Queen are spoilin' for another fight. All the same they won't leave Tad Jorth heah alone."

Then Colter leaned in at the door and whispered: "Ellen, I cain't boss this outfit. So let's y'u an' me shake 'em. I've got your dad's gold. Let's ride off to-night an' shake this country."

Colter, muttering under his breath, left the door and returned to his comrades. Ellen had received her first intimation of his cowardice; and his mention of her father's gold started a train of thought that persisted in spite of her efforts to put all her mind to attending her uncle. He grew conscious enough to recognize her working over him, and thanked her with a look that touched Ellen deeply. It changed the direction of her mind. His suffering and imminent death, which she was able to alleviate and retard somewhat, worked upon her pity and compassion so that she forgot her own plight. Half the night she was tending him, cooling his fever, holding him quiet. Well she realized that but for her ministrations he would have died. At length he went to sleep.

And Ellen, sitting beside him in the lonely, silent darkness of that late hour, received again the intimation of nature, those vague and nameless stirrings of her innermost being, those whisperings out of the night and the forest and the sky. Something great would not let go of her soul. She pondered.

Attention to the wounded man occupied Ellen; and soon she redoubled her activities in this regard, finding in them something of protection against Colter.

He had waylaid her as she went to a spring for water, and with a lunge like that of a bear he had tried to embrace her. But Ellen had been too quick.

"Wal, are y'u goin' away with me?" he demanded.

"No. I'll stick by my uncle," she replied.

That motive of hers seemed to obstruct his will. Ellen was keen to see that Colter and his comrades were at a last stand and disintegrating under a severe strain. Nerve and courage of the open and the wild they possessed, but only in a limited degree. Colter seemed obsessed by his passion for her, and though Ellen in her stubborn pride did not yet fear him, she realized she ought to. After that incident she watched closely, never leaving her uncle's bedside except when Colter was absent. One or more of the men kept constant lookout somewhere down the cañon.

Day after day passed on the wings of suspense, of watching, of ministering to her uncle, of waiting for some hour that seemed fixed.

Colter was like a hound upon her trail. At every turn he was there to importune her to run off with him, to frighten her with the menace of the Isbels, to beg her to give herself to him. It came to pass that the only relief she had was when she ate with the men or barred the cabin door at night. Not much relief, however, was there in the shut and barred door. With one thrust of his powerful arm Colter could have caved it in. He knew this as well as Ellen. Still she did not have the fear she should have had. There was her rifle beside her, and though she did not allow her mind to run darkly on its possible use, still the fact of its being there at hand somehow strengthened her. Colter was a cat playing with a mouse, but not yet sure of his quarry.

Ellen came to know hours when she was weak—weak physically, mentally, spiritually, morally—when under the sheer weight of this frightful and growing burden of suspense she was not capable of fighting her misery, her abasement, her low ebb of vitality, and at the same time wholly withstanding Colter's advances.

He would come into the cabin and, utterly indifferent to Tad Jorth, he would try to make bold and unrestrained love to Ellen. When he caught her in one of her unresisting moments and was able to hold her in his arms and kiss her he seemed to be beside himself with the wonder of her. At such moments, if he had any softness or gentleness in him, they expressed themselves in his sooner or later letting her go, when apparently she was about to faint. So it must have become fascinatingly fixed in Colter's mind that at times Ellen repulsed him with scorn and at others could not resist him.

Ellen had escaped two crises in her relation with this man, and as a morbid doubt, like a poisonous fungus, began to strangle her mind, she instinctively divined that there was an approaching and final crisis. No uplift of her spirit came this time—no intimations—no whisperings. How horrible it all was! To long to be good and noble—to realize that she was neither—to sink lower day by day! Must she decay there like one of these rotting logs? Worst of all, then, was the insinuating and ever-growing hopelessness. What was the use? What did it matter? Who would ever think of Ellen Jorth? "O God!" she whispered in her distraction, "is there nothing left—nothing at all?"

A period of several days of less torment to Ellen followed. Her uncle apparently took a turn for the better and Colter let her alone. This last circumstance nonplused Ellen. She was at a loss to understand it unless the Isbel menace now encroached upon Colter so formidably that he had forgotten her for the present.

Then one bright August morning, when she had just begun to relax her eternal vigilance and breathe without oppression, Colter encountered her and, darkly silent and fierce, he grasped her and drew her off her feet. Ellen struggled violently, but the total surprise had deprived her of strength. And that paralyzing weakness assailed her as never before. Without apparent effort Colter carried her, striding rapidly away from the cabin into the border of spruce trees at the foot of the cañon wall.

"Colter—where—oh, where are y'u takin' me?" she found voice to cry out.

"By God! I don't know," he replied, with strong, vibrant passion. "I was a fool not to carry y'u off long ago. But I waited. I was hopin' y'u'd love me! . . . An' now that Isbel gang has corralled us. Somers seen the half-breed up on the rocks. An' Springer seen the rest of them sneakin' around. I run back after my horse an' y'u."

"But Uncle Tad! . . . We mustn't leave him alone," cried Ellen.

"We've got to," replied Colter, grimly. "Tad shore won't worry y'u no more—soon as Jean Isbel gets to him."

"Oh, let me stay," implored Ellen. "I will save him."

Colter laughed at the utter absurdity of her appeal and claim. Suddenly he set her down upon her feet. "Stand still," he ordered. Ellen saw his big bay horse, saddled, with pack and blanket, tied there in the shade of a spruce. With swift hands Colter untied him and mounted him, scarcely moving his piercing gaze from Ellen. He reached to grasp her. "Up with y'u! . . . Put your foot in the stirrup!" His will, like his powerful arm, was irresistible for Ellen at that moment. She found herself swung up behind him. Then the horse plunged away. What with the hard motion and Colter's iron grasp on her Ellen was in a painful position. Her knees and feet came into violent contact with branches and snags. He galloped the horse, tearing through the dense thicket of willows that served to hide the entrance to the side cañon, and when out in the larger and more open cañon he urged him to a run. Presently when Colter put the horse to a slow rise of ground, thereby bringing him to a walk, it was just in time to save Ellen a serious bruising. Again the sunlight appeared to shade over. They were in the pines. Suddenly with backward lunge Colter halted the horse. Ellen heard a yell. She recognized Queen's voice.

"Turn back, Colter! Turn back!"

With an oath Colter wheeled his mount. "If I didn't run plump into them," he ejaculated, harshly. And scarcely had the goaded horse gotten a start when a shot rang out. Ellen felt a violent shock, as if her momentum had suddenly met with a check, and then she felt herself wrenched from Colter, from the saddle, and propelled into the air. She alighted on soft ground and thick grass, and was unhurt save for the violent wrench and shaking that had rendered her breathless. Before she could rise Colter was pulling at her, lifting her to her feet. She saw the horse lying with bloody head. Tall pines loomed all around. Another rifle cracked. "Run!" hissed Colter, and he bounded off, dragging her by the hand. Another yell pealed out. "Here we are, Colter!" Again it was Queen's shrill voice. Ellen ran with all her might, her heart in her throat, her sight failing to record more than a blur of passing pines and a blank green wall of spruce. Then she lost her balance, was falling, yet could not fall because of that steel grip on her hand, and was dragged, and finally carried, into a dense shade. She was blinded. The trees whirled and faded. Voices and shots sounded far away. Then something black seemed to be wiped across her feeling.

It turned to gray, to moving blankness, to dim, hazy objects, spectral and tall, like blanketed trees, and when Ellen fully recovered consciousness she was being carried through the forest.

"Wal, little one, that was a close shave for y'u," said Colter's hard voice, growing clearer. "Reckon your keelin' over was natural enough."

He held her lightly in both arms, her head resting above his left elbow. Ellen saw his face as a gray blur, then taking sharper outline, until it stood out distinctly, pale and clammy, with eyes cold and wonderful in their intense flare. As she gazed upward Colter turned his head to look back through the woods, and his motion betrayed a keen, wild vigilance. The veins of his lean, brown neck stood out like whipcords. Two comrades were stalking beside him. Ellen heard their stealthy steps, and she felt Colter sheer from one side or the other. They were proceeding cautiously, fearful of the rear, but not wholly trusting to the fore.

"Reckon we'd better go slow an' look before we leap," said one whose voice Ellen recognized as Springer's.

"Shore. That open slope ain't to my likin', with our Nez Perce friend prowlin' round," drawled Colter, as he set Ellen down on her feet.

Another of the rustlers laughed. "Say, can't he twinkle through the forest? I had four shots at him. Harder to hit than a turkey runnin' crossways."

This facetious speaker was the evil-visaged, sardonic Somers. He carried two rifles and wore two belts of cartridges.

"Ellen, shore y'u ain't so daid white as y'u was," observed Colter, and he chucked her under the chin with familiar hand. "Set down heah. I don't want y'u stoppin' any bullets. An' there's no tellin'."

Ellen was glad to comply with his wish. She had begun to recover wits and strength, yet she still felt shaky. She observed that their position then was on the edge of a well-wooded slope from which she could see the grassy cañon floor below. They were on a level bench, projecting out from the main cañon wall that loomed gray and rugged and pine fringed. Somers and Colter and Springer gave careful attention to all points of the compass, especially in the direction from which they had come. They evidently anticipated being trailed or circled or headed off, but did not manifest much concern. Somers lit a cigarette; Springer wiped his face with a grimy hand and counted the shells in his belt, which appeared to be half empty. Colter stretched his long neck like a vulture and peered down the slope and through the aisles of the forest up toward the cañon rim.

"Listen!" he said, tersely, and bent his head a little to one side, ear to the slight breeze.

They all listened. Ellen heard the beating of her heart, the rustle of leaves, the tapping of a woodpecker, and faint, remote sounds that she could not name.

"Deer, I reckon," spoke up Somers.

"Ahuh! Wal, I reckon they ain't trailin' us yet," replied Colter. "We gave them a shade better 'n they sent us."

"Short and sweet!" ejaculated Springer, and he removed his black sombrero to poke a dirty forefinger through a bullet hole in the crown. "Thet's how close I come to cashin'. I was lyin' behind a log, listenin' an' watchin', an' when I stuck my head up a little—zam! Somebody made my bonnet leak."

"Where's Queen?" asked Colter.

"He was with me fust off," replied Somers. "An' then when the shootin' slacked—after I'd plugged thet big, red-faced, white-haired pal of Isbel's—"

"Reckon thet was Blaisdell," interrupted Springer.

"Queen—he got tired layin' low," went on Somers. "He wanted action. I heerd him chewin' to himself, an' when I asked him what was eatin' him he up an' growled he was goin' to quit this Injun fightin'. An' he slipped off in the woods."

"Wal, that's the gun fighter of it," declared Colter, wagging his head. "Ever since that cowman, Blue, braced us an' said he was King Fisher, why Queen has been sulkier an' sulkier. He cain't help it. He'll do the same trick as Blue tried. An' shore he'll get his everlastin'. But he's the Texas breed all right."

"Say, do you reckon Blue really is King Fisher?" queried Somers.

"Naw!" ejaculated Colter, with downward sweep of his hand. "Many a would-be gun slinger has borrowed Fisher's name. But Fisher is daid these many years."

"Ahuh! Wal, mebbe, but don't you fergit it—thet Blue was no would-be," declared Somers. "He was the genuine article."

"I should smile!" affirmed Springer.

The subject irritated Colter, and he dismissed it with another forcible gesture and a counter question.

"How many left in that Isbel outfit?"

"No tellin'. There shore was enough of them," replied Somers. "Anyhow, the woods was full of flyin' bullets. . . . Springer, did you account for any of them?"

"Nope—not thet I noticed," responded Springer, dryly. "I had my chance at the half-breed. . . . Reckon I was nervous."

"Was Slater near you when he yelled out?"

"No. He was lyin' beside Somers."

"Wasn't thet a queer way fer a man to act?" broke in Somers. "A bullet hit Slater, cut him down the back as he was lyin' flat. Reckon it wasn't bad. But it hurt him so thet he jumped right up an' staggered around. He made a target big as a tree. An' mebbe them Isbels didn't riddle him!"

"That was when I got my crack at Bill Isbel," declared Colter, with grim satisfaction. "When they shot my horse out from under me I had Ellen to think of an' couldn't get my rifle. Shore had to run, as y'u seen. Wal, as I only had my six-shooter, there was nothin' for me to do but lay low an' listen to the sping of lead. Wells was standin' up behind a tree aboot thirty yards off. He got plugged, an' fallin' over he began to crawl my way, still holdin' to his rifle. I crawled along the log to meet him. But he dropped aboot half-way. I went on an' took his rifle an' belt. When I peeped out from behind a spruce bush then I seen Bill Isbel. He was shootin' fast, an' all of them was shootin' fast. That was when they had the open shot at Slater. . . . Wal, I bored Bill Isbel right through his middle. He dropped his rifle an', all bent double, he fooled around in a circle till he flopped over the Rim. I reckon he's layin' right up there somewhere below that daid spruce. I'd shore like to see him."

"Wal, you'd be as crazy as Queen if you tried thet," declared Somers. "We're not out of the woods yet."

"I reckon not," replied Colter. "An' I've lost my horse. Where'd y'u leave yours?"

"They're down the cañon, below thet willow brake. An' saddled an' none of them tied. Reckon we'll have to look them up before dark."

"Colter, what're we goin' to do?" demanded Springer.

"Wait heah a while—then cross the cañon an' work round up under the bluff, back to the cabin."

"An' then what?" queried Somers, doubtfully eying Colter.

"We've got to eat—we've got to have blankets," rejoined Colter, testily. "An' I reckon we can hide there an' stand a better show in a fight than runnin' for it in the woods."

"Wal, I'm givin' you a hunch thet it looked like you was runnin' fer it," retorted Somers.

"Yes, an' packin' the girl," added Springer. "Looks funny to me."

Both rustlers eyed Colter with dark and distrustful glances. What he might have replied never transpired, for the reason that his gaze, always shifting around, had suddenly fixed on something.

"Is that a wolf?" he asked, pointing to the Rim.

Both his comrades moved to get in line with his finger. Ellen could not see from her position.

"Shore thet's a big lofer," declared Somers. "Reckon he scented us."

"There he goes along the Rim," observed Colter. "He doesn't act leary. Looks like a good sign to me. Mebbe the Isbels have gone the other way."

"Looks bad to me," rejoined Springer, gloomily.

"An' why?" demanded Colter.

"I seen thet animal. Fust time I reckoned it was a lofer. Second time it was right near them Isbels. An' I'm damned now if I don't believe it's thet half-lofer sheep dog of Gass Isbel's."

"Wal, what if it is?"

"Ha! . . . Shore we needn't worry about hidin' out," replied Springer, sententiously. "With thet dog Jean Isbel could trail a grasshopper."

"The hell y'u say!" muttered Colter. Manifestly such a possibility put a different light upon the present situation. The men grew silent and watchful, occupied by brooding thoughts and vigilant surveillance of all points. Somers slipped off into the brush, soon to return, with intent look of importance.

"I heerd somethin'," he whispered, jerking his thumb backward. "Rollin' gravel—crackin' of twigs. No deer! . . . Reckon it'd be a good idee for us to slip round acrost this bench."

"Wal, y'u fellars go, an' I'll watch heah," returned Colter.

"Not much," said Somers, while Springer leered knowingly.

Colter became incensed, but he did not give way to it. Pondering a moment, he finally turned to Ellen. "Y'u wait heah till I come back. An' if I don't come in reasonable time y'u slip across the cañon an' through the willows to the cabins. Wait till aboot dark." With that he possessed himself of one of the extra rifles and belts and silently joined his comrades. Together they noiselessly stole into the brush.

Ellen had no other thought than to comply with Colter's wishes. There was her wounded uncle who had been left unattended, and she was anxious to get back to him. Besides, if she had wanted to run off from Colter, where could she go? Alone in the woods, she would get lost and die of starvation. Her lot must be cast with the Jorth faction until the end. That did not seem far away.

Her strained attention and suspense made the moments fly. By and by several shots pealed out far across the side cañon on her right, and they were answered by reports sounding closer to her. The fight was on again. But these shots were not repeated. The flies buzzed, the hot sun beat down and sloped to the west, the soft, warm breeze stirred the aspens, the ravens croaked, the red squirrels and blue jays chattered.

Suddenly a quick, short, yelp electrified Ellen, brought her upright with sharp, listening rigidity. Surely it was not a wolf and hardly could it be a coyote. Again she heard it. The yelp of a sheep dog! She had heard that often enough to know. And she rose to change her position so she could command a view of the rocky bluff above. Presently she espied what really appeared to be a big timber wolf. But another yelp satisfied her that it really was a dog. She watched him. Soon it became evident that he wanted to get down over the bluff. He ran to and fro, and then out of sight. In a few moments his yelp sounded from lower down, at the base of the bluff, and it was now the cry of an intelligent dog that was trying to call some one to his aid. Ellen grew convinced that the dog was near where Colter had said Bill Isbel had plunged over the declivity. Would the dog yelp that way if the man was dead? Ellen thought not.

No one came, and the continuous yelping of the dog got on Ellen's nerves. It was a call for help. And finally she surrendered to it. Since her natural terror when

Colter's horse was shot from under her and she had been dragged away, she had not recovered from fear of the Isbels. But calm consideration now convinced her that she could hardly be in a worse plight in their hands than if she remained in Colter's. So she started out to find the dog.

The wooded bench was level for a few hundred yards, and then it began to heave in rugged, rocky bulges up toward the Rim. It did not appear far to where the dog was barking, but the latter part of the distance proved to be a hard climb over jumbled rocks and through thick brush. Panting and hot, she at length reached the base of the bluff, to find that it was not very high.

The dog espied her before she saw him, for he was coming toward her when she discovered him. Big, shaggy, grayish white and black, with wild, keen face and eyes he assuredly looked the reputation Springer had accorded him. But sagacious, guarded as was his approach, he appeared friendly.

"Hello—doggie!" panted Ellen. "What's—wrong—up heah?"

He yelped, his ears lost their stiffness, his body sank a little, and his bushy tail wagged to and fro. What a gray, clear, intelligent look he gave her! Then he trotted back.

Ellen followed him around a corner of bluff to see the body of a man lying on his back. Fresh earth and gravel lay about him, attesting to his fall from above. He had on neither coat nor hat, and the position of his body and limbs suggested broken bones. As Ellen hurried to his side she saw that the front of his shirt, low down, was a bloody blotch. But he could lift his head; his eyes were open; he was perfectly conscious. Ellen did not recognize the dusty, skinned face, yet the mold of features, the look of the eyes, seemed strangely familiar.

"You're—Jorth's—girl," he said, in faint voice of surprise.

"Yes, I'm Ellen Jorth," she replied. "An' are y'u Bill Isbel?"

"All thet's left of me. But I'm thankin' God somebody come—even a Jorth."

Ellen knelt beside him and examined the wound in his abdomen. A heavy bullet had indeed, as Colter had avowed, torn clear through his middle. Even if he had not sustained other serious injury from the fall over the cliff, that terrible bullet wound meant death very shortly. Ellen shuddered. How inexplicable were men! How cruel, bloody, mindless!

"Isbel, I'm sorry—there's no hope," she said, low voiced. "Y'u've not long to live. . . . I cain't help y'u. God knows I'd do so if I could."

"All over!" he sighed, with his eyes looking beyond her. "I reckon—I'm glad. . . . But y'u can—do somethin' for me. Will y'u?"

"Indeed, yes. Tell me," she replied, lifting his dusty head on her knee. Her hands trembled as she brushed his wet hair back from his clammy brow.

"I've somethin'—on my conscience," he whispered.

The woman, the sensitive in Ellen, understood and pitied him then.

"Yes," she encouraged him.

"I stole cattle—my dad's and Blaisdell's—an' made deals—with Daggs. . . . All the crookedness—wasn't on—Jorth's side. . . . I want—my brother Jean—to know."

"I'll try—to tell him," whispered Ellen, out of her great amaze.

"We were all—a bad lot—except Jean," went on Isbel. "Dad wasn't fair. . . . God! how he hated Jorth! Jorth, yes, who was—your father. . . . Wal, they're even now."

"How—so?" faltered Ellen.

"Your father killed dad. . . . At the last—dad wanted to—save us. He sent word—he'd meet him—face to face—an' let thet end the feud. They met out in the road. . . . But some one shot dad down—with a rifle—an' then your father finished him."

"An' then, Isbel," added Ellen, with unconscious mocking bitterness, "your brother murdered my dad!"

"What!" whispered Bill Isbel. "Shore y'u've got—it wrong. I reckon Jean—could have killed—your father. . . . But he didn't. Queer, we all thought."

"Ah! . . . Who did kill my father?" burst out Ellen, and her voice rang like great hammers in her ears.

"It was Blue. He went in the store—alone—faced the whole gang alone. Bluffed them—taunted them—told them he was King Fisher. . . . Then he killed—your dad—an' Jackson Jorth. . . . Jean was out—back of the store. We were out—front. There was shootin'. Colmor was hit. Then Blue ran out—bad hurt. . . . Both of them—died in Meeker's yard "

"An' so Jean Isbel has not killed a Jorth!" said Ellen, in strange, deep voice.

"No," replied Isbel, earnestly. "I reckon this feud—was hardest on Jean. He never lived heah. . . . An' my sister Ann said—he got sweet on y'u. . . . Now did he?"

Slow, stinging tears filled Ellen's eyes, and her head sank low and lower.

"Yes—he did," she murmured, tremulously.

"Ahuh! Wal, thet accounts," replied Isbel, wonderingly. "Too bad! . . . It might have been. . . . A man always sees—different when—he's dyin'. . . . If I had—my life—to live over again! . . . My poor kids—deserted in their babyhood—ruined for life! All for nothin'. . . . May God forgive—"

Then he choked and whispered for water.

Ellen laid his head back and, rising, she took his sombrero and started hurriedly down the slope, making dust fly and rocks roll. Her mind was a seething ferment. Leaping, bounding, sliding down the weathered slope, she gained the bench, to run across that, and so on down into the open cañon to the willow-bordered brook. Here she filled the sombrero with water and started back, forced now to walk slowly and carefully. It was then, with the violence and fury of intense muscular activity denied her, that the tremendous import of Bill Isbel's revelation burst upon her very flesh and blood and transfiguring the very world of golden light and azure sky and speaking forestland that encompassed her.

Not a drop of the precious water did she spill. Not a misstep did she make. Yet so great was the spell upon her that she was not aware she had climbed the steep slope until the dog yelped his welcome. Then with all the flood of her emotion surging and resurging she knelt to allay the parching thirst of this dying enemy whose words had changed frailty to strength, hate to love, and the gloomy hell of despair to something unutterable. But she had returned too late. Bill Isbel was dead.

CHAPTER THIRTEEN

Jean Isbel, holding the wolf-dog Shepp in leash, was on the trail of the most dangerous of Jorth's gang, the gunman Queen. Dark drops of blood on the stones and plain tracks of a rider's sharp-heeled boots behind coverts indicated the trail of a wounded, slow-traveling fugitive. Therefore, Jean Isbel held in the dog and proceeded with the wary eye and watchful caution of an Indian.

Queen, true to his class, and emulating Blue with the same magnificent effrontery and with the same paralyzing suddenness of surprise, had appeared as if by magic at the last night camp of the Isbel faction. Jean had seen him first, in time to leap like a panther into the shadow. But he carried in his shoulder Queen's first bullet of that terrible encounter. Upon Gordon and Fredericks fell the brunt of Queen's fusillade. And they, shot to pieces, staggering and falling, held passionate grip on life long enough to draw and still Queen's guns and send him reeling off into the darkness of the forest.

Unarmed, and hindered by a painful wound, Jean had kept a vigil near camp all that silent and menacing night. Morning disclosed Gordon and Fredericks stark and ghastly beside the burned-out camp-fire, their guns clutched immovably in stiffened hands. Jean buried them as best he could, and when they were under ground with flat stones on their graves he knew himself to be indeed the last of the Isbel clan. And all that was wild and savage in his blood and desperate in his spirit rose to make him more than man and less than human. Then for the third time during these tragic last days the wolf-dog Shepp came to him.

Jean washed the wound Queen had given him and bound it tightly. The keen pang and burn of the lead was a constant and all-powerful reminder of the grim work left for him to do. The whole world was no longer large enough for him and whoever was left of the Jorths. The heritage of blood his father had bequeathed him, the unshakable love for a worthless girl who had so dwarfed and obstructed his will and so bitterly defeated and reviled his poor, romantic, boyish faith, the killing of hostile men, so strange in its after effects, the pursuits and fights, and loss of one by one of his confederates—these had finally engendered in Jean Isbel a wild, unslakable thirst, these had been the cause of his retrogression, these had unalterably and ruthlessly fixed in his darkened mind one fierce passion—to live and die the last man of that Jorth-Isbel feud.

At sunrise Jean left this camp, taking with him only a small knapsack of meat and bread, and with the eager, wild Shepp in leash he set out on Queen's bloody trail.

Black drops of blood on the stones and an irregular trail of footprints proved to Jean that the gunman was hard hit. Here he had fallen, or knelt, or sat down, evidently to bind his wounds. Jean found strips of scarf, red and discarded. And the blood drops failed to show on more rocks. In a deep forest of spruce, under silver-tipped spreading branches, Queen had rested, perhaps slept. Then laboring with dragging steps, not improbably with a lame leg, he had gone on, up out of the dark-green ravine to the open, dry, pine-tipped ridge. Here he had rested, perhaps waited to see if he were pursued. From that point his trail spoke an easy language for Jean's keen eye. The gunman knew he was pursued. He had seen his enemy. Therefore Jean proceeded with a slow caution, never getting within revolver range of ambush, using all his woodcraft to trail this man and yet save himself. Queen traveled slowly, either because he was wounded or else because he tried to ambush his pursuer, and Jean accommodated his pace to that of Queen. From noon of that day they were never far apart, never out of hearing of a rifle shot.

The contrast of the beauty and peace and loneliness of the surroundings to the nature of Queen's flight often obtruded its strange truth into the somber turbulence of Jean's mind, into that fixed columnar idea around which fleeting thoughts hovered and gathered like shadows.

Early frost had touched the heights with its magic wand. And the forest seemed a temple in which man might worship nature and life rather than steal through the dells and under the arched aisles like a beast of prey. The green-and-gold leaves of aspens quivered in the glades; maples in the ravines fluttered their red-and-purple leaves. The needle-matted carpet under the pines vied with the long lanes of silvery grass, alike enticing to the eye of man and beast. Sunny rays of light, flecked with dust and flying insects, slanted down from the overhanging brown-limbed, green-massed foliage. Roar of wind in the distant forest alternated with soft breeze close at hand. Small dove-gray squirrels ran all over the woodland, very curious about Jean and his dog, rustling the twigs, scratching the bark of trees, chattering and barking, frisky, saucy, and bright-eyed. A plaintive twitter of wild canaries came from the region above the treetops—first voices of birds in their pilgrimage toward the south. Pine cones dropped with soft thuds. The blue jays followed these intruders in the forest, screeching their displeasure. Like rain pattered the dropping seeds from the spruces. A woody, earthy, leafy fragrance, damp with the current of life, mingled with a cool, dry, sweet smell of withered grass and rotting pines.

Solitude and lonesomeness, peace and rest, wild life and nature, reigned there. It was a golden-green region, enchanting to the gaze of man. An Indian would have walked there with his spirits.

And even as Jean felt all this elevating beauty and inscrutable spirit his keen eye once more fastened upon the blood-red drops Queen had again left on the gray moss and rock. His wound had reopened. Jean felt the thrill of the scenting panther.

The sun set, twilight gathered, night fell. Jean crawled under a dense, low-spreading spruce, ate some bread and meat, fed the dog, and lay down to rest and sleep. His thoughts burdened him, heavy and black as the mantle of night. A wolf mourned a hungry cry for a mate. Shepp quivered under Jean's hand. That was the call which had lured him from the ranch. The wolf blood in him yearned for the wild. Jean tied the cowhide leash to his wrist. When this dark business was at an end Shepp could be free to join the lonely mate mourning out there in the forest. Then Jean slept.

Dawn broke cold, clear, frosty, with silvered grass sparkling, with a soft, faint rustling of falling aspen leaves. When the sun rose red Jean was again on the trail of Queen. By a frosty-ferned brook, where water tinkled and ran clear as air and cold as ice, Jean quenched his thirst, leaning on a stone that showed drops of blood. Queen, too, had to quench his thirst. What good, what help, Jean wondered, could the cold, sweet, granite water, so dear to woodsmen and wild creatures, do this wounded, hunted rustler? Why did he not wait in the open to fight and face the death he had meted? Where was that splendid and terrible daring of the gunman? Queen's love of life dragged him on and on, hour by hour, through the pine groves and spruce woods, through the oak swales and aspen glades, up and down the rocky gorges, around the windfalls and over the rotting logs.

The time came when Queen tried no more ambush. He gave up trying to trap his pursuer by lying in wait. He gave up trying to conceal his tracks. He grew stronger or, in desperation, increased his energy, so that he redoubled his progress through the wilderness. That, at best, would count only a few miles a day. And he began to circle to the northwest, back toward the deep cañon where Blaisdell and Bill Isbel had reached the end of their trails. Queen had evidently left his comrades, had lone-handed it in his last fight, but was now trying to get back to them. Somewhere in these wild, deep forest brakes the rest of the Jorth faction had found a hiding place. Jean let Queen lead him there.

Ellen Jorth would be with them. Jean had seen her. It had been his shot that killed Colter's horse. And he had withheld further fire because Colter had dragged the girl behind him, protecting his body with hers. Sooner or later Jean would come upon their camp. She would be there. The thought of her dark beauty, wasted in wantonness upon these rustlers, added a deadly rage to the blood lust and righteous wrath of his vengeance. Let her again flaunt her degradation in his face and, by the God she had forsaken, he would kill her, and so end the race of Jorths!

Another night fell, dark and cold, without starlight. The wind moaned in the forest. Shepp was restless. He sniffed the air. There was a step on his trail. Again a mournful, eager, wild, and hungry wolf cry broke the silence. It was deep and low, like that of a baying hound, but infinitely wilder. Shepp strained to get away. During the night, while Jean slept, he managed to chew the cowhide leash apart and run off.

Next day no dog was needed to trail Queen. Fog and low-drifting clouds in the forest and a misty rain had put the rustler off his bearings. He was lost, and showed that he realized it. Strange how a matured man, fighter of a hundred battles, steeped in bloodshed, and on his last stand, should grow panic-stricken upon being lost! So Jean Isbel read the signs of the trail.

Queen circled and wandered through the foggy, dripping forest until he headed down into a cañon. It was one that notched the Rim and led down and down, mile after mile into the Basin. Not soon had Queen discovered his mistake. When he did so, night overtook him.

The weather cleared before morning. Red and bright the sun burst out of the east to flood that low basin land with light. Jean found that Queen had traveled on and on, hoping, no doubt, to regain what he had lost. But in the darkness he had climbed to the manzanita slopes instead of back up the cañon. And here he had fought the hold of that strange brush of Spanish name until he fell exhausted.

Surely Queen would make his stand and wait somewhere in this devilish thicket for Jean to catch up with him. Many and many a place Jean would have chosen had he been in Queen's place. Many a rock and dense thicket Jean circled or approached with extreme care. Manzanita grew in patches that were impenetrable except for a small animal. The brush was a few feet high, seldom so high that Jean could not look over it, and of a beautiful appearance, having glossy, small leaves, a golden berry, and branches of dark-red color. These branches were tough and unbendable. Every bush, almost, had low branches that were dead, hard as steel, sharp as thorns, as clutching as cactus. Progress was possible only by endless detours to find the half-closed aisles between patches, or else by crashing through with main strength or walking right over the tops. Jean preferred this last method, not because it was the easiest, but for the reason that he could see ahead so much farther. So he literally walked across the tips of the manzanita brush. Often he fell through and had to step up again; many a branch broke with him, letting him down; but for the most part he stepped from fork to fork, on branch after branch, with balance of an Indian and the patience of a man whose purpose was sustaining and immutable.

On that south slope under the Rim the sun beat down hot. There was no breeze to temper the dry air. And before midday Jean was laboring, wet with sweat, parching with thirst, dusty and hot and tiring. It amazed him, the doggedness and tenacity of life shown by this wounded rustler. The time came when under the burning rays of the sun he was compelled to abandon the walk across the tips of the manzanita bushes and take to the winding, open threads that ran between. It would have been poor sight indeed that could not have followed Queen's labyrinthine and broken passage through the brush. Then the time came when Jean espied Queen, far ahead and above, crawling like a black bug along the bright-green slope. Sight then acted upon Jean as upon a hound in the chase. But he governed his actions if he could not govern his instincts. Slowly but surely he followed the dusty, hot trail, and never a patch of blood failed to send a thrill along his veins.

Queen, headed up toward the Rim, finally vanished from sight. Had he fallen? Was he hiding? But the hour disclosed that he was crawling. Jean's keen eye caught the slow moving of the brush and enabled him to keep just so close to the rustler, out of range of the six-shooters he carried. And so all the interminable hours of the hot afternoon that snail-pace flight and pursuit kept on.

Halfway up the Rim the growth of manzanita gave place to open, yellow, rocky slope dotted with cedars. Queen took to a slow-ascending ridge and left his bloody tracks all the way to the top, where in the gathering darkness the weary pursuer lost them.

Another night passed. Daylight was relentless to the rustler. He could not hide his trail. But somehow in a desperate last rally of strength he reached a point on the heavily timbered ridge that Jean recognized as being near the scene of the fight in the cañon. Queen was nearing the rendezvous of the rustlers. Jean crossed tracks of horses, and then more tracks that he was certain had been made days past by his own party. To the left of this ridge must be the deep cañon that had frustrated his efforts to catch up with the rustlers on the day Blaisdell lost his life, and probably Bill Isbel, too. Something warned Jean that he was nearing the end of the trail, and an unaccountable sense of imminent catastrophe seemed foreshadowed by vague dreads and doubts in his gloomy mind. Jean felt the need of rest, of food, of ease from the strain of the last weeks. But his spirit drove him implacably.

Queen's rally of strength ended at the edge of an open, bald ridge that was bare of brush or grass and was surrounded by a line of forest on three sides, and on the fourth by a low bluff which raised its gray head above the pines. Across this dusty open Queen had crawled, leaving unmistakable signs of his condition. Jean took long survey of the circle of trees and of the low, rocky eminence, neither of which he liked. It might be wiser to keep to cover, Jean thought, and work around to where Queen's trail entered the forest again. But he was tired, gloomy, and his eternal vigilance was failing. Nevertheless, he stilled for the thousandth time that bold prompting of his vengeance and, taking to the edge of the forest, he went to considerable pains to circle the open ground. And suddenly sight of a man sitting back against a tree halted Jean.

He stared to make sure his eyes did not deceive him. Many times stumps and snags and rocks had taken on strange resemblance to a standing or crouching man. This was only another suggestive blunder of the mind behind his eyes—what he wanted to see he imagined he saw. Jean glided on from tree to tree until he made sure that this sitting image indeed was that of a man. He sat bolt upright, facing back across the open, hands resting on his knees—and closer scrutiny showed Jean that he held a gun in each hand.

Queen! At the last his nerve had revived. He could not crawl any farther, he could never escape, so with the courage of fatality he chose the open, to face his foe and die. Jean had a thrill of admiration for the rustler. Then he stalked out from under the pines and strode forward with his rifle ready.

A watching man could not have failed to espy Jean. But Queen never made the slightest move. Moreover, his stiff, unnatural position struck Jean so singularly that he halted with a muttered exclamation. He was now about fifty paces from Queen, within range of those small guns. Jean called, sharply, *"Queen!"* Still the figure never relaxed in the slightest.

Jean advanced a few more paces, rifle up, ready to fire the instant Queen lifted a gun. The man's immobility brought the cold sweat to Jean's brow. He stopped to bend the full intense power of his gaze upon this inert figure. Suddenly over Jean flashed its meaning. Queen was dead. He had backed up against the pine, ready to face his foe, and he had died there. Not a shadow of a doubt entered Jean's mind as he started forward again. He knew. After all, Queen's blood would not be on his hands. Gordon and Fredericks in their death throes had given the rustler mortal wounds. Jean kept on, marveling the while. How ghastly thin and hard! Those four days of flight had been hell for Queen.

Jean reached him—looked down with staring eyes. The guns were tied to his hands. Jean stared violently as the whole direction of his mind shifted. A lightning glance showed that Queen had been propped against the tree—another showed boot tracks in the dust.

"By Heaven, they've fooled me!" hissed Jean, and quickly as he leaped behind the pine he was not quick enough to escape the cunning rustlers who had waylaid him thus. He felt the shock, the bite and burn of lead before he heard a rifle crack. A bullet had ripped through his left forearm. From behind the tree he saw a puff of white smoke along the face of the bluff—the very spot his keen and gloomy vigilance had descried as one of menace. Then several puffs of white smoke and ringing reports betrayed the ambush of the tricksters. Bullets barked the pine and whistled by. Jean saw a man dart from behind a rock and, leaning over, run for another. Jean's swift shot stopped him midway. He fell, got up, and floundered behind a bush scarcely large enough to conceal him. Into that bush Jean shot again and again. He had no pain in his wounded arm, but the sense of the shock clung in his consciousness, and this, with the tremendous surprise of deceit, and sudden release of long-dammed overmastering passion, caused him to empty the magazine of his Winchester in a terrible haste to kill the man he had hit.

These were all the loads he had for his rifle. Blood passion had made him blunder. Jean cursed himself, and his hand moved to his belt. His six-shooter was gone. The sheath had been loose. He had tied the gun fast. But the strings had been torn apart. The rustlers were shooting again. Bullets thudded into the pine and whistled by. Bending carefully, Jean reached one of Queen's guns and jerked it from his hand. The weapon was empty. Both of his guns were empty. Jean peeped out again to get the line in which the bullets were coming and, marking a course from his position to the cover of the forest, he ran with all his might. He gained the shelter. Shrill yells behind warned him that he had been seen, that his reason for flight had been guessed. Looking back, he saw two or three men scrambling down the bluff. Then the loud neigh of a frightened horse pealed out.

Jean discarded his useless rifle, and headed down the ridge slope, keeping to the thickest line of pines and sheering around the clumps of spruce. As he ran, his mind whirled with grim thoughts of escape, of his necessity to find the camp where Gordon and Fredericks were buried, there to procure another rifle and ammunition. He felt the wet blood dripping down his arm, yet no pain. The forest was too open for good cover. He dared not run uphill. His only course was ahead, and that soon ended in an abrupt declivity too precipitous to descend. As he halted, panting for breath, he heard the ring of hoofs on stone, then the thudding beat of running horses on soft ground. The rustlers had sighted the direction he had taken. Jean did not waste time to look. Indeed, there was no need, for as he bounded along the cliff to the right a rifle cracked and a bullet whizzed over his head. It lent wings to his feet. Like a deer he sped along, leaping cracks and logs and rocks, his ears filled by the rush of the wind, until his quick eye caught sight of thick-growing spruce foliage close to the precipice. He sprang down into the green mass. His weight precipitated him through the upper branches. But lower down his spread arms broke his fall, then retarded it until he caught. A long, swaying limb let him down and down, where he grasped another and a stiffer one that held his weight. Hand over hand he worked toward the trunk of this spruce and, gaining it, he found other branches close together down which he hastened, hold by hold and step by step, until all above him was black, dense foliage, and beneath him the brown, shady slope. Sure of being unseen from above, he glided noiselessly down under the trees, slowly regaining freedom from that constriction of his breast.

Passing on to a gray-lichened cliff, overhanging and gloomy, he paused there to rest and to listen. A faint crack of hoof on stone came to him from above, apparently farther on to the right. Eventually his pursuers would discover that he had taken to the cañon. But for the moment he felt safe. The wound in his forearm drew his attention. The bullet had gone clear through without breaking either bone. His shirt sleeve was soaked with blood. Jean rolled it back and tightly wrapped his scarf around the wound, yet still the dark-red blood oozed out and dripped down into his hand. He became aware of a dull, throbbing pain.

Not much time did Jean waste in arriving at what was best to do. For the time being he had escaped, and whatever had been his peril, it was past. In dense, rugged country like this he could not be caught by rustlers. But he had only a knife left for a weapon, and there was very little meat in the pocket of his coat. Salt and matches he possessed. Therefore the imperative need was for him to find the last camp, where he could get rifle and ammunition, bake bread, and rest up before taking again the trail of the rustlers. He had reason to believe that this cañon was the one where the fight on the Rim, and later, on a bench of woodland below, had taken place.

Thereupon he arose and glided down under the spruces toward the level, grassy open he could see between the trees. And as he proceeded, with the slow step and wary eye of an Indian, his mind was busy.

Queen had in his flight unerringly worked in the direction of this cañon until he became lost in the fog; and upon regaining his bearings he had made a wonderful and heroic effort to surmount the manzanita slope and the Rim and find the rendezvous of his comrades. But he had failed up there on the ridge. In thinking it over Jean arrived at a conclusion that Queen, finding he could go no farther, had waited, guns in hands, for his pursuer. And he had died in this position. Then by strange coincidence his comrades had happened to come across him and, recognizing the situation, they had taken the shells from his guns and propped him up with the idea of luring Jean on. They had arranged a cunning trick and ambush, which had all but snuffed out the last of the Isbels. Colter probably had been at the bottom of this crafty plan. Since the fight at the Isbel ranch, now seemingly far back in the past, this man Colter had loomed up more and more as a stronger and more dangerous antagonist than either Jorth or Daggs. Before that he had been little known to any of the Isbel faction. And it was Colter now who controlled the remnant of the gang and who had Ellen Jorth in his possession.

The cañon wall above Jean, on the right, grew more rugged and loftier, and the one on the left began to show wooded slopes and brakes, and at last a wide expanse with a winding, willow border on the west and a long, low, pine-dotted bench on the east. It took several moments of study for Jean to recognize the rugged bluff above this bench. On up that cañon several miles was the site where Queen had surprised Jean and his comrades at their campfire. Somewhere in this vicinity was the hiding place of the rustlers.

Thereupon Jean proceeded with the utmost stealth, absolutely certain that he would miss no sound, movement, sign, or anything unnatural to the wild peace of the cañon. And his first sense to register something was his keen smell. Sheep! He was amazed to smell sheep. There must be a flock not far away. Then from where he glided along under the trees he saw down to open places in the willow brake and noticed sheep tracks in the dark, muddy bank of the brook. Next he heard faint tinkle of bells, and at length, when he could see farther into the open enlargement of the cañon, his surprised gaze fell upon an immense gray, woolly patch that blotted out acres and acres of grass. Thousands of sheep were grazing there. Jean knew there were several flocks of Jorth's sheep on the mountain in the care of herders, but he had never thought of them being so far west, more than twenty miles from Chevelon Cañon. His roving eyes could not descry any herders or dogs. But he knew there must be dogs close to that immense flock. And, whatever his cunning, he could not hope to elude the scent and sight of shepherd dogs. It would be best to go back the way he had come, wait for darkness, then cross the cañon and climb out, and work around to his objective point. Turning at once, he started to glide back. But almost immediately he was brought stock-still and thrilling by the sound of hoofs.

Horses were coming in the direction he wished to take. They were close. His swift conclusion was that the men who had pursued him up on the Rim had worked down into the cañon. One circling glance showed him that he had no sure covert near at hand. It would not do to risk their passing him there. The border of woodland was narrow and not dense enough for close inspection. He was forced to turn back up the cañon, in the hope of soon finding a hiding place or a break in the wall where he could climb up.

Hugging the base of the wall, he slipped on, passing the point where he had espied the sheep, and gliding on until he was stopped by a bend in the dense line of willows. It sheered to the west there and ran close to the high wall. Jean kept on until he was stooping under a curling border of willow thicket, with branches slim and yellow and masses of green foliage that brushed against the wall. Suddenly he encountered an abrupt corner of rock. He rounded it, to discover that it ran at right angles with the one he had just passed. Peering up through the willows, he ascertained that there was a narrow crack in the main wall of the cañon. It had been concealed by willows low down and leaning spruces above. A wild, hidden retreat! Along the base of the wall there were tracks of small animals. The place was odorous, like all dense thickets, but it was not dry. Water ran through there somewhere. Jean drew easier breath. All sounds except the rustling of birds or mice in the willows had ceased. The brake was pervaded by a dreamy emptiness. Jean decided to steal on a little farther, then wait till he felt he might safely dare go back.

The golden-green gloom suddenly brightened. Light showed ahead, and parting the willows, he looked out into a narrow, winding cañon, with an open, grassy, willow-streaked lane in the center and on each side a thin strip of woodland.

His surprise was short lived. A crashing of horses back of him in the willows gave him a shock. He ran out along the base of the wall, back of the trees. Like the strip of woodland in the main cañon, this one was scant and had but little underbrush. There were young spruces growing with thick branches clear to the grass, and under these he could have concealed himself. But, with a certainty of sheep dogs in the vicinity, he would not think of hiding except as a last resource. These horsemen, whoever they were, were as likely to be sheep herders as not. Jean slackened his pace to look back. He could not see any moving objects, but he still heard horses, though not so close now. Ahead of him this narrow gorge opened out like the neck of a bottle. He would run to the head of it and find a place to climb to the top.

Hurried and anxious as Jean was, he yet received an impression of singular, wild nature of this side gorge. It was a hidden, pine-fringed crack in the rock-ribbed and cañon-cut tableland. Above him the sky seemed a winding stream of blue. The walls were red and bulged out in spruce-greened shelves. From wall to wall was scarcely a distance of a hundred feet. Jumbles of rock obstructed his close holding to the wall. He had to walk at the edge of the timber. As he progressed, the gorge widened into wilder, ruggeder aspect. Through the trees ahead he saw where the wall circled to meet the cliff on the left, forming an oval depression, the nature of which he could not ascertain. But it appeared to be a small opening surrounded by dense thickets and the overhanging walls. Anxiety augmented to alarm. He might not be able to find a place to scale those rough cliffs. Breathing hard, Jean halted again. The situation was growing critical again. His physical condition was worse. Loss of sleep and rest, lack of food, the long pursuit of Queen, the wound in his arm, and the desperate run for his life—these had weakened him to the extent that if he undertook any strenuous effort he would fail. His cunning weighed all chances.

The shade of wall and foliage above, and another jumble of ruined cliff, hindered his survey of the ground ahead, and he almost stumbled upon a cabin, hidden on three sides, with a small, bare clearing in front. It was an old, ramshackle structure like others he had run across in the cañons. Cautiously he approached and peeped around the corner. At first swift glance it had all the appearance of long disuse. But Jean had no time for another look. A clip-clop of trotting horses on hard ground brought the same pell-mell rush of sensations that had driven him to wild flight scarcely an hour past. His body jerked with its instinctive impulse, then quivered with his restraint. To turn back would be risky, to run ahead would be fatal, to hide was his one hope. No covert behind! And the clip-clop of hoofs sounded closer. One moment longer Jean held mastery over his instincts of self-preservation. To keep from running was almost impossible. It was the sheer primitive animal sense to escape. He drove it back and glided along the front of the cabin.

Here he saw that the cabin adjoined another. Reaching the door, he was about to peep in when the thud of hoofs and voices close at hand transfixed him with a grim certainty that he had not an instant to lose. Through the thin, black-streaked line of trees he saw moving red objects. Horses! He must run. Passing the door, his keen nose caught a musty, woody odor and the tail of his eye saw bare dirt floor. This cabin was unused. He halted—gave a quick look back. And the first thing his eye fell upon was a ladder, right inside the door, against the wall. He looked up. It led to a loft that, dark and gloomy, stretched halfway across the cabin. An irresistible impulse drove Jean. Slipping inside, he climbed up the ladder to the loft. It was like night up there. But he crawled on the rough-hewn rafters and, turning with his head toward the opening, he stretched out and lay still.

What seemed an interminable moment ended with a trample of hoofs outside the cabin. It ceased. Jean's vibrating ears caught the jingle of spurs and a thud of boots striking the ground.

"Wal, sweetheart, heah we are home again," drawled a slow, cool, mocking Texas voice.

"Home! I wonder, Colter—did y'u ever have a home—a mother—a sister—much less a sweetheart?" was the reply, bitter and caustic.

Jean's palpitating, hot body suddenly stretched still and cold with intensity of shock. His very bones seemed to quiver and stiffen into ice. During the instant of realization his heart stopped. And a slow, contracting pressure enveloped his breast and moved up to constrict his throat. That woman's voice belonged to Ellen Jorth. The sound of it had lingered in his dreams. He had stumbled upon the rendezvous of the Jorth faction. Hard indeed had been the fates meted out to those of the Isbels and Jorths who had passed to their deaths. But no ordeal, not even Queen's, could compare with this desperate one Jean must endure. He had loved Ellen Jorth, strangely, wonderfully, and he had scorned evil repute to believe her good. He had spared her father and her uncle. He had weakened or lost the cause of the Isbels. He loved her now, desperately, deathlessly, knowing from her own lips that she was worthless—loved her the more because he had felt her terrible shame. And to him—the last of the Isbels—had come the cruelest of dooms—to be caught like a crippled rat in a trap; to be compelled to lie helpless, wounded, without a gun; to listen, and perhaps to see Ellen Jorth enact the very truth of her mocking insinuation. His will, his promise, his creed, his blood must hold him to the stern decree that he should be the last man of the Jorth-Isbel war. But could he lie there to hear—to see—when he had a knife and an arm?

CHAPTER FOURTEEN

Then followed the leathery flop of saddles to the soft turf and the stamp of loosened horses.

Jean heard a noise at the cabin door, a rustle, and then a knock of something hard against wood. Silently he moved his head to look down through a crack between the rafters. He saw the glint of a rifle leaning against the sill. Then the doorstep was darkened. Ellen Jorth sat down with a long, tired sigh. She took off her sombrero and the light shone on the rippling, dark-brown hair, hanging in a tangled braid. The curved nape of her neck showed a warm tint of golden tan. She wore a gray blouse, soiled and torn, that clung to her lissome shoulders.

"Colter, what are y'u goin' to do?" she asked, suddenly. Her voice carried something Jean did not remember. It thrilled into the icy fixity of his senses.

"We'll stay heah," was the response, and it was followed by a clinking step of spurred boot.

"Shore I won't stay heah," declared Ellen. "It makes me sick when I think of how Uncle Tad died in there alone—helpless—sufferin'. The place seems haunted."

"Wal, I'll agree that it's tough on y'u. . . . But what the hell *can* we do?"

A long silence ensued which Ellen did not break.

"Somethin' has come off round heah since early mawnin'," declared Colter. "Somers an' Springer haven't got back. An' Antonio's gone. . . . Now, honest, Ellen, didn't y'u heah rifle shots off somewhere?"

"I reckon I did," she responded, gloomily.

"An' which way?"

"Sounded to me up on the bluff, back pretty far."

"Wal, shore that's my idee. An' it makes me think hard. Y'u know Somers come across the last camp of the Isbels. An' he dug into a grave to find the bodies of Jim

Gordon an' another man he didn't know. Queen kept good his brag. He braced that Isbel gang an' killed those fellars. But either him or Jean Isbel went off leavin' bloody tracks. If it was Queen's y'u can bet Isbel was after him. An' if it was Isbel's tracks, why shore Queen would stick to them. Somers an' Springer couldn't follow the trail. They're shore not much good at trackin'. But for days they've been ridin' the woods, hopin' to run across Queen. . . . Wal now, mebbe they run across Isbel instead. An' if they did an' got away from him they'll be heah sooner or later. If Isbel was too many for them he'd hunt for my trail. I'm gamblin' that either Queen or Jean Isbel is daid. I'm hopin' it's Isbel. Because if he ain't daid he's the last of the Isbels, an' mebbe I'm the last of Jorth's gang. . . . Shore I'm not hankerin' to meet the half-breed. That's why I say we'll stay heah. This is as good a hidin' place as there is in the country. We've grub. There's water an' grass."

"Me—stay heah with y'u—alone!"

The tone seemed a contradiction to the apparently accepted sense of her words. Jean held his breath. But he could not still the slowly mounting and accelerating faculties within that were involuntary rising to meet some strange, nameless import. He felt it. He imagined it would be the catastrophe of Ellen Jorth's calm acceptance of Colter's proposition. But down in Jean's miserable heart lived something that would not die. No mere words could kill it. How poignant that moment of her silence! How terribly he realized that if his intelligence and his emotion had believed her betraying words, his soul had not!

But Ellen Jorth did not speak. Her brown head hung thoughtfully. Her supple shoulders sagged a little.

"Ellen, what's happened to y'u?" went on Colter.

"All the misery possible to a woman," she replied, dejectedly.

"Shore I don't mean that way," he continued, persuasively. "I ain't gainsayin' the hard facts of your life. It's been bad. Your dad was no good. . . . But I mean I can't figger the change in y'u."

"No, I reckon y'u cain't," she said. "Whoever was responsible for your make-up left out a mind—not to say feeling."

Colter drawled a low laugh.

"Wal, have that your own way. But how much longer are y'u goin' to be like this heah?"

"Like what?" she rejoined, sharply.

"Wal, this stand-offishness of yours?"

"Colter, I told y'u to let me alone," she said, sullenly.

"Shore. An' y'u did that before. But this time y'u're different. . . . An' wal, I'm gettin' tired of it."

Here the cool, slow voice of the Texan sounded an inflexibility before absent, a timber that hinted of illimitable power.

Ellen Jorth shrugged her lithe shoulders and, slowly rising, she picked up the little rifle and turned to step into the cabin.

"Colter," she said, "fetch my pack an' my blankets in heah."

"Shore," he returned, with good nature.

Jean saw Ellen Jorth lay the rifle lengthwise in a chink between two logs and then slowly turn, back to the wall. Jean knew her then, yet did not know her. The brown flash of her face seemed that of an older, graver woman. His strained gaze, like his waiting mind, had expected something, he knew not what—a hardened face, a ghost of beauty, a recklessness, a distorted, bitter, lost expression in keeping with her fortunes. But he had reckoned falsely. She did not look like that. There was incalculable change, but the beauty remained, somehow different. Her red lips were parted. Her brooding eyes, looking out straight from under the level, dark brows, seemed sloe black and wonderful with their steady, passionate light.

Jean, in his eager, hungry devouring of the beloved face, did not on the first instant grasp the significance of its expression. He was seeing the features that had haunted him. But quickly he interpreted her expression as the somber, hunted look of a woman who would bear no more. Under the torn blouse her full breast heaved. She held her hands clenched at her sides. She was listening, waiting for that jangling, slow step. It came, and with the sound she subtly changed. She was a woman hiding her true feelings. She relaxed, and that strong, dark look of fury seemed to fade back into her eyes.

Colter appeared at the door, carrying a roll of blankets and a pack.

"Throw them heah," she said. "I reckon y'u needn't bother coming in."

That angered the man. With one long stride he stepped over the doorsill, down into the cabin, and flung the blankets at her feet and then the pack after it. Whereupon he deliberately sat down in the door, facing her. With one hand he slid off his sombrero, which fell outside, and with the other he reached in his upper vest pocket for the little bag of tobacco that showed there. All the time he looked at her. By the light now unobstructed Jean descried Colter's face; and sight of it then sounded the roll and drum of his passions.

"Wal, Ellen, I reckon we'll have it out right now an' heah," he said, and with tobacco in one hand, paper in the other he began the operations of making a cigarette. However, he scarcely removed his glance from her.

"Yes?" queried Ellen Jorth.

"I'm goin' to have things the way they were before—an' more," he declared. The cigarette paper shook in his fingers.

"What do y'u mean?" she demanded.

"Y'u know what I mean," he retorted. Voice and action were subtly unhinging this man's control over himself.

"Maybe I don't. I reckon y'u'd better talk plain."

The rustler had clear gray-yellow eyes, flawless, like crystal, and suddenly they danced with little fiery flecks.

"The last time I laid my hand on y'u I got hit for my pains. An' shore that's been ranklin'."

"Colter, y'u'll get hit again if y'u put your hands on me," she said, dark, straight glance on him. A frown wrinkled the level brows.

"Y'u mean that?" he asked, thickly.

"I shore do."

Manifestly he accepted her assertion. Something of incredulity and bewilderment, that had vied with his resentment, utterly disappeared from his face.

"Heah I've been waitin' for y'u to love me," he declared, with a gesture not without dignified emotion. "Your givin' in without that wasn't so much to me."

And at these words of the rustler's Jean Isbel felt an icy, sickening shudder creep into his soul. He shut his eyes. The end of his dream had been long in coming, but at last it had arrived. A mocking voice, like a hollow wind, echoed through that region—that lonely and ghost-like hall of his heart which had harbored faith.

She burst into speech, louder and sharper, the first words of which Jean's strangely throbbing ears did not distinguish.

"—— —— you! . . . I never gave in to y'u an' I never will."

"But, girl—I kissed y'u—hugged y'u—handled y'u—" he expostulated, and the making of the cigarette ceased.

"Yes, y'u did—y'u brute—when I was so downhearted and weak I couldn't lift my hand," she flashed.

"Ahuh! Y'u mean I couldn't do that now?"

"I should smile I do, Jim Colter!" she replied.

"Wal, mebbe—I'll see—presently," he went on, straining with words. "But I'm shore curious. . . . Daggs, then—he was nothin' to y'u?"

"No more than y'u," she said, morbidly. "He used to run after me—long ago, it seems. . . . I was only a girl then—innocent, an' I'd not known any but rough men. I couldn't all the time—every day, every hour—keep him at arm's length. Sometimes before I knew—I didn't care. I was a child. A kiss meant nothing to me. But after I knew—"

Ellen dropped her head in brooding silence.

"Say, do y'u expect me to believe that?" he queried, with a derisive leer.

"Bah! What do I care what y'u believe?" she cried, with lifting head.

"How aboot Simm Bruce?"

"That coyote! . . . He lied aboot me, Jim Colter. And any man half a man would have known he lied."

"Wal, Simm always bragged aboot y'u bein' his girl," asserted Colter. "An' he wasn't over-particular aboot details of your love-makin'."

Ellen gazed out of the door, over Colter's head, as if the forest out there was a refuge. She evidently sensed more about the man than appeared in his slow talk, in his slouching position. Her lips shut in a firm line, as if to hide their trembling and to still her passionate tongue. Jean, in his absorption, magnified his perceptions. Not yet was Ellen Jorth afraid of this man, but she feared the situation. Jean's heart was at bursting pitch. All within him seemed chaos—a wreck of beliefs and convictions. Nothing was true. He would wake presently out of a nightmare. Yet, as surely as he quivered there, he felt the imminence of a great moment—a lightning flash—a thunderbolt—a balance struck.

Colter attended to the forgotten cigarette. He rolled it, lighted it, all the time with lowered, pondering head, and when he had puffed a cloud of smoke he suddenly looked up with face as hard as flint, eyes as fiery as molten steel.

"Wal, Ellen—how aboot Jean Isbel—our half-breed Nez Perce friend—who was shore seen handlin' y'u familiar?" he drawled.

Ellen Jorth quivered as under a lash, and her brown face turned a dusty scarlet, that slowly receding left her pale.

"Damn y'u, Jim Colter!" she burst out, furiously. "I wish Jean Isbel would jump in that door—or down out of that loft! . . . He killed Greaves for defiling my name! . . . He'd kill *y'u* for your dirty insult. . . . And I'd like to watch him do it. . . . Y'u cold-blooded Texan! Y'u thieving rustler! Y'u liar! . . . Y'u lied aboot my father's death. And I know why. Y'u stole my father's gold. . . . An' now y'u want me—y'u expect me to fall into your arms. . . . My Heaven! cain't y'u tell a decent woman? Was your mother decent? Was your sister decent? . . . Bah! I'm appealing to deafness. But y'u'll *heah* this, Jim Colter! . . . I'm not what y'u think I am! I'm not the—the damned hussy y'u liars have made me out. . . . I'm a Jorth, alas! I've no home, no relatives, no friends! I've been forced to live my life with rustlers—vile men like y'u an' Daggs an' the rest of your like. . . . But I've been good! Do y'u heah that? . . . I *am* good—an', so help me God, y'u an' all your rottenness cain't make me bad!"

Colter lounged to his tall height and the laxity of the man vanished.

Vanished also was Jean Isbel's suspended icy dread, the cold clogging of his fevered mind—vanished in a white, living, leaping flame.

Silently he drew his knife and lay there watching with the eyes of a wildcat. The instant Colter stepped far enough over toward the edge of the loft Jean meant to bound erect and plunge down upon him. But Jean could wait now. Colter had a gun at his hip. He must never have a chance to draw it.

"Ahuh! So y'u wish Jean Isbel would hop in heah, do y'u?" queried Colter. "Wal, if I had any pity on y'u, that's done for it."

A sweep of his long arm, so swift Ellen had no time to move, brought his hand in clutching contact with her. And the force of it flung her half across the cabin room, leaving the sleeve of her blouse in his grasp. Pantingly she put out that bared arm and her other to ward him off as he took long, slow strides toward her.

Jean rose half to his feet, dragged by almost ungovernable passion to risk all on one leap. But the distance was too great. Colter, blind as he was to all outward things, would hear, would see in time to make Jean's effort futile. Shaking like a leaf, Jean sank back, eye again to the crack between the rafters.

Ellen did not retreat, nor scream, nor move. Every line of her body was instinct with fight, and the magnificent blaze of her eyes would have checked a less callous brute.

Colter's big hand darted between Ellen's arms and fastened in the front of her blouse. He did not try to hold her or draw her close. The unleashed passion of the man required violence. In one savage pull he tore off her blouse, exposing her white, rounded shoulders and heaving bosom, where instantly a wave of red burned upward.

Overcome by the tremendous violence and spirit of the rustler, Ellen sank to her knees, with blanched face and dilating eyes, trying with folded arms and trembling hand to hide her nudity.

At that moment the rapid beat of hoofs on the hard trail outside halted Colter in his tracks.

"Hell!" he exclaimed. "An' who's that?" With a fierce action he flung the remnants of Ellen's blouse in her face and turned to leap out the door.

Jean saw Ellen catch the blouse and try to wrap it around her, while she sagged against the wall and stared at the door. The hoof beats pounded to a solid thumping halt just outside.

"Jim—thar's hell to pay!" rasped out a panting voice.

"Wal, Springer, I reckon I wished y'u'd paid it without spoilin' my deals," retorted Colter, cool and sharp.

"Deals? Ha! Y'u'll be forgettin'—your lady love—in a minnit," replied Springer. "When I catch—my breath."

"Where's Somers?" demanded Colter.

"I reckon he's all shot up—if my eyes didn't fool me."

"Where is he?" yelled Colter.

"Jim—he's layin' up in the bushes round thet bluff. I didn't wait to see how he was hurt. But he shore stopped some lead. An' he flopped like a chicken with its—haid cut off."

"Where's Antonio?"

"He run like the greaser he is," declared Springer, disgustedly.

"Ahuh! An' where's Queen?" queried Colter, after a significant pause.

"Dead!"

The silence ensuing was fraught with a suspense that held Jean in cold bonds. He saw the girl below rise from her knees, one hand holding the blouse to her breast, the other extended, and with strange, repressed, almost frantic look she swayed toward the door.

"Wal, talk," ordered Colter, harshly.

"Jim, there ain't a hell of a lot," replied Springer, drawing a deep breath, "but what there is is shore interestin'. . . . Me an' Somers took Antonio with us. He left his woman with the sheep. An' we rode up the cañon, clumb out on top, an' made a circle back on the ridge. That's the way we've been huntin' fer tracks. Up thar in a bare spot we run plump into Queen sittin' against a tree, right out in the open. Queerest sight y'u ever seen! The damn gunfighter had set down to wait for Isbel, who was trailin' him, as we suspected—an' he died thar. He wasn't cold when we found him. . . . Somers was quick to see a trick. So he propped Queen up an' tied the guns to his hands—an', Jim, the queerest thing aboot that deal was this—Queen's guns was empty! Not a shell left! It beat us holler. . . . We left him thar, an' hid up high on the bluff, mebbe a hundred yards off. The hosses we left back in a thicket. An' we waited thar a long time. But, sure enough, the half-breed come. He was too smart. Too much Injun! He would not cross the open, but went around. An' then he seen Queen. It was great to watch him. After a little he shoved his rifle out an' went right fer Queen. This is when I wanted to shoot. I could have plugged him. But Somers says wait an' make it sure. When Isbel got up to Queen he was sort of half hid by the tree. An' I couldn't wait no longer, so I shot. I hit him, too. We all began to shoot. Somers showed himself, an' that's when Isbel opened up. He used a whole magazine on Somers an' then, suddenlike, he quit. It didn't take me long to figger mebbe he was out of shells. When I seen him run I was certain of it. Then we made for the hosses an' rode after Isbel. Pretty soon I seen him runnin' like a deer down the ridge. I yelled an' spurred after him. There is where Antonio quit me. But I kept on. An' I got a shot at Isbel. He ran out of sight. I follered him by spots of blood on the stones an' grass until I couldn't trail him no more. He must have gone down over the cliffs. He couldn't have done nothin' else without me seein' him. I found his rifle, an' here it is to prove what I say. I had to go back to climb down off the Rim, an' I rode fast down the cañon. He's somewhere along that west wall, hidin' in the brush, hard hit if I know anythin' aboot the color of blood."

"Wal! . . . that beats me holler, too," ejaculated Colter.

"Jim, what's to be done?" inquired Springer, eagerly. "If we're sharp we can corral that half-breed. He's the last of the Isbels."

"More, pard. He's the last of the Isbel outfit," declared Colter. "If y'u can show me blood in his tracks I'll trail him."

"Y'u can bet I'll show y'u," rejoined the other rustler. "But listen! Wouldn't it be better for us first to see if he crossed the cañon? I reckon he didn't. But let's make sure. An' if he didn't we'll have him somewhar along that west cañon wall. He's not got no gun. He'd never run thet way if he had. . . . Jim, he's our meat!"

"Shore, he'll have that knife," pondered Colter.

"We needn't worry about thet," said the other, positively. "He's hard hit, I tell y'u. All we got to do is find thet bloody trail again an' stick to it—goin' careful. He's layin' low like a crippled wolf."

"Springer, I want the job of finishin' that half-breed," hissed Colter. "It'd give ten years of my life to stick a gun down his throat an' shoot it off."

"All right. Let's rustle. Mebbe y'u'll not have to give much more'n ten minnits. Because I tell y'u I can find him. It'd been easy—but, Jim, I reckon I was afraid."

"Leave your hoss for me an' go ahaid," the rustler then said, brusquely. "I've a job in the cabin heah."

"Haw-haw! . . . Wal, Jim, I'll rustle a bit down the trail an' wait. No huntin' Jean Isbel alone—not fer me. I've had a queer feelin' about thet knife he used on Greaves. An' I reckon y'u'd oughter let thet Jorth hussy alone long enough to—"

"Springer, I reckon I've got to hawg-tie her—" His voice became indistinguishable, and footfalls attested to a slow moving away of the men.

Jean had listened with ears acutely strung to catch every syllable while his gaze rested upon Ellen who stood beside the door. Every line of her body denoted a listening intensity. Her back was toward Jean, so that he could not see her face. And he did not want to see, but could not help seeing her naked shoulders. She put her head out of the door. Suddenly she drew it in quickly and half turned her face, slowly raising her white arm. This was the left one and bore the marks of Colter's hard fingers.

She gave a little gasp. Her eyes became large and staring. They were bent on the hand that she had removed from a step on the ladder. On hand and wrist showed a bright-red smear of blood.

Jean, with a convulsive leap of his heart, realized that he had left his bloody tracks on the ladder as he had climbed. That moment seemed the supremely terrible one of his life.

Ellen Jorth's face blanched and her eyes darkened and dilated with exceeding amaze and flashing thought to become fixed with horror. That instant was the one in which her reason connected the blood on the ladder with the escape of Jean Isbel.

One moment she leaned there, still as stone except for her heaving breast, and then her fixed gaze changed to a swift, dark blaze, comprehending, yet inscrutable, as she flashed it up the ladder to the loft. She could see nothing, yet she knew and Jean knew that she knew he was there. A marvelous transformation passed over her features and even over her form. Jean choked with the ache in his throat. Slowly she put the bloody hand behind her while with the other she still held the torn blouse to her breast.

Colter's slouching, musical step sounded outside. And it might have been a strange breath of infinitely vitalizing and passionate life blown into the well-springs of Ellen Jorth's being. Isbel had no name for her then. The spirit of a woman had been to him a thing unknown.

She swayed back from the door against the wall in singular, softened poise, as if all the steel had melted out of her body. And as Colter's tall shadow fell across the threshold Jean Isbel felt himself staring with eyeballs that ached—straining incredulous sight at this woman who in a few seconds had bewildered his senses with her transfiguration. He saw but could not comprehend.

"Jim—I heard—all Springer told y'u," she said. The look of her dumfounded Colter and her voice seemed to shake him visibly.

"Suppose y'u did. What then?" he demanded, harshly, as he halted with one booted foot over the threshold. Malignant and forceful, he eyed her darkly, doubtfully.

"I'm afraid," she whispered.

"What of? Me?"

"No. Of—of Jean Isbel. He might kill y'u and—then where would I be?"

"Wal, I'm damned!" ejaculated the rustler. "What's got into y'u?" He moved to enter, but a sort of fascination bound him.

"Jim, I hated y'u a moment ago," she burst out. "But now—with that Jean Isbel somewhere near—hidin'—watchin' to kill y'u—an' maybe me, too—I—I don't hate y'u any more. . . . Take me away."

"Girl, have y'u lost your nerve?" he demanded.

"My God! Colter—cain't y'u see?" she implored. "Won't y'u take me away?"

"I shore will—presently," he replied, grimly. "But y'u'll wait till I've shot the lights out of this Isbel."

"No!" she cried. "Take me away now. . . . An' I'll give in—I'll be what y'u—want. . . . Y'u can do with me—as y'u like."

Colter's lofty frame leaped as if at the release of bursting blood. With a lunge he cleared the threshold to loom over her.

"Am I out of my haid, or are y'u?" he asked, in low, hoarse voice. His darkly corded face expressed extremest amaze.

"Jim, I mean it," she whispered, edging an inch nearer him, her white face uplifted, her dark eyes unreadable in their eloquence and mystery. "I've no friend but y'u. . . . I'll be—yours. . . . I'm lost. . . . What does it matter? . . . If y'u want me—take me *now*—before I kill myself."

"Ellen Jorth, there's somethin' wrong aboot y'u," he responded. "Did y'u tell the truth—when y'u denied ever bein' a sweetheart of Simm Bruce?"

"Yes, I told y'u the truth."

"Ahuh! An' how do y'u account for layin' me out with every dirty name y'u could give tongue to?"

"Oh, it was temper. I wanted to be let alone."

"Temper! Wal, I reckon y'u've got one," he retorted, grimly. "An' I'm not shore y'u're not crazy or lyin'. An hour ago I couldn't touch y'u."

"Y'u may now—if y'u promise to take me away—at once. This place has got on my nerves. I couldn't sleep heah with that Isbel hidin' around. Could y'u?"

"Wal, I reckon I'd not sleep very deep."

"Then let us go."

He shook his lean, eagle-like head in slow, doubtful vehemence, and his piercing gaze studied her distrustfully. Yet all the while there was manifest in his strung frame an almost irrepressible violence, held in abeyance to his will.

"That aboot your bein' so good?" he inquired, with a return of the mocking drawl.

"Never mind what's past," she flashed, with passion dark as his. "I've made my offer."

"Shore there's a lie aboot y'u somewhere," he muttered, thickly.

"Man, could I do more?" she demanded in scorn.

"No. But it's a lie," he returned. "Y'u'll get me to take y'u away an' then fool me—run off—God knows what. Women are all liars."

Manifestly he could not believe in her strange transformation. Memory of her wild and passionate denunciation of him and his kind must have seared even his calloused soul. But the ruthless nature of him had not weakened or softened in the least as to his intentions. This weather-vane veering of hers bewildered him, obsessed him with its possibilities. He had the look of a man who was divided between love of her and hate, whose love demanded a return, but whose hate required a proof of her abasement. Not proof of surrender, but proof of her shame! The ignominy of him thirsted for its like. He could grind her beauty under his heel, but he could not soften to this feminine inscrutableness.

And whatever was the truth of Ellen Jorth in this moment, beyond Colter's gloomy and stunted intelligence, beyond even the love of Jean Isbel, it was something that held the balance of mastery. She read Colter's mind. She dropped the torn blouse from her hand and stood there, unashamed, with the wave of her white breast pulsing, eyes black as night and full of hell, her face white, tragic, terrible, yet strangely lovely.

"Take me away," she whispered, stretching one white arm toward him, then the other.

Colter, even as she moved, had leaped with inarticulate cry and radiant face to meet her embrace. But it seemed, just as her left arm flashed up toward his neck, that he saw her bloody hand and wrist. Strange how that checked his ardor—threw up his lean head like that of a striking bird of prey.

"Blood! What the hell!" he ejaculated, and in one sweep he grasped her. "How'd y'u do that? Are y'u cut? . . . Hold still."

Ellen could not release her hand.

"I scratched myself," she said.

"Where? . . . All that blood!" And suddenly he flung her hand back with fierce gesture, and the gleams of his yellow eyes were like the points of leaping flames. They pierced her—read the secret falsity of her. Slowly he stepped backward, guardedly his hand moved to his gun, and his glance circled and swept the interior of the cabin. As if he had the nose of a hound and sight to follow scent, his eyes bent to the dust of the ground before the door. He quivered, grew rigid as stone, and then moved his head with exceeding slowness as if searching through a microscope in the dust—farther to the left—to the foot of the ladder—and up one step—another—a third—all the way up to the loft. Then he whipped out his gun and wheeled to face the girl.

"Ellen, y'u've got your half-breed heah!" he said, with a terrible smile.

She neither moved nor spoke. There was a suggestion of collapse, but it was only a change where the alluring softness of her hardened into a strange, rapt glow. And in it seemed the same mastery that had characterized her former aspect. Herein the treachery of her was revealed. She had known what she meant to do in any case.

Colter, standing at the door, reached a long arm toward the ladder, where he laid his hand on a rung. Taking it away he held it palm outward for her to see the dark splotch of blood.

"See?"

"Yes, I see," she said, ringingly.

Passion wrenched him, transformed him. "All that—aboot leavin' heah—with me—aboot givin' in—was a lie!"

"No, Colter. It was the truth. I'll go—yet—now—if y'u'll spare—*him!*" She whispered the last word and made a slight movement of her hand toward the loft.

"Girl!" he exploded, incredulously. "Y'u love this half-breed—this *Isbel?* . . . Y'u *love* him!"

"With all my heart! . . . Thank God! It has been my glory. . . . It might have been my salvation. . . . But now I'll go to hell with y'u—if y'u'll spare him."

"Damn my soul!" rasped out the rustler, as if something of respect was wrung from that sordid deep of him. "Y'u—y'u woman! . . . Jorth will turn over in his grave. He'd rise out of his grave if this Isbel got y'u."

"Hurry! Hurry!" implored Ellen. "Springer may come back. I think I heard a call."

"Wal, Ellen Jorth, I'll not spare Isbel—nor y'u," he returned, with dark and meaning leer, as he turned to ascend the ladder.

Jean Isbel, too, had reached the climax of his suspense. Gathering all his muscles in a knot he prepared to leap upon Colter as he mounted the ladder. But Ellen Jorth screamed piercingly and snatched her rifle from its resting place and, cocking it, she held it forward and low.

"Colter!"

Her scream and his uttered name stiffened him.

"Y'u will spare Jean Isbel!" she rang out. "Drop that gun—drop it!"

"Shore, Ellen. . . . Easy now. Remember your temper. . . . I'll let Isbel off," he panted, huskily, and all his body sank quiveringly to a crouch.

"Drop your gun! Don't turn round. . . . Colter!—*I'll kill y'u!"*

But even then he failed to divine the meaning and the spirit of her.

"Aw, now, Ellen," he entreated, in louder, huskier tones, and as if dragged by fatal doubt of her still, he began to turn.

Crash! The rifle emptied its contents in Colter's breast. All his body sprang up. He dropped the gun. Both hands fluttered toward her. And an awful surprise flashed over his face.

"So—help—me—God!" he whispered, with blood thick in his voice. Then darkly, as one groping, he reached for her with shaking hands. "Y'u—y'u white-throated hussy! . . . I'll . . ."

He grasped the quivering rifle barrel. Crash! She shot him again. As he swayed over her and fell she had to leap aside, and his clutching hand tore the rifle from her grasp. Then in convulsion he writhed, to heave on his back, and stretch out—a ghastly spectacle. Ellen backed away from it, her white arms wide, a slow horror blotting out the passion of her face.

Then from without came a shrill call and the sound of rapid footsteps. Ellen leaned against the wall, staring still at Colter. "Hey, Jim—what's the shootin'?" called Springer, breathlessly.

As his form darkened the doorway Jean once again gathered all his muscular force for a tremendous spring.

Springer saw the girl first and he appeared thunderstruck. His jaw dropped. He needed not the white gleam of her person to transfix him. Her eyes did that and they were riveted in unutterable horror upon something on the ground. Thus instinctively directed, Springer espied Colter.

"Y'u—y'u shot him!" he shrieked. "What for—y'u hussy? . . . Ellen Jorth, if y'u've killed him, I'll . . ."

He strode toward where Colter lay.

Then Jean, rising silently, took a step and like a tiger he launched himself into the air, down upon the rustler. Even as he leaped Springer gave a quick, upward look. And he cried out. Jean's moccasined feet struck him squarely and sent him staggering into the wall, where his head hit hard. Jean fell, but bounded up as the half-stunned Springer drew his gun. Then Jean lunged forward with a single sweep of his arm—and looked no more.

Ellen ran swaying out of the door, and, once clear of the threshold, she tottered out on the grass, to sink to her knees. The bright, golden sunlight gleamed upon her white shoulders and arms. Jean had one foot out of the door when he saw her and he whirled back to get her blouse. But Springer had fallen upon it. Snatching up a blanket, Jean ran out.

"Ellen! Ellen! Ellen!" he cried. "It's over!" And reaching her, he tried to wrap her in the blanket.

She wildly clutched his knees. Jean was conscious only of her white, agonized face and the dark eyes with their look of terrible strain.

"Did y'u—did y'u . . ." she whispered.

"Yes—it's over," he said, gravely. "Ellen, the Isbel-Jorth feud is ended."

"Oh, thank—God!" she cried, in breaking voice. "Jean—y'u are wounded . . . the blood on the step!"

"My arm. See. It's not bad. . . . Ellen, let me wrap this round you." Folding the blanket around her shoulders, he held it there and entreated her to get up. But she only clung the closer. She hid her face on his knees. Long shudders rippled over her, shaking the blanket, shaking Jean's hands. Distraught, he did not know what to do. And his own heart was bursting.

"Ellen, you must not kneel—there—that way," he implored.

"Jean! Jean!" she moaned, and clung the tighter.

He tried to lift her up, but she was a dead weight, and with that hold on him seemed anchored at his feet.

"I killed Colter," she gasped. "I *had* to—kill him! . . . I offered—to fling myself away. . . ."

"For me!" he cried, poignantly. "Oh, Ellen! Ellen! the world has come to an end! . . . Hush! don't keep sayin' that. Of course you killed him. You saved my life. For I'd never have let you go off with him. . . . Yes, you killed him. . . . You're a Jorth an' I'm an Isbel . . . We've blood on our hands—both of us—I for you an' you for me!"

His voice of entreaty and sadness strengthened her and she raised her white face, loosening her clasp to lean back and look up. Tragic, sweet, despairing, the loveliness of her—the significance of her there on her knees—thrilled him to his soul.

"Blood on my hands!" she whispered. "Yes. It was awful—killing him. . . . But—all I care for in this world is for your forgiveness—and your faith that saved my soul!"

"Child, there's nothin' to forgive," he responded. "Nothin' . . . Please, Ellen . . ."

"I lied to y'u!" she cried. "I lied to y'u!"

"Ellen, listen—darlin'." And the tender epithet brought her head and arms back close-pressed to him. "I know—now," he faltered on. "I found out to-day what I believed. An' I swear to God—by the memory of my dead mother—down in my heart I never, never, never believed what they—what y'u tried to make me believe. *Never!*"

"Jean—I love y'u—love y'u—love y'u!" she breathed with exquisite, passionate sweetness. Her dark eyes burned up into his.

"Ellen, I can't lift you up," he said, in trembling eagerness, signifying his crippled arm. "But I can kneel with you! . . ."

The Thundering Herd

CHAPTER ONE

AUTUMN WINDS HAD long waved the grass in the vast upland valley and the breath of the north had tinged the meandering lines of trees along the river bottoms. Gold and purple, and a flame of fire, shone brightly in the morning sunlight.

Birds and beasts of that wild open northland felt stir in them the instinct to move toward the south. The honk of wild geese floated down upon the solitudes and swift flocks of these heralds of winter sped by, sharply outlined against the blue sky.

High upon the western rampart of that valley perched an eagle, watching from his lonely crag. His telescopic eye ranged afar. Beneath him on the endless slope and boundless floor of the valley, moved a black mass, creeping with snail-like slowness toward the south. It seemed as long as the valley and as wide. It reached to the dim purple distances and disappeared there. The densest part covered the center of the valley, from which ran wide straggling arms, like rivers narrowing toward their sources in the hills. Patches of gray grass, dotted with gold, shone here and there against the black background. Always the dark moving streams and blots seemed encroaching upon these patches of grass. They spread over them and covered them. Then other open spaces appeared at different points. How slow the change! Yet there was a definite movement.

This black mass was alive. The eagle was gazing down upon leagues and leagues of buffalo. Acres of buffalo, miles of buffalo, millions of buffalo! The shaggy, irregular, ragged herd had no end. It dominated slopes, and bottomlands, and the hazy reaches beyond.

The vision of the eagle was an organ for self-preservation, not capable of appreciating the beauty and sublimity of the earth and its myriads of wild creatures. Yet with piercing eye the eagle watched from his lonely crag. Boundless void, with its moving coverlet of black, the wide space of sky keen with its cool wind—valley of leagues, with its living heritage of a million years! Wild, primitive, grand was the scene. It was eloquent of the past. The future stretched away like the dim, strange, unknown purple distances, with an intimation of tragedy. But the hour was one of natural fruition, wild life in the open, with the sun like an eye of the Creator, shining over the land. Peace, silence, solitude attended the eagle in his vigil.

Yet a brooding sadness, like an invisible mantle, lay over the valley. Was it the dreamy, drowsy spell of autumn? Was it the pervading spirit of a dying season, reluctant to face the rigor of snow and ice? The fact was that autumn lingered, and nature brooded over some mystery, some problem, some blunder. Life was sweet, strong—scented on the wind, but there was death lurking somewhere, perhaps in the purple shadow of distance to the southward. The morning was bright, golden, glorious, yet it did not wait, and night was coming. So there was more than the melancholy languor of autumn in the still air. A mighty Being seemed breathing there, invisible and infinite, all-encompassing. It kept its secret.

Suddenly the eagle plunged like a thunderbolt from his crag and shot down and down, at last to spread his closed wings, and sail slowly and majestically round and round, over an open grassy patch encircled by buffalo.

In this spot, well toward the center and front of the vast herd, appeared about to be enacted a battle between a monarch and his latest rival for supremacy.

The huge leader, shaggy, brown, ragged, was not a creature of beauty, but he was magnificent. He had twice the bulk of an ox, and stood as high as a horse. His massive head, with the long shaggy hair matted with burrs, was held low, muzzle almost to the ground, showing the big curved short horns widely separated. Eyes of dark fire blazed from beneath the shaggy locks. His great back slowly arched and his short tufted tail rose stiffly erect. A hoarse rumble issued from the cavern of his chest—a roar at the brazen effrontery of this young bull that dared to face him.

Many and many had been the battles of this old monarch. For years he had reigned, so many that he had forgotten the instinct of his youth, when he, like the rival before him, had bearded the king of the buffaloes. He had to fight again, in obedience to that law which respected only the survival of the fittest.

The bull that had challenged the king to battle was also magnificent. He too lowered his huge head, and with short prodigious strokes he pawed tufts of grass and heaps of earth up into the air. His color was a glossy seal brown and he did not have the ragged, worn appearance of the monarch. His shaggy hair hung thick and woolly from head and shoulders and knees. Great rippling muscles swelled on his flanks as he pawed and moved round his enemy. He meant to attack. He shone resplendent. He seemed the epitome of animal vigor and spirit. The bawl with which he answered the roar of the monarch rang clear and hard, like a blast. He possessed something that the old warrior had lost. He had beauty and youth.

The surrounding buffalo did not appear concerned over this impending battle. They were aware of it, for they would raise their shaggy heads from the grass and gaze a moment at the king and his jealous aspirant. Then they would return to their feeding. It was noticeable, however, that the circle did not narrow; if anything, it gradually widened.

The king did not wait for his foe to begin the struggle. He charged. His dash was incredibly fast for so heavy a beast and his momentum tremendous. Square against the lowered head of the young bull he struck. The shock sent forth a sodden crash. The bull staggered under the impact. His whole bulk shook. Then he was lifted, head up, forefeet off the ground, higher, and with grinding clash of horns he was hurled heavily upon his back.

Under the great force of that charge the old monarch went to his knees, and the advantage which might have been his was lost. He heaved in his rage.

Nimbly the young bull rolled over and bounded to his feet, unhurt. Nature had by this time developed him to a perfect resisting force. His front was all bone, covered by matted hair. Swifter than a horse, as quick as a cat, he launched his bulk at his antagonist, and hit him with a shock no less terrific than the one that had opened the battle. But the old warrior received it as if he had been a great oak rooted in the earth.

Then with heads pounding and horns grinding, these beasts, relentless as nature itself, settled down to the wonderful and incredible battle of buffalo bulls. Bent and bowed, always head to head, they performed prodigious feats of ramming and butting, and endeavoring to give each other a fatal thrust with horn.

But under that heavy mat of wool was skin over an inch thick and tougher than hardened leather. These bulls were made to fight. They had extraordinary lung capacity and very large nostrils. Their endurance was as remarkable as their physical structure.

In a cloud of dust they plowed up the prairie, driving the grazing buffalo back and forth, and covering acres of ground in their struggle. The crash of heads and rattle of horns gradually diminished in vigor of sound, indicating that the speed and strength of the rivals were wearing down. Not so their ferocity and courage! It was a battle to death or complete vanquishment. In time the dust cloud blew away on the wind, and then the bulls could be seen in action less strenuous but still savage.

The old monarch was near the end of his last battle. His race was run. Torn and dirt-covered and bloody, he backed before the onslaughts of his foe. His lungs, like great bellows, sent out gasps that were as well utterances of defeat. He could not withstand the relentless young bull. Age must go down. He was pushed to his knees and almost bowled over. Recovering, he wearily fronted that huge battering black head, and then was shoved to his haunches. Again, narrowly, he escaped the following lunge. That was the moment of defeat. He was beaten. The instinct for life took the place of the instinct for supremacy. Backward, step by step, he went, always facing the bellowing young conqueror. There came intervals when he was free of that lowered battering head; and during the last of these he sheered away among the stragglers of the herd, leaving the field to the victor. The old monarch had retired to the ranks and there was a new leader of the herd.

The eagle soared back to his lonely perch, there to clutch the crag with his talons and sweep the valley with crystal eye.

Out to the front of the black mass of buffalo a whirlwind twisted up a column of dust. Funnel-shaped it rose, yellow and spreading, into the air, while it raced across the valley. That, or something as natural, stirred a movement in the foreranks of buffalo. All at once the leaders broke into a run, heading south. The movement, and the growing pound of their hoofs, ran through the herd as swiftly as a current. Then, magically and wondrously, the whole immense mass moved as if one spirit, one mind, dominated it. The throbbing pound of hoofs suddenly increased to a roar. Dust began to rise and blow back, like low clouds of yellow smoke, over the acres, and then the miles of bobbing black backs. The vast herd seemed to become a sea in swift and accelerating action.

Soon a rising pall of dust shrouded the thousands of buffalo, running under what seemed an obscure curtain. The volume of sound had swelled from rhythmic pound and beat to a mighty and appalling roar. Only the battlements of the upper air, assailed in storm by the ripping of lightning, could send back such thunder as now rose from the shaking earth. But this was one long continuous roll. The movement of buffalo in unison resembled a tidal wave and the sound was that of an avalanche. The ground trembled under the thundering herd.

The eagle perched motionless on his crag, indifferent to the rolling chaos beneath him. The valley-wide cloud of dust floated low down. Time passed. Halfway to the zenith rose the sun. Then gradually the tremor of the earth and the roar of hoofs diminished, rolled, and died away. The herd had passed. On his lofty perch the eagle slept, and the valley cleared of dust and movement. Solitude, loneliness, and silence reigned at the solemn noontide.

It was spring of an era many years after the lone eagle had watched the buffalo herd.

An upland prairie country rolled and waved down from snow-capped Rocky Mountains to spread out into the immense eastern void. Over the bleached white grass had come a faint tinge of green. The warm sun had begun its renewal of the covering of the earth. A flock of wild geese, late on their annual pilgrimage, winged swift flight toward the northland. On the ridges elk grazed, and down in the hollows, where murmuring streams rushed, clouded with the blue color of melted snow, deer nibbled at the new tender shoots of grass.

Below the uplands, where the plain began, herds of buffalo dotted the patches and streaked the monotony of the gray vastness. Leagues and leagues it spread, always darker for the increase of buffalo, until all was a dense black that merged into the haze of distance.

A river wended its curving way out across the plains, and in a wooded bend an Indian encampment showed its white tepees, and red blankets, and columns of blue smoke lazily rising.

Hidden in the brush along the river half-naked red men lay in wait for the buffalo to come down to drink. These hunters did not need to sally forth for their game. They had only to wait and choose the meat and the hide that best served them for their simple needs. They did not kill more than they could use.

Along the river bank, far as eye could see, the shaggy monsters trooped down to drink. Bulls and cows and calves came in endless procession. In some places, where the bank was steep, the thirsty buffalo behind pushed the row ahead into the water, whence rose a splashing *mêlée.* The tawny calves, still too young to shed their coats and turn the seal brown of their mothers, bawled lustily as they were shoved into the river.

Near the encampment of the Indians, where trees and brush lined the shore, the buffalo were more wary. They liked the open. But stragglers came along, and the choicest of these fell prey to the deadly arrows of the red men. A shaggy young bull, sleek and brown, superb in his approaching maturity, passed within range of the chieftain of that hunting clan. He rose from his covert, a lean, dark Indian, tall and powerful of build, with intense face and piercing eyes turned toward his quarry. He bent a bow few Indians could have drawn. He bent it till the flint head of the arrow touched his left hand. Then he released the arrow. Like a glint of light it flashed and, striking the bull behind the shoulder, buried half its length there. The animal grunted. He made no violent movements. He walked back as he had come, only more and more slowly. The chief followed him out to the edge of the timber. There other buffalo coming in saw both Indian and wounded bull, but they only swerved aside. The bull halted, and heaving heavily, he plunged to his knees, and then rolled over on his side.

After the hunters came the squaws, with their crude flint and bone implements, to skin the buffalo and cut up the meat and pack it to the encampment.

There the chief repaired to rest on his buffalo hide under a tree, and to think the thoughts and dream the dreams of the warrior. Beyond the white-peaked mountain range lived enemies of his, red men of a hated tribe. Other than remembrance of them he had no concern. His red gods could not tell him of the future. The paleface, who was to drive him and his people into the fastnesses of the arid hills, was unknown and undreamed of. Into his lofty serene mind no thought flashed of a vanishing of the buffalo while yet his descendants lived. The buffalo were as many as the sands of the river bottoms. They had always been; they would always be. The buffalo existed to furnish food, raiment, shelter for the red man.

So the chief rested in his camp, watching beaver at work on the river bank, as tame as were the buffalo. Like these animals, he and his tribe were happy and self-sufficient. Only infrequent battles with other tribes marred the serenity of their lives. Always the endless herds were to be found, to the south or the north. This chief worshiped the sun, loved his people and the wild, lonely land he believed was his; and if there was in his tribe a brave who was liar or coward or thief, or a squaw who broke the law, death was his or her portion.

A straggling band of white men wearily rode and tramped across the great plains centuries before that wonderful level prairie was to be divided into the Western states of America.

These white travelers were the Spanish explorers under the command of the intrepid Coronado. It was a large band. Many of them rode horses—Arabian horses of the purest breed, from which the Western mustang was descended. But most of them walked, wearing queer apparel and armor not suitable to such arduous travel. They carried strange weapons.

Hardy, indomitable, and enduring, this first band of white men to penetrate the great plains and the deserts of the South and West, recorded for history something of their marvelous adventures and terrible experiences and strange sights.

Many hundreds of leagues they traveled, according to their historian, Castaneda, over tremendous plains and reaches of sand, stark and level, and so barren of trees and stones that they erected heaps of the ox dung they found, so that they could be guided back by the way they had come. They lost horses and men.

All the way across these great plains of grass and sand the Spaniards encountered herds of crooked-back oxen, as many as there were sheep in Spain. But they saw no people with the crooked-back cattle. These weary and lost travelers, almost starved, found in the oxen succor they so grievously needed. Meat gave them strength and courage to go on through obstacles none save crusaders could have overcome. Sometimes in this strange country it rained great showers of hailstones as big as oranges; and these storms caused many tears and injuries.

Castaneda wrote:

> These oxen are the bigness and color of our bulls. . . . They have a great bunch of hair on their fore shoulders, and more on their fore part than their hinder part, and it is like wool. They have a horse-mane upon their backbone, and much hair, and very long from their knees downward. They have great tufts of hair hanging down their foreheads, and it seemeth they have beards because of the great store of hair hanging down at their chins and throats. The males have very large tails, and a great knob or flock at the end, so that in some respects they resemble the lion, and in some others the camel. They

> push with their horns; they run; they overtake and kill a horse when they are in their rage and anger. The horses fled from them, either because of their deformed shape, or else because they had never before seen them. Finally it is a foul and fierce beast of countenance and form of body.

Coronado and Castaneda, with their band of unquenchable spirits, were the first white people to see the American buffalo.

CHAPTER TWO

All during Tom Doan's boyhood, before and through the stirring years of the Rebellion, he had been slowly yielding to the call that had made so many young men adventurers and pioneers in the Southwest.

His home had not been a happy one, but as long as his mother lived and his sisters remained unmarried he had stayed there, getting what education there was available at the little Kansas village school, and working hard on the farm. When Kansas refused to secede to the South at the beginning of the Rebellion, Tom's father, who was a rebel, joined Quantrill's notorious band of guerillas. Tom's sisters were in sympathy with the South. But Tom and his mother held open leaning toward the North. It was a divided family. Eventually the girls married and left home. Tom's mother did not long survive her husband, who was shot on one of Quantrill's raids.

Tom outlived the sadness and bitterness of his youth, but they left their mark upon him. His loyalty to his mother had alone kept him from the wildness of the time, and their poverty had made hard work imperative. After the war he drifted from place to place, always farther and farther toward the unsettled country. He had pioneer blood in him, and in his mind he had settled the future. He meant to be a rancher, a tiller of the soil, a stockman and a breeder of horses, for these things he loved. Yet always there was in him the urge to see the frontier, to be in the thick of wild life while he was hunting and exploring for that wonderful land which would content him. Thus Tom Doan had in him a perfect blending of the dual spirit that burned in the hearts of thousands of men, and which eventually opened up the West to civilization.

Not, however, until the autumn of 1874 did he surrender to the call. The summer of that year had been a momentous one in the Southwest. Even in years of stress this one stood out as remarkable, and the tales drifting up from the frontier had thrilled Tom's heart.

A horde of buffalo-hunters, lured by the wild life and the development of a commercial market for buffalo hides, had braved the Indians in their haunts and started after the last great herds. This had resulted in an Indian war. The Cheyennes, Kiowas, Arapahoes, and the Comanches had gone on the war-path. A thousand warriors of these tribes had made the memorable siege of a small band of buffalo-hunters and their soldier escort, and after repeated and persistent charges had been repulsed. The tale of this battle was singularly thrilling to Tom Doan.

Particularly had the hunting of buffalo appealed to him. Not that he had ever hunted a buffalo, for in fact he had never seen one. But stories told him as a boy had fixed themselves in his mind, never to be effaced.

Early spring found Tom Doan arriving at the outfitting post from which an army of buffalo-hunters were preparing to leave for the long haul to the south.

The atmosphere of this frontier fort and freighting station was new to Tom, and affected him deeply. The stir of youthful love of wild tales was here revived. At a step, almost, he had found himself on the threshold of the frontier. Huge freighting wagons, some with six horses attached, and loaded with piles and bales of green buffalo hides, lumbered in from the level prairie land. The wide main street of the town presented a continual procession of men and women, mostly in rough garb of travel, and all intent on the mysterious something that seemed to be in the air. There was a plentiful sprinkling of soldiers, and pale-faced, frock-coated gamblers, and many stylishly dressed women who had a too friendly look, Tom thought. There were places of amusement, saloons and dance halls, that Tom found a peep into sufficient. Dust lay inches deep in the street, and the horses passing along continually raised clouds of it.

The camp on the outskirts of this town soon drew Tom. Here, ranged all around, it appeared, were the outfits of the buffalo-hunters, getting ready to travel south. Tom meant to cast his lot with one of them, but the tales he had heard about the character of some of these outfits made him decide to be careful. According to rumor some of them were as bad as the Comanches.

The first man Tom accosted was a tall, rugged, bronzed Westerner, with a stubby red beard on his lean face. He was encamped under a cottonwood, just bursting into green, and on the moment was busy jacking up the hind wheel of his huge canvas-covered wagon.

"I'll give you a lift," offered Tom, and with one heave he raised the rear end of the wagon.

"Wal!" ejaculated the Westerner, as he rapidly worked up his jack to meet the discrepancy occasioned by Tom's lift. "Reckon you're husky, stranger. Much obliged."

Tom helped him complete the job of greasing the wagon wheels and then asked him if he were a buffalo-hunter.

"I am thet," he replied. "An' what're you?"

"I've come to join one of the outfits. Are there really good wages to be made?"

"Wal, you are new heahaboots," returned the other, grinning. "My early fall hunt netted me five hundred dollars. Late fall then I made four hundred. An' this winter I hunted down on the Brazos, cleanin' up six hundred an' eighty."

Tom was amazed and excited over this specific information, direct from the hunting grounds.

"Why, that's wonderful!" he replied. "A fellow can make enough to buy and stock a ranch. Did you have a helper?"

"Shore—my two boys, an' I paid them wages."

"How much?" inquired Tom.

"Twenty-five a month. Are you lookin' fer a job?" rejoined the Westerner, with an appreciative glance at Tom's broad shoulders.

"Yes, but not for such wages as that. I'd like to go in for myself."

"It's the way to do, if you can buy your own outfit."

Upon inquiry Tom found that outfits were high, and with his small savings he could hardly hope to purchase even an interest in one. It would be necessary for him to hire out to the best advantage, and save his earnings toward buying horses, wagon, and equipment for himself. Nevertheless, opportunity seemed indeed knocking at his door. The rewards of buffalo-hunting, as set forth by the Westerner, were great enough to fire the blood of any young man. Tom experienced a sudden lift of his heart; a new and strong tide surged through him.

At the end of the road Tom came to a small grove of cottonwoods, just beyond the edge of the town; and here he caught the gleam of more canvas-covered vehicles. He found three outfits camped there, apart from one another, and the largest one was composed of several wagons. A camp fire was burning. The smell of wood smoke assailed Tom's nostrils with more than pleasurable sense. It brought pictures of wild places and camp by lonely streams. A sturdy woman was bending over a washtub. Tom caught a glimpse of a girl's rather comely face peering out of the front of a wagon. Two young men were engaged at shoeing a horse. Under a cottonwood two men sat on a roll of bedding.

As Tom entered the grove one of the men rose to a lofty stature and showed himself to be built in proportion. He appeared past middle age, but was well preserved and possessed a bearded, jovial face, with frank blue eyes that fastened curiously upon Tom. The other man had remarkable features—sharp, hard, stern, set like a rock. Down his lean brown cheeks ran deep furrows and his eyes seemed narrowed inside wrinkled folds. They were gray eyes, light and singularly piercing.

Tom had an impression that this was a real plainsman. The giant seemed a man of tremendous force. Quick to form his likes or dislikes, Tom lost no time here in declaring himself.

"My name's Tom Doan," he said. "I want a job with a buffalo-hunter's outfit."

"Glad to meet you. I'm Clark Hudnall an' this is my friend, Jude Pilchuck," replied the giant.

Whereupon both men shook hands with Tom and showed the interest common to the time and place. Hudnall's glance was a frank consideration of Tom's stalwart form and beardless face. Pilchuck's was a keen scrutiny associated with memory.

"Doan. Was your father Bill Doan, who rode with Quantrill?" he inquired.

"Yes—he was," returned Tom, somewhat disconcerted by this unexpected query.

"I knew your father. You favor him, only you're lighter complexioned. He was a hard rider and a hard shooter. . . . You were a boy when he got—"

"I was fifteen," said Tom, as the other hesitated.

"Were you on your dad's side?" asked Hudnall curiously.

"No. I was for the North," returned Tom.

"Well, well, them days were tough," sighed Hudnall, as if he remembered trials of his own. Then he quickened with interest. "We need a man an' I like your looks. Have you any hankerin' for red liquor?"

"No."

"Are you alone?"

"Yes."

"Ever hunt buffalo?"

"No."

"Can you shoot well?"

"I was always a good shot. Have hunted deer and small game a good deal."

"What's your idea—throwin' in with a hide-hunter's outfit?"

Tom hesitated a moment over that query, and then frankly told the truth about his rather complicated longings.

Hudnall laughed, and was impressed to the point of placing a kind hand on Tom's shoulder.

"Young man, I'm glad you told me that," he said. "Back of my own reason for riskin' so much in this hide-huntin' is my need to make money quick, an' I've got to have a ranch. So we're two of a kind. You're welcome to cast in your lot with us. Shake on it."

Then Tom felt the mighty grip of a calloused hand that had known the plow and the ax. Pilchuck likewise offered to shake hands with Tom, and expressed himself no less forcibly than Hudnall.

"Reckon it's a good deal on both sides," he said. "The right kind of men are scarce. I know this buffalo-huntin'. It's a hard game. An' if skinnin' hides isn't tougher than diggin' coal, then I was a meathunter on the U. P. an' the Santa Fe for nothin'."

Hudnall called the two younger men from their task of shoeing the horse. Both appeared under thirty, stocky fellows, but there the resemblance ended.

"Burn, shake hands with Tom Doan," said Hudnall, heartily. "An' you, too, Stronghurl. . . . Doan is goin' to throw in with us."

Both men greeted Tom with the cordial good will and curiosity natural to an event of importance to them. It was evident that Burn, from his resemblance to Hudnall, was a son. Stronghurl had as remarkable a physiognomy as his name, and somehow they fitted each other.

"Burn, you'll take Doan with your wagon," said Hudnall. "That fills our outfit, an' we'll be pullin' to-morrow for the Panhandle. . . . Hey, you women folks," he called toward the wagons, "come out an' meet my new man."

The stout woman left off washing at the tub and came forward, wiping her red hands on her apron. She had a serious face that lighted with a smile.

"Wife, this is Tom Doan," went on Hudnall, and next in order he presented Tom to Burn's wife, whom Tom recognized as the young woman he had seen in the wagon. Last to emerge was a girl of eighteen or thereabouts, sister of Burn and manifestly Hudnall's pride. She was of large frame, pleasant faced, and she had roguish eyes that took instant stock of Tom.

Thus almost before he could realize his good fortune, Tom found himself settled with people of his own kind, whom he liked on sight. Moreover, Hudnall had the same pioneer urge which possessed Tom; and the fact that Pilchuck, an old buffalo-hunter, was to accompany them down into Texas, just about made the deal perfect. To be sure, Tom had not mentioned wages or shares, but he felt that he could safely trust Hudnall.

"Where's your pack?" inquired Burn. "An' what have you got in the way of outfit?"

"I left it at the station," replied Tom. "Not much of an outfit. A bag of clothes and a valise."

"Nary horse or gun. Have you any money?" went on Burn, with cheerful interest.

"I've got two hundred dollars."

"Good. Soon as we get this horse shod I'll go uptown with you."

"Well, son," spoke up Hudnall, "I reckon Tom had better let Pilchuck buy gun an' horse an' what else he needs."

"Humph!" ejaculated Mrs. Hudnall. "If I know men you'll all have a say about horses an' guns."

"Mr. Doan, wouldn't you like me to help you pick out that horse?" inquired Burn's sister, mischievously.

"Why, yes," replied Tom, joining in the laugh. "I'd like you all to help—so long as I get one I can ride."

The women returned to their tasks while Hudnall went off with Pilchuck toward the town. Left to his own devices, Tom presently joined Burn and Stronghurl, who were not having any easy job shoeing the horse. It was a spirited animal.

"Doan, would you mind fetchin' that bay horse back?" asked Burn, presently pointing toward the other side of the grove, where several canvas-covered wagons gleamed among the trees.

Tom picked up a halter and strode away under the trees, at once pleasantly preoccupied with thought of the most satisfying nature. He came up with the bay horse, which he found eating out of a girl's hand. Tom saw and heard other people close by, but he did not notice them particularly. Intent on the horse, he did not take a second glance at the girl, until she spoke.

"I've caught your horse twice to-day," she said.

"Much obliged. But he's not mine," replied Tom, and as he put the halter over the neck of the animal he looked at the girl.

Her eyes met his. They were large, black as midnight, and they gazed up from a face almost as dark as an Indian's. Her hair was brown and appeared to have a sheen or light upon it.

Tom's glance became what hers was—steady, almost a stare without consciousness, a look of depth and gravity for which neither was responsible.

Then Tom withdrew his glance and attended to knotting the halter. Yet he could see her still. She was of medium height, neither robust nor heavy, yet giving an impression of unusual strength and suppleness for a girl. She was young. Her dress of homespun material looked the worse for wear.

"He's a pretty horse," she said, patting the sleek nose. "Yes, he is. I hope the horse I've got to buy will be like him," replied Tom.

"Are you a buffalo-killer, too?" she inquired, in quicker tone.

"I expect to be."

"Milly," called a gruff voice, "you're not a hoss thief and you're not makin' up with strangers."

Tom turned hastily to see a big man looming across the camp fire. He wore a leather apron and carried a hammer in his brawny hand. It was impossible that this blond giant could be the girl's father. Even in that moment of surprise and annoyance Tom felt glad of this conviction. The man's face bore a thin yellow beard that could not hide its coarseness and brutality. He had bright, hard blue eyes.

"Excuse me," said Tom, stiffly. "I had to come after Mr. Hudnall's horse." Then turning to the girl, he thanked her. This time her eyes were cast down. Tom abruptly started off, leading the animal.

It did not occur to him that there was anything significant about the incident, except a little irritation at the coarse speech and appearance of the blond man. Nevertheless, that part of it slipped from his mind, and the vague, somehow pleasurable impression of the girl persisted until the serious and thrilling business of choosing horse and gun precluded all else.

The fact that Hudnall and his men left off work, and Pilchuck insisted on being the arbiter of these selections, attested to the prime importance with which they regarded the matter. Hudnall argued with Pilchuck that he knew the merits of horses as well as the latter knew guns.

So they journeyed into town, up the dusty motley-crowded street, rubbing elbows with Indians, soldiers, hunters, scouts, teamsters, men who bore the stamp of evil life upon their lean faces, and women with the eyes of hawks. Pilchuck knew almost everybody, it seemed. He pointed out many border celebrities to Tom's keen interest. One was Colonel Jones, a noted plainsman, who in the near future was to earn the sobriquet "Buffalo Jones," not like his contemporary, Buffalo Bill, for destroying buffalo, but for preserving calves to form the nucleus of a herd. Another, and the most striking figure of a man Tom had ever seen, was Wild Bill, perhaps the most noted of all frontiersmen. He was a superb giant of a man, picturesquely clad, straight as an Indian, with a handsome face, still, intense, wonderful in its expression of the wild spirit that had made him great. Tom thought he had never before seen such penetrating, alert eyes. Pilchuck mentioned casually that not long since, Wild Bill had fought and killed twelve men in a dugout cabin on the plains. Bill got shot and cut to pieces, but recovered. Tom was far from being a tenderfoot, yet he gaped at these strange, heroic men, and thrilled to his depths. Seeing them face to face stimulated and liberated something deep in him.

The supply store where Pilchuck conducted Tom and the others was full of purchasers, and except for absence of liquors in bottles it resembled a border barroom. It smelled of tobacco in bulk; and Tom saw shelves and stacks of plug tobacco in such enormous quantity that he marveled to Hudnall.

"Golly! man, we gotta have chaw tobacco," replied that worthy.

A counter littered with a formidable array of guns and knives appeared to be Pilchuck's objective point.

"We want a big fifty," he said to the clerk.

"There's only one left an' it ain't new," replied this individual, as he picked up a heavy gun. It was a fifty-caliber Sharps rifle. Pilchuck examined it and then handed it over to Tom. "I've seen better big fifties, but it'll do for a while. . . . Next you want a belt an' all the cartridges you can lug, an' both rippin' an' skinnin' knives."

When these purchases were made Tom had indeed about all he could carry. Hudnall then ordered the supplies needed for his outfit, and when that was accomplished Pilchuck led them down the street to the outskirts of town, where there was a corral full of dusty, vicious, kicking horses. It took an hour for Pilchuck and Hudnall to agree on a horse that Tom could ride. Having been a farm hand all his days, Tom was a good horseman, but he was not a bronco-buster. Finally the selection was made of horse, saddle, bridle, blanket, and spurs. When this purchase was paid for Tom laughed at the little money he had left.

"Things come high, an' they ain't worth it," complained Pilchuck. "But we haven't any choice. That's a good horse—young enough, strong, easy gait, but he never saw a buffalo."

"What of that?" asked Tom, with a little check to his elation.

"Nothin'. Only the first buffalo he sees will decide a lot."

Tom regarded this rather ambiguous remark with considerable misgiving and made a mental note of it, so he would not forget.

What with their purchases, and Tom's baggage, which they got at the station, the party had about all they could take back to camp. The afternoon then was a busy one for all concerned. Tom donned rough garb and heavy boots, suitable to life in the open. The change was not made without perception of an indefinable shifting in his spirit. He was about to face the perils of the frontier, and serious and thoughtful as he endeavored to make himself, he could not repress an eager, wild response. He tried out his horse, which he named Dusty, because at that time nothing but a bath could have removed the dust from him. Dusty gave a creditable performance and won the approval of all save Pilchuck. Hudnall, and his daughter Sally, particularly liked the horse. Tom saw that he could sell or trade at his discretion, and so for the time was well pleased.

The rest of the afternoon he spent helping Burn Hudnall arrange and pack the big wagon that was to transport their precious outfit, and later, out on the plains, haul the hides they expected to get.

"I was tellin' father I'd like to pick up a boy somewhere," said Burn.

"What for?" inquired Tom. "We can take care of this outfit."

"Sure, for the present. But when we get out among the buffalo we'll need some one to drive the wagon an' keep camp while we chase an' kill an' skin buffalo."

"I see. Then the idea will be a main camp kept by your father, and the rest of us in pairs with wagons and outfits will range all over?"

"I reckon that's Pilchuck's idea. From what I can gather there'll be a lot of hustlin' an' movin' when we strike the herds of buffalo."

"I should think it'd be a chase with no time for camp," said Tom.

"Reckon so. Anyways we're bound to know soon," replied Burn, grimly.

At sunset Tom heard the cheery call of the women folk to supper; and he was not far behind Burn in getting to the table, which was a canvas spread on the ground. They all appeared hungry. Hudnall loaded his tin plate, filled his cup, and then repaired to the wagon, and set his supper upon the seat. He was too big to squat on the ground, cross-legged and Indian fashion, but his stature enabled him to stand and eat from the wagon seat. Pilchuck, too, had his peculiar habit. He set his plate down, and knelt on one knee to eat.

They were all excited, except Pilchuck, and though this in no wise distracted from a satisfying of hunger, it lent a sparkle and jollity to the occasion. Tom was not alone in having cut away from the humdrum of settled communities and in cherishing dreams of untrammeled country and future home and prosperity.

After supper he again walked into the town, purposely going alone. He did not pry into his reason. This third visit to the main street did not satisfy his vague longing, whatever it was, and he retraced his steps campward.

When he reached the end of the street passersby became scarce, and for that reason more noticeable. But Tom did not pay attention to any one until he heard a girl's voice. It came from behind him and had a note of annoyance, even anger. A man's reply, too low and husky for coherence, made Tom turn quickly.

A young woman carrying a heavy parcel was approaching, a step or two in advance of a man. It required only a glance to see that she was trying to get away from him.

Tom strode to meet her, and recognized the girl with whom he had exchanged words at the camp adjoining Hudnall's.

"Is that fellow bothering you?" demanded Tom.

"He insulted me," she replied.

Tom broke into swift strides toward the offender.

"Say, you!" he called, forcibly. But the man hurried away, at a pace that would have necessitated running to catch him.

"Never mind. Let him go," said the girl with a little laugh of relief.

"This town is full of ruffians. You should not have come in alone," was Tom's reply.

"I know. It's happened before. I wasn't afraid—but I'm glad you came along."

"That package looks heavy. Let me carry it," offered Tom.

"Thank you, I can manage very well," she returned.

But he took it away from her, and in so doing touched her hand. The effect on Tom was sudden and profound. For the moment it destroyed his naturalness.

"Well—I—it is heavy—for a girl," he said, awkwardly.

"Oh, I'm very strong," she rejoined.

Then their eyes met again, as they had when Tom had reached for the horse and looked at her. Only this time it seemed vastly different. She looked away, across the open toward the grove where fires gleamed in the gathering twilight. Then she moved. Tom fell into step beside her. He wanted to talk, but seemed unable to think of anything to say. This meeting was not an ordinary incident. He could not understand himself. He wanted to ask her about who she was, where she was going, what relation she bore to the rude man who had called her Milly. Yet not a word could he utter. He could have spoken surely, if he had not been concentrating on the vagueness and uncertainty of himself.

Before they had quite reached the edge of the grove she stopped and confronted him.

"Thank you," she said, softly. "I'll carry it now."

"No. We're still a long distance from your camp."

"Yes—that's why," she returned, haltingly. "You must not go with me. . . . He—my stepfather, you heard him. I—I can't tell you more."

Tom did not yield up the parcel with very good grace. "I may never see you again!" he burst out.

She did not answer, but as she relieved him of the package she looked up, straight and clear into his face. Her eyes held him. In them he read the same thought he had just exclaimed aloud. Then she bade him good night, and turning away, vanished in the gloom of the grove.

Not until she was gone did Tom awake to a realization that this chance meeting, apparently so natural on her part and kindly on his, just an incident of travel, two strangers exchanging a few civilities, was the most significant and appealing and thought-provoking experience of his life. Why had he not detained her, just a moment, to ask for the privilege of seeing her again? Still, he could see her to-morrow. That last look of her big black eyes—what did it mean? His mind revolved many useless questions. He found a seat at the edge of the grove and there he pondered. Night came, dark and cool. The stars shone. Behind him sounded the crackle of camp fires and the voices of men and the munch of horses at their grain.

A strange thing had happened to him, but what was it? A girl's eyes, a few words, a touch of hands! Had they been the cause of this sudden melancholy one moment and inexplicable exaltation the next, and his curiosity about her, and this delving into himself? But he did not call it silly or foolish. Tom was twenty-four years old, yet this condition of mind was new. Perhaps the thrill, the excitement of the prospects ahead, had communicated themselves to an otherwise ordinary incident. The thought, however, he ridiculed. Every moment of his musing tended toward consciousness of a strange, dreamy sweetness inspired by this girl.

CHAPTER THREE

When Tom roused next morning to Burn Hudnall's cheery call he found that he had slept later than usual for him.

He rolled out of his bed of blankets under the wagon, and pulling on his boots and washing his face and hands, was ready for breakfast and the eventful day.

The sun had just risen above the eastern horizon. West and southwest the rolling prairie-land shone green and gold under the bright morning light. Near at hand horses and cattle grazed. Far down the clearly defined road canvas-covered wagons gleamed white. Some of the buffalo-hunters were already on their way. Tom stood a moment, watching and thinking, as he drew a deep full breath of the fresh crisp air, feeling that whatever lay in store for him beyond the purple horizon—adventure, hardship, fortune—he was keen to face it.

While at breakfast Tom suddenly remembered his meeting with the girl, Milly. In the broad light of day he did not feel quite the same as in the gloaming of last night. Yet a sweetness stole pervadingly upon him. Glancing through the grove toward the camp where the first meeting with her had taken place, he missed the white wagons. That end of the grove was empty. The wagons were gone—and with them the girl. Tom experienced a blankness of thought, then a sense of loss and a twinge of regret. After this moment he thoughtfully went on eating his breakfast. Nothing was to come of the meeting. Still, her people were buffalo-hunters, too, and somewhere down in that wild country he might see her again. What a forlorn hope! Yet by cherishing it he reconciled himself to the fact that she was gone.

After breakfast his curiosity led him to walk over to where her camp had been; and he trailed the wagon tracks out into the road, seeing that they headed toward the southwest. His grain of comfort gathered strength.

"Our neighbors pulled out early," he remarked, halting where Pilchuck and Hudnall were packing.

"Long before sunup," replied Hudnall. "Did you hear them, Jude?"

"Huh! They'd waked the dead," growled Pilchuck. "Reckon Randall Jett had his reason for pullin' out."

"Jett? Let's see. He was the man with the yellow beard. Come to think of it, he wasn't very civil."

"I heard some talk about Jett uptown," went on Pilchuck. "'Pears I've met him somewheres, but it's slipped my mind. He's one of the hide-hunters that's got a doubt hangin' on him. Just doubt, it's only fair to say. Nobody knows anythin'. Jett has come out of the Panhandle twice with thousands of hides. He's made money."

"Well, that's interestin'," replied Hudnall. "He's just been married. My wife had some talk yesterday with a woman who must have been Mrs. Jett. She was from Missouri an' had a grown daughter. Married a few weeks, she said. My wife got a hunch this woman an' daughter weren't keen about the hide-huntin' business."

"Well, when you get down on the Staked Plains, you'll appreciate Mrs. Jett's feelings," remarked Pilchuck, dryly.

Tom listened to this talk, much interested, recording it in memory. Then he asked if all the buffalo-hunters followed the same line of travel.

"Reckon they do," replied Pilchuck. "There's only one good road for a couple of hundred miles. Then the hunters make their own roads."

"Do they scatter all over the plains?" went on Tom.

"Well, naturally they hang round the buffalo. But that herd is most as big as the Staked Plains."

Tom had no knowledge of this particular part of Texas, but he did not fail to get a conception of magnitude.

"When do we pull out?" he concluded.

"Soon as we hitch up."

In less than an hour the Hudnall outfit, with three good wagons drawn by strong teams, were on the move. The women rode with the drivers. Tom had the job of keeping the saddle horses in line. They did not want to head out into the wilderness, and on the start were contrary. After a few miles, however, they settled down to a trot and kept to the road.

Soon the gleam of the town, and groves of trees, and columns of smoke, disappeared behind a rolling ridge, and all around appeared endless gray-green plain, bisected by a white road. No other wagons were in sight. Tom found the gait of his horse qualified to make long rides endurable. The lonely land was much to his liking. Jack-rabbits and birds were remarkable for their scarcity. The plain appeared endlessly undulating, a lonesome expanse, mostly gray, stretching away on all sides. The soil was good. Some day these wide lands would respond to cultivation.

The Hudnall outfit traveled steadily until about four o'clock in the afternoon, making about twenty-five miles. A halt was called in a grove of elm trees that had long appealed to Tom's eye. It amused him to see the amiable contention between Pilchuck and Hudnall. The former, like all guides and scouts long used to outdoor life, wanted to camp at the first available spot where others had camped. But Hudnall sought a fresh and untrammeled place, driving some distance off the road to a clean glade under spreading elms just beginning to green. A shallow creek ran under the high bank. Birds and rabbits were plentiful here, and cat and coyote tracks showed on the muddy shore.

There was work for everybody and something of confusion. Further experience in making camp was essential before things could be done smoothly and expeditiously.

"I laid out jobs for everybody. Now rustle," was Hudnall's order.

The teams were unhitched and turned loose to drink and graze. Harness and collars were hung upon the front wheels. Tom scouted for firewood, which appeared plentiful, and the ring of his ax resounded through the glade. Hudnall and his son lifted the cook stove and mess box from a wagon, then the cooking utensils and tableware. A level spot was cleaned off, a fire started on the ground and also in the stove, then the meal preparations were turned over to the women. Hudnall erected a tent for himself and his wife. Sally's bed was made in the wagon. Pilchuck helped Stronghurl pitch a tent beside their wagon, but he spread his own bed, consisting of blankets on a tarpaulin, outside under the trees. Burn Hudnall put up a tent for himself and his wife, and Tom unrolled his bed under Burn's wagon.

At sunset they ate supper. The gold and pink of western sky appeared to send a reflection upon the winding stream of water. Everybody was hungry, and even Pilchuck seemed to feel something good in the hour and the place. If there had been any misgivings on the part of the women, they had now vanished. The talk was jolly and hopeful. Sally Hudnall made eyes at Tom, and then, seeing her advances were apparently unobserved, she tried the same upon Stronghurl.

After supper Tom chopped and carried wood for the camp fire that night and for next morning. This done, he strolled along the creek toward the grazing horses. Fresh green grass grew abundantly on the banks and insured reasonably against the horses' straying that night. Tom decided not to hobble Dusty.

A few hundred yards from camp the creek circled through a grove of larger elms and eddied in a deep pool. Here on a log Tom lingered and indulged in rest and musings. His thoughts seemed to flow and eddy like the stream, without any apparent reason. But when thought of the girl, Milly, recurred, it abided with him. Here in the solitude of this grove he seemed to remember more vividly, and after reviewing gravely all the details concerning her it seemed to him not improbable that she was unhappy and unfortunately situated. "I—I can't tell you more," she had said, hurriedly, in a tone he now realized held shame and fear. Tom meditated over that, and at the end of an hour, when dusk was creeping under the trees, he threw off the spell and retraced his steps toward camp. There was little chance of his ever seeing her again. With resignation to that, and the vague sadness attending it, he put her out of his mind.

Soon a camp fire blazed through the dusk, and seen from afar, with the black shadows of men crossing its brightness, it made a telling picture. Tom joined the circle sitting and standing round it. The air had grown cold, making the warmth most agreeable.

"That 'tarnal smoke follows me everywhere I turn," said Sally Hudnall, as she moved to a seat beside Stronghurl.

"Elm wood ain't so good to burn," observed Pilchuck. "Neither is cottonwood. Smoke smells an' makes your eyes smart."

"Mary has a likin' for hickory," said Hudnall. "Golly! I'll bet I'll never again have apple pie baked over a hickory fire."

"Unless you go back to Illinois," added his wife, dryly.

"Which'll never be, Mary," he replied, with finality.

His words, tinged with a suggestion of failure back there in Illinois, checked conversation for a moment. They all had places dear to look back upon. Pioneers had to sacrifice much. Tom gazed at the circle of quiet faces with more realization and kindness. Buffalo-hunting was but to be an incident. It had dominated his thought. In the background of his mind, in the future, had been the idea of a ranch. With these people home and farm were paramount. Tom wondered if they were not starting out upon an ill-advised enterprise. Not to think of its peril!

Day by day the Hudnall outfit traveled over the prairie, sometimes west, and then south, yet in the main always southwest. They made from fifteen to twenty-five miles a day, according to condition of the road and favorable places to camp. Now and then they passed a freighting outfit of several wagons, heavily loaded with buffalo hides. The days passed into weeks, until Tom lost track of them.

Down here on the great plains spring had surely come. All was green and beautiful. The monotony of the country had been broken up by streams winding away between wooded banks, yet the rolling level seemed to hold generally, viewed from afar. On clear mornings a gray heave of higher ground appeared to the south. What farther north had been an openness and sameness of country now assumed proportions vast and striking.

One sunset, when halt was made for camp in an arroyo, Pilchuck waived his usual work and rode off up a slope. Reaching the summit, he dismounted and, elevating a short telescope, he looked long to the southward. Later, when he returned to the camp, all eyes fixed upon him.

"See anythin'?" queried Hudnall, impatiently.

Tom felt a thrill merely from the look of the scout.

"Buffalo!" announced Pilchuck.

There was a moment's silence. The women responded more quickly to this good news. Hudnall seemed slow and thick. Burn Hudnall threw down a billet of wood he had held in his hand.

"Buffalo!" he echoed, and the quick look of gladness he flashed upon his father proved how much he had been responsible for this trip.

"How many?" demanded Hudnall, with a long stride toward the scout.

"Reckon I couldn't say, offhand," replied Pilchuck. "Herd is another day's ride south."

Sally Hudnall interrupted her father as he was about to speak again: "Oh, I'm crazy to see a herd of buffalo. Are there lots of them?"

"Tolerable many," replied Pilchuck, with a look of professional pride. "Reckon this herd is about fifteen miles long an' three or four deep!"

Then Hudnall let out a stentorian roar, and that was a signal for equally sincere if not so exuberant a rejoicing from the others.

Next day's travel was the longest Tom had ever endured. The ground was dusty, the sun hot, the miles interminable, and there appeared ahead only the gray-green stretch of plain, leading the eyes with false hopes. But at last, toward sunset, a fringe of winding foliage marked the course of a stream. It seemed a goal. Beyond that water the great herd of buffalo must be grazing. An hour more of weary travel over uneven prairie—for Pilchuck had turned off the road early that morning—brought the outfit down into a coulee, the wildest and most attractive camp site that had yet fallen to them.

Tom made short work of his camp duties that evening, and soon was climbing the highest ridge. He climbed fast in his eagerness. Abruptly, then, he reached the top and, looking westward, suddenly became transfixed.

The sun was setting in a golden flare that enveloped the wide plain below. Half a mile from where he stood was an immense herd of huge woolly beasts, wild and strange to his sight, yet unmistakably buffalo. Tom experienced the most tingling thrill of his life. What a wonderful spectacle! It was not at all what he had pictured from tales he had heard. This scene was beautiful; and the huge straggling bulls seemed the grandest of big game beasts. Thousands of buffalo! Tom reveled in his opportunity and made the most of it. He saw that the herd circled away out of sight beyond the other end of the ridge upon which he stood. Long he gazed, and felt that he would never forget his first sight of a buffalo herd.

Upon his return to camp he found that he was not the only one late for supper. Hudnall had been out with Pilchuck. Burn was on the moment coming in with his wife and sister, who were talking excitedly about what they had seen.

"How many did you see?" asked Hudnall of Tom.

"Oh, I've no idea—all of five thousand—and I couldn't see the end of the herd," replied Tom.

"We saw ten thousand, an' that on the other side of the ridge from you," added Hudnall, tensely. His big eyes were alight and he seemed to look afar. Tom sensed that Hudnall had not responded to the wildness and beauty of the spectacle. He saw thousands of hides to sell.

"Reckon I heard shootin' down the river a couple of miles," said Pilchuck. "There's another outfit on the trail. We'll be lucky if we don't run into a dozen."

"Is this the main herd you spoke of?" inquired Tom.

"No. This is only a little bunch," returned Pilchuck.

Mrs. Hudnall broke up the colloquy. "Are you all daffy about buffalo? Supper's gettin' cold."

"Mary, you'll be fryin' buffalo steak for me to-morrow night," rejoined her husband, gayly.

After supper Hudnall called the men aside for the purpose of consultation.

"Pilchuck an' me are pardners on this deal," he said. "We'll pay thirty cents a hide. That means skinnin', haulin' the hide to camp, an' peggin' it out. No difference who kills the buffalo."

"That's more than you'll get paid by most outfits," added Pilchuck.

Stronghurl and Burn agreed on that figure; and as for Tom he frankly admitted he thought thirty cents a hide was big pay.

"Huh! Wait till you skin your first buffalo," said the scout, grinning. "You'll swear thirty dollars too little."

"Well, my part of this deal is settled. I furnish supplies an' pay for hides," said Hudnall. "Jude here will boss the hunt."

"Not much bossin'," said that individual. "We're a little farther south than I've hunted. I rode through here with some soldiers last fall, an' know the country. This bunch of buffalo is hangin' along the river. Reckon there's buffalo for miles. They'll hang around here, unless too many outfits get chasin' them. A good way to hunt is to catch them comin' to drink. Aim to hit behind the shoulder, an' shoot till he drops. Sometimes it takes two or three bullets, an' sometimes five on the old bulls. When you hunt out in the open you've got to ride like hell, chase them, an' keep shootin' till your cartridges are all gone."

"That's easy, an' ought to be heaps of fun," said Burn.

"Reckon so. An' don't forget it's dangerous. Keep out of their reach. The real hard work comes in skinnin' an' peggin' out. Before you get good enough at that to make three dollars a day, you'll be sick of the job."

"Three dollars!" echoed Burn, in scorn. "I expect to make five times that much."

Tom had much the same aspiration, but he did not voice it. Pilchuck looked amused and mysterious enough to restrain undue enthusiasm.

"Finally—an' this is a hunch you want to take serious," went on Pilchuck, lowering his voice so the women could not hear. "We might run on to Indians."

That sobered all the listeners.

"Last summer was bad an' fall was worse," he continued. "I don't know now how conditions are or what the Indians are doin'. Reckon somebody, hunters or soldiers, will happen along an' tell us. My belief is there'll be some tough fights this year. But, of course, the redskins can't be everywhere, an' these buffalo are thick an' range far. We may be lucky an' never see a Comanche. But we'll have to keep our eyes peeled all the time an' mustn't get far apart. If we see or hear of Indians, we'll move camp an' stand guard at night."

"Jude, that's stranger talk than you've used yet," responded Hudnall, in surprise and concern.

"Reckon so. I'm not worryin'. I'm just tellin' you. There'll be a heap of hunters in here this summer. An' like as not the soldiers will see what women there are safe to the fort or some well-protected freightin' post."

Tom thought of the dark-eyed girl, Milly. Almost he had forgotten. How long ago that meeting seemed! Where was she now? He convinced himself that Pilchuck's assurance of the protection of soldiers applied to all the women who might be with the hunting bands.

No more was said about Indians. Interest reverted strongly to the proposed hunt to begin on the morrow. Tom fell in with the spirit of the hour and stayed up late round the camp fire, listening to the talk and joining in. Once their animated discussion was silenced by a mournful howl from the ridge-top where Tom had climbed to see the buffalo. It was a strange sound, deep and prolonged, like the bay of a hound on a deer scent, only infinitely wilder.

"What's that?" asked somebody.

"Wolf," replied Pilchuck. "Not a coyote, mind you, but a real old king of the plains. There's a lot of wolves hang with the buffalo."

The cry was not repeated then, but later, as Tom composed himself in his warm blankets, it pealed out again, wonderfully breaking the stillness. How hungry and full of loneliness! It made Tom shiver. It seemed a herald of wilderness.

Tom was the first to arise next morning, and this time it was the ring of his ax and the crash of wood thrown into the camp-fire circle that roused the others. When Stronghurl sallied forth to find the horses, daylight had broken clear; and by the time breakfast was ready the sun was up.

Pilchuck, returning from the ridge-top, reported that buffalo were in sight, all along the river, as far as he could see. They were a goodly distance out on the plain and were not yet working in for a drink.

"I'll take my turn hangin' round camp," said Hudnall, plainly with an effort! "There's a lot to do, an' some one must see after the women folks."

"It'd be a good idea for you to climb the ridge every two hours or so an' take a look," replied Pilchuck, casually. But his glance at Hudnall was not casual. "I'll leave my telescope for you. Don't miss anythin'."

The men saddled their horses and donned the heavy cartridge belts. They also carried extra cartridges in their pockets. Tom felt weighted down as if by a thousand pounds. He had neglected to buy a saddle sheath for his gun, and therefore would have to carry it in his hand—an awkward task while riding.

They rode behind Pilchuck down the river, and forded it at a shallow sand-barred place, over which the horses had to go at brisk gait to avoid miring.

"How're we ever goin' to get the wagons across?" queried Burn Hudnall.

"Reckon we've no choice," replied Pilchuck. "The hides have to be hauled to camp. You see the actual chasin' an' killin' of buffalo doesn't take much time. Then the real work begins. We'll have all the rest of the day—an' night, to skin, haul to camp, an' peg out."

This side of the river bank was more wooded and less precipitous than the other. Buffalo tracks were as thick as cattle tracks round a water-hole. The riders halted at the top of the slope where the level plain began. Out on the grassy expanse, perhaps a mile or more, extended a shaggy dark line like a wall.

"Reckon there's your buffalo," said the scout. "Now we'll scatter an' wait under cover for an hour or so. Hide in the brush or behind a bank, anywhere till some come close. Then burn powder! An' don't quit the buffalo you shoot at till he's down. When they run off, chase them, an' shoot from your horses. The chase won't last long, for the buffalo will run away from you."

Pilchuck stationed Tom at this point, and rode on down the edge of the plain with the other men. They passed out of sight. In that direction Tom could not see far, owing to rising ground. To the southwest, however, the herd extended until it was impossible to distinguish between vague black streaks of buffalo and dim distance.

"Pilchuck said this was only a little bunch!" soliloquized Tom, as he scanned the plain-wide band of beasts.

Dismounting, he held his horse and stood at the edge of the timber, watching and listening. It was a wonderfully satisfying moment. He tried to be calm, but that was impossible. He recognized what had always been deep in him—the love of adventure and freedom—the passion to seek these in unknown places. Here, then, he stood at his post above the bank of a timber-bordered river in the Panhandle of Texas with a herd of buffalo in sight. He saw coyotes, too, and a larger beast, gray in color, that he was sure was a wolf. Hawks and buzzards sailed against the blue sky. Down through the trees, near the river, he espied a flock of wild turkeys. Then, in connection with all he saw, and the keenness of the morning which he felt, he remembered the scout's caution about Indians. Tom thought that he ought to be worried, even frightened, but he was neither. This moment was the most mysteriously full and satisfying of his life.

Opposite his point the buffalo did not approach more closely; he observed, however, that to the eastward they appeared to be encroaching upon the river brakes.

Suddenly then he was thrilled by gun-shots. Boom! Boom! . . . Boom-boom! His comrades had opened the hunt.

"What'll I do now?" he mused, gazing down the river, then out toward the herd. It presented no change that he could distinguish. "I was told to stay here. But with shooting begun, I don't think any buffalo will come now."

Soon after that a gun roared out much closer, indeed, just over the rise of plain below Tom.

"That's a big fifty!" he ejaculated, aloud.

Far beyond, perhaps two miles distant, sounded a report of a Sharps, low but clear on the still morning air. Another and another! Tom began to tingle with anticipation. Most likely his comrades would chase the buffalo his way. Next he heard a shot apparently between the one that had sounded close and the one far away. So all three of his fellow hunters had gotten into action. Tom grew restive. Peering out at the herd, he discovered it was moving. A low trample of many hoofs assailed his ears. Dust partially obscured the buffalo. They appeared to be running back into the gray expanse. Suddenly Tom became aware of heavy and continuous booming of guns—close, medium, and far-away reports mingling. As he listened it dawned on him that all the reports were diminishing in sound. His comrades were chasing the buffalo and getting farther away. After a while he heard no more. Also the dust-shrouded buffalo opposite his position had disappeared. His disappointment was keen.

Presently a horseman appeared on the crest of the ridge that had hidden the chase from him. The white horse was Pilchuck's. Tom saw the rider wave his hat, and taking the action as a signal he mounted and rode at a gallop to the ridge, striking its summit some few hundred yards to the right. Here he had unobstructed view. Wide gray-green barren rolling plain, hazy with dust! The herd of buffalo was not in sight. Tom rode on to meet Pilchuck.

"Tough luck for you," said the scout. "They were workin' in to the river below here."

"Did you kill any?" queried Tom, eagerly.

"I downed twenty-one," replied Pilchuck. "An' as I was ridin' back I met Stronghurl. He was cussin' because he'd only got five. An' Burn burned a lot of powder. But so far as I could see he got only one."

"No!" ejaculated Tom. "Why, he was sure of dozens."

"Reckon he knows more now," returned Pilchuck. "You ride down there an' see how many you can skin. I'll go back to camp, hitch up a wagon, an' try to come back across the river."

The scout rode away, and Tom, turning his horse eastward, took to a trot down the immense gradual slope. After searching the plain he espied a horse grazing, and then a dark shaggy mound which manifestly was a slain buffalo. Tom spurred his horse, rapidly covering the distance between. Soon he saw Burn at work skinning the buffalo.

"Good for you!" shouted Tom, as he galloped up.

"Helluva job—this skinnin'!" yelled Burn, flashing a red and sweaty face toward Tom. "Hey! Look out!"

But his warning came too late. Tom's horse snorted furiously, as if expelling a new and hateful scent, and, rearing high, he came down and plunged so violently that Tom flew one way and his gun another.

Tom landed hard and rooted his face in the grass. The shock stunned him for a second. Then he sat up and found himself unhurt. The surprise, the complete victory of the horse, and the humiliation of being made to root the ground like a pig stirred Tom to some heat.

"Hope you ain't hurt?" called Burn, anxiously, rising from his work.

"No, but I'm mad," replied Tom.

Whereupon Burn fell back and rolled over in the grass, roaring with mirth. Tom paid no attention to his comrade. Dusty had run off a hundred or more paces, and was now walking, head to one side, dragging his bridle. Tom yelled to stop him. Dusty kept on. Whereupon Tom broke into a run and caught him.

"You're a fine horse," panted Tom, as he mounted. "Now you'll—go back—and rub your nose—on that buffalo."

Dusty appeared placable enough, and trotted back readily until once again close to the buffalo. Tom spurred him on and called forcibly to him. Dusty grew excited as he came nearer. Still he did not show any ugliness.

"Don't hurry him," remonstrated Burn. "He's just scared."

But Tom, not yet cooled in temper, meant that Dusty should go right up to the buffalo. This he forced the horse to do. Then suddenly Dusty flashed down his head and seemed to propel himself with incredible violence high into the air. He came down on stiff legs. The shock was so severe that Tom shot out of the saddle. He came down back of the cantle. Desperately he clung to the pommel, and as Dusty pitched high again, his hold broke and he spun round like a top on the rump of his horse and slid off. Dusty ceased his pitching and backed away from the dead buffalo.

Only Tom's feelings were hurt. Burn Hudnall's "Haw! haw! haw!" rolled out in great volume. Tom sat where he had been dumped, and gazing at the horse, he gradually induced a state of mind bordering upon appreciation of how Dusty must have felt. Presently Burn got up, and catching Dusty, led him slowly and gently, talking soothingly all the while, nearer to the buffalo, and held him there.

"He's all right now," said Burn.

Tom rose and went back to the horse and patted him.

"You bucked me off, didn't you?"

"Tom, if I were you I'd get off an' lead him up to the dead buffalo till he gets over his scare," suggested Burn.

"I will," replied Tom, and then he gazed down at the shaggy carcass on the ground. "Phew! the size of him!"

"Looks big as a woolly elephant, doesn't he? Big bull," Burn said. "He's the only one I got, an' sure he took a lot of shootin'. You see the buffalo was runnin' an' I couldn't seem to hit one of them. Finally I plunked this bull. An' he kept on runnin' till I filled him full of lead."

"Where are those Pilchuck got?" queried Tom, anxious to go to work.

"First one's lyin' about a quarter—there, to the left a little. You go tackle skinnin' him. It's an old bull like this. An' if you get his skin off to-day I'll eat it."

"I've skinned lots of cattle—steers and bulls," replied Tom. "It wasn't hard work. Why should this be?"

"Man, they're buffalo, an' their skin's an inch thick, tougher than sole leather—an' stick! Why it's riveted on an' clinched."

"Must be some knack about the job, then," rejoined Tom, mounting Dusty. "Say, I nearly forgot my gun. Hand it up, will you? . . . Burn, I'll bet you I skin ten buffalo before dark and peg them out, as Pilchuck called it, before I go to bed."

"I'll take you up," said Burn, with a grim laugh. "I just wish I had time to watch you. It'd be a circus. But I'll be ridin' by you presently."

"All right. I'm off to win that bet," replied Tom, in cheery determination, and touching Dusty with the spurs he rode rapidly toward the next fallen buffalo.

CHAPTER FOUR

Dusty evinced less fear of the second prostrate buffalo, which was even a larger bull than the huge tough old animal Burn was engaged in skinning.

This time Tom did not take any needless risks with Dusty. Riding to within fifty feet of the dead beast, he dismounted, led the nervous horse closer, and round and round, and finally up to it. Dusty behaved very well, considering his first performance; left to himself, however, he edged away to a considerable distance and began to graze.

Tom lost no time in getting to work. He laid his gun near at hand, and divesting himself of his coat he took ripping and skinning knives from his belt. Determination was strong in him. He anticipated an arduous and perplexing job, yet felt fully capable of accomplishing it and winning his bet with Burn. This buffalo was a monster; he was old and the burrs and matted hair appeared a foot deep at his forequarters; he was almost black.

First Tom attempted to turn the beast over into a more favorable position for skinning. He found, however, that he could scarcely budge the enormous bulk. That was a surprise. There appeared nothing to do but go to work as best he could, and wait for help to move the animal. Forthwith he grasped his ripping knife and proceeded to try following instructions given him. It took three attempts to get the knife under the skin and when he essayed to rip he found that a good deal of strength was required. He had calculated that he must expend considerable energy to make any speed, until practice had rendered him proficient. The considerable energy grew into the utmost he could put forth. After the ripping came the skinning, and in very short time he appreciated all Burn had said. "Helluva job is right!" Tom commented, remembering his comrade's words. But he did not spare himself, and by tremendous exertions he had the buffalo skinned before Burn finished his. Tom could not vouch for the merit of the job, but the skin was off. He could vouch, however, for his breathlessness and the hot sweat that bathed his body. Plowing corn or pitching wheat, jobs he had imagined were hard work, paled into insignificance.

"Say—wonder what pegging out the hide—will be like," he panted, as he sheathed his knives and picked up his gun. Mounting Dusty he rode eastward, scanning the plain for the next dead buffalo.

Presently he espied it, and galloping thither he found it to be another bull, smaller and younger than the others, and he set to work with renewed zeal. He would have to work like a beaver to win that bet. It took violence to make a quick job of this one. That done, Tom rode on to the third.

While he was laboring here Burn rode by and paid him a hearty compliment, which acted upon Tom like a spur. He could not put forth any greater zeal; indeed, he would do wonders if he kept to the pace he had set himself. But as he progressed he learned. This advantage, however, was offset by the gradual dulling of his knives. He had forgotten to bring his steel.

He toiled from one dead buffalo to another. The breeze died away, the sun climbed high and blazed down upon the plain. His greatest need was water to drink. Hour by hour his thirst augmented. His shirt was so wet with perspiration that he could have wrung it out. The heat did not bother him so much. Gradually his clothes became covered with a lather of sweat, blood, grease, and dust. This, and the growing pangs in his body, especially hands and forearms, occasioned him extreme annoyance. He did not note the passing of time. Only now and then did he scan the plain for sign of his comrades. Indians he had completely forgotten. Burn and Stronghurl were to be seen at intervals, and Pilchuck, driving the wagon, was with them. Once from a high knoll Tom thought he espied another wagon miles down the river, but he could not be sure. He did, however, make out a dim black blur to the southward, and this he decided was the buffalo herd, ranging back toward the river.

During this strenuous time there were incidents of much interest, if he could only have given them due attention. Buzzards swooped down over him, closer and closer, till he felt the wind of their wings. A lean gray wolf came within range of his gun, but Tom had no time for shooting. He toiled on and the hours flew.

When, late in the afternoon, he tore off the hide that assured him of winning the wager, he was exultant. He was now two miles from the wagon, which he made out was approaching. Only one more buffalo did he find, and this he skinned by the time Pilchuck drove up.

"Wal, if you ain't a Kansas cyclone!" ejaculated the scout, with undisguised admiration. "Seventeen skinned your first day! Doan, I never seen the beat of it."

"I had a bet with Burn," replied Tom, wiping his hot face.

"If you can keep that lick up, young man, you'll make a stake out of this hide-huntin'," returned Pilchuck, seriously.

"Wait till I learn how!" exclaimed Tom, fired by the praise and the hopes thus engendered.

"Reckon I'll cut the hump off this young bull," remarked the scout, as he climbed out of the seat. "Buffalo steak for supper, hey?"

"I could eat hoofs. And I'm spitting cotton," said Tom.

"You forgot a canteen. Son, you mustn't forget *anythin'* in this game," admonished Pilchuck. "Rustle back to camp."

Tom was interested, however, to learn how Pilchuck would cut the desirable hump from the carcass. Long had Tom heard of the savory steaks from the buffalo. The scout thrust his big knife in near the joining of the loin, ripped forward along the lower side as far as the ribs ran; then performed a like operation on the upper side. That done, he cut the ends loose and carved out a strip over three feet long and so thick it was heavy.

"Reckon we can rustle back to camp now," he said, throwing the meat on the pile of hides in the wagon.

"Is that the herd coming back?" queried Tom, pointing from his horse.

"Yes. They'll be in to-night yet to drink. We'll find them here to-morrow mornin'. Did you hear the big fifties of the other hunters?"

"You mean others besides our outfit? No, I didn't."

"There's a couple of outfits down the river. But that's lucky for us. Probably will be hunters all along here soon. Reckon there's safety in numbers an' sure the buffalo are plenty enough."

Tom rode back to camp facing a sunset that emblazoned the western ramparts in gold and purple. The horizon line was far distant and lifted high, a long level upland, at that moment singularly wild and beautiful. Tom wondered if it could be the eastern extension of the great Staked Plains he had heard mentioned so often. Weary as he was from his extraordinary exertions, he yet had spirit left to look and feel and think. The future seemed like that gold-rimmed horizon line.

He reached camp before dusk, there to receive the plaudits of his comrades and also the women folks. Burn was generous in his eulogy, but he created consternation in Tom's breast by concluding, "Wait till you try peggin' out a hide!"

"Aw! I forgot there was more. I've not won that bet yet," he rejoined, dejectedly.

After attending to his horse Tom had just about enough energy left to drink copiously and stretch out with a groan under a tree. Never before in his life had he throbbed and ached and burned so exceedingly. An hour's rest considerably relieved him. Then supper, which he attacked somewhat as if he were a hungry wolf, was an event to be remembered. If all his comrades had not been equally as ravenous he would have been ashamed. Pilchuck got much satisfaction out of the rapid disappearance of many buffalo steaks.

"Meat's no good when so fresh," he averred. "After bein' hung up a few days an' set, we call it, an' fried in tallow, it beats beef all hollow."

Before darkness set in Tom saw Pilchuck peg out a hide. First the scout laid the hide flat and proceeded to cut little holes in it all around the edge. Next with ax and knife he sharpened sticks nearly a foot long. Three of these he drove through the neck of the hide and deep enough into the ground to hold well. Then he proceeded to the tail end and stretched the skin. Tom could well see that skill was required here. Pilchuck held the skin stretched, and at the same time drove one peg, then another, at this end. Following that, he began to stretch and peg the side, eventually working all around. The whole operation did not take long and did not appear difficult.

Tom essayed it with a vim that made up for misgivings. Like the skinning, it was vastly more difficult than it looked. Cutting the holes and making the pegs was easy; however, when it came to stretching the hide and holding it and pegging it all by himself, he found it a most deceiving and irksome task.

Sally Hudnall offered to help Tom, but he declined with thanks, explaining that he had a wager to win. The girl hovered round Tom and curiously watched him, much to his annoyance. He saw that she was laughing at him.

"What's so funny?" he queried, nettled.

"You look like a boy tryin' to play mumbly-peg an' leap-frog at once," she replied with a giggle.

Tom had to laugh a good-natured acknowledgment to that; and then he deftly turned the tables on her by making a dry, casual remark about Stronghurl. The girl blushed and let him alone to ponder over the intricacies of this hide pegging. No contortionist ever performed more marvels of stretching his body than Tom achieved. Likewise, no man ever so valiantly stifled back speech that would have been unseemly, to say the least, in the hearing of women. His efforts, however, were crowned with the reward of persistence. By midnight he had the job done, and utterly spent he crawled into his bed, where at once his eyes seemed to glue shut.

Next morning he readily answered Pilchuck's call, but his body was incapable of a like alacrity. He crawled out of his blankets as if he were crippled. A gradual working of his muscles, however, loosened the stiffness and warmed the cold soreness to the extent that he believed he could begin the day with some semblance of service.

It was again, in Pilchuck's terse terms, every man for himself. Tom welcomed this for two reasons, first that he could go easy, and secondly that he wanted to revel in and prolong his first real encounter with the buffalo.

Hudnall changed Tom's plans somewhat by relegating him to watch camp that day, while he went out with the other men. He modified this order, however, by saying that if any buffalo came near camp Tom might go after them.

Breakfast was over at sunrise. Pilchuck brought out his heavy ammunition box, with which each hunter was provided, and told Tom he could help a little and learn while he helped. His belt contained more than thirty empty shells that were to be reloaded.

"Reckon I ought to have done this last night," he explained to Hudnall, who was impatient to be off. "You fellows go on down the river. I'll catch up with you."

The three hunters rode off eagerly, and Pilchuck got out his tools for reloading. Tom quickly learned the use of bullet-mold, swedge, lubricator, primer, extractor, tamper, and patch-paper.

"Reckon I'm all set now," affirmed the scout. "You put these tools away for me. An' keep a good lookout. I'm not worryin', but I'd like to know if there's Indians huntin' this herd. Take a look from the ridge with my glass, an' there'll be buffalo on the other side of the river to-day, you can keep in sight of camp an' get a shot."

With that Pilchuck mounted his horse and trotted away through the timber. Tom leisurely set about the few tasks at hand. It pleased him when he was able to avoid Sally's watching eyes. She seemed to regard him with something of disapproval. When the camp chores were finished Tom took the telescope and climbed to the ridge-top. Apparently more buffalo were in sight than on the previous day and about in the same latitude. Tom swept the circle of surrounding country, gray-green rolling plain, the low ridges, the winding river depression, with its fringe of trees. Some miles down the river rose a column of smoke, marking, no doubt, another camp. Far away to the south and west loomed the strange upheaval of land. Clearly defined by the telescope, it appeared to be an escarpment of horizon-wide dimensions, gray and barren, seamed by canyons, standing in wild and rugged prominence above the plains.

Not until late in the morning did Tom's watchful gaze espy buffalo approaching camp. Then he was thrilled to see a number of what appeared to be bulls grazing riverward opposite the camp. Hurrying down from the eminence whence he had made this observation, he got his gun and cartridges, and crossing the river he proceeded up the thickly wooded slope some distance to the west of his first stand of yesterday. It looked to him as if the bulls might work down into a coulee which opened into the river depression. He was quite a little time reaching the point desired—the edge of woodland and brink of the ravine—and when he peered from under the last trees he was moved with such an overwhelming excitement that he dropped to his knees.

Out on the open plain, not a hundred yards distant, grazed nine buffalo bulls, the leader of which appeared larger than the largest he had skinned the day before. They had not scented Tom and were grazing toward him, somewhat to the right, manifestly headed for the coulee.

Trembling and panting, Tom watched with strained sight. He forgot he held a "big fifty" in his hands, and in the riotous sensation of that moment he did not remember until from far down the river came a dull boom—boom of guns. It amazed him to see that the buffalo bulls paid no attention to the shooting. He made up his mind then to take his time and await a favorable opportunity to down the leader. They were approaching so slowly that he had ample time to control the trembling of his muscles, though it was impossible to compose himself.

Several of the bulls piled over the little bank into the coulee, and while they were passing within fifty yards of Tom the others leisurely began the descent, the huge bull nodding along in the rear. The near ones passed into the timber, getting farther away from Tom. He had difficulty in retaining his eagerness. Then one bull began to crash in the brush. He made as much noise as an elephant. Tom watched with an intense interest only second to the hot-pressed lust to kill. This bull was crashing against thick brush, and it soon became plain to Tom that the beast was scratching his shaggy hide, tearing out the matts of burrs and the shedding hair. It came away in great tufts, hanging on the sharp broken ends of the brush. This old bull knew what he was about when he charged that thicket of hackberry.

Suddenly Tom was electrified by a puff which assuredly came from the nostrils of a buffalo close to him. He turned cautiously. Behind and below him, closer than fifty yards, the other bulls were passing into the timber. He plainly heard the grinding of their teeth. They were monsters. Instinctively Tom searched for a tree to climb or a place to run to after he fired. What if they should charge his way? He would scarcely have time to reload, and even if he had, of what avail would that be?

Then the monarch wagged his enormous head in line with Tom's magnifying vision. What a wide short face! His eyes stood out so that he could see in front or behind. His shaggy beard was dragging. Tom could see only the tips of the horns in all that woolly mass. Puff! came the sound of expelled breath.

Tom felt he hated to kill that glorious and terrifying beast, yet he was powerless to resist the tight palpitating feverish dominance of his blood. Resting the heavy rifle on a branch, he aimed behind the great shaggy shoulder, and with strained muscles and bated breath he fired.

Like a cannon the old Sharps roared. Crashings of brush, thudding of heavy hoofs, sounded to the right of the cloud of smoke. The other bulls were running. Tom caught glimpses of broad brown backs cleaving the brush down the river slope. With shaking hands he reloaded. Peering under the drifting smoke, he searched fearfully for the bull he had fired at, at first seeing only the thick-grassed swelling slope of the coulee. Then farther down he espied a huge brown object lying inert.

The wildness of the boy in Tom conquered all else. Leaping up, he broke out of the woods, yelling like an Indian, and charged down the gentle slope, exultant and proud, yet not quite frenzied enough to forget possible peril. From that quarter, however, he was safe. The monarch was heaving his last breath.

Pilchuck rode in at noon that day, in time to see Tom stretch the hide of his first buffalo.

"You got one, hey?" he called, eying the great shaggy hide with appreciation. "Your first buffalo! Wal, it's a darned fine one. They don't come any bigger than that fellow."

Tom had to tell the story of his exploit, and was somewhat discomfited by the scout's remark that he should have killed several of the bulls.

"Aren't you back early?" queried Tom, as Pilchuck dismounted.

"Run out of cartridges," he said, laconically.

"So quick!" exclaimed Tom, staring. "You must have seen a lot of buffalo."

"Reckon they *was* thick this mornin'," returned the scout, dryly. "I got plumb surrounded once an' had to shoot my way out."

"Well! . . . How many did you down?"

"Twenty-one. I think when we count up to-night we'll have a good day. Burn is doin' better than yesterday. . . . Wal, I want a bite to eat an' a drink. It's warm ridin' in the dust. Then I'll hitch up the wagon an' drive down for the hides. Come to think of it, though, I've a job to do before. You can help me."

Later Pilchuck hailed Tom to fetch an ax and come on. Tom followed the scout down into the thickets.

"Cut four strong poles about ten feet long an' pack them to camp," said Pilchuck.

Tom did as he was bidden, to find that the scout had returned ahead of him, carrying four short poles with forks at one end. He proceeded to pound these into the ground with the forks uppermost, and then he laid across them the poles Tom had brought, making a square framework. "We'll stretch a hide inside the poles, loose so it'll sag down, an' there we'll salt our buffalo humps."

Pilchuck then brought in a team of horses and hitched it to the big wagon. "Wal, son," he said to Tom, "I ain't hankerin' after skinnin' hides. But I may as well start. We're goin' to kill more buffalo than we'll have time to skin."

He drove out of camp down the slope into the shallow water. The horses plunged in at a trot, splashing high. Pilchuck lashed out with the long whip and yelled lustily. Any slowing up there meant wheels stuck in the sand. Horses, driver, and wagon were drenched. From the other side Pilchuck looked back. "Fine on a day like this," he shouted.

Not long after he had gone Tom heard one of the horses up the river neigh several times. This induced him to reconnoiter, with the result that he espied a wagon coming along the edge of the timber. It appeared to be an open wagon, with one man in the driver's seat. Another, following on horseback, was leading two extra horses.

"More hide-hunters," Tom decided as he headed toward them. "Now I wonder what's expected of me in a case like this."

When the driver espied Tom come into the open, rifle in hand, he halted the horses abruptly.

"Dunn outfit—hide-hunters," he announced, with something of alarmed alacrity, as if his identity and business had been questioned. He appeared to be a short, broad man, and what little of his face was visible was bright red. He had bushy whiskers.

"I'm Tom Doan, of Hudnall's outfit," replied Tom. "We're camped just below."

"Clark Hudnall! By all that's lucky!" exclaimed the man. "I know Hudnall. We talked some last fall of going in together. That was at Independence. But he wasn't ready and I come ahead."

Tom offered his hand, and at this juncture the horseman that had been behind the wagon rode forward abreast of the driver. He was a fat young man with a most jocund expression on his round face. His apparel was striking in its inappropriateness to the rough life of the plains. His old slouch hat was too small for his large head, and there was a tuft of tow-colored hair sticking out of a hole in the crown.

"Ory, shake hands with Tom Doan, of Hudnall's outfit," said Dunn. "My nephew, Ory Tacks."

"Much obliged to meet you, Mister Doan," replied Tacks, with great aplomb.

"Howdy! Same to you," greeted Tom, in slow, good humor, as he studied the face of this newcomer.

Dunn interrupted his scrutiny.

"Is Hudnall in camp?"

"No. He's out hunting buffalo. I'm sure you're welcome to stop at our camp till he comes in. That'll be around sundown."

"Good. I'm needing sight and sound of some one I know," replied Dunn, significantly. "Lead the way, Doan. These horses of mine are thirsty."

When the travelers arrived at Hudnall's camp, Tom helped them unhitch in a favorable camping spot, and unpack the necessary camp duffle. Once during this work Ory Tacks halted so suddenly that he dropped a pack on his foot.

"Ouch!" he cried, lifting his foot to rub it with his hand while he kept his gaze toward Tom's camp. It was an enraptured and amazed gaze. "Do I see a beautiful young lady?"

Thus questioned, Tom wheeled to see Sally Hudnall's face framed in the white-walled door of Hudnall's prairie wagon. It was rather too far to judge accurately, but he inclined to the impression that Sally was already making eyes at Ory Tacks.

"Oh! There!" ejaculated Tom, hard put to it to keep his face serious. "It's a young lady, all right—Miss Sally Hudnall. But I can't see that she—"

"Uncle Jack, there's a girl in this camp," interrupted Ory, in tones of awe.

"We've got three women," said Tom.

"Well, that's a surprise to us," returned Dunn. "I had no idea Hudnall would fetch his women folks down here into the buffalo country. I wonder if he . . . Tom, is there a buffalo-hunter with you, a man who knows the frontier?"

"Yes. Jude Pilchuck."

"Did he stand for the women coming?"

"I guess he had no choice," rejoined Tom.

"Humph! How long have you been on the river?"

"Two days."

"Seen any other outfits?"

"No. But Pilchuck said there were a couple down the river."

"Awhuh," said Dunn, running a stubby, powerful hand through his beard. He seemed concerned. "You see, Doan, we've been in the buffalo country since last fall. And we've sure had it rough. Poor luck on our fall hunt. That was over on the Brazos. Kiowa Indians on the rampage. Our winter hunt we made on the line of Indian Territory. We didn't know it was against the law to kill buffalo in the Territory. The officers took our hides. Then we'd got our spring hunt started fine—west of here forty miles or so. Had five hundred hides. And they were stolen."

"You don't say!" exclaimed Tom, astonished. "Who'd be so low down as to steal hides?"

"Who?" snorted Dunn, with fire in his small eyes. "We don't know. The soldiers don't know. They *say* the thieves are Indians. But I'm one who believes they are white."

Tom immediately grasped the serious nature of this information. The difficulties and dangers of hide-hunting began to assume large proportions.

"Well, you must tell Hudnall and Pilchuck all about this," he said.

Just then Sally called out sweetly, "Tom—oh, Tom—wouldn't your visitors like a bite to eat?"

"Reckon they would, miss, thanks to you," shouted Dunn, answering for himself. As for Ory Tacks, he appeared overcome, either by the immediate prospect of food, or by going into the presence of the beautiful young lady. Tom noted that he at once dropped his task of helping Dunn and bent eager energies to the improvement of his personal appearance. Dunn and Tom had seated themselves before Ory joined them, but when he did come he was manifestly bent on making a great impression.

"Miss Hudnall—my nephew, Ory Tacks," announced Dunn, with quaint formality.

"What's the name?" queried Sally, incredulously, as if she had not heard aright.

"Orville Tacks—at your service, Miss Hudnall," replied the young man, elaborately. "I am much obliged to meet you."

Sally took him in with keen, doubtful gaze, and evidently, when she could convince herself that he was not making fun at her expense, gravitated to a perception of easy conquest. Tom saw that this was a paramount issue with Sally. Probably later she might awake to a humorous appreciation of this young gentleman.

Tom soon left the newcomers to their camp tasks, and went about his own, which for the most part consisted of an alert watchfulness. Early in the afternoon the distant boom-boom of the big buffalo guns ceased to break the drowsy silence. The hours wore away. When, at time of sunset, Tom returned from his last survey of the plains, it was to find Hudnall and his hunter comrades in camp. Pilchuck was on the way back with a load of fifty-six hides. Just as twilight fell he called from the opposite bank that he would need help at the steep place. All hands pulled and hauled the wagon over the obstacle; and hard upon that incident came Mrs. Hudnall's cheery call to supper.

Tom watched and listened with more than his usual attentiveness. Hudnall was radiant. This day's work had been good. For a man of his tremendous strength and endurance the extreme of toil was no hindrance. He was like one that had found a gold mine. Burn Hudnall reflected his father's spirit. Pilchuck ate in silence, not affected by their undisguised elation. Stronghurl would have been dense indeed, in the face of Sally's overtures, not to sense a rival in Ory Tacks. This individual almost ate out of Sally's hand. Dunn presented a rather gloomy front. Manifestly he had not yet told Hudnall of his misfortunes.

After supper it took the men two hours of labor to peg out the hides. All the available space in the grove was blanketed with buffalo skins, with narrow lanes between. Before this work was accomplished the women had gone to bed. At the camp fire which Tom replenished, Dunn recounted to Hudnall and Pilchuck the same news he had told Tom, except that he omitted comment on the presence of the women.

To Tom's surprise, Hudnall took Dunn's story lightly. He did not appear to grasp any serious menace, and he dismissed Dunn's loss with brief words: "Hard luck! But you can make it up soon. Throw in with me. The more the merrier, an' the stronger we'll be."

"How about your supplies?" queried Dunn.

"Plenty for two months. An' we'll be freightin' out hides before that."

"All right, Clark, I'll throw in with your outfit, huntin' for myself, of course, an' payin' my share," replied Dunn, slowly, as if the matter was weighty. "But I hope you don't mind my talkin' out straight about your women."

"No, you can talk straight about anyone or anythin' to me."

"You want to send your women back or take them to Fort Elliott," returned Dunn, brusquely.

"Dunn, I won't do anythin' of the kind," retorted Hudnall, bluntly.

"Well, the soldiers will do it for you, if they happen to come along," said Dunn, just as bluntly. "It's your own business. I'm not trying to interfere in your affairs.

But women don't belong on such a huntin' trip as this summer will see. My idea, talking straight, is that Mr. Pilchuck here should have warned you and made you leave the women back in the settlement."

"Wal, I gave Hudnall a hunch all right, but he wouldn't listen," declared the scout.

"You didn't give me any such damn thing," shouted Hudnall angrily.

Then followed a hot argument that in Tom's opinion ended in the conviction that Pilchuck had not told all he knew.

"Well, if that's what, I reckon it doesn't make any difference to me," said Hudnall, finally. "I wanted wife an' Sally with me. An' if I was comin' at all they were comin' too. We're huntin' buffalo, yes, for a while—as long as there's money in it. But what we're huntin' most is a farm."

"Now, Hudnall, listen," responded Dunn, curtly. "I'm not tryin' to boss your outfit. After this I'll have no more to say. . . . I've been six months at this hide-huntin' an' I know what I'm talkin' about. The great massed herd of buffalo is south of here, on the Red River, along under the rim of the Staked Plain. You think this herd here is big. Say, this is a straggler bunch. There's a thousand times as many buffalo down on the Red. . . . There's where the most of the hide-hunters are and there the Comanches and Kiowas are on the war-path. I've met hunters who claim this main herd will reach here this spring, along in May. But I say that great herd will never again get this far north. If you want hide-huntin' for big money, then you've got to pull stakes for the Red River."

"By thunder! we'll pull then," boomed Hudnall.

"Reckon we've got some good huntin' here, as long as this bunch hangs around the water," interposed Pilchuck. "We've got it 'most all to ourselves."

"That's sense," said Dunn, conclusively. "I'll be glad to stay. But when we do pull for the Staked Plain country you want to look for some wild times. There'll be hell along the Red River this summer."

In the swiftly flying days that succeeded Dunn's joining Hudnall's outfit Tom developed rapidly into a hunter and skinner of buffalo. He was never an expert shot with the heavy Sharps, but he made up in horsemanship and daring what he lacked as a marksman. If a man had nerve he did not need to be skillful with the rifle. It was as a skinner, however, that Tom excelled all of Hudnall's men. Tom had been a wonderful husker of corn; he had been something of a blacksmith. His hands were large and powerful, and these qualifications, combined with deftness, bade fair to make him a record skinner.

The Hudnall outfit followed the other outfits, which they never caught up with, south along the stream in the rear of this herd of buffalo. Neither Dunn nor Pilchuck knew for certain that the stream flowed into the Red River, but as the days grew into weeks they inclined more and more to that opinion. If it was so, luck was merely with them. Slowly the herd gave way, running, when hunted, some miles to the south, and next day always grazing east to the river. The morning came, however, when the herd did not appear. Pilchuck rode thirty miles south without success. He was of the opinion, and Dunn agreed with him, that the buffalo had at last made for the Red River. So that night plan was made to abandon hunting for the present and to travel south in search of the main herd.

Tom took stock of his achievements, and was exceedingly amazed and exultant. How quickly it seemed that small figures augmented to larger ones!

He had hunted, in all, twenty-four days. Three hundred and sixty buffalo had fallen to his credit. But that was not all. It was the skinning which he was paid for, and he had skinned four hundred and eighty-two buffalo—an average of twenty a day. Hudnall owed him then one hundred forty-four dollars and sixty cents. Tom had cheerfully and gratefully worked on a farm for twenty dollars a month. This piling up of money was incredible. He was dazzled. Suppose he hunted and skinned buffalo for a whole year! The prospect quite overwhelmed him. Moreover, the camp life, the open wilderness, the hard riding and the thrill of the chase—these had worked on him insensibly, until before he realized it he was changed.

CHAPTER FIVE

There was just daylight enough to discern objects when Milly Fayre peeped out of the wagon, hoping against hope that she would be able to wave a farewell to the young man, Tom Doan. She knew his name and the names of all the Hudnall party. For some reason her stepfather was immensely curious about other outfits, yet avoided all possible contact with them.

But no one in Hudnall's camp appeared to be stirring. The obscurity of the gray dawn soon swallowed the grove of trees and the prairie schooners. Milly lay back in her bed in the bottom of the wagon and closed her eyes. Sleep would not come again. The rattle of wagon trappings, the roll of the crunching wheels, and the trotting clip-clop of hoofs not only prevented slumber, but also assured her that the dreaded journey down into the prairie had begun in reality.

This journey had only one pleasing prospect—and that was a hope, forlorn at best, of somewhere again seeing the tall, handsome stranger who had spoken so kindly to her and gazed at her with such thoughtful eyes.

Not that she hoped for anything beyond just seeing him! She would be grateful for that. Her stepfather would not permit any friendships, let alone acquaintances, with buffalo-hunters. Five weeks with this stepfather had taught her much, and she feared him. Last night his insulting speech before Tom Doan had created in Milly the nucleus of a revolt. She dared to imagine a time might come, in another year when she became of age, that would give her freedom.

The meeting with Tom Doan last night had occasioned, all in twelve hours, a change in Milly Fayre. His look had haunted her, and even in the kindly darkness it had power to bring the blood to her face. Then his words so full of fear and reproach—"I may never see you again!"—they had awakened Milly's heart. No matter what had inspired them! Yet she could harbor no doubt of this fine-spoken, clear-eyed young man. He was earnest. He meant that not to see her again would cause him regret. What would it mean to her—never to see him again? She could not tell. But seeing him once had lightened her burden.

So in Milly Fayre there was born a dream. Hard work on a farm had been her portion—hard work in addition to the long journey to and from school. She did not remember her father, who had been one of the missing in the war. It had been a tragedy, when she was sixteen, for her mother to marry Randall Jett, and then live only a few months. Milly had no relatives. Boys and men had tormented her with their advances, and their importunities, like the life she had been forced to lead, had not brought any brightness. Relief indeed had been hers during those months when her stepfather had been absent hunting buffalo. But in March he had returned with another wife, a woman hard featured and coarse and unreasonably jealous of Milly. He had sold the little Missouri farm and brought his wife and Milly south, inflamed by his prospects of gaining riches in the buffalo fields.

From the start Milly had dreaded that journey. But she could not resist. She was in Randall Jett's charge. Besides, she had nowhere to go; she knew nothing except the work that fell to the lot of a daughter of the farm. She had been apathetic, given to broodings and a growing tendency toward morbidness. All the days of that traveling southward had been alike, until there came the one on which her kindness to a horse had brought her face to face with Tom Doan. What was it that had made him different? Had the meeting been only last night?

The wagon rolled on down the uneven road, and the sudden lighting of the canvas indicated that the sun had risen. Milly heard the rattling of the harness on the horses. One of the wagons, that one driven by Jett, was close behind.

Movement and sound of travel became more bearable as Milly pondered over the difference one day had wrought. It was better that she was going on the road of the hide-hunters, for Tom Doan was one of them. Every thought augmented something vague and deep that baffled her. One moment she would dream of yesterday—that incident of casual meeting, suddenly to become one of strangely locked eyes—how all day she had watched Hudnall's camp for sight of the tall young man—how she had listened to Jett's gossip with his men about the other outfits—how thrilled she had been when she had met Tom Doan again. It had not been altogether fear of her stepfather that had made her run off from this outspoken, keen-eyed young man. She had been suddenly beset by unfamiliar emotions. The touch of his hands—his look—his speech! Milly felt again the uplift of her heart, the swell of breast, the tingling race of blood, the swift, vague, fearful thoughts.

The next moment Milly would try to drive away the sweet insidious musing, to ponder over her presence there in this rattling wagon, and what might be in store for her. There had been a break in the complexity of her situation. Something, a new spirit, seemed stirring in her. If she was glad of anything it was for the hours in which she could think. This canvas-topped wagon was her house of one room, and when she was inside, with the openings laced, she felt the solitude her soul needed. For one thing, Jett never objected to her seeking the privacy of her abode; and she now, with her new-born intuition, sensed that it was because he did not like to see the men watching her. Yet he watched her himself with his big hard blue eyes. Tom Doan's eyes had not been like that. She could think of them and imagine them, so kindly piercing and appealing.

This drifting from conjectures and broodings into a vague sort of enchanting reverie was a novel experience for Milly. She resisted a while, then yielded to it. Happiness abided therein. She must cultivate such easy means of forgetting the actual.

Milly's wagon lumbered on over the uneven road, and just when she imagined she could no longer stand the jolting and confinement, it halted.

She heard Jett's gruff voice, the scrape of the brakes on the wagon behind, and then the unsnapping of harness buckles and the clinking thud of heavy cooking-ware thrown to the ground. Milly opened the canvas slit at the back of her wagon, and taking up the bag that contained her mirror, brush and comb, soap, towel, and other necessities, she spread the flaps of the door and stepped down to the ground.

Halt had been made at the edge of a clump of trees in a dry arroyo. It was hot, and Milly decided she would put on her sunbonnet as soon as she had washed her face and combed her hair.

"Mawnin', girl," drawled a lazy voice. It came from the man, Catlee, who had driven her wagon. He was a swarthy fellow of perhaps forty years, rugged of build, garbed as a teamster, with a lined face that seemed a record of violent life. Yet Milly had not instinctively shrunk from him as from the others.

"Good morning, Mr. Catlee," she responded. "Can I get some water?"

"Shore, miss. I'll hev it for you in a jiffy," he volunteered, and stepping up on the hub of a front wheel he rummaged under the seat, to fetch forth a basin. This he held under a keg that was wired to the side of the wagon.

"Dry camp, Catlee," spoke up a gruff voice from behind. "Go easy on the water."

"All right, boss, easy it is," he replied, as he twisted a peg out of the keg. He winked at Milly and deliberately let the water pour out until the basin was full. This he set on a box in the shade of the wagon. "Thar you are, miss."

Milly thanked him and proceeded leisurely about her ablutions. She knew there was a sharp eye upon her every move and was ready for the gruff voice when it called out: "Rustle, you Milly. Help here, an' never mind your good looks!"

Milly minded them so little that she scarcely looked at herself in the mirror; and when Jett reminded her of them, which he was always doing, she wished that she was ugly. Presently, donning the sunbonnet, which served the double duty of shading her eyes from the hot glare and hiding her face, she turned to help at the campfire tasks.

Mrs. Jett, Milly's stepmother, was on her knees before a panful of flour and water, which she was mixing into biscuit dough. The sun did not bother her, apparently, for she was bareheaded. She was a handsome woman, still young, dark, full faced, with regular features and an expression of sullenness.

Jett strode around the place, from wagon to fire, his hands quick and strong to perform two things at once. His eyes, too, with their hard blue light, roved everywhere. They were eyes of suspicion. This man was looking for untoward reactions in the people around him.

Everybody worked speedily, not with the good will of a camp party that was wholesome and happy, bent on an enterprise hopeful, even if dangerous, but as if dominated by a driving spirit. Very soon the meal was ready, and the men extended pan and cup for their portion, which was served by Mrs. Jett.

"Eat, girl," called Jett, peremptorily.

Milly was hungry enough, albeit she had been slow and, receiving her food and drink, she sat down upon a sack of grain. While she ate she watched from under the wide rim of her sunbonnet.

Did she imagine a subtle change had come over these men, now that the journey toward the wild buffalo country had begun? Follonsbee had been with Jett before and evidently had the leader's confidence, as was evinced by the many whispered consultations Milly had observed. He was a tall, spare man, with evil face, red from liquor and exposure, and eyes that Milly had never looked into twice. Pruitt had lately joined the little caravan. Small of stature, though hardy, and with a sallow face remarkable in that its pointed chin was out of line with the bulging forehead, he presented an even more repulsive appearance than Follonsbee. He was a rebel and lost no opportunity to let that fact be known.

These men were buffalo-hunters, obsessed with the idea of large sums of money to be made from the sale of hides. From what little Milly had been able to learn, all the men except Catlee were to share equally in the proceeds of the hunt. Milly had several times heard argument to that effect—argument always discontinued when she came within hearing.

Milly had become curious about her stepfather and his men. This interest of hers dated back no farther than yesterday, when her meeting with Tom Doan, and a few words exchanged with the pleasant Mrs. Hudnall, and her eager watching of the Hudnall camp, had showed her plainly that Jett's was a different kind of outfit. No good humor, no kindliness, no gay words or pleasant laughs, no evidence of wholesome anticipation! Jett had never been a man she could care for, yet up to the last few weeks he had been endurable. The force of him had changed with the advent of these other men and the journey into unsettled country. In him Milly now began to sense something sinister.

They did not speak often. The business of eating and the hurry maintained by Jett were not altogether cause for this taciturnity. Catlee was the only one who occasionally made a casual remark, and then no one appeared to hear him.

"Rustle along, you-all," ordered Jett, gruffly, as he rose from the meal.

"Do you aim to camp at Wade's Crossin' to-night?" queried Follonsbee.

"No. We'll water an' get wood there, an' go on," returned Jett, briefly.

The other men made no comment, and presently they rose, to set about their tasks. The horses were hitched up while munching their grain out of the nose bags. Milly wiped the plates and utensils that Mrs. Jett hurriedly and silently washed.

"Mother, I—I wish we were not going on this hunt," ventured Milly, at last, for no other reason than that she could not stand the silence.

"I'm not your mother," replied the woman, tersely. "Call me Jane, if the name Mrs. Jett makes you jealous?"

"Jealous? Why should I be jealous of that name?" asked Milly, in slow surprise.

"You're no more related to Jett than I am," said Mrs. Jett, pondering darkly. She seemed a thick-minded person. "For my part, I don't like the hunt, either. I told Jett so, an' he said, 'Like it or lump it, you're goin'.' I reckon you'd better keep your mouth shut."

Milly did not need such admonition, so far as her stepfather was concerned. But from that moment she decided to keep both eyes and ears open. Jett's domineering way might be responsible for the discontent of his wife and the taciturnity of his men.

When all was in readiness to resume the journey Milly asked Jett if she could ride on the seat with the driver.

"Reckon not," answered Jett, as he clambered to his own seat.

"But my back gets tired. I can't lie down all the time," remonstrated Milly.

"Jane, you ride with Catlee an' let Milly come with me," said Jett.

"Like hob!" sneered his wife, with a sudden malignant flash of eyes that was a revelation to Milly. "Wouldn't you like that fine now, Rand Jett?"

"Shut up!" returned Jett, in mingled anger and discomfiture.

"You're mighty afraid some man will look at that girl," she went on, regardless of his gathering frown. "How's she ever goin' to get a husband?"

Jett glared at her and ground his teeth.

"Oh, I see," continued Mrs. Jett, without lowering her strident voice. "She *ain't* goin' to get a husband if *you* can help it. I've had that hunch before."

"Will you shut up?" shouted Jett, furiously.

Whereupon the woman lifted herself to the seat beside him. Jett started his team out toward the road. As Pruitt and Follonsbee had driven ahead in their wagon, Milly was left alone with Catlee, who seemed to be both amused and sympathetic.

"Climb up heah, miss," said he.

Milly hesitated, and then suddenly the new turn of her mind obstructed her old habit of obedience and she nimbly stepped to a seat beside the driver.

"Reckon it'll be warmer out heah in the sun, but there's a breeze an' you can see around," he said.

"It's much nicer."

Catlee plied his long lash, cracking it over the horses without touching them, and they moved off in easy trot. The road lay downhill, and ahead the gray prairie rolled in undulating vast stretches to the horizon.

"Are we going to Indian Territory?" Milly asked the driver.

"Miss, we're in the Territory now," he replied. "I don't know when, but in a few days we'll cross the line into the Panhandle of Texas."

"Is that where the buffalo are?"

"I ain't shore aboot that. I heard Jett say the big herd would be comin' north an' likely run into the hunters somewheres near Red River?"

"Will all the hunters go to the same place?"

"Shore they will, an' that'll be where the buffalo are."

Milly did not analyze the vague hope that mounted in her breast. She felt surprised to find she wanted to talk, to learn things.

"Is this strange country to you?" she asked.

"Shore is, miss. I never was west of the Missouri till this trip. Reckon it's goin' to be hard. I met some hunters last night. They was celebratin' their arrival in town, an' I couldn't take too great stock in their talk. But shore they said it was bad down heah where we're goin'. I'm afraid it ain't no place for a girl like you."

"I'm afraid so, too," said Milly.

"Jett ain't your real father?" queried Catlee.

"He's my stepfather," replied Milly, and then in a few words she told Catlee about herself, from the time her mother had married Jett.

"Well, well, that accounts," rejoined Catlee, in tones unmistakably kind. But he did not vouchsafe to explain what he meant. Indeed, her simple story seemed to have silenced him. Yet more than before she felt his sympathy. It struck her singularly that he had stopped talking because he might have committed himself to some word against her stepfather.

Thereafter Milly kept the conversation from personalities, and during the afternoon ride she talked at intervals and then watched the dim horizon receding always with its beckoning mystery.

Sunset time found Jett's caravan descending a long gradual slope ending in a timbered strip that marked the course of a stream. Catlee pointed out two camps to Milly. White wagons stood out against the woodland; fires were twinkling; smoke was rising. The place appeared pleasant and sheltered. Jett drove across the stream, unhitched the horses, and he and Follonsbee watered them and filled the kegs while Pruitt and Catlee gathered firewood, which was tied on behind the wagons.

One of the campers below the crossing came out in the open to halloo at Jett, more in friendly salutation than otherwise. Jett did not reply. He lost no time hooking up traces and harness and getting under way. He led on until nearly dark and halted at a low place where grass appeared abundant.

"Why didn't my stepfather camp back there with the other outfits?" queried Milly, as Catlee halted his team.

"Shore he's not sociable, an' he's bent on travelin' as far every day as possible," replied the driver.

While Milly was busily engaged helping Mrs. Jett round the camp fire, darkness settled. Coyotes were yelping. A night wind rose and, sweeping down into the shallow coulee, it sent the white sparks flying. The morose mood of the travelers persisted. After supper was over and the tasks were finished Milly climbed to the seat of her wagon and sat there. It was out of earshot of the camp fire. Jett's wagon had been drawn up close beside the one she occupied. Heretofore camp had always been pitched in a sheltered place, in a grove or under the lea of a wooded hill. This site was out on the open prairie. The wind swept around and under the wagon, and it needed only a little more force to make it moan. But few stars lightened the cloudy sky. Lonesome, dismal, and forbidding, this prairie land increased Milly's apprehensions. She tried not to think of the future. Always before she had been dully resigned to a gray prospect. But now a consciousness grew that she could not go on forever like this, even if her situation did not grow worse. Of that, she had no doubt. Someone had told her that when she was eighteen years old she would be free to look out for herself. Yet even so, what could she do? She worked as hard for the Jetts as she would have to work for anyone else. Perhaps eventually she might get a place with a nice family like the Hudnalls. Suddenly the thought of Tom Doan flashed into her mind, and then of marriage. Her face burned. She hid it, fearful that even under cover of night someone might see her and read her thoughts. No use to try to repudiate them! She yearned for the companionship of women who would be kind to her, for a home, and for love.

These thoughts became torture for Milly, but only so long as she strove against them. She had awakened. She could not be deprived of her feelings and hopes. Thus her habitual morbid brooding came to have a rival for the possession of her mind. When she went to bed that night she felt not only the insidious inception of a revolt, but also a realization that strength was coming from somewhere, as if with the magic of these new thoughts.

Days passed—days that dragged on with the interminable riding over the widening prairie—with the monotony of camp tasks, and the relief of oblivion in sleep.

Milly always saw the sun rise and set, and these were the only incidents of the day in which she found pleasure. She had exhausted Catlee's fund of stories and his limited knowledge of the frontier. He was the only one in the outfit that she could or would talk to. Follonsbee was manifestly a woman-hater. Pruitt had twice approached her, agreeably enough, yet offensive through his appearance; and she had cut his overtures short. Mrs. Jett's hawk eyes never failed to take note of any movement on her husband's part in Milly's direction, which notice finally had the effect of making Jett surlily aloof. Yet there was that in his look which made Milly shrink. As days and miles passed behind, Jett manifestly grew away from the character that had seemed to be his when Milly's mother married him. Here in this environment harshness and violence, and a subtle menace, appeared natural in him.

Not a day went by now that Jett did not overtake and pass an outfit of two or more wagons bound for the hunting fields. These he passed on the road or avoided at camping grounds. When, however, he met a freighter going out with buffalo hides, he always had spare time to halt and talk.

Jett pushed on. His teams were young and powerful, and he carried grain to feed them, thus keeping up their strength while pushing them to the limit. The gray rolling expanse of Indian Territory changed to the greener, more undulating and ridged vastness of the Panhandle of Texas. Where ten days before it had been unusual to cross one stream in a day's travel, now they crossed several. All of these, however, were but shallow creeks or washes. The trees along these stream bottoms were green and beautiful, lending contrast to the waving level of the plains.

Milly conceived the idea that under happy circumstances she would have found a new joy and freedom in riding down into this wilderness.

One afternoon, earlier than usual, Jett turned for good off the road, and following a tree-bordered stream for a couple of miles, pitched camp in a thick grove, where his wagons and tents could not readily be seen. Evidently this was not to be the usual one-night stand. If it were possible for Jett to be leisurely, he was so on this occasion. After helping unpack the wagons he gave orders to his men, and then saddling one of the horses he rode away under the trees.

It was dusk when he returned. Supper had been timed for his arrival. About him at this moment there was an expansion, an excitement, combined with bluff egotism. Milly anticipated what he announced in his big voice.

"Bunch of buffalo waterin' along here. We've run into the stragglers. It'll do to hang at this camp an' hunt while we wait to see if the big herd runs north."

The announcement did not create any particular interest in his comrades. No one shared Jett's strong suppressed feeling. After supper he superintended the loading of shells and sharpening of knives, and the overlooking of the heavy rifles.

"The old needle gun for me!" he exclaimed. "Most hunters favor the big fifty."

"Wal, the fifty's got it all over any other guns fer shootin' buffs at close range," responded Follonsbee.

"We might have to shoot some other critters at long range—redskins, for instance," commented the leader, sardonically.

Jett's superabundant vitality and force could not be repressed on this occasion. Apparently the end of the long journey had been cause for elation and anticipation, and also for an indulgence in drink. Milly had known before that Jett was addicted to the bottle. Under its influence, however, he appeared less harsh and hard. It tempered the iron quality in him. Likewise it roused his latent sentimental proclivities. Milly had more than once experienced some difficulty in avoiding them. She felt, however, that she need not worry any more on this score, while Mrs. Jett's jealous eyes commanded the scene. Still, Mrs. Jett could not be everlastingly at hand.

It turned out that Milly's fear was justified, for not long after this very idea presented itself, Jett took advantage of his wife being in the wagon, or somewhere not visible, to approach Milly as she sat in the door of the wagon.

"Milly, I'm goin' to be rich," he said in low hoarse tone.

"Yes? That'll be—good," she replied, bending back a little from his heated face.

"Say, let's get rid of the old woman," he whispered. His eyes gleamed in the flickering firelight, with what seemed devilish humor.

"Who—what?" stammered Milly.

"You know. The wife."

"Mrs. Jett! Get rid of her. . . . I—I don't understand."

"Wal, you're thicker 'n usual," he continued, with a laugh. "Think it over."

"Good night," faltered Milly, and hurriedly slipped into her wagon and tried with trembling fingers to lace up the flaps of the door. Her head whirled. Was Jett merely drunk? Pondering over this incident, she was trying to convince herself that Jett meant no more than ill humor toward his wife, when she heard him speak a name that made her heart leap.

"Hudnall, yes, I told you," he said, distinctly. "His outfit is somewhere in this neck of the woods. I saw his wheel tracks an' horse tracks."

"Wal, how do you know they're Hudnall's outfit?" queried Follonsbee.

"Huh! It's my business to know tracks," replied Jett, significantly. "There's two outfits camped below us. I saw horses an' smoke."

"Rand, if I was runnin' this outfit I wouldn't hunt buffalo anywhere's near Hudnall."

"An' why not?" demanded Jett.

"Say, you needn't jump down my throat. I jest have an idee. Hudnall's pardner, Pilchuck, is a plainsman, an'—"

"Huh! I don't care what the hell Pilchuck is," retorted Jett, gruffly ending the discussion.

CHAPTER SIX

Jett had chosen this secluded camp site, as he had all the others on the way down into the buffalo country, to render his whereabouts less liable to discovery. Anyone hunting for camps along the river would have found him, but the outfits traveling casually by would not have been aware of his proximity.

Next morning he had everybody up at dawn, and never had his dominating force been so manifest.

"Catlee, your job is horses," he said, curtly. "Keep them on this side of the river. The road's on the other side. You'll find the best grass along this strip of timber. Some time to-day I'll ride in an' help you hitch up to haul hides."

To his wife he gave a more significant order.

"Jane, I don't want any fire burnin' except when I'm in camp with the men. You an' Milly keep your eyes open, an' if you see Indians or anybody, slip off in the brush an' hide."

With that he rode off, accompanied by Follonsbee and Pruitt. Manifestly the hunt was on.

Milly, despite apprehension at the possibility of Indians, was glad to see the buffalo-hunters ride away. From what she had heard, this hide-hunting was an exceedingly strenuous business, consuming all of the daylight hours and half of the night. She had accepted her stepmother's sulky aloofness, finding relief also in that. The work given her to do she performed speedily and thoroughly. Then with a book and her sewing she slipped away from camp into the dense growth of underbrush.

By taking time she threaded a way without undue difficulties, and finally came out upon a beautiful grass-covered and flower-dotted bank above the stream. The place delighted her. The camp was within call, yet might have been miles away; the brush leaned over the fragrant shady nook, and above spread the giant elms; the stream widened here at a turn and formed a pool, the only one she had seen on the ride. A wide strip of sand ran along the opposite slope. On that side the wood appeared open, and led gently up to the plain. Milly could see the bright sky line barred by black trunks of trees. The road ran along the edge of the timber, and if any travelers passed she could see them. What would she do if she recognized the Hudnall outfit? The very thought made her tremble. Perhaps such hope dominated her watching there. For the rest, she could have hours alone, to think and dream, or to sew and read, and all the time she could see everything opposite her without being seen herself.

It did not take long for her to discover that this place had much to distract her from meditation or work. Suddenly it awoke in her a feeling that she did not know she possessed. Solitude she had always yearned for, but beauty and nature, the sweetness of sylvan scene and melody of birds, as now revealed to her, had not heretofore been part of her experience. They seemed strangely harmonious with the vague and growing emotion in her heart.

Milly did not read or sew. Wild canaries and song-sparrows and swamp blackbirds were singing all around her. A low melodious hum of many bees came from the flowering brush above. Somewhere under the bank water was softly rippling. A kingfisher flew swiftly downstream, glinting in the sunlight. At the bend of the stream, on a jutting sandbar, stood a heron, motionless and absorbed, gazing down into the water. The warm fragrant air seemed to float drowsily toward her.

The peace and music of this scene were abruptly dispelled by crashing, thudding sounds from the slope opposite. Milly gazed across. Shaggy dark forms were passing from the open plain down into the woods.

"Oh!—buffalo!" cried Milly, at once delighted and frightened. Her heart beat high. Gathering up her book and sewing, she was about to answer to the instinct to run when it occurred to her that she was on a steep bank high above the stream, out of danger. She decided to stand her ground. Sinking low behind a fringe of grass and flowers, she peeped over it, with bated breath and wide eyes.

Everywhere along the sky line of the wooded slope she saw the dark forms, not in a thick troop, but straggling in twos and threes. Lower down the foremost buffalo appeared, scattering dead leaves and raising the dust. A hundred yards below Milly the first buffalo came out of the woods upon the sand and crossed it to drink. Then gradually the line of bobbing brown humps emerged from the trees and grew closer and closer to Milly until she began to fear they would come right opposite to her. What wild, shaggy, ox-like beasts! If she had been fearful at first, she now grew frightened. Yet the wonder and majesty of these buffalo were not lost upon her. On they crashed out of the woods! She heard the splashing of the water. Like cattle at a long trough they lined up to the stream and bent huge woolly black heads.

"If any come close—I'm going to run!" whispered Milly to herself.

It did not appear, however, that she would have to resort to flight. The line of buffalo halted some fifty yards below her position. Thus she managed to avert utter panic, and as the moments passed her fears began to subside. A number of buffalo broke ranks and turned again to the woods, leaving open spaces where tawny little buffalo calves could be seen. Milly experienced a feeling of utmost pleasure. All her life on the farm she had loved the little calves. These were larger, very wild looking, fuzzy and woolly, light in color, and did not appear, like the calves she had seen, weak and wabbly in their legs. These young animals were strong and nimble. Some left their mothers' sides and frisked along the sand a little way, in an unmistakable playfulness, yet unlike any play Milly had ever seen. They lifted themselves off their front feet and gave their heads a turning, butting movement, quite agile, and nothing if not aggressive. Then they fled back to their mothers. Only a few of these calves drank from the stream, and they did not appear thirsty, as did the matured buffalo. Gradually the ranks thinned, and then the last of the grown buffalo turned to the slope. The calves, though loath to leave that enchanting spot, did not tarry long behind. The herd leisurely trooped up the slope and disappeared.

To Milly it did not seem possible that she had actually seen buffalo close at hand. The reality was strikingly different from the impression she had gathered. Huge beasts, yet not ugly or mean! They seemed as tame as cattle. Certainly if unmolested they would never harm anyone. Suddenly the bang of heavy guns rang from far over the slope.

"Oh, Jett and his hunters!" she exclaimed, in quick comprehension. "They are killing the buffalo!"

Not until that moment had the actual killing of buffalo—the meaning of it—crossed Milly's mind. Bang—bang—bang came the shots. They made her shrink. Those splendid beasts were being killed for their hides. Somehow it seemed base. What would become of the little calves? There dawned in Milly's mind an aversion for this hide-hunting. If the meat was to be used, even given to the hungry people of the world, then the slaughter might be condoned. But just to sell the hides!

"Tom Doan is a hide-hunter, too," she soliloquized. "Oh, I'm sorry! . . . he looked so nice and kind. I guess I—I don't care much about him."

What a man's vocation happened to be was really a serious matter to a woman. Milly recalled that one of the troubles between her mother and Jett had been his hatred of farm labor. Manifestly this hunting buffalo was to his liking, and perhaps he did not call it work.

Thus the incident of the buffalo coming down to drink had upset Milly's short period of revel in the sylvan place. Even when the muddy water cleared out of the stream, and the dust clouds disappeared from the woods, and the melody of birds and bees was renewed Milly did not recover the happy trend of feeling. Realization of the fact that Tom Doan was a hide-hunter had spoiled everything. Milly tried to read, and failing that she took up her sewing, which occupation had the virtue of being both necessity and pastime. For an hour or more the bang-bang of guns upon the plain above disturbed her. These reports appeared to get farther and farther away, until she could not hear them any more.

Some time after this, when she was returning to the dreamy mood, she heard a crashing of brush opposite and below her. Listening and peering in this direction, where the wood was thicker, she waited expectantly for buffalo to appear. The sound came at regular intervals. It made Milly nervous to become aware that these crashings were approaching a point directly opposite her. A growth of willows bordered the bank here, preventing her from seeing what might be there.

Then she heard heavy puffs—the breaths of a large beast. They sounded almost like the mingled panting and coughing of an animal strangling, or unable to breathe right.

Another crash very close sent cold chills over Milly. But she had more courage than on the first occasion. She saw the willows shake, and then spread wide to emit an enormous black head and hump of a buffalo. Milly seemed to freeze there where she crouched. This buffalo looked wild and terrible. He was heaving. A bloody froth was dripping from his extended tongue. His great head rolled from side to side. As he moved again, with a forward lurch, Milly saw that he was crippled. The left front leg hung broken, and flopped as he plunged to the water. On his left shoulder there was a bloody splotch.

Milly could not remove her eyes from the poor brute. She saw him and all about him with a distinctness she could never forget. She heard the husky gurgle of water as he drank thirstily. Below him the slow current of the stream was tinged red. For what appeared a long time he drank. Then he raised his great head. The surroundings held no menace for him. He seemed dazed and lost. Milly saw the rolling eyes as he lurched and turned. He was dying. In horror Milly watched him stagger into the willows and slowly crash out of sight. After that she listened until she could no longer hear the crackling of brush and twigs.

Then Milly relaxed and sank back into her former seat. Her horror passed with a strong shuddering sensation, leaving in her a sickening aversion to this murderous buffalo hunting.

The sun mounted high and the heat of the May day quieted the birds. The bees, however, kept up their drowsy hum. No more buffalo disturbed Milly's spasmodic periods of sewing and reading and the long spells of dreaming. Hours passed. Milly heard no horses or men, and not until the afternoon waned towards its close did she start back to camp. To retrace her steps was not an easy matter, but at last she wound her way through the brush to the open space. Camp was deserted, so far as any one stirring about was concerned. Milly missed one of the wagons.

Some time later, while she was busy making her own cramped quarters more livable, she heard the voices of men, the thud of hoofs, and the creak of wheels. With these sounds the familiar oppression returned to her breast. Jett would soon be there, surly and hungry. Milly swiftly concluded her task and hurried down out of her wagon.

Presently the men came trooping into camp on foot, begrimed with dust and sweat and manifestly weary. Catlee was carrying a heavy burden of four guns.

Jett looked into his tent.

"Come out, you lazy jade," he called, roughly, evidently to his wife. "A buffalo wolf has nothin' on me for hunger." Then he espied Milly, who was in the act of lighting a fire. "Good! You'd make a wife, Milly."

"Haw! Haw!" laughed Follonsbee, sardonically, as he threw down hat, gloves, vest, and spread his grimy hands. "No water! Gimme a bucket. If I had a wife there'd be water in camp."

"Huh! You hawk-faced Yankee—there ain't no woman on earth who'd fetch water for you," taunted Pruitt.

"Wal, if Hank thinks he can teach Jane to fetch an' carry he's welcome to her," responded Jett.

This bluff and hearty badinage, full of contention as it was, marked a change in the demeanor of Jett and his men. Catlee, however, took no part in it. He was connected with Jett's outfit, but did not belong there.

Mrs. Jett then appeared among them, and her advent, probably because of Jett's remark, occasioned ill-suppressed mirth.

"I heard what you said, Rand Jett," she retorted, glaring at him. "You can't make me welcome to any man, much less a hide thief like Hank Follonsbee."

"Shut your face," returned Jett, in an entirely different tone. "You know your job. Rustle to it."

That ended the approach to humor. When Follonsbee fetched the water they all washed and splashed with great gusto. This pleasant task finished, they showed plainly what little leisure was now possible to them, for they got their kits and began reloading shells and sharpening knives.

"Catlee, you clean the guns," ordered Jett.

While thus busily engaged they talked of the day's hunt—of the half hour of shooting that was fun and the eight hours of skinning that was labor—of the hide-stretching still to do before sleep could be thought of. Milly listened with keen ears in the hope they might drop some word of the Hudnall outfit, but she spent her attention in vain.

Presently Mrs. Jett called, "Come to supper."

"Or you'll throw it out, huh?" queried Jett, rising with alacrity.

They ate hurriedly and prodigiously, in silence, and each man reached for what he wanted without asking. Jett was the first to finish.

"Fill up, you hawgs," he said to his comrades; "we've work to do.—Jane, you an' Milly clean up—then go to bed. We'll be just outside the grove, stretchin' hides."

Milly lay awake a long while that night, yet did not hear the men return. Next day they had breakfast before sunrise and were off with a rush. Milly spent quiet hours on the shady bank, where the sweetness and music were undisturbed. Another day passed in which she saw nothing of the men except at the morning and evening meal hours. Jett and his helpers were settling into the strenuous routine of hide-hunting.

On the fourth day they broke camp and traveled twenty miles down the same side of the river, to halt in the only clump of trees Milly had noted for hours. Next morning Jett's men were again hunting buffalo. That night they did not return until long after dark. Milly had gone to bed, but she heard their gruff, weary voices.

The following day was again one of breaking camp and traveling south. Milly observed that the country changed, while yet it seemed the same; and she concluded that it was the vastness and wildness which grew. Next morning she heard shooting up until noon. She was so grateful to be left alone that the hours seemed to fly. There was always a place where she could hide near camp, and Jett seldom forgot to mention this. As they journeyed farther south his vigilance as well as his excitement increased day by day. From the camp-fire talk Milly gathered that both the number of buffalo and of hunters were augmenting. Yet Jett appeared to have established the rule of traveling one day and hunting the next. As he progressed the work grew more arduous. There was no road over this endless plain, and the level stretches were cut up, sometimes necessitating the unloading and reloading of the wagons. May warmed to June. The plain was now one wide rolling expanse of green, waving gently to every breeze; the stream courses were marked by a line of deeper green, trees now in full foliage. Herds of buffalo began to show to the east of this stream Jett was following. His hunting, however, he did on the west side, where Milly understood the buffalo ranged in larger numbers.

At length Jett traveled two days southward and then crossed the stream to its west bank. Following it down on that side, he was halted by a large river.

"Ha, boys, here's the Red, an' it's our stampin' ground this summer," he rolled out, sonorously.

For a camp he chose a spot hard to reach, as well as hard to espy from above. A forest of timber and brush bordered both sides of this Red River, and once down in it neither river nor plain could be seen. Jett spent the remainder of that day making permanent camp. Follonsbee, whom he had sent on a reconnoitering ride up the river, returned about sunset.

"Believe I saw fifty square miles of buffalo," he announced, impressively, sitting in his saddle and gazing down at the leader.

"Huh! I took that for granted," replied Jett. "How far did you go?"

"Reckon about five miles up an' climbed a big bluff above the river. Could see for miles. An' shore that sight stumped me. Why, Rand, I couldn't see the end of buffalo, an' I was usin' the telescope, too!"

"That's more to the point—how many outfits could you spot?" demanded Jett, impatiently.

"Wal, I spotted enough, an' some to spare," drawled the other. "West of the bluff I seen camp smokes all along the river, as far as I could see."

"Any camps close?"

"Only two between ours an' the bluff," replied Follonsbee. "Then there's one on the point across the creek. Reckon outfits are strung down the river, too. Buffalo everywhere."

"Ahuh! It's the main herd. Now, I wonder will they run north."

"Reckon so. But if they do they'll turn back."

"You figger on their bein' blocked by the gang of hide-hunters behind us?"

"Prezactly. We couldn't be in a better stand. This big herd is massed in a triangle. River on the south; Staked Plain on the west, an' on the third side thousands of hunters."

"Yes. It's seems that way. Mighty big bit of country, but it *is* a trap."

"Where do the Indians come in your calculatin'?" queried Follonsbee.

"Nowhere. If they get mean the buffalo-hunters will band together an' do what the soldiers couldn't do—chase the damned redskins up in their Staked Plain an' kill them."

"Wal, it looks like a hell of a summer, huh?"

"I reckon so, all around. It means the end of the buffalo, an' that means peace with the Indians, whether they fight or not."

"Rand, this is the huntin' ground of Comanches, Cheyennes, Kiowas, an' Arapahoes. The land an' the buffalo are theirs."

"Theirs—hell!" exploded Jett in contempt.

"Shore I know your sentiments," returned Follonsbee, rather shortly. "Like most of these hide-hunters, you say wipe the redskins off the earth. To me it looks like a dirty trick. I'd rather steal from a white man than an Indian. . . . But I'm givin' you my idee for what it's worth. We'll have to fight."

Jett appeared for the moment in a brown study, while he paced up and down, swinging a short rope he had in his hand.

"If the Indians are on the war-path, as we hear, won't they wait till this bunch of hunters has a big store of hides on hand—before startin' that fight?" he queried, shrewdly.

"I reckon they would," admitted Follonsbee.

"An' when they do come raidin', we're goin' to get the hunch in plenty of time, aren't we?" went on Jett.

"We shore have a fine stand. With hunters east an' west of us, an' millions of buffalo out there, we can't hardly be surprised."

"Wal, then, what's eatin' you?" growled Jett.

"Nothin'. I was just gettin' things clear. We're agreed on the main points. Now one more. The sooner we make a big stake, the better?"

Jett nodded a significant acquiescence to that query, and then went about his tasks. Follonsbee, dismounting, took the saddle off his horse. Soon after that Mrs. Jett called them to supper.

At this camp Milly lost her wagon as an abode, a circumstance, on the moment, much to her displeasure. The wagon, being high off the ground, and with its box sides, had afforded more of protection, if not comfort. Jett had removed hoops and canvas bodily and had established them as a tent, a little distance from the main camp. Milly pondered apprehensively over this removal by some rods from the rest of the tents. Perhaps Mrs. Jett had inspired this innovation, and if so, Milly felt that she would welcome it. But she had doubts of every move made by the leader of the outfit.

Upon entering the improvised tent Milly found that she could not stand erect, but in all other particulars it was an improvement. She could lace both doors tightly, something impossible when the tent was on the wagon. She unrolled her bed and made it up. Then she unpacked and unfolded her clothes and hung them conveniently at the back. Her bag, with its jumbled assortment of things she had thought so poor, now, in the light of this wild travel, assumed proportions little short of precious. She could have been worse off—something which before had never crossed her mind. Without soap, linen and muslin, a sewing kit, mirror, a few books, and many other like articles, she would have found this camp life in the wilderness something formidable to face.

When she went outside again daylight was still strong and the afterglow of sunset was spreading in beautiful effulgence over the western sky. Milly gazed about her. It appeared that a jungle lay between camp and the river. Jett and his men were in earnest and whispered council, with guns and tools and ammunition for the moment forgotten. Mrs. Jett sat a forlorn and sullen figure in front of her tent. Milly needed and wanted exercise. She began to walk around the camp. No one paid any heed to her. Indeed, since reaching the buffalo fields, she had become a negligible attraction, for which she was devoutly thankful.

Summer had indeed come to this northern part of Texas. The air was drowsy and warm. She found a few belated flowers blossoming in a shaded place. A spring bubbled from under a bank, and as she passed it frogs plumped into the water. She heard the mournful cooing of turtledoves.

Milly found a trail that evidently made short cut of the distance up to the plain, and she followed it, not without misgivings. Jett, however, did not call her, and emboldened by this she ventured on. The slope was gradual and covered by heavy timber. Her heart began to beat and her breath to come and go quickly. She felt her stagnant blood enliven to the call made upon it. She saw a flare of gold and rose sky beyond the black tree trunks. It was not so very far from camp—this first level of the plain. She wanted to see the great herd of buffalo. Thus engrossed, she went on to the edge of the timber, and halted there to gaze outward. A wonderful green plain stretched away to the west, rising gradually. It was barren of animals. The rich colors of the afterglow were fading. Was that a level purple-gray bank of cloud along the horizon or a range of upland hills?

A clip-clop of trotting horse made her start sharply. Wheeling, she espied a rider close upon her. He had come from round a corner of the wooded slope.

Milly took backward steps, meaning to slip out of sight. But the rider had seen her. Coming on so quickly, while she was slow in moving, he rode right upon her, and uttering an exclamation of surprise, he leaped from the horse.

Sight of him down on the ground where Milly could see him better gave her a galvanizing shock. Was this tall young man the image of her dreams? She stared. He took a step forward, his ruddy face lighting. He seemed strange somehow, yet she knew him. His eyes pierced her, and she suddenly shook with a sure recognition of them.

"Milly!" he cried, incredulously. His tone held the same wonderful thing that was in his look.

"Oh—it is you!" burst out Milly, all at once beside herself. She ran straight to meet him.

"Milly! Say—what luck!—I'd given up ever seeing you again," he said, trying to hold her hands.

"Tom—Doan!" she ejaculated in realization. She felt the hot blood flame in her face. Shamed and frightened, yet tingling with a joy nothing could check, she backed falteringly away. His glad eyes held her gaze, though she strove to avert it. Had he changed? His face was thinner, darker, a red bronze where it had been clear tan.

"Sure it's Tom Doan," he replied in delight. "So you remembered me?"

"Remembered—you?" faltered Milly. "I—I—"

A loud halloo from the wooded slope below interrupted her. It was Jett's voice, calling her back to camp.

"That's Jett," she whispered, hurriedly. "He must not see you."

"Go back. You've time. He's far off," replied Doan.

"Oh yes—I must go."

"Listen—just a second," he whispered, following her, taking her hand. He seemed intense. "Hudnall's camp is only a few miles up the river. I'm with him, you know. Meet me here to-night when the moon comes up. That'll be early."

"Here—at night?" murmured Milly, tremulously. The idea was startling.

"Yes. At moonrise. Promise!" he entreated.

"I'll come."

"Don't be afraid. I'll be waiting for you—right here. . . . Go back to camp now. Don't give yourself away."

Then he shot her a bright, intent look and strode noiselessly away, leading his horse into the grass.

Milly wheeled to run down into the woods, almost coming to disaster in her excitement. It was farther to camp than she thought and some parts of the trail necessitated care in the gathering twilight. Jett did not appear to be coming after her. In a few moments she recovered from her breathless headlong precipitation. The flicker of a camp fire shone through the woods, and that would have guided her had she lost the plain trail. Thoughts and emotions relative to the meeting with Tom Doan were held in abeyance. She must hurry back to camp and allay Jett's suspicions or fears concerning her. Dusk had fallen when she reached camp, which she approached leisurely. She saw Jett and all his outfit grouped round the camp fire.

"Where've you been?" he asked, gruffly.

"Walking under the trees," she replied, easily.

"Why didn't you answer me?"

"Do I have to yell because you do?" she returned.

"Haw! Haw! Haw!" roared Follonsbee, and he gave Pruitt a dig in the ribs.

"Wal," continued Jett, evidently satisfied, "when it gets dark that's your bedtime. Jane can set up all night if she likes."

"Because I've no need of sleep, eh?" demanded the woman, sarcastically.

"Why, you're a handsome jade," responded Jett.

Milly found in the situation a development of her own resourcefulness. She did not want this hour after supper to appear different from any other; so she stood a moment back of the circle of light, watching the camp fire, and then going to where the water pail stood she took a drink. Leisurely then she moved away to her tent. How fortunate now that it stood apart from the others!

Milly crawled inside to flop down on her bed. For a moment the self-restraint under which she had been taut lingered by reason of its very intensity. Then suddenly it broke. In the darkness of her tent she was safe. Thought of Jett and his outfit flashed into oblivion.

"Oh—what has happened? What have I done? What am I going to do?" she whispered to herself.

It all rushed back, strong and sweet and bewildering. She had to fight feeling in order to think. Some incredibly good instinct had prompted her to stray away from camp. Tom Doan! She had met him. In all that wide vast wilderness the one and only person she had met was the one she yearned for. She had spoken to him; she had promised to meet him later when the moon rose.

Tremendous as was the import of these facts, it did not seem all. What had happened? With mounting pulse she forced herself to recall everything, from the moment she had heard the horse. How she strung out the sensations of that meeting! Had she felt them all then? No—some of them, the deeper ones, were an augmenting of those which had been thoughtless. Could she ever gather into one comprehensive actuality the wildness of amaze, joy, and hope that had constituted her recognition of Tom Doan? What had gone on in her mind all these endless days? Futile to try to understand why! She had almost run straight into his arms.

"Oh, I—I had no time to think!" she whispered, with her burning face buried in the blankets.

Night and darkness and silence and loneliness could not help Milly now. She was in the throes of bursting love. Unawares it had stolen insidiously into all her waking and perhaps sleeping hours—and then, in an unguarded moment, when chance threw Tom Doan again into her presence, it had brazenly surprised her into betrayal. She knew now. And she lay there suffering, thrilling, miserable, and rapturous by turns. It was a trying hour. But it passed and there followed another mood, one wanting only proof, assurance of her wild dream, to border on exquisite happiness. She forgot herself and thought of Tom.

She saw him as clearly as if she had been gazing at him in the light of the sun. Older, thinner, graver, harder his face came back to her. There were lines he had not had, and a short fuzzy beard, as fair as his hair. There had been about him the same breath of the open plain and the buffalo and gunpowder and sweating brown that characterized Jett and his men. This could account for the hardness, perhaps for every change in him.

Only his eyes and the tone of his voice had seemed the same. And in recalling them there flooded over her a consciousness of the joy he had expressed at meeting her again. He had been as happy as she. It was impossible to doubt that. Without thought of himself or of what he was doing he had answered as naturally to the meeting as she had. Friendlessness, loneliness always had engendered a terrible need for love; and this raw life in the buffalo-fields, in the company of hard men and a woman who hated her, had but added a yearning for protection. Milly could understand; she could excuse herself. Yet that did not help much. It was all so sudden.

Absorbed in her new-born emotions, Milly had no cognizance of the passing of the hours. But when the gloom inside of her tent lightened and the canvas showed shadows of leaves moving and waving, she realized that the moon had risen. Trembling all over, she listened. The camp was silent. When had the men gone to bed? Only the murmur of insects and soft rustle of wind kept the silence from being dead. She peeped out. Low down through the trees a silvery radiance told of a rising moon. As Milly watched, with a growing palpitation in her breast, a white disk appeared and almost imperceptibly moved upward, until half the great beautiful moon sailed into her sight, crossed by black branches of trees.

"It's time to go," she whispered, and felt a cold thrill. She realized her danger, yet had no fear. If discovered in the act of meeting a lover she would surely be severely beaten, perhaps killed. But nothing could have kept Milly from keeping that tryst.

Cautiously she crawled out on hands and knees, and then away from the tent, keeping in the shadow. A log on the camp fire flickered brightly. She saw the pale gleam of the tents and her keen ear caught heavy breathing of one of the tired sleepers. At length she rose to her feet and, moving away silently, she lost sight of all round the camp except the fire. Then she circled in the direction of the trail that led up the slope.

Her nervous dread of being caught passed away, leaving only excitement. She did not know where to look for the trail, except that it started somewhere at the base of the slope behind the camp. She would find it. How big and black the elms! Shadows lay thick. Only here and there showed the blanched patches of moonlight. A stealthy step, a rustling, halted her and gave a different tingle to her pulse. Some soft-footed animal stole away into the obscurity. Relieved, she moved slowly to and fro, peering in the grass at her feet, searching for the trail. She remembered that it had led down to the spring and not to Jett's camp. As the spring lay east she worked that way. At last she stepped into the trail and then her heart throbbed faster. He would be waiting. What should she say?

As she climbed with swift steps the shadows under the trees grew less dense. Then she faced a long aisle where her own shadow preceded her. Beyond that she passed into thicker timber where it was dark, and she had to go slowly to hold to the trail. An incautious step resulted in the sharp cracking of a twig. It startled her. How lonely and wild the woods!

Milly reached level ground, and there not far was the end of the trees, now standing out clear and black against a wide moonlit plain. She glided faster, drawn in spite of herself, hurrying to meet him. Vague were her conjectures: sweet were her fears. She ran the last few yards.

As she entered the zone of moonlight and stood expectantly, peering everywhere, she felt the terrible importance of that moment. He was her only friend. Where was he? Had she come too early? If he had not . . . Then a tall dark form glided out into the moonlight.

"Milly!" came the low, eager voice. He hurried to her, drew her back into the shadow.

Milly's strained eagerness and the intensity of purpose that had brought her there suddenly succumbed to weakness. His presence, his voice, his touch changed her incomprehensibly. In desperation she tried to cling to her resolve not to be like she had been at that first meeting there.

"I thought you'd never come," he said.

"Am I—late?" she whispered.

"It's no matter, now you're here," he replied, and took her into his arms.

"Oh—you mustn't," she entreated, pushing back from him.

"Why, what's wrong?" he queried, in sudden concern.

In a silence fraught with exquisite torture for Milly she stood there, quivering against him. He put a hand under her chin and forced her head up, so that he could see her face.

"Girl, look at me," he ordered, and it was certain that he shook her a little. "Don't you know what I mean?"

Milly felt that she must drop then. Almost the last of her strength and courage had vanished. Yet she was impelled to look up at him, and even in the shadow of the trees she saw the fire in his eyes.

"How could I know—when you've never told—me?" she whispered, haltingly.

"I love you—that's what," he flung at her. "Do you have to be told in words?"

How imperative that was he could never have understood. It quite robbed her of will. She swayed to him with her head on his breast.

"Milly, did I take you in the wrong way?" he asked, bending over her.

"How—did you take—me?"

"That you must care for me." Fear and anxiety vied with a happy masterfulness in his voice.

"Do *you* have to be told in words?"

"No," he answered, low, and bent to her lips. "But tell me both ways."

Milly might have yielded to his importunity had his ardor left her any force. But she could only lean against him and cling to him with weak hands, in happiness that was pain. For a while then he held her in silence.

"What's your name?" he asked, suddenly.

"Mildred Fayre," she found voice to reply.

"How old are you?"

"Seventeen—nearly eighteen."

"Did you ever love any other man before me?"

"Oh no!"

"Ah, then you do?" he queried, bending to kiss her cheek.

"Don't you know that I do?"

"Will you be my wife?" he flashed.

"Yes," she whispered.

"When?"

"The very day I am of age—if you want me so soon."

"Want you!—I've wanted you so badly I've been sick, miserable. It was not so terrible at first. It grew on me. But I loved you from the moment I said I might never see you again. Do you remember?"

"Yes, Tom Doan, I remember as well as you."

"Oh, you do? Well, when did you love me. I'm curious. It's too good to be true. Tell me when."

"Since the instant I looked over that horse to see you standing there."

"Milly!" He was incredulous, and as if to make sure of his good fortune he fell to caressing her.

Later then, sitting against one of the trees, with his arm round her waist, Milly told him the story of her life. She did not dwell long on the poverty and hard work of her childhood, nor the vanishing hopes and ideals of her school days, nor the last sordid months that had been so hard to endure.

"You poor girl! Well, we must have been made for each other," he replied, and briefly told his own story. Life had been hard work for him, too, full of loss, and lightened by little happiness. Evidently it hurt him to confess that his father had been a guerilla under Quantrill.

"I always was a farmer," he concluded. "I dreamed of a fine ranch, all my own. And I'm going to have it. Milly, I'm making big money in this buffalo-hide business. I'll be rich. I'll have you, too!"

Milly shared his rapture and did not have the heart to speak of her disapproval of his killing buffalo, nor of her fear of Jett. She embraced joy for the first time.

The night hours wore on and the moon soared high in the heavens, full, silvery white, flooding the plain with light. Out there coyotes were yelping their sharp wild notes. From the river bottom came the deep bay of a wolf. An owl hooted dismally. All of this wildness and beauty seemed part of Milly's changed and uplifted life.

"Come, you must go back to your camp," said Doan at length.

"Oh—must I? I may never see you again!" she whispered.

"Plague me with my own words, will you?" he retorted, and his kisses silenced her. "Will you meet me here to-morrow night, soon as your folks are asleep?"

"Yes."

"Come then. It grows late. Lead the way down, for I'm going as far as I dare with you."

Within sight of the pale gleam of the tents he bade her good-by and silently stole back into the shadow of the slope. Milly as stealthily reached her tent and slipped into it, full of heart and wide awake, to lie in her bed, realizing that in gratefulness for the changed world and the happiness she would now never relinquish, she must go back to the prayers of her childhood.

CHAPTER SEVEN

At dawn the singing of wild canaries awakened Milly Fayre. There must have been a flock of them that had alighted on the elm tree which sheltered her tent. She listened, finding in the sweet treble notes an augury for her future. How good to awaken to such music and thought.

A loud hoarse yawn from the direction of camp proclaimed the rising of one of the men. Soon after that a sharp ring of Jett's ax drove away the canaries. Rays of rosy light penetrated the slit of Milly's tent, final proof that another day had come. Milly felt a boundless swell of life within her. Never before had any day dawned like this one! She lingered in her bed long after the crackling of the camp fire and the metallic clinking of Dutch oven and skillet attested to the task of breakfast.

"Hey, Milly, you're gettin' worse than the old lady!" called out Jett, in voice for once without gruffness. "Are you dead?"

"I'm very much alive," replied Milly, almost in glee at the double meaning of her words.

"Pile out, then," added Jett.

Milly did not hurry so much as usual; a subtle courage had stirred in her; she felt inspired to outwit Jett. Yet she meant to pretend submission to his rule. Her hope was strong that the arduous toil of hunting and skinning buffalo would continue to leave Jett little time in camp, and none to molest her with evil intentions. He was too obsessed to make money to spare time for drinking.

"Wal, the bombardin' has begun," Follonsbee was heard to say.

"Some early birds that's new to buffalo huntin'," replied Jett. "My experience is you get only so much shootin' in a day. I reckon, though, with the stragglin' bunches of this big herd rompin' to an' fro, we'll hear shootin' all day long."

The men were gone when Milly presented herself at the camp fire. She ate so little that Mrs. Jett noted the absence of her usual appetite.

"Are you sick?" she asked, with something of solicitude.

"No. I just don't feel hungry," replied Milly.

"You've got a high color. Looks like a fever," said the woman, her bright bold eyes studying Milly's face. "Better let me mix you a dose of paregoric."

"Thanks, no. I'm all right," returned Milly. But despite her calm assurance she was intensely annoyed to feel an added heat in her flushed cheeks. It might not be so easy to fool this woman. Milly divined, however, that it was not beyond the bounds of possibility for Mrs. Jett to be sympathetic regarding Tom Doan. Still, Milly dare not trust such impulsive premonition. She performed her accustomed tasks more expeditiously and even better than usual, then repaired to her tent.

After that the interminable hours faced her. How many till moonrise! They seemed everlasting and insupportable. She could neither read nor sew; all she could do was to sit with idle hands, thinking. At length, however, she discovered that this very thinking, such as it had come to be, was happiness itself. She had only the short morning and evening tasks now, and all the hours to wait here in this permanent camp for the stolen meetings with Tom Doan. Hours that would become days and weeks, even months, all to wait for him! She embraced the fact. Loneliness was no longer fearful. She had a wonderful secret.

The morning was still and warm, not so hot as on other days, by reason of a cloudily hazed sky. The birds had gone away, and there was not a sound close at hand. But from the plain above and from across the stream that flowed into the Red River, and from all around it seemed, when she concentrated her attention, there came the detonations of guns. None were close by, and most appeared very distant. They had no regularity, yet there were but few intervals of perfect silence. On the other hand, sometimes a traveling volley of reports would begin away in the distance and apparently come closer and then gradually withdraw to die away. A few shots together appeared a rare occurrence.

"At every shot perhaps some poor buffalo falls—dead—or dying like that great crippled bull I saw. Augh!" exclaimed Milly, in revulsion at the thought. "I'd hate to have Tom Doan grow rich from murdering buffalo. . . . But he said he did not kill many—that he was a skinner."

Then her ears seemed to fill with a low murmur or faint roar, like the rumble of distant thunder. At first she thought a storm was brewing out toward the Staked Plain, but the thunder was too steady and continuous. In surprise, she strained her hearing. Long low roar! What could it be? She had heard about the rumble of an earthquake and for a moment felt fear of the mysterious and unknown force under the earth. But this was a moving sound that came on the still summer air. It could be made only by buffalo.

"The thundering herd!" exclaimed Milly in awe. "That's what Jett called it."

She listened until the roar very slowly receded and diminished and rolled away into silence. Still the shooting continued, and this puzzled Milly because it was reasonable to suppose that if the hunters were pursuing the herd the sound of their guns would likewise die away.

Milly wandered round the camp, exploring places in the woods, and several times resisted a desire to go up the trail to the edge of the plain. Finally she yielded to it, halting under cover of the last trees, gazing out over the green expanse. It was barren as ever. The banging of guns appeared just as far away, just as difficult to locate. Milly wished she could climb high somewhere so that she might see over the surrounding country.

Near by stood a tree of a kind she did not know. It had branches low down and rose under one of the tall elms. Milly decided she would be much less likely to be seen up in a tree; besides, she could have her desire gratified. To this end she climbed the smaller tree, and from it into the elm, working to a high fork not easily attained. Then she gazed about her, and was so amazed and bewildered by the panorama that she had to exert her will to attend to any particular point of the compass.

Westward the green prairie rose in a grand fan-shaped slope of many leagues, ending in the horizon-wide upheaval of bold gray naked earth which the hunters called the Staked Plain. It was as level-topped as a table, wild, remote, austere, somehow menacing, like an unscalable wall.

In the middle of that vast stretch of green plain there were miles and miles of black patches, extending north and south as far as eye could see. Though they seemed motionless at that distance Milly recognized them as buffalo. Surely they could not be parts of the herd whence came the low, thundering roar.

Far to the left, along the shining green-bordered river, there appeared a belt of moving buffalo, moving to the southwest, and disappearing in what seemed a pall of dust. By turning her ear to that direction and holding her breath Milly again caught the low roar, now very faint. Much banging of guns came from that quarter. Out on the plain from this belt were small herds of buffalo, hundreds of them, dotting the green, and some were in motion.

Then Milly espied thin threads of black moving across the river. Buffalo swimming to the southern bank! These were several miles away, yet she saw them distinctly, and line after line they extended, like slender bridges, across the river until they, too, vanished in the curtain of dust. South of the river the boundless plain showed irregular ragged areas of black, and meandering threads, leading into the haze of distance. Eastward Milly gazed over a green river-bottom jungle, thick and impenetrable, to the level prairie blackened with buffalo. Here were straggling lines moving down toward the river. Altogether, then, the surrounding scene was one of immense openness, infinite waving green prairie crossed by widely separated streams, and made majestic by the domination of buffalo—everywhere buffalo, countless almost as the grasses of the prairie.

"What a pity they must die!" murmured Milly. For in the banging of the guns she heard the death knell of this multiplicity of beasts. She had seen the same in the hard, greedy, strong faces of Jett, and buffalo-hunters like him. Nature with its perfect balance and adjustment of the wild beasts was nothing to Jett. He would kill every buffalo on the plains for the most he could get, if it were only a bottle of rum.

Milly pondered over vague ideas in her developing mind. God might have made the buffalo to furnish the Indians and white men with meat and fur, but surely not through the sordidness of a few to perish from the earth.

Above Milly, in the blue sky, and westward till her sight failed, were huge black birds, buzzards, sailing high and low, soaring round and round, till the upper air seemed filled with them. Buzzards! Birds of prey they were—carrion-eaters, vultures that were enticed from their natural habits, from the need for which nature created them, to fall foul on this carnage left by the hunters.

Some of these uncanny birds of prey swooped down over Milly, and several alighted in a tree not far distant. Solemn, repulsive, they inspired in Milly a fear of the thing called nature. Were they necessary?

She did not long remain up there in her perch; and she discovered that descent was not so easy as climbing. Nevertheless she got by the worst of it without mishap, and then she breathed easier.

The thud of hoofs below caused her to stop abruptly. Horsemen were somewhere close at hand. Owing to the thick foliage she could not see what or where they were. Circling the trunk of the tree with her arm she leaned against it, making sure of her balance. She was still thirty feet from the ground, adequately hidden by bushy leaves, unless some one looked upward from directly beneath her. It was natural to suppose these riders were buffalo-hunters. Presently she espied them, indistinctly through the network of branches. They were riding from the north, evidently having come along the stream. To Milly's consternation they halted their horses almost directly under her. Then she made out that they were soldiers. She need have no fear of them, yet she did not like the idea of being discovered.

"Captain," spoke up one, "there's a good spring down this trail. I'd like a drink of fresh cold water.—Here, one of you men take some canteens down and fill them. The trail leads to the spring."

One of the half dozen soldiers dismounted, and collecting several canteens from his companions he lounged off out of sight.

"Ellsworth, you know this Red River country?" spoke up another soldier.

"Reckon I do, though not very well down this far," came the reply. "This is God's country compared to the Staked Plain. I know that well enough."

"Well, I figure we're on a wild-goose chase," said another, evidently an officer. He had dismounted to fling himself under one of the trees. He removed his sombrero to reveal a fine, strong, weather-beaten face, with mustache slightly gray. "We can never persuade these hide-hunters to go to the fort on account of Indian raids."

"Reckon not. But we can persuade them to send their women to a place of safety. Some of the fools have their women folk. For my part, I'd like to see these hunters band together against the Indians."

"Why?"

"Well, they're a hard lot and Lord only knows how many there are of them. They'll do what we soldiers never could do—whip that combination of redskin tribes."

"Better not say that in the colonel's hearing," said the officer, with a laugh.

"I wouldn't mind. Reckon I've hinted as much. I'm serving on scout duty, you know. But one thing's sure, these hide-hunters have started a bloody mess. And it's a good thing. This section of Texas is rich land. It's the stamping-ground of the Indians. They'll never give it up till the buffalo are gone. Then they'll make peace. As it is now they are red-headed as hell. They'll ambush and raid—then run back up into that devil's place, the Staked Plains."

"I'll bet you we get a taste of it before this summer ends."

"Like as not. If so, you'll remember the campaign," said the other, grimly.

Presently the soldier returned with the canteens, which manifestly were most welcome.

"There's a camp below, sir," said the soldier.

"Buffalo outfit, of course?"

"Yes. Three wagons."

"Did you ask whose outfit it is?"

"No one about camp, sir."

The officer got to his feet, and wiping his heated face, he stepped to his horse.

"Ellsworth, we've passed a good many camps of hide-hunters, all out in the open or along the edge of the timber. What do you make of an outfit camped way down out of sight. That's a hard pull for loaded wagons."

"Hunters have notions, same as other men," replied the scout. "Maybe this fellow wants as much protection as possible from storm and dust. Maybe he'd rather get out of the beaten track."

"Colonel's orders were to find trace of hide thieves," said the officer, thoughtfully. "That stumps me. They're hundreds of these outfits, all traveling, killing, skinning together. How on earth are we going to pick out thieves among them?"

"You can't, Captain," returned the scout, decidedly. "That'll be for the hunters themselves to find. As I said, they're a hard lot and jumbled one. Outlaws, ex-soldiers, adventurers, desperadoes, tenderfeet, plainsmen, and pioneers looking for new ground, and farmers out on a hunt to make money. I reckon most of them are honest men. This hide-hunting is something like the gold rush of '49 and '51, of course on a small scale. Last summer and fall there were hide thieves operating all through the Panhandle. A few of them got caught, too, and swung for it. This summer they'll have richer picking and easier. For with the Indian raids to use as cover for their tracks how can they be apprehended, unless caught in the act?"

"But, man, you mean these robbers waylay an outfit, kill them, steal the hides, burn the camp, and drive off to let the dirty work be blamed on Indians?"

"Reckon that's exactly what I do mean," replied Ellsworth. "It's my belief a good many black deeds laid to the Indians are done by white men."

"Did you tell the colonel that?"

"Yes, and he scouted the idea. He hates Indians. Got a bullet in him somewhere. I reckon he'd rather have bad white men on the plains than good Indians."

"Humph!" ejaculated the officer, and mounting his horse he led the soldiers west along the edge of the timber.

Milly waited a good while before she ventured to descend from her perch; and when she reached the ground she ran down into the woods, slowing to a walk when within sight of camp. She repaired to her tent, there to lie down and rest and think. She had something to ponder over. That conversation of the scout and officer had flashed grave conjectures into her mind. Could her stepfather be one of the hide thieves? She grew cold and frightened with the thought; ashamed of herself, too; but the suspicion would not readily down. Jett had some queer things against him, that might, to be sure, relate only to his unsociable disposition, and the fact, which he had mentioned, that he did not want men to see her. Milly recalled his excuse on this occasion, and in the light of the soldiers' conversation it did not ring quite true. Unless Jett had a personal jealous reason for not wanting men to see her! Once she had feared that. Of late it had seemed an exaggeration.

Fearful as was the thought, she preferred it to be that which made him avoid other camps and outfits, than that he be a hide thief and worse. But her woman's instinct had always prompted her to move away from Jett. She was beginning to understand it. She owed him obedience, because he was her stepfather and was providing her with a living. Nothing she owed, however, or tried to instil into her vacillating mind, quite did away with that insidious suspicion. There was something wrong about Jett. She settled that question for good. In the future she would listen and watch, and spy if chance offered, and use her wits to find out whether or not she was doing her stepfather an injustice.

The moon took an unconscionably long time to rise that night, Milly thought. But at last she saw the brightening over the river, and soon after, the round gold rim slide up into the tree foliage.

Her task of safely leaving camp this evening was rendered more hazardous by the fact that Jett and his men were near the camp, engaged in laborious work of stretching and pegging hides. They had built a large fire in a wide cleared space to the left of the camp. Milly could both see and hear them—the dark moving forms crossing to and fro before the blaze, and the deep voices. As she stole away under the trees she heard the high beat of her heart and felt the cold prickle of her skin; yet in the very peril of the moment—for Jett surely would do her harm if he caught her—there was an elation at her daring and her revolt against his rule.

Halfway up the trail she met her lover, who was slowly coming down. To his eager whispered "Milly" she responded with an eager "Tom," as she returned his kiss.

Tom led her to a grassy spot at the foot of a tree which was in shadow. They sat there for a while, hand in hand, as lovers who were happy and unafraid of the future, yet who were not so obsessed by their dreams that they forgot everything else.

"I can't stay long," said Tom, presently. "I've two hours pegging out to do to-night. Let's plan to meet here at this spot every third night, say a half hour after dark."

"All right," whispered Milly. "I always go to my tent at dark. Sometimes, though, it might be risky to slip out at a certain time. If I'm not here you wait at least an hour."

So they planned their meetings and tried to foresee and forestall all possible risks, and from that drifted to talk about the future. Despite Tom's practical thought for her and tenderness of the moment, Milly sensed a worry on his mind.

"Tom, what's troubling you?" she asked.

"Tell me, do you care anything for this stepfather of yours?" he queried, in quick reply.

"Jett? I hate him. . . . Perhaps I ought to be ashamed. He feeds me, clothes me, though I feel I earn that. Why do you ask?"

"Well, if you cared for him I'd keep my mouth shut," said Tom. "But as you hate him what I say can't hurt you. . . . Milly, Jett has a bad name among the buffalo outfits."

"I'm not surprised. Tell me."

"I've often heard hints made regarding the kind of outfits that keep to themselves. On the way south some freighter who had passed Jett ahead of us gave Pilchuck a hunch to steer clear of him. He gave no reason, and when I asked Pilchuck why we should steer clear of such an outfit he just laughed at me. Well, to-day Pilchuck found Jett skinning a buffalo that had been killed by a big-fifty bullet. Pilchuck knew it because he killed the buffalo and he remembered. Jett claimed he had shot the buffalo. Pilchuck told him that he was using a needle gun, and no needle bullet ever made a hole in a buffalo such as the big fifty. Jett didn't care what Pilchuck said and went on skinning. At that Pilchuck left, rather than fight for one hide. But he was mad clear through. He told Hudnall that hunters who had been in the Panhandle last summer gave Jett a bad name."

"For that sort of thing?" inquired Milly, as Tom paused.

"I suppose so. Pilchuck made no definite charges. But it was easy to see he thinks Jett is no good. These plainsmen are slow to accuse any one of things they can't prove. Pilchuck ended up by saying to Hudnall: 'Some hunter will mistake Jett for a buffalo one of these days!'"

"Some one will shoot him!" exclaimed Milly.

"That's what Pilchuck meant," rejoined Tom, seriously. "It worries me, Milly dear. I don't care a hang what happens to Jett. But you're in his charge. If he *is* a bad man he might do you harm."

"There's danger of that, Tom, I've got to confess," whispered Milly. "I'm afraid of Jett, but I was more so than I am now. He's so set on this hide-hunting that he never thinks of me."

"Some one will find out about you and me, or he'll catch us. Then what?" muttered Tom, gloomily.

"That would be terrible. We've got to keep any one from knowing."

"Couldn't you come to Hudnall's camp to live? I know he'd take you in. And his wife and daughter would be good to you."

Milly pondered this idea with grave concern. It appealed powerfully to her, yet seemed unwise at this time.

"Tom, I could come. I'd love to. But it surely would mean trouble. He could take me back, as I'm not of age. Then he'd beat me."

"Then I'd kill him!" returned Tom, with passion.

"He might kill you," whispered Milly. "Then where would *I* be? I'd die of a broken heart. No, let's wait a while. As long as he's so set on this hunting I have little to fear. Besides, the women out here with these buffalo-hunters are going to be sent to the fort."

"Where'd you hear that?" demanded Tom, in amaze.

Milly told him of the impulse that had resulted in her climbing the tree, and how the soldiers had halted beneath her, and the conversation that had taken place. She told it briefly, remembering especially the gist and substance of what the officer and scout had said.

"Well! That's news. I wonder how Hudnall will take it. I mustn't give way where I heard it, eh, little girl. It'd be a fine thing, Milly. I hope the soldiers take all you women to the fort quick. I wouldn't get to see you, but I could endure that, knowing you were safe."

"I'd like it, too, and, Tom, if I am taken I'll stay there until I'm eighteen."

"Your birthday is to be our wedding day," he said.

"Is it?" she whispered, shyly.

"Didn't you say so? Are you going back on it?"

His anxiety and reproach were sweet to her, yet she could not wholly surrender her new-found power or always give in to her tenderness.

"Did I say so? Tom, would you quit murdering these poor buffalo for me, if I begged you?"

"What!" he ejaculated, amazed.

"Would you give up this hide-hunting business for me?"

"Give it up? Why, of course I would!" he responded. "But you don't mean that you will ask it."

"Tom dear—I might."

"But, you child," he expostulated, "the buffalo are doomed. I may as well get rich as other men. I'm making big money. Milly, by winter time—next year surely, I can buy a ranch, build a house, stock a farm—for you!"

"It sounds silly of me, Tom. But you don't understand me. Let's not talk of it any more now."

"All right. Only tell me you'll never go back on me?"

"If you only knew how I need you—and love you—you'd not ask that."

Milly, upon her stealthy approach to camp, observed that the men had finished their tasks and were congregated about the fire, eating and drinking. The hour must have been late. Milly sank noiselessly down in her tracks and crouched there, frightened, and for the moment unable to fight off a sense of disaster. She could do nothing but remain there until they went to bed. What if Jett should walk out there! He and his comrades, however, did not manifest any activity.

"No—not yet. We'll wait till that Huggins outfit has more hides," declared Jett, in a low voice of finality.

"All right, boss," rejoined Follonsbee, "but my hunch is the sooner the better."

"Aw, to hell with buffalo hides," yawned Pruitt. "I'm aboot daid. Heah it's midnight an' you'll have us out at sunup. Jett, shore I'm sore, both body an' feelin'. If I knowed you was goin' to work us like this heah I'd never throwed in with you."

"But, man, the harder we work the more hides, an' the less danger—"

"Don't talk so loud," interrupted Follonsbee.

"It shore ain't me shoutin'," replied Pruitt, sullenly. "If I wanted to shout I'd do it. What's eatin' me is that I want to quit this outfit."

Jett shook a brawny fist in Pruitt's face, that showed red in the camp-fire light.

"You swore you'd stick, an' you took money in advance, now didn't you?" demanded Jett in a fierce whisper.

"I reckon I did. I'm square, an' don't you overlook that," retorted Pruitt. "It's you who's not square. You misrepresented things."

"Ahuh! Maybe I was a little overkeen in talkin'," admitted Jett. "But not about what money there is in this deal. I know. You'll get yours. Don't let me hear you talk quit any more or I'll know you're yellow."

For answer Pruitt violently threw a chip or stick into the fire, to send the sparks flying, and then rising, with one resentful red flash of face at Jett, he turned and swaggered away towards his tent, without a word.

"Bad business," said Follonsbee, shaking his head pessimistically. "You've no way with men, Rand. You'd get more out of them if you'd be easy an' patient, an' argue them into your opinions."

"Reckon so, but I can't stand much more from that damned rebel," growled Jett.

"He's harder to handle than Catlee," went on Follonsbee. "He's beginnin' to see a hell of a risk in your way of hide-huntin'. Catlee ain't wise yet. He's as much a tenderfoot as Huggins or a lot more of these jay-hawkers who're crazy to get rich off the buffalo. I was afraid of these two fellars, an' I said so."

"We had to have men. We'd lost a week waitin'," complained Jett.

"Yes, but it'd have been better to wait longer, till you got the right men."

"Too late now. I'll make the best of it an' try to hold my temper."

"Good. Let's turn in," replied Follonsbee, and rose to go toward the tents. Jett spread the fire and followed him. Soon the camp appeared dark and deserted.

Milly crouched there under the big elm until she was sure Jett had crawled into his bed, and then swiftly and noiselessly she covered the ground to her own tent. In the interest of this colloquy among the men she had forgotten her fright. That, in her opinion, had been strange talk for honest hunters. Yet she could only surmise. While she was revolving in her mind the eventful disclosures of the day sleep overtook her.

Days passed. They flew by, it seemed to Milly. The idle hours that fell to her lot were yet not many nor long enough for these ravenous hide-hunters. She watched in the daytime and listened at night, yet the certainty of what she feared did not come.

Her meetings with Tom Doan continued regularly as the third nights rolled round, without hitch or mishap; and in them Milly seemed to grow into the fullness of a woman's feeling. They talked of their love, of their marriage, and their plans for a home. There was little else to talk about except the buffalo, and the status of Jett and his men. Milly always suffered a pang when Tom, forgetting her love of all animals, raved about how many buffalo he had killed and skinned. Once she got blood on her hand from one of his boots, which she had inadvertently touched, and she was so sick and disgusted over it that she spoke sharply. Almost they quarreled. As for the truth concerning Jett, all Milly's observation and Tom's inquiry could not satisfy them as to what was the actual truth.

* * *

More days went fleeting by, ushering in hot July, more hide-hunters along the river brakes, and, what seemed incredible, more buffalo.

"They're massin' up an' makin' ready for a hell of a stampede one of these days," declared Jett, in his booming voice.

One night Milly was awakened by an unusual sound. Horses were snorting and stamping in camp. She peeped out. A wagon with two teams hitched to it stood just beyond the waning camp fire. Jett's burly form held the driver's seat; Follonsbee, rifle in hand, was in the act of climbing beside him; Pruitt stood on the ground, evidently intent on Jett's low, earnest voice. Milly could not distinguish what was being said. Jett drove away into the gloom of the woods. Where could he be going at this hour of the night? Milly could only conclude that he was driving out for another load of hides. Perhaps Jett had made trips before, unknown to her.

Next day disclosed the odd fact that Jett had not returned. Pruitt and Catlee evidently pursued the hunting as heretofore, and did not commit themselves to any words in Milly's presence. Sunset and supper time found Jett still absent. On the following morning, however, Milly learned that he had returned in the night and was asleep in his tent. She repaired to her own quarters and remained there till noon, when she saw him ride away. That afternoon Milly wandered around, as usual, with apparently no object in view, and eventually approached the glade where Jett kept his hides. She hated to go near it because of the unpleasant odor, the innumerable flies, and the sickening evidence of slaughtered buffalo.

The glade had been cleared farther on the side toward the stream, and everywhere were buffalo hides, hundreds and hundreds of them, some pegged out to dry, others in piles shaded by cut branches. Milly, because of her former reluctance to visit this place, had no record in her mind of quantity of hides, so she could not tell whether or not there had been a sudden and suspicious addition.

The day after that Jett loaded two wagons with hides, and with Catlee driving one of them they set off for a freighting station. They were gone five days, during which Milly had the most peaceful time since she had left the settlements. Twice she was with Tom, and they made the best of their opportunity. Mrs. Jett during this period was almost amiable. Follonsbee and Pruitt worked about as before.

When Jett returned, his presence, or something connected with it, seemed to spur his men to renewed efforts. Early and late they were toiling at this game. Tom Doan had told her that the great drive of buffalo was on. Milly, however, had not needed this information. She could see and hear.

No daylight hour was without its trampling thunder! Somewhere on one side of the river or other a part of the great herd was always in motion. Dust blew thick over the sky, sometimes obscuring the sun. And an unfavorable breeze, which fortunately occurred but seldom, brought a stench that Milly could not endure. By day the guns banged east, north, south, west, as if a battle were raging. Crippled buffalo limped by the camp, with red tongues hanging out, making for the brakes of the river, to hide and die. By night the howl of coyotes was sleep-preventing and the long-drawn deep, wild bay of wolves filled Milly with a haunting fear.

CHAPTER EIGHT

One day in July a band of soldiers rode into Hudnall's camp. The officer in charge got off his horse and appeared to be a lithe, erect man of forty, with a stern bronzed face.

"Who's the owner of this outfit?" he inquired.

Hudnall strode forward. "I am. Clark Hudnall's my name."

"Glad to meet you," replied the officer. "I'm Captain Singleton of the Fourth Cavalry, stationed at Fort Elliott. This is my scout, Ellsworth. We've been detailed to escort buffalo-hunters to the fort or one of the freighting posts. The Indians are raiding."

"But I don't want to go to the fort," protested Hudnall, obstinately.

"You'll stay here at your own risk," warned Singleton.

"We never expected anything else," returned Hudnall, bluntly. "If you want to know, you're the first soldiers we've seen."

"Have you women with you?" inquired the officer.

"Yes. My wife an' daughter an' my son's wife."

"Didn't you know any better than to fetch women out here in this Indian country?" went on Singleton, severely.

"We heard bad rumors, sir, but didn't believe them, an' I may say we've had no trouble so far."

"You've been lucky. Did you know Huggins?"

"Can't say I do—by name," rejoined Hudnall, reflectively.

"Huggins had the outfit several miles below here. One helper at least with him, maybe more. Their camp was raided, burned—hides stolen. No trace of Huggins or his helper."

"Indians?" queried Hudnall, sharply.

"Very likely. We've found no trace of Huggins or his man. They might have escaped to some other outfit or to a freighting post. But that's doubtful. West of here twenty miles or more a band of Comanches attacked some hunters, and were driven off. Unless you buffalo men camp together some of you are going to be killed."

"We'll fight," declared Hudnall, determinedly.

"But you must take your women to a place of safety," insisted the officer.

Hudnall called his wife and daughter. They came forward from their quarters, accompanied by Burn Hudnall's wife. Evidently they had heard something of the conversation; fear was manifest in their faces.

"Ladies, pray do not be frightened," said the officer, courteously. "There's no need for that right now. We're here to escort you to a place where you will be safe while your men folks are hunting. It is *not* safe for you here. Any day Indians might ride down on you when you are alone in camp.

Despite Singleton's courtesy and assurance, the women were alarmed, and gathering round Hudnall they began to talk excitedly.

"Captain, you an' your men make yourselves at home while we talk this over," said Hudnall.

Pilchuck and Tom Doan, just in from skinning buffalo, stood near during this conversation. Tom welcomed sight of soldiers, and he intended to inform Captain Singleton of the two women in Jett's camp.

"Say, Ellsworth," said Pilchuck to the soldier scout, "if this Huggins outfit was killed by Indians they'd not have disappeared. Comanches don't bother to bury or hide white men they've killed."

Ellsworth leaned close to Pilchuck. "Reckon it doesn't look like redskin work to me, either."

Pilchuck swore under his breath, and was evidently about to enter into earnest consultation with the soldier scout when Hudnall called him and Tom. They held a brief council. It was decided that Stronghurl and Pilchuck, with the addition of the outfit, Dunn and Tacks, would remain in camp, while Hudnall, Burn Hudnall, and Tom, accompanied by the women, would go with the soldiers. Hudnall did not consider it needful to send them all the way to Fort Elliott; the nearest freighting post, Sprague's, some three days' journey, would be safe and far enough. Hudnall intended to take advantage of this opportunity to freight out his buffalo hides, of which he had a large number.

"Reckon it may work out best, after all," he averred, brightening. "I'll run no risk losing the hides, an' then we'll soon be in need of supplies, 'specially cartridges."

How dense he seemed to the imperative side of the issue—safety for the women! But he was not a frontiersman. He was brave, though foolhardy.

"We'll pack an' leave early to-morrow," he informed Singleton.

"We'll catch up with you, perhaps before you get to the military road," said the officer.

"I don't know that road, an' with Pilchuck stayin' here I might lose my way," returned Hudnall in perplexity.

"The military road runs from Fort Elliott to Fort Dodge. You'll strike it about eighteen miles northwest."

"Reckon you can't miss it," added Pilchuck. "An' there's water aplenty."

Hudnall invited Captain Singleton and his soldiers to have supper, which invitation was accepted, much to Tom Doan's satisfaction. He wanted to think over what was best to say to Captain Singleton about the Jett outfit.

There was indeed bustle and rush around the Hudnall camp that afternoon, part of which work was the preparation of a hearty supper. It was cooked and eaten long before sunset. Afterward Tom found occasion to approach the officer.

"Captain, may I have a—a word with you—about something very important?" he inquired frankly, despite a certain embarrassment he could not help.

"Certainly, young man. What can I do for you?" he replied, with keen gray eyes on Tom.

As they withdrew a little, Tom lost his hesitation and briefly told who he was, what he was doing in Hudnall's outfit, and thus quickly reached the point.

"Captain, please let what I tell you be confidential," he went on, earnestly. "It's about a girl with the Jett outfit. She's Jett's stepdaughter. They're camped below the bluff at the mouth of White Creek, several miles down."

"Jett outfit," mused the officer. "I've heard that name. I know where his camp is—down in the woods. Hidden."

"Yes. Well, I—I'm in love with this girl, Milly Fayre—engaged to her. We expect to be married when she's eighteen. And I'm afraid for her—afraid of Jett more than the Indians. So is Milly. He'll not like this idea of sending his women to the fort or anywhere away from him. You see, he's got a wife, too, no relation to Milly—and he has them do the camp work. He's a hog for this hide-hunting. Then there are two hard nuts with him, Follonsbee and Pruitt. It's not an outfit like ours, Captain, or most any along the river. I can't honestly bring anything bad against Jett, unless it's that he's a brute and is after Milly. I know that. She won't admit it, but I can feel how she feels. She ought to be taken to the fort or wherever our women go—and please, Captain, don't fail to bring her. If you ask her you'll find out quick that she knows what's best for her."

"Suppose you ride down there with us," suggested Singleton.

"I'd like to, but I'd better not," replied Tom. "Jett knows nothing of me yet. Milly thinks it best he doesn't know until she's free. He might harm her. And if he ever lays a hand on her I'll kill him."

"What'd you say your name is?" inquired the officer.

"Tom Doan."

"All right, Tom, I'm for you and Milly. Here's my hand on it."

"Then you'll fetch her along?" queried Tom, trying to content himself, as he gripped the hand of this fine and soldierly man.

"If she's still there."

"I saw her last night—we've been meeting secretly. She's there."

"Then you will see her to-morrow again, for we'll catch you on the road," replied the officer, with a smile.

"We can never thank you enough," returned Tom, with emotion.

It was indeed with a thankful heart that he saw Singleton and his soldiers, leading their pack-horses, ride off down the river. After that Tom worked as never before, and not only got all his work done, but considerable of the others'. The Hudnall outfit went to bed late and got up early. By the time the July sun was blazing over the prairie the three heavily laden wagons were moving toward the northwest. Tom had the biggest load of hides in his wagon. The women rode on the drivers' seats with Hudnall and his son.

The route lay along the swell of the slope as it gently dipped to the river, then up on the level prairie and northwest toward the far escarpment of the Staked Plain, a sharp gray landmark on the horizon. Tom followed fairly good wagon tracks until they all appeared to converge in one well-trodden road. Here for hours good time was made. Tom did not mind the heat or the flies or the dust. Over and over again he had counted the earnings Hudnall owed him, and the sum staggered him. Hundreds of dollars! But splendid as that was, it shrank into insignificance at the good fortune of having Milly safely away from Jett and the Indians.

Hudnall made a noon stop at a shady crossing of a little stream. Here the horses were watered and fed and the travelers partook of a light meal. When the journey was resumed Tom could no longer resist the desire to look back along the road in the hope that he might see the soldiers coming. Really he did not expect them before camp that night, yet he was unable to keep from looking back.

All through this morning's travel they had skirted the ragged edge of the buffalo herd. Long, however, had they passed out of hearing of the guns of the hunters. Then early in the afternoon they ran into a large herd coming from the north. It was not a grazing herd, nor could it be called a stampeding herd; but the movement was steady and rapid. Hudnall drove way off the road to try to get round the leaders; this move, however, resulted in the three wagons being caught and hemmed in, with a stream of buffalo passing on both sides.

Tom believed it was a rather ticklish situation. The herd did not appear to be more than a mile wide, but the end toward the north was not in sight. The wagons were halted to wait until the herd had passed. The buffalo split round the wagons, probably fifty yards on each side, and they loped along lumberingly, not in any sense frightened. They raised dust enough to make the halt very uncomfortable, and noise enough to make it necessary to shout in order to be heard.

Tom's dissatisfaction had to do solely with the fact that Hudnall had gotten far enough off the road to miss the soldiers, if they came up presently. Hudnall, however, did not mind the halt, the discomfort, the loss of time, or the probable risk, should the buffalo become frightened.

To Tom's utter amaze, Hudnall presently took up his gun, and picking out bulls running somewhat away from the massed herd, he dropped four in as many shots. On that side the herd swerved away, the inside ranks pressing closer toward the middle, but they did not stampede. Then Burn Hudnall, not to be outdone by his father, dropped three buffalo on his side. The shooting served only to widen the oval that encompassed the wagons. Then the intrepid and indefatigable hunters proceeded to skin the slain beasts, regardless of the trampling mass passing so closely by.

Tom, contrary to his usual disposition, did not offer to help; and when Hudnall yelled something unintelligible he waved his hand at the herd.

It required two hours for this herd to pass the wagons, and another hour for the Hudnalls to complete skinning the seven they had shot. The women complained of the hot sun and the flies and the enforced wait. Tom spent a good deal of that last hour standing on top of the huge pile of hides in his wagon, scanning the horizon in the direction of the Red River camps.

"Hey, Tom, you might have helped along," said Hudnall, as he threw the wet hides up on his wagon.

"You might have been run down, yourself," retorted Tom.

"Father, I think Tom's scared of the Indians the soldier talked about," remarked Sally Hudnall, a little maliciously. She had never quite forgiven Tom for being impervious to her charms.

"Tom afraid? Nope, I can't savvy that," replied her father, in his hearty way.

"Well, he's looking back all the time," said Sally, with conviction.

Her tone, more than the content of her words, brought to Tom's mind a thought that when the soldiers did come along with Milly, there might result an embarrassing situation. What was he to say in explanation of his acquaintance with Milly? A moment's reflection convinced him that no explanation was necessary, nor need the Hudnalls know just yet of his engagement to her. Still, Milly had not been consulted; she would be overjoyed to see him and to meet the Hudnalls; and she was young, impulsive. How would she act? Tom told himself that he did not care the least what she said or did, but all the same an unusual situation for him seemed impending.

As Hudnall led off toward the road, Tom allowed Burn to fall into second place, leaving him to take up the rear, and from this position he could look back to his satisfaction.

Soon they were in the road again, and late in the afternoon turned into the military road Captain Singleton had indicated. Here the horses could travel, mostly at a trot. Tom had craned his neck sidewise so many times looking backward that he had put a crick in it, all to no avail. The soldiers did not put in an appearance. Tom began to worry. Suppose Jett had gotten wind of their coming and had moved camp! Might not the Comanches have raided Jett the same as Huggins! Tom had rather a bad hour along the military road.

At sunset the Hudnall wagons began to draw near a richly green depression of the prairie, where a stream wound its way. And when Hudnall, now far in the lead, turned off the road, Tom was suddenly compelled to pay some attention to the foreground.

Horses were grazing in the grass; tents shone white against the background of green trees; a camp fire sparkled, and round it stood men. Soldiers! Tom's heart gave a leap. Captain Singleton had forged ahead, probably during the delay caused by the buffalo herd.

Tom urged his team to a trot and soon caught up with Burn Hudnall, who turned off the main road towards the camp. Tom followed closely, to be annoyed by the fact that Burn's wagon obstructed his view. Once or twice Tom caught a glimpse of the tents and the fire; yet, peer keenly as he could, he did not discern any women. His heart sank. If Milly was there she would be out watching the wagons drive up. Tom passed from joy to sadness. Yet hope would not wholly die. He kept looking, and all the time, up to the very halt, Burn's wagon prevented him from seeing everything. Therein lay his one hope.

"Hey, Burn, don't you an' Tom drive smelly hides right in camp," yelled Hudnall.

Thus admonished, Tom wheeled his team away from the camp. Burn turned also, thus still obstructing Tom's vision. But there had to be an end to it some time. The next time Tom looked up, after he had halted the team, he was probably fifty yards from the camp fire.

He saw soldiers in dusty blue, Hudnall's stalwart form, all three of the Hudnall women, and then a girl in gray waving an excited hand at him. Tom stared. But the gray dress could not disguise the form it covered. Milly! He recognized her before he saw her face.

With surging emotions Tom leaped off the wagon and strode forward. In the acute moment, not knowing what to expect, trying to stifle his extraordinary agitation, Tom dropped his head until he came to the half circle of people before him. Their faces seemed a blur, yet intent, curious on him. Milly stepped into clear sight toward him. She was pale. Her eyes shone large and dark as night. A wonderful smile transfigured her. Tom felt the need of an effort almost beyond him—to greet Milly without betraying their secret.

But Milly was not going to keep any secrets. He felt that, saw it, and consternation routed his already weakened control.

"Oh, Tom!" she cried, radiantly, and ran straight into his arms.

Only this was terrible, because she forgot everybody except him, and he could not forget them. She almost kissed him before he had wit enough to kiss her first. With that kiss his locked boyish emotions merged into one great gladness. Realizing Milly, he stepped beside her and, placing his arm round her, moved to face that broadly smiling, amazed circle.

"Mrs. Hudnall, this is my—my girl, Milly Fayre," he said.

"Tom Doan! For the land's sake!" ejaculated the kindly woman. "Your girl! . . . Well, Milly Fayre, I'm right happy to make your acquaintance."

She warmly kissed Milly and then introduced her to Sally and Mrs. Burn Hudnall. That appeared to be sufficient introduction for all present.

Hudnall was the most astonished of men, and certainly delighted.

"Wal, Milly, I reckon Tom Doan's boss is sure glad to meet you," he said, and shook her hand with a quaint formality. "Would you mind tellin' me where this scallywag ever found such a pretty girl?"

"He found me—out here," replied Milly, shyly.

"Ah!" cried Sally Hudnall. "Now I know why Tom used to slip away from camp almost every night."

"An' leave off peggin' buffalo hides till the gray mornin'," swiftly added Hudnall. "I always wondered about that."

Amid the laughter and banter of these good people Tom stood his ground as long as possible; then, seeing that in their kindly way they had taken Milly to their hearts, he left her with them and hurried to unhitch the team he had driven.

Burn Hudnall followed him. "You buffalo-skinnin' son of a gun!" he exclaimed, in awe and admiration. "She's a hummer! By gosh! you're lucky! Did you see Sally's face? Say, Tom, she was half sweet on you. An' now we know why you've been so shy of women."

Upon returning to camp, Tom met Captain Singleton, who had a smile and a cordial handshake for him.

"Well, lad, I fetched her, but it was no easy job," he said. "She's a sweet and pretty girl. You're to be congratulated."

"Was Jett hard to manage?" queried Tom, intensely interested.

"Yes, at first, I had trouble with him. Rough sort of man! Finally he agreed to let her come to the freighting post until the Indian scare quieted down. He wouldn't let his wife come and she didn't want to. She struck me as being almost as able to take care of herself as any man."

"Well!" exclaimed Tom, blankly.

"Lad, don't worry," replied the officer, understanding Tom's sudden check of enthusiasm and warmth. "This Indian scare will last. It'll grow from scare to panic. Not until the buffalo are gone will the Indians quit the warpath. Maybe not till they're dead."

On the second day following, about noon, the Hudnall outfit, with their escort, arrived at Sprague's Post, which was situated on a beautiful creek some miles below Fort Elliott. Here the soldiers left the party and went on their way.

Sprague was one of the mushroom frontier posts that had sprung up overnight. It consisted mainly of a huge one-story structure built of logs, that served as sutler's store, as well as protection against possible Indian attacks. The short street was lined with cabins, tents, and shacks; and adjacent to the store were acres and acres of buffalo hides piled high. There were a dance hall, several saloons, a hotel and restaurant, all in the full blast. Buffalo outfits, coming and going, freighters doing the same, in considerable number, accounted for the activity of this post. The sutler's store, which was owned by Sprague, was a general supply center for the whole northern section of Texas.

Hudnall engaged quarters for the women folk, including Milly, that seemed luxurious after their camping experience. Sally Hudnall was to share her room, which had board floor and frame, roofed by canvas, with Milly; and the other Hudnall women had two rooms adjoining, one of which would serve as a kitchen. Hudnall had only to buy stove, utensils, supplies and fuel, to establish his wife and companions to their satisfaction.

Tom could hardly have hoped for any more, and felt that he would be always indebted to the Hudnalls. Fortune had indeed favored him by throwing his lot in with theirs.

Hudnall sold his hides to Sprague, getting three dollars each for the best robe cowhides, two dollars and a half for the bulls, and one dollar and seventy-five cents for the rest. His profits were large, as he frankly admitted, and he told Tom he thought it only fair to pay more for skinning. As for Tom, the roll of bills given to him for his earnings was such that it made him speechless. At the store he bought himself much-needed clothing and footgear, and a new rifle, with abundance of cartridges. Nor did he forget to leave some money with Mrs. Hudnall, for Milly's use, after he had gone. But he did not tell Milly of this.

"Tom," said Hudnall, seriously, when they had turned the horses loose in the fine grama grass outside of town, "I never saw the beat of this place right here for a ranch. Did you? Look at that soil!"

Tom certainly had not. It was rich prairie land, rolling away to the horizon, and crossed by several winding green-lined streams.

"Gee! I'd like to shove a plow into that," added Hudnall, picking up the turf. "Some day, Tom, all this will be in wheat or corn, or pasture for stock. Take my hunch, boy, we haven't seen its beat. We'll run up a cabin, at the end of this hunt, an' winter here. Then by another spring we can tell."

Tom found Sprague's Post the most interesting place that he had ever visited, and considerably much too wild, even in daytime. Dance hall and gambling hall, however, had only momentary attraction for him. Sprague's store was the magnet that drew him. Here he learned a great deal.

The buffalo south of the Brazos and Pease Rivers had at last turned north and would soon fall in with the great herd along the Red River. This meant that practically all the buffalo in the Southwest would concentrate between the Red River and the Staked Plain—an innumerable, tremendous mass. The Comanches were reported to be south of this herd, traveling toward the Red; and the Kiowas were up on the Staked Plain, chasing buffalo east; Cheyennes and Arapahoes, whose hunting ground had always been north of this latitude, were traveling south, owing to the fact that the annual migration of buffalo had failed this year. Failed because of the white hunters! An Indian war was inevitable.

Tom heard that Indian Territory was now being guarded by United States marshals; Kansas had passed laws forbidding the killing of buffalo; Colorado had done likewise. This summer would see all the buffalo hunters congregated in Texas. That meant the failure of the great herds to return north into Indian Territory, Kansas, and Colorado. The famous hunting grounds along the Platte and Republican Rivers would be barren. It seemed a melancholy thing, even to Tom, who had been so eager to earn his share of the profits. It was a serious matter for the state legislatures to pass laws such as this. No doubt Texas would do the same.

Tom reasoned out this conclusion before he learned that at this very time the Texas Legislature was meeting to consider a bill to protect buffalo in their state. So far it had been held up by remarks credited to Gen. Phil Sheridan, who was then stationed at San Antonio, in command of the military department of the Southwest. Sprague gave Tom a newspaper to read, and spoke forcibly.

"Sheridan went to Austin an' shore set up thet meetin'. Told the Senators an' Representatives they were a lot of sentimental old women. They'd make a blunder to protect the buffalo! He said the hunters ought to have money sent them, instead of discouragement. They ought to have medals with a dead buffalo on one side an' a dead Injun on the other."

Tom was strongly stirred by the remarks credited to General Sheridan, and he took the newspaper to the Hudnalls and read the passage:

> "These buffalo-hunters have done more in the last year to settle the Indian trouble than the entire regular army has done in thirty years. They are destroying the Indians' commissary. Send them powder and lead! . . . Let them kill, skin, and sell until the buffalo

are exterminated. Then the prairie can be covered with speckled cattle!"

"Great!" boomed Hudnall, slapping his big hand down. "But darn it—tough on the Indians!"

Tom was confronted then with a strange thought; he, like Hudnall, felt pity for the Indians, yet none for the buffalo. There was something wrong in that. Later, when he told Milly about what he had heard, and especially Hudnall's expression of sympathy, she said:

"Tom, it's because of the money. You men can't see right. Would you steal money from the Indians?"

"Why, certainly not!" declared Tom, with uplift of head.

"You are stealing their food," she went on, seriously. "Their meat—out of their mouths. Not because you're hungry, but to get rich. Oh, Tom, it's wrong!"

Tom felt troubled for the first time. He could not laugh this off and he did not have any argument prepared to defend his case.

"Tom Doan," she added, very sweetly and gravely, "I'll have something to say to you—about killing buffalo—when you come to me on my eighteenth birthday."

Tom could only kiss her for that speech, subtle, yet wonderful with its portent as to her surrender to him; but he knew then, and carried away with him next morning, the conviction that Milly would not marry him unless he promised to give up buffalo-hunting.

CHAPTER NINE

As Tom drove his team after the Hudnalls, southward along the well-beaten military road, he carried also with him a thought of his parting from Milly and something about her words or looks was like the one bitter drop in his sweet cup.

Early as had been the hour, Milly with the Hudnall women had arisen to prepare breakfast and see their men folk off. Hudnall and Burn were having their troubles breaking away from wives, daughter, and sister, so they had no time to note the poignancy of Milly's farewell to Tom.

At the last she had come close to Tom, fastening her trembling hands to his hunting coat. She looked up into his eyes, suddenly wonderful, strange.

"Tom, you are all I have in the world," she said.

"Well, dear, I'm all yours," he had replied, tenderly.

"You must not stay away long."

"I'll come back the very first chance," Tom had promised.

"You should not leave me—at all," she had whispered then, very low.

"Why Milly, you're safe here now," he expostulated.

"I'll never be safe until—until Jett has no right over me."

"But he will not come for you. Captain Singleton and Sprague say the Indian scare has just begun."

"Tom—I'll never be safe—until *you* take me."

"Dearest . . ." he had entreated, and then Hudnall boomed out, "Come on, break away, you young folks." And there had been only time for a last embrace.

Milly's last look haunted Tom. How big, black, tragic her eyes! How beautiful, too—and their expression was owing to love of him. His heart swelled until it pained. Was it right to leave her? He could have found work at Sprague's. A remorse began to stir in him. If he had only not been so poor—if he had not been compelled to hunt buffalo! He realized that he was returning to the buffalo fields no longer free, bearing the weight of a great responsibility,—a lonely girl's happiness, perhaps her life.

The summer morning was warm, colorful, fragrant with soft breeze off the prairie, full of melody of birds, and bright with the rising sun. But Tom did not respond as usual. The morning passed, and the hot afternoon was far spent before he could persuade and argue himself into something of his old mood. Common sense helped him. The chances of his returning to find Milly safe and well were very much greater than otherwise; yet he could not forget the last few moments they had been together, when under stress of fear and sorrow she had betrayed Jett's real status and her own fatalism. All that day Milly was in his thoughts, and afterward, when he lay in his bed, with the dark-blue, star-studded sky open to his sleepless gaze.

It took Hudnall only two days and a half, hauling light wagons, to return to the Red River camp. Conditions were identically the same as before the trip. Pilchuck and his three helpers had killed and skinned three hundred and twenty five buffalo during Hudnall's absence. The chief of the outfit was delighted; and late in the afternoon as it was, he wanted to go right at the slaughter.

"Take it easy," growled Pilchuck. "We want some fresh grub an' some news."

Manifestly, Pilchuck and his associates had not fared well since the departure of the women folk. "Dam the pesky redskins, anyhow," he complained to Hudnall. "Who's goin' to cook?"

"We'll take our turn," replied Hudnall, cheerfully.

"Lot of fine cooks we got in this outfit," he growled. "Wal, there's one consolation, anyway—reckon we won't have to eat much longer."

"An' why not?" demanded Hudnall, in surprise. "I fetched back a wagon load of grub."

"Wal, we're goin' to be scalped by Comanches directly."

"Bosh!" boomed Hudnall, half in anger. "You plainsmen make me sick. You're worse than the soldiers. All this rant about Indian raids! We've been out over two months an' haven't seen a single Indian, tame or wild."

The scout gazed steadfastly at Hudnall, and the narrow slits of his eyes emitted a gray-blue flash, cold as light on steel.

"It's men like you who can't savvy the West, an' won't listen, that get scalped by Indians," he said, with a ring in his voice.

Hudnall fumed a moment, but his good nature prevailed and he soon laughed away the effect of Pilchuck's hard speech. Dread he seemed to lack.

Next morning Tom followed the others of the Hudnall outfit out to the chase, which they returned to with redoubled energy and a fiercer determination. Concrete rewards in shape of gold and greenbacks paid to them by Hudnall were the spurs to renewed effort.

Tom started that day badly. Just as he came within range of the first buffalo and aimed at it he thought of Milly's reproachful dark eyes and he wavered so that he crippled the beast. It escaped into the herd. Tom was furious with himself for wounding a buffalo that could only limp away to die a lingering death. After that he put squeamishness out of his mind and settled down into the deadly and dangerous business of hide-hunting.

The day was one of ceaseless and strenuous labors, extending long after dark. Bed was a priceless boon; memory had little opportunity; sleep was something swift and irresistible.

Thus was ushered in the second phase of Tom Doan's buffalo-hunting.

The vast herd of buffalo, reported by Pilchuck to be several miles wide and more miles in length than any conservative scout would risk estimating, never got farther north than the vicinity of the Red River.

Gradually it was driven west along the river to the North Fork, which it crossed, and then, harassed by the hunters behind and flanked on the west by the barren rise of the Staked Plain, it turned south, grazing and traveling steadily, to make the wide and beautiful Pease River divide in ten days.

Here began a fearful carnage. Hudnall's outfit fell in with the thick of the buffalo-hunters, many of whom had been a year at the game. They were established in name and manifestly proud of that fact. "Raffert's, Bill Stark's, Nebraska Pete's, Black and Starwell, Bickerdyke's, Uncle Joe Horde, Old Man Spaun, Jack and Jim Blaise," and many other names became household words in the Hudnall camp.

Tom kept eyes and ears open for news of the Jett outfit, but so far had not been successful in learning its whereabouts. There were hundreds of gangs strung along the rivers for many miles, and by far not all of the buffalo were in the great massed herd.

On a tributary of the Pease it was decided by Pilchuck and Hudnall to make permanent camp until fall.

"I want four thousand hides by November," boomed Hudnall, rubbing his huge hands.

"Easy. I'll show you how to kill a hundred to-morrow in three hours," replied Pilchuck.

"When we'll freight back to Sprague's?" queried Tom, anxiously.

Thus each man voiced the thing most in his thoughts.

Next day Pilchuck outdid his boast in the estimated time, killing one hundred and eighteen buffalo—a remarkable feat. But he had a fast, perfectly trained horse; he was daring and skillful; he rode his quarry down and made one shot do the work.

Day by day Tom Doan killed fewer buffalo. He did not notice the fact until it was called to his attention. Then, going over his little book of record, which he kept faithfully, he was amazed and chagrined to discover that such was the case. He endeavored to right the falling off, only to grow worse. He wavered, he flinched, he shot poorly, thus crippling many buffalo. It made him sick. The cause was Milly. She dominated his thoughts. The truth was that Milly had awakened him to the cruelty and greed of this business and his conscience prevented him from being a good hunter.

Hudnall solved the knotty problem for Tom, very much to his relief.

"Tom, you've lost your nerve, as Pilchuck says," said the chief. "But you're the best skinner he ever saw. You're wastin' time chasin' an' shootin' buffalo. We're killin' about as many as we can skin, an' we could kill more. Pilchuck can, anyhow. Now you follow us an' skin buffalo only. We'll pay you thirty five cents a hide."

"You bet I take you up," declared Tom, gladly. "I didn't know I'd lost my nerve, but I hate the killing."

"Wal, it's begun to wear on me, to be honest," sighed Hudnall. "I'd rather push a plow."

Next moment he was asking Tom to make accurate estimate of the stock of ammunition on hand. Tom did his best at this calculation and reported: three hundred forty six pounds of St. Louis shot-toner lead in twenty-five pound bars; about five thousand primers; five cans of Dupont powder, twenty-five pounds to a can; and three cans of six pounds each.

"Jude, how long will that last us?" inquired Hudnall of Pilchuck, who had heard Tom's report.

"Wal, let's see. I reckon August, September, October—unless we have to fight Indians," replied the scout.

"Ho! Ho! There you go again," derided Hudnall. "This Injun talk is a joke."

With this skinning job Tom soon found himself in better spirits, and worked so effectively that he won golden praise from his employers.

"Shucks! What a scalper of redskins that boy would make!" declared Pilchuck. "He can keep a knife sharp as a razor an' cut with it like a nigger."

If Tom had been able to get some leisure he would have found much enjoyment in the permanent camp. It was situated on a beautifully wooded bench above the wild brakes of a tributary to the larger river near by, and game abounded there. Down in the brakes were bear, panther, wildcats in numbers too plentiful for wandering around without a gun. The wide belts of timber appeared to be full of wild turkey and deer. Antelope, tame as cattle, grazed on the prairie; and in the wake of the buffalo slunk hordes of howling coyotes. Bands of big gray wolves, bold and savage, took their toll of the buffalo calves.

The diet of buffalo steak was varied by venison and antelope meat, and once with wild turkey. This last trial of a changed menu resulted disastrously for Tom. It happened to be his turn as cook and he had killed several wild turkeys that day. Their flesh was exceedingly bitter, owing to a berry they lived on, which was abundant in the brakes. Pilchuck, who suffered with indigestion, made sarcastic remarks about Tom's cooking, and the other men were vociferous in their disapproval. Unfortunately Tom had not cooked any other meat.

"Tom, you're a valuable member, but your cookin' is worse than your shootin'," remarked Hudnall, finally. "We'll relieve you of your turn an' you can put that much time to somethin' else. . . . No offense, my lad. You just can't cook. An' we can't starve to death out here. Reckon when you come to ranchin' you'll be lucky to have that pretty black-eyed Milly!"

"Lucky!" exploded Burn Hudnall, who it was hinted suffered a little from being henpecked. "Say, he *is* an' he doesn't savvy it."

"Wal, we're all pretty lucky, if you let me get in a word," said the scout, dryly. "Here we've been days in hostile country, yet haven't been molested."

"There you go again!" protested Hudnall, who had become wearied of Indian talk.

"Wal, am I scout for this outfit or just plain plugger of buffs?" queried Pilchuck.

"You're scout, an' pardner, an' everythin', of course," replied Hudnall. "Your scoutin' for buffalo couldn't be beat, but your scoutin' for redskins, if you do any, hasn't worried me."

"Wal, Hudnall, I don't tell you everythin'," rejoined Pilchuck. "Yesterday, ten miles below on the river, I met a bunch of Kiowas, braves, squaws, kids, with ponies packed an' travois draggin'. They didn't look sociable. To-day I saw a band of Comanches tearin' across the prairie or I'm a born liar! I know how Comanches ride."

"Jude, are you tryin' to scare me into huntin' closer to camp?" asked Hudnall.

"I'm not tryin' or arguin'," responded the scout. "I'm just tellin' you. My advice to all of you is to confine your huntin' to a radius of five or six miles. Then there'd always be hunters in sight of each other."

"Jude, you an' Burn an' I killed one hundred ninety-eight buffalo yesterday on ground no bigger than a fifty acre farm. But it was far off from camp."

"I know. Most hunters like to kill near camp, naturally, for it saves work, but not when they can kill twice as many in the same time farther out."

"I'll kill mine an' skin them an' haul them in," replied the leader.

"Wal, wal," said Pilchuck, resignedly, "reckon advice is wasted on you."

Tom, in his new job, worked out an innovation much to Hudnall's liking. He followed the hunters with team and wagon, and through this hit by accident upon a method of skinning that greatly facilitated the work. Taking a forked stick, Tom fastened it to the middle of the hind axletree, allowing the other sharpened end to drag. Tying a rope to the same axle and the other end to the front leg of a dead buffalo, Tom would skin the upper side down. Next he would lead the horses forward a little, moving the beast. The stick served the purpose of holding the wagon from slipping back. Then he would skin down the center of the sides, and stop to have the team pull the carcass over. Thus by utilizing horse power he learned to remove a hide in half the time it had taken him formerly.

Often the hunters would kill a number far exceeding Tom's ability to haul to camp. But with their help all the hides were removed generally the same day the buffalo were slain. If Tom could not haul all back to camp, he spread them fur side up, to collect the next day. Tom particularly disliked to skin a buffalo that had been killed the day before; because the bloating that inevitably occurred always made the hide come off with exceeding difficulty. Like all expert skinners, Tom took pride in skinning without cutting holes in a hide.

Tom often likened the open ground back of camp on the prairie side to a colossal checkerboard, owing to the many hides always pegged out in regular squares. Five days from the pegging process these hides would be turned fur side up for a day, and turned again every day until dry. They had to be poisoned to keep the hide bugs from ruining them. As the hides dried they were laid one over the other, making as huge piles as could be handled. To tie these bundles strips of wet buffalo hide were run through the peg-holes of the bottom and top hides, and pulled very tight. All bull hides were made into one bundle, so marked; and the others sorted according to sex, age, and quality. Taken as a whole, this hunting of buffalo for their hides, according to the opinion of all hunters, was the hardest work in the world.

One morning a couple of drivers, belonging to Black and Starwell's outfit, halted their teams at Hudnall's camp, and spread a rumor that greatly interested the leader. They were freighting out thirteen hundred hides to Sprague's. The rumor had come a few days before, from hunters traveling south, to the effect that Rath and Wright of Dodge City was going to send freighters out to buy hides right at the camps. This would afford the hunters immense advantage and profit. The firm was going to pay regular prices and do the hauling.

These loquacious drivers had more news calculated to interest Hudnall. It was a report that the Kansas City firm, Loganstein & Co., one of the largest buyers of hides in the market, were sending their hides to Europe, mostly to England, where it had been discovered that army accouterments made of leather were much better and cheaper when made of buffalo hide. This would result in a rise in prices, soon expected, on the buffalo hides.

All this excited Hudnall. He paced the camp-fire space in thought. Ordinarily he arrived at decisions without vacillation, but this one evidently had him bothered. Presently it came out.

"I'll stay in camp an' work," he said, as if answering a query. "Tom, you an' Stronghurl shall haul all the hides we have to Sprague's. You can see our women folks an' bring back the straight of this news. Let's rustle, so you can go with Starwell's freighters."

The journey to Sprague's Post was an endless drive of eight long, hot glaring days; yet because each day, each hour, each minute, each dragging step of weary horses bore Tom closer to Milly, he endured them joyfully.

Making twenty-five miles the last day, Tom and his companions from the Pease River reached Sprague's late at night, and camped in the outskirts of the settlements, where showed tents and wagons of new outfits. Early next morning Tom and Stronghurl were besieged by prospective buffalo-hunters, intensely eager to hear news from the buffalo fields. Invariably the first query was, were the buffalo really herded by the millions along the Red, Pease, and Brazos Rivers? Secondly, were the Indians on the warpath? Tom answered these questions put to him in the affirmative; and did his best with the volley of other interrogations, many of them by tenderfoot hunters. He remembered when he had been just as ignorant and raw as they were now.

Thus, what with bringing in the horses, breakfast, and satisfying these ambitious newcomers, Tom was held back from rushing to see Milly. Stronghurl said he would see the Hudnalls later. At last, however, Tom got away, and he had only to hurry down the almost deserted street of the post to realize that the hour was still early. He was not conscious of anything save a wonderfully warm and blissful sense of Milly's nearness—that in a moment or so he would see her.

Tom's hand trembled as he knocked on the canvas door of the Hudnall quarters. He heard voices. The door opened, to disclose Mrs. Hudnall, wary-faced and expectant.

"For the land's sake!" she cried, her expression changing like magic. "Girls, it's Tom back from the huntin' fields."

"You bet, and sure glad," replied Tom, and could hardly refrain from kissing Mrs. Hudnall.

"Come right in," she said, overjoyed, dragging him into the kitchen. "Never mind Sally's looks. She just got up. . . . Tom, I know from your face all's well with my husband."

"Sure. He's fine—working hard and making money hand over fist. Sent you this letter. Stronghurl came, too. He'll see you later."

Sally Hudnall and Mrs. Burn Hudnall welcomed Tom in no less joyful manner; and the letters he delivered were received with acclamations of delight.

Tom looked with eager gaze at the door through which Sally had come, expecting to see Milly. But she did not appear.

"Where's Milly?" he asked, not anxiously, but just in happy eagerness.

His query shocked the Hudnall women into what seemed sudden recollection of something untoward. It stopped Tom's heart.

"Milly! Why, Tom—she's gone!" said Mrs. Hudnall.

"Gone!" he echoed, dazedly.

"Yesterday. Surely you met her on the road south?"

"Road south? . . . No, no," cried Tom, in distress. "Jett! Did he take her away?"

"Yes. He came night before last, but we didn't know until mornin'," continued Mrs. Hudnall, hurriedly. "Had his wife an' two men with him. Jett sold thirty-four hundred buffalo hides an' had been drinkin'. . . . He—well, he frightened *me,* an' poor Milly. I was never so sorry for any one in my life."

"Oh, I was afraid he'd come!" burst out Tom, in torture. "Milly said I shouldn't leave her. . . . Oh, why, why didn't I listen to her?"

"Strange you didn't meet Jett," replied Mrs. Hudnall. "He left with three wagons yesterday afternoon. They went straight down the military road. We watched them. Milly waved her scarf for a long time. . . . She looked so cute an' sweet in her boy's clothes."

"Boy's clothes?" ejaculated Tom, miserably. "What do you mean?"

"Jett came here in the mornin'," went on Mrs. Hudnall. "He was soberin' up an' sure looked mean. He asked for Milly an' told her that she was to get ready to leave with him in the afternoon. His wife wasn't with him, but we met her later in Sprague's store. She struck us as a fit pardner for Jett. Well, Milly was heart-broken at first, an' scared. We could see that. She didn't want to go, but said she'd have to. He could take her by force. She didn't say much. First she wrote you a letter, which I have for you, an' then she packed her clothes. When Jett came about three o'clock he fetched boy's pants, shirt, coat, an' hat for Milly. Said on account of Indians scarin' the soldiers the military department were orderin' women out of the buffalo fields. Jett was disguisin' his women in men's clothes. Milly had to have her beautiful hair cut. Sally cut it. Well, Milly dressed in that boy's suit an' went with Jett. She was brave. We all knew she might come to harm, outside of Indians. An' we felt worse when Sprague told us last night that this Mrs. Jett had been the wife of an outlaw named Hardin, killed last summer at Fort Dodge. That's all."

"Good heavens! it's enough!" declared Tom, harshly, divided by fear for Milly and fury at himself. "What can I do? . . . I might catch up with Jett. But then what?"

"That's what I'd do—hurry after her," advised Mrs. Hudnall. "Somehow you might get her away from Jett. Tell my husband. He'll do somethin'. . . . Tom, here's Milly's letter. I hope it tells you how she loves you. For you're all the world to that child. She was cryin' when she gave it to me."

"Thank you," said Tom, huskily, taking the letter and starting to go.

"Come back before you leave," added Mrs. Hudnall. "We'll want to send letters an' things with you."

"An' say, Tom," called Sally from the doorway, "you tell Dave Stronghurl if he doesn't run here to me pronto it'll be all day with him."

"I'll send him," returned Tom, and hurried back to camp, where he delivered Sally's message to Dave.

"Aw, I've all the time there is," drawled Dave, with an assured smile.

"No! We'll be leaving just as quick as I can sell these hides for Hudnall."

"Wal, I'll be goshed! What's the rush, Tom? . . . Say, you look sick."

"I am sick. I'm afraid I'm ruined," replied Tom, hurriedly, and told Dave his trouble.

His comrade swore roundly, and paced a moment, thoughtfully. "Tom, mebbe it ain't so bad as it looks. But it's bad enough. I'd hate to see that girl fall into the hands of the Indians."

"Indians? Dave, it's Jett I'm afraid of. He's bad and he means bad. . . . I—I think I'll have to kill him."

"Wal, quite right an' proper, if he's what you say. An' I'll back you. Let's see. We'd better rustle. You tend to sellin' the hides an' what else Hudnall wanted. An' I'll tend to Sally."

With that Stronghurl paid some elaborate though brief attention to his personal appearance, then strode off toward the post. Left alone, Tom hurriedly tore open Milly's letter. It was written in ink on good paper, and the handwriting was neat and clear. Tom thrilled at his first sight of Milly's writing.

SPRAGUE'S POST
July 19.

DEAR TOM:

It is my prayer you get this letter soon—surely some day. Jett has come for me. I must go. There isn't anything else I can do. But if you or Mr Hudnall were here I'd refuse to go and let Jett do his worst.

He'll surely take me back to the buffalo camps, and where they are you will be somewhere. I know you will find me.

I'm scared now and my heart's broken. But I'll get over that and do my best to fool Jett—to get away from him—to save myself. I've bought a little gun which I can hide, and if I have to use it to keep him from harming me—*I will do it.* I love you. You're all I have in this world. God surely will protect me.

So don't feel too badly and don't lose hope. Don't ever give up looking for me. Whenever you pass a camp you haven't seen before, look for a red scarf tied somewhere in sight. It'll be mine.

MILLY.

Tom sat there with clenched hands and surging heart. The letter at once uplifted him and plunged him into the depths. He writhed with remorse that he had ever left her alone. The succeeding moments were the most bitter of his life. Then another perusal of Milly's letter roused his courage. He must be true to the brave spirit that called to him; and he must hope for the best and never give up seeking her, though he realized how forlorn it was.

Tom sold Hudnall's hides at a higher figure than Hudnall had received for his first batch. Sprague not only corroborated the rumors that had been the cause of Hudnall sending Tom out, but also added something from his own judgment. The peak of prices for hides had not been reached. He offered so much himself that Tom wondered whether or not Hudnall would sell at all to the buyers from Dodge City. Tom gathered that there was now great rivalry among the several firms buying hides, a circumstance of profit to the hunters.

"I'll give you another hunch," said Sprague. "After the hides, the bones of the carcasses will fetch big money. I just heard that a twenty-mile pile of buffalo bones along the Santa Fe railroad sold for ten dollars a ton. For fertilizer!"

"You don't say!" exclaimed Tom, in surprise. "What'll Hudnall think of that? But, Sprague, it isn't possible to haul bones from the Red River country in quantity enough to pay."

"Reckon that seems far fetched, I'll admit. But you can never tell."

"Now about the Indian scare," went on Tom, anxiously. "What's your honest opinion? Is it serious?"

"Doan, listen," replied Sprague, impressively. "Believe what the scouts an' plainsmen say. They know. The whole half of Texas is bein' run over by a lot of farmers—hide-hunters for the time bein'. They don't know the West. An' some of them will be killed. That's the least we can expect."

"Then—these hide thieves. What do you know about them?" inquired Tom.

"Not much. That's not my business. I'm buyin' hides from anybody an' everybody. I can't afford to be suspicious of hunters."

"Did you know the little girl, Milly Fayre, who was staying with Mrs. Hudnall?"

"Shore did, an' I took to her pronto. Mrs. Hudnall told me aboot Jett bein' her stepfather, an' was packin' her off with him, togged out as a boy. I sold Jett the boy's clothes, but didn't know then what he wanted them for."

"She's engaged to marry me. She hates Jett and is afraid of him."

"So thet's the story!" ejaculated the sharp-featured Westerner, with quick gesture of comprehension. "Doan, I ain't sayin' much, but this deal looks bad."

"It looks terrible to me. Is Jett just a—a rough customer?"

"Doan, what he may be doesn't matter, I reckon," returned Sprague, in a low voice. "But take this hunch from me. Follow Jett an' get your girl out of his clutches—if you have to kill him. Savvy?"

Tom had seen the same dancing light gleam, sharp as fiery sparks, in the eyes of Pilchuck, that now shot from Sprague's.

"Yes—I savvy," replied Tom, swallowing hard.

An hour later he was driving his team at a brisk trot south on the military road, and Stronghurl was hard put to it to keep up with him.

CHAPTER TEN

Rising early and driving late, Tom Doan, with Stronghurl keeping in sight, traveled southward over the prairie toward the buffalo fields. He made it a point always to reach at night the camp of outfits that had been ahead of him. Thus every day was a dragging one of anxious hope to catch up with Jett, and every sunset was a time fraught with keen, throbbing excitement. Always, however, his search among the outfits ended in bitter disappointment.

A remarkable thing about this journey was that every outfit he passed on the way put on more speed and tried to keep him and Stronghurl in sight. Tom considered it just as well that they did so, for they were fast penetrating into the Indian country.

Early on the ninth morning of that long journey Tom and Stronghurl forded the Pease River, at a dangerous crossing, and entered the zone of slaughter. No live buffalo were in sight, but the carcasses left by the advancing hunters polluted the summer air and made of the prairie a hideous shambles. They passed thousands and thousands of bone piles and rotten carcasses; and as they advanced the bone piles became fewer and the solid carcasses more. Coyotes in droves, like wild dogs, fought along the road, regardless of the wagons. Indeed, many of them were so gorged that they could not run. And as for buzzards, they were as thick as crows in a Kansas cornfield in October, likewise gorged to repletion.

The wake of the hide-hunters was something to sicken the heart of the stoutest man and bring him face to face with an awful sacrifice.

Tom verified another thing that had long troubled him and of which he had heard hunters speak. For every single buffalo that was killed and skinned there was one which had been crippled and had escaped to die, so that if ever found its hide would be useless. In every ravine or coulee or wash off the main line of travel Tom knew, by investigation of those near where he and Stronghurl camped or halted at noon, there lay dead and unskinned buffalo. If he saw a hundred, how many thousands must there be? It was a staggering arraignment to confront the hide-hunters.

Toward noon of that day herds of live buffalo came in sight, and thereafter grew and widened and showed movement. Tom eventually overhauled a single wagon drawn by four horses, and drew up beside it, asking the usual query.

"Whoa, thar!" called the stout old driver to his team. "Jett? No, I ain't heard that name. Hev you, Sam?"

His companion likewise could not remember such a name as Jett.

"We've met up with lots of outfits an' never heerd nary name a'tall," added the former.

Then Tom asked if they had seen an outfit of three large wagons, three men, a woman, and a boy.

"Big outfit—wal, I reckon. Was the boss a yaller-bearded man?"

"Yes, that's Jett," replied Tom, eagerly.

"Passed us this mawnin' back a ways. I recollect sure, 'cause the boy looked at us an' waved a red kerchief. He had big black eyes."

"Milly!" breathed Tom, to himself. "Thank you, men. That's the outfit I'm after."

He drove on, urging the tired horses, and he was deaf to the queries his informants called after him upon their own account. Hope and resolve augmented in Tom as he traveled onward. Jett was hurrying back to the main camps, and he would not be hard to locate, if Tom did not catch up with him on the road. Milly's letter lay in the breast pocket of Tom's flannel shirt, and every now and then he would press his hand there, as if to answer Milly's appeal. He drove so persistently and rapidly that he drew far ahead of Stronghurl and the string of outfits which followed.

Miles farther, with straggling herds on each side, and then the boom-boom-boom of heavy guns! From the last ridge above the river he saw a pall of dust away to the west. Here there was action. But it must have been miles away. The river meandered across the prairie, a wide strip of dark green cottonwood and earth. In an hour Tom reached it. Not yet had he come in sight of a three-wagon outfit. With keen eyes he searched the dusty road to make sure that no wheel tracks swerved off without his notice.

Not long after this time he drew near the zones of camps, and presently passed the first one, new since he had come by that way about two weeks before. It was now August.

Tom's misery had diminished to a great extent, and he could contain himself with the assurance that Milly would be somewhere along this tributary of the Pease River.

Boom-boom-boom boomed the big fifties, not louder than at first, yet more numerous and on both sides of the river. Tom rolled by camp after camp, some familiar to him, most of them new. But no red scarf adorned any tent or wagon to gladden his eye. Miles he drove along the river, passing many more camps, with like result. The hunters were returning from the chase; a gradual cessation in gunfire marked Tom's approach to Hudnall's outfit. It was now impossible to see all the camps; some were too far from the road; others down in the widening brakes of the river. There were wagon tracks that turned off the main road to cross the river. Tom found no sign of Jett's outfit; yet, though much disappointed, it did not discourage him. Jett would be among the hunters after this main herd.

Before sunset he drove into Hudnall's camp.

"If it ain't Tom!" yelled Burn, who was the first to see him.

But Hudnall was the first to get to Tom, and almost embraced him, so glad and amazed was he.

"Back so soon? Gosh! you must have come hummin'!" he rolled out, heartily. "Say, we've had great huntin'. Hard, but just like diggin' gold. What'd you get for my hides?"

"Fifty cents more on every hide," replied Tom, producing an enormous wad of bills. "Maybe I'm not glad to get rid of that! And here's letters. There are newspapers, magazines, and other stuff in a basket under the seat."

"How's my women folks?" asked Hudnall, fingering the greenbacks.

"Just fine. You couldn't hope for better. But my—but Milly was gone," answered Tom.

"Milly? Who's she? Aw yes, your girl. I'd forgotten. . . . Say, Doan, you're thin, you look used up. Trip wear you out?"

Hudnall was all kindliness and solicitude now.

"No. Worry. I'll tell you presently. . . . Dave is somewhere along behind, heading a whole caravan of new hide-hunters."

"The more the merrier. There's room an' we don't see any slackin' up of buffalo," said Hudnall. "Pilchuck got two hundred an' eighty-six day before yesterday. That's his top notch. But he says he'll beat it. Tom, I forgot to tell you we'll pay you for drivin' out the hides. Five dollars a day, if that's all right?"

"Much obliged," replied Tom, wearily, as he sank down to rest. "Guess I'm fagged, too. You see, I tried to catch up with Jett. He left Sprague's a day ahead of me with Milly."

"The hell you say!" ejaculated Hudnall, suddenly losing all his animation. "We've heard bad rumors about that Jett outfit. You must take Milly away from them."

"Couldn't get track of Jett until to-day," went on Tom. "He was just ahead of me, though I couldn't see his wagons. He hit the river along about mid-afternoon and he's somewhere."

"Wal, we'll find him, an' don't you worry. These camps are no place for women folks. I've come to seein' that, Tom."

"What's happened since I left?" queried Tom.

"Son, if I believed all I heard I'd be pullin' stakes for Sprague's," declared Hudnall. "Reckon some of it's true, though. All I seen for myself was some Kiowas that got killed at the forks of the river above. They raided a camp, an' was crossin' the river when some hunters on the other side piled them up, horses an' all."

"Believe I expected to hear worse," replied Tom, soberly.

"Wash up an' take a rest," advised Hudnall. "I'll look after the horses. Reckon we'd better hold off supper a little. Pilchuck's always late these days. He likes the evenin' hunt an' I don't see any sign of Stronghurl."

"Dave was in sight when I struck the river," said Tom. "Then I slowed up. So he can't be far behind, unless he broke down."

Later, after a bath and shave and the donning of clean clothes, Tom felt somewhat relieved in body. His mind, however, was busy, pondering, clouded; and so it must continue until he had found Milly.

Pilchuck rode in after sunset, a dust-covered, powder-begrimed figure, ragged, worn, proven, everything about him attesting to the excessive endeavor that made him a great hunter. His jaded horse was scarcely recognizable; froth and sweat and dust had accumulated in a caked lather, yellow and hard as sun-baked mud, over front and hind quarters.

"Howdy, Doan!" was his greeting to Tom, with the offer of a horny, grimy hand. "As a freighter you're A number one. Reckon you look sorta washed out—an' washed up, too. Shore you're spick an' span. I'll go fall in the crick, myself."

"Did you have a good day?" asked Tom, after returning his greeting.

"Huh! Not much. I dropped fourteen bulls early, then got jammed in a herd an' had to quit shootin'. Wasn't no stampede or mebbe my story would never have been told. But the pesky bunch took me more'n twenty miles along Soapberry, an' when I did get clear of them I run plumb into some mean-lookin' Kiowas. They was between me an' camp. I had to head off west a little. They rode along for a couple of miles, keepin' on the wrong side for me, an' then seein' I was sure alone, they took after me."

The scout abruptly ended his narrative there, and went about his tasks. Tom, strange to realize, took the incident with a degree of calmness that seemed to him to be an acceptance of times grown heroic and perilous.

A little later Dave Stronghurl drove into camp with weary team, and tired himself, yet unusually loquacious and robustly merry for him. Tom could tell that Dave had something on his mind, and awaited results with interest. Hudnall greeted Dave in the same cordial way as he had Tom, asked the same questions, made the same statements about the hide-hunting and news of camp. And he also took charge of Dave's team.

"Get any line on Milly?" asked Dave, as he peeled off his shirt. "By gum! you shore rustled across the prairie to-day."

Tom was glad to acquaint his comrade with the trace he had obtained of Jett's outfit. Dave vented his satisfaction in forceful, though profane, speech.

While he was performing his ablutions Dunn and Ory Tacks drove in with the day's total of hides, eighty-six, not a good showing. Dunn threw the folded hides out on the open ground some rods from camp, while Tacks unhitched the team.

Hudnall, swift and capable round the camp fire as elsewhere, had a steaming supper soon ready, to which the six men sat down hungry as wolves and as talkative as full mouths would permit.

Ory Tacks had now been some weeks in the buffalo fields. Not in the least had it changed him, except that he did not appear to be quite so fat. Toil and danger had no power to transform his expression of infantile glee with life and himself. He wore the old slouch hat jauntily and, as always, a tuft of tow-colored hair stuck out through a hole in its crown.

Ory plied Tom with queries about Sprague, obviously leading up to something, but Tom, being both hungry and thoughtful, did not give him much satisfaction.

Forthwith Ory, between bites, turned his interest to Stronghurl, with the difference that now he was more than eager.

"Mr. Strongthrow," he began, as usual getting Dave's name wrong, "did you see my—our—the young lady at Sprague?"

"No, she was gone with Jett, I'm shore sorry to say," replied Dave.

"Miss Sally gone!" ejaculated Ory.

"Naw, I meant Tom's girl, Milly Fayre," replied Dave, rather shortly.

"But you saw Miss Sally?"

"Shore did."

"Haven't you a letter for me from her?" inquired Ory, with astonishing naïveté.

"What?" gaped Dave, almost dropping a large bite of biscuit from his mouth.

"You have a letter for me from Sally," said Ory, now affirmatively.

"Boy, do you reckon me a pony-express rider, carryin' the mail?"

"Did you see much of her?" inquired Ory, with scrupulous politeness.

"Nope. Not a great deal."

"How long were you with her? I'm asking, because if you saw her for even a little she'd have given you a message for me."

"Only saw her about thirty minutes, an' then, 'cause Tom was shore rarin' to leave, Sally an' me was busy gettin' married," replied Dave, with vast assumed imperturbability.

It had the effect to crush poor Ory into bewildered silence; he sank down quite staggered. Tom wanted to laugh, yet had not quite the meanness to let it out. Hudnall looked up, frowning.

"Dave, that's no way to tease Ory," he reproved, severely. "Ory's got as much right to shine up to Sally as you. Now if she sent him a letter you fork it over."

Dave got red in the face.

"She didn't send none," he declared.

"Are you sure?" added Hudnall, suspiciously. "I ain't placin' too much confidence in you, Dave."

"So it 'pears. But I'm not lyin'."

"All right. An' after this don't make any fool remarks about marryin' Sally, just to tease Ory. It ain't good taste."

"Boss, I wasn't teasin' him or talkin' like Ory's hair sticks through his hat," returned Dave, deliberately.

"What?" shouted Hudnall.

"Me an' Sally was married."

"You was married!" roared Hudnall, in amaze and rage.

"Yes, sir. There was a travelin' parson at Sprague, an' Sally an' me thought it a good chance to marry. So we did."

"Without askin' leave of me—of her dad?"

"You wasn't around. Sally was willin'—an' we thought we could tell you afterward."

"Did you ask her mother? She was around."

"Nope. I wanted to, but Sally said her mother didn't think I was much of a match."

"So you just run off with my kid an' married her?" roared Hudnall, beside himself with rage.

"Kid! Sally's a grown woman. See here, Hudnall, I didn't reckon you'd be tickled, but I shore thought you'd have some sense. Sally an' me would have married, when this huntin's over. I wanted some one to take care of my money, an' keep it, case I get killed out here. So what's wrong about it?"

"You big Swede!" thundered Hudnall. "You didn't ask *me*. That's what. An' I'm a mind to pound the stuffin's out of you."

Stronghurl was not profoundly moved by this threat.

"If you feel that way, come on," he replied, coolly. He was a thick, imperturbable sort of fellow, and possibly, Tom thought, he might be a Swede.

Pilchuck was shaking in silent mirth; Ory Tacks was reveling in revenge; Burn Hudnall sat divided between consternation and glee; old man Dunn looked on, very much amazed; and as for Tom, he felt that it looked mightily like a fight, yet he could not convince himself it would go that far.

"Come on, huh?" echoed Hudnall, boomingly, as he rose to his lofty height. He was twice the size of Stronghurl. He could have broken the smaller, though sturdy, bridegroom in short order. Slowly Stronghurl rose, at last seriously concerned, but resigned and forceful.

"Reckon you can lick me, Hudnall," he said, "an' if it's goin' to make you feel better let's get it over."

For answer Hudnall seemed to change, to expand, and throwing back his shaggy head he let out a stentorian roar of laughter. That eased the situation. Pilchuck also broke out, and the others, except Dave, joined him to the extent of their mirth. Hudnall was the last to recover, following which he shoved a brawny hand at Stronghurl.

"Dave, I was mad, natural-like, but you takin' me serious about fightin' over Sally was funny. Why, bless your heart, I'm glad for Sally an' you, even if you didn't ask me, an' I wish you prosperity an' long life!"

Stronghurl's armor of density was not proof against this big-hearted and totally unexpected acceptance and approval, and he showed in his sudden embarrassment and halting response that he was deeply moved. Nor did he take the congratulations of the rest of the outfit as calmly as might have been supposed he would, from his announcement of the marriage. Ory Tacks showed to advantage in his sincere and manly overture of friendliness.

What with this incident, and the news of Sprague to be told to Hudnall and Pilchuck, and their recital of the hunting conditions to Tom and Dave, the outfit did not soon get the day's hides pegged down, or to their much-needed beds.

Next morning Hudnall made the suggestion that each and all of the outfit would ride out of their way to look over new camps and to inquire of hunters as to the whereabouts of Randall Jett.

"Tom, we can't stop work altogether, but we can all spare some time," he said. "An' I'll drive the wagon out an' back, so you'll have time to ride along the river. It's my idea we'll find Milly pronto."

"Then what?" queried Tom, thrilling deeply with this good man's assurance.

"Wal, you can leave that to me," interposed Pilchuck, dryly. Tom was quick to sense something in the scout's mind which had not been spoken.

But that day and the next and the following passed fleetly by without any trace of Jett's outfit. Ten miles up and down the river, on the west bank, had been covered by some one of Hudnall's outfit. No three-wagon camp had been located.

"Shore Jett must be across the river," averred Pilchuck. "There's outfits strung along, an' enough buffalo for *him.*"

"What'll I do?" queried Tom, appealingly.

"Wal, son, you can't work an' do the job right," replied the scout. "I'd take a couple of days off. Ride down the river twenty miles or so, then cross an' come back on the other side. If that don't fetch results ride up the river, cross an' come back. Ask about Indians, too, an' keep your eyes peeled."

Tom's saddle horse, Dusty, had been ridden by Burn Hudnall and Pilchuck also during Tom's absence, and had developed into a fleet, tireless steed only second to Pilchuck's best buffalo chaser. Next morning Tom set off, mounted on Dusty. Well armed, with a small store of food, a canteen of water, and a field-glass, he turned resolute face to the task before him.

In less than two hours he had passed the ten-mile limit of his search so far, and had entered unfamiliar country where camps were many, and buffalo apparently as thick as bees round a hive. But very few of the camps had an occupant; at that hour all the men of each outfit were engaged up on the prairie, as the incessant boom of guns proved. How Tom's eyes strained and ached to catch a glimpse of the red scarf Milly said she would put up wherever she was! What bitter disappointment when he espied a blanket or anything holding a touch of red!

From each camp Tom would ride up the prairie slope to a level and out toward the black-fringed, dust-mantled moving medium that was buffalo. Thus he came upon hunters, skinners, teamsters, all of whom gave him less cordial greeting than he had received from hide-hunters before he went north. It took some moments for Tom to make his sincerity felt. These men were rushed for time, and a feeling of aloofness from strangers had manifestly passed south from camp to camp. Not one of them could or would give him any clue to Jett's outfit.

"Air you lookin' fer hide thieves?" queried one old grizzled hunter.

"No. I'm looking for a girl who has been brought down here by a man named Jett."

"Sorry. Never heard of him. But if you was lookin' fer hide thieves I'd be damn interested," replied the hunter.

"Why?" asked Tom, curiously.

"Because I had eleven hundred hides stole from my camp," he replied, "an' ain't never heerd of them since, let alone seein' hide or hair."

"Too bad. Is there much of this dirty work going on?"

"How 'n 'll can we tell thet?" retorted the man. "Thar's forty square miles of buffler, millin' an' movin', too. Nobody can keep track of any one. It's all mad rush. But some dirty sneaks air gittin' rich on other men's work."

Very few men Tom encountered, however, had any words to spare; and before that day was over he decided not to interrogate any more. It went against his grain to be regarded with hard, cold, suspicious eyes. There was no recourse for him but to search till he met Jett or found his camp. That struck him as far from a hopeless task, yet his longing and dread were poignant. He went on until he had passed the zone of camps and had drawn out of hearing of the boom-boom-boom of the big fifties. Not by many miles, though, had he come to the end of the buffalo herd.

It was the middle of the afternoon, too late for Tom to reach camp that day. He crossed the stream, now a clear shallow sandy-bottomed little watercourse, running swiftly. He was probably not many leagues from its source up in the bluffs of the Staked Plain, stark bald-faced heave of country, frowning down on the prairie.

Tom took the precaution to sweep the open stretches in front with his field-glass. All that he saw there were buffalo, near and far, everywhere, dots and strings and bands, just straggling remnants of the immense herd back over the stream.

A good trail, with horse tracks in it, followed the course of the water east, and led along the edge of the timber and sometimes through open groves. But Tom did not come to a road or see a camp or man or horse. The prairie was a beautiful grassy level, growing brown from the hot sun. Bands of antelope grazed within range of his gun, as tame as cattle; deer trotted ahead of him through the timber; wild turkeys by the hundreds looked up at his approach and made no effort to run. He saw bear and panther tracks in the dust of the trail.

Sunset overtook Tom and still he rode on. Before dark, however, he espied a thick clump of timber in which he decided to spend the night. Finding a suitable place well down from the trail, he unsaddled Dusty and led him to the stream to drink, then picketed him with a long lasso on a grass plot.

Twilight stole down into the grove while Tom ate some of the meat and bread he had taken the precaution to bring. No fire was necessary, as the air was close and sultry; besides, it might have attracted attention. He spread his saddle blankets for a bed, placed his saddle for a pillow, and with weapons at his side he lay down to sleep.

This was the first night he had been alone on the Texas prairies. It was novel, strange, somehow exhilarating, and yet disturbing. His anxiety to find Milly had led him far from the hunters' camps, into wild country, where he must run considerable risk. His state of mind, therefore, rendered him doubly susceptible to all around him.

Dusk mantled the river brakes. The night insects had begun their incessant song, low, monotonous, plaintive. And frogs joined in with their sweet, mellow, melodious trill. In spite of these sounds silence seemed to reign. Solitude was omnipresent there. Tom found it hard to realize that the extermination of America's most numerous and magnificent game beast was in frenzied operation along this river; that bands of Indians were on the warpath, and hide-robbers foraging secretly. Here the night and place were lonely, sad, provocative of such thoughts as had never before disturbed Tom.

By and by his attention was attracted at intervals by soft padded steps somewhere near, and the cracking of twigs down in the brakes, and the squealing of raccoons. Once a wild cry startled him, so nearly like a woman's scream was it, and he recognized it as the rare cry of a panther. He had heard hunters at the camps tell of it. Gradually his nervousness wore away. These creatures of the wilderness would not harm him; he had only to fear those beings made in his own image.

The night, the stars, the insects, the stealthy denizens of the brush, the soft, drowsy, sultry summer darkness with its dim flare of sheet lightning along the horizon, the loneliness and freedom of the open country—these worked on Tom's mind and from them he gathered a subtle confidence that there was something stronger than evil in men. Milly would not be lost to him.

At last Tom slept. He was awakened by the scratching and clucking of wild turkeys, so close that he could have tossed his hat among them. The sun was red in the east. He had slept late. To eat his meager breakfast, water and saddle his horse, fill his canteen, were but the work of a few moments, and then he was on his way again, alert, cautious, not to be misled by his ardor.

Tom traveled ten miles farther east before his ears again throbbed to the boom of the big buffalo guns. Scattered herds grazed out on the prairie, but appeared unmolested by hunters. The shooting came from across the river. Five miles farther on, however, Tom reached the zone of camps on that side, and heard the boom of guns.

Between that point and the river bluffs, which he recognized as landmarks near Hudnall's present location, he found and rode through seven camps of buffalo-hunters. Wagons, tents, reloading kits, mess boxes, bales of hides, squares and squares of hides pegged out—these were in no wise different from the particulars of the camps opposite.

But Tom did not find what he sought. He crossed the river and rode toward Hudnall's with a heavy heart.

The afternoon was far spent, still it was too early for Tom not to be surprised to see his comrades in camp. There appeared to be other hunters—a group, talking earnestly.

Tom urged his tired horse to a trot, then a lope. Something was wrong at Hudnall's. He felt it. There came a cold tightening round his heart. Reaching camp, Tom flung himself out of the saddle.

Ory Tacks, the nearest to Tom, as he advanced toward the men, was crying. Dunn sat near him, apparently dazed. Burn Hudnall's head was buried in his arms.

Stronghurl and Pilchuck were in conversation with a group of seven or eight men, among whom Tom recognized hunters from adjoining camps. It was significant to behold these men all carrying rifles. More significant was Pilchuck's face, hard, cold, forbidding, with his thin lips set in tight line and his eyes almost narrowed shut.

"What's—happened?" burst out Tom, breathlessly.

Burn Hudnall raised a face Tom could never forget.

"Father was murdered by Indians."

"Oh, my God—no!" cried Tom, in distress.

"Yes. . . . I saw him killed—an' I just got away—by the skin of my teeth," replied Burn, in a dreadful voice.

"How? When? Where?" panted Tom, shocked to his depths.

"It was father's carelessness. Oh, if he had only listened to Pilchuck. . . . Mebbe two hours ago. I was west of here four or five miles when I saw a band of Indians. They were ridin' towards us. I was skinnin' a bull an' was concealed behind the carcass. Father was off a quarter of a mile, ridin' round a small bunch of buffalo, shootin' fast, an' blind to anythin' else but buffalo. I yelled my lungs out. No use! He couldn't hear. I got to my horse an' was thinkin' of runnin' over to save father, when I saw I was too late. . . . The Indians rode like the wind. They ran down on father. I saw puffs of smoke an' heard shots. Father fell off his horse. Then the Indians circled round him, shootin', yellin', ridin' like naked painted devils. . . . Presently they quit racin', an' rode into a bunch, round where he lay. Some of them dismounted. Others rode toward the wagon an' team. These Indians saw me an' started for me. I tell you I had to ride, an' they chased me almost into camp. . . . Tom, I know what it is to hear the whistle of bullets!"

"He's out there—on the prairie—dead?" gasped Tom.

"Certain as death," replied Burn, solemnly. "Who's to tell mother an' Sally?"

"But—but we must go out there—to see—to find out—."

"Pilchuck's taken charge, Tom," replied the other. "He says the Indians were Comanches an' in pretty strong force. We're to wait till morning, get a bunch of men together, an' then go out to bury father."

Tom was stunned. The catastrophe as persistently portended by Pilchuck and corroborated by Sprague had at last fallen. Splendid, fine, kindly Hudnall was dead at the hands of revengeful savages. It was terrible. To be warned of such a thing was nothing, but the fact itself stood out in appalling vividness.

"Let's rustle supper while it's daylight," said Pilchuck, coming over. "We don't want a camp fire to-night. Reckon there's hardly any danger of attack, but we want to stand guard an' not take any chances."

Camp tasks had to go on just the same, and Tom helped Dunn and Ory Tacks. The other hunters turned to leave with an understanding that they were to stand guard at their camps, and return in the morning.

"Starwell, we'll plan to-morrow after we bury Hudnall," said the scout.

"One only plan," replied the other, a lean, dark, forceful looking Westerner whom Tom felt he would not care to cross. "We buff-hunters must band together an' trail them Comanches."

"Reckon you're right, Star," returned Pilchuck, grimly. "But there's no rush. Them redskins have done more'n kill Hudnall, I'll bet you. They've been raidin'. An' they'll strike for the Staked Plain. That means we've got to organize. If there's a hell of a place in the world it's shore the Staked Plain."

Supper without the cheerful presence of Hudnall would have been a loss, but the fact that he lay dead, murdered, surely mutilated, out there on the prairie, was monstrous to Tom. He could not eat. He wandered about camp, slowly realizing something beyond the horror of the calamity, a gradual growth from shock to stern purpose. No need to ask Pilchuck what was in his mind! The plainsman loomed now in Tom's sight big and strong, implacable and infallible.

Tom stood guard with Stronghurl during the earlier watches of the night; and the long-drawn mournful howl of the prairie wolf had in it a new significance. This wild West was beginning to show its teeth.

CHAPTER ELEVEN

Morning came, and Pilchuck had the men stirring early. When Tom walked out to the camp fire dawn was brightening, and there was a low roll of thunder from the eastward.

"We're in for a thunderstorm," he said to the scout, who was cooking breakfast.

"Storm, mebbe, but not thunder-an'-lightnin' storm," replied Pilchuck. "That sound you hear is new to you. It's a stampede of buffalo."

"Is that so? . . . Say, how like thunder!"

"Yep, we plainsmen call it the thunderin' herd. But this isn't the main herd on the rampage. Somethin', most likely Indians, has scared the buffalo across the river. They've been runnin' south for an hour. More buffalo over there than I had an idee of."

"Yes, I saw miles of scattered herds as I rode up the river," said Tom.

"I smell smoke, too, an' fact is, Doan, I don't like things a damn bit. If the main herd stampedes—holy Moses! I want to be on top of the Staked Plain. Reckon, though, that's just where we'll be."

"You're going after the Comanches?" inquired Tom, seriously.

"Wal, I reckon. It's got to be done if we're to hunt buffalo in peace."

Burn Hudnall presented himself at the camp fire, his face haggard with grief; but he was now composed. He sat at breakfast as usual, and later did his share of the tasks. Not long afterward Starwell and his men rode into camp, heavily armed and formidable in appearance.

"Jude, what you make of that stampede across the river?" he asked, after greetings were exchanged.

"Wal, I ain't makin' much, but I don't like it."

"We heerd shootin' yesterday at daylight down along the river from our camp," returned Starwell. "Small-bore guns, an' I don't calkilate hunters was shootin' rabbits for breakfast."

"Ahuh! Wal, after we come back from buryin' Hudnall we'll take stock of what's goin' on," said Pilchuck. "By that time camp will be full of hunters, I reckon."

"Hardy rode twenty miles an' more down the river, gettin' back late last night. He said there'd be every outfit represented here this mornin'."

"Good. We kept the horses picketed last night, an' we'll be saddled in a jiffy."

Burn Hudnall led that band of mounted men up on the prairie and southwest toward the scene of yesterday's tragedy. The morning was hot; whirlwinds of dust were rising, like columns of yellow smoke; the prairie looked lonesome and vast; far out toward the Staked Plain showed a dim ragged line of buffalo. Across the river the prairie was obscured in low covering of dust, like rising clouds. The thunder of hoofs had died away.

Tom Doan, riding with these silent, somber men, felt a strong beat of his pulse that was at variance with the oppression of his mind. He was to be in the thick of wild events.

In perhaps half an hour the trotting horses drew within sight of black dots on the prairie, and toward these Burn Hudnall headed. They were dead and unskinned buffalo. Presently Burn halted alongside the first carcass, that of a bull, half skinned.

"Here's where I was, when the Indians came in sight over that ridge," said Burn, huskily. "Father must be lyin' over there."

He pointed toward where a number of black woolly dead buffalo lay scattered over the green plain, and rode toward them. Presently Pilchuck took the lead. His keen eye no doubt had espied the corpse of Hudnall, for as he passed Burn he said, "Reckon it'd be more sense for you not to look at him."

Burn did not reply, but rode on as before. Pilchuck drew ahead and Starwell joined him. The riders scattered somewhat, some trotting forward, and others walking their horses. Then the leaders dismounted.

"Somebody hold Burn back," shouted Pilchuck, his bronze face flashing in the sunlight.

But though several of the riders, and lastly Tom, endeavored to restrain Burn, he was not to be stopped. Not the last was he to view his father's remains.

"Reckon it's Comanche work," declared Pilchuck, in a voice that cut.

Hudnall's giant body lay, half nude, in grotesque and terrible suggestiveness. He had been shot many times, as was attested to by bullet holes in his torn and limp limbs. His scalp had been literally torn off, his face gashed, and his abdomen ripped open. From the last wound projected buffalo grass which had been rammed into it.

All the hunters gazed in silence down upon the ghastly spectacle. Then from Burn Hudnall burst an awful cry.

"Take him away, somebody," ordered Pilchuck. Then after several of the hunters had led the stricken son aside the scout added. "Tough on a tenderfoot! But he would look. Reckon it'd be good for all newcomers to see such a sight. . . . Now, men, I'll keep watch for Comanches while you bury poor Hudnall. Rustle, for it wouldn't surprise me to see a bunch of the devils come ridin' over that ridge."

With pick and shovel a deep grave was soon dug, and Hudnall's body, wrapped in a blanket, was lowered into it. Then the earth was filled in and stamped down hard. Thus the body of the careless, cheerful, kindly Hudnall was consigned to an unmarked grave on the windy prairie.

Pilchuck found the tracks of the wagon, and the trail of the Comanches heading straight for the Staked Plain.

"Wal, Star, that's as we reckoned," declared the scout.

"Shore is," replied Starwell. "They stole wagon, hosses, gun, hides—everythin' Hudnall had out here."

"Reckon we'll hear more about this bunch before the day's over. Must have been fifty Indians an' they have a habit of ridin' fast and raidin' more'n one place at a time."

"Jude, my idee is they'd not have taken the wagon if they meant to make another raid," said Starwell.

"Reckon you're right. Wal, we'll rustle back to camp."

More than thirty hunters, representatives of the outfits within reaching distance of Hudnall's, were assembled at camp when the riders returned from their sad mission. All appeared eager to learn the news, and many of them had tidings to impart.

An old white-haired hunter declared vigorously: "By Gord! we air goin' to give the buffalo a rest an' the Injuns a chase!"

That indeed seemed the prevailing sentiment.

"Men, before we talk of organizin' let's get a line on what's been goin' on," said Pilchuck.

Whereupon the hunters grouped themselves in the shade of the cottonwoods, like Indians in Council. The scout told briefly the circumstances surrounding the murder of Hudnall, and said he would leave his deductions for later. Then he questioned the visiting hunters in turn.

Rathbone's camp, thirty miles west, on a creek running down out of the Staked Plain, had been burned by Comanches, wagons and horses stolen, and the men driven off, just escaping with their lives. That had happened day before yesterday.

The camp of two hunters, names not known, had been set upon by Indians, presumably the same band, on the main branch of the Pease. The hunters were out after buffalo. They found wagons, hides, tents, camp destroyed; only ammunition and harness being stolen. These hunters had made their way to the main camps.

An informant from down the river told that some riders, presumably Indians, had fired the prairie grass in different widely separated places, stampeding several herds of buffalo.

Most of the representatives from the camps up the river had nothing particularly important to impart, except noticeable discontent in the main herd of buffalo, and Starwell's repetition of the facts relating to the shots he and his camp-mates had heard yesterday morning.

Whereupon a lanky man, unknown to Pilchuck's group, spoke up:

"I can tell aboot that. My name's Roberts. I belong to Sol White's outfit across the river. We're from Waco, an' one of the few outfits from the South. This mawnin' there was a stampede on our side, an' I was sent across to scout around. I crossed the river aboot two miles above heah. Shore didn't know the river an' picked out a bad place. An' I run plumb on to a camp thet was so hid I didn't see it. But I smelled smoke an' soon found where tents, wagons, an' hides had been burnin'. There was two daid men, scalped, lyin' stripped, with sticks poked into their stomachs—so I hurried up this way to find somebody."

"Men, I want a look at that camp," declared Pilchuck, rising. "Some of you stay here an' some come along. Star, I'd like you with me. Roberts, you lead an' we'll follow."

Tom elected to remain in camp with those who stayed behind; he felt that he had seen enough diabolical work of the Comanches. Burn Hudnall likewise shunned going. Ory Tacks, however, took advantage of the opportunity, and rode off with Pilchuck. Tom tried to find tasks to keep his mind off the tragic end of Hudnall and the impending pursuit of the Indians.

Pilchuck and his attendants were gone so long that the visiting hunters left for their own camps, saying they would ride over next day. Worry and uncertainty were fastening upon those men who were not seasoned Westerners. They had their own camps and buffalo hides to consider. But so far as Tom could ascertain there was not a dissenting voice against the necessity for banding together to protect themselves from Indians.

About mid-afternoon the scout and newcomer from across the river returned alone. Pilchuck was wet and muddy from contact with the river bank; and his mood, if it had undergone any change, was colder and grimmer.

"Doan, reckon I'm a blunt man, so get your nerve," he said, with his slits of piercing eyes on Tom.

"What—do you mean?" queried Tom, feeling a sudden sinking sensation of dread. Bewildered, uncertain, he could not fix his mind on any effort.

"This camp Roberts took me to was Jett's. But I think Jett got away with your girl," announced Pilchuck.

The ground seemed to fail of solidity under Tom; his legs lost their strength, and he sat down on a log.

"Don't look like that," ordered Pilchuck, sharply. "I told you the girl got away. Starwell thought the Indians made off with her. But I reckon he's wrong there."

"Jett! Milly?" was all Tom could gasp out.

"Pull yourself together. It's a man's game we're up against. You're no tenderfoot any more," added Pilchuck, with a tone of sympathy. "Look here. You said somethin' about your girl tyin' her red scarf up to give you a hunch where she was. Do you recognize this?"

He produced a red scarf, soiled and blackened.

With hands Tom could not hold steady to save his life he took it.

"Milly's," he said, very low.

"Reckoned so myself. Wal, we didn't need this proof to savvy Jett's camp. I'd seen his outfit. These dead men Roberts happened on belonged to Jett's outfit. I recognized the little sandy-haired teamster. An' the other was Follonsbee. Got his name from Sprague."

Then Tom found voice poignantly to beg Pilchuck to tell him everything.

"Shore it's a mess," replied the scout, as he sat down and wiped his sweaty face. "Look at them boots. I damn near drowned myself. Wal, Jett had his camp in a place no Indians or buffalo-hunters would ever have happened on, unless they did same as Roberts. Crossed the river there. Accident! . . . Doan, this fellow Jett is a hide thief an' he had bad men in his outfit. His camp was destroyed by Comanches all right, the same bunch that killed Hudnall. But I figure Jett escaped in a light wagon, before the Indians arrived. Follonsbee an' the other man were killed *before* the Indians got there. They were shot with a needle gun. An' I'm willin' to bet no Comanches have needle guns. All the same they was scalped an' mutilated, with sticks in their bellies. Starwell agreed with me that these men were killed the day or night before the Indians raided the camp."

"Had Jett—gotten away—then?" breathlessly asked Tom.

"Shore he had. I seen the light wheel tracks an' Milly's little footprints in the sand, just where she'd stepped up on the wagon. I followed the wheel tracks far enough to see they went northeast, away from the river, an' also aimin' to pass east of these buffalo camps. Jett had a heavy load, as the wheel tracks cut deep. He also had saddle horses tied behind the wagon."

"Where'd you find Milly's scarf?" asked Tom, suddenly.

"It was tied to the back hoop of a wagon cover. Some of the canvas had been burned. There was other things, too, a towel an' apron, just as if they'd been hung up after usin'."

"Oh, it is Milly's!" exclaimed Tom, and he seemed to freeze with the dreadful significance it portended.

"So much for that. Shore the rest ain't easy to figure," went on Pilchuck. "I hate to tell you this part, Doan, because—wal, it *is* worryin' . . . I found trail where a bleedin' body, mebbe more'n one, had been dragged down the bank an' slid off into the river. That's how I come to get in such a mess. The water was deep there an' had a current, too. If we had hooks an' a boat we could drag the river, but as we haven't we can only wait. After some days corpses float up. I incline to the idee that whoever killed Follonsbee an' the other man is accountable for the bloody trail leadin' to the river. But I can't be shore. Starwell thinks different from me on some points. Reckon his opinion is worth considerin'. In my own mind I'm shore of two things—there was a fight, mebbe murder, an' *somebody* rode away with the girl. Then the Comanches came along, destroyed the camp, an' scalped the men."

"An' say, scout," spoke up Roberts, "you're shore forgettin' one important fact. The Indians left there trailin' the wagon tracks."

"Ahuh, I forgot that," replied the scout, averting his gaze from Tom's. "Jett had a good start. Now if he kept travelin' all night—"

"But it looks as if he had no knowledge of the Indians comin'," interrupted Tom, intensely.

"Shore. All the same, Jett was gettin' away from somethin'. He'd rustle far before campin'," continued the scout, doggedly bent on hoping for the best.

This was not lost on Tom nor the gloomy cast of Pilchuck's lean face. Tom could not feel anything save black despair. Either Jett had the girl or the Indians had her—and the horror seemed that one was as terrible as the other.

Tom sought his tent, there to plunge down and surrender to panic and misery.

Next morning the hunters round their early camp fires were interested to hear a low thunder of running buffalo. It floated across the river from the south and steadily grew louder.

"That darned herd comin' back," said Pilchuck, uneasily. "I don't like it. Shore they're liable to cross the river an' stampede the main herd."

An hour later a hunter from below rode in to say that buffalo by the thousands were fording the river five miles below.

Pilchuck threw up his hands.

"I reckoned so. Wal, we've got to make the best of it. What with raidin' Comanches an' stampedin' buffalo we're done for this summer—as far as any big haul of hides is concerned."

Men new to the hunting fields did not see the signs of the times as Pilchuck and the other scouts read them; and they were about equally divided for and against an active campaign against the Indians.

A good many hunters along the Pease continued their hide-hunting, indifferent to the appeal and warning of those who knew what had to be done.

The difficulty lay in getting word to the outfits scattered all over northern Texas. For when the buffalo-hunters organized to make war upon the marauders, that meant a general uprising and banding together of Comanches, Kiowas, Arapahoes, and Cheyennes. Also there were Apaches on the Staked Plain, and they, too, according to reports, were in uneasy mood. Therefore buffalo-hunters not affiliated with the war movement, or camping in isolated places unknown to the organizers, stood in great peril of their lives.

Investigation brought out the fact that a great number of hunters from eastern Texas were on the range, not in any way connected with the experienced and time-hardened band camped on the trail of the main herd. Effort was made to get word to these eastern hunters that a general conference was to be held at Double Fork on a given date.

Over three hundred hunters attended this conference, including all the scouts, plainsmen, and well-known frontier characters known to be in the buffalo country. Buffalo Jones, already famous as a plainsman, and later known as the preserver of the buffalo, was there, as strong in his opinion that the Indian should be whipped as he was in his conviction that the slaughter of buffalo was a national blunder.

It was Jones's contention that the value and number of American buffalo were unknown to the world—that the millions that had ranged the Great Plains from Manitoba to the Rio Grande were so common as to be no more appreciated than prairie-dogs. Their utilitarian value was not understood, and now it was too late.

The Indians knew the value of the buffalo, and if they did not drive the white hunter from the range, the beasts were doomed.

"Only the buffalo-hunters can open up the Southwest to the farmer and cattleman," averred Jones. "The U.S. army can't do it. . . . But what a pity the buffalo must go! Nature never constructed a more perfect animal."

The buffalo, according to Jones, was an evolution of the Great Plains, and singularly fitted to survive and flourish on its vast and varied environment. He estimated the number as ten million. The blizzard of Montana or the torrid sirocco of the Staked Plain was no hindrance to the travel of the buffalo. His great, shaggy, matted head had been constructed to face the icy blasts of winter, the sand-storms and hot gales of the summer. A buffalo always faced danger, whatever it might be.

Different men addressed the council, and none were more impressive than Pilchuck.

"Men, I've lived my life on the plains. I've fought Indians all down the line from Montana. I've seen for a long time that we buffalo-hunters have got to fight these Southern tribes or quit huntin'. If we don't kill off the buffalo there'll never be any settlin' of northern Texas. We've got to *kill* the Comanches, an' lick the Kiowas, Cheyennes, an' Arapahoes. I reckon we'll have to deal with Apaches, too. . . . Now the Indians are scattered all over, same as the buffalo hunters. We can't organize one expedition. There ought to be several big outfits of men, well equipped, strikin' at these Indians already on the warpath. . . . We hunters along the Pease River divide will answer for that section. There's a bunch of Comanches been raidin', an' are now hidin' up in the Staked Plain. Outfits ought to take care of the Brazos River district an' also the Red River. . . . Now there's one more point I want to drive home. Camps an' outfits should be moved close together in these several districts that expect to send out fightin' men. An' an equal or even strong force should be left behind to protect these camp posts. Last, I shore hope the tenderfoot hunters will have sense enough to collect at these posts, even if they won't fight the Indians. For there's goin' to be hell. This will be a fight for the buffalo—the Indians fightin' to *save* the buffalo an' the white men fightin' to *kill* the buffalo. It'll be a buffalo war, an' I reckon right hereabouts, halfway between the Brazos an' Fort Elliott, will see the hottest of it. I just want every man of you who may be on the fence about fightin', an' mebbe doubtin' my words, to go out an' look at the *acres an' acres* of buffalo hides, an' then ask himself if the Indians are goin' to stand that."

The old scout turned the tide in favor of general arming against the tribes on all points of the range. Then Pilchuck, with his contingent from the Pease River, left for their own camps, four days' travel, determined to take the field at once against the Comanches.

They visited every camp on the way south and solicited volunteers, arriving at Pease River with twenty-seven men ready to follow Pilchuck to the end. One of these was a friendly Osage Indian scout called Bear Claws by the men; another a Mexican who had been a scout in the United States army service and was reported to know every trail and water hole in the wild Staked Plain.

But Pilchuck, elated by his success in stirring up the hunters to the north, was fated to meet with a check down on the Pease River. Seventy-five of the hundred hunters who had agreed to take part in the campaign backed out, to Pilchuck's disgust. Many of these had gone back to hunting buffalo, blind to their danger or their utter selfishness. Naturally this not only held up Pilchuck's plan to start soon on the campaign, but also engendered bad blood.

The site of Hudnall's camp was now the rendezvous of from twenty to thirty outfits, most of which had failed the scout. At a last conference of hunters there Pilchuck, failing to persuade half of these men to fall in line, finally delivered a stinging rebuke.

"Wal, all I got to say is you're hangin' behind to make money while some of us have got to go out an' fight to protect you."

One of these reluctants was a young man named Cosgrove, a hard-drinking, loud-mouthed fellow with whom Tom Doan had clashed before, on the same issue.

Tom had been a faithful and tireless follower of Pilchuck, as much from loyalty to the cause as from desire for revenge on the Comanches, whom he was now convinced had either killed or carried off Milly Fayre. No authentic clew of Jett's escape or death had been found, but vague rumors of this and that, and more destroyed camps to the north, especially a one-night-stand camp with a single wagon and but few horses, had at last stricken Tom's last remnant of hope.

Accordingly, Tom's state of mind was not conducive to tolerance, especially of such greed and selfishness as was manifested by some of the hunters.

Cosgrove was louder than usual in voicing his opinions.

"Aw, to hell with the Indians," he said. "I'm a-goin' to keep on huntin' buffalo. It's nothin' to me who goes off on wild-goose chases."

"Cosgrove, you won't be missed, that's sure," retorted Tom.

"What d'ye mean?" demanded the other, his red, bloated face taking on an ugly look. He swaggered over to Tom. There was a crowd present, some thoughtful, many indifferent.

"I mean we don't want such fellows as you," replied Tom.

"An' why not? Didn't Pilchuck just ask me?"

"Sure. He's asked a couple of hundred men, and lots of them are like you—*afraid to go!*"

"What!" shouted Cosgrove, hotly.

"We'll be better off without cowards like you," returned Tom, deliberately standing up, strung for any move.

"You're a liar!" flashed Cosgrove, advancing threateningly.

Tom knocked him down. Then, as Cosgrove, cursing with rage, scrambled to his knees and drew his gun, the crowd scattered away on each side. All save Pilchuck, who knocked the half-leveled gun out of Cosgrove's hand and kicked it far aside.

"Hyar!" yelled the scout, sternly. "You might get hurt, throwin' a gun that way. I'm advisin' you to cool down."

"He needn't, far as I'm concerned," spoke up Tom, ringingly. "Let him have his gun."

Pilchuck wheeled to see Tom standing stiff, gun in hand.

"You young rooster!" ejaculated Pilchuck, in surprise and disapproval. "Put that gun up an' rustle back to camp."

Thus had Tom Doan at last answered to the wildness of the buffalo range.

Worse, however, grew out of that incident, though it did not affect Tom Doan in any way.

One of Pilchuck's lieutenants was a Texan known on the range as Spades Harkaway, a man to be feared in a quarrel. He had been present when Tom had knocked down young Cosgrove, and later he had taken exception to the talk of a man named Hurd, who was in the same outfit with Cosgrove.

Rumor of a fight reached Hudnall's camp that night, but not until next day were the facts known. Hurd had denounced Pilchuck's campaign, which had brought sharp reply from Harkaway. Bystanders came between the two men at the moment, but later the two met again in Starwell's camp. Hurd had been imbibing red liquor and Harkaway had no intention of avoiding trouble. Again the question of Pilchuck's Indian campaign was raised by Hurd and coarsely derided. To this Harkaway had answered, first with a flaming arraignment of those hunters who meant to let Pilchuck's company stand the brunt of the fighting, and secondly with short, cutting contempt for Hurd. Then the latter, as the story came, had shot at Harkaway from behind other men. There followed a bad mess, in which the Texan killed Hurd and crippled one of his friends.

These fights traveling along the shortened lines of camp, brought the question to a heated pitch and split the hunters in that district. The majority, however, turned out to be on the side of the Hurd and Cosgrove type. Pilchuck had over fifty men to take on his campaign, and about the same number to remain behind to protect camps and hides. These men were to continue to hunt buffalo, but only on limited parts of the range near the camps, and always under the eyes of scouts patrolling the prairie, with keen eyes on the lookout to prevent surprise. Over twenty outfits, numbering nearly seventy-five men, who had not the nerve to fight Indians or to remain on the range, left that district for Fort Elliott and Sprague's Post, to remain until the Indian trouble was ended.

CHAPTER TWELVE

Pilchuck's band contained fifty-two men, most of whom owned, or had borrowed, Creedmoor Sharps 45-caliber rifles for this expedition. These guns were more reliable and of longer range than the big fifties. Each man took at least two hundred loaded cartridges. Besides that, reloading tools and extra ammunition were included in the supplies. Four wagon loads of food and camp equipment, grain for horses, and medical necessities, were taken in charge of the best drivers.

This force was divided into three companies—one of twenty men under Pilchuck, and two, of sixteen men each, under old buffalo-hunters. This was to facilitate camping operations and to be in readiness to split into three fighting groups.

Tom Doan was in Pilchuck's company, along with Stronghurl, Burn Hudnall, Ory Tacks, Starwell, Spades Harkaway, the Indian called Bear Claws, Roberts, and others whom Tom knew. There were at least eight or ten hunters, long used to the range, and grim, laconic men who would have made any fighting force formidable.

Pilchuck, Bear Claws, Starwell, and Tom formed an advance guard, riding two miles ahead of the cavalcade. Both the scout and Starwell had powerful field-glasses. The rear guard consisted of three picked men under Harkaway. The route lay straight for the Staked Plain and was covered at the rate of fifteen miles a day. At night a strong guard was maintained.

On the fourth day the expedition reached the eastern wall of the Staked Plain, a stark, ragged, looming escarpment, notched at long distances by canyons, and extending north and south out of sight. This bold upheaval of rock and earth now gave at close hand an inkling of the wild and inhospitable nature of the Staked Plain.

The tracks of Hudnall's wagon led into a deep-mouthed canyon down whose rugged bottom poured a clear stream of water. Grass was abundant. Groves of cottonwood trees filled the level benches. Game of all kinds abounded in these fastnesses and fled before the approach of the hunters. Before noon of that day a small herd of buffalo, surprised in an open grassy park, stampeded up the canyon, completely obliterating the wagon tracks Pilchuck was following, and all other signs of the Comanches.

This flight of the buffalo, on the other hand, helped to make a way where it was possible to get the four wagons of supplies up on the Staked Plain. Many horses and strong hands made short work of this labor.

Tom Doan gazed in fascination at the wild, strange expanse before him, the Staked Plain, which though notorious of reputation, was so little known. He had expected to find it a gray level plain of sand. Sand there was, assuredly, but many other things at the same time, as appeared manifest in the sand dunes and bluffs and the ragged irregular brakes, and patches of grass, and wide areas of brush. In Tom's opinion, hunting Indians up there was indeed the wild-goose chase which the expedition had been stigmatized by many of the hunters who had remained behind.

Nevertheless, the Mexican scout led straight to the spot where there had recently been a large encampment of Comanches. They had been gone for days, no doubt having gotten wind of the campaign against them. The tracks of Hudnall's wagon were found again.

As it was now late in the day, camp was pitched here, with the three forces of hunters close together. By dark, supper was finished, the horses were picketed and herded, guards were on duty, and Pilchuck was in council with two of his scouts and the more experienced of his men. It was decided to hold that camp for the next day, and send out detachments with the scouts to try and locate the Comanches.

Round the camp fire that night Tom made the further acquaintance of Spades Harkaway, and found him an unique character, reticent as to himself, but not unwilling to talk about Texas, the buffalo, and the Indians. He had twice crossed the Staked Plain from its western boundary, the Pecos River, to the headwaters of the Brazos on the east.

"Thet name Llano Estacado means Staked Plain," said the Texan. "It comes from the early days when the Spanish Trail from Santa Fe to San Antone was marked by *'palos,'* or stakes. There was only two trails across in them days an' I reckon no more now. Only the Indians know this plain well an' they only run in heah to hide awhile. Water an' grass are plentiful in some parts, an' then there's stretches of seventy miles dry an' bare as a bone. Reckon aboot some of the wildest an' roughest holes in Texas are up heah, as shore you-all will find oot."

Harkaway claimed the Llano Estacado was shaped like a ham, with a north-to-south trend, about four hundred miles long, and more than half as much wide. It was a tableland, resembling more the Russian steppes than the other upland districts known in the West. Its height above the prairie was perhaps a thousand feet. Some of its most pronounced characteristics, that had helped to make its ill fame, were enumerated and described by the Texan as tremendous obstacles to overcome on an expedition like Pilchuck's.

"Thar's bare patches too big to see across," he specified, "an' others growed over with mesquite so thick thet ridin' it is impossible. Thar's narrow deep canyons thet can only be crossed in places miles apart. Then I've seen, myself, canyons thet opened out wide an' full of jumbles of broken cliff, where no man could go."

Higher up on the Staked Plain there were levels of a hundred miles in length, like a gravel floor, treeless, grassless, waterless, where the wind swept all before it. There were zones where ponds of water lay at times, a few of them permanent, sulphurous, or salty, and at dry seasons unfit to drink for man or beast. Near the southern end of this strange steppe was a belt of glistening white sand dunes, many miles wide, impassable for a horse, and extremely perilous for a man. Not, however from lack of water! For here the singular nature of the Staked Plain was more than unusually marked. Permanent ponds lined by reeds and rushes existed in the very region of sand dunes. Along the whole eastern escarpment of the Staked Plain, for three hundred miles, the bold rock rim was cut and furrowed by the streams that had their sources in this mysterious upland.

Late next day the Mexican scout returned with the information that he had found the main encampment of the Comanches. He had been on a reconnoiter alone. Bear Claws and Pilchuck, who had essayed to follow the tracks of Hudnall's wagon, had actually lost all sign of them. For miles they had trailed the marks of the iron-shod wheels over an area of hard-packed gravel, only to lose them further on in tough, short, springy grass that after the recent rain left no trace.

"The Indian says he can find the wagon tracks by making a wide circle to get off the grass," Pilchuck informed Starwell, "but that might take days. Besides, the Indians sent the wagon off their main trail. Reckon they expected pursuit. Anyway, we'll not risk it."

When Pilchuck made this decision he did not yet know that the Mexican had located the Comanches. Upon consulting with him the information came out that a large band of Indians had been encamped in a canyon, and undoubtedly their lookouts had seen him.

This was verified next day, after a hard ride. An Indian band, large enough to have hundreds of horses, had hastily abandoned the encampment in the canyon and had climbed up on the plain, there to scatter in all directions. Plain trails were left in several cases, but these Bear Claws would not pay any attention to. The Mexican sided with him. They concentrated on dimmer trails over harder ground to follow.

It was after dark when Pilchuck and his men got back to camp, hungry and weary from a long day in the saddle. Next morning camp was moved ten miles to the west, to a secluded spot within easy striking distance of the place where Bear

Claws had left off trailing the night before.

That day the Osage Indian lost track of the Comanches for the reason that the trail, always dim, finally vanished altogether. Three days more of searching the fastnesses within riding distance of this camp availed nothing. Camp had to be moved again, this time, at the Indian's suggestion, across the baffling stretch of plain to a wild and forbidding chaos of ruined cliffs, from which center many shallow canyons wandered for some leagues.

"Reckon we've got to rely on our field-glasses to see them before they see us," said Pilchuck.

When the sun rose high enough next morning to burn out the shadows Pilchuck stood with his scouts and some of his men on the crest of the rocky wilderness.

"Shore that's a hole!" he ejaculated.

Far and wide heaved the broken billows of gray rock, like an immense ragged sea, barren, monotonous, from which the heat veils rose in curtains. Here and there a tufted cedar raised its dwarfed head, but for the most part there was no green to break the stark nudity. Naked eyes of white men could only see the appalling beauty of the place and enable the mind to grasp the deceiving nature of its distance, size and color. Pilchuck took a long survey with his field-glass.

"Reckon all them meanderin' gorges head in one big canyon way down there," he said, handing the glass to Starwell.

"I agree with you, an' I'm gamblin' the Comanches are there," replied Starwell, in turn handing the glass to the man nearest him.

Tom had a good look at that magnified jumble of rocks and clefts, and the wonder of its wildness awed and thrilled him.

Standing next to Tom was Bear Claws, the Osage Indian, and so motionless, so striking was he as he gazed with dark, piercing eyes across the void, that Tom marveled at him and felt the imminence of some startling fact. Pilchuck observed this, also, for as he stood behind the Indian he watched him steadily.

Bear Claws was over six feet tall, lithe, lean, erect, with something of the look of an eagle about him. His bronze, impassive face bore traces of vermilion paint. Around his neck was the bear-claw necklace from which the hunters had nicknamed him. In the back of his scalp-lock, a twisted knot of hair, he had stuck the tail feathers of a prairie bird. Bright bracelets of steel shone on his wrists. He was naked to his beaded and quilled breech-clout.

"Me," he grunted, reaching for Pilchuck's field-glass, without taking his fixed gaze from what held him. With both hands then he put the glass to his eyes.

"Ugh!" he exclaimed, instantly.

It was a moment of excitement and suspense for the watching men. Pilchuck restrained Starwell's impatience. Tom felt a cold ripple run over his body, and then as the Indian said, "Comanches!" that ripple seemed suddenly to be strung with fire. He thought of Milly Fayre.

Bear Claws held the glass immovable, with stiff hand, while he stepped from behind it, and drew Pilchuck to the exact spot where he had stood. His long-reaching arm seemed grotesque while his body moved guardedly. He was endeavoring to keep the glass leveled at the exact spot that had held him.

Pilchuck fastened hard down on the glass, that wavered slightly and then gradually became still. To the watching men he evidently was an eternity. But at last he spoke: "By thunder! he's right. I can just make out . . . Indians on trail—goin' down—head of that canyon all these rock draws run into. . . . Starwell, take a look. . . . Hold there, over that first splinter of cliff, in a line with the high red bluff—an' search at its base."

Other glasses were now in use and more than one of the hunters caught a glimpse of the Comanches before they disappeared.

A council was held right there. The distance was approximately ten miles, yet incredibly the Osage Indian had seen something to make him take the field-glass and verify his wonderful keenness of vision. The Mexican scout knew the topography of the rough rock waste and guaranteed to place Pilchuck's force within striking distance of the Comanches by dawn next day.

Thereupon the hunters retraced their steps from that high point and returned to camp. Pilchuck took the scouts to search for a well-hidden pocket or head of a box canyon where wagons and horses not needed could be concealed to advantage and protected by a small number of men. This was found, very fortunately, in the direction of the Indian encampment, and several miles closer. The move was made expeditiously before dark.

"Reckon this is pretty good," said Pilchuck, with satisfaction. "We're far enough away to be missed by any scout they send out to circle their camp. That's an old Indian trick—to ride a circle round a hidin' place, thus crossin' any trail of men sneakin' close. It hardly seems possible we can surprise a bunch of Staked Plain Comanches, but the chance shore looks good."

In the darkest hour before dawn forty grim men rode out of camp behind the Mexican and Pilchuck.

Tom Doan rode next to Bear Claws, the fifth of that cavalcade, and following him came Spades Harkaway. No one spoke. The hoofs of the horses gave forth only dull, sodden sounds, inaudible at little distance. There was an opaque misshapen moon, orange in color, hanging low over the uneven plain. The morning star, white, luminous, like a marvelous beacon, stood high above the blanching velvet of the eastern sky.

They traveled at walk or trot, according to the nature of the ground, until the moon went down and all the stars had paled, except the great one in the east. This, too, soon grew wan. The gray of dawn was at hand. Dismounting in the lee of a low ledge, where brush grew thick and the horses could be tied, Pilchuck left two men on guard and led the others on foot behind the noiseless Mexican.

In less than a quarter of a mile the Mexican whispered something and slipped to his hands and knees. Pilchuck and his followers, two and three abreast, kept close to his heels. The fact that the Mexican crept on very slowly and made absolutely no sound had the effect of constraining those behind him to proceed as stealthily. This wrought upon the nerves of the men.

Tom Doan had never experienced such suspense. Just ahead of him lay the unknown ground never seen by him or any of his white comrades, and it held, no one knew how close, a peril soon to be encountered.

The dawn was growing lighter and rows of rocks ahead could be distinguished. The ground began to slope. Beyond what seemed a gray space, probably a canyon, rose a dim vague bulk, uneven and woolly. Soon it showed to be canyon slope with brush on the rim.

Tom, finding that he often rustled the weeds or scraped on the hard ground, devoted himself to using his eyes as well as muscles to help him crawl silently. Thus it was that he did not look up until Pilchuck's low "Hist!" halted everybody.

Then Tom saw with starting eyes a deep bend in a wonderful gully where on a green level of some acres in extent were a large number of Indian tepees. A stream wound through the middle of this oval and its low rush and gurgle were the only sounds to accentuate the quiet of the morning. Hundreds of Indian ponies were grazing, standing, or lying down all over this meadow-like level. Not an Indian appeared in sight. But as the light was still gray and dim there could not be any certainty as to that.

Pilchuck raised himself to peer over a rock, and he studied the lay of the encampment, the narrow gateways of canyon above and below, and the approaches from the slope on his side. Then he slipped back to face the line of crouching men.

"By holdin' high we're in range right here," he whispered, tensely. "Starwell, take ten men an' crawl back a little, then round an' down to a point even with where this canyon narrows below. Harkaway, you take ten men an' go above, an' slip down the same way. Go slow. Don't make noise. Don't stand up. We can then see each other's positions an' command all but the far side of this canyon. That's a big camp—there's two hundred Indians, more if they have their families. An' I reckon they have. Now Indians always fight harder under such conditions. We're in for a hell of a fight. But don't intentionally shoot squaws an' kids. That's all."

With only the slightest rustle and scrape, and deep intake of breath, the two detachments under Starwell and Harkaway crept back among the stones out of sight. Then absolute silence once more reigned.

Pilchuck's men lay flat, some of them, more favorably located than others, peering from behind stones. No one spoke. They all waited. Meanwhile the gray dawn broadened to daylight.

"Ugh!" grunted Bear Claws, deep in his throat. His sinewy hand gripped Tom's shoulder.

Tom raised his head a couple of inches and he espied a tall Indian standing before a tepee, facing the east, where faint streaks of pink and rose heralded the sunrise. Tom felt a violent start jerk over his whole body. It was a hot burst of blood. This very Comanche might have been one of the murderers of Hudnall or, just as much a possibility, one of the despoilers of Jett's camp, from which Milly Fayre had disappeared. That terrible loss seemed to Tom far back in the past, lengthened, changed by suffering. It was nothing less than hate with which Tom watched that statuesque Indian.

Presently another Indian brave appeared, and another, then several squaws, and in a comparatively short time the camp became active. Columns of blue smoke arose lazily on the still air. The ponies began to move about.

What an endless period it seemed to Tom before Harkaway and Starwell got into their positions! Tom wondered if Pilchuck would wait much longer. His blood beat thick at his temples; his throat was dry; and a dimness of eye bothered him every few seconds.

"Ugh!" exclaimed Bear Claws, and this time he touched Pilchuck, directing him toward a certain point in the encampment.

At that juncture there pealed out a singularly penetrating yell, most startling in its suddenness and nerve-racking with its terrible long-drawn and sustained wildness.

"Comanche war-cry!" hissed Pilchuck. "Some buck has glimpsed our men below. Wait! We want the shootin' to begin below an' above. Then mebbe the Indians will run this way."

Scarcely had the scout ceased his rapid whisper when a Sharps rifle awoke the sleeping echoes. It came from Starwell's detachment below.

In an instant the Indian camp became a scene of wild rush and shrill cry, above which pealed sharp quick shouts—the voice of authority. A heavy volley from Starwell's men was signal for Harkaway's to open up. The puffs of white smoke over the stone betrayed the whereabouts of both detachments. A rattle of Winchesters from the camp told how speedily many of the Indians had gotten into action.

Despite Pilchuck's orders, some of his men began to fire.

"All right, if you can't wait. But shoot high," he shouted.

Twenty Creedmoors thundered in unison from that rocky slope. It seemed to Tom then that hell had indeed broken loose. He had aimed and shot at a running brave. What strange fierceness he felt! His hands shook to spoil his aim and his face streamed with cold sweat. All the men were loading and firing, and he was in the midst of a cracking din. Yet above it all rose a weird piercing sound—the war-cry of the Comanches. Tom thought, as he shuddered under it, that he understood now why hunters had talked of this most hideous and infamous of all Indian yells.

In a few moments the first blending roar of guns and yells broke, and there intervened a less consistent din. Pandemonium reigned down in that encampment, yet there must have been many crafty Indians. Already the front line of tepees was in flames, sending up streaks of smoke, behind which the women and children were dimly seen running for the opposite slope. A number of frightened mustangs were racing with flying manes and tails, up and down the canyon, but the majority appeared to be under control of the Indians and coralled at the widest point. Soon many braves, women and children, dragging packs and horses, were seen through or round the smoke on the opposite slope.

The Comanche braves below then lived up to their reputation as the most daring and wonderful horsemen of the plains. To draw the fire of the hunters numbers of them, half naked demons, yelling, with rifles in hand, rode their mustangs bareback, with magnificent affront and tremendous speed, straight at the gateway of the canyon. They ran a gauntlet of leaden hail.

Tom saw braves pitch headlong to the earth. He saw mustangs plunge and throw their riders far. And he also saw Indians ride fleet as the storm winds under the volleys from the slope, to escape down the canyon.

No sooner had one bunch of rider braves attempted this than another drove their mustangs pell-mell at the openings. They favored the lower gate, beneath Starwell's detachment, being quick to catch some little advantage there. The foremost of four Indians, a lean wild brave, magnificently mounted, made such a wonderful target with his defiance and horsemanship that he drew practically all the fire. He rode to his death, but his three companions flashed through the gateway in safety.

"Hold men! Hold!" yelled Pilchuck, suddenly at this juncture. "Load up an' wait. We're in for a charge or a trick."

Tom Doan drew a deep breath, as if he were stifling. His sweaty powder-begrimed hands fumbled at the hot breech of his Creedmoor. How many times had he fired? He did not know, nor could he tell whether or not he had shot an Indian.

Following with sharp gaze where the scout pointed, Tom saw through smoke and heat the little puffs of white, all along behind the burning front line of tepees. There were many braves lying flat, behind stones, trees, camp duffle, everything that would hide a man. Bullets whistled over Tom's head and spanged from the rocks on each side of him.

"Watch that bunch of horses!" called Pilchuck, warningly. "There's fifty if there's one. Reckon we've bit off more'n we can chew."

Dimly through the now thinning smoke Tom could see the bunch of riders designated by Pilchuck. They were planning some audacious break like that of the braves who had sacrificed themselves to help their families escape. This would be different, manifestly, for all the women and children, and the young braves with them, had disappeared over the far slope. It was war now.

"Jude, they're too smart to charge us," said a grizzled old hunter. "I'll swear thet bunch is aimin' to make a break to git by an' above us."

"Wal, if they do we'll be in a hell of a pickle," replied the scout. "I'll ask Bear Claws what he makes of it."

The Osage readily replied, "No weyno," which Tom interpreted as being anything but good for the hunters.

The Mexican urged Pilchuck to work back to higher ground, but the scout grimly shook his head.

Suddenly with remarkable swiftness the compact bunch of Indian horsemen disintegrated, and seemed to spill both to right and left.

"What the hell!" muttered Pilchuck.

One line of Comanche riders swerved below the camp, the other above, and they rode strung out in single file, going in opposite directions. Starwell and Harkaway reserved their fire, expecting some trick. When halfway to each gate the leader of each string wheeled at right angles to head straight for the slope.

"By God! they're goin' between us!" ejaculated Pilchuck. "Men, we've shore got to stick now an' fight for our lives."

At two hundred yards these incomparable riders were as hard to hit with bullets as birds on the wing. Starwell's detachment began to shoot and Harkaway's followed suit. Their guns were drowned in the dreadful war-cry of the Comanches. It seemed wilder, more piercing now, closer, a united sound, filling the ears, horrid yet not discordant, full of death, but for all that a magnificent blending of human voices. It was the cry of a wild tribe for life.

It lifted Tom's hair stiff on his head. He watched with staring eyes. How those mustangs leaped! They crossed the open level below, the danger zone of leaden hail, without a break in their speeding line. When they reached the base of the slope they were perked to their haunches, and in a flash each one was riderless. The Comanches had taken to the rocks.

"Ahuh! I reckoned so," growled Pilchuck. "Pretty slick, if I do say it. Men, we've got crawlin' snakes to deal with now. You shore have to look sharp."

This sudden maneuver had the same effect upon the Starwell and Harkaway detachments as it had on Pilchuck's. It almost turned the tables on the white men. How grave it was perhaps only the experienced plainsmen realized. They all reserved their fire, manifestly directing attention to this new and hidden peril. The Comanches left in camp, a considerable number, redoubled their shots.

"Men, reckon it ain't time yet to say every one for himself," declared Pilchuck. "But we've shore got to crawl up to the level. Spread out, an' crawl flat on your bellies, an' keep rocks behind you."

Thus began a retreat, fraught with great risk. Bullets from the Winchesters spanged off the rocks, puffing white powder dust into the air. And these bullets came from the rear. The Comanches on each side had vanished like lizards into the maze of bowlders. But every hunter realized these Indians were creeping, crawling, worming their way to places of advantage, keeping out of sight with the cunning natural to them.

Tom essayed to keep up with Bear Claws, but this was impossible by crawling. The Osage wriggled like a snake. Pilchuck, too, covered ground remarkably for a large man. Others crawled fast or slowly, according to their abilities. Thus the detachment, which had heretofore kept together, gradually disintegrated.

It had been a short two hundred yards from the top of this slope to the position the hunters had abandoned. Crawling back seemed interminable and insurmountable to Tom. Yet he saw how imperative it was to get there.

Some one was close behind Tom, crawling laboriously, panting heavily. It was

Ory Tacks. As he was fat and round, the exertion was almost beyond his endurance and the risks were great. Tom had himself to think of, yet he wondered if he should not help Ory. Roberts crawled a little to Tom's left. He too was slow. An old white-haired buffalo-hunter named Calkins had taken Pilchuck's place on Tom's right. The others were above, fast wriggling out of sight.

A bullet zipped off a stone close to Tom and sang into the air. It had come from another direction. Another bullet, striking in front of him, scattered dust and gravel in his face. Then bullets hissed low down, just over the rocks. The Comanches were not yet above the hunters. Calkins called low for those back of him to hurry, that the word had been passed back from Pilchuck.

Tom was crawling as flat as a flounder, dragging a heavy gun. He could not make faster time. He was burning with sweat, yet cold as ice, and the crack of Winchesters had the discordance of a nightmare.

"Doan," called Roberts, sharply. "The fellow behind you's been hit."

Tom peered around. Ory Tacks lay with face down. His fat body was quivering.

"Ory! Ory! Are you hit?" flashed Tom.

"I should smile," he groaned, lifting a pale face. His old slouch hat was still in place and a tuft of tow-colored hair stuck out through a hole. "Never mind—me."

"Roberts, come help me," called Tom, and began to back down toward Ory. Roberts did likewise, and they both reached the young man about the same time.

"Much obliged to see you," said Ory, gratefully, as they took hold of his arms, one on each side.

Up to that moment Tom had been mostly stultified by emotion, utterly new to him. It had been close to panic, for he had found himself hard put to it to keep from leaping up to run. But something in connection with Ory's misfortune strung Tom suddenly and acutely to another mood. Grim realization and anger drove away his fear.

"Drag him; he cain't help himself," panted Roberts.

Then began what Tom felt to be the most heart-breaking labor imaginable. They had to crawl and drag the wounded Ory up hill. Tom locked his left arm under Ory's, and dragging his rifle in his right hand he jerked and hunched himself along. Bullets now began to whistle and patter from the other side, signifying that the Comanches to the right had located the crawling hunters. Suddenly above Tom boomed a heavy Creedmoor—then two booms followed in succession.

"Good!—It was—aboot time," panted Roberts.

Tom felt the coldness leave his marrow for good. It was fight now. Pilchuck, Bear Claws, the Mexican, and some of the old plainsmen had reached the top of the slope and had opened on the Comanches. This spurred him, if not to greater effort, which was impossible, at least to dogged and unquenchable endurance. Roberts whistled through his nose; his lean face was bathed with sweat. Ory Tacks struggled bravely to help himself along, though it was plain his agony was tremendous.

The slope grew less steep and more thickly strewn with large rocks. Tom heard no more bullets whiz up from direction of the encampment. They came from both sides, and the reports of Winchesters, sharp and rattling above the Creedmoors, covered a wide half circle. Farther away the guns of the Starwell and Harkaway forces rang out steadily, if not often. It had become a hot battle and the men were no longer shooting at puffs of white smoke.

Not a moment too soon did Tom and Roberts drag Tacks over the top of the slope into a zone of large bowlders from behind which Pilchuck and his men were fighting. For almost at the last instant Tom heard a dull spat of lead striking flesh.

Roberts' left arm, on which he was hunching himself along, crumpled under him, and he dropped flat.

"They—busted—me," he declared, huskily, then let go of Tacks, and floundered behind a rock.

Tom by superhuman exertion dragged Ory farther on, behind a long low ledge, from which a hunter was shooting. Then Tom collapsed. But as he sank flat he heard the boy's grateful, "Much obliged, Tom." For a few moments then Tom was deaf and blind to the battle. There was a bursting riot within his breast, an overtaxed heart fluttering to recover. It seemed long that he lay prostrate, utterly unable to lift face or hand. But gradually that passed. Pilchuck crawled close, smelling of sweat, dust, and powder.

"Tom, are you hurt?" he queried, shaking him.

"No—only—all in," whispered Tom, huskily, between pants. "We had to—drag Ory—up here. He's hit; so's Roberts."

"I'll take a look at them," said the scout. "We're shore in better position here. Reckon we can hold the red devils off. Lucky Starwell an' Harkaway are behind them, on both sides. We're in for a siege. . . . Bullets flyin' from east an' west. Peep out mighty careful an' look for an Indian. Don't shoot at smoke."

Tom crawled a little to the left and cautiously took up a position where he could peer from behind the long flat rock. He could see nothing move. An uneven field of bowlders, large and small, stretched away, with narrow aisles of gray grass and ground between. The firing had diminished greatly. Both sides were conserving ammunition. Not for several moments did Tom espy a puff of white smoke, and that came from a heavy Creedmoor, four hundred yards or more away, from a point above where Starwell's men had guarded the gateway of the canyon.

Meanwhile as he watched for something to shoot at he could hear Pilchuck working over the wounded men, and ascertained that Roberts had been shot through the arm, not, however, to break the bones, and Ory Tacks had a broken hip. Tom realized the gravity of such a wound, out there in the wilderness.

"I'd be much obliged for a drink of water," was all Tom heard Ory say.

Pilchuck crawled away and did not return. Ory Tacks and Roberts lay at the base of the low ledge, out of range of bullets for the present. But they lay in the sun and already the sun was hot. The scout had chosen a small oval space irregularly surrounded by bowlders and outcroppings of rough ledges. By twisting his head Tom could espy eight or ten of Pilchuck's force, some facing east behind their fortifications, others west. Tom heard both profanity and loquacious humor. The Mexican and the Osage were not in sight.

Then Tom peeped out from behind his own covert. This time his quick eye caught a glimpse of something moving, like a rabbit slipping into brush. Above that place then slid out a red streak and a thin blue-white cloud of smoke. Sputt! A bullet hit the corner of his rock and whined away. Tom dodged back, suddenly aghast, and hot with anger. A sharp-eyed Indian had seen him. Tom wormed his way around back of the long rock to the other end. Behind the next rock lay the old white-haired hunter, bare-headed, with sweat and tobacco stains upon his grizzled face.

"Take it easy an' slow," he advised Tom, complacently. "Comanches can't stand a long fight. They're riders, an' all we need is patience. On the ground we can lick hell out of them."

The old plainsman's nonchalance was incredible, yet vastly helpful to Tom. He put a hard curb on his impetuosity, and forced himself to wait and think carefully of every action before he undertook it. Therefore he found a position where he could command a certain limited field of rocks without risk to himself. It was like peeping through a knot hole too small for any enemy to see at a distance. From this vantage point Tom caught fleeting glimpses and flashes of color, gray and bronze, once a speck of red. But these vanished before he could bring his rifle into play.

"If you see suthin' move shoot quick as lightnin'," said the old plainsman. "It might be a gopher or a cottontail, but take no chances. It's likely to be a two-legged varmint."

Intense concentration, and a spirit evolving from the hour, enabled Tom to make considerable progress toward the plainsman's idea of fighting Comanches. Tom fired again and again, at the flit of a bird across a narrow space, at the flash of a gun, a gleam of a feather. But he could never see whether or not he hit an Indian. Strange to note, however, was the fact that these fleeting movements of something were never repeated in the same place. Concentration brought to Tom the certainty that he was seeing a faint glimpse now and then of these elusive Comanches. This, with the crack of Winchesters and hum of bullets, in time bred in him some semblance of the spirit of the old plainsman. It was indeed a fight. He had his part to perform. Life was here, and an inch away sped death. Grim, terrible, but exalting, and strangely memorable of a vague past! Tom Doan realized the inheritance he had in common with men, white or red.

The hours passed swiftly for the fighters. Another wounded man joined Roberts and Ory Tacks, and the ordeal must have been frightful for them. Tom forgot them; so did all the defenders of that position. The glaring sun poured down its heat. Stones and guns were so hot they burned. No breeze stirred. And the fight went on, favorable for the buffalo-hunters because of their fortifications, unfavorable in regard to time. They were all parching for thirst. By chance or blunder the canteens had been left on the saddles and water had come to be almost as precious as powder. The old plainsman cursed the Staked Plain. Tom's mouth appeared full of cotton paste. He had kept pebbles in his mouth till he was sick of them.

Noon went by. Afternoon came. The sun, hotter than ever, began to slope to the west. And the fight went on, narrowing down as to distance, intensifying as to spirit, magnifying peril to both sides. The Creedmoors from the Starwell and Harkaway forces kept up the bulk of the shooting. They were directing most of their fire down into the encampment, no doubt to keep the Comanches there from joining their comrades on the slope. Mustangs showed on the farther points, and evidently had strayed.

Presently Pilchuck came crawling on hands and knees, without his rifle or coat. A bloody patch showed on his shoulder.

"Tom, reckon I got punctured a little," he said. "It ain't bad, but it's bleedin' like hell. Tear my shirt sleeve off an' tie it round under my arm over my shoulder tight."

An ugly bullet hole showed angrily in the upper part of the scout's shoulder, apparently just through the flesh.

"Notice that bullet come from behind," said Pilchuck. "There shore was a mean redskin on your side. He hit two of us before I plugged him. There—good. . . . Now how's the rest of your hospital?"

"I don't know. Afraid I forgot," replied Tom, aghast.

"Wal, I'll see."

He crawled over to the wounded man and spoke. Tom heard Roberts answer, but Ory Tacks was silent. That disturbed Tom. Then the scout came back to him.

"Roberts's sufferin' some, but he's O.K. The young fellar, though, is dyin', I'm afraid. Shot in the groin. Mebbe—"

"Pilchuck! . . . Ory didn't seem bad hurt—"

"Wal, he is, an' if we don't get some water he'll go," declared the scout, emphatically. "Fact is, we're all bad off for water. It's shore hot. What a dumbhead I was to forget the canteens!"

"I'll go after them," returned Tom, like a flash.

"It's not a bad idee," said Pilchuck, after a moment's reflection. "Reckon it'd be no riskier than stayin' here."

"Direct me. Where'd you leave the horses?"

The scout faced south, at right angles with the cross-fire from the Comanches, and presently extended his long arm.

"See that low bluff—not far—the last one reachin' down into this basin. It's behind there. You can't miss it. Lucky the rocks from here on are thick as cabbages."

"I can make it," declared Tom, doggedly. "But to get back! That stumps me."

"Easy. You've got to go slow, pickin' the best cover. Just lay a line of little stones as you crawl along. Reckon the Comanches are all on these two sides of us, but there *might* be some tryin' to surround us."

"Anything more?" queried Tom, briefly.

The scout apparently had no thought of the tremendousness of this enterprise to Tom. It was as if he had naturally expected of Tom what he would do himself if he had not been partially incapacitated. Tom realized he had never in his life received such a compliment. It swelled his heart. He felt light, hard, tense, vibrating to a strange excitation.

"Wal, I can't think of anythin'," replied the scout. "Comin' back be slower'n molasses, an' get the drift of the fight. We're holdin' these redskins off. But I reckon Starwell an' Harkaway have been doin' more. If I don't miss my guess they've spilled blood down in the canyon. Comanches are great on horseback, but they can't stick out a fight like this. If they rush us we're goners. If they don't they'll quit before sunset."

CHAPTER THIRTEEN

Milly Fayre rode out of Sprague's Post on the front of a freighter's wagon, sitting between Jett and his wife. The rest of Jett's outfit followed close behind, Follonsbee and Pruitt in the second wagon, and Catlee driving the last.

For as long as Milly could see the Hudnalls she waved her red scarf in farewell. Then when her friends passed out of sight, Milly turned slowly to face the boundless prairie, barren of life, suddenly fearful in its meaning, and she sank down, stricken in heart. What she had dreaded was now an actuality. The courage that had inspired her when she wrote the letter to Tom Doan, leaving it with Mrs. Hudnall, was a courage inspired by love, not by hope. So it seemed now.

"Milly, you ain't actin' much like a boy, spite them boy's clothes," said Jett, with attempt at levity. "Pile over in the back of the wagon an' lay down."

Kindness from Jett was astounding, and was gratefully received by Milly. Doing as she was bidden, she found a comfortable place on the unrolled packs of bedding, with her head in a shade of the wagon seat. It developed then that Jett's apparent kindness had been only a ruse to get her away so he could converse with his wife in low, earnest tones. Milly might have heard all or part of that conversation, but she was not interested and did not listen.

Dejectedly she lay there while the steady trot of the horses carried her back toward the distant buffalo range. To be torn from her kind and loving friends at the post and drawn back into the raw hard life led by her stepfather was a bitter and sickening blow. Her sufferings were acute; and as she had become used to hope and happiness she was now ill fitted to cope with misery and dread. She did not think of the future or plan to meet it; she lived in the present and felt the encroaching of an old morbid and fatalistic mood, long a stranger to her.

The hours passed, and Jett's deep, low voice appeared never to rest or cease. He did not make a noon stop, as was customary among the buffalo-hunters. And he drove until sunset.

"Forty miles, bedam!" he said, with satisfaction, as he threw the reins.

Whether Milly would have it so or not, she dropped at once back into the old camp life, with its tasks. How well she remembered! The smoke of the camp fire made her eyes smart and brought tingling as well as hateful memories.

The other wagons drove up rather late, and once more Milly found herself under the hawk eyes of Follonsbee and the half-veiled hidden look of the crooked-faced Pruitt. Her masculine garb, emphasizing her shapely slenderness, manifestly drew the gaze of these men. They seemed fascinated by it, as if they both had discovered something. Neither of them spoke to her. Catlee, however, gave her a kindly nod. He seemed more plodding in mind than she remembered him.

One by one the old associations returned to her, and presently her fleeting happiness with the Hudnalls had the remoteness and unreality of a dream and she was again Jett's stepdaughter, quick to start at his harsh voice. Was that harshness the same? She seemed to have a vague impression of a difference in his voice, in him, in all of his outfit, in the atmosphere around them.

A stopping place had been chosen at one of the stream crossings where hundreds of buffalo-hunters had camped that year, a fact Jett growled about, complaining of the lack of grass and wood. Water was plentiful, and it was cold, a welcome circumstance to the travelers. Jett had an inordinate thirst, probably owing to his addiction to rum at Sprague's.

"Fetch some more drinkin' water," he ordered Milly.

She took the pail and went down the bank under the big, rustling, green cottonwoods. Catlee was at the stream, watering the horses.

"I seen you comin', an' I says who's that boy?" he said, with a grin. "I forgot."

"I forgot, too," she replied, dubiously. "I don't like these—these pants. But I've made a discovery, Catlee. I'm more comfortable round camp."

"Don't wonder. You used to drag your skirts round. . . . Gimme your bucket. I'll fill it where the water's clear."

He waded in beyond where the horses were drinking and dipped the pail. "Nothin' like good cold water after a day's hot ride."

"Jett drank nearly all I got before and sent me for more."

"He's burnin' up inside with red liquor," returned Catlee, bluntly.

Milly did not have any reply to make to that, but she thanked Catlee, and taking the pail she poured out a little water, so she would not spill it as she walked.

"Milly, I'm sorry you had to come back with Jett," said Catlee.

She paused, turning to look at him, surprised at his tone. His bronze face lacked the heat, the dissolute shades common to Jett and the other men. Milly remembered then that Catlee in her opinion had not seemed like the rest of Jett's outfit.

"Sorry? Why?" she asked.

"I know Sprague. He's from Missouri. He told me about you, an' your friend Tom Doan."

"Sprague told you—about—about Tom!" faltered Milly, suddenly blushing. "Why, who told him?"

"Mrs. Hudnall, he said. Sprague took interest in you, it 'pears. An' his wife is thick with the Hudnall women. Anyway, he was sorry Jett took you away—an' so'm I."

Milly's confusion and pain at the mention of Tom did not quite render her blind to this man's sympathy. She forced away the wave of emotion. Her mind quickened to the actuality of her being once more in Jett's power and that she had only her wits and courage to rely upon. This hard-faced, apparently dull and somber man might befriend her. Milly suddenly conceived the inspiration to win him to her cause.

"So am I sorry, Catlee," she said sadly, and her quick tears were genuine. Indeed, they had started to flow at mention of Tom's name. "I—I'm engaged to Tom Doan. . . . I was—so—so happy. And I'd never had—any happy times before. . . . Now I've been dragged away. Jett's my stepfather. I'm not of age. I had to come. . . . And I'm terribly afraid of him."

"I reckon," rejoined Catlee, darkly, "you've reason to be. He an' the woman quarreled at Sprague's. He wanted to leave her behind. For that matter, the four of them drank a good deal, an' fought over the hide money."

"For pity's sake, be my friend!" appealed Milly.

The man stared at her, as if uncomprehending, yet somehow stirred.

"Catlee," she said, seeing her advantage and stepping back to lay a hand softly on his arm, "did you ever have a sister or a sweetheart?"

"I reckon not or I'd been another kind of man," he returned, with something of pathos.

"But you're not bad," she went on, swiftly.

"Me not bad! Child, you're crazy! I never was anythin' else. An' now I'm a hide thief."

"Oh, it's true, then? Jett is a hide thief. I knew something was terribly wrong."

"Girl, don't you tell Jett I said that," replied Catlee, almost harshly.

"No, I won't. I promise. You can trust me," she returned, hurriedly. "And I could trust you. I don't think you're really bad. Jett has led you into this. He's bad. I hate him."

"Yes, Jett's bad all right, an' he means bad by you. I reckon I thought you knowed an' didn't care."

"Care! If he harms me I'll kill him and myself," she whispered, passionately.

The man seemed to be confronted with something new in his experience, and it was dissipating a dull apathy to all that concerned others.

"So that's how a good girl feels!" he muttered.

"Yes. And I ask you—beg you to be a man—a friend—"

"There comes Pruitt," interrupted Catlee, turning to his horses. "Don't let him or any of them see you talkin' to me."

Milly bent over the heavy bucket and, avoiding the dust raised by Pruitt with his horses, she hurried back to camp. Her return manifestly checked hard words between Jett and his wife. Milly took up her tasks where they had been interrupted, but with this difference, that she had become alive to the situation among these hide thieves. Jett's status had been defined, and the woman was no doubt culpable with him. Catlee's blunt corroboration of Milly's fears had awakened her spirit; and the possibility of winning this hardened man to help her in her extremity had inspired courage and resolve. All in a flash, then, it seemed she was the girl who had written that brave letter to Tom Doan.

Supper was cooked and eaten. The men, except Catlee, were not hungry as usual, and appeared to be wearing off the effects of hard drinking. They spoke but seldom, and then only to ask for something out of reach on the spread canvas. Darkness settled down while Milly dried the pans and cups. Catlee came up with a huge armload of wood, which he dropped with a crash, a little too near Pruitt to suit his irascible mood.

"Say, you Missouri hay seed, can't you see my feet?" he demanded.

"I could if I'd looked. They're big enough," retorted Catlee. "I ain't wonderin' you have such a care of them."

"Ain't you? Shore I'd like to know why?" queried Pruitt.

"I reckon what little brains you've got are in them."

"You damn Yank!" ejaculated the little rebel, as amazed as enraged. "I've shot men for less'n thet."

"Reckon you have," rejoined Catlee with slow, cool sarcasm. "But in the back! . . . An' I'm lookin' at you."

There was not the slightest doubt of Catlee's emergence from the character of a stolid dull teamster into something incalculably otherwise. Jett rolled out his loud, harsh laughter. It amused him, this revolt of the stupid farmer. Likewise it showed his subtle change. Was there reason for him to invite antagonism among his men? Assuredly there was strong antagonism toward him. Follonsbee gazed in genuine amaze at Catlee, and slowly nodded his lean buzzardlike head, as if he had before in his life seen queer things in men. As for the fiery little rebel, he was instantly transformed, in his attitude toward Catlee, from a man who had felt a raw irritation, to one who hated and who doubted. However Follonsbee read the erstwhile Missouri farmer, Pruitt got only so far as a cold and waking doubt. Enmity was thus established and it seemed to be Pruitt's natural mental attitude, and to suit Catlee better than friendliness.

Milly heard and saw this byplay from the shadow beyond the camp-fire circle. If that were Catlee's answer to her appeal, it was a change, sudden and bewildering. The thrill she sustained was more like a shudder. In that moment she sensed a far-reaching influence, a something which had to do with future events. Catlee stalked off into the gloom of the cottonwood, where he had made his bed.

"Rand, are you sure thet feller is what you said he was—a Missouri farm hand, tired of workin' for nothin'?" demanded Follonsbee.

"Hank, I ain't sure of anythin' an' I don't give a whoop," replied the leader.

"Thet's natural, for you," said the other, with sarcasm. "You don't know the West as I know it. Catlee struck me queer. . . . When he called Pruitt, so cool-like, I had come to mind men of the Cole Younger stripe. If so—"

"Aw, it's nothin'," cut in Pruitt. "Jett spoke my sentiments aboot our Yankee pard. It r'ils me to think of him gettin' a share of our hide money."

Jett coughed, an unusual thing for him to do. "Who said Catlee got a share?" he queried, gruffly.

Follonsbee lifted his lean head to peer at the leader. Pruitt, who was sitting back to a stump, his distorted face gleaming red in the camp-fire light, moved slowly forward to gaze in turn. Both men were silent; both of them questioned with their whole bodies. But Jett had no answer. He calmly lit his pipe and flipped the match into the fire.

"Shore, now I tax myself, I cain't remember thet anybody said Catlee got a share," replied Pruitt, with deliberation. "But I thought he did. An' I know Hank thought so."

"I'd have gambled on it," said Follonsbee.

"Catlee gets wages, that's all," asserted the leader.

"Ahuh! . . . An' who gets *his* share of the hide money?" demanded Pruitt.

"I do," rejoined Jett, shortly.

"Jett, I'm tellin' you that's in line with your holdin' out money for supplies at Sprague," said Follonsbee, earnestly. "You was to furnish outfit, grub, everythin', an' share even with all of us, includin' your woman. You got your share, an' her share, an' now Catlee's share."

"I'm willin' to argue it with you, but not on an equal divvy basis."

There followed a long silence. The men smoked. The fire burned down, so that their faces were but pale gleams. Milly sought her bed, which she had made in the wagon. Jett had sacrificed tents to make room for equal weight of buffalo hides. He had unrolled his blankets under the wagon, where the sullen woman had repaired soon after dark. Milly took off her boy's shoes and folded the coat for a pillow, then slipping under the blankets she stretched out, glad for the relief.

How different, lying out under the open starry sky! She liked it. The immense blue dome was alight, mysterious, beautiful, comforting. Milly said her short prayer, childish and loyal, somehow more than ever helpful on this eventful night. Often, before she had met the Hudnalls and Tom Doan, she had omitted that little prayer, but never since she had learned from them the meaning of friendship and love.

The night was warm; the leaves of the cottonwoods near by rustled softly in the breeze; insects were chirping and a night bird was uttering plaintive notes.

Jett, Follonsbee, and Pruitt remained around the camp fire, quarreling in low voices; and that sound was the last Milly heard as slumber claimed her.

Milly's eyes opened to the bright light of day, and pale-blue sky seemed canopied over her. Not the canvas roof of her tent! Where was she? The smell of cottonwood smoke brought her with surging shock to realization. Then Jett's harsh voice, that had always made her shrink with fear, sent a creeping fire along her veins.

She lay a moment longer, calling to the spirit that had awakened last night; and it augmented while she seemed to grow strangely older. She would endure; she would fight; she would think. So that when she presented herself at the camp fire she was outwardly a quiet, obedient, impassive girl, inwardly a cunning, daring woman.

Not half a dozen words were spoken around the breakfast canvas. Jett rushed the tasks. Sunrise shone on the three wagons moving south at a brisk trot.

Milly had asked Catlee to fix her a comfortable place in the back of Jett's wagon. He had done so, adding of his own accord an improvised sun shade of canvas. She had watched him from the wagon seat, hoping he would speak to her or look at her in a way that would confirm her hopes. But the teamster was silent and kept his head lowered. Nevertheless, Milly did not regard his taciturnity as unfavorable to her. There had been about Catlee, last night when he had muttered: "So that's how a good girl feels," a something which spoke to Milly's intuition. She could not prove anything. But she felt. This man would befriend her. A subtle unconscious influence was working on his mind. It was her presence, her plight, her appeal.

Milly thought of a thousand plans to escape, to get word to Doan, to acquaint buffalo-hunters with the fact of her being practically a prisoner, to betray that Jett was a hide thief. Nothing definitely clear and satisfactory occurred to her. But the fact of her new knowledge of Jett stood out tremendously. It was an infallible weapon to employ, if the right opportunity presented. But a futile attempt at that would result fatally for her. Jett would most surely kill her.

It seemed to Milly as she revolved in mind plan after plan that the wisest thing to do would be to play submissive slave to Jett until he reached the end of the drive south; and there to persuade Catlee to take her at once to Hudnall's camp, where she would betray Jett. If Catlee would not help her, then she must go alone, or, failing that, wait for Tom Doan to find her.

Before the morning was far advanced Jett gave wide berth to an oncoming outfit. Milly was not aware of this until the unusual jolting caused her to rise to her knees and look out. Jett had driven off the main road, taking a low place, where other drivers had made short cuts. Four freight wagons, heavily laden with hides, were passing at some distance to the right. The foremost team of horses was white—Milly thought she recognized it as Hudnall's. Her heart rushed to her lips. But she had seen many white teams, and all of them had affected her that way. If she leaped out and ran to find she was mistaken, she would lose every chance she had. Besides, as she gazed, she imagined she was wrong. So with a deep sigh she dropped back to her seat.

The hours passed quickly. Milly pondered until she was weary, then fell asleep, and did not awaken until another camp was reached. And the first words she heard were Jett's speaking to Follonsbee as he drove up abreast the leader, "Wasn't that Hudnall's outfit we passed?"

"First two teams was," replied Follonsbee. "That young skinner of Hudnall's was leadin', an' that ugly-face cuss was drivin' the second team. I didn't know the other outfits."

Milly had to bite her lips to repress a scream. Jett was clamboring down from the seat above. The woman, grumbling under her breath, threw out the canvas bags of utensils, that clinked on the ground. Milly hid her face as Mrs. Jett descended from the seat. Then, for a moment, she shook like a leaf with the violence of her emotions. So near Tom! Not to see his face! It was heartrending. She lay prostrate, with her mind in a whirl. Of the many thoughts one returned—that Tom would reach Sprague's Post next day and get her letter. That thought had strength to impart. He would lose no time following, perhaps would catch up with Jett before he got to the Pease River, and if not then, soon afterward. This thought sustained her in a trying moment.

The weakness passed, leaving her somewhat thick witted, so that as she climbed out of the wagon she nearly fell, and later her clumsiness at her assigned camp tasks fetched a reprimand from Mrs. Jett. Soon the men were back from attending to the horses, and this evening they were hungry. Meeting outcoming freighters with buffalo hides had for the moment turned the minds of Jett and his two lieutenants from their differences.

"How many hides in them outfits?" queried Jett.

"It weren't a big haul," replied Follonsbee.

"Shore was big enough to make us turn off the road," said Pruitt, meaningly.

Jett glared at him. Then Catlee drawled: "Funny they didn't see us. But we went down on our side some. That first driver was Hudnall's man, Tom Doan."

"Ahuh! Well, suppose it was?" returned Jett, nonplussed at this remark from the habitually unobserving Catlee.

"Nothin'. I just recognized him," replied Catlee, casually, as he lowered his eyes.

When he raised them, a moment later, to look across the canvas supper cloth at Milly, she saw them as never before, sharp as a dagger, with a single bright gleam. He wanted her to know that he had seen Tom Doan. Milly dropped her own gaze and she spilled a little of her coffee. She dared not trust her flashing interpretation of this man's glance. It seemed like a gleam of lightning from what had hitherto been dead ashes. Thereafter he paid no attention to her, nor to any of the others; and upon finishing the meal and finishing his chore of cutting firewood, he vanished.

Jett and his two disgruntled men took up their quarrel and spent a long, noisy, angry hour round the camp fire.

The next day came and passed, with no difference for Milly except that Catlee now avoided her, never seemed to notice her; and that she hung out her red scarf, with a hopeful thrill in its significance. Then one by one the days rolled by, under the wheels of the wagons.

Seven days, and then the straggling lost bands of buffalo! The hot, drowsy summer air was tainted; the gently waving prairie bore heaps of bones; skulking coyotes sneaked back from the road. A thousand times Milly Fayre looked back down the endless road she had traveled. No wagon came in sight!

Noon of the ninth day brought Jett within sight of the prairie-wide herd of buffalo. He halted to point it out to his sullen unseeing men; and later he reined in again, this time to turn his ear to the hot stinking wind.

"Aha! Listen," he called back to Follonsbee.

Milly heard the boom-boom-boom-boom of guns, near and far, incessant and potent. Strangely, for once she was glad to hear them!

All that hot midday she reclined on the improvised seat in her wagon, holding her scarf to her nostrils and looking out occasionally at the sordid ugliness of abandoned camp sites. The buffalo-hunters had moved on up the river, that now showed its wandering line of green timber.

Milly took a last backward gaze down the prairie road just as Jett turned off to go into the woods. Far away Milly saw a dot on the horizon—a white and black dot. Maybe it was Tom Doan's horses and wagon! He could not be far behind. It was as well now, perhaps, that he had not caught up with Jett. The buffalo range had been reached; and it could not be long before her situation was changed.

Jett drove off the prairie, into the timber, along a well-defined shady road where many camps had been pitched, and then down into the brakes. Brutal and fearless driver that he was, he urged his horses right through the tangled undergrowth, that bent with the onslaught of the wagon, to spring back erect after it had passed. Follonsbee came crashing next. Jett drove down into the bottom lands, thick and hot and aromatic with its jungle of foliage. He must have had either wonderful judgment as to where it was possible for horses to go, or an uncanny luck. For he penetrated the heavily wooded brakes clear to a deep shining river.

Milly would not allow herself to be unduly distressed because Jett meant to hide his camp, for she knew that any one hunting wagon tracks and camps would surely not miss his. In a way Milly was glad of the shade, the murmur of the river, the songs of birds, the absence of the stench. A camp on the edge of the prairie, with the rotten carcasses of buffalo close at hand, the dust and heat, the flies and bugs, would be well-nigh unendurable.

Jett halted his team in a shady glade of cottonwoods just back from the river and Milly then discovered that this was the scene of Jett's previous encampment. His tents and fireplace, boxes and bales, evidently had not been molested during his absence.

"Turn horses loose an' unload the wagons," he ordered his men. "I'll take a look for my saddle horses."

"No fear of hosses leavin' grass an' water," rejoined Follonsbee. "But there might be hoss thieves on the range."

"Haw! Haw!" laughed Pruitt, in his mean way. "Shore you know these heah buff-hunters are all honest men."

Jett strode off into the green brakes. The men unloaded the wagons and set the boxes and bags of supplies under a cottonwood. Mrs. Jett opened a tent near the fireplace.

"Miss," said Catlee, "the canvas wagon cover you had before got ripped to pieces. There ain't any tent for you till that one's mended."

"Can't I stay in the wagon?" she asked.

"Don't see why not. We'll hardly be movin' or haulin' very soon."

It was late in the afternoon when the rays of the sun began to lose heat. Milly was sorely in need of a little freedom of limbs. She had been cramped and inactive so long. This camp was the most secluded Jett had ever chosen—far from the prairie, down in the brakes at the edge of the river, hidden by trees from the opposite densely foliaged bank. If it had not hinted of a sinister meaning and was not indeed a prison for Milly she could have reveled in it. If she had to spend much time there she would be grateful for its quiet, cleanliness, and beauty. She strolled along the green bank until Mrs. Jett curtly called her to help get supper.

About the time it was ready Jett returned, with muddy boots and clothes covered with burrs and bits of brush.

"Found all the horses except the bay mare," he announced. "An' to-morrow we can go back to work. I'm aimin' at hard work, men."

"Huh! I'd like to know what you call all we've done," returned Follonsbee.

"Wal, Jett, there shore won't be *any* work aboot heah till you settle up," added Pruitt, crisply.

Jett's huge frame jerked with the shock of surprise and fury he must have felt.

"So that's it?" he queried, thickly. "Waited till you got way down here!"

"We shore did, boss," returned Pruitt.

In sullen silence then Jett began and finished his supper. Plain it was he had received a hard, unexpected blow, that he seemed scarcely prepared to cope with. He had no further words with his men, but he drew his wife aside; and they were in earnest conversation when Milly fell asleep.

Next day brought forward a situation Milly had not calculated upon. Jett had no intercourse whatever with his men, and saddling his horse rode off alone. The woman sulked. Follonsbee and Pruitt, manifestly satisfied with their stand, played cards interminably, now and then halting to talk in low tones over something vital to them. Catlee rigged himself a crude fishing tackle and repaired to the river bank, where he found a shady seat within sight of the camp.

Milly was left to herself. Her first act, after the tasks of the morning were ended, was to hang up her red scarf in a conspicuous place. Then she had nothing to do but kill time. With the men in camp, this was not easy. Apparently she had liberty. No orders had been given her, but perhaps this was owing to the timid meekness she had pretended. She might have wandered away into the brakes or have trailed the wagon tracks up to the prairie. But she could not decide that this was best. For the present she could only wait.

Already the boom of guns floated in on the summer air from all sides, increasing for a while, until along the upriver prairie there was almost continuous detonation. Every boom, perhaps, meant the heart or lungs of a noble animal torn to shreds for the sake of his hide. As Milly settled down again to the actual presence of this slaughter she accepted the fact with melancholy resignation.

In the course of her strolling round the camp Milly gravitated toward Catlee, where he sat contentedly smoking his pipe and fishing. She watched him, trying to make up her mind to approach him on the subject nearest her heart. But she knew the men and Mrs. Jett could see her and that any such action might arouse suspicion. Therefore she desisted. Once Catlee turned, apparently casually, and his gray gaze took her in and the camp. Then he winked at her.

That droll action established anew Milly's faith in an understanding between her and this man. She had no assurance that he would help her, but there was a secret between them. Milly felt more than she could prove. The incident made the long day supportable.

CHAPTER FOURTEEN

Jett's outfit fell into idleness for more days than Milly could remember. She waited for time to pass, and no one would have suspected her longing. When Jett returned to camp from one of his lonely rides Milly would hear his horse breaking the brush along the trail, and she could never repress a wild throb of hope. It might be Tom! But it was always Jett.

One day Jett returned in great perturbation, apparently exhausted. His horse was jaded. Follonsbee and Pruitt were curious, to no end, for Jett did not vouchsafe any explanation. Whatever had happened, however, brought about a change in him and his habits. He stayed in camp.

The business of hide-hunting had been abandoned; not improbably in Jett's mind for a temporary period, until his men weakened. But they did not weaken; they grew stronger. More days of this enforced idleness crystallized a growing influence—they would never again follow the extraordinary labors of hunting and skinning buffalo. Whatever had been Jett's unity of outfit was destroyed.

Milly heard the woman tell Jett this, and the ensuing scene had been violent. It marked, further, the revealment of Mrs. Jett's long-hidden hand in the game. She was the mainspring of Jett's calculated mechanism, and when the other men realized it, it precipitated something darkly somber into the situation. Follonsbee and Pruitt had manifestly been playing a hand they felt sure would win. Jett could no longer hunt hides, or steal them, either, without his men. All of these lonely rides of his had been taken to find other accomplices, whom Follonsbee and Pruitt knew could not be obtained there on the buffalo range.

Milly heard the bitter quarrel which ensued, between Jett and his wife, and the two lieutenants. Catlee was always there, listening, watching, but took no part in any of their talks or quarrels. He was outside. They did not count him at all. Yet he should have been counted immeasurably, Milly concluded. Like herself, Catlee was an intense, though silent, participator in this drama.

The content of that quarrel was simple. Jett had weakened to the extent of wanting to settle in part with his men. Follonsbee and Pruitt were not willing to take what he offered, and the woman, most tenacious and calculating of all of them, refused to allow Jett to relinquish any share of their profits.

There was a deadlock, and the argument put aside for the present. Follonsbee and Pruitt walked away from camp; Jett and his wife repaired to their tent where they conversed heatedly; Catlee and Milly cooked the supper. Milly did not know when the absent men returned.

Next day the atmosphere of Jett's outfit had undergone further change. The leader was a worried and tormented man, beset by a woman with will of steel and heart of hate; and he saw opposed to him Westerners whose reaction now seemed formidable and deadly. That had roused an immovable stubbornness in him.

Milly saw the disintegration of this group, and what she could not divine herself she gathered from study of Catlee. Indeed, he was the most remarkable of the outfit—he whom the others never considered at all. Not that Milly could understand her impressions! If she tried to analyze Catlee's effect upon her it only led to doubt. As for Jett and his men, they were a divided outfit, wearing toward dissolution, answering to the wildness of the time and place. The evil that they had done hovered over them, about to enact retribution.

Milly began to dread the issue, though the breaking up of this outfit augured well for her. Then any day Tom Doan, with Hudnall and his men, might ride into Jett's camp. That meant deliverance for her, in one way or another. If Jett refused to let her go she had but to betray him. Milly held her courage all through this long ordeal, yet she felt more and more the looming of a shadow.

Toward the close of that afternoon the tension relaxed. Follonsbee and Pruitt sauntered off with their heads together; Jett fell asleep under a cottonwood and his sullen wife slouched into her tent; Catlee sat on a log by the river bank, not fishing or smoking, but deep in thought.

Milly, answering the long-resisted impulse, slipped to his side.

"Catlee, I must tell you," she whispered. "This—all this I've gone through has got on my nerves. I've waited and hoped and prayed for Tom Doan. . . . He doesn't come. He has missed this road. I might have stood it longer, but this fight between the Jetts and his men wears on me. I'm scared. Something awful will happen. I can't stand it. . . . I know you're my friend—oh, I know it! . . . But you must help me. Tell me what you think. Tell me what to do. It's all so wild—so strange. . . . That awful woman! She eyes me so—as if she guessed what the men are not thinking of *now,* but would be soon. . . . Catlee, you're no—no—you're not like these people. But whatever you were—or are—remember your mother and save me before—before—"

Milly's voice failed her. Liberating her fears and hopes had spent her force in expression.

"Lass, have you said all you want to?" queried Catlee, in tense undertone.

"Yes—yes—I could only repeat," faltered Milly, but she held out trembling hands to him.

The man's face underwent a change not on the surface. It seemed light, agitation, transpiring beneath a mask.

"Don't go out of my sight!" he said, with ringing sharpness that made her gasp. Then he turned away, imperturbable as ever.

But Milly had seen or heard something terrible. She backed away from Catlee, sensing this was what he wanted her to do. Yet not out of his sight! What had he meant by that? It signified a crisis nearer than even her fears had presaged, and infinitely worse. All the time he had known what was to happen and all this time he had been her friend. This was what had been on his mind as he watched and listened.

Returning to the wagon that was her abode, she climbed to the seat and sank there, with wide eyes and beating heart. She could see Catlee sitting like a statue, staring into the river. Mrs. Jett came out of her tent, with slow, dragging step, and a face drawn, pale, malignant. Her eyes were beady, the corners of her hard mouth curved down. Heavy, slovenly, she moved to awaken Jett with a kick of foot no less gentle than her mien.

"Come out of it, you loafer," she said. "My mind's made up. We'll break camp at daylight to-morrow. . . . As you ain't got nerve to kill these men, you can have it out with them to-night. But I'm keepin' the money an' we're goin' to-morrow."

"Ahuh!" ejaculated Jett, with a husky finality.

The habit of camp tasks was strong in her, as in all of her companions. Methodically she bestirred herself round the boxes of supplies. Catlee fetched firewood as if he had been ordered to do so. Follonsbee and Pruitt returned to squat under a cottonwood, with faces like ghouls. Jett went into his tent, and when he came out he was wiping his yellow beard. He coughed huskily, as always when drinking.

For once Milly made no move to help. No one called her. It was as if she had not been there. Each member of that outfit was clamped by his or her own thoughts. Supper was prepared and eaten in a silence of unnatural calm. Lull before the storm!

Catlee brought Milly something to eat, which he tendered without speaking. Milly looked down into his eyes, and it seemed to her that she had been mistaken in the kindly nature of the man. As he turned away she noticed a gun in his belt. It was unusual for buffalo-hunters to go armed in such manner.

After supper Mrs. Jett left her husband to do her chores, and slouched toward her tent with a significant, "I'm packin' an' I want to get done before dark."

Milly saw Follonsbee motion for Pruitt and Catlee to draw aside. When they had gone, in separate directions, Follonsbee approached Jett.

"Rand, it's the last deal an' the cards are runnin' bad," he said.

"Ahuh!" ejaculated the giant, without looking up.

"Your woman has stacked the deck on us," went on Follonsbee, without rancor. "We ain't blamin' you altogether for this mess."

"Hank, I'm talked out," replied Jett, heavily.

"You've been drinkin' too much," went on the other, in conciliatory tones, "but you're sober now an' I'm goin' to try once more. Will you listen?"

"I ain't deaf."

"You'd be better off if you was. . . . Now, Rand, here's the straight of it, right off the shoulder. You've done us dirt. But square up an' all will be as before. We've got another chance here for a big haul—four thousand hides if there's one, an' easy. Use your sense. It's only this greedy woman who's changed you. Beat some sense into her or chuck her in the river. It's man to man now. An' I'm tellin' you, Pruitt is a dirty little rebel rattlesnake. He'll sting. I'm puttin' it to you honest an' level-headed. If this goes on another day it'll be too late. We're riskin' a lot here. The hunters will find out we're not killin' buffalo. We ought to load up an' *move.*"

"We're goin' to-morrow," replied Jett, gloomily.

"Who?"

"It's my outfit an' I'm movin'. If you an' Pruitt want to stay here I'll divide supplies."

"You're most obligin'," returned Follonsbee, sarcastically. "But I reckon if you divide anythin' it'll be money, outfit, an' all."

"There's where the hitch comes in," snarled Jett.

"Are you plumb off your head, man?" queried the other, in weary amaze. "You just can't do anythin' else."

"Haw! Haw!" guffawed Jett.

Follonsbee dropped his lean vulture face and paced to and fro, his hands locked behind his back. Suddenly he shouted for Pruitt. The little rebel came on the run.

"Andy, I've talked fair to Jett, an' it ain't no use," said Follonsbee. "He an' the woman are breakin' camp to-morrow."

"Early mawnin', hey?" queried Pruitt.

"Yes, an' he's offered to let us stay here with half the supplies. I told him if he divided anythin' it'd be money, outfit, an' all."

"Wal, what'd he say then?"

"That here was just where the hitch come in. I told him he couldn't do anythin' else but divide, an' then he haw-hawed in my face."

"You don't say. Wal, he ain't very perlite, is he? . . . Hank, I'm through talkin' nice to Jett. If I talk any more I'll shore have somethin' hard to say. Give him till mawnin' to think it over."

Pruitt's sulky temper was not in evidence during this short interview. Milly could not see his face, but his tone and the poise of his head were unlike him.

"Will you fellars have a drink with me?" asked Jett, in grim disdain.

They walked off without replying. Milly peered round. Catlee leaned against a tree close by, within earshot, and the look he cast at Jett was illuminating. Jett was new to the frontier, though he had answered quickly to its evil influence. But otherwise he had not developed. The man's quick decline from honest living had been the easiest way to satisfy a naturally greedy soul. Drink, the rough life of the open, had paved the way. His taking to this frontier woman was perhaps the worst step. And now the sordid nature of him lowered him beneath these thieves, who had probably put the evil chances in his way. But Jett did not understand Western men, much less desperadoes such as Follonsbee and Pruitt manifestly were.

Darkness settled down over the camp and the river. The crickets and frogs were less in evidence with their chirping and trilling. The camp fire had died out, and soon the dim light in Jett's tent was extinguished. The lonely night seemed to envelop Milly and strike terror to her soul. What was the portent of the wild mourn of the wolves? Yet there came a mounting intuitive, irresistible hope—to-morrow she might be free. Somewhere within a few miles Tom Doan lay asleep, perhaps dreaming of her, as she was thinking of him.

Milly heard Catlee's stealthy tread. He had moved his bed near her wagon, and his presence there was significant of his unobtrusive guardianship. It relieved her distraught nerves, and soon after that her eyelids wearily closed.

Milly awoke with a start. The stars above were wan in a paling sky; a camp fire crackled with newly burning sticks; the odor of wood smoke permeated the air. The wagon in which she lay was shaking. Then she heard the pound of hoofs, the clink and rattle of harness, a low husky voice she recognized. Jett was hitching up.

With a catch in her breath and a gush of blood along her veins Milly raised herself out of her bed and peered over the side of the wagon. The dark, heavy form of Mrs. Jett could be discerned in the flickering light of fire; contrary to her usual phlegmatic action, she was moving with a celerity that spoke eloquently of the nature of that departure. Apparently none of the others were stirring. Milly moved to the other side of the wagon and peered down, just making out Catlee's bed under the cottonwood. A dark form appeared against the dim background. Milly saw it move, and presently satisfied herself that Catlee was sitting on his bed, pulling on his boots.

Jett's huge figure loomed up, passing the wagon. Milly dropped down, so she would not be seen. He spoke in the low, husky voice to the woman. She did not reply. Presently Milly heard again the soft thud of hoofs, coming closer, to cease just back of her wagon. Next she heard the creak and flop of leather. Jett was saddling the fast horses he used in hunting. Again Milly cautiously raised her head. She saw Jett in quick, sharp, decisive, yet nervous action. He haltered both horses to the back of the wagon, and slipped nose bags over their heads. The horses began to munch the oats in the bags.

In a moment more Jett approached the wagon and lifted something over the footboard, just as Milly sank back into her bed. His quick heavy breathing denoted a laboring under excitement. She smelled rum on him. He disappeared, and soon returned to deposit another pack in the back of the wagon. This action he repeated several times. Next Milly heard him fumbling with the wire that held the water keg to the wagon. He tipped the keg, and the slap and gurgle of water told of the quantity.

"Half full," he muttered to himself. "That'll do for to-day."

His heavy footsteps moved away, and then came sound of his hoarse whisper to the woman. She replied:

"Reckon they'll show up. We'll not get away so easy, if I know men in this country. You'd better keep a rifle in your hand."

"Boh!" burst out Jett, in disgusted doubt of her, himself and the whole situation.

"Eat an' drink now, pronto," she said. "We won't stop to wash an' take these things. I packed some."

The boil of the coffee pot could be heard, and then a hot sizzle as the water boiled over into the fire. Some one removed it. Again Milly peeped out the wagon side. Dawn was at hand. All was gray, shadowy, obscure beyond the trees, but near at hand it was light enough to see. Jett and the woman were eating. His rifle leaned against the mess box. They ate hurriedly, in silence.

Just then a low rumble like thunder broke the stillness of the morning. Deep, distant, weird, it denoted a thunderstorm to Milly. Yet how long and strangely it held on!

Jett lifted his big head like a listening deer.

"Stampede, by gosh! First one this summer. Lucky it's across the river."

"Stampede!" echoed the woman, slowly. "Hum! . . . Are there lots of buffalo across here?"

"They'd make a tolerable herd if they got bunched. I ain't in love with the idee. They might start the big herd on this side. We're aimin' to cross the prairie to the Red River. An' even if we had two days' start, a runnin' herd would catch us."

"I don't agree with you, Jett," remarked the woman. "Anyway, we're goin', buffalo or no buffalo."

Milly listened to the low, distant rumble. What a strange sound! Did it not come from far away? Did she imagine it almost imperceptibly swelled in volume? She strained to hear. It lessened, died away, began again, and though ever so faint, it filled her ears.

Imperceptibly the gray dawn had yielded to daylight. The Jetts had about finished their meal. Whatever was going to happen must befall soon. Milly strove to control her fearful curiosity. Her heart beat high. This issue mattered mightily to her. Peeping over the far side of her wagon, she saw Catlee sitting on his bed, watching the Jetts from his angle. He saw Milly. Under the brim of his sombrero his eyes appeared to be black holes. He motioned Milly to keep down out of sight. Instinctively she obeyed, sinking back to her bed; and then, irresistibly impelled, she moved to the other side, farther up under the low wagon seat, and peeped out from under it.

At that juncture Pruitt and Follonsbee strode from somewhere to confront the Jetts. Milly would have shrunk back had she not been as if chained. The little rebel struck terror to her heart. Follonsbee resembled, as always, a bird of prey, but now about to strike.

"Jett, you ain't bravin' it out?" asked Pruitt, cool and laconic. "Shore you ain't aimin' to leave heah without a divvy?"

"I'm leavin' two wagons, six hosses, an' most of the outfit," replied Jett, gruffly. He stared at Pruitt. Something was seeking an entrance into his mind.

"You're lucky to get that," snapped the woman.

"Listen to her, Hank," said Pruitt, turning to Follonsbee.

"I'm listenin', an' I don't have to hear no more. She stacked this deal," replied Pruitt's comrade, stridently. Only the timbre of his voice showed his passion; he was as slow and easy as Pruitt.

"Talk to me," shouted Jett, beginning to give way to the stress of a situation beyond him. "Let my wife—"

"Wife? Aw, hell," interposed Pruitt, contemptuously. "This Hardin woman ain't your wife any more'n she's mine. . . . Jett, you're yellow, an' you're shore talkin' to men who ain't yellow, whatever else they are."

Jett cursed low and deep fumed in his effort to confront these men on an equality. But it was not in him. Fiercely he questioned the woman. "Did you tell them we wasn't married—yet?"

"Reckon I did. It was when you was silly over this black-eyed step-daughter of yours," she replied suddenly.

Assuredly Jett would have struck her down but for the unforgetable proximity of Pruitt and Follonsbee. The latter laughed coarsely. Pruitt took a stride forward. His manner was careless, casual, but the set of muscles, the action of him, indicated something different.

"Jett, did *you* tell your woman you wanted to get rid of her—so's you could have your black-eyed wench?" demanded the little rebel, with all his insolent meanness. "You shore told us—an' you wasn't so orful drunk."

The woman seemed to tower and her face grew black.

"I didn't," yelled Jett.

Wordlessly the woman turned to question these accusers.

"Jett's a lyin' yellow skunk," declared Pruitt. "He shore meant to give the girl your place. 'Cause he wouldn't give her to me or Hank heah!"

"It's true," corroborated Follonsbee. "It's Jett an' not us who's lyin'. Why, I wouldn't lie to save both your dirty lives."

That convinced the woman, and she turned on Jett with incoherent fury. He tried to yell a break into her tirade; and not till he had seized her in brutal hands, to shake her as if she had been a rat, did she stop. Then, after a pause, in which she glared at him with the hate of a jade, she panted: "I'll put—that little hussy's eyes out. . . . An' Rand Jett—*you'll* never—get a dollar of this hide money!"

"Shut up or I'll mash your jaw!" he shouted, hoarsely.

"Haw! Haw!" laughed Follonsbee, in glee that seemed only in his tones. He did not move hand or foot.

"Jett, I'm shore hopin' we can leave you to this sweet lady," cut in Pruitt, "for you deserve it. But I'm feared your bull-headedness will aboot force our deal. . . . Once more an' last time, damn you—will you divvy hide-money, outfit, an' supplies, as you agreed?"

"Naw, I won't," declared Jett, fiercely. He looked a driven man; and strangely his gaze of hate was for the woman and not the man who menaced him.

"Then we'll take it all!" flashed Pruitt, ringingly.

In violent shock Jett wheeled to face Pruitt, at last with comprehension. What he saw turned his skin white back of his yellow beard. His large, hard, bright blue eyes suddenly fixed in wild stare on Pruitt. And he began to shake. Suddenly he dove for his rifle.

Milly's gaze had been riveted on Jett. Dimly she had seen Pruitt, but not to note look or action. Her fascinated spell broke to a horror of what was coming. Swiftly she dropped down to cover and wrapped her head in the blankets of her bed. Tightly she pulled them over ears and eyes, and twisted and rolled. And deep concussions seemed to beat at her brain. The wagon lurched. The blackness that enveloped her was not all from the blankets. Her senses seemed whirling dizzily. Then heart, pulse, thought returned to degree of discrimination.

She listened. There was no sound she could discern while under the folds of blankets. She was suffocating. She threw them off. Then, fearfully she lay there. All was still. No sound! A low thunder of stampeding buffalo floated across the river. Milly listened for voices. The camp appeared deserted. Had these men run off into the brakes? Sullen, sousing splashes in the river under the bank transfixed her into blank, icy horror. Something was ended. She could only wait, lying there in a tremble.

Suddenly she heard a soft step close to the wagon. Then Catlee's hat and face appeared over the side. He looked down at her with eyes the like of which Milly had never seen in a human.

"Lass, it's half over, but the worst's to come," he whispered, and with dark, gray gleaming gaze on her, bright, almost smiling, he dropped down out of her sight. He had not seen her desperation. He had not appealed to her to bear up under this tragedy. His look, his whisper, had made of her a comrade, brave to stand the outcome. Likewise they were a warning for herself to interpret, a suggestion of his imminent part in this terrible affair. They strung Milly's nerves to high tension. What might her part be? Compared with this experience, the West had dealt to women fatality and catastrophe which dwarfed hers. Life was sweet, never more so than at that moment, when memory of Tom Doan flashed back to her. She felt the grim and somber presence of death; she felt the imminence of further developments, sinister, harrowing, revolving more around her. Must she surrender to her emotions? Milly bit and choked them back. She needed all the strength, will, nerve possible to a woman; and in her extremity, with a racked heart, and unseeing eyes on the cottonwoods above, she propelled her spirit with the thought of Tom Doan, to endure or achieve anything.

Low voices diverted the current of her mind. Some persons, at least two, were returning from the river bank. Milly sat up, to look over the wagon-side. Follonsbee and Pruitt were entering the camp clearing. Neither Jett nor the woman was to be seen. Milly suffered no shock, she had not expected to see them. Pruitt was wet and muddy to his hips.

". . . Shore may as well stay heah an' hunt hides, same as the other outfits," he was saying.

"I'm ag'in' stayin'," replied Follonsbee.

"Wal, we won't argue aboot it. Shore I ain't carin' much one way or other," responded Pruitt.

They reached the camp fire, the burned-out sticks of which Pruitt kicked with a wet boot. Follonsbee held his hands over the heat, though they could not have been chilled. The morning was warm. Milly saw his hands quivering very slightly.

"Shore we ought to have got that job off our hands long ago," said Pruitt. "Wal, Hank, heah's my idee. Let's pull out, ford the river below, an' strike for the Brazos. There's buffalo, an' this main herd won't be long comin'."

"Suits me good," responded the other, in relief. "Now let's have everythin' clear. We've shared the hide money Jett's woman had. How about the rest of the outfit?"

"Same way, share an' share alike."

"Ahuh. The deal's made. Shake on it," said Follonsbee, extending his hand.

Pruitt met it halfway with his own.

"Hank, we stuck together for aboot two years, an' I reckon we're a good team."

"How about the girl?" suddenly demanded Follonsbee.

Their backs were turned to Milly, who heard this query with the sharp ears of expectation. She was fortified by her own resolve and the still hidden presence of Catlee.

"Wal, if I didn't forgit aboot our black-eyed wench!" ejaculated Pruitt, slapping his leg.

"Toss you for her—or cut the cards?" asked Follonsbee, with his sleek, narrow, beak-like head lowered.

"No, you won't. Yo're shore too lucky. . . . We'll share the girl same as the rest of the outfit."

"All right. It'll be a two-man outfit, half of everythin' for each—even the girl. Then we can't squabble. . . . But say, we forgot Catlee. Where the hell's he been?"

"Reckon he was scared. Mebbe he's runnin' yet."

"Nope. I tell you, Andy, your hate of Yanks has got you figgerin' this Catlee wrong," protested Follonsbee.

"That farm hand!" retorted Pruitt, with infinite disgust.

"Farm hand nothin'," replied the other bluntly. "I don't know *what* he is, but he's got me figgerin'. We'd better give him a hoss an' pack an' turn him loose."

Pruitt pondered this suggestion for a moment and then somberly shook his head. That idea did not appeal to him, while at the same time it manifestly introduced another and uncertain element into the situation.

Milly heard quick, rustling footsteps behind her. Catlee appeared round the wagon, with a gun leveled low in his right hand. Follonsbee saw him first and let out a startled exclamation. Pruitt jerked up. Then he froze.

"Howdy, men!" was Catlee's greeting, in voice these companions evidently had never heard him use before.

Follonsbee uttered a gasp of amazed conviction.

"Andy! I *told* you!"

Pruitt scarcely moved a muscle, unless in the flicker of an eyelash. He did not change expression. He hissed out, "Who'n hell are you *now?*" That was his swift acceptance of Follonsbee's reiterated hints.

"Small matter," replied Catlee, as with weapon quiveringly extended he sheered round squarely in front of Pruitt, "but if it'd please you to be acquainted with me at this late day—you can bow to Sam Davis."

"Ahuh! Late pard of the Youngers," retorted Follonsbee, going white in the face.

"Reckon I'm used to hard company," whipped out Catlee, stingingly, "but never yet took to sharin' innocent little girls!"

Pruitt suffered no suggestion of Follonsbee's weakening to the power of a name, whatever it was. The leveled weapon, covering him and his comrade, was the great factor in his reaction. Not for the slightest fraction of a second did he take his dancing, furious gaze from Catlee. The uselessness of more words seemed marked in his almost imperceptible gathering of muscular force. All the power of sight and mind was transfixed on Catlee's eyes, to read there the intent that preceded action. He chose an instant, probably the one in which Catlee decided, and like a flash threw his gun.

As it left his hip and snapped, Catlee's gun crashed. The force of the bullet knocked Pruitt flat.

"Hur-ry Hank!" he yelled, in fierce, wild tone of terrible realization, and flinging the empty weapon he had forgotten to load he lurched like a crippled panther to get his hands on Jett's rifle.

Milly saw only the intrepid Pruitt, but she heard Catlee's second shot and the sodden thud of Follonsbee falling. He made no outcry. Pruitt's actions were almost too swift to follow—so swift that Catlee missed him, as with spasmodic dive he grasped and carried Jett's rifle over the mess box. Up he sprang, grotesque, misshapen, yet wonderfully agile, to discharge the heavy rifle even as he received Catlee's fire square in his chest. Staggering backward, he dropped the weapon, his arms spread, and he seemed falling step by step. An awful blankness blotted out the ferocity of his crooked face. Step by step, he fell backward over the bank into the river. A sounding splash followed his disappearance.

Milly's set gaze wavered. A silence intervened. Her lungs seemed to expand. The appalling fixity of her attention broke with a shock and she looked for Catlee. He lay on the ground beside the camp fire. His hand twitched—released the smoking gun. Milly leaped out of the wagon and ran to him.

She knelt. His hat was off, his face vague, changing. The gray storm of his eyes seemed fading.

"Oh—oh—Catlee!" cried Milly, poignantly.

"Good luck," he whispered. His lips set, his eyelids fluttered—all his body quivered to a relaxation. He had been shot through the breast.

"My God! how awful! . . . He's dead! They're all dead. I'm left—alone. It's over. . . . Brave Catlee! Oh, he saved me! . . . But what can I do? I—"

Milly's outburst was silenced by the shrill neigh of one of the horses hitched to the wagon. It was a neigh that heralded sight or scent of another horse. Wild and sharp then pealed out a whistling answer from across the river.

Milly bounded erect to peer out under the cottonwoods, thrilling with joy. But her joy sustained a bewildering check, and it died when steadier glance revealed mounted Indians riding down into the river. For one moment Milly stared, biting her fingers in her horror; then the spirit born of these trying hours ran through her like a white flame, and climbing to the seat of the wagon she whipped up the reins.

Her instinct was to escape. She had no time to think of a better way. And the horses, restive, not wholly recovered from fright, needed no urging. They broke into trot, dragging the saddled animals behind the wagon. Out of the clearing, into the brakes they crashed, and were hard to hold. Road there were none, but a wide lane of crushed weeds and brush marked where Jett had driven the wagon in, and later had ridden to and fro on horseback. The team followed it and they tore through the bending clumps of brush that hung over it and bumped over logs.

Branches of trees struck Milly as she passed, blinding her for a moment. When she could see clearly again the horses were no longer in the lane through the brush. They had swerved to one side or the other, she did not know which. But she kept her sense of direction: to the right was down river, and to the left was the prairie, the main herd of buffalo, and the camps of the hunters.

She must get out into the open quickly. If the Indians had not heard her drive away there would be a little time before they would strike out on her trail through the brakes.

"Oh, I forgot," she cried. "They heard the horse neigh." And with a sinking of her daring spirit she let the horses have free rein. They quickened their gait, but showed no sign of bolting. They wanted to get out of that jungle, and they broke a path through thickets, over rotten logs, and under matted hanging vines. Milly had all she could do to keep from being torn from her seat.

They got by the worst of the brakes and Milly saw light ahead low down through the trees, but it seemed to be in the wrong direction. She should turn more to the left. Her efforts to head the iron-jawed team in that direction were unavailing. They kept to a straight course, out into the light. But this open had deceived Milly, and probably the horses also. It was a wide bare strip of sand where a tributary of the Pease flowed in wet season. Here the horses slowed to a dragging walk, yet soon crossed the sand to enter the brakes again.

Here in the shade and dust, and the *mêlée* of threshing branches round her face, Milly lost all sense of the right direction. She realized her peril, yet did not despair. Something had always happened; it would happen to save her again.

Suddenly a crashing of brush in front of her stopped her heart. She almost fell back into the wagon. A huge brown buffalo bull tore ahead of her, passing to the left. Milly recovered. Then again she heard crashing ahead of her, to one side, and more at a distance. There were buffalo in the brakes.

Above the swish of brush and rattle of wagon and pound of hoofs she began to hear a low, rumbling thunder, apparently to the fore and her right.

"They said stampede!" she cried fearfully.

Her horses heard it and were excited, or else the scent and proximity of stray buffalo had been the cause of their faster, less regular gait. Milly essayed again to swerve them to the left, but in vain. And indeed that left side grew more and more impractical, owing to obstructions which shunted the horses in an opposite direction. Quite unexpectedly then they burst out of the brakes into open prairie.

Milly was as amazed as frightened. The plain was so dusty she could not see a mile, and strings of buffalo were disappearing into a yellow broken pall. They appeared to be loping in their easy, lumbering way. The thunder was louder now, though still a strange low roar, and it came out of the dust curtain which obscured the prairie. The horses, snorting, not liking dust or buffalo, loped for a mile, then slowed to a walk and halted. Milly tried to get her bearings. The whole horizon to fore and right was streaky with dust and moving buffalo. From behind her the line of river timber extended on her right to fade in the obscurity of dust. This established her position. She had crossed the brakes of the tributary and was now headed east. The buffalo were then coming out of the south and they were crossing the Pease. Milly realized that she was far out of her proper course and must make a wide turn to the left, cross the dry stream-bed, and then go up the river to the camps of the hide-hunters.

Suddenly she missed something. The two saddle horses! They had broken off in the rough ride. Milly looked back at the dark, ragged line of the timber from where she had come. The air was clearer that way. Movement and flash attracted her gaze.

She saw animals run out into the open. Wild, lean, colored ponies with riders! They stretched out in swift motion, graceful, wild, incomparably a contrast to the horses of white hunters.

Milly realized she was being pursued by Indians.

CHAPTER FIFTEEN

Milly screamed at the horses and swung the lash, beating them into a gallop. The lightly loaded wagon lurched and bounced over the hummocky prairie, throwing her off the seat and from side to side. A heavy strain on the reins threatened to tear her arms from their sockets.

It was this physical action that averted a panic-stricken flight. The horses broke from gallop into run, and they caught up with scattered groups and lines of buffalo. Milly was in the throes of the keenest terror that had yet beset her, but she did not quite lose her reason. There were a few moments fraught with heart-numbing, blood-curdling sensations; which on the other hand were counteracted by the violence of the race over the prairie, straight for the straggling strings of the buffalo herd. The horses plunged, hurtling the wagon along; the wind, now tainted with dust and scent of buffalo, rushed into Milly's face and waved her hair; the tremendous drag on the reins, at first scarcely perceptible, in her great excitement, began to hurt hands, wrists, arms, shoulders in a degree that compelled attention. But the race itself, the flight, the breakneck pace across the prairie, with stampeding buffalo before and Comanche Indians behind—it was too great, too magnificent, too terrible to prostrate this girl. Opposed to all the fears possible to a girl was the thing roused in her by love, by example of a thief who had died to save her, by the marvel of the moment.

Milly gazed back over her shoulder. The Comanches had gained. They were not half a mile away, riding now in wide formation, naked, gaudy, lean, feathered, swift and wild as a gale of wind in the tall prairie grass.

"Better death among the buffalo!" cried Milly, and she turned to wrap both reins round her left wrist, to lash out with the whip, and to scream: *"Run! Run! Run!"*

Buffalo loped ahead of her, to each side and behind, in straggling groups and lines, all headed in the same direction as the vague denser bunches to the right. Here the dust pall moved like broken clouds, showing light and dark.

She became aware of increasing fullness in her ears. The low rumble had changed to a clattering trample, yet there seemed more. The sound grew; it came closer; it swelled to a roar; and presently she located it in the rear.

She turned. With startled gaze she saw a long, bobbing, black, ragged mass pouring like a woolly flood out over the prairie. A sea of buffalo! They were moving at a lope, ponderously, regularly, and the scalloped head of that immense herd crossed the line between Milly and the Comanches. It swept on. It dammed and blocked the way. Milly saw the vermillion paint on the naked bodies and faces of these savages as they wheeled their lean horses to race along with the buffalo.

Then thin whorls of rising dust obscured them from Milly's sight. A half mile of black bobbing humps moved between her and the Comanches. She uttered a wild cry that was joy, wonder, reverence, and acceptance of the thing she had trusted. Thicker grew the dust mantle; wider the herd; greater the volume of sound! The Comanches might now have been a thousand miles away, for all the harm they could do her. As they vanished in the obscurity of dust so also did they fade from Milly's mind!

Milly drove a plunging maddened team of horses in the midst of buffalo as far as the eye could see. Her intelligence told her that she was now in greater peril of death than at any time heretofore, yet, though her hair rose stiff and her tongue clove to the roof of her mouth, she could not feel the same as when Pruitt had parceled her, share and share with Follonsbee, or when those lean wild-riding Comanches had been swooping down on her. Strangely, though there was natural terror in the moment, she did not seem afraid of the buffalo.

The thick massed herd was on her left, and appeared to have but few open patches; to the fore and all on the other side there was as many gray spaces of prairie showing as black loping blotches of buffalo. Her horses were running while the buffalo were loping, thus she kept gaining on groups near her and passing them. Always they sheered away, some of the bulls kicking out with wonderful quickness. But in the main they gave space to the swifter horses and the lumbering wagon.

The dust rose in sheets now thin, now thick, and obscured everything beyond a quarter of a mile distant. Milly was surrounded, hemmed in, carried onward by a pondering moving medium. The trampling roar of hoofs was deafening, but it was not now like thunder. It was too close. It did not swell or rumble or roll. It roared.

A thousand tufted tails switched out of that mass, and ten times that many shaggy humps bobbed in sight. What queer sensation this action gave Milly—queer above all the other sensations! It struck her as ludicrous.

The larger, denser mass on the left had loped up at somewhat faster gait than those groups Milly had first encountered. It forged ahead for a time, then gradually absorbed all the buffalo, until they were moving in unison. Slowly they appeared to pack together, to obliterate the open spaces, and to close in on the horses. This was what Milly feared most.

The horses took their bits between their teeth and ran headlong. Milly had to slack the reins or be pulled out of the seat. They plunged into the rear of the moving buffalo, to make no impression otherwise than to split the phalanx for a few rods and be kicked from all sides. Here the horses reared, plunged, and sent out above the steady roar a piercing scream of terror. Milly had never before heard the scream of a horse. She could do nothing but cling to the loose reins and the wagon seat, and gaze with distended eyes. One of the white horses, Jett's favorite, plunged to his knees. The instant was one when Milly seemed to be clamped by paralysis. The other white horse plunged on, dragging his mate to his feet and into the race again.

Then the space around horses and wagons closed in, narrowed to an oval with only a few yards clear to the fore and on each side. Behind, the huge, lowered, shaggy heads almost bobbed against the wagon.

The time of supreme suspense had come to Milly. She had heard buffalo would run over and crush any obstruction in their path. She seemed about to become the victim of such a blind juggernaut. Her horses had been compelled to slacken their gait to accommodate that of the buffalo. They could neither forge ahead, nor swerve to one side or other, nor stop. They were blocked, hemmed in, and pushed. And their terror was extreme. They plunged in unison and singly; they screamed and bit at the kicking buffalo. It was a miracle that leg or harness or wheel was not broken.

A violent jolt nearly unseated Milly. The wagon had been struck from behind. Fearfully she looked back. A stupid-faced old bull, with shaggy head as large as a barrel, was wagging along almost under the end of the wagon-bed. He had bumped into it. Then the space on the left closed in until buffalo were right alongside the wheels. Milly wrung her hands. It would happen now. A wheel would be broken, the wagon overturned, and she. . . . A big black bull rubbed his rump against the hind wheel. The iron tire revolving fast scraped hard on his hide. Quick as a flash the bull lowered head and elevated rear, kicking out viciously. One of his legs went between the spokes. A crack rang out above the trample of hoofs. The bull went down, and the wagon lifted and all but upset. Milly could not cry out. She clung to the seat with all her strength. Then began a terrific commotion. The horses plunged as the drag on the wagon held them back. Buffalo began to pile high over the one that had fallen, and a wave of action seemed to permeate all of them.

Those rushing forward pounded against the hind wheels, and split round them until the pressure became so great that they seemed to lift the wagon and carry it along, forcing the horses ahead.

Milly could not shut her eyes. They were fascinated by this heaving mass. The continuous roar, the endless motion toward certain catastrophe, were driving her mad. Then this bump and scrape and lurch, this frightful proximity of the encroaching buffalo, this pell-mell pandemonium behind, was too much for her. The strength of hands and will left her. The wagon tilted, turned sidewise, and stopped with a shock. An appalling sound seemed to take the place of motion. The buffalo behind began to lift their great heads, to pile high over those in front, to crowd in terrific straining wave of black, hideous and irresistible, like an oncoming tide. Heads and horns and hair, tufted tails, a dense, rounded, moving, tussling sea of buffalo bore down on the wagon. The sound was now a thundering roar. Dust hung low. The air was suffocating. Milly's nose and lungs seemed to close. She fell backward over the seat and fainted.

When she opened her eyes it was as if she had come out of a nightmare. She lay on her back. She gazed upward to sky thinly filmed over by dust clouds. Had she slept?

Suddenly she understood the meaning of motion and the sensation of filled ears. The wagon was moving steadily, she could not tell how fast, and from all sides rose a low, clattering roar of hoofs.

"Oh, it must be—something happened—the horses went on—the wagon did not upset!" she cried, and her voice was indistinct.

But she feared to rise and look out. She listened and felt. There was a vast difference. The wagon moved on steadily, smoothly, without lurch or bump; the sound of hoofs filled the air, yet not loudly or with such a cutting trample. She reasoned out that the pace had slowed much. Where was she? How long had she lain unconscious? What would be the end of this awful race?

Nothing happened. She found her breathing easier and her nostrils less stopped by dust and odor of buffalo. Her mouth was parched with thirst. There was a slow, torrid beat of her pulse. Her skin appeared moist and hot. Then she saw the sun, quite high, a strange magenta hue, seen through the thin dust clouds. It had been just after daylight when she escaped from Jett's camp. Ah! she remembered Catlee!—Sam Davis, one of Younger's clan! . . . Hours had passed and she was still surrounded by buffalo. The end had not come then; it had been averted, but it was inevitable. What she had passed through! Life was cruel. Hers had been an unhappy fate. Suddenly she thought of Tom Doan, and life, courage, hope surged with the magic of love. Something had happened to save her.

Milly sat up. She saw gray prairie—and then, some fifty yards distant, the brown shaggy bodies of buffalo, in lazy lope. The wagon was keeping the same slow speed. Milly staggered up to lean against the seat and peer ahead. Wonderful to see—Jett's white team was contentedly trotting along, some rods in the rear of straggling buffalo. She could scarcely believe what she saw. The horses were no longer frightened.

On the other side wider space intervened before buffalo covered the gray prairie. She could see a long way—miles, it seemed—and there were as many black streaks of buffalo as gray strips of grass. To the fore Milly beheld the same scene, only greater in extent. Buffalo showed as far as sight could penetrate, but they were no longer massed or moving fast.

"It's not a stampede," Milly told herself in sudden realization. "It never was. . . . They're just traveling. They don't mind the wagon—the horses—not any more. . . . Oh, I shall get out!"

The knotted reins hung over the brake, where she had left them. Milly climbed to the driver's seat and took them up.

The horses responded to her control, not in accelerated trot, but by a lifting of ears and throwing of heads. They were glad to be under guidance again. They trotted on as if no buffalo were near. It amazed Milly, this change. But she could tell by the sweat and froth and cakes of dust on them that they had traveled far and long before coming to this indifference.

Milly did not drive the horses, though she held the reins taut enough for them to feel she was there; she sat stiff in the seat, calling to them, watching and thrilling, nervously and fearfully suspicious of the moving inclosure which carried her onward a prisoner. Time passed swiftly. The sun burned down on her. And the hour came when the buffalo lumbered to a walk.

They were no different from cattle now, Milly thought. Then the dust clouds floated away and she could see over the backs of buffalo on all sides, out to the boundless prairie. The blue sky overhead seemed to have a welcome for her. The horses slowed down. Gradually the form of the open space surrounding the wagon widened, changed its shape as buffalo in groups wandered out from the herd. Little light tawny calves appeared to run playfully into the open. They did not play as if they were tired.

Milly watched them with a birth of love in her heart for them, and a gratitude to the whole herd for its service to her. No doubt now that she was saved! Nearly a whole day had passed since the Indians had seen her disappear, and leagues of prairie had been covered. The direction she was being taken was north, and that she knew to be favorable to her. Sooner or later these buffalo would split or pass by her; then she would have another problem to consider.

But how interminably they traveled on! No doubt the annual instinct to migrate northward had been the cause of this movement. If they had stampeded across the Pease, which had not seemed to her the case, they had at once calmed to a gait the hunters called their regular ranging mode of travel. Her peril at one time had been great, but if this herd had caught her in a stampede she would have been lost.

The stragglers that from time to time came near her paid no attention to horses or wagon. They were as tame as cows. They puffed along, wagging their big heads, apparently asleep as they traveled. The open lanes and aisles and patches changed shape, closed to reopen, yet on the whole there was a gradual widening. The herd was spreading. Milly could see the ragged rear a couple of miles back, where it marked its dark line against the gray prairie. Westward the mass was thick and wide; it was thin and straggly on the east. Northward the black creeping tide of backs extended to the horizon.

Milly rode on, escorted by a million beasts of the plain, and they came to mean more to her than she could understand. They were alive, vigorous, self-sufficient; and they were doomed by the hide-hunters. She could not think of anything save the great, shaggy, stolid old bulls, and the sleeker smaller cows, and the tawny romping calves. So wonderful an adventure, so vast a number of hoofed creatures, so strangely trooping up out of the dusty river brakes to envelop her, so different when she and they and the horses had become accustomed to one another—these ideas were the gist of her thoughts. It was a strange, unreal concentration on buffalo.

The afternoon waned. The sun sank low in the west and turned gold. A time came when Milly saw with amaze that the front leagues of buffalo had disappeared over the horizon, now close at hand. They had come to edge of slope on river brake. What would this mean to her?

When the wagon reached the line where the woolly backs had gone down out of sight Milly saw a slope, covered with spreading buffalo, that ended in a winding green belt of trees. In places shone the glancing brightness of water. Beyond, on a level immense plain, miles and miles of buffalo were moving like myriads of ants. They were spreading on all sides, and those in the lead had stopped to graze. The immensity of the scene, its beauty and life and tragedy, would remain in Milly's memory all her days. She saw the whole herd, and it was a spectacle to uplift her heart. While the horses walked on with the buffalo streaming down that slope Milly gazed in rapt attention. How endless the gray level prairie below! She understood why the buffalo loved it, how it had nourished them, what a wild lonely home it was. Faint threads of other rivers crossed the gray; and the green hue was welcome contrast to the monotony. Duskily red the sun was setting, and it cast its glow over the plain and buffalo, stronger every moment. In the distance purple mantled the horizon. Far to the northwest a faint dark ruggedness of land or cloud seemed limned against the sunset-flushed sky. Was that land? If so it was the Llano Estacado.

Milly's horses reached the belt of trees, and entered a grove through and round which the buffalo were traveling. She felt the breaking of the inclosure of beasts that had so long encompassed her. It brought a change of thoughts. She was free to let the remainder of the herd pass. Driving down, behind a thick clump of cottonwoods she turned into a green pocket, and halted. Wearily the horses stood, heaving, untempted by the grass. On each side of Milly streams and strings and groups of buffalo passed to go down into the river, from which a loud continuous splashing rose. She waited, watching on one side, then the other. The solid masses had gone by; the ranks behind thinned as they came on; and at last straggling groups with many calves brought up the rear. These hurried on, rustling the bush, on to splash into the shallow ford. Then the violence of agitated water ceased; the low trample of hoofs ceased.

Silence! It was not real. For a whole day Milly's ears had been filled and harassed by a continuous trample, at first a roar, then a clatter, then a slow beat, beat, beat of hoofs, but always a trample. She could not get used to silence. She felt lost. A rush of sensations seemed impending. But only a dreamy stillness pervaded the river bottom, a hot, drowsy, thick air, empty of life. The unnaturally silent moment flung at her the loneliness and wildness of the place. Alone! She was lost on the prairie.

"Oh, what shall I do now?" she cried.

There was everything to do—to care for the horses, and for herself, so to preserve strength; to choose a direction, and to travel on and on, until she found a road that would lead her to some camp or post. Suddenly she sank down in a heap. The thought of the enormous problem crushed her for a moment. She was in the throes of a reaction.

"But I mustn't *think,*" she whispered, fiercely. "I must *do!*"

And she clambered out of the wagon. The grove sloped down to the green bench where she had waited for the buffalo to pass. Grass was abundant. The horses would not stray. She moved to unhitch them, and had begun when it occurred to her that she would have to hitch them up again. To this end she studied every buckle and strap. Many a time she had helped round horses on the farm. The intricacies of harness were not an entire mystery to her. Then she had watched Jett and Catlee hitch up this team. Still, she studied everything carefully. Then she unbuttoned the traces and removed the harness. The horses rolled in a dusty place which the buffalo had trampled barren, and they rose dirty and yellow to shake a cloud from their backs. Then with snorts they trotted down to the water.

Milly was reminded of her own burning thirst, and she ran down to the water's edge, where, unmindful of its muddy color, she threw herself flat and drank until she could hold no more. "Never knew—water—could taste so good," she panted. Returning to the wagon, she climbed up in it to examine its contents. She found a bag of oats for the horses, a box containing utensils for cooking, another full of food supplies, a bale of blankets, and lastly an ax and shovel.

"Robinson Crusoe had no more," said Milly to herself, and then stood aghast at her levity. Was she not lost on the prairie? Might not Indians ride down upon her? Milly considered the probabilities. "God has answered my prayer," she concluded, gravely, and dismissed fears for the time being.

In the box of utensils she found matches, which were next to food in importance, and thus encouraged she lifted out what she needed. Among the articles of food were a loaf of bread and a bag of biscuits. Suddenly her mouth became flooded with saliva and she had to bite into a biscuit. There were also cooked meat and both jerked venison and buffalo. Salt and pepper, sugar, coffee, dried apples she found, and then did not explore the box to the uttermost.

"I'll not starve, anyway," murmured Milly.

Next she gathered dry bits of bark and wood, of which there was abundance, and essayed to start a fire. Success crowned her efforts, though she burned her fingers. Then, taking up the pail, she descended the bank to the river and filled it with water, which was now clarifying in the slow current. Returning, she poured some into the coffee pot and put that in the edge of the fire. Next, while waiting for the water to boil she cut strips of the cooked buffalo meat and heated them in a pan. She had misgivings about what her cooking might be. Nevertheless, she sat down presently and ate as heartily as ever before in her life.

Twilight had fallen when she looked up from the last task. The west was rose with an afterglow of sunset. All at once, now that action had to be suspended, she was confronted with reality. The emotion of reality!

"Oh, I'm lost—alone—helpless!" she exclaimed. "It's growing dark. I was always afraid of the dark."

And she shivered there through a long moment of feeling. She would be compelled to think now. She could not force sleep. How impossible to fall asleep! Panthers, bears, wildcats, wolves lived in these river brakes. She felt in her coat for the little derringer. It was gone. She had no weapons save the ax, and she could not wield that effectively.

Yet she did not at once seek the apparent security of her bed in the wagon. She walked about, though close by. She peered into the gathering shadows. She listened. The silence had been relieved by crickets and frogs. Slowly the black night mantled the river bottom and the trains of stars twinkled in the blue dome.

The presence of the horses, as they grazed near, brought something of comfort, if not relief. She remembered a dog she had loved. Rover—if she only had him now! Then she climbed into the wagon, and without removing even her boots she crawled into the blankets. They had been disarranged in the rough ride. She needed them more to hide under than for warmth. The soft night seemed drowsily lulling.

Her body cried out with its aches and pains and weariness, with the deep internal riot round her heart, with throb of brain. Not all at once could she lie still. But gradually began a slow sinking, as if she were settling down, down, and all at once she lay like a log. It was too warm under the blanket, yet when she threw it back and saw the white stars, so strange, watchful, she grew more aware of her plight and covered her face again. At length her body relaxed to the point where it was no longer dominating with its muscular sensations. Then her mind grew active—reverted to the terrible tragedy of Jett's outfit. Catlee! . . . All the time he had watched over her. He had killed for her—and died for her. A man who confessed he had never been anything else than bad! Something great loomed in Milly's mind. Could Jett have had any good in him? . . . She prayed for their souls.

They had left her alone, and she must find her way—whither? And into that dark gulf of mind flashed the thought and the vision of Tom Doan. Milly began to weep. It was too terrible, the remembrance of him, and his love and kisses, of his offer of marriage and his plan for their home. Terrible to dwell upon when she was lost in the prairie. She might never see him again! But she must try with all her power to find her way out.

"I—will try—for him!" she sobbed, and remembered her prayers. Then grief and worry succumbed to exhaustion; she drifted into slumber.

The singing of birds awakened Milly. The sun had risen; the green leaves were fluttering with a silken rustle. It took a moment for realization of her situation to rush into thought. Yet the darkness of mind, the old reluctance to return to consciousness, was absent this morning.

When she got to her knees, and knelt there, stretching her bruised and cramped muscles, she looked over the wagon to see the white horses grazing near under the cottonwoods. Sleek gray deer were grazing with them, as tame as cattle. A rabbit crossed the aisle of green. The morning held a strange bright beauty and peace.

Milly brushed out her tangled short curls. Her face was burned from the wind and sun of yesterday's ride. Then she climbed out of the wagon, ready for the day. She did not have to dress, and she thought bathing her face might make the sunburn worse.

First she put a quart of oats in each nose bag, and carried them out to the horses. She did not need to go far. Both horses saw her and came to meet her; and slipping the nosebags in place, she led them to the wagon and haltered them. Breakfast did not take long to prepare and eat. Then she cleaned the utensils, packed them away in the box, shook out her blankets, and rolled them. This left the task which worried her—that of hitching up.

But when she came to undertake it she found that she remembered where every part of the harness belonged. To lift the heavy wagon tongue and hold it while she snapped the hooks into rings required all her strength.

"There!" she muttered, with something of pride and wonder. "Now what?"

Was the wagon all right? She walked round it, as she had seen Jett do. One spoke had been broken out of the left hind wheel; other than that she could not see any damage. Jett had greased the wagon wheels the day before his intended departure. Nothing more to do but start! Milly was almost overcome at the thought. It seemed incredible that she would dare to drive across the prairie.

"I can't stay here. I'd be as badly off as on the move," she burst out, desperately. "Oh, I must go! But where—how?"

She wrung her hands and fought her fears. A terrible problem confronted her. Yet was it as perilous as when she was practically a prisoner in Jett's outfit. Again she remembered that her prayers had been answered. Suppose she was only a timid weak girl? Could she not make herself do what any boy might do? Once and for all she drove herself passionately into a spirit of daring and faith. She resolved to feel these, even though she had to endure agonies of dread.

Then she plumped to her knees before a little bare spot of sand, and gazing down at it she thought with all her might. Not for nothing had she been keen to observe men in camp, when they talked about roads, trails, places. Jett had been poor at direction and location, but Follonsbee had the whole buffalo country in his mind. Milly had seen him draw maps in the dirt. To this end she took up a stick.

"The west is there," she said, thoughtfully. "I saw the sun set. Then the north is there. Northwest is my direction. It was ten days' travel from Pease River to Sprague's Post. . . . Here's the Pease."

And she drew a line in the sand.

"Yesterday I came thirty miles—maybe forty, almost due north, to this stream. Then I'm here." She made a dot in the sand, and another line representing this stream. "I don't dare try to find my way back to the buffalo camps. I might meet the Indians. I must not follow this stream west. I must cross it and head northwest. I must cross every stream I meet. When I reach one too deep to ford I must follow along it till I find a place."

Milly's reasoning was the result of her experience with the Jett outfit. It took no particular degree of intelligence to calculate about where she was on the prairie and what to do to get out. The great task was to accomplish what her judgment dictated. She had traveled enough over the untrodden prairie to have some faint conception of the enormity of what faced her. Thought of meeting with buffalo-hunters persistently flaunted hopes. They encouraged her, but she could not trust to them. This Texas prairie covered a vast space, and in it she was lost.

"That's all!" she said, blankly.

The moment of decision had come. Milly drew a deep breath and flung wide her arms, with hands clenching. How she hated to leave the apparent protection of these friendly cottonwoods! Then, with a great throb in her breast, she turned to mount the wagon.

Not reluctant indeed were the horses. They had grazed and drunk their fill and they knew their noses were pointed homeward, away from the buffalo fields. Milly had all she could do to hold them. She drove out of the grove, to the right where the buffalo had worn a wide trodden belt down to the stream. The last fifty yards were quite downhill. Milly reined in to scrutinize her first obstacle of the day.

Thousands of buffalo had forded the stream here. Far as she could see, the banks on both sides were trodden fresh and dark with tracks. At this point the stream was perhaps three feet deep and forty wide; nothing for strong and nimble buffalo to ford. But these buffalo had not been hampered with a wagon. Still, the crossing was not especially bad. Jett would not have given it a second glance. He would have plunged across. The sandy bottom would assuredly be hard packed. Milly had only to start right, not too carefully, and to keep the horses going.

She threw on the brake and called to the horses. "Get up! Whity! Specks! . . . Easy now!"

They trotted down the slope—faster—faster. Milly leaned back on the reins. Her face blanched. Her teeth clenched. It was fearful, yet it roused defiance. She could drive them. They were eager, unafraid. The wagon propelled them. Plunge! the water crashed and splashed high. And the wagon bounced after them, to souse into the stream, over the front wheels. Milly was deluged. For an instant she could not see for water in her eyes, for the flying spray. But she called to the horses. They took the stream at a trot. It was no deeper than their knees, and they sent sheets of muddy water ahead of them. The opposite bank was low, easy for them; and Milly, before she realized it, pulled up on the level open prairie.

"Easy, and I got a bath!" she cried, exultantly. "Oh, Whity and Specks, I love you!"

She searched for her scarf to wipe her wet face and hair. But it, too, like her little gun, was gone. She had lost it. No! She recalled that she had left it tied on the hoop of the wagon cover in Jett's camp. The memory startled her. Suppose Tom Doan should at last find Jett's camp and see her red scarf. But that misery for him could never be. The Indians would have made blackened embers of that camp.

Milly took her direction from the sun and drove out upon the prairie. It was a gray, beautiful plain, luxuriant with ripened grass, sloping very gently to the north. Far to the eastward she espied the black horizon—wide line of buffalo. They had grazed down the stream. In the bright sunlight the whole panorama was splendid and stirring to Milly.

The horses started at a trot, and in the thick grass slowed to a steady brisk walk. The wagon was light, the ground level; and this powerful team had no serious task ahead of them, if they were only guided aright. Milly was excited, thrilled, and yet troubled. The adventure was tremendous, but the responsibility too great except for moments of defiance or exaltation. She could not all the time remain keyed up with a spirit that was unquenchable.

Several miles of travel brought her to the summit of the gradual slope of valley, and here, as on the side from which she had come, she obtained commanding view of the surrounding country. It was grand, but she had eyes only for the northwest. Across the leagues of billowy prairie, so gray and monotonous and lonely, there stood a purple escarpment, remote and calling. It was the Llano Estacado. Milly recognized it, and seemed for an instant to forget the sense of being lost. But it was far away, and the northern end disappeared in purple haze. On the other hand it was a landmark ever present from high points, and somewhere between it and her present position ran the road of the buffalo-hunters.

To her left meandered the green line of trees, like a fringed ribbon on the soft gray of prairie, and it headed toward the Staked Plain, where she knew all these Texas streams had their source.

"I could reach the road to-day or to-morrow, if I drove straight west," soliloquized Milly.

It was a sore temptation, but her good sense forbade her to take such added risk. The Comanches were between her and the buffalo camps. She must aim diagonally across the prairie, toward the extreme northwest corner of the escarpment, and perhaps four or five days she would strike the road. Then she would know the camping grounds, and would surely fall in with oncoming hunters or outgoing freighters. To find water at night, and to cross such streams as she met—these were her present problems.

Meanwhile, as she drove on, thinking only of this incredible journey, she could not help seeing and being momentarily thrilled by the wild creatures of the prairie.

Sleek gray, white-rumped antelope scarcely bothered to trot out of her path, and with long ears erect they watched her pass. Wild? These beautiful prairie deer were not wild. Milly believed she could in time have had them eating out of her hand, like she had the squirrels and birds at the Pease River camp. It was men who made animals wild.

She ranged the wide gray expanse for sight of buffalo. There were none. She saw a band of coyotes sneaking round the antelope. Farther on she espied a gaunt wolf, almost white, watching her from a ridge-top. Rabbits were always scurrying from before the horses, and prairie birds flitted out of the grass. Once Milly saw a red hawk poised in midair, fluttering its wings with marvelous rapidity, and then it shot down like a streak, to strike the grass and rise with a tiny animal in its talons. Always beauty and life present, and with them, cruelty—death!

Milly drove from early morning until an hour before sunset, when she reached the only water of the day. It was a pond in a sandy stream-bed. There were fringes of hackaberry brush along the banks, but no sheltering trees. Farther west some six or eight miles she thought she espied the green of timber, but that was far away and off her line of direction. She must take what afforded; and to this end she unhitched, turned the horses loose, and made the simple preparations for her own wants.

Whity and Specks, as she had christened the horses, after drinking at the pond returned to linger near the wagon. They manifested extraordinary interest in Milly and even got in her way.

"What's the matter with you white-faced beggars?" she asked. "It's oats you want, yes? Well, I'm not going to let you eat all the oats right away."

Yet she was not proof against their nosing round her. Long had she been gentle and kind to these horses—the more so because of Jett's brutality. They knew her well, and now that she was master they began to prove the devotion of dumb brutes. Milly gave them sparingly of the oats, and petted them, and talked the more because solitude had begun to impinge upon her mind.

This sunset hour found her tired after the long day's drive. With change of action, followed by food and drink she needed, there came a rally of spirits. Darkness soon hid the lonely, limitless expanse from Milly's gaze, and then it seemed the night was lonelier. Only a faint murmur of insects! She would have welcomed a mourn of wolf, or even a cry of panther. A slight breeze fanned the red embers of the meager fire. She went to bed afraid of the silence, the night, afraid of sleep, yet she could not keep her eyes open or stay the drowsy fading away of senses.

Next morning Milly was up early, and on the way before sunrise. She started well. But at the end of the first hour she ran into rough prairie, hindering travel. The luxuriant prairie grass failed and the gray earth carried only a scanty covering. The horses plowed up dust that rose and blew back upon her; the sun grew hot and glaring; and there was a wide area of shallow washes, ditches, gullies, like the depressions of a washboard. Having plodded miles into this zone, she could not turn back, unless absolutely balked, so she applied herself to careful driving, and kept on, true as possible to the distant purple landmark.

The strong horses, used to a heavy hand, could not altogether be controlled by Milly, and they plunged into many places without her sanction. What with holding the reins as best she could, and constant heed to brake and distance, and worry lest she would damage a wheel, she was in grievous straits most of that day. It passed swiftly, swallowed up in miles of hard going, and left no time for scanning the prairie or fearful imaginings. It was work.

Toward evening she drew out of this zone and came presently to good grass once more, and just at dusk hauled up to a timber belt that bordered water. The thirsty horses stamped to get down to it. Milly labored to unhitch them, and when the task was done she sank to the ground to rest. But she was driven to secure firewood while there was light enough. She felt too tired to eat, yet she knew she must eat, or else fail altogether of strength. The long hanging to the reins was what had exhausted Milly. Her hands hurt, her arms ached, her shoulders sagged. Driving that iron-mouthed team was a man's job. Milly was no weakling, but her weight and muscular force were inadequate to the demand of such driving.

Supper, bed, night, sleep—they all passed swiftly, and again the sun rose. Milly could not find a place to ford the stream. It was not a depth of water that prevented, but high banks unsafe to attempt. For miles she drove along it, glad of the green foliage and singing birds and wild creatures, and especially glad that its course for most of the morning ran a little west of north. When, however, it made an abrupt turn to the west, she knew she must cross. She essayed the best ford she could find, made it safely, wet, shaken, frightened, and nearly pulled apart. On that far side she rested in the shade, and wept while she ate.

When about to start again she remembered that the men had never passed a stream or pond without watering the horses. Whereupon she took the bucket and went down to fill it. Four trips were necessary to satisfy the thirst of Whity and Specks. She had done well.

"We had two dry camps between Sprague's and the Pease," she said, and thought she must not forget that.

The afternoon drive began favorably. The sun was somewhat hazed over, reducing the heat; a level prairie afforded smooth travel; the horses had settled down into steady stolid work. The miles came slowly, but surely.

Milly's courage had not failed, but she was beset by physical ills, and the attendant moods, fancies, thoughts that could not everlastingly be overcome. She grew to hate the boundless prairie-land, so barren of life, of any color but gray, of things that might mitigate the deceit of distance. Nothing save gray level and purple haze! It wore on her, ever flinging at her the attributes of the prairie openness, a windy vastness, empty of sound, movement, the abode of solitude, the abode of loneliness. Lonely, lonely land! She was as much lost as ever. There was no road, no river, no camp, no mountain, only the dim upflung false Llano Estacado, unattainable as ever.

But while Milly succumbed to her ills and her woes the horses plodded on. They knew what they had to accomplish, and were equal to it. They crowded the hours and miles behind them, and bore Milly to another watercourse, a wide glade-bordered enlargement of a stream, where ducks and cranes and kingfishers gave life to the melancholy scene.

While she performed her tasks the lake changed from blue to gold, and at last mirrored the rose of sunset sky. Then dusk fell sadly, and night came, dark, lonely, pierced by the penetrating trill of frogs and the dismal cry of a water fowl. They kept Milly awake and she could not shake the encroachment of morbid thoughts. Where was she? What would become of her? The vast gloomy prairie encompassed her, held her a prisoner, threatened her with madness. She had feared Indians, rivers, accidents, but now only the insupportable loneliness. Would she not die of it and be eaten by buzzards? The stars that had been so beautiful, watching, helpful, now seemed pitiless, remote, aloof, with their pale eyes on her, a girl lost on the endless prairie. What was beyond those stars? Not a soul, no kindly great spirit to guide her out of this wilderness? Milly prayed once more.

She dragged herself from bed next day, long after sunrise, and had spirit to begin the ordeal, if her flesh was weak.

Whity and Specks waited in camp for their oats. Milly scorned herself for dreading they would run away, leaving her utterly alone. She fed them and caressed them, and talked as if they were human. "You belong to me," she said. "I was Jett's stepdaughter. He's gone. And you're mine. . . . If you ever get me out of this—"

But she did not think she would ever get out now, unless Providence remembered her again. She had no hunger. A fever consumed her and she drank copiously of water. Hitching up was a dragging job. The heavy wagon tongue nearly broke her back. At last she was in the driver's seat. Whity and Sparks started of their own accord, splashed across the shallow lake, and pulled up on the gray flat expanse.

Milly was either ill or almost spent, she did not know which. She had power to sit up, hold the reins, guide the horses toward that futile illusive landmark days away on the horizon, but she could not control her mind.

The wandering roll of prairie-land mocked her with its shining gray distances, its illusive endlessness, its veils of heat. The hot sun rose, glared down, slanted to the west, and waned. She found no water that sunset. The horses had no drink. Milly mixed their oats with water from the keg. Hunger exceeded all her sensations, even the pains; and tenaciously she clung to her one idea of effort, to keep trying, to follow judgment she had made at the outset. She ate, and crawled into her wagon-bed, no longer afraid of night and loneliness. So tired—so tired she wanted to die!

But the sun awakened her and the will to go on survived. The faithful horses waited, whinnying at her approach. Mechanically she worked, yet was aware of clumsiness and pain, that she must water them that day. The prairie smoked with heat. It beckoned, flaunted, slanted to the hot steely sky. She closed her eyes and slept with the reins in her hands; she awakened to jolt of wagon and crunching of stone. Thunder rumbled out of the sky and clouds obscured the sun. She drove into a storm, black, windy, with driving sheets of cool rain and white zigzag ropes of lightning, crashing thunder, long roll across the heavens. She was drenched to the skin and strangely refreshed. That fiery band round her head had snapped and gone. The horses splashed into a buffalo-wallow and drank of the fresh rain water.

Away the storm rolled, purple clouds and pall of drifting gray and sheets of flame. The north showed blue again, and presently the sun shone. The horses steamed, the prairie smoked. Milly's clothes dried as the gray miles passed behind the tireless team.

The day's journey ended at a river, and as if her troubles need be multiplied, it was unfordable at that point. Milly camped. And the morning found her slower, stiffer, yet stern to go on. This river, too—could it have been the Louisiana Red?—had a northwest trend. All day she followed it, often in the shade of trees. No tracks, no trails, no old camps—the region was like a luxuriant barren land.

Next morning she found a disused buffalo ford. The tracks were old. They stirred her sluggish blood, her submerged hopes. She gained a little therefrom. If only she could drop the reins and rest her hands, her arms! But the faithful horses had to be guided. Would she ever come to a road? Was this whole world devoid of the manifestations of travel? Miles and miles, as gray, as monotonous as a dead sea!

Then she drove into a zone of buffalo carcasses, and was startled into wonder, hope, wild thought. Where was she? Fifty—maybe a hundred miles east of the Staked Plain, and still lost! These carcasses were black and dried; they had no odor; they were ghastly heaps of bones and hides. She drove ten miles across this belt of death and decay; and no sign of horse or wagon cheered her aching sight.

Milly lost track of hours, days, time. Sunset, a camp by water, black night with hateful stars, the false dawn, day with its gray leagues and blistering sun, the white horses forever moving on and on and on, night, blackness, light once more, and horrible weary pangs.

"What's this?" cried Milly, and wide flew her eyes. She was lying back in the wagon, where she had fallen from faintness. She remembered. It had been early morning. But now the sun was high. The wagon creaked, swayed, moved on to strange accompaniment—*clip-clop, clip-clop, clip-clop*. The horses were trotting on hard road. Was she dreaming? She closed her eyes the better to listen. Clip-clop, clip-clop, clip-clop! This was no lying trick of her jaded ears, worn out from silence.

"Oh—thank Heaven!" panted Milly. "It's a road—a road!" And she struggled to rise. Gray endless prairie, as always, but split to the horizon by a white hard road! She staggered to the seat. But driving was not necessary. The reins were looped round the brake. Whity and Specks needed no guidance now, no urging, no help. They were on the homeward stretch. With steady clip-clop they trotted, clicking off the miles. Whity was lame and Specks had a clanging shoe, but these were small matters.

Milly sank down overwhelmed with joy. On the Fort Elliott road! The Llano Estacado showed no longer the deceiving purple of distance. It showed gray and drab, shadowy clefts, rock wall and canyons. She forced herself to eat and drink, though the dried meat and bread were hard to swallow. She must brace up. Many were the buffalo-hunters who traveled this road. Surely before the hour was gone she would see a white wagon on the horizon. Milly lifted her head to gaze backward, toward the south, and then forward toward the north. The prairie was still a lonely land. Yet how different!

She rested, she thought, she gazed the hours away; and something came back to her.

Afternoon waned and sunset came; and with the fading of rosy and golden light the horses snorted their scent of water. Milly was stronger. Hope had wonderfully revived her. And she called to the horses.

Another horizon line reached! It was the crest of one of the prairie slopes. Long had it been unattainable, hiding while it beckoned onward. A green-mantled stream crossed just below. Milly's aching and exhausted heart throbbed to sudden recognition. She had camped here. She knew those cottonwoods. And strong sweet wine of renewed life fired her veins.

Whity and Specks remembered. This was the cold sweet water from the uplands, well loved by the buffalo. They snorted and lifted dusty, shaggy hoofs, to plod on and stop. Milly looked down on the green bank where Catlee had voiced his sympathy.

Another sunset, one of gold and red out of purple clouds, burned over the prairie-land. The sloping shadows crept along the distant valleys; the grassy undulating expanse shone with dusky fire. And a winding river, like a bright thread, lost itself in the far dim reaches.

Milly Fayre drove Whity and Specks across the cattle-dotted pasture which flanked the river banks outside of Sprague's Post.

Horses mingled with the cattle. Between the road and the cottonwoods camps sent up their curling columns of blue smoke. Tents gleamed rosily in the sunset glow. Dogs ran out to herald the coming of another team. Curious buffalo-hunters, on the way south, dropped out to halt Milly. Natives of the Post strolled across from the store to question the traveler from the buffalo fields.

"Howdy, sonny!" greeted a white-haired old Westerner, with keen blue eyes flashing over weary horses, and wagon with its single occupant. "All by yourself?"

"Yes," replied Milly, amazed to hear her husky voice.

Men crowded closer, kindly, interested, beginning to wonder.

"Whar you from?" queried the old man.

"Pease River," replied Milly.

"Aw, say now, sonny, you're—" Then he checked his query and came closer, to lay a hand on the smoking horse nearest to him. The rugged faces, some bronzed, some with the paleness that was not long of the prairie, were lifted to Milly. They seemed beautiful, so full of life, kindness, interrogation. They dimmed in Milly's sight, through her tears.

"Yes, Pease River," she replied, hurriedly and low. "My outfit fought—killed one another. . . . Comanches swam the river. . . . I drove Whity and Specks through the brakes. . . . The Indians chased us. . . . We ran into stampeded buffalo. . . . Driven all day—surrounded—dust and roar. . . . Oh, it was terrible! . . . But they slowed up—they carried us all day—forty miles. . . . Since then I've camped and driven—camped and driven, days, days, days, I don't—know—how—many!"

A silence ensued after Milly's long poignant speech. Then the old Westerner scratched his beard in perplexity.

"Sonny, air you jest foolin' us or jest out of your haid? You shore look fagged out."

"It's—gospel—truth," panted Milly.

"My boy," began the kindly interrogator, with graver voice, and again his keen gaze swept over grimy horses, and travel-worn wagon.

"Boy!" exclaimed Milly, as spiritedly as her huskiness would permit. "I'm no boy! . . . I'm a girl—Milly Fayre."

CHAPTER SIXTEEN

Tom raised himself as high as he dared and studied what he could see of the field in the direction of the bluff. A man might trust himself boldly to that jumble of rocks. Accordingly he crawled on hands and knees to the end of this stone-like corral, and there, stretching on his left side, with left hand extended and right dragging his rifle, he crawled as swiftly and noiselessly as possible. He peered only ahead of him. There was no use to look at the aisles between the rocks at the right and left, because he had to pass these openings, and looking was not going to help him. Trusting to luck and daring he went on, somehow conscious of a grim exultance in the moment. Fear had left him. At the outset he had a few thoughts of himself—that he could only die once, and if he had to do so now it would be for his comrades. Milly Fayre's dark haunting eyes crossed his memory, a stabbing, regretful pain; and for her he would have embraced any peril. Some way these Comanches had been the cause of Milly's flight, if they had not caught her. To them he owed loss of her. And he wanted to kill some of them. But all he asked was luck and strength enough to get back with the water.

After those few flashing thoughts all his senses were fixed on the physical task ahead of him. He had to go swiftly and noiselessly, without rest. His efforts were supreme, sustained. Coming back he would adhere to Pilchuck's advice, but on the way out he could not take it, except in the matter of laying a line of small stones as he progressed.

After the first ten or a dozen rods were behind him there came an easing of a terrible strain. His comrades behind him were shooting now something like a volley, which action he knew was Pilchuck's way of diverting possible discovery from him. The Indians were shooting more, too; and he began to draw considerably away from the cross-fire. He heard no more bullets whiz over his head. As it was impossible to crawl in a straight line, owing to rocks impeding his progress, he deviated from the course set by Pilchuck. This entailed a necessity of lifting himself every few moments so that he could peep over the rocks to keep the direction of the bluff. These wary brief actions were fraught with suspense. They exposed him perilously, but were absolutely imperative.

Bolder he grew. He was going to succeed in this venture. The sustained exertion threatened collapse, yet he still had strength to go on. A few more rods might safely earn rest! The burning sun beat down pitilessly. Tom's tongue hung out, dripping a white froth. His heart expanded as if trying to burst bands of steel. Despite the sternest passion of will he could not help the low gasping intake of air or the panting expulsion. A listening Indian within fifty yards could have heard him. But he kept on. His wet hand and wrist gathered a grimy covering of dust. His rifle grew slippery from sweat from his other hand. Rocks obstructing his advance, the narrow defiles he had to squeeze through, the hard sharp edges tearing his shirt, the smell of the hot earth, the glaring sun—all seemed obstacles that put the fact of Indians in the background.

Again Tom lost his direction. He was coming to a zone more open, and surely not far from the bluff that was his objective point. Usually he had chosen a high and large stone from which to peep. At this juncture not one of such size was available. Low down along the side of a flat stone he peered out. All he could see was a rather wide space, not thickly studded with rocks. But from that angle the bluff was not in sight.

Almost spent from his long crawl, with both muscle and will about played out, he raised himself to locate the bluff. Not on the right side! Dropping down, he crawled the few feet to the left end of this rock, and kneeling sidewise he raised himself again to look over.

Something like a sharp puff of wind whipped by. He heard a hiss. Then he felt a shock, solid, terrific, followed by a tearing burning pain across his back. Almost the same instant came the bursting crack of a rifle. Swift as light Tom's sight took in the open ahead. A half-naked Indian, red skinned, snake-like, stood with smoking rifle, a wild and savage expectation on his dark face.

Tom fell flat behind the rock, all the power of his mind in supreme and flashing conflict against the stunning surprise. It galvanized him. One second he gripped his rifle hard, cocked it, while his muscles gathered and strung for a mighty effort.

Tom leaped up and shot in the same action. It seemed he did not see the Indian clearly until after the discharge of the rifle. The Indian's gun was leveled. But it flew aside, strangely, as if propelled. And on the same instant there was a metallic crack. Tom's bullet had struck the breach of the Indian's gun and had glanced.

The Indian gasped and staggered. He seemed to push his gun away from him. It fell to the ground. Blood gushed from his mouth. He had been mortally wounded. His dark face was terrible to look upon. He was swaying, yet he snatched out a knife and made at Tom. A black flame of hate burned from his eyes.

For a second Tom stood transfixed. The Indian came lurching with the knife. Then Tom jumped just in time to avoid its sweep. Horror gave place to fury. He had no time to reload, so he whirled his rifle, making a club of it. But he missed the Indian, and such was the force of the blow he had aimed that he nearly lost his balance. As it was he righted himself to find the Indian lunging down with the knife.

Like a flash Tom's left hand caught the descending wrist and gripped it. Then he tried to swing the rifle with his right. But the Indian intercepted the blow and held the rifle.

Thus on the moment both were rendered helpless to force the issue. They held each other grimly.

"No—weyno!" gasped the Indian, thickly.

"Comanche! You're—no good—yourself!" panted Tom.

It was a deadlock. Tom exerted himself to the utmost to hold that quivering blade back from his body. He saw the advantage was on his side. Blood poured from a wound in the Indian's throat. The nearness of it, the terrible nature of the moment, the unabatable ferocity and courage of his red adversary were almost too much for Tom. He all but sank under the strain.

Then came a sudden shuddering convulsion on the part of the Indian, a last supreme effort. It was so great that it broke Tom's hold. But even as the Indian wrenched free his strength failed. The corded strung muscles suddenly relaxed. His working, fiercely malignant visage as suddenly set somberly. He dropped the knife. He swayed and fell.

Tom bent over him. The Indian gazed upward, conscious. Then the hate in his dark eyes gave way to a blankness. He was dead. Tom stared, slowly realizing.

In a moment more he was alive to the situation. He had conquered here. But he was not yet out of danger. Still, if any Indians had seen this encounter they would have shot him before this.

Crouching down, Tom peered round until he had again located his objective point. Then he ran as fast as his spent strength permitted and soon reached the red bluff. But he did not locate the hiding place of the horses until Jake Devine saw him and called. Tom staggered round the bluff and into the pocket where the horses were concealed.

Devine came rattling down from a ledge where evidently he had been watching. Then Al Thorndyke, the other guard, appeared from the opposite quarter. They ran to Tom.

"Say, you're all bloody!" declared Jake, aghast.

"Tom, I seen thet fight," added Thorndyke, sharply. "But I couldn't shoot fer fear of hittin' you."

"I'm hit—I don't know—how bad," panted Tom. "But it can't—be very bad. . . . Hurry, boys. I came after water. Tie me up. I've got to rustle back."

"We'll shore go with you," said Devine.

They tore Tom's shirt off. It was wringing wet and as red as a flag.

"Reckon you sweat a heap," put in Thorndyke, encouragingly.

Tom winced as one of them ran a finger in the wound on his back.

"Nothin' bad. Long deep cut," said Devine. "Fetch water, Al."

The two men washed Tom's wound and bandaged it tightly with a scarf.

"I've got to take some canteens back," declared Tom.

"I'll go. You stay with Al," replied Devine.

"Wal, I ain't a-goin' to stay. I've got to git in thet fight," asserted Thorndyke.

"Listen to the shootin'," exclaimed Devine.

Tom heard a rattling volley of Creedmoors, punctuated by the sharper, lighter cracking of Winchesters. It was certainly an exciting sound.

"But I wasn't told to fetch you," protested Tom.

"Thet don't make no difference. What's the use of us hidin' here? If the Comanches found us we couldn't hold the horses. We'd just be goners. Out there we can git in the fight."

Devine's logic was unanswerable. So Tom made no further objection. The three men took two canteens each, and their rifles, and hurried forth.

Tom led the way. It was easy walking, but when he reached the point where he thought it needful to stoop, the hard work commenced. The heavy canteens swung round and hung from his neck.

He reached the spot where he had fought the Comanche, and here he crouched down. Devine and Thorndyke came up with him. The Indian lay stark—his eyes wide open—his hands spread.

"Fellars, I'll fetch thet Indian's gun an' belt," said Devine, practically.

Tom wondered how Devine could pack these in addition to the load he already carried. But the stocky little man appeared equal to the occasion. Soon Tom lay flat to crawl like a snake. It was well that he had laid a trail. Tom kept the lead, ten feet in front of Thorndyke, who was a like distance ahead of Devine. Tom had to stop every little while to rest. His lungs appeared to stand the test, but his muscles were weak. Still he knew he could make the distance. The long drink of water he had taken had revived him.

Whenever Tom halted to rest he would listen to the shooting. His followers would creep up to him and make some comment. They were eager to join the fray.

"Tom, I reckon you're tuckered out," whispered Thorndyke, on the last of these occasions. "But do your damndest. For we're shore needed."

Thus admonished, Tom did not rest again, though he crawled less violently, trying to husband what strength he had left. The return had not been so exciting, and for that reason was harder work. It was different. Nothing but bullets could have stopped him.

They had crawled close to where Pilchuck and his men were shooting, and therefore within the zone of the Indians' fire, when a bullet kicked up the dust in front of Tom. He hesitated. Then a bullet clipped the crown of his hat. This spurred him to a spasmodic scrambling forward to cover behind a bowlder. From there Tom squirmed round to look back. Jake Devine was kneeling with leveled rifle, which on the instant belched fire and smoke. Jake dropped down and crawled forward. His face was black and his eyes blazed.

"Thet redskin is feed fer lizards," he said, grimly. "Go on, Tom."

Tom recalled the fact that Devine was a frontiersman, used to fighting Indians. So he crawled on, inspired by a sense of such companionship. Bullets now began to sing and hum overhead, and to spang from the rocks. Jake prodded Tom's feet.

"Tom, you're slower'n molasses," said Jake. "Reckon you don't mind this sort of thing. But, by golly! I'm scared. An' Al is hangin' on to my boots!"

Sometimes Jake would give Tom a shove, rooting his face in the dust. "Crawl, you belly-whopper!" he whispered, gayly. And then he would call back to Thorndyke. "Come on, Al. Dy'e you want to git plugged all to yourself?"

At last Tom and his comrades reached the smoky place that marked Pilchuck's position.

"I ain't hankerin' fer this part of the job," said Devine. "Suppose they take us fer redskins."

But Pilchuck was too wise a leader to allow blunders of that nature. He was on the lookout, and his grimy, sweaty, stern face relaxed at sight of Tom.

"Shore was good work, Tom," he said. "It's next door to hell here. Hurry to Ory an' Roberts."

Tom hurried to where the young man lay, under a sunshade Roberts had rigged up with his shirt and a stick. Roberts gave Tom a husky greeting. Manifestly his voice was almost gone. Ory's face was pale and clammy. When Tom lifted his head he opened his eyes and tried to speak. But he could not.

"Ory, here's water," said Tom, and held a canteen to the boy's pale lips.

Never until that moment had Tom appreciated the preciousness of water. He watched Ory drink, and had his reward in the wan smile of gratitude. "Much obliged, Tom," whispered Ory, and lay back with a strange look. Then he shut his eyes and appeared to relax. Tom did not like the uneasy impression he received on the moment, but in the excitement he did not think any more about it.

Roberts handed the canteen to the other wounded fellow and watched him drink. Then he slaked his own thirst.

"Say!" he ejaculated, with a deep breath. "Thet shore was all I needed."

The white-headed old plainsman crawled over for his share.

"Son, them canteens will lick Nigger Horse," he said.

"What! Are we fighting that chief?" queried Tom, in amaze.

"Accordin' to Pilchuck we're doin' jest that," responded the plainsman, cheerfully. "Old Nigger an' a thousand of his redskins, more or less."

Then Tom crawled to the vantage point behind the rock he had used before, and gave himself up to this phase of the fight. It did not take longer than a moment to realize what Pilchuck had meant. There was scarcely a second without its boom of Creedmoor or crack of Winchester. A little cloud of white smoke hung above every bowlder. Tom exercised the utmost vigilance in the matter of exposing himself to the Indians' fire. He was almost spent, and suffering excruciating pain from his wound. How infernally hot the sun burned down! His rifle and the stones were as fire to his hands. But as he began to peer out for an Indian to shoot at, and worked back into the fight, he forgot his pangs, and then what had seemed the intolerable conditions.

Tom grew intensely absorbed in his own little part in this battle. With the smell of gunpowder and smoke clogging his nostrils, with the thunder of the Creedmoors behind him, with the circling rattle of the Winchesters out there in the hot haze of the sun, he gave them but vague attention. He applied himself to an intent watchfulness, and a swift aim and shot at every moving thing in the direction he covered. It grew to be a grim duel between him and Indians he knew saw him. Like him they had to expose themselves somewhat to get in a shot. But as it was imperative to be swift their aim was necessarily erring. Nevertheless, bullets spat the dust from Tom's rock, sometimes within a few inches of his head. What a tingling sense of justice and deadly wrath these roused in Tom! It made the fight even. He welcomed these bullets, because they justified his own. He caught glimpses of shiny rifle barrels, of black sleek heads, of flashes of brown; and toward these, whenever possible, he directed his aim. Whether or not he ever hit his mark he could not tell. But he believed his bullets were making it hot for several Comanches.

Slowly the pitch of the fight augmented, until it was raging with a reckless fury on part of the Comanches, and a desperate resistance on that of the besieged. Sooner or later Tom was forced to realize in his own reactions the fact that the fighting and the peril had increased to an alarming extent. A stinging bullet crease in his shoulder was the first awakening shock he sustained. He had answered to the Indians' growing recklessness. He had been exposing himself more and redoubling his fire. He had missed Indians slipping stealthily from bowlder to bowlder—opportunities that only intense excitement and haste had made him fail to grasp. Then, when he crouched back, forced to cover, aghast at this second wound, he became fully aware of the attack.

The Comanches had pressed closer and closer, now better concealed by the pall of smoke that overhung the scene.

"Hold your fire! Look out for a charge!" yelled Pilchuck in stentorian voice.

The booming of Creedmoors ceased, and that permitted a clearer distinguishing of the Indians' fire. Their Winchesters were rattling in a continuous volley, and a hail of lead whistled over and into the bowlder corral. Manifestly the Indians had massed on the west side, between Starwell's position and Pilchuck's. This occasioned the leader to draw up his men in line with Tom's fortification. Closer and hotter grew the Indians' fire. Through the blue haze of smoke and heat Tom saw dim swiftly moving shapes, like phantoms. They were Comanches, gliding from covert to covert, and leaping from bowlder to bowlder. Tom's heart seemed to choke him. If the Indians were in strong enough force they would effect a massacre of Pilchuck's men. Suddenly, as Tom dwelt fearfully on such contingency, the firing abruptly ceased. A silence fraught with suspense ensued, strange after the heavy shooting.

"It's a trick. Look sharp!" Pilchuck warned his men.

"Wal, seein' this fight's ag'in' the exterminatin' of the buffalo, I reckon old Nigger Horse will do or die," said Jake Devine.

"If you'd ask me I'd say these hoss-ridin' redskins was up to their last dodge on foot," averred the old white-headed plainsman.

"Look out it's not *our* last dodge," replied Pilchuck.

Scarcely had he spoken when the Indians opened up with a heavy volley at alarmingly close range. Pilchuck shouted an order that was not intelligible in the cracking of firearms. But only its content was needed. The big buffalo guns answered with a roar. In another moment the firing became so fast and furious that it blended as a continuous thundering in Tom's ears. He saw the rush of Indians, incredibly swift and vague through the smoke, and he worked his rifle so hard that it grew hot. Above the roar of guns he heard the strange ear-splitting yell of the Comanches. Almost at the same instant smoke veiled the scene, more to the advantage of the white men than the red. The Creedmoors thundered as continuously as before, and the volume of sound must have been damning to the desperate courage of the Comanches. Perhaps they had not counted on so strong a force and resistance. Their war-cry pealed to a shrill pitch and ceased; and following that the rattling volleys fell off. Then Pilchuck ordered his men to stop shooting.

Tom saw the old white-haired plainsman stand up and survey the smoke-hazed slope. Then he dropped down.

"Fellars, they're draggin' off their dead an' crippled," he said. "They're licked, an' we ought to chase them clear to their hosses."

"Right," replied Pilchuck, grimly. "But wait till we're sure."

Tom could not see anything of the retreat, if such it was. The smoke mantle was lifting above the bowlders. With the sudden release of strain the men reacted according to their individual natures. Those new to such fighting were silent, as was Tom, and lay flat. Jake Devine was loquacious in his complaints that he had not downed any Comanches. The old plainsman urged Pilchuck to chase the Indians. Then when the receding fire of the enemy ceased altogether Tom heard yells close at hand.

"That's Harkaway," said the scout, eagerly, and he called out a reply.

Soon Harkaway and his men came stooping and crawling to join Pilchuck. They were panting from exertion.

"Boss—they're—workin' down," he said, breathlessly.

"Mebbe it's a trick," replied the wary scout. "I'll sneak out an' take a look."

Tom drew back from his position and eased his cramped limbs. His shirt was wet with blood. Examination showed his second bullet wound to be a slight one, but exceedingly annoying. He got Devine to tie it up, running a scarf under his arm and over his shoulder.

"Wal, a couple more scratches will make an old residenter out of you, Tom," he said, dryly.

Tom was about to make some fitting reply when Pilchuck returned in haste.

"Men, it's goin' to be our day," he said, his gray eyes alight with piercing intensity. "If we rout old Nigger Horse it'll be the first victory for the whites in this buffalo war. Us hunters will have done what the soldiers couldn't do. . . . Harkaway, you stay here with two of your men to guard these cripples. All the rest of you grab extra cartridges an' follow me."

Tom was not the last to get his hands into that cartridge bag, nor to fall in line after the scout. Once out of the zone of smoke, he was thrilled to see Indians disappearing over the edge of the slope. There was a good deal of shooting below, and the unmistakable booming reports told of Creedmoors in action. From the sound Tom judged Starwell had changed his position. But this could not be ascertained for sure until the brow of the slope was reached. Pilchuck advanced cautiously, gradually growing bolder as ambush appeared less probable, and the time came when he broke into a run.

"String out, an' come fast," he called back.

Tom fell in behind Jake Devine, and keeping some paces back he attended to the difficulty of running over the rough ground. Thus it was he did not look up until he reached the edge of the slope. Here he found Pilchuck and some of the men in a group, gazing, talking, and gesticulating all at once. Tom's breast was heaving from the hard run. He was hot and wet. But it was certain that a reviving thrill ran over him. The Comanches were in retreat. There was no doubt of that. It was still an orderly retreat, with a line of warriors guarding the rear. Tom saw Indians dragging and carrying their wounded and dead; others were gathering in the horses; and the mass was centered in the middle of the encampment, where there were signs of great haste.

One by one Pilchuck's arriving men added to the group on the slope.

"Starwell has the idea," declared Pilchuck. "See. He's moved this way an' down. He can still cover that gate an' also reach the camp."

"Jude, we shore hev our chance now," spoke up the old white-haired plainsman.

"I reckon," replied the scout. "Now listen, men. When I give the word we'll charge down this hill. Each an' every one of you yell like the devil, run a dozen jumps, drop down on your knee an' shoot. Then load, get up, an' do the same over again. Head for that pile of rocks this side of Starwell's position."

Silence followed the scout's trenchant speech. Then ensued a tightening of belts, a clinking of cartridges, a rasping of the mechanism of the Creedmoors. Tom was all ready, quivering for the word, yet glad of a few moments' rest. Pilchuck and the old plainsman stood close together, keen eyes on the Indian encampment. The sun was low over the escarpment to the west and it was losing its heat. The canyon seemed full of golden lights and blue haze, through which flashed and gleamed moving objects, horses, Indians, collapsing tepees, a colorful and exciting scene. The rear guard of Indians backed slowly to the center of the encampment. Their horses were being brought in readiness. Tom could not help but see the execution of a shrewd Indian brain. Still, there were signs of a possible panic. Already the Comanches had suffered in this fight, as was manifested by the number of those incapacitated, and which had to be packed off. Already the far slope of the canyon was covered by ponies dragging travois.

The sudden breaking up of the rear guard, as these Indians leaped for their horses, was a signal for Pilchuck.

"Charge, men!" he yelled, harshly, and plunged down the slope.

"Hi, fellars," shouted Jake Devine, "old Nigger Horse is my meat!"

In a moment Pilchuck's men were spread out on the jump, yelling like fiends and brandishing their weapons. Tom was well to the fore, close behind Devine and Pilchuck. Their heavy boots sent the loose stones flying and rattling down the hill. White puffs of smoke showed suddenly down in the encampment and were followed by the rattle of Winchesters. Presently Pilchuck plunged to a halt and, kneeling, leveled his Creedmoor. His action was swiftly followed by his men. His Creedmoor boomed; that of Devine and the plainsman next, and then the others thundered in unison. It was a long range-shot and Tom aimed generally at the commotion in the encampment. Pandemonium broke loose down there. All order seemed to vanish in a rushing *mêlée.* Pilchuck leaped up with a hoarse command, which his men answered in wild exulting whoops. And they plunged again down the slope, faster, rendered reckless by the success of their boldness.

Tom felt himself a part of that charging line of furious buffalo-hunters, and had imbibed the courage of the mass. Like the others, he had calculated on the Indians charging back to meet them, thus precipitating a pitched battle. But this was not the case. The Indians began returning the fire from all parts of the canyon. It was a hasty action, however, and did not appear formidable. They were now bent on escape. That gave irresistible momentum to the charge of Pilchuck's force. Starwell and his men, seeing the Indians routed, left their covert and likewise plunged down, firing and yelling as never before.

Tom, following the example of the men before him, ran and knelt and fired four times in rapid succession on the way down to the level floor of the canyon. By this time all the Indians were mounted and the mass of them abandoned the idea of a slow climb up the opposite slope. They broke for the canyon gate. This meant they had to lessen the long range between them and Pilchuck's force, a fact that did not daunt them. Their lean, racy mustangs were quickly in a running stride, and each rider was presenting a rifle toward the enemy.

"HOLD HERE, MEN!" bawled Pilchuck, stridently. "If they charge us take to the rocks!"

Tom no longer heard the bang of any individual gun, not even his own. And he was loading and firing as fast as possible. A roar filled his ears, and the ground seemed to shake with the furious trample of the mustangs racing by. How long and low they stretched out—how lean and wild these riders! What matchless horsemen these Comanches! Even in the hot grip of that fighting moment Tom thrilled at the magnificent defiance of these Indians, courting death by that ride, to save their burdened comrades climbing up the slope. Some of them met that death. Tom saw riders throw up their arms and pitch headlong to the ground. Mustangs leaped high, in convulsive action, and plunged down to roll over and over.

Tom seemed aware of the thinning of Pilchuck's ranks. And when the order came to run down the canyon to prevent a possible massacre of Starwell and men, who had impetuously advanced too far, some were left behind. From that moment Tom lost clear perception of the progress of the fight. The blood rage that obsessed the frontiersmen was communicated to him. He plunged with the others; he felt their nearness; he heard their hoarse yells and the boom of the guns; but he seemed to be fighting alone for the sake of the fight itself. The last of that mounted band of Comanches swooped across toward Starwell's men, driving them to the rocks. Pilchuck's force, charging down the level, came abreast of them, and there in the open a terrible, brief, and decisive battle ensued.

If the Comanches had not halted in the face of the booming Creedmoors there would have been an end to Pilchuck's buffalo-hunters. They would have been run down. But the Indians were not equal to victory at such cost. They shot as they had ridden, furiously, without direct attention. As for the white men, fury made them only the more efficient. They advanced, yelling, cursing, shooting and loading as men possessed of devils. The smoke and din seemed to envelop Tom. His gun scorched his hands and powder burned his face. When he reloaded he seemed to reel and fumble over his breech-lock. The compact mass of Indians disintegrated to strings and streams, vague, not so close, lean wild savage figures hard to aim at. Then something struck Tom and the vagueness became obscurity.

When Tom returned to consciousness he felt a dull pain, and a thickness of mind that did not permit him to establish a clear conception of his whereabouts or what had happened. He was being carried; voices of men fell upon his ears; daylight seemed fading into a red duskiness. A blankness intervened, then again he dizzily awoke. He was lying on his back and a dark bluff rose above him. Then he became aware of cold water being dashed in his face, and a familiar voice.

"Tom's not bad hurt," said Jake Devine. "Thet last bullet bounded off'n his skull. He shore is a hard-headed fellar."

"Aw! I reckon I'm glad," replied Pilchuck. "Looked to me like he'd gone."

"Nope. He'll come round tip-top. . . . I'm a son-of-a-gun if he ain't come to right now! Hey, Tom!"

"I'm all right, thanks," said Tom, weakly. "How'd we make out?"

Whereupon Devine began an eloquent account of how they had stood off Nigger Horse and two hundred braves, had whipped them, and finally routed them completely with a considerable loss. But Devine omitted to mention what Pilchuck's force had suffered.

Though feeling considerable pain and much weakness through loss of blood, Tom was able to eat a little, after which effort he fell asleep.

Daylight brought clear consciousness to him, and one glance round at his lame and bandaged comrades gave an inkling of what the victory over Nigger Horse had cost. Not a man had escaped at least one wound! Burn Hudnall had escaped serious injury. Tom missed familiar faces. But he did not make inquiries then. He submitted to a painful treatment of his wounds. Then he was glad enough to lie quietly with closed eyes.

Later that morning he had strength enough to mount his horse and ride with the slow procession back to the permanent camp. He made it, but prayed he would have no more such ordeals. The shady, cool camp with its running water was a most soothing relief. One by one the injured were made comfortable. It was then Tom learned that seven of Pilchuck's force had been killed in the fight. Ory Tacks had been the first to succumb. Thus Tom had verification of his fears. Poor, brave, cheerful Ory! These heroic men would find graves on the spot where they had helped to break forever the backbone of the Comanches' hostility.

Pilchuck visited with the injured men that day. His sternness had vanished.

"Boys," he said, "I never expected any of us to get out of that fight alive. When those yellin' devils charged us I thought the game was up. We did well, but we were mighty lucky. It's sad about our comrades. But some of us had to go an' we were all ready. Now the great good truth is that this victory will rouse the buffalo-hunters. I'll go after more men. We'll shore chase the Comanches an' Kiowas off the Staked Plain, an' that will leave us free to hunt buffalo. What's more important, it will make Texas safe for settlers. So you can all feel proud, as I do. The buffalo-hunters will go down in history as havin' made Texas habitable."

CHAPTER SEVENTEEN

In 1876 more than two hundred thousand buffalo hides were shipped east over the Santa Fe railroad, and hundreds of thousands in addition went north from Fort Worth, Texas.

For this great number of hides that reached eastern and foreign markets there were at least twice the number of hides sacrificed on the range. Old buffalo-hunters generally agreed on the causes for this lamentable fact. Inexperienced hunters did not learn to poison the hides, which were soon destroyed by hide bugs. Then as many buffalo were crippled as killed outright and skinned, and these wounded ones stole away to die in coulees or the brakes of the rivers. Lastly, a large percentage of the buffalo were chased by hunters into the quagmires and quicksands along the numerous streams, there to perish.

1877 saw the last of the raids by Comanches and Kiowas, a condition brought round solely by the long campaign of united bands of buffalo-hunters, who chased and fought these Indians all over the Staked Plain. But this campaign was really a part of the destruction of the buffalo, and that destruction broke forever the strength of these hard-riding Indians.

In the winter and spring of that year the number of hide-hunting outfits doubled and trebled and quadrupled; and from the Red River to the Brazos, over that immense tract of Texas prairie, every river, stream, pond, water-hole and spring, everywhere buffalo could drink was ambushed by hunters with heavy guns. The poor animals that were not shot down had to keep on traveling until the time came when a terrible parching thirst made them mad. Then, when in their wanderings to find some place to drink they scented water, they would stampede, and in their madness to assuage an insupportable thirst would plunge over one another in great waves crushing to death those underneath.

* * *

Tom Doan, during the year and a half of the Indian raids, fought through three campaigns against Comanches, Kiowas, and Llano Estacado Apaches.

Pilchuck's first organizing of buffalo-hunters into a unit to fight Comanches drove the wedge that split the Indians; and likewise it inspired and roused the hide-hunters from the Territory line to the Rio Grande. Thus there was a war on the several tribes, as well as continued slaughter of the buffalo.

In the spring of 1877, when, according to the scouts, the backbone of the Southwest raiding tribes had been broken, Tom Doan bade good-by to Burn Hudnall, his friend and comrade for so long. Dave Stronghurl had months before gone back to Sprague's Post to join his wife, and Burn, now that the campaign had ended, wanted to see his wife and people.

"I reckon I'm even with the Comanches," he said, grimly. That was his only reference to his father's murder.

"Well, Burn, we've seen wild life," mused Tom, sadly. "I'm glad I helped rout the Comanches. They've been robbed, I suppose, and I can't blame them. But they sure made a man's blood boil for a fight."

"What'll you do, Tom?" queried Burn.

Doan dropped his head. "It'd hurt too much to go back to Sprague's Post—just yet. You see, Burn, I can't forget Milly. Of course she's dead long ago. But then, sometimes I see her in dreams, and she seems alive. I'd like to learn the truth of her fate. Some day I might. Pilchuck and I are going south to the Brazos. The last great hunt is on there."

"I'm goin' to settle on a ranch at Sprague's," said Burn. "Father always said that would be center of a fine cattle an' farmin' district some day."

"Yes, I remember. It used to be my dream, too. But I'm changed. This roving life, I guess. The open range for me yet a while! Some day I'll come back."

"Tom, you've money saved," returned Burn, thoughtfully. "You could buy an' stock a ranch. Isn't it risky carryin' round all your money? There's worse than bad Comanches now in the huntin' field."

"I've thought of that," said Tom. "It does seem risky. So I'll ask you to take most of my money and bank it for me."

"It's a good idea. But see here, old man, suppose you don't come back? You know, we've seen things happen to strong an' capable men down here. Think how lucky we've been!"

"I've thought of that, too," said Tom, with gravity. "If I don't show up inside of five years invest the money for your children. Money's not much to me any more. . . . But I'm likely to come back."

This conversation took place at Wheaton's camp, on the headwaters of the Red River, in April. A great exodus of freighters was taking place that day. It was interesting for Tom to note the development of the hide hauling. The wagons were large and had racks and booms, so that when loaded they resembled hay wagons, except in color. Two hundred buffalo hides to a wagon, and six yokes of oxen to a team and twenty-five teams to a train! Swiftly indeed were the buffalo disappearing from the plains. Burn Hudnall rode north with one of these immense freighting outfits.

Tom and Pilchuck made preparations for an extended hunt in the Brazos River country, whence emanated rumors somewhat similar to the gold rumors of '49.

While choosing and arranging an outfit they were visited by a brawny little man with a most remarkable visage. It was scarred with records of both the sublime and the ridiculous.

"I'm after wantin' to throw in with you," he announced to Pilchuck.

The scout, used to judging men in a glance, evidently saw service and character in this fellow.

"Wal, we need a man, that's shore. But he must be experienced," returned the scout.

"Nary tenderfoot, scout, not no more," he grinned. "I've killed an' skinned over four thousand buffs. An' I'm a blacksmith an' a cook."

"Wal, I reckon you're a whole outfit in yourself," rejoined Pilchuck, with his rare broad smile. "How do you want to throw in?"

"Share expense of outfit, work, an' profit."

"Nothin' could be no more fair. I reckon we'll be right glad to have you. What's your handle?"

"Wrong-Wheel Jones," replied the applicant, as if he expected that cognomen to be recognized.

"What the hell! I've met Buffalo Jones, an' Dirty-Face Jones an' Spike Jones, but I never heard of you. . . . Wrong-Wheel Jones! Where'd you ever get that?"

"It was stuck on me my first hunt when I was sorta tenderfooty."

"Wal, tell me an' my pard here, Tom Doan," continued the scout, good-humoredly. "Tom, shake with Wrong-Wheel Jones."

After quaintly acknowledging the introduction Jones said: "Fust trip I busted a right hind wheel of my wagon. Along comes half a dozen outfits, but none had an extra wheel. Blake, the leader, told me he'd passed a wagon like mine, broke down on the Cimarron. 'Peared it had some good wheels. So I harnessed my hosses, rode one an' led t'other. I found the wagon, but the *left hind wheel* was the only one not busted. So I rode back to camp. Blake asked me why I didn't fetch a wheel back, an' I says: "What'd I want with *two* left hind wheels? I got one. It's the right one thet's busted. Thet left hind wheel back thar on thet wagon would do fust rate, but it's on the wrong side.' An' Blake an' his outfit roared till they near died. When he could talk ag'in he says: 'You darned fool. Thet left hind wheel turned round would make your right hind wheel.' An' after a while I seen he was right. They called me Wrong-Wheel Jones an' the name's stuck."

"By gosh! it ought to!" laughed Pilchuck.

In company with another outfit belonging to a newcomer named Hazelton, with a son of fifteen and two other boys not much older, Pilchuck headed for the Brazos River.

After an uneventful journey, somewhat off the beaten track, they reached one of the many tributaries of the Brazos, where they ran into some straggling small herds.

"We'll make two-day stops till we reach the main herd," said Pilchuck. "I've a hankerin' for my huntin' alone. Reckon hide-hunters are thick as bees down on the Brazos. Let's keep out of the stink an' musketeers as long as we can."

They went into camp, the two outfits not far apart, within hailing distance.

It was perhaps the most beautiful location for a camp Tom had seen in all his traveling over western Texas. Pilchuck said the main herd, with its horde of hide-hunters, had passed miles east of this point. As a consequence the air was sweet, the water unpolluted, and grass and wood abundant.

Brakes of the tributary consisted of groves of pecan trees and cottonwoods, where cold springs abounded, and the deep pools contained fish. As spring had just come in that latitude, there were color of flowers, and fragrance in the air, and a myriad of birds lingering on their way north. Like the wooded sections of the Red River and the Pease River Divide had been, so was this Brazos district. Deer, antelope, turkey, with their carnivorous attendants, panthers, wildcats, and wolves, had not yet been molested by white hunters.

Perhaps the Indian campaigns had hardened Tom Doan, for he returned to the slaughter of the buffalo. He had been so long out of the hunting game that he had forgotten many of the details, and especially the sentiment that had once moved him. Then this wild life in the open had become a habit; it clung to a man. Moreover, Tom had an aching and ever-present discontent which only action could subdue.

He took a liking to Cherry Hazelton. The boy was a strapping youngster, freckle faced and red headed, and like all healthy youths of the Middle West during the 'seventies he was a worshiper of the frontiersman and Indian fighter. He and his young comrades, brothers named Dan and Joe Newman, spent what little leisure time they had hanging round Pilchuck and Tom, hungry for stories as dogs for bones.

Two days at this camp did not suffice Pilchuck. Buffalo were not excessively numerous, but they were scattered into small bands under leadership of old bulls; and for these reasons offered the conditions best suited to experienced hunters.

The third day Tom took Cherry Hazelton hunting with him, allowing him to carry canteen and extra cartridges while getting valuable experience.

Buffalo in small numbers were in sight everywhere, but as this country was rolling and cut up, unlike the Pease prairie, it was not possible to locate all the herds that might be within reaching distance.

In several hours of riding and stalking Tom had not found a position favorable to any extended success, though he had downed some buffalo, and young Hazleton, after missing a number, had finally killed his first, a fine bull. The boy was wild with excitement, and this brought back to Tom his early experience, now seemingly so long in the past.

They were now on a creek that ran through a wide stretch of plain, down to the tributary, and no more than two miles from camp. A large herd of buffalo trooped out of the west, coming fast under a cloud of dust. They poured down into the creek and literally blocked it, crazy to drink. Tom had here a marked instance of the thirst-driven madness now common to the buffalo. This herd, numbering many hundreds, slaked their thirst, and then trooped into a wide flat in the creek bottom, where trees stood here and there. Manifestly they had drunk too deeply, if they had not foundered, for most of them lay down.

"We'll cross the creek and sneak close on them," said Tom. "Bring all the cartridges. We might get a stand."

"What's that?" whispered Cherry, excitedly.

"It's what a buffalo-hunter calls a place and time where a big number bunches and can be kept from running off. I never had a stand myself. But I've an idea what one's like."

They crept on behind trees and brush, down into the wide shallow flat, until they were no farther than a hundred yards from the resting herd. From the way Cherry panted Tom knew he was frightened.

"It is sort of skittish," whispered Tom, "but if they run our way we can climb a tree."

"I'm not—scared. It's—just—great," rejoined the lad, in a tone that hardly verified his words.

"Crawl slow now, and easy," said Tom. "A little farther—then we'll bombard them."

At last Tom led the youngster yards closer, to a wonderful position behind an uprooted cottonwood, from which they could not be seen. Thrilling indeed was it even for Tom, who had stalked Comanches in this way. Most of the buffalo were down, and those standing were stupid with drowsiness. The heat, and a long parching thirst, then an overcharged stomach, had rendered them loggy.

Tom turned his head to whisper instruction to the lad. Cherry's face was pale and the freckles stood out prominently. He was trembling with wild eagerness, fear and delight combined. Tom thought it no wonder. Again he smelled the raw scent of buffalo. They made a magnificent sight, an assorted herd of all kinds and ages, from the clean, glossy, newly shedded old bulls down to the red calves.

"Take the bull on your right—farthest out," whispered Tom. "And I'll tend to this old stager on my left."

The big guns boomed. Tom's bull went to his knees and, grunting loud, fell over; Cherry's bull wagged his head as if a bee had stung him. Part of the buffalo lying down got up. The old bull, evidently a leader, started off.

"Knock him," whispered Tom, quickly. "They'll follow him." Tom fired almost simultaneously with Cherry, and one or both of them scored a dead shot. The buffalo that had started to follow the bull turned back into the herd, and this seemed to dominate all of them. Most of those standing pressed closer in. Others began to walk stolidly off.

"Shoot the outsiders," said Tom, quickly. And in three seconds he had stopped as many buffalo. Cherry's gun boomed, but apparently without execution.

At this juncture Pilchuck rushed up behind them.

"By golly! you've got a stand!" he ejaculated, in excited tones for him. "Never seen a better in my life. Now, here, you boys let me do the shootin'. It's tough on you, but if this stand is handled right we'll make a killin'."

Pilchuck stuck his forked rest-stick in the ground, and knelt behind it, just to the right of Tom and Cherry. This elevated him somewhat above the log, and certainly not hidden from the buffalo.

"Case like this a fellow wants to shoot straight," said the scout. "A crippled buff means a bolt."

Choosing the bull the farthest outside of the herd, Pilchuck aimed with deliberation, and fired. The animal fell. Then he treated the next in the same manner. He was far from hurried, and that explained his deadly precision.

"You mustn't let your gun get too hot," he said. "Over-expansion from heat makes a bullet go crooked."

Pilchuck picked out buffalo slowly walking away and downed them. The herd kept massed, uneasy in some quarters, but for the most part not disturbed by the shooting. Few of those lying down rose to their feet. When the scout had accounted for at least two dozen buffalo he handed his gun to Tom.

"Cool it off an' wipe it out," he directed, and taking Tom's gun returned to his deliberate work.

Tom threw down the breech-block and poured water through the barrel, once, and then presently again. Taking up Pilchuck's ramrod Tom ran a greasy patch of cloth through the barrel. It was cooling rapidly and would soon be safe to use.

Meanwhile the imperturbable scout was knocking buffalo down as if they had been tenpins. On the side toward him there was soon a corral of dead buffalo. He never missed; only seldom was it necessary to take two shots to an animal. After shooting ten or twelve he returned Tom's gun and took up his own.

"Best stand I ever saw," he said. "Queer how buffalo act sometimes. They're not stupid. They know somethin' is wrong. But you see I keep knockin' down the one that leads off."

Buffalo walked over to dead ones, and sniffed at them, and hooked them with such violence that the contact could be heard. An old bull put something apparently like anger into his actions. Why did not his comrade, or perhaps his mate, get up and come? Some of them looked anxiously round, waiting. Now and then another would walk out of the crowd, and that was fatal for him. Boom! And the heavy bullet would thud solidly; the buffalo would sag or jerk, and then sink down, shot through the heart. Pilchuck was a machine for the collecting of buffalo hides. There were hundreds of hunters like him on the range. Boom! Boom! Boom! boomed out the big fifty.

At last, after more than an hour of this incredible stolidity to the boom of gun and the fall of their numbers, the resting buffalo got up, and they all moved round uneasily, uncertainly. Then Pilchuck missed dead center of a quartering shot at a bull that led out. The bullet made the beast frantic, and with a kind of low bellow it bounded away. The mass broke, and a stream of shaggy brown poured off the flat and up the gentle slope. In a moment all the herd was in motion. The industrious Pilchuck dropped four more while they were crowding behind, following off the flat. A heavy trampling roar filled the air; dust, switching tufted tails, woolly bobbing backs, covered the slope. And in a few moments they were gone. Silence settled down. The blue smoke drifted away. A gasp of dying buffalo could be heard.

"Reckon I never beat this stand," said the scout, wiping his wet, black hands. "If I only hadn't crippled that bull."

"Gosh! It was murder—wusser'n butcherin' cows!" ejaculated the boy Cherry. Drops of sweat stood out on his pale face, as marked as the freckles. He looked sick. Long before that hour had ended his boyish sense of exciting adventure had been outraged.

"Lad, it ain't always that easy," remarked Pilchuck. "An' don't let this make you think huntin' buffalo isn't dangerous. Now we'll make a count."

One hundred and twenty-six buffalo lay dead in space less than three acres; and most of them were bulls.

"Yep, it's my record," declared the scout, with satisfaction. "But I come back fresh to it, an' shore that was a grand stand. Boys, we've got skinnin' for the rest of to-day an' all of to-morrow."

The two outfits gradually hunted down the tributary towards its confluence with the Brazos. As the number of buffalo increased they encountered other hunters; and when May arrived they were on the outskirts of the great herd and a swarm of camps.

Hide thieves were numbered among these outfits, and this necessitated the consolidation of camps and the need for one or more men to be left on guard. Thus Tom and Cherry often had a day in camp, most welcome change, though tasks were endless. Their place was at a point where the old Spanish Trail from the Staked Plain crossed the Brazos; and therefore was in line of constant travel. Hunters and freighters, tenderfeet and old timers, soldiers and Indians, passed that camp, and seldom came a day when no traveler stopped for an hour.

Cherry liked these days more than those out on the range. He was being broken in to Pilchuck's strenuous method and the process was no longer enticing.

Once it happened that Cherry and Dan Newman were left together. Tom had ridden off to take up his skinning, in which he had soon regained all his old-time skill, but he did not forget to admonish the boys to keep out of mischief. Wrong-Wheel Jones, who had been recovering from one of his infrequent intemperate spells, had also been left behind. When Tom returned he found Jones in a state of high dudgeon, raving what he would do to those infernal boys. It was plain that Wrong-Wheel had very recently come out of the river, which at this point ran under a bank close to camp. Tom decided the old fellow had fallen in, but as the boys were not to be found, a later conclusion heaped upon their heads something of suspicion. At last Tom persuaded him to talk.

"Wal, it was this way," began Wrong-Wheel, with the air of a much-injured man. "Since I lost them two hundred hides—an' I know darn well some thief got them—I been drinkin' considerable. Jest got to taperin' off lately, an' wasn't seein' so many queer things. . . . Wal, to-day I went to sleep thar in the shade on the bank. Suthin' woke me, an' when I opened my eyes I seed an orful sight. I was scared turrible, an' I jest backed off the bank an' fell in the river. Damn near drowned! Reckon when I got out I was good an' sober. . . . An', say, what d'ye s'pose them boys done?"

Wrong-Wheel squinted at Tom and squirted a brown stream of tobacco into the camp fire.

"I haven't any idea," replied Tom, with difficulty preserving a straight face.

"Wal," went on Jones, "you know thet big panther Pilchuck shot yestiddy. Them boys hed skinned it, shot-pouched it, as we say, an' they hed stuffed it with grass, an' put sticks in fer legs, an' marbles fer eyes. An' I'm a son-of-a-gun if they didn't stand the dummy right in front of me, so when I woke I seed it fust, an' I jest nat'rally went off my head."

Another day an old acquaintance of Tom's rode in and halted on his way to Fort Worth.

"Roberts!" exclaimed Tom, in glad surprise.

"Just come from Fort Sill," said Roberts, evincing equal pleasure. "An' I have shore some news for you. Do you remember old Nigger Horse, the chief of that band of Comanches we fought—when I had this heah arm broke?"

"I'm not likely to forget," replied Tom.

"Wal, the Comanches that are left are slowly comin' in to Fort Sill an' goin' on the reservation. An' from some of them we got facts aboot things we never was shore on. The soldiers lately had a long runnin' fight with old Nigger Horse. Some sergeant killed the old chief an' his squaw, an' that shore was a good job."

"Nigger was a bad Comanche," agreed Tom. "Did you ever hear any more about Hudnall's gun?"

"Shore. We heerd all aboot it, an' from several bucks who were in our fight where I had my arm broke, an' other fights afterwards. . . . I reckon you remember Hudnall had a fine gun, one shore calculated to make redskins want it. An' possession of that rifle was bad medicine to every consarned Indian who got it. Nigger Horse's son had it first. He was the brave who led that ride down the canyon to draw our fire. He shore had spunk. Wal, I reckon he was full of lead. Then an Injun named Five Plumes got it. 'Pears we killed him. After that every redskin who took Hudnall's rifle an' cartridges got his everlastin'. Finally they quit usin' it, thinkin' it was bad medicine. Now the fact is, those Comanches who used Hudnall's gun got reckless because they had it, an' laid themselves open to our fire. But they thought it had a spell of the devil."

CHAPTER EIGHTEEN

The middle of July found Tom Doan and Pilchuck far down on the Brazos, in the thick of the slaughter. Thirty miles of buffalo-hunters drove the last great herd day by day toward extermination.

If the weather had been uncomfortable in mid-summer on the Pease River Divide, here it was worse than hot. Moreover, up there in earlier days the hunting had been comparatively easy. Here it was incessant toil. The buffalo had to be chased.

The prairie was open, hot, dusty, and vast. Always the buffalo headed to the wind; they would drink and graze, and go on, noses to the breeze. If the wind changed overnight, in the morning they would be found turned round, traveling toward it. All day they grazed against it. They relied on their scent more than on sight or hearing; and in that open country the wind brought them warning of their foes. But for the great number of hide-hunters these buffalo might have escaped any extended slaughter.

The outfits were strung along the Brazos for many miles; and as the buffalo had to drink they were never far from water. Thus a number of hunters would get to them every day, kill many on the chase, and drive them on to the next aggregation of slayers.

Tom Doan had been in hard action for over two months; and he and Pilchuck and Jones had killed thirty-nine hundred and twenty buffalo, losing only a small percentage of skins. Their aim was to last out the summer and fall if endurance could be great enough. They had no freighting to do now; they sold their hides in bales on the range.

The days grew to be nightmares. As the buffalo were driven up the river, then back down, and up again, the killing was accomplished for weeks in comparatively small area. It got to be so that Tom could not ride many rods without encountering either a pile of bones, or rotten carcass, or one just beginning to decompose, or a freshly skinned one torn over the night before by the packs of thousand of coyotes that followed the herd. Some days hundreds of newly skinned buffalo shone red along with the blackened carcasses over a stretch of miles. Buzzards were as thick as bees. And the stench was unbearable. The prairie became a gruesome, ghastly shambles; and the camps were almost untenable because of flies and bugs, ticks and mosquitoes. These hunters stuck to a job that in a worthy cause would have been heroic. As it was they descended to butchers, and each and all of them sank inevitably. Boom! Boom! Boom! All day long the detonation filled the hot air. No camp was out of hearing of the guns. Wagons lumbered along the dusty roads. All the outfits labored day and night to increase their store of hides, riding, chasing, shooting, skinning, hauling, and pegging, as if their very lives depended upon incessant labor. It was a time of carnage.

Long had Tom Doan felt the encroachment of a mood he had at one time striven against—a morbid estimate of self, a consciousness that this carnage would debase him utterly if he did not soon abandon it. Once there had been a wonderful reason for him to give up the hunting. Milly Fayre! Sometimes still her dark eyes haunted him. If she had not been lost he would long ago have quit this bloody game. The wound in his heart did not heal. Love of Milly abided, and that alone saved him from the utter debasement of hard life at a hard time.

One morning when he drove out on the dust-hazed, stinking prairie he found a little red buffalo calf standing beside its mother, that Tom had shot and skinned the day before. This was no new sight to Tom. Nevertheless, in the present case there seemed a difference. These calves left motherless by the slaughter had always wandered over the prairie, lost, bewildered; this one, however, had recognized its mother and would not leave her.

"Go along! Get back to the herd!" yelled Tom, shocked despite his callousness.

The calf scarcely noticed him. It smelled of its hide-stripped mother, and manifestly was hungry. Presently it left off trying to awaken this strange horribly red and inert body, and stood with hanging head, dejected, resigned, a poor miserable little beast. Tom could not drive it away; and after loading the hide on the wagon he returned twice to try to make it run off. Finally he was compelled to kill it.

This incident boded ill for Tom. It fixed his mind on this thing he was doing and left him no peace. Thousands and thousands of beautiful little buffalo calves were rendered motherless by the hide-hunters. That was to Tom the unforgivable brutality. Calves just born, just able to suck, and from that to yearlings, were left to starve, to die of thirst, to wander until they dropped or were torn to shreds by wolves. No wonder this little calf showed in its sad resignation the doom of the species!

August came. The great herd massed. The mating season had come, and both bulls and cows, slaves to the marvelous instinct that had evolved them, grew slower, less wary, heedless now to the scent of man on the wind.

At the beginning of this mating time it was necessary to be within a mile or less to hear the strange *roo roo roo—ooo.* This sound was the bellow of a bull. Gradually day by day the sound increased in volume and range. It could be heard several miles, and gradually farther as more and more bulls bellowed in unison. ROO ROO ROO—OOO!—It began to be incessant, heard above the boom! boom! boom! of guns.

The time came when it increased tremendously and lasted day and night. Tom Doan's camp was then ten miles from the herd. At that distance the bellow was as loud as distant thunder. ROO ROO ROO—OOO! It kept Tom awake. It filled his ears. If he did fall asleep it gave him a nightmare. When he awoke he heard again the long mournful roar. At length it wore upon him so deeply that in the darkness and solitude of night he conceived the idea that he was listening to the voice of a great species, bellowing out for life—life—life.

This wild deep *Roo—ooo* was the knell of the buffalo. What a strange sound, vastly different from anything human, yet somehow poignant, tragic, terrible! Nature had called to the great herd; and that last million of buffalo bellowed out their acceptance of the decree. But in Tom's morbid mind he attributed vastly more to this strange thunder, which was not the trampling thunder of their hoofs. In the dead of night when the guns were silent he could not shake the spell. It came to him then how terribly wrong, obsessed, evil were these hide-hunters. God and nature had placed the wonderful beasts on earth for a purpose, the least of which might have been to furnish meat and robe for men in a measure of reason. But here all the meat was left to rot, and half the hides; and the remaining half went to satisfy a false demand, and to make rich a number of hunters, vastly degraded by the process.

Roo—ooo—ooo! Tom heard in that the meaning of a futile demand of nature.

Tom Doan and Pilchuck reined their horses on the crest of a league-sloping ridge and surveyed the buffalo range.

To their surprise the endless black line of buffalo was not in sight. They had moved north in the night. At this early morning hour the hunters were just riding out to begin their day's work. No guns were booming, and it appeared that Tom and the scout had that part of the range to themselves.

"Wal, we spent yesterday peggin' hides in camp, an' didn't think to ask Jones if the buffalo had moved," remarked Pilchuck, reflectively.

"The wind has changed. It's now from the north," said Tom.

"Shore is. An' the buffs will be grazin' back pronto. That is, if they *are* grazin'!"

"Any reason to doubt it?" asked Tom.

"Wal, the breedin' season's just about ended. An' that with this muggy, stormy, electric-charged mornin' might cause a move. Never in my huntin' days have I seen such a restless queer herd of buffalo as this one."

"No wonder!" exclaimed Tom.

"Wal, it ain't, an' that's a fact. . . . Do I see hosses yonder?"

Tom swept the prairie with his glass.

"Yes. Hunters riding out. I see more beyond. They're all going downriver."

"Come to think of it, I didn't hear much shootin' yesterday. Did you?"

"Not a great deal. And that was early morning and far away," replied Tom.

"Buffs an' hunters have worked north. Let's see. The river makes a bend about ten miles from here, an' runs east. I'd be willin' to bet the herd hasn't turned that bend."

"Why?"

"Because they'll *never* go north again. For two months the trend has been south, day by day. Some days a wind like yesterday would switch them, but on the whole they're workin' south. This ain't natural for midsummer. They ought to be headed north. 'Course the mob of hunters are drivin' them south."

"But how about to-day?" inquired Tom.

"Wal, I'm shore figgerin'. Reckon I can't explain, but I feel all them outfits ridin' north will have their work for nothin'."

"What will we do?"

"I'm not carin' a lot. Reckon I've sickened on this job, an' I shore know that, when I stay a day in camp."

Tom had before noted this tendency in the scout. It was common to all those hunters who had been long in the field. He did not voice his own sentiment.

"I've been wantin' to ride west an' see what that next ford is goin' to be like," said the scout, presently. "We'll be breakin' camp an' movin' south soon. An' the other side of the river is where we want to be."

For the first time Tom experienced a reluctance to a continuation of the old mode of traveling south. Why not turn north once more? The thought was a surprise. There was no reason to start north, unless in answer to the revulsion of hide-hunting. This surely would be his last buffalo hunt. But he did not think it just to his partners to quit while they wanted to keep on. His reflection then was that Pilchuck was wearing out, both in strength and in greed.

They rode west, aiming to reach the river some four or five miles farther on.

It was a cloudy, sultry summer morning, with storm in the air. The prairie was not here a beautiful prospect. Tom seemed to gaze over it rather than at it. Westward the undulating gray rise of ground stretched interminably to a horizon bare of landmarks. Far in the east rays of sunlight streamed down between sullen, angry, copper and purple-hued clouds. The north threatened. It was black all along the horizon. Still, oppressive, sultry, the air seemed charged.

From time to time Pilchuck turned in his saddle to gaze backward along the empty range, and then up at the cloudbank. It appeared to Tom as if the scout were looking and listening for something.

"What're you expecting?" queried Tom, yielding to curiosity. "A thunderstorm?"

"Wal, I'll be darned if I know," ejaculated Pilchuck. "Shore I wasn't thinkin' about a storm. Wasn't thinkin' at all! Must be just habit with me. . . . But now you tax me, I reckon I'm oneasy about that herd."

Pilchuck led west farther than he had calculated, and struck the river at a wonderful place where the prairie took a sudden dip for miles, sheering steeply to the shallow water. Here was the buffalo ford, used by the herds in their annual migrations. Trees were absent, and brush and grass had not the luxuriance common to most stretches of river bank. From prairie rim to margin of river sloped a long steep bank, even and smooth; and at one point the wide approach to the ford was split and dominated by a rocky eminence, the only high point in sight along the river.

The place seemed dismal and lonely to Tom, as he sat on his horse while Pilchuck forded the river. Contrary to most river scenes, this one was lifeless. Not a bird or animal or a fish or turtle in sight! Loneliness and solitude had their abode in this trodden road of the buffalo.

At length the scout returned and rode up to Tom.

"Wal, I wouldn't care to get a team stuck in that sand," he remarked. "It shore ain't packed none. . . . Lend me your glass."

The scout swept a half circle of the horizon, and finally came to a halt westward, at a point on the prairie some distance from the river.

"See some small bunches of buffalo," he said. "Let's ride up on them, make our kill, skin what we get, an' pick them up with the wagon on our way south tomorrow."

"You're the boss," replied Tom.

"Wal, I wish some one was bossin' me," returned Pilchuck, enigmatically.

They trotted off over the gray prairie, and after traveling a couple of miles, could see the buffalo plainly. Meanwhile a slight breeze began to blow from the south.

"I'll be darned!" ejaculated Pilchuck, with annoyance. "Wind's turned again. If it blows stronger we'll not slip up on this bunch."

Another mile brought increase of wind, and the wary buffalo, catching the scent of the killers, loped away over the prairie. Pilchuck watched them in disgust. "Run, you old dunder-heads! Run clear across the Rio Grande! . . . Tom, I reckon we're all spoiled by the past easy huntin'. It'll never be easy again. An' somehow I'm glad. Let's work back."

They turned about to face the breeze, now quite strong, cooler, with a heavy scent of rotting buffalo carcasses.

"Faugh!" exclaimed the scout. "I'd rather have nose an' eyes full of cottonwood smoke."

Tom's quick ear caught a very low rumble of thunder. He turned his head. The sound had ceased. It had come on a stronger puff of wind.

"What'd you hear?" inquired the scout, whose eye never missed anything.

"Thunder."

"Wal, it does look stormy. But I never trust thunder in this country," replied the scout, significantly.

He halted his horse; and Tom did likewise. They gazed at the north. Dull, leaden mushrooming clouds were moving toward them, not rapidly, but steadily, in heavy changing forms. They merged into a purple-black mass down which streaked thin zigzag ropes of lightning.

"Storm all right," observed Pilchuck. "Listen."

After a moment in which nothing was heard save the heaving of horses, the rattle of bridle, and creak of leather, the scout dismounted.

"Get off, Tom, an' walk away from the horses. . . . Listen now."

Presently Tom again heard the low dull rumble.

"There," he said.

"Shore. That's genuine thunder, an' it means rain for this stinkin' dusty hot range. . . . Listen some more, Tom."

The two men stood apart, Pilchuck favoring his right ear, Tom his left; and they remained motionless. Several times the mutter of thunder, distinct now to Tom, caused the scout to nod his head.

"Reckon that's not what I'm expectin'," he said, gloomily. "An' we've no time to stand here all day. . . . Listen hard, Tom. You're younger than me."

Tom's sluggish blood quickened a little. He had been two years with this old plainsman, during which there had been numberless instances of his sagacity and vision, and remarkable evidences of experience. Pilchuck was worrying about that herd of buffalo. Thereupon Tom bent lower, held his breath, and strained his ear with all intensity possible. Again he heard the muttering long rumble—then the beat of his heart, the stir of his hair over his temple—the sweep of wind. Thunder again! That was all; and he abandoned the strain.

"Nothing but storm," he told Pilchuck.

"I reckon my ears are old, an' my imagination makes me think I hear things," returned the scout. "But a moment ago . . . Try again. I want to be *shore.*"

Thus incited, Tom lent himself to as sensitive and profound listening as was possible for him. This time he seemed to hear the thunder as before, somewhat louder; and under it another, fainter sound, an infinitely low roar that did not die out, that went on and on, deadened by another mutter of thunder, and then, when this was gone, beginning again, low, strange, unceasing.

Then he straightened up and told Pilchuck what he had heard. How sharply and intelligently the scout's gray eyes flashed! He made no reply, except to raise one of his brawny hands. Leaving it extended, he froze in the attitude of an Indian listening. Tom again lent his ear to the strengthening breeze. Thunder—then long low menacing roar—thunder again—and roar! He made his own deductions and, lifting his head, waited for the scout to speak. Long did Pilchuck maintain that tense posture. He was a slow, deliberate man on occasions. Sometimes he would act with the most incredible speed. Here he must have been studying the volume, direction, distance of this thrilling sound, and not its cause. Suddenly his big brown hand clenched and shot down to crack into the palm of the other. He wheeled to Tom, with gray lightning in his eyes.

"Stampede! . . . The whole herd!" he ejaculated. "I've been expectin' it for days."

Then he gazed across the northern horizon of the prairie round to a point due east.

"You notice we can see only four or five miles," he said. "The prairie rises slow for about that distance, then dips. That'd deaden sound as well as hide any movin' thing. We can't be shore that herd is far away. . . . Funny how we run into things. Reckon we'd better ride!"

They mounted, and were off at a gallop that gave place to a run. Tom had lost his fleet, faithful Dusty, and was now riding a horse strong and sound and fairly fast, but no match for Pilchuck's hunter. So Tom fell behind gradually. He did not goad the horse, though he appreciated Pilchuck's brief hint of danger.

The scout rode east, quartering toward the river, and passed a couple of miles out from where he and Tom had stopped at the ford. Tom gradually fell behind until he was fully a quarter of a mile in the rear. As long as he could keep Pilchuck in sight he did not have any anxiety about the separation. The horse could run, and he was sure-footed. Tom believed he would acquit himself well even in a grueling race with the buffalo. It seemed strange to be running away from an unseen danger. While riding he could not hear anything save the rhythmic beat of hoofs and rush of wind. He observed that the direction Pilchuck had chosen was just a point east of the center of the black storm cloud. Far to its right showed the dim fringe of river timber. There was a wide distance between the end of that cloud and the river, most of which was gently sloping prairie. He had a keen eagerness to know what could be seen beyond the long ridge-top.

Next time he gazed at Pilchuck he was amazed to see him pulling his horse to a halt. Tom rode on with eyes now intent. The scout reined in and leaped out of the saddle. He ran a few paces from the horse, and stopped to lie flat on the ground. Tom realized that Pilchuck was listening with ear close to the earth. The action startled Tom. Not improbably this situation was growing serious. Pilchuck lay a moment, then got up and stood like a statue. Then he abruptly broke his rigid posture and leaped astride. But instead of riding off he waited there, face to the north. Tom rapidly overhauled him and pulled his mount to a stand.

"Jude, what's wrong?" he called, sharply.

"I ain't shore, but I'm damned scared," replied the scout.

"Why? I can't see or hear anything."

"See that yellow dust way to the right of the black sky. Look! It's movin'!—I'm afraid if we go farther this way we'll get headed off an' run into the river. We could cross, but it'd take time, an' when we got over we might have to run south. That'd never do. We've got to go east or west."

"Jude, I hear a roar," said Tom.

"Shore. So do I. But it was the movin' dust that stopped me. . . . Keep still now an' let me figger. If I've any prairie cunnin' left we're in a hell of a fix. We've got to do what's right—an' quick."

Therefore Tom attended to sight of the low, rounded, yellow cloud of dust. It did move, apparently slowly, and spread to the right. Against the background of purple sky it held something ominous. Tom watched it rise gradually to the left, though in this direction it did not spread along the prairie so rapidly. The ground sloped that way, and the ridge-top stretched higher than the level to the east, where the dust now rolled plainly. The roar was a dull distant rumble, steady and ear-filling though not at all loud. It was a deceiving sound, and might be closer than it seemed or farther away.

Suddenly it became loud. It started Tom. He turned to see what Pilchuck made of that. The scout sat his fidgety horse, with his head extended, his long neck craned forward. Suddenly he jerked back as if struck.

"Doan, look!" he shouted, in a tone Tom had never heard. His voice seemed to merge into a rolling rumble.

Tom wheeled. Along the whole of the prairie horizon had appeared a black bobbing line of buffalo. Above them rose the yellow dust, and beyond that spread the storm-cloud of purple. The ragged front of the herd appeared to creep over the ridge-top, like a horizon-wide tide, low, flat, black. Toward the west the level gray horizon was being blotted out with exceeding swiftness, as the herd came in sight. It spread like a black smoke, flying low. To the east the whole space before noted by Tom had been clouded with black and yellow. The front line of the herd, then, did not appear to be straight across: it was curving from the right.

One moment Tom gazed, rapt, thrilling, then his blood gushed hot. The great herd was at last on the stampede. Not five miles distant, running downhill!

"By God! we're in a trap!" yelled Pilchuck, hoarsely. "We've only one chance. Follow me an' ride!"

He spurred and wheeled his horse and, goading him into a run, headed for the river ford. Tom spurred after him, finding now that his horse, frightened by the roar, could keep up with Pilchuck's. They ran straight away from the eastern front of the herd, that was curving in and quartering away from the western front. Tom had ridden fast before, but Pilchuck's start bade fair to lead him into the swiftest race of his experience on the range. He was aware of drawing away somewhat from the roar in the rear; on his right, however, the sound augmented. Tom gazed around. His eyes, blurred from the rush of wind, showed a league-wide band of black, sliding down the prairie slope, widening, spreading. He did not look behind.

Pilchuck's fleet horse began to draw ahead. The old scout was riding as he had never ridden away from Comanches. Tom remembered what fear these old plainsmen had of the buffalo stampede. It was the terror of the plains, more appalling than the prairie fire. Comanches could be fought; fires could be outridden or back-fired, but the stampede of buffalo was a rolling sea of swift insane beasts. With spur and fist and voice Tom urged his horse to its utmost, and kept the distance between him and Pilchuck from widening further.

Both horses now were on a headlong run strained to the breaking point. The wind hissed by Tom's ears, swayed him back in his saddle. On both sides the gray prairie slid by, indistinct, a blurred expanse, over which he seemed to sail. He could not see the river depression, but before long he made out the rocky eminence that marked the site of the ford. Pilchuck's intention now was plain. At first Tom had imagined the scout meant to try to cross the river ahead of the herd; now, however, he was making for the high point of rock. This realization unclamped Tom's cold doubt. If the horses did not fall they could make that place of safety. Pilchuck was fifty feet ahead, and not only was he driving the horse at breakneck speed, but he was guiding him over what appeared to be the smoother ground. Tom caught the slight variations in the course and the swervings aside; and he had only to follow.

So they flew. The gray mound of rock seemed close, the prairie flashing by, yet how slowly the distance lessened. Tom saw Pilchuck turn. His brown face gleamed. He waved his hand. A beckoning and an encouragement! Peril was not over, but safety was in sight. Then the scout leaned back, pulling the horse to his haunches, on which he slid to a stop. Over Pilchuck's head Tom saw the pale brightness of water. The river! Behind Tom rolled a rumbling thunder, strange to hear with his ears full of rushing wind. He dared not look back.

The straining horse broke his stride, caught it again, stretched on, and plunged to the bare rise of rocky ground. Tom hauled with all his strength on the bridle. He checked the maddened animal, but could not stop him. Pilchuck stood ten feet above the bank. He had dismounted. Both hands were uplifted in gesture of awe. Tom leaped off just as his horse slowed before the first rocky bench. Dragging him up, Tom climbed to Pilchuck, who seemed to yell at him. But Tom heard no voice.

The rocky eminence was about half an acre in extent, and high enough above the bank to split the herd. Tom dropped the bridle and whirled in fear and wonder.

His first thought when he saw the ragged, sweeping tide of beasts, still a third of a mile distant, was that he would have had time to spare. The herd had not been so close as his imagination had pictured.

Pilchuck dragged at Tom, pulling him higher on the rock. The scout put his mouth close to Tom's ear and manifestly yelled. But Tom heard no voice; felt only a soundless, hot breath. His ears were distending with a terrific thunder. His eyes were protruding at an awful spectacle.

Yet he saw that sweep of buffalo with a marvelous distinctness, with the swift leap of emotion which magnified all his senses. Across the level front of his vision spread a ragged, shaggy black wall of heads, humps, hoofs, coming at the speed of buffalo on the stampede. On a hard run! The sea of bobbing backs beyond disappeared in a yellow pall of dust curled aloft and hung low, and kept almost the speed of the front rank. Above the moving mantle of dust, farther back, showed the gray pall of storm. Lightning flashed in vivid white streaks. But there was no thunder from above. The thunder rolled low, along the ground.

Spellbound Tom gazed. He was riveted to the rock. If he had not been he would have fled, up, back, away from that oncoming mass. But he could only gaze, in a profound consciousness of something great and terrifying. These buffalo might not split round the higher ground; those in line might run over the rock. What an end for hide-hunters! Killed, crushed, trampled to jelly, trampled to dust under the hoofs of the great herd! It would be just retribution. Tom felt the awful truth of that in his lifting heart. It was mete. The murderous hide-hunters, money-grubbers, deserved no pity. He could not feel any for himself. How furiously angry that curling surf of woolly heads and shiny horns and gleaming hoofs! On! On! On! The thundering herd! How magnificent and appalling!

Suddenly his ears ceased to function. He could no longer hear. The sense had been outdone. There was no sound. But he saw yet the mighty onsweep, majestic, irresistible, an army of maddened beasts on the stampede, shaking the earth. The rock under his feet began to tremble. It was no longer stable. He felt the queer vibrations, and the sensation added to his terror.

Transfixed, Tom awaited the insupportable moment for the rolling front ranks to reach the rock, either to roll over it like a tidal wave, or split round it. The moment was an age. Pilchuck was holding to him. Tom was holding to Pilchuck. The solid earth seemed about to cave in under them. Shaggy black heads bobbing swiftly, gleam of horns, and flash of wild eyes, hoofs, hoofs, hoofs sweeping out, out, out—and the awful moment was at hand.

The shaggy flood split round the rock and two streams of woolly rounded backs, close-pressed as water, swift as a mill-race, poured over the bank toward the river.

Pilchuck dragged Tom away from the back position to the front of the rock. As if by supernatural magic the scene was changed. Below, far on each side, the mass of buffalo spilled over the embankment to plunge into the river. Up and down the water line spread white splashes; and over and into them leaped the second ranks of buffalo, too close to miss the first. Then what had momentarily been ranks on the slope closed up into solid mass of black. Bulge and heave—great sheets of muddy water—a terrible writhing massing forward along that irregular front! Then the tide of buffalo swept on, over, once more a flat, level multitude of heads and humps, irrepressible as an avalanche. They crossed the river on the run; the stampede had been only momentarily retarded. Downriver, below the ford, far as eye could see, stretched lines of buffalo swimming, swiftly, like an endless flock of enormous geese. Upriver stretched the same, as far as eye could see. The slope of the prairie to the water was one solid mass of buffalo, moving as one beast, impelled by motive as wild as the action. Above swept the dust, blowing as a storm wind from the prairie, and, curling like a yellow curtain of smoke, it followed the buffalo across the river, up the long slope, and out upon the prairie.

Tom and Pilchuck were on that level between the moving dust above and the moving buffalo below. All view back toward the prairie whence the herd rolled was soon obliterated. Likewise the front ranks of the great mass disappeared on the opposite side, under this accompanying mantle. But the river, for a while, lay clear to their gaze, miles up and miles down, and all visible space of water and ground was covered with buffalo. Buffalo more numerous than a band of ants on the march!

Tom sank down, overcome by the spectacle, by the continuous trembling of the earth under him, by the strangulation which threatened, by the terrible pressure on his ear-drums.

Suddenly night seemed to intervene. A gale swooped the dust away across the river; and in place of yellow curling curtain of dust there came a slanting gray pall of rain. It blackened as the light grew less. Blazing streaks of lightning played through the gray gloom. But if there was thunder above, it could not be heard in the thunder below.

Pilchuck drew Tom under a narrow shelf of rock, where, half protected from the deluge, they crouched in the semi-darkness. What seemed hours passed. Yet there was no end to the passing of the great herd. The rain ceased, the sky lightened and cleared, and clearer grew the black mantling of prairie and river. All was buffalo, except the sky. Then the sun broke out of the clouds.

Tom's stunned senses rallied enough for him to appreciate the grandeur and beauty suddenly given the scene by a glorious sheen of gold and purple, streaming down from the rifts between the clouds. The dust was gone. The thousands of shining black backs moved on and on, rapidly, ponderously, swallowed up by the haze of the disappearing storm. And still the buffalo came over the prairie, obscuring the ground.

But at last the time came when the mass showed breaks in the ranks, and then, in the rear line, more ragged than had been the fore. Tom's hearing seemed gradually to be restored. That, he realized, was only the diminishing of the vast volume of sound to the point where it was no longer deafening. It was a blood-deadening thunder that gradually lessened as the end of the herd rolled on from the prairie, down over the bank, and across the river.

The thundering herd swept on out of sight. And the thunder became a roar, the roar a rumble, and the rumble died away.

Pilchuck rose to his lofty height and peered across the river, into the gray haze and purple distance that had swallowed up the buffalo. He seemed to be a man who had lived through something terrible.

"The last herd!" he said, with pathos. "They've crossed the Brazos an' they'll never come back. . . . The storm of rain was like the storm of lead that'll follow them."

Tom also got dizzily to his feet and faced the south. What he felt about the last herd could not be spoken. He had been spared a death he felt he deserved; and he had seen a mighty spectacle, incalculable in its spiritual effect. All in vain was the grand stampede of that thundering herd. It must drink, it must graze—and behind would troop the ruthless hunters of hides. But Tom had seen and felt its overpowering vitality, its tremendous life, its spirit. Never would he kill another buffalo! And a great sadness pervaded his mind. As he stood there, trying to form in words something to say to Pilchuck, a huge old buffalo bull, one of the many that had been mired in the sand, floundered and wallowed free, and waddled to the opposite shore. Stupidly he gazed about him, forlorn, alone, lost, a symbol of the herd that had gone on without him. Then he headed south out into the melancholy gray of the prairie.

"Jude, I'm—going—north!" exclaimed Tom, haltingly, full of words that would not come.

"Shake!" replied the old scout, quick as a flash, as he extended his brawny hand.

CHAPTER NINETEEN

From the crest of the long prairie slope, beginning to color brown and gold in the September sun, Tom Doan gazed down at the place that had been Sprague's Post. It had grown so as to be almost unrecognizable. Ranches dotted the beautiful sweep of fertile land. Near at hand, the river wound away, hidden in green foliage, and far out on the plain it glistened in the sunlight.

Despite the keen pang in Tom's heart, and the morbid reluctance to return that had abided with him, strangely he found he was glad. The wildness of the buffalo range, loneliness and silence and solitude, and the loss that he felt was irreparable—these had dwarfed his former kindliness and hopefulness, and his old ambition to know the joy of his own home and ranch. But might there not be some compensation?

The long wagon train of hides and camp outfits lumbered across the prairie to enter the outskirts of the Post and haul up on the green square between the town and the river. Still there were new wagons and outfits belonging to hunters bound for the buffalo range. Tom wanted to cry out about the pains and blunders they were so cheerfully and ignorantly traveling to meet.

Big wagon trains such as this one were always encountered at the Post. News traveled ahead of such large caravans; and there was a crowd on the green. There were half a dozen wagons ahead of the one Tom drove, and the last of these was Pilchuck's. The lean old scout was at once surrounded by hunters eager to learn news of the buffalo range.

Tom saw Burn Hudnall and Dave Stronghurl before they saw him. How well they looked—fuller of face and not so bronzed as when they had ridden the open range! Eager and excited also they appeared to Tom. They would be glad to see him. If only he could avoid meeting their women folk! Then Burn espied him and made at him. Tom dropped the knotted reins over the brake with a movement of finality, and stepped down out of the wagon.

"Howdy, boys! It's sure good to see you," he said, heartily.

They grasped him with hands almost rough, so forceful were they; and both greeted him at once in a kind of suppressed joy, incoherent and noisy, all the more welcoming for that. Then they hung on to him, one at each side.

"Say, have you boys taken to drink?" retorted Tom, to conceal how their warmth affected him. "I haven't just come back to life."

"Tom, I—we—all of us was afraid you'd never come," burst out Burn. "You look fine. Thin, mebbe, an' hard. . . . My Gawd! I'm glad!"

"Tom—I've got a baby—a boy!" beamed Dave, his strong smug face alight.

"You don't say! Dave, shake on that. . . . I'm sure glad. How time flies! It doesn't seem so long—"

"We've got other news, but the best of it'll keep till we get to the ranch," interrupted Burn. "Tom, I've got that five hundred acres father liked so well. Remember? You can buy next to me, along the river. Dave has thrown in with Sprague. The town's boomin'! We've a bank, a church, and a school. An' wait till you see the teacher! She's—"

He rambled on, like a boy, to be silenced by Dave's look. Then Dave began, and being more practical he soon got out Tom's bag and gun and roll of blankets.

"You're comin' with us this hyar very minnit," he concluded, as Tom tried to make excuses. "Burn, grab some of his outfit. Reckon this team an' wagon belongs to Pilchuck?"

"Yes, it does," replied Tom.

"Come along then, you buffalo-chasin', Comanche-ridin' Llaner Estacador," went on Dave. "We've orders to fetch you home before these hyar town girls set eyes on you."

They dragged Tom and his belongings out of the crowd, pushed him up into a spring-wagon, and while Burn piled his baggage in the back, Dave climbed up beside him and started a team of spirited horses out along the river road.

If the welcome accorded Tom by Burn and Dave had touched him, that given by their women folk reached deeply to his heart. They were all at the front of Burn's fine ranch house. Burn's wife was weeping, it seemed for joy; and Sally Hudnall gave Tom a resounding kiss, to his consternation. Mrs. Hudnall, whose motherly face showed the ravages of grief, greeted him in a way that made Tom ashamed of how he had forgotten these good people. She took possession of him and led him indoors, ahead of the others. They had all seemed strange, hurried, suppressing something. They were not as Tom remembered. Alas! had he grown away from wholesome simplicity? They wanted to welcome him to their home.

Mrs. Hudnall shut the door. Tom had a sense that the room was large, lighted by windows at each end. Clearing his throat, he turned to speak. But Mrs. Hudnall's working face, her tear-wet eyes, made him dumb. There was something wrong here.

"Tom, you're changed," she began, hurriedly. "No boy any more! I can see how it hurts you to come back to us."

"Yes, because of—of Milly," he replied, simply. "But you mustn't think I'm not glad to see you all. I am. You're my good friends. I'm ashamed I never appreciated you as I should have. But that hard life out there—"

"Don't," she interrupted, huskily. "You know how it hurt me. . . . But, Tom, never mind the past. Think of the present."

"My heart's buried in that past. It seems so long ago. So short a time to remember! I—"

"Didn't you ever think Milly might not have been lost?" she asked.

"Yes, I thought that—till hope died," replied Tom, slowly.

"My boy—we heard she wasn't killed—or captured—or anything," said Mrs. Hudnall, softly.

"Heard she wasn't? My God! That would only torture me," replied Tom, poignantly. He felt himself shaking. What did these people mean? His mind seemed to encounter that query as a wall.

"Tom, we *know* she wasn't," flashed the woman, with all the ecstasy in face and voice.

He staggered back suddenly, released from bewilderment. He realized now. That had been the secret of their excitement, their strangeness. His consciousness grasped the truth. Milly Fayre was not dead. For an instant his eyes closed and his physical and spiritual being seemed to unite in a tremendous resistance against the shock of rapture. He must not lose his senses. He must not miss one word or look of this good woman who had given him back love and life. But he was mute. A strong quiver ran over him from head to foot. Then heart and pulse leaped in exquisite pain and maddening thrill.

"Milly is here," said Mrs. Hudnall. "We tried again and again to send you word, but always missed you. Milly has lived here—ever since she escaped from Jett—and the Indians. She has grown. She's taught the school. She is well—happy. She has waited for you—she loves you dearly."

Voice was wrenched from Tom. "I see truth in your face," he whispered, huskily. "But I can't believe. . . . Let me *see* her!"

Mrs. Hudnall pushed back the door and went out. Some one slipped in. A girl—a woman, white of face, with parted lips and great, radiant black eyes! Could this be Milly Fayre?

"Oh—Tom!" she burst out, in broken voice, deep and low. She took a forward step, with hands extended, then swayed back against the door. "Don't you—know me?"

"I'd lost all hope," whispered Tom, as if to himself. "It's too sudden. I can't believe. . . . You ghost! You white thing with eyes I loved!"

"It's your Milly, alive—alive!" she cried, and ran to envelop him.

Later they stood by the open window watching the sun set gold over the dim dark line of the Llana Estacado. She had told her story. Tom could only marvel at it, as at her, so changed, so wonderful, yet sweet and simple as of old.

"You shall never go back to the buffalo range," she said, in what seemed both command and appeal.

"No, Milly," he replied, and told her the story of the stampede of the thundering herd.

"Oh, how wonderful and terrible!" she replied. "I loved the buffalo."

Mrs. Hudnall called gayly to them from the door. "Tom—Milly, you can't live on love. Supper is ready."

"We're not hungry," replied Milly, dreamily.

"Yes, we are," added Tom, forcefully. "We'll come. . . . Milly, I'm starved. You know what camp grub is. A year and a half on hump steak!"

"Wait. I was only teasing," she whispered, as with downcast eyes, like midnight under their lashes, she leaned a little closer to him. "Do you remember my—my birthday?"

"I never knew it," he replied, smiling.

"It's to-morrow."

"You don't say. Well, I did get back at the right time. Let's see, you're eighteen years old."

"Ah, you forget! I am nineteen. You lost me for over a year."

"But, Milly, I *never* forgot what was to have been on your eighteenth birthday, though I never knew the date."

"What was to have been?" she asked, shyly, with a slow blush mantling her cheek.

"You were to marry me."

"Oh, did I promise that?" she questioned, in pretended wonder.

"Yes."

"Well, *that* was for my eighteenth birthday. You never hunted me—you hunted only buffalo. You might have had me. . . . But now you shall wait till—till I'm twenty."

"Milly, I hunted for you all through summer, fall, winter. And my heart broke."

"But—but I can only marry you on a birthday," she replied, shaken by his words, and looked up at him with dusky, eloquent eyes.

"Dear, I'm so happy to find you alive—to see you grown into a beautiful woman—to know you love me—that I could wait for ten birthdays," he said, earnestly. "But why make me wait? I've had a lonely hard life out there in the buffalo fields. It has taken something from me that only you can make up for. I must go back to my dream of a ranch—a home, cattle, horses, tilling the soil. Have you forgotten how we planned when we met in secret under the cottonwoods? Those moonlight nights!"

"No, I never forgot anything," she whispered, her head going down on his shoulder.

"Well—since to-morrow is your nineteenth birthday, and I've lost you for an endless hateful year—marry me to-morrow. Will you?"

"Yes!"

The Hash Knife Outfit

[illegible]

firepl[illegible]
the [illegible]
showe[illegible]
the [illegible] The men [illegible]
finished supper [illegible]
"Reckon the [illegible]

[illegible]
low [illegible] was [illegible]
recognize him [illegible]
the bright [illegible]
dressed of be[illegible]
[illegible]
in [illegible] shado[illegible]

[illegible] up an[illegible]

CHAPTER ONE

IT WAS A rainy November night down on the Cottonwood. The wind complained in the pines outside the cabin and whispered under the eaves. A fine cold mist blew in the open chinks between the logs. But the ruddy cedar fire in the huge stone fireplace gave the interior of the cabin a comfortable aspect and shone brightly upon the inmates scattered around. A coffee-pot steamed on some coals; browned biscuits showed in an open iron oven; and thick slices of beef mingled a savory odor with the smoke. The men, however, were busy on pipes and cigarettes, evidently having finished supper.

"Reckon this storm looks like an early winter," remarked Jed Stone, leader of the outfit. He stood to one side of the fire, a fine, lithe figure of a man, still a cowboy, despite his forty years and more of hard Arizona life. His profile, sharp in the fire glow, was strong and clean, in no way hinting of the evil repute that had long recorded him an outlaw. When he turned to pick up a burning ember for his pipe the bright blaze shone on light, rather scant hair, on light eyes, and a striking face devoid of beard.

"Wal, early or late, I never seen no bad weather down hyar," replied a man back in the shadow.

"Huh! Much you know about the Mogollans. I've seen a hell of a winter right here," spoke up another, in a deep chesty voice. "An' I'll be trackin' somethin' beside hoofs in a couple of days." This from the hunter Anderson, known to his comrades as Tracks, who had lived longer than any of the others in this wild section, seemed to strengthen Stone's intimation. Anderson was a serious man, long matured, as showed in the white in his black beard. He had big deep eyes which reflected the firelight.

"I'll bet we don't get holed up yet awhile," interposed Carr, the gambler of the outfit. He was a gray-faced, gray-haired man of fifty. They called him Stoneface.

"What do you say, Pecos?" inquired the leader of a long-limbed sandy-mustached Texan who sat propped against the wall, directly opposite the fire.

"Me? . . . Shore I don't think nothin' aboot it," drawled Pecos.

"We might winter down in the Sierra Ancas," said Stone, reflectively.

"Boss, somethin's beein eatin' you ever since we had thet fight over Traft's drift fence," spoke up Croak Malloy, from his seat against some packs. His voice had a peculiar croaking quality, but that was certainly not wholly the reason for his significant nickname. He was the deadliest of this notorious outfit, so long a thorn in the flesh of the cattlemen whose stock ranged the Mogollans.

"I ain't denyin' it," replied Stone.

"An' why for?" complained the croaker, his crooked evil face shining in the red light. "We got off without a couple of scratches, an' we crippled them two Diamond riders. Didn't we lay low the last nine miles of thet fence?"

"Croak, I happen to know old Jim Traft. I rode for him twenty years ago," answered Stone, seriously.

"Jed, as I see it, this drift fence of Traft's has split the range. An' there'll be hell to pay," snapped the other.

"Do you reckon it means another Pleasant Valley War? That was only seven years ago—thereabouts. An' the bad blood still rankles."

Croak Malloy's reply was rendered indistinguishable by hot arguments of Carr and Anderson. But the little rider's appearance seemed silently convincing. He was a small misshapen man of uncertain age, with pale eyes of fire set unevenly in a crooked face, and he looked the deadliness by which he had long been known to the range.

Just then the sodden beat of hoofs sounded outside.

"Ha! that will be Madden an' Sonora," said Stone, with satisfaction, and he strode to the door to call out. The answer was reassuring. He returned to the fire and held his palms to the heat. Then he turned and put his hands behind his back.

Meanwhile the horses thumped on the other side of the log wall. Then the sliddery sound of wet leather and heavy packs, and the low voice of men, attested to what was going on out there. Stone went again to the door, but evidently could not see in the stormy gloom. His men smoked in silence. The rain beat on the roof, in some places leaking through. The wind mourned hollowly down the stone chimney.

Presently a man entered the cabin, carrying a heavy pack, which he deposited against the wall, then approached the fire, to remove dripping sombrero and coat. This action disclosed the swarthy face and beady bright eyes of the Mexican whom Stone had called Sonora.

"Glad you're back, Sonora," said the leader, heartily. "How about things?"

"No good," replied Sonora, and when he shook his head drops of rain water sputtered in the fire.

"Ahuh," ejaculated Stone, and he leaned against the stone chimney, back in the shadow.

The other rider came in, breathing heavily under another pack, which he let fall with a thud, and approached the fire, smelling of rain and horses and the woods. He appeared to be a nondescript sort of man. Water ran off him in little streams. He hung his coat on a peg in the chimney, but did not remove his battered black sombrero from which the rain drops dripped.

"Wal, boss, me an' Sonora got here," he said, cheerfully.

"So I see," returned Stone, quietly.

"Bad up on top. Snowin' hard, but reckon it won't last long. Too wet."

"What you want to bet it won't last?" queried Carr.

Madden laughed, and knelt before the fire, his huge spurs prodding his hips.

"Lemme eat," he said. "It'll be the first bite since yestiddy mornin'."

Whereupon he drew the coffee-pot away from the fire at the same moment that Sonora removed the biscuits and meat. Stone, though nervously burning to ply questions, respected their hunger, which appeared to be of a ravenous nature. He paced the cabin floor, out of the shadow and into the light, and back again, ponderingly, as one who had weighty thoughts. The firelight struck glints from the bone-handled gun which swung in a belt-sheath below his hip. The other men of the gang smoked in silence.

The youngest of the group, a cowboy in garb and gait, rose to put more wood on the fire. It blazed up brightly. He had a weak, handsome face, with viciousness written all over it, yet strangely out of place among these hardened visages. No one need have been told why he was there.

The returned members of the outfit did not desist from appeasing their appetites until all the drink, bread, and beef were gone.

"Cleaned the platter," ejaculated Madden. "Gosh! there's nothin' like a hunk of juicy salty meat when you're starved. . . . An' here's a real cigar for everybody. Nice an' dry, too." He tossed them to eager hands, and taking up a blazing stick he lighted one for himself, his dark face and steaming sombrero bent over the fire. Then he sat back, puffed a huge cloud of white smoke, and exclaimed: "Aghh! . . . Now, boss, shoot."

Stone kicked a box nearer the fire and sat down upon it. Then from a shadowed corner limped a stalwart man, scarred of face and evil of eye, with a sheriff's badge glittering like a star on the front of his vest. Some of the others edged closer. All except Croak Malloy evinced keen eagerness. Nothing mattered to this little outlaw.

"Maddy, did you fetch all the supplies?" asked Stone.

"Yep. An' kept them dry, too. There's four more packs out in the shed. The tobacco, whisky, shells—all that particular stuff is in the pack Sonora fetched in. An' I'm here to state I don't want to pack down Cottonwood any more in the snow an' rain. We couldn't see a hand before our eyes. An' just follered the horses."

"Any trouble at Flag?" went on Stone.

"Nary trouble," answered Madden, brightly. "All our worryin' was for nothin'."

"Ahuh. Then neither of those drift-fence cowboys we shot up died?"

"Nope. Frost was around with a crutch. An' Hump Stevens will live, so they told me."

"How did Jim Traft take the layin' down of nine miles of his drift fence?"

"Which Jim Traft do you mean?"

"The old man, you fool. Who'd ever count that tenderfoot of a nephew?"

"Wal, boss, I reckon you'll have to count him. For he's shore countin' in Flag. . . . Of course I could only get roundabout gossip in the saloons an' stores, you know. But we can gamble on it. That nine-mile drop of Traft's drift fence didn't make him bat an eye, though they told me it riled young Jim somethin' fierce. Jed, the old cattle king, is goin' through with that drift fence, an' with more'n that, which I'll tell you presently. As I got it the drift fence is comin' more to favor with cattlemen as time goes on. Bambridge is the only big rancher against it, an' shore you know why he is. But the fence ain't the only thing talked about. . . . Boss, the Cibeque outfit is busted."

"No!—You don't say?" ejaculated Stone.

"Shore is. Most owin' to that cowpuncher Hack Jocelyn who left the Diamond outfit an' throwed in with the Cibeque. That split the Cibeque. It seems Jocelyn lost his head over that little Dunn girl, Molly, sister to Slinger Dunn. You've seen her, Jed, at West Fork."

"Yes. Prettiest kid in the country."

"Wal, Jocelyn was after her hard, an' he double-crossed the Haverlys an' Slinger Dunn by tryin' to play both ends against the middle. He hatched a low-down deal, if I ever knowed one. But it fell through. He got away with the girl, Molly, however, an' thet precipitated hell. Slinger quit the Cibeque, trailed them to a cabin in the woods. Back of Tobe's Well somewhere. Must have been the very cabin Anderson put up there years ago. Wal, Jocelyn an' the rest of the Cibeque had kidnapped young Jim Traft for ransom. But Jocelyn meant to collect the ransom an' then murder the boy. The Haverlys wasn't in on this, so the story goes. Anyway, things worked to a hot pitch at this cabin. Jocelyn had a drink too many, they say, an' wanted to drag the little girl Molly off 'n the woods. An' she, like what you'd expect of Slinger Dunn's sister, raised hell. Jocelyn tried to shoot young Jim. An' she fought him—bit him like a wildcat. Wal, Slinger bobbed up, Injun as he is, an' killed Jocelyn. Then he had it out with the Haverlys, killin' both of them. He was terrible shot up himself. They fetched him to Flag. But he'll live."

"I'm dod-blasted glad, though there ain't any love lost between me an' Slinger," said Stone, forcibly. "No wonder Flag wasn't excited over our little brush with Stevens an' Frost."

"Wel, thet's all of thet news," went on Madden, importantly. "Some more will interest you-all. Bambridge lost his case against Traft. He had no case at all, accordin' to the court. It seems Traft got this Yellow Jacket Ranch an' range from Blodgett, years ago. Bambridge didn't even know the deeds were on record in Flag. He was hoppin' mad, they said, an' he an' Traft had it hot an' heavy after the court proceedin's. Traft jest about accused Bambridge of shady cattle deals down here. Bambridge threw a gun, but somebody knocked it out of his hand. Wal, that riled the old cattle king. What do you think he said, boss? I got it from a fellar I know, who was in the court-room."

"Maddy, I'll bet it was a heap," replied Stone, wagging his head.

"Heap! Reckon you hit it. Traft swore he'd run Bambridge off the Arizona ranges. What's more, he made a present of this Yellow Jacket Ranch, which Bambridge an' you reckoned you *owned* yourselves, to his nephew, young Jim, an'—but guess who?"

"I'm not guessin'. Out with it," rejoined Stone, hardily.

"No one less than Slinger Dunn," announced Madden, with the triumphant tone of the sensation-lover.

"What?" bellowed Stone.

"I told you, boss. Old Traft gave this ranch an' range to young Jim an' Slinger—half an' half. Providin' thet Slinger throwed in with the Diamond outfit an' helped them clean up Yellow Jacket."

"Haw! Haw!" croaked Malloy, with vicious humor.

"Slinger Dunn an' the Diamond!" exclaimed Stone, incredulously. Evidently it was a most astounding circumstance, and one fraught with bewildering possibilities.

"Thet's it, boss, an' they're ridin' down here after Thanksgivin'," ended Madden, and took a long pull on his cigar.

Stone once more leaned in the shadow, his dim profile bent toward the fire. Madden stretched himself, boots to the heat, and gave himself over to the enjoyment of his cigar. All except the leader puffed white clouds of smoke which rose to catch the draught and waft through the chinks between the logs.

"What do you make of it, boss?" finally queried Anderson.

Jed Stone vouchsafed no reply.

"Humph!" grunted the hunter. "Wal, Frank, you're the green hand in this outfit. What you make of Maddy's news?"

The cowboy stirred and sat up. "I reckon it can't be done," he replied.

"What can't?"

"Cleanin' up Yellow Jacket."

The hunter took a long draw at his cigar and expelled a volume of smoke, while he thoughtfully stroked his black beard.

"Whar you from, Frank?"

"Born in Arizonie."

"An' you say thet? Wal. . . . Reckon it ain't no wonder you ended up with the Hash Knife outfit," said Anderson, reflectively. Then he turned his attention to the Mexican, who sat nearest. "Sonora, you been herdin' sheep for years on this range?"

"Si, señor."

"You've seen a heap of men shot?"

"Many men, señor."

"Did you talk to sheep-herders in Flag?"

"Si. All say *mucho malo.* Old Traft bad medicine. If he start job he do job."

Whereupon Tracks Anderson, warming as to a trail, set upon the long-limbed, sandy-mustached Texan. "Pecos, what was you when you rode thet river you're named fer?"

"Me? Much the same as I am now," drawled the rustler, with an easy laugh. "Only I wasn't ridin' in such good safe company."

"Safe, huh? Wal, thet's a compliment to Jed an' the Hash Knife. But is it sense? . . . To my way of thinkin' this—drift fence has spelled a change fer Arizona ranges. There's a mind behind that idee. It's big. It throws the sunlight on trails thet have been dim."

Croak Malloy did not wait to be interrogated. He spat as he emitted a cloud of smoke, which hid his strange visage.

"If you ask me I'll tell you Maddy's talk is jest town talk," he croaked. "I've heard the same fer ten years. An' Yellow Jacket is wilder today than it ever was. There's more cattle runnin' than then. More rustlers in the woods. More crooked ranchers. An' one like Bambridge wasn't ever heard when I first rode into the Tonto. . . . An' what's a bunch of slick-ridin' cowboys to us? I'll kill this young Traft, an' Sonora can do fer Slinger Dunn. Thet'll be the last of the Diamond."

"Very pretty, Croak. It might be done, easy enough, if we take the first step. I ain't aimin' to class thet wild Diamond outfit with the Hash Knife. It ain't no fair fight. Boys ag'in' men. An' this is shore allowin' fer Slinger Dunn an' thet Prentiss fellar."

"Tracks," spoke up Pecos, dryly, "you're plumb fergettin' there's a Texan in the Diamond. Lonestar Holliday. An' you can bet the Texas I come from wouldn't be ashamed of him."

"Humph!—Lang, you swear you come honest by thet sheriff badge," went on the hunter, in a grim humor. "Let's hear from you."

"There ain't no law but might in the Mogollans an' never will be in our day," replied the ex-sheriff.

"Kirreck," snapped Anderson. "Thet's what I'm drivin' at. *Our* day may be damn good an' short."

"Aw, hell! Tracks, you need some licker," croaked Malloy. "Let's open the pack an' have some."

"No," came from Stone with sharp suddenness, showing how intent he was on the colloquy.

"Wal, it narrows down to Stoneface," continued Anderson, imperturbably. "But seein' he's a gambler, you can't ever get the straight from him."

"Tracks, I'll bet you them gold wheels you'll be hibernatin' fer keeps when spring comes," said Carr, clinking gold coins in his palms.

"Quién sabe? But I won't bet you, Stoneface. You get hunches from the air, an' Gawd only knows—you might be communicatin' with the dead."

A silence ensued, during which the hunter gazed with questioning eyes at the shadowed leader, but he did not voice his thought. He returned diligently to the cigar that appeared to be hard to smoke. The rain pattered on the roof; the wind moaned under the eaves; beyond the log wall horses munched their feed; the fire sputtered. And presently Jed Stone broke the silence.

"Men, I rode on the first Hash Knife outfit, twenty years ago," he began. "An' Arizona never had a finer bunch of riders. Since then I've rode in all the outfits. Some had good men an' bad men at the same time. Thet Texas outfit in the early 'eighties gave the Hash Knife its bad name. Daggs, Colter, an' the rest didn't live long, but their fame did. Yet they wasn't any worse than the cattlemen and sheepmen who fought thet war. I've never had a real honest job since."

Stone paused to take a long pull on his cigar and to blow smoke. He kicked a stick into the fire and watched it crackle and flame.

"An' thet fetches me down to this day an' the Hash Knife outfit here," he went on. "There's a heap of difference between fact and rumor. Old Jim Traft knows we're rustlin' his stock, but he can't prove it—yet. Bambridge knows we are stealin' cattle, but he can't prove it because he's crooked himself. An' same with lesser cattlemen hereabouts. If I do say it myself, I've run this outfit pretty slick. We've got a few thousand head of cattle wearin' our brand. Most of which we jest roped out on the range an' branded. We knowed the mothers of these calves had Traft's brand or some other than ours. But no posse or court can ever prove thet onless they ketch us in the act. We're shore too old hands now to be ketched, at least at the brandin' game. But . . . an', men, here's the hell of it, we can't go on in the old comfortable way if Traft sends thet Diamond outfit down here. Yellow Jacket belongs to him. An' don't you overlook this Diamond bunch if Slinger Dunn is on it. Reckon thet will have to be proved to me. Slinger is even more of an Indian than a backwoodsman. I know him well. We used to hunt together. He's run a lot in the woods with Apaches. An' no outfit would be safe while he prowled around with a rifle. I'm tellin' you—if Slinger would ambush us—shoot us from cover like an Indian, he'd kill every damn one of us. But I'll gamble Slinger wouldn't never do thet kind of fightin'. An' we want to bear thet in mind if it comes to a clash between the Diamond an' the Hash Knife."

"If," exploded Anderson, as the leader paused. "There ain't no ifs. Any kind of reasonin' would show you thet Traft has long had in mind workin' up this Yellow Jacket. It'll run ten thousand head, easy, an' shore will be a fine ranch."

"Wal, then, we got to figger close. Let me make a few more points an' then I'll put it to a vote. I wish I hadn't always done thet. For I reckon I see clear here. . . . We've had more'n one string to our bow these five years. An' if we wasn't a wasteful outfit we'd all be heeled right now. Bambridge has been playin' a high hand lately. How many thousand unbranded calves an' yearlin's we've drove over to him I can't guess. But shore a lot. Anyway, he's figgerin' to leave Arizona. Thet's my hunch.

An' he'll likely try to drive some big deals before he goes. If he does you can bet he'll leave the Hash Knife to bear the brunt. Traft has come out in the open. He's on to Bambridge. There's no slicker cowman on the range than Traft's man, Ring Locke. They'll put the Diamond down here, not only to watch us, but Bambridge too. An' while we're at it let's give this young Jim Traft the benefit of a doubt. They say he's a chip of the old block. Wal, it'd jest be a hell of a mistake for Croak to kill thet young fellar. Old Traft would rake Arizona from the Little Colorado to the Superstitions. It jest won't do. Slinger Dunn, yes, an' any of the rest of the outfit. But not young Jim. . . . Wal, I reckon it'd be wise fer us to make one more drive, sell to Bambridge, an' clear out pronto."

"My Gawd!" croaked Malloy, in utter amaze.

"Boss, do I understand you to hint you'd leave the range your Hash Knife has run fer twenty years?" demanded Stoneface Carr.

And the Texan rustler Pecos asked a like question, drawling and sarcastic.

"Men, I read the signs of the times," replied the leader, briefly and not without heat. "I'll put it up to you one by one. . . . Anderson, shall we pull up stakes fer a new range?"

"I reckon so. It ain't the way of a Hash Knife outfit. But I advise it fer thet very reason."

Sonora, the sheep-herder, leaned significantly and briefly to Stone's side. But the gambler was stone cold to the plan. Malloy only croaked a profane and scornful refusal. The others came out flat with derisive or affronted objections.

"Wal, you needn't blow my head off," declared Stone, in like tone. "If you do there shore won't be a hell of a lot of brains left in this outfit. . . . It's settled. The Hash Knife stays until we are run out or wiped out."

That ultimatum seemed to be final. The force of Stone's grim voice had a thought-provoking effect, except upon the cold Malloy, and perhaps the silent Texan. One by one they unrolled their beds, talking desultorily and sleepily. Madden had already fallen asleep with his head on a sack. His sombrero had slipped back, exposing a heavy tired face, dark with shadows.

Jed Stone still stood in the darkening shadow by the chimney. Presently, when the members of his gang had quieted down he stepped out to seat himself on a box by the fire, and took to throwing chips on the red embers, watching them burn.

Outside, the storm appeared to be letting up. The wind moaned faintly and intermittently; the rain pattered softer; the trees ceased to lash their branches against the roof.

Stone must have been thinking of the past. He had the look of a man who saw pictures in the glowing embers. Twenty years ago he had been a cowboy riding the ranges, free, honest, liked, with all the future before him. The dark sad eyes told that then there had been a girl. Only twenty years! But the latter number of them were black and must be expiated. He had seen cattlemen begin honestly and end by being hanged. Sighing, he evidently dispelled something familiar yet rare and troublesome, and rising he began to pace the floor before the fire.

The replenished embers glowed fitfully, augmenting the shadows on the walls, playing on the sinister faces of the sleeping men. Malloy's had a ghastly sardonic mockery. Even in sleep he showed his deadliness. What were life and death to him? Young Reed, the cowboy lately come to the outfit, lay flat, his weak handsome face clear in the ruddy light. Stone pitied him. Did he have a mother living—a sister? He was an outlaw now at twenty-two. That should have meant nothing to Jed Stone, considering how many cowboys he had seen go to the bad. But somehow for the moment it meant a good deal. Stone saw with eyes grown old in the wild ways of the West. Sonora there—he had a dark sleek face, inscrutable like an Indian's, that did not betray he was thief and murderer. The gambler Carr, too, wore a mask. Pecos was the only other member of the gang who lay with face exposed to the firelight. Silent, mysterious Texan, he had always fascinated Stone. Pecos was a deadly foe, and to a friend true as steel. He cared little for money or drink, not at all for cards, and he shunned women. Could that be his secret?

Stone went to the door and looked out. It had cleared somewhat. Stars shone in the open spaces between the black clouds. A misty rain from the pines wet his face. A mountain to the East stood up wild and black. Out there a wolf bayed a deer. A chill in the air—or was it the haunting voice of the wolf? struck down Stone's spine. He had an honest love for this lonely range, which sooner or later, and one way or another, he must leave.

He went back to unroll his bed near the fire, and he for one pulled off his boots. Throwing more chips and bits of bark on the coals, he stretched his long length, feet to the warmth, and his head high, and watched the blaze rise and fall, the red glow pale, the ruddy embers darken, and the shadows dim and die.

CHAPTER TWO

That same stormy night in early November, when the members of the Hash Knife gang had their fateful colloquy in the old log cabin on the Yellow Jacket range, Jim Traft sat with his nephew in the spacious living-room of the big ranch-house on the edge of Flagerstown.

It was a bright warm room, doubly cosy owing to the whine of wind outside and the patter of sleet on the windowpanes. Old Traft had a fondness for lamps with rosy globes, and the roaring fire in the great stone fireplace attested to his years on the open range. A sleek wolfhound lay on the rug. Traft occupied an armchair that looked as ancient as the hills, and he sat back with a contented smile on his fine weather-beaten face, occasionally to puff his pipe.

"Dog-gone-it, Jim, this is somethin' like home," he said. "You look so good to me these days. An' you've come through a Westerner. . . . An' the old house isn't lonesome any more."

He nodded his gray head toward the far end of the room, where Molly Dunn curled in a big chair, her pretty gold-brown head bent over a book. Opposite Molly on the other side of the table sat Mrs. Dunn, with eager expectant look of enchantment, as one who wanted to keep on dreaming.

Young Jim laughed. It looked more than something like home to him, and seldom was there a moment his eyes did not return to that brown head of Molly Dunn.

"Shore is, Uncle," he drawled, in the lazy voice he affected on occasions. "You wouldn't think we're only a few weeks past that bloody fight. . . . Gosh! when I think! . . . Uncle, I've told you a hundred times how Molly saved my life. It seems like a dream. . . . Well, I'm back home—for this *is* home, Uncle. No work for weeks! No bossing that terrible bunch of cowboys! You so pleased with me—though for the life of me I can't see why. Molly here for the winter to go to school—and—and then to be my wife next spring. . . . And Slinger Dunn getting well from those awful bullet wounds so fast. . . . It's just too good to be true."

"Ahuh. I savvy how you feel, son," replied the old rancher. "It does seem that out here in the West the hard knocks and trials make the softer side of life—home an' folks—an' the girl of your heart—so much dearer an' sweeter. It ought to make you keen as a whip to beat the West—to stack cunnin' an' nerve against the wild life of the range, an' come through alive. I did. An', Jim, if I'd been a drinkin', roarin' cowpuncher I'd never have lasted, an' you wouldn't be here tonight, stealin' looks at your little Western girl."

"Oh, Uncle, that's the—the hell of it!" exclaimed Jim. "I'm crucified when I realize. Those weeks building the drift fence were great. Such fun—such misery! Then that fight at the cabin! O Lord! I could have torn Hack Jocelyn to pieces with my hands. Then when Molly was fighting him for possession of his gun—hanging to him like grim death—with her *teeth,* mind you—when he lifted and swung her and beat her—I was an abject groveling wretch, paralyzed with horror. . . . Then when Slinger leaped past me round the cabin, as I sat there tied and helpless, and he yelled like an Indian at Jocelyn. . . . I thrill and shiver now, and my heart stops. . . . Only since I've been home do I realize what you mean about the West. It's wonderful, it's glorious, but terrible too."

"You've had your eye teeth cut, son," said Traft, grimly. "Now you must face the thing—you must fight. I've fought for forty years. An' it will still be years more before the range is free of the outlaw, the rustler, the crooked cattleman, the thieving cowboy."

"Uncle Jim," called Molly, plaintively, "please hush up aboot the bad West. I want to study, an' I cain't help heahin'."

"Wal, wal, Molly," laughed Traft, in mild surprise. "Reckon I thought you was wrapped up in that school book."

"An', Jim—shore the West's not as wicked as Uncle makes out," went on Molly. "He wants you to be another Curly Prentiss—or even like Slinger."

"Ha! Ha!" roared the rancher, rubbing his hands. "That's funny from Molly Dunn. My dear, if *you* hadn't had all the Western qualities I'm tryin' to inspire in Jim, where would he be now?"

Even across the room Jim saw her sweet face blanch and her big dark eyes dilate; and these evidences shot an exquisite pleasure and happiness through him.

"Uncle, I'll answer that," he said. "I'd be in the Garden of Eden, eating peaches."

"Maybe you would, Jim Traft," retorted Molly. "A little more bossin' the Diamond outfit an' your chances for the Garden of Eden are shore slim."

Mrs. Dunn spoke up, exclaiming how strange and delightful it was to hear the sleet on the pane.

"Wal, this is high country, Mrs. Dunn," replied Traft. "Down on the Cibeque where you live it's five thousand feet lower. There's seldom any winter in the Tonto. But she's shore settin' in here at Flag."

"Will there be snow on the ground, tomorrow?" asked Molly, wonderingly.

"I reckon, a little. Couple of feet."

"How lovely! I can go to school in the snow."

"I'm sorry, Molly," interposed Jim. "Tomorrow is Saturday. No school. It will be very tame for you, I'm afraid. Only wading out to the corrals with me. A snowball fight or two. Then a sleigh ride into town."

"Jim!" she exclaimed, ecstatically. "I never had a sleigh ride in all my life."

Her rapture was reflected in the old cattleman's face. Jim imagined it must be pure joy for his uncle to see and hear Molly. What a lonely hard life the old fellow had lived! And now he wanted young folk around, and the children that had been denied him. Jim's heart swelled with longing to make up to his uncle for all that he had missed.

Mrs. Dunn rose to come forward and take a chair nearer the fire. "It's getting chilly. Such a big room!"

"Molly, come over an' be sociable," called Traft.

"But my study, Uncle. I—I've missed so much," replied the girl, wistfully.

"Molly, I'll not allow you to wear your pretty eyes out," declared Jim, authoritatively. "Learning is very good for a girl, but beauty should not be sacrificed."

"You won't allow me?" she asked, demurely, and resumed her study.

Whereupon Jim walked over, picked her up bodily, and carried her back to set her, blushing and confused, in his own chair.

"You're such a slip of a girl, Molly," he said, wonderingly. "In size I mean. You're heavy as lead and strong as the dickens. But you're so little. There's quite room enough in that chair for me, too."

And Jim slipped into it beside her, not quite sure how she would take this. But his fear was unfounded.

"Now, Uncle, tell us the story about the time you came West as a boy. How you rode in a caravan across the plains and were attacked by Indians at Pawnee Rock. I was six years old when you told me that story. I've never forgotten. It'll make Molly think the Cibeque a quiet, peaceful country."

Later, when the ladies had retired, Ring Locke came in with his quiet step and his intent eye. Since Jim's return from the disastrous failure of the drift fence (so he considered it, in contrast to his uncle's opinion) and the fight at the cabin below Cottonwood, he had seemed to be in the good graces of this Westerner, Ring Locke, a fact he hugged with great satisfaction. Locke was a keen, strong, and efficient superintendent of the old cattleman's vast interests.

"Some mail an' some news," he announced, handing a packet of letters to Traft.

"How's the weather, Ring?" asked the rancher.

"Clearin' I reckon, but we won't see any green round Flag till spring."

"Early winter, eh? Wal, we got here first. . . . Son, letter for you from home—two. An' in a lady's fancy hand. You better look out Molly doesn't see them. . . . Ring, help yourself to a cigar an' set down."

Jim stared at the first letter. "By gosh! Gloriana has written me at last. It's coming Christmas, the little devil. . . . And the other from Mother. Fine."

"Glory must be growed into quite a girl by now," remarked his uncle.

"Quite? Uncle, she's altogether," declared Jim with force.

"Wal, I hardly remember her, 'cept as a pretty little kid with curls an' big eyes. Favored your mother. She shore wasn't a Traft."

Locke lit a cigar. "Some of the Hash Knife outfit been in town," he announced, calmly.

Jim forgot to open his letters. Old Traft bit at his cigar. "Nerve of 'em! Who was it, Ring?"

"Madden and a greaser whose name I've forgot, if I ever knowed it. Reckon there was another of the gang in town, but I couldn't find out who. They bought a lot of supplies an' left Thursday. I went around to all the stores an' saloons. Dug up what

I could. It wasn't a lot, but then again it 'pears interestin'. One thing in particular. Curly Prentiss swears he saw Madden comin' out of Bambridge's, after dark Wednesday, he says. But Curly has had a ruction with his gurl, an' he's been drinkin', I'm sorry to say. That cowboy would be the grandest fellar, if he didn't drink. Still drunk or no, Curly has an eye, an' I reckon he did see Madden."

"Funny, his comin' out of Bambridge's," growled Traft, and the bright blue eyes narrowed.

"Awful funny," agreed Locke, in a dry tone, which acquainted the listening Jim with the fact that the circumstance was most decidedly not funny. "Anyway, it started me off. An' the upshot of my nosin' around was to find out that the Hash Knife crowd are at Yellow Jacket an' all of a sudden oncommon interested in you an' young Jim, an' the Diamond, an' Slinger Dunn."

"Ahuh. Wal, they'll be a heap more so by spring," replied Traft. "Funny about Bambridge."

"The Hash Knife have friends in Flag, you bet, an' more'n we'd ever guess. Shore, nobody knows our business, onless the cowboys have talked. I'm afraid Bud an' Curly have bragged. They do when they get to town an' guzzle a bit. Madden did darn little drinkin' an' none 'cept when he was treated. Another funny thing. He bought all the forty-five caliber shells Babbitt's had in stock. An' a heap of the same kind, along with some forty-fours for rifles, at Davis's. He bought hardware, too. Some new guns. An' enough grub to feed an outfit for a year."

"Winter supplies, I reckon. An' mebbe the Hash Knife are in for another war, like the one it started in 'eighty-two. Ha! Ha! . . . But it ain't so funny, after all."

"It shore don't look like peaceful ranchin'," drawled Locke.

"Damn these low-down outfits, anyway," growled the rancher. "I fought them when I rode the range years ago, an' now I'm fightin' them still. Locke, we'll be runnin' eighty thousand head of stock in a year or two."

"Eighty thousand!— Then you can afford to lose some," replied Locke.

"Humph. *I* couldn't lose a calf's ear to those thievin' outfits without gettin' sore. They've kept me poor."

"Uncle, we appear to have the necessities of life around the ranch. Nice warm fires, and some luxury," remarked Jim, humorously.

"Just you wait," retorted his uncle. "Just you wait! You'll be a darn sight worse than me, pronto."

"Locke, who is this Madden?" asked Jim, quietly, with change of tone.

"One of Jed Stone's gang. Hard-ridin', hard-drinkin' an' shootin' hombre. Come up from the border a few years ago. The murder of Wilson, a rancher out of Holbrook, was laid to Madden. But that was only suspicion. In this country you have to catch a man at anythin' to prove it. Personally, though, I'd take a shot at Madden an' ask questions afterward."

"Tough outfit, Uncle tells me," went on Jim, reflectively.

"Boy, the Cibeque was a summer zephyr to thet Hash Knife outfit. Stone used to be a square-shootin' cowboy. Rode fer your uncle once. That was before my day here. He's outlawed now, with crimes on his head. An intelligent, dangerous man. He's got a Texas gun-fighter in his outfit. Pecos something or other, an' I reckon he's 'most as bad as any of the killers out of Texas. Croak Malloy, though, is Stone's worst an' meanest hand. Then, there's Lang an' Anderson, who've been with him for years."

"Is Slinger Dunn the equal of any of these men?" queried Jim.

"Equal? I reckon. Yes, he's ahaid of them in some ways," replied Locke, thoughtfully. "Slinger could beat any one of them to a gun, unless mebbe this

Pecos feller. But Slinger is young an' he has no crimes on his haid. That makes a difference. None of this Hash Knife outfit could be arrested. They hang together, an' you bet they'll die with their boots on."

"Then we're in for another fight?" mused Jim, and though he sustained a wonderful thrill—cold as a chill—he did not like the prospect.

"Traft," said Locke, turning to the rancher, "strikes me queer that Stone hangs on in this part of Arizona. He's no fool. He shore knows he can't last forever. If the Diamond doesn't drive him out it'll break up his outfit. An' other riders will keep on his track."

"Wal, you know, Stone will never be run out of anywhere. But he's an Arizonian, an' this range is home, even if it has outlawed him. He's bitter an' hard, which is natural enough. Stone ought to be a rich cattleman now. I—I feel sorry for him, an' that's why I've let Yellow Jacket alone."

Jim thought his uncle spoke rather feelingly.

"Wouldn't it be better to drive off what stock's left there an' let the land go?" went on Locke.

"Better? Humph! It can't be done. We've got to organize against these rustlin' outlaws or they'll grow bolder an' ruin us. Take that case over in New Mexico when a big cattleman—crooked, of course—hired Billy the Kid an' his outfit to steal cattle, an' he sold them to the government. That deal lasted for years. Everybody knew it, except the government officials. Wal, I'm inclined to think there's *some* ranchin' man backin' Stone."

"Ahuh. I know how you incline, Traft," returned Locke, dryly. "An' it's likely to get us into trouble."

"Wal, if Bambridge is buyin' in our stock we ought to find it out," said Traft, testily.

"Suppose your suspicions reach Bambridge's ear? He *might* be honest. In any case he's liable to shoot you. An' I say this Yellow Jacket isn't worth the risk."

"Ring, I don't like the man. I suspect him. We've clashed from the first. He was hoppin' mad when he found out I owned Yellow Jacket an' had the range rights there. It'll be interestin' to see what move he makes."

"Like watchin' a game of checkers," rejoined Locke, with a laugh. "All right, Boss. I'm bound to admit you've made some sharp guesses in my days with you. Reckon I'll go to bed. Good night."

In the silence that succeeded after he had gone, Jim slowly opened the letters he had been idly holding.

"Uncle, I'm afraid Locke is against this Yellow Jacket deal, especially the Bambridge angle."

"Locke is cautious. He hates this sort of thing as much as I do. But what can we do? I take it as my duty to rid Arizona of this particular outfit, an' I'm goin' to do it."

"Then it isn't a personal grudge against Bambridge?"

"Not at all. I shore hope we find out my suspicions are wrong. An' I'm relyin' on your Slinger Dunn to find out. He's the man we need, Jim. I shore appreciate your gettin' hold of him."

Jim spread out one of the letters on his knee and read it.

"Good heavens!" he ejaculated, blankly.

"Son, I hope you've no bad news. Who's the letter from?"

"Mother," replied Jim, still blankly.

"Wal?"

"Uncle, what do you think? Mother is sending my sister, Gloriana, out here to stay with us a while. . . . Doctor's orders. Says Gloriana has a weak lung and must live a year or more in a high dry climate. . . . By gosh! Glory is on her way right now!"

"Wal, wal! I'm shore sorry, Jim. But Arizona will cure her."

"Cure! . . . Cure nothing!" snorted Jim. "Gloriana has no more lung trouble than I have. She's the healthiest girl alive. It's just a trick to get her out here."

"Wal, I reckon there ain't no need of tricks. We'll be darn glad to have her, won't we?"

"Uncle, you don't understand," replied Jim, in despair.

"Tell me, then."

"Gloriana will upset the ranch, and break the Diamond and drive me crazy."

"Haw! Haw! Haw!"

"It's no laughing matter."

"But, Jim, you've been away from home 'most a year. Your sister could have failed in health in much less time."

"That's so. . . . Oh, I hope not. . . . Of course, Uncle, I'll be glad to have her, if she's really sick. But . . ."

"Son, don't you care for this little sister?"

"Gosh, Uncle, I love her! That's the worst of it. I can't help but love her. Everybody loves her, in spite of the fact she's a perfect devil."

"Humph! How old is Gloriana?"

"She's eighteen. No, nearly nineteen."

"Wal, the Trafts were all good-lookin'. How does she stack up?"

"Glory is the prettiest girl you ever saw in all your life."

"Shore then it'll be fine to have her," replied the rancher. "An I'll tell you what, Jim. When we once get her out heah we'll keep her."

"What?" queried Jim, weakly.

"We'll never let her go back again. We'll marry her to some fine Westerner."

Jim felt it his turn to laugh. "Ha! Ha! Ha! . . . Uncle, there're not enough men in Arizona to marry Glory. And I'm afraid not one she'd wipe her feet on."

"Sort of stuck up, eh? Thet ain't a Traft trait."

"I wouldn't say she was stuck up. But she's certainly no plain everyday Traft, like you and I, or Dad or Mother. She's not conceited, either. Glory is a puzzle. She changes each moon. I wonder what she's like now. . . . Jerusalem! Suppose she doesn't take to Molly!"

"See heah, young man," spoke up Traft, gruffly. "Mebbe it'll be the other way round. Molly mightn't take to her."

"Molly? Why, Uncle, that adorable child would love anybody, if she had half a chance."

"Ahuh. Wal, that accounts fer her lovin' you. . . . Jim, it'll work out all right. Remember your first tenderfoot days. Would you go back East now to live?"

"Gosh, no!"

"Wal, the West will do the same for Gloriana, if she has any red blood. It'll go tough, until she's broke in. An' if she's a high-steppin' Easterner, it'll be all the tougher. But she must have real stuff in her. She's a Traft, for all you say."

"Gloriana May takes after Mother's side of the family, and some of them are awful."

"She's got to have some Traft in her. An' we'll gamble on that. For my part, I'm glad she's comin'. I hope she burns up the ranch. I've been so long without fun and excitement and deviltry around heah that I could stand a heap."

"Uncle Jim, you're going to get your desire," exploded Jim, dramatically.

"You'll see these cowboys walk Spanish and perform like tame bears with rings in their noses. You'll see the work on the ranch go to smash. The roundups will be a circus. As for dances—holy smoke! every one of them will be a war!"

"Wal, I'll be gol-darned if I wouldn't like the girl all the more," declared Traft, stoutly. "These cowpunchers make me awful sick with their love affairs. Any girl will upset them. An' if Glory is all you say—my Gawd, but I'll enjoy it! . . . Good night, son."

Jim slid down in his chair and eyed the fire. "Gosh! It's a good bet Uncle Jim will be apple pie for Glory. But if she really loves him, why, I reckon, I'll be glad. And I might get along with her, in a pinch.—But there's Molly. . . . Heigho! I'd better dig into Glory's letter."

He held it to the dying glow of the fire and read:

> DEAR BROTHER JIM:
>
> Don't let Mother's letter worry you. I'm not very sick. I've planned to start west the day after I mail this letter, so you won't have time to wire me not to come. I'm just crazy about the West. Your letters have done it, Jim. I've devoured them. Dad is so proud of you he almost busts. But Mother thinks it's terrible. I'm sorry to spring this on you so sudden. I hope you will be glad to see me. It seems ages since you left. You'll never know your Gloriana May.
>
> Expect me on the Western Special, November 7th, and meet me with a bunch of cowboys, a string of horses, and one of those tally-ho things you call a chuck-wagon. I'm starved to death.
>
> Love.
>
> GLORIANA.

Jim read the letter twice and then stared into the fire. "Sounds like Glory, yet somehow it doesn't. . . . I wonder if she *is* really ill. . . . Or in any kind of trouble. . . . It was Glory's affairs with boys that stuck in my craw. . . . Well. November the seventh. By jinks! it's Monday! What shall I say to Molly?"

The difficulty, it seemed to Jim, would be serious. Glory was bright and clever. She had graduated from high school at seventeen. She could do 'most anything well, and had a genius for designing and making modish dresses and bonnets. Molly, on the other hand, was a shy little woodmouse. She had never had any advantages. Two years at a backwoods school had been all the opportunity for education that had ever come to her. She was exceedingly sensitive about her lack of knowledge and her crudeness. The situation would be a delicate one, for Molly, in her way, was quite as proud as Gloriana was in hers.

"I'll trust to Molly's generous heart and the western bigness of her," soliloquized Jim. "In the end Glory will love her. That I'll gamble on."

CHAPTER THREE

Jim lay in bed longer than usual next morning, and when he finally rolled out, convinced that his problem was not so terribly serious after all, a white glistening world of snow greeted him from his window. The storm had gone and a clear blue sky and bright sun smiled coldly down upon the white-fringed pines and peaks. He did not take more than a glance, however, because his room seemed full of zero weather. He had to break the ice in his bucket to get water to wash, and he was far from lethargic about it. "I don't know about this high dry altitude," he soliloquized. "It'd freeze the nose off a polar bear."

The halls of the big ranch-house were like a barn. Jim rushed to the living-room. A fine fire blazed in the wide fireplace. How good it felt to his numb fingers! Jim thought the West brought out so much more of a man's appreciation. It was harsh, violent, crude, but it brought home to a man a full value of things.

"Mawnin', Jim," came in Molly's drawling voice from somewhere.

"Hello! . . . Oh, there you are!" exclaimed Jim, gladly, as he espied her at the corner window, gazing out upon the wintry scene. "I was sure you'd be snug in bed. Come here, darling."

Molly had not yet grown used to the impelling power of that word, and she seemed irresistibly drawn. She wore a red coat over her blouse, the color of which matched her cheeks. In the few weeks since her arrival at the ranch she had lost some of the brown tan of the backwoods, which only added to her attractiveness. The gold glints in her dark curly hair caught the sunshine as it streamed through the window. Her eyes had that dark, shy, glad light that always thrilled Jim. And her lips, like red ripe cherries, were infinitely provocative.

"Oh—Jim—" she gasped, "some one might come in."

"Kiss me, Molly Dunn," he replied, giving her a little shake. "I'll have to get like Curly or Bud in my lovemaking."

"If you do, Mister Missouri, you'll never get nowhere with me," she returned.

"Not 'nowhere,' Molly. Say, anywhere."

"Very well. Anywhere," she obeyed.

"I'll take that back about Curly and Bud."

"You don't need to learn from them. You're somethin' of a bear yourself."

"Don't you love me this morning?"

"Why, Jim—of course!"

"Then?"

Molly's kisses were rather few and far between, which made them so much more precious. Jim both deplored and respected her restraint. She had been raised in a hard school, and often she had regretted to Jim that her lips had not been kept wholly for him. She was strong and sweet, this little girl of the Cibeque, and she had earned Jim's worship.

"There!" she whispered, shyly, and slipped out of his arms. "Gee, your hands are cold. An' your nose is like ice."

"Molly, I've news for you," he said, thinking it wise to broach the subject in mind.

"Yes?"

"My sister is coming out here." He tried not to be sober, but failed. It seemed lost upon Molly, however, who smiled her surprise and gladness.

"Oh, how lovely!—Gloriana May! You told me aboot her—how pretty she is an' what a little devil. . . . Jim, thet'll be nice for you to have her heah. I'm glad."

Jim hugged her quite out of all reason. "Lord! but you're a sweet, fine, square kid! I just love you to death."

"J-Jim—let me go. . . . I see no call for rastlin' me."

"No, I dare say you don't. Please excuse my violence. . . . Molly, my sister is in poor health, so Mother writes. And she's sending Glory out to get well."

"I'm sorry. What ails her, Jim?"

"Weak lung, Mother said. It's hard to believe. But Glory said in her letter for me not to let Mother's letter upset me. Uncle Jim was tickled. Began figuring right away on marrying Glory to some Westerner. Isn't he the old match-maker?"

"He's the dearest, goodest man in Arizona," returned Molly, warmly.

"Sure he is. But all the same he's a son-of-a-gun for some things."

"When is Gloriana to be heah?" asked Molly, becoming thoughtful.

"Monday, on the Western Special."

"So soon? Oh! . . . I—I wish I'd had time to study more. . . . Jim, suppose she doesn't like me?"

"Molly! She can't help but adore you."

"Jim, I never noticed that any of these Flag girls went ravin' crazy over your Molly Dunn of the Cibeque," replied Molly, a little satirically.

That was perfectly true, thought Jim, and she might have mentioned how green with envy some of them were. But Molly Dunn was generous.

"Gloriana isn't like these Flag girls. She has more breeding. She couldn't be jealous or catty."

"She's a queer girl, then," mused Molly. "After all, Jim, you're only a big overgrown boy who knows nothin' aboot females. . . . Reckon it's thet breedin' you speak of thet scares me."

Jim reflected that, as usual, he had made a tactless remark.

"Molly, don't distress yourself. I'm sure you will love Glory and—and she'll adore you. Naturally, since you're going to marry me, you'll have to meet all my family sooner or later."

"Yes, Jim, but I—I wanted a little time to study—to improve myself—so they wouldn't be ashamed of me," replied Molly, plaintively.

Jim could only assure her by tender word and argument that she was making a mountain out of a molehill, with the result that Molly's heart seemed satisfied, if her mind was not. They went out to breakfast, and Jim hugged her disgracefully in the dark cold corridor. When Molly escaped into the dining-room a less keen eye than that of the old rancher, who stood back to the blazing fire, could have made amusing deductions.

"Mawnin', Uncle Jim. I—I been chased by a bear," laughed Molly.

"Good mornin', lass. Shore I seen thet. . . . Howdy, son! What do you think of Arizona weather?"

"Terrible. And you're sending me to camp out after Thanksgiving!" protested Jim. It seemed to him there was going to be good reason for him to stay in Flagerstown.

"Wal, Yellow Jacket is five or six thousand feet lower, an' if it snows it melts right off. Molly can vouch for thet. An' the valley of the Cibeque is higher than Yellow Jacket."

"I've seen snow every winter I can remember, most up on the Diamond. Down at my home it never lasted a day," replied Molly.

"That's some consolation."

"Jim, I think it's grand. I shore hope you won't go back on your promise," said Molly.

"What promise?"

"Aboot takin' me to town in a sleigh, with bells ringin'. An' snowballin' me. Oh, I'm shore I'll love this winter."

"Yes, I'll keep my promise, and I bet you beg for mercy."

"Me!"

Uncle Jim laughed heartily. His interest in their talk and plans, in all that concerned them, hinted of the loneliness of his life and what he felt he had missed.

"I like a little winter, too. Shore makes this here beef steak taste good. . . . Son, have you told the little lady your news?"

"Yes. And there's further proof she's an angel."

"Oh, Jim, such nonsense!" she protested. "Bein' glad with you don't—doesn't make me no angel. I keep tellin' you thet I'm shore not related to no angel yet."

"Haw! Haw! I'll bet he finds thet out, Molly," put in the rancher, heartily. "Reckon if I'd ever been keen on girls I'd have wanted one thet would scratch an' bite."

Molly blushed. "Uncle, I hope I've not got thet much cat in me," she said, anxiously.

Jim made good his promise, and when he had Molly bundled in the sleigh beside him, her cheeks like roses and her dark curls flying, he was as proud as she was delighted. Much to his satisfaction, all the young people of Flagerstown appeared to be out sleigh-riding also; and many a girl who had made Jim uncomfortable when he was a tenderfoot saw him now with Molly.

They had lunch at the hotel and drove home in the brilliant sunshine, with all the white world so glaring that they could hardly face it. All too soon they arrived at the ranch.

"That was glorious," said Molly, breathing deeply. "Jim, I'm shore a lucky girl. I'm so—so happy it hurts. I'm afraid it won't last."

"Sure it'll last," replied Jim, laughing. "Unless you're a fickle little jade."

"Jim Traft, I'm as—as true as steel," she retorted, vehemently. "It's only you may tire of me—or or your family won't accept me."

"Say, you're not marrying my family."

The word marriage or any allusion to it always silenced Molly. She betrayed that she saw the days fleeting by toward the inevitable, and her joy submerged any doubts.

Jim drove around to the barn, having in mind the latter half of his promise to Molly, which surely she had forgotten. As they went by the big bunk-house Bud Chalfack poked his ruddy cherub face out of the door and yelled, "Hey, Boss, thet ain't fair."

Jim yelled back, "Get yourself a girl, you cowboy."

At the barn he handed the reins to a Mexican stable boy, and helped Molly out. Then he led her into the lane toward the ranch-house. She was paddling along beside him through the deep snow and babbling merrily. When fully out of sight of the hawk-eyed cowboys Jim snatched up a big handful of snow, and seizing Molly he washed her rosy face with it.

"Jim Traft—you—you—" she sputtered, as he let her go. Then before she could recover her sight and breath he snatched up a double handful of snow and pitched that at her. His aim was true. It burst all over her in a white shower. She screamed, and bending quickly she squeezed a tight little snowball and threw it at Jim. He managed to save his eye, but it struck him on the head. Molly, it appeared, was no mean antagonist. Then fast and furious came the little snowballs. Never a one missed!

"Hey, you said—you'd never had a snowball fight," he panted.

"Shore never had. But I can lick you, Missouri," she replied, her high gay laugh pealing out.

Jim realized that she would make good her word unless he carried the battle to close range. Wherefore he rushed her, getting a snowball square on the nose for his pains. She dodged.

"Aw, Jim—stand up—an' fight square," she squealed.

But he caught her, tumbled her into the snow, rolled her over and over, and finally swept a great armful upon her. Then he ran for dear life, tinglingly aware of the snowy cyclone at his heels.

Later Jim emerged from concealment and walked down to the bunk-house. He had not seen the boys for several days. He stamped on the porch.

"Hey, don't pack no snow in hyar," yelled a voice. "I gotta do the sweepin' fer this outfit."

Jim opened the door and went in. The big room was cheerful with its crackling fire, and amazingly clean, considering it harbored the hardest cowboy outfit in Arizona.

"Howdy, boys!" he sang out.

"You needn't come an' crow over us," answered Bud. "Sleighridin' with Molly Dunn!"

Jackson Way looked askance at Jim's snowy boots, his lean young face puckered and resentful. "Boss, I reckon you had this snow come on purpose."

Hump Stevens spoke from his bunk, where he lay propped up, cheerful and smiling.

"How are you, Hump?"

"Rarin' to go, Boss. I been walkin' around this mornin'. An' I won all the money the boys had."

"Good work," said Jim, and turning to Uphill Frost, who sat before the fire in a rocking-chair, with a crutch significantly at hand. "And you, Up?"

"Boss, I ain't so damn good, far as disposition goes. But I could fork a horse if I had to."

"Great! Where're Cherry and Lonestar?" went on Jim.

"They hoofed it in town to see Slinger," replied Frost.

"I haven't been to the hospital for three days," said Jim. "How's Slinger coming around?"

"He was up, walkin' around, cussin' Doc fer not lettin' him smoke all he wants. Reckon time hangs heavy on Slinger. He can't read much, an' he says he wants to get back in the woods. Asked why you didn't come to see him. Didn't he, Bud?"

"Sure. Slinger complained like hell of your neglect, Boss. I seen him yestiddy. An' I told him thet no one never seen you no more. Then he cussed Molly fer not fetchin' you."

"I'm sorry. I'll see him tomorrow," replied Jim, contritely.

Curly Prentiss, the handsome blond young giant of the Diamond outfit, sat at a table, writing with absorbed violence. He alone had not appeared to note Jim's entrance.

"Curly, I've news for you."

But Curly gave no sign that he heard, whereupon Jim addressed Bud. "What ails Curly?"

"Same old sickness, Boss. I've seen Curly doubled up with that fer five years, about every few months. Mebbe it's a little wuss than usual, fer his girl chucked him an' married Wess Stebbins."

"No!"

"Sure's a fack. They run off to Winslow. You see, Curly come the high an' mighty once too often. Caroline bucked. An' they had it hot an' heavy. Curly told her to go where it was hot—so she says—an' he marched off with his haid up. . . . Wal, Carrie took him at his word. Thet is—he'd unhooked her bridle. Wess always was loony over her, an' she married him, which we all reckon was a darned good thing. Now Curly is writin' his funeral letter, after which he aims to get turrible drunk."

"Curly," spoke up Jim, kindly.

"Cain't you leave me alone heah?" appealed the cowboy.

"Yes, in a minute. Sorry to disturb you, old man. But I've news about Yellow Jacket, Jed Stone and his Hash Knife outfit."

"To hell with them! I'm a ruined cowboy. Soon as I get this document written I'm goin' to town an' look at red licker."

"Nope," said Jim, laconically.

"Wall, I jest am. Who says I cain't?"

"I do, Curly."

"But you're not my boss. I've quit the Diamond. I'll never fork a hoss again."

"Curly, you wouldn't let us tackle that Hash Knife gang without you?"

"Jim, I cain't care aboot nothin'. My heart's broke. I could see you all shot. I could see Bud Chalfack hung on a tree an' laugh."

"Curly, didn't you and I get to be good friends?"

"Shore. An' I was durn proud of it. But friendship's nuthin' to love. Aw, Boss, I'm ashamed to face you with it. . . . Caroline has turned out to be false. Chucked me fer thet bowlegged Stebbins puncher! Who'd ever thought I'd come to sech disgrace?"

"Curly, it's no disgrace. Wess is a good chap. He'll make Caroline happy. You didn't really love her."

"Wha-at!" roared Curly. And when his hearers all greeted this with a laugh he sank back crestfallen.

"Curly, there's some good reasons why you can't throw down the Diamond at this stage," said Jim, seriously, and placed a kindly hand on the cowboy's shoulder.

"Jest you give me one, Jim Traft," blustered Curly, and he lay down his pencil.

Jim knew perfectly well that this wonderful young Westerner could not be untrue to anyone. "First, then, Curly. You've already got a few head of stock on the range. In a few years you'll be a rancher on your own account."

"No reason atall. I don't want thet stock. I'd have given it to Bud if he hadn't been so nasty aboot Caroline. Swore she'd finally come to her senses. Then I gave the cattle to Hump, heah."

"Well, Hump can give them back. . . . Another reason is Uncle Jim is throwing us plumb against the Hash Knife outfit. Now what would the Diamond amount to without Curly Prentiss?"

"I don't give a—a damn," rejoined Curly. But it was a weak assertion.

"See here, Boss," yelled Bud, red in the face. "He hates us all jest because thet red-headed Carrie Bambridge chucked him."

"Curly, it's just as well," went on Jim. "Listen, and all of you. This is a secret and not to be spoken of except among ourselves. Uncle Jim is sure Bambridge is crooked. Making deals with the Hash Knife."

All the cowboys except Curly expressed themselves in different degrees of exclamation.

At length Curly spoke. "Even if Bambridge was crooked—that'd make no difference to me."

"Did you ask Caroline to marry you?" queried Jim, kindly.

"Dog-gone-it, no," replied Curly, and here his fine, frank face flamed. "Boss, I never was sure I cared that much, till I lost her."

"Curly, it wasn't the real thing—your case on Caroline."

"Ahuh.—Jim, you haven't given me any argument why I shouldn't go out an' drown my grief in the bottle—an' shoot up the town—an' kill somebody or get put in jail."

"No? All right. Here's another reason," replied Jim, and he drew a photograph out of his pocket and laid it on the table in front of Curly.

The cowboy started, bent over, and became absorbed in the picture.

Bud Chalfack started, too, but Jim waved him back.

"My Gawd! Boss, who is this?" asked Curly.

"My sister, Gloriana May Traft."

"Your sister?—Jim, I shore ought to have seen the resemblance, though she's ten million times better-lookin' than you. . . . But how is she a reason for my not goin' to the bad?"

"Curly, it's as simple as pie," said Jim. "Gloriana is a sick girl. She's coming West for her health. She'll arrive on Monday, on the Western Special. Now, I ask you, have you the heart to bust up the Diamond—to get drunk and worry me to death—when I've this new trouble on my hands?"

Curly took another long look at the photograph, and then he turned to Jim with all the clouds vanished from eyes and face. To see Curly thus was to love him.

"Boss, I haven't got the heart to throw you down," he replied. "It's my great weakness—this heah heart of mine. . . . I reckon I wasn't goin' to—anyhow. . . . An' I'll go down to meet the Western Special with you."

Jim, if he had dared, could have yelled his mirth. How well he had known Curly.

"Lemme see thet pictoore?" demanded Bud, advancing.

Curly handed the photograph back to Jim, and said, blandly, "Bud, gurls of high degree shouldn't interest you."

"Boys, I want you all to see Glory's picture," said Jim, calmly, though he reveled in the moment. "Come, take a look."

Bud and Jackson Way leaped forward; Uphill Frost forgot his crutch; Hump Stevens hopped out of his bunk; and they all, with Curly irresistibly drawn, crowded around Jim.

The long silence that ensued attested to the beauty of Gloriana Traft.

Finally Bud exploded: "Lord! ain't she a looker?"

"Prettier even than Molly Dunn," added Way, as if that was the consummation of all beauty.

"I never seen no angel till this minnit," was Uphill Frost's encomium.

"Ef I jest wasn't a crippled cowpuncher an' had a million dollars!" exclaimed Hump Stevens, with a sigh. "Boss, her name fits her."

Curly Prentiss reacted peculiarly to all this. It seemed he resented the looks and sighs and fervid comments of his comrades, as if they had profaned a sacred face already enshrined in his impressionable heart.

"Wal, I'm informin' you gentlemen of the range thet I saw her first," he said, loftily.

Bud took that as an insult. Frost swore his surprise. Hump Stevens stared in silence. Jackson Way laughed at the superb and conceited cowboy. Then Curly addressed Jim. "Boss, it's shore plain the Diamond will be busted now."

CHAPTER FOUR

Jim did not see much of Molly on Sunday. She kept to her room except at meal hours. He found opportunity, however, to ask her to go in to town with him on Monday to meet his sister.

"I'd rather not, Jim," she replied, as if her mind had long been made up. "She'd rather you didn't fetch any girl, especially *your* girl, to meet her, thet's shore."

"But why, Molly?" he queried.

"It'll be a surprise to her—the way things are with you an' me. An' it oughtn't come the minute she gets heah."

"We don't need to tell her—right away."

"She'd see it. . . . Jim, you should have written home weeks ago—to tell your folks aboot me."

"I suppose I ought. Really I meant to. Only I just didn't write."

"Wall, I reckon it'd be better not to let her know right away. I could hide it. But I'm shore afraid you couldn't. Uncle Jim will blurt it out."

"Molly! The idea—not telling Gloriana we're engaged," he protested, mystified by her gravity.

"Jim, it'll be all right if only she takes to me, but if she's like you when you first struck Flag—she won't."

"I was pretty much of a snob," he admitted. "Molly, I'm the better for all I've gone through. . . . You realize, don't you, how much I—"

The entrance of Molly's mother prohibited the rest of that tender speech. And Jim presently left the living-room perturbed in mind. He could not rid himself of a premonition that Gloriana's coming heralded disaster. No further opportunity to speak privately to Molly presented itself that day; and early Monday morning Molly trudged off to school like any country girl, wading through the snow. How serious she was about her studies!

In the afternoon Jim sent for Curly Prentiss, who appeared as if by magic, most gorgeously arrayed in the gayest and finest of cowboy habiliments.

"For goodness sake! Why this togging up?" exclaimed Jim.

Curly appeared to be laboring under stress.

"Had hell with the outfit," he said. "Come near punchin' Bud. He swore I ought to wear a plain suit—which is somethin' I don't own—but I'm no business man, or even a rancher yet. An' I want to look what I am."

"Oh, you mean you want my sister Gloriana to see you're a real cowboy?"

"Shore do."

"Big hat, gun, spurs and all?"

"I reckon."

"Well, Curly, she'll see you, all right. She could see you a mile away."

"Jim, don't you give me any of your chin aboot how I look. I had enough from

Bud an' Jack an' Uphill. An' my feelin's are hurt. . . . They're goin' to meet thet train, all of them except Hump. He wanted us to carry him on a stretcher. Up is goin' on a crutch—the damn fool!"

"Fine. The sooner you all see Gloriana May the sooner you'll be miserable. . . . I've ordered the buckboard to meet the train. Let's walk in, Curly, and stop to see Slinger."

"It's a good idea. A little movin' around might steady me. I'd shore hate to meet Jed Stone or thet Pecos gun-thrower."

So they strode out into the snow. The weather had moderated somewhat and the day was superb, with crisp tangy air. Curly manifestly was on the eve of a great adventure. Jim had to laugh when he thought again of how Glory would affect these simple, sentimental cowboys. It would be murder. He reflected that she would very likely be more Gloriana May at nineteen than she had been at eighteen. Worry over them he had no room for; all that seemed centered upon Molly. Curly stalked like a centaur, his spurs clinking, and talked like a boy engaged upon some lofty venture.

Meanwhile their long steps soon brought them to the edge of town and eventually the modest hospital, which, unpretentious as it was, had become the boast of cowboys.

They found Slinger Dunn the only inmate, besides an attendant or two, and he was limping up and down a warm and comfortable room. His dark face, bronze and smooth like an Indian's, wreathed into a smile at sight of his visitors. He had gained since Jim had last seen him. His long hair, black as the wing of a crow, hung down over the collar of the loose woolen dressing-gown he wore, in which obviously he felt ill at ease. Jim always thrilled at the sight of Slinger, and had reason to do so, beyond appreciation of his striking figure and piercing eyes. Anyone who had ever seen Molly Dunn would at once connect Slinger with her.

"Howdy, boys! It's aboot time you was comin'," he drawled. "Molly came in on her way to school, or I'd shore be daid now."

"Patience, Slinger. Why, you've made a marvelous recovery!" said Jim, cheerily.

"Slinger, you backwoods son-of-a-gun, only five weeks ago you was a sieve of bullet holes," declared Curly. "An' heah you can walk aboot."

"Wal, it's easy fer you fellars to talk, but I'd like to see you stand stayin' heah. Day after day—night after night. Thet damn Doc won't give me any more cigarettes an' only a nip of whisky. Set down, boys, an' tell me some news."

"Slinger, just as soon as you can ride we're off for Yellow Jacket," announced Jim.

"Wal, pack up fer tomorrow mawnin'."

"Not till after Thanksgiving. Three weeks yet. And now listen." Whereupon Jim related all the late news and rumors about the Hash Knife outfit.

"Shore, I'd expect thet of Jed Stone," said Dunn. "An', Boss, if you want to know, I've long had a hunch Bambridge is back of the Hash Knife."

"No!" ejaculated Jim, aghast at so definite a statement from this backwoodsman.

"Slinger, we reckon you mean Bambridge ain't above buyin' a few haid of stock from Stone now an' then?" queried Curly, slow and cool, but his blue eyes flashed fire.

"Hellno! Buyin' a few steers nuthin'," drawled Dunn, forcibly. "Bambridge's outlayin' ranch is across the divide from Yellow Jacket. Thirty miles around by road. But by the canyon—Doubtful, we call it—there's less'n ten miles. An' Bambridge is gettin' stock through Doubtful an' drivin' it to Maricopa."

Curly whistled his amazement. Jim simply stared. This was getting down to hard pan. It did not occur to either of them to question Slinger Dunn.

"Shore, I cain't prove it, Jim," he continued. "But it's what I reckon. An' my hunch is fer us to keep our traps shet—an' go down to Yellow Jacket to make shore."

"Right, you bet," agreed Curly. "But if it's true, the Hash Knife will stop operations until either they or the Diamond are settled."

"We've got to find out," interposed Jim, emphatically. "Ring Locke advised against Uncle sending the Diamond on that job. Said we could do easier and more important work. He's afraid Bambridge might shoot Uncle."

"Wall, there's shore risk of thet," rejoined Dunn. "But Traft could keep out of the way. When we get the trick on these fellars we can do a little shootin' ourselves. . . . You know, Boss, there ain't no other way oot of it."

"So Uncle says," assented Jim, gloomily. "Slinger, you don't think it'll be another Pleasant Valley War?"

"Lord, no," declared Dunn, showing his white teeth. "Thet war hed hundreds of sheepmen an' cattlemen behind it, with rustlers on the side of the sheep fellars. This heah deal is a matter of a little gun-play."

"Slinger, you've got a lot of time to think it over," said Jim. "Do so, and I'll come in after a few days. I'm a little upset just now. My sister is coming today. She's ill. They say the climate will agree with her."

"Thet's too bad, Boss. But mebbe it'll all turn oot right. . . . Molly never told me you hed a sister. I reckon I know how you feel."

"Here's her picture, Slinger," said Jim, producing the photograph and handing it over.

Dunn bent his piercing eyes upon the likeness of Gloriana May. He was not a volatile cowboy. His expression did not change. Only he gazed a long time.

"Wal, I never before seen any gurl or a pictoor of one thet could beat Molly. But this heah shore does."

"Molly is totally unlike Gloriana. Just as pretty in her way, I think," he said, stoutly.

"Boss, you're loco. Molly is a slick, soft, pretty little woodmouse. But this sister of yourn is like the sun in the mawnin'."

Jim felt a surprise he did not betray. The compliment to Gloriana at Molly's expense did not find great favor with him. Receiving the picture back, he took a look at it, somehow seeing Glory differently, and then he returned it to his pocket.

"It was taken a year ago," he explained. "And if Gloriana has improved in looks since I've been gone as much as she did the year before—whew! but she'll be something to look at. I hardly expect improvement, though, since she has been ill."

"Huh! Thet gurl couldn't be ailin'," returned Dunn, positively.

Conversation reverted to other channels then—the Diamond, the incompleted drift fence, winter, horses, until finally Jim rose to go, with Curly following suit.

"Slinger, I'm awful glad you're doing so well," said Jim.

"Wal, you fellars have cheered me right pert. Come again soon. . . . An', Jim, would you mind lettin' me borrow thet pictoor fer a spell? I get hellsrattlin' lonesome—an' it'd be good to look at."

"Why, certainly, Slinger," declared Jim, hastily producing it. "I'm sure Glory will be flattered."

"Thanks, Boss," drawled Slinger. "Your havin' a sister, too, kinda makes us closer, huh? Wal, adios."

All the way out Jim heard Curly growling under his breath. This ebullition came out in force once they reached the street.

"Jim, what'n hell did you want to let Slinger Dunn borrow Gloriana May's picture fer?" demanded Curly.

"Why, cowboy, I never thought not to. What could I say? It was a perfectly innocent request of Slinger's."

"Shore. It was innocent enough. But cain't you see straight? The dam' backwoodsman was shot plumb through the heart."

"What! By Glory's picture?"

"Shore. It did the same fer me. An' I've no call to kick. But, my Gawd! Boss, I couldn't stand for a rival like Slinger Dunn. Now aboot Bud an' the rest of the Diamond, I'm not carin'. But Dunn is darned handsome, an' shore fascinatin'. Any girl would lose her heart to him—if he let himself go. . . . I'd hate to have to shoot it out with Slinger."

"Ha! Ha! Ha! I should think you would," replied Jim, after a hearty laugh. "But, Curly, don't be a jackass. Let me give you a hunch. Glory will be sweet to you cowboys—let you saddle her horse or carry something for her. And she *might* dance with you. But she could never see one of you seriously, even through a microscope."

Curly looked crestfallen, yet sustained a little dignity.

"Jim, you're her brother an' you fell in love with Molly Dunn."

The remark was thought-provoking, but Jim could not keep it before his consciousness.

"True, Curly, old boy. But I'm not Glory. Wait till you see her!"

"I'm a-waitin' best I can," averred Curly, "An' I'll bet a handful of gold eagles against two bits, thet Bud an' Up an' Jack are waitin', too, right now at the station. Let's rustle."

For a cowboy who had been born on a horse and who had spent most of his life in a saddle, Curly Prentiss could certainly walk. He might have had on seven-league boots. In quick time they arrived at the station, to find Zeb there with the buckboard; Bud, Jackson, Lonestar Holliday, Cherry Winters, and Uphill in a state of vast excitement, that seemed strange in their plain business suits, at least three of which were brand new; and lastly that the Western Special was two hours late.

Curly groaned. Jim did not know whether this expression of pain was due to the lateness of the train or the presence of the cowboys. Probably it was for both.

"Zeb, drive over to the stable and keep the horses there till you hear the train whistle," directed Jim. "And, boys, what do you say to a game of pool at Raider's?"

"I ain't dressed fer thet," objected Bud, eyeing his nice clean cuffs. "You-all go an' I'll hang around here. Mebbe the train will make up some time."

"Wal, you're a rotten pool-shot," remarked Curly, "an' you cain't be missed."

"Say, rooster, I beat you last time we played," retorted Bud.

"Cowboy, you couldn't beat a carpet," put in Jim, knowing full well how to work Bud.

"Got any money with you, Boss?" asked Bud, sarcastically.

It was noticeable that when the company reached Raider's, Bud was following along. This Raider place, a saloon, gambling-den, as well as pool-hall, did not bear a very respectable name. But as the other places were uptown, Jim thought he could take a chance on it.

"No drinks, boys," said Jim.

"What?" demanded Curly, who was edging toward the bar.

"Not a drop of anything. You're meeting my sister," replied Jim, sharply.

"You big hunk of cheese," added Bud, scornfully. "All dressed up as for a rodeo, an' now you want to soak in a gallon of licker."

"Curly, jest because you're a good-lookin' cuss you cain't meet the boss's sister with a whisky breath. Why, you plumb ought to be ashamed!" said Uphill Frost.

"Where's your manners, Curly?" asked Cherry Winters. "You get wusser every day."

Jim was inclined to revel in the situation. Never would he recover from the innumerable and infinitely various tricks these boys had perpetrated upon him when he had come to them a tenderfoot. They were still capable of the same, if he was not sharp enough to detect them. Molly had helped him circumvent them—had given him something of revenge. And Gloriana May would surely fill his cup to the brim. They were such a devilishly lovable lot.

"Nope. There'll be no more drinking for the Diamond," said Jim, simulating cheerful satisfaction. "Glory hates drink. And I want her to be happy out here. She's a sick girl, you know."

"Aw!" breathed out Bud Chalfack, enigmatically. He might have been profoundly impressed or only regretting the ban on liquor.

"Haw! Haw! Haw!" roared Curly Prentiss, in derision of something or somebody.

"Laff, you dressed-up kangaroo," shouted Bud. "Fine chanct *you'll* have!"

"Shut your faces, you cowboys," ordered Jim, genially. "Now let's see. There are seven of us. . . . Reckon Uphill can't play, with his game leg. We'll—"

"The hell I can't. I can beat any of you with only one leg," remarked Frost, speaking for himself.

"Ex-cuse me, Up. . . . We'll each put in a dollar. Play rotation pool. Every time one of us misses his shot he puts in two bits. And whoever gets the most shots takes the pot."

"Great stuff!" agreed Curly, who imagined he divided honors with Jim in pool.

"Turrible stiff game," said Bud.

"You might jest as well stick your hands in my pockets," added Uphill, derisively.

"I'm game, but it's highway robbery," put in Cherry Winters.

"Suits me. I can jest aboot pay fer these heah new clothes," said Lonestar Holliday.

So the game began. Probably it never could have been started but for the state of mental aberration the boys were in. Not often had Jim prevailed upon them to play, after they had a sample of his game. They were atrocious shots. With fifteen balls on the table, all numbered, it was no easy task sometimes to hit the number called for, and Bud never did it once during that whole game. He had to produce nine two-bits, two dollars and a quarter in all, and he was perfectly furious. Jim won the game and pocketed the cash. Then they began another. Curly appeared to be next to Bud in poor playing. In fact, he was away off in his game, a fact the others boys soon made much of. Jim won this time also.

"Might as well steal our wages and be done with it," said Bud.

But in the third game, when Bud started off by pocketing three balls in succession and Curly began to miss, he changed his tune. This time Jim deliberately made poor shots, which, playing along with other retarding chances of the game, prolonged it. Bud played beyond his actual ability and altogether got nine balls, which won him the money and recovered his good humor.

"Curly, I told you I could beat you all holler," he said. "Same in poker. An' likewise in affairs of the heart."

"Bah, you little bow-legged runt," scoffed Curly.

"I can lick you, too," concluded Bud, belligerently.

Jim consulted his watch. "Whoopee! she's due in two minutes. Don't forget to pay the bill, you losers." He ducked out of the hall and ran across to the station, thrilling at the whistle of the train. And he found the boys at his heels, except poor Uphill, who had to labor behind on his crutch. Jim knew perfectly well that his partners in the pool game had not tarried to pay their score.

The Special roared into the station, all ice and snow, with the steam hissing and the smoke obscuring the platform lights. It was almost dark. When the engine and mail and baggage cars passed the air cleared, and the bright lights shone again. In his excitement Jim quite forgot his comrades. The second coach stopped opposite his position and he was all eyes. A porter began sliding bags and suitcases off the step. Then a slim form emerged from the car upon the vestibule. The furs proclaimed it feminine. But there was too much shadow. Then she stepped down and paused in the bright light. It was Gloriana, Jim said to himself, conscious of inward tumult. The tall slim shape, with its air of distinction, the cut of the long fur coat, the set of the stylish little hat, would have been enough. But Jim stared a moment longer. Gloriana's face shone like a white flower out of the black furs, and her great eyes, dark in that light, strained eagerly to and fro, and then fixed on him.

"Jim!" she cried in a rapture. When had she ever called him with a voice like that? He ran to the steps and lifted her down in a bearish hug. She did not appear as substantial and heavy as he remembered his sister.

"Glory!—Dog-gone, I'm glad to see you!" he said, and certainly returned the warm kiss she gave him, which struck him even more unusual than the poignant tone of her voice. Something had changed Jim Traft's value in the eyes of his sister.

"Jim, you can't be—half as glad—as I am to see—you," she panted, gayly, clinging to him. "Is this the—North Pole? Who are these young men? . . . Jim, I thought Arizona was desert—sunny, hot—all golden ranges and pine trees."

"Hey, boys, grab the bags," ordered Jim, with a laugh. "Fetch them into the waiting-room." Then he led Gloriana into the station, where it was light and warm. "The rig will be here in a minute. . . . Gosh! . . . I just don't know you, Glory. Your eyes, maybe."

No one, not even a brother, would ever have been likely to forget Gloriana May's eyes. At this moment they were traveling over Jim, brilliant with amaze.

"I know you and I don't. You great big handsome man. O, Jim, you're so wonderfully different. Arizona has improved you. . . . I'll bet you've fallen in love with some Western cowgirl."

Jim should have said she had guessed right the very first time, and he would have done so but for the something familiar and disconcerting that was merely Gloriana. Then the cowboys came bustling in with bags and suitcases. Even Uphill carried one with an air of importance. Curly disengaged himself from the excited group and strode forward. Sight of him filled Jim with glee, and a quick glance at Glory took in her eyes, fixed and beautiful. Now it was a natural function of Glory's eyes, even in her most casual glance, to shine and glow and give illusion of a thousand thoughts that were not in her head at all. They were so alive, so speaking, so eloquent, so treacherously lovely, that Jim sustained a second thrill at the sight of them.

"A cowboy!" she whispered. "Jim, I believe you now."

It probably was a magnificent moment for Curly, but he did not betray that in the least.

"Boss, Zeb is heah with the buckboard," he announced, in his cool lazy way.

"Gloriana, this is Curly Prentiss, one of my cowboys—and quite a cattleman in his own right," introduced Jim. "Curly—my sister."

Curly doffed his sombrero and made a gallant bow that, though easy and slow like his voice, was as singularly pleasing.

"Miss Traft, I shore am glad to meet you-all," he said.

"How do you do, Mr. Prentiss. I'm pleased to meet you," she replied, with a dazzling smile. "You are my very first cowboy."

Gloriana May probably did not mean she had taken possession of Curly at first sight, but Jim saw that this identical circumstance had come to pass.

"Wal," drawled Curly, not in the least knocked off his balance, "I'm shore happy to be the first an' I'll see to it I'm the last."

"Oh," laughed Glory, merrily, and turned to Jim with her first appreciation of a cowboy.

The other boys lined up, with Uphill Frost hanging a little behind to hide his crutch. They presented a bright-eyed, shiny-faced coterie, at the moment devoid of any trace of devilment or horns and hoofs.

"Boys, this is my sister Gloriana," announced Jim. "Glory, meet the rest of the Diamond, except two that are laid up for repairs. . . . Bud Chalfack."

Bud took a step out and his smile was cherubic. "Miss Gloriana I reckon there ain't no one any gladder to welcome you to Arizonie."

"Thank you, Mr. Chalfack. I'm happy to meet you," replied Gloriana.

"And this is Lonestar Holliday," went on Jim. Lonestar in his eager confusion stepped on Bud's foot and could not find words to answer Glory's bright acknowledgment.

"And Jackson Way . . . and Cherry Winters . . . and Uphill Frost. . . . There, Glory, you've made the acquaintance of most of the Diamond, which, according to Uncle Jim, is the most terrible cowboy outfit in Arizona."

"Oh, I'm sure Uncle Jim is wrong," said Gloriana, sweetly. "They look very nice and mild to me—except Mr. Prentiss—who *is* quite terrifying with his gun and those awful spurs."

Somehow Jim got the impression from Glory's speaking eyes that she meant Curly's handsome presence was something calculated to stop the heart of a girl fresh from the East.

Bud looked disgustedly at Curly, as if to say he had gone and done it again. If there was anything a cowboy hated it was to be thought nice and mild.

"Miss Glory," he spoke up, most winningly, and Jim made certain that the next time Bud addressed her it would be Glory minus the prefix, "there's some cowpunchers who pack hardware all the time an' sleep in their spurs. But they ain't the dangerous kind."

Thus Jim saw with delight a new species of men and life dawn upon his bewildered sister. Likewise he perceived with fiendish glee that he was going to get even with the Diamond.

"Carry the baggage out, boys," he said. "We'll go home to the ranch. . . . Curly, you can ride with us, so in case we meet any desperadoes or Indians they won't get Glory."

CHAPTER FIVE

On the way out Jim did not say anything to Glory about the room he had fixed up for her. In fact, he did not have much chance to talk, for Glory addressed her curiosity to Curly. Jim drove fast, so the wind would pierce through his sister, furs and all. It did.

"F-f-fine f-for a g-girl with o-one lung," chattered Gloriana as Jim lifted her out of the buckboard. "G-good n-night—Mr. Curly. If I don't—f-f-freeze to death I'll see you—to-tomorrow."

"I shore pray for a moderation of temperature," replied Curly, gallantly. "Good night, Miss Traft."

"Set the bags on the porch," said Jim, "and hurry those horses into the barn. . . . Glory, I reckon you'll want to get warm before you see Uncle Jim."

Gloriana stood in the cold starlight, looking out at the spectral pine forest and the pure white peaks that notched the sky. "W-w-wonderful!"

Jim almost carried her to her room, which was in the west end of the rambling ranch-house. When he opened the door a blaze of light and warmth and color greeted Gloriana's eyes. Jim had spent a whole day on making this room different from any Glory had ever seen, and one that would be livable, even for a sick girl in zero weather. It had an open fireplace where logs were snapping and blazing; Navajo rugs covered the floor; Indian ornaments of bead, basket and silver work hung on the walls; a fine elk head, with massive horns, stood out over the mantel; the bed had a coverlet of deep, woolly, soft red, most inviting to the eye. Even the lamp had a shade painted with Indian designs.

Gloriana gasped with delight, threw off her furs and hat, and rushed to the fire, where she stretched her gloved hands.

"Pretty nifty, huh?" asked Jim.

"Just lovely. But wait a minute until I can see."

Jim went out to fetch in the luggage. He had to make three trips to the porch and back. "Glory, from the looks of this you've come to stay awhile."

"I've three trunks, too," rejoined Gloriana.

"Is that all? Gee! I didn't figure on trunks when I worked over this room. But there's a big closet. . . . Turn round, Glory, so I can look at you."

She did so, and he saw his sister strangely changed, but how he could not tell at once. She appeared taller, which might have accounted for her slimness. But Jim looked in vain for a frail, flat-chested girl bordering on consumption. Her face, however, was exceedingly white, and herein lay the change that struck him. She looked more than her age. She wore her dark chestnut hair in a fashion new to him, and very becoming. But Glory's great purple eyes were as he had them pictured in a loving memory.

"Well, how do I look?" she asked, soberly.

"Prettier than ever, Glory, only different. I can't figure it yet," said Jim.

"Thanks. I didn't hope for compliment. . . . Jim, you've been away almost a year."

"So long? Gee! time flies. Well, sister, it has been a terrible and a wonderful year for me. I've sure got a story to tell you. But that can wait. Sit down. You look fagged. And tell me about yourself. Mother's letter scared me."

She did not take the chair he indicated, but sat down on the arm of his, and rather timidly took his hand. Jim remembered how seldom Gloriana had ever touched him voluntarily. They had never gotten along well together. Gloriana could not bear criticism of her actions or any antagonism to her freedom. And Jim had always been the bossy older brother, until she reached eighteen, when he had been flatly rebuffed. After that there had been a slowly widening breach. It all returned to him now, a little sadly, and he wondered at her. Perhaps she really had cared something for him. Gloriana had never been shallow; quite the reverse. Jim began to feel a deeper significance in her coming West, in her presence now, than at first had occurred to him.

"Jim, you're my last bet," she said, frankly.

"Glory! . . . I don't understand," exclaimed Jim, blankly. "You were a belle when I left home. You had so many friends that *I* never saw you. Then all that money Aunt Mary left you. . . . And now I'm your last bet!"

"Funny, isn't it, Jim? . . . Retribution, I guess."

"For what?"

"I was never—a—a real sister."

Jim caressed the soft thin little hand while he gazed into the fire and pondered. A chill of fear of he knew not what crept over him. Glory had always worried him. Her childish pranks—then her girlish escapades—but now she seemed a woman!"

"Perhaps that was my fault," he replied, regretfully.

"Jim—you're changed," said his sister, quickly.

"Sure. I'd not been much good if this Arizona hadn't changed me."

"I hope it does as well by me," she continued, wistfully.

"Glory . . . what're you driving at?" burst out Jim, no longer able to repress a mounting anxiety.

"Please—ask me questions."

That from Gloriana May was indeed a strange request. Jim felt an uncomfortable constriction of his throat.

"Glory, have you really lung trouble?" he queried, sharply.

"No. Mother and Dad think so because I got so white and thin. I coaxed Dr. Williamson to hint of that. I wanted to come West."

"Thank goodness!—But, you deceitful girl!—Why such an extreme? And are you really ill?"

"Only run down, Jim."

"From what?"

"Worry—unhappiness."

Jim imagined his ears were deceiving him. Yet there his sister sat, slipping closer to him. She was now half off the arm of his chair and her head rested on his shoulder. A faint fragrance came from her hair. He let a long silence ensue. He could not ask just then what was forming in his mind.

"Love affair?" he finally asked, lightly.

"Affair—but not love," she replied, scornfully.

"So that's it?"

"No, that's not it. Still, it had a lot to do with it."

"Gloriana!" That was how he had used to address her when he was on his dignity or wished to reprove. She laughed a little, remembering it.

"Jim, I—I have disgraced the family," she admitted, with a catch in her breath, and suddenly she sat up.

"My God! . . . Oh, Glory—you can't be serious!" he exclaimed, distressed, yet uncertain.

"I wish to heaven I wasn't serious."

Jim tried to prepare himself for a blow. Contact with the rough and wholesome West had knocked pride and prejudice out of his head. Nevertheless, something of the former reared its hydra head. In his gathering apprehension and horror he sensed that he was on trial. He must react differently to this revelation. Glory had come to him in her trouble. If he repulsed or scorned her! If he showed any of the old outraged brotherly disfavor! Suddenly he happened to think of Curly Prentiss—that cool, easy, careless firebrand of a Texas cowboy. How would he take such a confession from a once loved sister? Beloved still, he discovered, poignantly! But that thought of Curly was sustaining. Its content typified the West.

"Well, so little sister has kicked over the traces?" he queried, as coolly as ever Curly could have said it.

"Jim, don't misunderstand," she said, quickly. "I've been wild, crazy, out of my head. But I can still look you in the eyes."

And she sat up to give him a straight full glance, that was as searching as it was revealing. Jim hid his relief. And he realized the moment gave birth to his existence as a brother. The purple blaze of Gloriana's eyes failed to hide her sadness, her hunger.

"Shore, I never had any notion you couldn't," he replied, essaying Curly's drawl. Then he put his arm around her, which action brought Glory slipping into his lap. Her head went down with a suspicious haste. Her nervous hand tightened on his. "Tell me all about it."

"Jim, you remember when I was sixteen the Andersons took me up," began Glory, presently. "That began my gadding about, my desire for fine clothes—excitement, dancing—and so forth. Then Aunt Mary left me that money. And you remember the summer I graduated—how gay I was—what a wonderful time I had! . . . Even before you left I was traveling with a pretty fast set. But we younger girls hadn't really gotten into it yet. After you left home I was about ready for it, I guess. But something happened. I met a man named Darnell—from St. Louis. He was handsome—and all the girls were crazy over him. That tickled me. I—I thought I was in love with him. It *might* have been just as well—the way things turned out. I could have done worse. Mother wanted me to marry Mr. Hanford—you know him—the dry goods merchant."

"Not Henry Hanford?" broke out Jim, incredulously.

"Yes, Henry Hanford. He was more than old enough to be my father. But Mother nagged me nearly to death. I dare say she wanted me to be—safe. Dad hated my running around—and he didn't like Ed Darnell. So we had a bad time for some months. . . . I thought I was engaged to Ed. So did everybody else. All the same, I wasn't. He said he was mad about me, but he didn't ask me to marry him. . . . He borrowed a lot of money from me. He was a gambler. Then he embezzled money from Dad. Oh, how wretched it was! He left town, without a word to me. The truth came out—and—and the Andersons, the Loyals, the Millers—all my old friends dropped me. Cut me dead! . . . That broke Mother's heart. And it went hard with Dad. . . . Well, I had reached the end of my rope. You know what gossip is in a little town. And gossip made it a great deal worse than it actually was. I had been a fool over Ed Darnell. I had snubbed some of the boys because of him. I had been wild as a partridge—so far as parties, dancing, running around were concerned. But I wasn't as bad as I looked. Still that queered me at home, when the crash came. . . . And, Jim, it knocked me out. I began to go downhill. I realized I was done for there. I worried myself sick. Many and many a night I cried myself to sleep. I went downhill. . . . And then I got to thinking about the West—your West. I read all your letters to Mother. You never wrote *me.* And I thought, if I could get out West, far away, it'd be my salvation . . . and here I am."

"Well, is *that* all?" drawled Jim, true to his imitation of Curly. "You shore had me plumb scared."

"Jim!" she cried, and then she kissed his cheek in mute gratitude. By that Jim felt how hard it had been for Gloriana to confess to him—how little of a brother he had been in times past. Then before he could say more she burst into tears, which was another amazing thing, and Jim could do no more than hold her. There must have been much dammed-up misery in Gloriana, for when she succumbed to weeping it gradually grew uncontrollable. Jim thought, to judge by her emotion, that the situation at home had been insupportable for the proud, vain young lady. She had come to him as a last resource, doubtful of her reception, and he had overwhelmed her by making light of her trouble. As a matter of fact Jim felt exceedingly relieved, and even happy that what he had suspected had been wrong. Glory had been on the verge of disaster. That seemed enough for him to know. There might have been details which would have hurt him to hear. Pity and tenderness welled up in his heart for his sister. Indeed, there had been cause for her to come West and throw herself upon his protection. The very idea was incredible, yet here she was, sobbing softly now, and gaining control of herself.

"Thank God I—I had the—courage to come," she said, speaking a thought aloud. "I—I never knew how—good Jim was!"

That established a character Jim regretted he hardly deserved, and one to which he felt he must live up.

"Glory, I've got a little confession to make, myself," he said, with a happy laugh. "Not that I've actually fallen by the wayside. But I've gone back on the East. And I'm—"

"Wait," she interrupted, sitting up to dry her eyes. "I haven't told all—and what seems the worst to me."

"Gosh!" ejaculated Jim, with a sinking sensation in his chest. "Perhaps you'd better not tell me more."

"Jim, I met Ed Darnell in the station at St. Louis," went on Glory, hastily, as if eager to impart what seemed important. "Quite by accident. I had to change trains there and wait five hours. And it was my bad luck to run into him first thing. . . . Well, he raved. He made a thousand excuses. . . . The liar! The thief! . . . I absolutely refused to have any more to do with him. Yet I was scared stiff at him. He had some queer power over me. But I had the sense enough to realize I despised him. Then he threatened me—swore he'd follow me. And Jim—that's exactly what he'll do. He knew, of course, about Uncle Jim, the rich ranchman. Mother gabbed a lot. At first she was fascinated by Ed. I didn't tell him where I was going, but he could find out easily. And he'll come. I saw it in his eyes. . . . And that'd be dreadful."

"Let him come," replied Jim, grimly. "I hope he does. It would be a bad move for Mr. Darnell."

"What would you do?" queried Gloriana, with all a woman's curiosity.

"Glory, you're out West now. It'll take you some time to realize it. . . . I'd impress that fact upon Mr. Darnell pretty pronto. And if it wasn't enough, I'd tell Curly Prentiss."

"That wonderful-looking cowboy!" exclaimed Gloriana. "He seemed so kind and nice. He wouldn't hurt anyone."

Jim laughed outright. Gloriana would be the tenderfoot of all tenderfeet who ever struck Arizona.

"Glory, I'm engaged," he blurted out suddenly, with a gulp.

"Jim Traft!—You've kept up with that catty Sue Henderson," exclaimed Glory, aghast.

At first Jim could not connect any of his Missouri attachments of bygone days with that particular name. When he did he laughed, not only at Glory's absurd guess but at the actual realization. Ten times ten months might have elapsed since he left home.

"No, Glory. My girl is a real Westerner," he replied.

"Real Westerner? What do you mean by that? Uncle Jim was born in the East. He couldn't be Western."

"He's pretty much so, as you will discover. Molly was born in Arizona. She's about eighteen. Twice in her life she has been to Flagerstown, and that is the extent of her travels. She lives down in the Cibeque, one of the wildest valleys in Arizona."

"Molly.—Molly what?" queried Glory, her white smooth brow wrinkling and her fine eyes dilating and changing, as she bent them upon Jim.

"Molly Dunn. Isn't it pretty?" rejoined Jim, warming to his subject. He had need to.

"Rather. But sort of common, like Jones or Brown. Is *she* pretty?"

"Glory, I reckon there's only one prettier girl in the world, and that's you."

It was a subtle and beautiful compliment, but somehow lost upon Gloriana May.

"You were always getting a case on some girl—back home. It never lasted long," said his sister, reflectively.

"This will last."

"How about her family?" came the inevitable interrogation.

"Arizona backwoods. And that's as blue-blooded as the skies out here," replied Jim, rising to the issue. "Her father was ruined by a range feud between cattlemen and sheepmen. Her mother has been a hard-working pioneer. You will learn what that means. Molly has one brother. Slinger Dunn. I don't know his first name. But the Slinger comes from his quickness and use with a gun. He has killed several men—and shot up I don't know how many."

"Desperado?" gasped Gloriana.

"Of course an Easterner would call him that. I did at first. But now he's just Slinger to me—and the very salt of the earth."

Dismay, consternation, and sincere regret succeeded one another on Gloriana's expressive face.

"Dad called me the black sheep of our family," she said. "But I'm afraid there are two. . . . It'd kill Mother. . . . Jim, they have no idea whatever of all this. Dad brags to his friends about you. How you are in charge of his brother's big cattle ranch. Nothing of this—this you tell me ever crept into your letters. I know them by heart."

"That's true, Glory. I left out the real stuff which was making me over. And besides, it all sort of bunched just lately. . . . Look here." Jim unbuttoned his flannel shirt at the neck, and pulled his collar back to expose a big angry scar on his breast.

"My heavens! what's that?" she queried, fearfully.

"My dear sister, that's a bullet hole," he replied, not without pride.

"You were shot?"

"I should smile."

"My God!—Jim, this is awful! You might have been killed."

"Shore I might. I darn near was. I lay in the woods two days with that wound. Alone!"

"And you can smile about it!" she ejaculated, her eyes dark with awe and fading terror.

"It helped make a man of me."

"Some desperado shot you?"

"Yes, one of the real bad ones."

"Oh, Jim," she cried. "I hope—I pray you—you didn't kill him."

"It turned out I didn't, Glory—which was darn lucky. But at the time I'd have shot him to bits with great pleasure."

"This terrible West has ruined you. Mother always said it would. And Dad would only laugh."

"Nope, Glory. You've got it wrong. I'm not ruined by a long shot. And I hope you've sense and intelligence enough left to see it."

"Jim, I've nothing left," she replied. "You're wild, strange to me—sort of cool and indifferent like that Prentiss fellow. I'm just terribly sorry this West has made you rough—crude. I know I'll hate it."

"Glory, you just misunderstand," rejoined Jim, patiently. "It'll jar you at first—more than it did me. You were always a sensitive, high-strung thing. And your trouble has only made you worse. But please give the West—and me—the benefit of a doubt, before you condemn. Wait, Glory. I swear you will gain by that. Not have any regrets! Not hurt any of these Westerners."

But he saw that he made no impression on her. He had shocked her, and it nettled him. She had quite forgotten already how kindly he had taken her dereliction.

"Where is this Molly Dunn?" asked Gloriana, curiosity strong.

"She's here."

"In this house?"

"Yes. She and her mother. I fetched them up from the Cibeque. Molly is going to school. It's great—and a little pathetic—the way she goes at study. Poor kid—she had so little chance to learn. . . . I expect to marry her in the spring, if I can persuade her."

"Persuade her!" echoed Gloriana, with a wonderful flash of eyes. "I dare say that will be extremely difficult."

"It probably will be," replied Jim, coolly. "Especially after she meets you. But Uncle Jim adores her and he's keen to see me married."

"Well, I deserve it," mused Gloriana.

"What?"

"A dose of my own medicine."

"Glory, I don't want to lose patience with you," said Jim, slowly, trying to keep his temper. "I can understand you, for I felt a little like you do when I landed out here. . . . Now listen. I'm glad you've come to me. I'm sorry you've made mistakes and suffered through them. But they are really nothing. I predict the West will cure them in less than a year. You won't know yourself. You could not be dragged back to Missouri."

Gloriana shook her beautiful head in doubt and sorrow.

"If you only hadn't engaged yourself to this backwoods girl!" she said, mournfully.

"But she saved my life," declared Jim, hotly. "She fought a fellow—one of those desperadoes you mentioned—fought him like a wild cat—*bit* him—hung on him with her teeth to keep him from murdering me as I sat tied hand and foot. . . . Saved my life until her brother Slinger got there to kill Jocelyn."

"The wretch!" exclaimed Gloriana, in passion and horror. Her face was white as alabaster and her eyes great dark gulfs of changing brilliance. "Did this Slinger Dunn really kill him?"

"You bet he did. And two other desperadoes. They shot Slinger all up. He's in the hospital at Flag. I'll take you in to see him."

"Wonderful!" breathed Gloriana, for the moment thrilled out of her disgust and horror. "But, Jim, why all this bloody murdering? I thought you worked on a cattle range."

"I do. That's the trouble," said Jim, and forthwith launched into a brief narrative of the drift fence and subsequent events which led up to his capture by the Cibeque gang, of Hack Jocelyn's arrival with Molly, who had consented to sacrifice herself to save Jim, of Jocelyn's treachery and how Molly fought to keep him from killing Jim until Slinger got there.

When Jim concluded there was ample evidence that Gloriana did not lack heart and soul, though they were glossed over by restraint and sophistication. This reassured Jim in his stubborn hope that Gloriana was undeveloped and needed only the hard and wholesome contacts she was sure to get in Arizona.

"But, Jim, you can't *marry* a girl who bites like a little beast, no more than I could the brother who kills men," was Gloriana's grave reply.

"I can't—can't I?" retorted Jim goaded at the regurgitation of a forgotten phrase of the Traft boy he had once been. "Well, I am going to marry her, and I think myself the luckiest fellow on earth."

Plainly she thought he was out of his head or that Arizona had broken down his sense of values. But she did not voice either conviction.

"Gloriana, I think I'd better take you in to meet Uncle Jim—and the Dunns," concluded Jim.

"Yes, since it has to be," she replied, soberly. "Give me time to make myself presentable. Come back for me in fifteen minutes."

"Sure. I'm curious to see what *you* call presentable," said Jim, and went out whistling. Nevertheless, his heart was heavy as he proceeded down the hall toward the living-room.

CHAPTER SIX

Jim found his uncle alone in the living-room. "Hey!" he said, "when are you going to trot my niece in?"

"Pretty soon. She was tired and wants to clean up after the long ride."

"How is she, Jim?" he asked, anxiously.

"White and thin. Looks wonderful, though. You could have knocked me over with a feather, Uncle."

"Wal, I reckon I'm plumb ready for mine."

At this juncture Molly and her mother came in, and it was certain Jim had never seen Molly so pretty, so simply and becomingly attired. He did not see how Gloriana could help admiring her.

"Oh, Jim, did your sister come?" she asked, eagerly.

"You bet. Curly and the boys were there with me. It was a circus."

"I shore reckon," agreed Molly, her eyes round and bright. She was excited, trembling a little.

"I'll fetch Glory in pronto."

"Does she look sick, Jim?"

"Well, you won't be able to see it," laughed Jim. "She'll dazzle you. But when I remember Glory a year ago—how tanned and strong—I confess she looks ill to me. She's white as the snow out there. She has dark circles under her eyes and that makes them bigger. She's very slender."

"Oh, I—I'm crazy to see her," exclaimed Molly. "What did the boys say an' do? Was Curly knocked silly?"

"They were funny, Bud especially. Curly wore his best cowboy outfit, gun and all. The other boys had new suits and they looked most uncomfortable. Curly had the best of them. . . . Well, I'll go fetch Glory in."

Jim went out and thoughtfully wended his way to the west wing of the huge ranch-house. In a certain sense this event was a thrilling and happy one, but in the main it was shadowed by misgivings. He tapped at Gloriana's door, and at her call he entered.

He stared. Was this lovely white creature Gloriana Traft? She wore a pale blue dress, without sleeves, and cut somewhat low. She was slender, but there was not an ungraceful line about her. And she had a little color in her cheeks, whether from excitement or from artificial means Jim could not tell.

"Glory, if you let the boys see you in that rig—we can't go on ranching," he said, with grave admiration.

"Why not?" she asked, not knowing how to take him.

"Because this place would beat the Pleasant Valley War all hollow. You just look like—like some beautiful sweet flower."

His genuine praise brought more color to her cheeks. "Thank you, Jim. It's nice to hear I look well. But this dress is nothing. I've some new ones and I'll have to wear them, even if your ranching can't go on. . . . Guess I'd better put my coat around me. That hall was like Greenland's icy mountains."

"This house is a big old barn. But the living-room is comfortable," said Jim as he replaced the screen before the fire.

"Jim, if I catch cold again it'll be the end of little Glory."

"Don't talk nonsense. This is a beginning for you, Glory," he replied, warmly, and he kissed her. Gloriana caught his hand and clung to it. Her action and the sudden flash of her face toward him gave Jim a clue to something he had not before guessed. Glory might resemble a proud, cold, aloof young princess, but she really was unconsciously hungering for love, kindness, and sympathy. By that Jim judged how she had been hurt, and through it he divined he could win her. Right there Jim decided on the attitude he would adopt with his sister.

"Jim, my failure and disgrace do not alter the fact that I represent your family out here," she said, as they went out.

The remark rather flustered Jim. He was not used to complexity, and he could find no words in which to reply. He hurried her down the hall to the living-room, and opened the door for her to enter. When he followed and closed it Gloriana had let her coat fall to the floor and was advancing quickly to meet the rancher.

"Oh, Uncle Jim, I know you," she said, happily, as if she had expected not to.

"Wal—wal! So you're my niece, Gloriana?" he replied, heartily, yet with incredulity. "I remember a big-eyed little girl back there in Missouri. But you can't be her."

"Yes, I am, Uncle. I've merely grown up. . . . I'm so glad to see you again." She gave him her hands and kissed him.

"Wal, it can't be, but if you say so I'll have to believe," he said, quaintly. "I reckon I'm powerful pleased to have you come West. . . . Gloriana, meet some friends of ours—Arizona folks from down country. . . . Mrs. Dunn and her daughter Molly."

The mother appeared embarrassed at the introduction; Gloriana graciousness itself. Then Jim experienced a sort of fright as this lovely sister and the little girl so precious to him faced each other. Probably Jim was unaware of his intense scrutiny of both. But as a matter of fact he held them both on trial.

"Gloriana, I'm shore happy to welcome you heah," said Molly, with simple sweet warmth. She was tremendously impressed—Jim had never seen her so pale—but there was no confusion for her in this meeting. Her eyes had a shining, earnest light. Jim could not have asked more. She was true to Molly Dunn. She was Western. She had stuff in her. Never in her life had she been subject to such an intense and penetrating look as Gloriana gave her. Jim's heart leaped to his throat. Was Glory going to turn out a terrible snob?

"Molly Dunn! I'm glad to meet you," replied Gloriana, cordially, and she was quick to accept the shy advance of the Western girl. She met Molly's kiss halfway. Jim almost emitted audibly a repressed breath of relief. But he was not sanguine. Gloriana appeared the epitome of perfect breeding, and she was too fine to let the Western girl outdo her in being thoroughbred. Yet heart and soul were wanting. And Jim thought that if he felt it Molly must have, too.

Uncle Jim beamed upon Gloriana and then upon Molly, and lastly upon his constrained nephew.

"Jim, shore there's such a thing as luck," he said. "I reckon I didn't believe so once. But look there. An' think of your havin' a sister an' a sweetheart like them."

It was a simple warm tribute from a lonely old bachelor who had given his heart to Molly and now shared it with Gloriana. But the compliment brought a blush to Gloriana's pale cheek and broke Molly's composure.

"Wal, I don't know aboot it, as Curly would say," drawled Jim, far from feeling like Curly. "A man can have enough luck to kill him."

This unexpected sally from him made the girls laugh and eased the situation. All took seats except Molly, who stood beside Gloriana's chair, plainly fascinated. It gave Jim a pang to see that Molly had already fallen in love with his sister. If Gloriana would only give the Western girl the smallest kind of a chance!

"You shore don't look sick to me," said Molly, her dusky eyes on Gloriana.

"Perhaps Jim exaggerated," returned Gloriana, with a smile. "I'm not on my last legs, but neither am I so very well."

"You look like you didn't eat an' sleep enough, an' run aboot in the sun."

"I don't. That's just what ails me." It would have been hard for anyone human to resist Molly's sweet simplicity.

"You're lovely right now," murmured Molly. "But in six months out heah. . . ." She could not find words to express her conviction, and they were not needed.

"It's fine pneumonia weather just now. I had that last winter. The doctor said once more and it would be flowers for Gloriana May."

Molly did not quite assimilate this speech, and turned to Jim.

"You mustn't roll her in the snow, like you did me."

"Glory will love even winter in Arizona," said Jim. "It's so dry you never feel the cold. But if Glory freezes too much at first we might send her to Tucson for a while."

"Take her down to Yellow Jacket," interposed the rancher.

Molly clapped her hands. "Thet would be fine. We never have any winter down in the Tonto. It snows a little, then melts right off. Sunny days to ride. The air full of cedar an' pine an' sage. Camp fires at night. . . . Gloriana, you would get well quick down at Yellow Jacket."

Jim spoke up seriously: "Next summer we will have both you girls down. But it'd never do now, even down in that low country. We'll have the Hash Knife outfit to entertain."

Gloriana was all interest. "Pray what is Yellow Jacket? And what is the Hash Knife outfit?"

Uncle Jim hawhawed. "Glory, don't let them tease you. Yellow Jacket is a cattle range, wildest left in Arizona. An' the Hash Knife outfit is a gang of cattle thieves."

"Now you've made me want to go," exclaimed Gloriana. "More than anything I want to see a desperado. I—I want to be scared. And I want to go to some lonely place. And when I'm strong again I want to ride. . . . Jim, have you a horse you will let me have?"

"A horse? Glory, you've grown amazingly modest. I have a hundred horses you can ride—that is, as soon as you can stick in a saddle."

"You will take me on trips into the desert?" queried Gloriana, breathlessly, her great eyes shining like stars.

Jim concealed his thrill of satisfaction. Added to Gloriana's need of love there seemed a thirst for something she had never had. Perhaps this was merely for excitement. But if she showed an innate leaning toward the beauty and wildness of nature then Arizona would claim her, and change her body and soul.

"Glory, I reckon I'll have to take you, if we want any work done," replied Jim.

Gloriana was as delighted as nonplussed. "But I don't quite understand your reference to work. I can't do very much."

"Could you bake sour-dough biscuits?"

"Gracious no!"

Molly laughed merrily. "Could you call wild turkeys?"

"I could eat a whole one, anyhow. . . . Oh, I'll be the greenest tenderfoot who ever came West."

"Glory, I'll teach you to make biscuits an' call wild turkeys," volunteered Molly.

"You're very good. I'm afraid you'll find me stupid."

"Glory, I didn't mean work for you, though I dare say a little would be good for you. I meant that the cowboys said there wouldn't 'never be no more ranchin' now.'"

"And why not?" queried Gloriana, vastly puzzled.

"I showed them a photograph of you."

Gloriana joined in the laugh at her expense.

"That horrid picture of me! I have some really good ones."

"For Heaven's sake, don't let anybody see them!" exclaimed Jim, plaintively.

Thereupon followed a half-hour of pleasant conversation, mostly for Gloriana's edification, and received by her with undisguised enthusiasm. Then she said she was very tired and begged to be excused.

"Jim, take me back to my Indian wigwam. I'd never find it," she begged, and bade the others good night.

When back in Gloriana's room Jim stirred the fire and put on a few fresh sticks of wood.

"Well?" he queried, presently, rising to face his sister, and he was quite conscious of the anxious gruffness of his voice.

To Jim's surprise she placed a hand on each of his shoulders.

"Jim, your Western girl is distractingly pretty, sweet as a wild flower, honest and good as gold—and far braver than I could have been. I saw what you couldn't see. Probably it was harder for her to meet me than that Hack fellow she—she bit to save your life. I'm your family, so to speak."

"Thanks, Glory," replied Jim, somewhat huskily. "I—I was afraid—"

"I'd not like her? Jim, I don't blame you for loving her. I *did* like her. . . . But—and here's the rub—she is illiterate. She comes from an illiterate family. She's only a very common little person—and certainly not fit to be the wife of James Traft."

"That's your Eastern point of view," returned Jim. "It might—though I don't admit it—be right if we were back home. But we're out West. I love the West. It has made me a man. It is now my home. I worship this 'common little person,' as you call her. *I* think she is farthest removed from that. She's strong and true and big, and crude like this great raw West. And as I've thrown in my fortunes here I consider myself most lucky to win such a girl. . . . All of which, Glory, dear, is aside from the fact that but for her I'd be dead. . . . But for Molly *you* wouldn't have had any brother to come to!"

"Don't think me ungrateful," she rejoined, in hurried, shuddering earnestness. "I am . . . and indeed you talk like a man. I admire and respect you. But I had to tell you the ethics of it. I wouldn't be a Traft if I failed to tell you."

"Then—you're not against us?" queried Jim, hopefully.

"Jim, I disapprove. But it would be absurd for me to oppose. I have come to you for help—for a home—to find *my* chance in life, if there be one. Besides, I like Molly. . . . The trouble will come not from me, but from *her*. Can't you see it? I don't think I ever was subjected to such study. Yet no trace of jealousy or bitterness! She was just being a woman seeing *you,* your family, your position through me. I saw fear in her eyes as she bade me good night. That fear was not of me, or that I might come between you. It was a fear of realization, of love. She ought not marry you because she is Molly Dunn of the Cibeque! And, Jim, if she's really as strong and fine as it seems she is, she will not marry you."

"I've had the very same fear myself," admitted Jim. "But I always laughed myself out of it. Now you—"

"Make it worse," she interposed. "I'm sorry. I ought not to have come. . . . I could go away somewhere, I suppose, and work. . . . But, Jim, the damage is done."

"I wouldn't let you go. I think we're making a mountain out of a molehill. It'll sure come out all right, if you'll help."

"Jim, I promise. I'll do my utmost for you. I'll be nicer to that little girl than I ever was to any one in my life. I *can* make people like me. But the worst of me is I'm cold. I've been frozen inside since Ed Darnell deceived me. I can't promise to love Molly, though it'd appear easy enough."

She seemed so eloquent, so moving, so beautiful that Jim could have decried aloud her intimation of her indifference.

"Glory, I couldn't ask any more," he concluded. "It's more than I had hoped for.

You have made me feel—oh, sort of warm deep down—glad you've come West. We'll win out in the end. We've got the stuff. . . . And now good night. You're worn out. Be sure to put the screen in front of the fire."

"Good night, brother Jim," she said, and kissed him. "I'm glad I came."

Jim left her with her kiss lingering on his lips. Gloriana had never been the kissing kind, and it was easy to tell now that she had not changed. She was older, deeper, more complex, with a hint of sadness about her which he wanted to eradicate. The cowboys would do that. They would change even the spots of a leopard. He went toward his room, and on the way tapped on Molly's door.

"Are you in bed?" he called.

"No, Jim—not quite," she replied, and presently opened the door a few inches to disclose a sweet agitated face.

"I just wanted to ask. . . . Do you like her?"

"Like!—I shore fell in love powerful deep. She's—she's—" But Molly could find no adequate word to express herself.

Jim darted his head downward to give her a quick kiss. "Darling, I'd gamble my soul on you," he whispered, gratefully. Then louder, "Did your mother like Glory?"

"Shore. But she was aboot scared stiff. . . . An', Jim, me too—a little."

"Well now, you mustn't be. Glory said some mighty sweet things about you."

"Oh, Jim—tell me," she begged, breathlessly.

"Not much. I'll keep them until I want something special out of you. Ha! Ha!—But they're awfully nice. . . . Good night, Molly."

Jim found his uncle dozing before the living-room fire. "Wake up and tell me what I'm to do?"

"Huh?" grunted Uncle Jim.

"Wake up and talk to me," replied Jim. "Did you like Glory? What on earth am I to do with two such girls on my hands? How can I keep the cowboys from murdering each other? Tell me what—"

"One at a time, you Missouri rooster. . . . Wal, Glory is the most amazing girl I ever saw. Bright an' smart as beautiful! She's got a haid on her, Jim. An' only nineteen. I reckon she'll be a bitter pill for Molly. But Molly is true blue. She'll be Western. In the end she an' Glory will be sisters. Not soon, but you can bet on it. An' your part is goin' to be harder'n buildin' the drift fence. Shore, Glory will upset the cowboys. Because she's sweet, she's nice, she'll be interested in them—an' the poor dumbhaids will reckon they can win her. At that she could do worse than be won by Curly or Bud or Jackson Way."

"I've come somewhere near that conclusion myself," rejoined Jim, thoughtfully. "Confidentially, Uncle, I want to tell you Gloriana has come West for good."

"Fine!" ejaculated the rancher. "Is she thet sick? Or what—"

"She's not so sick as it appeared. Only run down. She got involved in an unfortunate affair back home. Took up with some flashy fellow—thought she loved him when she didn't—and he turned out bad. Borrowed money from her and cheated money out of Dad. It hurt Glory with her crowd, which she was pretty sick of, anyhow, I guess. She's the proudest of the whole raft of Trafts. . . . So she has turned to me, poor kid."

"Ahuh!—Wal, dog-gone! . . . Jim, you ain't implyin' some scoundrel ruined your sister?"

"No, thank God," returned Jim, fervently. "But he ruined her reputation, at least. Fellow named Ed Darnell. And Glory is sure he'll show up out here."

"Wal, if he does I reckon it'll be aboot the last place he ever shows up," replied the cattleman, grimly.

"I said as much. . . . So, Uncle, we've got the happiness and future of two wonderful girls to make. I swear I'm stumped. I'm scared. I'm struck pretty deep."

"Wal, it's a problem, shore. But you're young an' you want results too quick."

"I can be patient. I'll do everything under the sun. But suppose Molly gets upset by Glory? Scared of my family, so to speak."

"Wal, in thet case I'd put Glory up against the real stuff out *heah*. An' have Molly with her. Thet'll square the balance. Then they'll learn from each other."

"It's a good idea," agreed Jim, almost with enthusiasm. "You mean put Glory up against rough outdoor life—horses, cowboys, camp, cold, heat, rain, dust and hail? Hard beds, poor feed, privation—danger—and so on?"

"Shore, an' so on. Put her up against everythin' thet Molly knows."

"It's risky, Uncle. Glory is not strong. It might kill her."

"Wal, you'd have to go slow an' easy till she could just aboot stand it, an' thet's all."

"But, if it *didn't* kill her—" mused Jim, fascinated by the memory of how terrible and wonderful the raw West had been to him. It was that which had won him for Molly Dunn; and now he regarded the stronger and primitive in him more desirable than any development he might have had in the East. The thing had to be gone through to be understood. Gloriana would succumb to it sooner than he had done, despite or probably because of her sensitive, feminine nature. And during this transition of his sister he was going to have trouble holding on to his sweetheart. Jim regretted that he had not persuaded Molly to marry him before Gloriana had come out. Could he do it yet? His mind whirled and his blood leaped at the suggestion. But it would not do, because Molly might suspect the reason. All of a sudden he realized that his uncle was talking.

"Beg pardon, Uncle, I was lost."

"Wal, I was changin' the subject," replied the rancher. "Locke was in awhile ago an' he's got wind of Bambridge shippin' steers tomorrow from Winslow. We was figurin' thet it might be a good idea for you to run down there an' look 'em over."

"Gee! In this weather?"

"Wal, you forget we're up high heah on the mountain slope. Winslow is down in the desert. Reckon there won't be any snow. Anyway, weather never phases this Bambridge cattleman, thet's shore."

"What's the idea, Uncle?" asked Jim, soberly.

"Bambridge doesn't know you, nor none of his outfit, so Locke reckons. An' you've never been in Winslow. You could look them steers over without bein' recognized. An' for thet matter it wouldn't make a whole lot of difference if you were. . . . Whatever is comin' of this Bambridge deal is shore comin'."

"Uncle Jim, you expect trouble with him?"

"Son, I've seen a hundred Bambridges come an' go. I know the brand. I've been forty years raisin' steers. . . . Ten years ago a fine-spoken most damn likable fellow named Stokes drifted into Flag. Had money. Began to buy stock an' sell. Soon was operatin' big. Everybody his friend. But there was somethin' aboot Stokes thet stuck in my craw. An', Jim, I seen him hangin' to a cottonwood tree—by the neck."

"Queer business, this cattle-raising," mused Jim, darkly.

"Wal, so long's there are big open ranges there'll be rustlers. An' I reckon when the ranges are fenced the cattleman of my type an' Bambridge, an' Jed Stone, too, all will have passed. It's a phase of the West."

"You regard Jed Stone as a cattleman?" queried Jim, in surprise.

"Shore do. He's a factor you've got to regard. Yellow Jacket belongs to you, legally, because I bought it, an' *gave* it to you. But Stone shore thinks it belongs to him," replied Traft, with a dry laugh.

"Humph! And for what reason?"

"He's just been ridin' it for years, thinkin' it free range, same as the rest. But it's a ranch, an' two sections of land, twelve hundred acres, have been surveyed. The best water—an' by the way, Jim, Yellow Jacket Spring is the wonderfulest in Arizona—an' level ground are in thet surveyed plot. The corners were hid pretty well by the man who first owned the ranch. I haven't been down there for years. But Locke has an' he's seen them. So we can prove our claim."

"Good heavens, Uncle!" exclaimed Jim. "Do you mean we may have to prove to an outlaw that we have a right to a piece of land you bought?"

"Not Stone. You'll have to prove it to him with guns. Haw! Haw! . . . But Bambridge, an' mebbe thet cattleman who's in with him—I forget the name—may want to see our proofs. Of course, son, nothin' but a little fight may ever come of this. But I've a hunch Yellow Jacket will catch your eye. It did mine. It's the wildest an' most beautiful place to live I ever seen in Arizona. Yellow Jacket isn't a valley, exactly. Really it's a great wide canyon, with yellow walls. Protected from storms. Best place to hunt in Arizona. Bear, deer, turkey just thick. An' very few hunters ever get in there, because it's a long way an' there's plenty good huntin' ranges closer. Lots of beaver left in Yellow Jacket an' where there's beaver you bet it's wild."

"Well, I've set my heart on Yellow Jacket, Uncle Jim Traft," declared Jim, forcefully. "And Slinger Dunn has a half interest in the stock running there. That was the deal I made with him, you know, to get him into the Diamond."

"Shore, an' you don't know how good a deal it was. Wish Dunn could go to Winslow with you. . . . An' come to think of it, Jim, you take Curly along."

"Fine. We'll hop the early train."

In the nipping frosty dawn, Jim, clad in jeans and boots, and heavy leather jacket, stamped into the bunkhouse, and yelled, "Curly Prentiss!"

Not a sound. The bunks might have been empty, only they were not. Jeff, the cook, stirred out in the kitchen, and asked through the door, "Boss, is the ranch-house on fire?"

"No. I've got to go to Winslow. Fix some breakfast for two, Jeff. And rustle . . . Curly."

"I'm daid."

"Get up and into your jeans."

"Aw, Jim, I was oot late last night."

"Hurry, or I'll ask Bud," returned Jim, tersely.

That fetched a lithe clean-limbed young giant thudding to the floor, and in the twinkling of an eye, almost, Curly was in his clothes. He stalked into the kitchen. "Water, Jeff, you sleepin' cook, an' if it's not hot I'll shoot at your toes."

Bud poked his cherub face above the blankets and blinked at Jim.

"Funny how this reminds me of camp," he said. "What's wrong, Boss?"

"I'm going to Winslow. Bambridge is shipping cattle, and I want to look over the bunch."

"Dog-gone-it, Jim, don't go," rejoined Bud, seriously.

"I'm not stuck on going, but Uncle says go, and that settles it. . . . What do you know, you mum little geezer?"

"Me? Aw, hell, I don't know nuthin' this early in the mawnin'. . . . Let me go along?"

"I reckon I can't, Bud. Uncle said take Curly."

"An' why thet hombre especial? Looks ain't everythin' in a cowpuncher."

"Well, Bud, I think Uncle is worried about you and the other boys. You need sleep and rest, he says."

"Like hell he does! . . . Jim, I don't like this hyar deal atall," complained Bud.

"I asked you what you knew."

"Sure, I heerd you," replied Bud, innocently. "Jim, are my eyes pore or is thet a gun you're packin'?"

"Yep. I've got in the habit, you know, since I bossed the Diamond."

"But some of these days you'll be throwin' it, sure. Jim, you've got a rotten temper. An' you oughtn't be trusted with a gun, unless the outfit was around."

Curly came in, his tawny hair damp and tousled, his cheeks rosy as a girl's.

"Shet up, you little monkey," he admonished, glaring at his bosom friend.

"All right," said Bud, sinking back in his blankets. "It shore won't be on my haid. But I'm tellin' you, Boss, Curly has been plumb crazy since—"

Bud narrowly escaped a well-aimed bootjack, which thumped hard on the wall, and he succumbed. But the noise awoke other of the cowboys.

"Injuns! We're attacked," ejaculated Uphill Frost, still half asleep.

"I smell ham," said Lonestar Holliday. "What'n'll's goin' on around heah?"

Jim and Curly went into the kitchen, shutting the door, and they warmed their palms over Jeff's fire until breakfast was ready. Curly was not his usual bright self, which might have been owing to the night before, of which he had hinted, but also it might have been the portent of Jim's early call. They had breakfast and hurried out into the snow. The morning was still, with the frost crackling, and the fence posts glittering with sunshine on the snow. Curly had little to say until they reached the station.

"Ring Locke was in last night," announced Curly, "an' he shore had bad news."

"Thought you were out late?" queried Jim, gruffly.

"Wal, I wasn't. Ring got wind of this heah Bambridge shippin'. Dog-gone-it, Ring's always gettin' tipped off aboot things we don't want to heah. He has too many friends."

"Wait till we're on the train," replied Jim, tersely. The station-room and platform were not the places just then for indiscriminate speech. Cowboys, cattlemen, Mexican laborers, and other passengers for this early train, were noisily in evidence.

When they got into the train, to find a seat somewhat isolated from those occupied, Jim whispered, "What did Locke hear?"

"Some darn fool sent him word there were Diamond steers in thet bunch of stock Bambridge is shippin'."

"So that's it? Uncle didn't tell me Locke said that. . . . The nerve of this Bambridge! . . . Curly, what're you growling about?"

"Locke ought to have kept his big mouth shet. . . . We shore cussed him last night."

"And why?"

"'Cause we all knew what'd come off pronto. Old Traft would send you down there, an' if you saw any steers with our brand you'd go right to Bambridge an' tell him."

"I should smile I would."

Curly threw up his hands, an expressive gesture of his when he was helpless, which in truth was not often.

"Why shouldn't I tell him, cowboy?" queried Jim, somewhat nettled. How long it took to understand these queer cattlemen!

"Wal, we reckon Bambridge oughtn't know we're suspicious, till we've had a spell at Yellow Jacket."

"But, Curly, surely Locke and Uncle Jim know more what is best than you cowboys."

"Hellyes. But they don't have to do the fightin'."

The way Curly spat out those words, as well as their content, gave Jim a breath-arresting moment. Indeed it was true—Locke was an aggressive superintendent, and the old rancher a stern and ruthless dealer with crooked cattlemen. No more was said then, and Jim gazed out at the speeding white and black landscape. The pines had given place to cedars and piñons, and these soon made way for sagebrush. The snow thinned out, and when the train got down on the open desert the white began to give way to the yellow of grass and occasional green tuft of sage or greasewood.

CHAPTER SEVEN

The Hash Knife were back from a drive, the nature of which showed in their begrimed, weary faces, their baggy eyes, and the ragged condition of their garb.

"Home!" croaked Malloy, flinging his crooked length down before the fire Stone was building.

"My Gawd!" ejaculated Stone, staring at the little gunman. And his men simulated his look if not his speech. The idea of Croak Malloy giving expression to such a word as home was so striking as to be incongruous, not to say funny.

"Did you ever have a home?" added the outlaw leader, more curious than scornful.

"Aw, you can't gibe me," replied Malloy, imperturbably. "What I mean is hyar's rest an' comfort—after a hell of a job."

"It shore was," agreed Pecos.

"An' ain't it good to be down out of the snow an' thet damn Tonto wind," said Madden. "Like spring down hyar at Yellow Jacket. It smells different."

"Wal, we'll sit tight till spring, you can gamble on thet," spoke up the gambler, Carr.

"Mebbe we will," interposed Jed Stone, sarcastically, yet not without pathos.

"Aw hell!" bit out Malloy. "Jed, don't begin your bellyachin', now we're home. We've got supplies till spring, plenty of drink an' money to gamble with. Let's forget it an' be happy."

Sonora came in dragging a pack, and young Frank Lang, the ex-sheriff, also appeared heavily laden. It was about midday, and outside the sun shone brightly warm. The air was cool and sweet with sage and cedar, and had a hint of spring, though the time was early December.

"Reckon Jed built thet fire 'cause he's so absent-minded," remarked some one.

"No, I want a cup of coffee. I'm soured on whisky. . . . At that it ain't bad to be back in the old cabin. . . . Bambridge anyhow!"

"He shore pulled a rummy deal," said Pecos, his tone harmonizing with Stone's.

"Wal, no one much ain't a-goin' to connect the Hash Knife with thet winter shippin' of stock. So what the hell?" replied Malloy. "But it wasn't a slick trick to turn."

For Malloy to show disapproval of a cattle-steal seemed to prove it was the last word in bold and careless rustling.

"Bambridge will skip Arizona pronto," put in Anderson, wagging his shaggy head. "I'd have give my pipe to see thet young Traft call him."

"So would I—an' some more," said Stone, thoughtfully. "Nervy youngster. . . . Frank, tell me about it again."

"Boss, I told you twice," complained Reed.

"Sure. But we was on the trail an' it was cold an' windy. You made it short an' sweet, too. . . . Here's a cigar."

Thus importuned the young cowboy rustler lighted the cigar, smiling his satisfaction, and settled himself comfortably.

"I was in Chance's saloon after the shippin', an' I heard a man say, 'damn funny about thet Bambridge cattle-drive. I went by the railroad stockyards late last night, 'cause I live out thet way. There wasn't no cattle there. An' next mornin' at daylight the pen was full of bawlin' steers.'"

"Haw! Haw!" croaked Malloy, gleefully, rubbing his thin brown hands.

"Laugh, you frog!" exclaimed Stone, darkly. "Thet drive was another blunder. We ought to have left the cattle at Bambridge's ranch, which I wanted to do. But he got sore. . . . An' well—Frank—"

"We drove the stock in at midnight, as you-all ain't forgettin'," resumed Reed, puffing his cigar. "It was a slick job fer any cowpunchin' outfit. An' next mornin' at ten o'clock them steers was all on a stock train, ready to move. Thet was another slick job. . . . I stayed at Chance's, sleepin' in a chair, an' went out to the yards after breakfast. Already the railroad men was movin' the cars to the pen. There wasn't no cowboy in sight 'till thet mornin' train from Flag come in. Then I seen Curly Prentiss. Used to ride under him when he had charge of the U Bar. He had a young fellar with him thet turned out to be Jim Traft. They watched the cattle fer about two minutes. No more! An' young Traft jumped right up an' down. You could see Prentiss talkin' turkey to him. I made it my business to foller them back to the station. An' you bet your life Curly Prentiss seen me. There ain't much thet hombre doesn't see. But it was safe, I reckon, 'cause nobody knows I'm with the Hash Knife. Prentiss an' Traft went in the freight office, an' I ducked in the station. As luck would have it, Bambridge came in with a dark-complected fellar, sporty dressed, an' good-lookin'. I edged over an' heard Bambridge ask: 'Where you from?' The fellar said St. Louis. 'What do you know about cattle?' He said nuthin', but he happened to know a stock-buyer in Kansas City who told him to hunt up George Bambridge, if he was goin' to Arizona. 'An' who's this stockman?' asked Bambridge, quick like. He said, 'Darnell'—I got thet name straight. 'Come to my office up town later in the day. I'm busy now with this cattle shipment.' . . . He was shore goin' to be damn busy in a minnit, only he didn't guess it. Just then Prentiss an' Traft come in. They was both packin' guns, which was funny only for Traft, I reckon. Prentiss sleeps in a gun. They looked kinda fire-eyed, an' Traft stopped Bambridge right in the middle of the station, an' he was in a hurry, too."

Reed leisurely drew on his cigar, and puffing out a white cloud of smoke he looked at Stone and Malloy and Lang and Pecos and the others, as if to note if his story was having any effect. Malloy had a sardonic grin. Lang was pale for a weather-beaten outdoor man. Anderson wore an intent anxious expression.

"Talk, an' come to the point," ordered Stone, in cold, testy voice.

"Not much more," replied Reed, casually. "Traft asked, 'Are you George Bambridge?'—an' he got a short answer.

"'You're shippin' some of my steers,' snapped Traft.

"Bambridge turned red as a turkey gobbler's comb. 'The hell you say, my young cowpuncher! An' who may you be?'

"'My name is Traft,' said thet young cowpuncher, an' he said it loud.

"Bambridge went white now. 'Jim Traft's nephew?'

"'Yes, an' you're shippin' steers with my brand.'

"'What brand is thet?' jerked out Bambridge, sort of husky. He was madder'n hellsfire.

"'Diamond brand.'

"'Ahuhm, I see.' . . . Bambridge sort of pulled himself together. 'Sorry, Mr. Traft. Mistakes happen. This is a rush order. An' them Yellow Jacket steers of yours overrun my range. An' I'm runnin' some new cowhands. Send me a bill.'

"'No, Mr. Bambridge, I'll not send you a bill now, but I'll send a telegram East to have a count made of the Diamond steers in this shipment,' said Traft, an' he shore looked a lot.

"'You call me a liar—an' a cattle thief?' busted out Bambridge, movin' a hand back.

"'No. An' don't pull a gun. This gentleman with me is Curly Prentiss. . . . I didn't *say* you was a liar an' a thief. But this shipment has a queer look an' I'll not be satisfied till it's been counted over.'

"'I tell you if there's Diamond steers on that train it's only a mistake. Any rancher makes mistakes when he's rushed,' yelled Bambridge.

"'No, any rancher doesn't make *such* mistakes!'

"'Every cattleman drives stock sometimes thet ain't his.'

"'But not branded stock.'

"'Your Uncle does it. An' fer thet matter he's as much of a cattle thief as Blodgett, or Babbitt, or me—or any—'

"'Don't you call my uncle a thief,' broke in young Jim. An' he cracked Bambridge square on his ugly mug. You ought to have heard thet fist. Sounded like hittin' a beef with an ax. Bambridge fell all over himself—damn near knockin' down the stove, an' he didn't get up. It was a good thing he was knocked out, fellars, for when I looked at Traft again there he was waitin' with a gun, an' Prentiss was standin' far over to one side."

"Pretty," croaked Malloy, with relish.

"Is thet all?" asked Stone, tersely.

"Just about. Some men got around Bambridge an' helped him up. I seen Prentiss eyein' me sort of sharp, so I ducked back to Chance's an' hid there till early next mornin'."

"Bambridge is a damn fool," burst out Stone. "An' I was the same for dealin' with him."

"Looks like young Traft has done us a good turn," said Anderson, with satisfaction.

"It shore does, Boss," added Pecos, quietly. "He throwed the light on Bambridge."

Others of the group attested to the same conviction.

"Well, yes, I reckon—mebbe," agreed the leader. "But it'll only make old Jim Traft sorer."

"Jed, the fact that you once rode fer Traft an' stood well with him sticks by you like a fish-bone in the throat," observed Anderson. "We've all seen better days. We was all different once—onless mebbe Croak there, who hasn't changed a damn iota since he was born."

"What's a iota?" inquired the subject of this remark. "Sounds somethin' like I-O-U, which you'll all be doin' pronto."

"Men," said Stone, "I'll split this money I got fer this last job, an' let myself out."

"Thet ain't fair," objected Malloy, who was strict in regard to shares of spoil. He had been a bandit at an earlier stage of his career. "You did thet last time."

"An' spoiled my settin' in for you an' Carr to fleece? It's jest as well. I'd be broke soon, anyhow."

"Reckon thet four-flush rancher owes you quite a wad?"

"Ten thousand."

"— — —!" cursed Malloy, in consternation. "Jed, he's goin' to do you. Sure as shootin'!"

"He'd better not, or there'll *be* a little shootin'," declared the chief, grimly. "But I don't mind admittin' thet the Hash Knife has struck a snag in this same high-talkin' crooked cattleman."

Stone left his men to their profanity and humor, both of which expended some force over the debt Bambridge owed him, and he went outside to walk around the familiar grounds.

December was on the way, but it was like spring down here in this protected spot. The air was crisp and full of tang. Blue jays were squalling and black squirrels chattering. A faint sound of wind from the pines above came down, and was almost drowned by the mellow roar of the brook that ran through the boulder-strewn, sycamore-lined glen just below the cabin. There were gold and green leaves still on the sycamores, which was another proof of the peculiar climate of Yellow Jacket.

Stone strolled under the great checker-barked junipers. Bear signs not yet old showed on the brown matted earth, and gave him peculiar satisfaction with its suggestion of the loneliness of this canyon. That feeling did not survive long. He had a premonition that the race of the long notorious Hash Knife was about run. None of his men shared that with him, and not improbably the big ranchers of the Mogollans and the Little Colorado Range would have scouted the idea. But Stone knew better than any of them; and this home-coming, as he bitterly called it, back to Yellow Jacket, had made him pretty sick. He was weary with the toil, the devious crooked ways, the sweat and blood, and, yes, the ignominy of the Hash Knife. He confessed it to himself for the first time, and realized it as a factor that would lead to something drastic.

He walked under the pines and spruces, across the log bridge over the brook, where many a time he had angled for trout in the amber water, and under the vine-covered, fern-fringed walls. In places he waded through leaves up to his knees, brown, dry, rustling oak leaves that gave up an acrid dust. And he went back and along the high bank to the beautiful glen where Yellow Jacket Spring poured its amber flood from under huge mossy rocks. From that high point he surveyed the gray-green valley, with its rock walls, its open range of bleached grass, silver in the sunlight, its many groves of cedar and pine, its numberless slopes of shaggy oaks which the bear and deer and turkey haunted in the early fall, its black timber belt along the rims. All these features presented the isolated confines of the canyon itself. Below, the gray-walled gateway opened into the wildest and most rugged range in Arizona, a wilderness of rock and brush and forest, grassy ridges, brawling streams, thickets of manzanita and mescal, towering cliffs and canyons where no sunlight entered—altogether a big country which only the Apaches had ever thoroughly explored.

Toward the lower end of this country, perhaps forty miles as a crow flies, it was barred from the open range by Clear Creek Canyon. Beyond lay the Little Colorado Range, where the rich cattlemen operated.

Yellow Jacket possessed a very singular feature. High and isolated and inclosed as it was, it yet looked down, at least through that narrow gateway, upon the desert which sloped away into purple infinitude. For that country it had the right altitude, neither too high nor too low, and its walls held back the winds and reflected the sunlight.

Some years back Stone had indulged in the illusion that he was going to own Yellow Jacket. Bambridge had promised to give it to him. But Bambridge had failed to get possession, and Stone's dream of quitting the outlaw game and settling down to honest ranching had been dispelled. He hated Bambridge for that, though he blamed himself for indulging in dreams. Hunted man as he was, the plan could have been carried out. Arizona was quick to recognize a cattleman whose shady dealings were in the past.

From that hour Jed Stone was more than ever a preoccupied man, wandering around the canyon during sunny hours, sitting in favorite places, or smoking by the camp fire. His gambling comrades, intent on their daily gains or losses, saw nothing of the almost imperceptible change in their leader. Anderson hunted every day, supplying the camp with fresh meat, while he stuck to his trade of trapping fur, even though he had been an outlaw for years. Sonora was the trusted scout of the band, always watching the trails. Pecos, the Texan, dreamed away his life. The rest of them staked their ill-gotten gold on the turn of a card.

Stone had something on his mind, and it was not only the slow disintegration of the once virile Hash Knife outfit, and therefore the decline of his leadership, but a realization that for the first time in his life he leaned towards betrayal of those who trusted him. And loyalty was the predominating trait of his personality. It was loyalty to a friend that had lost him his place among honest cattlemen.

One afternoon, Jed, returning from a walk up the brook, heard a shot. Rifle-shots were not rare around camp, but this came from a small gun of heavy caliber. It had a dull, ominous sound that echoed from the walls. Upon reaching the cabin he saw some of his men standing in a group—the kind of group he had seen so often and which suggested so much.

"Croak jest shot Carr," said Pecos, coolly and slowly; but there was a glint in his eyes.

"What for?" demanded Stone.

"Ask him."

Stone hesitated at the threshold of the cabin door. He did not trust Malloy, or was it that he did not trust himself? Then he entered. The little outlaw sat at the rude table, smoking a cigarette and shuffling a deck of cards. Carr lay humped over a bench, his head resting on the floor.

"Is he dead?" queried Stone, asking a superfluous question.

"Thet's funny," replied Malloy, with his little croaking laugh.

"Not so damn funny!" retorted the leader. "What'd you shoot him for?"

"Boss, he cheated at cairds," returned Malloy, almost plaintively.

It was Stone's turn to laugh. Malloy's statement was preposterous, if not in fact, then certainly in significance.

"Sure he cheated. But you all turn a trick when you can. Carr was the slickest. You had no call to kill him for what you do yourself."

"Wal, he won all the money. Thet's the difference."

"Ahuh. I see. It's shore a big difference. An' where's all this money Carr won?"

"He was stuffin' his pockets an' laughin' at us," said Malloy, with heat. "Thet made me sore. An' I cussed him fer bein' a caird sharp. Then, Boss, he got mean an' personal. He swore I stacked the cairds, which you all know is a lie, 'cause I can't do it. The best trick I know is to slip an ace from the pack or hold out a hand. An' the damn gambler threw thet in my face."

Stone called the men in from outside. "Search Carr an' put what he has on the table. Then take him out an' bury him—an' make it a good long way from this cabin."

"Boss, what're you goin' to do with it?" asked Malloy, as the heaps of gold coin and rolls of greenbacks were thumped upon the table.

"Divide it, accordin' to what each of you lost."

Then arose an argument among the gamesters over what amounts Carr had won from them. Lang and Madden, and especially young Reed, lied about it. Malloy frankly admitted he did not know how much he had lost, but certainly all that he had. Stone finally adjusted the difficulty by giving each the exact sum he had portioned out to them as their share of the recent cattle-drive. This caused some grumbling. And it turned out that Stone himself, with the aid of Pecos, had to carry Carr out into the woods and bury him.

"Much good his stone face done him," said the outlaw leader, wiping the sweat from his face.

"Shore not much," agreed the Texan. "Boss, I reckon Carr got his deserts. He was aimin' to slope with all thet money."

"You don't say? Who told you?" asked Stone, in surprise.

"Carr told me aboot it. Made no bones of braggin' he'd quit the outfit soon as he'd won our pile."

"Did he ever say thet before Croak?"

"Shore. We all heahed him."

"Then thet was why Croak shot him."

"I reckoned so myself."

"Pecos, do you hold this job as good or bad for the Hash Knife?"

"Wal, both, I reckon. Carr riled the fellars, most of the time. He was a disorganizer. Bad hombre for a business like ours. On the other hand, the fact that he meant to double-cross us an' thet Croak killed him in cold blood shore is serious. . . . Boss, the Hash Knife is ailin' from dry rot."

"Ahuh. . . . Money too easy—no hard work like we used to have—this two-faced Bambridge—"

Pecos nodded his lean hawklike head, acquiescing silently to the leader's unfinished speech.

Two mornings later, rather early, for Madden and Lang were cleaning up after breakfast, Stone was surprised by Sonora darting in the cabin door with his noiseless swift step.

"Boss, somebody comin'," he whispered.

"Who?"

"Cowboy—on foot."

"Sit tight, all of you," ordered Stone, and faced the door. Then Sonora told him that there was a camp somewhere down outside the gateway of the canyon. He had smelled smoke and had started to hunt for it when he had espied this lone cowboy approaching up the trail.

After a long wait a leisurely footfall was heard outside. A shadow fell across the sunny threshold. Then came a knock.

"Hello! Anybody home?" called a clear voice.

"Come in," replied Stone.

A tall, lithe-limbed, broad-shouldered young man stepped into sight. He was bareheaded, and the sun shone on a tanned open countenance.

"I'm looking for Jed Stone," he announced, frankly.

"Wal, you're lookin' at him," replied the outlaw, tersely. "An' who may you be, stranger?"

"Boss, it's young Jim Traft," spoke up Reed, excitedly.

"Yes. But I can talk for myself," returned the young visitor, with a flash of sharp hazel eyes at Reed.

"Jim Traft! . . . What you want?" exclaimed Stone, in slow amaze.

"I want a straight talk with you."

"Wal, young fellar, thet ain't hard to get, though most ranchin' folks reckon they'd get straight shootin' instead."

"I'd like to talk to you alone," said Traft, eagerly.

"No. What you have to say to me you'll say in front of my outfit.

"Very well, then," rejoined Traft, slowly, and he sat down on a box in the broad sunlight that flared through the wide door. He did not appear to be hurried or nervous; indeed, for an Easterner not long in the West he was exceedingly cool. Stone liked his face, the keen curious light of hazel eyes, and his manner. And the thought stung Stone that twenty years ago he was very like this young man. Traft glanced casually over the Hash Knife outfit, his gaze lingering longest on Croak Malloy, who sat on the floor, leaning against a pack, and for once his expression was one of interest. Though the little gunman did not realize it, he had respect for courage.

"First off, my Uncle Jim didn't advise me to call on you. I've done that on my own hook," said Traft.

"Wal, you needn't of told me thet," observed Stone.

"I've made up my mind ever since I got out of that fight at Tobe's Well—to try common sense."

"It ain't a bad idea, if the other party has any."

"Stone, would it surprise you to learn my uncle speaks well of you?" queried the young rancher.

"Reckon it would," replied Stone, slowly. And a pang rent his heart.

"He has done so. To me, and I've heard the same to others. He said twenty years ago he knew you and you rode for him—and there wasn't a finer or squarer cowboy in Arizona. He said you must have been driven to outlawry. Anyway, you never had been and you never would be a cattle thief at heart. . . . And it was a damn pity."

Stone felt a rush of hot blood to his face, and a cold tightness of skin as the wave receded. His breast seemed to cave with a sickening pain. So old Jim Traft spoke openly that way about him? Somehow it had a terrible significance, almost a fatality, coming at this hour. Malloy's hollow croaking laugh jarred on him.

"Wal—thet was—good of Jim—but I reckon—wasted sympathy," he replied, rather hoarsely.

"I'm not concerned with the truth of it—though I believe my uncle," went on Traft. "It just encouraged me to call on you and have a talk."

"No harm done, young fellar, but shore a little risky."

"I didn't see it. Curly Prentiss called me a crazy tenderfoot. And Slinger Dunn swore it was ten to one I'd not come back. But I couldn't see it that way. I'm not packing a gun or looking for trouble."

"Wal, Traft, I reckon if you'd happened to miss me here—you'd run into trouble all right."

"I took the chance. . . . But, Stone, before I make you the—the proposition I have, I want to talk some more. Making the best of my opportunity." He had to laugh at that, and once more glanced over Stone's men, particularly at Malloy, who appeared to fascinate him. "I went down to Winslow to look over a cattle shipment. Prentiss and I. We saw a big herd of stock being loaded on a freight train. Wildest bunch of steers Prentiss ever saw. . . . Well, we only watched the loading for about two minutes. A good many unbranded cattle—and some wearing the Diamond brand. . . . That's my mark, Stone. They were my cattle, and that was all I wanted to know. . . . I met Bambridge at the station and told him he was shipping some of my steers. He laughed it off as a mistake. I needed only one look at him to see he was as crooked as a rail fence. And that *any* man who dealt with him would get the worst of it. So you can bet my talk was pretty sharp. He got nasty and said old Jim Traft had made many such mistakes—or words to that effect, and—but, Stone, what do you think of him accusing my uncle of stealing cattle?"

"Kinda funny," replied Stone. "But the fact of ranchin' is, every cattleman appropriates cattle thet ain't his. It can't be helped. The dishonest cattleman takes advantage of this. All owin' to the custom of the range. No rancher has ever thought of anythin' better than the individual brand. An' thet shore has its defects."

"Bambridge didn't mean in that way," resumed Traft. "Anyway, I got mad and swung on him—but, Stone, maybe you're a friend of Bambridge's?"

The sly quick query was that of a boy and fetched a hollow croak from Malloy, and a smile to the hard face of the outlaw leader.

"Nope. He's shore no friend of mine, an' I'd have liked to see you slug him."

"I was sorry for it afterward. My outfit regretted it. Said it'd lead to worse. But I got hot under the collar, and saw red—"

"Traft, if I don't miss my guess some one will make you *spill* red before you're much older," returned the outlaw, significantly.

"Lord! I hope not," said Traft. "But I don't know what's come over me. Prentiss told me that after I hit Bambridge I pulled my gun and waited. . . . Well, the other thing I wanted particularly to tell you is that we can't find any of my three thousand head of stock. We're camped down among the rocks, and of course we haven't ridden over the Yellow Jacket. But Ring Locke told me we'd find my cattle down there in the brakes. But he was wrong. There are a few bulls and steers, wilder than the deer or bear. . . . I'd like to ask—not insinuating anything—if you know where that three thousand head have gone?"

"Wal, Traft, I shore don't," replied Stone, and he was telling the truth.

"Bambridge could tell me, I'll bet a hundred. He hired some one to rustle my stock. I don't accuse you, Stone. I know there is more than one gang in the Tonto Basin. Take the Cibeque outfit, for instance. So if you tell me straight out that the Hash Knife didn't rustle my Diamond cattle—why, I'll believe you."

Then ensued a queer little silence. Stone's men seemed as much concerned with him as the audacity of this young visitor.

"Wal, thet would be kind of you, Traft, an' I reckon foolish. But I'm not tellin' my business, one way or another," replied the Hash Knife leader.

"Which is answer enough for me," returned Traft, with a shrewd, almost merry twinkle in his clear eyes. "Well—my job here is to clean up Yellow Jacket."

"Uhuh.—Clean it up of what?"

"Wild cattle, rattlesnakes, cow-eating grizzlies and cougars, brush and cactus—and anything else not good for the making of a fine ranch."

"Your Uncle Jim hasn't give you no job atall," said Stone, with a grin. "Where's the common sense comin' in?"

"This visit to you is my first move, except ride around below to look for stock," rejoined the young man, seriously. "I've made up my mind—that if I live through this job I'll build me a fine big room log house here and make this place my home."

"Home! . . . Marry some Western gal, I reckon?" went on the outlaw, with interest.

"I've already found her, Stone. . . . No one else than Molly Dunn."

"Molly Dunn!—You don't say? Thet little brown beauty of the Cibeque!—Wal, Traft, I'll say you're a good picker an' a fast mover. I happen to know Molly. Used to run into her at Enoch Summer's store in West Fork. Last time scarce a year ago. . . . Me an' Slinger, her brother, was friends once. She's the prettiest lass an' the best little woman south of Flag."

"Or north, either," said Traft, happily. "Thanks for your compliment. I'll tell her. . . . And see here, Stone, don't you agree with me that it'd be pretty tough for me to get killed now or shot up bad—with marriage with Molly coming next spring?"

"Shore would be for Molly. She never had nothin' but tough luck. . . . If you feel thet way about her, why go lookin' up chances?"

"I'm not. I'm trying to avoid them. But this Yellow Jacket is a fine ranch. It belongs to me. It's my job.—What can I do?"

Stone shook his head as if the problem was a knotty one.

"Now here's another reason I want to—well, keep my health. Ha! Ha! . . . My sister, nineteen years old, arrived in Flag a few weeks ago. Came to make her home in the West. With me. She's not so well. The doctors think Arizona will make her strong again. So do I. Already she has begun to improve. . . . She wasn't very happy when she first got here. But that's passing. Stone, she's a lovely girl. Full of the devil—and, I'm afraid, stuck up a little—Eastern, you know, but the West will cure her of that, you bet. . . . Now, she's in my charge, not to say more, and even if there wasn't a Molly Dunn to make life so sweet, I'd hate like sixty to fail my sister. . . . So there you are, Jed Stone."

"Thanks. You're shore kind spoken, confidin' in me. . . . It's a hell of a situation for a young man."

"I wanted you to know exactly how I stand," went on Traft, earnestly. "I'm not afraid of a fight. I'm afraid when I get into one I almost like it. But common sense is best. I'm down here to tell you and your outfit to get out of Yellow Jacket. I want to tell you in a decent way, and that I appreciate this range has been like your own. But business is business. You'd do the same. . . . If you don't move off I'll have to try to put you off. And that's no fair deal. The Diamond, even with Slinger Dunn, is no match for the Hash Knife. I may still be a tenderfoot, but I'm no damn fool. A clash will mean a lot of blood spilled. I'd like to avoid it. Not only for my own sake, but for my men, and for that matter for you, too. . . . So I'm putting it up square to you. I can raise ten thousand dollars. That's my limit. Uncle Jim won't help me buy anybody out. I'll give you that to move off, fair and square, like the good fellow I believe you are."

"Traft, I couldn't accept your offer, nohow," returned Stone, pacing the floor with grave face and intent eyes. He made his last move look casual, but he did not like the gleam in Croak Malloy's pale eyes, and wanted to be within reach of the little rattlesnake. Croak did not have to be stepped upon to show his fangs. "Much obliged to you, but shore I couldn't take the money. I'll say, though, thet Jed Stone ain't the man to stand in the way of a young fellar like you. . . . I'll get out of Yellow Jacket for nothin'."

"You will!" cried Traft, in amaze and gladness. "Well, that's darn fine of you, Stone. . . . Uncle Jim *was* right. I—I just can't thank you enough."

"Shore you needn't thank me atall."

"Gosh!—" The young man arose in relief and with shining face stepped forward to offer a hand to Stone. "Shake. I'll always remember you as one of the big lessons the West has taught me, and already they've been more than a few."

Stone gripped hands with him, with no other reply. Then Traft moved back into the sunlight, and halting at the door proceeded to roll a cigarette, in Western fashion and with deft fingers.

"It'll be great to tell the boys. Good day and good luck to you, Stone. . . . And same to your men."

If he had glanced at these men he might not have expressed such good will. As he struck the match and held it to the cigarette there came a ringing crack of a gun. The match vanished. A bullet thudded into the dark logs. Traft suddenly changed into a statue, his empty fingers stiff, his face blanched in a fixed consternation. Then followed another shot. The cigarette whipped out of his mouth and another bullet thudded into the wood.

"Them's my compliments, Mister Jim Traft, junior," croaked Malloy, in a stinging, sarcastic speech full of menace.

Slowly Traft lost his rigidity and turned his head, as if on a pivot, to fix staring eyes upon the little gunman.

"Good God!—Did you shoot that match—and cigarette—" he exclaimed, hoarsely.

"Yep. I didn't want to see you leave without somethin' from the rest of the Hash Knife," replied Croak, significantly.

"But you—you might have shot me—at least, my hand off!" expostulated Traft, the white beginning to leave his face for red.

"Me? Haw! Haw! Haw! . . . I hit what I shoot at, an' you can go back an' tell your Slinger Dunn an' Curly Prentiss thet."

"You—crooked-faced little runt!" burst out Traft, furiously.

At this juncture Stone took a noiseless and unobtrusive step closer to the sitting Malloy.

It had chanced that of all opprobrium, of all epithets which could have been directed at Croak Malloy, the young rancher had chosen to utter the worst to inflame the gunman. His lean body vibrated as if a sudden powerful current had contracted every muscle, and his face flashed with a hideous deadly light.

As he raised his gun Stone kicked his arm up. The gun went off as it flew into the air. Malloy let out a bellow of rage and pain, and leaped erect, holding his numbed arm.

"Croak, I reckoned you'd done shootin' enough fer one day," said Stone, coolly.

The little outlaw had no time to reply. Traft sprang at him and in three bounds reached him. He was like a whirlwind. One swift hand fastened in Malloy's shirt and swung him off his feet. The other, doubled into a big fist, swung viciously the other way round. But it missed Malloy's head by an inch. He flung the outlaw, who went staggering over the floor to crash into the door. Traft, light and quick as a cat, was again upon him, even before he could fall, which he surely was going to do. Traft gave him a terrific slap alongside the face, which banged his head against the door. Then he held him there.

"You dirty—little snake!" panted Traft. "You may be a good shot—but you're a damned yellow—coward."

A hard blow from Traft's right sent Malloy's head with sodden thump against the door post. The outlaw swayed forward, only to meet Traft's left swing, which hurtled him through the doorway, out on the ground, where he rolled clear over and lay still.

Traft stood on the threshold, glaring out. Then he stepped back, produced another cigarette and match. His fingers shook so he could hardly light the cigarette. His ruffled hair stood up like a mane. Presently he turned, to give Stone another thrill. It was something for the outlaw to look again into furious blazing honest eyes.

"Reckon I was a little previous," he said, in a voice that rang. "All the same, Stone, I'm wishing *you* good luck."

As he swept out the door Malloy appeared to be attempting to get up, emitting a strange kind of grunt. He was on his hands and knees, back to the cabin. Traft stuck out a heavy boot and gave him a tremendous shove. The little outlaw plunged face forward and slid into the brush.

Stone stood in the doorway and watched Traft's lithe, erect, forceful figure disappear in the trees. Then he laid a humorous and most satisfying gaze upon Malloy. And he muttered, "Somebody will croak for this, an' I hope it's Malloy."

CHAPTER EIGHT

Jim Traft did not pause in his rapid stride until he had passed through the walled gateway which permitted egress from Yellow Jacket to the rough brakes of the basin below. Then he slowed up along the brawling brook, waiting to compose himself before he arrived at camp. The fire and tumult within him did not soon die down. "Gosh!" he ejaculated. "I get worse all the time. . . . I'm going to kill somebody, some day—sure as the Lord made little apples." And thoughtful review of the experience he had just passed through in the old Yellow Jacket cabin made him correct his exclamation by adding, "if I don't get killed myself."

The trail followed the brook. No one could have guessed from the environment that the season approached mid-winter. White cottonwood trees, with gold and russet leaves, and even some tinged with green, lined the amber stream, sending out gnarled and smooth-barked branches across from one bank to the other. Wild turkeys and deer scarcely made an effort to move into the green brush. Jays were squalling, woodpeckers hammering on dead trees, black squirrels barking shrilly. And there was a dreamy hum of murmuring water mingled with a low sough of wind in the great silver spruces and pines. The wildness and ruggedness of this country increased the farther Traft got down the stream. Grass grew luxuriantly in every open patch of ground, mostly bleached, yet some of it still green.

Jim soon left trail and stream to plunge into the forest toward a mighty wall of red and gray rock which towered above the highest pines. A wild steer, ugly as a buffalo bull, crashed into the brush ahead of him. It afforded Jim amusement to have proof that the remnant of his cattle were wilder than the bears and lions. He had met several bears, one a cinnamon and another a grizzly, without making any attempt to run. But sight of a wild Diamond steer always engendered in him a desire to climb a tree.

He reached the wall and flung himself down in a sunny spot surrounded by green on three sides and dominated by the cracked and caverned cliff. If he was compelled to leave Arizona he would always remember it and cherish it by pictures in mind of this marvelous Yellow Jacket country. If the Tonto Basin, the Cibeque Valley, and especially the Diamond Mesa, across which he had built the now famous drift fence, had fascinated him, what had this wilderness of canyon and forest done? It brought into expression some deep, long-latent force of joy. Hours he had spent alone like this, not worrying over some problem, nor dreaming of Molly—which happened often enough—but not thinking of anything at all. It was a condition of mind Jim had not inquired into, because he realized it was pure happiness, and he feared an analysis would dispel it. And the enchantment fastened down strong upon him, so that it alternated with a serious consideration of what he had just passed through at the outlaw camp.

"I've made another blunder," he soliloquized, regretfully. "Stone proved to be a decent fellow, as Uncle Jim vowed he was. . . . But Stone is not all of the Hash Knife. Whew! . . . That little hatchet-faced ruffian!—Sure he scared me, and I reckon I wasn't in any danger from his playful bullets. But, my God! when I cursed him—if Stone hadn't kicked his arm up—I'd be dead now! . . . That was Croak Malloy, sure as hops. Reckon I'll remember his face. And any of them. Sure a hard crowd! . . . They'll probably buck against Stone about leaving Yellow Jacket. But he struck me as a man who'd be dangerous to cross. . . . Anyway, I made a good impression on him. . . . I'll put the matter up to the boys and see what they say."

If Jed Stone did really keep his word and abandon Yellow Jacket, how would that simplify the big task there! Jim would put the boys to cutting, peeling, and dragging pine logs down to the site where he wanted to erect a wonderful house. He had meant to clean up that ragged brushy end of Yellow Jacket, but after seeing it he had changed his mind. He would not even tear down the old log cabin where the Hash Knife outfit had held forth so long. In time this cabin would become a relic of Arizona's range days. It would take all winter to cut the logs, rip-saw the boards, split the shingles, and pack in the accessories for the ranch-house Jim had planned.

If Stone moved off peacefully and took his men—about whom Jim was most dubious—then it would be possible for Jim to go back to Flag for Christmas. What a thrilling idea! It warmed him into a genial glow. But another thought followed swiftly—the cowboys of his outfit would go back to Flag also. And that would be terrible. He groaned when he recalled the Thanksgiving dinner and dance which his Uncle Jim had given in honor of Gloriana May Traft. It had been a marvelous occasion, attended by everybody in or around Flagerstown, and something about which the cowboys raved more and more as time passed. Or was it Gloriana about whom they raved! What havoc that purple-eyed, white-faced girl had wrought! She had looked like a princess—and had flirted like a—a—Jim did not know what. She had even enticed Slinger Dunn to dance—a feat Molly avowed was without parallel. And she had showed open preference for handsome Curly Prentiss, which fact had gone to the head of this erstwhile gay and simple cowboy. He had made life for Bud and Cherry, not to mention the others, almost insupportable. Yet it all—the whole situation following that unforgettable dance—was so deliciously funny. All except the stunned look of Molly's eyes—as Jim recalled it! Molly had not been jealous. She, too, had been carried away by Gloriana's lovely face and charming personality. But there was something wrong with Molly. And Jim had been compelled to leave Flag almost before he realized that the advent of his sister had brought about some strange change in Molly's happiness.

It required submission to the dream of love and of the future to dispel Jim's dread, and his regret. His faith in Molly's tenderness was infinitely stronger than all doubt. He knew he had won her and that always he could prevail. This imperious sister, Gloriana, with her charm, and the distinction of family and class which seemed to hang upon her words and every action, might cause the sincere and simple Arizona lass the mortification and realization of what she considered her own humble station, but they were really chimeras, and would pass in time.

Jim had only to recall the last moments he had spent with Molly, her betrayal of self, her utter devotion, and her passionate love, to which she was gradually surrendering. These sufficed here, as they had before in moments of gloom, to lift him buoyantly to the skies again.

At last he got up and wended a devious way toward camp, preoccupied and tranquil. He was so absent-minded that when Slinger Dunn appeared as if by magic, right out of the green wall of foliage, he sustained a violent shock that was not all thrill.

"You darned Injun!" he ejaculated, in relief, "always scaring me stiff."

"Howdy, Boss. I reckon you spend a heap of time heah-aboots—sittin' in the sun," replied Dunn.

There was no help for it—Jim could not leave camp or approach it, or hide, or in any way escape the vigilance of this backwoodsman. It rather pleased Jim, who recognized in it a protective watchfulness. His cowboys were always concerned, sometimes unduly, when he was absent. And the acquisition of Slinger Dunn to the outfit had been hailed with loud acclaim.

Slinger leaned on his rifle and regarded Jim with eyes like Molly's, only darker and piercing as the points of daggers. He was bareheaded, as he went usually, and his long hair almost lay upon his shoulders. He wore buckskin, which apparel singularly distinguished him from the cowboys. In his backwoods way Slinger was fastidious, or so it seemed. His simple woodsman's costume partook of the protective hue of foliage and rock, according to which furnished a background.

"Jim, you look sorta worried," he observed.

"Huh! Small wonder, Slinger."

"How'd Jed treat you?"

"Fine. He's a good fellow, even if he is an outlaw."

"Shore I reckoned you'd like Jed. But I was skeered of Croak Malloy, an' thet slippery greaser sheep-herder."

"I didn't get a line on the Mexican you called Sonora. But, Slinger, I formed the acquaintance of Mister Malloy, croak and gun and all. I did! . . . Wait till we reach camp. I don't want to have to tell it twice. . . . How are the boys? I swear I'm afraid to leave them alone these days."

"Hell to pay," grinned Slinger, showing his white teeth, and his black eyes had a gleam of fun.

"Now what?" demanded Jim, perturbed.

"Curly busted Bud one on the nose."

"Oh! . . . Is that all?"

"Wal, it shore was enough, leastways for Bud."

"Aw, they're pards, the best of friends. They worship each other, even if they do scrap all the time. What was it about this time?"

"Somethin' aboot Gloriana's laigs," drawled Slinger.

"Wh-hat!" exclaimed Jim, astounded and furious.

"I didn't heah Bud. But you could have heahed Curly a mile. He roared like a mad bull. An' I near died laffin'. I'll shore have fun tellin' Gloriana aboot it."

"Oh, the —— you will?" queried Jim, constrainedly. Slinger was an entirely new element in the Diamond outfit and assuredly an unknown quantity. He was naïve to the point of doubt, and absolutely outspoken. "Better tell me first."

It appeared, presently, that Bud Chalfack, as frank and innocent in his cowboy way as Slinger was in his backwoods fashion, had been talking about Gloriana's pretty feet, ankles, and so on, much to Curly's disgust. And when Bud nonchalantly added that Gloriana was not wholly blind to the grace and beauty of her nether extremities Curly had taken offense. He could allow no insult to his young lady friend from the East, and despite Bud's protest he punched him on the nose.

Jim held himself in until he reached camp. He did not know whether to explode in wrath or glee. But the incident might prove to have advantages. Gloriana had upset the outfit; and Jim had found himself at a loss to combat the situation. He grasped at straws.

The camp site, assuredly the most beautiful Jim had seen, was in a break of the wall, where a little brown brook ran crystal clear over stones and between grassy banks. A few lofty silver spruces lorded it over an open glade, which the sun touched with gold. Huge blocks of cliff had fallen and rolled out. Boulders as large as houses stood half hidden by pines. Ferns and amber trailing vines colored the rock wall behind. Camp paraphernalia lay around in picturesque confusion that suited the lounging cowboys.

Jim stalked toward the boys. He must maintain tremendous dignity and make all possible use of this opportunity. Curly got up, his fine face flushing, and made a half-hearted advance, which he checked. Jim divined that this young man was not sure of his stand. Bud sat apart, disconsolate, and nursing a bloody nose.

"What's this Slinger tells me?" Jim demanded, in a loud voice. "You insulted my sister?"

"Aw no, Boss. Honest t'Gawd I never did," burst out Bud in distress.

"Is Slinger a liar, then?"

"Yes he is, dog-gone-it, if he says so," retorted Bud.

"And Curly slugged you for nothing?"

"Not egzactly nuthin', Boss," replied Bud. "I—I did say somethin', but I meant nuthin'."

"Bud Chalfack, did you dare to speak of my sister's legs—here in this camp of low-down cowboys?" demanded Jim, as he leaned over to jerk Bud to his feet.

"Aw, Jim. Fer Heaven's sake—listen," begged Bud. "Shore I—I said somethin', but it was compliment an' no insult."

Jim placed a boot behind Bud and tripped him, spread him on the grass, and straddling him, lifted a big menacing fist.

"Aw, Jim, don't hit me. I got enough from Curly. An' he cain't hit as hard as you."

"I'll smash your wagging jaw!"

"I'm sorry, Boss. I—I was jest excited, an' talkin' aboot how pretty Miss Gloriana is. An' I reckon I was jest seein' if I could rile Curly. It shore did. . . . I swear I didn't mean nuthin'. An' I apologize."

"What'd you say?" demanded Jim, his fist still uplifted.

"Aw, I forget. It wasn't nuthin' atall."

"Curly, come here," called Jim, sharply, and as the red-faced cowboy advanced reluctantly Jim went on: "Since you had the gall to constitute yourself my sister's champion you can tell me just what this blackguard did say. Don't you dare lie!"

Curly seemed to be in a worse predicament than Bud, though for no apparent cause, unless it was Jim's great displeasure. He did not look like the chivalrous defender of a young girl. But presently he got it out, thereby acquainting Jim with the exact words and nature of Bud's offense. Jim could have shrieked with glee, though he acted the part of an avenging Nemesis. Curly was the deceitful one who had taken advantage of Bud's ravings; and Bud was the innocent victim, scared terribly by Jim's wrath and a dereliction he could not quite understand.

"Ahuh. So this is the kind of a cowboy you are," shouted Jim, raising his fist higher. "I'll beat you good, Bud Chalfack. . . . Do you crawfish? Do you take it back?"

"No—damn' if I do!" cried Bud, righteous anger rising out of his grief. "You can beat all you want. What I said I *said,* an' I'll stick to it. . . . 'Cause it's true, Jim Traft."

Jim solemnly regarded the prostrate cowboy, while poising aloft the clenched mace of retribution. Bud's true spirit had flashed out. In his code of honor he had not transgressed. But Jim did not like the familiarity with which the boys bandied about Gloriana's charms. It was absolutely inevitable, it was Western, and there was not any harm in it; nevertheless, he was inconsistent enough to see the humor of it and still resent.

Suddenly an idea occurred to Jim and in an instant he accepted it as a way of escape out of the dilemma. He certainly had not intended to strike Bud, unless there was real offense. He released the cowboy and got up.

"Bud, you are hopeless," he said, with pretense of sorrow and resignation. "No use to beat you! That'd be no adequate punishment. I'll make you an example. . . . I'll *tell* Glory what you said about her!"

"Aw—Boss!" gasped Bud.

"I shall, Bud Chalfack. Then we'll see where you get off."

"But Jim, for Gawd's sake, think! You'd have to tell her Curly punched me for it. Then I'd be wuss'n a coyote an' he'd be a hero. Thet'd be orful, Jim, an' you jest cain't be so mean."

"Curly never talked exactly that same way about Gloriana, did he?"

"No, I never heerd him, but I reckon he thinks it, an' more'n thet, too, you bet."

"Bud, if you admire a girl and *must* gab about her, why not confine yourself to her eyes, her hair, or mouth? Couldn't you be satisfied to say her eyes were like wells of midnight, her hair spun gold, and her lips sweet as red cherries?"

"Hellyes, I could. But I never swallered no dictionary. An' dog-gone-it, any bootiful girl has more'n eyes an' hair an' lips, hasn't she?"

"Nevertheless, I shall tell Gloriana," returned Jim, inexorably.

"Boss, I'll take the beatin'," implored Bud.

"No, you won't, Bud. You'll take your medicine. And pretty soon, too. We're all going back to Flag for Christmas. Jed Stone agreed to get off Yellow Jacket and that leaves us free, for the present, anyway."

"Whoop-ee!" yelled the outfit, in a united chorus.

Only Bud was not radiant. "I'll get drunk an' disgrace the outfit," he avowed.

"Listen, men, and tell me what you make of this deal," said Jim, and seating himself on a pack while the cowboys gathered around, he began a detailed account of his visit to the Hash Knife outfit. He took longer than usual in the telling of an incident, because he wanted to be specific and not omit a single impression. When he had finished there was a blank silence, rather perturbing. At length Slinger Dunn broke it:

"My Gawd! Boss, you're as good as daid!" he ejaculated, with the only expression of concern Jim had ever seen on his dark impassive face.

Curly Prentiss broke out: "Jim! You've slugged the dangerousest gunman in Arizona!"

One by one the others vented similar opinions, until only Bud was left to express himself.

"Boss, you're a tenderfoot, same as when you come West," declared that worthy. "You cain't be trusted with a job like thet. Didn't I ast to go? Didn't I *tell* you to take Curly? You dod-blasted jackass! Now you've played hell!"

"So it appears," returned Jim, sober-faced.

"If you'd only shot Malloy when you had the chanct," said Slinger, moodily.

"But I didn't pack a gun," expostulated Jim. "I went unarmed so that I couldn't shoot anybody."

"Wal, Boss, you shore made another mistake," spoke up Curly. "Jed Stone is square. He'll keep his word. But he's only the brains of the Hash Knife. Croak Malloy haids the gun end of thet outfit. An' if he doesn't shoot up Arizona now, I'll miss my guess."

"Well, it's too late. I'm sorry. I sure was mad. And I'd have slammed that dirty little rat around if it was the last thing on earth. . . . But let's get our heads together. What'll we do? Slinger, you talk first."

"Better lay low an' wait while I watch the trails. Jed will go, but he might go alone. An' I'm shore tellin' you *if* he goes alone the Hash Knife will be ten times wuss'n ever."

"I reckon he'll get off Yellow Jacket an' persuade the outfit to follow," said Curly. "Stone is a persuasive cuss, I've heahed men say. An' Yellow Jacket is cleaned out of cattle. They've made way with your Diamond stock, Jim, an' once more you're a poor cowboy. Haw! Haw!"

"They're welcome to my stock, if they only vamoose," returned Jim, fervently.

"Boss, they shore ain't welcome to the half of thet stock you gave me," declared Dunn, darkly. "I was pore, an' all of a sudden I felt rich. An' now—"

"Slinger, you still have your half interest in what cattle are left and what I'll drive in," replied Jim. "My uncle won't see us left stripped."

"Wal, thet's different," said Slinger, brightening.

"You stay off the war-path, you darned redskin," interposed Curly. "We're shore goin' to need you. . . . Now, Boss, heah's the deal in a nutshell, as I see it. An' I know these rustlin' outfits. Jed Stone will change his base. But he won't get out of the brakes. There's rich pickin' on the range below. The Hash Knife will hide down heah an' then go to operatin' big an' bold. Stone will throw thet outfit down or I don't read the signs correct. An' as Slinger says, then the Hash Knife will be worse. Somebody will have to kill Malloy or we cain't do any ranchin' in these parts. Shore everythin' will be quiet till spring."

Jim maintained a long, thoughtful silence. He respected Curly Prentiss' judgment, and could not recall an instance when it had been wrong. Curly was young, but old in range wisdom. Then his intelligence and education were far above that of the average cowboy.

"Very well," finally said Jim. "We'll stick close to camp, with two guards out day and night. Slinger will watch the Hash Knife gang and report. So until then—I guess we'll have to play mumbly-peg."

"Say, Boss, I ain't a-goin' to stop fishin' fer all the dog-gone rustlers in Arizonie," declared Bud, rebelliously.

"Fishing? You're crazy, Bud. Something has affected your mind. I declare I don't wonder at Curly's effort to make you think. Fishing in December!"

"Boss, I ain't the only one whose gray matter is off," replied Bud, and from the way he got up and hitched his overalls Jim knew something was coming. Bud's glance had distinctly charged Jim with an affection of the brain. Bud stalked to a spruce tree, reached in the foliage, and drew forth a string of trout that made Jim's eyes bulge and the cowboys yell.

"Jim, you know a heap aboot the West—aboot wild turkeys an' deer an' trout—an' cowboys an' cowthieves—an' Western gurls—now, don't you?"

"Bud, I—I don't know much," admitted Jim, weakly. "Trout in December! . . . Gosh! that's one on me. I thought it was winter. Boy, I'll give you a new gun if you'll show me where you caught them."

"I should smile not," returned Bud. "An' there ain't another fellar in this locoed outfit who could show you, either."

"Shore is a fact, Boss," said Curly. "Bud's a rotten hunter, but as a fisherman he's got us trimmed to a frazzle. Fish just walk out on the bank an' die at his feet."

Jim was studying the disfigured face of the disgruntled Bud. He could read that worthy's mind. Bud would move heaven and earth to keep him from telling Gloriana about the disrespectful gossip.

"Stay in camp. You hear me?" said Jim, sternly.

"I heah you, Boss. I ain't deaf."

Two lazy idle yet watchful days passed. Slinger did not return until long after dark of the second day, so long that it took persuasion by Curly to allay Jim's anxiety. Slinger came in with Uphill Frost, who had been on guard down the trail and who had missed the supper hour.

"The Hash Knife gang is gone," announced Frost, loudly. "I seen the whole caboodle ride by, an' I damn near took a peg at thet Croak Malloy."

"What!—You sure, Up?" shouted Jim, leaping excitedly to his feet.

"Yep. I wisht I was as sure of heaven. It was aboot two o'clock this afternoon. I'd come back sooner, but Slinger slipped up on me an' told me to wait till he got back. There was eight of 'em an' they had a string of pack-horses."

"Slinger, where'd they go?" asked Jim, breathlessly.

"I followed them ten miles, an' when I turned back they was travelin'," returned Dunn. "Tomorrer I'll take a hoss. I reckon they're makin' fer the Black Brakes."

"How far is that?"

"Aboot twenty miles as the crow flies."

"Too close for comfort."

"Boss, I sneaked up almost within earshot of the cabin," went on Dunn. "Fust off this mawnin' I seen the greaser Sonora wranglin' their hosses. An' as he's the only one of thet outfit I'm skeered of I went up the crick an' crawled up in the brush. I got close enough to heah voices, but not what they said. Shore was a hell of a argyment, though. They'd pack awhile, then fight awhile. Reckon I didn't need to heah. All as plain as tracks to me. Malloy kicked on quittin' Yellow Jacket an' most of the outfit was with him. But Stone was too strong. An' along aboot noon they rode off."

"Yippy-yip!" yelled Jim, in wild elation. "Gone without a scrap. Gosh! but I'm glad."

"Boss, you shore air previous," spoke up Bud, with sarcasm. "Thet Hash Knife gang hev only rid off aways to hide till you throw up a fine big cabin. Then they'll come back an' take it away from you."

"They will like—h-hob," stammered Jim.

"Thet'll be like Malloy," admitted Slinger. "I'm afeered they went off too willin'."

"Shore is aboot the deal to expect," chimed in Curly, cheerfully. "But life is short in Arizona an' who knows?—Malloy may croak before spring."

"Curly Prentiss, you've somethin' on your mind," declared Jim, darkly.

"Humph! It's only curly hair an' sometimes a sombrero," said Bud.

"Shore. I'm a thoughtful cuss. Always reckonin' fer my friends an' my boss."

"An' your next sweetheart."

"Bud, old pard, for me there'll never be no next one."

"Boys, we'll build the house," interposed Jim, with decision that presupposed heretofore he had been only dreaming. "Jeff, we'll break camp at daylight. Better pack some tonight. We'll hit the trail for Yellow Jacket. Gosh! I'm glad! . . . We'll keep Slinger on watch, and the rest of us will cut, peel, an' make pine poles out of the woods."

"Swell job fer genuine cowpunchers," observed Bud, satirically.

"I've ridden all over Yellow Jacket, Jim," spoke up Curly. "Some years ago. But shore there's timber to build a town. Grandest place for a ranch! It'd be tough to spend a lot of coin on it, an' work a good outfit to death, an' haul in stuff to make a nice home, an' fetch your little Western bride down fer your honeymoon—an' then stop one of Croak Malloy's bullets. . . . Shore would be tough!"

"Curly, you're a blamed pessimist," burst out Jim. "Don't you ever have any dreams?"

"Me?—Never once in my life," drawled Curly.

"Boss, he's dreamin' now—an' if you knowed what it's aboot you'd punch *him* on his handsome nose," said Bud, revengefully.

"Bud, you surprise me," rejoined Jim, mildly. Then he advised the outfit to turn in and be up at daylight.

Jim rode through the colorful rock-wall gateway of Yellow Jacket, imagining himself Vercingetorix riding his black stallion at the head of his army into one of the captured cities.

On his hurried visit to Jed Stone he had scarcely noted details of this wild and beautiful retreat. But now he had eyes for everything.

"Wal, we'll shore have hell cuttin' a road in heah," Curly was observing. "Reckon it'll have to be at the up end of the canyon."

The trail wound among big sycamores and spruces, a remarkable combination for contrast, of green and white, and silver, and of gold. The brook brawled between mossy banks of amber moss, and at the ford it was deep enough and swift enough to make the horses labor.

"Cain't cross heah in a spring an' fall freshet, thet's shore," went on Curly. "By golly! this place gets under my skin."

Blocks of red and yellow rock lay scattered beyond the gateway, with tall pines and spruces shading them, except in occasional grassy open sunlit nooks. The gray walls converged from the gate, sculptured by nature into irregular and creviced ramparts, festooned with bright-red vines and bronze lichens, and with ledges supporting little spruces, and with crags of every shape lifting weathered tops to the fringe of pines on the rim.

There was a long slow ascent thinning from forest to parklike ground, up to the old cabin. Indeed, Jim meant to preserve this relic of rustler and outlaw days.

"What's thet white thing stuck on the door? Looks like paper to me," said the sharp-eyed Bud.

Curiously they rode up to the cabin, dismounting one by one. Jim saw a dirty page of a lined notebook pegged into the rotten woodwork of the door. Upon it was scrawled in a crude but legible handwriting the word "Mañana." And under it had been drawn the rude sketch of a hash knife, somehow compelling and suggestive.

"Dog-gone! What'd they mean?" exclaimed Jim, in perplexity.

"Clear as print," replied Curly, tersely.

"Wal, heah's four bits thet Croak Malloy left thet," added Slinger.

"Well?" demanded Jim, impatiently.

"Boss, yore mind's so full of ranch an' house an'—wal, an' so forth, thet it ain't workin'," explained Bud. "Mañana means tomorrer. An' the knife says they'll come back pronto to make hash out of us."

"Oh, is that all?" returned Jim, with a laugh. "Bud, life does not seem very bright and hopeful for you just now."

"Hellno! I got brains an' six-sense eyesight," replied the gloomy cowboy.

"We'll throw the packs under the pine trees there. No sleeping in that buggy cabin for me," said Jim. "Jeff, I'd rather you didn't cook here unless it storms. You can build a fireplace under the extension of roof there. . . . Say, there's an open-roofed extension at the back, too. Used for horses. Well, here we are. Let's rustle. Slinger, your job is to use your eyes."

"Boss, there's two holes to this burrow," spoke up Bud.

"Where's the other?"

"Reckon it's aboot three miles west, where the canyon boxes," replied Curly, pointing. "Higher an' not so rough. If I recollect, the trail grades down easy. We'll cut the road through there. It'll take some blastin'."

"We'll take a chance on that end," said Jim. "Bud, I tell you what you can do. While we pitch camp you ride up and find the best place to cut our poles. But remember, it must be back in the woods, out of sight. No defacing the beauty of this property!"

"Funny how some fellars are," observed Bud, philosophizing. "Beooty first an' last, an' always in wimmen."

Then he rode away. Jim gazed after him in perplexity. "What's wrong with Bud?" he asked.

"His nose an' his feelin's are hurt," replied Cherry Winters.

"You forget, Boss. You swore you'd give him away," drawled Curly. "An' the poor kid is in love. I've seen him like this sixty-nine times."

"Rustle, you gazabos," ordered Jim, rather sharply, as he dismounted. It scarcely pleased him—the implication that Bud was in love with his sister. How true it might be and probably was! Everybody fell in love with Gloriana, who certainly was not worth such wholesale homage. Right there Jim eradicated the last remnant of foolish pride or vanity of family or whatever it was, and acknowledged to himself that Gloriana could do far worse than marry a fine, clean, fire-spirited cowboy like Curly Prentiss. Suppose Curly had looked at a good deal of red liquor—had shot a number of men, some fatally—and had been generally a wild harum-scarum cowboy? That was the way of the West—the making of a pioneer rancher. Jim was beginning to appreciate the place cowboys held in the settling of the rangeland. It could not be overestimated by any intelligent man. Thus he leaned a little, perhaps almost unconsciously, toward Curly in the vague and grave problem of his sister's future.

Jim set the outfit to work, and had no small hand in the cutting and trimming of pine poles. Bud had located a fine stand of long straight trees, growing so close together that there was scarcely any foliage except at the top. This particular grove would benefit by a good thinning out. The peeling of the green bark was no slight task. Some of the boys proved adept at that. And Bud and Lonestar were good at snaking the logs down to the cabin site. Jim had tried this "snaking" job more than once, and he simply could not do it. All it consisted of appeared to be a lasso around the pommel of the saddle, with the other end tied to the small end of the pole, and then dragging through the woods. The trick was, to keep the small sharp end of the pole off the ground, and from catching under roots and rocks. By sunset that first day there were a dozen or more skinned pines, yellow and sticky and odorous, lying in a row in the grass where Jim intended to build his wonderful house. It was an actual start. He thrilled, and thought of the dusky-eyed girl for whom he was going to make a home there.

Ten days of uninterrupted labor followed. Slinger Dunn had trailed the Hash Knife outfit to Black Brakes, the very retreat to which he had surmised they would go; and according to him they had stayed there, or at least had not ridden north on the trail toward Yellow Jacket. When Jim allowed himself to think of it he was vastly concerned. The prospect of a ranch and a home within twenty miles of the hardest and most notorious gang in Arizona was almost unthinkable. They would have to be dealt with. Nevertheless, Jim nursed a conviction that Jed Stone would turn out to be the kind of man Uncle Jim had vowed he was. To be sure, all Jim had to substantiate such faith was the fact of Stone's leaving Yellow Jacket, and an undefinable something Jim felt.

One night Jim overheard Curly and Bud talking. It was late, the fire had died down so that it cast only ruddy flickering shadows, and no doubt the boys thought Jim was sound asleep. Bud had seemed more like his true self lately, and had forgiven the blow on his nose and the affront to his vanity. He worshiped Curly like a brother.

"It's a fool job, I tell you, Curly," Bud was saying, almost in a whisper. "Like as not Malloy will burn this pile of logs while we're in Flag."

"Shore he will, or more like wait till the house is half up," agreed Curly. "But, dog-gone-it, Bud, I cain't go against the boss. He has a way of makin' me soft. Shore as hell he'll stop my drinkin'. I' jest a-rarin' fer a bust. It's due in Flag this heah trip, an' honest to God, Bud, I'll be afraid to take a drink."

"I feel the same, but I'm gonna get orful drunk onct more or die tryin'. . . . Curly, if you don't watch out Jim will argue you or coax you to stop gun-throwin'. An' then you'll be slated for a quiet rest under a pine tree!"

"Uh-ugh. I practice just the same as ever, Bud, only on the sly."

"Wal, I'm glad. If I don't miss my bet we're gonna need some gun-throwin'. Slinger don't like this 'possum-playin' of the Hash Knife. He knows. Curly, what do you think? Slinger was tellin' me he reckoned he oughta dog them rustlers, an' pick them off one at a time, with a rifle."

"Slinger cain't do thet, no more than I could. Shore I'm not Injun enough. But you know what I mean.—What'd you say, Bud?"

"I ast him why he oughta. An' he said for Molly's sake."

"Shore. Thet same thing worries me a lot. I never seen a girl love a fellar like she loves Jim. Dog-gone! It'd shore be . . . Wal, Croak Malloy will shoot Jim the first time he lays eyes on him, no matter where."

"Curly, I agree with you. Croak would. But I bet you Slinger gets to him first. Because, Curly, old pard, our backwoods cowboy is turrible in love with Gloriana May. Did you get thet?"

Curly swore surprisingly for him, and not under his breath by any means.

"Not so loud. You'll wake up somebody," admonished Bud, in a fierce whisper.

"Shore he is, Bud," admitted Curly. "But thet's nothin'. I've lost my haid. So've you, an' all the boys. The hell of it is Glory is in love with Slinger."

"Wow! You *are* out of your haid. He amuses Glory—fascinates her, mebbe, 'cause she's crazy aboot desperadoes, but thet's all, pard," returned Bud, with all the heart-warming loyalty of his nature.

"Shore sounds queer—for me to say that aboot Glory," went on Curly. "Lord knows I mean no disrespect. She's a thoroughbred. But, Bud, jest consider. She's an Easterner. She's young. She's full of sentiment an' romance. An' she's had some kind of trouble. Deep. An' it's hurt her. Wal, this damn Slinger Dunn is far better-lookin' than any of us—than any cowpuncher I ever seen. He's a wonderful chap, Bud. If I wasn't so jealous of him that I want to shoot him in the back—I—I'd love him myself. It wouldn't be so strange for a gurl like Glory to fall haid over heels in love with him. An', honest, I'm scared so I'm afraid to go to Flag."

"Nonsense! Any damn fool could hev seen you had the inside track with Glory. Sure, if you back out an' show yellow, Slinger, or somebody else, will beat you. Don't you think I'm backin' out. I reckon Glory couldn't see me with a spy-glass, but I'm in the race an' I got a flyin' start. When I raved aboot Slinger havin' her picture she gave me one, an' a darn sight newer an' prettier than his."

Curly swore again. "Wal, can you beat thet? Shore she wouldn't give one to me. . . . Women are no good, Bud."

"I wouldn't say it's thet bad, Curly," replied Bud. "They're damn hard to figger. I reckon Glory jest *likes* me. Why, she laughs an' cuts up with me. She's sorta shy with you."

"Shy nothin'. Shore I haven't seen her a lot of times—that is, to talk to. Twice at the corral—three times in the livin'-room, when I went in to see Jim—once at Babbitt's store—an' at the dance. That was the best. My Gawd! I cain't get back my breath. . . . Bud, she was only curious aboot my gun-play. It makes me sick as a dog to remember the fights I've been in, let alone talk aboot them. But she kept at me till I got mad. Then she froze an' said she guessed I wasn't much of a desperado, after all."

"Haw! Haw!" laughed Bud, low and mellow. "Curly, what thet little lady needs is a dose of Croak Malloy."

CHAPTER NINE

Jim blazed a road out of Yellow Jacket. His authority was not questioned by any one of the cowboys, but his ability as an engineer certainly was.

"You gotta drive wagons up this grade," asserted Bud, repeatedly. "You wasn't so pore runnin' a straight-line drift fence, but this hyar's a different matter. You don't savvy grades."

"All right, Bud. Maybe I'm not so darn smart as I think I am," replied Jim, laying a trap for Bud. "Suppose we go back and run it all over. You can be the engineer. That'll cut two days off our Christmas vacation in Flag. Too bad, but that road must be right."

The howl that went up from the Diamond was vociferous and derisive, and it effectually disposed of Bud.

"Aw, Boss, mebbe it ain't. I reckon it'll work out—an' any little grade can be eased up after," he rejoined, meekly.

Twenty miles on through the slowly ascending forest they struck a cattle trail which afforded good travel, and in due course led them to the Payson road, and eventually the ranch where they had left the chuck-wagon. They stayed there all night, and the following night camped at the edge of the snow, only one more day's ride to Flag.

Next afternoon late a tired, cold, dirty, unshaven, but happy group of cowboys rode into town, and there they separated. Jim had reasons to shake Curly and Bud, and they manifested no great desire to continue on with him.

Flagerstown was windy and bleak. The snow had been shoveled or had blown off the streets, down which piercing dusty gusts whipped in Jim's face. But it would have taken an unfaceable blizzard or an impassable prairie fire to have daunted Jim's soaring spirits. He had two important errands before rushing out to the ranch, and he did not want them to take long, for his horse was pretty warm. Dismounting in front of the jeweler's, Jim hurried in. The proprietor, with whom Jim had left an order, was not in, but his son was, a young Westerner whom Jim did not like.

"Mr. Miller in?" he asked.

"No. Father's out of town. But I can wait on you. . . . The diamond ring is here—if you still want it," returned the young man.

Jim stared. What in the devil did this nincompoop mean?

"Certainly I want it. I paid in advance. Let me have it, quick, please," retorted Jim.

The jeweler produced a little white box, from which glistened a beautiful diamond. Jim took it, trying to be cool, but he was burning and thrilling all over. Molly's engagement ring! It was a beauty—pretty big and valuable, he thought, now he actually saw what he had ordered. Molly would be surprised. She did not even know Jim had ordered it. And sight of her eyes, when they fell upon it, would be worth ten times the price.

"Thanks. I reckon it's all right. I was careful about size," said Jim, and pocketing the ring he strode out to his horse, which he led down the street. "Funny look that gazabo gave me," he soliloquized, thoughtfully, and he dismissed the incident by admitting to himself he must have been rather amusing to the clerk. Then he went into Babbitt's, where he had left another order, for a Christmas present for his uncle, and one for Molly. Securing the packages, which were rather large and heavy, and which he did not trouble to open, he hurried out through the store. In the men's-furnishing department a bright red silk scarf caught his eye, and he swerved to the counter.

"I'd like that red scarf," he said to the girl clerk, "and a pair of buckskin gloves."

The girl neither spoke nor moved. Then Jim looked at her—and there stood Molly Dunn, with white and agitated face. Jim was perfectly thunderstruck. Could he be dreaming? But Molly's gasp, "Oh—Jim!" proved this was reality.

"What—what does this mean?" he stammered.

"I'm workin' heah, Jim," she whispered. "Mawnin's I go to school an' afternoons I'm heah."

"For Heaven's sake!—A clerk in Babbitt's?" he exclaimed.

"Di-didn't you—get my letter?" she faltered, her eyes unnaturally large and frightened.

"Letter? No, I didn't. How could I get a letter when I've been three weeks in the woods?"

"I—I left it—with your uncle."

"Molly, I just rode in. Haven't been home. What's wrong? Why are you here?" Jim leaned against the counter, fighting to check the whirl of his thoughts. Molly's eyes suddenly expressed a poignant dismay.

"Oh, Jim—I'm so sorry—you had to come in heah—not knowin'," she cried, piteously. "I wouldn't have hurt you. . . . But I—I've left your home. . . . I've broke our engagement."

"Molly!" he ejaculated, in hoarse incredulity.

"It's true, Jim. . . . But you mustn't stand there—"

"Why, for God's sake?" he burst out.

"Please go, Jim. I—I'll see you later—an' tell you—"

"No. You can tell me here why you jilted me," he interrupted harshly.

"Missouri—I—I didn't," she said, huskily, tears streaming down her cheeks.

"Was Gloriana mean to you?" Jim suddenly demanded.

"She was lovely to me. Kind an' sweet. An' she—she tried to meet me on my own level—so I wouldn't see the difference be—between us . . . but I did. I—I wasn't fit to be her sister. I shore wasn't goin' to disgrace you. So I—I left an' come heah to work. Mother went back home to the Cibeque."

"You swear Glory didn't hurt you?"

"No, Jim, I cain't swear thet. But she never hurt me on purpose. There's nothin' mean aboot your sister. . . . I just loved her an' thet made it worse."

"Molly Dunn, you're a damn little fool," exploded Jim, overcome by a frenzy of pain and fury. "You were good enough for *any* man, let alone me. . . . But if you're as fickle—as that—"

Jim choked, and gathering up his packages he gave Molly a terrible look and rushed out of the store.

In an ordinary moment he could not have mounted his horse, burdened as he was, but he leaped astride, scarcely feeling the weight of the packages. And he spurred Baldy into a run, right down the main street of Flagerstown. The violence of action suited the violent tumult in his breast. But by the time he reached the ranch-house the furious anger had given away somewhat to consternation and a stunned surprise. That simple, honest, innocent child! But even so she might be protecting Gloriana. Jim left his horse at the barn, and taking his bundles he ran into the house and into the living-room, bursting in upon the old cattleman like a hurricane.

"Jim! Good Lord! I thought it was Injuns," exclaimed Traft. "Wal, I expected you along soon. How are you, son?"

"Howdy, Uncle?" replied Jim, throwing aside his bundles and meeting the glad hand extended. "I *was* fine, till I struck town. . . . Glad to report the Hash Knife got off Yellow Jacket without a fight."

"Jim Traft!—You're not foolin' the old man?"

"No, I'm happy to say. It's a fact, Uncle."

"Wal!—You long-headed, big-fisted tenderfoot son-of-a-gun from Mizzouri! . . . Jim, I'm clear locoed. I'm dead beat. I'm—wal, I don't know what. How'n hell did you do it?"

"I went straight to see Jed Stone."

"You braved thet outfit?" yelled Traft.

"Sure. Jed Stone was sure decent. He agreed to get out. But Croak Malloy shot a match out of my fingers, then a cigarette out of my mouth. I sure was mad. I cussed him—called him a crooked-faced little runt. He'd shot at *me* then, but Stone kicked his gun. It went off in the air. Then I piled into Croak. I banged him around—then knocked him about a mile out of the door. He was trying to get up when I went out, and I gave him a good stiff kick, and left."

"My Gawd!—Son, don't tell me you punched thet gunman, same as these cowboys?" ejaculated Traft.

"I reckon I did, Uncle. It was foolish, of course. But I was mad. And I didn't know then that the little runt was Malloy. It mightn't have made any difference."

"Croak Malloy! Beat an' kicked around by a Mizzouri tenderfoot! . . . Jim, my boy, you're as good as dead," wailed the old rancher.

"Don't you believe it," retorted Jim. "And how long do I have to serve as a tenderfoot. . . . Well, no more about the Hash Knife now. We moved up to Yellow Jacket and went to cutting poles. And on our way out we blazed a line out to the road. After the holidays we'll go back, and by spring be ready—"

Suddenly it dawned upon him that something had happened which made the home-building at Yellow Jacket a useless and superfluous task. His heart contracted and sank like cold lead.

"Wal, you're an amazin' youngster," said Traft, with his keen blue eyes full of admiration and pride. "You scare me, though. I reckon it's a more Christian thing to slug a man than to shoot him. You 'pear to have a hankerin' to use your fists. I heard aboot your hittin' Bambridge in the station at Winslow. You never told me that, you sly young dog. Didn't want to worry your old uncle, huh? . . . Wal, I can see you've more on your mind. An' I'll wait to hear aboot Bambridge, the Hash Knife deal, an' Yellow Jacket."

"Uncle, I ran into Babbitt's, and there, behind a counter, was Molly," burst out Jim, and the mere telling of it aloud caused a regurgitation of fierce emotions. "She's broken our engagement. . . . She's gone to work. . . . I'm stunned."

"Jim, don't take it too hard," replied the old rancher, soothingly. "Don't imagine it a permanent break. Why, she done it because she loves you so much. She came to me an' told me, Jim. How she wasn't good enough for you—she hadn't the courage to marry you—your family would stick up their noses at her, an' all that sort of thing. I tried to argue her out of goin'. But she's a stubborn little minx. Independent, an' proud, too, in her way. So I jest told her thet you'd understand, but you'd never take her at her word. She cried at thet. Jim, she couldn't hold out against you for five minutes. So don't let it break you all up."

"My word, Uncle, but you're a life-saver," replied Jim, with intense relief. "It's bad enough. Lord knows, but if there's any hope I can stand it. Do you think Glory made it hard for Molly?"

"Wal, I reckon she did," said Traft, seriously. "An' all the time she was tryin' to put poor Molly at her ease. But she couldn't. An' that'll never come until Molly gets Glory on her own ground. Then there'll be a balance struck. Glory an' I have got on fine, Jim. She's a comfort to me, an' has been confidin' a little of her troubles at home. I reckon we'll never let her go back."

"No, we'll keep her out West. Uncle, how is she? Has her health improved?"

"Wal, Glory's got thet bad cough yet, an' she gains but slow. I reckon she has improved. It'll take summer an' outdoors among the pines an' cedars to make her strong again. Suppose you hunt her up. Then after supper you can get the rest off your chest."

"All right, Uncle, but just one word more," returned Jim, eagerly. "You tell me not to fear a permanent break with Molly. When she's made it, already! I'm sick. I'm dumbfounded. I was so furious I called her a damn little fool."

"So she is. An' thet won't hurt your cause none. Now, Jim, don't fall into this broken-heart cowboy style an' go to drinkin'. I tell you Molly worships the ground you walk on. An' if I was you I'd jest go an' pack her back home here to the ranch."

"Pack her?" echoed Jim, aghast.

"Shore. She won't come willin', not very soon. So I'd jest fetch her back by force. A good spankin' wouldn't do no harm. But I reckon you haven't the nerve enough for thet. Molly has given the town people lots to gossip about. Glory will tell you. An' you in turn can give them somethin' to gossip about."

"Ahuh. . . . Thanks, Uncle," rejoined Jim, soberly. "I'll consider your advice. It appeals to me, especially the spanking part."

Jim left the living-room, absent-mindedly fingering the ring box in his pocket. He did not take all his uncle had said as absolute gospel, but it had surely checked the riot of his feelings. Then he knocked at Gloriana's door.

"Who's there?" she called, in rather a startled voice.

Some devil beset Jim, perhaps the besetting sin of his joke-loving cowboys, and without reflection he announced in a gruff voice:

"Darnell."

He heard an exclamation, followed by quick footsteps, and a sudden locking of the door.

"You nagging scoundrel!" called Gloriana, her voice ringing. "The nerve of you! I'm sick of your chasing after me. Get out of this house or I'll scream for my uncle. You'll reckon with Jim and his cowboys for the way you've treated me."

Jim was thunderstruck again, though in a vastly different way.

"Oh, Glory," he cried, "it's only Jim. I thought I was being funny."

"Jim!"

"Sure. Don't you know my voice? I just rode in. Had a word with Uncle and here I am."

"Are you—alone?" she asked, fumbling at the lock.

Wherewith she opened the door to disclose a lovely though most agitated countenance. Jim went in, stricken at the scare he had evidently given her.

"Glory, I'm darn sorry. I don't know what possessed me—to think of that fellow Darnell. Please forgive me."

"Have you heard—anything?" she asked, searching his face with darkly troubled eyes.

"About Darnell? I think I did hear that name. Before I left for Yellow Jacket. But I only just got back. Saw Molly! . . . Imagine my luck! I ran in Babbitt's—and almost fell over her. We had a few words, sister. . . . Then I came home. Saw Uncle for a minute. . . . Aren't you glad to see me?"

"Glad!" she echoed, with a deep rich note. A flash of light, like a golden warmth, seemed to erase the havoc from her face. She closed the door and enveloped Jim. Her embrace, her kisses, were inexpressibly sweet to him that moment. And he hugged her in a way which left no doubt about his own gladness.

"You great big handsome hairy—bear!" she cried, breathlessly. "You look like a tramp. You smell like horses and smoke. . . . Oh, Jim, I'm so glad to see you!"

"We're square on that, then," he said. "Come to the fire. Gee! I'm nearly frozen. I've been so knocked out I hardly knew it was cold. Let me look at you." Turning his back to the cheerful blazing logs, he placed a hand on each of her shoulders and ran searching eyes over her face and form, and back again to her face. It was lovelier than ever—with a subtle change not wholly of more rounded contour and a hint of color, but of less strain. She had rested. She had gained, as he ascertained mostly by the feel of her shoulders.

"Well, what's your verdict?" she asked, meeting his gaze with a wistful smile. Gloriana's eyes had the inscrutable quality of beauty that was a blending of purple hue and a light which anyone might well mistake. But Jim saw deeper, and he was satisfied.

"I couldn't ask more. You're on the mend."

"Jim, I was fine until that damned Darnell turned up here in Flag," she replied. "I told you he would. It was a couple of weeks ago. But I found out before I saw him. He came here—coaxed and threatened. I told him I would have absolutely nothing more to do with him. He has bobbed up every time I went downtown, to stores, post-office, everywhere. Finally I stayed home. And you bet I was angry when I took you for him."

"What's he doing out here, Glory?" asked Jim.

"He followed me. But he'll have more than one string to his bow. Said he had gone to work for a rancher named Bambridge—"

"Oh, I remember now," interrupted Jim. "I saw him that day at the station. So your erstwhile beau has thrown in with Bambridge? Interesting—and funny."

"Jim, it's not funny to me," she spoke up, hurriedly. "I'm afraid of Darnell. He's a two-faced slicker. But he has become acquainted in town. He's already popular with the girls, I'm deathly afraid."

"Of what?" laughed Jim. He was in fact a little amused at the way he found his Western development disposed of Mr. Darnell.

"He'll talk about me—disgrace you, hurt you in Flag."

"Talk about you, will he? Glory, what do you suppose Curly Prentiss or Slinger Dunn would do—if he so much as spoke one slighting word of you?"

"I—I can't imagine, Jim," she replied, her great eyes dilating.

"Well, it will be funny—unless I get to him first. . . . Glory dear, this Darnell has no claim on you?"

"No, Jim, on my honor," she replied.

"Then dismiss him from your mind. He has struck the wrong place to hound a girl."

"I'm afraid he'll wheedle Uncle out of money," went on Gloriana, slowly yielding to relief.

"Ha! Ha! That's funny. He can't do it, Glory. He's not slick enough. Besides, he has gotten in with the wrong rancher. Bambridge is a cattle thief. We know it, and we can prove it presently. Darnell will have to step mighty slow and careful."

"Oh-h!" sighed Gloriana, and leaned her head against him. Jim could feel the quick beat of her pulse. How sensitive, how highly organized she was!

"Have you had any other trouble, sister? Come out with it."

"Yes, with Molly. Jim, she's the sweetest kid. Honestly, I just fell in love with her. But I made a tactless start. I wanted only to help her. She misunderstood. She thought I was stuck up, and she got the idea she wasn't good enough for you. When she told me she was leaving here I begged and I scolded. I talked sense to her. I argued myself hoarse. I was sincere, too. Only she imagined me afraid of you and lying to her. Then I lost my temper—I have one, if you remember, Jim—and I—well, I made it worse by telling her how lucky she was—that you meant to marry her. . . . But she has a will of her own. She left. And I haven't been able to get her back. I've been to that store I don't know how many times. Then I heard Molly had met Darnell—one of the Flag girls, Elsie Roberts, told me. And she went to a dance with him. I—"

"Molly went to a dance with this Darnell?"

"Yes, she did. But, Jim, you mustn't hold it against her," entreated Gloriana. "She's only a child. I went right downtown and told Molly who and what Darnell was. She didn't believe me. Darnell is attractive and smooth. She doesn't care a rap for him, because she worships you, Jim. But in her present state of mind she'd do anything. And Darnell is dangerous and unscrupulous. If I had not been pretty wise—despite my infatuation—he'd have ruined me. You mustn't lose any time getting Molly out of his clutches."

"My God! . . . Do I want her?" groaned Jim, dropping his head.

"Yes, you want her. So do I. And so does Uncle Jim. Molly is a treasure. No matter *what* she does, you must stand it, bear with her, and get her back."

Jim raised his head to kiss Gloriana gratefully. "Thanks, Glory. You couldn't have said anything that would mean so much to me. I love that kid. It'd *kill* me to lose her. . . . But Uncle Jim bucked me up, and now so have you. . . . Here's her engagement ring. Isn't it a beauty?"

Gloriana looked at the jewel with eyes that sparkled like it.

"She wouldn't be human if that didn't fetch her. . . . But, Jim, Molly is Western. Diamonds might mean nothing at all to her. Still, I know she loves pretty clothes. She told me she went in debt for a new dress to wear at the Christmas dance."

"Molly certainly must be human and wholly feminine," said Jim, with a tinge of bitterness. "In love with me last month—engaged to me. Now she's going to a dance with another fellow. I call it pretty raw."

"She wrote you—begged Uncle Jim to send it by a rider. But Uncle wouldn't do it. . . . And Molly is just wild with regret and pain and wounded love. Any girl is in peril under a mood of that kind. She wants the town people to *believe* she's no good, so that they can't think she jilted you. It's a sad little story, Jim. But now you're here it will be all right. I *know* it, Jim, unless you're an utter jealous fool. Trust me. I know girls. Molly only needs to learn that you do love her for herself and that neither you, nor I, nor anyone could be ashamed of her—to be the sweetest and happiest girl in the world. That's your job, brother mine. And it beats building the drift fence."

"Glory, I can prove it—with you and Uncle to help. Gosh! I feel as if a mountain had been lifted off my heart. . . . Now what festivities are in order for the holidays?"

"Oh, Flag is quite a social place," laughed Gloriana. "But the dance Christmas Eve, and the party here on the following Wednesday night, are the outstanding events. Uncle is giving that for Molly. She, of course, thinks it's off because she left. But Uncle says no. Wait till Jim comes."

"It's not off, Glory," declared Jim, grimly. "Molly will be here if I have to pack her."

"Romantic, to say the least," replied Gloriana, with a trill of laughter. "I approve. . . . And now, Jim, tell me about Slinger and Curly. And don't forget Bud. He's a dear."

"Your Three Guardsmen, eh?" rejoined Jim, dryly. "They've managed to live together without actual murder. Slinger looks at his rivals and listens in silent contempt, as down upon lesser men who did not share his secret of power."

Because of the whiteness of Gloriana's face even a little wave of color appeared a startling blush.

"Do they talk about me, among themselves?" she asked, a little confused.

"For three weeks you have shared conversation honors with the Hash Knife."

"How flattering! And what do they say?"

"I've forgotten most of it. At first I got kind of sore. They talked right out before me, with the utmost candor. They were all going to marry you, I gathered. To be sure, murder must be committed. It was funny. You should have been around to listen."

"They are the most amusing fellows—just fascinating to me."

"So I've gathered. Well, dearest, out West you reap as you sow. . . . One day I came back to camp and found Bud with a bloody nose. Curly, his pard, his almost brother, had punched him for talking about your legs."

"Wha-at!" gasped Gloriana.

"Sure. I ascertained that Bud said you had pretty legs and you knew it. Curly took that as an insult and bloodied Bud's nose. When I got there Bud was nursing his nose and his wounded vanity. I thought it a good opportunity for an object lesson, so I pretended tremendous anger, when I really wanted to split with laughter. I threw Bud down on the grass, straddled him, and threatened to smash his face unless he recognized his offense, apologized, and took it back. Do you know, Glory, he couldn't see any offense, although he apologized. But he swore it was true and he wouldn't take it back. Then I conceived the idea of greater punishment for Bud by giving him away to you. He almost wept at this, begged me to beat him, said he could stand anything except you thinking Curly a hero and him a low-down skunk, or something."

"I—I don't know what to say," replied Gloriana, but it was plain to Jim that she wanted to laugh.

"Glory, I told you—gave you fair warning. If you flirt with these cowboys you must pay dearly for it. And of course you have flirted, if not intentionally, then some other way. It won't do out here. These boys have hearts of gold. Every last one of them would die for you. They seem like some kind of inflammable tinder. So easy, cool, droll, yet underneath all fire. Curly Prentiss is the highest type of cowboy I know. He is a prince. All the same he's a strutting, conceited jackass who needs a lesson. Bud is the best-hearted of the lot, honest as the day. He speaks right out what he thinks. A raw, crude, common sort of person to any superficial observer from the East, but to me, or Uncle Jim, or anyone who sees clearly, he's a boy to love. The rest of the outfit trail along somewhat similarly, except Slinger Dunn. He's not a cowboy. He's a strange mixture of woodsman and Indian, of country boy and chivalrous gentleman. All the same, if I were you I'd be careful of what I said or did before him."

"I'm afraid it's too late," replied Gloriana, with gravity. "You took us to the hospital to see him. He had my picture under his pillow. Told me right out he'd gazed at it until he was terribly in love with *me.* That you had taken Molly from him and he was going to take me from you."

"Well, I'm a son-of-a-gun!" ejaculated Jim.

"I should have squelched him at once," admitted Gloriana. "But I didn't. I didn't take him seriously. Thought that was just Western. And at a dance here I'm afraid I made it worse. He—"

"Glory, darling," interrupted Jim, plaintively, "I don't want to know any more. I've trouble of my own. I need your help—not to be staggered with your love affairs."

"Silly! My love affairs? The idea!" she retorted, but her cheeks were red.

"But you can't dodge them. I *told* you how to handle these cowboys. Did you listen? I should smile not."

"Misery loves company. We are in a mess, Jim. Only yours is serious. Molly is stubborn as a mule. I forgot to tell you that some of the Flag girls became very friendly to me, but they snubbed poor Molly. That hurt her— and somehow she associates it with her relation to you and me."

"Ahuh. I see. Glory, those same girls snubbed me, too, at first. Then when they found out I was old Jim Traft's nephew they changed their tune. But nix—I wasn't interested. They were jealous of Molly—the cats. . . . Well, I shall move mountains to make them worse."

Gloriana laid her cheek against Jim's rough and grimy face, oblivious of that or indifferent to it, and she gave vent to a long sigh.

"I'm glad you're back," she said. "I've been lonely, only I didn't guess it. You're a comfort. . . . Jim, when spring comes you must take me to your camp. I'll get well there—and be safer, if you want to know."

CHAPTER TEN

Next morning Jim awakened very early, and lay in bed pondering his problem and mapping out a deliberate course of what he intended to do. He fortified himself against mortification, embarrassment, against all possible contingencies liable to inflame him, and set the limit short of heartbreak. He simply would not and could not face the thought of losing Molly.

It was the 23rd of December, less than two days before the Christmas Eve dance. His leave of absence from work on Yellow Jacket would expire on New Year's day, following which he and the Diamond outfit must ride back to the range for a long and surely trying stay. Wherefore he had no time to lose. But first he must consult his uncle and Locke, report every detail pertaining to what had happened down at Yellow Jacket, and, consistent with their advice, plan future work.

After breakfast, at which Gloriana was not present, Jim asked for a conference with his uncle and Locke. They repaired at once to the living-room. Jim began with his discovery of Diamond-branded cattle going aboard the train with Bambridge's shipment from Winslow, and slighted nothing in his narrative of what had followed, nor any of his conjectures and convictions, and lastly, the opinions of his men. After he had concluded, his superiors smoked furiously, which appeared their only indication of mental disturbance. Locke was the first to break silence: "I advise givin' up Yellow Jacket."

"Naw," replied Traft, laconically.

"I don't want to," added Jim. "It's a wild, lonely, wonderful wilderness. I want to own it—improve it—and live there part of the year, at least."

"Wal, aside from Jim's leanin' to Yellow Jacket, I wouldn't let it go now," went on Traft. "It'd be givin' in to Bambridge, an' I'll see him in hell first."

"Short an' sweet," said Locke, with a dry cackle. He knew his employer of old. "Then I suggest we arrange some plan of transportin' Mr. Bambridge to the place you name."

"Aw, Ring, don't get funny. This is business. . . . How many head of unbranded stock can you round up this spring?"

"Matter of ten thousand, more or less, countin' new calves."

"Wal, slap the Diamond brand on half of them, this comin' round-up," ordered the rancher, brusquely.

Locke wrote in his notebook, then said: "I'd advise no cattle drive to Yellow Jacket till spring. Let the rustlers have a chance at the lower range."

"Reckon thet's a good idea. Put it down. Now, Jim, tell Locke what you want for the house. He'll order it. Meanwhile the sleddin' will be good an' we'll haul all supplies such as hardware, cement, tools, powder, down to Cottonwood Ranch, an' store it there. Lumber, framework, bricks, and all such to follow fast as it gets here. When the ground dries in the spring you can haul in over your new road. . . . As for the present, wal, stick to our original plan. Take the Diamond back to Yellow Jacket an' clean it up—of varmints, rubbish, an' such, includin' any rustlers who might come burnin' your good firewood. . . . Savvy?"

"Yes, sir," replied Jim, quickly.

"Got thet down, Locke?" queried the old rancher, as he rose and knocked the ash off his cigar.

"I'll put it down," replied the superintendent.

"Wal, don't pester me with this two-bit stuff any more," replied Traft, testily. "Help Jim all you can. It's up to him." And he stalked out sturdily, his shaggy head erect, leaving Jim alone with the superintendent.

"Shorter an' sweeter," said Locke, tapping his book with his pencil.

"Gosh!—I never heard Uncle talk like that. What ails him?"

"He's sore at Bambridge. Small wonder. He's had forty years buckin' the crooked side of cattle-raisin', an' he hates it. . . . Jim, he's given you a man-size job. But you've got a hard crew in the Diamond. They're good fer it. Jed Stone's movin' off your range strikes me deep. It means a lot, besides his bein' decent. I've a hunch he's about through, some way or another. But Malloy will have to be reckoned with. If you ever meet him, anyhow, under *any* circumstances, shoot quick an' think afterwards. Don't ever fail to pack a gun, an' keep Slinger or Curly close to you."

"Ring—you mean here—at home—in town?" queried Jim, aghast.

"I should smile."

"Whew!—When will I ever learn?"

"You've been shot once, an' shot at a number of times. Don't you savvy what it means? Come down on the hard ground, Jim."

After that conference, which left Jim with a keen poignant sense of responsibility, he stayed in his room until after dinner and then started for town on foot. Any sharp observer, at least a Westerner, could have detected the bulge of a gun back of his hip, and the tip of a leather sheath projecting an inch or two below his coat. How he longed for the cool imperturbability of Curly Prentiss or the aloof unapproachableness of Slinger Dunn! But these he could never attain, for he had not been born to the West. Jim had to make determination do for confidence. And when, in accordance with his plan, he walked into Babbitt's store, no one would have guessed the sinking sensation he had in his vitals. He was terribly afraid of Molly Dunn, not to mention the gunman Croak Malloy. Jim knew he was something of a lion when under the sway of righteous anger, but most assuredly he could not muster that at will.

Molly stood behind the counter, and from her wide startled eyes he gathered that she had seen him first. It was early and he appeared to be the only customer present, and at once the object of much interest, both of which facts did not confuse him one whit.

"Good day, Molly," he said, doffing his sombrero. "Yesterday I forgot what I wanted to buy."

"Howdy—Jim," she faltered, huskily, the scarlet coming up from neck to face.

How the sight made Jim's blood leap! She could not be indifferent to his presence.

"I want that red silk scarf and a pair of buckskin gloves," he said.

Molly produced the scarf, and then, with the other clerks snickering openly, she had to try glove after glove on Jim's hand, until he was satisfied with the fit. Her little brown fingers trembled so that she was scarcely able to perform the task; and Jim gloated over this manifestation of weakness, instead of feeling sorry for her.

"Thanks. I reckon these will do," he said, at length. "Please charge to the Traft account. . . . I shall tell Mr. Babbitt you are a very beautiful clerk, but a poor saleswoman."

Molly was staring at the gun-sheath under his coat. Her eyes had been quick to see it.

"Jim!—You're packin' a gun!" she exclaimed, breathlessly and low.

"I should snigger I am, as Bud would say," he replied, facetiously.

"Who for?" she whispered, and it was significant that she did not say what for.

"Well, if you care to know, that Hash Knife gunman, Croak Malloy, is looking for me—and *I* am looking for a fellow named Ed Darnell," concluded Jim, and heartless though he knew himself, it was impossible to look into her eyes then. He took his parcels and went out, most acutely conscious of bursting veins and thrilling nerves.

Jim walked down the street, dropping in at all the business places where his uncle had dealings. Then he visited the saloons, which were more numerous and to him vastly more interesting. He acted, too, like a man who was looking for some one. Next he called at the post-office and the hotel, after which he returned to Babbitt's store.

Molly did not see him enter. She was busy with a customer, which occupation permitted Jim a moment to devour her sweet face with hungry eyes. She looked paler and thinner than he had ever seen her; and these evidences of trouble were dear to Jim's heart. She had not done this cruel thing without suffering. Presently she finished with her customer and espied Jim.

"You again?" she queried, blushing furiously.

"I forgot something, Molly," he drawled.

"Somethin' you wanted to buy?" she went on, a little sarcastically.

"Yes, but I forget. Whenever I see your sweet face I forget everything. . . . Oh yes, buckskin gauntlets for the cowboys—the fringed ones with a horseshoe design on the back. Christmas gifts, you know. My size will do."

"How many pairs?" she asked.

"Have you forgotten how many cowboys in my outfit?"

She did not reply and presently sorted out the gloves, wrapped them into a parcel and handed it to him. This time he fixed upon her reproachful piercing eyes.

"Molly, you are to understand that I do not accept my dismissal," he said, deliberately. "I am sorry you feel so. I—I forgive you, I guess. . . . And I'll not give you up."

"But, Jim, everybody heah knows," she said, shrinkingly.

"What?"

"Thet I gave—you up—'cause I wasn't good enough—for you."

Jim could scarcely refrain from leaning over the counter and snatching her to his breast.

"I know, Molly. But you're terribly mistaken. Uncle Jim knows you're good enough for me. I know you're too good for me or anyone else. And Glory, she's heart and soul for you."

"Jim, I reckon you're somethin' of a liar," she returned, a red spot forming on each cheek.

"Ordinarily, yes, but not in this," he said, cheerfully. "Anyway, it doesn't make the slightest difference who and what you are. You're going to be Mrs. James Traft."

"I—I am—not."

"You bet you are. . . . Oh yes, that reminds me. I forgot something else. Look here." He slipped the little ring-box out of his pocket, and bending over the counter opened the lid. The big blue-white diamond seemed to leap up. Jim glanced quickly at Molly's face. And that was enough, almost even for him.

"I thought you'd like it," he said, remorsefully, but not now meeting her tragic eyes. "We'll try it on first chance. . . . So long, till tomorrow."

Taking up his purchases, Jim hurried out, his pulse tingling, his heart singing. Molly loved him still. And all the way out the bleak cold road he could have danced. Upon arriving home he went in to see Gloriana, who was gorgeously arrayed in a dressing-gown and demonstratively glad to see him. Jim recounted his adventure to Glory.

"Men are brutes, devils, fiends," responded his sister. "But since the female of the species is what she is and self-preservation the first law of life, I don't see what else you can do. Hurry and get Molly back here."

"Give me a little time, Glory," declared Jim, somewhat daunted.

"Get her here before she goes to the dance with that darn Darnell," advised Gloriana, with a wonderful purple flash of eyes.

"Reckon I don't want to, till afterwards. I sure am curious to see how she acts—and, Darnell too—and what the cowboys do."

"Will you tell them?"

"I will, you bet, and between you and me, Glory, I wouldn't be in Darnell's boots for a million."

"You are beginning to make me feel the same way. . . . Jim, you showed the ring to Molly?"

"Yes—and you should have seen her eyes. Oh!—I felt like a coyote, but, gosh! I was happy."

"It's a lovely ring, Jim. Let me have it a little—just to look at. I won't put it on."

"Sure. But wait till I come back from the bunk-house. I want to show it to the boys."

"Jim, if you're going to tell them about Darnell, put it strong."

"Huh! Trust me. I've already told them something. . . . Glory, I don't feel so sick this afternoon."

"You loving goose!—Heigho! I wish somebody loved *me* that way."

"That's funny. As if you hadn't had and didn't have more love than any girl ever had."

"But, Jim, only to be loved because you're pretty!" she exclaimed. "Would even these sentimental cowboys love me—if they knew I couldn't cook, sew, bake, darn a sock—that I'm a useless ornament—that the thought of babies scares me stiff?"

"Sure they would. Men *are* loving geese, Glory. Don't worry. Only begin to deserve it."

He made his way to the bunk-house, finding all the boys in, as he had expected, and recovered from any indulgence they might have treated themselves to the night before.

"Fellars, hyar's the boss, lookin' like a thundercloud," announced Bud.

"Packin' a gun, too, the Mizzouri hayseed," added Curly.

Their separate greetings were all in the nature of comment upon his appearance. The moment seemed propitious and Jim chose to act upon it.

"Boys, friends, pards," he began, dramatically, "if it weren't for my sister and you I'd blow my brains out."

Silence! Staring eyes and awed lean faces attested to the felicity of his acting.

"Why, Jim, what the hell?" uttered Curly, without his drawl.

"Listen. Let me tell it quick," he announced, hurriedly. "We go back to Yellow Jacket after New Year's. No more town till spring, if then. The old man is sore at Bambridge—at this two-bit rustling. We've got the job of clearing the range of varmints, rubbish, rustlers, and so forth. He'll throw five thousand head of cattle on to Yellow Jacket in less than a year. That's that, and it isn't a marker to what I'm going to tell you."

As he paused, Curly interposed, coolly: "Wal, Boss, maybe it isn't a marker, whatever thet is, but it's sure rattlesnake poison, gunpowder, and bad whisky, all mixed up."

"Let me get it off my chest," went on Jim. "Maybe you remember I hinted of a fellow named Darnell, who made trouble for my sister back in Missouri. Anyway, he's here in Flag. Has taken a job with Bambridge. He has been hounding poor Glory until she has stopped going to town. She is deathly afraid of him. Afraid he will disgrace me by talking about her. Mind you—Glory is straight and fine and good. So don't get the wrong hunch. She was only a crazy girl and this Darnell is a man, handsome, slick as the devil, a gambler and cheat at cards, and crooked otherwise. He beat Glory out of money, and my father, too. She thinks he'll beat Uncle Jim the same way. But you all know Darnell can't fool the old man. . . . Now does that sink in?"

"Wal, it shore doesn't sink very deep in me, Boss," drawled Curly. "Mister Darnell has shore picked an awful unhealthy climate."

"You saw Darnell with Bambridge that day at the station."

"Shore. An' thet was enough fer me an' Bud an' all of the outfit."

"All right . . . here's the worst—Lord! how am I to get—it out?" continued Jim, and now he did not need to simulate trouble. He was genuine. He felt clammy and nauseated. He paced a step here and there, flung himself upon the chair before the fire, and all but tore his hair in his distress and shame.

"Molly Dunn has—jilted me. Broken her engagement—left my uncle's house. . . . Says she's not good enough to marry me. And it's just the other way around. Poor kid! Just let that sink in, will you? . . . She's a clerk in Babbitt's store in the afternoons. Mornings she goes to school. All that's tough, boys. But listen to this. She's going around with that — — — Darnell! . . . I can't realize it, let alone understand it. But Glory says Molly is only distracted—out of her head—that it's really because she loves me she's done it. Wants everybody in Flag to *see* she's not good enough for us! That's why she's carrying on with this Darnell. I'm so sorry for her I—I could cry. And so mad I could bite nails. And so scared I can't think."

Jim paused for breath. What relief to get this confession made! When he looked up he gathered a singular conception of the regard in which he was held by the Diamond. It was rather a big moment for him.

Slinger Dunn, without a word, put on his cap and glided noiselessly toward the door.

"Hold on, Slinger. Where are you going?"

Dunn turned. At any moment his sloe-black eyes were remarkable; just now they made Jim shiver.

"I was shore wonderin' why my sister hadn't sent fer me to come up to the house," he said. "An' I reckon it's aboot time I hunted her up. Then I'll take a look round fer this Darnell fellar."

"Slinger, by all means go see Molly, but let Darnell alone for the present," rejoined Jim, earnestly.

"Jim, air you electin' to boss me aboot Molly?" asked Slinger.

"No indeed, Slinger. Only asking you to wait."

"What fer?"

There did not appear to be much to wait for, Jim admitted to himself, and he felt he had been hasty in stating the case to these firebrands.

"Listen, Slinger, and all of you," said Jim. "Tomorrow night is this Christmas Eve dance. We'll all go. We'll look this Darnell over. I won't do anything and I ask you not to—until after that. But understand me. I—I couldn't stick it out here in the West without Molly. You all know how I care for her. It's far more serious for me than the Hash Knife deal. . . . I've confided my intimate feelings because I believe you all my pards. I reckon I'll be laughed at and ridiculed by the Flagerstown young people, as I was at first. But I don't care. All I care for is to get Molly back, to make a home for Glory, and to have the Diamond stick to me."

Curly might have been spokesman for the outfit. Usually in critical cases he assumed that position. Now he laid a lean brown pressing hand upon Jim's shoulder.

"Jim, all this heah Diamond cares for is thet you grow a little more Western overnight," he drawled, in his careless, cool, inflexible tone, that seemed to carry such moment. Curly's ultimatum intimated so much. It embodied all of Jim's longings. He divined in that cowboy's droll words an unutterable and unquenchable loyalty, and more, the limitless spirit and the strength of all that the wild range engendered.

"By Heaven—I will!" cried Jim, ringingly, as he leaped to his feet.

CHAPTER ELEVEN

Jim had resisted an impulse to bribe the cowboys to call in a body and singly at Babbitt's store to make purchases of Molly and incidentally remind her of him.

In his own case, he went downtown late, and everywhere except Babbitt's, trying to screw up his courage. It was not that overnight he had not become transposed to a thorough Arizonian, but that his genuine tenderness for Molly had asserted itself. This he knew he should not yield to. Still he did. On several occasions he espied some of his cowboys, laden with bundles, mysteriously gay and full of the devil. They had not required prompting to do the very thing he had so sneakingly desired. He could just imagine the drawling, persuasive Curly telling Molly she was out of her "haid." And Bud—what that cherubic volcanic friend would say was beyond conjecture. And Slinger! Jim had forgotten that Slinger was Molly's brother, her guardian, in his own estimation, at any rate. It rather frightened Jim to guess what Slinger would do, considering he was not given to much speech. And the rest of the cowboys—they would drive Molly frantic in their Western fashion.

Ruminating thus, Jim lounged in the lobby of the hotel. All of a sudden he saw Molly go into Davis' store, on the far corner. He jumped. It was only four o'clock, and she should have at least another hour of work. What a chance! It quite took his breath. He went out, crossed the street, and stood back in a hallway, close to the door of the store, where he could see and scarcely be seen. Once he had to dodge back to escape detection when Lonestar and Cherry passed, each with a load of packages. "Gosh!" ejaculated Jim. "They've been in Babbitt's. I can tell by the wrapping-paper on those parcels."

He had to wait what seemed an endless while before Molly appeared. Then he stepped out as if by magic, and Molly bumped into him. It startled her so that she uttered a cry and dropped some of her bundles. Jim picked them up, and rising he coolly faced the scarlet Molly and appropriated the rest of her parcels.

"I reckon I'll carry these. Where are you going?" he said, naturally, with a smile.

Molly looked both furious and helpless. Evidently this was the last straw. "You—you—"

"Careful, honey, this is the main thoroughfare of Flag. People all about. If you want to swear, wait till we get somewhere."

"Jim Traft—I could swear—a blue streak," she replied, and her appearance certainly verified her words.

"Shore, but it ain't ladylike, as Bud would say," he drawled. "Molly, I'm going to talk to you or die in the attempt. Where are you going?"

"Home. To my boardin'-house," she said, a little mockingly.

"Well, I'll pack your load for you," returned Jim. He dropped one of them, and in securing it let several others slip, and had quite a time recovering them all. As he rose he thought he detected Molly averting dusky hungry eyes. Just on the moment Sue Henderson passed. She gave them a bright smile and said: "Hello, you-all! Everybody Christmasing. See you tonight."

Jim answered with a cheerful, "Howdy!" but Molly's response was unintelligible. Then she said: "If you must make it wuss for me—"

"Darling, don't say wuss. Say worse. . . . Come—which way?"

That epithet had the desired effect. Jim had discovered its potency and had used it sparingly. Just now it caused Molly's blaze to dim and pale. She started off. Jim caught up with her at the corner, which she turned into the side street. They walked in silence. The bleak wind swept straight down this street from the mountains and it was like icy blades. Molly did not look warmly clad. Her coat was wholly inadequate for such weather. Jim longed to speak of the fur coat he had bought for her, but this was not the moment.

"You played me a low-down trick," she said, presently, coldly.

"Me? I sure did not. How so?"

"You set thet Diamond outfit onto me."

"Molly! I swear I didn't. Honest. You know I wouldn't lie," replied Jim, most earnestly.

"You shore would. You'd do anythin'."

"But I protest my innocence."

"Innocence?—You!" She gave him her eyes for a second. Jim felt shot through with black and gold arrows.

"Sure I'm innocent. I thought how good it'd be to send the gang in on you—if for nothing else than to remind you of my existence. But I didn't. Not only that, Molly, but yesterday I actually kept Slinger from hunting you up."

"Wal, you shore didn't this heah day. . . . Oh, it was—turrible!" Her voice broke, close to a sob.

"Molly!—I'm sorry. What'd Slinger do?"

"I wouldn't tell you. I—I wouldn't give you the satisfaction. But I'll never forgive him—or you, either."

"Gee! he must have given you 'most as much as you deserve," said Jim, laconically.

Molly's recollection, coupled with Jim's good-natured sarcasm, proved too much for her reticence. "He disgraced me," she burst out, almost weeping. "Right there in the store—before two of the clerks, an' thet gabby old Mrs. Owens—who'll tell it all over."

"What'd Slinger say, honey?"

"Stop callin' me them sweet names," flashed Molly, in desperation. "I cain't stand it. I'll run away from heah or do somethin' turrible."

"You have already done something 'turrible,' only you don't know it," responded Jim. "I'll try to remember not to be sentimental. . . . Tell me what Slinger said."

"Nothin' 'cept, 'come heah, you moon-eyed calf!' . . . I was paralyzed when I seen him come in. I couldn't run. Slinger's eyes are shore turrible. He reached over the counter an' said—what I told you. Then he grabbed me by my blouse—it's a way he has—only this time he pulled me half over the counter—face down—an'—an' smacked me so hard you could have heahed it out in the street. . . . I won't be able to—to set down at dinner! . . . An' then he said he'd see me later."

Jim kept a straight face, gazing ahead on the wintry street. How he wanted to shout!

"Turrible," he agreed. "For a grown girl. . . . And what did the cowboys do?"

"Drove me mad. One by one, in two an' threes—the whole outfit," said Molly, woefully. "Not one single word aboot you, Jim Traft, but all the same it was all for you. The sweet things they said to me aboot the dance tonight—aboot the party Unc—Mr. Traft was goin' to give me—Christmas presents—"

"Uncle *is* going to give the party for you," interposed Jim.

"They were darned nice," went on Molly, ignoring his statement. "You know durin' the holidays Mr. Babbitt gives us clerks ten percent on all sales. Curly Prentiss heahed aboot thet. An', Jim, the sons-of-guns cleaned me out. Bought every last thing in my department. Mr. Babbitt was thunderstruck an' tickled to death. He complimented me, as if *I* had anythin' to do with the idiots squanderin' their money. They spent all the cash they had, an' went in debt for hundreds of dollars. They'll never get the money to pay up. An' thet Bud Chalfack! . . . I cain't tell you aboot him."

"Sure you can, Molly. Go on. It's very thrilling. And maybe telling me will make it easier for you," persuaded Jim.

"I've only Curly's word for it," returned Molly. "But he swore Bud bought the finest set of furniture—a bedroom set—Babbitt's had on hand. For *me.* For a Christmas present—an'—an' weddin' present together. Bud said he's shore be daid or broke when thet weddin' comes off. . . . An' I'm afraid he'll be daid."

"The extravagant sons-of-guns!" ejaculated Jim, amazed and chagrined. "They had to go overdo it. Buyin' you some presents—or even buyin' out the store—was all right. But I reckon the—the rest was tactless, to say the least. Molly, you'll have to excuse it. They can't take you seriously, any more than can I."

Molly stopped before a modest little brown cottage, almost at the end of the street. Jim made a note of the single large pine tree in the yard, for future emergency, when he wished to find Molly after dark.

"This is where I board," she said, simply.

"Are you comfortable here?" asked Jim, anxiously.

"I'm used to cold. But there's a stove in the parlor. Come in."

Jim was elated that she should trust him so far as to ask him inside. The modest little parlor was warm and comfortable indeed, compared with the blustery outdoors. Jim deposited Molly's bundles in a chair, and turning discovered that she had removed her hat and coat and was warming her hands over the stove. She looked healthy and pretty, yet somehow forlorn. What was to prevent him taking her in his arms then and there? He longed to. That had been his intention, should opportunity offer. Nevertheless, something inhibited him. Probably it was a divination that Molly, during the few minutes' walk with him, had unconsciously been drawn to him again. She betrayed it now. That was what he had prayed for, but he could not act upon it.

"Thanks for asking me in, Molly," he said. "I suppose you expect me to get my trouble off my chest—then let you alone. . . . Well, I won't do it now. When that time comes we'll have a grand row. And I just won't spoil your Christmas. . . . But I ask you—will you send word to Darnell that you will not go to the dance with him tonight?"

"Thet'd be a low-down trick," replied Molly, quickly.

"It does appear so. There are good reasons, however, why it would be wise for you to do so—unless you want to lose your good name in Flag."

"Glory said thet. I don't believe either of you. An' it's not square of you to—"

"You needn't argue the point. Answer me. Will you go with me instead?"

She hung her head, she clenched her little trembling hands, she shook all over. What a trial that must have been! Jim sought to add to it.

"With me and Glory, of course. She wants you. And she thinks *this* is the time for you to come back. Before you've made me the laughing-stock of Flag."

"But it cain't do thet," she cried.

"Yes it can. And it will. Not that I care a hang for what people think or say. We want you to avoid—well, Molly, being misunderstood, not to say worse."

"You hit it on the haid, Jim," she replied, with spirit. "Thet's what I'm not goin' to avoid."

Jim regarded her speculatively. If he had had a vehicle of some kind out in the street he would have picked her up right there, as she was, and packed her out, and carried her off home. But this drastic action could scarcely be undertaken now, though his finger tips burned to snatch her.

"I am not angry with you now, but I shall be presently," he said.

"Who cares?" she rejoined, flippantly, and he realized he had brought her reply on himself.

"Oh, I see. . . . Do you then care—something for this gambler and embezzler, Ed Darnell?"

"How dare you?" retorted Molly, but she was shocked. Jim realized that Gloriana had not told her a great deal, after all.

"I'm a darin' cowpuncher," said Jim.

"I'll tell Mr. Darnell. Then mebbe you won't be so darin'."

Jim, despite self-control, grew a little hot under the collar. There was not anything soothing in Molly's championship of a cheap adventurer.

"By all means tell him. . . . You're a queer kid, Molly. Just to hurt me you'll flirt with this stranger, forgetting or pretending to forget that Slinger Dunn, your brother, perhaps the hardest nut in Arizona next to Croak Malloy, is my partner."

"Jim Traft, I'm no flirt—an' Slinger isn't a hard nut," she retorted, pugnaciously.

"Well then, you're going to do it?"

"Do what?"

"Make me an object of scorn. These Flag girls never cottoned to me. The young fellows, except cowboys, have no use for me. The old women don't like me. When they all see—actually see you've jilted me—"

"They won't. I'll make it the other way round," she interrupted, passionately.

Jim saw this tack was useless. The only thing that would move Molly at this particular moment, and perhaps at any other time, was physical force. Slinger knew how to handle her. Jim essayed another argument.

"You saw one of my Christmas presents—for you. What you think of it?"

"Gave me nightmare."

"Have you any curiosity about the other?"

"Nope. I may be a poor little country girl, but you cain't buy me—you Mizzouri villain."

"You used to call me Mizzouri, with a kiss. Do you remember when we went wild-turkey hunting?"

"I'm tryin' to forget. Oh, Jim, you've been so good—I—I—I" She bit her tongue. "An' I will forget, if I have to go to the bad."

"You've made a fair start, Molly Dunn," replied Jim, curtly. "Say, has this Darnell so much as laid a hand on you?"

"No! You insult me," she cried, with flaming face.

"But, Molly, be reasonable. You hinted that you'd encourage such things," protested Jim, justly nettled.

"I will—if you drive me."

Then there was a deadlock. Molly and Jim glared at each other across the stove, above which their extended hands almost met. Jim found it hard to tear himself away, especially in view of her anger. He pondered a moment. Finally he said, gently: "Darling, do you have *any* idea to what extremes you may drive me?"

She shook her head dubiously.

"Don't you know I worship you?"

Her glossy head drooped.

"Don't you realize you'll ruin me if you persist in this madness? I can't believe it. But you might convince me, eventually."

Then she covered her face with her hands and the tears trickled through her fingers.

Jim grasped at the right moment to make his escape.

"I won't distress you any more," he said. "Don't cry and make your eyes red. I'll see you tonight. Please save a dance for me."

Then he rushed out to find the cold wind soothing to a heated brow. He trudged home, his mind in a whirl. It was nearly dark when he arrived. Gloriana was not in the living-room. Wherefore Jim threw himself into the armchair and reclined there until he had reestablished the Western character he had recently adopted.

Before supper he went out to the bunk-house, to find the place a bedlam of jolly cowpunchers and a storeful of the men's furnishings, goods which they had bought so indiscriminately. All of the boys were sober—a remarkable circumstance on the eve of Christmas. When he entered—and he had stood in the open door a moment—they whooped and began to throw packages at him.

"Merry Christmas!" yelled Bud.

"Son-of-a-gun from Mizzouri!" yelled Curly.

"Whoopee, you diamond-buyer!" yelled Cherry.

"You lovesick, dyin' duck!" yelled some one Jim did not pick out, for the reason that he had to dodge. And so it went until they had exhausted their vocabularies and their missiles.

"Am I to understand that this fusillade is kindly meant?" he asked, with mock solemnity.

"Means we shore went broke on you an' Molly Dunn," replied Bud.

"Boys, that was a cowboy stunt—your buying out Babbitt's," said Jim. "I'm broke, too, but I'll share the debt."

Some one observed that he would, like the old lady who kept tavern out West, and as Jim had learned that that was a very disreputable thing, he made no further comment.

"Slinger, I hope you didn't tell these wild men what *you* did in Babbitt's," he returned.

"I shore did, an' the outfit's with me, Mister Traft," answered Dunn.

"Boss, Slinger had an inspurashun," observed Bud, sagely. "Soon as a feller learns to treat bull-halded sisters an' fickle sweethearts thetaway he'll get some obedience."

"I'm afraid it won't work on high-spirited girls like Molly and my sister."

"It shore would. Wimmen is all the same. What you say, pard Curly?"

"But, on this heah Christmas Eve my heart is shore sad," rejoined Curly. "Peace on earth an' good will toward men is a lot of guff. There's battle an' murder in the air. Some of us won't ever see another Christmas."

"Then we oughta get turrible drunk," said Bud.

Approval of this statment was not wanting.

"Curly, what's eating you?" asked Jim, grasping that his favorite cowboy had something besides the festivities of the season on his mind.

"Ask Bud," replied Curly, gloomily.

"Wal, Boss, it ain't nuthin' much, leastways oughtn't fuss us till after Christmas," replied Bud. "Curly an' I made a round of the gamblin'-places this afternoon. I didn't know what was in Curly's mind. Anyway, the doorkeeper at Snell's tried to bar Curly out. Shore it's a swell place, but we reckoned it wasn't none too good fer the Diamond. After I got in I seen why Curly pushed his gun against the doorkeeper's bread-basket. A bartender friend of Curly's had tipped him off thet there was a big game goin' on at Snell's. Wal, there was. Bambridge, Blodgett, another rancher we didn't know, an' Blake, a hotel man from Winslow, an' last this hyar Darnell hombre, was sittin' in. You should of seen the coin of the realm on thet table. Wal, we watched the game. I seen Bambridge was bettin' high an' losin'. Looked like he'd whoop up the pots, an' Darnell would rake them in. Blake is no slouch of a gambler, an' he was shore sore at the game, either from losin' or somethin'. All I seen about Darnell was thet he was mighty slick with the cards. They jest flew out of his hands. Curly, you know, is a card sharp hisself, an' he swore Darnell stacked the deck on every deal he had. An' Blodgett an' the strange rancher, anyhow, was gettin' a hell of a fleecin'."

"Ahuh. So that's it," returned Jim, seriously. "Curly, I don't see anything in that to make you sad on Christmas Eve."

"Boss, there's shore two things," drawled Curly. "I've got to raise enough money to set in that game at Snell's. An' I'm wonderin' if Darnell is as slick with a gun as he is with the cairds."

"Life is orful hard fer a cowpuncher when he's in love," observed Bud. "Sky so blue an' grass so green, flowers an' birds, dance an' holdin' hands, an' kisses sweeter'n ambergris—an' jest round the corner bloody death lurkin'."

"What's the idea, Curly?" asked Jim, quickly interested.

"Boss, it's a fine chance to get rid of Mister Darnell without involvin' any of our lady friends, you know. Flag is such a hell of a place for gossip. An' I reckon there's shore enough right now."

"Get rid of Darnell!" ejaculated Jim, curiously.

"Shore. I can set in thet game if I've a good-sized roll. Shore I'd flash it an' let on I was a little drunk. Savvy? Wal, I can nail Darnell at his cheatin' at cairds. If he pulls a gun—well an' good. If not he'll shore find Flag too hot a town in winter."

"Curly, it's a grand idea, except the possibility of Darnell's throwin' a gun. I hardly believe he'd have the nerve. He's an Easterner."

"We don't know for shore," said Curly. "He might even be from Texas."

"Aw, guff an' nonsense!" burst out Bud. "Thet handsome, white-mugged sharper won't go fer a gun. But whatinhell's the difference if he does? Save us the trouble of stringin' him up to a cottonwood. . . . An', Boss, an' Curly, an' all you galoots, thet's what Darnell is slated fer. I seen it—I felt it. . . . Now I ask you, knowin' how few my hunches are—do you recollect any of them far wrong? What's more, Bambridge ain't genuine Western. He's too cock-sure. He reckons us all easy marks."

"Curly, I'll dig up the money and go with you to Snell's," said Jim.

The Diamond immediately voted upon a united presence at that occasion. Curly made no objection, provided they dropped in unobtrusively.

"I heahed this poker game has been goin' on most in the afternoons," he said. "An' of course it's kind of private—Snell's is—an' you may not get in. But don't start a fight. Aboot four o'clock would be a good hour, Jim."

"How much money will you require?" queried Jim.

"Wal, I ought to have a roll of greenbacks big enough to choke a cow, with a century as a wrapper. Shore I'll have to flash this roll or they'd never let me set in. But you can gamble I won't lose much of it."

"That makes it easier," said Jim. "I can manage somehow. . . . Now, fellows, about this dance tonight. It's at the hotel and the big bugs in town are back of it. No knock-down and drag-out cowboy dance. Savvy? . . . I—I tried to coax Molly not to go with this Darnell, but she's stubborn. She's going. And we can't help it. I'm curious to see what comes off. Also a little worried about you boys. Anything up your sleeves?"

"Nope. We're layin' low, Boss, honest Injun," averred Bud.

"Jim, I met Sue Henderson this afternoon," spoke up Curly, "an' she asked me if it was true that Molly wasn't goin' with *you.* Sue's the biggest gossip in Flag, except her ma, so I tried to use my haid. I said yes it was true—that Molly an' Jim had a tiff an' she got mad an' dished Jim fer this dance. Sue looked darned queer an' asked me if that also applied to your engagement. I said Lord, no. But I didn't convince Sue. I reckon it's goin' to look bad fer Molly."

"Serve her darn right," said Slinger.

"You see, Jim, Molly's picked the quickest way to queer herself with Flag folks," went on Curly. "But the crazy kid—she's not smart enough to see that Darnell won't queer himself with these Flag girls fer her. Shore as shootin' Molly Dunn of the Cibeque will be a wall-flower at the dance.

"But you boys—" began Jim, haltingly.

"Shore we'll cut her daid," interrupted Curly, and his drawling voice had a steel ring. "Molly's a darlin', but she cain't play didoes with the Diamond."

When Jim related this bit of conversation to Gloriana, after supper, he was amazed to note she did not show any surprise. He had been shocked at

Curly's ultimatum. These loyal cowboys whom Molly could wind round her little finger! But this was only another proof to Jim how little he knew the cowboys and the West. Gloriana, with her feminine perspicacity, saw much more clearly than he.

"It'll be a good lesson, Jim," said Glory. "If only Ed Darnell runs true to form!"

"And what's that?"

"Molly is only pretty game for him. He'll play with her, but he won't champion her. He's keen after Sue Henderson. All these Flag girls have regular beaus who take them to dances. Darnell couldn't get any one except Molly. And you can bet he won't dance exclusive attendance on her."

"I don't like it, Glory," returned Jim, moodily.

"No wonder. It'll be a beastly Christmas Eve for you, Jim. Small return for your affection and generosity. But life is like that. I'm sure, though, this dance will settle Molly's hash, to be slangy, and work to your interest. . . . I think you'd better vamoose now, so I can dress."

"What are you going to wear, Glory?" asked Jim, with interest.

"Well, it's an occasion not to overlook. I want your town of Flag to see you have a sister you can be proud of, anyway."

"Good! Knock 'em dead, Glory. And that goes for the cowboys, too."

"I shall avail myself of the opportunity, to my utmost. . . . Jim, how are we to go? In that breezy buckboard?"

"Yes; we have to. The snow's 'most gone. But we might use the sleigh in a pinch."

"I'd like that, with the buffalo robe. And, Jim, don't forget a couple of hot stones in a burlap sack. It'll save me from pneumonia."

Jim ran into the living-room to have a word with his uncle before dressing.

"Son, I'm goin' to pass on this dance," said the rancher, with a chuckle. "I reckon it wouldn't be any fun for me. I'll wait for Molly's party hyar next Wednesday. An' you see to it she's back home by then."

"Uncle, I'll do it or die."

"Fetch Glory in before you leave. I can stand havin' my eye knocked out once more."

While Jim dressed his mind was active. If his cowboys and acquaintances snubbed Molly that night it might give him an opening for the wild plot he meant to carry out. And if Darnell played up to it as Gloriana had declared he would play—then the hour would be ripe for Jim's coup. He had to choke down his shame, his resentment that he must resort to such means to recover his sweetheart. Whatever he was going to do must be done quickly, for Molly's sake more than his.

Molly's room at the ranch-house had been kept precisely as she had left it. Jim went to the kitchen and gave the housekeeper instructions to light Molly's lamps about midnight, to start a fire in the grate, and to be careful about the screen. Lastly Jim took from his closet the fur coat he had bought for Molly, and with this on his arm, and his own overcoat he made the stone-floored corridor ring with his footsteps. Gloriana's room was dark, except for the flicker of wood fire behind the screen. Whereupon Jim hurried to the living-room.

Glory stood in the bright flare of lamps and fire, her furs on the floor, and she was pivoting for the benefit of her uncle.

Jim was not prepared for this vision of loveliness. Glory, in white gown with flounces of exquisite lace, and a hint of blue, her beautiful arms and neck bare, with a smile of pure joy on her face, and that dancing purple lightning in her eyes, was an apparition and a reality that sent the blood thrilling from Jim's heart.

"Glory, you look a little like your mother," Uncle Jim was saying. "But I reckon, only a little. . . . Lass, I—I hope we Western folks are not too rough an' plain to—to make you happy. It shore makes *me* happy, an' almost young again, to look at you."

"Thank you, Uncle; that *is* a sweet compliment," said Glory, and she stepped out of her furs to kiss him. "Don't you worry about me and all my finery. It'll wear out—and by that time I hope I'll deserve to be happy in your great West."

It was late according to Western custom when Jim and Gloriana arrived at the hotel, and the lobby was crowded. Red and green decorations, upon which shone bright lights, lent the interior of the hotel the felicitous color of the season. Entrance to the dining-hall, from which emanated strains of Spanish music and the murmur of gay voices, was blocked by a crowd of lookers-on, some of whom surely had the lithe build of cowboys.

Jim saw Gloriana to the wide stairway which led to the ladies' dressing-room, and then went in search of his own. Curly and Bud were there, immaculate in dark suits and white shirts, which rendered them almost unrecognizable to Jim. Curly, particularly, looked handsome and clean-cut, and he did not appear uncomfortable, as did Bud. Slinger also showed up on Jim's entrance, sleek and dark and impassive, as striking in his black suit as when he wore the deerskin of the forest.

"Where's the gang?" asked Jim.

"Wal, they're shore out there hoofin' it. Up an' Lonestar an' Cherry an' Jack all dug up gurls somewhere. Hump says he's too crippled yet an' will only look on."

"Boss, you oughta see the lady who came in on the arm of Jackson Way," observed Bud. "Out-of-town gurl an' she'll run Molly close fer looks. Jack never seen us atall. Son-of-a-gun! We gotta get a dance with her."

"Sure. I'll fit it, boys," Jim assured them.

"Jim, I see you've disobeyed Ring Locke's orders," drawled Curly, disapprovingly.

"Curly, darn it, I couldn't pack a gun with this rig," complained Jim, designating the trim suit of black. "Where'd I wear that cannon you insist on my carrying?"

"Wal, if you went slappin' around me you'd shore hurt your hand. An' if you watch me you'll notice I don't turn my back to nothin'."

Jim sighed. Almost he had forgotten the menace of the time and place.

"I'll risk it. And if Croak Malloy shows up I'll dive somehow."

"Wherever you are you want to see Croak first," returned Curly. "He's not liable to show up heah, but he might. An' to look fer him is the idea."

"Slinger, you're going to dance?" asked Jim.

"I shore ain't hankerin' to make a slidin' fool of myself. But I promised this mawnin', an' I reckon I cain't back out."

Curly looked rather fierce, and chewed at his cigarette, something unusual for the cool Texan.

"Well, come on, you Diamond," said Jim, at length. "Let's go get Glory."

She was waiting for Jim on the stairway, queenly and beautiful, her great eyes brilliant with excitement and interest.

"My Gawd! Curly, lemme hold on to you," whispered Bud.

Curly let out a little gasp, which was not lost on Jim, but Slinger showed no sign of being transfixed by Gloriana's loveliness. She came down to meet them, with just a hint of eager gaiety, and apparently unconscious of the gaping crowd. After a moment of greeting Curly elbowed an entrance for the others into the colorful hall.

"Pretty nifty, I'll say," observed Bud. "What do you think of the style

Flag's been puttin' on, since you come, Miss Glory?"

"Very different from Jim's letter descriptions of Western dance-halls," laughed Gloriana. "I like this."

"Jim, hurry an' dance with your sister so we can get a chanct," added Bud, very business-like.

"Say, don't you gazabos fight over Glory or dance her off her feet," replied Jim. "That happened last time. Glory came West to get well, and not to be buried. . . . Come on, Glory, see if boots and chaps have made me clumsy."

When he swung his sister out into the eddying throng of dancers she said: "Jim, I saw Molly in the dressing-room. Sue Henderson and her mother cut her dead. Mrs. Henderson, you know, is the leading social light of Flag. Molly looked wonderfully sweet and pretty in her new dress. But scared, and dazed in spite of her nerve. Jim, she won't be able to carry it through. Darnell will fail her. Then your chance will come."

"Poor crazy kid!" choked Jim. "This'll be a rotten night for her—and sure a tough one for me. . . . Glory, if it wasn't for that, I'd be the proudest escort you ever had at any dance. Even as it is I just want to bust with pride. I'll bet you Curly squeezed my arm black and blue when he saw you on the stairs. And Bud whispered: 'My Gawd! Curly, lemme hold on to you!'"

"They are dears," replied Gloriana, dreamily. "Only—just too much in earnest. . . . Slinger scares me."

"Well, enjoy yourself. These affairs are few and far between. . . . It ought to be a great night for you. All eyes are on you, Glory. . . . How terribly pretty you are!—Gosh! pretty isn't the word. . . . And you dance like—like a dream. . . . Glory, dear, haven't you wasted a good deal of your life doing this?"

"Yes, I have, Jim," she replied, regretfully.

At the expiration of that waltz they were at the far end of the large room, and had to make their way through a whispering, staring crowd of dancers. Jim espied Jackson Way with a very pretty brunette girl. Jack tried to escape in the press, but Jim nailed him gaily. "Where you going, cowboy?" And so the blushing Jack and his fair damsel were captured and led across to Curly and Bud and Slinger.

"Glory, I'll leave you to the tender mercies of the Diamond," said Jim, after there had been a pleasant interchange of introductions and some gay repartee. "But I'll keep an eye on you. . . ."

"Jim, there are Ed Darnell and Molly," interrupted Gloriana, suddenly. Her voice had an icy edge.

Before Jim glanced up he felt a jerk of his whole frame, as released blood swelled along his hot veins. He saw Molly first, and knew her, yet seemed not to know. As he met her dusky eyes, unnaturally large and bright, with almost a wild expression, his passion subsided. He smiled and bowed to her as if nothing untoward had happened. And it pleased him that Gloriana did likewise. The others of Jim's company, however, pointedly snubbed Molly. Then Jim's glance switched to Darnell. In this good-looking and elegant gentleman Jim scarcely recognized the man he had seen with Bambridge in the station at Winslow. At least that was a first impression, which had not the test of proximity or consistence; and he concluded it would be wiser to be deaf to his jealousy and await developments.

That moment, however, was the beginning of a most miserable experience. Jim left Gloriana with the gathering group of young people, and strolled away on his vigil. His purpose was fixed and unalterable; his embarrassment and humiliation now actual pain; and not all of these states of mind could render him oblivious to his position there. He had only to make the rounds of the dance-hall, the corridors and lobby, to realize his status. His cowboys, and his other friends, and Flagerstown folk who were close to old Jim Traft, had shown and were still showing their contempt for Molly Dunn. These people represented the rather small élite of the Arizona town. A majority of those present, however, were made up of cowboys, and young men about town, all accompanied by the girls of their choice; and it was plain gossip had run rife among them, and they did not conceal their curiosity and satisfaction. Little Molly Dunn of the Cibeque, sister of the gun-thrower, and a plain girl of the Arizona backwoods, had jilted the young Easterner, the favorite nephew of rich old Jim Traft. It was all as plain as print, and it grew so much plainer, as time progressed, that Jim might have been reading it through a microscope. There was only one good thing about the miserable situation, and that was that Molly Dunn could not fail to see the humiliation she had brought upon her lover.

Jim danced with Sue Henderson, and two others of the Flagerstown girls who had been friendly to Gloriana, and it was an ordeal, for they were both sympathetic and vindictive. Common little hussy—Molly Dunn! And Jim had to resent that, and try to make excuses for Molly.

Darnell did precisely what Gloriana had predicted. He neglected Molly for the girls of higher social standing, and it seemed to Jim that when Darnell grasped the significance of the situation he showed his true colors. He left Molly to the cowboys and the clerks. She danced and flirted wildly. She was too gay, too indifferent, and before long she broke and went to the other extreme. Jim watched her sit out three dances alone, trying to hide in a corner. But Molly Dunn could not hide at that dance.

Jim thought it was time to do something, and approaching Gloriana, who sat with Curly, he said, "Come on, you." And he dragged them up.

"You're going to dance with Molly," replied Gloriana, gladly. "It is high time."

"Yes, if she will. But, anyway, we can show this crowd where we stand."

As they approached Molly she appeared to shrink, all except her big dark eyes. Gloriana sat down beside her and said something nice about Molly's new dress and how sweet she looked.

"Molly, won't you dance the next with me?" asked Jim.

Curly gazed down upon her, his fair handsome face clouded, and his flashing blue eyes full of sorrow.

Molly Dunn, you've shore played hell heah tonight," he said.

Molly surely was ready to burst into tears when the music started again. Dancers from all sides rushed upon the floor, and Curly, with a gay call to Jim, drew Gloriana into the thick of the whirling throng. Jim did not wait for Molly's consent; he took her hand, and pulled her to her feet and led her out into the maze. Then when he had her close and tight in his arms, he felt that he had surely understood himself.

"Oh—Jim," she whispered, "it's been awful! . . . An' the worst was when Glory came to me jest now—before them all—an' spoke so sweet—as if nothin' had happened. . . . Oh, I wanted the ground to open an' swallow me."

Jim thought that a strange speech, full of contrition and shame as it was. What about him! But Gloriana had been the great factor in Molly's downfall.

"Glory is true blue, Molly," Jim whispered back. "That ought to prove it. You've doubted her."

Jim felt a gradual relaxing of Molly's stiff little hand and then a sinking of her form against him.

"I'm ashamed," she replied, huskily. "I'll go drown myself in the Cibeque.

"Yes, you will!" In the press of the throng it seemed to Jim that he had her alone and hidden safe from the inquisitive eyes. He could hug her without restraint and he did. Molly hid her dusky head on his shoulder and danced as one in a trance.

CHAPTER TWELVE

All too soon that dance ended, and Jim got Molly into an out-of-the-way corner, where a few other couples, evidently lovers, were too concerned with themselves to look at anyone else.

Jim believed the tide had turned in his favor, though tragic little Molly was unconscious of it. She gazed up at him as if fascinated, with almost a terrible yearning and hopelessness. "Don't do it," whispered Jim, "or I'll kiss you right here."

"Do—do what?"

"Look at me like that. . . . Molly, you've sure made a mess of Christmas Eve, but it's not too late."

"Oh yes, Jim dear, it *is* too late," she sighed, mournfully. "They all gave me the cold shoulder. Except Glory, bless her! I—I cain't realize she didn't take me at my word."

"Not Glory. And what do you care for the others? You won't have to live with them. . . . Molly, you were mistaken in this Darnell. He's no good. He very nearly ruined Gloriana. What she told you was true. Look how he has treated you—"

"Jim, I don't need to be told now," she interrupted, bitterly. "He's made a fool out of me. . . . But only tonight did I learn he's no good. Before we got here. He—he insulted me, Jim."

"Did he?—Well, that's not surprising. Just how?" returned Jim, in cool, hard query. "I hope he didn't lay a hand on you."

"He laid two hands on me," she said, frankly. "An' he was 'most as bad as Hack Jocelyn, if you remember, Jim. . . . I was aboot ready to bite when some one came into the hall."

"Ahuh!—Why did you come with him, then?" queried Jim, serenely.

"I had to come to this dance or die. Besides, I reckon I was some to blame. I told Darnell I wasn't good enough for the Trafts an' their crowd."

"Molly, you're generous, but you can't save him now."

"You leave him alone," flashed Molly. "He carries a gun. He might hurt you—an' thet'd shore kill me. . . . I'll tell Slinger. Honest, I will. But Slinger has never even looked at me tonight. He must despise me."

"No. Slinger is just angry with you. . . . Now, Molly, you must not let Darnell take you home. Promise you won't—or I'll go right out now—"

"I promise, Jim. Please ask Slinger to take me away. I'm sick of this dance. I want to go home."

"Out to the ranch?" he asked, hopefully.

"Home to the Cibeque, where I belong."

"All right, I'll find Slinger," rejoined Jim, thinking fast and furiously. "But let's dance again. There goes the music."

Jim did not break the sweet tumultuousness of that dance by a single word. When it was over he asked Molly to wait near the door, and left her back somewhat out of the throng. Then he instituted a wild search for Gloriana, whom he found presently with Curly.

"Gee! you two must be having the time of your lives!" he exclaimed, surprised at

Gloriana's radiance and something indescribable about Curly.

"Jim, I am enjoying myself," admitted Gloriana, with a blush.

"Boss, this heah is aboot as near heaven as I ever hope to get," drawled Curly.

"Fine. Then you see Glory home. I'm going to be—engaged. . . . Glory, don't stay late." And Jim rushed away to find Slinger. In this he was also fortunate, as he found him in the smoking-room, alone and watchful. His dark face wore a rather sad expression. He was out of his element at a dance.

"Slinger, I want you. What're you doing? Dancing any?"

"I had one with Glory. Thet'll be aboot all fer me. If I wasn't worried about the kid I'd chase myself back to the ranch. I've been hanging around heah listenin' to this fellar Darnell." Slinger spoke low and indicated a noisy group of young men. They had a flask and were exchanging it. Darnell had here the same ingratiating manner, the same air of good fellowship, which Jim had noted in the dance-hall. He appeared to be a man nearing thirty, well set up, handsome in a full-faced, sensual way, and unmistakably egotistical. He would go far with young people.

"What of him?" whispered Jim.

"Wal, I shore ain't crazy aboot him. Strikes me sort of tincanny. . . . Jim, he's packin' a gun. Can you see thet?"

"No, Slinger, I'll be hanged if I can."

"Wal, he is, an' thet's kind of funny. If I could find a reason, I'd mess up this heah place with him. But it'd look all the wuss fer Molly—"

"Yes, it would. Let Darnell alone. And, Slinger, listen. Molly has had enough of this. She sent me to ask you to take her home. But I've got an idea. You run over to the stable and send a boy with a sleigh. Pronto. I'll let Molly think you're going to take her. But I'll take her myself, and out to the ranch. Savvy, pard?"

"I shore do. An' damn if you ain't a good fellar," declared Slinger. "Molly had better sit tight this time. . . . Jim, this heah deal eases my mind."

"Rustle, then, you Indian."

Jim saw Slinger glide out with his inimitable step, and then he went to get his overcoat and hat. For the moment he had forgotten the fur coat, which he had folded inside his. But there it was. With these he hurried back to the hall, eager and thrilling, afraid, too, that Molly might have bolted or that Darnell might have come out. To his relief, however, he found her waiting, strained of face, her eyes like burnt holes in a blanket. They leaped at sight of him.

"Slinger has gone for a sleigh," said Jim, as he reached her, and he tried to be natural. "Here, slip into this. You won't need to go upstairs. I'll get your coat tomorrow. And no one will see you as you go out."

"Whose coat is this? . . . Oh, what lovely fur!—Glory's?"

"Hurry!" he replied, holding it for her.

"Slinger can fetch it right back."

Jim turned up the high collar of the coat, and against the dark fox fur Molly's eyes shone beautifully. What a difference fine feathers made!

"Come," he said, taking Molly's arm. He led her out, relieved that but few dancers paid attention to their departure. In the lobby entrance they ran squarely into Darnell, gay, heated of face.

"Hello, kid!—Where the deuce are you going?" he shot out, and his gaiety suddenly fled. Two men behind him came up, evidently his companions, and curious. Jim did not recognize either.

"Home," replied Molly, and she flashed by.

Darnell took a step forward to confront Jim.

"We've met before?" he said, and both voice and look were uncertain.

"Yes, I happen to be Jim Traft—Miss Dunn's *fiancé*. And if you don't step aside this meeting will be somewhat like the one you spoke of."

It was certain that long before Jim completed this deliberate speech Darnell had recognized him. One of the strangers drew him aside, so Jim could pass. And as Jim went out he heard Darnell curse. Molly was already out in the corridor. As Jim joined her Slinger came up the steps.

"Any ruction heah?" he queried, sharply. "I seen Darnell stop you."

"No. I got out of it all right, Slinger. Come on," replied Jim, grimly, and he laughed inwardly at the thought of what this Ed Darnell had happened upon. His luck, at least, was out.

A two-seated sleigh, with a Mexican driver, stood at the curb. Jim bundled Molly into the back seat, and stepping in he tucked the heavy robe around her and himself. Molly uttered an exclamation which was surely amazed protest.

"Slinger, I'll see Molly—home," said Jim, and for the life of him he could not keep the elation out of his voice.

"Shore, Jim, you see her home," drawled Slinger, meaningly. And he leaped over the side of the sleigh. "Sister, you've messed up things considerable. But somehow Jim still loves you, an' I reckon I do, too. We jest cain't help it. All the same, don't go triflin' with strange fellars no more. I'll see you in the mawnin'."

"Slinger, you lay off Darnell," insisted Jim, forcefully.

"All right, Boss. But I'll jest watch him a little. Shore is an interestin' cuss. I seen him gettin' gay with one of them rich gurls."

Jim laughed and told the Mexican boy to drive straight out the main street.

"It's closer, turnin' heah," spoke up Molly, a little alarmed. As yet, however, she had no inkling of the plot.

"More snow out this way. This bare ground is hard on the runners," replied Jim, and indeed the rasping sound of iron on gravel was irritating to nerves as well. Jim felt for Molly's hand under the robe, and found it, an ungloved cold little member. She started and tried to draw it away. In vain! Jim held on as a man gripping some treasure he meant to keep. Soon they were on the snow, and then the sleigh glided smoothly with the merry bells ringing. Soft heavy flakes were falling, wet and cool to the face.

"Heah—turn down heah," called Molly, as they reached the last side street.

"Boy, drive straight out to the Traft ranch," ordered Jim.

Molly stood up, and would have leaped out of the sleigh had not Jim grasped her with no uncertain hands, and hauled her down, almost into his arms. She twisted round to look up at him. The darkness was thick, but he could see a pale little face, with great staring eyes.

"You—you want to get somethin' before takin' me home?" she asked.

"Why, of course, Molly. This is Christmas, you know," he returned, cheerfully.

"I—I didn't know you could be like this." And Jim imagined he had more cause to be happy.

No more was said. Jim endeavored to secure Molly's hand again, but she had hidden it somewhere. Thwarted thus, Jim put an arm round her. When they reached the big pine trees, black against the snow, Jim knew they were nearing the ranch. He nerved himself for the crisis. There was no use of persuasion or argument or subterfuge. Then the ranch-house loomed dark, with only one light showing. The bells ceased jangling in a crash.

"Molly, come in for—a minute," said Jim, easily, as he stepped out.

"No, thanks, Jim," she replied, with pathos. "I'll stay heah. Hurry, an' remember—I—I cain't accept no Christmas presents."

Jim leaned over, as if to rearrange the robe, but he snatched her bodily out of the sleigh.

"All right, boy, drive back," he ordered, and as the bells clashed again he turned with the kicking Molly in his arms. He heard her voice, muffled in the furs, as he pressed her tight, and he feared she used some rather strong language. Up the steps, across the wide veranda and into the dark ranch-house he packed her, fighting all the while, and on into the dim-lighted living-room, where he deposited her in his uncle's big armchair. Then he flew to lock the door. It was done. He felt no remorse—only a keen, throbbing, thick rapture. He turned up the lamp, and then lighted the other one with the red shade. Next he removed the screen from before the smoldering fire, to replenish it with chips of cedar and pine cones.

"Jim Traft—what've you done?" cried Molly, huskily.

Jim turned then, to see her in the chair, precisely as he had bundled her.

"Fetched you home, Molly," he said, with emotion.

"It was a trick."

"Reckon so."

"You didn't mean to take me to my boardin'-house?"

"I'm afraid I never thought of that."

"An' thet damn Slinger! He was in the deal with you?"

"Yes. Slinger was implicated—to the extent of getting the sleigh."

"Wal, now you got me heah—what you think you're goin' to do?" she demanded.

"Oh, wish you a merry Christmas and a happy New Year."

"Jim—honest I wish—you the same," she responded, faltering a little.

"Thanks. But it's not Christmas yet," rejoined Jim, consulting his watch. "Only eleven o'clock. At midnight I'll give you the other Christmas present."

"Other?—Jim Traft, are you loony? Or am I dreamin'? You didn't give me nothin'. You tantalized me with thet—thet ring, which was shore low-down. But thet's all."

"Molly, you have one of your presents. You've got it on. . . . That fur coat."

Uttering a cry of surprise and consternation, she bounced out of the chair to slip out of the rich, dark, fragrant coat. She handled it with awe, almost reverence, stroked it, and then with resignation laid it over the table.

"Pretty nice, don't you think?" queried Jim, pleasantly. "Becomes you, too."

"I'm findin' out you're as much of—of a brute as any cowboy," she asserted, tearfully. "How'm I to get back to my boardin'-house? When Glory comes? You'll send me then, Jim?"

"Molly, you're not going back to your boarding-house—tonight—or ever again," he replied, confronting her and reaching for her, so that Molly backed into the armchair and fell into it.

"I am—too," she retorted, but she was vastly alarmed.

"No, this is home, till you've grown out of your schoolgirl days."

"Kidnappers—you an' Slinger!"

"I reckon we are, Molly."

"You're wuss than Hack Jocelyn," she cried, wildly. "Are you goin' to hawg-tie me heah?"

"No. I don't believe you'll want to leave, after tomorrow when you see Uncle Jim and Glory."

"Jim—I cain't see them. It'd hurt too bad. Please let me go."

"Nope. . . . You hurt me, didn't you?"

"All fer your good, Jim. . . . Cain't you see thet?"

"Indeed I can't. You just almost broke my heart, Molly Dunn. If it hadn't been for Uncle and Glory— Well, never mind. I don't want to heap coals of fire upon your head."

"What did Uncle Jim an' Glory do?" she asked, poignantly.

"They both have faith in you. Faith!"

"I cain't stand thet, Jim. I cain't," she wailed.

He slipped into the big chair and gathered her in his arms. What a tight, quivering little bundle!

"Molly, both Uncle and Glory love you."

"No—no. Thet's not so," she cried, half smothered. "Let me go, Jim."

"Ha, ha! I see myself. . . . Hold up your head, Molly."

"If you dare kiss me—Jim Traft—I—I. . . . Oh—"

"Don't you dare me, Molly Dunn, " added Jim, quite beside himself now. Molly's lips were sweet fire, and she could not control them. But she was strong, and as slippery as an eel. Jim had to confine his muscular efforts to holding her merely.

"Molly, you are mussing a perfectly beautiful little dress," he said, mildly, "besides, darling, you're making a very indecorous, not to say immodest, display of anatomy."

"I don't care," panted Molly, red of face, blazing of eye. But she did care. She was weakening.

"Darling." Jim divined this word had considerable power; at least enough to make Molly hide her face.

"Sweetheart," he went on.

And this appeared to end her struggling.

"Don't you love me, Molly?"

"Thet has been—all the trouble. . . . Too much—to disgrace you," she replied, haltingly, and she looked up with wet eyes and trembling lips. Jim was quick to kiss them, and when he desisted this time, she lay back upon his arm, her eyes closed, heavy-lidded, her face pale and rapt.

"Don't you *want* to stay, Molly," he went on, tenderly.

"No—no. . . . But I'm a liar," she replied, brokenly, without stirring.

"To be my wife?"

She was mute and therefore won. Jim found the little box in his pocket, and extracting the diamond ring from it he slipped it upon her finger, where it fitted tight and blazed triumphantly.

"There!"

Moreover, it had a potency to make her eyes pop open. She stared. Slowly a transformation set in. She became ecstatic and ashamed, filled with sudden wild misery and joy, all at once.

"Oh, I—I've been—jest what Slinger called me," she cried.

"What was that?"

"It's too turrible to tell. . . . How can you be so good—to make me love you more? . . . Jim, honest I thought I was thinkin' only of you. If I was fit for you I wanted to—an' sometimes deep down in me I reckoned I was, because love ought to count—I wanted to make myself unfit. . . . Yet when thet mouthin', pawin' Darnell laid hold of me—when I had my chance to disgrace you an' degrade myself—I couldn't. My very soul went sick. An' then I only wanted to get free of him at any cost. I did. An' afterward he begged so hard, an' I longed so to go to the dance, thet I went."

"Well, I'm glad you did, since we had to have this ruction. But don't mention

Darnell to me again, at least tonight."

"After all, people won't know how bad it was," she said, with a passion of hope and regret.

"They'll think it only a lovers' quarrel," replied Jim, happily, and he was glad to believe that himself.

"If only Glory will forgive me!"

"Glory! Why, she has already."

"You don't know thet lovely sister of yours, Jim. . . . The more she persuaded me I was doin' wrong, the kinder an' sweeter she talked, the proud way she looked—the more I wanted to do somethin' awful. I wanted to hide thet I loved her, too. . . . Oh, she seemed so wonderful—so far above me. But if she'll forgive I'll never do wrong again, so help me Gawd!"

"Molly, that's a vow. I'll hold you to it. . . . And now, honey, make up to me for all I suffered—for every miserable moment."

"I cain't, Jim," she replied, mournfully. "What's done is done. Oh, if I only could."

"Well, then for every wretched moment you spent with *him.* Could you count how many?"

"I reckon I could," she said, thoughtfully. "What's a moment? Same as a minute?"

"More like a second. Some are utterly precious, like this one. Others are horrible."

"Wal, with sixty seconds to the minute and sixty minutes to the hour—an' I reckon aboot five hours, all told—thet would be how much?—A lot to make up for!"

"Will you try? That will be your repentence."

"Yes," she promised, shyly, yet fearfully, as if remembering.

"Put your arms up round my neck. . . . There!—Now start kissing me once for every one of those heart-broken minutes."

Molly was not very far on this tremendous penance, considering sighs and lulls, and spasms of quick tender passion to make amends, when a knock on the living-room door startled her violently.

"Well, if that isn't tough!" ejaculated Jim, and putting Molly down he arose to go to the door. "Must be Gloriana May."

And she it was who entered, radiant and beautiful, with a swift hopeful flash of purple eyes that moved from Jim to Molly, and back again. Curly stepped in beside her.

"Jim, dear, I hope we didn't intrude," she said, sweetly, with mischief and gaiety underlying her speech. "Were you aware that this is Christmas?"

"Jim, many happy returns of this heah evenin'—I mean the last of it," drawled Curly, as he came forward so cool and easy, and already within possession of the facts. "Molly, I've been shore daid sore at you. But I'm an understandin' cuss. . . . Suppose I kiss you my Christmas greetin's."

And he did kiss her, gallantly, though withal like a brother, while Molly stood stiff, blushing and paling by turns.

"Curly Prentiss, do you kiss *every* girl on Christmas?" she had the spirit to retort.

"Nope. Thet privilege I reserve fer particular gurls," he drawled, and turned to Jim with extended hand. "Boss, I'm shore glad. This is the second time the Diamond's near been busted. Never no more! . . . Good night, all. I'll see you in the mawnin'."

When Jim had closed the door upon him there was an eloquent silence in which

Gloriana and Molly gazed into each other's eyes. Certain it was that Jim trembled. Yet his hopes ran high. Molly approached Gloriana and stood bravely, without trace of the shame Jim knew she felt.

"Glory, I'm heah again—to stay," she said, simply. "Jim kidnapped me—an' I reckon saved me when he did it. . . . I'm shore powerful sorry I've been such a dumbhaid. But you cain't doubt my love for Jim, at least. . . . Will you forgive me?"

Gloriana took Molly into her arms, and bending over her spoke with emotion. "I do indeed, Molly, as I hope to be forgiven. . . . Come with me to my room. . . . Good night, brother Jim; it's late. We'll see you in the morning."

CHAPTER THIRTEEN

Snell's gambling-hall was crowded on the afternoon of Christmas Day, when Jim Traft and Curly Prentiss arrived rather late. Evidently no open sesame was required on this occasion, and no doortender. Curly said this was because the business men of Flagerstown, who liked to buck the tiger, would be conspicuous for their absence on this holiday. But there would be a big game going, and Darnell would be in it.

Curly appeared to be under the influence of liquor, which Jim knew he was most decidedly not. But Curly excited no interest whatever, for the good reason that he differed very little in garb and manner from other cowboys present. Some, in fact, were hilariously drunk.

They strolled around to watch the faro game, the roulette wheel, and other games of chance, more or less busy with customers, until they approached a ring of lookers-on which surrounded the heavy poker game Curly wanted to sit in, provided Darnell was one of the players.

By looking over the heads of spectators they ascertained that Darnell was indeed there, and also Bambridge. Then Curly whispered to Jim that the other three gamblers were precisely the same he and Bud had watched yesterday afternoon.

"All set," concluded Curly, his blue eyes flashing like a northern sunlit sky. "Big game an' all daid sore. Darnell is ridin' them high an' handsome."

Then he turned to the circle of watchers and lurched into it. "Heah, lemme in, you geezers," he called out, in a loud and good-natured drawl. "I'm a-rarin' to set in this heah game."

But Curly's action was more forceful. Without waiting for the men to open up he swept them aside. Jim followed until he secured a place just back of the front row, where he could see and yet keep out of sight.

"Gennelmen, I wanta set in," said Curly. "There's only five of you heah. Thet shore ain't no good game. You oughta have six. An' heah I am."

Darnell looked up and gave Curly a hard glance. But if it were one of recognition he certainly did not connect Curly with the little meeting in Winslow some time previous.

"This is poker for men of means and not casino for two-bit cowpunchers," he said.

"Hell you shay," replied Curly, without offense, as he wiped a hand across his face, after the fashion of the inebriated. "Reckon you don't savvy I ain't no two-bit cowpuncher."

"Get out or I'll have you thrown out," snarled Darnell. His concentration on the game was such that an interruption jarred him. Yet even in anger there was no heat in the sharp dark eyes. His cheek and the line of his chin were tight. Here Jim saw the man as a handsome cold-faced gambler.

"My Gawd! man, you must be a stranger heahaboots," drawled Curly, and he clumsily pulled out the one vacant chair and fell into it, knocking against the table. With one hand he dropped his sombrero beside the chair and with the other he slammed down a huge roll of greenbacks, the outside one of which bore the number one hundred.

"My money ain't counterfeit, an' I reckon it's as good as anybody's," said Curly, lolling over the table in the careless laxity of a drunken man. His curly hair, wet and dishevelled, hid his eyes. He gave his mouth and chin the weakness characterizing the overindulgence in drink.

At sight of the roll of greenbacks Darnell's eyes leaped, but before he could speak, which it was evident he intended to do, Bambridge came out with: "Sure your money's as good as anybody's, cowboy. Sit in an' welcome."

"Much obliged, Mister," replied Curly, gratefully, as he snapped the rubber band off his roll. "What's the game, friends?"

"You make your own game. No limit," replied the dealer, who happened to be the man from Winslow. "Your ante."

"Make it five call ten," drawled Curly, but he labored long over the huge roll of greenbacks trying to find one of small numeration. "Doggone!—This heah legacy of mine is shore dwindlin' of change."

The game proceeded then with Curly apparently a lamb among wolves. Still, though betting with reckless abandon, he did not risk much. "Dog-gone-it! Wait till I get some cairds," he complained, "an' I'll show you fellars how a cowboy bets."

Altogether he carried out his pretense of a drinking range-rider come into possession of much money that was destined to make rich pickings for one of the gamblers presently. Once or twice the Winslow man kindly cautioned Curly about betting, which act incurred the displeasure of Bambridge.

"I'm two thousand out," he growled. "This cowpuncher insisted on joining us. Now let him play his own game."

"Bambridge, I'm out more than that," replied the Winslow rancher, sarcastically. "But I reckon it's low-down to rob this boy."

"Rob!—Are you casting any reflections?" spoke up Darnell, sharply.

"Not yet," answered the rancher, steadily, his eyes veiled.

"See heah, Boss," began Curly, to the Winslow man. "I'm shore appreciatin' your advice. But since it 'pears to rile this gamblin' couple, you let me play my own game. I ain't so dumb. But at thet I only started in fer fun."

Jim was all eyes when the deal passed to Darnell. He had long slim white hands, flexible, and they manipulated the cards marvelously. Yet when he dealt them out he was very slow and deliberate, as if to show his antagonists that his deal was open and fair. There was some stiff betting on that hand, which Curly passed and which Bambridge won. The game seesawed on. Finally Curly won his first hand, and he was jubilant. After that he staked his winnings recklessly. He had injected something of humor into the game, from a spectator's point of view, judging from the comments round the circle. Jim heard a cowboy whisper: "Thet's Curly Prentiss, an' you wanta look out."

Upon Darnell's next deal the play was a jack-pot, with the dealer's privilege of making the ante.

"Throw in one of your hundreds, cowboy," he said, as he chipped in one hundred dollars.

"Wal, century plants ain't nothin' in my young life," drawled Curly. "There you air, my Mississippi River gazabo."

Darnell gave a slight start, and eyed the cowboy intently. Curly's head was bent rather low, as usual, with his eyes hidden under that wave of bright hair any girl might have envied. He was smiling, easy, and happy in the game. Perhaps his remark was merely a chance one and meant nothing. But Jim's reflection was that Darnell certainly did not know cowboys of the Arizona-range stripe.

The Winslow man opened the jack-pot, the two players between him and Curly stayed, and then Bambridge raised before the draw. Presently they were all in, in a jack-pot carrying more than six hundred dollars. The watchers of the game looked on with intense interest. Each player called for what cards he wanted. Darnell said casually: "Three for myself—to this little pair." And he slid the three cards upon the table and laid the deck aside.

Suddenly like a panther Curly leaped. His left hand shot out to crack down upon Darnell's and crush it flat on the table. Then his right followed, clutching a big blue gun, which he banged on the table, making the players jump, then freeze in their seats. Curly sank back and threw up his head to show blazing eyes as clear as crystal. His frank young face set cold. How vastly a single moment had transformed him!

Darnell turned a greenish livid hue. He had been trapped. Malignance and fear betrayed him.

"You—low-down — — — —— of a caird sharp!" drawled Curly, in a voice with a terrible edge. "You reckoned I was drunk, eh?"

The circle of men back of Darnell split and spread, with shuffling feet and hoarse whispers, in two wings, leaving the space there clear. That act was as significantly Western as Curly's. Jim had seen it before.

"Don't anybody move a hair," ordered Curly, and the pivoting of his gun indicated the other players. Bambridge gasped. Only the Winslow man remained cool. Perhaps he knew or guessed the nerve behind that gun-hammer, which plainly rose a trifle, sank back, to rise again, almost to full cock.

"Gentlemen, look heah," went on Curly, bitingly, and he turned Darnell's crushed hand over. Bent and doubled in his palm were three cards that dropped out. Aces!

"Pretty raw, I must say," spoke up the Winslow man. "At that, I had a hunch."

"Darnell, we Westerners don't often hang caird sharps, like we do cattle thieves. But on second offense we throw a gun," said Curly, and the menace of him seemed singularly striking. Then in the same cool, careless voice he called Darnell all the profane epithets, vile and otherwise, known to the range. "You get out of Flag. Savvy? . . . An' any time anywhere after this—if you run into me—you pull a gun!"

Darnell whirled on his chair, knocking it to the floor, and he rushed through the opening in the crowd to disappear.

Curly moved the gun, by accident or intent—no one could tell—until it had aligned itself with Bambridge.

"Mister Bambridge, you've laid yourself open to suspicion round heah—long before this poker game," said Curly, as cutting as before. "I told your daughter thet, an' naturally it riled her. I reckon she's a fine girl who doesn't savvy her Dad."

"Who the hell is this hyar lyin' cowpuncher?" demanded Bambridge, yellow of face, as he appealed to the other players.

Curly's arm moved like a snake. "Don't you call me a liar twice! . . . I'm Curly Prentiss, an' I belong to the Diamond. *We* are on to you, Bambridge, if no other outfit round heah is. *We* know you're a damn sight crookeder cattle thief than Jed Stone himself. . . . Now listen closer. What I said aboot gun play, to your gamblin' new hand, Darnell, goes for you, too. Savvy? . . . Right now an' heah, or anywhere after."

"You—you drunken puncher—you'll pay for this hold-up of an innocent—and unarmed man," panted Bambridge, as he got up, his face ghastly, sweating, and his eyes bulging with a fury of passions. He swept the edge of the crowd aside and thumped away.

"Gentlemen, I apologize for breaking up your game," said Curly, sheathing his gun. "But I reckon I saved you money. Suppose we divide what's on the table an' call it quits."

"Agreed," replied the Winslow man, gruffly. "Prentiss, we sure owe you a vote of thanks."

It was Jim, and not Curly, who told the rest of the Diamond what had happened at Snell's late on Christmas Day.

Bud and Cherry, who had already been surreptitiously looking upon red liquor, promptly went on the rampage, eventually getting Lonestar and Up Frost with them. Jackson Way, owing to his new girl, manfully refused to drink more than one glass with his comrades.

"No, siree," avowed Jack, seriously. "Sometime in a man's life he parts with bad whiskey—an' company."

"You disgrash to Diamond," roared Bud.

Jim, learning of this from Ring Locke, rode back to town, perturbed in mind, but the cowboys could not be located, at least in a hasty search. So he went home to supper. Later Curly came in, serene and drawling. "They're shore a bad bunch of punchers. They've busted out. In the mawnin' we better go find them an' hawg-tie them an' pack them in, or they'll never be fit fer Molly's party."

It seemed incredible to Jim that the quiet evening at home was real. How strange to glance at Curly now and recall the tremendous force he had exhibited at Snell's only a few hours before! He was so easy-going, so droll and tranquil, as he unmercifully teased Molly, subtly including Gloriana in his philosophy.

"You cain't never tell aboot girls, Jim," he said, sorrowfully. "I've shore had a deal of experience with all kinds. Red-headed girls, I reckon, are best to gamble on. Blondes are no good. Brunettes are dangerous. They're like mules, an' fer a spell will be powerful good, just to get a chance to kick you. Christmas an' birthdays, though, a fellar's girl can be relied upon to stand without a halter. But these girls between blondes an' brunettes, the kind with hair like the ripple of amber moss, an' eyes like violets under water—they're scarce, thank the Lord. . . . I've heahed of a few, only never saw but one."

Uncle Jim roared, Molly threw something at Curly, while Gloriana was convulsed with laughter. Curly evidently was a perpetual source of surprise, delight, and mystery to Gloriana. There dawned in Jim a hope that she would grow to find more.

They had a pleasant hour in the bright living-room, then the rancher left the young folk to themselves. Curly stayed awhile longer.

"Wal," he said, presently, "I'll say good night, Miss Glory."

"What's your hurry?" queried Gloriana, in surprise. "Don't be so outlandishly thoughtful of my brother. He and Molly don't know we exist. . . . Oh, maybe you want to go to town."

"Wal, I had thought aboot it," drawled Curly.

"And maybe join in the general painting the Diamond is giving Flag?" went on Gloriana.

"Wal, they shore cain't do much paintin' or anythin' without me," he admitted, his keen blue eyes studying Gloriana.

Despite Gloriana's conviction of Jim's utter absorption, he still had eyes and ears for his sister and his best friend. Molly saw nothing except the ruddy coals of the fire, until Jim gave her a nudge.

"Very well, Mister Prentiss, good night," said Gloriana, icily, as she rose.

"Say, do you care a whoop aboot whether I get drunk or not?" demanded Curly, his face flaming. Gloriana was the one person who could stir him out of his nonchalance or coolness.

"Certainly not," replied Gloriana, in amaze. "Why should I? . . . But you are my brother's right-hand man. And I had hoped you would develop some character, for his sake."

"Cain't a man take a drink an' still have some character?" asked Curly, stoutly.

"Some men can," replied Gloriana, with emphasis that excluded Curly from her generalization.

"Wal, I reckon I'll go get awful drunk. Good night, Miss Traft."

"Good-by! . . . Mister Prentiss."

Curly departed hastily. His heavy steps sounded faster and faster, until they died away.

"Jim, this Curly cowboy irritates me," remarked Gloriana, coming to the fire.

"What?—Oh, I'm sorry, Glory. I thought you liked him," replied Jim, innocently.

"I do. He's a fine upstanding chap, so kind, easy-going, and big-hearted. He worships you, Jim. And of course that goes a long way with me. But it's the *other* side of him I can't—savvy, isn't it? It's that plagued cowboy side. . . . For instance, just a moment ago he saw you holding Molly's hand. So he possessed himself of mine. And I give you my word I could hardly get it away from him."

How sweet to hear Molly's laugh trill out! And the perplexity of Glory's expressive face, with its suggestion of color, likewise pleased Jim.

"Glory, the way to get along with Curly—and amuse yourself—is to let him hold your hand," said Jim.

"Don't be silly. I—I did that very thing, at the dance, until I got scared. In fact, I scarcely knew I *was* letting him."

"Glory, I told you Curly was the finest fellow I ever knew, for a man's friend, or a pard, as they call it out West. If you could stop his drinking he'd be that for a woman, too."

"I want to stop his drinking," admitted Gloriana, now gravely, "but I—I am not prepared to—to—"

"Sure you're not," interposed Jim, apologetically. "Don't misunderstand me, Glory. On the other hand, don't be cold to Curly just because you wasted some admiration—and sentiment—perhaps some kisses and caresses that would have raised poor Curly to the seventh heaven—on that Ed Darnell. . . . By the way, Glory, Curly threw a gun on Darnell today. Cussed him!—Whew! I never heard such language. He cast our cook, Jeff Davis, in the shade. And he drove Darnell out of Flag!"

"My—heavens! . . . Jim!" cried Gloriana, and Jim could find no suggestion of indifference now.

"Yes, by heavens—and any other place," nodded Jim, emphatically. He had the satisfaction also of seeing Molly come out of her trance.

"Not on my account?" queried Gloriana, breathlessly. "Oh, I hope not. I had all the slander and gossip I could stand—back home."

"Your name will never be heard of in connection with Darnell," said Jim. "And fortunately he chased half a dozen girls more than Molly. He—"

"The big liar!" interrupted Molly, disgustedly. "He swore *I* was the only one. . . . Aren't men low-down, Glory?"

"Some of them are assuredly," agreed Gloriana. "But tell us, Jim. What happened? How did Curly do it?"

Whereupon Jim, warning the girls not to tell Uncle Jim just yet, related the experience of the afternoon, punctuating the story with mention of his own thrills and fears. He wanted to do justice to Curly's nerve—to that side of his character which seemed so incomprehensible to Gloriana. She was as horrified and fascinated as she was relieved.

"This was no trick for Curly Prentiss," went on Jim. "He had Darnell sized up. Knew he was a bluff, as well as a cheat. That there was not the slightest chance of a fight. And never will be so far as Darnell risking an even break."

"What's that?" asked Gloriana, her eyes still large and full of wondering awe.

"An even break is where two men go out, with intention to fight, and each has his chance to draw."

"Draw!—Draw what?" queried Gloriana, bewildered.

"Gosh! how dumb you are, Glory. Do you think I mean to draw pictures on the side of a barn?—The draw means to pull, throw, jerk a gun."

"Oh, I see. . . . I guess I am very stupid. . . . Then you don't think Curly will have one of those draws—even breaks with Darnell?"

"Not a chance in the world. Curly says Darnell will come to the end of his rope pretty pronto—and that will be swinging from a cottonwood tree."

"Hanged!"

"I reckon that was what Curly was driving at.—Glory, it shocks you terribly, I see. But please realize that Darnell has come to Arizona, first hounding a girl who happens to be my sister. Then he affiliates himself with a crooked cattleman—Bambridge. In Arizona, mind you! . . . Try to steel yourself to facts. The West is still raw, hard, sudden, bloody. It sickened me for months and even now I get a jar occasionally. But it's grand with all its stings. You'll find that out."

"I'm afraid I'm finding out a good deal already," murmured Gloriana, still with that fixed look in her beautiful eyes. "And some of it is—maybe I'm not big enough for this West. . . . Well, I'll go to bed and leave you to yourselves. . . . Good night, Molly, little Western sister. This Christmas Day has been a happy one, after all. *'Quién sabe?'* as Curly says. Forget all the rest, Molly. . . . Good night, brother Jim. After all, you're smiled upon by the gods."

After Gloriana had gone Molly whispered, dreamily: "She called me sister! . . . Oh, I adore her! . . . Jim, shore as beans she's fallin' in love with Curly. Only she doesn't even dream of it. An' Curly is ravin' crazy aboot her. He'll get drunk, Jim. Jest you wait an' see. I know these heah cowboys. . . . An' Bud—he's as bad. An' poor Slinger!—Lordy! what's to become of us?"

"Love is indeed a very destructive agent, my dear," replied Jim, dreamily.

"It darn near destroyed me, Mizzouri," she said, plaintively. "Oh, Jim, it'll shore do it yet—if you make me love you more an' more."

"Well, sweetheart, if you want to know, I'm quite satisfied and happy now. And I'd rather not risk another of your demonstrations—if it were to take the form of another Ed Darnell."

"You're makin' fun of me now," returned Molly, reproachfully, and then she slipped back into his arms. "I'm heah—for good."

Next morning the bunk-house was incredibly quiet when Jim knocked and stamped in. Jeff was cooking a lonely breakfast. "Outfit's stampeded, Boss. I seen it comin'."

"Dog-gone their hides!" complained Jim. "Now I'm afraid to go downtown."

Before he started, however, he consulted his uncle and advised a postponement of Molly's party until New Year's Eve.

"Fine idee," agreed the rancher. "But don't be hard on the boys, Jim. Remember that Diamond was the toughest outfit in Arizona. Lovable punchers, if I ever knew any, but sure blue hell on holidays. Better go downtown an' drag them out. Reckon thet four-flush Sheriff Bray had his chance at us last night. Don't tell the girls."

Jim had no intention of that, though so far as Molly was concerned she would know. He had a talk with Ring Locke and told him about the affair at Snell's. The foreman seemed both vastly concerned and pleased. "Son-of-a-gun, thet Prentiss boy. . . . Jim, thet'll settle Bambridge. He'll have to shoot or git out. An' he ain't the shootin' kind. All the same, I wish the Diamond was out of town."

Some of the cowboys might as well have been out of town, for all Jim could find of them. Jackson Way, of course, had gone to Winslow with his girl. Hump, Cherry, and Uphill had disappeared, after a bloodless and funny fight with some rival cowboys over a pool game. Lonestar Holliday was discovered lurching out of a cheap Mexican lodging-house, almost speechless, and certainly lost to a sense of direction. Jim bundled him into the buckboard. "Sit on him, Charley," ordered Jim, "and take him home. Then hurry back."

Bud was in jail, and all Jim could find out, in the nature of offense, was a charge of disorderly conduct, including unusual profanity. Bray, the sheriff, was not to be found on the moment, and probably that was a good thing for all concerned. Bud was locked up with a tramp, two Mexicans, and a Navajo, and a madder cowboy Jim never had seen. "Boss, I'm gonna shoot thet — — — coyote of a sheriff!" he asserted. Jim paid his fine and got him out, greatly relieved that it had been no worse.

"Where's Curly?" demanded Jim.

"Shore haven't the slightest idee. I reckoned *he'd* stay home on Christmas—considerin'."

"When'd you see him last?"

"Yestiddy sometime, I think it was, but I ain't shore. The last time I seen him was when he was helpin' Miss Glory in the sleigh, after the dance. My Gawd! you'd took him for the Prince of Wales."

"Then you went an' got drunk?"

"Must have, Boss, or suthin' like. My haid feels sorta queer."

"Fine lot of cowboys!" ejaculated Jim, meaning the expression literally. He had lived long enough in the West to learn that such derelictions of the Diamond were now the exception instead of the rule, which had been the case before his uncle put the outfit in his charge. Bud, however, took the assertion as a calumny and proceeded to burst forth. "Boss, celebratin' Christmas an' Fourth of July are religus duties every cowpuncher holds sacred. An' this hyar is the fust time the Diamond, all together, has busted out since last Fourth. You don't appreciate us. We oughta get pulverized every Saturday night."

"I'd fire every last man jack of you," averred Jim, stoutly.

"Dog-gone-it! When you was a tenderfoot you had some human feelin's. But now thet you're a moss-backed Westerner—an' turrible in love—you're wuss'n a sky pilot. If I fell in love I'd do somethin' won-n-derful."

"If *you* fell in love!—Why, you moon-eyed, dying-duck, tenor-singing lovesick calf—everybody knows what ails you," declared Jim, dryly.

"Hellyousay?" replied Bud, good-naturedly. "News to me. I'd like to know who she is. An' say, Boss, I'm not tellin' you what I'd do to anyone else for such disrespectful talk."

"Shut up, and think, if you're capable of it. I'm worried. I want to find Curly."

But that was impossible. Jim went back to the ranch considerably concerned over Curly's disappearance. Lonestar and Bud were back, and late that night Uphill came, so Ring Locke informed Jim. The next day and the next passed. On the third day Hump and Cherry rolled in, more or less dilapidated. But no Curly! Jim discovered that he was not the only one who missed the drawling-voiced cowboy. Gloriana passed from coldness to disdain and then to pique, and from that to a curiosity which involved her own state of mind as well as interest in Curly's whereabouts.

"Curly is a proud fellow," observed Jim, for Gloriana's benefit, though he directed the remark to his uncle. "Belongs to a fine old Southern family. Rich before the war. He has taken offense at something or other. Or else he's just gone to the bad. I don't know what the Diamond will do without him."

Later, Gloriana, with one of those rare flashes of her eyes, said to Jim: "Brother mine, your remarks were directed at me. Very well. The point is, not what the Diamond will do without Curly, but what *I* will."

"Glory!—What are you saying?" expostulated Jim, both thrilled and shocked. "It's just pique. You don't care a rap for Curly. But because he bucked against your imperious will your vanity is hurt."

"Some of your deductions are amazingly correct," retorted Gloriana, satirically. "But you're off on this one. And I'm afraid your prediction about my bucking up the Diamond must be reversed. If you were not blind you'd see that."

"Glory, hang on to this strange new sweet loving character you've developed, won't you?"

"I'll hang on for dear life," laughed Gloriana, finally won over.

The last day of the old year dawned—the day of Molly's party. The cowboys, excepting Bud, had given up ever expecting to see Curly Prentiss again, who, they claimed, had eloped. Bud, however, was mysterious. "You cain't ever tell aboot thet son-of-a-gun. He'll bob up, mebbe."

Jim was not sanguine, and felt deeply regretful. Had he unduly lectured Curly? But he could not see that he had, and he resigned himself to one of those inexplicable circumstances regarding cowboys which he had come to regard as inevitable.

Jim's small family were all in the living-room early that morning, planning games for the party, when there came a familiar slow step outside, and a knock on the door. Jim opened it.

There stood Curly, rosy-cheeked as any girl, smiling and cool as ever.

"Mawnin', Boss," he drawled.

"How do, Curly! . . . Come in," replied Jim, soberly. It was too sudden for him to be delighted.

Curly sauntered in. He wore a new colored blouse, new blue jeans, and new high top boots, adorned with new spurs. He did not have on a coat or vest, the absence of which brought his worn gun-belt and gun into startling prominence.

"Mawnin', folks. I dropped in to wish you-all a happy New Year," he drawled.

Uncle Jim, Molly, and Gloriana all replied in unison. The old rancher's face wreathed itself into smiles; Molly looked delighted; and Gloriana tranquil, aloof, with darkening eyes.

"Where you been—old-timer?" queried Jim, coolly. Curly's presence always steadied him, whether in amaze, anger, or indecision.

"Wal, I took a little holiday trip to Albuquerque—to see a sweetheart of mine," replied Curly. "Shore had fun. I wanted particular to brush up on dancin'. An' my girl Nancy shore is a high stepper. I got some new steps now that'll make Bud green."

"Albuquerque!" exclaimed Jim, beginning to realize this was Curly Prentiss.

"Curly, I never heahed of no Albuquerque girl before," said Molly, bluntly.

"Molly, this was one I forgot to tell you aboot."

"Did you fetch her down for my party?"

"No. I couldn't very well. Nancy's married an' her husband's a jealous old geezer. But I shore would have loved to fetch her."

It was the expression in Molly's big dark eyes that gave Jim his clue. The cowboy did not live who could deceive Molly Dunn. Curly's story was a monstrous fabrication to conceal his drunken spree. Yet how impossible to believe this clear-faced, clear-eyed cowboy had ever been drunk! Not the slightest trace of dissipation showed in Curly's handsome fair face. He looked so innocent that it was an insult to suspect such a degrading thing. Suddenly Molly shrieked with mirth, which had the effect of almost startling the others.

"Say, anythin' funny aboot me?" queried Curly, mildly.

"Oh, Curly Prentiss!—You're so funny I—I could kiss you."

"Wal, come on. I've shore been in a particular kissable spell lately."

Gloriana was the quiet, wondering one of the group. She had been gullible enough to believe Curly's story, and had no inkling from Molly's mirth. Moreover, the growing light in her beautiful eyes gave the lie to cool indifference to Curly's presence. She was too cool. Gloriana could never wholly hide her true feelings. That was part of the price she had to pay for those magnificent orbs of violet.

"Molly," put in Jim, "if you have an urge to kiss anybody, you can come to me. I won't have you wasting kisses on this handsome, heartless cowboy. . . . Well, let's get back to our plans for the party. . . . Curly, we'd be glad to have you sit in with us on this discussion—that is, of course, if you're coming to the party."

"Wal, you shore flattered me, postponin' Molly's party once on my account," he drawled, with a blue flash of eyes upon Gloriana. "An' I wouldn't want you to do thet again. I gave up the society of a wonderful damsel to come to this heah party."

"You dog-gone lovable fraud!" burst out Molly, unable longer to conceal her feelings.

CHAPTER FOURTEEN

If ever a cowboy outfit needed to get out of town and back to hard food and hard work the Diamond was surely it—so said Ring Locke. By New Year's they were a spoiled bunch. Bud went round looking for somebody to fight; Jackson Way got married on the sly and broke the outfit in more ways than one; Lonestar grew lonesome and sad, and swore he was pining for Texas; Uphill and Hump developed acute hysteria over some trick or joke which only they seemed to share; Cherry scoured the town for a girl; and Curly, according to united verdict, became a star-gazing idiot. Nevertheless, they had daily uproars in the bunk-house, drove Jim and Molly nearly crazy with their pranks, and Gloriana to her wit's end; and at the last, as if to make amends, they made Molly's party a huge success.

The day after New Year's they rode forty miles ahead of the chuck-wagon, down out of the snow and cold, to the sunny cedared and piñoned forest. Back to saddle and chaps, to sour-dough biscuits and flapjacks, to chopping wood and smoky campfires—in a word—back to the range! And as if by magic they were all in a day the same old Diamond. Jim felt that he could burst with pride and affection. Where was there to be found another group like this? Yet that was only his personal opinion, for Uncle Jim and Locke had laughed at his conceit and told him of other noted Arizona outfits. "You get an outfit that sticks together for a spell—anywhere in Arizona—an' you have the makin's of another Diamond," declared Locke.

But Jim had his doubts. He took the Cibeque for example, and he shuddered in his boots. They, however, had been a rustling outfit. Jim gazed at the lean, quiet, youthful faces around the campfire, and he just gloried in the fact that he was one of them. Perhaps the dual characters of these boys were the secret of their fascination for him.

Next camp they were in the pines, and once more Jim lay awake at night, listening to that mighty roar of the wind in the tree tops. It was a storm wind from the north, from the mountains, and it swelled and lulled, moaned and sighed its requiem. Sometimes it sounded like an army approaching on horses.

And the fourth day they rode along their blazed trail, down into wild and beautiful Yellow Jacket. All the long way down that zigzag trail Jim whistled or stopped his horse at the turns to gaze down. Once he heard Bud remark, laconically: "My Gawd! it must be great to be in love like the boss. Jest soarin'. He'll come down with a hell of a thump pronto."

Jim laughed at Bud, but a couple of hours later, when he gazed at a huge blackened, charred mass, all that remained of the wonderful peeled pine logs which had been cut to build his ranch-house, he did come down with a sickening thump.

"Haw! Haw!—Reckon the Hash Knife has had a party, too," yelled Bud, shrilly.

"Croak Malloy's compliments, Boss. See the latest cut in the aspen there," added Curly, grimly, pointing to the largest of the beautiful white-barked quaking-asps near at hand.

Curly had sharp eyes. Jim dismounted and walked over to the tree. The crude, yet well-fashioned outline of a hash knife had been cut in the bark, and inside the blade was the letter M. Jim had seen enough of these hash knife symbols to be familiar with it, but not before had he noticed the single letter. That was significant. It seemed to eliminate Jed Stone. In a sudden violent burst of temper

Jim wheeled to his men and cursed as never before in his life.

"Wal, Boss, thet's shore fine," drawled Curly.

"Dog-gone! The boss is actooly riled," observed Up, in delight.

"Pard Jim, you aboot hit plum center, thet time," cut in Slinger Dunn's inimitable voice, something to make the nerves tingle.

"Jim Traft, so help me Gawd, I've got an inspirashun," chimed in Bud. "I'll cut down thet aspen, split out thet section an' dress it up fer Croak Malloy's grave."

"Yippy—yip—yippee!" yelled some of the cowboys, in unison.

Jim caught the infection of their grim and merry mood, but gave no further indication.

"Boys, throw the packs. And three of you go back to the wagon for another load. The rest of us will pitch camp."

According to Slinger the tracks around the cabin site and pile of charred logs were old, and probably had been made the day after the Diamond rode home to Flagerstown before Christmas.

"Which means the Hash Knife had a scout watching us," asserted Jim, quickly.

"Boss, you shore hit it on the haid," remarked Curly, admiringly.

"Dog-gone if he ain't gettin' bright," agreed Bud.

"Speaks kinda bad fer me, but I shore do think jest thet," went on Slinger.

"Slinger, all you could hope to do heah is to watch the trails down in the canyon," said Curly. "Thet greaser of Jed Stone's, the sheep-herder Sonora, has been keepin' tab on us from the rim."

"Shore. I was afeered of jest thet. Wal, I hate to kill a man when he ain't out in the open. But he's spyin' on my pardner."

"Slinger, don't be so sorrowful an' apologetic aboot it," replied Curly. "He's a greaser. He's a low-down skunk, a murderer. Next trick he'll shoot one of us in the back. Don't forget he's Croak Malloy's pard, an' not Jed Stone's."

"Smoke him up, Slinger," added Bud, with a sting in his flippant speech. "We've had all our parties an' dances an' spoonin' bees—leastways *I* have, an' thet's no joke. This hyar Sonora better keep out of my sight, fer I'll take him fer a deer or a turkey or a bob-cat."

Jim drew a deep hard breath that actually hurt his lungs. "God, it *is* hell—to wake up to this! . . . Boys, my softy days are past. We'll start this long job slow, and watch as much as we work. Slinger, your job is the same as before, only it's more. Bud, you hunt meat for camp, and I don't need to tell you what else."

"Now you're shore talkin', Boss," drawled Curly, with fire in his eye. "We'll fall down on this job if we don't forget home an' mother an' sweetheart."

"Say wife an' baby, too," added Bud, indicating the sober-faced Jackson Way. "Jack's so damn sudden an' mysterious I reckon—"

"Shet your loud trap," yelled Jackson, not seeing any humor in Bud's talk, "or I'll beat your head into a puddin'."

"Aw, Jack, I was only tryin' to be funny, to cheer up the boss," explained Bud, contritely.

Thus began the Yellow Jacket task of the Diamond. They set grimly to it, like pioneers with Indians lurking in the woods, wary and watchful. Here Jim sensed the tremendous pride of the members of the Diamond. Even Curly's carelessness now vanished, he glided at a task with the steps of a hunter and always his matchless eyes had the roving, searching look of a hawk. Rifles took precedence of axes, or any other working tools. When one of the cowboys went forth to pack in some firewood or a bucket of water, he did not leave his rifle behind. They changed the open camp to a wide dry cavern in the side of the yellow cliff, the only ingress to which was by a pine tree dropped across the brook.

Nevertheless, the new pile of peeled pine logs slowly grew as the days passed.

Slinger spied upon the Hash Knife camp, reporting several of their number absent. They were inactive, waiting for spring. "I couldn't get no closer than top of a rock wall," said Slinger. "But I seen Stone, walkin' to an' fro, his haid bent, as if he had a load on his back. Couldn't make out Malloy, an' reckon he's away. Same aboot the greaser."

"Take my field-glasses next time," said Jim, tersely. "We want to know who's there and what they're doing."

When more days, that lengthened into weeks, passed without any sign on the part of Stone's gang that they were even aware of the return of the Diamond to Yellow Jacket, Jim felt the easing of a strain.

"Wal, we'll heah from them when Malloy comes back," said Curly, meditatively. "He'll come. I cain't conceive of thet hombre bein' daid or quittin' this range. Can you, Slinger?"

"Not till he raises some more hell," returned the backwoodsman. "Malloy an' thet Texan an' the greaser must be down-country, hatchin' up somethin', or huntin' up cattle to rustle in the spring."

"Wal, spring will be heah some fine mawnin'," replied Curly. "An', dog-gone-it, Jim, your uncle will be shovin' all thet stock down in heah. He's in too darn big a hurry."

"Anyway, Uncle can't be stopped," rejoined Jim. "This rustler nest has long been a sore spot with him. And really, he doesn't see any more than a scrap or two for us, like we had with the Cibeque. The Hash Knife outfit simply doesn't phase Uncle Jim."

"He's shore a tough old cattleman an' he's been through the mill. But I cain't quite agree with him aboot only a little scrap or two. Shore there may be aboot only *one.*"

In spite of these convictions and misgivings, the weeks went on without any untoward happening at Yellow Jacket. And while vigilance did not relax there was a further lulling of apprehension. It was not wholly improbable for the Hash Knife outfit to be through. Other Arizona gangs had come to an end. In the past the Hash Knife itself had rounded out both meritorious and vicious cycles.

March brought spring down into the brakes under the giant rim of the Mogollans; violets and bluebells and primroses, as well as trout rising to flies, and the bears coming out of their hibernation, to leave muddy tracks on all the trails. The brown pine needles floated down to make room for fresh green, the sycamores showed budding leaves, long behind the cottonwoods. Smoky blue water ran in the hollows, and that was proof of snow melted off the uplands. And lastly the turkey gobblers began to gobble; early and late they kept up their chug-a-lug, chug-a-lug-chug-a-lug chug.

March also brought the vanguard of Mexican laborers to blast out and grade the road down into Yellow Jacket. Already the road was cut and leveled through the forest to the rim. And at the nearest ranch lumber and framework, cement and pipe, bricks and hardware, had begun to arrive.

Coincident with this arrived also more food supplies, and mail and news, all of which were avidly devoured by the cowboys. Curly had received a letter which rendered him oblivious to his surroundings, even to Bud's sly intrusions into his dream. Jim's uncle had taken Gloriana to California, while Molly went to stay with Mrs. Locke and diligently pursued her studies.

"Jim, lemme see thet letter from Miss Glory," asked Bud, casually. "I jest want to admire thet lovely handwritin'."

And the innocent Jim handed over the letter.

"I knowed it," declared Bud, after a quick glance, but on the moment he did not explain what it was he knew. Jim guessed readily enough that Bud had seen the handwriting on Curly's letter, and now he was in possession of the secret of Curly's trancelike abstraction.

News from Uncle Jim and Ring Locke, from friends of the cowboys, from the weekly newspaper recently started in Flagerstown, furnished debate, not to mention endless conversation, for many a camp fire.

Bambridge had sent his family away from Flagerstown, no one knew where, and had moved to Winslow to conduct his cattle business. Darnell had not been seen in town since Christmas, when he boarded a late eastbound train, after buying a ticket for Denver. But a cowboy friend of Uphill's had seen Darnell in Holbrook right after New Year's, and hinted that he kept pretty well hidden there. Croak Malloy had shot a man in Mariposa, according to range rumor. Blodgett, who operated a ranch south of the brakes, complained of spring rustling.

"Uncle Jim says to expect our five thousand head of cows and calves, with a sprinkling of steers, just as soon as the road dries up. . . . Darn his stubborn hide!"

"Then he's back from California?" asked Curly, with a naïve hopefulness.

"Sure; long ago. Says he's rarin' to come down. I'll bet he comes, too. And Glory—she raved about California. Let me read you gazabos some of her letter." And Jim sorted over the closely written pages, and finding one, he read aloud a beautiful tribute to the sunny golden state. Then he went on: "And Jim, dear, something will have to be done or I'll sure go back on Arizona for California. I didn't meet any boys out there that can compare with our cowboys. But I can't be loyal forever, without any reward. Tell the outfit that, will you, Jim? And tell them Molly and I are coming down there just as soon as ever Uncle Jim will let us. We're making life almost unendurable for him now. . . . Tell Bud he must take me hunting—(no, Molly is going to teach me to call wild turkeys)—but fishing for trout and gathering flowers. Tell Lonestar, who's the best rider in the outfit, that *he* is to teach me the flying mount, not to say how to get on a horse any old way at first. Tell Jackson—but I forgot, Jack is married, and of course, having become friends with his wife, who's a dear girl, I can't ask him to take me on long lonely walks, and climb up cliffs, where it would be necessary to support me—at least. . . . Come to think of it, I don't know that there is any other in the outfit I'd ask to fill such capacity. . . . Oh yes, Bud must show me how to carve my name on aspen trees. . . . I have favors to ask of Cherry and Up and Hump. And lastly, *somebody* must show me a real live desperado."

Not a word about Curly or Slinger! It was an omission which the impassive faces of these two individuals did not betray. Nevertheless, no violence was needed on the part of Curly and Slinger to raise pandemonium in camp. The other cowboys had incentive enough. After they had finished their remarkable demonstration Jim calmly remarked: "Certainly I would never allow Glory and Molly to visit this wild camp, even if Uncle Jim would, which I greatly doubt."

"Haw! Haw! Haw!" roared Bud, derisively, to the four winds.

"Boss, shore it'll be safe when summer comes," said Curly, eagerly, without the drawl.

"How'll it be safe?" asked Jim, bluntly.

"'Cause, dog-gone-it, Slinger an' I will make it safe—if we have to kill off the whole durned Hash Knife outfit."

"I wasn't thinking of danger to my sister and my sweetheart—from that source," remarked Jim, subtly—and he felt deeply gleeful at the glaring glances of the suspicious cowboys.

"Jim, the outfit has aboot given up whisky and fighting, not to say the society of questionable women—all for you. Don't rub it in," rejoined Curly, in cool, curt drawl, and he stalked away rather too stiff and erect to look his usual graceful self.

It was a rebuke Jim acknowledged he deserved, but he did not take occasion then to explain he had been exercising the cowboys' privilege of being cryptically funny.

The road came on down into Yellow Jacket, and all too soon the horde of bawling cattle followed, to spread over the great wild canyon and to go on down into the brakes below, and on their heels rolled the wagons with materials for Jim's ranch-house. It took days to transport the lot. And meanwhile the two builders Jim's uncle had sent down drove the cowboys to desperation with log-lifting. Jim labored mightily with them, and had the joy of the primitive pioneer, in seeing his habitation go up in the wilderness. Bud ran a pipe-line from Yellow Jacket spring, and had water on the place before the house was up. The canyon had never resounded to such unfamiliar noise. Its tranquillity had been disrupted. And this kept on while the log house grew, one log above the other, and the high-peaked, split pine-shingle roof went on, with its wide eaves sloping out over wide porches. Then while the carpenters were busy with the floors and windows and inside finish, the big barn was started, and long slim poles cut and hauled for corrals.

It was well on in May when the expert workmen left to go back to Flagerstown, leaving Jim possessed of a spacious new pine house that flashed yellow in the sunlight. But much labor there was still, and Jim realized it would take months before that habitation coincided with the picture in his mind.

"Jim, heah you have a log-cabin palace aboot ready," drawled Curly, and did not add whether he meant ready for furniture or a bride or for another bonfire for the rustlers.

After the workmen left, the old vigilance was observed. Spring was at its height, and up and down the wild canyon, and far down in the brakes, cows and steers and unbranded calves roamed at will, an irresistible temptation to range men of Croak Malloy's type. Then came the spring round-up—the first ever ridden at Yellow Jacket—and for days the yells of cowboys, the bawl of calves, and the acrid smell of burning hair filled the canyon. The Diamond brand went on hundreds of calves and yearlings. Whether he liked it or not, Jim had begun his ranching, and the cowboys had settled down once more to life in the saddle.

"Wal, the longer thet Hash Knife waits the wuss they'll ride over us," summed up the pessimistic Bud.

"Boss, it's shore the range twenty miles an' more down in the brakes that'll take our cattle," added Curly. "You can pen up a few hundred haid heah in the canyon. But your range is below. An' thet damned country is big, an' lookin' for a lost cow will be huntin' fer a needle in a haystack. It's yours, though, an' worth fightin' fer. You can double your stock in two years. Grass an' water mean a fortune to a rancher. To find 'em an' hang on to 'em—thet's the ticket."

"Aw, you gotta hang on to the *cattle,*" rejoined Bud. "I've known many a rancher who'd made his pile—if he could only have hanged on."

"Wal, it's lucky fer Jim thet the Hash Knife is peterin' out."

"Shore. . . . Say, did you fellars heah a rifle-shot?" Curly threw up his head like a listening deer.

"By gum, I heerd somethin'," replied Bud.

"What's strange about it—if you did?" queried Jim, uneasily.

"Get back under the porch," ordered Curly, sharply. "We made one mistake aboot buildin' this cabin. A good rifle could reach you from thet cliff."

"Wal, it's a safe bet Hump heerd somethin'. Look at him."

The cowboy designated by Bud's speech and finger appeared hurrying under the pines toward the cabin.

"Shot came from high up," observed Curly, warily. "Back a ways from the rim. I wonder would Slinger be up there?"

"Slinger'd be anywhere where he ought to be," said Lonestar.

They waited for Hump.

"Fellars," he said, sharply, running up on the porch, "I heerd a forty-four crack up on the rocks."

"We heahed a rifle-shot, Hump. But I couldn't swear to it's bein' a forty-four. . . . Thet would be Slinger."

"Mebbe shot a deer on the way to camp."

"An' pack it around an' down? Not much. Somethin' wrong. You could hear it in thet shot."

The Diamond waited, with only one member absent; and every moment increased speculation. When Slinger appeared down the trail there was only one exclamation, which was Curly's "Ahuh!"

They watched the backwoodsman glide along. He had the stride of the deer-stalker. But there seemed to be force and menace, something sinister, in his approach.

"Packin' two rifles," spoke up the hawk-eyed Curly. "An' what's thet swingin' low?"

"Pard, it's a gun-belt," declared Bud.

"By Gawd! so it is!" ejaculated Curly, and then as they all watched Slinger come on, he sat down to light a cigarette. "Boss," he said, presently, now with his lazy drawl, "I reckon you have one less of the Hash Knife to contend with."

"Wal, it's been some time comin'," added Bud, as if excusing a flagrant omission.

Slinger soon reached the porch. His dark face betrayed nothing, but his glittering eyes were something to avoid. He laid a shiny, worn carbine on the ground, muzzle pointing outward. It was the kind of rifle range-riders liked to carry in a saddle sheath.

"Wal, Slinger, what'd you fetch it heah thet way fer?" demanded Curly, sharply.

"Dog-gone if it ain't cocked!" exclaimed Bud. Jim, too, had just made this discovery.

"Jest the way he left it," replied Slinger. "I wanted to show you-all how near somethin' come off."

He bent over to touch the trigger, which action discharged the rifle with a spiteful crack.

"Funny it didn't go off up there," observed Slinger. "Hair trigger, all right." Then he laid a gun-belt full of shells, and also burdened with a heavy bone-handled gun, at Jim's feet on the edge of the porch. But Jim did not have any voice just then. He sensed the disclosure to come.

"Slinger, whose hardware are you packin' in?" demanded Curly.

"Belonged to thet Hash Knife greaser, Sonora," replied Slinger, who now removed his cap and wiped his wet face. "I struck his fresh track this mawnin' down the trail, an' I followed him. But I never seen him till a little while ago, up heah on the rim. He was lyin' flat on his belly, an' he shore had a bead on Jim. Pretty long shot for a greaser, but I reckon it was aboot time I got there."

Jim stood stricken, as he gazed from the porch steps where he had been sitting up to the craggy rim. Surely not a long shot! He could have killed a deer, or a man, at that distance. He suddenly felt sick. Again a miraculous accident, or what seemed so to him, had intervened to save his life. Would it always happen? Then he became conscious of Curly's cold voice.

"You — — —!" cursed that worthy, red in the face, and with a violence that presupposed a strong emotion. "Heah I've been tellin' you to keep under cover! Is it goin' to take a million years of Arizona to teach you things? . . . My Gawd! boy—thet greaser shore would have plugged you!"

CHAPTER FIFTEEN

Jed Stone regarded his Texas confederate with a long unsmiling stare of comprehension.

"Shore, Jed," repeated Pecos, "you're goin' to draw on Croak one of these days. You cain't help yourself. . . . I'd done it myself if I hadn't been afeered of him."

"Pecos, you tell me thet?" queried Stone, harshly. "You know then? He's got you beat on the draw? You're not hankerin' to *see?*"

"Not a damn hanker, Jed," drawled Pecos. "I'd shore like to see him *daid*—the crookedest little rattlesnake—but I still love life."

"Ahuh. . . . An' thet's why you're leavin' the Hash Knife?"

"Not by a long shot, Jed. I'd gone with Anderson, but for you. An' I'd gone when Malloy killed thet cowboy Reed, who throwed in with us. But I stuck on, hopin' Malloy had spit out his poison. I'm goin' because I reckon the Hash Knife is done. Don't you know thet, too, Jed?"

"Hell!—If we are done, what an' who has done us?"

"Reckon you needn't ask. You know. Malloy was the one who took up Bambridge. Arizona will never stand a cattle thief like Bambridge. She shore hates him most as bad as Texas. It's Bambridge's pretense of bein' honest while makin' his big cattle deals thet riles Jim Traft, an' other ranchers who are the real thing. Mark my words, Bambridge won't see out this summer."

"Huh! If he doesn't fork over the ten thousand he owes me he shore won't, you can gamble on thet," returned Stone.

"Wal, all those deals thet have brought us up lately were instigated by Bambridge. Runnin' off the Diamond brand up at Yellow Jacket an' shippin' the stock from Winslow—of all the damn-fool deals, that was the worst. We could have gone on for years heah, appropriatin' a few steers now an' then, an' livin' easy. No, Malloy has done us. These last tricks of his—they make me sick an' sore."

"You mean thet cattle-drive in April, without me knowin'?"

"Not thet particular. I mean buildin' this heah cabin, fer one thing. Shore it's a fort. An' only twenty miles from Yellow Jacket!"

"Ha! Ha!—Croak runs up this cabin, he said, because he liked the view down over the brakes, an' the wall of the Mogollans standin' away there so beautiful."

"Wal, I ain't gainsayin' the view. But to take Malloy serious, except regardin' life an' death, is sheer nonsense. He aims to hang on heah whether you like it or not."

"Mebbe he will hang—an' from a rope," muttered the outlaw.

"Not Croak Malloy! He'll die with his boots on, sober an' shootin'. Don't have vain hopes, Jed. . . . Malloy will run the Hash Knife—an' run it to hell. Take, for instance, these two hombres he's lately rung in on us. Just a couple of town rowdies, drinkin' up what they steal. No stuff for the Hash Knife!"

"I had the same hunch when I seen them," said Stone, pacing to and fro.

"Wal, heah's Lang an' Madden, both scared of Croak, an' they'd double-cross you any day. An' Sonora, he's Croak's man, as you know. Right now, Jed, the Hash Knife, outside of you an' me, is done."

"I reckon so. It's been keepin' me awake nights."

"Wal, then, shake the onery outfit an' come away with me?"

"Where you goin', Pecos?"

"Reckon I'll lay low fer a spell."

"Shore. But where? I want to know."

"Jed, I'll ride straight for the haid of the Little Colorado. I told you I had word last fall from an old Texas pard who's layin' low up there."

"Uh-huh. Pecos, have you got any money?"

"Shore. Malloy hasn't won all I had."

Stone turned with a jerk of decision. "All right, Pecos, if I don't join you up there before the snow flies, you can reckon Malloy's done fer *me,* as he has fer the Hash Knife."

"Jed, shore there's no call fer you to risk an even break with Croak," said the Texan, gravely. "He's no square gunman. He'd have murdered young Traft over there at Yellow Jacket thet day."

"Yes, I remember. An' my kickin' his gun up made him hate me. . . . Honest to Gawd, Pecos, the only reason I'd ever risk an even break with Croak—if I did—would be just to see if he could beat me to a gun."

"I savvy. I had the same itch. It's the one weakness of a gunman. It's plain vanity, Jed. Don't be a damn fool. Come away with me now."

Stone thought for a long moment. "No, not yet. I'm broke. I want thet money from Bambridge. An' I want to—" His pause and the checking of his thought suggested an ominous uncertainty of himself rather than meaning not to confide in the Texan. "But, Pecos, I'll promise you, barrin' ordinary accidents, thet I'll meet you at the haid of the Little Colorado sometime before the summer's over."

"Thet shore sounds good," replied Pecos, rising to his lofty stature. "Shake on thet."

Stone gripped his lieutenant's hand, and their eyes locked as well. It was one of the moments that counted with men of the open. Then Pecos strode out to his horse, and while he mounted Stone untied the halter of the pack-mule.

"Reckon you'd better work out through the woods," he said casually. "If Croak happened to meet you on the trail he'd be curious. He took Anderson's desertion as a slap in the face. . . . Good luck, Pecos."

"Same to you, Jed. I'll shore be countin' the days."

Pecos rode out from under the shadow of the great cliff, keeping to the grass, and soon headed into the fringe of timber below. Stone watched him go with mingled regret and relief. Pecos was the last of the old Hash Knife, except himself. Malloy represented a development of a later type of Arizona rustler. There was such a thing as straight rustling, about which the ranchers had never made any great hullabaloo. But these new fellows, who had corrupted some of the old, stealing cattle barefaced and wholesale, were marked for a bullet or a rope. Of course Malloy would get a bullet.

And that thought focused Stone's plodding mind on the hint he had given Pecos. The Texan had admitted as much. That was a strange coincidence, and it shamed Stone a little. Pecos, no doubt, was as good a man with a gun as Malloy. But he rode away and now he would never be certain. The outlaw leader acknowledged to himself that he was not built that way. He hated Malloy, the same as every square shooter in the Tonto. Likewise he shared their fear of the notorious gunman.

Stone sat down on the rude seat which had been fashioned by Malloy, and where he sat so often, to smoke and watch the sunset over the Mazatzals. What a grand wild view it was out and down over the black brakes to the purple ranges! But did the crooked-faced little murderer really care anything about the beauty and grandeur of that scene? Stone, inquiring into the intricacies of his own habits, was constrained to admit that most probably Croak Malloy loved Arizona and particularly this wild and lonely and colorful corner of the Tonto. It was an amazing conviction to dawn upon Stone.

Malloy had certainly selected this site for a cabin with more than its superb view in mind. It stood high up, above a long fan-shaped bare slope of grass, and had been built in a notch of the great wall of rock. It could only be approached from the front, facing downhill. The spruce logs, of which it had been constructed, had been cut right on the spot. They were heavy, too green to burn for a long time, and significant indeed were the narrow chinks left open between the logs, some close to the floor, others breast high, and not a few in the loft. A spring of clear cold water ran from under the cliff, and the cabin had been erected right over it. The wall above bulged far out, so far that neither avalanche nor bullets from any point above could reach the cabin. With store of meat and provisions a few vigilant and hardened outlaws could hold that cabin-fort indefinitely. No Arizona posse of sheriff's sworn-in deputies, or any reasonable outfit of cowboys, were going to rush that retreat, if it sheltered the Hash Knife. Stone conceded Malloy's sagacity. But it was a futile move, simply because he and his new accomplices would spend very little time there. They had made three cattle-drives already this spring, one of which was as bold and as preposterous as the raiding of the last of the Diamond stock on Yellow Jacket. Bambridge, with his new man, Darnell, was back of these. Stone had not needed to meet Darnell more than once to get his status. Darnell would hardly bother the Hash Knife long. He was too sharp a gambler. Presently, if he won too much from Croak Malloy, very suddenly he would turn up his toes.

But it was Malloy who stuck in Jed Stone's craw. Jed had never before admitted even to himself that he meant to kill the gun-thrower. When, however, he had intimated so much to Pecos, he realized the grim thing that gripped him. He did mean to kill Malloy. It had been in his dreams, in that part of his mind which worked when he was asleep, and now it possessed him. How and when to do the deed were matters of conjecture; the important thing was the decision, and Stone imagined he had arrived at it. Nevertheless, conscience awakened a still small voice. Bad as Malloy was, he trusted Stone, had fought for him, would do so again at the drop of a card, and that meant, of course, he stood ready to die for him. Stone faced the issue uneasily.

"An' the little cuss likes to set here fer the view," soliloquized the outlaw.

Stone did not blame him. Where in Arizona was there a more wonderful scene for a fugitive from justice? The black expanse of tangled rock and timber sloped many miles down, and on each side the high unscalable walls stood up with bold protection. Four days' hard riding from Winslow or Flagerstown, and more from points south, Malloy's cabin retreat seemed safe from intrustion. Moreover, it would have to be found, which task would be no slight one. Slinger Dunn probably knew of it already, and perhaps more of the backwoodsmen and hunters of the Cibeque. Stone took satisfaction in convincing himself that the Hash Knife had no more need of concern about the Diamond. Still, an afterthought was that he no longer controlled the Hash Knife. Suppose that doughty old cattleman, Jim Traft, did throw a few thousand head of steers down into Yellow Jacket! He was fool enough, and bull-headed enough, to do it. And if he did, nothing but death could ever prevent Croak Malloy from stealing them. Wherefore the ghastly idea of death for Malloy again held sway over Jed Stone.

It was a beautiful morning in May, and the brakes were abloom with fresh foliage and spring flowers. All the way down the slope bright blossoms stood up out of the grass. And the voices of birds were rich and sweet on the morning air. Pecos had ridden away, and Stone was left alone to fare for himself, as had so often been the case of late. Somebody had to stay here, and it might better be he. Any day now Malloy would return with his new men; and Madden, who had taken a message to Winslow for Stone, ought to be back. Sonora rode to and fro over the trails of the brakes, in accordance with Malloy's orders, which for once coincided with Stone's judgment.

This section of Arizona, so long a refuge, would be hard to leave. Stone did not know the headwaters of the Little Colorado, except that it was a very thickly forested country, inhabited only by Apaches and a few straggling outlaws and trappers.

But Jed Stone loved the rock walls, the colored cliffs, the canyons, the byways of the rims of the Mogollans. There was no other country like that—none so full of hiding-places—none with the labyrinth of gorge and thicket and cavern, where the wild game was tame, and where men of his kind could sleep of nights. That was the shibboleth Stone hugged to his breast. But was it all?

He confessed, as he gazed away down the sea of tree-tops, so green and tufted and bright, at the gray crags standing up as if on sentinel duty, at the wandering lines of the insulating walls, that there might be more to his obsession than just a sense of security.

"Never will be no different," he muttered. "They can't fence these brakes, or cut the timber or live down here. It belongs to us—and the Indians. Fire could never run wild down here. Too green and rocky! Too many streams! . . . All they can do is throw cattle in, and even then a thousand head would be lost. Nope, this corner of the Tonto never will be no different. . . . Reckon thet's another reason why I hate to leave."

Jed Stone had been twenty years a fugitive—a criminal in sight of the law. But he knew in his heart that the crime which had outlawed him had not been his. He held no bitterness, no resentment. Never in all those hard years would he have changed that sacrifice. Nevertheless, it was natural for him to resent the encroachment of civilization, as if he had an actual right. He had arrived at a time in his life when he balked at things as they were, at things he must do.

Stone's quick eye, ever roving from habit, detected movement of gray down in the foliage. He thought it was a deer until he saw brown and heard a distant thud of hoofs. Horses! Probably Malloy was returning. But Stone took no chances with suppositions, and his hand went to the rifle leaning against the bench.

When three horses emerged from the green below he recognized the first of the riders to be Madden, but they were halfway up the hill before he made out that the second was Bambridge. The outlaw's thought changed, and conjecture that was not friendly to this visit took the place of hard vigilance. Bambridge riding down into the Black Brakes must certainly have something to do with Malloy. It was unwise, especially for this pseudo rancher. Stone arose and walked to the high step.

The dusty horses limped wearily up the hill, to be halted before the cabin. The men were travel-stained and tired. Bambridge's big face appeared haggard, and it did not express any pleasure.

"Hullo, Boss! I fetched a visitor," called out Madden, busy with saddle packs.

"So I see. . . . Howdy, Mr. Bambridge!" replied Stone, coolly.

"Mornin', Stone. I expect you're surprised to see me," said Bambridge, bluntly.

"Shore am. Glad, though, for more'n one reason," answered the rustler.

Bambridge unstrapped a coat from his saddle, and mounted to the porch, heavy of step and dark of eye. He flopped down on the bench, dropping his coat and sombrero. Evidently he had not slept much, and it was plain his sweaty and begrimed apparel had not been changed for days. He packed a gun, which Stone had taken note of first.

"Malloy failed to show up," he said shortly.

"Ahuh. It's a way Croak has. But he'll show up when you least expect him an' don't want him. Where'd you go to meet him?"

"Tanner's out of Winslow," returned Bambridge, shortly, his dull gray eyes studying the outlaw, as if he was weighing that remark about Malloy.

"Tanner's. So Malloy meets you there, eh?—Wal. I reckon he might as well go into Winslow or Flag," said Stone, dryly.

Bambridge seemed uncertain of his ground here, but was indifferent to it. Stone grasped the fact that the cattle dealer did not take him for the dominant factor in the Hash Knife.

"You can bet I'd rather he had. Eighty miles ride, without a bed, an' practically nothin' to eat, is enough to make a man bite nails."

"What's the reason you undertook it?"

"It concerns me an' Malloy," said the other.

Whatever sense of fair play Jed Stone felt toward this man—and he confessed to himself that it was little—departed here.

"Any deals you make with Malloy concern me. I'm boss of this Hash Knife outfit."

"Not so any one would notice it," rejoined Bambridge, with scant civility.

The man was on dangerous ground and had no intimation of it. Steeped in his absorption of his greedy sordid plans, if he had the wit to understand Jed Stone he did not exercise it. Stone paced the narrow porch, gazing out over the brakes. For the moment he would waive any expression of resentment. Bambridge was in possession of facts and plans that Stone desired to know.

"Wal, mebbe you're right aboot Croak bossin' the outfit pretty generally," he said, at length. "But only in late deals that I had little to do with. What I don't advise I shore don't do. Thet deal of Diamond cattle last winter—thet was an exception. I've kicked myself often enough. . . . By the way, you can fork over thet ten thousand you've owed me on thet deal. I sent Madden in to get it."

"Man alive! I gave the money to Darnell, with instructions to hand it to Malloy for you," ejaculated Bambridge, in genuine surprise.

"You did? When?"

"Weeks ago. Let's see. It was the ninth of April that I drew that ten thousand.

Next day Darnell was to ride out to Tanner's. He met Malloy there and delivered your money."

"Not to me," declared Stone.

"Why!—the man is reliable," replied Bambridge, in exasperation. "Are you quite—honest, about it? . . . Have you seen Malloy since?"

"Wal, Bambridge, I've seen Malloy several times since then. He never mentioned no money—for me. Appeared to be pretty flush himself, though. . . . An' much obliged for the hint about my honesty."

Bambridge let the caustic rejoinder go by without apology.

"Honesty is not your trade, Stone. I'll say, though, you've kept your word to me, which is more than Malloy has. . . . You suspect this new man of mine, Darnell?"

"No, I don't suspect him. I *know* him to be a Mississippi River gambler, run out of St. Louis—accordin' to his own statement. I've seen a few of his kind hit the raw West. They didn't savvy us Westerners an' they didn't last. Darnell has double-crossed you. He'll try it on Croak Malloy, which will be bad for his health."

"No wonder Darnell can't savvy you Westerners. Who the hell can, I'd like to know?"

"Wal, not you, thet's shore."

"Give me proof Darnell has done me dirt," demanded the other, impatiently.

"Wal, I saw him right here after the tenth of April—along aboot the twentieth, I reckon, for it was after Malloy made a raid on Blodgetts' range. . . . Darnell did not give me any money. He had a big roll, for I saw him flash it when he was gamblin' with the men. . . . Thet was the day Croak shot young Reed."

"Aw. I'd want more proof than that," returned Bambridge. "You might have been drunk when Darnell gave it to you."

"Shore. I might have been anythin'. Us outlaws are pretty low down, I reckon. But I, for one, am not as low-down as some who call themselves cattlemen. . . . Bambridge, am I to hold you or Darnell responsible fer thet ten thousand?"

"Not me, you can bet. Or Darnell, either. Malloy is your man. He seems to be runnin' your outfit now, an' no doubt appropriated your money."

"Nope. Croak is square aboot money," said the outlaw, meditatively.

"Bah!—What you givin' me?" retorted Bambridge, harshly. "Stone, you talk queer for a rustler. Here you are hidden down in this God-forsaken wilderness—afraid to go near any town—with a price on your life, yet you talk of honesty in yourself an' men. Thet's a joke about honor among thieves."

"Wal we needn't argue aboot it," replied Stone. A Westerner would have gauged something from the cool quality of his voice and the averting of his eyes. "I've served your turn. An' now thet Malloy is doin' it, why, you've no call to get nasty. What I'd like to know is—how'd you come to ride out here? Shore is a long hard ride fer anyone."

"I want action. That's why I came," almost yelled Bambridge, red in the face. "Malloy has failed me twice, both times because I didn't pay first. Here I have a chance to sell ten thousand head of cattle—to the government buyer in Kansas City—an' I haven't the cattle."

"Chance to sell quick an' get out of Arizona, huh?"

"You've hit it, Stone. An' that's why I'm here. I want cattle. Old Traft lately drove a big herd down into Yellow Jacket. I'm after it. Malloy agreed to drive it. I've built a corral along the railroad, halfway between Winslow an' Holbrook. Short-cut idea, see? An' I can load there. He also agreed to make away with this damned young smart Alec, Jim Traft. Took the money quick enough, by damn."

"Took what money?" queried Stone, with no apparent interest.

"What I offered for the job," fumed the cattleman. "Then afterward he said it was the kind of job Croak Malloy couldn't do. But he'd put his man Sonora on it. A Mexican."

"Job to do away with young Jim Traft," mused Stone, drumming the bench with his fingers. "Wal, I reckon thet's a fine idee—fer *you.* I'll tell you somethin', though. Sonora will never do it."

"More double-crossin', eh?"

"No. The greaser is straight. Funny fer a greaser, ain't it? But he simply won't, because Slinger Dunn will kill him. I wouldn't go prowlin' around Yellow Jacket for anythin', an' you can gamble Malloy wouldn't, either."

"So that's why he's slow about drivin' the Diamond cattle. Damn his crooked mug! . . . Stone, did you know Malloy was in with that Tanner outfit an' has been workin' on Blodgett's stock?"

"No. Thet's news to me. Who told you?"

"Darnell. In fact, he made the deal. This was against my orders, I'm bound to admit. I am pretty sore at him an' I'm through with him. But Malloy has got to square himself with me."

"Your man is playin' both ends against the middle," observed the outlaw, thoughtfully. "He's smart enough to try to use Malloy—same as you—an' get a big raid off. Then he, too, can jump Arizona. Wal, my advice is to be jumpin' quick. We decent rustlers don't work thet way. We never rob any cattleman of enough stock to ruin him. Thet's why the Hash Knife has lasted twenty years."

"My daughter married a cowboy in Flag last winter," said Bambridge. "An' I'm ready to get out quick, without any advice from you. Can you jack up Malloy on this job?"

"Shore I can, if I like," replied the outlaw, easily. "I can handle Croak on any deal, providin' I give him the big share. I'm not keen, though, to egg him along—for nothin'."

Bambridge was no match for Stone in subtlety. He had been led on to tell his business with Malloy; now all the outlaw leader wanted to know was whether or not he had brought the money.

"Malloy wanted twenty thousand dollars," said Bambridge. "That was out of all reason. He can't deliver cattle enough. So we jawed about it. He came down to fifteen—an' I've got ten thousand with me. Suppose you persuade Malloy to make the drive—with as few men as can possibly be needed. An' the day you land the cattle at my corral I'll fork over the other five thousand."

"How many cattle?" asked Stone, tremendously interested, but not in any case in the query he made.

"I don't stipulate any number. Only as many as can be rounded up quick an' driven out quick."

"Ahuh. . . . Suppose you let me see the color of thet ten thousand," suggested the rustler, as if he needed a little more material persuasion.

Bambridge unbuttoned his bulging vest, and from an inside pocket drew forth a packet of clean new greenbacks, with the bank wrapper still round them. He flipped it upon the bench. Money was only so much paper to him! His large features worked.

"You've as much right to doubt me as I have you," he said, blandly. "There you are!—Nice fresh green color!"

"Wal, it ain't so much money, after all, considerin'," reflected Stone.

The cattleman's face fell. He had calculated upon this last card.

"I've got about five hundred more in gold. I'll throw that in. Will you pull off the deal?" And he jingled the heavy coins, which evidently were what had made his vest bulge.

Stone's veins leaped as the released blood gushed hot and bursting along them. All his talk had been pretense, except wherein he had wanted to find out if Bambridge really carried the money with him.

"Let me see thet, too. . . . The gold! The good old yellow stuff with the music—an' the hell hid in it."

Bambridge reacted slowly to that suggestion. Something wedged into his eager one-ideaed mind. Instead of complying with Stone's request he ceased jangling the gold and snatched up the packet of bills, which he returned to his pocket. Then he buttoned up his vest.

"Fork it all over!" suddenly called the outlaw, and in a single second such a remarkable transformation occurred in him that Bambridge's eyes popped wide.

"Wha-at?" he stammered.

"Hand me thet money."

"I will not. No pay in advance. Malloy—"

"Pay hell! I wouldn't drive a steer fer you. But I want the ten thousand. You owe it to me."

"See you in hell first," burst out Bambridge, furiously. He stood up, and stepped out as if to go off the porch.

Stone gave him a sudden hard shove, which staggered him backward. "You—fool! You will brace me on my own ground? Fork over thet money or—"

"You're a low-down thief! No wonder Malloy's quit standin' for you. . . . An' if you want to know it—there's talk of collectin' the reward on your head."

Bambridge's ignorance of such men as Jed Stone could not have been better expressed. And if he had known how to inflame this outlaw it was doubtful if he could have done so more subtly. For years that price on Stone's head had been a thorn in his flesh. There were still a mother and a father living, not to forget a sacrificed sweetheart; and the thought of them hearing of this reward was torture.

Stone drew his gun and struck Bambridge over the forehead. Not a violent blow, though it brought blood! The cattleman fell over the bench, against the wall.

"Get that through your thick skull?" demanded Stone, as he menacingly straddled the bench. *"Hyar!* Don't pull—"

But Bambridge, like a madman, his face ablaze, reached back toward his hip.

"Take it then!" hissed the outlaw. His shot broke Bambridge's draw. The gun slipped out on the floor and spun round. Bambridge uttered a horrible groan, sagged back, his huge face going out, like an extinguished light.

Stone stood an instant. Then with swift movement he picked up the gun from the floor, fired it into the wall, and dropped it again. Then, bending over the dead man, he ripped open his vest and extracted the money, which he transferred to his own pocket. That done, he stepped to the porch. The gun in his hand still smoked. Sheathing it, he glanced along the wall of the cliff to see Madden coming on a run. His next move was to light a cigarette, and his fingers were as steady as a rock. He had shot Bambridge as he would have a hydrophobia skunk, than which there was no more despised beast of the wilderness.

CHAPTER SIXTEEN

Madden thumped up to the cabin, breathless and alarmed. "Boss, I heerd—shootin'," he panted.

"Reckon you did," replied Stone, removing his cigarette to puff a cloud of smoke.

The right-hand man of Croak Malloy took his cue from that—no need for concern!

"What come—off?"

"Wal, you can see fer yourself."

Madden stamped up the high porch steps, his beady eyes working as if on points, until suddenly they fixed on the dead man, the little stream of blood running out toward the gun lying on the floor. It seemed to be an accusing finger.

"—! Throwed on you?" ejaculated Madden, in amaze.

Stone nodded.

"What's thet cut on his haid?" asked the other, curiously.

"Wal, he fell all over the place," replied Stone, casually. "I reckon he hit the bench. . . . Better search him, Madden."

The outlaw picked up the gun, took a look at the chamber, and laid it on the bench. Then he extracted watch, papers, and a handful of gold coins from the pockets, which he placed beside the gun. His next move was to look for a money-belt.

"Wasn't well heeled," he remarked, in disgust. "I recollect he an' Croak had a hell of a row at Tanner's. There was a game on. An' Bambridge lost. Swore he'd never fetch any more money where there was a lot of robbers. Haw! Haw!"

"You're welcome to thet, Madden. I shore don't want it."

"Thanks, Boss. An' what about all these papers?"

"Wal, I reckon you can keep them for Croak," said Stone, with humor. "By the way, Madden, when do you expect him?"

"Today, sure. Thet's why I near rode Bambridge off his laigs gettin' hyar. . . . What'd you an' Bambridge fight aboot?"

"Wait till Croak comes," replied the rustler leader. "I don't want to tell it all over again."

"Shall we drag Bambridge an' bury him, or wait fer thet, too?"

"Reckon we'd better wait. Put thet gun back on the floor where you found it. An' cover him over."

"Haw! Haw! Pertickler on Coark seein' the evidence, huh? . . . Don't blame you. Croak will be a-rarin'. But at thet he wasn't so fond of Bambridge, an' don't you overlook it."

Stone sat down on the porch steps and smoked a cigarette, while Madden fetched a tarpaulin from the canyon corral where the horses were fenced in. The tight cold tension within Stone slowly relaxed its grip, but did not disappear. He felt that he might as well make a day of it, if opportunity afforded. Malloy would undoubtedly be rancorous at the killing of Bambridge. Stone did not concern himself even to think out an explanation. What did he care what the little rattlesnake thought? The hard fierce creed of outlaws had not been transgressed—that Stone knew in his heart. It might be, presently, but that was another matter. He would wait to see how Malloy took the situation.

"Firewood runnin' low," said Madden. "I'll pack up some. Funny how we all hate to lug wood up the hill."

Stone watched the short, sturdy figure in its dust-crusted garb go down the hill to the edge of the timber, and come staggering up again, under a load of faggots. He wondered how soon Croak Malloy would come, and still felt sure of himself. There was no time like the first moments of the inception of a resolve. Who would be with Malloy? Perhaps a new man or so, and surely that hulking specimen of town-dive riffraff, Blacky Reeves, as Malloy called him. Stone reflected that he might as well have a shot at him, too, while he was at it, and the thought was pleasing.

But the afternoon wore on, and the croaking Nemesis of the Hash Knife did not appear. Stone sat for hours on Malloy's seat on the porch, waiting and watching.

The long shadows crept out over the brakes, the purple veils drooped into the canyons, the high rims caught the gold of sunset and shone in winding zigzag lines. Then dusk intervened, the air chilled, the night-hawks began their piercing-noted quest. Gloom settled down over the wilderness, and silence, and soon night. Malloy would not come up that rough trail in the dark.

Call to supper at last brought the outlaw leader inside the cabin, where bright fire and smoking pans and pots attested to Madden's practical application of duties surely neglected by others of the Hash Knife.

"No sign of Croak?" he asked.

"Nary. An' mebbe it's jest as well," replied Stone.

"Shore. Tomorrer you'll feel less testy. . . . Wal, Croak's been in a fight, you can lay to thet. Else he'd been hyar. I seen him at Tanner's about a week ago—yep, jest seven days, an' we set the day for me to get hyar with Bambridge. . . . Thet feller Darnell has messed things up again, I reckon."

"Madden, I appreciate your cookin', if not your company," said Stone.

"Shore kind of you, Boss," replied the other, sarcastically. "But when the final row between you an' Croak comes don't take any of it out on me. I was Croak's pard before we come to the Hash Knife. An' if I do see some queer deals I hardly approve of, I can't do nothin'."

"I'll remember thet, Madden," rejoined Stone, in a surprise he did not show. "Thet's straight talk. I didn't think it was in you."

They finished the meal, after which Stone smoked in front of the fire, where Madden presently joined him.

"Forgot aboot thet dead hombre out there," he said. "We ought to have planted him."

"Maddy, you've slept before where there was a dead man lyin' around."

"Shore. But I ain't crazy about it."

After a while, which was mostly silence, they sought their blankets. Stone's bed happened to be in the corner just inside where Bambridge lay, and he could smell the blood. Sleep did not come readily, so presently he got up, and carrying his blankets to another unoccupied bough-couch in the cabin, he spread them in that. It was a quiet night, with no sound except a low moan of wind in the caverns of the great overhanging cliff. And some hours elapsed before Stone fell into slumber.

Next morning he was up with the sun, and something as black and uncanny as the vanished night, had left him. Stone walked along the wall, as far as the intersecting canyon which the rustlers used as a corral for the horses. He reminded himself that he did this quite often. There seemed no sense in deceiving himself—he would soon be riding away from the rendezvous and the brakes. Which presupposed that he did not mean to give Malloy a chance to kill him!

On his return he heard a halloa, and quickening his steps soon turned a corner of wall to see riders coming up the slope. Three—with pack-animals!

Madden hailed him from the door. "Croak comin' with Blacky an' some fellar I cain't make out yet."

Stone, in action of which he was unaware, hitched his heavy belt, as if about to mount a horse or undertake something physical. As he went up the porch steps his quick eye took in the tarpaulin that hid Bambridge. The body looked like some covered packs.

"Maddy, no hurry aboot tellin' Croak," said Stone, indicating the dead man.

"All right, Boss. I'd jest as lief see Croak cheerful as long as possible."

Then they both went into the cabin. Madden to bustle around the fire, and Stone to watch through one of the chinks between the logs. The three rustlers came very slowly up the slope, to halt before the cabin. A lean dark rider, the stranger, sagged in his saddle. A bloody bandage showed from under his sombrero. He was the last to dismount, but they were all ridden out. Without speaking they threw saddles and packs, and left the weary horses standing.

"Wal, if thar's anybody home they shore ain't powerful glad to see us," said Malloy, gruffly.

Madden ran out, his hands white with flour. "Howdy, men! We seen you comin', but didn't think it no call fer a brass band."

"Haw!—I should smile not. . . . Anybody hyar?" returned Malloy.

"Only the boss."

Whereupon Stone stalked out, and a singular incomprehensible fact was that he was glad to see the gunman. Croak radiated the raw hard force of the range. He was, at best, an ally to depend upon in times that tried men. On the other hand, Stone certainly had a wavering thought—this was the moment! Nevertheless, he did not take advantage of it.

"Mornin', Croak. How's tricks?" he said, cheerfully.

"Hullo there, you old son-of-a-gun!" replied Malloy. "Got news fer you—an' somethin' else."

Malloy limped. Something beside sweat and dust had caked on his worn yellow chaps—something dark and sinister. Stone's sharp eye caught a bullet-hole in the leather. Malloy carried a rifle, saddle-bag, and an extra gun-belt, minus shells. His leather jacket looked as if he had slept in wet clay that had hardened. His crooked face somehow appeared wonderful to look at, or else Stone's mind at the moment was steeped in strong feeling. Malloy might have been wearing a death mask, yet his eyes were alight, and it seemed that in them was a smile. His boots dragged across the floor, his spurs jangled, as he went into the cabin, to deposit wearily what he carried.

"Howdy, you cook!" he called. "Then the four-flush cattle thief didn't come out?"

"Croak, I've shore got bad news," returned Madden. "But s'pose you rest a little—an' eat somethin'—before I spring it on you."

"Good idee. I'm mad as a tarantula-wasp anyhow. . . . I reckoned Bambridge wouldn't come. . . . An' mebbe I like it jest as well as if he did. No more deals fer me with thet —— —— ——!"

"Sounds good to me, Croak," returned Stone, with satisfaction. "Reckon I can give you a reason why you can't take up any more deals with Bambridge. But it's bad news. An' suppose you have a shot at my bottle first."

Malloy took a long drink of fiery liquor that made him cough huskily and brought color to his ashen cheeks.

"Uggh!—If I'd hed thet two days ago—mebbe I'd never got hyar," he said, enigmatically.

"Where's Lang?"

"Ha!—Feedin' the buzzards."

"You don't say," returned the outlaw leader, coolly, though the statement had struck fire from him. Another of the original Hash Knife gone! Lang was not loyal, but he belonged to the old school, and once he had been respectable.

Slow footfalls thudded up the steps outside, across the porch. The bar of light from the door darkened. Reeves entered with the lean-jawed stranger.

"Hed to shoot thet bay. She was bad crippled," announced Reeves.

"Should have been done before," replied Malloy. "Boss, shake hands with Sam Tanner. . . . Cousin of Joe's from up Little Colorado way."

"Howdy, Tanner," said Stone, civilly, though he did not move toward Malloy's new man. Perhaps this omission was not noticed, as table and packs and also Malloy stood between. Tanner merely bowed his bandaged head, which, with sombrero removed, showed matted hair, and dark stains extending down over the left temple and ear.

"Must have jagged your haid on a snag or somethin'," went on Stone.

"Nary snag. I got sideways to a lead slug," returned Tanner. He had a low voice, and a straight, level look from his black eyes. Stone gauged men of the range with speed and precision. This fellow, since he was kin to Joe Tanner, and in the company of Croak Malloy, could be only another of their ilk, but he seemed a man to consider thoughtfully.

"Croak, I reckon you'll be tellin' me you've had a little brush with somebody," said Stone, dryly.

"Brush?—Haw! Haw!" rejoined the gunman, and his flaring glance, his crisp query, and his deadly little croak of a laugh made Stone's flesh creep. He guessed there were some dead men somewhere who would never tell the tale of what had happened.

"Wal, take your time tellin' me," drawled the leader.

"Come an' get it," yelled Madden.

They sat at the rude table, upon which the cook thumped steaming utensils. The keen-eyed Stone remarked that all three men were ravenously hungry, yet only Malloy could eat. That to Stone was most significant. So far as Malloy was concerned, however, it would take a great deal to sicken him.

"A good stiff drink with some hot grub—an' a fellar's able to go on," he said, as he rose. "But I'll shore sleep most like our pard Lang hangin' down there on thet cottonwood."

Stone did not reveal his curiosity; he knew he would soon be enlightened, and if his intuition was not at fault most weighty things had happened. But when Malloy drew a heavy roll of soiled greenbacks from his pocket and tossed it over, Stone could not hide a start.

"Bambridge sent thet money he owed you," said Malloy. "Like the muddlehaid he is he trusted it to Darnell. . . . An' I'm tellin' you, pard, if it hadn't been fer me you'd never seen it."

"I reckon. Thanks—Croak," replied the outlaw chief, halting. This was one of the surprising attributes of the little gunman. Vicious and crooked as he was, he yet had that quality which forced respect, if not more, from Stone's reluctant mind.

Malloy laboriously took off his chaps and flapped them into his corner of the cabin. Then a bloody wet spot showed on the leg of his jeans. "Some hot water, Maddy, an' a clean rag. I've a crease on my laig."

"What's the fellar got who gave you thet cut, Croak?" queried Stone.

"He got nothin', wuss luck. I was shore damn near my everlastin', Jed, an' don't you overlook it. . . . Sam, you better have Madden wash thet bullet hole of yours. He's pretty handy."

Stone curiously watched the deft Madden dress the wounds of the injured rustlers.

"Ouch!—What'd you put in it, you idjet? Feels like salt," shouted Malloy.

"Croak, you're wuss'n a baby aboot little hurts. What'd you do if you got shot bad?"

"Haw! Haw! Thet's a good one. I can show more bullet scars than any damn rider in these brakes. An' I know who made each one. Some of the men are livin' yet, which speaks pore fer me. I never lived up to my reputation."

In due time the ministering was ended, after which Malloy asked for another drink. "Reckon I'd better get some of my news off my chest. Then after I hear yours I'll have a nap of about sixteen hours. . . . Boss, would you mind comin' out on the porch where I can set down an' talk?"

They went outside, and Stone experienced a qualm when Malloy hobbled to his favorite seat. The foot of his injured leg rested upon what he must have thought was a pack, but it happened to be Bambridge's head under the tarpaulin.

"Jed, you know thet trapper's cabin down hyar a ways—reckon aboot three hours stiff ridin'?—Thet old one under the wall, where a spring runs out by a big white sycamore?"

"Shore. I know it. Slept there often enough. Full of mice an' bugs."

"Wal, it ain't no more," said Malloy, with a grim chuckle. "It's a heap of ashes."

"Burnt, eh? What you fellars doin'—burnin' all the cabins around?"

"Hellno. We didn't do it. That tarnel Slinger Dunn!"

"Ah, I see. . . . Wal, Slinger is a bad hombre. Too much like an Apache! . . . Hope you didn't brush with the Diamond."

"Jed, your hopes air only born to be dashed. Me an' you left of the Hash Knife, 'cept Maddy hyar—an' you can lay it to thet damned slick tracker. Dunn an' the outfit he's throwed in with. You oughta have killed him long ago."

"Not so easy to do as to say," replied Stone, sarcastically.

"Ha—you're talkin'. Wal, I had a chanct to kill Slinger, but it'd have meant me gettin' it too."

"You're learnin' sense late—mebbe too late, Croak. . . . I hope to God, though, you didn't raid this new stock of Jim Traft's."

"No, Jed, we didn't," replied Malloy, frankly. "I was sore at you fer talkin' ag'in' it, but after I got away an' seen what a mess Bambridge an' his card sharper got me into I changed my mind. Not that I wouldn't of druv the cattle later! But this hyar wasn't the time. An' if Bambridge had come to meet me hyar, as he promised, with a new deal on fer this Diamond stock, I'd shore have taken the money, but I wouldn't have made a single move. Not now."

"Wal, you puzzle me. Suppose you quit ridin' round in a circle," declared Stone, impatiently.

"Fust aboot the money Bambridge sent you by Darnell," began Malloy. "I seen he was flush at Tanner's, an' he was losin' fer a change. Joe is pretty keen himself with the cairds. I set in till I was broke. We hung round Joe's ranch fer a week, waitin', an' finally I got wind of this backhand game Darnell was playin'. He was the mouthpiece between me an' Bambridge. But all the time he was hatchin' a deal on his own hook. An' this one was to make a raid on Blodgett's range without lettin' Bambridge in on it. Joe Tanner never was no smart fellar, an' shore he was always greedy. So he double-crossed us, too. Wal, it was Sam hyar who put me wise. An' after figgerin' some an' snoopin' around I seen the deal. Funny I didn't shoot Darnell. But I jest held him up. Then he swore the big roll he had was fer you from Bambridge. I reckoned thet was the truth. . . . Wal, a day or so after they druv the lower end of the brakes an' got some odd thousand head of Diamond stock up on the open range below Tanner's. I was hoppin' mad when I found out, but neither Darnell or Joe came back to Tanner's. Sam's sweet on the sawmill man's daughter, an' thet's how he come to be out of what followed. He told me, an' also thet Darnell, Joe, Lang, an' some riders he didn't know were comin' up to get another whack at the Diamond cattle. Then I was a-rarin' to get at them. I seen it all too late. Bambridge, by playin' on my hopes, had got me in on his deals. He was aimin' fer a big stake—then to duck out of Arizona. Now Darnell carried his messages to an' fro, an' he seein' a chance himself, double-crossed Bambridge an', as I said, persuaded Joe Tanner to throw in with him."

Malloy refilled his pipe and called for Madden to fetch him a light. After puffing thoughtfully, his cramped, wrinkled brow expressive of much, he went on:

"I took their trail with Sam. Night before last, jest before sundown we come damn near gettin' run down by a stampede of cattle. We rustled to thet trapper's cabin, an', by Gawd! we hadn't hardly hid our horses an' slipped in there when hyar come Joe, Lang, Darnell, an' his seedy-lookin' outfit. Some of them had sense enough to ride on. But both Darnell an' Tanner had been shot an' found ridin' hard. I never seen a madder man than Tanner, nor a scareder one than Darnell. We'd jest started to have hell there—with me readin' it to them, when we found out who an' what was chasin' them. . . . No less than the Diamond outfit, Jed, led by Slinger Dunn an' thet Prentiss cowpuncher.—Dog-gone, I'd always wanted to run ag'in' him! . . .Wal, there they had us, an' you can bet we didn't sleep much thet night. When daylight come I took a look out, an' was surprised when the bullets begun to fly. Them darned punchers all had rifles!—An' there we was, with only our guns, no shells to spare, little grub, an' no water atall. We was stuck, an' you bet I told them. Thet glade is open in front of the cabin, as you can recollect, an' there them daredevil cowboys dodged along the edge of the timber, like a bunch of Apaches, an' kept shootin'. We couldn't do nothin'. Say, wasn't I hot under the collar? Worried, too, Jed, an' don't you overlook thet. . . . Wal, they was cute enough to guess it, an' this Prentiss hombre yelled for us to throw out all guns an' belts, an' to come after, hands up, an' line up ag'in' the cabin wall. . . . Haw! Haw!"

Malloy laughed in grim recollection of the images or ideas his words called up. Stone could not divine any humor in them. Probably Malloy laughed at the suggestion for him to put up his hands.

"I yelled back," resumed Malloy, "'Hey, Prentiss, what'll you do to us—in case we surrender?'

"'Wal, we'll shore hang you an' thet caird sharp, anyways,' called back the cowboy. Orful cheerful he was, an' sort of cocky. . . . Gawd! but I wanted to get out there to throw a gun on him. Then I yelled back, 'Reckon you'll have to come take us.'

"It wasn't long after thet when I smelled smoke," resumed Malloy, after a pause. "Thet damned redskin Dunn had set fire to the cabin roof. It was an old roof of shacks an' brush, an' shore dry. Burn? You should have heerd it! We didn't have a hell of a lot of time. Fire began to drop on us. Lookin' out, I seen thet the cowboys had bunched over at the edge of the woods, jest out of gunshot. I seen also thet the smoke from the cabin was blowin' low an' gettin' thicker. 'Men,' I says, 'we've got one chanct an' a slim one. Take it or leave it. I'm gonna run out under cover of thet smoke, an' make a break fer cover. Anyway, it's better to be shot than burn up or hang. Take your choice. But whoever's comin' with me start when I yell.'"

Malloy took another long pull at his pipe, and his wonderful eyes, flaring with lightning, swept down over the wild brakes and along the wandering gray wall of rock.

"I waited till a thick lot of smoke rolled off the roof," went on Malloy, "an' then I yelled, 'Let 'er rip!' An' I run fer it, a gun in each hand. To do 'em credit, every last man in the cabin charged with me. But what'n hell could they do? . . . Wal, I got a bullet in the laig fust thing, an' I went down. But I got up an' run as best I could. You'd thought an army had busted loose—there was so much shootin'. An' bullets—say, they was like bees! But we had the smoke with us, or not one man jack of us would have escaped. Shore I was shootin', but bein' crippled an' on the run, I was shootin' pore. I nailed one of them punchers, though, an' I seen another one fall. Thet one was daid before he hit the ground. But some one else allowed fer him. . . . I got to the timber an' fell in the brush, where you bet I laid low. I reckoned my laig was broke. But I wasn't even bad shot, an' when I got it tied up I felt better. The shootin' an' yellin' soon ended. I peeped through the brush . . . an' what do you reckon I seen?"

"Some rustler swingin'," returned Stone, hazarding a guess.

"Nope. It was thet caird sharp, Darnell. But when I seen him fust they hadn't swung him up. I could hear him beggin'. But thet Diamond bunch was shore silent an' swift. They jerked him clear, till he kicked above their haids. I seen his tongue stick out . . . then his face go black. . . . An' next went up Lang an' Joe Tanner. They had their little kick. . . . I watched, but seen no more rustlers swing. But shore Prentiss an' Dunn would have nailed some of them on the run. I crawled away farther an' hid under a spruce thet had branches low on the ground. I lay there all day, till I was shore the cowpunchers had rid away. Then I went into the spruces where me an' Blacky had hid our horses. His was gone, but mine was there. I sneaked him off into the woods, an' worked round to the trail. All night! This mawnin' I run into Blacky, who'd got away without a scratch. An' Sam, who hadn't been in the cabin, seen us from his hidin'-place, an' whistled. . . . An' wal, hyar we air."

"Croak, you might have reckoned on some such mess as thet," said Stone, gravely.

"Shore I might, but I didn't. Jed, I've had too damn much money lately. Thet gambler het up my blood. I'm sorriest most thet I didn't plug him. But it was a hell of a lot of satisfaction to see him kick."

"No wonder. I'd like to have been there. . . . So the Hash Knife is done!—Croak, what do you aim at now?"

"Lay low an' wait," replied the gunman. "We shore can find men to built up the outfit again."

"Never—if young Traft got killed in thet fight," retorted Stone, vehemently. "Old Jim would rake the Tonto with guns an' ropes."

"Course I don't know who got shot, outside of the two cowboys I see drop. The one I shot wasn't young Traft, an' neither was the other. An' they wasn't Slinger Dunn or Prentiss, either. . . . Boss, have you seen Sonora?"

"No. He hasn't been in fer days," replied Stone.

Malloy held his pipe far away from him and sniffed the air.

"Damnit, am I loony, or do I smell blood?"

"I reckon you smell blood all right, Croak, old boy," returned Stone, jocularly.

"How so? I'm shore washed clean." Suddenly, with his gaze on Stone, narrowing and shrewd with conjecture, he felt with his foot the pack upon which it had rested. "What the hell?"

Then with a singularly violent action he swept away the tarpaulin, to disclose Bambridge, a ghastly sight for even calloused men; and the pool of blood, only partly dried up; and the gun lying near on the floor.

"Bambridge!" he exclaimed, in cold and ringing speculation. "Boss, you done fer him?"

"I reckon. He throwed a gun on me, Croak," replied Stone, rising to go to the wall, where he poked a finger in a bullet hole in one of the yellow logs. "Look here."

"Ahuh. . . . Wal, you saved me the trouble, mebbe. . . . Shot yestiddy, I reckon. What'd he have on him?"

"Ask Madden. He searched him."

"Hyar, Maddy, come out pronto," he yelled, and when the cook ran out breathless and anxious, he went on. "This was your bad news, eh?"

"Nope, I didn't reckon thet bad. But he had only aboot five hundred on him, an' some papers."

"Huh. Five hundred what?" demanded Malloy.

"Dollars—in gold double-eagles."

"An' this two-bit cattle thief reckoned he'd bribe me with thet!" he ejaculated, in disgust. "Wal, Maddy, give me one of them gold birds fer luck, an' keep the rest. . . . An' say, somebody'll have to plant this stiff. . . . Blacky, you an' Madden gotta dig a grave fer our departed guest. Dig it right out hyar alongside the porch, an' put up a stone or somethin', so when I see it I'll be reminded of what a foolish galoot I am."

"Reckon you'd better search him again, Madden," added Stone. "Bambridge was the kind of hombre who'd sew bills up inside his clothes."

The two outlaws, enthusiastic in obedience, lost no time complying. Stone turned away from the gruesome sight. But Malloy watched with a sardonic grin.

"Jed, I don't notice thet you've gone back any on the draw," he remarked. "You shore hit him plumb center. . . . An', wal, I guess I gotta take it as friendly act on your part, though I seen red fust off."

Malloy had his strong fascination for all men who came in contact with him, and never had Jed Stone felt it more certainly than now. Over all men he exerted a fascination of fear, but this was hardly what influenced the rustler leader here. He still bore the hatred for Malloy, because the gunman had broken up the Hash Knife; nevertheless, his deadly intent began to lose the keenness of its edge. A deep resolve, however, was something so fixed in Stone that to change it, let alone eradicate it, was a slow, painful process.

It had its inception at this hour, however, and began its gradual disintegration.

Malloy went to bed and to sleep. His slumber, however, was as strange a thing as any other connected with him. He slept, yet seemed to be awake. The slightest sound would make him wide awake in a second. This was not conscience or fear, for the man possessed neither; it was the defensive instinct of the gunman most highly developed.

That day and the night passed. Stone grew more thoughtful. It did not surprise him to see Sam Tanner saddle a horse and ride away while Malloy lay asleep. These two men would never have gotten along.

Stone walked under the wall, and found his way into the hidden recesses of a wide fissure which opened out into a canyon, choked with green thicket and splintered sections of cliff, where silence and peace reigned. He could not stay longer at the cabin. Any hour that wild Diamond outfit might ride up there. Stone realized that Malloy expected it and certainly would not remain. Tanner had taken no chances. But Stone was reluctant to relinquish his revenge.

He lay on the pine-needle mat of brown, and fought the thing out. Malloy, so far as was possible for one of his character, had certain virtues worthy of respect, if not regard. He had not approved of the leadership of the Hash Knife and had openly opposed it. On the other hand he was not an enemy of Stone's. He trusted him. He would not have cheated him. And so Stone beat down the insistent voice that called to him to murder Malloy in cold blood. He would be truer to the old creed of the Hash Knife. Let Malloy go his way, build up another rustler outfit, and meet his inevitable end. That must come soon. These young Arizonians like Dunn and Prentiss were not to be stopped, or if they were, others as resourceful and deadly would arise. Arizona was slow but sure. Jed Stone would disappear and never be heard of again. That idea had its strong attraction. The range rumor would go abroad—the Hash Knife leader gone.

Stone felt an amazing relief at the joint renunciation of his desperate resolve and the sense of his vanishing from the Tonto. As he lay under its spell the pain at giving up these wild lonely canyons and tangled brakes he loved so, seemed to mitigate. There were other places where wilderness survived—where the forest was sweet and insulating.

And from that strange hope it took only a single leap of consciousness to land him on the verge of abandoning forever the crooked trail of the rustler, the outlaw. Almost before he realized it the transformation happened—not to character, for he was too old to change, but to its objective—to the necessity of stealing to live, and of fighting to survive. He had in his possession now more money than he had ever had at one time, enough to start ranching as he had dreamed of it twenty years before. Something had clarified his intelligence. Where were the clamoring fears attendant on the fugitive from justice? Vanished. It was a joke that he might be apprehended for that old crime of which he bore the stigma. And outside of Arizona who would know him or want to pry into his past? Many a successful cattleman or sheepman had gotten his start by questionable means. Stone knew this because he knew such men.

No—there was nothing to prevent him—nothing to fear. When he gave up his intention to kill his most notorious partner he had freed himself from intricate and subtle fetters. That was the secret of his surprise, his relief, his elation. Because when he abandoned that bloody revenge on Malloy he was in reality abandoning his position as a leader of outlaws.

Pecos would be waiting for him up at the headwaters of the Little Colorado. Stone decided that the sooner he started the better for him. There was a shadow over the yellow cabin built by Malloy, and more than that cast by the bulk of the looming wall. Besides he hardly trusted himself, so long as he remained in propinquity to the remnant of the Hash Knife.

Upon Stone's return to the cabin, at sunset, he found it deserted. Malloy and his two comrades had departed in a hurry, leaving the interior of the cabin in a state of confusion. He felt no surprise. It had happened before. Still, there might have been good reason for such a departure. Sonora might have returned or anything could have happened. Hastily packing some food supplies and a blanket, Stone made his way under cover of the wall to the corral. His horse was among the several horses left. In a few moments Stone rode down the slope into the darkening forest.

CHAPTER SEVENTEEN

Three mornings later, in the first rosy flush of sunrise, when the black squirrels were chattering and the blue jays screeching, Jed Stone struck into a blazed trail new to him and which led to a newly graded road. This he concluded was the road recently cut down into Yellow Jacket.

He would have suffered a pang for this desecration of the wilderness but for the satisfaction and even melancholy happiness which had increased during his slow and wary working up towards Clear Creek and Cottonwood Canyon, from which junction he could find his way to the Little Colorado. He had meat and salt, hard biscuits and coffee, enough to last him for the journey.

Up out of the canyon country now, on the level of the slowly rising plateau, where forest of pine began to be sprinkled with open patches of desert of cedar and piñon and sage, he relaxed something of vigilance and made much faster time. Because of this he discovered, presently, that he had ridden some distance over fresh horse tracks before he had observed them.

"That's queer," he soliloquized, halting. "They shore weren't in the road back there a ways."

Riders had come along here that very morning, and they had certainly cut off into the woods somewhere between this point and back where Stone had noticed the clean untracked road.

The fact was disturbing, but after he had reflected a moment he made sure that he would have heard and seen them long before they could have discovered him. For he had been alone, and though relaxed somewhat from strain he still exercised keen eyes and ears. They had turned off not to avoid him, but for reasons of their own.

Stone spurred on and rode at a brisk canter for a while, anxious to get to the Cottonwood country, where again he could take to the deep forest. But when he came to the junction of the new road with the old one he was halted by plain evidences of a hold-up. A vehicle of some sort had come along here headed south and had gone no farther, along either road. Stone found a canvas bag, open and rifled of its contents, and thrown aside. The ground about had been so cut up with hoofs that he could read but little from the tracks. But soon he ascertained that the wheel tracks turned back the way they had come.

"Wal, now, jest what comes off heah?" he muttered. He was accustomed to read the signs of the open. These might have meant little, and again they might have meant a great deal. Stone sensed the latter, and he searched the roadside until he found along the wheel tracks a bloody glove that had fallen into the weeds.

"Ahuh. I smelled it—as Croak would say," declared Stone. "I'm jest curious now to catch up with whatever had these wheels."

Whereupon he put his horse to a gallop, walk and trot, and lope, according to the stretches of road open far ahead or turning through the cedars. And in an hour or less he sighted a buckboard with one occupant driving slowly north. Stone kept on. He would have a look at that driver and his vehicle. A strong instinct prompted this, not all curiosity. He did not need to come to close quarters with the driver. This individual wore no hat; he had gray hair; he sagged in his seat, now with his head hunched between square shoulders and again with it lifted doggedly. Stone, after the manner of riders of his kind, like hounds on scent, caught the color of blood on stones along the roadside. Then he spurred his horse into a run.

Before he caught up with the buckboard it stopped, and the man turned, evidently having heard the thudding hoofs behind. As Stone flashed up, to haul his horse to a sliding halt, he caught sight of the dark face of a Mexican lying on the floor behind the back seat. Stone had seen too many dead men not to know this was one.

"Hey, old-timer—" Then he experienced a violent heart-stabbing start. He was staring into the hard convulsed visage of a man he had not seen for twenty years, yet whom he instantly recognized. A wrench tore Stone. "Dog-gone-me if it ain't Jim Traft!"

"Howdy, Jed!" replied the rancher, grimly. "An' what do *you* want?"

"Me!—Hell, nothin', except to ask what's happened? I run across your tracks a ways back. Looked like a hold-up to me. An' I knew it when I found this glove."

Stone pulled out the stained glove, which he had tucked under the pommel of his saddle.

"Belonged to my driver, Pedro, lyin' there," said Traft, nodding at the dead man. "But, shore, you know what come off."

"I don't. I know nothin'. I've been three days ridin' out of the brakes. I jest run across you."

"Jed Stone, can you expect me to believe thet?" queried Traft, incredulously.

"Reckon I expect it, Jim, 'cause I swear it's true," replied Stone, and gazed straight into the steel-blue eyes bent so piercingly and accusingly, and yet so strangely, upon him. That look bridged the long cruel years back to the dim cowboy days.

"You don't know I've been held up an' robbed by Croak Malloy?" demanded Traft, derisively.

"By God! . . . You have? . . . No, Jim, I didn't know."

"Nor thet he killed my driver?"

"I didn't know, Jim," repeated Stone, now with terrible earnestness to be believed by this old rancher.

"Jed, I reckon I don't see any reason for you lyin' to me. Many years ago you lied to me—an' that lie ruined you an' saved me. But don't lie now."

"Jim, I'm not lyin'. I swear to God! . . . I'd quit the Hash Knife. I left our hole down in the brakes three days ago. My outfit's done. Malloy broke it up. I'm leavin' Arizona forever—an' this life I've led."

After a protracted study of Stone's face the rancher burst out: "My Gawd! Jed, I'm glad. An' it's shore a queer meetin' for me an' you. . . . But listen. I was goin' down to Yellow Jacket to surprise my nephew Jim. I had his sweetheart, Molly Dunn, with me, an' his sister, Gloriana. We slept last night at Miller's sheep-ranch, I reckon some fifteen miles up the road. An' at the turn-off down there we got held up by three men. I didn't know Malloy till one of his pardners called him Croak. . . . Wal, when Pedro drove on, at my order, Malloy rode up an' shot him. An' you bet he'd have done fer me but fer an idee he got. Anyway, they robbed me an' yanked the girls out of the buckboard. They had to hawg-tie Molly. She shore fought. Malloy says, 'Traft, I'll give you three days to come to Tobe's Well with ten thousand dollars. Put the money in the loft of the cabin, next the chimney. We'll see you come, or whoever you send. An' these girls will be set free. Mebbe a little wuss fer love-makin'!' . . . The little ruffian said jest thet, an' grinned aboot it. I agreed. An' he let me go."

"Jim, if I know Malloy he let you off easy," declared Stone, sharply, and he reined his horse over close to the buckboard. "I struck their tracks down by the new road. An' I know aboot where they cut off into the woods. . . . Jim, I'll trail Malloy, an' go round an' haid him off, or come up on him at Tobe's Well. Mebbe I better make a short cut an' beat him there. . . . But I'll come up on him before dark. An' I'll get the girls."

"Jed Stone, are you aimin' fer thet ten thousand?" demanded Traft.

"I don't want a dollar. I'll do this because, wal, because I liked young Jim an' because I'd starve before I'd do you another dirty deal. At thet Malloy an' Bambridge rung me into the only one. An' I killed Bambridge fer doin' it."

"You killed Bambridge?" ejaculated the rancher.

"I shore did. An' Croak told me he'd seen thet gambler Darnell kickin' at the end of a rope. But, Jim, you'll hear all thet pronto. I'll have to rustle. . . . One thing more. Malloy may kill me. I reckon I can outfigger him, but to be on the safe side you'd better send a trusty rider with thet money, an' after you do, make a bee line for Yellow Jacket. For I'll fetch the girls there."

"Jed Stone, by—heaven! . . . wait!" faltered the old cattleman.

But Stone had spurred away, to call over his shoulder, "So long, Jim—old pard!"

Like the wind Stone raced back down the road, and as soon as he was sure of direction he cut across the cedared desert and into the woods, where gallop and trot soon brought him upon Malloy's tracks. He followed them, and marveled in mind at the inscutability of chance, at the inevitableness of life—at this meeting with Jim. After all, he was not to ride away from the brakes without the blood of Croak Malloy on his hands. How his heart leaped at the just cause! For as surely as his keen eyes were finding the tracks over moss and pine needles, he realized he would kill Malloy. Very likely all three of the rustlers! He must come up to them before night, otherwise the young women would be subjected to abuse and worse. Malloy had always made much of his few opportunities to degrade women. Probably owing to his misshapen body and repulsive face all women, even the slatterns of the towns, had wanted none of his acquaintance, which had made the little gunman a woman-hater.

The hours of the day were as moments. Forest and ravine, pine and spruce, rock and log, all looked alike to Stone. Yet he recognized familiar country when he rode into it. By mid-afternoon he had approached the vicinity of Tobe's Well, a wonderful natural hollow in the high escarpment overlooking the Cibeque. Stone left the trail he was hounding, and going around came up on the rim from the south. Horses rolling below in the sandy patches! Smoke curling from the stone chimney of the log cabin! Saddles and packs under the great silver spruce!

Jed Stone led his horse around the rim and down a dim seldom-trodden trail to the opening into the circular gorge. And never in all his twenty years of hard wild life had he been more Jed Stone.

No one hailed him as he strode along the mossy bank of the brook, under the stately pines, and on toward the cabin. The lonely isolation of the place invited carelessness. But Stone muttered: "They must be powerful keen on what's inside. Reckon I didn't get here too soon."

Dropping the bridle reins, he strode on to the open door. It was a big bright cabin, open on the lee side. And as he glanced in he heard a girl's low cry, deep, broken with emotion. He saw a dark little girl with gold-brown hair, all tossed and tangled, lying bound half upright against a pile of packs. That was Molly Dunn. He did not need to look twice. His eyes swept on.

Madden was on his knees, his hand white with flour, but on the moment he appeared riveted. Reeves stood back, his face set toward Malloy, who manifestly had just torn the blouse off a white-faced, white-shouldered girl, shrinking before him.

The moment had been made for Jed Stone. He recognized it, and saw, as if by magic, how far in the past it had its incipiency and now had reached fulfillment. He gloried in it. What debts he would pay here!

He stepped inside to call out, harshly, "What the hell's goin' on?"

It was the first occasion on which he had ever seen Malloy surprised, but perhaps the thousandth when he had seen him angry. Stone felt his sudden presence had been decidedly inopportune for his erstwhile partner and his accomplices.

"Aw, it's the boss!" gasped Madden, in explosion of breath that suggested relief.

"Who's been chasin' *you?"* burst out Malloy, and with gesture of impatience he flung down the torn blouse.

"Jed Stone!" screamed Molly Dunn, and if ever a voice thrilled Stone this one did then. She had recognized him. Even on the moment he remembered the times he had patted Molly's curly head when she was a mere tot, had bought her candy at the store in West Fork, had often lifted her upon his horse, and in later years, when she was grown into a pretty girl, he had talked with her on occasions when he rode to and fro from the Cibeque to the Tonto.

"Wal, I reckon ten thousand devils might be chasin' me, fer all you'd care, Croak," replied Stone. "I jest happened in on you here."

"Damn queer, an' I call it tough. You're wuss'n an old woman," complained Malloy.

"Who're these girls an' what're you doin' with them?"

"Jed, we got into another brush down in the brakes," replied Malloy. "Damn if it wasn't full of cowpunchers. But we give them the slip. An' comin' out we run plumb into old Jim Traft an' these gurls. It gave me a great idee. An' hyar air the gurls while old Jim is raisin' the dust back to Flag."

"My Gawd!—Not old Jim Traft—the rancher?" burst out Stone, loudly, in pretended consternation.

"Shore. I said old Jim, didn't I?"

"An' these girls are friends or kin of his?"

"Shore. I reckon you'd know Molly Dunn if you'd look. She knowed you all right. The other is young Jim Traft's sister."

"An' you aim to make money out of them?"

"I shore do."

"An' make game of them while the money's comin'?" demanded Stone, harshly.

"Wal, thet's none of your bizness, Jed," rejoined Malloy, testily. Habit was strong upon him. This interruption had upset him and he had scarcely adapted himself to it.

But Stone, acting his part, intense and strung, saw already that Malloy's mind had not grasped the situation.

"Man, are you crazy?" shouted Stone. "Jim Traft will have a hundred cowboys ridin' on your trail. You couldn't hit it—with nine horses. They'll catch you—they'll hang you."

"Hang nothin'. Jed, you're the one who's crazy. What's got into you lately?" replied Malloy, in plaintive amaze and disgust. "You're gettin' old or you've lost your nerve."

"Croak, you've done fer the Hash Knife, an' now this deal will set the whole country ablaze."

Malloy stared his amaze. Stone, seizing the instant, strode to and fro in apparent despair, and wringing his hands, he wheeled away. But when he turned, swift as light, he held a gun spouting red. The little gunman died on his feet, without a movement, even of that terribly sensitive right hand. But he fell face down, showing where the bullet had blown off the back of his head.

Madden, with a bawling curse, swept one of his flour-covered hands for his gun. Too late, for Stone's second shot knocked him over as if it had been a club.

Reeves leaped for the door, just escaping the bullet Stone fired after him. And he was visible running madly in the direction of the horses. Stone let him go. Then he surveyed the cabin. A glance sufficed for Madden and Malloy, but it was a dark and terrible one, of reckoning, of retribution.

The girl Malloy had half stripped had slipped to the floor in a faint, her white arms spread. Then on the instant Molly Dunn's eyes opened, black and dilated with terror.

"How do, Molly!" said Stone, as he bent over her to slash the thongs of buckskin round her boots. He had to roll her over to free her hands. "I reckon I got here none too soon, but not too late, either."

"Oh, Jed—you've come—to save us?" cried Molly.

"Shore. An' as I said I hope not—too late."

"We're all right, Jed. But, oh, I was scared. Thet croakin' devil! . . . Is he daid?"

"Malloy has croaked his last, Molly," went on Stone. "I happened to run across old Jim out on the road. Thet's how I got on your trail. Brace up, now, Molly. Why, this little affair shouldn't phase Molly Dunn of the Cibeque."

"I knowed—knew you at first sight, Jed. An' oh, my heart leaped! . . . Jed, thank God you came in time. I was aboot ready to die. I'd fought Malloy till he hawg-tied me. . . . Oh, how can I ever thank you enough? How will Jim ever do it?"

Her passion of gratitude, her wet eloquent eyes, her trembling little hands, so prodigal of their pressure on his, warmed all the ghastly deadliness out of Jed Stone's veins. Happy moments had vanished forever, for him, he had imagined. But this one was reward for all the lonely starved past.

"Wal, you needn't try to thank me, Molly," he replied. "Now let's see. . . . It's 'most dark already. We'd better camp here tonight. An' tomorrow we'll start for

Yellow Jacket. . . . Reckon I'd better pull these disagreeable-lookin' hombres outside."

Madden was of heavy build and took considerable strength to drag out, but Malloy was slight and light.

"With your boots on, Croak, old man!" ejaculated Stone, as he let the limp body flop down. Then Stone possessed himself of the bone-handled gun and the belt with its shiny shells. As an afterthought he rifled the dead man's pockets, to extract considerable money, watch and knife, and the one golden double-eagle Malloy had taken from Madden for luck.

Inside the cabin Stone saw that Molly had somehow gotten the torn blouse on the unconscious girl, and was now trying to bring her to.

"Let nature take its course, Molly," he advised. "She'll come to presently of her own accord, an' mebbe the shock to her will be less. . . . Lord! what a pretty girl! I never seen her like. . . . An' she's young Jim's sister?"

"Yes. An' isn't she just lovely?"

"Here, we'll lift her up on this bed of spruce. Somebody cut it nice an' fresh. You can both sleep there tonight."

"Jed, fetch me some cold water. I'm near daid of thirst. Thet wretch tried to make us drink whisky. Ughh!"

Stone found a pail and went to fill it at the spring. His mind seemed full of happy yet vague thoughts. He felt sort of boyish, and warm deep down within. Going back inside, Stone filled a cup with water and watched Molly drink. What a glossy head she had! Two such pretty girls at once quite took his breath. One Western and the other Eastern! Stone regarded them with interest, with a growing sense of the importance he had played in their lives, with an assurance of the food for memory that would be in the future.

"Glory—you called her?"

"Shore. But her name's Gloriana."

"An' she's a city girl from the East?"

"Yes. An', Jed, she's come to live out West always."

"Fine, if you can keep her. Proud-lookin' lass! Won't this little adventure sicken her on the West?"

"It'll be the best thing thet ever happened to her," avowed Molly, with bright eyes. "Jed, she shore was aboot the proudest girl I ever met. An' Jim's sister. His family, really! Gosh! it was hard on me. I made a mess of things. Jed, I went back on Jim because I thought I wasn't good enough for him—for his aristocratic family. But he kidnapped me—thank the good Lord. I reckon I was jealous, too."

"Small wonder, Molly. It was tough on you—to stack up against these Trafts, you just fresh from the Cibeque. But you're good enough fer anybody, Molly Dunn. I shore hope it'll come out all right."

"Oh, it will, Jed," replied Molly, hopefully. "Glory has a heart of gold. I love her—an' indeed I believe she's comin' to love me. But she can't savvy me. Heah I've had only two years' schoolin', an' lived all my life in a log cabin no better'n this, almost. Never had any clothes or nothin'. An' she has had everythin'. Uncle Jim says the West will win her an' thet she an' I will get along an' be sisters soon as Glory is broke in. He says she must get up against the real old West—you know, an' thet will strike the balance. I don't savvy jest what Uncle Jim means, but I believe him."

"Molly, I reckon I savvy what Uncle Jim is drivin' at," replied Stone, smiling thoughtfully at the earnest girl. "The real old West means hard knocks, like this one she's gettin', cowboys an' cattle, work when you want to drop, an' no sleep when you're dyin' fer it. Cold an' wet an' dust an' wind! To be starved! To be scared stiff! . . . A hundred things thet are nothin' at all to *you,* Molly Dunn, are what this city girl needs."

"Jed, thet's exactly what Uncle says. . . . I'm to marry Jim soon," she went on, with a blush. "They all wanted it this spring, but I coaxed off till fall."

"Ahuh. I reckon you love him heaps, Molly?"

"Oh!—I'm not really Molly Dunn any more. I've lost myself. I'm happy, though, Jed. I'm goin' to school. An' if only Glory could see me as I see her!"

"Wal, I'll help her see you true, Molly," returned Stone, patting her hand. "Now, I'd better go outside while you fetch her to. Sight of the desperado who came a-rarin' in here, swearin' an' shootin', mightn't be good."

"Jed, she was simply crazy aboot desperadoes," said Molly. "An' I honestly believe she was tickled when Malloy carried us off. Leastways, she was till he got to pawin' her."

"Dog-gone! Thet's good. . . . Now, Molly, don't you say one word aboot me till I think it over. I'll go outside an' see to my horse. An' when she's all right, you come out to tell me. Mebbe by then I'll have a plan."

"Jed Stone, never in my life—an' I've always known you—did I ever think of you as a rustler, a killer, a bad man. An' now I *know* you're not really."

"Thanks, Molly; thet'll be sweet to remember," he replied. "Fetch her to, now, an' say nothin'."

Stone went outside, unsaddled his horse and turned him loose, then walked to and fro, in his characteristic way when deep in thought. Presently Molly came running to him. What pleasure that afforded the outlaw whose life had been lived apart from the influence of women!

"She's come to, Jed. An' she's not so knocked out as I reckoned she'd be," said the girl, happily. "I darn near exploded keepin' our secret—thet we're safe with you an' will start in the mawnin' fer Yellow Jacket."

"Wal now, Molly Dunn, you stick to me," rejoined Stone, eagerly. "We'll let on I'm wuss than Croak—thet I jest killed them fellars an' drove the third off so I could have you girls to myself. It's a good three-day ride to Yellow Jacket, fer you, anyhow. Thet gives us time to cure Miss Gloriana of all her bringin'-up. I'll be a real shore-enough desperado—up to a certain point. Savvy, Molly?"

"Oh, Jed, if I only dared do it!" exclaimed Molly, pale with excitement. How her dark eyes glowed! "But she'll suffer. An'—an'I love her so!"

"Shore. All the same, if she's got the real stuff in her thet's the way to fetch it out. It's the only way, Molly, to strike thet balance between you an' her which your Uncle Jim meant. If you've got the nerve, girl, an' do your part, you'll never regret it."

"Jed, you don't mean never to tell Glory you're good instead of bad. I couldn't agree to thet."

"Wal, of course, she's bound to find out sometime thet I'm not so bad, after all. But I'd advise you to put Uncle Jim wise an' keep the secret for a while. Molly, I'll be disappointed in you if you fall down on this chance. I'll bet you young Jim would jump at it."

"He would—he would," panted Molly. "Jed, Heaven forgive me—I'll do it. I'll trust you an' do my part."

"Thet's like a girl of the Cibeque," replied Jed, heartily. "Go back, now, an' tell her you both have fallen out of the fryin'-pan into the fire."

CHAPTER EIGHTEEN

Life played even an outlaw queer pranks, thought Jed Stone, as he stalked toward the cabin, conscious of a strange elevation of spirit. When a young man he had shouldered the sin of his friend, for the sake of the girl they both loved—and the noble deed had earned him twenty years of loneliness, misery, and infamy. Just now he had actually committed a crime—he had murdered his confederate, who, vile as he was, had yet the elements of loyalty, the virtue of trust; and out of this circumstance, again in the interest of woman, he divined that he would climb out of the depths. It was an enigma.

Stone entered the cabin, as once he had seen the villain in a melodrama. The Traft girl was sitting up, with Molly fluttering around her. He sustained a shock—like wind rushing back through his veins to his heart. It was as if he had not before seen this girl. In all his life such eyes had never before met his. They were large, dark violet, strained with an expression which might have been horror or terror, or fascination. How wondrously lovely! Stone doubted that he could play his part before their gaze.

"Wal, what'd this Dunn kid tell you?" he demanded, with a fierce glare.

"Oh—sir—she said you—you were Jed Stone, the desperado," faltered the girl, in haste. "That we'd fallen out of the frying-pan into the fire—that you killed those men so you could have us all—to yourself."

"Correct. An' now what do you think?" queried Stone, studying the girl. She was frightened, and still under the influence of shock, but she was no fool.

"Think? About—what?"

"Why, your new owner, of course. Reckon I always was jealous of Croak Malloy—of his gun-play an' his way with wimmen."

"Mister Stone, when you came in this cabin—when that little beast was tearing my clothes off—I *knew* you were going to save me from him."

"Wal, you're the smart girl," he replied, and almost wavered before those searching, imploring eyes. "Shore I was." Then he reached down with a slow hand and clutched the front of her blouse and jerked her to her feet. Holding her to the light, he bent his face closer to her. "You're a beautiful thing, but are you good?"

"Good? . . . I think so—I hope so."

"Wal, you gotta know—if *I* ask you. Are you a *good* girl?"

"Yes, sir, if I understand you."

"Wal, thet's fine. I've shore been hungry fer one of your kind. Molly Dunn there, she's a Western kid, an' a little wildcat thet's not afraid of desperadoes. She comes of the raw West, same as me. She'll furnish game fer me. But you're different. You belong to the class that made me an outlaw. An' I'm gonna take twenty years of shame an' sufferin' out on you. . . . Make you slave for me! . . . Make you love me! Beat you! Drag you down."

She sagged under his grasp, without which she would have fallen. Her face could not have been any whiter. "I—I am at your mercy. . . . But, for God's sake—if you had the manhood to kill those brutes—can't you have enough to spare us?"

Stone let her sink down upon the couch. Tenderfoot as she was, she had instinctively recognized or at least felt the truth of him. He would need to be slow, careful, and probably brutal to convince her.

"If you're gonna flop over an' faint every time I grab you or speak to you this'll be a picnic fer me," he said, disgustedly. "Where's your Traft nerve. Thet brother of yours, young Jim, has shore got nerve. He braced me an' my whole outfit. Come right to us, an' without a gun. I shore liked him. Thet was the day he knocked the stuffin's out of Croak Malloy. . . . No, Gloriana, you ain't no real Traft."

That stung red into her marble cheeks and a blaze to her wonderful eyes.

"I haven't had half a chance," she flashed, as much to herself as to him.

"You'd never make a go of the West, even if you hadn't had the bad luck to run into Jed Stone," he went on. "You're too stuck up. You think you're too good fer plain Western folks, like Molly there, an' her brother, an' me, an' Curly Prentiss. An' you really ain't good enough. Because here it's what you can *do* thet counts. Wal, I'll bet you cain't do much. An' I'm shore gonna see. Come hyar!"

He dragged her across the floor to the fireplace, where Madden had opened packs and spread utensils and supplies.

"Get down on your knees, you white-faced Easterner," he ordered, forcing her down. "Bake biscuits fer me. If they ain't good I'll beat you. An' fry meat an' boil coffee Savvy?"

With trembling hands she rolled up her sleeves and began to knead the flour Madden had left in the pan. Stone observed that she was not so helpless and useless as he had supposed. Then he turned to Molly.

"Wal, my dusky lass, you can amoose me while Gloriana does the housework."

"I shore won't. Stay way from me!" shouted Molly, bristling like a porcupine. When Stone attempted to lay hold of her person she eluded him, and catching up a pan she flung it with unerring aim. Stone dodged, but it took him on the back of the head with a great clang, and then banged to the floor.

"You'll pay fer thet, you darned little hussy," he roared, and made at her.

Then followed a wild chase around the cabin, that to an observer who was not obsessed with fear, as was Gloriana, would have been screamingly funny. As an actor Jed was genuine, but he was as heavy on his feet as an ox, and he had to face the brunt of missiles Molly threw, that never failed to connect with some part of his anatomy. When she hit him on the knee with a heavy fruit-can he let out a bawl of honest protest. Molly finally ran behind the half-partition which projected out from the wall, and here allowed Jed to catch her. The partition was constructed of brush. He tore out a long bough and cracked the wall with it.

"Take thet—you darned—little Apache squaw," he panted, and he whacked away with his switch. Then he bent over Molly, who was convulsed on the pine-needle floor, and whispered in her ear, "Yell—scream!"

Whereupon Molly obeyed: "Ah! . . . *Oh!* . . . Ouu!"

Stone paused for effectiveness, while he peeped through the screen. Gloriana knelt erect, her breast heaving, her eyes wildly magnificent. They were searching round for a weapon, Jed concluded.

"Now—Molly Dunn—mebbe thet'll learn you not to monkey with Jed Stone. . . . Come hyar, an' kiss me."

He had to shake her to keep her remembering her part. Stone made smacking sounds with his lips, capital imitations of lusty kisses.

"Oh—you crazy—desperado!" burst out Molly, choking. "Jim Traft—will kill you—for this!"

"Haw! Haw! Thet's funny. . . . Now, you be good fer a minnit." Whereupon he picked her up and carried her, along with the wicked whip, out to the couch, where he dropped her like a sack of potatoes. Molly's face was a spectacle. It was wet and working. She hid it on the green spruce boughs and then she kicked like a furious colt. Her smothered imprecations sounded like: "Brute! Beast! Coyote! Skunk!"

Stone had made a discovery. His keen sight caught Gloriana concealing the butcher knife, clutched in her hand and half hidden in the folds of her dress. She, too, was a spectable to behold, but beautiful and marvelous to him—her spirit so much greater than her strength.

"Say, what're you goin' to do with thet knife?" demanded Stone.

"You're no desperado! You're a dog," she cried. "If you lay hand on Molly again I—I'll kill you."

Here indeed was a quick answer to the primitive instincts which Stone and Molly had wished to rouse in the Eastern girl. Indeed, Stone thought she might develop too fast and spoil the game. Most assuredly she had to be intimidated. "You'd murder me—you white-faced panther?" he shouted, ferociously. "Drop thet knife!" And whipping out his gun he fired, apparently pointblank at her; but he knew the bullet would hit the bucket of water. The crash in the encompassing cabin walls was loud. Gloriana not only dropped the knife—she dropped herself. However, she did not quite faint. Stone lifted her up, with feelings vastly different from what he pretended, and then he made a show of collecting everything around which she might have used as a weapon.

"Get back to work," he ordered.

Just then Gloriana was a pitiful sight, verging on collapse. It quite wrung Molly's heart, as Jed saw. But he was adamant. He had divined the thing had gone beyond them both. It was serious, earnest business; and if they kept on, simply making situations for Gloriana to react to, the benefit to her would be incalculable. She had a surprising lot of courage for a tenderfoot placed, as she believed she was, in a terrible, irremediable situation. She weakly brushed back her amber hair, leaving a white blot of flour on it and her forehead, and then went at the biscuit dough again.

"Say, darlin', did you wash them slim little paws of yourn?" asked Stone, suddenly.

"No. I—I never thought to," she faltered.

"Wal, you wash them. There's the washpan. . . . What're you tryin' to do—poison me with dirty hands? I'll have you know, Gloriana Traft, thet I'm a clean desperado, an' any woman who cooks fer me has gotta be spick an' span."

Suddenly Molly, with an almost inarticulate cry, leaped off the bed and bolted out the door. Stone did not understand her move, but yelling, he thudded after her. But she was not trying to escape. Manifestly she had to get outside, away from Gloriana. She waited behind the young spruces for Stone.

"What's the matter, lass?" he asked, anxiously. "It's shore goin' fine. You're a grand aktress. You'd beat thet Siddons woman all holler."

Molly had a hand pressed into her heaving bosom. Her eyes were distended.

"Oh, Jed—I—I cain't bear it!" she wailed. "I'm afraid it'll do her some harm. . . . Please, Jed, let me tell her you're not the—the devil you seem?"

"An' spoil it all!—No, Molly, I jest won't," he replied, stubbornly. "Cain't you see the good it'll do? Look at the spunk she showed. She'd knifed me, too!—Molly, fer Heaven's sake, stick it out. We'll make a man out of her."

"But—but you'll overdo it," cried Molly.

"You dog-gone little simpleton," he retorted. "I cain't overdo it with thet girl. She'll lick us both yet, if we don't watch out."

"Wasn't she jest—wonderful? When I seen her with thet knife I aboot went stiff. . . . Jed, what we're doin' is turrible wrong. Heah you've killed two men. Right before her eyes! There's blood all over the floor yet. . . . You've pretended to beat me—an' *kiss me*—which I didn't reckon was in the play. An' you've shot at her! . . . Jed, people can die of fright. You scare me into thinkin' you're not actin'—you *mean* it all. . . .An' oh, I'm sick—sick."

"Molly, I swear to Gawd I wouldn't harm one hair of thet girl's haid," he avowed, earnestly. "But I had a hunch. I seen what *she* needs—an', by thunder, if you don't show yellar, she'll get it! . . . Molly, I've knowed you since you was a baby, an' I used to call you 'Little wood-mouse.' Slinger got thet name from me. Shore you can trust me. It's hard to do—an' the hardest of all is to come fer her. But, honest, Molly, I reckon this deal's a Godsend to her, an' to you, an' to *me.*"

"You!—How come, Jed?" she queried, sharply.

"Dog-gone-it, Molly, I cain't tell all in a minnit. But I feel it's somethin' big an' wonderful fer me—to remember all my life after as the thing which helped change me."

"Jed!—You're goin' to give up rustlin'?" she asked, breathlessly.

"I shore am, Molly Dunn."

"Gawd! I'm glad! 'Most as glad as when my brother quit. I reckon it's gettin' through my thick haid. . . . Go on, Jed, with our play. I'll stick, but fer my sake don't—don't hurt her."

"You're shore real Arizona," returned Stone, feelingly. "Run back in, now. I've some diggin' to do before dark."

"But you'd better drag me back," objected Molly.

Wherefore Stone presently heaved a kicking rebellious young woman into the cabin, with a fiercely appropriate command. And he followed that with an order to put some pine cones on the fire. Then Stone searched among the packs to find a short-handled shovel, with which he proposed to dig Croak Malloy's grave. The thing was monstrously impelling. Jed Stone digging Croak Malloy's grave! Arizona would learn that some day, and the range-riders would marvel as they talked about the campfires, adding bit by bit to the story of the doom of the Hash Knife.

Stone had sense enough of the dramatic to choose the most striking spot at Tobe's Well, and that was under the monarch of a silver spruce which dominated the place, and where the cowboys, hunters, trappers, as well as outlaws, always camped in pleasant weather. Stone found the ground soft. He dug a deep grave, and dragging Madden over he tumbled him into it, with scant ceremony. While performing a like office for Malloy he got blood on his hands. It seemed to burn, and before filling up the grave he went to the brook to wash it off.

"Wal, Croak, you shore didn't end as you always swore you would," mused the outlaw, as he plied the shovel. "You shore wasn't back against the wall—your guns shootin' red. . . . You an' Madden were pretty close these late years. Now you can rot together an' go to hell together."

The job done, he placed a huge rock at the foot of the grave, with the prophetic remark: "Shore some wag of a cowpuncher will plant a haidpiece."

Whereupon Jed's active mind reverted to the issue in the cabin, and on the way back he picked up a good-sized stone which he concealed under his coat. The light of blazing pine cones revealed the two girls working frantically to get supper for him. He caught the tail end of Molly's conversation: "—an' no use lyin', Glory—I'm as scared as you."

"O Heaven! how false men are!" sighed Glory. "When this desperado came in I had a wild thought he was a hero."

"Hey, don't talk aboot me," put in Stone. I'm a sensitive man."

Silence ensued then. The girls did not look up. And Stone, profiting by this, threw some sacks over the blood pools on the hard-packed clay floor. Also he surreptitiously laid the stone on the box seat where he intended to sit at the rickety old rough-hewn table. This he cleared by piling Malloy's trappings on the ground, and covering it with the cleanest piece of canvas he could find. Then he sat down to watch and wait. He realized he had fallen upon the most delicious situation of his life—if he had ever had one before—and he wanted to live every second of it to the full. Finally the girls put the supper on the table.

"Thet's right, wait on me, Gloriana," he said. "An' you, Molly, set down an' eat. . . . Gimme one of them turrible-lookin' biscuits. . . . Ou! Hot!"

He contrived to drop the biscuit and at the same instant push the heavy rock off the box seat. It fell with a solid thump. Gloriana actually jumped. Her eyes opened wide.

"Golly! Did you heah thet biscuit hit?" ejaculated Stone, as if dumbfounded.

"I heahed somethin' heavy," corroborated Molly, serious-faced, but her sweet red lips slightly twitched.

"Say, gurl, air you aimin' to poison me?" demanded Stone, suspiciously. "What'n hell did you put in thet biscuit?"

Gloriana stammered something, and then walking round the table, she espied the rock, which, unfortunately, had fallen upon the biscuit.

"It was a rock," she said slowly.

"Wal, dog-gone! So it was. Must have been on the box. I shore didn't see it. . . . I offer my humble apologies, Miss Traft."

No doubt Gloriana's mind was so steeped in fright that it could not function normally, yet she gazed with dubious tragic eyes at the desperado.

Stone then devoted himself to the meal, which he soon discovered was the best he had sat at for many a weary moon. Days on end he had prepared frugal meals for himself, and the last few he had lived on dried meat, hard biscuits, and coffee. This was a repast—a feast, to which he did ample justice.

"Wal," he drawled, when he could eat no more, as he transfixed Gloriana with eyes he tried to make devouring, "if you can love as well as cook, I'm shore a lucky desperado. . . . Get out now and I'll wash up. No sweethearts of mine ever had to do the dirty work round my camp."

While he was noisily banging pans, cups, and other utensils around his trained ear caught Gloriana's whisper, "Now—let's run!"

"An' get lost in the woods—for bears to eat!" whispered Molly.

Stone dried the camp utensils and placed them on the shelf, after which he washed his hands in hot water.

"Put some wood on the fire," he said, filling his black pipe. "Pass me a red coal on a chip. . . . Thet's it, darlin'; you're shore learnin' fast."

The interior of the cabin brightened with blazing cones and sticks. Molly sat as in a trance. Gloriana stood awaiting another command, nervous, with great blank eyes. She might have been a bird fascinated by a snake.

"Spread some blankets on the bed there," he said, pointing to the pack he had opened. While this order was being complied with he puffed his pipe, and opened his big hands to the fire with an air of content. Molly's reproachful glance might have been lost upon him. Jed reasoned it out that the little Cibeque girl had lived too long among Western men to trust him wholly. That gave Stone more thrills.

He would fool Molly, too. At length he got up to view the bed.

"Kinda narrow fer three to sleep comfortable," he said, laconically. "I always wear my boots an' spurs to bed—in case I have to hurry to a hoss—an' I kick when I have nightmare. But I reckon there's room fer two. Now, Molly, you an' Gloriana draw lots to see who'll sleep fust night with me."

"Jed Stone, I'll see you in hell before I'd do it," cried Molly, passionately. "You'll have to tie me, hand an' foot."

"Wal, you needn't take my head off. I kinda lean to Glory, anyhow."

Gloriana gazed at him with eyes full of a sickening horror and desperate defiance.

"You'll have to kill me—you monster!" she said, hoarsely.

"Wal, both buckin' on me, huh," replied Stone, as if resigned to the nature of women. "All right, I don't want no tied gurl sleepin' with me, an' shore no daid one. So I'll pass. You can sleep together, an' I'll be a gentleman an' go outdoors. But you gotta entertain me before. Molly, you sing, 'Bury me not on the Lone Prairie.'"

"I cain't sing a note an' I wouldn't if I could," avowed Molly.

"Gloriana, my duckie, can you sing?"

"I used to sing hymns, in Sunday school. But they would scarcely be to your taste, Mister Stone," was the partly satiric reply.

"Say, where'd you think I was brought up?" queried Stone, as if deeply insulted. "I used to go to church. I had a gurl once who took me to prayer-meetin'."

"You did? Impossible to believe! I wish she were here now to pray for us."

"Ahuh. So do I. . . . But she's daid—these many years," replied Stone, and was lost in reverie for a moment. He saw that girl, and the little church, and the gate where he bade her good night. "I bet you can dance," he went on, looking up. "You've shore got dancin' feet an' ankles. I never seen such bootiful laigs, if you'll excoose me bein' familiar."

"Yes, I can dance, and I'll try," replied the girl, as if relieved to get off so easily. Whereupon she began a swaying of her graceful body, a sliding of her little feet. But she appeared unsteady.

"Hold on. You need a bracer," said Stone, and going to his pack he took out a black bottle, from which he emptied some liquor into a cup. This he diluted with water and offered her with the curt word, "Drink."

"No!"

"Say, it's fine old stuff. It'll do you good. An' when you get to be a grandma you can tell your grandchildren you once drank out of Jed Stone's flask."

"The honor does not appeal to me."

"Glory, he's gettin' mad," spoke up Molly, in alarm. "An' it shore won't hurt you."

"I—I won't," replied Gloriana, backing away weakly.

"Gurl, I'll pour it down your lily throat," said Stone, in a terrible tone, while he reached for her. But Gloriana eluded him. Then Stone whipped out his gun and aimed at her feet. "You drink an' you dance—or I'll shoot at your feet."

At this dire threat Gloriana took the cup with trembling hands and drank the contents.

"Ag-hhh!" she choked, and then stood with distended eyes, with hand on her breast, as if feeling fire within. "Oh, Molly—such stuff! . . . Is there no way out of this nightmare?"

"Dance!" thundered Stone.

And then he was to see the girl waltz fantastically over the open space of the clay floor, with the firelight shining fitfully on her wan face, until she gave out and collapsed upon the bed.

"Thanks, Glory," he said, huskily. "You're shore a fairy on your feet. . . . Now, I reckon, I'll let you go to bed. You gotta sleep, for we have a long tough ride tomorrow."

Stone picked up one of the bed rolls, and carrying it out back through the open side of the cabin he unrolled it in the gloom of the cliff and stretched himself as if he never meant to move again. He could see the flicker of the firelight on one wall of the cabin, but the girls were out of his sight. He heard their low voices for what seemed a long time.

Sleep did not come readily. He doubted if it would that night, and welcomed wakefulness. When had he lain down in such strange sweet sense of security? Was it peace? What had happened to him? And he rested there trying to understand the vast change. It was not the little service he had rendered these young women, or the strenuous and agonizing experience he meant to give Gloriana Traft, out of which would come wholesome good. No—it was that he was free. The Hash Knife outfit was dead—every one dead, since he, too, Jed Stone, was dead to all that strife. He had no enemy in the world, it seemed, except every honest rancher and cowboy. But they were no longer enemies. He had squared himself. He could lie down without fear, without one eye kept open, without distrust of comrades, of the morrow, of the future. Without certainty of inevitable death at the crack of a gun or the end of a rope! For years Malloy had been the dark shadow over him—the step on his trail. And Malloy would never awaken again—never ruin another rancher—never spread fear and hate about him—never exercise that fatal draw—never by reason of his personality cause better men to lose poise and serenity in their desire to kill him.

The flicker of the fire died out, as did also the low voices. They slept—those two pretty girls, destined to make two lucky cowboys happy and Arizona the better for their worth. Arizona! The name lingered in Stone's consciousness. He had been born and bred in this country of arid zones, of canyon and forest, of the clear streams with the gray salt margins along the sand. But who—what Arizonian had ever loved a country more than had he?

The night wind arose, mournful as always, cold off the heights. Yet it seemed a different music, as if it blew from far-off forests, as yet unknown to the fame of Jed Stone.

CHAPTER NINETEEN

Jed Stone awoke with the first pink streak of dawn flushing the sky. The old somber distrust of the new day had departed. He seemed young again.

Going to the door of the cabin, he called: "Hey, babes in the woods! Roll out an' rustle."

He heard a gasp, and then a low moan, but he did not look in. He went out to fetch the horses. There had been nine in the canyon the night before; now he could see but six, including his own. One was a pretty pinto mare which he selected for

Gloriana, with a chuckle at the thought of how all her life she would remember this ride. He drove four horses in, haltered them, and chose the best saddles for the girls, the stirrups of which he shortened to fit them. It tickled him to see blue smoke curling up from the cabin, and a little later his keen nostrils took note of the fragrance of coffee. When he got a pack-saddle strapped on the fourth horse he was ready to go in, but he tarried a moment. How sweet, rich, melodious, and rose-green the sunrise-flushed canyon! Henceforth Tobe's Well would be famous as the last resting-place of the great Croak Malloy.

Presently he repaired to the cabin.

"Mawnin', gurls," he bawled, stalking in.

Gloriana had been listlessly brushing her lustrous hair, while Molly attended to the breakfast chores.

"Ha, makin' yourself look pretty," remarked Stone. "Wal, you can't bamboozle the boss of the Hash Knife. An' you ought to be ashamed—lettin' Molly do all the work."

"I started the fire and made the biscuits," she retorted. Stone had grasped before that she seemed peculiarly susceptible to criticism, and decided he would work on her sensitiveness to the limit.

"Wal, we can't pack much of this outfit," observed Stone. "You gurls pick out what belongs to you."

Molly designated two duffle-bags and one small grip. Stone carried them outside. Then returning, he rolled some blankets. He remembered that he had some hard bread and dried meat in his saddle-bags, which supply he would add to without letting the girls know. His plan precluded an insufficiency of food on this three-day ride down to Yellow Jacket. When he had packed the horse Molly called from the cabin, "Come an' get it!"

"You come hyar yourself an' get somethin'," he replied.

Molly came running, anxious and big-eyed. "What—Jed?"

"Pitch in now, an' show this Eastern gurl what a Western lass is made of. Savvy?"

"I reckon."

"I'm givin' you the chance, Molly. Don't fall down. Take everythin' as a matter of course. Help her, shore, but give her a little dig now an' then."

"Jed, you're a devil," returned Molly, slowly, and turned away.

Stone stamped into the cabin, upon her heels: "Feed me, now, ladylove. An' then we gotta rustle. I'm a hunted desperado, you know. Soon as your Uncle Jim gets back to Flag the woods will be full of cowboys, sheriffs, deputies, an' a lot of gallants who'd like to win the hearts of my captives. Haw! Haw!"

The breakfast was even more tasteful than had been the supper the night before. Stone ate with the appetite of an Indian, and the wisdom of a range-rider who had to go far.

"You ain't eatin' much," he observed, addressing Gloriana.

"I'm not hungry," she replied.

"Wal, you eat. Heah me? Or I'll be givin' you another drink."

This threat had the desired result.

"Gurls, I've gotta hurry, so can't pack much grub," said Stone, rising to gather up a few utensils, some coffee and meat, and what biscuits had been left. These he tied up securely, and took them out to put upon the pack-animal. The rest of the outfit he would leave until his return that way. His last service to Croak Malloy was pounding and smoothing the grave.

Presently the girls appeared. Molly had taken the precaution to don a riding-skirt and boots, but Gloriana wore the thin dress which Malloy had torn considerably.

"Where's your hat?" asked Stone.

"It blew off, yesterday. . . . I—I forgot to look in my bag—and change. If you'll give me time—"

"Nope. Sorry, Gloriana. Didn't I tell you I was a hunted man? You'll have to ride as you are. Strikes me the Lord made you wonderful to look at, but left out any brains. You'll do fine in Arizona. . . . Here, wear Croak's sombrero. . . . Haw! Haw! If your ma could see you now!"

She had to be helped upon the pinto, which promptly bucked her off upon the soft sward. What injury she suffered was to her vanity. She threw off the old sombrero, but Stone jammed it back on her head.

"Can't you ride?" inquired Stone, gazing down upon her.

"Do you think I was born in a stable?" she asked, bitterly.

"Wal, it'd be a darn sight better if you was. An' far as thet is concerned the Lord was born in a stall, so I've heerd. So it ain't no disgrace. . . . I'm curious to know why you ever come to Arizona?"

"I was a fool."

"Wal, get up an' try again. This little mare isn't bad. She was jest playin'. But don't let her see you're afraid. An' don't kick her in the ribs, like you did when you got up fust."

"I—I can't ride this way," she said, scarlet of face.

"Wal, you are a holy show, by golly!" observed Stone. "I never seen so much of a pretty gurl, You shore wouldn't win no rodeo prizes fer modesty."

"Molly, I can't go on," cried Gloriana, almost weeping. "My skirt's up round my neck!"

"Glory, I don't see what else you can do. You'll *have* to ride," replied Molly.

"Thet's talkin'. Glory, you'll get some idee of the difference between a no-good tenderfoot from the East an' a healthy Western cowgurl. . . . Now, you follow me, an' you keep up, or there'll be hell to pay."

The ease with which Molly mounted her horse, a wicked black animal, was not lost upon Gloriana, nor the way she controlled him.

"Molly, you better lead this pack-hoss. I'll have to keep my eye on our cultured lady-friend hyar," drawled Stone, and he started off. At the gateway of the canyon, where a rough trail headed up toward the rim he turned to caution Gloriana. "Hang on to her mane."

When they reached the top he had satisfaction in the expression of that young woman's face. Stone then struck out along the rim, and he did not need to pick out a rough way. The trail was one seldom used, and then only by riders who preferred to keep to the wilder going. It led through thickets of scrub oak, manzanita, and dwarf pine, with a generous sprinkling of cactus. To drag Gloriana Traft through them was nothing short of cruelty. Stone kept an eye on her, though he appeared never to turn his head, never to hear her gasps and cries. Molly, who came last, often extricated her from some tangle.

Stone, from long habit, was a silent and swift traveler, and did not vary his custom now. But he had to stop more often to let the girls catch up. The condition of Gloriana's dress—what was left of it—seemed satisfactory to the outlaw. She had lost one of the sleeves that Malloy had almost torn from her blouse, and her beautiful white arm showed the red and black of contact with brush. What a ludicrous and pathetic figure she made, hunched over her saddle, with the gunman's battered and bullet-marked sombrero on her head! She had pulled it down now, to protect her eyes and face, thankful for it. Where was her disgust and horror? Nothing could have better exemplified the leveling power of the wilderness. Before Gloriana Traft got through this ride she would give all her possessions for a pair of blue jeans.

About the middle of the morning Jed came out on the high point of the Diamond Mesa. And he halted. The girls came up, to gaze out and down.

"Oh-h!" cried Miss Traft, her voice broken, yet deep and rich with feeling. She did not disappoint Stone here.

"The Tonto!" screamed Molly, suddenly beside herself. "Jed, why didn't you *tell* me you were comin' heah?" . . . Oh, Glory, look—look! It's my home."

"Home!" echoed Gloriana, incredulously.

"Yes. *Home!* . . . An', oh, how I love it! See thet thin line, with the white? Thet's the Cibeque windin' away down through the valley. See the big turn. Now look, Glory. There's a bare spot in the green. An' a gray dot in the middle. Thet's my home. Thet's my cabin. Where I was born."

"I see. But I can hardly believe," replied Gloriana. "That tiny pin-point in all the endless green?"

"Shore is, Glory. You're standin' on the high rim of the Diamond, a mile above the valley. But it looks close. You should see from down there. All my life I've looked up at this point. It was the Rim. But I was never heah before. . . . Oh, look, look, Glory, so you will never forget!"

The Eastern girl gazed silently, with eyes that seemed to reflect something of the grandeur of the scene. Stone turned away from her, glad in his heart that somehow she had satisfied him. Then he had a moment for himself—to gaze once more and the last time over the Tonto.

The Basin was at its best at sunrise or sunset, or in storm. Tranquil and austere now, it withheld something which the outlaw knew so well. The dotted green slopes from the Rim merged in the green-black forest floor, so deceivingly level, but which in reality was a vast region of ridges and gorges. Molly called it home, and so it was for backwoodsmen, deer, bear, and wild turkeys, and outlaws such as he. He liked best the long sections of yellow craggy Rim stepping down into the Basin toward the west. They showed the ragged nature of the Tonto. Away beyond them rose the purple range, spiked as a cactus plant, and to the south, dim on the horizon, stood up the four peaks that marked the gateway of the Cibeque, out into the desert. But nowhere was the desert visible. Doubtful Canyon called to Stone. He had killed a man there once, in an argument over spoil, and he had never been sure of the justice of it. Doubtful had been well named. It was deep and black and long, a forest and cliff-choked rent in the vast slope of the mountain.

"Molly, don't forget to show Gloriana some other places," said Stone, with a laugh. "There's West Fork, the village I used to ride through an' see you at Summer's store. An' buy you a stick of candy. . . . Not for years now. . . . An' never again. . . . There's Bear Flat an' Green Valley. An' Haverly's Ranch, an' Gordon Canyon. An' see, far to the east, thet bare yellow patch. Thet's Pleasant Valley, where they had the sheep an' cattle war which ruined your dad, though he was only a sympathizer, Molly. I reckon you never knew. Wal, it's true. . . . Miss Traft, you're shore the furst Eastern gurl ever to see the Tonto."

Though they wanted to linger, Stone ordered them on. Momentarily he had forgotten his rôle of slave-driver. But Gloriana had been too engrossed in her own sensations to notice his lapse.

Straight back from the Rim he headed, through trailless forest of stunted pines and wilderness of rock and cactus, toward the far side of the mesa, which sloped to the east, and gradually varied its rough aspect with grassy levels and healthier growth of pine. When Stone crossed the drift fence, which along here had been cut by the Hash Knife, he halted to show the girls.

"Traft's drift fence. Gloriana, this is what the old man saddled on your brother Jim. There's nine miles of fence down, which Jim an' his uncle can thank Croak Malloy fer. But I will say the buildin' of this fence was a big thing. Old Jim has vision. Shore I'm a cattle thief, an' the fence didn't make no difference to me. I reckon it was a help to rustlers. But Malloy hated fences. . . . Wal, it'll be a comfort to Traft an' all honest ranchers to learn he's dead."

"Jed Stone, you—you seem to be two men!" exclaimed Gloriana.

"Shore. I'm more'n thet. An' I reckon one of them is some kin to human. But don't gamble on him, my lovely tenderfoot. He's got no say in my make-up."

Molly Dunn lagged behind, most intensely interested in that drift fence, the building of which had made her lover, young Traft, a marked man on the range, and which had already caused a good deal of blood-spilling. Stone had to halloa to her, and wait.

"What's ailin' you, gurl?" he queried, derisively. "Thet fence make you lovesick fer Jim? Wal, I reckon you won't see him again very soon, if ever. . . . Get off an' straighten thet pack."

While Molly heaved and pulled to get the pack level on the pack-saddle again, Stone rolled a cigarette and watched Gloriana. Her amaze at Molly Dunn amused him.

"Wal, Glory, she used to pack grub an' grain from West Fork on a burro, when both of them wasn't any bigger'n jack-rabbits."

"There's a lot I don't know," observed Gloriana, thoughtfully, as for the hundredth time she tried to pull her town skirt down to hide her bare legs.

"Shore," agreed the outlaw. "An' when a feller finds thet out there's hope fer him."

He led on, calling for his followers to keep up, as they were losing time and the way was rough and long. As a matter of fact, Stone could have led down into Yellow Jacket that very day, but this was not his plan. He intended to ride these girls around, through the forest, up and down canyons, across streams, and among the rocks until one of them, at least, could no longer sit in the saddle. He was enjoying himself hugely, and when he saw how Gloriana had begun really to suffer he assuaged his conscience in the same way that a surgeon excused his cruel bright blade. Stone believed now that the Eastern girl would come off in the end with flying colors, even if she went down flat on her back. She had something, he began to divine, and it would come out when physically she was beaten.

The rest of that day he rode through a maze of wild country, at sunset ending up on a weathered slope where he had to get off and walk.

"Hey, there!" he called back. "Fall off an' walk. If your hoss slides, get out of his way. An' step lively so you won't go down in one of these avalanches."

All of which would have given a cowboy something to do. Molly had to stop often to rescue her friend, and more than once a scream rent the air. But at length they got across and down this long slant of loose shale, and entered a grassy wooded flat where water ran. Here Stone halted to make camp.

Gloriana came staggering up, sombrero in hand, leading her horse, and her appearance would have delighted even the most hardened Westerner who was inimical to tenderfeet. Her face was wan where it was not dirty, her hair hanging dishevelled and tangled with twigs, her bare arms all black and red, and her dress torn into tatters. One stocking hung down over her shoe, exposing a bloody leg, and the other showed sundry scratches.

"Wat-er!" choked Gloriana, huskily, as she sank down on the sward.

"Aha! Spittin' cotton, my proud beauty?" ejaculated the outlaw.

"Reckon you'd better have a drink out of my bottle." But she waved the suggestion aside with a gesture of abhorrence. And when Molly came carrying a dipper of water, Gloriana's great tragic eyes lit up. She drank the entire contents of the rather large vessel.

"Wal, Glory, you have to go through a good deal before you find the real value of things," remarked Stone, thoughtfully. "You see, most folks have life too easy. Take the matter of this drink of cold pure spring water. Sweet, wasn't it? You never knowed before how turrible sweet water could be, did you? It's the difference between life an' death."

"Thanks, Molly," said Gloriana, gratefully. "Aren't you—thirsty?"

"Not very. You see, out heah we train ourselves to do without water an' food. Like Indians, you know, Glory," replied Molly.

Plain indeed was it that Gloriana did not know; and that she was divided in emotion between her pangs and the surprise of this adventure.

"Hey, Molly, stop gabbin' an' get to work," ordered Stone, dryly. "Our St. Louis darlin' here will croak on us, if we ain't careful."

He slipped the ax out from under a rope on the pack, and proceeded to a near-by spruce, from which he cut armloads of the thick fragrant boughs. These he spread under an oak tree, and went back for more, watching the girls out of the tail of his eye. Once he caught Gloriana's voice in furious protest—"The lazy brute! Look at the size of him—and he makes you lift those packs!" And Molly's reply: "Aw, this heah's easy, Glory. An' I'm tellin' you again—don't make this desperado mad."

Then Stone slipped behind the spruce and peered through the branches. Molly did lift off those heavy packs, and unsaddled the animal. Next she turned to remove the saddle from her horse. At this Gloriana arose with difficulty, and limping to the horse she had ridden she tugged at the cinches, and labored until she got them loose. Then she slid the big saddle off. It was a man's saddle and heavy, which of course she had not calculated upon, and down she went with it, buried almost out of sight. Molly ran to lift it off. Stone saw the Eastern girl wring her helpless hands. "Dog-gone tough on her," he soliloquized, and proceeded to get another load of spruce boughs, which he carried over to the oak tree.

"Hey, Gloriana, fetch over thet bed roll," he called.

She paid no attention to him. Then he bellowed the order in the voice of a bull. He heard Molly advise her to rustle. Whereupon Gloriana lifted the roll in both arms and came wagging across the grass.

"Untie the rope," he said, not looking at her, and went on spreading the boughs evenly. Presently, as she was so slow, he looked up. She was wearily toiling at the knot.

"I—I can't untie it," she said.

"Wal, you shore are a helpless ninny," he returned, in disgust. "What in Gawd's name *can* you do, Miss Traft? Play the concertina, huh? An' fix your hair pretty, huh? It's shore thunderin' good luck for some fine cowboy thet I happened along an' saved him from marryin' you."

The marvel of that speech lay in its effect upon Gloriana, whose piteous mute appeal to Molly showed she had been driven to believe it was true.

"See heah, Jed Stone," demanded Molly, loyally, "how could Glory help the way she was brought up? Everybody cain't be born in Arizona."

"Misfortune, I call thet. . . . But see heah, yourself, Molly Dunn. The more you stick up fer this wishy-washy tenderfoot the wuss I'll be. Savvy?"

"You bet I savvy," rejoined Molly, resignedly.

"Wal then, rustle supper. I'm tired after thet ride. My neck's stiff from turnin' round to watch Miss Traft. It was a circus, though. . . . Gather some wood, start a fire, put on the water to boil, mix biscuits, an' so forth."

No one could ever have guessed that Molly Dunn had packed a horse and led him, and had ridden over thirty miles of rough wilderness during the hours of daylight. She was quick, deft, thorough in all camp tasks; and it gave the outlaw pleasure to watch her, outside of his diabolical plot to subjugate the Eastern girl.

"Say, if this heah's all the grub you fetched we'll eat it tonight," said Molly.

"Go light on grub, I tell you. Mebbe I didn't pack enough. But I was a-rarin' to get away from Tobe's Well."

"Molly, I'll help you—or die trying," offered Gloriana. "But if that queer pain comes to my side again—farewell."

"What pain, honey?"

"Reckon she's got appendixitis," drawled Stone, who allowed no word to get by him unheard.

"It was in my left side—and, oh, it was awful!"

"Thet comes from ridin' a hoss when you're not used to it. But it'll not kill you."

"Yes, it will, if I live long enough to mount that wild mustang again," avowed Gloriana. Then in a lower tone she added. "Molly, I thought Ed Darnell was a villain. But, my, oh!—he's a saint compared with this desperado."

"Oh no, Glory. Jed Stone is an honest-to-Gawd desperado," expostulated Molly.

"What's she sayin' aboot thet fellar Darnell an' me?" demanded Stone, going to the fire.

"Jed, she knew Darnell back in Missouri," explained Molly.

"You don't say. Wal, thet's interestin'. Hope she didn't compare me to him. Two-bit caird-sharp before he hit the West. An' then, like a puff of smoke, he lit into crooked cattle-dealin'. . . . An' did he last longer than any of them dude Easterners who reckon they can learn us Westerners tricks? He did not."

"What do you mean, Jed?" queried Molly, who divined when he was lying and when he was not.

"Croak Malloy was in thet outfit Traft's cowboys rounded up in a cabin down below Yellow Jacket. They'd been rustlin' the new Diamond stock an' had to ride fer their lives. Wal, they didn't ride fer, not with your red-skin brother an' Curly Prentiss an' thet rodeo-ridin' bunch after them. Croak said they set fire to the cabin, an' burned them out, an' he got shot in the laig. But he escaped, an' it was when he was hidin' in the brush thet he seen the cowboys string up Darnell along with two rustlers. Croak said he never seen a man kick like thet white-cuff caird-slicker, Darnell."

Gloriana's eyes were great black gulfs.

"Mr. Stone, among other things you're a liar," she said, deliberately.

"Wal, I'll be dog-goned!" ejaculated the outlaw, genuinely surprised and not a little hurt. "I am, am I? Wal, you'll see, Miss Traft."

"You're trying to—to frighten me," she faltered, weakening. "Have you no heart—no mercy? . . . I was once engaged to—to marry Darnell, or thought I was. He followed me out here."

"Ahuh. What'd he foller you out heah fer?"

"He swindled my father out of money, and I suppose he thought he could do the same with Uncle Jim."

"Not old Jim Traft. Nix come the weasel! Old Jim cain't be swindled. . . . Wal, Miss Gloriana, I must say you was lucky to have Darnell stack up against Curly Prentiss. I remember now thet Madden was in Snell's gamblin'-den when Curly ketched Darnell cheatin' an' drove him out of Flag. Funny he didn't bore thet caird-sharp. Reckon he savvied how soon Darnell would come to the end of his rope. He did come soon—an' it was a lasso."

"I don't believe you," replied Gloriana, steadily.

"Sweet on him yet, huh?"

"No. I despite him. Any punishment, even hanging, would be too good for him," retorted Gloriana, with passion.

"See there, Molly She's comin' round," drawled Stone. "We'll make a Westerner of her yet."

"Jed, was there a—a fight down below Yellow Jacket?" asked Molly, with agitation.

"Shore was. Malloy said he seen two cowboys shot, one of which he accounted fer himself. But he didn't know either. An' so they couldn't have been Jim or Slinger or Prentiss."

"Oh—how'll we find out?" cried Molly, in honest agony. And the tone of her voice, the look of her, about finished Gloriana, who fell in a heap.

"Wal, what difference does it make," queried Stone, "to one of you, anyhow? One of you gurls is shore goin' with me, an' cowboys won't never be no more in your young life. Haw! Haw!"

"I could stick this in you, Jed Stone," cried Molly, brandishing the wicked butcher knife.

The outlaw reached down and lifted Gloriana upright. Gloriana's head rolled. "Brace up," he said, and shook her. She found strength left to resist. Then he clasped her in his arms and hugged her tight. And while he did this he winked and grinned at Molly, who stood there aghast. "You need a regular desperado hug to stiffen your spine. . . . There! Now you stand up an' do your work."

She did keep her feet, too, when he released her, and such eyes Jed Stone had never seen. If he had been the real desperado he pretended, he would have flinched and quailed under their magnificent fury.

"Call me when supper's ready," he ordered Molly. "I smelled a skunk out there, an' I'm afeerd it's one of them hydrophobia varmints. They shore stink wuss."

As he stroke off he heard Gloriana ask in Heaven's name what he would think of next, and what was a hydrophobia skunk anyway. Luckily Stone had smelled a skunk, and any kind of one would serve his purpose, so presently he fired his gun twice, and then went back to camp.

"Missed him, by gosh!" he said, greatly annoyed. "An' it shore was a hydrophobia, all right. Molly, you gurls will have to sleep with me tonight. 'Cause thet skunk will come round camp, an' it'd be shore to bite Glory's nose. Hydrophobia skunks always pick out a fellar with a big nose. An' I'll have to be there to choke it off."

"I'd be eaten up by skunks with hydrophobia and lions with yellow fever before I'd obey you," declared Gloriana.

"Haw! Haw! Yes, you would. Wait till it gets dark an' you smell thet varmint."

While they sat at the meager supper, Stone bedeviled Gloriana in every way conceivable, yet to his satisfaction it did not prevent her from eating her share. That was the answer. Let even the effete Easterner face the facts of primal life and the balance was struck.

Darkness soon settled down, and twice Gloriana fell asleep beside the fire. "Let's sit up—all night," she begged, of Molly.

"I'd be willin', if he'd let us. But, Glory, dear, you jest couldn't. You'd fall over. An' by mawnin' you'd be froze. We'll *have* to sleep with Stone. He's put all the blankets on thet bed. An' I'll sleep in the middle—so he cain't touch you."

"You'll do nothing of the sort," retorted Gloriana. And when they reached the wide bed under the oak tree she crawled in the middle and stretched out, as if she did not care what happened.

"Wal, now, thet's somethin' like," declared the outlaw, as he saw the pale faces against the background of blankets. He sat down on the far side of the bed and in the gloom contrived to remove his boots and spurs. "Gurls, I'm liable to have nightmare. Often do when I'm scared or excited. An' I'm powerful dangerous then. Shot a bedfellow once, when I had nightmare. So you wanta kick me awake in case I get to dreamin'. . . . An', Molly, don't forget if thet skunk gets its teeth fastened in Glory's nose you must choke it off."

It was not remarkable that almost before he had ceased talking Gloriana was asleep. He knew what worn-out nature would do. Nevertheless, as soon as Molly had dropped off he made such a commotion that he would almost have awakened the dead. Then he began to snore outrageously, and between snores he broke out into the thick weird utterance of a man in a nightmare.

"Molly—Molly!" cried Gloriana, in a shrill whisper, as she clutched her friend madly. "He's got it!"

"Sssh! Don't wake him. He won't be dangerous unless he wakes," replied Molly.

Jed made the mental reservation that his little ally was all right, and began to rack his brain for appropriate exclamations: "AGGH! I'll—carve—your—gizzard!" And he sprang up to thump back. Then he gave capital imitations of Malloy's croaking laugh. Then he shouted: "You can't have the gurl! She's mine, Croak, she's mine! . . . I'll have your heart's blood!" After which he snored some more, while listening intently. He did not hear anything, but he thought he felt the bed trembling. Next he rolled over, having thrown the blankets, to bump hard into Gloriana. But that apparently did not awaken him. He laid a heavy arm across both the girls and went on snoring blissfully.

"Molly," whispered Gloriana, in very low and blood-curdling voice. *"Let's—kill him—in his sleep!"*

"Oh, I wish we could, but we're not strong enough," replied Molly, horrified. "Don't you dare move!"

Stone could scarcely contain himself, and wanted to roar his mirth and elation. So his acting had been so good, so convincing that it had driven this lovely tenderfoot to consider murder! He could not have asked more. She was responding nobly to the unplumbed primitive instincts which, happily for her and those who loved her, she shared in common with the less sophisticated characters of the West.

Lastly Jed thought he would try the love-making of a man suffering from delusions in a nightmare. This rather taxed his capacity. His actual experience had never gone so far. But he bawled out endearments of every kind, and he hugged both girls until they appeared to be squeezed into one. Suddenly there came a terrific tug at his hair. He bawled in earnest. A tight little fist was fast in his hair and pulling fiercely. It was Molly's, and he had trouble in tearing it loose. After that rebuke Jed rolled back against the tree, and pulling his blanket free he composed himself to slumber.

In the gray of dawn he got up, pulled on his big boots, and went at the camp-fire tasks, careful not to make noise. His two babes in the woods were locked in sleep, also in each other's arms. Stone cooked the last of the meat and boiled the last of the coffee. A few biscuits were left, hard as rocks. Then he went to awaken the girls. Their heads were close together, one dark, the other amber, and their sweet pale faces took the first flush of the sunrise. It was a picture the outlaw would carry in his memory always, and he found himself thanking God that he had come upon Croak Malloy before they had suffered harm.

"Gurls, roll out," he called.

Molly awakened first and was bright and quick in an instant. She smiled, and Jed thought he would treasure that smile. Then Gloriana's eyes popped open. Dim gulfs of sleep! Stone turned away from them with a conscience-stricken pang.

"Rustle an' eat. I gotta hunt the hosses," he said.

Upon his return they had finished eating. Molly said: "Glory's bag is missin'. With all her outdoor clothes!"

"Shore. I hid it. I don't want her dressin' up. She looks so cute in thet outfit," he replied. "Saddle your hoss, you starin' idgit," he said to Gloriana. "An', Molly, rustle with the bed an' packs while I eat."

Molly proved as capable as any cowboy, but poor Gloriana could not get the saddle up, and when the pinto bit and kicked at her, which was no wonder, she gave up coaxing and struck it smartly with a branch.

"Hyar! Don't beat thet pony," expostulated Stone. "Who'd ever think you'd show cruelty to a dumb beast?"

"Dumb! He sure is," replied Gloriana, "and he's not the only be— thing around that ought to be beaten."

"Molly, you cain't never tell aboot people till you get them in the woods," said Stone, reflectively. "Their real natoor comes out. I reckon Glory, hyar, would have murdered Croak Malloy in cold blood if he'd got away with her. It's turrible to contemplate."

Soon they were mounted and riding in single file, as on the day before. Stone led them out of this gorge, miles and miles through the forest, out into the sunny desert, and back again, and finally, without a halt to the rim of the Black Brakes. He followed along that until mid-afternoon, when he came to a trail he knew, which was seldom used even by rustlers, unless pressed. Here they had to walk down and it was no fun. "Don't let your hoss fall on you," was all Stone said. At a particularly bad descent Gloriana and her pinto both fell, and she miraculously escaped being rolled on. "Whew!" ejaculated Stone. "I reckoned you was a goner then. The Lord shore watches over you."

"I don't—care," panted the girl. "I'd sooner die—that way—than some other way." Her spirit was hard to break. She seemed to recover her courage after each successive trial. But her strength was almost spent. Once down in the brakes Stone eased up on rough going, and wended a leisurely course through the labyrinthine glades and aisles, groves and fields of broken cliff. The gold slants from the westering sun fell across their path, and the wilderness appeared more than usually beautiful. Stone calculated their position at that hour was less than a dozen miles below Yellow Jacket. And his intention was, if Gloriana could stand it, to climb out of the brakes, and ride to the head of Yellow Jacket, where he could show the girls their way and then take leave of them. There was a risk of being held up along the trail by one or more of the Diamond outfit, but since he had the girls to credit him with their rescue he had little to worry about. Still he did not want that to happen. He had planned a climax to his plot.

The sun set behind the western wall of the brakes; a mellow roar of running water filled the forest with dreaming music. Stone thought it about time to choose a place to camp, and he desired it to be remote from the trail, which he believed ran somewhat to his left along the stream. With this end in view he wormed his way through the woods toward the wall they had long since descended.

It loomed above him, gray and lofty, always silent and protective. And suddenly he emerged into an open space where tall spruces and wide-spreading sycamores dominated the green. The glade appeared familiar, and as Gloriana and Molly rode out of the forest he reined his horse.

"O my God—look!" cried Molly, in accents of horror.

Simultaneously then Stone's senses accounted for a smell of burned wood, the pile of charred logs that was once the trapper's cabin, and three grotesque and hideously swaying figures of men, hanging limp by their necks from a prominent branch of a sycamore.

Stone's shock had its stimulus in Gloriana's shriek. She swayed and slid out of the saddle. He caught her and lifted her in front of him, a dead weight.

"Jed—this heah is too much," expostulated Molly, hoarsely. She looked as if she, too, would faint.

Cursing under his breath, he turned to the girl. "I swear it was accident," he avowed, earnestly. "We were east of the trail, an' if I thought aboot it at all, I reckoned we were far from thet old cabin. By Gawd! I'm sorry, Molly, It *is* too much."

"Jed, I'll be—keelin' over, too," gasped Molly. "Thet's a hard sight for *me,* let alone Glory. . . . If I recognized Darnell, *she* recognized him, you bet."

"Shore she did. I never seen him but once, an' I knew him. An' there's my old Sheriff Lang, his star still a-shinin' on his vest. An' Joe Tanner. . . . Wal, thet's shore a cowboy job, slick an' clean. Thet's the way of the West!"

Darnell's distorted and discolored features had been stamped by an appalling surprise and terror, something wholly wanting from the visages of the other two dead men. They swayed as the evening breeze moved the sycamore branch. Darnell's watch fob dangled from his vest.

"Jed, come on—fetch her," implored Molly. "I'll hate you forever—if she doesn't get over this."

"Molly, it's shore sickening', but mebbe jest as well she seen it."

"I—I wasn't above bein' took in myself—by thet handsome gambler," admitted Molly, with intense humility. "What an end! . . . An' Jim an' Slinger were responsible. I'll never get—"

"Don't you believe it," interrupted Stone. "Thet's the work of Arizona range-riders. Prentiss an' his pards are back of thet. . . . An' see there. Graves! But wait, Molly."

The outlaw's sharp eyes, in further survey of the glade, had fallen upon freshly made graves.

"Wal, there are no cowboys buried here, thet's shore. . . . Ride on, Molly."

Stone halted in the first likely spot for camp, and slipping out of his saddle with Gloriana in his arms, he laid her down on a soft pine-needle mat. She was conscious.

"Tend to her, Molly," said Stone, briefly, and he turned to look after the horses. Then he cut ample spruce boughs for two beds, and made them, one of which, for the girls, he laid in a protected niche of the cliff. Having finished these tasks, he approached his prisoners.

"There's nothin' to eat."

"Small matter, Jed. Our appetites are shore not a'rarin'," replied Molly.

Gloriana transfixed him with solemn tragic eyes.

"I take back—calling you a liar," she said, simply.

"Thanks. I accept your apology."

"Who—who did that?" she asked, with a gesture to indicate the tragedy down the valley.

"What? Who did what?"

"Hanged those men?"

"I reckon thet was Curly Prentiss an' his pards. Shore young Jim had a hand in it, onless, of course, Curly an' Jim got killed by the rustlers. Some of the Diamond were done for, thet's shore."

"But—you—said—" she faltered, piteously.

"Shore. I said I reckoned it wasn't Jim or Curly. I forgot thet. Must have been one or more of them dare-devils. Bud or Lonestar—an' mebbe Slinger. I seen where blood had dripped on the leaves, about saddle-high, along the trail. Some cowboys packed out, shore."

That surely finished Gloriana and all but did the same for Molly. She just had strength left to help Stone carry Gloriana to bed. The outlaw then sought his own rest, and the meditations inspired by the latest developments. This adventure had not lost its sting, despite the knocking at the gate of his conscience. Tomorrow would see the end of it and he must not fail in the task he had set himself.

Morning disclosed Molly to be herself again, and Gloriana able to get up, though she could not stand erect. She could do nothing but watch the others saddle and pack. Still, her perceptions were all the keener, and she paid Molly mute and eloquent tribute of appreciation.

"I'm made of straw and water," she said, humbly.

"Wal, Gloriana, darlin', a thing of beauty is a joy forever," rejoined Stone, with gallant cheerfulness.

Once more they were mounted and off. Stone led up out of the brakes through a narrow hidden crack in the east wall, a secret exit known only to outlaws. It was a long gloomy ascent which took an hour of labored climbing on foot. From the outlet Stone made his way along the rim, north, and in the direction of Yellow Jacket. He led the pack-horse, while Molly supported Gloriana in her saddle. Stone kept close to them, fearing Molly might weaken and betray him. But she did not. And the outlaw recalled what she had confessed about her brother giving up rustling. Slinger had once belonged to the Cibeque outfit, and the years were not many since Stone had tried to get him into the Hash Knife. Molly could be generous and strong.

Before they reached the head of Yellow Jacket, which Stone was approaching, he had fears the Eastern girl would not make it. Yet a little rest enabled her to go on, without complaint, without appeal for mercy.

At last Stone espied the new road, where it turned to go down into the canyon. He halted before the girls noticed it and dismounted near the rim.

"Wal, we've reached the partin' of the trails," he said. "There's a ranch down heah where one of you can go an' send word to the cowboys. 'Cause I cain't take you both with me any farther. I'm a hunted desperado, you know. An' I've gotta hole up till all this blows over. One of you goes with me."

"Take us both—Jed," implored Molly, and that plainly was her last word in this trick perpetrated upon an innocent tenderfoot.

"No, Molly, *I* will go," interposed Gloriana. "You love Jim. He worships you. . . . There's no one cares for me or—or whom I care for. . . . And I'm not strong, as you've seen from my miserable frailty on this ride. I won't live long, so it'll not matter much."

Molly, with eyes suddenly full of tears, averted her gaze. Stone regarded the Eastern girl with poignant emotion he gladly hid.

"Ahuh. So you'll go willin'?"

"Yes, since you compel me. But on one condition."

"An' what's thet?"

"You must—marry me honestly. I have religious principles."

"Wal, I reckon I could fetch a padre down into the brakes—where we'll be hidin'," replied Stone. "An' so—Miss Gloriana Traft—you'd marry me—Jed Stone of the Hash Knife—thief, killer, outlaw, desperado—to save your friend?"

"Yes, I'll do even that for Jim and Molly."

Suddenly Jed Stone turned away, gripped by a whirlwind of passion. It had waylaid him, at this pathway of middle life, like a tiger in ambush. All the hard bitter years of outlawry rose like a hydra-headed monster to burn his soul with the poison of hate, revenge, lust, and the longing to kill. To wreak his vengeance upon civilization by despoiling the innocence and crushing the life of this young girl! The thing roared in his brain, a hell-storm of fury. He had never realized the depths into which he had been thrust until this madness wrapped him in a whirling flame.

But the instant he understood that this was actual temptation—that it had tripped him with surprise and feeling he never dreamed he possessed—he rejected it with the hard stern courage of the outlaw who had survived baseness. That kind of crime was for Croak Malloy—never for Jed Stone.

He stepped through the brush to the rim and gazed down into Yellow Jacket. The canyon seemed to lift to meet his eye, with all the gold and green beauty, the noble gray cliffs, the singing amber stream, and with some indefinable peacefulness of solitude that he grasped then and there, forever to be a possession of his lonely soul.

Then he returned in thought to the issue at hand. Far beyond his hope had he succeeded in forcing latent good into being. This Eastern girl had really defeated him. What could be greater than sacrificing virtue and life itself for her friend? Stone bowed under that. Gloriana Traft had love—which was greater than all the fighting instincts he had meant to rouse. It would have been an error of nature to have created such a beautiful being as this girl and not have endowed her with unquenchable spirit. She was as noble, in her extremity, as she was beautiful. Her eyes and lips, the turn of her face, were no falsehoods. And so Jed Stone divined how he was to profit by the courage of a girl he had driven to such desperate straits. The lesson, the good would rebound upon him.

"Ride over hyah a step," he said to the girls, and he pointed down into the canyon. "This is Yellow Jacket, an' thet new house you see way down there in the green is Jim Traft's."

While they stared he went back to mount his own horse and turn to them again.

"The road is right hyar," he went on, as coolly and casually as if that fact was nothing momentous. "Shore you can make it thet fer."

Then he patted Molly's dusky tousled head: "Good-by, little wood-mouse. Be good—"

"Oh, Jed," cried Molly, wildly, with tears streaming down her cheeks. "Remember aboot never—rustlin' no more!"

Stone turned to the Eastern girl. "Big-eyes!" he called her, for that was the most felicitous of all names for her then. "So long!—Marry Curly or Bud, an' have some real Western kids. . . . But don't never forget your desperado!"

As he spurred away he heard her poignant call: "Oh wait—wait!" But Jed Stone rode as never had he from sheriffs and posse, from vengeful cowboys who pursued with gun and rope.

CHAPTER TWENTY

"—— —— ——LUCK!" shouted Jim Traft, slamming down his pencil, and crumpling the white sheet of paper to fling it into the fire.

"Why, James!" exclaimed Curly, looking in grave surprise from his game of checkers, which he was playing with the crippled Bud, on his bed.

"Boss, thet shore's amazin' fine example fer us—on a Sunday night, too," added Bud, plaintively.

"Shore the way Jim can cuss now is somethin' frazzlin' on the nerves," put in Jackson Way, who, as usual during any leisure, was writing to his young wife.

"Aw, you weren't listening," returned Jim, exasperated. "I said, 'Dod blast the dog-gone luck.'"

"Yes, you did. Haw! Haw!"

"Jim, you're shore demoralizin' what's left of the Diamond."

"Next an' last it'll be red-eye, an' then good-by."

It was Sunday evening at the ranch-house down in Yellow Jacket. The big living-room shone bright and new with lamp and blazing fire. Jim had been endeavoring to write a letter to his uncle, reporting loss of two thousand head of Diamond-brand stock, and the fight at the cabin down in the brakes, which had entailed a more serious loss. But the letter for many reasons was difficult to write. For one thing, Molly and Gloriana would surely see it, and as Gloriana took care of her uncle's mail she would be very likely to read it first. And it had to be bad news. Jim could not gloss over the deaths of Uphill Frost and Hump Stevens, nor the serious condition of Slinger Dunn and Bud Chalfack. Moreover, he found it impossible to confess his part in that fight. On the moment Curly was trying to keep the fretful and feverish Bud from reopening wounds. Lonestar Holliday read quietly by the lamplight across the table from Jim, but he could not sit still, and as he moved his bandaged foot from one resting-place to another he betrayed the pain he was suffering. Jack Way wore the beatific smile which characterized his visage while writing to the absent bride.

"Jump, dog-gone you," said Curly, mildly, to his opponent. "Cain't you see a jump when you have one?"

Bud reluctantly made the required move, when Curly promptly jumped three men, practically winning the game. Bud gave the home-made checker-board a shove, sending the checkers flying.

"Skunked again! Thet's three games, without me gettin' a king," complained Bud, fiercely. "Of all the lucky gazabos I ever seen, you're the dingest. . . . Lucky in fights—lucky in good looks—lucky at games—lucky at shenanagin out of work—an' lucky with wimmen! It do beat hell!"

"Bud, what's eatin' you? I've got brains, which shore was left out of your make-up. I think aboot things. I don't yell an' run into a lot of bullets, like you do. I take care of my face, hair, teeth, an' so on. When I play cairds or checkers I use my haid an' figger out what the other fellar is aimin' at. An' it's a damn lie aboot me gettin' out of work. As fer the ladies—wal, I cain't help it if they like me."

"Go out an' drown yourself," shouted Bud, who plainly was angry for no reason at all, unless because he was all shot up.

"Wal, pard, you can gamble on this heah," drawled his handsome friend. "If I turn out as unlucky as you with a certain lovely person, I shore will drown myself in drink."

"Aw, I said wimmen. The way you talk, anyone would reckon there was no plural number of wimmen atall. Jest one woman in the world!"

"Which is correct."

Jim broke into the argument. "Shut up, you game-cocks. Listen. I can't write to Uncle Jim. If he doesn't show up here in a few days I'll have to ride to Flag."

"An' take Jack with you?" queried Bud, in a terrible voice.

"Yes. Jack has a wife, you know."

"An' leave the rest of us hyar fer Croak Malloy to wipe out, huh?"

Jim paced the floor. The matter was not easy to decide, and more than once he had convinced himself that the longing to see Molly had a good deal to do with the need to go to Flagerstown.

"Of course, if you boys think there's a chance of Malloy coming back—"

"Wal, Jim," interposed Curly, coolly. "As I see it you'd better wait. We've managed to get along without a doctor, an' I reckon we can do the same without reportin' to old Jim. He'll roar, shore, but let him roar. This last few weeks hasn't been any fun fer us. Somebody will get wind of thet fight an' Flag will heah aboot it."

"All right, I'll give up the idea about going, as well as writing. It'll be a relief," replied Jim, and indeed the outspoken renunciation helped him. "You know one reason I wanted to go was to block Uncle Jim's fetching Molly and Glory down here."

"Aw!" breathed Bud, reproachfully. "An' me dyin' hyar by inches."

"Let Uncle Jim fetch the girls," rejoined Curly, stoutly.

"Curly, you're a cold-blooded Arizonian," declared Jim, with both irritation and admiration. "Here's the deal. We had to take Slinger home to West Fork, shot to pieces. Bud's on his back, full of bullets and bad temper. Lonestar hobbles about making you grind your teeth. And out there under the pines lie two of the Diamond—in their graves!"

"Wal, it's shore sad," replied Curly, "but the fact is we got off lucky. An' we cain't dodge what's comin' because of what's past. I reckon thet fight aboot broke the Hash Knife fer keeps. I'm pretty shore I crippled Malloy. I was shootin' through smoke, but I seen him fall. An' then I couldn't see him any more. He got away, an' thet leaves him, Madden, an' Jed Stone of the Hash Knife. Stone won't stand fer the kind of rustlers Malloy has been ringin' in of late. Thet Joe Tanner outfit, let alone such hombres as Bambridge an' Darnell. So heah we are, not so bad off. An' I reckon we could take care of your uncle an' the girls."

Cherry Winters came in at that juncture, carrying a rifle and a haunch of venison. The cool fragrance of the night and the woods accompanied him.

"Howdy, all!" he said, cheerfully.

"What kept you late, Cherry?" asked Curly.

"Nothin'. I jest ambled along. Reckon I was pretty fur up the crick. G[illegible] watchin' the beaver."

"Jeff has kept supper on for you," added Jim. "You know how sore he gets wh[illegible] we're late? Rustle now."

Jim went out on the porch. Night down in Yellow Jacket was always dark, b[illegible] reason of the looming walls, which appeared so much closer and higher and blacker than by day. No air was stirring, consequently no sound in the pine and spruce tops, and the warm fragrant atmosphere of the sunny hours lingered in the canyon. The stream murmured as always, mellow and low; and the crickets were chirping. White blinking stars watched pitilessly out of the blue above.

The trouble with Jim was that he had not been weaned of his tenderfoot infancy; he had swallowed too big a dose of Arizona and he was sick. Beginning with Sonora's ambush—which only Slinger's timely shot had rendered futile—a series of happenings had tested Jim out to the limit. He had been found wanting, so far as stomach was concerned, and he knew it. Asleep and awake, that fight before the burning cabin had haunted him. No use to balk at the truth! He had taken cool bead with rifle at an oncoming and shooting, yelling rustler, and well he knew who had tumbled him over, like a bagged turkey. Afterward Jim had looked for a bullet-hole where he had aimed, and had found it. That was harsh enough. But the fact that he had, in common with his cowboys, turned deaf ear alike to the cursings and pleadings of the gambler Darnell, and had himself laid strong hands on that avenging rope, had like a boomerang rebounded upon him. All the arguments about rustlers, raids, self-preservation, had not been sufficient to cure him. Reality was something incalculably different from conjecture and possibility. In the Cibeque fight, rising out of the drift fence, he had been unable to take an active part; and so the killing of Jocelyn and the Haverlys by Slinger Dunn had rested rather easily upon his conscience. But now he was an Arizonian with blood on his hands. He still needed a violent and constant cue for passion.

Curly came outside presently: "Fine night, Boss. An' it's good to feel we can peek out an' not be scared of bullets. I reckon, though, thet feelin' oughtn't be trusted fer long. We'll heah from Croak Malloy before the summer is over."

"Yes, it's a fine night, I suppose," sighed Jim. "But almost—I wish I was back in Missouri."

"Never havin' seen Arizona an' Molly?" drawled the cowboy, with his cool, kindly tone.

"Even that."

"But more special—never havin' killed a man?"

"Curly!"

"Shore you cain't fool me, Jim, old boy. I was aboot when it come off. I seen you bore thet rustler. Fact is I had a bead on him myself."

"I—I didn't dream anybody knew," replied Jim, hoarsely. "Please don't tell, Curly."

"Wal, I cain't promise fer the rest of the outfit. Bud seen it, from where he fell. An' what's more, he seen thet rustler shoot Hump daid."

"He did!" cried Jim, a dark hot wave as of blood with consciousness surging to his head. A subtle change marked his exclamation.

"Shore. An' Lonestar reckoned he seen the same. Wal, thet rustler was Ham Beard. We searched him, before we buried him. Used to be a Winslow bartender till he murdered some one. Then he took to cattle-stealin'. Sort of a lone wolf an' shore a daid shot. If it hadn't been fer thet smoke he an' Croak might have done fer all of us. Though I reckon in thet case, if they'd charged us without the cover of

have stopped them with our rifles. . . . It was a mess, Jim, an' you
t yourself on the back instead of mopin' around."
ized this clearly, and in the light of Curly's cool illuminating talk he felt
ng of a gloomy shade.
lory an' Molly never hear of it—I guess I'll stand it," he said.
al, you can bet your last pair of wool socks in zero weather thet our beloved
will spring it on the girls."
'No!"
"Shore. An' not because of his itch to talk. It'll be pride, Jim, unholy pride in your addition to the toll of the Diamond."
"I'll beg him not to, and if that's not enough I'll beat him."
"Wal, Mizzouri, it cain't be did," drawled Curly.

The cowboys had given the brakes a wide berth for days, notwithstanding the pertinent and baffling fact that most of the Diamond stock had been driven or had stampeded as far south as Yellow Jacket. Jim was strong to ride down, at least as far as the burned cabin, and to bury the rustlers they had left hanging to the sycamore. But Curly took as strong exception to leaving crippled cowboys unprotected at the ranch-house; and as for the hanging rustlers, he said, "Let 'em sun dry an' blow away!"

Curly was not as easy in mind as might have appeared to a superficial observer. He was restless; he walked up and down the canyon trail. Jim noted that Curly's blue flashing eyes were ever on the alert. And when Jim finally commented about this, Curly surprised him with a whisper: "Nix on thet, Mizzouri. I don't want Bud or Lonestar to worry. They make fuss enough. But I'll tell you somethin'. This very day, when you were eatin' dinner, I seen a rider's black sombrero bobbin' above the rim wall there. On the east rim, mind you!"

"Curly! . . . A black sombrero? You might have been mistaken," replied Jim.

"Shore. It might have been a black hawk or a raven. But my eyes are pretty sharp, Jim."

Hours of uneasiness on Jim's part followed, and apparently casual strolling the porch on Curly's. Nothing happened, and at length Jim forgot about the circumstance. He went back to his account-books, presently to be disturbed by the nervous Bud.

"Boss, I thought I heerd a call a little while ago, but I didn't want to bother you. But now I shore heerd hosses."

"You did?" Jim listened with strained ears, while he gazed around the living-room. Lonestar was asleep, and so was Cherry, while Jack, writing as usual, could not have heard the crack of doom. But Jim distincly caught a soft thud, thud, thud of hoofs.

"Curly!" he called sharply. That jerked the sleepers wide awake, but it did not fetch Curly.

"Boys, something up. We hear horses. And Curly doesn't answer. Grab your rifles."

"Listen, Boss!" ejaculated Bud.

Then Jim caught a call from outside: "Jim—oh, Jim!"

"Molly!" he shouted wildly, and rushed out, to be followed by the three uninjured cowboys. No sign of horses down the trail. But under the pines in the other direction moved brown figures, now close at hand, emerging from the grove. Molly led, on a big raw-boned bay horse. Hatless, her dusky hair flying, she called again: "Jim—oh, Jim!"

Roused out of stupefaction, Jim rushed to meet her. "Molly! for Heaven's s how'd you get here?" he cried as she reined in the bay. She dropped a halter c pack-horse she was leading. Then Jim saw that she was brush-covered and trave stained. Her hair was full of pine needles, and her eyes shone unnaturally large an bright. Jim's rapture suffered a check. He looked beyond her, to see Curly supporting Gloriana in the saddle of a third horse. Her head drooped, her hair hung in a tawny mass.

"My God! what's happened?" he exclaimed, in sudden terror.

"Shore a lot. Don't look so scared, Jim. We're all right. . . . Help me down."

She slid into his arms, most unresisting, Jim imagined, and for once his kisses brought blushes without protest. If she did not actually squeeze him, then he was dreaming. He set her down upon her feet, still keeping an arm around her.

"What—what's all this?" he stammered, looking back to see Gloriana fall into Curly's arms. As Curly carried her up the porch steps Jim caught a glimpse of Gloriana's face. Then he dragged Molly with him into the house.

"Curly, let me down," Gloriana was saying.

But Curly did not hear, or at least obey. "For Gawd's sake, darlin', tell me you—you're not hurt or—or anythin'."

No longer was Gloriana's face white. "Let me down, I say," she cried, imperiously. Whereupon Curly became aware of his behavior, and he set her down in the big armchair, to gaze at her as at a long-lost treasure found.

"Glory!—What crazy trick—have you sprung on us?" gasped Jim, striding close, still hanging to Molly. He stared incredulously at his sister. Her flimsy dress had once been light-colored. It seemed no longer a dress, scarcely a covering, and it was torn to shreds and black from contact with burned brush. But that appeared only little cause for the effect she produced upon Jim and his comrades. One arm was wholly bare, scratched and dirty and bloody; her legs were likewise. To glance over these only forced the gaze back to Gloriana's face. The havoc of terrible mental and physical strain showed in its haggard outlines. But her eyes seemed a purple radiant blaze of rapture, or thanksgiving. They would have reassured a cynic that all was well with heart and soul—that life was good.

"Oh—Jim," she whispered, lifting a weak hand to him, and as he clasped it, to sink on one knee beside her chair, she lay back and closed her eyes. "I'm here—I'm safe—oh, thank Heaven!"

"Glory, dear, what in the world happened?" begged Jim.

On the other side of the chair Curly lifted her hand, which clung to a battered old sombrero, full of bullet holes.

"Jim, this heah's what I seen bobbin' above the rim," he said, in amazed conjecture. "Whose hat is this? Reckon it looks some familiar."

He could not remove it from the girl's tight clutch.

"Thet sombrero belonged to Croak Malloy," interposed Molly, who stood back of Jim, smoothing the pine needles out of her tangled hair.

"Holy Mackeli!" burst out Curly. "I knew it. I recognized thet hat. . . . Jim, as shore as Gawd made little apples thet croakin' gun-thrower is daid."

"Daid? I should smile he is," corroborated Molly, laconically. "Daid as a door nail."

The tremendousness of that truth, which no one doubted, commanded profound silence. Even Curly Prentiss had no tongue.

"Jed Stone killed Malloy, an' Madden, too," went on Molly, bright-eyed, enjoying to the full the sensation she was creating.

Jim echoed the name of the Hash Knife leader, but Curly, to whom that name more deadly significance, still could not speak.

Dunn, I'm a hurted cowpuncher," called Bud from his bed. "An' if you pronto what's come off, I'll be wuss."

na opened her eyes, and let them dwell lovingly upon her brother, and olly, after which they wandered to the standing wide-eyed cowboys, and to the stricken Curly, whose adoration was embarrassingly manifest.

ell them, Molly," she whispered. "I—can't talk."

'We planned to surprise you, Jim," began Molly. "It took some persuadin' to et Uncle Jim in on our job. But we did. An' let's see—five days ago—early mawnin' we left Flag in the buckboard, Pedro drivin'. That night we slept at Miller's ranch. Next mawnin' at the fork of the road we got held up by Croak Malloy, an' two of his pards, Madden an' Reeves. They'd jest happened to run into us. Uncle Jim didn't know Malloy until he shot Pedro. Malloy robbed Uncle, took our bags, an' threw us on horses. An' he told Uncle to go back to Flag, dig up ten thousand dollars, an' send it by rider to Tobe's Well, where it was to be put up in the loft by the chimney. Malloy drove us off then, into the woods, an' along in the afternoon we reached Tobe's Well. We'd jest been dragged in, an' they'd hawg-tied me, an' Malloy was tearin' Glory's clothes off, when in comes Jed Stone. He shore filled thet cabin. . . . Wal, Croak was sore at bein' interrupted, an' Jed raved aboot what Uncle Jim would do. Queer what stress he put on Uncle Jim! Called him Jim! . . . Croak got sorer at all the fuss Jed was makin' over nothin'. Then Jed stamped up an' down, wringin' his hands. But when quick as a cat he turned one of them held a boomin' gun. I shut my eyes. Jed shot two more times. I heahed one of the rustlers run out, an' when I looked again Malloy an' Madden were daid, an' Reeves had escaped."

"Wal, of all deals I ever seen in my born days!" ejaculated Curly Prentiss as Molly paused, gradually yielding to excitement engendered by her narrative. Her big eyes glowed like coals.

"Wal, it turned out we'd only fallen out of the fryin'-pan into the fire," went on Molly, presently. "Jed had run into Uncle Jim, an' learnin' aboot the hold-up, he'd trailed us, an' he killed them men jest to have us girls all to himself. It began then. . . . Whew, what a desperado Jed Stone was! He had to beat me with a switch. An' when he was fightin' an' kissin' me Glory grabbed up the butcher knife to kill him. She'd been put to makin' biscuits while Jed made love to me. He had to shoot at her, an' she fainted again. . . . Wal, Glory cooked his supper, an' afterward he made her drink whisky, an' then dance fer him. Thet played poor Glory out. He let us alone then. Next mawnin' we rustled off quick, without hardly any grub, an' he rode us all over the Diamond. He got lost, he said. We had two more days of ridin', up an' down, through the brush, over rocks. Oh, it was bad even for me. All the time Jed made me do the work an' near drove Glory crazy. One night he forced us to sleep in the same bed with him, an' gave us choice of who was to lie in the middle. Glory wouldn't let me. He had a nightmare, an' raved aboot hydrophobia skunks an' how we'd have to choke one off Glory's nose. . . . Yesterday, late afternoon, we slid an' rolled down into the canyon, an' soon we rode plumb into thet place where you hanged Darnell an' the two rustlers. . . . The sight near keeled me over. An' poor Glory— But enough said aboot thet. We camped above here, an' this mawnin' climbed out again. Glory was all in, starved, an' so sick after seein' those daid men, hangin', like sacks by their necks, thet she couldn't sit up in her saddle. I had to hold her. We went along the rim till we came to the road. An' there Jed said he'd located himself again, an' we'd have to separate, as he could take only one of us with him, the other goin' to a ranch he said was down heah. I begged him not to separate us . . . an' then Glory told Jed she w[illegible] go with him, *to save me!* . . . Thet flabbergasted Jed, as you could see. He ha[illegible] savvied Glory. He'd been daid set to make her squeal an' show yellow—which s[illegible] shore didn't. . . . An' then what do you reckon he said?"

Only questioning eyes made any return to that.

"He patted me on the haid, called me Wood-mouse, an' then to Glory, 'Big-eyes, go marry Curly or Bud, an' have some real Western kids, an' never forget your desperado.' . . . Then he rode off like mad. An' after Glory had braced up we found the road. An' heah we are!"

"Of all the strange things!" exclaimed Jim.

The cowboys were mystified. Curly ran his lean brown hand through his tawny locks, in action of great perplexity.

"Molly, was Jed drunk?"

"No. He had a bottle, an' he made Glory drink some of the stuff. But he didn't drink any."

"Bud, you heah Molly's story?" went on the nonplussed Curly.

"Yes, an' if she ain't lyin', Jed Stone was locoed. Thet happened, mebbe, when he seen Glory, an' it ain't no wonder."

"Bud Chalfack, don't you dare hint I'm not tellin' the truth," declared Molly, approaching his bed, and then seeing how white and drawn his face was, how prone his sunk frame, she fell on her knees, with a cry of pity.

"Wal, ain't you only a kid, an' turrible in love?" he growled. "You couldn't see straight, let alone tell anythin' straight. . . . I'm a dyin' cowpuncher, Molly. I reckon you'd better kiss me."

"Oh, Bud, I'm so sorry. Are you in pain?" she asked.

"I shore am, but you an' Glory might ease it some."

Whereupon she kissed his cheek and smoothed the damp hair back from his wrinkled brow. That fetched a smile to Bud's face, until it almost bore semblance to the cherubic visage he possessed when in good health and spirits.

"Glory, ain't you comin' over to kiss me, like Molly done?" he asked plaintively.

"I am, surely, Bud, as soon—as I'm able," she replied, smiling wanly. "I hope and pray you're not serious—about dying."

"Aw, I am, Glory. But I might be saved," he said, significantly. "If only I jest didn't want to croak."

"Hush, you sick boy. Molly and I will nurse you."

At that Curly arose with a disgusted look, muttering under his breath: "If it takes thet, I reckon I can get shot up some."

Jim came out of his trance. "Boys, in our surprise and joy we're forgetting the girls. . . . Curly, fetch hot water, and tell Jeff to fix something fit for starved people. Cherry, bring in the bags. . . . Now, Glory, I'll carry you upstairs. . . . Come, Molly."

"Oh, such a wonderful, sweet-smelling house!" murmured Gloriana as he carried her along a wide hall, into the end room, sunny and open. It was bare except for a built-in bed of sycamore branches, upon which lay a thick spread of spruce foliage. He gently deposited Gloriana there, only to find her arms round his neck.

"Jim, brother—my old world came to an end today," she murmured, dreamily.

"Yes. But you can tell me all when you're rested again," he replied, and kissing her cheek he disengaged himself and turned to meet Molly, who had followed. "Molly, you two use this room. Make her comfortable. Put her to bed. Feed her sparingly. And have a care for yourself. . . . What a kid you are! To go through all come out like this!—Damn Jed Stone. Yet I bless him! I can't make it

ıd the cowboys came up, packing things, and Curly lingered, unmindful Molly.

ry, I beg pardon for callin' you darlin', in front of the outfit," he said, ıy. "I was shore out of my haid. But they all know aboot me."

e transfixed him with eyes of awe and reproach, almost horror.

Curly, I—I ought to shudder at sight of you," she said, very low. "But I—I ɔn't."

"There! That'll be about all for you," interrupted Jim, and he shoved the shy and stricken cowboy out of the room, to follow on his heels.

"What'd she mean, Jim?" Curly asked, huskily.

"I don't know, but I imagine it's a lot—from Gloriana Traft."

Curly stalked downstairs and out into the open, like a man who did not see where he stepped. He remained absent until sunset. At supper, which was a silent meal, in deference to the sleeping girls up stairs, he ate but little, and that with a preoccupied air. Later he sought out Jim.

"Boss, I been thinkin' a heap aboot Molly's yarn," he said, ponderingly. "An' it's shore a queer one. The idee of Jed Stone bein' lost! . . . Heah's what I make of it—if you swear on your knees you'll never squeal on me."

"I promise, pard," returned Jim, feelingly.

"Wal, you remember how crazy Glory was to heah aboot desperadoes. Now she took Jed for one, an' I'll bet he was cute enough not to disappoint her. Jed must have hatched up some deal with Molly, to fool Glory, to scare her, to find out if she had any real stuff in her. Thet an' thet only can account fer Jed's queer doin's an' Molly's queer story."

"But, Curly, was that motive enough?" asked Jim, incredulously.

"No, I reckon it wasn't," admitted the cowboy. "They had to have a deeper one. Now, Jed knew Molly when she was a baby, always was fond of her. Molly is shore Arizona, Jim. So is Jed. But you cain't savvy thet because you're an Easterner. An' to boil it down I reckon Jed scared Glory an' starved her an' drove her jest fer Molly's sake. An' in the end Glory took the brim off their cup by meanin' to give herself up to save Molly's honor. Glory was plumb fooled, an' clean honest an' as big as life. It was great, Jim. An' if I hadn't been in love with her before, I shore would be now."

"If that's true, Molly is an awful little liar," said Jim, dubiously.

"Wal, yes an' no. It depends on how you see it. Molly worships Glory, an' she couldn't have meant anythin' but good. An' good it shore was an' is. Thet gurl is changed."

"Ahuh. I begin to savvy, maybe. I believe I did notice some little difference, which I put down to her joy at being safe again with us."

"Shore it was thet. But more. If I don't miss my guess, Gloriana will never see through Jed an' Molly. An' thet's jest as well. I hope the lesson wasn't too raw. But thet sister of yours has guts. . . . When she gets rested she'll appreciate things as they *are* out heah."

Next day Molly showed up downstairs, in changed garb, merry and shy by turns; and she surely was beleagured by the cowboys. Eventually Jim contrived to get her away from Bud, and to walk out to look over Yellow Jacket. She was enraptured.

"Molly, the end of the Hash Knife makes a vast difference," Jim was saying as he halted with her on the log bridge across the amber stream. "We can actually live down here, eventually. But not till next year, and then you must have frequent visits to Flag. . . . You haven't forgotten your promise to marry me this fall, have you?"

"Oh, did I promise, Jim?" she asked, in shy pretense of surprise.

"You sure did."

"Wal, then, say late November."

"But that's winter!"

"November? Oh no, thet's the last of fall."

"Gosh! how long to wait! . . . But I love you so and you're such a wonderful girl—I guess I can wait."

"Maybe—the middle of November," she whispered, whereupon Jim, with a glad shout, snatched her into his arms, to the imminent peril of their falling off the log that bridged the brook.

Next morning late a lovely and languid Gloriana trailed shakily down the winding stairs into the living-room. Dark shadows enhanced the depth and hue of her eyes. She wore white, and to Bud and Curly, at least, she might have been an angel. But to Jim she appeared spent and shaken, completely warped out of her old orbit. She was made much of by the cowboys, except Curly, who worshiped and glowered by turns, from afar. Bud took advantage of Gloriana's pledge of the day before and held her to it, after which he held her hand. At length Curly lunged out of the room, as if he meant to destroy himself, and then almost immediately he lunged back again. Jim understood his pangs, and when Curly gravitated to him, as always happened when he was cast down, Jim whispered:

"Pard, it doesn't mean anything!"

"Wal, I'll shore find out pronto," replied Curly, in heroic mood. "Never do to let her get hold of herself again."

Presently the other cowboys went out on the porch, to take up tasks, or to amuse Lonestar, who had a chair outside. This left Jim and Molly at the table. Gloriana sat on the edge of Bud's bed, which consisted of blankets over spruce boughs, laid on the floor. Curly, who had before wandered around like a lost dog, now watched his friend and his sweetheart with flashing blue eyes. They apparently were oblivious of the others.

"Glory, you're the beautifulest gurl," Bud was saying.

"Silly, you've seen prettier ones," she replied, but she was pleased, and she stroked his hair with her free hand.

"Nope. They don't walk on Gawd's green earth," returned her champion.

"Bud, I'm to be here all summer," she said, with a smile of enchantment. "Oh, it's so heavenly here. I didn't know. . . . Will you be all right soon—so you can ride with me—teach me how to handle a horse? I'm so stupid—so weak. Why, that pinto bucked me off!"

"She did? Son-of-a-gun! I'll beat her good fer thet."

"No you won't. I love her."

"Love a pinto! . . . Is thet all?"

"Bud, I love every horse—everything—everybody in Arizona."

"Aw, thet's wuss."

Jim, entranced at this byplay, suddenly felt a tug. "Look at Curly," whispered Molly.

Curly seemed to have become transformed back to the old cool, easy cowboy, an unknown quantity, potent with some secret of imperturbable assurance. Yet Jim divined his was the grandeur of despair.

"Glory," drawled Curly, as he sat down on the bed, opposite her, and possessed himself of Bud's other restless hand, "we've been like brothers for six years. . . . Bud an' I. . . . An' I reckon this last fight I evened up an old debt. When Bud went down, thet rustler woud have killed him but fer me."

"Pard, what's ailin' you—thet you never told me before?" demanded Bud, his voice deep and rich.

"No call fer it, Bud."

Gloriana looked from one to the other, fascinated, and vaguely troubled. Her intuition distrusted the moment.

"Dog-gone! I had a hunch you did. Shore as hell thet's why you missed the chance at Croak Malloy."

"I reckon." Then Curly looked up at the girl. "I jest wanted you both to know, in case I don't stay on heah."

"Stay on—heah?" faltered Gloriana, in her surprise actually imitating him. Then her eyes dilated with divining thoughts.

"Now what I want to know—seein' Bud an' I are the same as brothers—which of us is to call you sister?"

"Curly!" she entreated.

"Aw, pard!" burst out Bud.

"This son-of-a-gun ain't bad hurt," went on Curly. "I've seen him with more and worse gun-shot wounds. He's only workin' on your sympathy. Wal, thet's all right. But it makes me declare myself right heah an' now."

"Please, Curly—oh, don't."

"You know I love you, Glory," he continued, coolly and slowly. "Only it's more since I told you first. An' I asked you to marry me an' let me be the one to help you tackle this tough Arizona. . . . Wal, thet was Christmas-time, aboot. You promised to write your answer. But you never did. An' I reckon now I'm wantin' to heah it."

"But, Curly—how unreasonable! Wait, I beg of you. I—I'm upset by this adventure. I don't know myself."

"Wal, you know whether you love me or not. So answer pronto, lady."

She drooped her lustrous head a moment, then raised it, fearlessly, as one driven to the wall.

"Curly, you're not greatly different from Jed Stone," she said.

"I reckon thet a compliment."

"I'm not sure yet how or what I feel toward you, Curly, except that I know I'm not worthy. But since you insist—I—I say yes." And with wistful smile she held out her free hand to him. Curly clasped it in both his and carried it to his breast, his face pale, his eyes intense.

"Whoopee!" yelled Bud, in stentorian tones. "I knowed I could fetch him. All the time I knowed it—the handsome jealous geezer!"

Next day Uncle Jim Traft drove down into Yellow Jacket.

No suggestion of the hard old cattleman! He was merry and keen, full of energy to see and hear, and somehow mysteriously buoyant. At Jim's hurried report of the lost cattle he replied: "Pooh-pooh! Only an incident in a rancher's life!" But he gazed sorrowfully down at the graves of those cowboys who had died for the Diamond. They had not been the first, and perhaps they would not be the last.

Curly related the story of the fight at the trapper's cabin. Molly led him aside to tell her version of their adventure with Croak Malloy and Jed Stone. And Bud with rare pride exhibited the headpiece of carved aspen which he vowed he would place on Croak Malloy's grave.

"Wal, wal, we have our ups an' downs," replied the old rancher, when all was said. "An' I say you got off easy. . . . My news is good news. Blodgett's riders rounded up your stampeded stock. All the range knows Malloy is dead an' the Hash Knife no more. Spread like wildfire. Yellow Jacket will prosper now, an' my! what a gorgeous place! An', Jim you won't be lonesome, either, when you settle down with the little wife. Allen Blodgett is takin' charge of his father's range, an' he'll live there. Jack Way's wife's father will start him ranchin'. Miller is goin' to move down. An' in no time this valley will be hummin'. An' I near forgot. The doctor come back from West Fork, reportin' Slinger Dunn out of danger."

That, of all news, was the best for Jim, who found his joy and gratitude in Molly's brimming eyes.

"Rustlin' will go on," continued Uncle Jim, "but no more at the old Hash Knife rate. It'll be two-bit stealin' an' thet we don't mind."

After supper, when the old rancher had Jim, Gloriana, Molly, and Curly alone, he pulled a soiled paper from his pocket. His air was strikingly momentous.

West of the Pecos

CHAPTER ONE

WHEN TEMPLETON LAMBETH'S wife informed him that if God was good they might in due time expect the heir he had so passionately longed for, he grasped at this with the joy of a man whose fortunes were failing, and who believed that a son might revive his once cherished dream of a new and adventurous life on the wild Texas ranges west of the Pecos River.

That very momentous day he named the expected boy Terrill Lambeth, for a beloved brother. Their father had bequeathed to each a plantation; one in Louisiana, and the other in eastern Texas. Terrill had done well with his talents, while Templeton had failed.

The baby came and it was a girl. This disappointment was the second of Lambeth's life, and the greater. Lambeth never reconciled himself to what he considered a scurvy trick of fate. He decided to regard the child as he would a son, and to bring her up accordingly. He never changed the name Terrill. And though he could not help loving Terrill as a daughter, he exulted in her tomboy tendencies and her apparently natural preferences for the rougher and more virile pleasures and occupations. Of these he took full advantage.

Lambeth saw that Terrill had teachers and schooling beginning with her fifth year, but when she reached the age of ten he was proudest of the boyish accomplishments he had fostered, especially her skill in horsemanship. Terrill could ride any four-footed animal on the plantation.

Then came the Civil War. Lambeth, at that time in his middle thirties, obtained an officer's commission, and his brother, Terrill, enlisted as a private.

During this period of slow disintegration of the South's prosperity Mrs. Lambeth had her innings with Terrill. Always she had been under the dominance of her husband, and could not stress the things she desired to see inculcated in her daughter. She belonged to one of the old Southern families of French extraction, and after her marriage she had learned she had not been Lambeth's first love. Pride and melancholy, coupled with her gentle and retiring virtues, operated against her opposing Lambeth in his peculiar way of being happy by making Terrill's play as well as work those of a boy. But during the long and devastating war the mother made up greatly for those things she feared Terrill had lacked. Before the end of the war, when Terrill was fifteen, she died, leaving her a heritage that not all the girl's passionate thirst for adventure nor her father's influence could ever wholly eradicate. Lambeth returned home a Colonel, destined to suffer less grief at finding himself ruined as a planter, than at the certainty of his brother's early demise. Terrill had fallen victim to an incurable disease during the war, and had been invalided home long before Lee's surrender.

His wife's death and his ruin did not further embitter Lambeth, inasmuch as these misfortunes left the way unobstructed for tearing up root and setting out for the western frontier of Texas, where vast and unknown rangelands offered fortune to a man still young enough to work and fight.

Texas was a world in itself. Before the war Lambeth had hunted north as far as the Panhandle and west over the buffalo plains between the Arkansas and the Red Rivers. He had ideas about the future of the country. He was tired of cotton raising. Farther west he would roam to the land beyond the vague and wild Pecos, about which country alluring rumors had reached his ears.

Colonel Lambeth's first move upon arriving home was to free those slaves who still remained on his plantation despite the freedom for which the war had been waged. And the next, after selecting several favorite horses, a wagon and equipment, and a few possessions that would have been hard to part with, he put the plantation and everything on it under the hammer. Little indeed did he realize from this sale.

Then came news of his brother's death and with it a legacy sufficient to enable him to carry on. But Lambeth had had enough of a planter's ups and downs. The soil was poor and he had neither the desire nor the ability to try again. The West called. Texans impoverished by the war, and the riff-raff left over from the army, were spreading far and wide to the north and west, lured on by something magnetic and compelling.

Lambeth journeyed across the Mississippi, to return with sad and imperishable memories of his brother, and with the means to fulfill his old forlorn hope—to find and stock a ranch in the West.

Two of Lambeth's younger generation of slaves, out of the many who wanted to cleave to him, he listened to, appreciative of what their help would mean on such a hazardous enterprise as he was undertaking.

"But, Sambo, you're a free man now," argued Lambeth.

"Yes, suh, I sho knows I'se emancipated. But, Kuhnel, I don' know what to do with it."

This was a problem Sambo shared with the other slaves. He had been sold to the Lambeth plantation from the Texas plains, and was a stalwart, sober negro. Lambeth had taken Sambo on his latest buffalo hunts, finding in him a most willing and capable hand. Moreover he was one of the few really good negro vaqueros. It was Sambo who had taught Terrill to stick like a burr on a horse and to throw a lasso. And he had always been devoted to the girl. This last fact decided Lambeth.

"Very well, Sambo, I'll take you. But what about Mauree?" And Lambeth indicated the handsome negress who accompanied Sambo.

"Well, Kuhnel, we done got married when you was away. Mauree's a-devilin' me to go along wid you. There ain't no better cook than Mauree, suh." Sambo's tone was wheedling.

Lambeth settled with this couple, but turned a deaf ear to the other loyal negroes.

The morning of their departure, Terrill walked along the old road between the canal and the grove of stately moss-curtained oaks that surrounded the worn and weathered Colonial mansion.

It was early spring. The air was full of the sweet, fragrant languor of the South; mockingbirds were singing, full-throated and melodious; meadow larks and swamp blackbirds sang their farewell to the South for that season; the sky was blue and the sun shone warm; dewdrops like diamonds sparkled on the grass.

Beyond the great lawn a line of dilapidated old cottages faced the road, vacant-eyed and melancholy. From only a few rose the thin columns of blue smoke that denoted habitation. The happy, dancing, singing slaves were gone, and their whitewashed homes were falling to ruin. Terrill had known them all her life. It made her sad to say good-by to them, yet she was deeply glad that it was so and that slaves were no longer slaves. Four years of war had been unintelligible to Terrill. She wanted to forget that and all of the suffering and the bitterness.

When she returned from this, her last walk along the beloved old canal with its water-lily pads floating on the still surface, she found the horses in the yard, and Sambo carrying out her little brass-bound French trunk.

"Missy Rill, I done my best," said Sambo, as he shoved the trunk into the heavily laden canvas-covered wagon.

"Sambo, what're you sneakin' in on me heah?" demanded Lambeth, his sharp dark eyes taking in the situation.

"Missy's trunk, suh."

"Rill, what's in it?" queried her father.

"All my little treasures. So few, Dad! My jewelry, laces, pictures, books—and my clothes."

"Dresses, you mean? Rill, you'll not need them out where we're goin'," he replied, his gaze approving of her as she stood there in boy's garb, her trousers in her boots, her curls hidden under the wide-brimmed, soft hat.

"Never?" she asked, wistfully.

"I reckon never," he returned, gruffly. "After we leave heah you're the same as a real son to me. . . . Rill, a girl would be a handicap, not to speak of risk to herself. Beyond Santone it's wild country."

"Dad, I'd shore rather be a boy, and I will be. But it troubles me, now I face it, for really I—I'm a girl."

"You can go to your Aunt Lambeth," responded her father, sternly.

"Oh, Dad! . . . You know I love only you—and I'm crazy to go West. . . . To ride and ride! To see the buffalo, the plains, and that lonely Pecos country you tell me aboot! That will be glorious. . . . But this mawnin', Dad, I'm sorrowful at leavin' home."

"Rill, I am, too," replied Lambeth, with tears in his eyes. "Daughter, if we stayed heah we'd always be sad. And poor, too!—But there we'll take fresh root in new soil. We'll forget the past. We'll work. Everything will be new, strange, wonderful. . . . Why, Rill, if what I heah is true we'll have to fight Mexican hoss thieves and Comanche Indians!"

"Oh, it thrills me, Dad," cried Terrill. "Frightens me! Makes cold chills creep up my back! But I'd not have it otherwise."

And so they rode away from the gray, dim mansion, out under the huge live oaks with their long streamers of Spanish moss swaying in the breeze, and into the yellow road that stretched away along the green canal.

Sambo headed the six free horses in the right direction and rode after them; Mauree drove the big wagon with its strong team of speckled whites. Terrill came on behind, mounted on her black thoroughbred, Dixie. Her father was long in catching up. But Terrill did not look back.

When, however, a mile down the road they reached the outskirts of the hamlet where Terrill's mother was buried, she looked back until her tear-blurred eyes could no longer distinguish objects. The day before she had taken her leave of her mother's grave, a rending experience which she could not endure twice.

All that endless day memories of the happy and grievous past possessed Terrill as she rode.

CHAPTER TWO

Lambeth traveled leisurely. He meant to make this long-wished-for journey an education. Most of his life he had lived in that small part of Texas which adjoined Louisiana, and partook of its physical and traditional aspects. Now he wanted to find the real Texas—the Texas that had fallen at the Alamo and that in the end had conquered Santa Ana, and was now reaching north and west, an empire in the making.

To that end he traveled leisurely, halting at the occasional hamlets, making acquaintances on the way. Sometimes when sunset overtook his little cavalcade on the march he would camp where they were, usually near grass and water. Terrill grew to love this. Sambo made her bed in the wagon under the canvas, where she felt snug, and safe from prying eyes. To wear boy's clothes had once been fun for Terrill; now it augmented a consciousness that she was not what she pretended to be, and that sooner or later she would be found out. Otherwise as days and leagues lengthened between her and the old home she began keenly to live this adventure.

They stayed only one night in Austin, arriving after nightfall and departing at dawn. Terrill did not have much opportunity to see the city, but she did not like it. New Orleans had been the only large place she had visited, and it, with its quaint streets and houses, its French atmosphere, had been very attractive to her.

From Austin to San Antonio the road was a highway, a stage line, and a thoroughfare for travelers going south and west, and Terrill found it tremendously interesting. So long as she could be astride Dixie and her contact with people confined to the rôle of a looker-on, she was happy. To ride through the long days and at night to creep into her snug bed in the wagon brought her an ever-growing joy. She could have gone on this way forever.

When they arrived at San Antonio, however, Terrill seemed plunged into a bewildering, bustling world, noisy, raw, strange, repellent to her, and yet strangely stirring. If only she really were a boy! How anyone could take her for a boy seemed incredible. Her masculine garb concealed the feminine contours of her form, almost to her satisfaction, but her face discouraged her terribly. At the hotel where they stayed Terrill regarded herself in the mirror with great disapproval. Her sunny curls, her violet eyes, above all her smooth girlish skin—these features that had been the joy of her mother, and which somehow in the past had not been distasteful to Terrill—now accorded her increasing embarrassment, not to say alarm. She must do something about it. Nevertheless, reflection relieved her, inasmuch as it made clear there could be no particular annoyance while they were traveling. She would never see the same people twice.

She had to remain in her room, next to her father's, unless she was accompanied by him or Sambo. Lambeth was tremendously keen on the track of something, and he went everywhere; but he took Terrill along with him whenever she wanted to go. Or he would send her to a store with Sambo. This pleased Terrill, for she had money to spend, and that was a luxury vastly pleasant. Only Sambo was disconcerting. Boy's boots and pants did not change his adored young mistress to him.

"Sambo, stop callin' me Miss Rill," protested Terrill. "Call me Master Rill."

"I sho will, Missy Rill, when I thinks about it. But you is what you is an' you can't nebber be what you ain't."

One morning, accompanied by Sambo, she went farther down the main street than usual. The horsemen and wagons and the stage-coaches accorded Terrill an increasing delight. They smacked of the wild, vast open Texas land, about which she had heard so much.

A little store attracted her, but she did not go in the first time she passed it because it stood next to a noisy saloon, in front of which shaggy, dusty saddled horses gave evidence of riders within. But finally Terrill yielded to temptation and entered the store, very soon to forget all about Sambo. When she had indulged her fancy to the extent of compunction, and had started out, she suddenly remembered him. He was nowhere to be seen. Then loud voices outside augmented anxiety to alarm. She ran out. Sambo was not waiting for her.

Terrill started hurriedly down the street, aware that several men were moving violently just ahead of her. As she got even with the door of the saloon it swung open and a man, backing out, collided with her, sending her sprawling. Her packages flew out of her hands. Terrill indignantly gathered herself together, and recovering her belongings, stood up, more resentful than alarmed. But suddenly she froze in her tracks.

The man had a gun in each hand, which he held low down, pointing into the wide open door. All the noise had ceased. Terrill saw men inside, one of whom was squirming on the floor.

"Reckon thet'll be aboot all," announced the man with the guns, in a cold voice. "Next time you deal crooked cairds it shore won't be to Pecos Smith."

He backed by Terrill. "Kid, untie my hoss. . . . Thet bay. An' lead him heah," he ordered.

Terrill obeyed clumsily. Sheathing one of the guns the man retreated until he bumped into his horse. He had a young clear cut cold profile, set and ruthless. From the high curb he mounted his horse in a single step.

"Smith, we'll know next time you happen along," called a rough voice from the saloon. Then the door swung shut.

"What you shakin' aboot, boy?" queried Smith, in a cool, drawling voice, suggestive of humor.

"I—I don't know, sir," faltered Terrill, letting go the bridle. This was her closest contact with one of these tawny stalwart Texans. And this one had eyes too terrible for her to look into. A smile softened the set of his lean hard face, but did not change those light piercing eyes.

"Wal, I only shot his ear off," drawled Smith. "It stuck out like a jack rabbit's. . . . Much obliged, sonny. I reckon I'll be goin'."

Whereupon he rode off at a canter. Terrill watched the lithe erect figure with mingled sensations. Then she stepped back upon the pavement. At this juncture Sambo appeared. Terrill ran to meet him.

"Oh, Sambo!—I was so frightened," she cried, in relief. "Let's hurry. . . . Where did you go?"

"I'se done scared myself," replied the negro. "I was waitin' by dat do when one of dese wild Texans rode up an' got off. He seen me an' he sed, 'Niggah, move away from mah vecinnity.' An' I sho moved. He got into a fight in here, an' when he come backin' out wid dem big guns I was scared wuss."

"Santone," which was what its inhabitants called San Antonio, appeared crowded with Texans and hordes of other men. Terrill took the Texans to be the rangy, dusty-booted youths, tight-lipped, still-faced, gray-eyed young giants, and the older men of loftier stature who surely were the fathers of the boys. Terrill was suddenly crestfallen when she became aware that she had several times been interested at sight of handsome young men. And this Pecos Smith had strangely thrilled her. Despite the terror and revulsion he had roused, his memory haunted her.

The Mexicans, the teamsters, the soldiers, the endless hurrying, colorful throng of men, gave Terrill a vague and wonderful impression. These were men of the open, and according to her father they had come from everywhere. Buffalo-hunters on their way out to the plains to catch the buffalo herds on their spring migration north; horse-dealers and cattlemen in from the ranches; idle, picturesque Mexicans with their *serapes,* their tight-legged flared-bottom trousers, their high-peaked sombreros; here and there a hard-eyed, watching man whom Lambeth designated as a Texas Ranger; riders on lean, shaggy, wild horses; tall men with guns in their belts; black-coated, black-hatted gamblers, cold-faced and usually handsome; and last, though by far not least, a stream of ragged, broken, often drunken men, long-haired, unshaven, hard and wretched, whose wolfish eyes Terrill did not want to meet. These, according to Lambeth, were the riffraff left of the army, sacrificed to a lost cause. He also remarked emphatically that he desired to put such men and such reminders far behind him.

"Rill, I've an hour now," said her father, on their third day at San Antonio. "Reckon I won't let you miss the Alamo. As long as Texas exists the Alamo will be sacred. Every boy should stand once on that bloody altar of heroism and country."

Terrill knew the story as well as any Texas boy. She tripped along beside her father, whose strides covered a good deal of ground. And soon they were on the threshold of the historic edifice. Lambeth had been there before. A distant relative of his had fallen in that battle. He took Terrill around and showed her where and how the besiegers had been repelled so long and with such deadly loss.

"Santa Ana had four thousand Mexican soldiers under him," explained Lambeth. "They surprised the Americans by charging before daylight. But twice they were repulsed with terrific loss, and it looked as if the greasers would retreat. But Santa Ana drove them to another attack. They scaled the walls, and finally gained the top, from which they poured down a murderous fire. Then the Alamo doors were forced and a breach opened in the south wall. Hell broke loose. . . . In this room heah Bowie, who was ill, was murdered on his bed. . . . Over heah Travis died on his cannon. . . . And heah Davy Crockett went down with a ring of daid aboot him. . . . Rill, I could ask no more glory than that for my son. . . . The Texans perished to a man. One hundred and eighty-two of them. They killed sixteen hundred of Santa Ana's soldiers. Such were Texans of that day."

"Oh, how splendid!" cried Terrill. "But it horrifies me. I can see them fighting. . . . It must be in our blood, Dad."

"Yeah. . . . Never forget the Alamo, Rill. Never forget this heritage to Texans. We Southerners lost the Civil War, but we can never lose the glory of freein' Texas from Spanish rule."

Pensive and roused by turns, Terrill went back uptown with her father. Later that day she experienced a different kind of stimulation—something intimate and exciting. Lambeth took her to the large outfitting store, where he purchased a black Mexican saddle with *tapadores,* a silver-mounted bridle and spurs, *riata,* gauntlets, bandanas, and a sombrero so huge that when Terrill donned it she felt under a heavy cloud.

"Now you will be a vaquero," said Lambeth, proudly.

Terrill observed that he bought guns and ammunition, though he had brought along his English arms; also knives, belts, axes, a derringer for her, and in fact so many things that Terrill had her doubts that the wagon would carry them all. But she was to learn, presently, that he had acquired another and larger wagon which

Sambo was to drive with two teams.

"Rill, I may as well tell you now," announced her father, "that I've given up the plan of followin' the stage road. Too many travelers, not healthy to meet west of Santone! We'll start out with some buffalo-hunters I've met and travel with them for a while. You'll get to hunt buffalo with me. We'll see the country."

Two days later Terrill rode out with a fair-sized cavalcade, there being six wagons besides her father's, and eight men, none of whom, however, were mounted. They were experienced buffalo-hunters, knew the country, and hunted buffalo for meat and hides. Much to Terrill's relief, there was not a young man in the party.

They traveled in a northwesterly direction, along a stream where beautiful pecan trees lined the banks. These Texans were hard drivers. When sunset came the first day they must have made thirty miles. Sambo with his heavy wagon did not get in until after dark, a fact that had worried Lambeth.

The hunters took good-natured notice of Terrill, but she was sure none of them suspected her secret. This night she had courage to sit back at the edge of the camp-fire circle, and listen. They were a merry lot, mostly ranchers and horse-raisers. One of them had been a Texas Ranger, and he told bloody tales which made Terrill's flesh creep. Another of the group, a stockman from the Brazos River, talked a good deal about the Llano Estacado and the Comanche Indians. On a former hunt he, with comrade hunters, had been camping along the Red River, and had narrowly missed losing their scalps.

"Them Comanches air shore gettin' bad," he said, shaking a shaggy head. "An' it's this heah buffalo-huntin' thet's rilin' them. Some day Texas will have to whip off not only the Comanches, but the Arapahoes, the Kiowas, the Cheyennes, mebbe all the Plains Injuns."

"Wal, I reckon we're too early an' too fer south fer the Comanches at this time of year," remarked another. "Buffalo herds comin' up from the Rio Grande won't be as far as the Red River."

"We'll strike them this side of Colorado," replied the red-faced hunter. "Which is a darn good thing, fer thet river ain't no slouch to cross. Our friend Lambeth heah would have hell."

"No, he could haid the Colorado. Fair to middlin' road. But I don't know the country west."

Terrill might indeed have been a boy, considering the sensations aroused in her by this casual talk of hostile Indians, the Staked Plains, dangerous rivers, stampeding buffalo, and the like. But sometimes the lamentable fact that she was a girl forced itself upon her when she lay in bed unable to sleep, prey to feminine emotions that she could never dispel, yet all the while tingling with the wonder and zest of her existence.

Several days later, Terrill, riding with Sambo, somewhat behind the other wagons, imagined she heard something unusual.

"Listen, Sambo," she whispered, turning her ear to the south. Had she only imagined that she heard something?

"I doan heah nuffin'," replied the black.

"Maybe I was wrong. . . . No! There it comes again."

"Lud, Massa Rill, I sho hopes yo doan heah somethin' like thunder."

"That's just it, Sambo. . . . Rumble of low thunder. Listen!"

"I doan heah it yet. Mebbe storm down dat way."

"Sambo, it cain't be ordinary thunder," cried Terrill, excitedly. "It doesn't stop. It keeps right on. . . . It's getting louder."

"By gar! I heahs it now, Massa Rill," returned the negro. "I knows what dat is. Dar's de buffalo! Dat's de main herd, sho as I'se born."

"Main herd!—Oh, that hunter Hudkins was wrong, then. He said the main herd was not due yet."

"Dey's comin' an' dey's runnin', Massa Rill."

The rumble had grown appreciably louder, more consistent and deeper, with a menacing note. Lambeth and the saddle-horses had vanished in a dusty haze. Terrill thought she noted a quickening in the lope of the buffalo passing, closer pressing together of the lines, a gradual narrowing of the space around the wagons.

"Oh, Sambo, is it a stampede?" cried Terrill, suddenly seized by fright. "What has become of Dad? What will we do?"

"I dunno, Missy. I'se heahed a stampede, but I nebber was in one. Dis is gittin' bad. It sho is. We'se gotta be movin'."

Sambo ran and turned Mauree's team in the direction the buffalo were moving. Then he yelled for Terrill to get off her horse and climb into Mauree's wagon.

"What'll I do with Dixie?" screamed Terrill, as she dismounted.

"Lead him so long's yu can," yelled Sambo, and ran for his wagon.

Terrill thought she would have to mount Dixie again to catch up with Mauree. But she made the wagon, and vaulting high she got on, still hanging to the bridle. Fortunately it was long. Dixie loped behind, coming close so that Terrill could almost reach him. Then she saw Sambo's team gaining at a gallop. He did not pull them to accommodate Mauree's gait until at the heels of Dixie.

Then fearfully Terrill gazed from one side to the other. The streams of buffalo had closed in solid and were now scarcely a hundred yards from the wagons. The black and tawny beasts appeared to bob up and down in unison. Dust rolled up yellow and thick, obscuring farther view. Behind, the gap was filling up with a sea of lifting hoofs and shaggy heads. It was thrilling to Terrill, though her heart came up in her throat. The rumble had become a trampling roar. She saw that Sambo's idea was to keep his big wagon behind Mauree's smaller one, and try to run with the beasts, hoping they would continue to split behind it. But how long could the horses keep that gait up, even if they did not bolt and leave the wagons to be crushed? Terrill had heard of whole caravans being flattened out and trodden into the plain. Dixie's ears were up, his eyes wild. But for Terrill's presence right close, holding his bridle, he would have run away.

Soon Terrill became aware that the teams were no longer keeping up with the buffalo. That lumbering lope had increased to a gallop, and the space between the closing lines of buffalo had narrowed to half what it had been. Terrill saw with distended eyes those shaggy walls converging. There was no gap behind Sambo's wagon—only a dense, gaining, hairy mass. Sambo's eyes rolled till the whites stood out. He was yelling to his horses, but Terrill could not hear a word.

The trampling roar seemed engulfed in deafening thunder. The black bobbing sea of backs swallowed up the open ground till Terrill could have tossed her sombrero upon the shaggy humps. She saw no more flying legs and hoofs. When she realized that the increased pace, the change from a tame lope to a wild gallop, the hurtling of the blind horde, meant a stampede and that she and the two negroes were in the midst of it, she grew cold and sick with terror. They would be lost, smashed to a pulp. She shut her eyes to pray, but she could not keep them shut.

Next she discovered that Mauree's team had bolted. The wagon kept abreast of the beasts. It swayed and jolted, almost throwing Terrill out. Dixie had to run to keep up. Sambo's team came on grandly, tongues out, eyes like fire, still under control. Then Terrill saw the negro turn to shoot back at the charging buffalo. The red flame of the gun appeared to burst right in the faces of the maddened beasts. They thundered forward, apparently about to swarm over the wagon.

Clamped with horror, hanging on to the jolting wagon, Terrill saw the buffalo close in alongside the very wheels. A shroud of dust lifted, choking and half blinding her. Sambo blurred in her sight, though she saw the red spurt of his gun. She heard no more. Her eyes seemed stopped. She was an atom in a maelstrom. The stench of the beasts clogged her nostrils. A terrible sense of being carried along in a flood possessed her. The horses, the wagons, were keeping pace with the stampede. Dixie leaped frantically, sometimes narrowly missing the wagon. Just outside the wheels, rubbing them, swept huge, hairy, horned monsters that surely kept him running straight.

The agony of suspense was insupportable. Terrill knew she soon would leap out under the rolling hoofs. It could not last much longer. The horses would fall or fail, and then . Sambo's gun burned red through the dust. Again the wall on each side moved ahead, faster, and appeared to draw away. Little by little the space widened. Terrill turned to gaze ahead. The herd had split. Dimly she saw an X-shaped space splitting, widening away from a high gray object.

Terrill lost the clearness of her faculties then and seemed clutched between appalling despair and hope. But surely the wagon slowed, careened, almost upset. Then it stopped and Terrill closed her eyes on the verge of collapse.

But nothing happened. There was no crash—no pounding of her flesh. And again she could hear. Her ears registered once more the fearful trampling roar. She felt the wagon shaking under her. Then she opened her eyes. The wagon stood on a slant. Mauree had driven into the lea of a rocky knoll. Sambo's team, in a lather of froth and dust, heaved beside her, while Sambo, on foot, was holding Dixie. To Terrill's left the black woolly mass swept on. To the right she could not see for the knoll. But she sensed that the obstruction had split the herd and saved them. Terrill fell back spent and blind in her overwhelming reaction.

The roar rolled on, diminishing to thunder, then gradually lessening. The ground ceased to shake. In an hour the stampede was again a low rumble in the distance.

"De good Lawd was wif us, Missy Rill," said Sambo, leading Dixie to her. Then he mounted to the seat of his wagon and calling to Mauree he drove back through the settling dust along the great trail. It was long, however, before Terrill got into the saddle again. At last the dust all blew away, to disclose Lambeth far ahead with the horses.

CHAPTER THREE

The Colorado River from the far eastern ridge top resembled a green snake with a shining line down the center of its back, crawling over rolling, yellow plains. In this terrain ragged black streaks and spots, and great patches stood out clearly in the morning sunlight. Only a few were visible on the north side of the river; southward from the very banks these significant and striking contrasts to the yellow and gray of plain extended as far as the eye could see, dimming in the purple obscurity of the horizon.

These black patches were buffalo. There were thousands in the scattered head of the herd, and in that plain-wide mass far to the south there were millions. The annual spring migration north was well on its way.

The hunters yelled lustily. Lambeth rode back to speak to Terrill, his black eyes shining. He seemed a changed man. Already sun and wind and action had begun to warm out the havoc in his face.

"Rill, they're heah," he called, exultantly. "What do you think of that sight?"

"Glorious!" replied Terrill, under her breath. She was riding beside Sambo on the wagon seat. Dixie had fallen lame, and Terrill, after riding two of the harder-gaited horses, had been glad of a reprieve from the daily saddle.

"Missy Rill, yo sho will kill yo' first buffalo today," declared the negro.

"Sambo, I'm not crazy aboot firing that Henry rifle again," laughed Terrill.

"Yo didn't hold it tight," explained Sambo. "Mighty nigh kick yo flat."

Despite a downhill pull the wagons did not reach the Colorado until late in the afternoon. Hudkins, the leader of the expedition, chose a wooded bend in the river for a camp site, where a cleared spot and pole uprights showed that it had been used before. The leaves on the trees were half grown, the grass was green, flowers on long stems nodded gracefully, and under the bank the river murmured softly.

"Wal, you fellars fix camp while I go after a buffalo rump," ordered Hudkins, and strode off with what Terrill had heard him call his needle gun. She wondered what that meant, because the gun was almost as big as a cannon.

Terrill sat on the wagon seat and watched the men. This arriving at a new camp and getting settled had a growing attraction for her. Even if this life in the open had held no appeal for her, she would still gladly have accepted it because of the change it wrought in her father's health and spirits. How resolutely had he turned his back upon ruin and grief! He was not rugged, yet he did his share of the work. Sambo, however, was the one who had changed most. On the plantation he had not seemed different from the other negroes, except when on horseback. Here he appeared to be in his element and the laziness of a cotton-picker had departed. He wore boots and overalls. There was a gun belted around his lean hips. When he swung an ax and carried the heavy picks his splendid physique showed to advantage. He whistled as he worked, and like Mauree had fallen happily into this new way of life.

Presently Terrill's father came to her, carrying the Henry rifle.

"Rill, from now on you pack this on your hoss, in the wagon, by your bed, and everywhere."

"But, Dad, I'm afraid of the darned thing," expostulated Terrill.

Colonel Lambeth laughed, but he was inexorable. "Rill, farther west we'll hit the badlands. Indians, outlaws, bandits, Mexicans! And we may have to fight for our lives. Red Turner has been across the Pecos. He told me today what a wild country it was. Cattle by the thousand and just beginnin' to be worth somethin'. . . . So come out and practice a little. Stuff a towel inside your shirt aboot where the gun kicks your shoulder."

Terrill accompanied Lambeth down to the river bank, where he directed Terrill how to load, hold, aim, and fire the big Henry. Terrill had to grit her teeth, nevertheless there was a zest in the thing her father insisted upon—that she fill the boots of a son for him. Five shots from a rest she fired, squeezing the rifle with all her might. The first shot was not so terrible, after all, but the bullet flew wide of the target. She did better on the second and third. And the last two she hit the black across the river, to her father's sober satisfaction. How seriously he took all this! It was no game to him.

"Sambo will clean the rifle for you," he said. "But that you should learn also. Familiarize yourself with the gun. Get used to handlin' it. Aim often at things without shootin'. You can learn to shoot as well that way without wastin' too many bullets."

Hudkins returned with the hump of a buffalo, from which were cut the steaks these hunters praised so much. Lambeth appeared as greedy as any of them. They made merry. Some one produced a jug of liquor which went the rounds. For a moment Terrill's heart stood still. She feared her father might ask her to take a drink. But he did not overstep the bounds of reason in his obsession to see in Terrill a son.

"Sonny, how you like rump steak?" asked Hudkins, merrily, of Terrill.

"It's got a kind of wild flavor," replied Terrill. "But I certainly like it."

She went to bed early, tired out from the jolting she had undergone on the high wagon seat. There were sundry places on her anatomy sore to the touch. And soon slumber claimed her. Some time in the night she awoke, an unusual thing for her. A noise had disturbed her rest. But the camp was dark and silent. A low rustle of leaves and a tinkle of water could scarcely have been guilty. Then from across the river a howl that curdled her blood. She sat up quivering in every muscle, and her first thought was that the dreaded Comanches were upon them. The howl rose again, somehow different. It seemed like the bay of a hound, only infinitely deeper, wilder, stranger, with a fierce, mournful note. Answers came from above camp, and then a chorus of chirping, shrieking barks. These sounds she at once associated with the wolves and coyotes that the hunters said followed the buffalo in packs. So Terrill lay back in relief and listened. It was long, however, before she stopped shivering and fell asleep again.

After all, Sambo and not her father took Terrill out to see the buffalo and perhaps shoot one. Lambeth had gone with the hunters.

"Missy Rill——"

"Say Master Rill, you pestifercatin' nigger," interrupted Terrill, only half in fun.

"Sho I done forgot," replied Sambo, contritely. "Wal, Massa Rill, tain't goin' be no trick atall fo' yo' to kill a buffalo. An' it'll sho tickle the Kuhnel."

No boy could have been any more eager than Terrill, nor half so scared. She trotted along beside the striding negro, packing the heavy rifle, all eyes and ears. She saw birds and rabbits, and presently had her first view of wild turkeys and deer. The surprise to Terrill was their exceeding tameness. Then she heard the boom of guns far over the ridge of grassy ground. Sambo said the hunters were at it and that Terrill would soon see buffalo at close range.

Suddenly Sambo dragged her into the cover of the trees and along the edge of the woods to a log. This appeared to be at a bend of the river from where Terrill could discern a slope rising gradually to the high bank.

"Bunch a-comin', Massa Rill," said Sambo, examining his rifle.

"I heah slopping in the water," replied Terrill, excitedly.

"Sho. Det's some buffs. Dey'se wadin' across an'll come out on det sandbar."

Suddenly a shaggy, elephantine beast hove in sight directly in front of Terrill. Her tongue clove to the roof of her mouth. It was an enormous bull. Another climbed out of the shallow water, and then dozens of woolly, hump-backed buffalo swarmed over the dry sandbar. Some were black, some were tawny. Terrill thought she saw little ones in behind the others. Terrill heard them pant. She heard them rub together. She smelled them.

"Rest yo' gun heah, Miss Rill," whispered Sambo. "Hol' tight an' aim low."

"But—but it's like murdering cows," protested Terrill.

"Sho is. But it'll please yo' Dad."

"Won't they r-run o-over us?"

"Naw, Missy, dey won't run atall. Don't be afeared. We kin hide heah. . . . 'Member how. Hol' tight an' aim low."

Terrill seemed monstrously divided between two emotions. The stronger forced her down over her rifle, made her squeeze it tight, squint along the barrel, and align the sight generally on that wide, shaggy, moving mass, and pull the trigger. The recoil threw her to her knees and the smoke blinded her. Then Sambo's gun boomed.

"Oh, I hope I missed!" cried Terrill.

"Yo' sho didn't, Miss Rill. . . . Look! Dat bull tryin' climb. He's shooted through. . . . Dar he goes down, Missy Rill . . . he's sho a-rollin'. . . . Now he's kickin'. Ain't yo' gonna look, gal?"

Terrill wanted to look, but she could not. She let her rifle balance on the log on which she sank down, rubbing her shoulder, fighting her fears.

"Daid! . . . 'Em both daid. We sho is de hunters, Massa Rill, we sho is! Dat tickle yo' Dad 'most to death."

"Where are—the others?" gasped Terrill, fearfully.

"Dey's mozied round de bend. Look Massa Rill. . . . Dat big bull closest to us is yo's. Ain't he sho black an' shiny? Dar's yo' buffalo robe, Missy, an' we is gonna skin it off right now."

"We is—not," retorted Terrill, still shakily, though now she had the courage to peep over the log. There, scarcely a hundred steps away, lay a huge, black buffalo flat on the sand, motionless. Beyond and to the left was another. Terrill experienced a wild thrill, instantly checked by a pang.

"Yo' gonna help me skin off dat buffalo robe of yo's?" queried the negro.

"Skin the—poor creature!" cried Terrill. "No, indeedee, I'm not. It was awful enough to—kill it."

"Please yo'self, Missy. But I done tell yo' whar yo's gwine yo'll soon git over squackishness at daid things an' hair an' blood," replied Sambo, philosophically. Then bidding Terrill wait there, he made for the buffalo. She watched long enough to see him draw a bright blade and drop to his knees. Then she backed out of sight of that sandbar.

The grove seemed dreamy and silent. Presently Terrill found a grassy seat, and reclining there in the sun-flecked shade, with sweet fragrance all around and pale-blue flowers peeping up at her from the green, she felt the slow receding of excitement and fear and nausea. That buffalo was the first creature she had ever wittingly killed in all her life. She sensed the truth in Sambo's practical words, but not yet could she bear to dwell upon it. After all, she was not a man and she never would be a man.

Birds and squirrels and rabbits soon trusted her. Finding in her nothing to fear, they came close and pleased her with their soft-hued beauty and saucy barking and nibbling at the grass. She was distracted from these, however, by a rustling of brush, a queer sound like put-put, put, put, put. Then she heard a gobble. Wild turkeys near! This would be an event. And presently she espied a huge gobbler, bronzed and flecked, with a purple beard and red comb. How stately he strutted!

Then he stopped under a tree to scratch in the leaves and grass. Other turkeys appeared, some smaller, sleeker, with subdued colors and wild bearing. These were the hens. They came close to Terrill, eyed her with curiosity, and passed on, put-put, put, put, put. Terrill went back to lesser attractions, vaguely content. She was sorry when Sambo disrupted the spell, as he crashed along the edge of the brush, bowed under a heavy burden.

"Massa Rill, whar yo' is?" he called.

Terrill hurried up, and securing her rifle ran out to join him.

"Aw, dar yo' is. I done feared the Comanches had got yo'. . . . Heah's yo' robe, Missy. Look dar."

The heavy, black mass thumped on the ground. Sambo laid aside his rifle and spread the magnificent buffalo hide out on the grass. Terrill could not believe her eyes.

"Dey don't come any finer," he declared. "Now, Missy, yo' take my gun, so I kin pack dis dog-gone heavy hide to camp. Den I'll fetch in de meat."

Soon they reached camp, having been gone only a few hours. Mauree was still alone. When Sambo exhibited the hide and extolled Terrill's prowess the negress rolled the whites of her handsome eyes.

"Fer de land's sake! Yo' done dat, Rill? I sho is s'prised. I sho is! An' I sho is sorry—dat no-good niggah husband of mind done make a killer out of yo'."

About mid-afternoon several of the hunters returned to hitch up the wagons and drive back to fetch the proceeds of the hunt. At sunset Lambeth rode in, covered with dust and lather. His horse was spent. Hands and face were begrimed. He yelled for water. Presently, after he had washed, he espied the great buffalo hide which Sambo had carefully stretched where it must command instant attention.

"You hoss-ridin' nigger!" he exclaimed. "Been huntin' yourself."

"Yas, suh. Yas, Kuhnel, I ben. Ain' dat a mighty fine hide?"

"Best I ever saw," declared Lambeth, smoothing the glossy fur. "Biggest I ever saw, too. . . . Sambo, see heah. You give it to me."

"I'se powerful sorry, Kuhnel," replied Sambo, shaking his kinky head. "But I done cain't do it."

"Reckon you gave it to Rill?"

Sambo shook his head solemnly.

"No, sah. I didn't. Missy Rill killed de buffalo dat wore dat hide. Jest one shot, Kuhnel. Plumped over de biggest bull in de herd."

"Terrill!"

"Yes, Dad," replied Terrill, coming out from her hiding-place.

"Is this heah nigger lyin' to me? Did you shoot a buffalo?"

"Yes, Daddy," she returned, nonchalantly. "Aboot like murderin' a cow, I'd say. I don't think much of buffalo-huntin'."

Lambeth whooped and gave Terrill a tremendous hug. When the other hunters returned he proudly acclaimed Rill's achievement, which indeed immediately took precedence over many and eventful deeds of the day. Nineteen buffalo, selected for their hides, had been killed by the party, all, in fact, that could be skinned and cut up and hauled in that day. They could not leave the meat out on the prairie for the wolves to haggle. Lambeth had accounted for three of the slain beasts, and appeared elated. He loved the chase and had never indulged it as now appeared possible. If the camp had been a merry one before, it was this night a circus for Terrill. The hunters had too many drinks from the jug, perhaps, but they were funny. They stretched and pegged buffalo hides until midnight.

"A hunter's life for me!" sang Hudkins. "Too bad one more day will load us up. They shore come too easy."

On the morning of the third day after this successful start the hunters were packed and ready to return to San Antonio. Lambeth's horses were headed west from the Colorado. Here was the parting of the ways for the hunters and the pioneers. For Lambeth the real journey began from this camp.

"Stick to your direction an' don't git off. Four days . . . eighty miles to San Saba River," advised Red Turner. "Then haid west an' keep yore eye peeled."

Many were the gay and kindly good-bys directed at Terrill, one of which, from the old Texan, Hudkins, she thought she would never forget.

"Good-by, sonny. Hang on to thet rifle an' yore curly hair."

CHAPTER FOUR

Though Lambeth had struck away from the Colorado River he did not get rid of the buffalo. During that day the caravan was frequently held up by strings of the great, shaggy beasts. They grazed as they traveled. When the horses and wagons approached a bunch they would swerve ahead or behind, at a lope, and then drop back to feeding again. But when a large number barred the way there was nothing to do save halt and wait until they had passed.

A hundred times buffalo were within easy rifle range and showed less concern at sight of the travelers than the travelers did of them. They were not wild. The inroads of desultory hunting showed no effect whatever.

The horses grew accustomed to the great beasts and ceased to shy or balk. Dixie was the only one that stuck up his ears at every new straggling line. Sambo almost went to sleep over the reins. Lambeth rode out in front, ever watchful, at last a scout in reality. Terrill rode Dixie for some hours, then returned to the wagon seat beside Sambo.

It was while she was on the wagon that the largest contingent of buffalo met them. "We'se a-gwine to get corralled," observed Sambo. "An' if dat Kuhnel doan' be keerful he'll lose us."

"Sambo, is there still danger?" asked Terrill, anxiously, as she surveyed the straggling lines, with a black mass behind. "They are so tame now."

"Wal, I reckon we doan' need to worry. De main herd is back an' south."

"Golly! If this isn't the main herd, what must that be like?"

"Black as fur as eye kin see. . . . Dar! Dat is jes' what I sed. Yo' Dad is bein' cut off."

Lambeth, with the saddle horses, was far in the lead, and a line of buffalo intervened between him and the wagons. Then another line swerved back of the wagons, and presently Terrill saw they were surrounded. The belt of black, bobbing backs between her and Lambeth broadened until it was half a mile across. Sambo got off to step back and assure Mauree that there was no danger. Terrill, however, could scarcely accept that. Still her fears gradually subsided as nothing happened except a continual passing of buffalo to the fore and rear. The herd split a couple of hundred paces below the wagons and the two streams flowed by. Terrill could not help shuddering at the prospect of a stampede. But the gentle trampling roar went on uneventfully. Dust filled the air and a strong odor prevailed.

It took an hour for this branch of the herd to pass. Sambo drove on. When the dust blew away Lambeth was seen waiting with the horses, and the plain ahead appeared clear. Behind and to the south rolled the slow dust cloud, soon settling so that the stringy, black horde once more showed distinct against the gray.

Thereafter only occasional lines of buffalo were crossed, until at last, toward sunset, the herd appeared to have been passed. The undulating prairie appeared the same in every direction, except that there was a gradual uplift to the west. Lambeth disappeared over a ridge, and when the wagon topped it Terrill saw a willow-bordered swale where he had elected to make camp that night.

Twilight was stealing over the land when Sambo hauled up beside the willows where Lambeth was hobbling the horses. Terrill sat a moment longer on the seat. The perils of the day were past. Coyotes were barking at the far end of the swale. A melancholy solitude enfolded the place. Behind Terrill the weeks seemed years. They were dimming old associations. She sighed for them, yet she welcomed the future eagerly. What work and life lay ahead for her! Terrill leaped off the wagon, conscious of a subtle break as of something that had come between her and the old house. It was time she set brain and hand to help her father in the great task he had undertaken.

The ring of Sambo's ax in the gray dawn was Terrill's signal to arise and begin the momentous day. Sambo rolled his ox eyes at her. "Now what fur is yo' up so early, Miss Rill?"

"To work, Sambo. To help my Dad be a pioneer. To become a vaquero. . . . Nigger, never you Missy Rill me again. I'm a man!"

"Yo' is! Wal, dat am funny. How is yo' come aboot bein' a man?"

Terrill was abashed at the approach of her father, who had heard. His eyes took on a dark flash, burning out a sadness that had gloomed there. The kiss he gave Terrill then seemed singular in that it held an element of finality. He never kissed her again.

The rosy sunrise found them on their way, headed toward the purple horizon. There was no road. Lambeth led a zigzag course across the prairie, keeping to the best levels, heading ravines and creek bottoms.

Summer had come to the range. The bleached grama grass rose out of a carpet of green. Flowers bloomed in sheltered places. Deer trooped in the creek bottoms, and there was a varied life everywhere in the vicinity of water.

That day the vastness of Texas and the meaning of loneliness grew fixed in Terrill's heart forever. On all sides waved the prairie, on and on, in an endless solitude. The wild animals, the hawks and ravens, the black clouds of passenger pigeons that coursed by, the faint, dark lines behind in the Colorado valley,—all these only accentuated the solitude.

Hour after hour the wagon wheels left tracks in the rich soil, and the purple beckoning distance seemed ever the same. Terrill rode Dixie, drove Sambo's wagon, and she even walked, but nothing changed the eternal monotony of the Texas plains. She forgot the Comanches and other perils about which she had heard. And at times she caught a stealing vacancy of mind that had entranced her, for how long she could not tell. It was a strange and beautiful thing. But for the most part she watched and listened and felt.

The next day was like the one before, and then Terrill lost track of days. She could recall only events such as a rain that drenched her to the skin, and what fun it was to dry in the sun, and a hard wind which blew in their faces all one day, and the doubtful crossing of a sand-barred river that Lambeth was sure was the Llano, which Red Turner had claimed was a tributary to the Colorado, not many days south of the San Saba.

On the north side of the Llano they had crossed a road that ran east and west. Lambeth vacillated long here. It troubled him. A road led somewhere. But he had at length pushed on toward the San Saba.

Dry camps alternated with those at which water and grass were abundant. At night, round the camp fire, Lambeth and Sambo would discuss the growing problem. As they climbed out of the vast valley the springs and creeks grew scarcer. It would soon be imperative to follow rivers and roads, and that meant a greater risk than they had been incurring. The Comanches lived up on the Staked Plains, and the Kiowas farther north, and the Jicarillo Apaches west.

"Yas, suh," agreed Sambo, in relation to an unavoidable peril. "'Mos' a matter of luck, Kuhnel. But Texas done be as big as de whole Yankeeland."

It was July when they struck the San Saba, a fine river watering a beautiful country Lambeth did not want to leave. Pressing on on the left bank, they came to a crossing. This was the road Red Turner had informed Lambeth he would find. There were wheel tracks in it. He followed that road for days, and at last, where the forking of creeks with the San Saba indicated the headwaters, he sighted cattle on the plain.

They camped near a ranch that sunset. Lambeth made the acquaintance of the settler before night. His name was Hetcoff and he hailed from Missouri. He had neighbors, but they were few and far between. Their cattle had been unmolested, but it was hard to hide horses from the marauding Comanches. Lambeth was advised to pick his range somewhere along the San Saba. It had possibilities. At Menardsville, a day's ride west, there was a junction of roads and that point would be thickly settled some day. The Staked Plains to the north was a barren plateau, known only to the savages, and decidedly to be avoided by white men. A road staked out by the Spaniards across its sandy wastes had been the death of many a settler. Hetcoff knew little of the Pecos country, but the name Pecos itself had a sinister significance.

Terrill was excited at the prospect of entering a town again. But Menardsville was disappointing, as it consisted of but a few adobe houses surrounded by ranges. A Texan named Bartlett maintained a post there, freighting supplies at infrequent intervals. He was also in the cattle business, which at that time had only a prospective future. Cattle were plentiful and cheap.

Lambeth camped at Menardsville for a week, resting, buying supplies, mending harnesses, gaining information. When he left there he had both wagons loaded to capacity—a fine haul for Comanches, Bartlett averred.

Terrill still occupied the smaller canvas-covered wagon, but she had less room and comfort. She had ceased to suffer from sun and wind, and had become hard and strong. She did not lose weight because she was growing all the time. Increased height and a widening of her frame favored her disguise. Often she gazed in rueful wonder at her hands, still shapely, but hardening from work, growing callous of palm and a deep gold tan on the back. At intervals she cut her rebellious curly locks, though never very short. And she was troubled at the thinning of her cheeks and coarsening of her skin, which she had once desired; at the look in the dark blue eyes which watched her gravely from the little mirror.

West of Menardsville the road Lambeth chose to travel headed northwest over an increasingly difficult country, barren and fertile in patches. Settlers had drifted into this region, and a few ranches established before the war were accumulating more cattle than they took the trouble to brand.

Lambeth decided to buy cattle enough to make the nucleus of a herd. Wakefield, a rancher who did not know how many long-horn cattle he owned, sold Lambeth what he wanted at his own price, and to boot lent him a couple of vaqueros. He advised against the Pecos country. "Best of cattle ranges," he said; "but wild, hard, an' lonely, shore to be a hotbed of rustlers some day."

Terrill sustained a peculiar feeling at her first close sight of a Texas long-horn steer. The enormously wide-spreading, bow-shaped horns had inspired the name of this Mexican breed, and they quite dwarfed the other characteristics of the animal. Terrill was destined to learn the true nature of this famous Texas stock. All in a single day she became a vaquero.

At every ranch Lambeth added to his herd; and after every night stand some of them eluded the guards and departed for home. Nevertheless, the herd grew, and the labors of driving a number of long-horns increased in proportion. Necessarily this slowed down their daily travel to less than a fourth of what it had been.

The end of August found Lambeth's wagon train and cattle drive encroaching upon the bad lands of west Texas. They rimmed the southern edge of *Llano Estacado,* a treeless, waterless, sandy region faintly and fascinatingly indicative of its impassable and destructive nature.

They encountered a wandering, prospective settler and saved his life. He had come across the arid plateau from the Panhandle, how or where he could not explain. He was glad to throw in with Lambeth and help drive that growing herd For now Lambeth's steers, leisurely driven and as carefully looked after as was possible, had begun to pick up cattle along the way. Lambeth could not prevent this. He had no brand of his own. He could not pick out from his herd all stock he had paid for and all that had joined it of their own accord. So he became an innocent rustler, something which Wakefield had seriously warned him against; and had then removed the sting of his words by a laughing statement that all ranchers, at some stage or other of their careers, appropriated cattle not their own.

The two borrowed vaqueros had to work so hard that Terrill seldom came in direct contact with them. The Mexican was a sloe-eyed, swarthy rider no longer young, silent and taciturn, with whom conversation, let alone friendliness, was difficult. The white vaquero was a typical Texan who had been reared on the plains. He was rough and uncouth, yet likable and admirable to Terrill. She learned much from watching these two men. At the last ranch Lambeth had added a boy to the caravan, whose duty it was to drive the large wagon while Sambo helped with the herd. There was never a day dawned that Terrill did not expect to see the last of the herd. But they drove on and on into the west, always finding grass at the end of a day's travel, and seldom missing water. The frequent rains, summer storms they were, favored travel over this increasingly arid land.

September came. At least that was how Terrill calculated. And with it cooler nights and dawn with a nip in the air. Terrill often stood hours of the night guarding the herd with her father. These were wonderful hours. The Mexican vaquero sometimes sang to the herd, strange, wild Spanish songs of the range. While the cattle rested and slept, the guards took their turns of four hours on and four off, Sambo and Steve, the white vaquero alternating with Lambeth and the Mexican. Terrill did her share, which, however, had so far been only guarding. As luck would have it, nothing stampeded the long-horns.

For days on end dim blue hills had led Terrill's gaze on to dimmer and bluer mountains, like ghosts above the hazy horizon. Steve said those mountains lay across the Pecos, that they must be the Guadaloupes. The blue hills, however, were the brakes of the Pecos.

The white-and-yellow plain undulated on to meet these rising uplands. And the naked slope of the Staked Plains imperceptibly receded. Lambeth had been most fortunate in finding stream beds to follow. He grazed the herd along only a dozen miles a day, gradually slowing up as the harder country intervened.

October! Lambeth's caravan was lost in a forlorn and desolate country. They had no landmarks to travel by—no direction except west. And half the time that was impossible to follow, owing to the character of the country.

The blue hills they had sighted from a distance were the rock-and-ridge region through which the Pecos cut its solitary way. Lambeth had been told to strike the river wherever he could and then to travel west to Horsehead Crossing, a ford that had been used by the Spaniards a hundred years before.

When the situation began to be very serious they stumbled upon the Flat Rock Water Holes, and were thus accorded another reprieve. Two dry camps brought them to Wild China Water Holes. From there the dim road faded among the rocks. But the Mexican vaquero, upon whom had evolved the responsibility of getting them through, had his direction, and led on with confidence.

Grass grew plentifully over the scaly ridges, but so scattered in little patches that stock had to range far to get enough. That further slowed the caravan. Nevertheless, Lambeth pushed on with relentless optimism. He had a vision and it could not be clouded. He cheered on his hands by promise of reward, and performed miracles of labor for a man who had been a Southern planter. The adventure could not recall his youth, for that was irretrievably past, but it rehabilitated his strength and energy.

As for Terrill, the seven months in the open had transformed her physically. She was at home in the saddle or on the wagon seat. The long days under the blazing sun, or facing the whipping wind with its dust and sand, rain and chill, the lonely night watch when the wolves mourned and the coyotes wailed, the hard rides over stony ridges to head refractory old long-horns—these all grew to be part of the day to Terrill Lambeth.

Again the Mexican lost his way. Washes to cross, sandy and dragging, cattle that must graze, ravines deepening to gorges, which had to be headed, all these confused the guide. Lambeth preferred to corral the stock at night in one of the gorges or a bowl between two ridges. Ridge tops were less favorable places.

They drove two days without water, except enough for the horses. The cattle began to suffer. They grew harder to hold. The riders had little rest and no sleep. Next day they dropped down over a ridge into a well-defined trail coming up from the south. Rain had almost obliterated hoof tracks which might have been so very old.

Lambeth wanted to turn south. The vaquero shook his head. "Mucho bad, Señor. Ver seco. Water mañana. Rio Pecos," he said, and pointed north.

But the following night found them in a precarious predicament. Two canteens of water left! The horses were in bad shape. Cattle had fallen along the wayside. Another hot day without rain or water would spell the doom of the stock. And that meant horrible toil and suffering, probably death, for the travelers.

Terrill remembered her prayers that night and her mother's face came to her in a dream.

Lambeth had the caravan on the move at break of day, hoping to find water before the sun got high.

The road penetrated deeper into this wilderness of stone and cactus, greasewood and gray earth. Still there was always grass. The stock now, however, no longer grazed.

Notwithstanding the dangerous situation, Lambeth's luck seemed not wholly to have departed. Before the sun grew hot, clouds rolled up to obscure it. The riders, grasping at straws, mercilessly drove the cattle on.

A gloomy canopy overhead fitted the strange, wild country, which every mile appeared to take on more of its peculiar characteristics.

Terrill, driving the smaller wagon, noticed a developing uneasiness in the long column of cattle. They had been plodding along wearily, heads down, tongues out, almost spent. Suddenly a spirit seemed to run through the whole herd. Here and there a cow bawled. They quickened from a crawl to a trot. The Mexican and the other vaquero, far in front, were not succeeding in holding them back. Apparently they were not trying. They waved wildly back to Sambo and Lambeth, who had the rear positions. Something had gone wrong, Terrill feared. How would this terrible drive end?

Then the cattle, as if actuated by a single spirit, stampeded in a cloud of dust and disappeared. Lambeth rode on with dropping head. Sambo approached him as if to offer consolation for the loss.

It was a downgrade there. Terrill had to hold in the team, that had also become imbued with some quickening sense. Ahead where the dust cloud hung, a rugged line of rocks and ridges met the gloomy sky. Terrill could not see far. Where had the cattle gone? What had frightened them? They were gone, and hope was, too. It was over, the suspense of the endless weeks of driving longhorns. A sterner task now confronted her father—to save the horses and their own lives.

Terrill was plunged into an abyss of despair. Somehow she had kept up, believing her prayers would be answered. But now she succumbed. Theirs would be the fate of so many who had wandered off into that Godforsaken wilderness, lured on by the dream of the pioneer. It would have been better to meet a quick and fighting death at the hands of Comanches.

Terrill had caught up with her father and Sambo when she saw the Mexican turn in his saddle to cup his hands and yell. But she could not understand. She did not need to understand his words, however, to realize that some new peril impended. Then several strange riders appeared out of an arroyo. At first Terrill feared they were Indians, so dark, lean, wild were their horses.

It was only when the leader advanced alone that Terrill made out they were white men. But how sinister! The leader was suspicious. He had no rifle over his pommel. The vaquero, riding beside Lambeth, halted his horse.

"Massa, dat's a rustler, if I ebber seen one," said Sambo. "We'se held up, we sho is."

The rider approached to halt some paces from the wagons. Suddenly, with a violent start, Terrill recognized him. Pecos Smith! The young Texan who had backed out of the saloon in San Antonio with a gun in each hand!

"Who air you an' what you doin' heah?" he queried, curtly, his piercing eyes taking in all of the travelers, to go back to Lambeth.

"My name's Lambeth. We're lost. An' my cattle have stampeded," replied Lambeth.

"Where was you goin' when you got lost?"

"Horsehaid Crossin' of the Pecos."

"Wal, you're way off yore direction. Horsehaid is east from heah."

"We were told to travel north whether we lost the road or not."

Evidently the rider had his doubts about this outfit. Finally he called to Sambo: "Niggah, you get down an' come heah."

Sambo obeyed precipitately.

"Where'd I ever see you?"

"I dunno, sir, but I'se sho seen you," replied Sambo.

"Santone, wasn't it?"

"Yas, sir. I was standin' in front of a saloon an' you told me to move along."

"Reckon I remember you," returned the rider, and then directed his attention to Lambeth. "But thet don't prove nothin'. Lambeth, you may be all right. But this vaquero is not. I know him. How'd you come by him?"

Lambeth explained how the Mexican had been lent to him for the trip across the Pecos. And he added, stiffly: "I'm Colonel Templeton Lambeth. What are you takin' me for?"

"Howdy, Pecos Smith!" spoke up Terrill, feeling at this moment that she might well ease the situation.

"Wal! . . . An' who're you?" exclaimed the rider, amazed, as he bent eyes that bored upon her.

"He is my father."

"Ahuh. An' how'd you know me?"

"I was the—the kid you knocked over that day in Santone—when you came out of the saloon. . . . You made me fetch your horse. . . . And you said you'd only shot the man's ear off—that it stuck out like a jack rabbit's."

"Wal, I'll be dog-goned!" ejaculated the rider. "I remember, but you're shore changed a lot, boy." Then he turned to Lambeth. "We've been trailin' a rustler outfit up from the Rio Grande. Reckoned mebbe they'd run across somebody with wagons. Sorry to annoy you, Colonel. Turn yore wagons an' I'll lead you to the crossin'."

"Is it far?" asked Lambeth, anxiously.

"Wal, it's far enough, considerin' yore hosses. I reckon you'll just aboot make it."

The ensuing drive, short though it might have been, proved to Terrill that if they had not been led out of this maze of hot draws and ridges they would have been irrevocably lost. As it was, the weary horses were barely goaded to the gap in a summit of gray bluff. The rider sat his horse, waiting for the caravan to come up.

"Rio Pecos!" he called, and pointed down.

The riders galloped forward at his call. Terrill, with a wild start and a sob of thanksgiving, urged the team ahead. Sambo dismounted and turned back to wave at Terrill. She had all she could do to pull the horses up beside the riders.

"De good Lawd am delibbered us," said Sambo, and hurried back to meet Mauree.

"Rill—he has led us—to the river!" exclaimed Lambeth, with deep emotion. "Look! Heah is Horsehaid Crossin'—of the Pecos. And look there—the cattle!"

Terrill gazed down from a height. Just on the moment pale sunlight filtered through the drab clouds, to shine upon a winding silver river that formed a bend like the shape of a horse's head. It flowed out of gray and green wilderness, and probably came through a gap in the distant stone bluff.

The foremost cattle had reached the water. It had been the scent of water that had stampeded them. Sand bars gleamed white.

Terrill caught her breath. The joy of deliverance had momentarily blinded her to something that struck her like a blow, but which she could not yet grasp. She stared at her father, at the other riders. Pecos Smith was riding by. "Adios an' good luck!" he called, and galloped away. Sambo's deep voice pealed from behind, where he was rejoicing with his wife.

All along this trail, surely once a traveled road, lay skulls and bones of animals. Horses, cattle—a line of bones! From a rock stuck up the ghastly skull and weirdly long horns of a Texas steer—fit guidepost for that crossing. The place was desolate, gray, and lonely, an utter solitude, uninhabited even by beasts of the hills or fowls of the air. It stretched away to infinitude. In the east rose a pale streak—possibly the slope of *Llano Estacado*.

But it was to the west that Terrill forced her gaze. West of the Pecos! How, for what seemed a lifetime, had she lived on those words, with an added word—home! Could home have any place in this strange and terrific prospect?

The river changed its course with Horsehead Crossing, but soon veered back to its main trend southward. It dominated that savagely monotonous and magnificent scene. Miles were nothing in this endless expanse. The green and the gray along the river were but delusions. Back to the west and south mounted the naked ridges, noble and austere by reason of their tremendous size and reach, and between them gloomed the purple gorges, mysterious, forlorn, seemingly inaccessible for beast or man. No grassy pasturelands such as had existed in Terrill's hopeful dreams! All that was not gray stone, gray earth, were mere specks of cactus, of greasewood on the boundless slopes.

Terrill's heart sank. After all, she thought bitterly, she was only a girl. She had loved the open rangeland of Texas, over which she had ridden nearly a thousand miles, but could she ever do aught but hate this deceitful desert? She had loved the river bottoms of the Red, the Sabine, the Brazos, the Colorado, and the San Saba. They had openness, color, life, beauty. But this Rio Pecos, for all its pale silver gleam, its borders of white and green, seemed cold, treacherous, aloof, winding its desolate way down into the desolate unknown.

"Oh, Dad!" cried Terrill, voicing her first surrender. "Take me back! . . . This dreadful Pecos can never be home!"

CHAPTER FIVE

To the cowhands at Healds' ranch he called himself Pecos Smith. They were not long in discovering that he was the best horseman, the best shot, the best roper that had ever ridden up out of Southwest Texas. But that was about all they ever learned about his past.

Pecos had come up the river with a trail driver named McKeever, who had a contract to deliver cattle at Santa Fé, New Mexico. The Spanish towns of Santa Fé, Taos, Las Vegas, and Albuquerque furnished a growing market for beef. The Government forts added largely to this demand. Cattlemen, believing in future protection against the marauding bands of Indians, had followed the more adventurous settlers into southern New Mexico and western Texas. Most of the cattle at this period came from the Rio Grande.

McKeever, on his return, stopped at Healds' minus one of his rangy vaqueros, and it was observed that that rider was Smith.

"We left Smith behind at Santa Fé," explained the trail driver. "He pecosed another man an', like he always does after a shootin', he got drunk. We couldn't wait fer him. But I reckon he'll be along soon."

"Quarrelsome cowhand, this Smith?" asked Bill Heald, one of the brother ranchers.

"Not atall. He's aboot the best-natured boy you'd want to meet," returned McKeever. "But he gets picked at, seems like, or else he's everlastin' bustin' into somebody's trouble. An' he's shore hell with a gun."

That was Smith's introduction to the Healds. Several days after that he dropped in at the ranch, a clean-cut, smiling, devil-may-care Texas boy of the old stock. Bill Heald took a fancy to him, and being in need of riders offered him a job.

"Wal, I'll shore take ye up," drawled Smith. "Mac won't like it. But he was ornery up there at Santa Fé. Cussed me powerful."

"McKeever told me you shot a man," rejoined Heald, slowly, watching the rider. "In fact, he said *another* man."

"Damn Mac's pictures, anyhow," complained the rider, annoyed. "He's always talkin' aboot me."

Heald decided it would be wiser to waive personal inquiries, despite the curiosity Smith aroused. Heald's experienced eye, however, took in certain details about this rider that prompted one more query. "Ever work for a Mexican?"

"Yeah. Don Felipe Gonzales," admitted Smith, readily. "My father was killed in the war an' my family busted up. Don Felipe was an old acquaintance of ours. So I went across the Rio Grande an' rode his range four or five years. I'm not shore how many. Anyway, till I got chased back over the river."

Further than that Smith never vouchsafed information about himself, to the Healds or any of the hands.

Upon close scrutiny of Pecos Smith, Heald decided that his appearance belied the boyishness that seemed to be born of his careless, free insouciance. His age must have been between twenty and twenty-five years, which was not very young for a range rider in Texas. He was just above medium height, not so lean and rangy as most horsemen, having wide shoulders and muscular round limbs. He struck Heald as a remarkably able horseman, which opinion was soon more than verified. All the leather trappings about Smith and his horse were ragged and shiny from use, particularly the gun holster which hung low on his left thigh and the saddle sheath. The ivory handle of his gun was yellow with age. What metal showed, and this was also true of his rifle, shone with the bright, almost white luster of worn, polished steel. His saddle, bridle, and spurs, also his black sombrero, were of Spanish make, decorated with silver; and if they had not been so old might have made a thief out of many a vaquero.

"Smith, you're on," declared Bill Heald, finally, having been unaccountably slow in decision, for him. "Thet's a grand hoss you're forkin'. If he ain't Arabian I'll eat him. Have a care for him. What with this outfit an' the Comanches you'll have hell keepin' him."

"Wal, Cinco cain't be caught in a race, anyhow," drawled the rider, patting the tired and dusty horse. "Heald, I'm shore thankin' you for the job."

"Not atall. We're short-handed. An' you strike me right. But, Smith, if you've got thet queer hand-itch fer a gun, won't you doctor it with axle grease or somethin'?"

"Never no more, boss. I'm a sick hombre. Red likker an' me air on the oots," drawled the rider, his flashing smile answering the other's levity.

"Then you're set heah," concluded Bill Heald.

It chanced that Heald's sister, Mary, had watched this interview from the door, unobserved. She was only sixteen, and with the brothers had been made an orphan not so long ago. She was the pride of their eyes as well as the disturber of their peace.

"Oh, Billy!" she exclaimed, her black eyes shining roguishly. "That's the handsomest rider I've seen since I came West."

"Thunder an' blazes!" ejaculated Heald. "If I'd seen thet I'd never hev hired him. . . . Mary, if you make eyes at him ranchin' will shore stop heah."

The next time Heald saw Smith he remembered Mary's tribute and took keener note of the stranger. Smith was not an unusual type for a Texan, though he appeared to have Texas characteristics magnified. Many Texans were sandy-haired or tow-headed, and possessed either blue or gray eyes. This rider had flaxen hair and he wore it so long that it curled from under his sombrero. His face was like a bronze mask, except when he talked or smiled, and then it lightened. In profile it was sharply cut, cold as stone, singularly more handsome than the full face. His eyes assumed dominance over all other features, being a strange-flecked, pale gray, of exceeding power of penetration. His lips, in repose, were sternly chiseled, almost bitter, but as they were mostly open in gay, careless talk or flashing a smile over white teeth, this last feature was seldom noticed.

The *remudo* filed in that night, enlivening the ranch again, and next day Bill Heald asked his brother what he thought of the new cowhand.

"Strikes me fine. Likable cuss, I'll gamble," replied John Heald. "Real Texas stuff in thet fellar."

"Mary has fallen in love with him already."

"O Lord! What'll we do, Bill? Send her back to Auntie Heald?"

"Hell no! She stays if she puts the outfit up a tree. Mebbe this Pecos hombre can win her."

"I don't know aboot thet," replied John, soberly. "Mary's tryin' an' thet's no joke. I want her to settle out heah an' marry some good fellar. But this Pecos has a gun record, Bill. Did you know thet?"

"McKeever told me Smith had killed another man," admitted the elder brother, thoughtfully.

"Sandy told me more than thet," went on John, impressively. "Sandy says he sneaked a peep at this Pecos fellar's gun. It had six notches on the handle an' one of them was cut fresh."

"Six. . . . I reckoned it might be more. Let's not borrow trouble, John. Anyway, it's a shootin' country an' we might be most damn glad to have thet kind of a Texan among us."

"Shore. An' it ain't likely Mary will capitulate to a blood-spiller. She's squeamish for a Heald. But she might flirt with the fellar. Mary's the dod-blastedest flirt I ever seen."

"Flirtin' might be as bad as a real case," rejoined Bill. "What concerns me is the effect thet'd have on our outfit. You know, John, every last man Jack of them thinks he's goin' to wed with Mary."

Pecos Smith gave opportunity for various discussion among the brothers and their cowhands. It was a lonesome country, and strangers, that were not to be avoided, were few and far between. Their opinions, however, fell far wide of the mark, except as they had to do with Smith as a vaquero. The horse Cinco lived up to his looks and his rider's pride. Pecos was a whole outfit in himself. He never knew when work was done. His riding and roping might have been that of the famous vaquero, Rodiriquez. Every cowhand in the outfit had his sombrero full of bullet holes, proofs of Pecos' marksmanship. Pecos was most obliging and he could not resist any kind of a bet. He seldom missed a sombrero tossed into the air, and as often as not he put two bullets through it before it dropped. He would never let anyone handle his gun, which shared with Cinco in his affections. Pecos proved to be a round peg fitting snugly into a round hole. Riders were scarce, cattle growing plentiful, likewise rustlers, and always the horse-stealing Comanches.

Long before McKeever drove north again with a herd of steers Pecos had won the regard of the X Bar outfit, which was run by an adjoining rancher, as well as that of the H H outfit, belonging to the Healds.

The singular thing about Pecos, remarkable in view of the universal esteem in which he was held, was that he avoided contact with people, save the riders with whom he worked or those of the neighboring ranch. Mary Heald gave a party one night to which all the people in that part of the country were invited. Somebody had to be out with the cattle on that particular night, and Pecos took the job for another rider. Mary Heald was furious with him, and snubbed him on the following day when he happened to run into her at the corrals.

"Wal, I just cain't please the ladies, nohow," he drawled to Sandy McClain.

"Huh! Say, you mysterious cuss—you could have 'em eatin' out of your hand if you'd give 'em a chance."

"Sandy, yore what them Colorado chaps call loco."

"Am I? What's thet?"

"Wal, it's a kind of weed thet hosses eat an' go off their haids."

"Pecos, air you hitched to some gurl?—Married, I mean?"

"Me?—Santa Maria!"

"Air you a woman-hater then? Had yore heart broke? . . . Honest, Pecos, yore laughin' an whistlin' an' makin' fun don't fool this heah chicken none. You're a sad hombre."

"No, Sandy, my heart's shore not broke yet, but dog-gone me, it wouldn't take much."

Bill Heald and his brother satisfied themselves finally as to Pecos' peculiar aloofness.

"First off I figured Pecos was one of them Texas-Ranger-dodgin' hombres," said Bill. "But I've changed my mind. Thet fellar never did a shady thing in his life. He comes of a good family, you can tell thet, an' he's had trouble."

"Bill, I agree with you. More'n thet I'd say if there was a sheriff or a ranger huntin' Pecos he'd never dodge him. I'd shore hate to be the sheriff that tried to arrest him, provided it was an even break."

"He fooled us aboot Mary, didn't he? Darn good lesson fer thet little lady. Only I hope she doesn't fall daid in love with Pecos."

"Wal, if she did it wouldn't last. . . . No, Pecos is just one of them driftin', fascinatin' vaqueros. I've met as many as I have fingers. Texas is the only country thet could produce such a breed."

McKeever, on his return from Santa Fé spent a night at the Heald ranch and not only inquired about his lost vaquero, but wanted to see him. Pecos was not to be located.

"Reckon he likes it hyar an' wants to hang aboot," concluded the trail driver, with a sly look at Mary, which made her blush flamingly.

"I'm shore nobody hyar wants him hangin' aboot," she retorted, her chin tilting.

"My loss is your gain, folks," returned McKeever, resignedly. "They don't come any finer than Smith."

If there were any doubts at the H H ranch as to the status of Pecos Smith, that recommendation definitely dispersed them.

The time came when Pecos Smith justified the prefix to his name, if he had not already done so. Like an Indian, it was second nature for him to remember any trail, any thicket, any creek bottom, or canyon that he had ever seen. His brain instinctively photographed places.

The Rio Pecos from Castle Gap Canyon to the New Mexico border became his intimate possession. The Healds did not know whether they were running twenty thousand head of stock or thirty thousand. Pecos Smith had a more accurate estimate of their cattle than anyone, and his reports of unbranded calves and yearlings and steers hiding in the thickets of the creek bottoms or the brakes of the Pecos ran into the thousands.

Bill Heald took this with a grain of salt, while his brother pondered over it seriously. Like all ranchers of the period, they were careless branders. That was to say they did not have the hands nor the time to comb the range for unbranded stock. Cattle had begun to demand a price and the future looked promising. But money was scarce. Texas was in her first stage of recovery after the ruin left by the war. The Healds were doing about all that was possible for them.

Rustlers appeared on the Pecos range. The long-horns had come originally from south of the Rio Grande; so had the cattle thieves. Nowhere had there ever been such wholesale and tremendous thefts of cattle as along the Mexican border. That was one reason why Texans like the Healds had moved to isolated ranges.

But up to this period the X Bar, the H H, and other outfits had not suffered much from rustling. At least they had not been aware of it. Every rancher lost stock, the same as he appropriated a little that really did not belong to him. There had not been, however, any appreciable inroads upon the herds.

It was through the trail driver, McKeever, that the Healds found the opportunity they had planned and waited for, and this was a considerable market for their product. McKeever bought cattle from them in large numbers and drove them to the Spanish settlements in New Mexico and the Government headquarters. Extensive military operations against the Indians were already under way. Rumors of railroads through New Mexico and Texas were rife. Altogether the Healds looked forward to huge markets, to advancing prices, and trail herds of their own.

To this end Pecos Smith was promoted to be their outside man. He accepted the job with reluctance, and upon being asked why he was not keen about it he replied rather evasively that it held too much responsibility. His duty was to ride all over the country, to the farthest outlying ranges, not only to keep track of the Heald cattle, but to gauge general conditions, study the methods of other ranchers, and watch their round-ups. Thus Pecos Smith added to his already wide knowledge of the country.

Upon his return from one of these trips, in the autumn of his second year's service to the Healds, he ran into the inevitable trouble that had always hounded his trail.

Pecos had ridden into the ranch early in the morning, and after cleaning up was enjoying a much-needed rest and a smoke when Sandy McClain came hurrying over from the ranch-house. Pecos divined there was something up before Sandy drew near enough to distinguish his features. He could tell by that hurried yet suspensive stride. So that when Sandy arrived at the porch of the cabin, his hazel eyes full of fire and his lips hard, Pecos cursed under his breath.

"Pecos, thar's shore—hell to pay," declared Sandy.

"Who's payin' it?" queried Pecos, in his cool, lazy drawl.

"Nobody yit, but you'll have to. An' I'm gittin' this off my chest first. If it comes to a fight I'm with you."

"Thanks, Sandy, I shore appreciate thet. But usually I can tend to my own fights. Suppose you tell me aboot what's up?"

"You know thet Sawtell, foreman fer Beckman?" rushed on Sandy.

"Shore. I was at Marber's Crossin' not two months ago," replied Pecos, his boots coming down from a bench. "They had a round-up. I was there, you bet, an' I stayed, in spite of the cold shoulder from Sawtell."

"Pecos, it ain't so good. Sawtell is hyar, with three of his outfit. An' he's been hittin' the bottle, Pecos. He's loud an' nasty."

"What's it all aboot?"

"I didn't heah. But I can guess. Bill is all upset, an' madder'n hell under his hat, as I could see. He sent me to fetch you."

Pecos sat silent a moment with slowly contracting brows. His eyes were downcast. Presently he drew his gun, and flipping it open he extracted an extra cartridge from his vest pocket and inserted it in the one empty chamber. Then he arose to his feet, sheathing the gun. Without another word he strode off toward the ranch-house, with Sandy beside him, talking wildly.

Presently Pecos espied four saddled horses standing, bridles down, across the open space in front of the house. He sheered a little to the left so that he would not go abruptly around the corner.

"Keep out of this, Sandy," he ordered.

"But they're four to one, Pecos," expostulated Sandy. "An' thet red-faced Sawtell doesn't talk like he savvied you. I've got a hunch, Pecos. It won't do no harm to let them see you got a pard."

Pecos answered with a gesture that needed no speech. Sandy sheered widely to the right. Pecos heard a loud voice. Next moment he came into the open, where he had a clear view. Mary Heald was the first person he saw.

"Go in the house," Bill Heald ordered her.

"Oh, your grandmother!" retorted Mary. She was flushed and excited, and upon espying Pecos gave a violent start.

"Bill! . . . Hyar he is," she called.

Pecos took in the prospect. Sawtell, a tall cattleman wearing a bandana as red as his face, stood out before three cowhands whose posture was not easy. Bill Heald, turning from Mary, called to his brother: "This ain't no mix fer her. Drag her inside."

"Let her stay. Mebbe she'll hyar somethin'," declared John.

"I *did* hyar somethin' and it's a confounded lie," flashed Mary, hotly.

Upon seeing Pecos approaching, Bill Heald showed a subtle change of manner.

"Sawtell, hyar's Pecos now, to speak fer himself. We think you're on a wrong track. An' if you'll listen to reason, you'll go mighty slow."

"Hell!—Air you threatenin' me, Bill Heald?" returned the visitor, harshly.

"Not atall. I'm just advisin' you."

"Wal, I don't need any advice. I was ridin' these ranges long before you."

"Shore. But you don't know Pecos Smith."

"Pecos! Whar'd he git thet handle?"

"I don't know. He had it when he come."

Pecos halted some paces out.

"Boss, what's up heah?"

"I'm ashamed to tell you, Pecos, an' I swear I'd never done it if I could have persuaded Sawtell to ride off."

"Thanks, Heald. . . . Get back an' leave this to me."

Bill promptly acted upon that suggestion, and it was equally noticeable that the three cowhands behind Sawtell moved out of line with him.

Pecos eyed the cattleman and read him through. There would be no equivocation here. The matter had been settled in Sawtell's mind before he arrived at Healds' ranch, and he had fortified it with drink.

"You know me, Smith?" demanded Sawtell. He was loud, authoritative, but not of the braggart breed.

"I haven't the honor, Señor," replied Pecos, coldly. "When I called on you at Marber's Crossin' not long since you didn't give me the chance. An' I reckoned I didn't miss much."

"Wal, you might have missed hyarin' aboot the maverick-brandin' thet's goin' on."

"No. I didn't have to heah thet."

Bill Heald could not keep out of the colloquy.

"Pecos reported to me. The H H is losin' a dribble of mavericks."

"Is thet so?" sneered Sawtell. He was ugly and could not be conciliated.

"See hyar, Sawtell," retorted Heald, sharply, at last out of patience. "You come shore set to make trouble. An' by Gawd, you're liable to run into more'n you bargained fer."

"Air you defendin' maverick-brandin'?" demanded Sawtell, sarcastically.

"Boss, would you mind leavin' this deal to me?" interposed Pecos.

"All right, Sawtell. You're makin' your own bed. I've no more to say," concluded Heald, and he backed away.

Pecos made two strides which brought him within ten feet of the irate cattleman. Everyone present except Sawtell must have sensed the singular, cold menace of the vaquero. Only the false stimulus of whisky could have blinded a matured Texan to imminent peril. And at that Sawtell seemed confronted with an obstructing thought.

"Sawtell, you gave me a cold shoulder up at Marber's Crossin'."

"You bet I did."

"If it hadn't been fer my boss, I'd have called you then, in yore own back yard. I took thet as an insult."

"Wal, you took it proper. An' if it hadn't been fer the Healds hyar I'd run you off my ranch."

That was definite and it settled all but the conclusion of this meeting, which the cattleman was evidently too obtuse or bull-headed to sense. One of his men made a movement as if to intercede, but was restrained by a second. They edged nervously to one side, as if wary to get out of line with Pecos' piercing eyes. But they would have had to dissolve in thin air to accomplish that.

Pecos' silence, his strained intensity, the suspense of the moment penetrated Sawtell's befogged brain. But it was too late.

"Mr. Pecos Smith," Sawtell blustered, "you know them X Bar cowhands, Curt Williams an' Wess Adams?"

"Reckon I do."

"They rode fer thet greaser Felipe, down on the Big Bend."

"So did I."

"Wal, thet ain't any recommend fer them or you."

"Beggars cain't be choosers. I had to ride to live. . . . Yore beatin' aboot the bush. Come on!"

"I had Williams an' Adams fired off the X Bar."

"No news to me."

"They was seen brandin' mavericks on my range."

"Sawtell, it's not beyond the bounds of reason thet them mavericks wasn't yore'n," replied Pecos, coldly.

"No, it ain't. But I'm choosin' to claim them."

"Thet's yore affair. Tolerable unhealthy, I'd say—on the Pecos."

Sawtell's hurried speech apparently augmented his anger, but did not relieve the cramping effect of Pecos' front.

"I'm down hyar to have you fired off the H H," shouted the cattleman.

"Cain't be done. I quit."

"Ahuh. When?"

"Aboot two minutes ago."

"You're a slick hombre, Mr. Smith," retorted Sawtell, exasperated to derision. "Wal, then, I'll drive you off the Pecos range."

Pecos made a singular movement, too swift to discern, though it left him as if in the act of leaping. From his whole being suddenly emanated terrible suspense.

"You —— idiot! Drive *me* off the Pecos? . . . What's all yore gab aboot?"

Sawtell had again gone too far. There was no retreat. The red of his face receded in a marked line, leaving it a leaden gray.

"You was thick with them maverick-branders."

"Who accuses me?" cried Pecos, piercingly.

Sawtell let out an incoherent roar—rage at himself as well as at Pecos—at the realization that he had misjudged his man. His arm moved stiffly. His hand jerked at his gun.

The single, whipping throw of Pecos' gun discharged it. Sawtell's body lost its vibrant tension. It slumped. His head dropped forward. Then he swayed.

Pecos leaped like a tiger past the falling man to face the cowhands, his gun high, quivering to flash down with the force that would fire it.

"Any of you back him up?" he yelled, stridently.

"Smith, it weren't our mistake," hoarsely replied the one who would have importuned Sawtell. "Honest to Gawd—we wanted him—to go slow."

Pecos waved them off, and watched them go hurriedly toward their horses. When he turned, Bill Heald was kneeling beside Sawtell. Sandy was running over and John Heald was trying to drag the white-faced girl away.

"Daid! . . . Shot through the heart! . . . Pecos, this is shore bad bizness," ejaculated Bill.

"You heah him!" Pecos' voice cracked like steel on ice.

"Shore. But my Gawd, man, I didn't expect you to kill him," returned Heald, suddenly rising.

"You believe ——"

"No, Pecos! Not fer a second," protested Heald, hastily, lifting a hand. "An' thet's straight. John an' I think you're as clean an' fine as they come. McKeever swore by you. This damn fool Sawtell must have been drunk. I *told* him. . . . Pecos, don't hold any of it against the H H."

Pecos lowered the gun, but he kept up his pacing to and fro, his strange eyes pivoting like the oscillations of a compass needle. All his cold poise was gone. He had the lunge, the standing hair, the savageness of a wild animal. Sandy approached him, to halt in hesitation.

"Pecos, you had to bore him," he ejaculated. "You jest had to. We'll all stick up fer you. Sawtell brought it on himself."

One of the retreating cowhands, now mounted on their horses, called to Heald: "We'll send a wagon back fer him."

"All right. Make it pronto," Heald replied.

Pecos sheathed his gun, and with that motion appeared to sag. He ceased his cat-like stride. Freckles no one had ever seen stood out on his clammy face. His hair was wet. He stooped to pick up his sombrero, which had fallen when he leaped to confront Sawtell's men.

"Bill, didn't I tell you not to give me thet outside job?" he queried.

"You shore did, Pecos. I'm sorry. But I don't see what difference thet could have made."

"I seen too much, Bill. An' I tried to—wal, never mind aboot thet. . . . I'm shore thankin' you an' John fer keepin' me heah so long an' fer defendin' me to thet white-livered liar."

His implication must have been clear to Heald. At least he looked as if he had grasped at the truth—Pecos had come upon these roistering cowhands at some shady deal. He had tried to show them the error of their ways and had kept his mouth shut about it.

"Pecos, listen hyar. Sawtell must have had a show-down on Williams an' Adams. He was aimin' to bluff you into squealin'—shore he didn't know you."

"You heah somethin' aboot Curt an' Wess?"

"Yes. More'n once, an' I have my doubts, Pecos."

The vaquero threw up his hands. "—— the fools!"

At this juncture Mary Heald broke away from her brother and ran out to confront Pecos. She was still white, sick, trembling, but she was brave.

"Pecos, I know you're not a thief," she burst out.

His somber face lightened beautifully.

"Wal, Miss Mary, thet's shore good fer me to heah. . . . I've no home, no family, no friends, an' when I go out on the long trail again, it'll be good to remember you an' yore brothers believed in me."

"We do, Pecos. Oh, we do," she replied, brokenly. "Don't say you've no friends—no home. . . . Do not leave us, Pecos."

"I cain't stay. It might do yore brothers harm. Those cowhands will tell how Bill stuck up fer me. An' they'll add to it. If I stayed on ——"

"Mary, he's right," interposed Bill. "Much as I regret it, Pecos will have to leave the H H."

"Shore. An' I may as wal have the game as the blame," added Pecos, bitterly.

"Don't say thet, boy," entreated Heald who heard in this resignation the spirit and the hopelessness that had sent so many fine Texas boys down the wrong trail. It was cruel, because in that great state, depleted by wars and overrun with ruined boys and men, there seemed so slight a line of demarcation between the right trail and the wrong.

"Oh, you wild vaquero!" burst out Mary, passionately. "That is wrong—to yourself—to us . . . . to *me!* . . . Pecos, you're such a—a wonderful boy. Don't let the horror of—of killin' another man drive you to—to . . . He deserved it. He was mean. I—I could have shot him myself. . . . Bill—John—say somethin' ——"

The girl failed of utterance there. She had much excuse for agitation, but neither her youth nor the shock of seeing a man killed could wholly account for all she betrayed.

"Pecos, I reckon you'd better stay on," said Bill, huskily. "I'll ride up to

Marber's an' prove your innocence—explain how Sawtell was drunk an' forced this shootin'."

"No. Bill, you cain't do thet," returned Pecos. "I've riled up bad blood before an' I shore don't want to do it heah."

"Pecos!" whispered the girl.

The vaquero turned to her in a realizing amazement that almost hid his gratitude. "Miss Mary, I shore thank you. . . . An' I promise you—thet if *anythin'* can make me go straight from now on—it'll be you—yore faith—yore goodness. Adios."

He reached as if to take her hand, drew back, and wheeled away. Sandy McClain ran to stride beside him.

"Adios, Pecos!" called the girl. "Go straight—an' come—back—some—day."

CHAPTER SIX

But it developed quickly that neither the sweet memory of Mary Heald, nor the scorn Pecos Smith had for rustlers, nor the promise he had given could keep him straight.

Branding mavericks was not a crime in Texas at that early stage of cattle-raising. All ranchers did it more or less, without being absolutely sure that the calves belonged to them. There could be no positive identification, unless the calf accompanied a branded cow. And if a calf or a yearling or a two-year-old did not get the mark of one outfit, it would eventually find that of another.

But in his heart Pecos Smith knew that he had slipped, for the first time in his range life. Bitterly he regarded it as being shoved, rather than having slipped. Nevertheless, what could he do? The X Bar made the excuse that they did not require an extra hand; so did another outfit below the New Mexico line. Pecos' good sense urged him to work south and take up with McKeever again, or some other cattleman west of the Pecos, or even Don Felipe. But his pride and his bitter conviction that there was a step on his trail set his face the other way. He made up his mind to throw in with Curt Williams and Wess Adams, who were indeed trafficking in unbranded mavericks. There was no law against it. There was no obstacle, except that of a gun; and bold maneuvers like Sawtell's were the exception rather than the rule. Pecos argued that if he stuck to the branding of mavericks, and collected a herd of his own, or saved his share of the money he would not long need to do questionable work that was offensive to him.

Williams and Adams had not vouchsafed any information as to their market, except that it was unfailing. Pecos did not care to know. There were ranchers in New Mexico buying stock and asking no questions. There were Government buyers dealing directly with rustlers. The stage was almost set for a great cattle business in the Southwest. Pecos sensed it so well that he thought it a pity he had not already a sizable herd of his own to start with.

Wherefore he trailed the two X Bar cowhands down into the Pecos brakes and joined them.

This couple had a string of horses and a pack outfit. Strengthened by Pecos, they made a formidable band. Pecos knew where to locate more unbranded stock than any cowhand in Texas. The thicketed canyons were full of cattle, many of them that had never felt an iron. The operations of Williams and Adams were too loose to satisfy Pecos. He tightened them. These two riders were on their way to becoming rustlers very shortly. Pecos did not think he could afford to train with them very long. Still, he had to take risks.

"Listen, you footloose hombres," he said. "I can round up thousands of unbranded stock south of hyar. Hard work an' lots of time, but shore an' we cain't get in trouble."

"We'll take 'em as they come," replied Wess Adams, a craggy faced young rider, dissolute and forceful.

"Pecos has some good idees, Wess," interposed Williams, who was more amenable and less reckless. "So we gotta compromise."

"If you must work out these brakes—which is shore pore judgment—it'd be best to throw together a bunch of say a hundred haid or less, an' drive them to yore buyers once a month."

"A hundred haid an' once a month? Bah!" blurted Adams.

"I'm sidin' with Pecos," said Williams, thoughtfully. "An' then it ain't so damn safe."

"Wal, when it gits hot for us we'll change tactics," rejoined Pecos. "We'll clap on another brand thet nobody ever saw, an' throw the stock out on the range. None of the ranchers will know thet brand is ours. Later when the brands are old we can round up an' drive a big herd without much risk."

"Wess, it's a good idee," ventured Williams. Adams at length gave in with bad grace.

The trio set to work. They did their roping and branding alone; at least Pecos did, and he accounted for as many as both his comrades. In a few days they had a mixed herd of over five score. Williams and Adams started north with this bunch, expecting to drive twenty-five miles a day, which would get them to their market in less than a week. Pecos remained in camp and went on with his riding, roping and branding. He regretted that he had not been able to go into this game alone. However, that required horses and outfit and especially a market, unless he could afford to wait and watch his herd grow. He liked the lonely life and came to love the Rio Pecos. It was now a refuge.

His comrades returned in due course, and Pecos found himself the richer for something in excess of two hundred dollars, more money than he had ever possessed at one time in his life. His exuberance was short-lived; this money had been earned, but not by honest toil and sweat.

In far less than a month Wess Adams had prevailed upon Williams to make another drive north, with all the stock they and Pecos had burned brands on. Pecos entered strong objection, but in vain. He deliberated just which of two courses to pursue—the first, to pick a quarrel with Adams and shoot him, the second, to let his partners go on their perilous way without further resistance. Pecos found the latter more to his liking. He needed to resist this strange tendency to resort to his gun, and if he could keep strict watch in their absence, prepared for anything, so that if they were trailed back, as seemed most likely, he need not be caught. On the other hand, he reasoned that if they never returned, well and good; he would take the outfit and move to a wilder country farther south on the Pecos.

But Adams and Williams came back. They were hard riders, cunning and resourceful, driving mostly at night, and they must have had allies somewhere along the trail. Thus for Pecos the situation remained the same, except that he had another and a larger roll of greenbacks.

From late summer, through autumn and winter, those two indefatigable riders made ten drives to their market in New Mexico. Towards spring they grew bolder, as was inevitable for such characters and as a result of such success. Moreover, Adams returned smelling of strong drink. Therefore, when sometime in April, the two did not return from their drive on time, Pecos was not surprised. Nor was he worried or grieved. He had decided this drive was to be the last for him, under any circumstances.

Pecos had so much money that he did not dare count it; assuredly enough to start him with a ranch of his own somewhere. The Pecos near its junction with the Rio Grande took his fancy, but that had long been the seat of Mexican depredations, and he had had enough to do with Mexicans. He indulged in long cogitations about this future venture. He had been clever to allow Williams and Adams to make the cattle drives to their market—which, after all, was their own wish; nevertheless Pecos felt that he might be implicated, too, when these two riders had gone to the end of their tether. In that case he had only to lie low in hiding for a year or so to be forgotten. Texas was too enormous, too wild, too swiftly changing on its course to empire, for a few unbranded mavericks to be remembered. There were a thousand real rustlers to be contended with before considering that. Sometimes Pecos had his doubts as to the latest status of his comrades. What a slight step it was from branding mavericks to burning brands! Yet therein lay the actual dishonesty. When mavericks grew scarce, as they certainly were decreasing in number down the river as far as Pecos had ridden, Williams and Adams might be expected to resort to burning out of brands.

A week or more beyond the date Pecos had set as the latest for the return of his two partners, he became certain some untoward circumstance had befallen them. They might have been caught; they might have sold this last bunch of stock and departed for other fields, without the formality of returning to give Pecos his share of the proceeds. Adams would have done it, but Williams seemed hardly that kind of a man.

Anyway Pecos moved his camp, choosing a wild and almost inaccessible retreat some miles below. He packed most of the fast diminishing supplies, and he left the pack-horses there with Cinco. A dense thicket choked the mouth of the little side canyon, where it opened on the Pecos, and back of it there were water and grass in abundance. It could not be entered from the mouth, owing to the matted underbrush, and as there were no cattle or horse tracks leading into it there was little danger of pursuers bothering with the place. Pecos had no concern about its being discovered from above.

From here he went forth every day, carrying his rifle and a pocket full of ammunition, to make a slow, cautious way back to the old camp. When his comrades returned it would be time enough to explain his action to them.

On the fourth morning after Pecos had left the old camp, and the eleventh since his partners had been overdue, he sighted a bunch of Indians on the east bank of the river. He had only a glimpse of lean wild forms and ragged mustangs crossing a brake back from the high bank, but that was enough for Pecos Smith. His persistent and unerring watchfulness had at last earned its reward. With the arrival of spring Kiowas or Comanches might be expected to ride down off the Staked Plains to make a raid anywhere in West Texas.

Pecos deliberated awhile. These savages might be on their way upriver, returning from a raid. There was an Indian trail across on that side. The camp that the three maverick hunters had chosen was in a low-walled canyon, well hidden from the west side of the Pecos, but exposed to the other. If Williams and Adams had returned it would almost surely have been the night before, in which case their horses and camp-fire smoke would betray them to the Indians.

Keeping well out of sight, Pecos made his way toward the old camp. He had traveled more than two miles when his sharp eye detected movement and color at the mouth of a ravine on the eastern bank. A band of mounted Indians, that he made sure were Comanches, rode out of the ravine and into the river. A lone string of half naked savages! He counted eighteen. The river was shallow there and could be forded at this stage of the water. Pecos watched them with hard eyes. More than once he had nearly lost his scalp to these painted devils. They crossed without difficulty and disappeared.

Half a mile up the river opened the canyon in which lay the camp Pecos was approaching. He knew that horses could not be ridden up that far. There was a brake, however, between the impassable bank and where the Indians had crossed. Perhaps they would pass up that. At any rate, they were bent upon mischief.

Pecos retraced his steps to a brake where he could get up out of the river bottom. Once out of the ravine, he took to the rocks and brush, making fast time until he got into the vicinity of the gorge he expected the Comanches to work up, when he proceeded very warily. But they had not passed that way. This meant that their procedure must almost certainly be directed against the old camp.

This point was not now far distant, and it appeared certain that Pecos could arrive there ahead of the Comanches, if he chose to risk traversing rather open ground. His first impulse was to risk anything to warn his comrades, provided they had arrived. Sober reason, however, gave him pause. He could warn them as well from the rim of the canyon wall, and be in a much more advantageous position to help them ward off the impending attack.

Nevertheless the moments became fraught with uncertainty. Pecos hoped his comrades had not returned, but he had a queer intuitive conviction that they had. Adams would be sleeping off the effects of liquor and a long ride; Williams was certainly not a wary man around camp, at least this camp in the brakes of the Pecos.

Something not only held Pecos from hurried action, but forced him to make slow detours under cover. Once near the south wall of the canyon he would be secure, as it was exceedingly broken.

As he neared its vicinity he thought he heard a distant neigh of a horse. He waited in suspense. The morning was quite advanced, clear and bright, not a cloud in the sky, with the sun burning the herald of summer near at hand. Buzzards sailed high above the camp. These uncanny birds always annoyed Pecos. A sarcastic enemy had once told Pecos that he would be food for buzzards some day. The enemy had verified that presagement for himself, but Pecos had never forgotten. Buzzards had a strange prescience of death and carrion soon to be visited upon a certain locality. Bees hummed by Pecos as he crouched among the rocks, listening. Presently he went on, eyes and ears strained.

But it was his nose that gave first and sure proof of his sagacity. Smoke! "I shore smell smoke," he whispered.

That meant Williams and Adams were back. The fact shot a cold sense of tragedy through Pecos, which he could not explain on the score of imminent peril. He could not understand it, but it felt so. No more could he have explained his feeling about the buzzards. Three men under cover could stand off a larger force of Indians than this one Pecos had seen crossing the river.

At last Pecos gained the canyon, but some distance above camp, and round a bend. He had to work down along the broken rim among thick thorned bushes and gray sage, the treacherous dagger-spiked *lechuguilla* and the maze of broken rocks.

He soon got out of breath, not being accustomed to long climbs out of his saddle, and this going was very rough. Panting and sweating, he thought it best to rest a little. He imagined he might need the clearest of faculties and all his breath before so very long.

Still back and down from the ragged rim-wall he made his way, not at all sure of where he should peep over in to the canyon. Presently he espied a column of blue smoke lazily rising. He had passed the camp. That was all right, for it placed him between his comrades and the sneaking Comanches.

Pecos got down on his knees and one hand, to crawl toward the rim. He had not proceeded far when he was brought stockstill by a horrid scream abruptly cut off. Cold sweat now broke out over the hot sweat.

"What'n hell? Was thet a hoss or a man?" he whispered low. Then his sensitive ear caught loud angry voices. Whatever was going on down below, the Comanches had not yet made their presence known. Wherefore Pecos made short work of the remaining distance to the rim, coming out in a niche of the wall, covered by brush. He could not be seen; he could get away swiftly; and pursuit was impossible within a reasonable time.

Pecos raised himself to peep down, the voices guiding him. His eyes nearly popped out at sight of four men holding Adams on a horse. He was cursing, bellowing, entreating. They had a lasso round his neck, with an end thrown up over the branch of a tree.

This led Pecos' startled gaze to something dark and moving. It jerked. A man hung by his neck. Williams! He was kicking in a horribly grotesque manner. His distorted face, eyes distended, mouth wide, tongue out, was in plain sight across the canyon.

An instant of paralyzed staring was long enough for Pecos. Adams and Williams had been surprised by cattlemen, who were meting out the law to rustlers. They were hanging them. Pecos had heard of that summary justice coming to the Texas range. His blood froze, only to gush again in a bursting fire. No cattlemen would ever put a noose over his head.

All five men were shouting, but Adams' voice could be heard above the others. Pecos grasped that the coward was trying to beg off or buy his freedom. What a fool! He did not know Texans!

Suddenly Pecos had a lightning-swift realization of his complicity in this tragedy. He was an ally of Adams, though he had never liked or trusted the man. But he had thrown in with them, he had helped them brand mavericks; he had shared their ill-gotten spoils. He did not consider himself a rustler. But it was monstrously evident that these cowmen regarded Adams and Williams as rustlers.

This, then, was the inevitable climax Pecos had dreaded. He had killed Sawtell because he had been unjustly accused. But if he killed here, in defense of the comrades who had been outlawed by the range, he would be an outlaw himself.

Pecos made his choice instantly. His code left him no alternative. He cocked and raised his rifle, deadly sure of saving Adams' life.

"Stretch hemp!" yelled the leader, in a stentorian voice. And he heaved on the rope, while two of his men wheeled from the victim to assist.

Even as Pecos swerved the rifle to align its sights with this leader, Adams was jerked half out of the saddle.

Then from below Pecos, and to his right, boomed a buffalo gun. The leader of that hanging squad uttered a hoarse cry. Dropping the rope, he staggered, arms spread wide to fall into the grass.

Before Adams had sunk back into the saddle a roar of heavy rifles followed the first report, accompanied by the hideous war cry of Comanches.

Pecos went stiff in every muscle. He lowered his rifle, his gaze riveted on the terrible scene opposite. Another cattleman fell. The horse leaped up, throwing Adams off. It plunged down, to kick with all four hoofs in the air, suddenly to sag quiet. Adams had been crippled. Still with the noose around his neck he tried to crawl. The rope, which had been over a branch, caught up in the tree. While Adams frantically pulled to free it he received more bullets and slid face forward. The third cattleman leaped behind the tree. And the fourth was brought down before he could reach shelter behind the rocks. But he was not killed. With a broken leg at least, he flopped behind the fallen horse.

Puffs of blue smoke rose from behind the tree. Pecos saw the man behind the horse slide rifle out of its saddle-sheath to level it and fire.

Pecos crawled out of the niche to a point where he could see below. Fortune favored him, as it ruled disaster to the Comanches. Pecos watched them slipping, sliding, gliding, down among the rocks, into the thicket that fringed that side of the canyon. They filled the air with their wild cries of hate and exultance. Emboldened by the success of their surprise attack, they were charging. Still they kept shooting as fast as they could reload, and the din of the heavy rifles was so loud that Pecos could scarcely hear the rapid fire from the two cattlemen.

At this juncture Pecos grimly entered the engagement. He could not be seen and his lighter calibre rifle scarcely heard. The last line of the gliding Comanches appeared scarcely fifty feet below him. When Pecos drew a quick bead on a naked red back he pulled the trigger, then looked for another Indian. He fired seven shots in less than two minutes.

While he reloaded he saw the front line of savages spread to left and right. At least six of these, in their thirst for blood charged out of the thicket. Pecos discerned arrows flying like glints of light through the air, some to stick in the carcass of the horse, others in the tree.

Suddenly the cattleman who had been firing from behind the tree lunged into sight with an arrow through his middle. Evidently a cunning redskin far to the right had been able to hit him. One after another, he killed the three foremost charging Comanches. The others turned tail to flee.

Here Pecos got into action again, killing the Indian nearest him. But it was a blunder, for the other two, out in the open, discovered him, and fled along the edge of the thicket, screeching like demons. The remaining four or five flashed here and there among the rocks, in open patches in the brush. Pecos connected with another, but he was sure not fatally.

Suddenly the yelling ceased. Pecos saw that the attack had been turned into a rout. No doubt the Comanches supposed reinforcements had arrived. No sign, no sound! The canyon had become appallingly silent. Looking across, Pecos was in time to see the cattleman who had come out from behind the tree sink to his knees. His smoking gun dropped, and his hands pressed round the arrowshaft in his abdomen. He fell forward, which action could only have driven the arrow deeper. Pecos veered his searching gaze to the crippled man behind the horse. He could not be seen. But the rifle had slid over on this side of the horse—a significant and ominous sign. Then on the instant, proving the brevity of that fatal fight, Williams kicked his last in the hanging noose.

CHAPTER SEVEN

There was no fear that the remaining few Comanches would return. Nevertheless, Pecos got back up on the level rim and ran down to the wall that dropped off into the river. Several hundred yards below he espied them in great haste driving their ponies into the water. Presently Pecos made out five riders, one of whom was holding a sixth Indian, badly crippled, on his mount.

The range was too far for accurate shooting, nevertheless Pecos thought that while hurrying their retreat he might hit one. So from behind his covert he fired seven more shots. The bullets all fell short of a few feet, sending up white splashes, but they were almost as effective as if they had found their mark. The Comanches raced madly across the river, to disappear in a brake in the bank.

Reloading, Pecos retraced his steps to a point above camp where he could get down over the wall. He had satisfied himself fully that there were no crippled Indians, so he hurried to the scene of the hanging.

It was ghastlier than any Pecos had ever heard of, tragic and common as were fights in Texas. The swinging Williams, black in the face; the dead horse full of arrows; the cattleman lying on his face, with a bloody barb protruding far from his back—these were the details which lent most sinister and grisly aspect.

"All daid!" muttered Pecos. Then the choking rattle of blood in a man's throat informed Pecos that he was wrong. Not Adams, not the brained man behind the horse—it was the fellow with the arrow through his middle.

Pecos made haste to turn him over on his side. He was a stranger to Pecos, a man of middle age, apparently not a Texan, and he was alive, conscious, but dying. He called incoherently for water. Pecos rushed to the packs that he had stowed away under the wall, and seizing a vessel he dashed to fill it at the spring.

A moment later while Pecos held the man's head so he could drink it became more pitifully evident that he was mortally hurt.

"They're gone," he said, huskily.

"Shore. I saw the last of them crossin' the river."

"Comanche hell-hounds. . . . How many'd we do fer?"

"Eleven, I reckon, an' one crippled."

"You all alone?"

"Yes. I had the drop on them, as I was back up on the rocks."

"Wal, they spoiled our necktie party—an' you spoiled their game. . . . Reckon it—was fair. . . . Air my outfit all daid?"

"Yes, an' I'm afraid yore a gonner, too."

"Thet's a safe bet. . . . Gimme another drink?"

"Any message you want sent?" queried Pecos, presently.

"None, onless you happen to—meet this Pecos Smith," replied the other, his pale blue eyes steady on Pecos.

"Wal, thet's likely, as I happen to be Smith."

"I reckoned so. . . . But was you burnin' brands with Williams an Adams?"

"No! . . . So thet's what you was hangin' them fer. . . . They double-crossed me. The deal I made with them was maverick-brandin'."

"Wal, they shore been cheatin' you. The Heald boys spoke well of you, Smith. It's Breen Sawtell, brother of Beckman's foreman who you shot at Healds'—he's the fellar who's got it in fer you."

"Breen Sawtell? . . . Shore don't know him. What's he look like?"

"Daid ringer fer his brother. . . . An' see hyar, Pecos Smith, as I'm aboot to cash, it won't hurt me none to tell you somethin'. As I got it Breen Sawtell was stealin' his own brother's stock. Thet's why he put him on your trail, as he has—of others. . . . Want another—drink."

"Ahuh. An' why'd he pick on me?" returned Pecos, after he had given the failing man the last of the water.

"Wal, they do say Breen had a look in at Healds'—fer the gurl, you know—until you rode along."

"Bill never told me thet," exclaimed Pecos, aghast.

"Wal, it's true. . . . Smith, things air—gettin' sort of dark—an' I'm cold."

"It's kinda tough—to croak hyar, with an Indian arrow in yore gizzard," declared Pecos, feelingly.

"All in—the day's—ride," panted the dying man. "Gawd—I'm glad—thet burnin's over."

"Yeah, it's aboot all over."

"Smith, you strike me—as bein' too—good a fellar—fer rustlers like them—X Bar cowhands."

"If I'm a rustler, they made me one," declared Pecos, with passion.

"Wal, they're daid—an' nobody can hyar aboot this. . . . Chuck the game—Smith," gasped the other.

Pecos had a poignant cry on his lips, but it never left them. The cattleman's last conscious look was unforgettable, in that it changed from one of kindness to the stranger he had pursued, to a somber divination of his own lonely end. Then his senses failed, and a moment later he quivered with a cough and lay still. He had ceased to breathe.

Pecos got up to contemplate the scene. And his mind worked fast. These four cattlemen would eventually be trailed. The thing for Pecos to do was to leave everything precisely as he saw it then. Shrewd trackers might suspect the presence of an outside hand in this massacre, especially if they were keen enough to figure on the Comanches shot from the canyon wall; nevertheless Pecos considered it wisest to leave all the bodies as they lay.

There was nothing on them that he wanted, except the money he knew he would find on Adams and Williams. This he secured, in the latter's case by untying the rope and letting him down. On second thought, however, Pecos took Adams' gun, a box of ammunition, and a sack of fresh food supplies, all of which, with his rifle, made a pretty heavy burden to carry down to his own camp.

By resting frequently he made the three miles in somewhat less than two hours, which time brought the day to about noon.

Pecos decided to pack at once and strike south. A hundred miles down the Pecos would put him in another world, so far as Breen Sawtell and his ilk were concerned. He thought of Don Felipe, of McKeever, both of whom he wished to avoid, for very different reasons. Still, if he happened to encounter the trail driver it would be of no great moment, except that Pecos preferred to be unseen by anyone who knew him for a long time.

There was not a single settlement until Eagle's Nest, just above where the Pecos River joined the Rio Grande. That probably would have grown, in the years since Pecos had ridden north.

Saddling Cinco and packing the other horse were soon accomplished. What to do with all the money he had Pecos was at a loss to decide. He could not carry it all on his person, as it made too much bulk and would certainly be observed if he encountered any riders. Finally he selected out of the dozen rolls of bills all those of large denomination, and these he stowed away in deep pockets. The rest he secreted in the lining of his heavy coat, which he tied back of his saddle. Handling this money made Pecos sweat from sheer excitement. He could not persuade himself that he came by it in strict honesty, though he certainly had not stolen it. The facts narrowed down to this—some Texas ranchers had collectively lost a good many head of stock and he had amassed a small fortune.

Never had Pecos set out on a long ride with faculties more keenly alert. As soon as he had placed a score of miles between him and the camp of dead men he would breathe freer and look only ahead.

That night he camped across from Alkali Lake, a place on the east bank which he knew less well than the west side of the Pecos.

Adobe Wells, to which another day's travel brought him, was also on the opposite side of the river. Likewise Frazier's Crossing, which he was careful to pass at night, and Dapper's Bend and Red Bluffs, were to be feared more from the eastern shore. Another ten-hour ride gained Castle Gap Canyon, within striking distance of the most notable, dangerous, yet solitary point on the Rio Pecos, no less than the old ford of the Spaniards—Horsehead Crossing.

Much as Pecos loved lonesome places, he could not abide this haunted ford. He would not even camp there, but pushed on into the wilderness of twisted, swelling, greasewood-spotted ridges and the shallow ravines that ran between. Canyons were few along this somber reach of the Pecos, there being only at long intervals a break in the lofty walls. At times Pecos could see the opposite side of the canyon, with its high rim wall, and part of the shaggy-brushed and rock-ribbed slope; at other times the road curved far west of the river.

"Tough country on hosses an' cattle, Cinco," said Pecos. "But the grass is heah, an' the water is there. Nothin' on earth to keep a rancher from gettin' rich, 'cept hard work, greasers, an' redskins."

These were handicaps which Pecos discovered, two days later, had not deterred a rancher or ranchers from throwing cattle onto that rocky range. He did not see many cows or steers at one given point, but in the aggregate, after a day's ride, they amounted to a surprisingly large number. Not so surprising, but certainly more significant to Pecos was the fact that he saw few calves.

Of ranchers, however, there was no sign. Cowhands probably had to ride fifty miles or more to round up these cattle. Pecos did not envy them the job on that desolate range. But the farther he rode south, finding, if anything, an increase in cattle tracks, the more it was driven home to him that somewhere along these reaches of the Pecos, there was an ideal location for his own cherished plan to materialize. Still, he was not far enough south, though he calculated he had come somewhere near a hundred miles. The trails and roads, however, had been devious. Pecos pushed on. He must not forget another thing, that he should lie low for months before starting in the ranching game. And in the ensuing days he was to recognize that the road on which he traveled south was not the trail on which he had come north.

Therefore when he rode out of a great depression to higher ground to espy the red adobe and gray stone shacks of Eagle's Nest, half hidden by green trees, and the gigantic bluff of the Rio Grande beyond, he was neither surprised nor sorry. Perhaps it was just as well, or better: something unforeseen always guided his solitary steps.

There did not appear, at a moment's glance, any appreciable change in Eagle's

Nest; still, as he drew near he made out a number of adobe houses that he did not remember, and lastly a new gray structure, apparently a frame one, alongside the low flat stone and adobe post run by Dale Shevlin.

It was not an hour for the inhabitants, especially the Mexicans, to be stirring. Pecos espied a wagon far down the wide street, and there were half a dozen sleepy horses distributed from the corner of Shevlin's place past the new gray house.

Pecos got off in the shade of some trees, and tying his horses looked around for some one to question. Shevlin would scarcely remember him, and he was not likely to encounter Felipe there. Nevertheless, Pecos did not want to be recognized. There were difficulties, however, that stood in the way of his desires. He had about run out of food supplies and he was hungry; moreover, he could not avoid towns and people forever. It was here that his temper had to be encountered.

Finally he sat down in the shade. To all outward appearance Eagle's Nest was having a siesta. Presently Pecos espied a Mexican far down the street toward the Rio Grande, which flowed under the big bluff just back of the town. Then he became aware of voices in Shevlin's place. There were two doors, one opening into the post, the other into the saloon but Pecos could not tell from which the voices came. Several men were talking, evidently all at once. Pecos was amused. Men were a queer lot, always squabbling, particularly in the neighborhood of red liquor.

A moment later several persons emerged from the post, the foremost of whom was a barefooted boy who ran out into the street, gazing back over his shoulder. He did not appear exactly scared, but he certainly was excited.

Pecos accosted him. "Say, sonny, what's goin' on aboot heah?"

This did scare the youngster, as he had not observed the vaquero. He was bout to bolt when Pecos' friendly smile disarmed him.

"Aw, I—never seen you."

"No wonder, son. You shore was lookin' hard back there. What's goin' on in Dale Shevlin' place?"

"He ain't there no more."

"Wal, you don't say? What's become of Dale?"

"Somebody knifed him in the back."

"Too bad. Dale was a white man. Did he have any family?"

"Yes, but Don Felipe drove them off. He runs both store an' saloon now."

"Aho. He does? Wal, thet's news. . . . Is Don Felipe heah now?"

"No, sir. He stays a good deal in Rockfort, where they say he sells cattle to Chisholm trail drivers."

"Who runs these places?"

"Man from New Orleans. Frenchy, we call him. His name is Conrad Brasee. He has two Mexicans workin' for him, an' a white bartender. Don't know his name. He just got to Eagle's Nest."

"Come heah, Johnny," said Pecos, persuasively. "I'm a rider, a Texan, an' shore yore friend. Fact is I've got a dollar thet's burnin' a hole in my vest pocket. You want it?"

"Betcha," retorted the lad, with wide-open eyes, approaching with diminishing reluctance.

"There. Now tell me some more. I'm restin' an' darned lonesome. It's good to listen to some news," went on Pecos. "So Don Felipe's doin' things around Eagle's Nest? He must be a greaser, or a Mexican shore."

"He's more white than Mex. But he's a greaser, all right," replied the boy, his shrewd gray eyes, belonging unmistakably to the breed of Texans who hated anything Mexican, seeking Pecos' with subtle meaning.

"How's the Don stand in Eagle's Nest?"

"Mister, he 'most runs it. But nobody likes him. Why, he's killed seven men, three of them white."

"Holy smoke! He's a bad hombre," declared Pecos, in assumed wonder. As a matter of fact he was surprised, because Felipe, when Pecos left him, had a record of only four killings, just one of whom had been reputed to be a white man, and that a foreigner. "So Don Felipe is sellin' cattle to Chisholm trail drivers. What's become of McKeever? He used to drive up heah."

"He made his last trip 'most a year ago. My dad says McKeever is drivin' up the Chisholm trail now."

"Ah, I see. Cattle driftin' south from heah. . . . Don Felipe's ranch is down the Pecos, isn't it?"

"Yes, sir. Devil's River. But his vaqueros are rakin' the brakes farther up than Eagle's Nest."

"Does yore dad say whether Felipe's vaqueros are brandin' mavericks—or burnin' brands?" inquired Pecos, casually.

The lad hesitated at that, which was significant enough for Pecos.

"I—I— He never said," at length the lad faltered. "For goodness' sake, Mister, don't get the idee——"

"Son, I was just thinkin' out loud. Forget thet. . . . Any other cattleman workin' the river near heah?"

"Yes, sir. Hails from New Mexico. Calls himself Sawtell. Funny name."

A slight vibration, like a shooting spark, ran along Pecos' nerves. Sawtell! He had once had a presentiment that he was not through with that name. Certainly his questioning of the lad had not been idle, but it had scarcely been more than curiosity. He desired to avoid Don Felipe rather than be thrown across his path again. His queries, however, had led somewhere. Pecos grew soundly interested, and delved in his mind.

"Who's the big darky over there?" he asked, to keep the lad talking. "Is he drunk?"

"Oh no, sir! Thet's Sambo, a good nigger if there ever was one. He came hyar as vaquero to Kurnel Lambeth, who was killed a year or so ago."

"Lambeth. Wal! . . . I've heahed of him. . . . Wal, what's the nigger look so down aboot, if he isn't drunk?"

"It's because Brasee shet Terrill up—'cause he didn't have no money to pay what was owin'. That was yestiddy. Sambo got hyar this mawnin'. He cain't do nothin'. He wasn't packin' no gun. They throwed him oot fer makin' such a fuss aboot Terrill."

"Who's Terrill?"

"This Terrill is the finest young feller who ever come to Eagle's Nest. But he ain't hyar often. Once a month, mebbe. He's the son of thet Kurnel Lambeth, an' now boss of the nigger. They have a ranch somewhere up the Pecos; Dad says Lambeth was rich in cattle a couple of years ago. But he wouldn't sell at six dollars a haid. An' now most of his cattle are gone. An' they're so poor they cain't pay fer grub."

"Cattle gone. Seems like I've heahed such words before. Gone where, son?"

The boy laughed. "You're west of the Pecos, Señor."

"So I am! I shore 'most forgot," drawled Pecos. "Wal, heah's another peso."

"Oh sir, thank you. I—I never had so much money. You must be orful rich. . . . Oh, if you are—pay Terrill's bill an' get him oot!"

"Out of where? There's no jail heah."

"Yes there is—or what Brasee calls his jail. It's a red 'dobe back of the post. The bartender throws drunken greasers in there, too. Terrill is shet in with one now."

"Wal, this is gettin' warm, boy. Is this Brasee a sheriff, too?"

"Naw, sheriff nothin'. He plays at it. There ain't no law west of the Pecos, Señor. You jest bet Brasee never fools with a Texan."

"Ahuh. I savvy. Wal, I'll go over an' get your friend Terrill out," drawled Pecos, as he arose.

The lad gave him a wondering, grateful look, and bounded away, proving in his flight that whatever the issue might have been before, it was not something to lend wings to his feet.

Pecos sauntered across toward the downcast negro. Things happened to Pecos in every conceivable way. He never learned a lesson. At every turn he encountered selfishness, crookedness, greed, brutality, bloodshed, and murder. Wherever one of these attributes flourished there was some boy or man or woman suffering loss or pain or bereavement.

Pecos Smith had known negro slaves as worthy as any white man, though he had the Southerner's contempt for most of the black trash. This man, Sambo, had the build of a vaquero, and Pecos remembered him. His boots and spurs gave further proof to Pecos. Negro vaqueros were so rare that they were remarkable. If Pecos needed anything more than recognition to heighten his ever-ready sympathy, here it was.

"Howdy, Sambo! What's it all aboot?" he queried, kindly.

The negro started violently out of his dull misery and rolled his dark eyes at Pecos from head to foot, lingering a moment at the gun sheath so prominent and low on Pecos's left thigh.

"Yas, suh. I'se Sambo, suh. What yo say, suh?"

"A lad told me you were in trouble."

"Gawd, suh, I is, I is. Turrible trubble. . . . But 'scuse me, Mister, who yo' is? Don' I know yo'?"

"Wal, Sambo, I might be a friend in need," replied Pecos, putting a hand on the negro's shoulder. As he did so the Mexican and white man whom he had observed emerging from the post went back in rather precipitately.

"Man, yo' lend me dat gun an' I'll believe yose a friend," declared the negro, suddenly flaring.

"What'll you do, Sambo?"

"I'll kill dat cussed Brasee, sho as yore borned."

"But thet'll get you into more trouble, Sambo. . . . Come over away from thet door. . . . Now don't be afraid to talk. Tell me your story, quick an' straight."

Thus admonished, the negro seemed to collect his wits. "You ought to remember me, suh. I'se Sambo, vaquero fo' Kuhnel Lambeth, dat yo' found lost up on the Crossin'. We're from east Texas an' we come out heah 'mos' five years ago. We druv in a herd of cattle an' two years ago we had 'mos' ten thousand haid. . . . Marse Lambeth no sell when he ought. De rustlers done found us, suh, an' dey—or sumbody killed him. Now we's pore. . . . Marse Lambeth's b-boy, Massa Terrill, rid ovah heah yes'day alone. We never knowed till dis mawnin'. I rid my hawse 'mos' to deff. But Brasee hit me over de haid wid something. He got Massa Rill shet up in thet 'dobe shack wid a greaser. . . . Lemme dat gun, man, an' I show yo'."

"Hold yore hosses, Sambo. . . . What'd Brasee shet up young Terrill for?"

"He swears fo' money det Kuhnel Lambeth owes. But dat's only a 'scuse, stranger. Det —— —— Don Felipe an' his pardner, Breen Sawtell, air behin' it.

Dey was upriver—dey was gonna drive Marse Lambeth out. But dey couldn', an' Ah sho suspec's dat outfit made way wif de Kuhnel. My woman Mauree knows, suh. It come to her in a dream. . . . Dey stole mos' of our stock, suh, an' now it's Massa Rill they'se after."

"Wal, Sambo, come with me," replied Pecos, quietly, as he wheeled back toward the door of the post. In any case he had meant to buy young Lambeth's freedom, and he had asked for the negro's story just for verification. All at once the thing had assumed proportions, and that complex spirit of his had extracted stern purpose out of what had seemed trivial.

Pecos entered the store. It had been enlarged since his last visit to Eagle's Nest. A more complete stock of merchandise filled shelves and cluttered up the place so that there was scarcely room to move about. A Mexican made pretense of work, but the side slant of his beady black eyes told Pecos what he was interested in. Behind a counter stood a man in his shirt sleeves. He was fat and pale, and his dark thin hair fell over his brow, almost to his large, ghoulish eyes. For the rest he had a long, sharp nose, a small mouth, and a peaked chin with a dimple in the middle.

For years one of Pecos Smith's essential habits had been to look at men, to gauge them in one lightning-swift glance. The fact that he had been able to do so in some instances accounted for the fact that he was still alive.

"Howdy. Air you Brasee?" drawled Pecos.

CHAPTER EIGHT

This new keeper of Eagle's Nest's only store looked to Pecos more like a New Orleans creole gambler than anything else.

"Yes, I'm Brasee. What you want?" he returned, in a voice with a slight accent, which, however, did not hint of negro taint.

"Wal, I'm sort of close to the Lambeth family," announced Pecos, coldly. "Not exactly a blood relation. Just come from east Texas. An' I'm some concerned to hear the Colonel is daid an' young Terrill is shet up in a shed of yourn. How aboot thet last, Brasee?"

"That's none of your business."

"Shore it is, Mister Brasee," went on Pecos, softly. This man no more knew Texans of Pecos' stripe than he would have been able to contend with them. Pecos' careless, easy manner misled him. "I come a long way to see young Terrill. He must be growed to quite a boy by now. An' I want to see him."

"You can't see him."

"What right had you to shet him up in a shed with a drunken greaser?"

Brasee gazed hard at Pecos, unable to meet him on common ground. There was something about Pecos that obstructed his will, but he did not know it. He had not long been west of the Pecos.

"Matter of owin' yu money, Sambo heah says," went on Pecos, indicating the glaring negro.

"Yes, Lambeth owes for the winter's supplies."

"How much?"

"No matter, Señor."

"It matters a hell of a lot," retorted Pecos, subtly changing. "If yore a sheriff or a Texas Ranger, show yore badge."

This Brasee did not attempt to do, as Pecos had known very well he would not.

"Ahuh. Playin' the law, eh? I've seen thet done before in Texas. But it shore doesn't make for long life. . . . How much does this boy owe?"

"Two hundred—ten dollars," replied Brasee, swallowing hard.

Pecos counted out that amount from a generous roll of bills and pitched it to Brasee. He had not failed to catch the greedy glitter in this man's hungry eyes; nor had Pecos missed other significant things. Dale Shevlin's place had degenerated into a questionable den. There was another man listening, perhaps watching, just inside the half-closed door that opened into the saloon.

"Write out a receipt," said Pecos as he reached behind to grasp the first thing available to throw. It happened to be a sack of salt, at least ten pounds in weight. Quick as a flash Pecos flung it at the door. Then followed three distinct sounds—the bang of the bag striking the door, then a solid thump of the violently moved door colliding with something soft, and lastly a sodden slump of that something on the floor. The door, having swung wide, disclosed a man struggling to a sitting posture, one hand fumbling at his bloody, flattened nose.

"Say, yu," demanded Pecos. "How'n hell do I know what yu was listenin' for behind thet door? . . . What kind of a den air yu runnin', Brasee?"

Brasee rolled up the scattered bills with hands not perfectly steady. Then, using a pencil, he scribbled something on a piece of paper.

"There's your receipt, Señor. But I'm holding young Lambeth till Felipe comes."

"Yu just think yu air. Say, how do yu know I'm not a Texas Ranger?"

"Rangers don't come west of the Pecos," snapped Brasee, but he was wholly uncomfortable and uncertain.

"Wal, anythin' can happen west of the Pecos. An' thet's a hunch," flashed the vaquero. "Sambo, grab thet ax an' come with me."

Pecos backed out of the store. Contempt for such men as Felipe gathered around him did not make Pecos careless. Sambo had preceded him.

"I knowed it, boss, I sho knowed it," declared the negro, rolling his eyes.

"What'd you know, Sambo?"

"Dat Brasee wus yaller clean to his gizzard. But I sho kept my eye on de greaser. I'd 'a' busted him."

"Wal, I was watchin' him, too. Thet's a low-down outfit, Sambo. They cain't last hyar. . . . Show me this calaboose where they stuck yore young Lambeth."

Some little distance back of the store stood a new adobe hut, small and square, with a wooden door fastened by a chain and padlock. Pecos walked around the structure, wondering where any air could get in. Sambo banged on the door.

"Massa Rill, is yo' dar?" he called, his voice thick and rich.

"Oh, Sambo! . . . If you don't—get me out—I'll soon be daid," came a plaintive reply.

"Tell him to stand aside from the door. We've got to break it in," directed Pecos.

"Git away f'om dat do', honey, 'cause I'se a-gwine to busticate it."

Pecos rather expected some interference from Brasee, possibly a shot from the back of the store. But there was no sign from that direction that anyone was interested in Sambo's lusty blows with the ax. The powerful negro soon sent the door crashing in.

"Whar yo' is, Massa Rill?" he shouted, breathing like a huge bellows.

Pecos expected to recognize a boy he tried to remember, but he saw a slender, well-formed youth stagger out into the sunlight. He wore a ragged gray coat and overalls and top boots, all of which were covered with dirt and grass. His battered black sombrero was pulled well down, shading big, deep eyes of a hue Pecos could not discern, and a tanned, clean-cut face. The sombrero, however, showed a tuft of glossy hair through a hole in its crown, and also straggling locks from under the brim. Pecos thought Sambo could be excused for his anxiety over this fine-looking youth.

"Sambo, I almost—smothered," gasped young Lambeth.

"Whar's det greaser dey done throwed in wid yo'?"

"He was let out this mawnin', still drunk."

Then Lambeth espied Pecos and gave a slight start. Pecos felt those strange, big eyes sweep over him, back again to his face, to fasten there a moment, and then revert to Sambo.

"Massa Rill, yo' have to thank dis heah gennelman fo' gettin' yo' out," said the negro, warmly.

"Oh, thank you, sir," said the boy, staring strangely at Pecos. There was deep gratitude in his voice, although his demeanor was shy.

"Massa Rill, it was dis way. I nebber discubbered yo' had left home till dis mawnin'," spoke up Sambo. "Den I rid some. I sho did. But dat Brasee banged me ovah my haid an' throwed me out. I wus plannin' to kill him when dis old friend of ours come up. 'Pears yo' little friend Bobby tole him 'boot us. An' he sed he'd get yo' out, Massa Rill. So we goes in. An' det yaller Brasee sho tuk water. Yo' bill is paid at de sto' an' you see how we busticated dis do' heah."

"Paid! . . . Sambo, did you pay it?"

"Me? laws amassy! No, Massa Rill, it was him."

Pecos stood listening and watching with an amused smile at the eloquent Sambo and the excited youth. How little it took sometimes to make people happy! But when Lambeth wheeled suddenly with face flushed and eyes alight, Pecos quite lost his sense of the casualness of the moment. Somehow there was a significance in the occasion for which Pecos was unable to account.

"Pecos Smith! . . . I remember you. How very—good of you—sir!" exclaimed young Lambeth, extending his hand. It felt small and nervous to Pecos', but it nevertheless was hard and strong. "I am Terrill Lambeth. . . . You remember me?"

"Wal, I reckon I do—now," replied Pecos.

"Please tell me where you are staying—where I can find you. Else how can I ever repay the debt?"

"Wal, I reckon you needn't worry none aboot thet."

"But I shall. . . . You have befriended us both. Please tell me your address?"

"'Most the same, Lambeth. . . . Pecos Smith, Texas, west of the Pecos," he drawled.

"Oh, you're not serious," laughed Lambeth.

"Massa Rill, he sho looks Texas an' talks Pecos," interposed Sambo, with a huge grin.

"Indeed yes," replied Terrill. "Sambo, I rode my pinto pony in here yesterday. Left him in front of the store. Bobby might have him."

They walked across the wide street, with Pecos in advance. Presently, emerging from behind the post, he espied his horses as he had left them.

"Lambeth, I'd like to talk somethin' over with yu," said Pecos, presently. "We can set down over heah in the shade. How aboot it?"

"I'll be glad to," replied the youth. "Sambo, you run over to Bobby's. See if he's got my pony. . . . I'm starved and very thirsty."

An idea had taken root in Pecos' mind—one that refused several attempts to dislodge it. The boy Bobby, the negro Sambo, and recognition of young Lambeth had each in succession given it impetus. An opportunity knocked at Pecos' door.

"Wal, it's shore nice heah," began Pecos, when they had found shady seats on the grass not far from Pecos' horses. "Thet boy yu call Bobby told me things an' so did yore nigger. I'm plumb curious, Lambeth, an' I'd like to ask yu a few questions."

"Fire away. People do get curious aboot me. I don't wonder. Only I'm mum as an oyster. But you're shore different—and I'll tell you anything I—I can."

"Yu from eastern Texas?"

"Yes. We lived on a plantation near the Louisiana line. The war ruined my dad. . . . Mother died before he came home. There was nothing left. Dad decided to go west. When we were aboot ready to start my uncle died—he had been in the war, too—and left Dad some money. But we started west, anyhow. Dad had freed our slaves. Sambo and his wife, Mauree, refused to leave us. . . . We had a canvas-covered wagon and eight horses. I rode and I drove and I rode for eight months—all the way across Texas. Toward the end of that journey Dad picked up cattle. Texas longhorns! You found us lost up the Pecos. After you guided us to Horsehead Crossing we drove the Pecos and worked down this side of the river, heading the brakes until Dad found a place that suited him. . . . There we started ranching. Two years ago we had around ten thousand haid. We were rich. But Dad wouldn't sell. Aboot that time we began to see our stock fade away. There were riders in the brakes. Dad made an enemy of a half-breed cattleman named Don Felipe. Sambo was shot at twice. . . . Then . . . then . . . Oh, it hurts so—to bring it back."

"Yore dad was killed," interposed Pecos, gently, as the youth averted his face.

"Yes. . . . He was—murdered," went on Lambeth. "Found with an arrow through his body. Felipe and his vaqueros said it was the work of Comanches. But I *know* better. Many times the Indians rode out on the river bluff across from my home. They watched us. They shot guns and arrows into the river. But bullets and arrows could not reach halfway. The Indians could not get across for miles above and below. They never tried. So I *know* Comanches never killed my dad. . . . From that time our fortunes fell. Felipe took on a partner named Sawtell—a villain who had hounded me. Sambo and I could not keep track of stock. You see our range went twenty miles up river and more down. And in low water our cattle crossed the river. There are hundreds, maybe thousands of longhorns under the east wall of the Pecos. They are mine. But how can I ever get them? No doubt Felipe and Sawtell will get them eventually. . . . Oh, Mister Smith, I've been cautioned not to say that. Because I can prove nothing. . . . But I've seen Felipe's vaqueros steal our cattle. Brand-blotters! . . . Well, it's grown harder lately. We had to have supplies. Dad had gone in debt for them. And this last winter I had to. Brasee would not take cattle in payment. . . . Last and worse—they've waylaid me—tried to catch me alone. . . . Oh, I can't tell you the half. . . . But yesterday this Brasee dragged me—forced me into that stinking dungeon—locked me in. . . . There, Mister Smith, have I anticipated all your questions?"

"Yu can call me Pecos," responded the vaquero, thoughtfully. "Wal, wal, it's a tough story, Terrill, 'most as tough as mine. But dog-gone! What I cain't understand is why, yu bein' shore old Texas stock, yu didn't kill this half-breed greaser an' his partner. Yu must be all of fifteen years old, ain't you?"

"Si, Señor," replied Terrill, with a little laugh. "I'm all of fifteen."

"Wal, thet's old enough to handle a gun."

"I can. I've shot buffalo, deer, wolves, panthers, javelin, mean old mossy-horns. But never a—a man. I might have, lately, if all our guns hadn't been stolen."

"Wal, Terrill, I'll shore have to kill Don Felipe an' Breen Sawtell fer yu," mused Pecos, softly, marveling that he had not long ago decided that this deed was decreed for him.

"Mister Smith! . . . *Pecos,* you can't be serious!" cried the youth.

"Never was so serious before. . . . Would yu want to heah somethin' aboot me?" drawled Pecos.

"Yes," whispered Lambeth, evidently overcome.

"An' will yu swear yu'll never tell what I tell yu?"

"I—I swear, Pecos," said Terrill, excitedly.

"Wal, yore not the only orphan in Texas. . . . I come of one of the old families, Terrill. But I never had much schoolin' or home influence. An' so I just growed up a vaquero. The years I spent in Mexico were good an' bad fer me. . . . Wal, I rode through heah first a few years ago, with thet trail driver, McKeever. An' last time, up at Santa Fé, I got reckless with my trigger finger again. Dog-gone it, there was always some hombre thet needed shootin'. . . . My last job was on the H H outfit up the river. An' I was almost happy. There was a girl I liked awful well, but never had the nerve to say so. An' the day I had to go . . . Wal, thet's not goin' to interest yu, an' maybe I was wrong. . . . Anyway, I got accused of rustlin' by one Sawtell, brother of this same Breen Sawtell thet's been houndin' yu. Course I had to kill him. Thet made me so sore I got to feelin' I might as well have the game as the blame. So I throwed in with two shady cowhands an' took to rustlin'."

Terrill gasped at that. The boy in his excitement pulled off the old sombrero to crumple it in his hands. Whereupon Pecos had his first clear view of the lad. He was surprisingly young and his clean, tanned cheeks bore not a vestige of downy beard. Indded, he looked like a very pretty girl, notwithstanding the strong chin, the sad, almost stern lips. His eyes were large and a very dark blue, almost purple.

"Wal, it's my conscience that accuses me of rustlin'," went on Pecos, presently. "But as a matter of fact, Terrill, I wasn't no rustler. My game was brandin' mavericks, an' yu know thet's not crooked. Every cowman in Texas has done it. Only the drawback was thet I knowed damn well thet not one of those calves could be mine. There's the difference. A cowhand with a small herd grazin' aboot can brand a maverick with a kind of satisfaction. But shore I couldn't. . . . Wal, thet went on all last winter. My pardners drove stock to their market in New Mexico while I stayed in camp. The last time they were trailed to our camp. Shore I wasn't there. I happened to be watchin' a bunch of redskins thet were crossin' the river. To make it short, when I sneaked back to camp, there was four cattlemen very busy with my pards. They'd already hanged one an' had a rope on the other. They were haulin' him up when hell busted loose right under me. The Comanches had sneaked up on the camp. There was a pretty lively fight in which I took part from the hillside. When what was left of the Indians had run off I found only one white man alive an' he was dyin'. He told me my pards had been burnin' brands. Yu see, they double-crossed me, for I never saw a haid of stock they drove, except my mavericks. Thet deal made me a rustler when I'm really not one atall. Do yu reckon I am?"

"No, you're not a rustler—at heart," replied Terrill, soberly. "Dad used to put our brand on mavericks. He thought that was honest. So do I."

"Much obliged, boy. Thet shore makes me feel better, now it's off my conscience. An' I reckon I can hit yu for a job."

"Job!" echoed Lambeth.

"Shore. I hate to brag. But there's nothin' I cain't do with a rope. I'll bet I could find a thousand calves thet yu never dreamed of in those brakes."

"You mean ride for me? Be my—my vaquero?"

"Yeah. I'm reckonin' yu need one," drawled Pecos, pleased with the effect of his story and proposition.

"It would be—wonderful. . . . But I have no money."

"Wal, I'd trust yu."

"You'd *trust* me?"

"Shore, I would, if yu believed in me."

"What do you mean?"

"Thet I'm no thief. Thet I want to find a home in some lonely brake along the river, an' work, an' ferget a lot."

"I could believe that. If you tell me there will be no more cattlemen trailing you to hang you—I will believe you."

"Wal, Terrill, I'm not so dinged shore aboot thet. There's one man, an' he's this Breen Sawtell. The dyin' rancher told me Sawtell was stealin' his own brother's cattle. What aboot thet? An' it was he who sent thet brother down to have me fired an' run off the range. . . . So then this Breen Sawtell may turn up heah, like his brother did there. All of which doesn't mean anythin' to me, since I'm shore to kill him anyhow."

Pecos had been somewhat puzzled and nonplused over this Texas youth, and kept hoping he would overcome what seemed unusual agitations. Probably the soft-spoken lad had not recovered from the shock of his father's murder. Motherless, too—and he had lived alone with only a couple of negroes, harried by vaqueros and hounded by these crooked cattlemen. There was excuse for much. Besides, young Lambeth had not been brought up in the south and west of the wild Lone Star State.

"I hope you do kill Sawtell—and shore that Don Felipe," suddenly burst out Terrill, after a long pause. His face turned pearl gray, and such a blaze of purple fire flashed upon Pecos that he was surprised out of the very change he had wished for.

"Then I get the job with yu?" retorted Pecos, responding to the other's fire.

"You shore do. I think I've found a—a friend as well as a vaquero. Heah's my hand."

It was minus the glove this time, and the little calloused palm, the supple fingers that closed like steel on Pecos', shot a warm and stirring current through his veins.

"So far as friend is concerned, I hope it works the other way round," replied Pecos. "An' if we get along good an' I build up yore herd of cattle an' buy a half interest in yore ranch—do yu think yu'd take me on as yore pardner?"

"Pecos, I think God . . . Well, never mind what I think," replied Lambeth, beginning with eloquent heat, and suddenly faltering. "But, yes, yes, I will take you."

Sambo's arrival, leading a pony with the lad Bobby astride, put an end to this most earnest colloquy.

"Heah yo is, Massa Rill," called out Sambo, happily. "Our luck has done changed."

"Take all this grub so I can git down," piped up Bobby.

The advent of the lively Bobby and the exuberant Sambo, together with the generous supply of food and drink they brought, effectually silenced Terrill and brought back the singular aloofness Pecos had sensed. Still the lad could not be expected to be gay and voluble when he was half starved, with the means at hand to allay hunger and thirst. But there was something more.

Pecos shared a little of the food. He was thoughtful during this picnic and realized that he had made a profound and amazing decision. He could see no drawbacks. His mounting zeal had burned them away. He had not been caught burning brands. Williams and Adams were dead, as were all of the posse that had tracked them. He was free. What did a brawling cheat or two like Breen Sawtell matter to him? He was forewarned and forearmed. As for Don Felipe—the half-breed was dangerous like a snake in the grass was dangerous. Both of these men failed to raise the tiniest clouds on Pecos' horizon.

For ten years Pecos had lived more or less in an atmosphere of strife. That was Texas. It had to grow worse before it ever could grow better. And this range west of the Pecos was bound to see stirring life as the cattle herds augmented. Ranchers and settlers would trail grass and water like wolves on a scent. Vaqueros would throng to the Pecos. And likewise the parasites of rangeland. Pecos had a vision of the future. He had had his one, brief fling at outlaw life. No more! Let accusers flock in. No sheriff could put handcuffs on him, nor would any court in Texas uphold a sheriff who tried. A wonderful gladness flushed his veins. What a little incident could transform a career! He owed much to Bobby, to Sambo, and most to this strange orphaned lad, out of place there on the wild range. But for his plight Pecos might have gone on drifting. Somehow Terrill seemed a lovable lad. He needed a protector, a trainer, some one who could bring out the latent Texas qualities that must be in him. And Pecos felt eminently qualified for the position.

"Yo sho wuz starved," declared Sambo. "Whar yo put all dat grub?"

"I was hungry," admitted Terrill. "But I shore didn't eat it all, Sambo. Bobby was around. And so was Pecos, heah."

"Pecos? Thet's a funny handle fer a man," quoth Bobby. "Pecos means 'most anythin'. Hell an' killin' a man an' everythin' orful."

"Shore does, Bobby," drawled Pecos, fishing out another dollar. "Hyar's another peso."

"Aw! . . . I'm rich, Terrill, I'm rich! What's this one fer?" exulted Bobby.

"Wal, to keep mum aboot me bein' Pecos anythin' fer a while. Savvy?"

"Betcha I do," replied Bobby, his shrewd eyes bright. "I jest think you're wonderful."

"Folks, let's shake the dust of Eagle's Nest," suggested Pecos. "While we've been sittin' heah I've counted a dozen greasers snoopin' at us, along with Brasee an' his bartender. An' some white people down the street."

"Sambo, where's yore horse?" queried Lambeth.

"I dunno. Reckon he's eatin' his haid off out a ways."

"Wal, I ought to stock up on my supplies," said Pecos. "But I'm not crazy aboot buyin' from Brasee."

"We'll never deal with him again," spoke up Terrill, decidedly. "There's an army post upriver, aboot twenty miles from my home. Camp Lancaster. We seldom go there, because it's across the river and there were always Indians hanging around. But now it's preferable to Eagle's Nest."

"An' how far to yore ranch, Terrill?"

"Four hours, if we rustle along."

Pecos untied the halters of his horses and mounted. "Adios, Bobby. I won't forget yu."

"Aw, I'm sorry you're all goin', but gladder, too. Terrill, I'm 'most big enough to ride fer you."

"Some day, Bobby. Good-by."

Terrill got on the pony and led the way out of town, with the whistling negro following and Pecos bringing up the rear. Just before the road turned Pecos quickly glanced back. A crowd of people were standing before the store, with Brasee conspicuous among them.

CHAPTER NINE

Not many miles out of Eagle's Nest an unfrequented trail branched off the road toward the river. Here Sambo, who had found his horse and taken the lead, turned off into the brakes. And from that moment Pecos was lost.

No wheel had ever rolled along that trail, nor had a herd of cattle ever tramped its rocky, cactus-bordered course. At infrequent intervals cattle tracks crossed it, but no other trail for miles. Then a dim road intersected it from the west. Lambeth said this led down to Mortimer Spring.

For the most part Pecos rode down in washes and gulches, but occasionally he was up one of the snake-like, wandering ridges from which he could see afar. All the same was this wild Pecos country, bare grass spots alternating with scaly patches, greasewood and cactus contrasting with the gray of rocks, winding ridge and winding canyon all so monotonous and lonely, rolling endlessly down from the west to the river, rolling endlessly up toward the east, on and on, a vast wasteland apparently extending to infinitude. The course of the Pecos appeared only as a dark meandering line, its walls hidden, its presence sometimes mysteriously vanished.

Pecos was glad to have companions once again, though he little availed himself of the opportunity to talk. Young Lambeth rode a fast-gaited mustang and was hard to keep up with. Most of the time he and Sambo were out of sight, hidden by rock corners or a descent into a gorge. And Pecos' pack-horse was tired.

About mid-afternoon Pecos espied the first bunch of cattle, wilder than deer—an old mossy-horn, a cow, two yearlings and a calf, for all he could tell unbranded. This encounter was in a shallow rock-bottomed gorge where clear water ran. From that point on cattle tracks increased markedly, and mixed stock showed on the ridges. At length Pecos made out a brand T L, and concluded that must belong to Lambeth. Thereafter he kept sharp lookout for cattle and brands, the latter of which, to his growing surprise, he saw but few.

No doubt Colonel Lambeth had been one of the loosest of branders. But how could any cattleman, even an old stager, with only one vaquero and a boy, expect to brand one tenth of the calves and yearlings that belonged to him? Conditions were changing and such ranching as that was of the past. With cattle demanding a price, with markets increasing, this vast range west of the Pecos would in time produce a million head. Pecos saw fortune in the future for this Lambeth lad and himself. Pecos possessed the money to buy, to replenish what had been left of Lambeth's stock; he knew how to raise cattle; he had the will, and particularly the nerve to stop extensive rustling. Wherefore he rode this trail more nearly happy than he could recall.

At length, toward sunset, Sambo waited for Pecos in one of the shallow, rock-walled, rock-bedded draws. Evidently Lambeth had gone on. But Pecos failed to see where. There was no water, no sand or earth to mark tracks.

"Heah's whar we turns off," announced the negro. "Mos' deceivin' place."

"Wal, Sambo, I might have passed on heah myself," replied Pecos. "How far to the river?"

"Reckon not so fur as a crow flies. But we go round an' round aboot an' pilin' down an' down till yo sho t'ink it's miles."

The draw wound lazily down, turning back upon itself, keeping its narrow width, but heightening its rock walls. From an appreciable descent it fell off to jumps where the men had to dismount and lead the horses. It remained a gorge, however, never widening to the dignity of a canyon. Nevertheless, Pecos expected it to do so, for that was the nature of the brakes of the river. Down and down he went until the sky above appeared like a winding, blue stream. Water certainly poured down here in floods at certain seasons, but the bed of the gorge continued dry as a bleached bone in the sun. Gradually its dry fragrance failed, which fact came to Pecos' attention through the actions of the horses. They scented water. And presently Pecos smelled it, too, and felt in his face a warm, drowsy breath of air, moving, laden with sweet essence of greens and blossoms.

But Pecos was not prepared to turn a last corner suddenly and be confronted by a burst of golden sunlight and a blaze of open canyon.

"Heah yo is, boss," announced Sambo, with pride. "Dis is Massa Rill's ranch. An' it's sho de only purty place on dis ole Pecos ribber."

"Dog-gone!" ejaculated Pecos, and halted to revel.

The sun was setting behind him, far up over those rolling ranges, and it cast long rays of gold down across this canyon, to paint the gliding river and the huge, many-stepped wall of rock above. That wall appeared higher than any in view on this side of the river. It frowned forbiddingly, notwithstanding its front of glancing sunset hues.

"Up dar's whar de Comanches ride oot an' yell an' shoot at us," exclaimed Sambo, in his deep voice, pointing to the low center of the great cliff opposite. "But dey cain't reach us an' dey cain't git down."

"Dog-gone!" repeated Pecos, as he mopped his wet face.

From where Pecos stood the walls spread and curved on each side, lofty and perpendicular, craggy and impassable along the rims, rock-splintered and densely-thicketed at the bases, perhaps half a mile apart at the extreme width of the curve, and thereafter gradually closing to the mouth, which, however, was large enough to permit a lengthy view of the Pecos and the rugged wall opposite.

It was an oval canyon twice its breadth in length, remarkable in many ways, and strikingly so for a luxuriance of green. This charmed Pecos' eye, for he had never seen anything like it along this lonely, gray-walled river.

The center was an oval pasture inside an oval fringe of trees and cliffs. Horses dotted the green, and many cattle. The sunset had changed its gold for red, so that the eastern walls took on a rosy flush, while those nearer Pecos deeped their purple. In between, shafts of light slanted down across the canyon, rendering it ethereally lovely—a garden of fertile beauty lost in all that wilderness of gloomy, dismal, barren land.

"Dar's one big spring dat nebber goes dry," concluded Sambo, with importance. "It's so big it's a little ribber all by itself. So when de Pecos is low an' so full ob alkali dat de cattle cain't drink, why, dis water is pure as de good Lawd makes."

Sambo mounted again and rode down through the sections of broken cliff toward the canyon floor. And Pecos followed him, presently to emerge from the groves of willow and mesquite and blossoming brush to a trail that led on through the grass. A murmuring of many bees, buzzing and humming in the foliage mingled with a soft sound of an unseen, falling stream.

Here indeed Pecos rode by mossy-horns that were not wild. There were hundreds of cattle toward the lower end of the oval. This canyon alone, without the boundless ranges above, would support a rancher who was not ambitious to grow rich.

Meanwhile the sun set and with the fire and color changed to darkening gray, this isolated retreat returned to its true aspect as part of the hard Pecos country.

At length, just as twilight began to creep out of the larger canyon, gleaming cold on the steely Pecos, a cabin appeared on the edge of the fringe of trees that faced the river. It was fairly high on the bank and commanded a view across the river and down. A smaller cabin sat back and to one side.

"Heah we air an' I'se sho glad," sang out Sambo. "Mauree, yo unwelcomin', no-good woman, whar yo is?"

A negress, large of frame, comely of face, with a red bandana tied round her head, appeared in the doorway.

"So yo's back, yo lazy niggah," she ejaculated, rolling her eyes till the whites showed. "Yo sabed yo' life, man, fetchin' our Terrill home."

"Yas, I'se home, honey, thanks to dis gennelman," replied Sambo, happily. "Mauree, meet a real Texan, Mistah Pecos Smith."

"Wal, Mistah Smith, I'se sho happy to welcome yo," replied the negress. "Git down an' come in. Der's ham an' eggs an' milk—aplenty fo hungry men."

"Thanks, Mrs. Sambo," rejoined Pecos as he slid off his saddle. With swift, sure hands he untied his bulky coat from the cantle and slipped his rifle, to lay them upon the stone steps of the porch. Then he unsaddled Cinco while Sambo performed a like office for the pack-animal.

The cabin was long, with three doors opening out on the porch, and it had been crudely though strongly constructed of logs and poles, with sun-baked mud filling the chinks between. The several windows served equally for portholes. In the center it had a low-peaked roof, which shelved down to cover the porch. It did not, however, touch the side wall, thus leaving a considerable air space for the attic. When Pecos had deposited his saddle and pack on the porch he espied a bench upon which stood a wooden pail and an iron dipper, also a basin and soap, and above, hanging on pegs, clean, white towels. He laughed. When had he seen anything like this? The bucket was full of crystal water which proved to be as cold as ice and singularly free of taste. Pecos drank twice, verifying Sambo's claim for the water. Then he washed his hands and face, to feel a refreshment that equaled his enthusiasm. When he turned, Terrill stood bareheaded in the doorway.

"Pecos Smith," he said, shyly, "welcome to Lambeth Ranch."

"Terrill—our fortune's made!" he flashed, to express his appreciation of this welcome, and the opportunity a chance meeting had thrown to him.

"You think so? You like my lonely canyon?"

"Paradise! No man could have made me believe such a place could be found along the Pecos."

"Come in. Supper is ready. You wouldn't expect me to be hungry, after that lunch Bobby gave us. But I am."

"Wal, I wasn't particular hungry till Mrs. Sambo mentioned ham an' eggs. I shore fergot there were such things."

The interior was dark, like all log cabins, except in the neighborhood of the open fire. Evidently this large apartment was living-room and kitchen combined. A door at the end led into another room. Pecos sat down to a home-made table, upon which were a spotless white tablecloth, old silverware, and a supper the savory fragrance of which attested that it was good enough for a king.

Terrill had breeding, though he had not been used to company. If the situation was novel for Pecos, what must it have been for the lad? Here, more than at any other time since Terrill had been freed, that strange, rather aloof awkwardness, if not actual shyness, seemed noticeable to Pecos. It would not have been difficult for Pecos to burst into a hearty laugh and to slap the lad on the shoulder and ridicule him for such diffidence out on the west bank of the wildest river in Texas. But something inhibited Pecos. Lambeth must have had a sheltered childhood, a sad boyhood, and now he certainly was an orphaned youth. It would take time to get acquainted with him, and Pecos decided it would be worth some pains to keep much to himself and give familiarity time to grow. Vaqueros of his type were not usually rough and ready fellows, and Pecos was nothing if not quiet.

They did not exchange half a dozen words throughout the meal, to which Pecos did justice that assuredly flattered the cook.

"Wal, a few more suppers like thet an' I'll be spoiled," was Pecos' encomium.

"We have plenty to eat, even if we are poor," replied Terrill. "Raise 'most everything, I reckon. . . ."

"Wal, this has shore been an excitin' day, an' I'm sleepy. If yo don't mind I'd like to bunk up in thet hole under the roof. I'll get plenty of air there, and it's a good place for a lookout."

"That will be all right," the lad replied, quickly. "Sambo has been sleeping there since Dad was killed, so I wouldn't be afraid at night. Now he can go back to his cabin."

"Yeah. I shore hope my comin' will make things better all around."

"Oh, I know it will, Pecos," returned Lambeth. "I shore had some luck today, if never before."

"Thet reminds me. Yu 'pear far from starvin' hyar, yet yu had to take chances ridin' into Eagle's Nest for supplies. How aboot it?"

"Pecos, it wasn't food supplies that I went after, or I would have taken a pack-horse."

"I see. Wal, I'll turn in. Good-night."

"Wait. You said our fortune was made. . . . I cain't go to sleep if you don't explain."

Pecos laughed. "Yore a funny kid. Let me figure for yu. . . . This range is the best on the Pecos. What yu an' yore dad needed was a man who could ride this range. Sambo is a good nigger. But yu want a handy man with guns. He happens to have dropped in. Now takin' a ridiculous estimate, say yu have a thousand cows left. Thet number with the brandin' of mavericks will more than double this year. Thet means, say, twenty-five hundred haid. Followin' year five thousand haid. Third year ten thousand haid. Mind yu, we're allowin' for the brandin' of mavericks along this river as far up an' down as we can ride. Fourth year easy twenty thousand. An' so on. Wal, two-year-olds are sellin' now for six dollars a haid. Any Texan can see thet cattle-raisin' is goin' to save Texas. Prices will go up an' up. But suppose, for sake of bein' conservative, say prices go no higher. In four years we'll be worth way over a hundred thousand dollars. But I'd gamble it'll be double thet."

"Pecos!" cried Lambeth, his voice ringing high.

"Wal, don't Pecos me. Yu know thet Pecos means 'most anythin'. I'm tellin' yu straight, Terrill. For ten years I've been layin' for this chance."

"Oh, thank God you—came in time!" exclaimed the lad, poignantly.

"See heah, lad, yore still upset. Let's talk no more tonight," replied Pecos, surprised into keen solicitude. Terrill stood against the stone chimney just out of the light of the freshly blazing sticks Sambo had put on. The shadow somehow heightened the effect of large dark eyes.

"I'm not upset. It's—it's just—I cain't tell you. . . . But I can tell you—that if Brasee had kept me shut up much longer—I'd have hanged myself."

"Aw, son, yore exaggeratin'," ejaculated Pecos. "Why, he wouldn't have dared. He was tryin' to scare you into borrowin' money."

"That's all you know," retorted the lad, with passion. "Brasee is only one of Don Felipe's hands. But he does terrible things. Not so long ago he held a *girl* prisoner in that 'dobe shack."

"A girl! . . . What the hell is wrong with the white men in Eagle's Nest?"

"She was—a—Mexican," replied Terrill, haltingly, and ended as if biting his tongue.

"Makes no difference," growled Pecos. "Reckon I'll have to inquire into thet."

Pecos went out and called: "Hey, Sambo, you big molasses. Come heah an' help me."

Sambo appeared, so promptly as to give rise to a suspicion that he had been listening. It certainly seemed natural under the circumstances.

"Yo climb up de ladder an' I'll fro up yore bed," suggested Sambo.

"Hand up my coat an' rifle first," replied Pecos as he ascended to the roof and knelt on the uneven pole floor. It was so dark Pecos could not see back into the loft.

"Yo fro my quilts down, Pecos."

Pecos felt around until he found a bed, which consisted of no more than several heavy quilts. He gave these a pitch into space. Sambo let out a smothered ejaculation and was evidently thrown off his balance. Pecos, peering down, found that this was the case. Sambo floundered around to extricate himself. His language and the commotion that he had created brought Mauree to the scene.

"Fo' de land's sake! Yo crazy black man, what yo doin'?"

"Go long wid yo, woman."

"Ex-cuse me, Sambo," called Pecos. "I reckoned yu was lookin'."

"Sho I wuz lookin', but it done no good. Yo is a real vaquero, Mars Pecos, yo sho is."

Presently Pecos had his bed spread in that dark loft and his preciously laden coat folded for a pillow. Before stretching his frame at length he gazed out in the direction of the river. He could not see well, though the pale, wide, winding bar under the black wall must be it. Above the bold rim blinked white stars, cold and austere in their message to him. By listening intently he caught a faint murmur of water chafing by reedy shore. An owl hooted on the canyon side of the river, to be answered from a distance. Cattle and horses were silent.

Pecos felt of the bundles of money in his coat. His conscience discovered a still small voice. Had he been wholly honest with young Lambeth? Angrily he cast the query aside. He had fought that out. He could look any man in the eye, with a hand on his gun, and swear that he was not a thief. Nevertheless, if he had so long lived the free, wild lawless life of a vaquero that his sense of right and wrong had suffered, now was the time to correct it. Whereupon he lay down and slept, an indication that his conscience was not too burdened.

Pecos did not awaken until rather late for him, which perhaps was owing to a sense of security. The sun was crossing the gap far down the river and the Rio Pecos appeared a path of glory.

Sambo came into sight below, his arms full of split fagots.

"Fine mawnin'," called out Pecos, pulling on his boots.

"Sho is. An' once more I'se glad to be alibe."

"Me too. . . . Where's our boss, Sambo?"

"Sho he's in de land ob Nod. Mauree she call him twice. But mos' always he's up early."

Pecos lay flat on the floor, with his head over the edge. The open door of the cabin was a little to his right. *"Hey, Terrill!"* he yelled.

"Yes—yes," came a quick, bewildered cry from the distant room.

"Pile out. The mawnin's broke. We gotta hang today on a peg an' all the days thet come after. . . . Ridin' the brakes, boy! Who could ask a happier lot?"

Pecos descended the ladder to begin the day himself, surprised at something that made him want to sing. He washed his face and hands, and brushed his tangled hair, and felt of his stubby beard. Some day he might shave, if only for the comfort of a clean, smooth chin. There were gold and red ripples on the river, under a gentle wind. Ducks were winging flight upstream. Cattle spotted the green banks. Terrill's pinto mustang had come almost to the porch. Chickens were numerously manifest.

"Sambo, is there any other way in an' out of this canyon?" queried Pecos.

"They sho is. Yo can drive a wagon to the rim. It done ain't no shucks of a road, suh, but we've druv it many a time."

"Then we've got a wagon?"

"Sho—up thar on top. Harness, too, all nice hid in de brush. Kuhnel Lambeth done bought dat wagon t'ree years ago."

"Did you ever drive it to Eagle's Nest?"

"Yas, suh. But dat's a long pull around. We can get to de fort in two days."

"Wal, we're shore startin' pronto."

A jingling step caused Pecos to turn. Terrill had come out in clothes much the worse for wear.

"Mawnin', Pecos. You scared me stiff."

"So yore up, lad? Wal, I was gettin' worried. If yore gonna trail with me, Terrill Lambeth, yore shore gonna rustle. . . . Do yu sleep in thet old sombrero?"

"Sometimes," replied Terrill, with a laugh.

"Yo-all come an' eat," called Mauree, from within.

Pecos followed him in. The living-room was full of sunlight now. Pecos, sitting at table, gazed from the flushed Terrill around upon the walls, at Mauree's crude cupboard, at the pots and pans on the coals, at the homemade furniture, the skins and horns over the rude mantel, at the old Henry rifles—and his mental reservation was that the Lambeths had the spirit of the pioneer, but not the resourcefulness.

"Pecos, I heahed you tell Sambo you were startin' pronto somewhere," said Terrill, his deep eyes glancing up fleetingly.

"What you think aboot it? We'll ride hossback, an' Sambo—an' his wife, too ——"

"Mauree has a pickaninny."

"Ump-um! Wal, she can shore take it, if she wants. We'll drive to thet fort—what'd yu call it—campin' along easy, an' load yore wagon till it sags."

"Pecos, you're the—the most amazing vaquero *I* ever heahed of. You filled my head with dreams last night. But this mawnin' I'm awake."

"Dog-gone, boy, yu do seem brighter. Not so pale. . . . Wal, what's wrong with my idee?"

"Nothing. It's just inspiring. Only I have no credit at Camp Lancaster, even if I—I dared go in debt again."

"Wal, yore pardner's got some money," drawled Pecos.

"You would lend it to me?"

"No. I'm investin' in yore ranch. I'll buy supplies, tools, guns, shells, cattle, hosses, any darn thing we need thet *can* be bought in this heah Gawd-forsaken country."

Terrill dropped his head, though not so quickly but that Pecos caught a glimpse of flaming cheeks.

"Terrill, don't take offense an' don't be uppish," added Pecos, in change of tone. "I want to help yu an' I know I cain't lose nothin'. Yu said yu trusted me, though I don't see how yu can on such short notice. Not west of the Pecos!"

"I do—trust you. But I—it's only that I'm overcome. It's too good to be true. Don't think me uppish or—or ungrateful. . . . I—I could scream. I could swear!"

"Wal, thet's fine. Come out with a good old Texas cuss-word."

"—— ——!" swore Terrill, valiantly. But the profanity did not ring true, so far as familiarity was concerned.

Sambo burst into a roar. "Haw! Haw! Haw! . . . My Lawd!—Wife, did yo heah dat?"

"I sho did an' I'se scandalized," declared Mauree, resentfully. "Terrill never wuz a cusser an' he ain't a-gonna begin now."

"Wal, I'm sorry, Mrs. Sambo," said Pecos. "But it shore did me good to heah him. . . . Now, son, yu get a pencil an' paper. Say, can yu write?"

"I'm not quite so ignorant as I look and sound," protested Terrill.

"Boy, listen to me. Yu gotta know when I'm in fun, which is shore most of the time, an' when I'm mad, which ain't often. I wasn't mad atall yesterday. . . . Now if yu've lived out heah five years an' yore fifteen altogether, how'n the devil did yu get much schoolin'?"

"Who said I was fifteen?"

"Reckon I did. Yu shore cain't be older?"

"I reckon I am, a little," returned Terrill, dryly. "But never mind my age. . . . Only, Señor Pecos Smith, I'm no child to tease. . . . Now I'll get pencil and paper."

"Wal, if yu balk at teasin' we'll dissolve partnership right heah an' now. What yu say?"

"I'm not a bit balky."

"Dog-gone! I'll bet yu are."

When it came to enumerating supplies and necessities for the ranch, Terrill showed a long-formed habit of economy. After he set his list down Pecos said: "Put an X an' a four after thet."

"X and a four?"

"Shore. Thet means multiply by four. . . . Heah, Sambo, yu ought to know what yu've got an' what yu haven't. Answer my questions, an' yu, Terrill, write down what I say."

At the conclusion of this exercise, Sambo was jubilant and Terrill was awed. Pecos heard Sambo say to his wife: "Mauree, dat man take my bref. If he ain't crazy we'ze lookin' at hebben right dis minute."

Maurce elected to stay home with her pickaninny. "But yu, niggah, yu fetch me some stockin's an' shoes an' some clothes—an' if yu forgit my smokin' yu needn't come honeyin' around heah no mo."

What with climbing the gulch trail with saddle horses and team, and clambering over rocks and greasing the wagon and mending the harness, Sambo and Pecos were not ready to start until midday. Then Sambo drove off over rough ground where no sign of wheel tracks was visible. Terrill did not know the way, so he and Pecos followed behind the wagon.

"Boy, yu gotta pack a gun an' learn how to shoot it," advised Pecos.

"I told you I could shoot."

"Wal, take this an' show me," replied Pecos, handing over his gun—an action he had never done since that gun had become part of him. "Be careful. Yu have to thumb the hammer."

"Shoot from the horse?"

"Why, shore! If yu run into a bandit would yu git off polite an' plug him from the ground?"

"I did meet two bandits—and I ran for all I was worth."

"Wal, yore education is beginnin'. Hold the gun high with yore thumb on the hammer. Then throw it hard with a downward jerk. The motion will flip the hammer just as the gun reaches a level, an' it'll go off, yu bet. Yu gotta sort of guess instead of aimin'. Thet is at a man close to yu, but at some distance yu want to aim."

"Heah goes. If Spot hangs me in a tree it'll be on yore head," replied Terrill, and he threw the gun as directed, pointing it at a big rock. Bang! The mustang leaped straight up, almost unseating his rider. It took a moment to quiet him.

"Take your old gun," declared Terrill, returning it to Pecos. "It nearly kicked my arm off."

"Wal, yu hit the rock, anyhow, an' thet's fine. I'll let thet do till we git home."

Pecos was not long in discovering that Sambo kept to the ridge-tops, seldom crossing a wash. And the direction was away from the river. Once up on top, the horses made better time. They camped at the head of a ravine where water was to be had, having made, according to Sambo, more than fifteen miles. Soon after supper Terrill unrolled his bed in the wagon and crawled into it. Pecos talked to the negro for an hour, with the object of learning what Sambo knew about the country, cattle, rustlers, and all pertaining to the range.

Next day they struck into a road, well defined and lately used. It wound along the ridges, for the most part downhill, and late that evening they made camp on the west bank of the river. Pecos was relieved to hear a ripple of shallow water, denoting an easy ford on the morrow. Before the sky grew red next morning they were across and headed down a good road toward the military camp.

CHAPTER TEN

Pecos learned from an old army sergeant that Camp Lancaster was the post of the U.S.A. Fourth Cavalry, who were operating against hostile Indians along the river; and at the present time were up somewhere on the Staked Plains.

It was an old post. Lieutenant N. F. Smith had camped there as early as 1849; and Lieutenant Michler in 1863, had traced out the road which Pecos had struck west of the river. There was a trading-post besides an army supply-store inside the old stone walls. The high chimneys made visible landmarks for miles around.

While Pecos helped Terrill and Sambo buy their extensive list, he did not let anything escape him. Indians lounged around on the stone steps and inside the stores, sullen, greasy, painted savages supposed to be peaceful. They were not Comanches, but all the same Pecos would not have trusted some of them out on the range.

According to the sergeant, the Comanches seldom raided below Horsehead Crossing. That ford, owing to the more frequent passing of the trail drivers, had become a favorite spot for the Indians to waylay and attack cattlemen driving herds up from lower Texas.

"Only last month a bunch of Comanches massacred some cowhands at Horsehead," said the army man. "Tolerable big bunch of cattle scattered all down the river. The Pecos is treacherous an' many head of stock mire down in quicksand or drown in floods. But there's thousands of cattle in the brakes that no one will ever claim."

Pecos did not linger at the fort after their purchases had been packed in the wagon. He did not ask for an escort back to the ford, but the sergeant sent three troopers with him, jolly fellows who imparted much information. They saw him and his companion safely across the river, just before sunset. This was the last water for a long stretch, but Pecos pushed on west far into the night before halting for camp. Then he staked the horses close, he and Sambo keeping alternate guard. Their next camp was somewhere down on the rocky slopes. And afternoon of the third day saw them arriving safely on the rim above Lambeth Ranch. The following day Pecos conceived the idea of letting the supplies down over the cliff on lassos, a method which saved much time and labor.

South of Lambeth Ranch was a range claimed by Don Felipe before his association with Sawtell, after which time they openly challenged any claim clear down to Devil River. Several other cattlemen, according to Sambo, ran stock on both sides of the river. And as cattle strayed far up and down the Pecos there was a considerable mixing of brands, and always, for the persistent vaqueros, an unfailing number of mavericks.

Pecos said cheerfully to Terrill and Sambo: "Every time yu put a red-hot iron on a maverick we are six dollars richer right *then.*"

They left the north brakes alone because even Felipe's vaqueros had not penetrated them, and confined their efforts to riding the river canyon, the intersecting brakes, and up these as far as the heads, where dense thickets never failed to yield calves and yearlings that had never smelled burned hair.

They rode together, or at least Pecos never allowed Terrill to get out of his sight, with the result that the average of brandings a day was small, in the neighborhood of six. This number, however, was eminently satisfactory to Pecos, and it elated Terrill so that the lad daily lost something of his reserve. Pecos, reviewing the situation, seemed to gather that Terrill apparently lost some kind of a fear of him. Pecos did not concern himself much about anything now except the amassing of a herd. He knew where to find mavericks, and many there were that Felipe's outfit had not sweat hard enough to find.

Summer came, hot and drowsy, with its storms. As a consequence work became harder on the men and easier on the horses. Lambeth owned less than a dozen horses, and these, with the two of Pecos', were not half enough to stand the grind.

Therefore a day here and there was given the horses to rest, during which time Pecos and his two followers worked on the ranch. There was no end of repairs, and when these were attended to, Pecos began improvements. He was indefatigable, and he made Sambo's red tongue hang out like that of a driven calf in the brakes.

Terrill turned out to be less hardy and enduring than he looked. Still, for a youth who had not reached his full growth and who had never experienced the grueling drill common to vaqueros, he won praise from Pecos. Terrill lost a little of the fullness of his cheeks and the graceful roundness of form that even the loose and ill-fitting clothes he wore failed to hide.

One still, scorching noon in August, after a hard morning's toil in pursuit of some wild three-year-old steers, they flung themselves down in a shady place on the banks of the river. Pecos was hot, and Sambo heaved and sweat like a horse, but it was Terrill who had suffered most from the exertion and heat. He had become expert with the rope under Pecos' tutelage and was mightily proud of it. He could run down, lasso, throw, and tie a calf in short order. But either Sambo or Pecos had to apply the branding-iron. Pecos often took the lad to task for his squeamishness, and finally Terrill, who was easy to exasperate, made a surprising and unanswerable retort. "Aw, burning hair and flesh stink!"

Pecos had gaped at the lad.

This particular day Terrill's face was as red as fire and as wet as if it had been plunged under water.

"You darned little fool!" ejaculated Pecos. "Why don't yu ride in yore shirt sleeves?"

"I haven't any heavy shirts like yours. Mine are thin stuff. Mauree made them for me. If I rode through the brush without my coat I'd be torn to pieces."

The coat Terrill referred to and which Pecos had complained of was a short jacket much too full for Terrill.

There was a flat rock along the bank and the current of the river swirled green and cool beside it. Terrill lay down to drink. Suddenly Pecos, possessed of one of his teasing moods, leaped down noiselessly, and with a quick action plunged Terrill's head clear under. Terrill nearly lunged into the river; then bounding erect, he burst out furiously: "Damn fool! . . . Pushing me in when I can't swim!"

"By gosh! Thet's an idee. Swim! We'll go in," shouted Pecos. "I was too durned lazy to think of it."

"No *we* won't," declared Terrill.

"Don't yu ever bathe, yu dirty boy?"

"Yes, but I'm not doing it today," retorted Terrill, resentfully.

"Come on, Terrill. I promise not to duck yu," rejoined Pecos, beginning to strip. By the time he had gotten his shirt off Terrill had disappeared under the trees. Pecos laughed, thinking he had offended the sensitive lad. He removed the rest of his clothes and had his swim.

"Sambo, why don't you come in? It's shore nice an' cool," called Pecos.

"Too much work. An' I'se had one baf dis summer. I fell in a hole."

When Pecos emerged to dress Terrill was not in sight, and did not return until fully half an hour later.

"Terrill, old pard, I'm sorry I ducked yu. Cain't yu take a little fun? My Gawd! but yore a queer kind. Not wantin' to go in swimmin' on a day like this!"

"I'd like it well enough, but I—I couldn't strip before yu and Sambo."

"Ahuh. So thet's it. . . . Terrill, I didn't savvy yu was so modest. Heahafter Sambo an' I will go off an' let yu take a swim."

This incident recalled certain things about Terrill that had seemed peculiar to

Pecos. Of late weeks, however, the boy had grown less aloof, and had become so zealous in work, so evidently glad to be with Pecos, so thoroughly promising in every way, that Pecos had grown greatly attached to him. It was like bringing up a boy who stayed boyish. There appeared to be limits, however, that Pecos could not exceed; and an altogether hopeless task to make a rough vaquero out of Terrill.

Nevertheless, these convictions of Pecos' rather endeared Terrill the more to him, because of a sense of guardianship, almost parental, that Terrill inspired. The lad had lost his fear of being alone, and at times he seemed almost happy. Naturally this drew Pecos closer to him. And as the days slipped by, always full of work in the open, these two grew insensibly the closer.

Terrill could stand considerable teasing of certain kinds. But one day, during a rest hour, Pecos had come upon him lying flat on his stomach, so absorbed in contemplation of some flowers—a habit of Terrill's—that he did not hear Pecos' step. So that he was wholly unprepared for Pecos' swoop down upon him, to straddle his back and tickle him in the ribs with steel-like fingers. At first Pecos took the noise Terrill made and the amazing struggle he put up to be the natural outcome of extreme ticklishness. But presently it dawned upon Pecos that the boy was not laughing, or struggling in a sense of response to Pecos' fingers dug into his ribs. When Pecos got off, Terrill leaped up in a rage.

"If you ever do that again—I'll fire you!" cried Terrill.

"Fire me?" echoed Pecos, aghast.

"Yes, fire you! Have you no respect for a—a fellow's person? I told you once before it drives me crazy to be tickled."

"Shore I remember now. Dog-gone it, Terrill, cain't I treat yu as I would any other boy?"

"You bet you can't."

"An' yu'd fire me—honest to Gawd?"

"I—I've got to do something to—to protect myself," replied Terrill, choking up.

"It's got to be home to me—this hyar Lambeth Ranch, an' I'm shore powerful fond of yu."

"Shut up! That was a lie. I—I couldn't get along without you," flashed Terrill, with another kind of temper, and he ran away to the house, leaving Pecos relieved and glad, and uncomprehensibly moved. From that hour, nevertheless, Pecos realized he and Terrill were going to clash sooner or later. It only waited for the time and the place and the cause; and there was no use for Pecos to attempt to fend it off.

Terrill was subject to moods. He really was astounding in that way, but most of them did not interfere with the work, which, after all, was Pecos' heartfelt aim. Sometimes when Terrill thought he was alone on the rocks or the banks of the river he would sing at the top of his lungs. Pecos never got close enough to him on these occasions to hear distinctly, but he caught a sweet rising and falling contralto voice. Then again Terrill would be wildly gay, and if opportunity offered where he was safe from attack, he would torment Pecos unmercifully. At times he would be profoundly melancholy and unapproachable, so sad-lipped and somber-eyed that Pecos was glad to let him alone. Again, and this was unusual and rare, happening in the dusk or in shadow, when his face was not visible, he would be provokingly curious about Pecos' love-affairs.

"Dog-gone yu, boy, I told yu I hadn't had any," Pecos would reply, in good-humored impatience.

"Aw, you lie. A wonderful handsome vaquero like you! Pecos Smith, you cain't make me believe you haven't had ——"

"Wal, what? Yore so damn curious. Now just what?"

"A wife, maybe. Sweethearts, shore lots of them—and, like as not—more than one of those black-eyed, bewitching little Mexican hussies."

"Wal, I'll be jiggered! Thet last's fine talk for a clean-minded boy who cain't undress to go swimmin' in front of men! . . . You got me wrong, Terrill Lambeth. I never had no Mexican hussy, nor any other kind. Nor a wife. Gawd! thet's kinda funny. . . . An' the nearest I ever come to a sweetheart was up heah at the H H Ranch. . . . Mary Heald. I was a little sweet on her, but I never told her. Course she might have liked me—the boys swore she did—an' I knew I'd shoot some fellar sooner or later an' have to go on down the long trail. An' thet's just what happened."

"Forgive me, Pecos. I—I was just curious. . . . I suppose then—I—we've only to look forward to the day when you shoot Breen Sawtell or Don Felipe—and ride away from Lambeth Ranch?"

Pecos was not so dense but he caught a faint bitterness in the lad's words, and it touched him. In the shade of the trees—it was twilight under the canyon wall and they were riding home. Pecos reached out a hand to clasp Lambeth's shoulder.

"Terrill, didn't I say I'd never leave yu? Would it have been honest of me to go in partnership with yu when I might have to go on the drift? But it cain't happen now. An' if I shoot Sawtell an' Felipe—which I'm damn liable to do if they come foolin' in heah—it'll be for yu."

Terrill made no response to that unless riding on ahead could be construed as one.

Terrill had a sulky mood now and then, the only kind that Pecos found it trying to put up with. Without any reason whatever, that he could grasp, Terrill would get as sulky as a spoiled pup. It chanced one day that such a state of temper encroached upon an occasion when Pecos was as exasperated as he could well be. Things had gone wrong all day, even to the burning of his thumb with a branding-iron. This was serious. It was his trigger thumb! To be sure, he could shoot fairly well with his left hand, but if he ran into some of the vaqueros he suspected of brand-burning T L stock, he would be in a pretty pickle.

An argument arose over the matter of driving again to Camp Lancaster. Pecos wanted to put it off, and he was reasonable about it, though he did not mention the particular objection, which was his sore thumb. Terrill tossed his tawny head—happening for once to be without the omnipresent battered sombrero—and said he would be damned if he would not take Sambo and go alone.

"Yu will not," replied Pecos, shortly.

"I will!"

"Ump-umm."

"Who'll stop me?"

"Wal, if yore such a dumbhaid, this heah little old Pecos Smith."

"Dumbhaid! . . . I shall go. I'd like to know who's boss around Lambeth Ranch."

"I reckon yore the owner of the ranch, Terrill, 'cause I have only a half share in the stock. But yu cain't boss me."

"I *am* your boss."

"Say, go away an' leave me be. Yore pesterin' me. Cain't yu see this is a particular job."

Terrill snatched the article Pecos was working on—no less than a wide leather belt he meant to carry money in—and threw it far down the bank.

"Wal, yu little devil!" ejaculated Pecos, nettled.

"Don't call me names and don't think you can work when I'm talking business," declared Terrill, hotly.

"Call yu names? Shore I will. Heah's a couple more. When yu air like yu air this minnit yu air a dod-blasted mean little kickin' jackass. Yu heah me? . . . Yore cranky, too, an' turrible conceited aboot bein' a boss. Why, yu couldn't boss a lot of mavericks. Yu make me tired, Terrill, an' I've a mind to spank you."

"Spank me!" shrilled Terrill. "How dare you?" And he gave Pecos a stinging slap in the face.

That settled it. Out flashed Pecos' long arms. He seized Terrill by the shoulders, heartily disposed to carry out the spanking threat. But sudden pangs in his sore thumb changed his mind. Instead he gave Terrill a flip that spun him around like a top. Then he swung his boot in a lusty kick to Terrill's rear. In any case a vaquero's kick was no trivial thing. This one lifted Terrill a little off the grass and dropped him sprawling. With astounding celerity Terrill sprang erect. Then Pecos met blazing eyes that took his breath. Many as had been the wonderful eyes of different-hued fury that had flashed into his, Terrill's were the most magical.

"I'll kill you!"

"Run along, yu little bullhaid," drawled Pecos.

Terrill did run off, screaming incoherently, and that was the last Pecos saw of him until dusk. Pecos was watching the last ruddy glow of sunset down on the river when Terrill came out to edge closer to him.

"Pecos." It was an entreating voice.

"Yeah."

"I—I apologize. . . . You treated me just—just as I deserved. It was temper. I used to lose my haid at Dad. I'm sorry."

Pecos and his two helpers rode the brakes of the river for twenty miles below Lambeth Ranch, and out on the slopes of the range for as many miles west. And Pecos' hopes were more than fulfilled. They had burned the T L brand on more than seven hundred mavericks. What a grievous blow this would be to Don Felipe and his new partner, not to include several other ranchers who lived in Eagle's Nest and ran their stock up and down the river! Soon the vaqueros of all those cattlemen would be riding out on full round-ups. Then Pecos expected some burned-out brands, if nothing worse.

In these three hot months of summer Pecos' vigilant eye had not been rewarded by a single sight of Indians, or any tracks in the brakes or up on the ranges. Men who knew that country were partial to spring and fall for their operations. Before long now anything might be expected.

Toward the end of August the drought was broken by occasional rainstorms, most welcome to Lambeth Ranch. Even the well-watered canyon had begun to grow dusty and gray. But the rains worked magic.

When Pecos rode down from the desolate ranges or up the lonely, silent river with its drab walls, its never-changing monotony, back into the one green canyon within his range it was like entering another world. Months of riding the Pecos brakes could not but have its effect upon any man. The contrast of Lambeth's Canyon counteracted this, and the vaquero would gain by night what he lost by day. Sambo was not affected by seasons, by heat or cold, by loneliness, by anything. "So long's I'se got my chewin'-terbaccer I'se all right," the negro was wont to say. Terrill was a difficult proposition to figure, and Pecos gave it up. Nevertheless, the lad never made one complaint about the hard work, the loneliness, and the confinement of the brakes.

Before undertaking a long siege of upriver riding, from which Pecos expected so much, he advised a week's rest for the horses. During this interval Pecos and his helpers dammed the stream up near the canyon head, and formed a fine little lake, from which they dug an irrigation ditch, with branches almost the whole length of the ranch. This was something Terrill claimed his father had always wanted to do.

The change from the everlasting seat in a saddle, riding the rough, ragged, dreary brakes, to work on foot with clear running water while eyes were rested and soothed by soft greens, and the lines of goldenrod, and the autumn coloring of vines and willows, turned out to be something so beneficial that Pecos saw the wisdom of frequently resorting to it.

The white clouds sailed up back of the rims to fill the blue vault above, and to thicken and change and darken, until a heavy black one would come trailing veils of rain across the ranch. At the same time the sun would be shining through somewhere, and lakes of azure showed amidst both the white and the black clouds, and rainbows arched down from the ranges above to bend a gorgeous curve over the river, or drop a fading end far down the canyon.

"Shore the lovely time heah is coming," said Terrill. "Makes up for the rest."

"Pity we have to miss it," replied Pecos. "But I've an idee, if it isn't too ambitious. Let's pack grub an' beds an' work out two or three of them upriver brakes at a time, then come home to rest up a bit."

That met with Terrill's approval.

"Sho yo's gonna find det upribber tough sleddin'," predicted Sambo.

Pecos was destined to learn vastly more about the river from which he had been named.

The country with which he had grown familiar while trail driving for McKeever did not take in the brakes of the river, but mostly the rolling ridges that led up to the vast sweeping ranges.

From Heald's range, up and down the Pecos for miles, the strange river had worn a deep channel through dull red soil, and the places where cattle could get down to drink were not many.

The part of the river Pecos was now to explore proved to be the wildest and most dangerous reaches along its whole length. Nothing marked the course of the river. The cedar trees that grew sparsely were all down in the narrow deep-walled winding canyon. Cattle tracks led to the few breaks where it was possible to get down to water.

From time to time Sambo had told Pecos what he had learned personally about the river below Horsehead Crossing, and what had come to him through other riders. Whole herds of cattle had been drowned in the Pecos, and thousands had perished singly and doubly, and in small bunches. Fords were so few and far between that cowhands had often attempted a crossing at a bad place and a bad time, only to be carried down the swift current beyond a rocky wall to death.

The savages, lying in ambush at Horsehead Crossing, which was the most important and the most dreaded ford on the river, had often massacred an outfit of trail drivers and chased their cattle into the breaks. Even a repulsed attack seldom failed of a stampede, which added to the number of unknown strays.

Pecos was of the opinion that most of these lost cattle—for that matter all the cattle in this region were lost and not only had to be found, but caught—grazed gradually to the southward.

Three weeks of riding this hard country, allowing for weekend rests at home, did not account for many branded mavericks for Pecos' outfit, but the labor was most valuable in acquainting Pecos with the haunts of a surprising number of cattle, and in what could not be done and what could. There was enough unbranded stock along Independence Creek alone to make Pecos and Terrill rich ranchers, and that stream lay between Lambeth Ranch and Camp Lancaster. Pecos' visions of wealth and dreams of the future were not inconsistent with possibilities. At night, round the little camp fire, he would dwell on this and that aspect of the business, finding in Terrill a rapt listener.

"Listen pard," said Pecos once, voicing a growing belief. "I shore don't want to set up yore hopes way sky-high an' then see them take a tumble. But, dog-gone it, I just cain't see anythin' 'cept big money for us."

"Pecos, you've got my hopes so high now I'm riding the clouds instead of my saddle," replied Terrill.

"Wal, I'll stick by my guns," went on Pecos, doggedly. "By spring we'll have twenty five hundred haid wearin' the T L. We've got the ranch, the water, the range. This country will *always* run cattle, an' a hundred times more'n what's grazin' heah now. It's so darn big an' so wild. Why, there's no cattle range in Texas thet can come up to our West of the Pecos range. Grass doesn't fail heah. Thet damned gray-green-yellow alkali-bitten river never went dry in its life. . . . We're *heah*, boy, we're *heah!*"

"But, Pecos, you've forgotten Don Felipe and Sawtell. It's so easy to forget anything here. I cain't keep track of days. It's *you*, Pecos, with all your talk of riches, that makes me remember poor Dad and his hopes. And then I come back to these slick devils who not only stole my stock but tried to steal *me*. . . . It cain't last, Pecos. Before October comes and goes these happy days will get a jolt."

Pecos was silent a long time. The lad spoke sense, but then he had no idea who his partner was. And naturally Pecos was brought face to face with dire possibilities. He pondered over them, one by one, and added others as far-fetched and unlikely as he could conceive. Not one presented any great obstacle to him! Still, he could get shot in the back. If he would only sternly get down to the somber vigilance that had been natural to him in the past. But that was the opposite to being happy! He owed it to this orphaned lad, so lovable and fine, and so full of promise, to see that no tragedy ruined him.

"Terrill, yu handsome son-of-a-gun, listen," began Pecos, deliberately. "Yu don't know what I know. An' I've gotta brag some to convince yu. . . . Wal, I once rode for Don Felipe."

"Pecos! You did?" Terrill queried, in amaze, and he threw up his head so that the ruddy firelight played upon his tanned face.

"Shore did. An' when thet greaser sees me an' recognizes me, his black-peaked face will turn green, an' his little pig's eyes will pop out of his haid, an' them pigtails—shore yu seen how he braids his hair?—they'll stand up stiff. . . . Yu savvy, son?"

"Yes, I savvy," replied Terrill, soberly.

"Wal, to resoom. Don has got the same vaqueros he always had, 'cept two or three thet ain't ridin' for nobody no more. Ha! Ha! . . . An' do they know me? Wal, yu'll see some day, an' yu shore won't worry no more. . . . An' thet fetches us down to Breen Sawtell. . . . Terrill, thet man cain't cause me to lose the tiniest wink of sleep. Now do yu savvy thet, too?"

"No, I cain't. . . . Who *are* you, Pecos?"

"Wal, I'm yore partner, an' thet's enough. . . . Now listen to this new idee of mine. Next spring or fall, at the latest, *provided* we're free of worry aboot the Felipe-Sawtell outfit, we'll go south to the Rio Grande. We'll pick up some honest-to-

Gawd vaqueros thet I know how to find, an' we'll buy some fine hosses an' cows, an' particular some bulls, an' turn trail drivers ourselves long enough to get them heah."

"Oh, Pecos, there yu go again," declared Terrill, in despair. "Do you mean we'll drive and sell what cattle we have?"

"Not a darned hoof."

"But that would cost a lot of money."

"Shore it would, the way yu figure money. But I've got it, Terrill."

"Where?" gasped the lad, incredulously.

"Wal, I reckon yu ought to know," drawled Pecos. "'Cause somethin' might happen to me, an' in thet case I'd want yu to have the money. I hid all my small bills in a tin can back in the corner of thet loft where I sleep when we're home. The rest—the big bills—I pack around with me. Heah."

Pecos opened his shirt, and unlacing the wide leather belt he had made he handed it over to his partner.

"I reckon you remember this belt. It's to blame for my nearly kickin' the pants off yu thet day."

"I'm not—likely to forget that—Pecos Smith," returned the lad, in a low voice. "What'll I do with this?"

"Take a peep inside."

With eager trembling fingers Terrill complied; and then, utterly astounded, he fixed large dark dilated eyes upon Pecos.

"Fifty dollar bills! Hundred dollar bills! . . . I dare look no farther. . . . A fortune!"

"Not so bad, for a couple of young Texas vaqueros," replied Pecos, complacently, as he replaced the belt round his waist, and tucked in his shirt. "Yu 'pear more shocked than tickled."

"Pecos, if—if you turned out to—to be a—a thief—it'd *kill* me!"

"For Gawd's sake! I'm no bank-robber or rustler. I told yu," sharply returned Pecos, too keenly stung to weigh the strange significance of Terrill's words.

October waned. The sunny days were still hot, but no longer hot in comparison with those of midsummer. Lambeth Ranch presented a beautiful spectacle for that arid and rocky region.

The gray rock walls never changed. They were immutable in their drab insulation, though the sunrise and sunset took fleeting colorful liberties with them. But at their base a yellow-and-gold hue vied with the green, and circled the whole oval canyon, a warm fringe that had no regularity. In the notch of the walls, where the gulch opened, there were clinging vines with hints of cerise among the brown and bronze leaves. Across the green canyon floor shone lines and patches of goldenrod.

It was the season when birds and ducks had halted there on their southern migration; and there were splashes upon the blue lake and in the silver river, and flashes of myriads of wings, and music of many songsters.

Pecos was working the river canyon, with results that delighted Terrill and brought the rolling white to Sambo's ox eyes.

"I done tole yu," he averred, time and again. "I'se de darky dat knowed all aboot dem cattle. Dey libes on dem ribber banks, up an' down so furs dey can git. An' dat's furder den we can go."

Nevertheless, keen as Sambo was about most things, he was wrong in regard to Pecos, for that vaquero could take a horse where any steer could go. And so at the low stage of water, and wading or even swimming their mounts around sharp corners of wall the three maverick-branders found places no white man had ever tried, and unbranded cattle by the score, and old mossy horns that took a good deal of hard chasing. Pecos had a knack of running them into the river, and if they did not venture to cross, which happened frequently, he roped them, dragged them ashore, and with Sambo's assistance, burned the T L on their wet flanks. Terrill built the fires and heated the iron.

With few exceptions all these cattle were driven downriver toward the ranch. Pecos had far-seeing plans. There were twenty miles of brakes below Lambeth Canyon, and a vastly wider range west of the river, which would one day run thousands of T L stock. Every time Pecos threw a lasso, and every several times Sambo did likewise, and once in half a dozen throws for Terrill, meant an added six dollars for the Smith-Lambeth combination. It was amazing how the thing grew. And likewise their appetite for work, and daring to encompass it grew in proportion to their reward.

"Wal, in the mawnin' we'll ride up this heah side, an' Sambo an' I'll cross the river while yu stay behind," said Pecos, at supper one evening.

"Like hob I will," drawled Terrill.

Pecos deliberated a moment. Often difficulties arose in the way of keeping Terrill from sharing real perils. To hint of danger a little too risky for his strength or horsemanship was to invite failure. And it struck Pecos rather strangely that now he should seek to deter the lad from ordeals that months past he had thrust upon him. There had been several narrow escapes for Terrill.

"S'pose yu tackle thet little brake just below where we'll cross?" suggested Pecos. "It hasn't been ridden yet an' there'll shore be a maverick or two. See what yu can do alone."

"Ump-umm," replied Terrill, imitating his vaquero's laconic expression.

"Gosh! I wish I could make yu mind," said Pecos, impatiently.

"Make *me* mind? Mr. Smith, you're desiring the impossible. You should obey me, and you never do."

"But, damn it, Terrill, I'm an old hand an' yu're a kid. I gotta confess yu're shore gettin' good."

"Who's a kid?"

"Yu are."

"I'm—well, you never mind *how* old I am. You wouldn't believe it, anyhow. But I'm going wherever you go. Savvy?"

Pecos saw the hopelessness of that tack. So he adopted another.

"Very wal. Course yu're my boss," he replied, sadly. "I'll just give up brandin' them mavericks across the river. 'Cause I care too much for yu, Terrill, to let yu try things thet might give me an' Sambo our everlastin'."

That was tremendously effective. Terrill looked queer and averted his face, as always when embarrassed. Pecos saw a constriction of the round throat.

"Then you do—care something for me, Pecos," he asked.

"Wal, I should smile I do—when yu're good."

"Don't spoil it by whens and ifs. . . . I'll do as you want me to."

They were stirring long before the red burst of sun glorified the eastern wall. Sambo had the horses up before Mauree called them to breakfast. Soon they rode down to the river, in the flush of dawn, and headed up the shore, where they had worn a trail.

Flocks of ducks got up with a splashing start and winged swift flight up the canyon; the salt-cedar trees were full of singing birds; buzzards soared overhead; and cattle made a great bustle to climb out of sight or disappear in one of the brakes.

At last they arrived at the place Pecos had marked as an easy one to ford the river.

"Wal, bub, heah's the partin' of the ways," announced Pecos, jovially. "Yu can shore keep busy all day. An' meet us heah aboot sundown."

"Bub!" ejaculated Terrill, scornfully.

"Huh? . . . Aw, excuse me, Terrill. I shore do forget."

"Wal, you shore do forget," drawled Terrill, tantalizingly. "For instance, you forget Don Felipe and Sawtell are due any day now. Suppose while you're way across there, chasing mavericks, they trailed me up heah—and nailed me."

"No, I didn't forget thet," denied Pecos, vigorously. "They couldn't come up this river any distance without me seein' them."

"They might. And if they did and caught me—neither you nor anyone else would ever see me again."

"See heah, boy, what the hell kind of talk's thet?" demanded Pecos, roused by the singular look and tone of the lad. Terrill knew something that he did not know.

"Have yu been honest with me—about those calf thieves?" went on Terrill.

"Shore. As far as I went. Are yu tryin' to scare me so's you can go along with us?"

"No. But I'm scared myself. I've become used to being with you, Pecos. It's so—so comfortable."

"All right. Stay comfortable an' come on," rejoined Pecos, tersely. But he was not satisfied with himself or with Terrill. "Grab yore rifles if it gets deep over there."

Without more ado Pecos headed Cinco into the river, taking a diagonal course downstream toward the opposite shore. Cinco was a big and powerful horse; moreover he had enjoyed a rest of several days. And he liked water. He crossed without swimming. Pecos got only his feet wet. Sambo dismounted halfway over and waded, to ease his own horse and lead Terrill's. The pony was small. He broke away from Sambo and lunged back.

"Rake him good!" yelled Pecos. "Yu're goin' too low down! . . . It's deeper! . . . Dig him—come on!"

Sambo had to wade up to his neck to make it, and Terrill's pony had to swim. He was a poor swimmer. There was one moment when Pecos thought he would have to spur Cinco in to go to Terrill's assistance. But the pony floundered to a foothold and soon gained the bank, with Terrill in high glee.

Pecos had observed in crossing that the water was a little roily. And he thought this had been caused by the disturbance his horse had made in the stream; however, the water was flowing toward him, and a second glance discovered to him that it was slightly discolored as far as he could see. He did not like it, though perhaps cattle had been wading in above.

This side of the Pecos, at least as far up as he could see, differed considerably from the west shore. Rough wooded steps and benches rose to the rim wall, which was insurmountable though only one-tenth the height of the sheer cliff in other places.

They rode up along the edge of the water until halted by the usual barrier. This point was surely a couple of miles above where they had crossed. Pecos did not need to thresh out the brushy terraces to flush mavericks, as had been necessary in the thickets of the brakes below. Here it was possible to see calves, yearlings, two-year steers, and old mossy-horns.

"Build yore fire, boy, an' red up the irons," shouted Pecos, almost excited at the prospect. "Million mavericks along these benches. Looks hard to ride an' rope, but they'll be easy to corner."

The work began fast and furiously. Terrill had to run from one spot to another with the red-hot branding-iron. Soon the air grew rank with the odor of burnt hair and hide. Pecos cornered a miscellaneous bunch on a bench where they could not get by him. They were stupid or tame; they had never been chased by a vaquero. Only the old wide-horned steers made any trouble. Pecos branded them all in time and number that was record for him.

"Seventy-eight pesos in less than thet many minutes," he yelled. "Aw, I don't know. . . . Yippy-yip! . . . Yore fire's not hot enough, Terrill. If yu wasn't so slow we'd shore get rich faster."

Sambo likewise did the best work Pecos had ever seen him do. Terrill was not only supposed to heat and run with the irons, but also keep track of numbers. This he soon failed on. Pecos and Sambo came to the point of dragging calves down off the upper benches, thus saving time. To keep one iron heating all the time and dash hither and yon with the others was about the toughest job Pecos had ever seen Terrill attempt. They not only lost track of numbers, but likewise of time.

"All de whole day long," sang Sambo. "All de whole day lo-on-ng."

"Pecos, I'm about ready to drop," cried Terrill, and he looked it. "Let's rest and eat."

"Nope. We shore gonna be hawgs today. 'Cause we don't want to cross over hyar again till next summer," replied Pecos. "Stay with us, Terrill, old pard."

Thus stimulated, Terrill saved his breath and went his limit. They worked downriver, and to Pecos, absorbed and thrilled at this unparalleled day, the hours were as minutes. Most of the time he was back of the trees and brush, out of sight of the river.

The first indication that time was flying appeared to be a darkening of the light. Indeed, the sun had gone behind the western wall, and the day three-fourths spent. Pecos wiped his grimy, sweaty face so that he could see. Terrill was staggering back down off the wide bench with his smoking irons. He had built a score of fire this lucky day.

The river appeared black-streaked gold instead of green. But it struck Pecos that the sinking of the sun over the rim could scarcely account for the changed color. Suddenly his heart leaped, as his quick eye registered the muddy hue of the water, and his ear caught a low, sullen, chafing murmur. A flood had come down. That explained the roily water in the early morning. Pecos cursed as he spurred Cinco along the brushy bench.

"Jump on an' ride!" he yelled, piercingly, to Terrill.

Terrill dropped everything to run for his mustang. Leaping astride, he hurried to meet Pecos coming down.

"What's up?"

"The river, by Gawd! Look at it! . . . Ride now an' don't break yore hoss's leg."

Sambo had seen and heard from above. He was dragging a calf by his rope. He got off to release it.

"Rustle, Sambo! If thet river's up a foot we're shore stuck."

Pecos could not tell how much the water had risen. But he was scared. Besides, he had to guide Cinco over the roughest kind of going. They had half a mile to travel to reach the place where they had come over. Cinco sensed danger and his blood was up. He was hard to hold. He crashed through the brush and sent the rocks rolling. In a few minutes of perilous riding Pecos got off the lowest bench to the sandy shore. Already the water had half covered it. Looking back, he saw that Terrill was behind, and that Sambo was in sight. Pecos rode at a gallop the rest of the way to the ford.

When he halted to look at the river his excitement was augmented by dismay. The channel had wholly changed. It had been fairly swift when low, but now it was swollen and fast, with swirls and eddies, and ridges of current. Logs and sticks and patches of debris were floating down. Close at hand the low sullen roar had a growing ominous sound. It reflected a strange black-and-gold sky, where broken clouds were taking on stormy colors of sunset. The whole scene, river, sky, walls, seemed strangely unreal and full of menace.

"Damn yore greaser soul!" yelled Pecos, shaking a fist at the treacherous river.

He deliberated a moment, while Terrill was splashing toward him. To be cut off from the ranch was a serious matter. With meat and water they would scarcely starve, but the prospect of being marooned there for months, probably, was something Pecos could not entertain for a moment. At that season when the river got high it stayed high. Pecos saw the theft of their cattle and the ruin of their hopes, if they were barred from the west side of this river.

Terrill came galloping down to halt the mustang beside Pecos.

"Don't wait—Pecos!" he panted, pale with excitement.

"Boy, can yu make it?"

"Shore I can—if we start quick. . . . She's rising fast—Pecos."

"—— —— luck! . . . A foot rise, maybe, wouldn't been so bad," ejaculated Pecos. "Keep above me."

Pecos eyed the river again, to get his bearing, then with a word made Cinco take to the water. Terrill spurred the mustang to a point a few yards above Pecos. Soon they were off the shallow bar. Terrill's horse had to swim before Pecos' lost his footing. They breasted that deep channel. But Terrill got behind. Pecos could not hold the iron-jawed Cinco, but as it happened, the horse soon found bottom again. Another plunge took him to shallow water, on the edge of the big bar. Here Pecos held Cinco.

Terrill was in difficulties, and Pecos made about to go to his assistance when the mustang touched the bar. But the water was swift and there appeared a chance of his being swept below the bar. Pecos spurred Cinco, to snatch at Terrill's bridle just in time to drag the mustang out of danger.

"I'd have—made it, Pecos," shrilled Terrill.

"Maybe yu would. But thet's the worst place, unless the damn river's changed. . . . Work above me now, so if he founders I can grab yu."

Pecos turned to see that Sambo had arrived at the point to take to the river. "Haid upstream, Sambo!" he yelled. "Allow for current. Haid upstream!"

To Pecos' further dismay and increasing alarm he found that the water was fully two feet higher than normal and so swift and thick that the horses could not be kept to the line.

Halfway across the mustang slipped and rolled, dumping Terrill out of the saddle. There was a terrific floundering and splashing before the lad reappeared. Then he floated face up and inactive on the surface. In the struggle, the mustang had bumped or kicked him.

It took tremendous effort of arms and legs to turn Cinco in that current. But Pecos accomplished it in time to stretch a long arm and catch Terrill before he drifted out of reach. The ensuing wrench almost jerked Pecos out of his saddle. Cinco, up to his haunches in the dragging current, kept his feet. He appeared more thoroughly angered than frightened, and once headed right again he made a magnificent struggle to keep to the line Pecos wanted. But that was only possible where he could wade.

Pecos had not attempted to drag Terrill across the saddle, fearing to burden Cinco too greatly. With a powerful grip on Terrill's coat under his chin Pecos kept the pale face above water.

Then suddenly Cinco plunging into deeper water, went under, and was swept downstream. The water came up to Pecos' waist. Cinco came up, swimming vigorously.

"Stay with it, old boy!" rasped Pecos, hard as iron, as he pulled the horse a little to the right. "Steady! Nothin' for yu, Cinco!"

But it was increasingly manifest that the ordeal was a great one, almost too much for the wonderful horse. They were off the bar in deep water sweeping like a mill-race. If Cinco could keep from being carried out of line before they passed a shallow point Pecos was heading for they would be saved.

There was no use to beat him. Seeing that he would probably fail, Pecos slipped out of the saddle and with right hand holding Terrill up he dropped back to seize the tail of the horse with his left. That move relieved Cinco of the weight which had handicapped him. It did not impede him to drag Pecos behind.

Pecos had extreme difficulty in keeping Terrill above water. Already the lad's head had been under too often and too long.

Suddenly something jarred Cinco. He snorted and lunged. The yellow current roared in seething foam around him. He had struck the rocky shore. He lunged again, sending the water in flying sheets. Then his black shoulders heaved up. At this juncture, Pecos let go to find he was about waist-deep. As he gathered Terrill up in his arms he looked back to see that Sambo had fared better. He had started farther upstream and had kept to the bar.

Pecos carried Terrill up on the bank and laid him on the grass. Bareheaded, white, motionless, with eyes closed, the lad looked dead.

Pecos tore at the loose coat buttoned up to the neck.

"Damn this heah coat!" flashed Pecos, passionately. "No wonder you cain't swim. . . . Terrill! . . . Oh, lad, yore not daid!"

Frantically Pecos ripped open the wet shirt to feel for Terrill's heart. It beat. Terrill was still alive. A cold, sick horror left Pecos. But what was this?

With shaking hands he spread wide the lad's shirt, suddenly to be transfixed. His staring gaze fell upon round marble-white swelling breasts.

"My Gawd! . . . A woman!"

At that instant Terrill's beautiful breast heaved. There followed a gasping intake of breath. Consciousness was returning. Then Pecos awoke from his stupefaction. Emotion such as he had never known flooded over him. With wildly swift hands he closed and buttoned the shirt over that betraying breast, and likewise the coat.

Then he waited, on his knees, calling on all his faculties to keep Terrill's secret inviolate. He could meet that, as he had met so many desperate situations. But what of this strange and tumultuous rapture of his heart?

Terrill stirred. The long eyelashes quivered on the pale wet cheeks. Pecos fortified himself to look into eyes that must somehow be different. They opened. But he was scarcely prepared for the dark humid mystery of the reviving mind and soul—for the purple depths of beauty and of passion.

"Pecos," Terrill whispered, faintly.

"Heah," drawled the vaquero.

"The river—the flood! . . . I went under. . . . There was a gurgling roar. . . . All went black. . . . Oh, where are we?"

"Wal, Terrill, yu 'pear to be lyin' heah on the goldenrod, an' comin' out of yore faint," drawled Pecos. "But I ain't so damn shore whether I'm in heaven or not."

"Sambo!"

Pecos had forgotten the negro. But Sambo appeared, wading, his horse ashore some distance above.

"Good! Sambo made it fine, Terrill. . . . An' shore there's yore pony climbin' the bank below."

Terrill sat up dizzily, with an instinctive hand going to her breast, where her fingers fastened between the lapels.

"Pecos, I shore owe yu heaps," murmured Terrill, dreamily. "First at Eagle's Nest, from I—I don't know what . . . . Then at home—the black nights—the terrible loneliness . . . and now from this awful river. . . . I—I don't know how to ——"

"Wal, what's a pardner for?" interrupted Pecos, once more his cool drawling self. "I'll fetch yore hoss an' we'll meander home. . . . All in the day's ride, lad, it's all in the day's ride."

CHAPTER ELEVEN

It was mid-November. Early frost had severed yellow willow leaves from the branches, and seared the goldenrod and killed the scarlet of the vines on the rocks. The melancholy days had come. Birds and ducks had long bade farewell to Lambeth Canyon; and the coyotes were sneaking down off the bleak range. Wary of the watchful Sambo, they kept to the thickets and rocks until night, when they pierced the solitude with their wild barks.

A norther was blowing, the first of the season, and the wind moaned up on the rims. Drab clouds scudded low toward the south and scattering rain pattered on the cabin roof.

Terrill stood in the doorway, watching as always when she was alone, for Pecos. He was in the canyon somewhere. Sambo often rode or hunted out of reach of call, but Pecos, since the flooded river had ended branding operations for the season, worked around the ranch. It was time for vaqueros to ride in from Eagle's Nest or the several ranches below. And so long as Terrill could remember they had made use of the trail down the gulch. Her father had complied with the hospitable custom of the Southwest, even in case of vaqueros whom he suspected of stealing from him. It was safer not to appear suspicious.

But Pecos Smith would not be hospitable to Don Felipe's outfit, or any other questionable one. And long had Terrill dreaded the day.

Somewhere around this time came her birthday. She knew that it fell upon a Wednesday and that she would be nineteen years old, incredible as it seemed. But she did not know which day Wednesday was. Or was it her twentieth birthday? She had difficulty persuading herself that she was only nineteen, and over and over again she calculated events of the fleeting past. How swift the years! Yet what ages she had lived since the day she rode away from the old Southern home! Whenever she saw moss on a tree she suffered an exquisite pang.

"Mauree, how old am I?" she asked as the negress came by from her cabin.

"Honey, yo is eighteen."

"No. I'm more than that. Nineteen at least."

"How come yo tink ob dat, after all dese years?"

"I don't know. But I feel terribly old."

"Shucks, Rill, yo ain't old," replied Mauree, and then, after a careful glance around, to see if the coast was clear, she whispered, "Honey, is yo gonna keep on forebber bein' a—a boy when yo's a gurl?"

Terrill knew she had prompted this broaching of a long-forbidden subject. She could not scold Mauree and be honest, though the mere mention of her secret terrified her. But she had failed herself. After her father was gone she had accepted the deceit as the only defense possible to her. It had become endurable to live perpetually in fear of discovery—until that fateful day when she burst through the broken door of Brasee's abode prison to look into the face of Pecos Smith. What had she not lived through since then?

"Oh, Mauree! Don't whisper it! I'd fall dead in my tracks if—if *he* ever found me out."

"But, chile, fer de good Lawd's sake, it ain't natchell. It ain't right. Why yo's a woman! How yo gonna hide dat bosom any longer? It's heavin' right dis minnit like a plate of jelly."

Terrill pressed her hands to her tumultuous breast. Without and within that cried her sex. And it seemed to cry more than a physical secret, more than the lie she had lived—the strange emotion that had insidiously, imperceptibly grown upon her, until all-powerful, it had flung at her the terrifying truth of love.

"Mauree, I must hide it—I must," she cried, and she meant this consuming torture, this thing that made her hot and cold by turns, that toyed with her peace, that ambushed her every mood, that awakened in her longings she had never dreamed of.

"But, yo fool chile, yo cain't hide it," ejaculated Mauree. "Yo nebber growed up in mind, but yo sho is a woman in body. I sew till I'se mos blind makin' yo clothes to hide yo real self. But I can't do it much mo. Why, if dis Pecos wuzn't blind himself—a simpleminded boy who nebber knowed woman, he'd 'a' guessed it long ago."

"Oh, do—do you think he will—find me out?" faltered Terrill, in despair.

"He sho will, sooner or later."

"What on earth can I—I do?"

"I dunno. Why yo so scared he'll find you out?"

"It would be—terrible."

"Chile, yo lub dis Pecos. Dat's what ail yo so. De doomsday ob woman has done fell on yo."

"Hush!" whispered Terrill, and she fled.

In the darkness of her room Terrill suffered an anguish of fact that had been but a dream. Mauree had called her child. If that were true, she grew out of childhood in this hour of realization. And when the wild shame and the nameless pang had eased, Terrill tried to face the crisis of her life. If she confessed to Pecos that her claim of masculinity had been a hoax, that for years she had worn the garb of a boy, first to please her father, and later to protect herself in that wild country—if she confronted him with the truth, would he not be so disgusted and alienated that he would leave her? It seemed to her that he would. And anything would be better than to be abandoned to the old fears, the lonely nights, the dreaded days—and now to this incomprehensible longing to see Pecos, to hear him, to know he was near, to shiver at a chance contact and to burn for more. No—she could not bear to lose him.

She must keep her miserable secret as long as she could, and when the unforeseen betrayed her, if Pecos despised her unmaidenly conduct and left her—then there would be nothing to live for.

Terrill went back in retrospect to the last years of the war when her mother had trained her to meet the very part her father had forced her to play. Her mother had divined it. Hence the lessons and the talks and the prayers that had shaped Terrill's spiritual life, that had kept her a child. Terrill's sharpened intelligence told her that if she had not hidden her sex in the guise of a boy she never could have lived up to those aloof and noble teachings. To be a boy had earned the solitude she imagined she had hated. Her mother had the wise vision of the dying. Terrill would not have had it different.

But she was a woman now and this love had come upon her. What could she do to avert calamity? She had suffered through love of mother, love of father, and suffered still. This thing, however, was different. And she realized that now, with the scales dropped from her eyes, she would be uplifted to heaven one moment and plunged into hell the next. Still, if she were a woman she could find strength and cunning to hide that. Else what was it to grow into a woman? If she were clever Pecos might never find her out and never leave her.

Then came another startling thought, like a lightning flash in the night, and it was that she wanted him to find out she was a woman. Longed for it almost as terribly as she feared he might! Between these two agonies she must live and fight for what she knew not. A woman's intuition of hitherto unknown powers of subtlety or reserve, of incalculable possibilities, paralleled in her mind this sense of a tragic suspension between two states.

Outside on the porch a step sounded—a step that had never failed to thrill or shake her, and now set her stiff on her bed, with a heart that seemed to still its beats to listen.

"Mauree, where's thet darned Terrill?" drawled Pecos, at the door.

"I dunno," lied the negress, nonchalantly.

"Dog-goneit! Nobody knows nothin' aboot this hyar shack," complained Pecos. "Hyar I slave myself damn near daid while Sambo goes gunnin' around, an' thet boy sleeps or loafs on me. I'm gonna bust up the outfit."

Of late Pecos had talked in that strain, something unprecendented. Yet his solicitude, his unfailing watchfulness, and a something indefinable that was so sweet to Terrill—these belied his complaints. Terrill trembled there in the darkness on her little bed.

"Yo is?"

"Yas, I is," snorted Pecos.

"Pecos, yo done pretty good hyar wid us. Yo be a damnation idgit to throw us away lak rags now."

"Say, who said thet?"

"Not Mars Rill. No, suh. It was dat no-good yaller niggah of mine. He sed it."

"Ahuh. Wal, Mauree, it's true. An' I'm a liar. Why, I couldn't no more leave Terrill than go back to thet old life of driftin', drinkin', shootin'."

"Mars Pecos, I'se sho glad. For why yo talk dat way, den?"

"Wal, I gotta talk to somebody or I'll bust. Sambo runs off huntin' like a canebrake nigger. An' Terrill lays down on me, all day long."

"Nobody to lub yo, huh? Mars Pecos, what yo need is a woman."

"Ha! Ha! Thet's a good one. . . . Lord! who'd ever have me, Mauree?"

"Yo's a blame handsome vaquero, Pecos."

"Wal, if I am, it never did me any good. Mauree, I never really had a—a woman, in my life."

"Lawd amercy! Yo *is* a liar."

"Honest, Mauree."

"I believes no man, Pecos, white or black."

"Yu wouldn't believe this, either. I'd give my half of our T L cattle to have a decent pretty girl to love me. One yu know thet hadn't been pawed familiar by some man. I reckon I'd hug an' kiss her 'most to death."

"Pecos, I'se sho yo could git some black-eyed greaser wench fer less'n dat."

"Hullo, heah's Sambo," said Pecos, at the sound of heavy steps on the porch.

"Whar yo been, niggah?"

"I'se been huntin', woman."

"What fo' yo hunt when yo cain't hit nothin'?"

"Pecos, I'se hung up a fine fat deer."

"Good. I'm tired of beef. How's supper comin'?"

"'Mos' ready. Yo kin call Rill."

"Sambo, put on some wood so we can see to eat. . . . Hey, Terrill! . . . Are you shore he's in?"

"Yas, Mars Pecos."

Pecos called again, louder this time. But Terrill, secure in some delicious late-mounting sense of power, lay perfectly silent.

"Terrill!"

Ordinarily such a stentorian yell from Pecos would have scared Terrill out of her boots. All it did now was to send the blood rushing back to her heart.

"Ughh-huh," replied Terrill, drowsily.

"Yu come out heah."

Terrill got up, and slipping on a new blouse Mauree had given her that day, she stepped from the darkness of her room into the fire-lit living-room

"What's all the hollering aboot, Pecos?" inquired Terrill, demurely, and with a yawn she stretched her arms high, and looked him straight in the eyes, with her new-found duplicity.

But a glance was all he gave her. "I've been worried aboot you. An' supper is ready."

No meal had ever been so enjoyable as this one to Terrill, so fraught with the delicious peril of her situation, so monstrously intriguing with a consciousness of her falsehood.

"Boy, you don't eat much. What ails yu?" said Pecos, before they had finished.

"Can't I fall a little off my feed without worrying you?" demanded Terrill, petulantly.

"I reckon yu cain't do anythin' off color without worryin' me."

They got up presently. Terrill pulled a rustic armchair closer to the fire, while Pecos filled his pipe. Sambo and Mauree sat down to eat their meal. Pecos took a long look out into the black night, then closed the door.

"Yu hyar thet wind, boy?" queried Pecos, as he drew the other chair up. "Blowin' the real *del norte* tonight. Heah thet rain!—Dog-gone if it ain't nice an' homey hyar! Fire feels so good. . . . Terrill, if it wasn't for them damn rustlers I'm lookin' for I'd come darn near bein' happy heah with yu."

"Same heah," murmured Terrill, trusting her gaze on the fire. "But I'd 'most forgot Don Felipe's outfit. . . . Pecos, will those vaqueros of his dare to steal our stock *now?*"

"Shore. Even if they did know Pecos Smith was on the job they'd take watchin'. Yu see we've a string of old cattle and new branded mavericks for twenty miles an' more down the river. We've put our brand on aboot every maverick in the brakes. Thet's goin' to rile Felipe's outfit. They'll take to brand-burnin'."

"But we could recognize any burning out of our brand," protested Terrill.

"Shore we could—if we ever see it. There's the rub. Thet outfit won't burn a strange brand on our cattle an' turn them out, as has been the custom of brand-burners. They'll throw a herd together an' drive it pronto."

"Oughtn't we ride down the river and see? They don't have to come through our place to get down into the brakes."

"Shore we'll go, soon as this norther blows out. . . . Come to think of it, I'd better work some on yore rifle. I saved it from rustin', but thet darned sand is shore hard to get out."

"Say, I filled myself full of water and sand that day," retorted Terrill.

"Pretty close shave, son," responded Pecos, shaking his head.

Sambo fetched the rifle to Pecos, who worked the action. There was still a grating sound of sand inside.

"I reckon some boilin' water will do the trick."

"Pecos, can't you get me a smaller rifle? This one almost kicks the daylights out of me. Bad as that old Sharps of Dad's."

"Shore, when we take thet trip next spring with our herd of cattle."

"Oh, it's so terribly long. Let's go now."

"An' leave our stock for those outfits to clean up? Not much. We'll go next spring after we've done some cleanin' up ourselves."

When Pecos drawled one of his cool assumptions like that, Terrill had no reply ready. She could not repress a shudder. This vaquero spoke of a fight as carelessly as of a ride. That dampened Terrill's spontaneity for the time being, and rather than have Pecos see that she was downcast she went to bed. But sleep was not to be soon wooed. She had done nothing to make her tired physically, and her emotions seemed to have transformed her into another creature. Wherefore she lay snug in her warm blankets, wide eyes staring into the blackness, thinking, wondering about the future and Pecos. He filled her whole life now. There was no one else; there was nothing else.

Meanwhile her senses were alive to the *del norte.* The norther was a familiar thing to Terrill and she hated it, especially at night, when the conformation of the canyon and the structure of the cabin made sounding-boards for the gale. It moaned and shrieked and roared by turns. During these lulls Pecos could be heard talking to Sambo. After a while, however, this sound ceased and the cabin was silent. Then the monstrous loneliness of Lambeth Canyon assailed Terrill as never before, even in the far past, when she had first come there. She was not a man. It was solemn black night, full of weird voices of the storm, fraught with the menace of the wild range, and she had been forced into womanhood, with a woman's love and hunger, which she must cruelly hide, flooding her wakeful hours with the inexorable and inscrutable demands of life.

Next day the norther blew out of a clear sky, and the sheltered sunny spots in the canyon were the desirable ones.

Terrill got around to work again with Pecos, and no task frightened her. Moods were of no use. It had done her no good to brood, to sulk, or dream, unless to incur Pecos' solicitude, which was at once a torture and a delight to her. When he came searching for her, patient, kind, somehow different, she had to fight a wild desire to throw herself into his arms. She would do that some day; she knew she would. Then—the deluge!

She could do justice to any boy's labor for a day. And since she had discovered that what little peace of mind she achieved was when she was working with Pecos, she embraced it. She never did anything in moderation. And toward the close of this day she got scolded for overdoing.

"Say, I can pack a log with any boy," she retorted, secretly pleased at his observation, yet becoming conscious again of a slight difference in him. Perhaps she imagined it. Whereupon she reverted to a former character, just to see if she could rouse him as she used to. But Pecos did not lose his temper; he did not chase her, or slap her on the back, or make any objection to her omissions.

The norther passed and the warm days came again. Then it was delightful weather. Working about the ranch was pleasant. Terrill marveled at the improvements and wished her father had lived to see them. Pecos could turn his hand to anything.

"When are we going to ride down the river?" Terrill asked more than once. But Pecos was evasive about this. And she observed that though he had always been watchful, he seemed to grow more so these late November days.

Time slipped by. And every night Terrill said her prayers—as she had never ceased to do—and wept, and hugged her secret, and dreamed wild and whirling dreams. And every morning when she awakened she made new resolves not to be such a little fool this day and to avoid the crazy incomprehensible things she had done in the past. Only to find that she grew worse!

She could not leave Pecos alone. She was unhappy when he was out of her sight. She was unhappier when she was with him because the sweetness of it, the havoc that threatened, were harder to bear than loneliness. Lastly Terrill detected a new mood in Pecos, or one she had never noticed before. Either he was worried or melancholy, or both, but neither of these states of mind was evinced by him while Terrill was present. It was only when he thought he was alone that he betrayed them. Terrill got into the habit of peeping through a chink between the logs of her partition, when she was supposed to have gone to bed and when Pecos sat before the fire. Something was wrong with him. Was he growing sick of this tame life around Lambeth Ranch? Terrill grew cold all over, and longed for something to happen, for rustlers to raid their stock, for that horrid Breen Sawtell to come, and even Don Felipe. Everything, however, served only to add fuel to the fire of her love, until she felt that it was consuming her.

For a long while Terrill had kept faith in the belief that it was enough just to have Pecos there. But this grew to be a fallacy. One of her particularly impish moods betrayed this to her. A weakness of Pecos' had been hard to find but he had one. He simply could not bear to be tickled. Terrill had found it out by accident, and upon divers occasions had exercised the prerogative of a boy to surprise Pecos and dig strong little fingers into his ribs. The effect had been galvanizing; moreover, it proved to be something she could not resist.

Pecos was husking corn and did not know Terrill had stealthily stolen up behind him. He was sitting on a sack back of the corral. Sambo was packing the cornstalks up from the field and depositing them in front of Pecos. Both of them were tremendously proud of the little patch of corn they had raised. It was a fine warm day and Pecos sat in his shirt sleeves, husking the sheaths off the ears and tossing the latter into a golden pile.

Terrill's step was that of a mouse. She got right behind Pecos before he had the slightest inkling of her presence. Then, extending two brown hands with fingers spread like the claws of an eagle, she shot them out to rake his ribs with a fiendish glee.

Pecos let out a yelp. He fell off the sack in a spasmodic wrestling, with Terrill on top of him.

"You little devil!" he rasped, snatching at her.

Terrill would have been frightened if she had not been in the throes of other sensations. But her usual nimbleness failed her, although she got clear of Pecos. However, before she ran twenty feet she fell upon her face in the grass. Pecos pounced upon her. He knelt astride of her and dug his long steel-like fingers into her ribs. Terrill passed from one paroxysm to another. Even if she had not been exquisitely ticklish, such contact from Pecos' hands would have driven her well-nigh crazy. He was yelling at her all the time, but she could not distinguish what the words were. Then, letting up on her ribs, Pecos boxed her ears and got up.

Terrill lay there on her face until she had recovered. The wonder of it was that she was not furious, not outraged, not frightened, not anything but blissfully happy. Presently when she arose to flee she took good care that he did not see her face. She ran to the cabin and hid; then it was that she learned Pecos' mere presence no longer sufficed. Such a subterfuge as the tickling episode had been a shameless excuse to get her hands on him. In her heart, however, she knew she had not anticipated such a devastating response, and suddenly she found herself weeping violently.

Presently voices disturbed Terrill. She raised her head from a tear-wet pillow. Could Pecos have returned so early from that important task of corn-husking? She heard Sambo, then a strange voice, and finally Pecos. Terrill lost no time in getting to the living-room door.

Sambo was helping a rider off his horse. Evidently he was wounded or at least injured, for Terrill espied blood. She had seen the man somewhere, probably in Eagle's Nest. He must be one of the cattlemen who shared the range. Sight of Pecos then startled Terrill more than had the stranger. It had come, then—war over cattle that Pecos expected.

"Yu bad hurt?" queried Pecos.

"I reckon not," replied the man, rather weakly. "But I had to ride—bleedin' like a stuck pig. . . . Guess it's loss of blood."

"Help him to the bench, Sambo," directed Pecos. "Terrill, yu fetch some blankets, then yore dad's kit. . . . Mauree, we'll have to have water an' clean rags."

Terrill, having rushed to fulfill Pecos' order, did not stay out on the porch to look on, but stepped inside and listened. Despite what the man said, she was afraid he would die. She leaned against the door, quaking. That might happen to Pecos any day. What a coward she was!

"Wal," said Pecos, cheerfully, after a few moments, "yore pretty bloody for a gunshot no worse than thet. Shore there's nothin' else?"

"No."

"Yu bled a heap an' thet's what put yu off yore pins. I'm glad to say yu'll be all right in a few days. We'll take care of yu heah."

"Lucky I made it. Course I knowed where Lambeth's Ranch was, but it 'peared a damn long ways."

"Ahuh. How aboot some questions?"

"Okay. Gimme another drink."

"Water or whisky?" drawled Pecos.

"I'll take whisky, this time . . . thanks. My name's Watson. Hal Watson. Hail from the Gulf. Rockport. I've been runnin' stock out of Eagle's Nest fer a couple of years. Thet's how I come to get pinked."

"Hal Watson? Heahed the name somewheres?" replied Pecos.

"I reckon you're the fellar who got young Lambeth away from Brasee last spring?"

"Shore was. Smith's my name."

"You haven't dropped into Eagle's Nest since?"

"No. But never mind aboot me. Yu runnin' cattle below heah on the river?"

"Yes. I started in with a thousand head."

"What's yore mark?"

"It was a diamond, but it looks like a star now," replied Watson, meaningly.

"Diamond, eh? Wal, I shore saw a lot of yore stock last spring. Some close as five miles below heah. Reckon we might have branded a few of yore mavericks. Ha! Ha! But I didn't see any diamond brands burned into stars."

"All fresh done, Smith. I reckon thet outfit hasn't been operatin' long."

"What outfit?"

"I don't know. Some white cowhands an' greaser vaqueros. They come across the Pecos from the east."

"Wal. . . . Did yu see anythin' of Don Felipe's outfit?"

"They's workin' upriver, so I was told at Eagle's Nest. They're worryin' Stafford a lot. He sold out his Y stock an's runnin' only one brand, the old Double X X."

"Thet brand is mixed up with ours, too."

"Smith, there are some new brands that will make you think. But let me tell you how I happen to be here. . . . I left home a week or so ago with two of my boys, a Mexican an' a cowhand I recently hired. Said his name was Charley Stine. I'm satisfied now he was in with thet new outfit. We had two pack-hosses, an' we dropped off into the brakes above Stafford's. I hadn't ridden in there for months an' I was plumb surprised. More stock than I ever seen, but my brand was as scarce as hens' teeth. We found about fifty head fenced in a brake an' then my eyes were opened. My small diamond brand had been burned into a clumsy big star. You can bet I was red-headed. Stine advised goin' back, an' then's when I got leary about him. You know thet big brake down ten miles or more below here? It has two branches, shape of a Y. Well, we run plumb into runnin' hosses, bawlin' calves, flyin' ropes, an' burnin' hair. When I rode out of the brush into sight an' yelled that outfit was shore surprised."

"Man alive! Yu should have kept out of sight an' let yore gun do the yellin'," declared Pecos, severely.

"I quit packin' a gun for fear I'd kill some one. An' if I'd had one I'd shore done it then. Well, they didn't wait to see whether I had one or not, but began to shoot. Stine disappeared an' the Mexican was shot off his hoss. I had to ride for it, an' as they had me cut off from below I lit out for upriver. Two of them, both white cowhands, chased me a mile or more, shootin' to beat hell. They shore meant to kill me."

"Wal, yu don't say so," drawled Pecos, dryly. "It shore takes a lot to convince some men. I don't need to ask if yu're a Texan."

"No, that ain't hard to guess. I've been only about five years in Texas. . . . Well, I outrode those men an' got away by the skin of my teeth. Never knew I was shot till I grew wet an' felt all wet an' slippery. That's all. . . . Gimme another drink."

Pecos took to pacing the porch, his hands behind his back, his brow knitted in thought. Terrill was almost repelled. He was no longer her smiling, cool, and kindly Pecos. She stared as if fascinated. Vague recollection of the story he had related about himself now recurred. Either she had not believed it or had forgotten the bloody details. Then she did recall her first sight of him at Eagle's Nest, and somehow that picture faintly resembled this somber Pecos.

"Honey, yo is sho pale round de gills," remarked Mauree, drawing Terrill away from the door. "Now yo lissen to yo' Mauree. They ain't nothin' bad gonna happen. I'se got second sight, chile, an' yo can gamble on it."

Sambo came in at that juncture, apparently as unconcerned as usual.

"Yo lazy perdiculous wench! Whar's dar supper? We is hungry men."

"Sambo, I done had it 'mos' hot when dis Watson fellar come."

The early twilight soon fell. Sambo revived the smoldering fire and then helped Mauree hurry the evening meal. Terrill kept away from the door, but still she saw Pecos pass to and fro. Presently Sambo called him.

"Boss, is dat fellar able to eat?"

"I reckon, Sambo," replied Pecos, seating himself. "Terrill, I'm shore sorry I cain't lie to you."

"Don't ever lie to me, Pecos," she entreated.

"Wal, we're due to lose some stock."

"I heard every word he said to you," went on Terrill, hurriedly. "Pecos, if we don't lose anything but stock—I won't care. We're no better than other ranchers."

"Terrill, thet's shore sensible talk from yu. Maybe yu'll grow up yet."

Pecos spoke no more, ate sparingly, and soon went outside again.

"How yu feelin', Watson?" he queried.

"Not so bad when I lay still."

"Wal, yu'll be settin' up in the mawnin'. An' as I'm goin' to ride out early, I'd like to ask you some more questions."

"Where you goin', Smith?"

"I'm takin' the back trail, an' when the sun rises I'll be peepin' over my rifle down into thet Y Canyon."

"From the rim?"

"Shore. I can ride there in less than two hours."

"By Gawd! I'd like to go with you!"

"Nope. You need some rest. I'll be back before noon. Tell me where thet cow outfit is camped."

"Right in the middle below the forks."

"Ahuh. Thet's a long shot from the north rim, but I reckon I can burn some of them. I'll take two rifles an' scare 'em to jump in the river, if no more. Did yu see whether they had rifles or not?"

"Come to think of it, they wasn't usin' rifles, else I wouldn't be here."

"Ahuh. . . . Now what was yu aboot to tell me aboot Brasee?"

"He's dead. Killed by Jade, the barkeeper."

"I reckoned he'd not last long. Was it the same bartender I slammed the door on last spring?"

"No. Brasee or one of his greasers did for him. Place changed hands again. You wouldn't know Eagle's Nest."

"You don't say? What's happened? Somebody strike gold?"

"Stafford told me it was Texas gettin' a move on. Cattle have gone to ten dollars a head. Maybe it won't last, but Stafford thinks it will. Beginnin' of a new era, he says. You know when cattle were thick an' cheap there wasn't much movement, especially of rustlers. But this late summer an' fall all that changed. Trail herds drivin' north now, by Horsehead Crossin' in West Texas, an' the Chisholm Trail is a procession these days. Comanches on the war-path. Texans buyin' more stock than ever from Mexico, an' a hell of a lot of it is gettin' stolen right back again. Rustlers, gamblers, hoss thieves, gun-fighters, outlaws, loose women, all flockin' in with settlers, cattlemen, soldiers. It's one hell of a movement, Smith."

"Humph. I'm shore surprised. But yu cain't mean thet all this is affectin' it out hyar west of the Pecos?"

"Shore I do. Course nothin' like rumor has it for all the rest of cattle Texas. The Pecos has a hard name an' it's a far country. But if Texas is goin' to be a cattle empire—which Stafford swears is as shore as the sun shines—why, West Texas will soon be runnin' a hundred thousand head where now it's runnin' a thousand."

"Ten dollars a haid!" Pecos whistled long and low. "More'n ever damn good reason to hang onto yore cattle. I told my young partner, Lambeth, dog-gone near thet very thing."

"Smith, if you can hang on to half your stock, or one-third—you're rich."

"I'm not countin' any calves before they're branded, but this heah news shore . . . But, say, what's this done to Eagle's Nest?"

"Woke it up, Smith. There's twenty-odd families now, not countin' greasers. Another store. Freighters every week. An' last but not least there's law come in."

"Law! What you mean—law?" queried Pecos, sharply.

"Thet's all. Law."

"Rangers?"

"No."

"Sheriff?"

"No. There's a little fat old duffer come to Eagle's Nest. Calls himself Judge Roy Bean. He built a home aboot a block from the corner Brasee had, you remember. An' this newcomer put up a sign—a good big one you can see—an' it says on it: 'Judge Roy Bean—Law West of the Pecos.'"

"Law West of the Pecos," echoed Pecos, incredulously. "For Gawd's sake! . . . Is this hyar Bean out of his haid?"

"Smith, it shore 'pears so. He's constituted himself sheriff, judge, court, law. Nobody knows if he has any papers from the government. He's been asked to show 'em an' he showed that fellar a big six-shooter. Thet ain't the best. He runs a saloon an' he's his own bartender. He stops holdin' court to sell a drink an' he stops bartendin' to hold court. He runs a card game, an' he'll bust into that to arrest a fellar for cheatin'. An', by thunder, I 'most forgot. He marries people."

"A parson, too?" whooped Pecos.

"No, he hardly claims to be a parson. A judicial right, an' moral for the community, he calls it."

"Judge Roy Bean! . . . I'll shore call on thet hombre. . . . An' he marries people?—Dog-gone!—I reckon I could get a wife now—if thet Mary Heald would have me!"

CHAPTER TWELVE

Terrill had to clap her hand over her mouth to keep from shrieking. It might have been hysterical laughter, but only she would have known how mirthless it would be. Flying to her room, nearly knocking her brains out in the dark, she barred her door, and awoke to more astounding proclivities of a woman.

"Find a wife!" she whispered fiercely to herself as she tore at the bed covers in the dark and kicked at nothing. "That Heald girl?—Merciful God! I thought he'd forgotten her. . . . The cold-hearted faithless wretch! He's what my mother told me to beware of. . . . But I'm his boss. He's working for me. What's partnership? This is my land, my cattle. He can't marry anyone but . . . Oh! Oh!"

Terrill slipped to her knees and buried her head in the pillows. Pecos had no idea she was a girl—that she could be his wife. But how could he love her if he never knew she was a girl? Who was there to tell him that she, Terrill Lambeth, loved him, adored him, worshiped him more than any woman ever had or ever could worship him? And the old torment rushed over her again, augmented a thousandfold by a new instrument of this terrible thing, love—jealousy.

She was in the midst of the worst hour she had ever endured when a knock on her door sent her stiff and thrilling.

"Terrill, air yu in bed?" asked Pecos, in an anxious voice.

"I—I— Yes," choked Terrill.

"What's wrong with yore voice? Sounds sort of hoarse."

Terrill made a magnificent effort. "Must have had my haid under the blanket," she managed to enunciate clearly. "What do you want, Pecos?"

"Nothin' much. Only to talk a little. This man Watson upset me."

"Pecos, I'll get up and—and dress," returned Terrill, brazenly, anathematizing her silly falsehood.

"No. I'll come in," he replied, and to Terrill's horror and transfixing gush of blood, the bar of the door, which had evidently not slipped into place, dropped at Pecos' push and let him in.

"Shore dark as hell in this heah little cubbyhole of yores," he drawled. "First time I ever was in heah, come to think aboot it. Yu used to be such a queer lad."

Terrill never knew how she had accomplished the phenomenon, but when Pecos stumbled to her bed and sat down upon it she was lying on the far side with a blanket over her.

"Wal, son, I just wanted to tell yu thet I'm ridin' off before daylight an' won't see yu till I get back," said Pecos.

"But, Pecos—don't—you oughtn't go," cried Terrill.

"Listen, pard. We've struck some bad times. I reckoned we would. An' the thing for me to do is meet them. What's the use of us runnin' cattle if we cain't fight for them? If I needed yu or thought there was any risk leavin' yu behind I'd shore take yu along. But I'll be ridin' like hell in the dark. An' yu know Cinco. It's a thousand to one I'll get back pronto, but—an' see heah, Rill, I—I'm hatin' to give yu this hunch—if I lost out at such odds an' didn't come back, yu wait a reasonable time, then leave for Eagle's Nest with Watson an' the niggers. Savvy?"

Terrill's lips were mute. It was her arms she had to contend with—for they had a mad impulse to go up round his neck. To keep him home! She wondered if they would.

"Reckoned I'd jar yu," he went on. "Heah's my money belt. Hide it under yore bed. In case I don't show up, thet's yores. I'd advise yu to leave this Pecos country."

"Leave my—home!" gasped Terrill.

"Shore. Terrill, yu dunce, I'm only sayin' all this because somethin' *might* happen. . . . An' I've—I—I've been powerful fond of yu, lad. . . . Thet's all. Now adios, an' sleep tight."

His hand groped for her head, and finding it, fastened his fingers in her hair, as he had been wont to do, and gave it a tug. Then he was gone, leaving Terrill prey to such sensations that she made sure she would die with them. But they did not kill her then, and she concluded that she must be pretty tough.

The heavy money belt lay over her like a caressing arm. Terrill felt of it. How thick and soft! It was full of bills. Where had Pecos gotten all that money? She remembered Pecos' story of the two cowhands with whom he had gone to maverick-branding, and who had betrayed him by burning brands. There was all the difference in the world. A maverick belonged to anybody, at least anyone who owned cattle on the range. But these brand-burners and brand-blotters knew they were guilty.

Terrill undressed and went to bed, with the leather belt around her. The weight of it, or the consciousness that it belonged to Pecos, disturbed her, so she finally put it under her pillow. Then it gave rise to a fearful dream, in which Pecos was about to be hanged for rustling, and she rode up on thundering Cinco to snatch him out of the very noose. They escaped very romantically and satisfactorily, but when Terrill awakened the dream haunted her.

She was dropping off to sleep again when she heard a thud of soft feet outside on the porch. Pecos had jumped down from his loft. Her little window was a mere gray patch in the black wall. She got up on her knees to peep out. The stars were wan. It was a couple of hours before dawn. Pecos' steps sounded faintly, and after a considerable interval she heard a rapid beat of hoofs on the trail. Pecos had ridden away on his deadly errand. It gave her panic, yet in spite of that there came to her a sense of disaster for those thieving riders of the brakes. Neither her father, nor Sambo, nor any of the other cattlemen between Horsehead Crossing and the Rio Grande had ever presented any obstacle to rustlers. But Pecos seemed of another stripe.

She crawled back into bed, and lay awake until dawn, after which she fell into a doze. Mauree awakened her. "Rill, air yo daid or jest gettin' like them lazy white trash in the towns?"

Terrill would have been out promptly after that call, had it not been for the need to hide Pecos' money belt. How heavy it was! And in the light it looked fat and bulky. She wished Pecos was going to marry her and take her to Rockport on a honeymoon. Just at that moment Terrill did not care where Pecos had gotten the money.

After breakfast Terrill went out on the porch to see how their wounded guest had fared during the night. He was sitting up, drinking a cup of coffee.

"Mawnin', Mister Watson. How are you?"

"Hullo, lad!" replied the cattleman. "I'm pretty good, considerin'. Little dizzy, but that's passin'."

"I'm glad you got off so easy."

"Wal, luck shore was with me. But I was on a fast hoss. Reckon he could run away from anythin' on four laigs."

"Ump-umm! I saw your horse. He's fine. But he could never run away from Cinco."

"Cinco. Is he your hoss?"

"Oh no. Wish he were. Cinco belongs to Pecos."

"Who's Pecos?" queried Watson, with more interest.

"Why, Pecos Smith, my partner."

"Smith! Oh, I see. He never mentioned his front handle. Wal, wal!"

"Had you ever heard of Pecos?"

"Reckon I have. I'm tryin' to recollect. But my haid's sort of buzzy this mawnin'. . . . So you're young Lambeth, eh? I knew your father. We had some dealin' together. He was a fine man—too upright an' trustin' for this country. Is it true that he was killed by Indians?"

"No, Mister Watson," replied Terrill, sadly. "It was a Comanche arrow that killed Dad, but it was never shot by a Comanche."

"Indeed! That's news. Some more of this Pecos deviltry. Wal, we've a lot to go through before we can have peaceful ranchin'. It's got to get worse before it can get better."

"We ought to band together."

"Lambeth, that's not a bad idee. But we're not ready for it here yet. Country too sparsely settled. Only a few cattlemen an' riders. Range too big. Distances too long. An' we're all too poor to hire enough help. It 'pears to me we got all we can do to keep from bein' shot, for a while yet."

Terrill sighed. Perhaps this rancher was right. "Until you came yesterday we hadn't seen a single rider for months, and not an Indian all summer. I'd almost forgotten we lived on the wild Pecos."

"Wal, it never rains but it pours, lad," laughed Watson. "I hope I'm not a bird of ill omen, but I'm shore afraid. . . . Hullo, what's the matter with your nigger?"

Sambo appeared, running up from the direction of the corral. The instant Terrill saw him she knew something was amiss. Her first thought was of Pecos. But he would be returning at noonday, or later. Sambo lumbered up to the porch.

"Mars Rill—dar's riders—comin'," he panted, and pointed up the canyon toward the gorge trail.

Terrill stepped to the edge of the porch. She saw horses, riders. She counted four—five riders and several pack-horses. They had turned the curve of the canyon and were coming down the trail half a mile distant. It was a sight Terrill's father had always greeted with dread, a dread which had been transmitted to her. This time, however, after the first start of dismay, Terrill reacted differently. It would not help Pecos for her to be panic-stricken. She belonged to Texas, too, and she was his partner. As she watched the riders leisurely approach, speculating upon their character and purpose, she determined they should not get the best of her. To the outside world she was still young Terrill Lambeth, son of Colonel Lambeth, and she could act the part.

"Dey's no vaqueros," said Sambo, finally.

"I reckon there's nothin' to do but receive them," suggested Watson.

"I dunno, suh, I dunno. Sho it hed to happen jest when dat Pecos Smith rid off."

"They're shore not backward aboot ridin' up here," replied Terrill, thoughtfully. "Maybe they are some of the new cattlemen you told Pecos aboot."

"Wal, either they're honest or plumb nervy."

When the trees and the barn hid the approaching horsemen from sight Terrill ran to her room. She threw off the light blouse, and donning her loose coat she buttoned it up. Then she stuck her gun in her hip pocket. The long barrel protruded from a hole and showed below the edge of her coat. But that was just as well, perhaps. Then before going back she paused to consider. Sambo and Pecos, and she, too, had always been expecting unwelcome visitors. Well, let them come. Whatever their errand, Terrill's first care was to conceal her sex, and after that meet the exigencies of the case as Pecos' partner.

"Where are they?" she asked when she got outside.

"Must be havin' a parley or leavin' their hosses," returned Watson.

"Heah dey come on foot. An' dey's walkin' arsenals," said Sambo, who stood out from the porch. He returned to sit down on the step. "Mars Rill, dis is no friendly call."

Presently the men came into Terrill's range of vision. "I shore know that tall one," she flashed. "Breen Sawtell."

"So do I," rejoined Watson, not without excitement. "Met him at Eagle's Nest last summer. Talks big cattle deals. . . . Can't say I liked him, Lambeth."

Terrill uttered a little laugh, which got rid of the last of her nervousness. "I can't say I'm in love with him, myself."

"Has he been here before?"

"Twice. Last time I took to the brush till he left. He's a new partner of Don Felipe's."

Watson whistled significantly, and no more was said. Terrill watched her visitors approach. Well she remembered the tall Sawtell, even to his shirt sleeves, his black vest and sombrero, his long mustache and deep set black eyes. On his right stalked a short thick individual, ruddy of face and pompous of bearing. The other three men were cowhands, young, unshaven, hard-faced, not markedly different from any other cowhands of West Texas. They were all heavily armed, except Sawtell, who showed only a gun strapped to his hip. He halted some dozen or so steps from the porch and swept its occupants with his deep-set basilisk eyes.

"Howdy, folks."

Watson replied, but neither Terrill nor Sambo offered any greeting. Sawtell, after a moment, appeared most interested in Watson. He took a few more steps forward, while the stout man followed rather hesitatingly. Terrill had eyes for everything. She noted that only Sawtell looked over-eager.

"Don't I know you?" queried Sawtell, fixing Watson with his greedy eyes.

"Met you at Eagle's Nest last summer. My name's Watson," replied Watson, shortly.

"Sure. I remember. Talked cattle sale with you, but you wanted cash. . . . Say, sort of pale an' sickish, aren't you?"

"I ought to be. Got shot yesterday. Lookin' my stock over an' run plumb into some brand-blotters. They darn near did for me."

Sawtell's change of expression was not marked, but it was perceptible to Terrill.

"Shot! Brand-blotters! . . . Where aboot, Watson?"

"Downriver aboot ten miles. I outrode them an' got here, pretty much all in."

"So I see. All alone, eh?"

"No. I had two cowhands. A Mex an' fellow named Stine. I didn't see them after the first shots."

Sawtell seemed to proceed gropingly in thought. Terrill divined his next query.

"Downriver outfit?"

"I reckon not. There were several white cowhands mixed in with vaqueros. New outfit from across the Pecos."

"Like as not. They're driftin' in from all over." Then Sawtell turned abruptly to Terrill. "Howdy, Lambeth. I hear you lately went in partnership with one Hod Smith."

"Not Hod Smith. My partner's name is Pecos," rejoined Terrill.

"Where is he?"

"Out," replied Terrill, laconically.

"When'll he be back?"

"No telling. In aboot a week, maybe."

"Bill," said Sawtell to the stout man, "I reckon Smith is the hombre we want. Them cowhands at Heald's called him Pecos. But we never heard of it."

"'Pears to me there's a Hod Smith an' a Pecos Smith," replied the other, ponderingly. "We don't want to get our brands mixed. The man we're after is the Smith who shot your brother an' went to burnin' brands with Williams an' Adams."

"Shore. An' we're on the right track," replied Sawtell, confidently.

"Excuse me, gentlemen, but if you ask me I say you're shore on the wrong track," spoke up Watson.

"How so?" retorted Sawtell.

"Wal, that's aboot all from me."

"It's enough. Are you a friend of Hod Smith's?"

"I don't know any Hod Smith."

"Fellers, we might have known we'd get up against a stall like this," said Sawtell, spreading his hands to his men. "So just drape yourselves around an' be comfortable. . . . Get up, nigger," he went on, addressing Sambo, and giving him a kick. "You can feed us after a bit."

"Thet's up to Mars Lambeth," replied Sambo, sullenly.

"Boy, order your niggers to cook up a feed for us."

"You go to hell," drawled Terrill, from where she leaned in the doorway.

"No Southern hospitality here, huh?"

"Not to you."

"Wal, we'll help ourselves."

"Bill, meet young Terrill Lambeth. This is Bill Haines, sheriff from up New Mexico way."

Terrill eyed the stout man. He would not have been unprepossessing if he had been minus the odious prefix. Terrill was playing a boy's part, but she was looking out with a woman's intuitive gaze, with the penetration of love. Haines had a smug, bold front; he had a bluff laugh; but his shifty gray eyes did not meet Terrill's glazing ones for more than a fleeting instant.

"Glad to meet you, young feller," he said, in a hearty voice.

"Are you a Ranger?" queried Terrill.

"Used to be, sonny," was the reply. "I'm now an officer for private interests."

"Have you come heah to arrest Pecos Smith?"

"Wal, yes, if this Pecos Smith is Hod Smith."

"Then you might as well leave before you get into trouble, because Pecos Smith is shore Pecos Smith."

"Breen, this young jackanapes has got plenty of chin," growled Haines.

"Wal, you can arrest him, too," declared Sawtell, with a guffaw. "He's in with Smith."

"Arrest *me!*—You just try it," flashed Terrill.

"Listen to the kid!"

"Excuse me, gentlemen," spoke up Watson, evidently prompted by Terrill's spirit. "Is this a legal proceedin'? I never heard of a sheriff west of the Pecos. It's none of my business. I'm as much a stranger to Lambeth an' Smith as I am to you. But I've a hunch you're barkin' up the wrong tree."

"Wal, for your edification, Mister Watson," sneered Breen Sawtell, "an' as you're a Pecos River cattleman, I'll tell you. . . . This cowhand Smith rode for the Healds. He was implicated in shady deals with two riders named Williams an' Adams. My brother rode down to the H H an' asked the Healds to fire Smith. An' he got shot for his pains. Shot when he wasn't lookin', so it runs up on the Pecos. Wal, then Smith lit out for the brakes. His pards drove small herds of stock to a certain New Mexico market. They were fetchin' out herds of a hundred haid or so, part mavericks just branded, and the rest yearlin's an' steers thet had burned brands. Beckman, a cattleman I was foreman for a little while back, was the biggest loser. An' after six months or more of this thievin' he took three good riders an' trailed Williams an' Adams down in the thickets of the Pecos. This was in the Alkali Lake country across from Tayah Creek. . . . Wal, they never came back an' nothin' was ever heard of them. Then Haines an' I, with our men, took up the trail. We found the decomposed bodies of six men. One had a lariat round his neck. That one we figgered was Williams. Adams we identified by his front teeth. He had been shot. Beckman we recognized from his clothes. He had an arrow stickin' through his ribs. But, hell! no Comanche killed him. There was a dried-up hoss carcass with some arrows stickin' in it. . . . Now here's how we figger it. This man Smith was campin' alone. He never went anywhere with his pards. An' expectin' them back from a drive, he come in time to see Williams hangin' to a tree, an' no doubt Adams aboot ready for his. There was a fight, an' Smith was the only one left. He shot a lot of Comanche arrows around to make it look like the work of Indians. Then he searched all the dead men for money, took it, an' rode away. We kept on down the river trail to Eagle's Nest. There we learned a rider answerin' the description of Smith rode into town early last spring, broke open Brasee's jail, where this young Lambeth was locked up for somethin', an' left with him an' the nigger for this ranch. In this case it's shore easy to put two an' two together."

"Sawtell, take this from me," ejaculated Watson, feelingly. "This Pecos Smith is not your man."

"An' why not?"

"There's some mistake."

"Hell! didn't we find out thet he'd paid a big bill for young Lambeth? Two hundred dollars. Lambeth had been locked up for debt. The greaser said Smith had a roll of bills as big as his laig."

"That may very well be. But this *Pecos* Smith is some one else. He's not the kind of a Texan who'd burn brands an' murder for it."

"Say, how'n hell do you know this Pecos Smith ain't our Hod Smith?" demanded Sawtell, angrily.

"Wal, I can't prove it. But I'd gamble on it. An' what's more, I wouldn't be one of the outfit to accuse him of all this—not for a million dollars."

"Aw, you wouldn't? Watson, your talk ain't so convincin'. How do we know you ain't in cahoots with Smith?"

"Sawtell, you're a damned fool, among other things," declared Watson, in amazed heat. "I'm a respectable rancher, as everybody on this river knows."

"Ahuh. So you say. But *we* don't know ——"

"Breen, you're goin' a little too fast," interrupted Haines, sourly. "I told you we might be on a wild-goose chase. An' if we are we want to know it before makin' any moves."

Sawtell fell into a rage at this and stamped up and down, cursing. He was a passionate and headstrong man, evidently determined upon a certain line of conduct, and he meant to stick to it.

Terrill had suffered a horrifying conviction. Pecos really was the man they were after. He really was a rustler. All that money, surely thousands of dollars, part of which Terrill had in her possession—had been the combined profits of the three brand-burners. Pecos' story had omitted a few little details, but it dove-tailed with that told by Sawtell. Terrill could easily supply the discrepancies. She had a rending, sickening agony in her heart. Was it possible that the man she loved was a cow thief? Terrill's impulse was to run and hide to conceal her hurt, but she dared not act upon it, because any moment Pecos might ride in sight, and she had to see him meet these men. She shook at the very thought, and was hard put to it to stand there.

"Haines, are you afraid to go through with this job?" demanded Sawtell, after his tirade.

"No. But I'm not arrestin' any unknown vaqueros. You can lay coin on that," replied the sheriff, testily.

Sawtell plainly was handicapped by the presence of others. He fumed, and chewed his long mustache, and glared at his ally as if he suspected hitherto unconsidered possibilities.

"After all, the money is the main thing we're after," he burst out, as if unmasking. "Agree to thet?"

"Yes. There's some sense in makin' the money our issue. Why didn't you come to that long ago?"

"No matter. . . . Wal, I've a hunch this money is hid right in this cabin," went on Sawtell, with passion. "An' if we find it you can bet your life I'll have the truth of Hod Smith's identity."

"Yes? You're a positive man, Sawtell, but that ain't enough for me. How will you have it?"

"I was the market for Williams an' Adams. I paid them for all their stock. I know every greenback of thet money. Haw! Haw!—Now what do you say?"

Haines appeared not only thunderstruck, but slowly growing enraged.

"I'll say a hell of a lot if thet's a fact."

"Wal, it is, an' you can just swaller it, hook, line, an' sinker. I bought thet stolen stock cheap, you bet, knowin' I could realize on it. An' of course I meant to trail Williams an' Adams an' get all my money back. I kept advisin' them to stay out of towns, to rustle all the stock possible, to save all their money, an' they cottoned to thet. My plans would have worked out fine. But while I was away, one of Beckman's cowhands rid plumb on to Williams an' Adams with another bunch of cattle. They shot him. Thet put Beckman on their trail, with the result I told you."

"Sawtell, that deal doesn't hold water," protested Haines, red in the face.

"Wasn't I dealin' with rustlers?"

"Shore. An' buyin' in stolen stock once for evidence was all right. But keepin' it up! What'll the cattlemen whose stock you bought say to this?"

"Wal, to hell with them! If it came to a showdown I'd let them pick out their burned brands. . . . You got any more kicks to make?"

"Little good it'd do me if I had."

"We come down here to find that money an' hang thet Hod Smith, an', by Gawd, we're goin' to do it!" declared Sawtell, black in the face.

"Sawtell, I'd say there was little chance of either, with you holdin' the reins," returned Haines, with sarcastic finality.

Suddenly Sawtell whipped out his gun and presented it at Sambo. "Nigger, do you want to be shot?"

"No, suh. I'se not hankerin' fer dat," replied Sambo, rolling his eyes.

"Turn round an' stick your black snout against thet post," ordered Sawtell. . . . "Hey, Sam, fetch a rope. Rustle. . . . There's one on thet saddle. Take it. . . . Now a couple of you hawg-tie this nigger to thet post. Make a good job of it."

In a few moments Sambo was securely bound, after which Sawtell confronted Watson, as he sat pale and composed on the porch bed. He flinched as the gun was carelessly waved in his direction.

"Tie this feller hands an' feet."

"See here, Sawtell, that's goin' too far. I'm a crippled man. Besides, I'm absolutely neutral in this fight."

"Neutral be damned! . . . Tie him up!"

His further protestations were of no avail. The three cowhands roped him fast to the bed he sat upon.

"Now then," went on the leader. "Sam, you an' Jack go down by the river. There's a trail under thet far wall. Hide in the brush an' hold up any man who might ride alone. . . . You, Acker, hop your hoss an' ride up the canyon to thet thicket below where the trail comes out of the gorge. Hide your hoss an' yourself, an' you be damn shore to stop any rider comin' down. You all savvy?"

"Ahuh. But I reckon we all better have our hosses," replied Sam.

"Wal, yes, if it suits you. Now rustle," finished Sawtell, and sheathed his gun. "An' now, Bill, it's for you an' me to go through this cabin with a currycomb."

CHAPTER THIRTEEN

Terrill heard this byplay between the two men and watched them with clouded eyes, while almost sinking in the throes of stupefying misery at the renewed doubt of Pecos. But when Sawtell announced his intention of ransacking the cabin she conquered the blinding weakness. Whatever Pecos had been in the past, he was honest and fine now; he had saved her and he was her partner; but even if some of these things were true, she loved him so wonderfully that she would fight for him and share his fortune.

"Come on, Bill," sang out Sawtell, his heavy boots creaking the porch boards.

"Not me. Search the shack yourself," replied Haines, ill-temperedly. He did not like the situation. Terrill's hopes leaped at the chance of dissension between them.

"Wal, by thunder! if you ain't cross-grained all of a sudden," snorted Sawtell, in disgust.

"I hired out to arrest a criminal, an' not to risk pokin' around in his shack. Like as not, if there wasn't anybody here with sense enough to keep a lookout, you'd turn around presently to have a gun poked in your belly."

"But, you thick-headed ——! The boys are guardin' the only two trails into this canyon. We cain't be surprised."

"That's what you say. My idee of your judgment has changed."

"Ha! It's your nerve thet's changed. A few words from this peak-faced cowman an' you show your white liver."

"Sawtell, your remarks ain't calculated to help this deal," rejoined Haines.

"I shore see thet. Wal, in a pinch I can do the job myself."

"Haw! Haw!"

That sardonic ridicule widened the breach. Terrill made sure now that these two men would clash.

"Haines, this man has fooled you all the way and means to double-cross you in the end," interposed Terrill.

The sheriff's frame vibrated as if it had been surcharged with a powerful current.

"Kid, you don't say much, but when you chirp it's somethin' worth thinkin' about," returned Haines, with a harsh laugh.

"That'll do from you, Lambeth, or I'll slap the tar out of you," growled Sawtell. "Haines, I'll give you one more chance. Are you goin' help hunt for thet money?"

"Bah! You're loco, Sawtell. If this Hod Smith ever had any money it's gone by now. Why, it's 'most six months since that last cattle drive was made."

"Wal, it's a forlorn hope, I'll admit, but if I do find thet money you shore won't get a dollar of it."

"The hell I won't. Find it an' I'll show you."

Sawtell gave him a long gaze. "You may be surprised pronto," he said, in another tone. Then he wheeled to stamp toward the door.

"Get out of my way, Lambeth," he ordered.

For reply Terrill extended the gun, which she had drawn and cocked. Sawtell recoiled away from it.

"By Gawd! . . . Look here, Bill. . . . This kid has throwed a gun on me."

The sheriff showed a disposition to get out from behind Sawtell.

"You can't come in heah," rang out Terrill. The man's close, raw presence, his blood-red eyes, the hard amaze he showed, added a last force to her will. She meant to kill him if he tried to enter. And on the instant Terrill was thinking that the hammer of her gun would fall on an empty chamber.

"Ahuh. So, Lambeth, you're givin' yourself away. Cub partner of a rustler an' murderer, huh?"

"Breen Sawtell, you bet I'm Pecos' partner," flashed Terrill, and pulled the trigger. The hammer fell with a sharp metallic click. Sawtell flinched. Terrill cocked the gun again. "Look out for the next one. I'll kill you. . . . You can't ——"

Sawtell's hand flashed out to throw up the gun. Terrill screamed and pulled the trigger. The gun went off in the air, but it was a narrow escape for him. Holding her arm up, he wrenched the gun loose, and tossing it back he knocked Terrill into the cabin. As she went down her head struck hard.

When Terrill came to she found that she had been bound to a chair. Sawtell had taken down a jug of liquor that had stood on the shelf for years, and after smelling it he took a long gulp.

"Aggh! . . . Bill Haines don't know what he's missin'."

Whereupon Sawtell began a search of the room. This did not take many moments, for there were such few places to hide anything. Meanwhile Terrill had fully recovered her wits. She had been hastily tied with some soft rope hobbles that had hung just inside the door. She could twist one small and capable hand so as to reach the knot, which she believed she could loosen. There were two rifles in the living-room, of which hers was loaded. If she could get hold of that! Then she grasped the fact that her feet were bound to the legs of the chair. Even if she did free her hands she could not get up. Then she espied Sambo's hunting-knife on the table, within reach. After that she watched the ransacking ruffian while she redoubled her efforts to free her hands. She wondered what had become of Mauree. Probably the negress had run off in fright to her cabin and baby.

Sawtell got through searching the living-room. Then he gave the pole partition a vigorous shake. Terrill's door flew open and Sawtell entered her little room. No one was ever permitted to go in there. Any thorough search must discover that there was something strange about Terrill Lambeth. But on the moment Terrill had no qualms about this. It was the money Pecos had intrusted to her. Why had she not hid the belt in the barn or a crevice in the cliff. For Sawtell would most surely find it.

"Haw! Haw! Haw!" roared in husky accents from Terrill's room. Then Sawtell appeared with the money belt clutched in his hands. There was a radiance about him, but it appeared far from beautiful. His eyes emitted a wolfish hunger. "By Gawd! . . . I've got it," he crowed as he laid the belt on the table. His big shaking hand, with its tobacco-stained fingers, tore out sheafs of greenbacks that had been neatly and compactly folded. "Oho! I guess I didn't have a hunch. . . . All the big bills—fifties—hundreds! . . . Mister Hod Smith, you shore are a savin' hombre."

The doorway darkened to the wide frame of Haines, who suddenly halted, pop-eyed, at sight of Sawtell and what he was doing. As if by magic, then, astonishment appeared swept away.

"Breen, so help me Gawd, you found it!" he exclaimed.

"I shore did," replied the other, in grim exultance. "There's twenty thousand, anyway. An' that was worth comin' for." Whereupon he moved the belt and piles of bills back to his left on the table, interposing his body between it and Haines. Then he poured out a cupful of red liquor from the jug. "Here's to your bad luck, Haines, an' poor judgment!"

He tossed off the drink with a flourish. "Aggh!—That's stuff for you. Have a drink, Bill. It's as old as the hills."

Neither of the men seemed aware of Terrill. Haines took a stiff drink, though his gray eyes, now with a blaze in them, never left the belt and money for an instant.

"Good likker, all right," he coughed, and edged along the table. "Breen, I was wrong. You shore had a hunch. But I was only sore, an' worried aboot this Hod Smith mebbe bein' Pecos Smith. . . . Do you recognize the money?"

"Yes, if it's anythin' to you," responded Sawtell, dryly, and he began stowing the flat packets of bills back into the belt.

"Shore it's a lot to me. I'm as tickled as can be. If you know your own money we're justified in takin' it. An' I say let's let well enough alone an' rustle out of here before this Smith person gets back."

"An' why for, Bill?"

"He might be Pecos Smith?"

"Hell! S'pose he is? What do we care? Wouldn't he look as fine danglin' from a rope as anyone else?"

"You don't seem to savvy somethin'," retorted Haines. "If he is Pecos Smith he won't be easy to string up."

"Haw! Haw!"

"Man, you've lost your head completely."

"Nope. Thet applies to you, Bill. I'm figgerin' shore close. There's only two trails into this canyon, an' I've got two men hid on the river trail an' one man hid on the gulch trail. Smith will be held up either way."

"Then we ought to help guard. There's many a slip, you know. . . . Give up your crazy notion to hang Smith an' let's go."

"He shot my brother."

"What'n'hell if he did?" shouted Haines, stridently. "There's some who say that wasn't such a loss. You make me sick with your braggin' loyalty, when all the time you was double-crossin' him yourself."

"You're a —— liar!" returned Sawtell, ominously.

"Now, Breen, don't bluster that way an' go back on what you know."

"What I know is my business," returned Sawtell, doggedly. "What you think you know concerns me when you get to gabbin' in front of strangers. You forget that nigger tied up out there. An' this cattleman who calls himself Watson. You talk too much. You haven't one damned proof that I double-crossed my brother."

"No. It's just my hunch. But you can bet your pile this Smith vaquero knows. An' that's why you're so keen to hang him."

"Air you goin' to shet up?" demanded Sawtell, threateningly.

"Wal, there's no use in arguin' any more since we've got the money."

"We?" shouted Sawtell, derisively.

"You heard me correct, Breen. I consented to take up my old Kansas job as sheriff to serve your ends. I rode down in this Gawd-forsaken Pecos country with you. I'm riskin' my skin right this minute, an' you bet I'm in on everythin'."

"Haines, you're in on nothin'. I told you thet a while back. You shot your chin off once too often."

"You mean you're not goin' to divide that money?" yelled Haines, hoarsely, his ruddy face changing color.

"Get out! Your fat greedy face hurts my sensitive feelin's," retorted Sawtell, and he shoved Haines out of the cabin. For a moment his tall form obstructed the light. Terrill espied Sawtell's hand creeping down toward his gun. Her heart nearly burst. The fight was coming. These ghouls would destroy one another. Terrill's right hand came free. If she could only get up! She tore at the knots. The men had forgotten her. Her rifle leaned against the wall. Sawtell had left the money belt on the table.

"Breen Sawtell, you're as crooked as a rail fence," replied Haines. "But crooked or not, I want my share of that cattle money. You agreed to divide it."

Sawtell stepped out on the porch, so that all Terrill could see was his left side. His left hand was stiff, with the long fingers quivering.

"Shore. But you lost your nerve an' you wouldn't help me. So I'm justified in not makin' a divide."

"——! I'll show you up all over New Mexico," hissed Haines.

"No you won't, Bill."

"Of all the thick-skulled men I ever seen! Do you think you can soft-soap me out of this deal?"

"All I'm thinkin' now, Bill, is that you won't be goin' back."

"He-l—!" A shot cut short Haines' yelp of fury. The thundering report appeared to clamp Terrill's eyes tight shut. Then her ears vibrated to the crash—crash—crash of guns. Both men must have emptied their weapons. As Terrill opened her eyes she heard a groan that appeared to come from the left side of the door. Sambo or Watson had been hit. Then a boot grated, the porch boards creaked—and there followed another bursting report.

Terrill's strung faculties broke to sight of Sawtell stepping before the door. He was sheathing a smoking gun. Terrill had wit enough to grasp that Sawtell had not had time to reload the gun. His face was black and terrible. He felt of his left arm where blood showed near the shoulder.

"Barked me, huh," he soliloquized, and pulled a bandana from his pocket. Then as he stepped to the threshold he espied Terrill. "Ha! 'most forgot you, Lambeth."

"Is—he—dead?" gasped Terrill.

"Who? Bill? . . . I reckon so, for all intents an' purposes. . . . Tie this arm up for me." And taking the hunting-knife off the table, he cut the hobble that bound

Terrill's hands, not noticing that one of them was already free. "What you shakin' aboot, youngster? A little while ago you was steady enough. I thought my day had come."

Terrill at last succeeded in knotting the bandana securely. Sawtell stuck the knife upright in the table and made no move to retie Terrill's hands. "Now what?—Aha! Another little drink for my nerves."

When he threw back his head and tipped the jug to his lips, Terrill snatched the knife, and quick as a flash freed her feet. He saw her out of the corner of his eyes. Down the jug thumped. Terrill flashed her hand for the money belt, and securing it she whirled to flee.

But as she leaped through the door Sawtell's hand fastened on the back of her coat. He gave such a tremendous jerk that not only did he drag Terrill back across the threshold, but he ripped both coat and shirt almost off her body.

"You —— little devil! Must I kill you, too?" And with his free hand he twisted the belt out of her now nerveless hands and tossed it back on the table.

Terrill sank to her knees, almost fainting. To be suddenly snatched almost nude paralyzed her. Sawtell pulled at the split garments, which divided and slipped off Terrill's white shoulders.

"Fer Gawd's sake!" he rolled out, in breathless amaze, his bold eyes feasting on the curved white breast Terrill could not hide. "A *girl!*"

He let go the half of Terrill's garments, and dropping heavily into the chair he placed a hand on each of her shoulders. He shook her. Terrill's head wabbled back and forth. She was almost swooning.

"Come out of it!—You ain't hurt. . . . Let me look at you. . . . Terrill Lambeth, heh? . . . Wal, I'll be . . . ! I reckoned you was damned pretty for a boy."

"Let me—go!" wailed Terrill. The end had come. She would rather have died. This man's horny hands! His hot eyes! Her faintness left her. There was more horror than shame. She tried to get up. He held her down with hands like lead.

"All the time you've been a girl?" he ejaculated. "When I was here—twice before—you was a girl?"

"Yes—yes. I've always been. . . . It was Dad's fault. He—he hated girls. He would dress me as a boy—when I was little. . . . And so—out heah—I kept to boy's clothes. . . . For pity's sake—let me—cover myself!"

"That —— half-breed Felipe—he knows you're a girl," declared Sawtell. "I savvy now. *That's* why he wanted me to stay away from here. . . . Wal, if this ain't my lucky day!"

Terrill, with returning strength, plucked at her rent garments, so obviously agonized by her nudity that Sawtell let go and flung some of them in her face.

"Why, you damned little hussy!" he rasped in sudden passion. "Awful ashamed, ain't you, half undressed before a strange man? Puttin' it on thick, huh? . . . You damned lyin' cat. Livin' here with this rustler, Smith. Pretendin' to be a boy!—Why I ought to strip you an' drive you up an' down this canyon."

Something about this remarkable revelation, no doubt the sight of the girl, had inflamed Sawtell into a frenzy. He jerked the torn coat out of her hands and flung it aside. He pulled at the shirt, but she clung desperately to this.

"Kill me—and be—done!" she whispered.

"Kill nothin'. You're too pretty to kill. But I'll beat hell out of you if you try any more tricks with me."

Terrill would have sagged to the floor but for his pressing knees.

"You've been livin' here with this man Smith?"

She thought she understood him.

"Answer me," he went on, and cuffed her sharply over the head. "You're livin' with this man Smith?"

"Yes—I—I'm living—heah."

"You're not married to him? . . . An' you're in love with him? . . . Haw! Haw!—You bet you air. . . . An' you know he's a rustler—a cattle thief? He told you where all this money come from?"

"Yes. But he wasn't brand-burning. . . . He was only—branding mavericks."

"Aw, hell! You're not an idiot. You didn't swaller that old guff?"

"I did—I did. I believed him."

"Wal, I furnished thet money to him an' his pards. I paid it into his hands."

"But you—you said Pecos wasn't—with those men?"

"I lied to fool Haines. It served my turn. . . . Yes, you been livin' with a low-down rustler. Shore you're no lady to be proud. Sooner or later you'd seen him hanged. An' it's just as well that I come along when I did. You're young yet. You'll get over it. . . . Now when this Smith feller comes back we'll swing him up. An' I'm goin' to stay here all night—with you. An' tomorrow I'll be takin' you away with me."

Terrill was past speech and almost power of vision.

"Wal, if you ain't pretty ——"

He broke off suddenly. He seemed to listen, and his fondling hands dropped from her person.

"What the hell?" he muttered.

Terrill's ears—that had been strained to breaking all these interminable hours—caught a low swift rhythmic patter of hoofs.

"A hoss comin'. . . . Must be Sam."

When he got up Terrill slid forward, her head toward the door. Sawtell strode over her.

"Sam's shore tearin'. . . . What's he runnin' his hoss like thet for?"

Terrill tried to rise, rose to one elbow, slid back again. She recognized that horse. Cinco! And shuddering death seemed to run along her reviving nerves out of her body.

Sawtell leaped out of the door, off the porch, to face up the canyon. His legs stood wide and bowed. His hair bristled.

Terrill whispered: *"It's—Pecos!"* And she got up on one hand. Suddenly her stunned faculties reasserted themselves. But she was still so weak that she could scarcely slip into the two halves of the split shirt, and hold the front together.

That swift clatter had become a thrumming roar.

"My Gawd, it ain't Sam!" yelled Sawtell.

Terrill's sight caught the black Cinco against the gold of the sunset sky. He scattered dirt and gravel against the cabin. Then Pecos leaped out of the very air, his spurs jangling, his boots thudding, as he hit the ground to confront the stricken Sawtell.

Pecos was hatless. A white band spotted with blood bound his head. He was also coatless, vestless, and there were other stains of blood visible. His face was stone gray, except the leaping terrible eyes.

"Who'n hell are yu?" queried Pecos, piercingly.

"Sawtell. Breen Sawtell," replied the other hoarsely. He licked his lips.

"What are yu doin' heah?"

"We come down to arrest one Hod Smith."

"Ahuh. Who's we?"

"Haines there, an' my men. Maybe you met Sam—up at the gulch trail."

"Mebbe I did. Who shot these men?"

"There was a hell of a fight. Young Lambeth was in it."

"Terrill!"

"Oh, Pecos—I'm all right," replied Terrill to that devastating call.

"Sambo, you daid?"

"No, boss. I ain't daid atall. But I'se damn near daid."

"Watson! . . . Who killed him?" flashed Pecos.

"Must have stopped a stray bullet," replied Sawtell, his voice huskier.

"Haines, yu called him. . . . Shot to pieces. Who did thet?"

"Wal, me an' Bill had a little duel."

"If yu came down heah to arrest me, why'd yu fight?"

"We come to arrest Hod Smith."

"There's no Hod heah. I am Pecos Smith."

"Pecos—Smith!"

"I said so. Are you hard of heahin'?"

"Did you shoot my brother—at Healds' Ranch?"

"I beat him to a gun. He forced me to draw."

"Was you a partner to Williams an' Adams?"

"Yes. I'm the man."

"Then—Pecos Smith, you're the man I'm after."

"So I reckon. What're yu goin' to do aboot it?"

"Pecos, he swore he'd hang you," rolled out Sambo, passionately.

"Wal, Sambo, I'm wastin' a lot of time in gab, but I'm shore curious."

"Boss, dis white trash sho treated our Bill turrible low down."

"Terrill!—Yu said yu were all right?"

"I am, Pecos . . . only scared—and weak. He tore me—to pieces . . . and he found out I—I'm . . . Oh, Pecos, I can't tell you."

Sawtell quailed. His eyes had been locked with Pecos'. At last he sensed what Watson had hinted at and Haines had warned him of.

"Can't tell me what?" called Pecos.

Terrill was mute. If she had not been frozen there, leaning on her hand, she would have flopped down. But Pecos did not see her. His dancing gold-flecked eyes never oscillated a fraction from Sawtell.

"Smith, I'm on to your dodge," spoke up Sawtell. It was the brazen voice of desperation. "This Terrill Lambeth is a girl. You been livin' with her—pretendin' she was a boy. Don Felipe had a hunch. . . . If any more comes of this meetin'—you'll be spotted all over the Pecos country. . . . But you ought to marry the girl. She must have been a decent little thing once."

"Are yu—talkin' yet?" queried Pecos, in a strange, almost inaudible voice. And perhaps that weakness spurred the desperate Sawtell on. Perhaps his mind grasped at straws. If he infuriated this Pecos Smith beyond control he might gain an instant's advantage.

"But whatever she was—she's shore a hussy now," rasped on Sawtell, his body flexing.

"Ahuh."

"She knows you're a rustler—a brand-burnin' cow thief. She admitted that."

"Terrill—believed—thet?"

"Shore. She's on to you. That money now."

"Ahuh!" There might have been, to the strained sight of a madman, an indefinable break in Pecos.

"That money! *By—Gawd!*" Then Sawtell bawled and lunged.

There was a red flash, a burst, a boom. A cloud of smoke. Sawtell's gun went flipping high. He staggered back to fall upon the porch, a great spurt of blood squirting from his heart.

CHAPTER FOURTEEN

Pecos leaped out of his set posture. He glared around, particularly toward the mouth of the canyon. And on the instant he espied two men running along the thicket under the west wall. Their clumsy gait betrayed cowhands unused to such locomotion. They tallied with the number of saddle horses Pecos had counted.

"Ahuh. Thet's aboot all," he muttered, and slowly sheathed his gun, to turn to Sambo.

"Boss, if yo ain't speculatin' on nuthin' particular, jest cut me loose," spoke up that worthy, turning his head as far as possible.

Pecos drew a knife, and cutting the hard knot of the lasso he unwound it from Sambo's long frame. There appeared to be considerable blood from a gunshot high up on Sambo's shoulder.

"Hit any other place?" queried Pecos, sharply. "This heah is only an open cut."

"Boss, if I hadn't played 'possum I'd shore got more hits dan dat," replied the negro as he stepped free. "'Cause dat black mustached gennelman was sho out to kill eberybody."

"How many in the bunch, Sambo?"

"Five was all I seen."

"There's the last two—across under the cracked wall." Pecos pointed until Sambo had located them. "We don't want them hangin' around. Take my rifle, Sambo. Go down an' drive thet outfit of hosses up the trail. Let those men see you doin' it. Then take a few shots at them just for luck.—Rustle now an' get back pronto."

Cinco had edged back from the cabin and now had his head up as he nervously pawed the ground.

"Whoa dar, Cinco—whoa, old hoss," called Sambo, as he approached. The horse stood, allowing Sambo to unsheath the rifle. Whereupon Sambo lumbered away out of sight.

Pecos surveyed the ghastly scene, then he strode over Sawtell's body into the cabin.

Terrill sat on the floor, holding to a chair. With her other hand she was holding rent garments together over her breast.

"Pe-cos!" she whispered.

"Yu all right?" he demanded, sharply, as he knelt to take her by the shoulders and force her head up to the light. There was absolutely no color in her face. He gazed piercingly into her eyes. Stark horror was fading. A rapture of deliverance shone upon Pecos. After that one swift scrutiny his tight breast expanded in passionate relief. For the rest, he could not trust himself to gaze longer into those exquisite betraying depths.

Terrill let go of the chair and clung to him wildly. Her head dropped against him.

"Pecos! Pecos!" she whispered.

"Shore it's Pecos. What yu think? I reckon yu mean I didn't get back any too soon. . . . There's a bruise on yore temple."

"He—hit me."

"Ahuh. Hurt yu anywhere else?"

"My arm's wrenched."

"Yu fought him?"

"I threw my gun—on him," replied Terrill, growing stronger. "Meant to kill him. . . . But he knocked it—up . . . grabbed me. . . . I didn't quite faint. I felt him tying me—to the chair. . . . Later I worked my hands loose—and when he was drinking—I cut my legs free—snatched your belt and ran. . . . But he caught me. . . . It was then he tore my—my coat and—shirt off . . . found me—out. . . . Oh, Pecos!"

Mauree interrupted this scene. Her eyes were rolling.

"Mars Pecos, dem debils sho turned our home into a slotterhouse. . . . Rill honey, say yo ain't hurted."

"I'm all right, Mauree."

"Yu take charge of Terrill," said Pecos, rising.

"Oh, Pecos—don't go!" implored Terrill, hanging to his knees.

He could hardly look into the sweet havoc-shadowed face.

"Child, I won't go far," he said, hurriedly. "Thet mess out heah—an' Sambo's chasin' what's left of thet outfit."

He disengaged his knees from clinging arms and got outside, feeling shaken and dizzy. It took strong will to counteract the softer mood, to face stern issues still, to fortify himself against the sickening reaction sure to follow.

Pecos scanned the opposite side of the canyon. Cattle and horses were running in fright. Then he heard Sambo shooting. It would be just as well, he thought, to have a look. Cinco came whinnying to him, whereupon Pecos remembered to scan him for a possible wound. There was a welt on his flank, sensitive to the touch.

"Wal, it's darn good fer yu, old hoss, thet yu can run fast."

When Pecos got beyond the trees where he could look up the canyon he espied Sambo trudging back down the trail. Apparently the negro had driven the horses clear out of sight. Pecos waited for him, straining his eyes to catch a glimpse of the last of Sawtell's riders.

Sambo arrived presently, puffing hard.

"Boss—I—sho—winged—one of dem."

"Thet'll help, Sambo. But I reckon those cowhands wouldn't hang around heah now. I shore peppered thet one who was layin' fer me up the trail."

"Pecos, I wuz worried aboot dat. How yo see him? Sam, dat Sawtell skunk call him."

"I ran into fresh hoss tracks before I got within miles of our trail down the gulch. Those fellers had been to Eagle's Nest. When they turned off down our gulch I got leery. An' when I rose into the canyon Cinco either seen or smelled a hoss. So I cut off the trail by thet thorn-bush thicket. It's good I did, fer there was one of them hidin' in it, an' he shot at me. Wal, I shot back, you bet, an' plenty fer good measure. Then I loaded up an' sent Cinco down the trail hell-bent fer heah."

"All de time I prayed yo'd come. An' den when I'd gone back on de good Lawd den yo come, yo sho come, Pecos."

"Wal, I'll heah yore story after a bit," replied Pecos, thoughtfully. "I reckon we've gotta begin a graveyard on Lambeth Ranch. Some graves with haidstones, Sambo. Damn good idee— Up there on thet level bench. Shallow holes, Sambo, 'cause we shore ain't goin' to sweat more'n we have to to cover them stiffs."

While conversing thus they had once more approached the cabin.

"Search 'em, Sambo. Take papers, guns, watches, money, anythin' worth keepin' an' put them all in a sack. Relatives an' friends of theirs might ride in heah some day. An' if they don't come a rarin' fer trouble we'll turn the stuff over. . . . Too bad aboot this cattleman Watson."

"Boss, I'se a hunch dat was sho no accident," spoke up Sambo.

"What?"

"Dis killin' of Watson. 'Cause after all dat bunch shootin' when I got my shoulder barked I seen Watson was alive. Den come anudder shot an' he sagged in dat rope."

"Wal! Wal! . . . Sawtell figgered this Watson had heahed an' seen too much. Shot him an' laid it to accident."

"'Zackly. Dat Sawtell was a hell of a man, Pecos."

"I reckon—among his kind. . . . But save yore story, Sambo, till our work's done."

"You some shot up yo'self, boss?" queried the negro.

"I stuck my haid up over thet Y Canyon rim, an' one of them vaqueros grooved me. This other cut heah is from a snag ridin' the brush. They won't interfere with my appetite none. . . . Sambo, yu'll want a pack-hoss, also an old canvas yu can cut up. I'll take pick an' shovel, an' go dig the graves."

"Yas, suh. Heah's yo' rifle, boss. Don' leave dat behind. Yo can nebber tell. . . . 'Kin sabby,' as the greasers say."

"Ahuh. . . . An', Sambo, after yu move these men, have Mauree scrub away all thet blood."

Pecos did not think he would need the rifle, nevertheless he took it, and burdened with this and the heavy tools he approached the bench he had chosen for the graveyard. It chanced to be situated where ambush from the rim above was out of the question.

Pecos applied himself vigorously and in an hour or more had three shallow graves dug. The labor had caused him to sweat and pant. Moreover, it had begun to operate upon the dark grimness of mind and the sick icy sensation in the pit of his stomach, reactions which always succeeded deadly passion. He kept on working even after the job was sufficiently done. Indeed, he would have welcomed much toil. There must be other ordeals after this mood had passed.

Presently he was interrupted by the arrival of Sambo, leading a horse over the back of which bent the body of a man roped up in canvas.

"Which is this heah one?" asked Pecos.

"Dis is Sawtell," replied Sambo, unceremoniously tumbling the corpse off the horse. "Pecos, yo sho hit him whar hi libbed. . . . An' what yo tink! He wored a money belt chuck full."

"Did he?—Thet reminds me of mine. Where is it, Sambo?"

"Terrill got dat. . . . Boss, yo sho should hab seen ——"

"Rustle back after another daid man," interrupted Pecos. Still he had not arrived at the state of mind where he could listen.

"Wal, Sawtell," said Pecos, after Sambo had ridden away, "yu'll rot heah because you had no good in yore heart nor sense in yore haid."

Pecos had made a clean, swift job of killing the man, and he duplicated it in the burial. Then he searched about until he found an oblong stone, one end of which he imbedded at the head of the grave. Later he would cut a name in the stone.

Sambo made two more trips with gruesome burdens, and after the last one remained to help Pecos until the duty was accomplished.

It was mid-afternoon when Pecos wended a weary way back to the cabin. The shock had passed, as often it had before; the sickness lingered only faintly. Pecos had weathered another stern vicissitude of the wild Texas borderland. These things had to be. He counted himself a pioneer. He knew what had to be stood and done before a man could have peace along the length and breadth of that Pecos wilderness.

He must face another ordeal, a more difficult one for him, and he shirked it. He could not think how to meet the coming issue between him and Terrill. He could let only the exigencies of the hour decide for him. Only one certainty stood out clearly in his troubled mind, and it sustained him where otherwise he might have had no anchor at all. A wonderful affection for Terrill Lambeth as a boy had been transformed into a tremendous love for Terrill Lambeth as a girl. Pecos would far rather have had the inevitable revelation postponed indefinitely. He had grown happy with his secret. Terrill's sex, no longer hidden, might make a difference—he had no idea what. Certainly as a boy she had looked to him, trusted him, relied upon him, cared for him in a way, but as a girl ——

The first stranger who had wrung from Terrill the truth of her sex had likewise instilled in her a belief in Pecos' guilt. That was a blow. It stung, it flayed. It was bitter. It raked over the old sore. Perhaps his reasoning was vain, illogical, invalid, and he was indeed a rustler. That issue might be met, with himself and with Terrill; and he might as well face both at once.

To approach that cabin was now harder for Pecos than if it had contained ten men of Sawtell's ilk. Pecos made a stupendous effort, and he did not really know exactly what the effort was for. But he had to go on; he had to go back to that cabin, to work there, to eat and sleep there, to face Terrill a hundred times a day. And the prospect filled him with breathless tumult.

Sambo and Mauree had cleared and cleaned away every vestige of the fight. The old cabin looked as sleepy and lonely as always. Sambo had removed the rude bough couch that had been on the porch.

While Pecos lingered outside Sambo called from the door:

"Boss, what is I gwine do wif all dese waluables?"

Whereupon Pecos forced himself to enter. One end of the table was littered with guns, belts full of shells, watches, knives, wallets, and last a wide black money belt.

"Sawtell an' dat no-good sheriff 'peared to be well heeled," said Sambo. "But Watson had no money or nuthin'."

"Sambo, do yu think thet fat feller was a sheriff?" queried Pecos as he weighed the money belt.

"Wal, I tuk it he might have been once. I heahed them say somethin' aboot Kansas. But he sho wuz no mo' sheriff dan me. Dey gabe demselves away, boss. Dat was a trick."

"Ahuh. Wal, put all this stuff out of sight so we can forget the deal."

"Boss, I sho don't want to be 'sponsible fer dis money."

"All right. I'll hide it. Let's see." Pecos gazed about the room.

"Dere's a loose stone in de chimley low down," said Sambo, and kneeling he worked a large stone free.

"Just the place. Dig out behind it, Sambo," replied Pecos. Between them they soon disposed of the belt, and the other articles Pecos stowed upon a triangular shelf in a corner. That done, Pecos breathed still more freely. Mauree had begun to prepare for the evening meal: there were iron pots and tin pots on the fire.

"Mauree, is that water hot?" called a voice, somehow Terrill's voice, yet not the same.

"Yas, honey, it's sho hot. An' de salve yo ast fo is on de table. Yo better hurry, chile, an' fix Mars Pecos up 'cause supper 'mos' ready."

There happened to be a chair close to Pecos, which he backed into weakly. He heard a step.

"Pecos, will you let me dress your wounds?" asked the soft changed voice.

"Wounds!—Aw, why shore, if they're worth botherin' with."

"But you look so awful in that bloody bandage and shirt," protested Terrill.

"So I must. Reckon I forgot."

Terrill appeared coming around the table, upon which she deposited some articles. Pecos did not look up, yet he saw her. It was Terrill and still not Terrill. The same small boots with the worn trousers carelessly tucked in the tops! But instead of the omnipresent loose coat or shirt she wore something white. He caught that without really looking.

"Pecos, have you another shirt?" she asked, standing thrillingly close beside him, with a hand on his arm.

"Yes, it's up in the loft. I'll put it on after."

"This one is gone. Today has shore been rough on our shirts." She uttered a wonderful little low laugh, deep and rich, that tingled Pecos clear to his toes. What could have made all this difference in a boy he had known so well?

Terrill cut his ragged bloody sleeve off just below his shoulder.

"This can't be a bullet hole," she said.

"Cut myself on a snag."

With deft capable hands Terrill washed the wound, anointed it with salve, and bound it securely.

"This one on your haid!—I'm almost afraid to look at it."

"Wal, never mind, Terrill, if it'll sicken yu. Sambo'll do all right."

"*I* shall dress it." She wet a towel in hot water and soaked the stiff bandage off and bathed the wound, which Pecos was sure consisted only of a shallow groove. "O my God!" she whispered, very low, as if to her inmost soul. "One inch lower—and life would have been over for me!"

"But, Terrill, it's my haid," said Pecos, rather blankly. That speech of hers would require long cogitation.

Terrill appeared slow over this task. Her touch was not so sure, so steady. Pecos felt her fingers tremble upon his brow. She hovered over him, from one side to the other. There was a slight soft contact to which his over-sensitive nerves reacted outrageously. He never raised his half-closed eyes. He saw the white garments as a blur, too close for clear vision. But her round arms were bare to the elbows, golden brown at the wrists, then white as milk. Once, as she leaned over him, to work with the difficult bandaging on the far side of his head, she had only to drop her arms a trifle and they would be round his neck. Pecos longed for this so dreamily, so poignantly, that when he awoke to it he thought he was crazy.

"There! If you don't roll in your sleep it will stay," she was saying.

"Sleep!—I'll never sleep no more around heah. . . . Thanks, Terrill. I reckon yore a fair doctor."

Pecos stalked out upon the grass without any definite aim. If he had kept on he would have stalked over the bank into the river. But he stopped. The sun was setting in wondrous hues; the river gloomed, a winding purple band with silver edges; the great wall stood up, receiving the golden blast of sunset; and the canyon lay under a canopy of spreading rays and dropping veils.

Where had it gone—the menace, the peril, the raw wild life that hid behind the beauty, the solitude of the Pecos? A vision came to him, not unlike the dreams of the pioneer, of a time when the hard lives of vaqueros and cattlemen, the brutality of the range, the mingled blood of rustler and avenger, the raid of the Comanche, all would vanish in a sense of security in neighbors up and down the roads, in the tranquillity of homes, in the prosperity of endless herds of cattle. That was the promise of the glory of the sunset. Otherwise all hope and strife toward such an end would be futile.

But the vast Pecos range must ever be lonely, gray, brooding, hot as a furnace in the summers, cold in winters, when the bitter northers blew, a barren land of scaly ridges for leagues and leagues, a grazing wilderness for numberless cattle, from which the coyote and the buzzard would never disappear. It was what this country was that chained Pecos to it. But for men like Watson and women like Terrill, whose destinies had set them there, Pecos could have foregone the dream of the pioneer to write a bloodier name across that frontier. Better men than he had done no less. Texas had been a battleground, and was bloodsoaked from river to river. No Texans but had been born to fight—no Texans ever survived in the longing for homes. This era of guns and nooses, of the burned brand and the hard-eyed outlaw, would pass some day.

In that moment of exultation Pecos divined he had always been on the right trail. If he had lost the letter of it at times and had veered from it in spirit, yet he had always come back to plant his feet right. His past tracks had had to be bitterly reckoned with; there might be more and worse before the years covered them with dust, but he would never again make a false step.

A voice called him to supper and it was that same changed voice. As he turned to go back to the cabin he espied a gleam of white moving away from the door. Terrill had been watching him.

Pecos went in resolved to be natural. If he had been wise and great enough to forestall events, there would never have been any reason to blot out this tragic day. Sambo had put mesquite knots on the fire, as the bright ruddy light and sweet fragrance testified. Terrill sat at the other end of the table, as she had always done. But nothing else could ever have been so different.

Her hair was parted in the middle. It rippled and shone like the ripples of the river when the sunset fell upon them. Her face was as white as if it had never worn any golden tan. Her eyes were large, dark, luminous, windows of myriads of emotions. And under them shadows as deep and mysterious enhanced their havoc. But her features alone could not have accounted for the disturbing transformation from boy to girl. That white waist! It was old-fashioned—as compared with those Mary Heald had worn—and it fitted Terrill poorly. It had been a girl's waist and now it graced a budding woman. It was open a little at the top, no doubt because Terrill could not close it, and slightly exposed the graceful swell of her neck. For the rest there was the contour of breast that thrilled Pecos while it stabbed him with the memory of his unintentional sacrilege.

His prolonged stare, or something in his look, brought the vivid blood to

Terrill's face. She appeared nervous, timid, shy, yet her eyes hung upon him hauntingly. What had she to fear in him? He knew now, and she must never know that he had long been aware of her secret. Then he remembered what Sawtell had said, and there came a break in his feeling.

"I can't eat," she said, after she had tried. "I—I can't be natural, either. . . . Pecos, are you shocked—angry?"

"Don't think aboot things," he answered, rather gruffly. He was thinking about things himself. What could he do if she looked at him like that, with such strangely hungry eyes?

"But, Pecos—if I—if we don't talk—it'll be harder," she rejoined, with singular pathos.

Sambo, who sat before the fire, came to their rescue. "Boss, I'se powerful curious 'boot whar yo got dat bump on yo' haid."

"Wal, I'll tell yu," replied Pecos, never before so willing to talk.

"Please, Pecos, tell us," added Terrill, eagerly.

"Wait till I drink this coffee," he replied, and presently got up to light a Mexican cigarette, one of the few he had smoked since the trip to Camp Lancaster. "I got down to the Y Canyon aboot sunrise. An' I found thet outfit camped where Watson said they was. Wal, my idee was to scare them out, if I couldn't do more. An' I figgered the way to work it. If you remember it's a queer-shaped canyon. I shot seven times into thet bunch havin' breakfast. Long range, but I hit one greaser, anyhow. He squealed like a jack rabbit. Yu should have seen them pilin' over one another. Then I run back, hopped my hoss, an' rode like hell as far as I could along the rim. Thet was when I got snagged. Wal, I jumped off with the other rifle an' made for the rim. Heah, if anythin', I was even closer than where I first seen them. An' I began to shoot again, as fast as I could load the old rifle. My idee shore worked. Thet outfit reckoned they'd been set on by men surroundin' the canyon. Their hosses were ready for the day, an' they mounted an' made off through the thicket for the river. An' they kept shootin' steady. It was when I was climbin' along the rim thet one of them hit me. Wal, they shore rustled down the river, an' I reckon they won't come back very soon."

"Sambo, is yo' appetite done gone whar Rill's an' Pecos' is?" asked Mauree. "'Cause if it is dis supper am wasted."

"Doan trubble, woman, doan trubble," replied Sambo. "Dar won't be no grub left. I'se so happy I could eat a hoss."

A fugitive happiness seemed to hover over Terrill. One moment she radiated eager young life, and the next she grew blank, as if suspended between hope and fear. Pecos became guiltily aware of her unconscious appeal to him. While he told his story she sat wide-eyed and open-lipped, absorbing every word, betraying her fears and her thrills.

Presently Pecos, driven by wonder and cruel longing, went out on the porch to sit in the dusk. How serene the canyon! The river moaned low out of the shadow. A coyote wailed from the heights. If avarice and lust and death had stalked there this day, there were no ghosts of them abroad now. He wondered if Terrill would follow him out. What did her actions, her brave and wistful glances, betray? She realized she had failed in faith. Her conscience tortured her. Or was it something else? He might make a pretense of hardening his heart, of holding aloof, but it was sham. How many interminable hours since morning! His head throbbed from the bullet wound. At intervals a slight sigh, almost a gasp, escaped his lips, involuntary regurgitation of that hideous inward clamp on his vitals. Could he listen to the solitude, could he think of the tranquil dusk settling down, could he dwell upon this beautiful girl delivered into his keeping when he had ridden red death that very day? But that was hours, endless hours, past. Life seemed surging on, piling up, swelling to engulf him.

A light footfall creaked on the porch board. Terrill came out and sat beside him, close to where Sawtell had fallen that day.

"Pecos." She spoke low.

"Yeah."

"I—I'm nervous—that old fear of the dark. . . . Let me sit by you?"

"Yeah." He drawled it, but that was a lie, too. She sat down close beside him and gazed out into the gathering dusk. If she had any terrors of the place, of what she had escaped, these were not manifest. Her profile against the black cliff appeared chiseled out of marble, cold, pure, singularly noble, and as sad as her life had been. Pecos could not convince himself of the facts. His wandering rides, his ruthless hand, his unfailing service to the weak and unfortunate—these had landed him there in that lonely canyon, at the side of a girl as lovely as an angel—and as good.

"Terrill, go to bed," he broke out, abruptly.

He startled her. "Must I?" she asked, and the willfullness of the boy Terrill seemed gone forever. There was a suggestion of his word as law, never to be disobeyed.

"Suit yourself. But yu look so white—so spent. If yu'd sleep ——"

"Pecos, I cain't sleep this night unless you—unless I'm near you."

He could not reply. It was as hard for him to think clearly as to speak clearly. His nerves were on edge. His heart seemed thawing to an immense pity, and that meant a liberation of his love—which, surrendered to, while she sat so close, so tense and alive, meant only chaos.

"May I stay?" she asked.

"Yeah."

A bright line tipped the opposite canyon rim. The moon was rising behind them. Terrill edged a little closer to him. Once a timid hand slipped under his arm, to be quickly withdrawn. He caught her glancing up at his face, which he kept rigidly to the fore.

"Pecos, I'm all tight inside—on fire. . . . But feel my hands."

She put them in his and they were like ice. One lingered in his, and as no nerve or muscle of his responded, it slowly fell.

"Fever, I reckon," he said. "Terrill, it's been a tough day for a—a g—youngster."

"Horrible! . . . And just to think! If I'd had one more shell in my gun I'd have killed him! . . . I wish to God I had."

"Wal, Terrill, thet's queer. Why do you?"

"Then he couldn't have told."

"Ahuh." Pecos believed she meant that Sawtell could not have betrayed her sex. That seemed natural. Terrill over-exaggerated some kind of shame in this dual character she had lived.

She sat silent awhile and the warmth of her contact with him seemed strange in view of her ice-cold hands.

Across the canyon the moonlit line had grown to a broad white band creeping down, imperceptibly diminishing the darkness below. An owl hooted in the gloom and the insects kept up their low mournful hum. Sambo and Mauree came out, evidently having finished their work. Mauree bade Terrill good-night while Sambo tarried a moment.

"Folks, I sho gotta tell yo," he rolled out. "Yo know mah wife has second sight. An' she say good is comin' out of dis turrible day."

"Bless her, Sambo," cried Terrill.

"Shore there is, Sambo," drawled Pecos. "'Cause there was a lot of bad went under the ground."

"Dey sho did, Pecos. Dey sho did. . . . An' now good-night Mars Pecos. . . . An' Gawd bless an' keep yo, Missy Rill."

Sambo moved away toward his cabin and the moonlight tipped his black head.

"Oh . . . he has not called me Missy Rill since I was a child," murmured Terrill, in mingled joy and pain. Perhaps that chord of the past vibrated in her frozen and inhibited emotions, for suddenly she clutched his arm, she slipped to her knees and crept close and lifted her face. Pecos' heart leaped up in his breast.

"Pecos, my only friend—you are angry—cold—you freeze me when I want—I need so much to ——"

"Yeah, I reckon," blurted out Pecos. How long could he resist snatching her to him? What would she do? Was he only blind, mad, a blundering vaquero who had never learned to know women?

"But I can't endure that," she wailed, and clung to him. "Is it be-because that beast tore my clothes off—saw that I wasn't a—a boy?"

"Yeah," replied Pecos, dully, as if by rote.

"But I couldn't help that, Pecos, any more than I can help being a girl. I was fighting for you—to save your money. I got it, too, and ran. But he caught me by my coat and shirt—and they tore off."

"You mebbe wasn't to blame. But why yu was there an' he seen yu half-naked. A girl! . . . Yu cain't deny he meant to make a hussy of yu then," declared Pecos, knowing full well how wild and unreasonable his statements were.

"No, dear Pecos," she replied, gravely. "I saw too late it would have been far better to let him take the money. But I didn't. . . . And you came in time to—to save me."

In all Pecos' life there had never been anything a millionth part so sweet as this moment. What was she pleading for? It must come out. Could he deny her whatever she seemed entreating for, so as to prolong this growing suspicion of her love? Prolong it only to keep back the inevitable truth of her affection for a brother, a protector? After the whirling heights of his hopes, could he bear that? But he must goad her on.

"What if I hadn't come in time?"

"Then, when you did come you would have found me—daid."

"Wal, we're wastin' breath on thet. I did come an' yu ain't daid. . . . But I'd rather have seen yu daid than to live to believe me a low-down rustler."

"Oh, Pecos!" She wailed.

That was the mark. He had struck home. The thing which flayed him likewise flayed her. Almost rudely he shoved her back. Yet that was of no avail. She swayed again to catch at his hands.

"Terrill Lambeth, you believed me a thief?" he queried, sternly, and he laid rude hold of her.

"Yes—yes. I cain't lie aboot anything so terrible. I *did*. . . . But he was so shore. He seemed to know all. He recognized that money—the very bills you had. . . . He'd paid you, he swore. And God forgive me! I thought it the truth."

"Aw!" breathed Pecos, huskily.

"There! It's out. It was killing me. . . . But, Pecos—Pecos, dear Pecos, don't look so black and fearful. Listen. The minute I saw you again—the very instant—I knew Sawtell was the criminal and not you. I felt it. I saw it in your eyes. . . . Let that plead for me."

"But you believed!" he flashed, harshly.

"I did, but I don't. Cain't you be human?"

"I'm human enough to be powerful hurt."

"But what is a hurt?"

"You went back on me."

"Pecos!"

"You betrayed yore pard."

"Not truly."

"You double-crosser."

"No—no. I deny that. If—if it *had* been true, I would still have stuck to you."

Pecos gazed at her spellbound. The moon had long since topped the rim and had just then come out from behind the corner of the cabin, to shine in its silver radiance upon her face. Something sustained her in spite of the monstrous barrier Pecos had cruelly raised. There was no bottom to the tragic abyss of her eyes, as there was no limit to her loyalty. She belonged to him. She was a leaf in the storm. But her strength consisted in the bough from which she would not be separated. She clung.

"Yu failed me, Terrill Lambeth," he went on, hoarsely, and his true pain was easing out forever in these accusations. "In my hour of need yu failed me."

"In faith, but never in heart."

"I'm a Texan. An' I hate a cow thief as bad as a hoss thief. I've helped to hang both. An' yu believed I was one."

"But I confessed it to you. I could have lied," she cried, driven desperate.

"Yu never cared."

"O God—hear him! . . . Pecos Smith, I've loved you from the moment I laid eyes on you."

"As a big brother, mebbe."

"As a girl hungry for she knew not what. As a girl who must hide her longing and her sex. As a girl driven into womanhood. Oh, I could never have learned to love you so well but for my secret."

"Terrill, yu've been a bogus boy. Yu've lived so long untrue thet you cain't be true."

"Pecos, I love—you—now," she cried, brokenly, her spirit following her spent strength.

"Yu beautiful fraud!"

She made one last effort to clasp him in failing arms. "If you—do not—love me—there's nothing left—but the river."

"Liar!"

"Pecos, this flint man cain't be you. My Pecos ——"

"Yu double-crossed me."

"No—no!"

"Yu failed me."

"Have mercy, then!"

"Yu believed me a thief."

"Forgive me. My heart—is breaking. I have only you—in all this world."

Pecos could hold out no longer. He drew her to his breast and lifted her lax arms round his neck.

"Wal, I reckon thet'll be aboot all," he said, in a voice so vastly changed that it seemed a stranger had spoken. She lay still in his arms, but he knew she had not fainted. He could see those great dark eyes. He felt the slow-stealing warmth of her breast on his, and the quickening pound of her heart.

"Pecos," she whispered.

"Yeah."

"You forgive?"

"I reckon I was only punishin' yu for lack of faith. You poor kid."

"Oh, wait! Pecos. This *will* kill me. Don't tell me too quickly—you didn't mean all—those—horrible names."

"Wal, I meant them for the moment. I shore was mad. But I saved another for the last."

"Oh, Pecos—what?" she implored.

"Terrill darlin'."

"Then—you—love—me?"

He spent his answer on her cool sweet lips. It was then that his reward came unasked, unexpected as had been the treasure of her love. For all that had been innate in Terrill Lambeth, the femininity that had been suppressed, the emotion that had been denied so long, and the fostering of the lonely years of that wild country, where she had been kept as secluded as a cloistered nun, and the hunger which such a life must only magnify, now burst all bounds in an abandonment as pure as her thoughts had ever been, and which blindly sought his lips in kisses and his arms in embraces that broke off only to be renewed.

At last her lovely face fell back in the hollow of his arm and it was no longer white or tragically convulsed.

"Pecos, how can you love me so—so much as that, if only these few hours you've known me to be a girl?"

"Wal, it shore seems a whole lot of love on such short notice," he drawled. "But the fact is, honey, thet I've loved you more an' more all the time ever since I—I found you out."

Startled, she leaped up in his arms.

"Pecos Smith! . . . You deceitful wretch! . . . O Heaven—since when?"

"Darlin' Rill—since the day you nearly drowned."

"That day—that day!" She hid her hot face on his breast and hugged him tight. "But since you love me ——"

CHAPTER FIFTEEN

As far as Pecos was concerned Rockport or any town would have been good for a visit, but the Gulf cattle town in its heyday was no place for Terrill.

Pecos had not seen its like. It appeared to be surrounded on three sides by bawling cattle and on the other by the noisy Gulf. There was a main street upon which to ride or drive or walk at any hour of the day and far into the night, but to do so was a most strenuous and uncomfortable undertaking.

The Gulf Hotel, where Pecos engaged rooms at an exorbitant figure hummed like a beehive. Its patrons appeared to be the same as the surging crowds in the street—settlers, cattlemen, cowhands, buffalo-hunters, soldiers, nondescript travelers, desperadoes, and the motley horde of parasites who lived off them. It was hot and dusty on this December day. What would it have been in mid-August?

The spirit of the throng, the movement and meaning of it, permeated Pecos' blood. He had been only a riding vaquero, a gun-throwing adventurer. He had now become a part of this very thing. There were settlers' wives and daughters in that crowd, all of whom had embarked upon the great adventure Terrill was already living.

"Dog-gone it, Terrill," he drawled to her, "this heah is grand. Turrible for us to watch 'cause we shore know what those young men an' women are goin' up against. But we feel somethin' big an' wonderful with them. They'll *do* it, Terrill. Yu cain't fool me when I can see people's eyes. Thet's why I'm alive, 'cause I can see what men think."

"Pecos, it makes my heart come up in my throat. I'd like to go with them. Oh, I hope these young men can fight."

"I shore see a lot of Texans among them."

"But who are the white-faced men in black, an' the ghastly women all decked in flowery dresses?"

"Dog-gone if I know them, honey," replied Pecos, evasively. "But I reckon they ain't so good. Now, Terrill, don't yu leave me for a single minute. An' if I have to leave yu it'll be heah where yu can lock yoreself in yore room."

"Pecos Smith, you won't leave me even there for a single minute," she retorted. "Do you imagine I'd let a dashing, handsome vaquero, loaded down with money, go out in that crowd alone? Not much!"

"Say, thet ain't so turrible flatterin'," replied Pecos, dubiously. "You look like a kid, but yu got the mind of a woman."

"Pecos, I'm dependent upon you," she said, sweetly. "And aren't you dependent upon me?"

"My Gawd, yes! If I didn't have yu I'd be drinkin', gamblin', mebbe shootin', an' I don't reckon what else. But all thet's past an' I'm so happy I'm loco."

"I'm so happy I'm frightened."

"I shore wish thet Judge Roy Bean had been home. Then *I* wouldn't be so frightened, myself. Haw! Haw!"

"What do you mean, Pecos?" she asked, blushing scarlet. "We came here to buy cattle."

"Aw, I didn't mean nothin'. . . . Wal, come on. There are stores heah an' mebbe we can find some of those women's clothes you're cravin'."

But a breathless scramble through the crowd from one store to another failed to reveal any ready-made female attire that Terrill wanted. There was an abundance of material, some of it good, but it had to be made into dresses. So they had to resort to boys' apparel. After a mirthful foray they returned to the hotel with new fancy-topped Mexican boots, silver spurs, a buff sombrero in which Terrill looked so fetching that Pecos whooped, corduroys, shirts of various hues, a jacket, and other articles. While Terrill raved over these purchases like a boy, Pecos told her to change while he went downstairs to the office.

Pecos was perturbed because he had discovered that he was being followed by two men. This was no unusual thing in any crowded frontier post. But these men looked like Texas Rangers to Pecos. And he could not take any chances with such men. Why were they following him? Pecos decided his right move was to find out.

Wherefor he approached the hotel desk and asked if there were any Texas Rangers in town.

"Captain McKinney is here with some of his Rangers," replied the clerk.

"They're working on that Big Brewster cattle-steal."

"Where can I find him?"

"He's stopping here. Saw him here a moment ago."

The lobby was crowded with men. Presently Captain McKinney was pointed out to Pecos. He appeared to be about medium height, of the usual Texan complexion, had a fine stern face and piercing eyes. Pecos approached and stood respectfully waiting a break in the Captain's conversation with two men, evidently ranchers.

"Well, sir?" queried McKinney.

"Are you Captain McKinney?" replied Pecos.

It was characteristic of Texas and particularly of the Rangers that such a query invited a guarded reply.

Finally Captain McKinney replied.

"Yes."

"Wal, Captain, I reckon a couple of yore Rangers have been trailin' me all aboot town."

"Who are you?"

"Pecos Smith."

Well Pecos knew then that he had been wise to approach this Ranger Captain. Also he had further appreciation of the significance of his name.

"Come to my room," said McKinney, abruptly.

Pecos had the keenest of susceptibilities in his meetings with men. No matter what the issue, this meeting had been favorable, or most certainly a Captain of the Texas Rangers would not walk down a corridor in front of a suspected man.

Pecos was ushered into a well-lighted corner room.

"I'm glad you looked me up," said McKinney, inviting Pecos to a chair.

"What's the idee, Captain—Rangers trailin' me?" drawled Pecos, sitting back.

Then the two Texans locked glances. Pecos liked this man, saw in him the clean-fighting Ranger. He saw, too, that he was the object of such scrutiny as seldom fell upon him.

"Mind letting me see your gun?"

"Captain, thet's somethin' I don't do. But in yore case ——"

Pecos handed the gun over, butt foremost. McKinney received it with the thoughtful air of a man who knew what guns meant to Texans. He examined the butt.

"Seven notches—all old," he observed.

"Wal, Captain, reckon I could have added three more lately, but I had reason to quit."

The Ranger Captain returned the gun, also butt foremost.

"Smith, I've heard good and bad aboot you."

"I reckon. I've lived sort of a reckless vaquero life."

"Smith, could you by any chance be related to Bradington Smith? He was on the Ranger force before the war."

"Yes. Brad was my uncle."

"You don't say. That's interesting. You come of an old Texas family. . . . Smith, I have a letter here somewhere aboot you," said McKinney, searching among a pile of papers. "Here it is. From a cattleman who ranges over the New Mexico line. Sawtell—Breen Sawtell. Do you know him?"

"Wal, I reckon I *did,"* replied Pecos, coolly. In spite of his earnestness and his unforgettable relation and duty to Terrill, he reacted subtly and coldly to this approach.

"Like to read the letter?"

"No. I can tell yu just what's in it, Captain."

"Well, do so. Give me your angle. I don't mind telling you that it's through this letter you were shadowed by my men."

"I reckoned thet. How'd they know me?"

"Slinger knows you. Jeff Slinger. I'm glad to add that he swears he doesn't believe one word of this letter."

"Jeff Slinger!—Is he a Ranger?"

"He certainly is. Ten years' service."

"Wal, I'll be dog-goned. He never said so. I helped him in a scrape with some greaser hoss thieves some years ago. Just happened to run into him. We camped some days on the Rio Grande."

"It may stand you in good stead. What's your angle on this Sawtell letter?"

"He was tryin' to hide his tracks, Captain," replied Pecos, and briefly related Sawtell's relations to Williams and Adams, and how he operated.

"That fits in perfectly with some information I got not long ago from a trail driver. We'd better look this Sawtell up."

"Wal, Captain, if yu do yu'll have to *dig* him up," replied Pecos, with a grim laugh.

"How so?" queried the Ranger, though he understood perfectly well.

"Sawtell's daid."

"You shot him!"

"Captain, I'd like to deny the doubtful honor, but I cain't."

"Perhaps you better tell me aboot that—if you will."

Pecos necessarily had to make this a longer narrative and he slighted nothing, though he did not go into detail about the Lambeth Ranch nor did he care to give any impression of a large amount of money.

"There were witnesses to this visit of Sawtell's?"

"Yes. Before I arrived an' after."

"The negroes and this young Lambeth?"

"Yes, sir."

"That is well for you, in case there ever is a comeback. But that does not seem likely to happen. . . . Smith, is the boy my Rangers saw with you this young Lambeth?"

"It's young Lambeth, all right. I'd shore like to fetch him in, Captain."

"Do so, by all means."

In his relief and exuberance Pecos ran up to Terrill's room to bang upon the door.

"Who's there?"

"Pecos. Rustle."

Evidently Terrill had been sitting on the floor. She opened the door with a boot in one hand. All the rest of the new things she had on. And if she did not look bewitching, Pecos knew he had some magnifying ailment of his eyes.

"How do I look?" she beamed, eagerly.

"Wal, girl, I'd hate to say," he replied. "'Cause it might go to yore haid. . . . Heah, let me pull on thet boot."

"It's new—and a little tight. . . . Ouch! . . . Pecos, are you shore I'm ——"

"Heah. Don't climb all over me. You'll muss yoreself. Leave the jacket off. . . . There. Now you're a girl in spite of them pants. . . . Come to look at them, though, any man with eyes could see ——"

"I won't wear them," flashed Terrill.

"Honey, yu got to, or we cain't go on."

"Then don't hint and don't look," she pouted. "Here—where are you taking me?"

"Terrill, I've had some more good luck. There's a Ranger Captain heah. I went in to see him. Reckoned it a good idee to tell aboot Sawtell. Wal, he was fine. An' he asked to see young Lambeth."

"Young Lambeth!"

"Some of his Rangers saw you with me. Took you for a boy. An' I didn't give it away. Oh, this will be fun. Now, Terrill, you be just as sweet an' nice as you know how. Put on a lot of—of swank. Savvy? It won't do me no harm."

Terrill seemed quick to divine that there had been something amiss and her spirit rose to meet it.

At Pecos' knock he was bidden to come in. The Ranger sat at his table.

"Captain McKinney, heah's my pard, young Lambeth," announced Pecos, and he certainly reveled in McKinney's stare.

"How do you do, Captain McKinney?" said Terrill, with just the right tone of deference.

Hastily the Ranger stood up, as if his eyes were poor while sitting. He certainly used them. "Young Lambeth!—Ah! . . . Er. How do you do? . . . Say Smith, this is no boy!"

"Captain, I didn't say young Lambeth was a boy," drawled Pecos. "She's a girl, all right. Terrill Lambeth."

"Oh!—My mistake. Well, I—I am delighted to make your acquaintance, Miss Lambeth," he replied, making Terrill a gallant bow. His eyes shone with pleasure succeeding amaze. "Do you ride rodeo today?"

"I'm pleased to meet you, Captain McKinney," replied Terrill, shyly. "You see, I've been a boy for a long time, and we couldn't find any women's clothes to fit, so I kept right on."

McKinney was plainly mystified as well as captivated.

"Terrill Lambeth? . . . Well, I remember that name Lambeth. Are you any kin to Colonel Templeton Lambeth?"

"His daughter," replied Terrill.

"Well, of all things!" exclaimed the Captain, profoundly stirred. "His daughter! . . . Templeton Lambeth and I were friends. We went through the war together. I never heard of him afterward. Where is he?"

"He is daid, Captain," returned Terrill, gazing away through the window. "He was murdered. . . . After the war, my mother being daid, and Dad ruined, we drove to West Texas, and settled on the Pecos River below Horsehead Crossing. I was nearly fifteen then. . . . It was a lonely place, our ranch. But wonderful for cattle-raising, until the rustlers came. . . . Nearly two years ago they murdered Dad. Made it look like the work of Comanches. Of course I have no proof, but I believe Breen Sawtell and his partner, Don Felipe, were behind it. They tried to steal *me,* as they did my cattle, and they would have done so but for Pecos here."

"I am shocked, saddened," declared McKinney. "Yet so glad to get news of Temple. . . . What a story! Oh, that is Texas of these hard years. . . . And you lived on alone there in that wild Pecos country? It's almost incredible for a girl of your class."

"Alone except for my negroes, Sambo and Mauree, until Pecos came last spring. And you must remember, no one knew I was a girl."

Pecos drawlingly interposed: "Captain, young Lambeth is goin' to be Mrs. James Pecos Smith."

"I wondered. I had a hunch. . . . Of all the romances! Terrill, I congratulate you. I wish you happiness. But—but is this Pecos fellow ——"

The Captain halted in grave embarrassment.

"Captain McKinney, if he had not been Pecos Smith he never could have saved me," replied Terrill, lifting her head with pride. Love and faith did not need to be spoken.

"Terrill, I am glad he *is* Pecos Smith," returned McKinney, with strong feeling. "I believe my old friend would be glad, too."

Then he turned to Pecos to extend a hand.

"You will marry the best blood of Texas. . . . You will get one of the most lovely girls I ever saw. . . . I swear she is as good and fine as she is beautiful. . . . Do you realize your wonderful fortune? . . . You gun-throwing vaquero—come of an old Texas family, too! . . . What luck! What duty! Pecos, I hope to God you rise to your opportunity."

"Captain, I'm shore prayin' for thet myself," responded Pecos, slowly and with emotion.

Later Pecos went out to purchase guns, rifles, shells, knives, all of the newest designs, and sadly needed wearing apparel for himself, two new saddles and various other articles.

And Pecos met settlers, trail drivers, cattlemen, ranchers from whom he learned many things. The settlers, perhaps, profited as much from the meeting as Pecos. He encountered Jeff Slinger again and they became friends. Captain McKinney devoted himself to their service, and was especially kind to Terrill. When he went away, having ended his duties there, he left Slinger and another Ranger, an experienced Indian-fighter named Johnson, to go back with Pecos on the long drive with the cattle.

Slinger knew of a cattleman named Hudson who ran stock out on the Frio River, and could be bought out. He was a bachelor, getting well along in years, and wanted a little peace and freedom from rustlers. Slinger had happened to encounter this cattleman in Rockport during Pecos' stay. The result was a meeting. Hudson appeared to be a hawk-eyed old plainsman from Brazos country and at once inspired confidence.

"Wal, I got aboot two thousand haid left—the finest breed of long-horns I ever had," Hudson said.

"Would yu sell?" asked Pecos.

"Reckon I would long ago if I'd known what to do with the boys. I've got two nephews who've been brought up on hosses, an' ridin' cattle is their especial dish."

"Ahuh. How many cowhands besides these boys?"

"Two. They ben with me long an' I shore hate to see them go up the trail with the drivers. Dodge an' Abilene are bad medicine."

"Would these four hands fit in with the kind of outfit I want?"

"An' what's thet?"

"A young, sober, hard-ridin', straight-shootin' outfit to run cattle with me West of the Pecos."

"West of the Pecos! . . . Wal, Smith, I don't believe you could beat these four boys in all Texas."

"If I take them will yu sell?"

"Reckon I will. I can get ten dollars a haid at Dodge."

"Shore, but thet's there."

"Wal, to get down to bed-rock. . . . Eight dollars, Smith."

A deal was made. Slinger promised to find two more cowhands that he could absolutely guarantee. These were to go home with Hudson, and the herd was to be rounded up, and made ready for Pecos' arrival, when he would pay his debt and go on.

"Course thet means Horsehaid Crossin'," he pondered.

"Smith, it's your best bet. The west trail is not so good. Grazed off in places. Water little an' far between. My range is way at the haid of the Frio. You have a good road an' fine conditions this season all the way to the old Spanish trail thet takes off west for the Pecos. With eight good men beside yourself, all well armed, you needn't worry none aboot Indians. An' you won't lose a steer."

"Done. I'm much obliged, Hudson."

It took vastly more time to consider what else to buy and take back to Lambeth Ranch. Pecos wanted a home for Terrill and all the comforts possible to pack into the wilderness. For two days he had Terrill's pretty head buzzing. Yet in spite of her glee and enthusiasm, when it came down to selections she rendered a vast and sensible help.

Pecos bought three wagons, one new and the others second-hand, and twelve horses, all of which were acquired at a low figure. But when these three larger vehicles were loaded to the seats they represented several thousand dollars in value, not including Terrill's precious treasures. What with Pecos' armament, and food supplies for a year, furniture, tools, bedding, lumber, leather goods, boots, clothing, utensils, lamps, oil, and so many other needful articles that Pecos could not remember them all, the wagons were heavily laden.

"Gosh! My hair shore raises when I think of crossin' the river with these loads," ejaculated Pecos, in mingled concern and hope.

"Wal, yore hair might be raised afore we git thar," remarked Johnson, dryly.

At last they left Rockport early one morning with Slinger and Johnson each driving a wagon, and Pecos the third, with Cinco haltered behind. Terrill, back in her old blue jeans and jacket, and a battered old sombrero she had picked up somewhere, astride her buckskin mustang, rode beside Pecos for all the world, to his glad eyes, a boy again.

CHAPTER SIXTEEN

Hudson's range took in the headwaters of the Rio Frio, and it was a rugged beautiful country that captivated Pecos' eye.

The very day Pecos arrived with his three wagons buffalo were sighted in the wonderful sheltered valley where Pecos' two thousand long-horns had been grazing. Buffalo seldom traveled west so far as the Rio Pecos, but according to Hudson isolated herds, probably separated by the hunters from the main body, often wandered up the Frio. Even before Pecos had arrived a buffalo hunt had been planned for him.

Hudson's ranch-house betrayed the bachelor and one who was used to the elemental life. It was located up in a pass, between two round-top hills, where the wind blew eternally. Terrill vowed it would have driven her crazy.

"Why wind!" ejaculated the old Texan, in surprise. "It wouldn't be home without wind."

"Lord! what'd a norther do heah?" replied Pecos. "Hudson, we live down in a canyon where it seldom blows. No dust. Never very cold, even when the northers blow."

"Wal, no one man can hope to know the whole of Texas," returned the rancher.

On first sight Pecos formed a most satisfying estimate of the outfit he had hired through Jeff Slinger and Hudson. The brothers, John and Abe Slaughter, were typical Texans, born on the range, stalwart six-footers, almost like twins. Texas Jack was a bullet-headed, jolly-featured, bow-legged cowhand who appeared to be one it might be well to have as a friend, and never as an enemy. Lovelace Hall was an extremely tall Texan, red-headed, and dark-eyed, an unusual type in Pecos' experience, and said to be "hell on hosses, cows an' other ornery things." These two had been trail drivers and had been secured by Slinger. Hudson's other two cowmen were strikingly different, as one was a Mexican vaquero and the other a negro. Lano, the former, was a slim lizard-like rider, darker than an Indian, stamped all over with incomparable horsemanship. The negro answered to the name Louisiana. In fact, Hudson had no other for him. He was medium-sized, but magnificently muscled, and had a pleasing, handsome face. These completed the sextette, and Pecos, seldom at a loss to gauge men, was greatly pleased.

"Fellers," he said, intimately, "before we come to terms I have this to say. Accordin' to Hudson, none of yu know Texas West of the Pecos. I wouldn't be square with yu if I didn't say it's a hell of a tough nut to crack. Hard all the time, harder in winter, an' turrible in summer. Lonesome as no other part of Texas. Even Llano Estacado ain't so lonesome. Gray, rocky, scaly ridges runnin' forever down to the Pecos an' away on the other side. A buzzard now an' then, or a coyote, an' rarer a deer. Wild hosses on the lower reaches, but few along the fifty miles of my ranges. Comanches always, Kiowas an' Apaches occasionally. Soldiers few and far between. Rustlers bad an' comin' thicker. We'll have to fight. No law except an old geezer named Judge Bean at Eagle's Nest, an he's a highway robber."

Pecos rested a moment to catch his breath and to let all that sink in.

"But West of the Pecos it's the grandest cow-country on the face of the earth. I am aimin' big. I know the game. I have the grass, the water, the start in cattle. What I need is a fightin', hell-rattlin', hard-shelled outfit. I'd be grateful alone for yu drivin' this new herd out there for me. But I want yu all to *stick.* There is a future out there for the right kind of men. If I make out big—as I shore could do with yu fellers all keen an' hot on the prod—I will give yu an interest, or help you to make a start yoreselves. An' for the present I'll pay yu more than yu're earnin' heah. Thet's all. Think it over while we're gettin' acquainted."

Later Hudson told Pecos that he had overheard Lovelace Hall say to his comrades: "Fellers, we've nothin' to lose an' everythin' to gain. Thet talk of Pecos Smith's was as straight as Slinger says he can shoot."

Next day they hunted buffalo as shy as wild mules, which were the wildest animals Pecos had ever hunted. Six bulls were killed, two by the Ranger Johnson, who knew the game. The cowhands accounted for three, and the other fell to Pecos and Terrill.

Pecos disclaimed the credit and Terrill did likewise.

"Wal, if I didn't see Terrill stagger thet bull my eyes are pore," remarked Hudson, with a twinkle in those members. "An' it shore fell before it got near enough to Smith for a last shot."

"Terrill, yu get that robe," drawled Pecos.

"What aboot all the robes an' the meat? I cain't use any more. Besides, I'm leavin' for Santone."

"Dog-gone! I never thought of packin' hides an' meat," declared Pecos. "We just haven't got the room. Hudson, will yu sell me a wagon an' team?"

"No. But I'll throw them in the bargain."

Half of the next day was taken up in skinning and cutting up the buffalo. And on the following day, at sunrise, Pecos' caravan of wagons, riders, and cattle set out on the long slow drive.

It was a leisurely procedure for the wagons, at least. Pecos drove one of the teams and Terrill sat on the wagon with him. They talked and planned, and made love, and dreamed of the future, and marveled at the long string of cattle grazing ahead, not so wild a bunch as was usual with that breed. The slow pace made Terrill drowsy, and finally, when Pecos rested the horses at the foot of a hill, she went to sleep. When she awoke the first thing she did was to make sure that her precious trunk was still on the wagon, carefully hidden and protected.

"Pecos Smith, if we run into Comanches and they get my trunk—you lose me," she averred.

"If they go thet far you bet yore sweet life we'll all be daid."

"We're going to be raided. I feel it in my bones."

"Terrill darlin', Comanches ride usually in bunches of thirty or forty. What chance would such a bunch have with this outfit, heeled like we are?"

Long before sunset the day's drive ended. The camp site was ideal; Pecos could look afar to the west and see the dim ghosts of the mountains, somewhere beyond the lower brakes of the river. The cowhands, eating supper in relays of three, were happy, which augured well for the state of the herd. With this the case, with grass and water abundant, and wood for fire and Terrill singing, Pecos gazed at the evening star and thought it was rising for him.

The next day, as far as action and result were concerned, seemed like the first. And so, one after another the slow days accumulated with only minor mishaps that occasioned no delay. The weather stayed fine, cold at night, stinging at dawn, warm at midday.

"Pecos, do you ever stop to think how—how strange and natural a long drive gets to be?" queried Terrill, dreamily.

"Don't I? Ha! It's life, Terrill, an' with yu it's heaven."

"Pecos Smith, I don't believe I could bake biscuits without you getting sentimental," she retorted.

"Wal, yu'll have to show me aboot the biscuits."

But he understood her. There grew to be something beautiful in such a long ride into wild country. The anticipation and labor of preparation, the endless gossip of accident, weather, scant grass and water, savages, the worries about what might happen and never did happen, the gradual fading away of the influence of towns and people—these things ceased magically to loom and were eventually forgotten. Storms and floods, stampedes and Indians, certainly could and did disrupt the peaceful tenor of such days as these. Terrill ceased to mention them; she even forgot her trunkful of delights that revived the memories of her old home. And Pecos dreamed while he watched the horizon.

He would have preferred to dream in his saddle, because the wagon seat was hard and uncomfortable and he was a poor teamster. Nevertheless, no journeying of his down into the wilderness had ever been comparable to this. The sun rose red, shone pale at noon, gold at eventide, and that was another day. That long-horn herd might have been especially trained for him. What little trouble they gave! How few had strayed! He had to award all praise to his riders.

Day by day the landscape imperceptibly changed. A mile was an atom on that vast western upheaval of Texas, yet to keen eyes each mile told of the approach toward the more barren regions that sheered north to the Staked Plains, and west to the brakes of the Pecos. Yet still there was good water to be had, and fair grazing. Pecos' herd gained weight. Now and then a bleached skull of a steer, ghastly reminder of less fortunate drivers, gleamed under the pale sun.

A day came, however, that stood out like a landmark. The caravan cut off from old Fort McKavett toward the military road that stretched west toward the Horsehead Crossing of the Pecos. This sheering off was, of itself, a stirring change. But when Terrill came radiant of eye to cry out: "Oh, Pecos, I know this road! I remember the hills. I came by here . . . . I will show you the old camps . . . . It seems so long ago . . . . Oh, Pecos!"

Downgrade all day they drove, with the cattle moving faster, owing to a thinning of the grass. And that night they made dry camp, the first of the long drive. Next day they crossed water, and on the third made Dove Creek. A thicketed bottomland, with a clear stream, held the stock.

Terrill showed Pecos where she had slept in the wagon. She remembered a tree where she had sat at twilight, melancholy and sad, longing for home yet never wanting to go back, pondering doubtfully over the future, fearful of the ever-growing wildness of this dark-gray stone ledged land.

"Oh, I cried so hard," said Terrill, her eyes picturing that past hour. "It was a day when all had gone wrong. Dear old Dad—so seldom discouraged! But this day he was down, and I went down too. I could not see any hope in the future—anything but dreadful pain and loneliness. . . . Oh, Pecos, how terribly wrong I was! What a child! . . . Oh, if I had ever dreamed then that I was to meet you, love you, be loved by you—I would not have cried myself sick that day."

"Terrill, what do yu suppose *I* would have done in the past, if I'd ever dreamed I was to meet yu, love yu, be loved by yu?" returned Pecos, in a passion of regret. "I never dreamed of a yu, darlin', yet somethin' kept me from goin' plumb to hell."

Another day set Pecos' caravan on the old military road.

The sun hazed over. There was a chill in the air and a wind rustled the brush. No living creature of the wild crossed Pecos' vision. The coyotes had ceased following the herd. Something, perhaps an instinct, encroached the leisurely travel. Pecos felt a slight restlessness. Despite the weeks and leagues behind, the way still was long. The horses lagged less; the cattle plodded on sometimes without looking for grazing. That night at Kinway Creek, after the best and longest day's journey of the trip, the cowmen did not sing on guard or joke around the camp fire.

Johnson had picked up Indian mustang tracks not many days old.

Pecos decided to put Louisiana on the wagon and take to the saddle next day. He talked with Jeff and Johnson.

"Wal, it ain't anythin' to see Indian signs," said Slinger. "Not up heah, anyway. The land is shore heavin' an' grayin' for the Staked Plains."

Johnson was not sanguine. He did not appear to be a talkative man. Pecos decided the chances were ever that they would have a brush with the Indians. The Slaughter boys and Lovelace Hall were out on night guard. Texas Jack lay asleep in his blanket, his head on his saddle. Lano and Louisiana stood beside the fire, toasting one side, then the other.

Pecos walked away from camp toward where the herd rested and slept. In the main the steers were quiet. Calves born on the way bawled drearily. Travel was hard on them. The guards sat their horses, or rode to and fro, to edge in a stray. All seemed well. It was only the silent night, the cold winds, the encroaching monotony, the long, long way.

Terrill was still awake. She called to Pecos as he was passing. The little tent was just barely large enough for her bed and duffle.

"Lady, one bad thing aboot you, anyhow, is yu cain't sleep with yore boots on," said Pecos, reflectively, as he sat on the bed. Terrill had felt for his hand and found it.

"Pecos, you are worried," she whispered.

"Not atall, dear. But I'm just thoughtful."

"Well, the men are. I heard Johnson talking to Slinger. But how much easier we are than Dad's outfit when it camped here years ago. Pecos, I think the country grows on you."

"Ahuh. Wish we could drill right on instead of waitin' for the cattle."

"But we cain't. All our hopes are in that herd. Pecos, I feel like Mauree when she has 'second sight,' as Sambo calls it. We are going to get across."

"Shore we are, honey. Dog-gone, but yore a game kid. I don't mind admittin' thet it's yu I buckle on. But for yu, this drive would be apple pie. Last day or so it's come home to me. Yu're the real stuff, Terrill. But yu're a *woman,* an' no man ought to risk yu on this cussed Hosshaid Trail."

"Dad risked me. All the settlers risk their wives and daughters. We can't be left behind. Besides, Pecos dear, don't you exaggerate this woman idea? I can ride and I can shoot. I'm not the least bit afraid. I will not be in the way. And I'll bet I can keep my haid under better than you."

Pecos rose with a fervent: "Thet's just it, Terrill. Yore nerve, yore spirit, yore faith. Yu beat me all hollow. 'Cause yu have other an' finer feelin's. More courage. Thet's what kills me. . . . I'm prayin' Gawd to see yu through safe. . . . Good-night!"

Dead Man's Water Hole was the next camp, reached late in the evening of a dark and dismal day. If a norther threatened, it did not materialize. That night Pecos stood hours on guard at camp, giving way to Slinger after midnight. Wolves mourned from the ridges above the restless herd. There were four cowhands on duty. Terrill was awake when Pecos noiselessly crept past the little tent. She called a good-night to him. Then he sought his own bed under a tree.

One more day to Wild China Water Holes, then a long drive to Horsehead Crossing. That second day would be the rub. Again the signs of Indian mustangs had perturbed Pecos. And in the morning Johnson informed him that a score or more of Kiowas or Comanches had camped right on that spot two, or at the most, three, days ago.

"Take charge, Johnson," replied Pecos, curtly.

Lano was fetching in the saddle horses; it was Texas Jack's day with the cooking chores; Slinger was greasing the wagon wheels; Johnson strode off to a high point with his field-glass; the cattle grazed down the road.

A wintry sun shone fitfully through the dreary clouds and lighted the winding road down toward the Pecos. Out of the gray blur showed dark-spotted hills and blank spaces and white streaks, all forbidding, all the menace of the Pecos.

At breakfast Johnson unfolded his first surprise. "Men, we'll stay heah today, rest an' graze the stock. Everybody sleep some. We'll make the long drive into Hosshaid tonight."

It was a wise move, no doubt, but it enhanced suspense and wore upon all. Pecos had to find what work offered to counteract his restlessness. He was no trail driver, and he marveled at those doughty Texans who had endured the waits, the stampedes, the toils and fights of the Chisholm Trail.

Terrill, however, slept at least half the day. When she was about camp she seemed quiet, a little strained, but always that ready, beautiful smile flashed for Pecos.

At sunset the caravan was on the move, with the cattle far in the lead. Terrill rode her mustang and kept close to Pecos. Lano returned on a scout far back along the road. The sun came out dully red before setting and the barren world grew ruddy. Then it faded under a steely twilight and black night.

No stars showed. The black hills stood up against a dark sky. The wagon wheels rolled downgrade and sometimes the brakes creaked startlingly. The herd walked and trotted three miles an hour, never being allowed to graze. The dumb brutes were silent, as if they knew of the stampedes and massacres that had occurred on this lonely road.

Terrill sat her mustang for ten dark hours, without complaint, and when the gray dawn began to lighten she had a reassuring smile for the anxious Pecos.

Word came back to halt the wagons.

"Hosshaid Crossin', Terrill," exclaimed Pecos, huskily. "Now, if we can only cross I'll ask no more."

It was almost daylight when Johnson rode back alone. Pecos needed only one glance at the Ranger, even in the gloom.

"We cain't hold the herd," he said. "They smell water. They'll go down an' drink, scatter shore, an' mebbe stampede."

"What's the deal?" asked Pecos.

"Drive the wagons off the road, down behind thet bank of brush. Take Terrill, Louisiana, Jack, an' Lovelace, an' climb thet bluff there. Take water, grub, plenty of shells. An' hide in the rocks till we come back."

A few minutes later when the gray gloom began to show objects dimly at a distance, Pecos had his several followers upon the low bluff to which he had been directed.

The flat summit with its rim of broken rock and fringe of brush was just about large enough to afford protection to a party of six. Pecos was swift to appreciate it as a natural defense. A few good shots with an abundance of ammunition could hold it against a considerable force without undue risk. It stood somewhat above the road and about two hundred yards or more distant. Behind was a deep ravine. To the west the land dropped off to the gray thicket-patched valley of the Pecos. On the left sheered down the brushy ravine in which the wagons had been fairly well concealed. At least they would have to be searched for, and considering that they were close under the bluff, it would go rather hard for the discoverers.

"Terrill, yu lay low behind this rock," ordered Pecos. "An' if yu get careless I'll bang yu on the haid."

"Don't worry, Pecos," she retorted.

"Wal, I'm worried already. Cain't yu see this means a scrap? . . . Jack, yu watch the river side."

"Si Señor," replied Texas Jack, crawling toward his stand.

"Lovelace, yu an' Louisiana face the road. An' now let's all get set for whatever Johnson has a hunch aboot."

Day had broken, meanwhile, a morning with good visibility, but no indication of sunshine. It was still too early for sunrise, though by this time there should have been a ruddy glow on the horizon. But the east was black.

Pecos felt a reluctance to look at the river. If he had ever felt love for this God-forsaken secret river that feeling was in abeyance now. Nevertheless, he raised himself to peep over the rock, quite aware of Terrill's tugging remonstrance. There! The well-remembered river-sweep in the shape of a horse's head. It gleamed dark in the cold morning light. It meandered out of gray obscurity into the wide open break of the valley and meandered on into the gray confines. That river had a treacherous soul. It seemed to know that this ford was the only sure one for hundreds of miles, that in itself and the few fountains it drained out of the stony earth, there hid the only allaying of thirst for beast and man in all that aloof and inscrutable country.

It was this soul, this sublime arrogance in its power, that lay like a mantle over the endless banks of sand, its gray ridges, its patches of green. For that dominated.

Up from the river thin pale lines, broken here and there, paralleled the road. Bleached bones. Skulls of cattle. For three hundred years, ever since the Spaniards had staked off the stark and deadly *Llano Estacado,* cattle had perished there. They had dropped within sight of the river they had killed themselves to reach. It was a place where death stalked. No Indian teepee, no herder's tent, no cowman's stone shack, no habitation had ever marked Horsehead Crossing. Men had to cross the Pecos there, but they shunned it as a pestilence. As it had been, so would it always be, used but hated, a dire necessity. On the sunniest of days this place could not but repel. And on this dreary dawn the dominance of loneliness and solitude, with its attributes of ghastly gray, prevailed to weigh down the heart of man, to warn him that nature respected only survival; to appall his sight with desolation, to flaunt the invisible shadow of the Pecos over all.

"Look, boss," whispered Texas Jack.

There was that in the vaquero's voice which caused Pecos to start and duck down to roll over to the watcher's side, a matter of six feet.

"Kiowas," whispered Jack.

Through a crack in the rock they could see into a ravine that paralleled the road. It curved round the mound from behind and had a high fringe of brush on the left bank. In fact the narrow gully could not be seen from the road. Jack's finger indicated this place, which was no doubt one of the coverts the Indians used to ambush travelers.

"Bunch sneakin' up the gully," whispered Jack. "Leadin' their hosses. They're behind the brush now."

Pecos beckoned Lovelace and Louisiana to crawl over on this side of the narrow space. And he had to make a fierce gesture to keep Terrill from following suit.

"Where'nhell did Johnson an' his outfit go?" queried Pecos, impatiently.

"Boss, you can bet they're watchin' them Injuns," replied Texas Jack. "Johnson was a buffalo-hunter an' Injun-fighter before he became a Ranger. He's had fights with Comanches right heah, an' he's up to their tricks."

"Last night's drive put us right, boss," interposed Lovelace. "Shore as shootin' these redskins never expected us till tonight. An' they've just heerd an' seen our cattle. So they're sneakin' up to see what it's all aboot."

"Boss, I see color again," whispered Texas Jack, pointing. "Hey, keep your noodle low."

Pecos had been searching the lower end of the gully, which part was within rifle range of their position. But it was toward the farther end that Texas Jack pointed.

Suddenly Pecos' burning eyes caught a movement of something through the bushy bend of the gully.

"I see 'em, boss," whispered Lovelace, as cool as if he had just espied some deer they were hunting.

"How aboot you, Louisiana?"

"I'se sho waitin' fer orders, boss," replied the negro vaquero.

It increased Pecos' excitement and impatience to realize that all his men had gotten a line on these skulking savages before he had. Yet their positions behind the rocks were not markedly different. Pecos had kept his gaze glued to that brushy bend, behind which the movement and color had disappeared. Then so easily did a bunch of lean redskinned forms creep into view that Pecos had to stifle a yelp.

"Kiowas, all right," said Texas Jack, in a low voice. "Wasn't shore, but now I am. I know them birds. Suits me they ain't Comanches."

"Hold on, boys. Thet's a long shot for these rifles," warned Pecos. "We might spoil Johnson's idee, whatever thet is."

"There ain't so many in thet bunch," whispered Lovelace.

"Aboot a dozen, but shore there's more around thet bend," rejoined Jack. "Looks to me like it's taps fer these reddys."

"Taps. What's thet, Jack?" asked Pecos.

"Boss, I served three years in the army."

"Ahuh. An' thet's where yu had yore Injun-fightin'?"

"Most of it. But I rode with— Say, look, boss. *Look!*"

"Yes, I see. Somethin' scared 'em. They was leary enough before."

"More comin' along. Must be twenty. . . . Wal, if Johnson has draped his outfit where I reckon he has the boot will shore be on the other foot."

Pecos watched the dark line of Kiowas with mingled emotions.

"I see them, Pecos," whispered Terrill, tremulously.

"Be careful, yu little devil," ordered Pecos. He did not see how she could be any more careful, as she was lying flat and peeping low down between brush-screened rocks. She should have been thoroughly frightened, but she was not. She had her new rifle and did not look averse to breaking it in.

Then Pecos sheered his gaze back to the Kiowas. From some source they had become acquainted with imminent peril. Their first movements had indicated that they were bent on ambushing the drivers of the cattle herd now spilling over the banks of the river. But now there had come a great difference. First Pecos had noted the arrival of a lean tall Kiowa, evidently a leader, for as he glided round the bend the others wheeled to him. What violent, eloquent, significant gestures! They might have been surrounded, to judge from this chief's expressive arms and hand. From the ambushers they might have become ambushed. Still it was evident that they still believed that they were unseen. They were particularly apprehensive of the winding sweep of the ravine below. But to Pecos' position they paid scant attention. For one thing, it was too far distant to be a menace, and secondly it was from the river that they sensed danger.

"Funny deal, ain't it?" queried Texas Jack, amused. "The reds are goin' to get a dose of their own medicine, an' I'd say it was aboot time."

"If Johnson drives them down thet gully or up on the road this way it's ——"

"Boss," interrupted Louisiana, "I sho seen somethin' black bob up ober de bank. Sho's I libe it wuz one of dem Slaughter boys' noggins."

"Where?" queried Pecos. What was the matter with his eyes, anyway, that he could discover nothing? One distraction was caused by the slender Terrill lying prone behind him. His attention was divided.

"Way down de gully, boss," replied Louisiana.

"Look out yu don't take one of our outfit for a redskin," warned Pecos. "There! . . . My gosh! it's Abe Slaughter. He's wavin' his hat at us."

"So he is. Thet's to post us to his whereaboots. Wal, Abe, we're wise, but yu gotta guess it 'cause we cain't get up heah an' dance for yu."

"Two fellers thar, boss. Both the Slaughter boys," said Lovelace.

"Thet leaves Johnson, Slinger, an' Lano somewhere else," mused Pecos. Then he glanced back at Terrill. She gave him a bright look from her darkly purple eyes. "Terrill, somebody shore will open the ball soon, but we want to keep out of the dance at first."

"Thet's a good idee, boss," agreed Texas Jack. "'Cause if them Kiowas come pilin' either down the gully or the road under us it'll be most damn bad for them."

"They won't go down the gully," averred Lovelace. "They'll be quick to get lines on where the shootin' is comin' from. An' they'll break away in the other direction."

"Darn if Johnson didn't figger this nice," ejaculated Pecos, gratefully.

"Boss, them Kiowas has given up ambushin' us," rejoined Jack, gleefully. "If it just ain't too slick for anythin'!"

Pecos entertained something of the same enthusiastic acclaim of Johnson's coup. It was easy to see through the situation now.

The Kiowas had gotten wind of Pecos' caravan or some other, and had proceeded on to Horsehead Crossing, where the facilities for ambush were particularly favorable. All day long they would have had lookouts on the watch for cattle in the distance. But Johnson's night drive had been an innovation. These savages had been in camp somewhere back from the river and had been surprised by a vanguard of cattle at daybreak. Whereupon they had made haste for their ambush, only to meet with uncertain and puzzling circumstances which now had augmented to either hearing or sight of white men who were hunting instead of hunted men.

Obviously the three avenues of escape were up and down the gully, both of which the Kiowas showed a decided reluctance to approach, and the high brushy bank to the road, which they likewise feared because it might bring them into sight of enemies located behind the high bare bank toward the river.

Pecos' sharp eyes caught stealthy movement of one Kiowa scout working under the lea of the bank down the gully. No doubt the same reconnoitering was being done in the other direction.

"Ah—h!" came from Texas Jack.

Pecos saw a puff of bluish-white smoke spout from behind the bank at the head of the gully. Next instant, crack! went a rifle.

"She's opened, boys," said Pecos, grimly.

"Pick your partner," added Lovelace.

"No. Hold your fire. *Wow!* Listen to thet!"

Five or six heavy rifle-shots spread along the bank, and instantly pandemonium broke loose down in the gully. The horrid screams and snorts of wounded and frightened mustangs, the threshing, hideous war-cries and gunshots. Pecos saw Indians stagger and fall into the brush before a dust cloud obscured that bend of the gully behind which the Kiowas had concentrated.

"They'll break an' run, fellers," said Texas Jack, disgustedly, "an' we won't git a chance."

"Sho will. They're gonna come by heah," replied Louisiana.

"Let's pile down an' bust 'em comin' up," suggested Lovelace.

"Say, yu roosters, listen to the boss," declared Pecos. Indian-fighting had been out of his line. What a fire-eating outfit he had collected! It added mightily to the thrill of the moment.

"Pecos, come here," piped up Terrill, just as coolly as either of the three who had spoken. "I see horses breaking the brush down there."

He lost no time crawling to Terrill's side. After that first heavy volley the shooting from the gully had become desultory. Smoke and dust hid the bend. Johnson's men were pouring as rapid fire as possible into that cloud.

"Look out, Abe, old boy, or you'll git it," said Texas Jack, from his side.

"Damn fool! What's he want to show himself thet way for?" ejaculated Lovelace.

"I doan see no more arrers," added Louisiana.

Pecos had marked the flight of arrows, like swallows streaking up from the gully, but in the excitement he had not made note of when this defense ceased. From beside Terrill he could not see down into all the gully. She had a perfectly steady finger pointing toward the heavy thicket of brush that lined the road. It was not altogether Terrill's finger that directed Pecos' attention to the important spot, but a shaking of brush, and then lean, dark, wild heads of mustangs.

"Heah, boys, quick," called Pecos, sharply. "They're shore goin' to make a dash." The three men crawled swiftly to his side. "Now look. See thet yellow rock with the cow skull stickin' on top?—Look beyond it a hundred steps, mebbe, on this side of the road where ——"

"Whoopee! I got 'em," shouted Jack, under his breath.

"Me too!—Gosh, if they was only closer!"

"Dey's close enuff fer dis nigger," remarked Louisiana, dryly. "I sho doan lub dem red debbils."

"Terrill, yu shore did a good piece of scout work," said Pecos, with great pride. "Heah I been thinkin' aboot yore blueblooded grandmother an' the delicate feelin' yu inherited! An' all the time yu're one of them greatest of women—a Texas pioneer's wife-to-be!"

"Haw! Haw! She's shore Texas, all right, boss," declared Jack.

"I reckon from this heah day she'll be Texas Terrill," drawled Lovelace.

"She doan gib me no creeps," added the negro vaquero. And thus the status of Terrill seemed established by practical hard men during a time of stress, at the wildest place along the wild Pecos.

The shooting ceased. No doubt Johnson's men were expecting the Kiowa band to burst out somewhere from under that pall of dust.

All of a sudden the dark, lean mustangs leaped out of the brush into the road.

"They're comin'," called Pecos, stridently. "Wait!—It's a long shot. Wait till they're even with us!"

Shots pealed from across the gully.

"Fellers, there's ridin'!" ejaculated Texas Jack, admiration wrung from him.

"Move boys! To the left! Don't shoot over Terrill!" ordered Pecos.

"—seven—nine—eleven," Terrill was counting. "Heavens Pecos, look at them come!—Poor naked, skinny things!"

The Kiowas strung up the road with mustangs stretching low. No painted, feathered, colorful riders these! . . . They fitted the wildness of the place. The spirit of that ghastly country pervaded them. They strung out in single file, dark, gleaming faces glancing back, rifles and bows aloft, their lean figures erect with that incomparable horsemanship of the plains Indians.

"My Gawd! cain't they ride!" exclaimed Pecos. "Wal, boys, it'll be short an' sweet. . . . Get ready! . . . *Let drive!*"

With the heavy boom of guns the erect forms on the mustangs appeared to go over like tenpins. The Kiowas at the flash and bang from that quarter slid down on the off side of their mustangs and rode by magnificently, with only an arm and a foot visible over the backs of their racing steeds. In a few seconds they had passed the zone of danger. Bullets kicked up dust beyond. Then the string of Kiowas, as if by magic, flashed behind a projecting bank and were gone.

"Wal, the boss had it figgered," said Lovelace, who was the first to get up. "Short an' sweet."

"I never was no good at wing shootin'," declared Texas Jack. Pecos rose from his kneeling posture, to wipe the perspiration from his face.

"Didn't even skin one!" he ejaculated.

"Boss, it'd been a tolerable good shot to hit one of them reddys standin' still from heah. An' these was goin' like greased lightnin'."

"I never got a bead on nuthin'."

Pecos looked at Terrill, who had not moved. She lay with her rifle to her shoulder, pointing over the bank. "Get up, Terrill. It's all over. No scalps for us!—How many times did yu shoot?"

Terrill sat up. She was quite pale, but her eyes were dancing darkly.

"Pecos, couldn't they ride?—Oh, it was wonderful!—I guess I was too—too fascinated to shoot."

"Wal!—Say, young woman, just suppose they'd rode right up heah an' one of them was aboot to lift my hair! . . . What then?"

"You shore have beautiful hair, Pecos, and I wouldn't want you bald-haided. . . . Oh, my legs are weak!"

"Fellers, Johnson is yellin' fer us. An' there go the Slaughter boys down into the gully," said Texas Jack.

Pecos stood up to survey the scene.

"Yes, an' he means for us to rustle. Pile down to the wagons, men. . . . Terrill, give me yore hand. We'll make a run down for our horses."

In quick time Pecos and Terrill were in the saddle again. The horses were hard to hold. And the extra saddle horses, once unhaltered, broke and ran down the road. But the other men were appearing down there.

Presently the two factions of Pecos' party were reunited. Johnson, sweaty and dust-begrimed, talked while he tightened his saddle cinch.

"It worked jest as I'd planned. Must have been aboot twenty of them. We ain't hangin' around to see. Now drive the wagons right across. Tie them three saddle hosses behind the wagons. Leave the wagons over there an' come back to help us cross the stock. . . . Let's all work fast while our luck holds. I don't never feel good on this side of the river."

The wagons rolled downhill at a brisk trot. Pecos saw that the cattle had spread up and down the river, but none appeared to have strayed more than a quarter of a mile. They had drunk their fill and were now grazing. Watching the wagons splash into the water, Johnson said the river might be a little high, but would not give them any trouble. This was a wide, shallow, gravelly ford. The wheels scarcely sank over their hubs. In short order the wagons were across and up on the bank off the road.

"Come on, Texas Terrill; we gotta ride now," shouted Pecos, gayly, though anxiety vied with his hope. They joined the riders rounding up the herd. It proved to be far less trouble than Pecos had anticipated. They crowded the cattle gradually to the ford, then with ten riders in a half circle the wedge-shaped start was at last effected. Once the leaders had been forced into the water the greatest difficulty was passed. The river ran a little high and swift, with water slightly roiled.

"Look, Terrill, thet's the color of the water the day we got trapped. Remember?" called Pecos, as they splashed along in the rear of the herd.

"I reckon I've cause to remember, Pecos Smith," declared Terrill, dark meaning eyes on his.

Pecos had the satisfaction of crossing his herd in less than half an hour from the start.

"Say, Smith, do you know we picked up a couple hundred haid of stock over there?" queried Johnson, with a broad smile.

"No!"

"Wal, we shore did. There was a bunch on the downriver side. All wearin' an XS brand. I reckon some trail driver had a stampede here an' mebbe got wiped out. I seen burned wagons an' not so old."

Soon the long caravan was strung out on the west side of the river. From the highest point Pecos gazed back. The scene appeared the same as from the other side. Horsehead Crossing gleamed pale and steely under the wintry sun. There was no evidence of life. The white skulls of steers stood out distinctly, striking the deadly note of the place. It brooded there in its loneliness. Nature was inhospitable. It had allowed Pecos' caravan to pass; perhaps the next would be added to the tragedy of the past.

CHAPTER SEVENTEEN

All the way from Independence Creek to the head of the Gulch Trail that led down to the ranch Pecos distributed his stock. When the last batch of weary cattle were turned loose Pecos and his cowhands rode back towards the river to join the wagons.

Eight days' drive from Horsehead Crossing! Pecos had to recall the camps to make sure of the number. How the days had flown! The long, long drive was over. Before sunset the wagons would be on the rim above Lambeth Ranch.

"It shore makes one think—all this good luck," soliloquized Pecos, solemnly. "Ever since I met thet boy Terrill—who was a girl. . . . Gawd bless her an' make me keep her safe an' happy. . . . No more of some things for me, an' one of them is Hosshaid Crossin'!"

From a high point on a ridge Pecos came out where he could see down the river. The scene gave him both shock and thrill. He seemed to have been long absent, and all at once to be plunged into the old, wild atmosphere of the brakes. The wide, bone-dry jaws of the canyon yawned beneath him, and stretched away with the green river showing. There was a white rapid close enough for Pecos to hear its low roar. The river bottom held wide green bands of mesquite, salt cedar and arrow-weed, and from these the gray brush-spotted slopes rose gradually to the ragged cliffs. Above spread the land for leagues and leagues, with grass and stone prevailing far as the eye could see.

As always, Pecos tried to find a way to climb out of the brake. It was a habit which operated instinctively. On either slope there was no place to which he would have put Cinco. Trapped there, he would have to go up or down the river. He gazed again at the boundless rolling range, with its gray monotony, its endless physical manifestations of solitude. West of the Pecos for him! It filled every need of his adventurous soul. And down there, ahead of the wagons, rode the little woman who had taught him self-reverence, self-control. Life loomed so sweet, so great that it stung him to humility.

The sun was still above the range when the wagons reached the rim above Lambeth Ranch. But it was sunset down in the canyon.

Terrill had dismounted to run wildly to the rim, where suddenly she stood entranced. Pecos followed. He hoped to look down upon the old tranquil place unchanged. How his gaze swept the opposite rim, the golden cliff, the purple caves and thickets, and finally the green meadows dotted with cattle and horses, the brook that was a ruddy streak of sunset fire, and lastly the old green-roofed cabin with its column of blue smoke winding upward.

"Looks like all was well, Terrill," said Pecos, feelingly.

Terrill squeezed his arm, but she was mute. One by one the other members of Pecos' caravan lined up on the rim. And just at that moment a flare of gold deepened on the bold face of wall across the river, to reflect its wondrous warmth back into the canyon. Low down the purple veils appeared to intensify and show caverns and gilded foliage through their magic transparency. From the cracked and cragged rim of the opposite canyon wall down over the seamed face and the green-choked crevices shone the mystic light, down the grassy, boulder-strewn slope to the second wall, and then sheer down this cracked and creviced form to the shining foliage, and the gold-fired flags and rushes that fringed the blazing brook.

This ephemeral moment held the watchers entranced. Then the glory and the beauty began to fade. And with that the practical Texans turned to necessary tasks.

"Smith, you never could have convinced me there was such a pretty brake along this gray old Pecos," observed Johnson.

"More'n pretty. It's a gold mine," vowed Slinger.

"Skins the brakes of the Rio Grande all holler, boss," added Texas Jack. "We'll shore stay with you heah till the old mossyhorns come home."

"Thanks, boys," replied Pecos, finding speech difficult. "Unhitch an' spread around. We'll camp on top heah tonight."

"How'n hell are we ever goin' to git the wagons down?" asked Lovelace.

"We'll take the old one apart an' let it down piece by piece," replied Pecos. "The others we'll leave up heah. Reckon we'll build a shed for them. . . . Cut a long pole, somebody, a good strong one thet we can fasten the pulley an' rope to. I fetched them along so we can lower our outfit easy."

"Mauree-ee! Sambo-oo!" Terrill was screaming in wild sweet peal down into the canyon.

Pecos ran to the rim. The echoes pealed back, magnified in all their sweet wildness, to mourn away in the distance.

"Sambo!" yelled Pecos, with all his might. *Sam-m-mbooo!* cracked back the echo, wonderful and stirring, to bang across to the great wall, and roll on, on, on down the river.

"Mauree-ee!" cried Terrill, in ecstasy.

"There they are!" exclaimed Pecos, in great satisfaction.

"Oh! Oh! Oh!" screamed Terrill, beside herself.

"Boss, dat yo come back?" rolled up Sambo's deep bass.

"Yes, Sambo, we're heah."

"Ah, Missy Rill, is yo all right?" called Mauree.

"All safe and well, Mauree."

"Is yo done married to dat Pecos man?"

"No-o! Not yet, Mauree!"

"How's everythin', Sambo?" shouted Pecos, gladly.

"Boss, I'se done hab trubble. New calves an' colts an' pickaninnies ——"

Pecos let out a roar, but it did not drown Terrill's shrill cry of surprise and delight.

"What yo sayin', Sambo?"

Mauree had disappeared around the corner of her little cabin, and when she hove in sight again with a black mite of humanity in each arm Sambo awoke the slumbering echoes once more:

"Dar yo is, boss. Two mo' black cowhands!"

"Whoopee!" bawled Pecos, giving vent to all that was dammed up in him.

Louisiana, like the other cowhands, had come to the rim again, drawn by curiosity. When the echoes of Pecos' stentorian climax had died away the vaquero yelled down:

"Hey dar, niggah."

"Hey yo'self," replied Sambo, belligerently.

"Seems lak I know yo. Is yo' name Sambo Jackson?"

"Yas, it am."

"I sho yo how glad I is when I come down dar."

In the dusk Pecos and Terrill sat on the rim above the canyon. Lano was singing a Spanish love song, the men were joking around the camp fire, a cow was lowing in the dark meadow.

Terrill had her head on Pecos' shoulder and at last she was weeping.

"Wal, darlin', what yu cryin' for now?" he asked, softly, stroking her hair. "We're home."

"Oh—Pecos—I'm—so—so happy. . . . If only—Dad knows!"

The last gleam of the afterglow faded off the river. Shadowy rifts of blackness marked the brakes of the Pecos, in their successive and disappearing notches. Night fell upon the lonely land. A low murmur of running water soared upward. The air grew chill. Wind rustled the brush. And a crescent moon peeped over the dark bold canyon rim. The Pecos flowed on, melancholy and austere, true to its task, unmindful of the little lives and loves of men.

CHAPTER EIGHTEEN

Pecos moved the supplies down into the canyon the next day, a strenuous job that left no time for the sentiment that might have overcome him upon returning to the ranch. Another day dawned with him in the saddle, guiding this merry and bold outfit into the brakes of the river. And that evening, finding Terrill rested, he yielded to his yearning and faced the tremendous issue at hand. But he did not tell her then.

After Terrill had gone to bed, Pecos strolled up and down, listening to the wild night sounds, watching the moon slide down to the opposite wall, peering into the river gap, slowly surrendering to the emotion that had dammed up within him. He marveled why God had been so good to him. Forgotten prayers learned at his mother's knee came back to him. His happiness and his responsibility, realized so stupendously now in these lonely moon-blanched hours, magnified all the forces of his mind. On his lips still lingered the sweet fire of Terrill's kisses, and he gazed up at the watching stars with a breathless sense of his ecstasy, while all the time he had the eye and the ear of a hunted wolf. He had been trained in the open. He did not trust the dreaming solitude. If some raw wild spirit had spurred him to a tenacious grip on his life, when he had nothing but the bold, reckless pride of the vaquero, what now must transport him, make him invulnerable, to protect the beautiful and innocent life dependent upon him? He felt a mighty passion that swept him up and up, like a great storm wind, and rent asunder the veil of the mystery of love. He seemed to be illumined by the meaning of love, home, children, life, and death. He who had dealt death so ruthlessly!

In the gray dawn Pecos had met and solved his problem. He was a Texan. He was one of the moving atoms of the great empire he envisaged. He realized the chances; he knew the cost of success on that frontier. All could be met and vanquished, but only through an eternal vigilance, a lion heart and iron hand.

"Queer idees for a vaquero," he soliloquized, possessed with a sense of power.

The day broke beautifully to the melody of a mockingbird in the mesquite. The river slid on like a ribbon of red and gold. Pecos called the negroes and his riders to their tasks, while he went for the horses. Cinco came at a whistle, but the little buckskin mustang, as always, obeyed only a rope. It was when Pecos was on the back of one of these bewhiskered little beasts that his respect was roused. The mustang never tired, he lived on little grass and water, and he could climb or go down where even Cinco balked.

Pecos turned the horses in at the corral and strode on to the cabin. He smelled wood smoke and savory meat. Was Terrill really a girl? Had she been spirited away in the night? What queer pranks his imagination played him? He went in eagerly. After all, his eyes never deceived him.

"Terrill up?" he queried of Mauree.

"I done call her. Breakfast on de table."

There came a thumping of little hard boot-heels on the floor. Pecos wheeled from the fire. All was well with his world! Here was the glorious embodiment of all the night had brought in dreams, hopes, plans, beliefs.

"Mawnin' Pecos." The rich sweet voice had been the magic almost of a day.

"Sleepy-haid!" was all he said.

"Oh, I slept a thousand hours away."

"Thet's good. It takes yu a long way from yesterday. . . . Let's eat. We've shore got lots to do." And he placed a chair for her.

"Do?—I cain't do anything but run after you—all the livelong day."

"Thet'll be enough."

Where was the havoc wrought by the long trip? His keen eyes had to search for a little pallor, a little thinness in her cheeks. But youth had returned triumphant. Happiness shone in opal glow of skin and luminous eyes. She was hungry, she was gay, she was inquisitive. But Pecos gave her no satisfaction until the meal was finished, when with a serious air he led her out of the cabin, across the open grassy plot to his favorite seat under a tree. Here, surrendering momentarily to her charm, he drew her close.

"Pe-cos, some one might—see," she said, with what little breath he left her.

"See us? Heah?" He laughed and released her.

"Not that I object," she laughed. "But, you know, Comanches ride out on that rim sometimes. . . . If you want to—to hug me, let's go in."

"Terrill, we must rope an' tie up our problem," he said, earnestly.

"Problem? Why, we settled that all, didn't we?"

"It seems long ago an' I'm glad," agreed Pecos. "I stayed up all night. An' I thought, Terrill, I thought as never before in my life. . . . Come, sit heah by me, an' we'll talk aboot everythin'."

"Pecos dear—you're very—serious," she replied, almost faltering.

"Wal, don't yu reckon I've enough to be serious over? . . . When will yu marry me?"

She gave a sudden guilty start and red blushes waved from neck to cheek and brow. But he struck fire from her.

"Soon as we can ride to Eagle's Nest. Three hours if we push the horses, Pecos Smith," she flashed.

"Darlin', thet sounds like yu were callin' my bluff. But I'm in daid earnest. Yu will be my wife?"

"Si, Señor! . . . Oh, Pecos. . . . Yes—yes—yes."

"Wal, we won't run the hosses haids off, but we'll go today."

"Today!" she whispered, awed.

"Shore. Thet's the first step on our problem. Accordin' to thet—to what we heahed, this Judge Roy Bean can marry us. . . . By the way, Terrill, just how old air yu?"

"Guess."

"Wal, I said fifteen when I met yu an' I reckon I stick to thet yet."

"Way wrong, Pecos. I'm nineteen."

"No!"

"I am. Ask Mauree. I'm certainly my own boss, if that worries you."

"I'm yore boss, child. . . . So you're a grown-up girl, after all. Dog-gone! Thet accounts. I'm shore glad. Wal, thet's the second step on our problem. We're shore gettin' along fine. But the next's a sticker."

"Pooh!"

"Thet damned money. We've got a lot left. I've had a notion to burn it up. But thet's nonsense. Now Terrill Lambeth, use yore woman's haid an' decide for me. . . . I held it honest then an' I hold it honest now to brand mavericks. What brandin' I did with Williams an' Adams was straight. I never knew till it was all over thet they'd been burnin' brands. Then all the money fell to me. What could I do with thet any better than buildin' up a ranch for us? It all came from Sawtell. He was crookeder than Williams an' Adams. Made rustlers out of them. Led them on, meanin' to track them down, hang them, an' get his money back."

"Pecos, we shall keep what's left of that money and forget where it came from," replied Terrill, deliberately, almost without pause. "I know Dad would have done so."

"Honey, yu shore are a comfort," replied Pecos, huskily. "My conscience is clear on the moral side. There ain't any other. . . . So thet third step on our problem wasn't such a sticker, after all."

"Go on. We'll build a whole stairway, right to the sky."

"Terrill, we'll spend some of thet money."

"Spend it!" gasped Terrill.

"Shore. Squander a lot of it, if yu like," he drawled, watching her closely.

"Where?"

"Wal, say San Antonio."

She squealed in a frenzy of glee, mauled him with strong brown little fists, kissed him in a transport, all the while babbling wildly. Pecos could not keep track of the breathless enumeration of things to buy and do, but he gained a startling idea of what she had been used to back on the old plantation home. That gave him more insight into the family she had sprung from. He realized it had been one of blood and wealth.

"Say, sweetheart, if thet means so turrible much to you, we'd better hang on to most of this money, so we can go to town occasionally while we're gettin' rich."

"Oh, Pecos, I was just carried away. I would come to my senses and not buy everything. But I must have a woman's clothes."

"Shore. I savvy. Yu shall have all the damn linens, silks, laces, ribbons, all the flimsy stuff an' fine dresses yu want, a pack-saddle full of toothbrushes, hair combs, powders, an' all the jimcracks yu raved aboot."

"Oh, Pecos! . . . And to think I'll start off on my honeymoon in boy's pants!"

"Shore. An' yu'll come back in them, too."

"San Antonio!"

"Listen, honey, the seriousness is this, I reckon. We're goin' to stay heah always?"

"Why, Pecos!" she ejaculated, suddenly down to the earth of practical things.

"Yu love this place?"

"I love my Pecos River and my Pecos Vaquero.—Listen. I'll be serious, too. I suffered here. But I came to love the loneliness—all that makes this Pecos country. I have lived outdoors. I could never be happy in a city. I don't want to live among people. I couldn't think or be myself. . . . If it's for me to say, then this shall be our home—always."

"Terrill, yu've all to say aboot thet," returned Pecos, with strong feeling. "An' yu've settled it as I hoped yu would. . . . Now, little girl, let's face it as I see it. . . . As a cattle-raisin' proposition this range of ours cain't be beat in all Texas. The grass is scant, but the range is wide. We have pure water heah, an' a fine spring in Y Canyon. Halfway between an' back up on the rollin' ridges there's Blue Lake, a cold spring-fed waterhole where thousands of cattle drink. If cattle have pure water they don't need a lot of grass. When the river runs so salty the stock cain't drink, we have our other water, always steady an' pure. Thet means we can run fifty thousand haid of cattle in heah. It means what I so often joked you aboot when yu was a boy. Our fortune's made!"

"I believe you, Pecos. But, oh! the obstacles!"

"There's only one obstacle, honey, an' thet's the rustler," went on Pecos, thoughtfully. "He's heah an' he'll come more an' more. For years yet rustlin' will increase as the number of cattle an' prices increase. I could hold my own, mebbe, but as yu've consented to be my wife—bless yore brave heart!—I'm not goin' to take the risks I've taken in the past. . . . We'll go get married. . . . Gosh! it's sweet to see yu blush like thet! . . . We'll have our honeymoon an' our little squanderin' fit. I shore have an outfit of cowhands who are the real Texas breed. I'll drill them into the hardest-ridin', hardest-shootin' bunch thet ever forked hosses. We'll ride these Pecos brakes together an', by Gawd! we'll make it tough for rustlers."

"Oh, Pecos! All Dad's life that was his dream. Wouldn't it be strange if he realized it through me? . . . And *I* shall be your right-hand vaquero."

"Terrill, yu're goin' to be a wife," he replied, forcibly.

"Shore. But I want to ride, too," she said, spiritedly. "If I cain't, well, I won't be your wife. So there!"

"Yu can ride yore pretty little bull-haid off! . . . But, Terrill dear, yu're such a kid. Yu don't know what bein' married means. We—things come aboot, yu know—happen to married people."

"I—I dare say," she replied, dubiously, leaning away to look at him.

"Yu cain't go on bein' a vaquero for-forever," he protested.

"No-o?"

"We'd want—yu know, yu cain't never tell—I shore love the idee—we—yu might ——"

"What under the sun are you talking aboot?"

Pecos knew he was not much on beating about the bush.

"Terrill, shore yu'd want a—a little Pecos ——"

She uttered a smothered shriek, and rolling away she bounded up to run like a deer. Halfway to the cabin she stopped to turn a crimson face.

"Pecos Smith, I'll be ready in a half-hour for anything."

By midday Pecos and Terrill rode into Eagle's Nest.

Pecos had scarcely stepped off his horse when he realized that this hamlet had changed in the interval since he had been there. Half a dozen Texas faces turned to him right in front of the new store, and one of them he recognized just the instant it broke its still repose to a warm smile. The owner of that face stepped out, a Texan of about Pecos' age, sunburnt, tow-headed, blue-eyed, a fine strapping fellow who yelped:

"Pecos Smith or I'm shore loco!" he ejaculated, and Pecos laughed to think what the Heald outfit would have thought of that.

"Howdy, Jerry Brice. I'm shore glad to see yore darned old skinny snoot."

"Been hidin' oot, you rascal," returned Brice, hanging on to Pecos' hand. "Heahed somethin' aboot you, though. Whar you goin'? What you doin'? Who's this heah boy with the big eyes?"

"Boy? Huh! Thet's no boy, Jerry. Thet's my girl, Terrill Lambeth. We're goin' to be married, an' by golly yu've got to see me through it. . . . Terrill, hop off an' meet a real shore Texas pard, one I'd be scared to have yu meet if it wasn't our weddin'-day."

Terrill came sliding off to slip to his side. Pecos ran his arm through hers and felt it tremble.

"Pecos, you amazin' dod-blasted lucky cuss!" ejaculated Brice.

"Terrill, this heah is Jerry Brice, an old friend. . . . An' Jerry, meet the sweetheart I was always gonna find some day—Terrill Lambeth."

"Wal, Miss Lambeth, this is more than a pleasure," said Brice, bareheaded before her, making her a stately bow. "I shore am happy to meet you."

"Thank you. I—I'm very glad to meet you," replied Terrill, flushed and shy.

Brice gave their horses into the charge of some one he knew and dragged them into a restaurant, where he divided his pleasure between compliments to Terrill and wonder at Pecos. They had dinner together, during which Brice told him of a new ranching venture he and his brother had undertaken in New Mexico, and which was going to be slow but sure. After that there followed an abundance of news. Pecos expressed surprise at the way sleepy little Eagle's Nest had come to life. At which Brice laughed and bade him wait till he saw something. Texas steers were on the move north. Dodge City and Abilene, the two ends of the great Chisholm Trail, were roaring towns. Rockport, the southern terminus, was full of trail drivers, cattlemen, ranchers, traveling settlers, gamblers, desperadoes, which was no news to Pecos. Stock prices were on the rise. Pecos asked innumerable questions, and finally got down to the most important thing for Terrill and him.

"How aboot this Judge Roy Bean?"

"Funny old codger. Shore is a law unto himself. Justice of peace, magistrate, judge, saloon-keeper—he's shore the whole show."

"Can he marry us?"

"Course he can. Good an' fast, too, so Miss Terrill cain't get away from you."

"Thet's fine," retorted Pecos, with satisfaction. "But all the same, Jerry, just to make *shore* I'll have the weddin' service done over again when we get to San Antonio."

They made merry over that while Terrill tried to hide her blushes.

"Come on. Let's go an' get it over," drawled Pecos, and so they went out together.

Pecos did not need to see all the new houses to realize that Eagle's Nest had indeed grown. Even during the warm noon hour the streets were lined with vehicles, saddle horses hitched, riders, trail drivers, cattlemen, and idle sloe-eyed Mexicans. There were ten Mexicans to every white man, so that altogether there must have been a daily population at Eagle's Nest in excess of two hundred. Pecos saw a couple of familiar faces, the last of which dodged out of sight. It would be natural, he thought, to gravitate toward some incident calculated to be embarrassing on this wedding-day.

Terrill did not have a lagging step. Her face glowed and her eyes sparkled. When not directly drawn into conversation or especially noticed she was beginning to enjoy herself. She did not attract particular attention, though she clung to Pecos' arm.

"Say, Jerry, yu remember Don Felipe," said Pecos, suddenly reminded of his former employer. "Heah anythin' aboot him?"

"Shore. He got run oot of Rockport. Down on his luck, Pecos. I reckon he's run his rope."

"Thet so. It ain't such awful bad news," returned Pecos, ponderingly.

"I met a trail driver named Lindsay. He has a ranch on the San Saba. Told me Felipe had an outfit half white an' half greaser, workin' the east brakes of the Pecos. Lindsay also said Felipe had a mix-up with Rangers in the Braseda last summer."

"Ahuh. Dog-gone! Things do happen." But straightway the momentary ominous regurgitation passed as they reached the court-house of Judge Roy Bean. Evidently something was going on, for there were a number of Mexicans on foot, and several mounted on burros.

"This is the back of his place," said Brice. "We'll have to go round in front, where I reckon he's holdin' court or servin' drinks."

The structure Bean called his court-house had been built of clapboards, and stood on posts high off the ground. A stove-pipe protruded from the roof. Presently the front of the building stood revealed—a rather wide porch upon which court was apparently in session.

"Thet's the judge settin' on the box at the table," said Brice, pointing. "The rest are greasers."

Pecos bent most interested eyes upon the judge. He appeared to be a short stout man, well along in years, with a long gray beard, cut round in a half circle. He was in his shirt sleeves, wore a huge light sombrero, and packed a gun at his hip. A Mexican peon stood bareheaded before him. There were three other Mexicans, all sitting in the background. A rifle leaned against the post nearest the judge. Behind him on the corner post was a board sign upon which had been painted one word—Saloon. Above the wide steps, at the edge of the porch roof, was another and much larger one bearing the legend in large letters—*Law West of the Pecos.* Above that hung a third shingle with the judge's name. Although Pecos and his companions were on the edge of the front yard, they could not distinguish what was said.

At this juncture two cowhands rode into the yard and dismounted at the steps. Red and lean of face, gun-belted and wearing shaggy *chaparejos,* they fetched a drawling remark from Pecos. "Folks, this heah is better'n a show."

"Howdy, Judge," called out the foremost rider as he doffed his sombrero. "Will you adjurn court long enough to save two hombres' lives a-dyin' of thirst?"

"Step right up, boys," boomed the judge, kicking his box seat back as he rose. "There ain't no law heah but me, an' we adjurn."

He waved the two tall cowmen into the courthouse, and stamped after them. The peon on trial stood there and waited. The other Mexicans peered in as if they would not have minded being invited to drink.

"Dog-gone me!" ejaculated Pecos. "If thet doesn't beat the Dutch!"

"Isn't he a funny old fellow?" whispered Terrill. "Fancy our being married by him! Pecos, it's all so like a story."

Presently the thirsty couple came out, followed by the judge, who was certainly wiping his lips. The cowhands strode down to their horses, led them aside a few steps, and proceeded to light cigarettes.

When the judge had reseated himself on his box he banged the table with a force and finality that presupposed he had imbibed instant decision while in the barroom.

"Cinco pesos!" he shouted.

One of the Mexicans jingled silver upon the table. Then all of them left the porch. The Judge closed his big book.

"Now's our chance," whispered Pecos, squeezing Terrill's arm. "Jerry, be shore to stick to us."

Terrill giggled, though laboring under suppressed excitement. Pecos whispered to her. "Honey, this shore is aboot all."

Pecos strode up on the porch, holding Terrill to his side. She dragged a little the last few steps. Brice hung back a trifle. Judge Bean looked up. He had hard, shrewd blue eyes and a good-natured, smug face. Pecos' instant angle was that this gentleman who constituted within himself all the law west of the Pecos might be eccentric, but he was no fool.

"Howdy, Judge," drawled Pecos.

"Howdy yourself. Who might you happen to be?" he replied, sharply, his gaze growing speculative.

"I shore got a lot of names, Judge, but my right one is James Smith."

"All right, James Smith. What you want heah in court?"

"Can you marry me?"

"*Can* I? Say, young feller, I can marry you, divorce you, an' hang you."

"Wal, I only want the first."

"Where's your woman? I'm tolerable busy today. Why you come bellyachin' aboot gettin' married, takin' up my time when you've no woman?"

"Heah she is, Judge," replied Pecos, who, despite his cool audacity and the poignancy of his errand, wanted to howl his mirth.

"Where?"

"Heah." And Pecos had to indicate the drooping Terrill.

"Hell! Are you drunk, man? This heah's a boy."

"Nope. Yu're mistaken, Judge," returned Pecos as he removed Terrill's broad-brimmed hat. "Hold up your haid, Terrill."

She did so, struggling with mingled emotions. And her face resembled a red poppy.

Judge Bean stared. He slammed both hands on the table. He was astounded. Suddenly his smug face beamed.

"Wal, I should smile you are a girl. Prettiest who ever stepped into this court. . . . What's your name?"

"Terrill Lambeth."

"Lambeth? I've heard that name somewhere."

"My father was Colonel Templeton Lambeth."

"How old are you, Terrill?"

"Nineteen."

Then the Judge turned to Pecos. "I'll marry you, Smith. What's it worth to get spliced to this pretty girl? It cain't be done nowhere else in this country."

Pecos saw through this old robber. "Wal, it's shore worth aboot a million dollars to me," he drawled. "But I cain't afford much—no more'n say twenty."

"Fork it over," retorted the Judge, swiftly, extending one hand toward Pecos while with the other he felt for something in his desk.

Pecos was in an embarrassing position. He had forgotten to segregate a twenty dollar bill from the roll he had inside his vest. There was no help for it. When the Judge's eyes came up from a search for the little Bible in his hand and espied Pecos stripping a bill off that fat roll of greenbacks, they popped right out.

"Say, have you held up a bank?" he growled, snatching the bill Pecos dropped on the table.

"No. I been savin' up a long time for this heah occasion."

"I forgot to charge you for the certificate. That'll be ten more."

"Yeah. Make it twenty, Judge."

"All right, it's twenty," retorted Bean, and he took the second bill with alacrity. Then he opened the book and began to read a marriage service. He skipped some unimportant parts, but when he came to the vital points he was less hurried. The questions he put were loud and emphatic. But Pecos realized what was happening so fleetingly, and he choked over his "Yes," and heard Terrill's low reply.

"I pronounce you man and wife," finished the Judge. "Whom God has joined together let no man put asunder!"

Then he sat down at his desk to fumble in his drawer for the certificate which he soon filled out.

"Sign your names."

Pecos' hand was as steady as a rock, but Terrill's shook. Brice leaned over them and said, gayly: "Pecos, old boy, good luck an' long life! . . . Mrs. Smith, I wish you joy an' all ——"

A loud voice, slightly foreign, interrupted Brice.

"Señor Judge, stop da marriage!"

Brice exclaimed violently and wheeled to mark the intruder, a tall thin man in black sombrero. Pecos, who stood on the inside behind Terrill and his friend, froze in his tracks.

"What's eatin' you, Felipe?" boomed Bean, angrily. "A-rarin' into my court this way."

"I stop da marriage. Da Lambeth señorita ——"

"Hell, man! You'll stop nothin' heah, unless it's breathin'. . . . I've pronounced this young couple man an' wife."

"Oh, Pecos, it's Don Felipe," whispered Terrill.

"Jerry, take her aside," hissed Pecos, straightening up to push them toward the judge. Then in a single leap he landed in front of the steps.

His enemy, stalking swiftly, had reached the lower steps. His trim, small, decorated boot halted in mid-air, stiffened, slowly sank.

"Howdy, Don. The bridegroom happens to be Pecos Smith."

"Santa Maria!"

The half-breed's lean, small face, black almost as his stiff sombrero, underwent a hideous change that ended in a fixed yellow distortion. Fangs protruded from under his stretched lips. His slim frame vibrated under the thin black garments. And that vibration culminated in a spasmodic jerk for his gun. As it left the sheath Pecos fired to break his arm, but the heavy bullet struck the gun, spinning it away to the feet of the cowhands. Then a swifter and a different change transfixed the half-breed. He appeared to shrink, all except his beadlike eyes.

"Ump-umm, Don. Yu've got a bad memory," said Pecos, cold and sarcastic. "It's damn lucky for yu this is my weddin'-day."

Pecos aligned his gun a little higher, where it froze on a level, spurted red, and thundered. The bullet tore Felipe's stiff sombrero from his head and never touched a hair. Then Pecos aimed at the flowery silver-spurred boots.

"Dance, yu ——"

And he threw the gun down to fire again. This bullet cut more than leather. "Dance on my weddin'-day or I'll bore yore laig!"

Felipe made grotesque, almost pitiful dance steps until his will or flesh ceased to function.

"Wal, yu're as rotten a dancer as yu are a shot. . . . Stand still now ——! And heah me. I'm callin' yu before Judge Bean an' these cowmen, an' the rest of this outfit. . . . Yu're a low-down greaser-hirin' rustler. Yu hire pore ignorant vaqueros an' kill them to get out of payin' their wages. I rode for yu. I learned yore Braseda tricks. I know yu stole most of Colonel Lambeth's stock an' tried to steal his daughter. I chased yore new outfit across the river just a day or so ago. Brand-burnin' *my* stock. Watson caught yu an' got away, only to be shot by yore pard Breen Sawtell. An' before I killed Sawtell I got yore case from him."

Pecos spat as if to rid himself of the bitter restraint he must hold this day. "An' now yu yellow-faced greaser dog! Get out! Get across the river! Hide in the brakes! . . . 'Cause if I ever lay eyes on yu again I'll—*kill* yu!"

Amid a stunned silence the half-breed lunged around, head down like a blinded bull, and spreading the crowd, he disappeared. Pecos stood motionless a moment, until suddenly he relaxed. He flipped his gun. It turned over in the air to alight in his palm. Sheathing it, he turned to face the fuming judge.

"Not on our marriage program, Judge," he said, with the old drawl edging into the ring of his voice.

"Hell, no! Not on my court proceedin's at all. . . . Pecos Smith, whoever yu are, yu have a high-handed way."

"Yes, an' yu better savvy this," retorted Pecos. "I've done yore little community a good turn. Thet man has been the bane of Eagle's Nest. Yu heahed why I couldn't kill him."

"Smith, I'm not rarin' aboot yore drivin' Felipe off. But it'd been a better job if yu'd bored him instead of shootin' fancy didos around him."

"Ahuh. Wal, what's eatin' yu, then?"

"It's agin the law, shootin' heah. Contempt of court. An' I'm compelled to fine yu, suh."

"What?" ejaculated Pecos, completely floored.

Terrill came hurriedly from the door to catch his arm and press it. "Oh—Pecos!" was all she could falter.

"I said 'contempt of court,'" repeated the judge, imperturbably. "I'm compelled to fine you."

"Leapin' bullfrogs! . . . How much, Judge Roy Bean, Law West of the Pecos, Justice of the Peace, Saloon-keeper, Bartender, an' Parson, an' Gawd only knows what else? How much?"

"I was aboot to say fifty dollars. But it's seventy-five."

"What'd it cost me if I'd plugged the breed?" inquired Pecos, sarcastically.

"I reckon my law on the case now reads one hundred dollars."

"Yu got Don Felipe skinned to death!" yelled Pecos.

"Upon reflection the fine imposed for more contempt of court will be one hundred twenty-five dollars—not pesos."

"Robber! Road agent!"

"One hundred fifty!" shouted Judge Bean, purple in the face.

Terrill gave Pecos a wrench that fetched his face round to hers.

"Pay him before he ruins us!" cried Terrill, and Pecos did not know whether she was bursting with mirth or alarm or both.

"Hullo, honey. Dog-gone! I forgot aboot yu. . . . Shore I'll pay it," he declared, whipping out the roll with magnificent gesture, and peeling off bills galore. . . . "Reckon I'm never goin' to be married again. . . . Heah, Judge, buy yoreself some lawbooks an' paint another big signboard in big letters: 'Shell out, stranger, or yu cain't get west of the Pecos!'"